D0927838

American Local-Color Stories

American LOCAL-COLOR Stories

Edited, with an Introduction, by

HARRY R. WARFEL
Professor of English, University of Maryland

AND

G. HARRISON ORIANS
Professor of American Literature, University of Toledo

Cooper Square Publishers, Inc.
NEW YORK   1970

Originally Published and Copyright © 1941
Copyright Renewed 1968 by Harry R. Warfel
Published 1970 by Cooper Square Publishers, Inc.
59 Fourth Avenue, New York, N. Y. 10003
Standard Book No. 8154-0345-3
Library of Congress Catalog Card No. 72-127599

Printed in U.S.A. by
NOBLE OFFSET PRINTERS, INC.
NEW YORK 3, N. Y.

Table of Contents

Introduction ix

JAMES HALL (1793-1868)
The French Village (1829) 1

ALBERT PIKE (1809-1891)
The Inroad of the Nabajo (1834) 15

AUGUSTUS BALDWIN LONGSTREET (1790-1870)
The Horse-Swap (1835) 28
The Gander-Pulling (1835) 35

CAROLINE MATILDA KIRKLAND (1801-1864)
The Land-Fever (1845) 42
The Bee-Tree (1841) 54

HARRIET BEECHER STOWE (1811-1896)
The Minister's Housekeeper (1871) 72

ROSE TERRY COOKE (1827-1892)
Uncle Josh (1857) 84
Grit (1877) 99

RICHARD MALCOLM JOHNSTON (1822-1898)
How Mr. Bill Williams Took the Responsibility (1871) . . . 118

BRET HARTE (1836-1902)
Tennessee's Partner (1870) 139
The Romance of Madroño Hollow (1873) 147
The Iliad of Sandy Bar (1873) 157
How Santa Claus Came to Simpson's Bar (1873) 166

PHILANDER DEMING (1829-1915)
Lost (1873) 179

CONSTANCE FENIMORE WOOLSON (1840-1894)

Solomon (1873) 188
Peter, the Parson (1874) 206
King David (1878) 225

GEORGE WASHINGTON CABLE (1844-1925)

'Tite Poulette (1874) 242
Belles Demoiselles Plantation (1874) 260
Jean-ah Poquelin (1875) 275

MARY NOAILLES MURFREE (Charles Egbert Craddock) (1850-1922)

Taking the Blue Ribbon at the County Fair (1880) 294
Over on the T'other Mounting (1881) 311

SARAH ORNE JEWETT (1849-1909)

A Lost Lover (1878) 329
Miss Debby's Neighbors (1883) 344
A White Heron (1886) 354
The Gray Mills of Farley (1898) 363

MARY HARTWELL CATHERWOOD (1847-1902)

The Stirring-Off (1883) 383
Pontiac's Lookout (1894) 393

JOEL CHANDLER HARRIS (1848-1908)

Trouble on Lost Mountain (1886) 409
Ananias (1888) 430

THOMAS NELSON PAGE (1853-1922)

Polly: A Christmas Recollection (1886) 447
P'laski's Tunaments (1890) 470

ALICE FRENCH (Octave Thanet) (1850-1934)

The Mortgage on Jeffy (1887) 484
The Loaf of Peace (1888) 503

MARY E. WILKINS FREEMAN (1852-1930)

Gentian (1887) 514
A New England Nun (1891) 525
A Village Singer (1891) 536

JAMES LANE ALLEN (1849-1925)

Two Gentlemen of Kentucky (1888) 548

F. HOPKINSON SMITH (1838-1915)
Six Hours in Squantico (1890) 572

MARY HALLOCK FOOTE (1847-1938)
Maverick (1894) 583

HAMLIN GARLAND (1860-1940)
The Return of a Private (1890) 598
Lucretia Burns (1893) 613

GRACE ELIZABETH KING (1851-1932)
A Drama of Three (1892) 635
La Grande Demoiselle (1893) 640

KATE CHOPIN (1851-1904)
Désirée's Baby (1894). 646
A Gentleman of Bayou Têche (1894) 651
Nég Créol (1897) 657
Suzette (1897) 662

CHARLES W. CHESNUTT (1858-1932)
Sis' Becky's Pickaninny (1899) 666

MARGARET DELAND (1857-   )
The Child's Mother (1898) 677

THOMAS ALLIBONE JANVIER (1849-1913)
The Lost Mine (1884) 703

FRANK NORRIS (1870-1902)
The Third Circle (1895) 720

WILLIAM ALLEN WHITE (1868-   )
The Story of Aqua Pura (1893) 728

RUTH McENERY STUART (1849-1917)
Aunt Delphi's Dilemma (1891) 735

CHARLES F. LUMMIS (1859-1928)
Bogged Down (1897) 744

STEPHEN CRANE (1871-1900)
A Man and—Some Others (1897) 753

VIRGINIA FRAZER BOYLE (1863-1938)
    The Triumph of Shed (1901) 767

HARRY STILLWELL EDWARDS (1855-1938)
    His Defense (1899) 776

PHILIP VERRILL MIGHELS (1869-1911)
    The Tie of Partnership (1904) 788

ALICE BROWN (1857-   )
    Mis' Wadleigh's Guest (1895) 806

HELEN R. MARTIN (1868-1939)
    Ellie's Furnishing (1903) 819

ZONA GALE (1873-1939)
    Nobody Sick, Nobody Poor (1907) 831

Appendix
    Table of Contents Arranged by Regions Represented 843

Introduction

Amerıcan fiction has portrayed with ever-increasing fidelity the native scene in its manifold variety. Every section of the United States today has its writers who with photographic accuracy are recording local topography, architecture, manners, customs, history, dialect, and character types. The New Regionalism has called forth a hundred novels, each expressive of the characteristics of the people in a given setting. Amazing differences in modes of thought, in traditions, in dialect set apart the New Englander from the Southerner and from the Westerner, the city dweller from the farmer, the old English stock from the more recent immigrants. Small cultural islands retaining Old World folkways exist within the busiest metropolis and in open rural areas. Every effort to enfold this diversity within the covers of one novel or a series of novels has thus far failed. Despite the common tie of faith in fundamental democratic doctrines, despite the standardizing influence of school, radio, and nationwide syndication of newspaper information, despite the unity of religious mood fostered by church federations, despite the tendency to wear identical "store" clothes, Americans, region to region, slip the tether of uniformity.

These divergences result from racial heritage, from community and family traditions, and from the efforts of people in particular regions to adapt themselves to their environment. Since the shaping circumstances of man's life on this vast continent are not uniform, it is inevitable that the cultural responses will vary. Even where there was no difference in racial stock, there always occurred something more than a land change when settlers departed from the wooded areas of the Appalachian highland and debouched upon the broad, treeless plains of the trans-Mississippi area. Certainly the regions of heavy rainfall in the Ohio and Mississippi valleys and in the forested watersheds of the Adirondack, Allegheny, and Great Smoky regions evoked cultural responses widely different from those in the stony regions of New England or in the prairies of the Missouri River valley. Occupations, as well as topography and heritage, created distinguishable character types, such as the miners, the solitary shepherds, the cowboys, the lumberjacks, the rivermen, and the plains farmers. The many qualities necessary for gaining a livelihood in each region form no small part in local-color portraiture.

The first successful record of this cultural diversity was made in the nineteenth century by authors whose work has been denominated *local color*. These writers, perceiving the peculiarities of a community, wrote narratives whose vitality depended largely upon accurate portrayal of this setting, upon the delineation of provincial character types, and upon the use of dialect. Although the regionalists naturally strove to comply with all the demands of fictional art, they found understanding and verisimilitude to be special requisites for success. The characters must be true to their locale; their dialect must be recorded with phonetic accuracy and yet made intelligible to the reader unfamiliar with this speech. The topographical descriptions must introduce the reader to a scene unique in landscape and atmosphere. All these qualities need not be contained within a single story; yet they should emerge in the course of a volume devoted to one community.

Local color is one type of realism, if realism be defined as a graphic delineation of actual life. It is concerned with contemporary social truth. Yet it is not a realism that professes to present the whole truth and then proceeds to reveal only the nether side of life without its compensations: its sense of humor, its homiletic tendencies, its forthrightness, and its essential neighborliness. These, too, are the truth, if only partially so, and upon these truths the local colorist seized, sometimes with sentiment, sometimes with austerity. Occasionally these narratives possess an idyllic quality; at times they are frankly unsentimental; at other times they contain the caustic ingredients perceptible in Garland's "Lucretia Burns" and in Mrs. Freeman's unadorned stories. Generally the term *local color* has denominated a surface realism delighting in oddity, whimsicality, idiosyncrasy, and in those stubborn, inbred character traits which lend themselves to comic treatment or caricature. Merit depends upon an author's knowledge, insight, and artistry. The chief limitation of local color, in practice if not as a genre, is its frequent unwillingness to front some of the unpleasant facts of life. Yet it must be said that the strongest local-color areas have been those which longest resisted change, because

they are farthest removed from the blight of industrialism; and in \
such regions tragedy, when apparent, wears a softer aspect because)
ameliorated by community sympathy. Not all writers in the form were
superficial in psychological analysis or interpretation of life. If most
of them burrowed seldom into the intricacies of abnormal psychology,
they at least tried to give to their chronicles a touch of sympathy and
a regional atmosphere. The more commonplace the facts, the better
the local colorists liked them. "Evidently," wrote William Dean
Howells, "they believed that there was a poetry under the rude outside of their mountaineers, their slattern country wives, their shy
rustic men and maids, their grotesque humorists, their wild religion-
ists, even their black freedmen. . . . The range of this work is so
great as to include even pictures of the more conventional life, but
mainly the writers keep to the life which is not conventional, the life
of the fields, the woods, the cabin, the village, the little country town."

Commonest among the fictional practices of the local colorist is the
employment of an atmospheric setting which, although clearly related to the action and to characterization, intensifies both, and becomes a positive force in the narrative. Recognizing that many stories
are original only in their setting, those authors who made a direct
study of a neighborhood or who allowed their imaginations to picture
convincingly what the eye could not see, found in the selection and
arrangement of atmospheric detail a principle of emphasis from which
the truly local emerged. Thus environmental features were presented
not only for the purpose of stimulating interest, but also to add to the
forces influencing action and to produce a harmony between characters and their background. Sometimes the landscape assumed a greater
importance than the individual protagonists. When this overempha-
sis occurred, as it did in some early place stories, plot was submerged
and the narrative framework became a skeleton upon which to festoon
scenic effects. Certain early local colorists earned for the school a reputation for sheer connoisseurship in the exhibition of unusual material
or regions. Yet, with the realization that external background is justified only as it provides objective reality for the whole story, most
writers agreed with James Lane Allen that "fiction is not the proper
literary form in which to furnish the reader miscellaneous information of flora, climate, and other scientific features of an unknown
region."

The local colorist, simply because he had his eye upon a particular
locale, did not forget that he was under a reasonable necessity of
telling a good story and of creating vitalized characters. Although
the aim of the occasional local colorists did not always include the

invention of breathless narrative, nor demand loving devotion to incident, there was, in matters of plot, no general relaxation of literary
discipline. Not infrequently these writers liked slow-moving pieces or
restricted themselves to limited plot ingredients. An affinity seemed
to exist, as in Sarah Orne Jewett's *Country By-Ways,* between the
local-color story and the sketch. Yet the besetting temptation of the
regionalist to write sketches rather than close-grained stories arose
partly from a tendency noticeable from the first emergence of the form
in the work of Washington Irving, Catherine M. Sedgwick, and
James Hall. The artistic limitation resulting from the wedding of the
sketch and the tale was a weakness of the age, not one of the form.
Springing originally from a fictional period that did not distinguish
between short story and tale, the short story competed through much
of the nineteenth century with tales that substituted emotionalism for
scenery and plot. As the concept of plot improved, the local-color
story improved with it; in this respect local color was neither ahead
nor behind other forms.

Dialect has been used, to a greater or less extent, in all local-color
literatures since Sir Walter Scott pointed the way in his Scottish
stories. Variations in a dialect from the standard language include
provincial words, peculiar speech turns involving unfamiliar sentence
patterns and fresh imagery, and lapses from standard grammatical
forms. The following sentences from Mary Noailles Murfree's
"Taking the Blue Ribbon at the County Fair" illustrate some of
these peculiarities:

> " 'When I goes a-huntin' up yander ter Pine Lick, they is mighty perlite
> to me. They ain't never done nothin' ag'in me, ez I knows on. . . . Nor
> hev they said nothin' ag'in me, nuther.'
> "Cynthia took up her side: 'That thar Becky Stiles, she's got the freckled-
> est face—ez freckled ez any turkey-aig.' "

Or from Annie Trumbull Slosson's "A Local Colorist":

> "He said just what anybody anywheres that had took notice of the clouds
> would say, that it was goin' to be catchin' weather like the day afore, when
> he got soppin' wet over to the medder lot, and he cal'lated 'twould keep
> on thataway till the moon fulled. ' 'Tany rate,' he says, 'it's growthy weather
> for grass.' "

The first illustration is from Tennessee highlander talk, while the
latter is from Vermont. Once the reader has caught the mannerism,
little difficulty hinders an understanding of the words. In some of the
dialects, like the Louisiana Creole and the Pennsylvania German,

words are introduced from foreign languages; their meaning is made clear either through the context or by immediate translation. These words are inserted with sufficient frequency to lend piquancy and the appearance of verisimilitude to the narrative, the total number in any one story being small. The Negro dialects vary greatly because of the different origins of the speakers and partly because of the different national backgrounds of the white people with whom the Negroes have been in contact. Since the reader will take pleasure in recognizing dialects heard in conversation with natives of the various regions, it is not necessary here to enter upon the fascinating study of the many variations. Most of the stories in this volume reflect the linguistic individuality of the locale; in some communities the changes wrought by time have tended to alter the dialect from that here recorded, but by and large these provincial speech manners still exist.

Local color achieved wide popular acceptance only after Bret Harte's stories in 1870 enthralled an East unacquainted with the true conditions of Western mining camps, but a long background prepared the way for that acclaim, many forces contributing to the success of the movement which had had a generation of growth. Immediately after the Revolution a nationalistic spirit demanded a native literature by and about the people of the United States. The dramatists succeeded first; patriotic Americans strutted the stage continuously after 1787. Yet in spite of the example offered by the drama of native character types, no writer of prose fiction succeeded in achieving a satisfying Americanism until James Fenimore Cooper published *The Spy* (1821). Washington Irving's transplanted German legends, containing generalized descriptions of the Hudson River valley, gave impetus to landscape description and to the search for character types recognizable as native. Cooper, however, effectively demonstrated the feasibility of preparing narratives descriptive of everyday American life; although he wrote in a romantic mood, he paved the way for a vast literature of historical fiction founded upon American political and social experience.

Foreign models supplied techniques and patterns for the delineation of American life. Irving, Hawthorne, and Poe made good use of German materials; Cooper adapted Sir Walter Scott's devices of historical pageantry, topographical description, local character portrayal, and dialect; Catherine Maria Sedgwick frankly imitated Maria Edgeworth's *Castle Rackrent* (1800) and *Moral Tales for Young People* (1801), which pictured society by contrasting social virtues and vices; the humanized English countryside in Mary Mitford's *Our Village* (1824-1832) received a satirical sea change in the work of Caroline M. Kirkland. Later the methods of Charles Dickens were adopted by Harriet Beecher Stowe and Bret Harte, and in the 1880's Thomas Hardy's interweaving of setting and character, a formula borrowed by Mary Noailles Murfree, led to the representation of "subliminal influences of terrain and atmosphere." Since all art possesses both pattern and theme, and since theme is of more importance than pattern, emphasis should not be placed so much upon the influence of these oversea models as upon the native impulses compelling American writers to keep their eyes on the homeland in search of native materials.

Sir Walter Scott's formulae dominated early nineteenth-century serious fiction and led to imitation in three directions: first, the search for legends and traditions which could be localized on American streams, or in caves, or in hillside fastnesses; second, the search for American regions which could be portrayed with quaintness or distinction; and, third, a fictional representation of America's past. As a result a large body of legends, both foreign and native in origin, soon clustered about the Passaic, the Housatonic, and the Mohawk rivers, much as the Hudson River had been invested with a folklore borrowed from Germany by Irving. The whole area of Indian legend was explored by James Athearn Jones, William J. Snelling, William Gilmore Simms, Charles Fenno Hoffman, Henry R. Schoolcraft, and others. These tales, being largely unlocalized survivals of romantic imagination, have not been represented in this volume; yet their part was large in the development of a self-conscious national literature. Cooper's Scott-like regional scenic painting tended toward vastness and indefiniteness. Miss Sedgwick in *A New England Tale* (1822) successfully delineated the mountain country of Western Massachusetts and pointed the way to a blending of character with precise topographical background. Timothy Flint, James Hall, Morgan Neville, and William Leggett wrote colorful stories of the frontier settlements in the Ohio River valley. Albert Pike pictured Indians, Mexicans, and Americans in the Taos-Santa Fe district of New Mexico. James Kirke Paulding, chief tale-writer of the early thirties, though too devoted to supernatural ingredients and to digressions, sought to advance American types and homespun qualities in tales of Yankee schoolmasters, burghers of Nieuw Amsterdam, and Dutch damsels. Augustus Baldwin Longstreet humorously chronicled low life in Georgia. In *Swallow Barn* (1832) John Pendleton Kennedy traced the descent of the Virginia plantation from the feudal system in essay-sketches about lordly gentlemen surrounded by faithful dependents. In Cincinnati in 1834 Harriet Beecher Stowe won a story contest with "A New England Sketch," a dialect tale foreshadowing her later local-color writings. By 1835 the areas open for fictional exploitation and the native types were being charted by early local colorists.

Yet Scott's influence, as well as a continuous nationalistic enthusiasm, set writers delving into America's past to chronicle incidents in the early settlements and, especially, events in the American Revolution. Of the fourteen hundred books of fiction published before 1850, fully two thirds are historical in substance and most of these relate to the Revolution. Hawthorne, true to the romantic literary ideals of his generation, gave a Scott-like setting to *Fanshawe* (1827), and in his later writings placed most of his stories in the gloomy Puritan past. His fidelity to details of architecture, costume, and topography paralleled the verisimilitude sought by the local colorists. Historical novelists, while playing fast and loose with incident, accurately limned regional customs and unconsciously assisted in fostering a literature descriptive of contemporary manners. Best of these novels was Sylvester Judd's *Margaret* (1845), set in the period following the Revolution; despite a sermonic base it captured the flavor of New England's rural activities in a language saturated with dialect and queer turns of speech. James Russell Lowell's *Biglow Papers* (1848), dialect poems on contemporary political themes, earned critical sanction of dialect; later as editor of *The Atlantic Monthly* Lowell published many local-color stories and gave critical support to the movement.

While an increasingly large number of historical novelists was delving into the past, a faithful transcript of daily life in the United States was being prepared by agents humbler than these serious writers. Most stimulating, possibly, in sending patriots to their mirrors were the accounts of American customs as detailed by amused foreign travelers. As early as 1795 were printed samples of the various dialects which Noah Webster had lamented as "objects of reciprocal ridicule in the different States." These travelers guffawed over our alleged unintelligible speech, boorish manners, inadequate hotel accommodations, amazing democratic social system, careless dress, spare diet, and general intellectual insufficiency; they sneered at paltry humans dwelling in majestic scenery. In self-defense Americans sketched their native land in colors as favorable as those of Dickens and Mrs. Martineau were hostile. James K. Paulding's *Letters from the South* (1817), Timothy Flint's *Recollections of Ten Years in the Valley of the Mississippi* (1826), David Crockett's *Tour to the North and Down East* (1835), Eliza W. Farnam's *Life in the Prairie Land* (1846), and Frederick Law Olmsted's *A Journey Through Texas* (1857) typify the variety of writings designed to familiarize Americans with their own land. Government reports on exploring expeditions into the Far West lent impetus to the movement, for John C. Frémont's vivid narratives, in addition to their geographical, botanical, and zoological data, recited many thrilling encounters with Indians and also gave the first characterization of the noted hunter, Kit Carson. Somewhat similar was the immigration propaganda issued by states, land companies, and railroads to entice Easterners to settle in the land of golden opportunity. Although, as in *Illinois in 1839,* much of this writing aimed only to present favorable pictures of a little-known territory, it sharpened public awareness of the diversity of America.

Many tales and novels were composed to rebut Eastern prejudices against Western backwoodsmen and Southern slaveowners. John L. M'Connel in *The Glenns* (1851) portrayed ordinary life in Texas to overcome the detraction this State suffered from wild west yarns which gave the impression of a population of bandits, cutthroats, and untamable savages. *"The Mysteries of the Backwoods* [1845] has one object," declared Thomas Bangs Thorpe; "an effort has been made, in the course of these sketches, to give to those personally unacquainted with the scenery of the Southwest some idea of the country, of its surface and vegetation. In these matters the author has endeavored to be critically correct, indulging in the honest ambition of giving some information, as well as to lighten the lagging moments of a dull hour." In the preface to *Legends of the West* (1832), James Hall wrote: "The sole intention of the tales comprised in the following pages is to convey accurate descriptions of the scenery and population of the country in which the author resides." In Southern areas, especially after *Uncle Tom's Cabin* (1852), many attempts at a correction of Northern misconceptions were made. In *Marcus Warland* (1852) Caroline Lee Hentz stated: "If the domestic manners of the South were more generally and more thoroughly known at the North, the prejudices that have been gradually building up a wall of separation between these two divisions of our land would yield to the irresistible force of conviction." Through fiction the sprawling nation could learn the distinctive traits of its many sections and, through this increased awareness, prevent some of the misunderstanding which placed one region in opposition to another.

Possibly of greatest significance in the development of the local-color story pattern was the humorous literature of the tall-tale variety, which extended from the Down-East stories of Seba Smith to the humorous yarns of the Old Southwest. Early in the nineteenth century there emerged in the comic stories printed in almanacs and newspapers several distinct character types: the lean, lathy New England

Yankee, distinguished by the nasal twang of his speech and by cheating ways as a peddler or trader; the slow, taciturn, fat Holland Dutch burghers in New York State; the Pennsylvania Germans, wedded to cleanliness, good farming, parsimony, and superstitious beliefs; the Kentucky frontiersman, apt with rifle and liquor jug, fond of brawls, and bragging of exploits in dealing with wilderness creatures; the Virginia (and Southern) gentleman devoted to gambling, cock-fighting, and horse racing, and possessing elegant company manners in the presence of ladies, although a notorious domestic tyrant at home; the Irish immigrant, ignorant and easily imposed upon but shrewd in extricating himself when caught in escapades; and the Negro, faithful, jolly, religious, and musical. Later, as the nation expanded westward, the riverboatman, prairie dweller, squatter, trapper, Indian hater, bee hunter, miner, railroader, country doctor, schoolmaster, itinerant preacher-evangelist, wandering actor, country lawyer, and the callous mortgage holder emerged as distinct American types. About each of these types there clustered tales of extravagant action phrased in dialect. Here is a sample of Western tall talk about the daughter of Mike Fink, the famous riverman:

SAL FINK, THE MISSISSIPPI SCREAMER

I dar say you've all on you, if not more, frequently heerd this great she human crittur boasted of, an' pointed out as *"one o' the gals"*—but I tell you what, stranger, you have never really set your eyes on *"one o' the gals,"* till you have seen Sal Fink, the Mississippi screamer, whose miniature pictur I have here give, about as nat'ral as life, but not half as handsome— an' if thar ever was a gal that desarved to be christen—"one o' the gals," then this gal was that gal—and no mistake.

She fought a duel once with a thunderbolt, an' came off without a single scratch, while at the fust fire she split the thunderbolt all to flinders, an' gave the pieces to Uncle Sam's artillerymen, to touch off their cannon with. When a gal about six years old, she used to play see-saw on the Mississippi snags, and arter she were done she would snap 'em off, an' so cleared a large district of the river. She used to ride down the river on an alligator's back, standen upright, an' dancing *Yankee Doodle,* and could leave all the steamers behind. But the greatest feat she ever did, positively outdid anything that ever was did.

One day when she war out in the forest, making a collection o' wild cat skins for her family's winter beddin, she was captered in the most all-sneaken manner by about fifty Injuns, an' carried by 'em to Roast Flesh Hollow, whar the blood-drinkin' wild varmints datarmined to skin her alive, sprinkle a leetle salt over her, an' devour her before her own eyes; so they took an' tied her to a tree, to keep till mornin' should bring the rest o' thar ring-nosed sarpents to enjoy the fun. Arter that, they lit a large fire in the Holler, turned the bottom o' thar feet towards the blaze, Injun fashion, and went to sleep to dream o' thar mornin's feast; well, after the critturs got into a somniferous snore, Sal got into an all-lightnin' of a temper, and burst all the ropes about her like an apron-string! She then found a pile o' ropes, too, and tied all the Injuns' heels together all round the fire,—then fixin' a cord to the shins of every two couple, she, with a suddenachous jerk, that made the intire woods tremble, pulled the intire lot o' sleepin' red-skins into that ar great fire, fast together, an' then sloped like a panther out of her pen, in the midst o' the tallest yellin', howlin', scramblin' and singin', that war ever seen or heerd on, since the great burnin' o' Buffalo prairie!

The basis of this yarn is an anecdote, enlarged with joyous hyperbole by men sitting around campfires, riding slow river boats, or loafing in taverns. Exaggeration, unexpected word coinage, deliberate malapropism, dialect, and egregious misspelling combine to secure a comic effect. This form of humor, developed with conversation and description, became immensely popular; full-length character sketches were formed, as in the David Crockett legend, by the union of many incidents.

One other humor device frequently used by the dialect writers is the "horse-sense aphorism," a sententious utterance rich in homely, Franklinian wisdom pronounced by an uneducated or illiterate speaker. "Josh Billings" (Henry Wheeler Shaw) was the best of the one-sentence humorists, and the following examples illustrate the form:

"Natur never makes enny blunders; when she makes a phool she means it."

"I luv tew see an old person joyfull but not kickuptheheelsfull."

"A kicking cow never lets drive until just as the pail gets phull,—it is jiss so with sum mens blunders."

"Pity costs nothing,—and ain't wuth nothing."

Similar sentences stud the speech of strong characters in local-color stories. Although such pithiness is natural to quaint persons, the comparative absence of similar remarks in non-dialect fiction suggests the influence here of our native humor tradition.

This employment of humor in short tales was widespread in the mid-forties when frontier volumes by T. B. Thorpe, John S. Robb, Johnson J. Hooper, and others were issuing from the press of T. B. Peterson and Brothers in Philadelphia. Such humorists, with their tall tales, elaborate yarns, and droll touches, presented enough patterns of existence to make their works quite adequate pictures of regional pe-

culiarities in the South and the Southwest. In New England a similar
mixture of humor and social material was perceptible. When, as in
the case of J. W. McClintock and W. E. Burton, humor concerned
itself with local life and activities, the bridge to the purely regional
story was completed. That local color was not merely a handmaid
to humor became apparent in Harriet Beecher Stowe's *Mayflower*
(1843), a volume of stories almost wholly devoted to a formal presentation of manners in the aristocratic strata of New England society.
Two years later Caroline Matilda Kirkland combined humor and
satire in her pictures of the early Michigan settlements in *Western
Clearings* (1845). James Hall added three new tales to older frontier
material in *Wilderness and Warpath* (1846).

In the 1850's American fiction became vigorously aware of the contemporary scene; then began the vogue of stories describing local manners, customs, and incidents. Remarkable for its minute knowledge of
every phase of New York City is Cornelius Matthews's *Money-Penny*
(1850). Harriet Beecher Stowe dramatized life on a Southern plantation and provoked a dozen other writers to attempt the description
of the same scene; her *The Minister's Wooing* (1859), with its plain,
earthy characters, portrayed the warm hearts of Puritans in New
England. Day Kellogg Lee's *Merrimack, or Life at the Loom* (1854)
pictured factory life in a thriving, bustling, crowded, dusty, spinning
and weaving city. A romantic plot does not hide the salty actuality of
Joseph Reynolds's *Peter Gott, the Cape Ann Fisherman* (1856). Short
stories shared in this celebration of local areas. Despite its senti-
mentality Alice Cary's *Clovernook* (1851) touched vividly on many
village and rural attitudes. Charles Webber's *Tales of the Southern
Border* (1852), Caroline M. Kirkland's *Sketches of Western Life*
(1852), Joseph G. Baldwin's *Flush Times in Georgia* (1853), J. L.
M'Connel's *Western Characters* (1853), and Seba Smith's *'Way Down
East* (1854), when placed beside Irving's *Wolfert's Roost* (1855), demonstrate the great advance made in native fiction since the appearance
of *The Sketch-Book* (1819), and how true in 1853 was the dictum of
Putnam's Magazine: "Local reality is a point of utmost importance."
An event of significance in the development of local materials was
the founding late in the decade of *The Atlantic Monthly* under the
editorship of James Russell Lowell, who proved especially encouraging to the regionalists. The local-color story was, like all American
short stories, including those of Hawthorne, Poe, and Stockton, more
or less dependent upon publication facilities, for development in short
fiction came only· with expansion in the magazine field. Thus the

early domestic and frontier stories appeared first in the gift-books and early magazines, such as Hall's *Illinois Monthly Magazine* and Buckingham's *New England Magazine;* later, they found their way into *The Atlantic Monthly, Scribner's Monthly, Harper's New Monthly,* and *The Century.* This reliance upon the magazine was markedly true in 1857; Richard Malcolm Johnston published in *The Spirit of the Times* his "The Goosepond School"; Rose Terry contributed "Uncle Josh" to *Putnam's Magazine;* and for *The Atlantic* she wrote eight stories that attempted directness of opening, lively naturalness of dialogue, and a sense of local reality.

Even the Civil War did not impede the progress toward realism in the 1860's. Rebecca Harding Davis's "Life in the Iron Mills" (1861) and *Margaret Howth* (1862) describe industrial communities in Western Pennsylvania. Harriet Elizabeth Prescott departed once from her conventional romantic method to write a local-color story of New England, "Knitting Sale-Socks" (1861). Bayard Taylor portrayed the intense spirituality of Quakers in "Friend Eli's Daughter" (1862) and in *Hannah Thurston* (1863); of the latter he said, "I do not, therefore, rest the interest of the book on its slender plot, but on the fidelity with which it represents certain types of character and phases of society." Rural New England continued to be the popular setting for stories by Rose Terry, Elizabeth Barstow Stoddard, Louisa M. Alcott, and John T. Trowbridge; and Charles Nordhoff described fishermen's experiences in the stories of *Cape Cod and All Along the Shore* (1868). In martial fiction, the local was not forgotten. The Civil War called forth numerous novels by John W. DeForest, Sidney Lanier, John Esten Cooke, and other writers. These partisan tales, despite romantic fustian, present a social history of the sincerity animating both armies, and of the fumbling, corruption, and inefficiency undermining the success of both contestants.

The 1860's reached an astonishing climax in the stories of Bret Harte. Although Harte trod in the footsteps of many predecessors, he focused attention upon the short story as a medium for regional portraiture and enjoyed the distinction of being widely imitated in this country and abroad. "The Luck of Roaring Camp" in *The Atlantic Monthly* for August, 1868, fascinated the East, since this story was set in the comparatively unknown gold-mining area of the Sierra Nevada Mountains. Harte's material was absolutely new; it consisted of the coarse, lower phases of life in a region where the decencies of social restraint had been released and where only the law of human necessity imposed a check upon depravity. "Power of contrast in characterization, skill in heightening effects, the perception of oddity, combined with a happy faculty of engrafting it upon the recognized human types, the keen sense of humor of a new sort—a kind of devil's humor suited to the diabolism of the surroundings, a tender feeling for the essential goodness of the human heart, running over with the gospel of grace into the very mouth of the pit,—these were the chief qualities of the new writer. They were all Dickensy; yet original observation, impressibility, and a fine power of imitation had given them an individuality that was helped out by the wholly new atmosphere of the mining slopes." [1] Yet Harte never grew in power, intellectual depth, or in psychological insight; *The Luck of Roaring Camp* (1870), *Mrs. Skagg's Husbands* (1873), and *Tales of the Argonauts* (1875) differ only in freshness from *Colonel Starbottle's Client* (1892) and *Stories in Light and Shadow* (1898). He had discovered new fictional territory, but he was unable to do more than skim the surface of its possibilities.

Following Harte's success, writers in the 1870's delved into almost every area of the United States; with considerable minuteness and with no small amount of humor they sketched every layer of society. Sarah Orne Jewett touched the out-of-way customs and local scenery in the neighborhood of Berwick, Maine. George Washington Cable found in Creole Louisiana a quaintness hitherto unrevealed in American fiction. Adirondack characters were pictured by Philander Deming. Constance Fenimore Woolson portrayed the forested shores of Lake Michigan and Mackinac Island. Later Miss Woolson wrote of Ohio and the South; her work demonstrates both the ease with which authors on summer visits gathered fresh materials for story backgrounds, and the ultimate artistic inadequacy of fiction whose unique setting fails to contribute to the shaping of human lives.

Local color was not the sole literary tradition in the years after 1870, for such masters of technique as Aldrich, Twain, Howells, and Henry James were producing notable examples of the novel of manners. Yet it was the local-color group which continuously insisted upon including "poor, dear, real life" in all its phases in their stories. The 1880's became especially significant for fullness of national portraiture. The novels include Henry James's *Washington Square* (1881) and *The Bostonians* (1886); William Dean Howells's *A Modern Instance* (1882), *The Rise of Silas Lapham* (1885), and *A Hazard of New Fortunes* (1889); Mark Twain's *The Adventures of Huckleberry Finn* (1884); and Helen Hunt Jackson's *Ramona* (1884). In the

[1] James Herbert Morse, "The Native Element in American Fiction," *The Century Illustrated Monthly Magazine* (July, 1883), XXVI, 364.

same decade came Twain's *Life on the Mississippi* (1883) with its numerous isolated episodes of river life. Short stories meanwhile gained new dignity and popularity. Joel Chandler Harris's *Uncle Remus* (1880) gave scientific precision to the recording of Negro dialect; a similar accuracy prevails in his later volumes about white mountaineers in Georgia. Sarah Orne Jewett published *The Mate of the Daylight* (1883), and Rose Terry Cooke began the collection of her stories with *Somebody's Neighbors* (1881). Katherine McDowell imitated Harte in *Dialect Tales* (1883). Mary Noailles Murfree ("Charles Egbert Craddock") in *In the Tennessee Mountains* (1884) utilized the scenery of the Great Smokies with such seriousness that in these stories, as with Egdon Heath in Thomas Hardy's *The Return of the Native,* the mountains acquired the force of a character.

The year 1887 marked a high point in the publication of volumes of local-color stories, for then appeared Thomas Nelson Page's *In Ole Virginia,* idylls of aristocratic plantation life; Mary E. Wilkins Freeman's *A Humble Romance,* austere, controlled studies of cramped lives in New England; Rowland E. Robinson's *Uncle Lisha's Shop,* a humorous depiction of Vermonters' idiosyncrasies in the 1840's; Alice French's ("Octave Thanet") *Knitters in the Sun,* pictures of crude life in the canebrakes of Arkansas; Esther Bernon Carpenter's *South County Neighbors,* drab stories of Rhode Island; and Joel Chandler Harris's *Free Joe, and Other Georgian Sketches.*

From 1887 to 1900 more than a hundred volumes of local-color stories were published. Each of the authors mentioned above published one or more additional volumes, and many stories remain uncollected in magazines. Meanwhile new figures and new areas engaged the attention of the public. Continuing the New England tradition were Annie Trumbull Slosson and Alice Brown. New York City became the setting of stories by Henry Cuyler Bunner, Brander Matthews, Thomas Janvier, and Richard Harding Davis. F. Hopkinson Smith provided stories of New Jersey and Virginia. In North Carolina, Charles W. Chesnutt recounted authentic Negro folk superstitions, and Mary Carter wrote stories about poor whites. James Lane Allen and John Fox drew upon Kentucky for stories and character types that differed widely in mood and quality. In Georgia, William N. Harben and Maurice Thompson related stories about the mountaineers, while Harry Stillwell Edwards, with a broadly humorous touch, wrote tales of plantation life. In Louisiana, Grace Elizabeth King revised Cable's unfavorable interpretation of the Creoles, Kate Chopin realistically described the 'Cajans, and Ruth McEnery Stuart portrayed the less aristocratic inhabitants. The vast wheat country found a recorder in Hamlin Garland, whose two volumes of short stories exemplified the author's new literary theory, veritism, which demonstrated that local color, if not always realistic, is not opposed to realism. Distinctive, particularly in the blending of romantic history with local color, was Mary Hartwell Catherwood, who reintroduced the area of Mackinac and conveyed the spirit of early Illinois towns. Bret Harte kept the California slopes in the minds of readers by frequent publications; in 1892 he was joined by Gertrude Atherton in a slender volume, *Before the Gringo Came*. Other areas new and old were described: Davenport, Iowa, by Alice French; Idaho and the army camps by Mary Hallock Foote; Chinatown in San Francisco by Chester Bailey Fernald; the Puget Sound country by Ella Higginson; the arid West by Charles F. Lummis and Thomas A. Janvier.

In the years immediately after 1900 the temporary enthusiasm for historical romance caused a decline in the bulk of local-color fiction; yet the impulse of the movement was so strong that some new areas were added to the local-color picture: the cod fishing banks by J. B. Connolly; the Pennsylvania Deitsch by Helen R. Martin and Elsie Singmaster; Ontario by Herman Whitaker; Wisconsin by Zona Gale; Alaska by Jack London; Chicago by George Ade; Cape Cod by Joseph Crosby Lincoln. By 1920 local color was modified by the new mood of intense realism in such books as Willa Cather's *O Pioneers!* (1913) and *My Ántonia* (1918), Sherwood Anderson's *Winesburg, Ohio* (1919), Zona Gale's *Miss Lulu Bett* (1920), and Sinclair Lewis's *Main Street* (1920). Social motives now dominate fiction; authors write to support theses rather than to photograph a group of people against a setting. Yet these realistic stories, as well as recent Regionalist fiction—the novels of Mary Ellen Chase, Walter D. Edmonds, Marjorie Kinnan Rawlings, Walter S. Campbell ("Stanley Vestal"), H. L. Davis, among others—indicate clearly the progressive advance of our writers in achieving satisfactory patterns to portray American life minutely. Constantly at war with the realistic impulse has been that of unlocalized romance, airy nothing without a habitation or a name. In the history of American letters these two forces have always opposed each other, but it is interesting to note that, with very few exceptions, works achieving a lasting quality have survived in no small part because of their fidelity to a given locality. The New Regionalism, by applying the now acceptable technique of frank realism to the history, traditions, and character types of the many sections of the United States, is adding to the descriptive and dialect accuracy of the early regionalists deeper psychological insight, fuller portraiture, and high seriousness. The older regionalism, with less reliance upon folklore and without a program for enlightened sectionalism (the chief difference between the two), played its adequate part in making possible the full-bodied fiction of our own day.

II

In making selections for this volume the editors thoroughly examined the whole body of local-color fiction and chose the following sixty-three stories by thirty-eight authors to illustrate the history and form of this literary type. Although it has been impossible to represent every area and every author, preference has been given to those writers whose achievement is relatively high. Regretfully omitted are Indian legends and tales of Indian life; a comprehensive collection alone would afford adequate space for the part the Indian has played in our literature. Omitted also are verse local-color narratives; here, too, is a genre deserving a special volume. The omission of tales by Irving, Hawthorne, Poe, Twain, Howells, and Henry James, among others, must be justified on the ground that, in general, their approach to the art of fiction was not that of the local colorist. Hamlin Garland's stories appear here because his realism seems to fall within the bounds of local color. Drawing lines between the various moods in storytelling is difficult; the reader may take pleasure in testing how far each of these stories is romantic and how far each is realistic. A comparison of Zona Gale's local-color *Friendship Village* (1909) with her later realistic *Miss Lulu Bett* (1920) will indicate how fluid is narrative art and how helplessly the critic stands holding a yardstick.

An attempt has been made to portray each of the main sections of the United States, and, to facilitate the reader's tour of the various geographical areas, a table of contents arranged according to the settings of the stories has been added to the volume. Punctuation and spellings in all dialect passages have been maintained as found in the original texts.

JAMES HALL

★ ★ ★

Frontier life in Illinois, particularly of the French and English settlers, is graphically delineated in tales and sketches by James Hall (1793-1868) who, as editor of annuals and magazines, fostered the preparation of a local literature descriptive of the Ohio River Valley. Fidelity to fact and to the traditions of the people were his chief claim to merit, yet he romanticized his characters much as did James Fenimore Cooper. Born in Philadelphia and educated at home, Hall rejected a mercantile career for the law, served with distinction as an officer in the War of 1812, and, settling in 1820 in Shawneetown, Illinois, rose to be a circuit judge and state treasurer. His years after 1832 were spent in Cincinnati. "The French Village" is from *Legends of the West* (1832). His non-fictional books include *Letters from the West* (1828) and *Sketches of History, Life, and Manners in the West* (1834-1835).

★ ★ ★

The French Village

ON the borders of the Mississippi may be seen the remains of an old French village, which once boasted a numerous population of as happy and as thoughtless souls, as ever danced to a violin. If content is wealth, as philosophers would fain persuade us, they were opulent; but they would have been reckoned miserably poor by those who estimate worldly riches by the more popular standard. Their houses were scattered in disorder, like the tents of a wandering tribe, along the margin of a deep bayou, and not far from its confluence with the river, between which and the town was a strip of rich alluvion, covered with a gigantic growth of forest trees. Beyond the bayou was a swamp, which during the summer heats was nearly dry, but in the rainy season presented a vast lake of several miles in extent. The whole of this morass was thickly set with cypress whose interwoven branches, and close foliage, excluded the sun, and rendered this as gloomy a spot as the most melancholy poet ever dreamt of. And yet it was not tenantless—and there were seasons, when its dark recesses were enlivened by notes peculiar to itself. Here the young Indian, not yet entrusted to wield the tomahawk, might be seen paddling his light canoe among the tall weeds, darting his arrows at the paroquets, that chattered among the boughs, and screaming and laughing with delight, as he stripped their gaudy plumage. Here myriads of musquitoes filled the air with an incessant hum, and thousands of frogs attuned their voices in harmonious concert, as if endeavouring to rival the sprightly fiddles of their neighbours; and the owl, peeping out from the hollow of a blasted tree, screeched forth his wailing note, as if moved by the terrific energy of grief. From this gloomy spot, clouds of miasm rolled over the village, spreading volumes of bile and fever abroad upon the land; and sometimes countless multitudes of musquitoes, issuing from the humid desert, assailed the devoted village with inconceivable fury, threatening to draw from its inhabitants every drop of French blood, which yet circulated in their veins. But these evils by no means dismayed, or even interrupted the gaiety, of this happy people. When the musquitoes came, the monsieurs lighted their pipes, and kept up, not only a brisk fire, but a dense smoke, against the assailants; and when the fever threatened, the priest, who was also the doctor, flourished his lancet, the fiddler flourished his bow, and the happy villagers flourished their heels, and sang, and laughed, and fairly cheated death, disease, and the doctor, of patient and of prey.

Beyond the town, on the other side, was an extensive prairie—a vast unbroken plain of rich green, embellished with innumerable flowers of every tint, and whose beautiful surface presented no other variety than here and there a huge mound—the venerable monument of departed ages, or a solitary tree of stunted growth, shattered by the blast, and pining alone in the gay desert. The prospect was bounded by a range of tall bluffs, which overlooked the prairie, covered at some points with grooves of timber, and at others exhibiting their naked sides, or high, bald peaks, to the eye of the beholder. Herds of deer might be seen here at sun-rise, slyly retiring to their coverts, after rioting away the night on the rich pasturage. Here the lowing kine lived, if not in clover, at least in something equally nutritious; and here might be seen immense droves of French ponies, roaming untamed, the common stock of the village, ready to be reduced to servitude, by any lady or gentleman who chose to take the trouble.

With their Indian neighbours, the inhabitants had maintained a cordial intercourse, which had never yet been interrupted by a single act of aggression on either side. It is worthy of remark, that the French have invariably been more successful in securing the confidence and affection of the Indian tribes than any other nation. Others have had leagues with them, which, for a time, have been faithfully observed; but the French alone have won them to the familiar intercourse of social life, lived with them in the mutual interchange of kindness; and by treating them as friends and equals, gained their entire confidence. This result, which has been attributed to the sagacious policy of their government, is perhaps more owing to the conciliatory manners of that amiable people, and the absence among them of that insatiable avarice, that boundless ambition, that reckless prodigality of human life, that unprincipled disregard of public and solemn leagues, which, in the conquests of the British and the Spaniards, have marked their footsteps with misery, and blood, and desolation.

This little colony was composed partly of emigrants from France, and partly of natives—not Indians—but *bonâ fide* French, born in America; but preserving their language, their manners, and their agility in dancing, although several generations had passed away since their first settlement. Here they lived perfectly happy, and well they might, for they enjoyed to the full extent those three blessings on which our declaration of independence has laid so much stress— life, liberty, and the pursuit of happiness. Their lives, it is true, were sometimes threatened by the miasm aforesaid; but this was soon ascertained to be an imaginary danger. For whether it was owing to their temperance, or their cheerfulness, or their activity, or to their being acclimated, or to the want of attraction between French people and fever, or to all these together; certain it is, that they were blest with a degree of health, only enjoyed by the most favoured nations. As to liberty, the wild Indian scarcely possessed more; for although the "grand monarque" had not more loyal subjects in his wide domains, he had never condescended to honour them with a single act of oppression, unless the occasional visits of the commandant could be so called; who sometimes, when levying supplies, called upon the village for its portion, which they always contributed with many protestations of gratitude for the honour conferred on them. And as for happiness, they pursued nothing else. Inverting the usual order, to enjoy life was their daily business, to provide for its wants an occasional labour, sweetened by its brief continuance, and its abundant fruit. They had a large tract of land around the village, which was called the "common field," because it belonged to the community. Most of this was allowed to remain in open pasturage; but spots of it were cultivated by any who chose to enclose them; and such enclosure gave a firm title to the individual so long as the occupancy lasted, but no longer. They were not an agricultural people, further than the rearing of a few esculents for the table made them such; relying chiefly on their large herds, and on the produce of the chase for support. With the Indians they drove an amicable, though not an extensive, trade, for furs and peltry; giving them in exchange, merchandize and trinkets, which they procured from their country-men at St. Louis. To the latter place, they annually carried their skins, bringing back a fresh supply of goods for barter, together with such articles as their own wants required; not forgetting a large portion of finery for the ladies, a plentiful supply of rosin and catgut for the fiddler, and liberal presents for his reverence, the priest.

If this village had no other recommendation, it is endeared to my recollection, as the birth-place and residence of Monsieur Baptiste Menou, who was one of its principal inhabitants, when I first visited it. He was a bachelor of forty, a tall, lank, hard-featured personage, as straight as a ramrod, and almost as thin, with stiff, black hair, sunken cheeks, and a complexion, a tinge darker than that of the Aborigines. His person was remarkably erect, his countenance grave, his gait deliberate; and when to all this be added an enormous pair of sable whiskers, it will be admitted that Monsieur Baptiste was no insignificant person. He had many estimable qualities of mind and body which endeared him to his friends, whose respect was increased by the fact of his having been a soldier and a traveller. In his youth he had followed the French commandant in two campaigns; and not a comrade in the ranks was better dressed, or cleaner shaved on parade than Baptiste, who fought besides with the characteristic bravery of the nation to which he owed his lineage. He acknowledged, however, that war was not as pleasant a business as is generally supposed. Accustomed to a life totally free from constraint, the discipline of the camp ill accorded with his desultory habits. He complained of being obliged to eat, and drink, and sleep, at the call of the drum. Burnishing a gun, and brushing a coat, and polishing shoes, were duties beneath a gentleman, and after all, Baptiste saw but little honour in tracking the wily Indians through endless swamps. Besides, he began to have some scruples, as to the propriety of cutting the throats of the respectable gentry whom he had been in the habit of considering as the original and lawful possessors of the soil. He, therefore, proposed to resign, and was surprised when his commander informed him, that he was enlisted for a term, which was not yet expired. He bowed, shrugged his shoulders, and submitted to his fate. He had too much honour to desert, and was too loyal, and too polite, to murmur; but he, forthwith, made a solemn vow to his patron saint, never again to get into a scrape, from which he could not retreat whenever it suited his convenience. It was thought that he owed his celibacy in some measure to this vow. He had since accompanied the friendly Indians on several hunting expeditions towards the sources of the Mississippi, and had made a trading voyage to New Orleans. Thus accomplished, he had been more than once called upon by the commandant to act as a guide, or an interpreter; honours which failed not to elicit suitable marks of respect from his fellow villagers; but which had not inflated the honest heart of Baptiste with any unbecoming pride; on the contrary, there was not a more modest man in the village.

In his habits he was the most regular of men. He might be seen at any hour of the day, either sauntering through the village, or seated in front of his own door, smoking a large pipe, formed of a piece of buck-horn, curiously hollowed out, and lined with tin; to which was affixed a short stem of cane from the neighbouring swamp. This pipe was his inseparable companion; and he evinced towards it a constancy which would have immortalized his name, had it been displayed in a better cause. When he walked abroad it was to stroll leisurely from door to door, chatting familiarly with his neighbours, patting the white-haired children on the head, and continuing his lounge, until he had peregrinated the village. His gravity was not a "mysterious carriage of the body to conceal the defects of the mind," but a constitutional seriousness of aspect, which covered as happy and as humane a spirit, as ever existed. It was simply a want of sympathy between his muscles, and his brains; the former utterly refusing to express any agreeable sensation, which might happily titilate the organs of the latter. Honest Baptiste loved a joke, and uttered many, and good ones; but his rigid features refused to smile even at his own wit—a circumstance which I am the more particular in mentioning, as it is not common. He had an orphan niece whom he had reared from childhood to maturity,—a lovely girl, of whose beautiful complexion, a poet might say, that its roses were cushioned upon ermine. A sweeter flower bloomed not upon the prairie, than Gabrielle Menou.

But as she was never afflicted with weak nerves, fever, or consumption, and had but one avowed lover, whom she treated with uniform kindness, and married with the consent of all parties, she has no claim to be considered as the heroine of this history. That station will be cheerfully awarded by every sensible reader to the more important personage who will be presently introduced.

Across the street, immediately opposite to Mons. Baptiste, lived Mademoiselle Jeanette Duval, a lady who resembled him in some respects, but in many others was his very antipode. Like him, she was cheerful and happy, and single—but unlike him, she was brisk, and fat, and plump. Monsieur was the very pink of gravity; and Mademoiselle was blessed with a goodly portion thereof,—but hers was specific gravity. Her hair was dark, but her heart was light, and her eyes, though black, were as brilliant a pair of orbs as ever beamed upon the dreary solitude of a bachelor's heart. Jeanette's heels were as light as her heart, and her tongue as active as her heels, so that notwithstanding her rotundity, she was as brisk a French woman, as ever frisked through the mazes of a cotillon. To sum her perfections, her complexion was of a darker olive than the genial sun of France confers on her brunettes, and her skin was as smooth and shining, as polished mahogany. Her whole household consisted of herself, and a female Negro servant. A spacious garden, which surrounded her house, a pony, and a herd of cattle, constituted, in addition to her personal charms, all the wealth of this amiable spinster. But with these she was rich, as they supplied her table without adding much to her cares. Her quadrupeds, according to the example set by their superiors, pursued their own happiness without let or molestation, wherever they could find it—waxing fat or lean, as nature was more or less bountiful in supplying their wants; and when they strayed too far, or when her agricultural labours became too arduous for the feminine strength of herself, and her sable assistant, every Monsieur of the village was proud of an occasion to serve Mam'selle. And well they might be, for she was the most notable lady in the village, the life of every party, the soul of every frolic. She participated in every festive meeting, and every sad solemnity. Not a neighbour could get up a dance, or get down a dose of bark, without her assistance. If the ball grew dull, Mam'selle bounced on the floor, and infused new spirit into the weary dancers. If the conversation flagged, Jeanette, who occupied a kind of neutral ground, between the young and the old, the married and the single, chatted with all, and loosened all tongues. If the girls wished to stroll in the woods, or romp on the prairie, Mam'selle was taken along to keep off the wolves and the young men; and in respect to the latter, she faithfully performed her office, by attracting them around her own person. Then she was the best neighbour, and the kindest soul! She made the richest soup, the clearest coffee, and the neatest pastry in the village; and in virtue of her confectionery, was the prime favourite of all the children. Her hospitality was not confined to her own domicil; but found its way, in the shape of sundry savory viands, to every table in the vicinity. In the sick chamber she was the most assiduous nurse; her step was the lightest, and her voice the most cheerful—so that the priest must inevitably have become jealous of her skill, had it not been for divers plates of rich soup, and bottles of cordial with which she conciliated his favour, and purchased absolution for these and other offences.

Baptiste and Jeanette were the best of neighbours. He always rose at the dawn, and after lighting his pipe, sallied forth into the open air, where Jeanette usually made her appearance at the same time; for there was an emulation of long standing between them, which should be the earliest riser.

"Bon jour! Mam'selle Jeanette," was his daily salutation.

"Ah! bon jour! bon jour! Mons. Menou," was her daily reply.

Then as he gradually approximated the little paling, which surrounded her door, he hoped Mam'selle was well this morning; and she reiterated the kind enquiry, but with increased emphasis. Then Monsieur enquired after Mam'selle's pony, and Mam'selle's cow, and her garden, and everything appertaining to her, real, personal and mixed; and she displayed a corresponding interest in all concerns of her kind neighbour.—These discussions were mutually beneficial. If Mam'selle's cattle ailed, or if her pony was guilty of any impropriety, who so able to advise her as Mons. Baptiste; and if his plants drooped, or his poultry died, who so skilful in such matters as Mam'selle Jeanette. Sometimes Baptiste forgot his pipe, in the superior interest of the "tête-à-tête," and must needs step in to light it at Jeanette's fire, which caused the gossips of the village to say, that he purposely let his pipe go out, in order that he might himself go in. But he denied this; and, indeed, before offering to enter the dwelling of Mam'selle on such occasions, he usually solicited permission to light his pipe at Jeanette's sparkling eyes, a compliment at which, although it had been repeated some scores of times, Mam'selle never failed to laugh and curtsy, with great good humour and good breeding.

It cannot be supposed, that a bachelor of so much discernment, could long remain insensible to the galaxy of charms which centered in the person of Mam'selle Jeanette; and accordingly, it was currently reported that a courtship of some ten years' standing had been slyly conducted on his part, and as cunningly eluded on hers. It was not averred that Baptiste had actually gone the fearful length of offering his hand; or that Jeanette had been so imprudent as to discourage, far less reject, a lover of such respectable pretensions. But there was thought to exist a strong hankering on the part of the gentleman, which the lady had managed so skilfully as to keep his mind in a kind of equilibrium, like that of the patient animal between the two bundles of hay—so that he would sometimes halt in the street, midway between the two cottages, and cast furtive glances, first at the one, and then at the other, as if weighing the balance of comfort; while the increased volume of smoke which issued from his mouth, seemed to argue that the fire of his love had other fuel than tobacco, and was literally consuming the inward man. The wary spinster was always on the alert on such occasions, manœuvring like a skilful general according to circumstances. If honest Baptiste, after such a consultation, turned on his heel, and retired to his former cautious position at his own door, Mam'selle rallied all her attractions, and by a sudden demonstration, drew him again into the field; but if he marched with an embarrassed air towards her gate, she retired into her castle, or kept shy, and by able evolutions, avoided everything which might bring matters to an issue. Thus the courtship continued longer than the siege of Troy; and Jeanette maintained her freedom, while Baptiste, with a magnanimity superior to that of Agamemnon, kept his temper, and smoked his pipe in good humour with Jeanette and all the world.

Such was the situation of affairs, when I first visited this village, about the time of the cession of Louisiana to the United States. The news of that event had just reached this sequestered spot, and was but indifferently relished. Independently of the national attachment, which all men feel, and the French so justly, the inhabitants of this region had reason to prefer to all others the government which had afforded them protection, without constraining their freedom, or subjecting them to any burthens; and with the kindest feelings towards the Americans, they would willingly have dispensed with any nearer connexion, than that which already existed. They, however, said little on the subject; and that little was expressive of their cheerful acquiescence in the honour done them by the American people, in buying the country, which the Emperor had done them the honour to sell.

It was on the first day of the carnival, that I arrived in the village, about sunset, seeking shelter only for the night, and intending to proceed on my journey in the morning. The notes of the violin, and the groups of gaily-attired people who thronged the street, attracted my attention, and induced me to inquire the occasion of this merriment. My host informed me that a "King-ball" was to be given at the house of a neighbour, adding the agreeable intimation, that strangers were always expected to attend without invitation. Young and ardent, little persuasion was required to induce me to change my dress, and hasten to the scene of festivity. The moment I entered the room, I felt that I was welcome. Not a single look of surprise, not a glance of more than ordinary attention, denoted me as a stranger, or an unexpected guest. The gentlemen nearest the door, bowed as they opened a passage for me through the crowd, in which for a time I mingled, apparently unnoticed. At length, a young gentleman adorned with a large nosegay, approached me, invited me to join the dancers, and after inquiring my name, introduced me to several females, among whom I had no difficulty in selecting a graceful partner. I was passionately fond of dancing; so that readily imbibing the joyous spirit of those around me, I advanced rapidly in their estimation. The native ease and elegance of the females, reared in the wilderness, and unhacknied in the forms of society, surprised and delighted me, as much as the amiable frankness of all classes. —By and by, the dancing ceased; and four young ladies of exquisite beauty, who had appeared during the evening to assume more consequence than the others, stood alone on the floor. For a moment, their arch glances wandered over the company who stood silently around; when one of them advancing to a young gentleman, led him into the circle, and taking a large bouquet from her own bosom, pinned it upon the left breast of his coat, and pronounced him "KING!" The gentleman kissed his fair elector, and led her to a seat. Two others were selected almost at the same moment. The fourth lady hesitated for an instant, then advancing to the spot where I stood, presented me her hand, led me forward, and placed the symbol on my breast, before I could recover from the surprise into which the incident had thrown me. I regained my presence of mind, however, in time to salute my lovely consort; and never did king enjoy with more delight, the first fruits of his elevation—for the beautiful Gabrielle, with whom I had just danced, and who had so unexpectedly raised me, as it were, to the purple, was the freshest and fairest flower in this gay assemblage.

This ceremony was soon explained to me. On the first day of the carnival, four self-appointed kings, having selected their queens, give a ball, at their own proper costs, to the whole village. In the course of that evening, the queens select, in the manner described, the kings for the ensuing day, who choose their queens, in turn, by presenting

the nosegay and the kiss. This is repeated every evening in the week;—
the kings for the time being, giving the ball at their own expense;
and all the inhabitants attending without invitation. On the morning
after each ball, the kings of the preceding evening make small presents
to their late queens; and their temporary alliance is dissolved. Thus
commenced my acquaintance with Gabrielle Menou, who, if she cost
me a few sleepless nights, amply repaid me in the many happy hours,
for which I was indebted to her friendship.

I remained several weeks at this hospitable village. Few evenings
passed without a dance, at which all were assembled, young and
old; the mothers vying in agility with their daughters; and the old
men setting examples of gallantry to the young. I accompanied their
young men to the Indian towns, and was hospitably entertained. I
followed them to the chace; and witnessed the fall of many a noble
buck. In their light canoes, I glided over the turbid waters of the
Mississippi, or through the labyrinths of the morass, in pursuit of
water fowl. I visited the mounds, where the bones of thousands of
warriors were mouldering, overgrown with prairie violets, and thousands of nameless flowers. I saw the moccasin snake basking in the
sun, the elk feeding on the prairie; and returned to mingle in the
amusements of a circle, where, if there was not Parisian elegance, there
was more than Parisian cordiality.

Several years passed away before I again visited this country. The
jurisdiction of the American government was now extended over
this immense region, and its beneficial effects were beginning to be
widely disseminated. The roads were crowded with the teams, and
herds, and families of emigrants, hastening to the land of promise.
Steam boats navigated every stream, the axe was heard in every forest,
and the plough broke the sod whose verdure had covered the prairie
for ages.

It was sunset when I reached the margin of the prairie, on which
the village is situated. My horse, wearied with a long day's travel,
sprung forward with new vigour, when his hoof struck the smooth,
firm road, which led across the plain. It was a narrow path, winding
among the tall grass, now tinged with the mellow hues of autumn.
I gazed with delight over the beautiful surface. The mounds, and
the solitary trees, were there, just as I had left them, and they were
familiar to my eye as the objects of yesterday. It was eight miles across
the prairie, and I had not passed half the distance, when night set in.
I strained my eyes to catch a glimpse of the village, but two large
mounds, and a clump of trees, which intervened, defeated my purpose. I thought of Gabrielle, and Jeanette, and Baptiste, and the priest

—the fiddles, dances, and French ponies; and fancied every minute an hour, and every foot a mile, which separated me from scenes and persons so deeply impressed on my imagination.

At length, I passed the mounds, and beheld the lights twinkling in the village, now about two miles off, like a brilliant constellation in the horizon. The lights seemed very numerous—I thought they moved; and at last discovered, that they were rapidly passing about. "What can be going on in the village?" thought I—then a strain of music met my ear—"they are going to dance," said I, striking my spurs into my jaded nag, "and I shall see all my friends together." But as I drew near, a volume of sounds burst upon me, such as defied all conjecture. Fiddles, flutes, and tambourines, drums, cow-horns, tin trumpets, and kettles, mingled their discordant notes with a strange accompaniment of laughter, shouts, and singing. This singular concert proceeded from a mob of men and boys, who paraded through the streets, preceded by one who blew an immense tin horn, and ever and anon shouted, "Cha-ri-va-ry! Charivary!" to which the mob responded "Charivary!" I now recollected to have heard of a custom which prevails among the American French, of serenading at the marriage of a widow or widower, with such a concert as I now witnessed; and I rode towards the crowd, who had halted before a well-known door, to ascertain who were the happy parties.

"Charivary!" shouted the leader.

"Pour qui?" said another voice.

"Pour Mons. Baptiste Menou, il est marié!'

"Avec qui!"

"Avec Mam'selle Jeanette Duval—Charivary!"

"Charivary!" shouted the whole company, and a torrent of music poured from the full band—tin kettles, cow-horns, and all.

The door of the little cabin, whose hospitable threshold I had so often crossed, now opened, and Baptiste made his appearance—the identical, lank, sallow, erect personage, with whom I had parted several years before, with the same pipe in his mouth. His visage was as long, and as melancholy as ever; except that there was a slight tinge of triumph in its expression, and a bashful casting down of the eye; reminding one of a conqueror, proud but modest in his glory. He gazed with an embarrassed air at the serenaders, bowed repeatedly, as if conscious that he was the hero of the night—and then exclaimed,

"For what you make this charivary?"

"Charivary!" shouted the mob; and the tin trumpets gave an exquisite flourish.

"Gentlemen!" expostulated the bridegroom, "for why you make

this charivary for me? I have never been marry before—and Mam'selle Jeanette has never been marry before!"

Roll went the drum!—cow-horns, kettles, tin trumpets, and fiddles poured forth volumes of sound, and the mob shouted in unison.

"Gentlemen! pardonnez-moi—" supplicated the distressed Baptiste. "If I understan dis custom, which have long prevail vid us, it is vat I say—ven a gentilman, who has been marry before, shall marry de second time—or ven a lady have de misfortune to loose her husban, and be so happy to marry some odder gentilman, den we make de charivary—but 'tis not so wid Mam'selle Duval and me. Upon my honour we have never been marry before dis time!"

"Why, Baptiste," said one, "you certainly have been married, and have a daughter grown."

"Oh, excuse me, sir! Madame St. Marie is my niece; I have never been so happy to be marry, until Mam'selle Duval have do me dis honneur."

"Well, well! it's all one. If you have not been married, you ought to have been, long ago:—and might have been, if you had said the word."

"Ah, gentilmen, you mistake."

"No, no! there's no mistake about it. Mam'selle Jeanette would have had you ten years ago, if you had asked her."

"You flatter too much," said Baptiste, shrugging his shoulders;—and finding there was no means of avoiding the charivary, he with great good humor accepted the serenade, and, according to custom, invited the whole party into his house.

I retired to my former quarters, at the house of an old settler—a little, shrivelled, facetious Frenchman, whom I found in his red flannel nightcap, smoking his pipe, and seated, like Jupiter, in the midst of clouds of his own creating.

"Merry doings in the village!" said I, after we had shaken hands.

"Eh, bien! Mons. Baptiste is marry to Mam'selle Jeanette."

"I see the boys are making merry on the occasion."

"Ah, Sacré! de dem boy! they have play hell tonight."

"Indeed! how so?"

"For make dis charivary—dat is how so, my friend. Dis come for have d'Americain government to rule de countrie! Parbleu! they make charivary for de old maid, and de old bachelor!"

I now found, that some of the new settlers, who had witnessed this ludicrous ceremony, without exactly understanding its application, had been foremost in promoting the present irregular exhibition, in conjunction with a few degenerate French, whose ancient love of fun outstripped their veneration for their usages. The old inhabitants, although they joined in the laugh, were nevertheless not a little scandalized at the innovation. Indeed they had good reason to be alarmed; for their ancient customs, like their mud-walled cottages, were crumbling to ruins around them, and every day destroyed some vestige of former years.

Upon enquiry, I found that many causes of discontent had combined to embitter the lot of my simple-hearted friends. Their ancient allies, the Indians, had sold their hunting grounds, and their removal deprived the village of its only branch of commerce. Surveyors were busily employed in measuring off the whole country, with the avowed intention on the part of the government, of converting into private property those beautiful regions, which had heretofore been free to all who trod the soil, or breathed the air. Portions of it were already thus occupied. Farms and villages were spreading over the country with alarming rapidity, deforming the face of nature, and scaring the elk and the buffalo from their long frequented ranges. Yankees and Kentuckians were pouring in, bringing with them the selfish distinctions and destructive spirit of society. Settlements were planted in the immediate vicinity of the village; and the ancient heritage of the ponies was invaded by the ignoble beasts of the interlopers. Certain pregnant indications of civil degeneration were alive in the land. A county had been established, with a judge, a clerk, and a sheriff; a court-house and jail were about to be built; two lawyers had already made a lodgment at the county-seat; and a number of justices of the peace, and constables, were dispersed throughout a small neighbourhood of not more than fifty miles in extent. A brace of physicians had floated in with the stream of population, and several other persons of the same cloth were seen passing about, brandishing their lancets in the most hostile manner. The French argued very reasonably from all these premises, that a people who brought their own doctors expected to be sick; and that those who commenced operations, in a new country, by providing so many engines, and officers of justice, must certainly intend to be very wicked and litigious. But when the newcomers went the fearful length of enrolling them in the militia; when the sheriff, arrayed in all the terrors of his office, rode into the village, and summoned them to attend the court as jurors; when they heard the judge enumerate to the grand jury the long list of offences which fell within their cognizance, these good folks shook their heads, and declared that this was no longer a country for them.

From that time the village began to depopulate. Some of its inhabitants followed the footsteps of the Indians, and continue to this day to trade between them and the whites, forming a kind of link between civilized and savage men. A larger portion, headed by the priest, floated down the Mississippi, to seek congenial society among the sugar plantations of their countrymen in the South. They found a pleasant spot, on the margin of a large bayou, whose placid stream was enlivened by droves of alligators, sporting their innocent gambols on its surface. Swamps, extending in every direction, protected them from further intrusion. Here a new village arose, and a young generation of French was born, as happy and as careless as that which is passing away.

Baptiste alone adhered to the soil of his fathers, and Jeanette in obedience to her marriage vow, cleaved to Baptiste. He sometimes talked of following his clan, but when the hour came, he could never summon fortitude to pull up his stakes. He had passed so many happy years of single blessedness in his own cabin, and had been so long accustomed to view that of Jeanette, with a wistful eye, that they had become necessary to his happiness. Like other idle bachelors, he had had his day-dreams, pointing to future enjoyment. He had been for years planning the junction of his domains with those of his fair neighbour; had arranged how the fences were to intersect, the fields to be enlarged, and the whole to be managed by the thrifty economy of his partner. All these plans were now about to be realized; and he wisely concluded, that he could smoke his pipe, and talk to Jeanette, as comfortably here as elsewhere; and as he had not danced for many years, and Jeanette was growing rather too corpulent for that exercise, he reasoned that even the deprivation of the fiddles, and king balls, could be borne. Jeanette loved comfort too; but having besides a sharp eye for the main chance, was governed by a deeper policy. By a prudent appropriation of her own savings, and those of her husband, she purchased from the emigrants many of the fairest acres in the village, and thus secured an ample property.

A large log house has since been erected in the space between the cottages of Baptiste and Jeanette, which form wings to the main building, and are carefully preserved in remembrance of old times. All the neighbouring houses have fallen down; and a few heaps of rubbish, surrounded by corn fields, show where they stood. All is changed, except the two proprietors, who live here in ease and plenty, exhibiting in their old age, the same amiable character which, in early life, won for them the respect and love of their neighbours, and of each other.

ALBERT PIKE

★ ★ ★

Adventuring westward after teaching school six years in Massachusetts, Albert Pike (1809-1891) at St. Louis in 1831 joined a party of hunters and traders moving into New Mexico. This tall, brawny Yankee with poetic aspirations arrived at the great pueblo in Taos and at Santa Fe in time to gather first-hand accounts of the warfare between the Mexicans and Indians. With a social historian's insight he recorded, together with stirring frontier incidents, the manners, traditions, and customs of these peoples against the colorful background of semi-arid, majestic mountains. In 1833 he went to Arkansas, taught school, edited a newspaper, studied law, and rose to eminence as an attorney. He served in the Mexican War and as a brigadier general in the Confederate Army. His last years were spent in Washington, D. C. *Hymns to the Gods* (1839) contains his best verse. "The Inroad of the Nabajo" is from *Prose Sketches and Poems Written in the Western Country* (1834).

★ ★ ★

The Inroad of the Nabajo

IT was a keen, cold morning in the latter part of November, when I wound out of the narrow, rocky cañon or valley, in which I had, for some hours, been travelling, and came in sight of the village of San Fernandez, in the valley of Taos. Above, below, and around me, lay the sheeted snow, till, as the eye glanced upward, it was lost among the dark pines which covered the upper part of the mountains, although at the very summit, where the pines were thinnest, it

15

gleamed from among them like a white banner spread between them and heaven. Below me on the left, half open, half frozen, ran the little clear stream, which gave water to the inhabitants of the valley, and along the margin of which, I had been travelling. On the right and left, the ridges which formed the dark and precipitous sides of the cañon, sweeping apart, formed a spacious amphitheatre. Along their sides extended a belt of deep, dull blue mist, above and below which was to be seen the white snow, and the deep darkness of the pines. On the right, these mountains swelled to a greater and more precipitous height, till their tops gleamed in unsullied whiteness over the plain below. Still farther to the right was a broad opening, where the mountains seemed to sink into the plain; and afar off in front were the tall and stupendous mountains between me and the city of Santa Fe. Directly in front of me, with the dull color of its mud buildings, contrasting with the dazzling whiteness of the snow, lay the little village, resembling an oriental town, with its low, square, mud-roofed houses and its two square church towers, also of mud. On the path to the village were a few Mexicans, wrapped in their striped blankets, and driving their jackasses heavily laden with wood towards the village. Such was the aspect of the place at a distance. On entering it, you only found a few dirty, irregular lanes, and a quantity of mud houses.

To an American, the first sight of these New Mexican villages is novel and singular. He seems taken into a different world. Everything is new, strange, and quaint: the men with their pantalones of cloth, gaily ornamented with lace, split up on the outside of the leg to the knee, and covered at the bottom with a broad strip of morocco; the jacket of calico; the botas of stamped and embroidered leather; the zarape or blanket of striped red and white; the broad-brimmed hat, with a black silk handkerchief tied round it in a roll; or in the lower class, the simple attire of breeches of leather reaching only to the knees, a shirt and a zarape; the bonnetless women, with a silken scarf or a red shawl over their heads; and, added to all, the continual chatter of Spanish about him—all remind him that he is in a strange land.

On the evening after my arrival in the village, I went to a fandango. I saw the men and women dancing waltzes, and drinking whiskey together; and in another room, I saw the monte bank open. It is a strange sight—a Spanish fandango. Well-dressed women—(they call them ladies)—harlots, priests, thieves, half-breed Indians—all spinning round together in the waltz. Here, a filthy, ragged fellow with half a shirt, a pair of leather breeches, and long, dirty woollen stockings, and Apache moccasins, was hanging and whirling round with the pretty wife of Pedro Vigil; and there, the priest was dancing with La Altegracia, who paid her husband a regular sum to keep out of the way, and so lived with an American. I was soon disgusted; but among the graceless shapes and more graceless dresses at the fandango, I saw one young woman who appeared to me exceedingly pretty. She was under the middle size, slightly formed; and besides the delicate foot and ankle, and the keen black eye, common to all the women in that country, she possessed a clear and beautiful complexion, and a modest, downcast look, not often to be met with among the New Mexican females.

I was informed to my surprise, that she had been married several years before, and was now a widow. There was an air of gentle and deep melancholy in her face which drew my attention to her; but when one week afterward I left Taos, and went down to Santa Fe, the pretty widow was forgotten.

Among my acquaintances in Santa Fe, was one American in particular, by the name of L——. He had been in the country several years; was a man of much influence there among the people, and was altogether a very talented man. Of his faults, whatever they were, I have nothing to say. It was from him, some time after my arrival, and when the widow had ceased almost to be a thing of memory, that I learned the following particulars respecting her former fortunes. I give them in L.'s own words as nearly as I can, and can only say, that for the truth of them, he is my authority—true or not, such as I received them, do I present them to my readers.

"You know," said he, "that I have been in this country several years. Six or eight years ago, I was at Taos, upon business, and was lodging in the house of an old acquaintance, Dick Taylor. I had been up late one night, and early the next morning, I was suddenly awakened by mine host, Dick, who, shaking me roughly by the shoulder, exclaimed, 'Get up, man—get up—if you wish to see sport, and dress yourself.' Half awake and half asleep, I arose and commenced dressing myself. While employed in this avocation, I heard an immense clamor in the street; cries, oaths, yells, and whoops, resounded in every direction. I knew it would be useless to ask an explanation of the matter from the sententious Dick; and I therefore quietly finished dressing, and, taking my rifle, followed him into the street. For a time, I was at a loss to understand what was the matter. Men were running wildly about—some armed with fusees, with locks as big as a gunbrig; some with bows and arrows, and some with spears. Women were scudding hither and thither, with their black hair flying, and their naked feet shaming the ground by their superior filth. Indian girls were to be seen here and there, with suppressed smiles, and looks of triumph. Men, women, and children, however, seemed to trust less in their armor, than in the arm of the Lord, and of the saints. They were accordingly earnest in calling upon Tata Dios! Dios bendito! Virgen purisima! and all the saints of the calendar, and above all, upon Nuestra Señora de Guadalupe, to aid, protect, and assist them. One cry, at last, explained the whole matter,—'Los malditos y picaros que son los Nabajos.' The Nabajos had been robbing them; they had entered the valley below, and were sweeping it of all the flocks and herds—and this produced the consternation. You have never seen any of these Nabajos. They approach much nearer in character to the Indians in the south of the Mexican Republic than any others in this province. They are whiter; they raise corn; they have vast flocks of sheep, and large herds of horses; they make blankets, too, and sell them to the Spaniards. Their great men have a number of servants under them, and in fact, their government is apparently patriarchal. Sometimes they choose a captain over the nation; but even then, they obey him or not, just as they please. They live about three days' journey west of this, and have about ten thousand souls in their tribe. Like most other Indians, they have their medicine men who intercede for them with the Great Spirit by strange rites and ceremonies.

"Through the tumult, we proceeded towards the outer edge of the town, whither all the armed men seemed to be hastening. On arriving in the street which goes out towards the cañon of the river, we found ourselves in the place of action. Nothing was yet to be seen out in the plain, which extends to the foot of the hills and to the cañon, and of which you there have a plain view. Some fifty Mexicans had gathered there, mostly armed, and were pressing forward towards the extremity of the street. Behind them were a dozen Americans with their rifles, all as cool as might be; for the men that came through the prairie then were all braves. Sundry women were scudding about, exhorting their husbands to fight well, and praising 'Los Señores Americanos.' We had waited perhaps half an hour, when the foe came in sight, sweeping in from the west, and bearing towards the cañon, driving before them numerous herds and flocks, and consisting apparently of about one hundred men. When they were within about half a mile of us, they separated; one portion of them remained with the booty, and the other, all mounted, came sweeping down upon us. The effect was instantaneous, and almost magical. In a moment not a woman was to be seen far or near; and the heroes who had been chattering and boasting in front of the

Americans, shrunk in behind them, and left them to bear the brunt of the battle. We immediately extended ourselves across the street, and waited the charge. The Indians made a beautiful appearance as they came down upon us with their fine-looking horses, and their shields ornamented with feathers and fur, and their dresses of un-stained deer-skin. At that time, they knew nothing about the Ameri-cans; they supposed that their good allies, the Spaniards, would run as they commonly do, that they would have the pleasure of frightening the village and shouting in it, and going off safely. As they neared us, each of us raised his gun when he judged it proper, and fired. A dozen cracks of the rifle told them the difference; five or six tum-bled out of their saddles, and were immediately picked up by their comrades, who then turned their backs and retreated as swiftly as they had come. The Americans, who were, like myself, not very eager to fight the battles of the New Mexicans, loaded their guns with immense coolness, and we stood gazing at them as they again gathered their booty and prepared to move towards the cañon. The Mexicans tried to induce us to mount and follow; but we, or at least I, was perfectly contented. In fact, I did not care much which whipped. The Nabajos seemed thus in a very good way of going off with their booty unhindered, when suddenly the scene was altered. A consider-able body, perhaps sixty, of the Pueblo of Taos, a civilized Indian who are Catholics, and citizens of the Republic, appeared suddenly under the mountains, dashing at full speed towards the mouth of the cañon. They were all fine-looking men, well mounted, large, and exceedingly brave. These Pueblos (a word which signifies tribes—of Indians) are, in fact, all handsome, athletic men. There are about a dozen different tribes around here, each having a different language, and all very small in number. The Taos, the Picuris, the Poguaque, the Tisuqui, the Xemes, the San Domingo, the Pecos, (the two latter, however, though they live fifty miles apart, all speak the same language,) the San Ildefonso,* and one or two others; all these are close here. You need not go more than seventy miles from Santa Fe to find any of them. Some of their towns were formerly much larger than at present —for example, that of the Pecos tribe. Half their town is fallen to ruin. The wall which originally surrounded it, is now at a distance from the one little square which composes the present town. I say square, but it is an oblong, about forty yards by fifteen, surrounded by continuous houses of mud, three and four stories high, to which you generally ascend by ladders, and go down again from the top.

* The Abiquiu. [*Pike's note.*]

Everything is built for the purpose of defence. There is but one passage from the oblong, and this is about six feet wide. When the Spaniards first came up above the Pass and conquered the Indians, and founded Santa Fe, these tribes rose against them and drove them again below the Pass. Only the Pecos and San Domingo tribes remained faithful, and they were nearly exterminated by the other Indians, on account of it. In the Pecos tribe, there are not more than fifteen or twenty men. The Santa Fe tribe went into the mountains, and has disappeared, mingling, perhaps, with the Apaches. Another tribe is the one which the Indians and Spaniards call the Montezuma tribe. I cannot say, whether this be their proper name, or one which they have learned from the Americans; but the latter supposition would be improbable. This, too, is a small and diminishing tribe; they live in the mountains not far from Taos, and never intermarry with any other tribe. They worship a large snake, whose teeth, I suppose, they have extracted, and rendered it harmless. Not long ago, it was lost, and after a time, it was discovered by some of the Pueblo of Taos, who knew it by some ornaments it wears. They gave notice to the Montezuma tribe, and their priest came and took it back. But I am tiring you with this verbiage; shall I go back to my story?"

"Ho," said I, "go on with your account of these Indians first."

"Just as you please. They likewise keep a continual fire burning in a kind of cave; every year, a man is placed there to take care of it; and for the whole of that year, he does not see the sun;—they bring him food, wood and water. I have never seen this, but creditable Spaniards have told me that it was all true, and I am far from being inclined to doubt it. You will see between this and the Nabajo country, remains of vast buildings of rock and mud, which were evidently used for temples—by their insulated position, and their entire difference from the other ruins around them. One of these places, about two days' ride from here, is under a mountain, in which, they say, treasures are hid. In fact, many things concur to prove these Indians to be different from our Indians, and even from the Eutaws—(or, as the Spaniards write it, Llutas)—from the Apaches and from the Comanches. Their dances are very graceful and considerably complicated, and as regular as our contra dances; much handsomer than any dances and xarabes of these vagabond Mexicans. But sooth it is, they are accompanied by the same monotonous *hu a ha, hu a ha,* which all Indians sing, so far as I have ever seen them. I might say, too, that they have very little of that sententious gravity and unbending sobriety of appearance generally ascribed to Indians. They laugh, and chatter, and play; but so do all Indians—Mr. Cooper, and

Heckewelder, and any other person, to the contrary notwithstanding. The Osages play with their children before white men, laugh, chat and joke; the Choctaws laugh so much as frequently to appear silly; and you may look in vain for those specimens of dignity and gravity which are told of in many veritable books. Not that I mean to say that they are never grave—sometimes they are; but generally, an Indian is the most merry and apparently lighthearted thing in the world. Do you think that they are like Chingachgook, who would not embrace Uncas till they were alone by their camp-fire? No. An Osage chief will fondle his child, toss it in the air, and chatter to it like a childish woman, talking baby talk. So will a Comanche, or a Crow, or a Snake, and they are the gravest Indians I ever saw. But I was speaking of the difference between them and our Indians. They have woven blankets—heaven knows how long; and they have, and had before this continent was discovered, a considerable knowledge of pottery; witness the vessels of cookery, and also the bottomless jars, which they put one upon the other for their chimneys. They are probably a mixture of the Mexicans, (whether these latter were originally Phœnicians, Egyptians, or Aboriginals,) and of the Northern and Eastern Indians—the fiercer and ruder tribes who inhabit to the north, east and west of them. The Mexicans, in my opinion, penetrated at some day—heaven knows how long ago—into the United States, and were repulsed, leaving those fortifications, hieroglyphics, and other matter so curious to the learned. They likewise came towards the north and left colonies in New Mexico; but the cold kept them from going farther; they were no people for mountains and deserts. I incline to believe that they were Phœnicians; at any rate, they were an insulated portion of the human race, entirely distinct from, and far superior to, the natives of the east and north, as well as of California. As to the story of the Nabajos having a part of a Welsh bible, and a silver cup, it is all a matter of imagination. To be sure they have beards, and are whiter than the surrounding Indians, and they do speak a language which nothing can learn, and which is marvelously like the Welsh, in the respect of guttural and nasal unpronounceables. So much for Indians—and since I have ended where I began—with the Nabajos—I will return to my narrative.

"Upon seeing the Pueblo of Taos, between them and the mouth of the cañon, the Nabajos uttered a shrill yell of defiance, and moved to meet them. Leaving a few men to guard the cattle, the remainder diverging like the opening sticks of a fan, rushed to the attack. Each man shot his arrow as he approached, till he was within thirty or forty yards, and then wheeling, retreated, shooting as he went. They were steadily received by the Pueblo, with a general discharge of fire-arms and arrows at every charge, and were frustrated in every attempt at routing them. Several were seen to fall at every charge; but they were always taken up and borne to those who were guarding the cattle. During the contest, several Mexicans mounted, and went out from the village to join the Pueblos, but only two or three ventured to do so; the others kept at a very respectful distance. At length, finding the matter grow desperate, more men were joined to those who guarded the cattle, and they then moved steadily towards the cañon. The others again diverging, rushed on till they came within fifty yards, and then converging again, charged boldly upon one point; and as the Pueblo were unprepared for this manœuvre, they broke through, and again charged back. Drawing them together in this way to oppose them, nearly two thirds of the cattle were driven through the line, goaded by arrows and frightened by shouts. Many of the Nabajos, however, fell in the mêlée, by the long spears and quick arrows of the Pueblo. In the meantime, I had mounted, and approached within two hundred yards of the scene of contest. I observed one tall, and good-looking Spaniard, of middle age, who was particularly active in the contest; he had slightly wounded a large athletic Nabajo, with his spear, and I observed that he was continually followed by him. When this large chief had concluded that the cattle were near enough to the mouth of the cañon to be out of danger, he gave a shrill cry, and his men, who were now reduced to about sixty, besides those with the cattle, gathered simultaneously between the Pueblo and the cañon. Only the chief remained behind, and rushing towards the Spaniard who had wounded him, he grasped him with one hand and raised him from the saddle as if he had been a boy. Taken by surprise, the man made no resistance for a moment or two, and that moment or two sufficed for the horse of the Nabajo—a slight-made, Arabian-looking animal—to place him, with two or three bounds, among his own men. Then his knife glittered in the air, and I saw the Spaniard's limbs contract, and then collapse. A moment more sufficed for him to tear the scalp from the head; he was then tumbled from before him to the ground, and with a general yell, the whole body rushed forward, closely pursued by the Pueblo. In hurrying to the cañon, the Nabajo lost several men and more of the cattle; but when they had once entered its rocky jaws, and the Pueblo turned back, still more than half the plunder remained with the robbers; fifteen Nabajos only were left dead; and the remainder were borne off before their comrades. The Pueblos lost nearly one third of their number.

"It was this fight, sir, this inroad of the Nabajos, which brought me acquainted with the young widow of whom we have spoken before. She was then an unmarried girl of fourteen; and a very pretty girl too was La Señorita Ana Maria Ortega. I need not trouble you with descriptions of her; for she has saved me the trouble by appearing to your eyes in that sublime place, a fandango—when you first saw the charms of New Mexican beauty, and had your eyes ravished with the melody and harmony of a Spanish waltz—(I beg Spain's pardon)—a New Mexican waltz."

"Which waltz," said I, "I heard the next morning played over a coffin at a funeral; and in the afternoon, in the procession of the Host."

"Oh, that is common. Melody, harmony, fiddle, banjo, and all—all is common to all occasions. They have but little music, and they are right in being economical with it; and the presence of the priest sanctifies anything. You know the priest of Taos?"

"Yes. The people were afraid to get drunk on my first fandango night. I was astonished to find them so sober. The priest was there; and they feared to get drunk until he had done so. That event took place about eleven at night, and then aguardiente was in demand."

"Yes, I dare say. That same priest once asked me if England was a province or a state. I told him it was a province. He reads Voltaire's Philosophical Dictionary, and takes the old infidel to be an excellent Christian. Ana Maria was his god-daughter, I think, or some such matter; and I became acquainted with her in that way. He wanted me to marry her; she knew nothing of it, though; but I backed out. I did not mind the marrying so much as the baptism and the citizenship. I don't exchange my country for Mexico; or the name American for that of Mexican. Ana was, in truth, not a girl to be slighted. She was pretty, and rich, and sensible; her room was the best furnished mud apartment in Taos; her zarapes were of the best texture, some of them even from Chihuahua, and they were piled showily round the room. The roses skewered upon the wall, were of red silk; and the santos and other images had been brought from Mexico. There were some half dozen of looking-glasses, too, all out of reach, and various other adornments common to great apartments. The medal which she wore round her neck, with a cross-looking San Pablo upon it, was of beaten gold, or some other kind of gold. She had various dresses of calico and silk, all bought at high prices of the newcomers; and her little fairy feet were always adorned with shoes. That was a great extravagance in those days. Ana Maria had no mother when I first saw her; but she was still wearing the 'luto' for her, and she had transferred all the affection to her father, which she had before bestowed upon her mother; and when the knife of the Nabajo made her an orphan, I suppose that she felt as if her last hold upon life was gone. She appeared to, at least.

"Victorino Alasi had been her lover, and her favored one. He had never thought of any other than Ana Maria as his bride, and he had talked of his love to her a hundred times. But there came in a young trapper, who gave him cause to tremble, lest he should lose his treasure. Henry, or as he was most commonly called, Hentz Wilson, was a formidable rival. Ana knew not, herself, which to prefer; the long friendship and love of Victorino was almost balanced by the different style of beauty, the odd manners, and the name American, which recommended Hentz. Her vanity was flattered by the homage of an American, and Victorino was in danger of losing his bride. The bold, open bearing of Hentz, and his bravery, as well as his knowledge, which, though slight at home, was wondrous to the simple New Mexicans, had recommended him, likewise, to the father. Just before, his death suspended, for a time, all operations. They had each of them made application by letter (the common custom) for the hand of Ana Maria. In the course of a fortnight after the inroad of the Nabajo, each of the lovers received, as answer, that she had determined to give her hand to either of them who should kill the murderer of her father. And with this, they both were obliged to content themselves for the present.

"Directly after the inroad, I came down to Santa Fe. The Lieutenant Colonel of the Province, Viscara, was raising a body of men to go out against the Nabajo, and repay them for this and other depredations lately committed upon the people, and he was urgent for me to accompany him—so much so, that I was obliged to comply with his requests, and promised to go. Troops were sent for from below, and in the course of four months, the expedition was ready; and we set out upon the Nabajo campaign. We were a motley set. First there was a body of regular troops, all armed with British muskets and with lances. Here, there was a grey coat and leathern pantaloons; there, no coat and short breeches. But you have seen the ragged, ununiformed troops here in the city, and I need not describe them to you. Next there was a parcel of militia, all mounted; some had lances, some, old fusees; and last, a body of Indians of the different Pueblos, with bows and shields—infinitely the best troops we had, as well as the bravest men. Among the militia of Taos, I observed the young Victorino—and Hentz had likewise volunteered to accompany the expedition, and lived with me in the General's tent.

"It was in the dryest part of summer that we left Santa Fe, and marched towards the country of the Nabajo. We went out by the way of Xemes, and then crossing the Rio Puerco, went into the mountains of the Nabajo. We came up with them, fought them, and they fled before us, driving their cattle and sheep with them into a wide sand desert; and we being now out of provisions, were obliged to overtake them or starve. We were two days without a drop of water, and nearly all the animals gave out in consequence of it. On the third day, Viscara, fifteen soldiers, and myself went ahead of the army, (which, I forgot to say, was thirteen hundred strong.) Viscara and his men were mounted. I was on foot, with no clothing, except a cloth round my middle, with a lance in one hand, and a rifle in the other. That day I think I ran seventy-five miles, bare-footed, and through the burning sand."

"Viscara tells me that you ran thirty leagues."

"Viscara is mistaken, and overrates it. Just before night, we came up with a large body of Nabajos, and attacked them. We took about two thousand sheep from them, and three hundred cattle, and drove them back that night to the army. The Nabajos supposed, when we rushed on them, that the whole of our force was at hand, and they were afraid to pursue us. But it is the battle in which you are most concerned. When we attacked the Nabajo, they were drawn up, partly on foot, and partly on horseback, in the bed of a little creek which was dry. It was the common way of fighting, charge, fire and retreat; and if you have seen one fight on horseback, you have seen all. I observed, particularly, one Nabajo, upon whom three Pueblos charged, all on foot; he shot two of them down before they reached him. Another arrow struck the remaining one in the belly. He still came on with only a tomahawk, and another arrow struck him in the forehead. Yet still he braved his foe, and they were found lying dead together. I could have shot the Nabajo with great ease, at the time; for the whole of this took place within seventy yards of me.

"In the midst of the battle, I observed Victorino and Hentz standing together in the front rank, seeming rather to be spectators than men interested in the fight. They were both handsome men, but entirely different in appearance. Victorino was a dark-eyed, slender, agile young Spaniard, with a tread like a tiger-cat; and with all his nerves indurate with toil. His face was oval, thin, and of a rich olive, through which the blood seemed ready to break; and you could hardly have chosen a better figure for a statuary as he stood, now and then discharging his fusee, but commonly glancing his eyes uneasily about from one part of the enemy to the other. Hentz, on the contrary, was a tall, and well-proportioned young fellow, of immense strength and activity; but with little of the cat-like quickness of his rival; his skin was fair even to effeminacy, and his blue eyes were shaded by a profusion of chestnut hair; he, too, seemed expecting some one to appear amid the enemy; for though he now and then fired and reloaded, it was but seldom, and he spent more time in leaning on his long rifle, and gazing about among the Nabajos.

"On a sudden, a sharp yell was heard, and a party of Nabajos came dashing down the bank of the creek, all mounted, and headed by the big chief who had killed the father of Ana Maria. Then the apathy of the two rivals was at once thrown aside. Hentz quickly threw his gun into the hollow of his arm, examined the priming, and again stood quietly watching the motions of the chief, and Victorino did the same. Wheeling round several times, and discharging a flight of arrows continually upon us, this new body of Nabajo at length bore down directly towards Hentz and Victorino. As the chief came on, Victorino raised his gun, took a steady, long aim, and fired. Another moment, and the Nabajo were upon them, and then retreated again like a wave tossing back from the shore. The chief still sat on his horse as before; another yell, and they came down again. When they were within about a hundred yards, Hentz raised his rifle, took a steady, quick aim, and fired. Still they came on; the chief bent down over the saddle-bow, and his horse, seemingly frightened by the strange pressure of the rider, bore down directly towards Hentz, who sprang to meet him, and caught the bridle; the horse sprang to one side, and the wounded chief lost his balance, and fell upon the ground. Losing his hold upon the horse, he dashed away through friend and foe, and was out of sight in a moment. The Nabajo rallied to save the body of the chief, and Viscara himself rushed in with me to the rescue of Hentz. But the long barrel of Hentz's rifle, which he swayed with a giant's strength, and in which I humbly imitated him, the sword of Viscara, and the keen knife of Victorino, who generously sprang in the aid of his rival, would all have failed in saving the body, had not a band of the gallant Pueblo attacked them in the rear and routed them. Hentz immediately dispatched the chief, who was, by this time, half hidden by a dozen Nabajos, and immediately deprived his head of the hair, which is more valuable to an Indian than life.

"After our rout in the sand desert, the Nabajos sued for peace, and we returned to Santa Fe. Poor Victorino, I observed, rode generally alone, and had not a word to say to any one. Although formerly, he had been the most merry and humorous, now he seemed entirely buried in sorrow. He kept listlessly along, neither looking to the right hand or the left, with his bridle lying on the neck of his mule. I tried to comfort him, but he motioned me away. I urged it upon him, and he answered me gloomily, 'Why should I cheer up? what have I to live for? Had I lost her by any fault of my own, I would not have thought so hardly of it; but by this cursed old fusee, and because another man can shoot better than I—— Oh, sir, leave me to myself, I pray you, and make me no offers which do me no good. I think I *shall* be happy again, but it will be in my grave, and Dios me perdone! I care not how soon I am there.'

"As I fell back towards the rear where I generally marched, Hentz rode up by me and inquired what the young Spaniard had said. I repeated it to him. 'Do you think he is really that troubled?' inquired he. 'Yes,' said I—'the poor fellow seems to feel all he says.' Without a word, Hentz rode towards him, and reining up by him, tapped him on the shoulder. Victorino looked fiercely up, and seemed inclined to resent it, but Hentz, without regarding the glance, proceeded with a mass of immensely bad Spanish, which I know not how the poor fellow ever understood. 'Here,' said he, 'you love Ana better than I do, I know—you have known her longer, and will feel her loss more; and after all, you would have killed the chief if you could have done it—and you did help me save the body. Take this bunch of stuff,' holding out the hair, 'and give me your hand.' Victorino did so, and shook the offered hand heartily; then taking the scalp, he deposited it in his shot-pouch, and dashing the tears from his eyes, rode off towards his comrades like a madman. So much for the inroad of the Nabajos."

"But what became of Victorino?" inquired I.

"He married Ana Maria after she had laid aside the luto, (mourning,) and two years ago, he died of the small pox, in the Snake country. Poor fellow—he was almost an American."

AUGUSTUS BALDWIN LONGSTREET

★ ★ ★

Ante-bellum Georgia "Crackers" and "po' white trash" are immortalized by Augustus Baldwin Longstreet (1790-1870) in *Georgia Scenes, Characters, Incidents, etc., in the First Half Century of the Republic* (1835). This work portrayed the swearing, fighting, eye-gouging, horse-swapping, gander-pulling prowess of Southern mountaineers so realistically that, in later years when he became a college president, Longstreet attempted to suppress it. Frequently reprinted and widely accepted as a volume of humor, it is one of the finest early examples of the fictional portraiture of local manners. Born in Augusta, Georgia, Longstreet studied at Yale, read law in Litchfield, Connecticut, and became, in turn, a lawyer, preacher, writer, jurist, college president, farmer, and business man. Between the years 1840 and 1865 he served successively as president of Emory College and the universities of Mississippi and South Carolina.

★ ★ ★

The Horse-Swap

DURING the session of the Supreme Court, in the village of ——, about three weeks ago, when a number of people were collected in the principal street of the village, I observed a young man riding up and down the street, as I supposed, in a violent passion. He galloped this way, then that, and then the other; spurred his horse to one group of citizens, then to another; then dashed off at half speed, as if fleeing from danger; and, suddenly checking his horse, returned first in a pace, then in a trot, and then in a canter. While he was performing these various evolutions, he cursed, swore,

28

whooped, screamed, and tossed himself in every attitude which man could assume on horseback. In short, he *cavorted* most magnanimously (a term which, in our tongue, expresses all that I have described, and a little more), and seemed to be setting all creation at defiance. As I like to see all that is passing, I determined to take a position a little nearer to him, and to ascertain, if possible, what it was that affected him so sensibly. Accordingly, I approached a crowd before which he had stopped for a moment, and examined it with the strictest scrutiny. But I could see nothing in it that seemed to have anything to do with the cavorter. Every man appeared to be in good humour, and all minding their own business. Not one so much as noticed the principal figure. Still he went on. After a semicolon pause, which my appearance seemed to produce (for he eyed me closely as I approached), he fetched a whoop, and swore that "he could out-swap any live man, woman, or child that ever walked these hills, or that ever straddled horseflesh since the days of old daddy Adam."

"Stranger," said he to me, "did you ever see the *Yallow* Blossom from Jasper?"

"No," said I, "but I have often heard of him."

"I'm the boy," continued he; "perhaps a *leetle,* jist a *leetle,* of the best man at a horse-swap that ever trod shoe-leather."

I began to feel my situation a little awkward, when I was relieved by a man somewhat advanced in years, who stepped up and began to survey the *"Yallow Blossom's"* horse with much apparent interest. This drew the rider's attention, and he turned the conversation from me to the stranger.

"Well, my old coon," said he, "do you want to swap *hosses?*"

"Why, I don't know," replied the stranger; "I believe I've got a beast I'd trade with you for that one, if you like him."

"Well, fetch up your nag, my old cock; you're jist the lark I wanted to get hold of. I am perhaps a *leetle,* jist a *leetle,* of the best man at a horse-swap that ever stole *cracklins* out of his mammy's fat gourd. Where's your *hoss?*"

"I'll bring him presently; but I want to examine your horse a little."

"Oh! look at him," said the Blossom, alighting and hitting him a cut; "look at him. He's the best piece of *hoss*flesh in the thirteen united univarsal worlds. There's no sort o' mistake in little Bullet. He can pick up miles on his feet, and fling 'em behind him as fast as the next man's *hoss,* I don't care where he comes from. And he can keep at it as long as the sun can shine without resting."

During this harangue, little Bullet looked as if he understood it all, believed it, and was ready at any moment to verify it. He was a horse of goodly countenance, rather expressive of vigilance than fire; though an unnatural appearance of fierceness was thrown into it by the loss of his ears, which had been cropped pretty close to his head. Nature had done but little for Bullet's head and neck; but he managed, in a great measure, to hide their defects by bowing perpetually. He had obviously suffered severely for corn; but if his ribs and hip bones had not disclosed the fact, *he* never would have done it; for he was in all respects as cheerful and happy as if he commanded all the corn-cribs and fodder-stacks in Georgia. His height was about twelve hands; but as his shape partook somewhat of that of the giraffe, his haunches stood much lower. They were short, strait, peaked, and concave. Bullet's tail, however, made amends for all his defects. All that the artist could do to beautify it had been done; and all that horse could do to compliment the artist, Bullet did. His tail was nicked in superior style, and exhibited the line of beauty in so many directions, that it could not fail to hit the most fastidious taste in some of them. From the root it dropped into a graceful festoon; then rose in a handsome curve; then resumed its first direction; and then mounted suddenly upward like a cypress knee to a perpendicular of about two and a half inches. The whole had a careless and bewitching inclination to the right. Bullet obviously knew where his beauty lay, and took all occasions to display it to the best advantage. If a stick cracked, or if any one moved suddenly about him, or coughed, or hawked, or spoke a little louder than common, up went Bullet's tail like lightning; and if the *going up* did not please, the *coming down* must of necessity, for it was as different from the other movement as was its direction. The first was a bold and rapid flight upward, usually to an agle of forty-five degrees. In this position he kept his interesting appendage until he satisfied himself that nothing in particular was to be done; when he commenced dropping it by half inches, in second beats, then in triple time, then faster and shorter, and faster and shorter still, until it finally died away imperceptibly into its natural position. If I might compare sights to sounds, I should say its *settling* was more like the note of a locust than anything else in nature.

Either from native sprightliness of disposition, from uncontrollable activity, or from an unconquerable habit of removing flies by the stamping of the feet, Bullet never stood still; but always kept up a gentle fly-scaring movement of his limbs, which was peculiarly interesting.

"I tell you, man," proceeded Yellow Blossom, "he's the best live hoss that ever trod the grit of Georgia. Bob Smart knows the hoss. Come here, Bob, and mount this hoss, and show Bullet's motions." Here Bullet bristled up, and looked as if he had been hunting for Bob all day long, and had just found him. Bob sprang on his back. "Boo-oo-oo!" said Bob, with a fluttering noise of the lips; and away went Bullet, as if in a quarter race, with all his beauties spread in handsome style.

"Now fetch him back," said Blossom. Bullet turned and came in pretty much as he went out.

"Now trot him by." Bullet reduced his tail to *"customary;"* sidled to the right and left airily, and exhibited at least three varieties of trot in the short space of fifty yards.

"Make him pace!" Bob commenced, twitching the bridle and kicking him at the same time. These inconsistent movements obviously (and most naturally) disconcerted Bullet; for it was impossible for him to learn, from them, whether he was to proceed or stand still. He started to trot, and was told that wouldn't do. He attempted a canter, and was checked again. He stopped, and was urged to go on. Bullet now rushed into the wide field of experiment, and struck out a gait of his own, that completely turned the tables upon his rider, and certainly deserved a patent. It seemed to have derived its elements from the jig, the minuet, and the cotillon. If it was not a pace, it certainly had *pace* in it, and no man would venture to call it anything else; so it passed off to the satisfaction of the owner.

"Walk him!" Bullet was now at home again; and he walked as if money was staked on him.

The stranger, whose name, I afterward learned, was Peter Ketch, having examined Bullet to his heart's content, ordered his son Neddy to go and bring up Kit. Neddy soon appeared upon Kit; a well-formed sorrel of the middle size, and in good order. His *tout ensemble* threw Bullet entirely in the shade, though a glance was sufficient to satisfy any one that Bullet had the decided advantage of him in point of intellect.

"Why, man," said Blossom, "do you bring such a hoss as that to trade for Bullet? Oh, I see you're no notion of trading."

"Ride him off, Neddy!" said Peter. Kit put off at a handsome lope.

"Trot him back!" Kit came in at a long, sweeping trot, and stopped suddenly at the crowd.

"Well," said Blossom, "let me look at him; maybe he'll do to plough."

"Examine him!" said Peter, taking hold of the bridle close to the mouth; "he's nothing but a tacky. He an't as *pretty* a horse as Bullet, I know; but he'll do. Start 'em together for a hundred and fifty *mile;* and if Kit an't twenty mile ahead of him at the coming out, any man may take Kit for nothing. But he's a monstrous mean horse, gentlemen; any man may see that. He's the scariest horse, too, you ever saw. He won't do to hunt on, no how. Stranger, will you let Neddy have your rifle to shoot off him? Lay the rifle between his ears, Neddy, and shoot at the blaze in that stump. Tell me when his head is high enough."

Ned fired, and hit the blaze; and Kit did not move a hair's breadth.

"Neddy, take a couple of sticks, and beat on that hogshead at Kit's tail."

Ned made a tremendous rattling, at which Bullet took fright, broke his bridle, and dashed off in grand style; and would have stopped all farther negotiations by going home in disgust, had not a traveller arrested him and brought him back; but Kit did not move.

"I tell you, gentlemen," continued Peter, "he's the scariest horse you ever saw. He an't as gentle as Bullet, but he won't do any harm if you watch him. Shall I put him in a cart, gig, or wagon for you, stranger? He'll cut the same capers there he does here. He's a monstrous mean horse."

During all this time Blossom was examining him with the nicest scrutiny. Having examined his frame and limbs, he now looked at his eyes.

"He's got a curious look out of his eyes," said Blossom.

"Oh yes, sir," said Peter, "just as blind as a bat. Blind horses always have clear eyes. Make a motion at his eyes, if you please, sir."

Blossom did so, and Kit threw up his head rather as if something pricked him under the chin than as if fearing a blow. Blossom repeated the experiment, and Kit jerked back in considerable astonishment.

"Stone blind, you see, gentlemen," proceeded Peter; "but he's just as good to travel of a dark night as if he had eyes."

"Blame my buttons," said Blossom, "if I like them eyes."

"No," said Peter, "nor I neither. I'd rather have 'em made of diamonds; but they'll do, if they don't show as much white as Bullet's."

"Well," said Blossom, "make a pass at me."

"No," said Peter; "you made the banter, now make your pass."

"Well, I'm never afraid to price my hosses. You must give me twenty-five dollars boot."

"Oh, certainly; say fifty, and my saddle and bridle in. Here, Neddy, my son, take away daddy's horse."

"Well," said Blossom, "I've made my pass, now you make yours."

"I'm for short talk in a horse-swap, and therefore always tell a gentleman at once what I mean to do. You must give me ten dollars."

Blossom swore absolutely, roundly, and profanely, that he never would give boot.

"Well," said Peter, "I didn't care about trading; but you cut such high shines, that I thought I'd like to back you out, and I've done it. Gentlemen, you see I've brought him to a hack."

"Come, old man," said Blossom, "I've been joking with you. I begin to think you do want to trade; therefore, give me five dollars and take Bullet. I'd rather lose ten dollars any time than not make a trade, though I hate to fling away a good hoss."

"Well," said Peter, "I'll be as clever as you are. Just put the five dollars on Bullet's back, and hand him over; it's a trade."

Blossom swore again, as roundly as before, that he would not give boot; and, said he, "Bullet wouldn't hold five dollars on his back, no how. But, as I bantered you, if you say an even swap, here's at you."

"I told you," said Peter, "I'd be as clever as you, therefore, here goes two dollars more, just for trade sake. Give me three dollars, and it's a bargain."

Blossom repeated his former assertion; and here the parties stood for a long time, and the by-standers (for many were now collected) began to taunt both parties. After some time, however, it was pretty unanimously decided that the old man had backed Blossom out.

At length Blossom swore he "never would be backed out for three dollars after bantering a man;" and, accordingly, they closed the trade.

"Now," said Blossom, as he handed Peter the three dollars, "I'm a man that, when he makes a bad trade, makes the most of it until he can make a better. I'm for no rues and after-claps."

"That's just my way," said Peter; "I never goes to law to mend my bargains."

"Ah, you're the kind of boy I love to trade with. Here's your hoss, old man. Take the saddle and bridle off him, and I'll strip yours; but lift up the blanket easy from Bullet's back, for he's a mighty tender-backed hoss."

The old man removed the saddle, but the blanket stuck fast. He attempted to raise it, and Bullet bowed himself, switched his tail, danced a little, and gave signs of biting.

"Don't hurt him, old man," said Blossom, archly; "take it off easy. I am, perhaps, a leetle of the best man at a horse-swap that ever catched a coon."

Peter continued to pull at the blanket more and more roughly, and Bullet became more and more *cavortish:* insomuch that, when the blanket came off, he had reached the *kicking* point in good earnest.

The removal of the blanket disclosed a sore on Bullet's back-bone that seemed to have defied all medical skill. It measured six full inches in length and four in breadth, and had as many features as Bullet had motions. My heart sickened at the sight; and I felt that the brute who had been riding him in that situation deserved the halter.

The prevailing feeling, however, was that of mirth. The laugh became loud and general at the old man's expense, and rustic witticisms were liberally bestowed upon him and his late purchase. These Blossom continued to provoke by various remarks. He asked the old man "if he thought Bullet would let five dollars lie on his back." He declared most seriously that he had owned the horse three months, and had never discovered before that he had a sore back, "or he never should have thought of trading him," &c., &c.

The old man bore it all with the most philosophic composure. He evinced no astonishment at his late discovery, and made no replies. But his son Neddy had not disciplined his feelings quite so well. His eyes opened wider and wider from the first to the last pull of the blanket; and, when the whole sore burst upon his view, astonishment and fright seemed to contend for the mastery of his countenance. As the blanket disappeared, he stuck his hands in his breeches pockets, heaved a deep sigh, and lapsed into a profound revery, from which he was only roused by the cuts at his father. He bore them as long as he could; and, when he could contain himself no longer, he began, with a certain wildness of expression which gave a peculiar interest to what he uttered: "His back's mighty bad off; but dod drot my soul if he's put it to daddy as bad as he thinks he has, for old Kit's both blind and *deef,* I'll be dod drot if he eint."

"The devil he is," said Blossom.

"Yes, dod drot my soul if he *eint.* You walk him, and see if he *eint.* His eyes don't look like it; but he'd *jist as leve go agin* the house with you, or in a ditch, as any how. Now you go try him." The laugh was now turned on Blossom; and many rushed to test the fidelity of the little boy's report. A few experiments established its truth beyond controversy.

"Neddy," said the old man, "you oughtn't to try and make people discontented with their things. Stranger, don't mind what the little boy says. If you can only get Kit rid of them little failings, you'll find him all sorts of a horse. You are a *leetle* the best man at a horse-swap that ever I got hold of; but don't fool away Kit. Come, Neddy, my son, let's be moving; the stranger seems to be getting snappish."

The Gander-Pulling

IN the year 1798 I resided in the city of Augusta and, upon visiting the market-house one morning in that year, my attention was called to the following notice, stuck upon one of the pillars of the building:

"*advurtysement.*

"Those woo wish To be inform heareof, is heareof notyfide that edwd. Prator will giv a gander pullin, jis this side of harisburg, on Satterday of thes pressents munth to All woo mout wish to partak tharof.

"e Prator, thos wishin to purtak will cum yearly, as the pullin will begin soon.

"e.p."

If I am asked why "jis this side of harisburg" was selected for the promised feat instead of the city of Augusta, I answer from conjecture, but with some confidence, because the ground chosen was near the central point between four rival towns, the citizens of all which "*mout wish to partak tharof;*" namely, Augusta, Springfield, Harrisburg, and Campbellton. Not that each was the rival of all the others, but that the first and the last were competitors, and each of the others backed the pretensions of its nearest neighbour. Harrisburg sided with Campbellton, *not because she had any interest in seeing the business of the two states centre upon the bank of the river, nearly opposite to her;* but because, like the "Union Democratic Republican Party of Georgia," she thought, after the adoption of the Federal Constitution, that the several towns of the confederacy should no longer be "separated" by the distinction of local party; but that, laying down all former prejudices and jealousies as a sacrifice on the altar of their country, they should become united in a *single body,* for the maintenance of those principles which they deemed essential to the *public welfare.*

Springfield, on the other hand, espoused the State Rights' creed. She admitted that, under the Federal Compact, she ought to love the sister states very much; but that, under the *Social Compact,* she ought to love her own state a little more; and she thought the two compacts perfectly reconcilable to each other. Instead of the towns of the several states getting into *single bodies* to preserve the *public welfare,* her doctrine was, that they should be kept in *separate bodies* to preserve the *private welfare.* She admitted frankly, that, living, as she always had lived, right amid gullies, vapours, fogs, creeks, and lagoons, she was wholly incapable of comprehending that expansive kind of benevolence, which taught her to love people whom she knew nothing about, as much as her next-door neighbours and friends. Until, therefore, she should learn it from the practical operation of the Federal Compact, she would stick to the oldfashioned Scotch love, which she understood perfectly, and "go in" for Augusta, live or die, hit or miss, right or wrong. As in the days of Mr. Jefferson, the Springfield doctrines prevailed, Campbellton was literally *nullified;* insomuch that, ten years ago, there was not a house left to mark the spot where once flourished this active, busy little village. Those who are curious to know where Springfield stood at the time of which I am speaking, have only to take their position at the inter-section of Broad and Marbury streets, in the city of Augusta, and they will be in the very heart of old Springfield. Sixty steps west, and as many east of this position, will measure the whole length of this Jeffersonian republican village, which never boasted of more than four dwelling-houses; and Broad-street measures its width, if we exclude kitchens and stables. And, while upon this subject, since it has been predicted by a man for whose opinions I entertain the pro-foundest respect * (especially since the prediction), that my writings will be read with increased interest a hundred years to come; and as I can see no good reason, if this be true, why they should not be read a thousand years hence with more interest, I will take the liberty of dropping a word here to the curious reader of the year 1933. He will certainly wish to know the site of Harrisburg (seeing it is doomed, at no distant period, to share the fate of Springfield) and of Campbellton.

Supposing, then, that if the great fire in Augusta, on the 3d of April, 1829, did not destroy that city, nothing will; I select this as a permanent object.

In 1798, Campbell-street was the western verge of Augusta, a limit to which it had advanced but a few years before, from Jackson-street. Thence to Springfield led a large road, now built up on either side, and forming a continuation of Broad-street. This road was cut across obliquely by a deep gully, the bed of which was an almost impassable bog, which entered the road about one hundred yards

* The Editor of the "Hickory Nut." [*Longstreet's note.*]

below Collock-street on the south, and left it about thirty yards below Collock-street on the north side of now Broad-street. It was called Campbell's Gully, from the name of the gentleman through whose possessions and near whose dwelling it wound its way to the river. Following the direction of Broad-street from Springfield westward, 1347 yards, will bring you to Harrisburg, which had nothing to boast of over Springfield but a warehouse for the storage of tobacco, then the staple of Georgia. Continue the same direction 700 yards, then face to your right hand, and follow your nose directly across Savannah river, and, upon ascending the opposite bank, you will be in the busiest part of Campbellton in 1798. Between Harrisburg and Springfield, and 1143 yards from the latter, there runs a stream which may be perpetual. At the time just mentioned, it flowed between banks twelve or fourteen feet high, and was then called, as it still is, "Hawk's Gully." *

Now Mr. Prator, like the most successful politician of the present day, was on all sides in a doubtful contest; and, accordingly, he laid off his gander-pulling ground on the nearest suitable unappropriated spot to the centre point between Springfield and Harrisburg. This was between Harrisburg and Hawk's Gully, to the south of the road, and embraced part of the road, but within 100 yards of Harrisburg.

When *"Satterday of thes pressents munth"* rolled round, I determined to go to the gander-pulling. When I reached the spot, a considerable number of persons, of different ages, sexes, sizes, and complexions, had collected from the rival towns and the country around. But few females were there, however; and those few were from the lowest walks of life.

A circular path of about forty yards diameter had already been laid out; over which, from two posts about ten feet apart, stretched a rope, the middle of which was directly over the path. The rope hung loosely, so as to allow it, with the weight of a gander attached to it, to vibrate in an arc of four or five feet span, and so as to bring the breast of the gander within barely easy reach of a man of middle stature upon a horse of common size.

A hat was now handed to such as wished to enter the list; and they threw into it twenty-five cents each; this sum was the victor's prize.

The devoted gander was now produced; and Mr. Prator, having first tied his feet together with a strong cord, proceeded to the *neck-*

* It took its name from an old man by the name of Hawk, who lived in a log hut on a small knoll on the eastern side of the gully, and about 100 yards south of the Harrisburg road. [*Longstreet's note.*]

greasing. Abhorrent as it may be to all who respect the tenderer relations of life, *Mrs.* Prator had actually prepared a gourd of *goose*-grease for this very purpose. For myself, when I saw Ned dip his hands into the grease, and commence stroking down the feathers from breast to head, my thoughts took a melancholy turn. They dwelt in sadness upon the many conjugal felicities which had probably been shared between the greasess and the greasee. I could see him as he stood by her side, through many a chilly day and cheerless night, when she was warming into life the offspring of their mutual loves, and repelled, with chivalrous spirit, every invasion of the consecrated spot which she had selected for her incubation. I could see him moving with patriarchal dignity by the side of his loved one, at the head of a smiling, prattling group, the rich reward of their mutual care, to the luxuries of the meadow or to the recreations of the pool. And now, alas! an extract from the smoking sacrifice of his bosom friend was desecrated to the unholy purpose of making his neck "a fit object" for Cruelty to reach "her quick, unerring fingers at." Ye friends of the sacred tie! judge what were my feelings when, in the midst of these reflections, the voice of James Prator thundered on mine ear, "Darn his old dodging soul; brother Ned! grease his neck till a fly can't light on it!"

Ned, having fulfilled his brother Jim's request as well as he could, attached the victim of his cruelty to the rope, directly over the path. On each side of the gander was stationed a man, whose office it was to lash forward any horse which might linger there for a moment; for, by the rules of the ring, all pulling was to be done at a brisk canter.

The word was now given for the competitors to mount and take their places on the ring. Eight appeared: Tall Zubley Zin, mounted upon Sally Spitfire; Arch Odum, mounted on Bull and Ingons (onions); Nathan Perdew, on Hellcat; James Dickson, on Nigger; David Williams, on Gridiron; Fat John Fulger, on Slouch; Gorham Bostwick, on Gimlet; and Turner Hammond, on 'Possum.

"Come, *gentlemen,*" said Commandant Prator, "fall in. All of you git behind one another, sort o' in a row."

All came into the track very kindly but Sally Spitfire and Gridiron. The former, as soon as she saw a general movement of horses, took it for granted there was mischief brewing, and, because she could not tell where it lay, she concluded it lay everywhere, and therefore took fright at everything.

Gridiron was a grave horse; but a suspicious eye which he cast to the right and left, wherever he moved, showed that "he was wide awake," and that "nobody better not go fooling with him," as his owner sometimes used to say. He took a sober but rather intense view of things; insomuch that, in his contemplations, he passed over the track three times before he could be prevailed upon to stop in it. He stopped at last, however; and when he was made to understand that this was all that was required of him for the present, he surrendered his suspicions at once, with a countenance which seemed plainly to say, "Oh, if this is all you want, I've no objection to it."

It was long before Miss Spitfire could be prevailed upon to do the like.

"Get another horse, Zube," said one; "Sal will never do for a gander pullin."

"I won't," said Zube. "If she won't do, I'll make her do. I want a nag that goes off with a spring; so that, when I get a hold, she'll cut the neck in two like a steel-trap."

At length Sally was rather flung than coaxed into the track, directly ahead of Gridiron.

"Now, gentlemen," said the master of the ceremonies, "no man's to make a grab till all's been once round; and when the first man *are* got round, then the whole twist and tucking of you grab away as you come under (Look here, Jim Fulger! you better not stand too close to that gander, I tell you), one after another. Now blaze away!" (the command for an onset of every kind with people of this order).

Off they went, Miss Sally delighted; for she now thought the whole parade would end in nothing more nor less than her favourite amusement, a race. But Gridiron's visage pronounced this the most nonsensical business that ever a horse of sense was engaged in since the world began.

For the first three rounds Zubly was wholly occupied in restraining Sally to her place; but he lost nothing by this, for the gander had escaped unhurt. On completing his third round, Zube reached forth his long arm, grabbed the gander by the neck with a firmness which seemed likely to defy *goose-grease,* and, at the same instant, he involuntarily gave Sally a sudden check. She raised her head, which before had been kept nearly touching her leader's hocks, and for the first time saw the gander in the act of descending upon her; at the same moment she received two pealing lashes from the whippers. The way she now broke for Springfield "is nothing to nobody." As Zube dashed down the road, the whole Circus raised a whoop after him. This started about twenty dogs, hounds, curs, and pointers, in full chase of him (for no one moved without his dog in those days). The dogs alarmed some belled cattle, which were grazing on Zube's path, just as he reached them; these joined him, with tails up and a tremendous rattling. Just beyond these went three tobacco-rollers, at distances of fifty and a hundred yards apart; each of whom gave Zube a terrific whoop, scream, or yell as he passed.

He went in and out of Hawk's Gully like a trapball, and was in Springfield "in less than no time." Here he was encouraged onward by a new recruit of dogs; but they gave up the chase as hopeless before they cleared the village. Just beyond Springfield, what should Sally encounter but a flock of geese! the tribe to which she owed all her misfortunes. She stopped suddenly, and Zube went over her head with the last acquired velocity. He was up in a moment, and the activity with which he pursued Sally satisfied every spectator that he was unhurt.

Gridiron, who had witnessed Miss Sally's treatment with astonishment and indignation, resolved not to pass between the posts until the whole matter should be explained to his satisfaction. He therefore stopped short, and, by very intelligible looks, demanded of the whippers whether, if he passed between them, he was to be treated as Miss Spitfire had been? The whippers gave him no satisfaction, and his rider signified, by reiterated thumps of the heel, that he should go through whether he would or not. Of these, however, Gridiron seemed to know nothing. In the midst of the conference, Gridiron's eye lit upon the oscillating gander, and every moment's survey of it begat in him a growing interest, as his slowly rising head, suppressed breath, and projected ears plainly evinced. After a short examination, he heaved a sigh, and looked behind him to see if the way was clear. It was plain that his mind was now made up; but, to satisfy the world that he would do nothing rashly, he took another view, and then wheeled and went for Harrisburg as if he had set in for a year's running. Nobody whooped at Gridiron, for all saw that his running was purely the result of philosophic deduction. The reader will not suppose all this consumed half the time which has been consumed in telling it, though it might have been so without interrupting the amusement; for Miss Spitfire's flight had completely suspended it for a time.

The remaining competitors now went on with the sport. A few rounds showed plainly that Odum or Bostwick would be the victor; but which, no one could tell. Whenever either of them came round, the gander's neck was sure of a severe wrench. Many a half pint of Jamaica was staked upon them, besides other things. The poor gander withstood many a strong pull before his wailings ceased. At length, however, they were hushed by Odum. Then came Bostwick, and broke the neck. The next grasp of Odum, it was thought, would bear away the head; but it did not. Then Bostwick was sure of it; but he missed it. Now Odum must surely have it. All is interest and animation; the horses sweep round with redoubled speed; every eye is upon Odum; his backers smiling, Bostwick's trembling. To the rope he comes; lifts his hand; when, lo! Fat John Fulger had borne it away the second before. All were astonished, all disappointed, and some were vexed a little; for it was now clear that, "if it hadn't o' been for his great, fat, greasy paw," to use their own language, "Odum would have gained the victory." Others cursed "that long-legged Zube Zin, who was so high he didn't know when his feet were cold, for bringing such a nag as Sal Spitfire to a gander-pullen; for if he'd o' been in his place, it would o' flung Bostwick right where that *gourd* o' hog's *lard* [Fulger] was."

Fulger's conduct was little calculated to reconcile them to their disappointment.

"Come here, Neddy Prator," said he, with a triumphant smile; "let your Uncle Johnny put his potato stealer [hand] into that hat, and tickle the chins of them *are* shiners a little! Oh you little shining sons o' bitches! walk into your Mas' Johnny's pocket, and jingle so as Arch Odum and Gory Bostwick may hear you! You hear 'em, Gory? *Boys,* don't pull with *men* any more. I've jist got my hand in; I wish I had a pond full o' ganders here now, jist to show how I could make their heads fly. Bet all I've won, you may hang three upon that rope, and I'll set Slouch at full speed, and take off the heads of all three the first grab; two with my hands and one with my teeth."

Thus he went on, but really there was no boasting in all this; it was all fun; for John knew, and all were convinced he knew, that his success was entirely the result of accident. John was really "a good-natured fellow," and his *cavorting* had an effect directly opposite to that which the reader would suppose it had; it reconciled all to their disappointment save one. I except little Billy Mixen, of Spirit Creek; who had staked the net proceeds of six quarts of huckleberries upon Odum, which he had been long keeping for a safe bet. *He* could not be reconciled until he fretted himself into a pretty little *piney*-woods fight, in which he got whipped; and then he went home perfectly satisfied. Fulger spent all his winnings with Prator in treats to the company; made most of them drunk, and thereby produced four Georgia *rotations;* * after which all parted good friends.

---

* I borrowed this term from Jim Inman at the time. "Why, Jim," said I to him, just as he rose from a fight, "what have you been doing?" "Oh," said he, "nothing but taking a little *rotation* with Bob M'Manus." [*Longstreet's note.*]

CAROLINE MATILDA KIRKLAND

★　★　★

Michigan life in the late 1830's and 1840's seemed crude to the refined Easterner, Mrs. Caroline M. Stansbury Kirkland (1801-1864), whose romantic notions received rude shocks as she mingled with gossipy, ague-smitten neighbors. In realistic but good-natured sketches she drew unflattering portraits of overworked women, incompetent men, rustic belles, and impoverished schoolmasters engaged in ordinary occupations and in merrymaking. Not unsympathetic in her descriptions of the rude angularities of the frontier, she satirized these people because she saw their unfulfilled possibilities rather than because she disliked them. Born in New York City and married to a college professor, Mrs. Kirkland tried her fortunes in Michigan at the time of the land speculation and the depression of 1837. *A New Home—Who'll Follow?* (1839) and *Western Clearings* (1845), from the latter of which the following selections are made, won immediate fame for their humor and truthfulness to life. Her later works, ten in number, were chiefly on literary, travel, and inspirational topics.

★　★　★

The Land-Fever

THE wild new country, with all its coarseness and all its disadvantages of various kinds, has yet a fascination for the settler, in consequence of a certain free, hearty tone, which has long since disappeared, if indeed it ever existed, in parts of the country where civilization has made greater progress. The really fastidious, and those who only pretend to be such, may hold this as poor compensation for the many things lacking of another kind; but those to whose apprehension sympathy and sincerity have a pre-eminent and independent charm, prefer the kindly warmth of the untaught, to the icy chill of the half-taught; and would rather be welcomed by the woodsman to his log-cabin, with its rough hearth, than make one of a crowd who feed the ostentation of a *millionaire,* or gaze with sated eyes upon costly feasts which it would be a mockery to dignify with the name of hospitality. The infrequency of inns in a newly settled country leads naturally to the practice of keeping "open house" for strangers; and it is rare indeed that the settler, however poor his accommodations, hesitates to offer the best he has to the tired wayfarer. Where payment is accepted, it is usually very inconsiderable; and it is seldom accepted at all, unless the guest is manifestly better off than his entertainer. But whether a compensation be taken or refused, the heartiness of manner with which every thing that the house affords is offered, cannot but be acceptable to the visitor. Even the ever rampant pride, which comes up so disagreeably at the West, where the outward appearance of the stranger betokens any advantage of condition, slumbers when that stranger claims hospitality. His horse is cared for with more solicitude than the host ever bestows on his own; the table is covered with the best provisions the house affords, set forth in the holiday dishes; the bed is endued with the brightest patchwork quilt—the pride of the housewife's heart; and if there be any fat fowls—any white honey—any good tea—about the premises, the guest will be sure to have it, even though it may have been reserved for "Independence" or "Thanksgiving."

This habit was however reversed, or at least suspended, during the speculating times. The country was then inundated with people who came to buy land,—not to clear and plough, but as men buy a lottery-ticket or dig for gold—in the hope of unreasonable and unearned profits. These people were considered as public enemies. No personal violence was offered them, as might have been the case at the South-west; but every obstacle, in the shape of extravagant charges, erroneous information, and rude refusal, was thrown in their way. Few were discouraged by this, however; for they came in the spirit of the knights of romance when they had to enter enchanted castles—strong in faith of the boundless treasures which were to reward their perseverance.

To mislead an unpractised land-hunter was a matter of no great difficulty; for few things are more intricate and puzzling, at first, than the system which has been devised to facilitate the identifying of particular spots. Section-corners and quarter-stakes, eighties, and forties, and fractions, are plain enough when one is habituated to them, and they *seem* plain enough to the new man,—on paper. But when he finds himself in the woods, with his maps and his copious memoranda, he is completely at sea, with no guide but the compass. A friend who afterwards became quite a proficient in the mysteries of land-finding tells me that he twice lost himself completely in the woods. "The first time," he says, "my mishap was owing to the wandering habits of a wild Indian pony which I had chosen on account of his power of ceaseless travel. He had been accustomed to pick up his living where he could find it, and he took advantage of my jogging pace, just at dusk, when I did not feel *too* certain of my whereabout, to quit the scarce-defined road, in search of something tempting which he espied at a distance. My resource in this case was to abandon my horse, and fix my eyes on the North Star, which I knew would bring me to a certain State road, in due time. The other occasion was in broad daylight, but when there was only an occasional gleam of sunshine, so that I had no steady guide as to direction. The ground was so thickly strown with leaves that my horse's hoofs left no permanent track, and I found myself in a complete maze. The trees were all alike to my bewildered eyes (I had left my compass at the last lodging-place); and all I knew was that I was south of the road which I had quitted for the sake of saving some miles' distance. After many efforts at marking trees—very ineffectual without an axe—I bethought me of a newspaper, which I tore into pieces and affixed to bushes and low limbs as I went, and so obtained a straight line; by which means, after some hours' rather anxious wandering, I was finally extricated."

To pass a night in the woods is a small affair for a hunting party; but it is something quite different for a solitary individual, unprovided with axe or gun, and, of course, unable to make himself comfortable in any way. To sleep in a tree might do, if trees were not occasionally haunted by wild cats; or a lair in the heaped leaves of autumn, if there were not a chance of warming into activity a nest of rattlesnakes. These are no doubt partly useless fears, but to the stranger they are very real; and they tend not a little to the increase of his difficulties by discomposing his nerves when cool reflection would be his best friend.

Mistakes in "locating" land were often very serious, even where there had been no intention to deceive—the purchaser finding only swamp or hopeless gravel, when he had purchased fine farming land and maple timber. Every mile square is marked by blazed trees, and the corners especially distinguished by stakes whose place is pointed out by trees called Witness-trees, and so accurate and so minute is the whole system that it seems almost incredible that so many errors should have arisen. The backwoodsman made no mistakes, for to him a stump, or a stone, or a prostrate tree, has individuality; and he will never confound it with any other. One accustomed to wandering in the woods will know even the points of the compass, in a strange place, without sun or star to guide him. But the fact of the unwillingness of the actual settler to guide the speculator faithfully, became so well known, that purchasers often preferred relying on their own sagacity, backed by what seemed unmistakable rules, to trusting such disaffected guides. Innumerable stories are current in the woods of the perplexities of city gentlemen;—and the following, if not strictly true, will serve to illustrate somewhat the state of things in those wild times when sober prudence was forgotten, and delusion ruled the hour. I shall call it, for want of better title,

A REMINISCENCE OF THE LAND-FEVER

The years 1835 and 1836 will long be remembered by the Western settler—and perhaps by some few people at the East, too—as the period when the madness of speculation in lands had reached a point to which no historian of the time will ever be able to do justice. A faithful picture of those wild days would subject the most veracious chronicler to the charge of exaggeration; and our great-grand-children can hope to obtain an adequate idea of the infatuation which led away their forefathers, only by the study of such detached facts as may be noted down by those in whose minds the feeling recollection of the delusion is still fresh. Perhaps when our literary existence shall have become sufficiently confirmed to call for the collection of Ana, something more may be gleaned from the correspondence in which were embodied the exultings of the successful, and the lamentations of the disappointed.

"Seeing is believing," certainly, in most cases; but in the days of the land-fever, we, who were in the midst of the infected district, scarcely found it so. The whirl, the fervour, the flutter, the rapidity of step, the sparkling of eyes, the beating of hearts, the striking of hands, the utter *abandon* of the hour, were incredible, inconceivable. The "man of one idea" was everywhere: no man had two. He who had no money, begged, borrowed, or stole it; he who had, thought he made a generous sacrifice, if he lent it at cent per cent. The tradesman forsook his shop; the farmer his plough; the merchant his counter; the lawyer his office; nay, the minister his desk, to join the general chase. Even the schoolmaster, in his longing to be "abroad" with the rest, laid down his birch, or in the flurry of his hopes, plied it with diminished unction.

> "Tramp! tramp! along the land they rode,
> Splash! splash! along the sea!"

The man with one leg, or he that had none, could at least get on board a steamer, and make for Chicago or Milwaukee; the strong, the able, but above all, the "enterprising," set out with his pocket-map and his pocket-compass, to thread the dim woods, and see with his own eyes. Who would waste time in planting, in building, in hammering iron, in making shoes, when the path to wealth lay wide and flowery before him?

A ditcher was hired by the job to do a certain piece of work in his line. "Well, John, did you make any thing?"

"Pretty well; I cleared about two dollars a day: but I should have made more by *standing round;*" i.e., watching the land-market for bargains.

This favourite occupation of all classes was followed by its legitimate consequences. Farmers were as fond of "standing round" as any body; and when harvest time came, it was discovered that the best land requires sowing; and grain, and of course other articles of general necessity, rose to an unprecedented price. The hordes of travellers flying through the country in all directions were often cited as the cause of the distressing scarcity; but the true source must be sought in the diversion, or rather suspension, of the industry of the entire population. Be this as it may, of the wry faces made at the hard fare, the travellers contributed no inconsiderable portion; for they were generally city gentlemen, or at least gentlemen who had lived long enough in the city to have learned to prefer oysters to salt pork. This checked not their ardour, however; for the golden glare before their eyes had power to neutralize the hue of all present objects. On they pressed, with headlong zeal: the silent and pathless forest, the deep miry marsh, the gloom of night, and the fires of noon, beheld alike the march of the speculator. Such searching of trees for town lines! Such ransacking of the woods for section corners, ranges, and base lines! Such anxious care in identifying spots possessing particular advantages! And then, alas! after all, such precious blunders!

These blunders called into action another class of operators, who became popularly known as "land-lookers." These met you at every turn, ready to furnish "water-power," "pine lots," "choice farming tracts," or any thing else, at a moment's notice. Bar-rooms and street-corners swarmed with these prowling gentry. It was impossible to mention any part of the country which they had not personally surveyed. They would tell you, with the gravity of astrologers, what sort of timber predominated on any given tract, drawing sage deductions as to the capabilities of the soil. Did you incline to city property? Lo! a splendid chart, setting forth the advantages of some unequalled site, and your confidential friend, the land-looker, able to tell you more than all about it, or to accompany you to the happy spot; though that he would not advise; "bad roads," "nothing fit to eat," etc.; and all this from a purely disinterested solicitude for your welfare.

These amiable individuals were, strange to tell, no favourites with the actual settlers. If they disliked the gentleman speculator, they hated with a perfect hatred him who aided by his local knowledge the immense purchases of non-residents. These short-sighted and prejudiced persons forgot the honour and distinction which must result from their insignificant farms being surrounded by the possessions of the magnates of the land. They saw only the solitude which would probably be entailed on them for years; and it was counted actual treason in a settler to give any facilities to the land-looker, of whatever grade. "Let the land-shark do his own hunting," was their frequent reply to applications of this kind; and some thought them quite right. Yet this state of feeling among the Hard-handed was not without its inconvenient results to city gentlemen, as witness the case of our friend Mr. Willoughby, a very prim and smart bachelor, from ——.

It was when the whirlwind was at its height, that a gentleman wearing the air of a bank-director, at the very least—in other words, that of an uncommonly fat pigeon—drew bridle at the bars in front of one of the roughest log houses in the county of ——. The horse and his rider were loaded with all those unnecessary defences, and cumbrous comforts, which the fashion of the time prescribed in such cases. Blankets, valise, saddle-bags, and holsters nearly covered the steed; a most voluminous enwrapment of India-rubber cloth completely enveloped the rider. The gallant sorrel seemed indeed fit for his burden. He looked as if he might have swam any stream in Michigan

> "Barded from counter to tail,
> And the rider arm'd complete in mail;"

yet he seemed a little jaded, and hung his head languidly, while his master accosted the tall and meagre tenant of the log cabin.

This individual and his dwelling resembled each other in an unusual degree. The house was, as we have said, of the roughest; its ribs scarcely half filled in with clay; its "looped and windowed raggedness" rendered more conspicuous by the tattered cotton sheets which had long done duty as glass, and which now fluttered in every breeze; its roof of oak shingles, warped into every possible curve; and its stick chimney, so like its owner's hat, open at the top, and jammed in at the sides; all shadowed forth the contour and equipments of the exceedingly easy and self-satisfied person who leaned on the fence, and snapped his long cart-whip, while he gave such answers as suited him to the gentleman in the India-rubbers, taking especial care not to invite him to alight.

"Can you tell me, my friend, ——" civilly began Mr. Willoughby.

"Oh! *friend!*" interrupted the settler; "who told you I was your friend? Friends is scuss in these parts."

"You have at least no reason to be otherwise," replied the traveller, who was blessed with a very patient temper, especially where there was no use in getting angry.

"I don't know that," was the reply. "What fetch'd you into these woods?"

"If I should say 'my horse,' the answer would perhaps be as civil as the question."

"Jist as you like," said the other, turning on his heel, and walking off.

"I wished merely to ask you," resumed Mr. Willoughby, talking after the nonchalant son of the forest, "whether this is Mr. Pepper's land."

"How do you know it ain't mine?"

"I'm not likely to know, at present, it seems," said the traveller, whose patience was getting a little frayed. And taking out his memorandum-book, he ran over his minutes: "South half of north-west quarter of section fourteen— Your name is Leander Pepper, is it not?"

"Where did you get so much news? You ain't the sheriff, be ye?"

"Pop!" screamed a white-headed urchin from the house, "Mam says supper's ready."

"So ain't I," replied the papa; "I've got all my chores to do yet." And he busied himself at a log pig-stye on the opposite side of the road, half as large as the dwelling-house. Here he was soon surrounded by a squealing multitude, with whom he seemed to hold a regular conversation.

Mr. Willoughby looked at the westering sun, which was not far above the dense wall of trees that shut in the small clearing; then at the heavy clouds which advanced from the north, threatening a stormy night; then at his watch, and then at his note-book; and after all, at his predicament—on the whole, an unpleasant prospect. But at this moment a female face showed itself at the door. Our travel-ler's memory reverted at once to the testimony of Ledyard and Mungo Park; and he had also some floating and indistinct poetical recollec-tions of woman's being useful when a man was in difficulties, though hard to please at other times. The result of these reminiscences, which occupied a precious second, was that Mr. Willoughby dismounted, fastened his horse to the fence, and advanced with a brave and de-termined air, to throw himself upon female kindness and sympathy.

He naturally looked at the lady, as he approached the door, but she did not return the compliment. She looked at the pigs, and talked to the children, and Mr. Willoughby had time to observe that she was the very duplicate of her husband; as tall, as bony, as ragged, and twice as cross-looking.

"Malviny Jane!" she exclaimed, in no dulcet treble, "be done a-pad-dlin' in that 'ere water! If I come there, I'll—"

"You'd better look at Sophrony, I guess!" was the reply.

"Why, what's she a-doin'?"

"Well, I guess if you look, you'll see!" responded Miss Malvina, coolly, as she passed into the house, leaving at every step a full im-pression of her foot in the same black mud that covered her sister from head to foot.

The latter was saluted with a hearty cuff, as she emerged from the puddle; and it was just at the propitious moment when her shrill howl aroused the echoes, that Mr. Willoughby, having reached the threshold, was obliged to set about making the agreeable to the mamma. And he called up for the occasion all his politeness.

"I believe I must become an intruder on your hospitality for the night, madam," he began. The dame still looked at the pigs. Mr. Wil-loughby tried again, in less courtly phrase.

"Will it be convenient for you to lodge me to-night, ma'am? I have been disappointed in my search for a hunting-party, whom I had engaged to meet, and the night threatens a storm."

"I don't know nothin' about it; you must ask the old man," said the lady, now for the first time taking a survey of the new comer; "with *my* will, we'll lodge nobody."

This was not very encouraging, but it was a poor night for the woods; so our traveller persevered, and making so bold a push for the door that the lady was obliged to retreat a little, he entered, and said he would await her husband's coming.

And in truth he could scarcely blame the cool reception he had experienced, when he beheld the state of affairs within those muddy precincts. The room was large, but it swarmed with human beings. The huge open fire-place, with its hearth of rough stone, occupied nearly the whole of one end of the apartment; and near it stood a long cradle, containing a pair of twins, who cried—a sort of hopeless cry, as if they knew it would do no good, yet could not help it. The schoolmaster, (it was his week,) sat reading a tattered novel, and rocking the cradle occasionally, when the children cried *too* loud. An old grey-headed Indian was curiously crouched over a large tub, shelling corn on the edge of a hoe; but he ceased his noisy employment when he saw the stranger, for no Indian will ever willingly be seen at work, though he may be sometimes compelled by the fear of starvation or the longing for whiskey, to degrade himself by labour. Near the only window was placed the work-bench and entire paraphernalia of the shoemaker, who in these regions travels from house to house, shoeing the family and mending the harness as he goes, with various interludes of songs and jokes, ever new and acceptable. This one, who was a little, bald, twinkling-eyed fellow, made the smoky rafters ring with the burden of that favourite ditty of the west:

> "All kinds of game to hunt, my boys, also the buck and doe,
>   All down by the banks of the river O-hi-o;"

and children of all sizes, clattering in all keys, completed the picture and the concert.

The supper-table, which maintained its place in the midst of this living and restless mass, might remind one of the square stone lying bedded in the bustling leaves of the acanthus; but the associations would be any but those of Corinthian elegance. The only object which at that moment diversified its dingy surface was an iron hoop, into which the mistress of the feast proceeded to turn a quantity of smoking hot potatoes, adding afterward a bowl of salt, and another of pork fat, by courtesy denominated gravy: plates and knives dropped in afterward, at the discretion of the company.

Another call of "Pop! pop!" brought in the host from the pig-stye; the heavy rain which had now begun to fall, having no doubt, expedited the performance of the chores. Mr. Willoughby, who had established himself resolutely, took advantage of a very cloudy assent from the proprietor, to lead his horse to a shed, and to deposit in a corner his cumbrous outer gear; while the company used in turn the iron skillet which served as a wash-basin, dipping the water from a large trough outside, overflowing with the abundant drippings of the eaves. Those who had no pocket-handkerchiefs, contented themselves with a nondescript article which seemed to stand for the family towel; and when this ceremony was concluded, all seriously addressed themselves to the demolition of the potatoes. The grown people were accommodated with chairs and chests; the children prosecuted a series of flying raids upon the good cheer, snatching a potato now and then as they could find an opening under the raised arm of one of the family, and then retreating to the chimney corner, tossing the hot prize from hand to hand, and blowing it stoutly the while. The old Indian had disappeared.

To our citizen, though he felt inconveniently hungry, this primitive meal seemed a little meagre; and he ventured to ask if he could not be accommodated with some tea.

"Ain't my victuals good enough for you?"

"Oh!—the potatoes are excellent, but I'm very fond of tea."

"So be I, but I can't have every thing I want—can you?"

This produced a laugh from the shoemaker, who seemed to think his patron very witty, while the schoolmaster, not knowing but the stranger might happen to be one of his examiners next year, produced only a faint giggle, and then reducing his countenance instantly to an awful gravity, helped himself to his seventh potato.

The rain which now poured violently, not only outside but through many a crevice in the roof, naturally kept Mr. Willoughby cool; and finding that dry potatoes gave him the hiccups, he withdrew from the table, and seating himself on the shoemaker's bench, took a survey of his quarters.

Two double-beds and the long cradle seemed all the sleeping apparatus; but there was a ladder which doubtless led to a lodging above. The sides of the room were hung with abundance of decent clothing, and the dresser was well stored with the usual articles, among which a tea-pot and canister shone conspicuous; so that the appearance of inhospitality could not arise from poverty, and Mr. Willoughby concluded to set it down to the account of rustic ignorance.

The eating ceased not until the hoop was empty, and then the company rose and stretched themselves, and began to guess it was about time to go to bed. Mr. Willoughby inquired what was to be done with his horse.

"Well! I s'pose he can stay where he is."

"But what can he have to eat?"

"I reckon you won't get nothing for him, without you turn him out on the mash."

"He would get off, to a certainty!"

"Tie his legs."

The unfortunate traveller argued in vain. Hay was "scuss," and potatoes were "scusser;" and in short the "mash" was the only resource, and these natural meadows afford but poor picking after the first of October. But to the "mash" was the good steed despatched, ingloriously hampered, with the privilege of munching wild grass in the rain, after his day's journey.

Then came the question of lodging for his master. The lady, who had by this time drawn out a trundle-bed, and packed it full of children, said there was no bed for him, unless he could sleep "up chamber" with the boys.

Mr. Willoughby declared that he should make out very well with a blanket by the fire.

"Well! just as you like," said his host; "but Solomon sleeps there, and if you like to sleep by Solomon, it is more than *I* should."

This was the name of the old Indian, and Mr. Willoughby once more cast woful glances toward the ladder.

But now the schoolmaster, who seemed rather disposed to be civil, declared that he could sleep very well in the long cradle, and would relinquish his place beside the shoemaker to the guest, who was obliged to content himself with this arrangement, which was such as was most usual in those times.

The storm continued through the night, and many a crash in the woods attested its power. The sound of a storm in the dense forest is almost precisely similar to that of a heavy surge breaking on a rocky beach; and when our traveller slept, it was only to dream of wreck and disaster at sea, and to wake in horror and affright. The wild rain drove in at every crevice, and wet the poor children in the loft so thoroughly, that they crawled shivering down the ladder, and stretched themselves on the hearth, regardless of Solomon, who had returned after the others were in bed.

But morning came at last; and our friend, who had no desire farther to test the vaunted hospitality of a western settler, was not among the latest astir. The storm had partially subsided; and although the clouds still lowered angrily, and his saddle had enjoyed the benefit of a leak in the roof during the night, Mr. Willoughby resolved to push on as far as the next clearing, at least, hoping for something for breakfast besides potatoes and salt. It took him a weary while to find his horse, and when he had saddled him, and strapped on his various accoutrements, he entered the house, and inquired what he was to pay for his entertainment—laying somewhat of a stress on the last word.

His host, nothing daunted, replied that he guessed he would let him off for a dollar.

Mr. Willoughby took out his purse, and as he placed a silver dollar in the leathern palm outspread to receive it, happening to look toward the hearth, and perceiving the preparations for a very substantial breakfast, the long pent-up vexation burst forth.

"I really must say, Mr. Pepper—" he began: his tone was certainly that of an angry man, but it only made his host laugh.

"If this is your boasted western hospitality, I can tell you—"

"You'd better tell me what the dickens you are peppering me up this fashion for! My name isn't Pepper, no more than yours is! May be that *is* your name; you seem pretty warm."

"Your name not Pepper! Pray what is it, then?"

"Ah! there's the thing now! You land-hunters ought to know sich things without asking."

"Land-hunter! I'm no land-hunter!"

"Well! you're a land-shark, then—swallowin' up poor men's farms. The less I see of such cattle, the better I'm pleased."

"Confound you!" said Mr. Willoughby, who waxed warm, "I tell you I've nothing to do with land. I wouldn't take your whole state for a gift."

"What did you tell my woman you was a land-hunter for, then?"

And now the whole matter became clear in a moment; and it was found that Mr. Willoughby's equipment, with the mention of a "hunting party," had completely misled both host and hostess. And to do them justice, never were regret and vexation more heartily expressed.

"You needn't judge our new-country folks by me," said Mr. Handy, for such proved to be his name; "any man in these parts would as soon bite off his own nose, as to snub a civil traveller that wanted a supper and a night's lodging. But somehow or other, your lots o' fixin', and your askin' after that 'ere Pepper—one of the worst land-sharks we've ever had here—made me mad; and I know I treated you worse than an Indian."

"Humph!" said Solomon.

"But," continued the host, "you shall see whether my old woman can't set a good breakfast, when she's a mind to. Come, you shan't stir a step till you've had breakfast; and just take back this plaguey dollar. I wonder it didn't burn my fingers when I took it!"

Mrs. Handy set forth her very best, and a famous breakfast it was, considering the times. And before it was finished, the hunting party made their appearance, having had some difficulty in finding their companion, who had made no very uncommon mistake as to section corners and town-lines.

"I'll tell ye what," said Mr. Handy, confidentially, as the cavalcade with its baggage-ponies, loaded with tents, gun-cases, and hampers of provisions, was getting into order for a march to the prairies, "I'll tell ye what; if you've occasion to stop any where in the Bush, you'd better tell 'em at the first goin' off that you ain't land-hunters."

But Mr. Willoughby had already had "a caution."

The Bee-Tree

AMONG the various settlers of the wide West, there is no class which exhibits more striking peculiarities than that which, in spite of hard work, honesty, and sobriety, still continues hopelessly poor. None find more difficulty in the solution of the enigma presented by this state of things, than the sufferers themselves; and it is with some bitterness of spirit that they come at last to the conclusion, that the difference between their own condition and that of their prosperous neighbours, is entirely owing to their own "bad luck;" while the prosperous neighbours look musingly at the ragged children and squalid wife, and regret that the head of the house "ha'n't no faculty." Perhaps neither view is quite correct.

In the very last place one would have selected for a dwelling,—in the centre of a wide expanse of low, marshy land,—on a swelling knoll, which looks like an island,—stands the forlorn dwelling of my good friend, Silas Ashburn, one of the most conspicuous victims of the "bad luck" alluded to. Silas was among the earliest settlers of our part of the country, and had half a county to choose from when he "located" in the swamp,—half a county of as beautiful dale and upland as can be found in the vicinity of the great lakes. But he says there is "the very first-rate of pasturing" for his cows, (and well there may be, on forty acres of wet grass!) and as for the agues which have nearly made skeletons of himself and his family, his opinion is that it would not have made a bit of difference if he had settled on the highest land in Michi*gan,* since "every body knows if you've got to have the ague, why you've got to, and all the high land and dry land, and *Queen Ann* * in the world wouldn't make no odds."

Silas does not get rich, nor even comfortably well off, although

* Quinine. [*Mrs. Kirkland's note.*]

he works, as he says, "like a tiger." This he thinks is because "rich folks ain't willing poor folks should live," and because he, in particular, always has such bad luck. Why shouldn't he make money? Why should he not have a farm as well stocked, a house as well supplied, and a family as well clothed and cared for in all respects, as his old neighbour John Dean, who came with him from "York State"? Dean has never speculated, nor hunted, nor fished, nor found honey, nor sent his family to pick berries for sale. All these has Silas done, and more. His family have worked hard; they have worn their old clothes till they well nigh dropped off; many a day, nay, month, has passed, seeing potatoes almost their sole sustenance; and all this time Dean's family had plenty of every thing they wanted, and Dean just jogged on, as easy as could be; hardly ever stirring from home, except on 'lection days; wasting a great deal of time, too, (so Silas thinks,) "helping the women folks." "But some people get all the luck."

These and similar reflections seem to be scarcely ever absent from the mind of Silas Ashburn, producing any but favourable results upon his character and temper. He cannot be brought to believe that Dean has made more money by splitting rails in the winter than his more · enterprising neighbour by hunting deer, skilful and successful as he is. He will not notice that Dean often buys his venison for half the money he has earned while Silas was hunting it. He has never observed, that while his own sallow helpmate goes barefoot and bonnetless to the brush-heap to fill her ragged apron with miserable fuel, the cold wind careering through her scanty covering, Mrs. Dean sits by a good fire, amply provided by her careful husband, patching for the twentieth time his great overcoat; and that by the time his Betsey has kindled her poor blaze, and sits cowering over it, shaking with ague, Mrs. Dean, with well-swept hearth, is busied in preparing her husband's comfortable supper.

These things Silas does not and will not see; and he ever resents fiercely any hint, however kindly and cautiously given, that the steady exercise of his own ability for labour, and a *little* more thrift on the part of his wife, would soon set all things right. When he spends a whole night " 'coon-hunting," and is obliged to sleep half the next day, and feels good for nothing the day after, it is impossible to convince him that the "varmint" had better been left to cumber the ground, and the two or three dollars that the expedition cost him been bestowed in the purchase of a blanket.

"A blanket!" he would exclaim angrily; "don't be puttin' sich uppish notions into my folks' heads! Let 'em make comfortables out o' their old gowns, and if that don't do, let 'em sleep in their day-clothes, as I do! Nobody needn't suffer with a great fire to sleep by."

The children of this house are just what one would expect from such training. Labouring beyond their strength at such times as it suits their father to work, they have nevertheless abundant opportunity for idleness; and as the mother scarcely attempts to control them, they usually lounge listlessly by the fireside, or bask in the sunshine, when Ashburn is absent; and as a natural consequence of this irregular mode of life, the whole family are frequently prostrate with agues, suffering every variety of wretchedness, while there is perhaps no other case of disease in the neighbourhood. Then comes the two-fold evil of a long period of inactivity, and a proportionately long doctor's bill; and as Silas is strictly honest, and means to wrong no man of his due, the scanty comforts of the convalescents are cut down to almost nothing, and their recovery sadly delayed, that the heavy expenses of illness may be provided for. This is some of poor Ashburn's "bad luck."

One of the greatest temptations to our friend Silas, and to most of his class, is a bee-hunt. Neither deer, nor 'coons, nor prairie-hens, nor even bears, prove half as powerful enemies to any thing like regular business, as do these little thrifty vagrants of the forest. The slightest hint of a bee-tree will entice Silas Ashburn and his sons from the most profitable job of the season, even though the defection is sure to result in entire loss of the offered advantage; and if the hunt prove successful, the luscious spoil is generally too tempting to allow of any care for the future, so long as the "sweet'nin" can be persuaded to last. "It costs nothing," will poor Mrs. Ashburn observe, "let 'em enjoy it. It isn't often we have such good luck." As to the cost, close computation might lead to a different conclusion; but the Ashburns are no calculators.

It was on one of the lovely mornings of our ever lovely autumn, so early that the sun had scarcely touched the tops of the still verdant forest, that Silas Ashburn and his eldest son sallied forth for a day's chopping on the newly-purchased land of a rich settler, who had been but a few months among us. The tall form of the father, lean and gaunt as the very image of Famine, derived little grace from the rags which streamed from the elbows of his almost sleeveless coat, or flapped round the tops of his heavy boots, as he strode across the long causeway that formed the communication from his house to the dry land. Poor Joe's costume showed, if possible, a still greater need of the aid of that useful implement, the needle. His mother is one who thinks little of the ancient proverb which commends the stitch in time; and the clothing under her care sometimes falls in pieces, seam by seam, for want of the occasional aid is rendered more especially necessary by the slightness of the original sewing; so that the brisk breeze of the morning gave the poor boy no faint resemblance to a tall young aspen,

"With all its leaves fast fluttering, all at once."

The little conversation which passed between the father and son was such as necessarily makes up much of the talk of the poor,—turning on the difficulties and disappointments of life, and the expedients by which there may seem some slight hope of eluding these disagreeables.

"If we hadn't had sich bad luck this summer," said Mr. Ashburn, "losing that heifer, and the pony, and them three hogs,—all in that plaguy spring-hole, too,—I thought to have bought that timbered forty of Dean. It would have squared out my farm jist about right."

"The pony didn't die in the spring-hole, father," said Joe.

"No, he did not, but he got his death there, for all. He never stopped shiverin' from the time he fell in. *You* thought he had the agur, but I know'd well enough what ailed him; but I wasn't a goin' to let Dean know, because he'd ha' thought himself so blam'd cunning, after all he'd said to me about that spring-hole. If the agur could kill, Joe, we'd all ha' been dead long ago."

Joe sighed,—a sigh of assent. They walked on musingly.

"This is going to be a good job of Keene's," continued Mr. Ashburn, turning to a brighter theme, as they crossed the road and struck into the "timbered land," on their way to the scene of the day's operations. "He has bought three eighties, all lying close together, and he'll want as much as one forty cleared right off; and I've a good notion to take the fencin' of it as well as the choppin'. He's got plenty of money, and they say he don't shave quite so close as some. But I tell you, Joe, if I do take the job, you must turn to like a catamount, for I ain't a-going to make a nigger o' myself, and let my children do nothing but eat."

"Well, father," responded Joe, whose pale face gave token of any thing but high living, "I'll do what I can; but you know I never work two days at choppin' but what I have the agur like sixty,—and a feller can't work when he's got the agur."

"Not while the fit's on, to be sure," said the father; "but I've worked many an afternoon after my fit was over, when my head felt as big as a half-bushel, and my hands would ha' sizzed if I'd put 'em in water. Poor folks has got to work—but, Joe! if there isn't bees, by golly! I wonder if any body's been a baitin' for 'em? Stop! hush! watch which way they go!"

And with breathless interest—forgetful of all troubles, past, present, and future—they paused to observe the capricious wheelings and flittings of the little cluster, as they tried every flower on which the sun shone, or returned again and again to such as suited best their discriminating taste. At length, after a weary while, one suddenly rose into the air with a loud whizz, and after balancing a moment on a level with the tree-tops, darted off, like a well-sent arrow, toward the east, followed instantly by the whole busy company, till not a loiterer remained.

"Well! if this isn't luck!" exclaimed Ashburn, exultingly; "they make right for Keene's land! We'll have 'em! go ahead, Joe, and keep your eye on 'em!"

Joe obeyed so well in both points, that he not only outran his father, but very soon turned a summerset over a gnarled root or *grub* which lay in his path. This *faux pas* nearly demolished one side of his face, and what remained of his jacket sleeve, while his father, not quite so heedless, escaped falling, but tore his boot almost off with what he called "a contwisted stub of the toe."

But these were trifling inconveniences, and only taught them to use a little more caution in their eagerness. They followed on, unweariedly; crossed several fences, and threaded much of Mr. Keene's tract of forest-land, scanning with practised eye every decayed tree, whether standing or prostrate, until at length, in the side of a gigantic but leafless oak, they espied, some forty feet from the ground, the "sweet home" of the immense swarm whose scouts had betrayed their hiding-place.

"The Indians have been here;" said Ashburn; "you see they've felled this saplin' agin the bee-tree, so as they could climb up to the hole; but the red devils have been disturbed afore they had time to dig it out. If they'd had axes to cut down the big tree, they wouldn't have left a smitchin o' honey, they're such tarnal thieves!"

Mr. Ashburn's ideas of morality were much shocked at the thought of the dishonesty of the Indians, who, as is well known, have no rights of any kind; but considering himself as first finder, the lawful proprietor of this much-coveted treasure, gained too without the trouble of a protracted search, or the usual amount of baiting, and burning of honeycombs, he lost no time in taking possession after the established mode.

To cut his initials with his axe on the trunk of the bee-tree, and to make *blazes* on several of the trees he had passed, to serve as waymarks to the fortunate spot, detained him but few minutes; and with many a cautious noting of the surrounding localities, and many a charge to Joe "not to say nothing to nobody," Silas turned his steps homeward, musing on the important fact that he had had good luck for once, and planning important business quite foreign to the day's chopping.

Now it so happened that Mr. Keene, who is a restless old gentleman, and, moreover, quite green in the dignity of a land-holder, thought proper to turn his horse's head, for this particular morning ride, directly towards these same "three eighties," on which he had engaged Ashburn and his son to commence the important work of clearing. Mr. Keene is low of stature, rather globular in contour, and exceedingly parrot-nosed; wearing, moreover, a face red enough to lead one to suppose he had made his money as a dealer in claret; but, in truth, one of the kindest of men, in spite of a little quickness of temper. He is profoundly versed in the art and mystery of store-keeping, and as profoundly ignorant of all that must sooner or later be learned by every resident land-owner of the western country.

Thus much being premised, we shall hardly wonder that our good old friend felt exceedingly aggrieved at meeting Silas Ashburn and the "lang-legged chiel" Joe, (who has grown longer with every shake of ague,) on the way *from* his tract, instead of *to* it.

"What in the world's the matter now!" began Mr. Keene, rather testily. "Are you never going to begin that work?"

"I don't know but I shall;" was the cool reply of Ashburn; "I can't begin it to-day, though."

"And why not, pray, when I've been so long waiting?"

"Because, I've got something else that must be done first. You don't think your work is all the work there is in the world, do you?"

Mr. Keene was almost too angry to reply, but he made an effort to say, "When am I to expect you, then?"

"Why, I guess we'll come on in a day or two, and then I'll bring both the boys."

So saying, and not dreaming of having been guilty of an incivility, Mr. Ashburn passed on, intent only on his bee-tree.

Mr. Keene could not help looking after the ragged pair for a moment, and he muttered angrily as he turned away, "Aye! pride and beggary go together in this confounded new country! You feel very independent, no doubt, but I'll try if I can't find somebody that wants money."

And Mr. Keene's pony, as if sympathizing with his master's vexation, started off at a sharp, passionate trot, which he has learned, no doubt, under the habitual influence of the spicy temper of his rider.

To find labourers who wanted money, or who would own that they wanted it, was at that time no easy task. Our poorer neighbours have been so little accustomed to value household comforts, that the opportunity to obtain them presents but feeble incitement to that continuous industry which is usually expected of one who works in the employ of another. However, it happened in this case that Mr. Keene's star was in the ascendant, and the woods resounded, ere long, under the sturdy strokes of several choppers.

The Ashburns, in the meantime, set themselves busily at work to make due preparations for the expedition which they had planned for the following night. They felt, as does every one who finds a bee-tree in this region, that the prize was their own—that nobody else had the slightest claim to its rich stores; yet the gathering in of the spoils was to be performed, according to the invariable custom where the country is much settled, in the silence of night, and with every precaution of secrecy. This seems inconsistent, yet such is the fact.

The remainder of the "lucky" day and the whole of the succeeding one, passed in scooping troughs for the reception of the honey,— tedious work at best, but unusually so in this instance, because several of the family were prostrate with the ague. Ashburn's anxiety lest some of his customary bad luck should intervene between discovery and possession, made him more impatient and harsh than usual; and the interior of that comfortless cabin would have presented to a chance visitor, who knew not of the golden hopes which cheered its inmates, an aspect of unmitigated wretchedness. Mrs. Ashburn sat almost in the fire, with a tattered hood on her head and the relics of a bed-quilt wrapped about her person; while the emaciated limbs of the baby on her lap,—two years old, yet unweaned,—seemed almost to reach the floor, so preternaturally were they lengthened by the stretches of a four months' ague. Two of the boys lay in the trundle-bed, which was drawn as near to the fire as possible; and every spare article of clothing that the house afforded was thrown over them, in the vain attempt to warm their shivering frames. "Stop your whimperin', can't ye!" said Ashburn, as he hewed away with hatchet and jack-knife; "you'll be hot enough before long." And when the fever came his words were more than verified.

Two nights had passed before the preparations were completed. Ashburn and such of his boys as could work, had laboured indefatigably at the troughs, and Mrs. Ashburn had thrown away the milk, and the few other stores which cumbered her small supply of household utensils, to free as many as possible for the grand occasion. This third day had been "well day" to most of the invalids, and after the moon had risen to light them through the dense wood, the family set off, in high spirits, on their long, dewy walk. They had passed the causeway, and were turning from the highway into the skirts of the forest, when they were accosted by a stranger, a young man in a hunter's dress, evidently a traveller, and one who knew nothing of the place or its inhabitants, as Mr. Ashburn ascertained, to his entire satisfaction, by the usual number of queries. The stranger, a handsome youth of one or two and twenty, had that frank, joyous air which takes so well with us Wolverines; and after he had fully satisfied our bee-hunter's curiosity, he seemed disposed to ask some questions in his turn. One of the first of these related to the moving cause of the procession and their voluminous display of *containers*.

"Why, we're goin' straight to a bee-tree that I lit upon two or three days ago, and if you've a mind to, you may go 'long, and welcome. It's a real peeler, I tell ye! There's a hundred and fifty weight of honey in it, if there's a pound."

The young traveller waited no second invitation. His light knapsack was but small incumbrance, and he took upon himself the weight of several troughs, that seemed too heavy for the weaker members of the expedition. They walked on at a rapid and steady pace for a good half hour, over paths which were none of the smoothest, and only here and there lighted by the moonbeams. The mother and children were but ill fitted for the exertion, but Aladdin, on his midnight way to the wondrous vault of treasure, would as soon have thought of complaining of fatigue.

Who then shall describe the astonishment, the almost breathless rage of Silas Ashburn,—the bitter disappointment of the rest,—when they found, instead of the bee-tree, a great gap in the dense forest, and the bright moon shining on the shattered fragments of the immense oak that had contained their prize? The poor children, fainting with toil now that the stimulus was gone, threw themselves on the ground; and Mrs. Ashburn, seating her wasted form on a huge branch, burst into tears.

"It's all one!" exclaimed Ashburn, when at length he could find words; "it's all alike! this is just my luck! It ain't none of my neighbours' work, though! They know better than to be so mean! It's the rich! Them that begrudges the poor man the breath of life!" And he cursed bitterly and with clenched teeth, whoever had robbed him of his right.

"Don't cry, Betsey," he continued; "let's go home. I'll find out who has done this, and I'll let 'em know there's law for the poor man as well as the rich. Come along, young 'uns, and stop your blubberin', and let them splinters alone!" The poor little things were trying to gather up some of the fragments to which the honey still adhered, but their father was too angry to be kind.

"Was the tree on your own land?" now inquired the young stranger, who had stood by in sympathizing silence during this scene.

"No! but that don't make any difference. The man that found it first, and marked it, had a right to it afore the President of the United States, and that I'll let 'em know, if it costs me my farm. It's on old Keene's land, and I shouldn't wonder if the old miser had done it himself,—but I'll let him know what's the law in Michi*gan!*"

"Mr. Keene a miser!" exclaimed the young stranger, rather hastily.

"Why, what do *you* know about him?"

"O! nothing!—that is, nothing very particular—but I have heard him well spoken of. What I was going to say was, that I fear you will not find the law able to do any thing for you. If the tree was on another person's property—"

"Property! that's just so much as you know about it!" replied Ashburn, angrily. "I tell ye I know the law well enough, and I know the honey was mine—and old Keene shall know it too, if he's the man that stole it."

The stranger politely forbore further reply, and the whole party walked on in sad silence till they reached the village road, when the young stranger left them with a kindly "good night!"

It was soon after an early breakfast on the morning which succeeded poor Ashburn's disappointment, that Mr. Keene, attended by his lovely orphan niece, Clarissa Bensley, was engaged in his little court-yard, tending with paternal care the brilliant array of autumnal flowers which graced its narrow limits. Beds in size and shape nearly resembling patty-pans, were filled to overflowing with dahlias, china-asters and marigolds, while the walks which surrounded them, daily "swept with a woman's neatness," set off to the best advantage these resplendent children of Flora. A vine-hung porch, that opened upon the miniature Paradise, was lined with bird-cages of all sizes, and on a yard-square grass-plot stood the tin cage of a squirrel, almost too fat to be lively.

Mr. Keene was childless, and consoled himself as childless people are apt to do if they are wise, by taking into favour, in addition to his destitute niece, as many troublesome pets as he could procure. His wife, less philosophical, expended her superfluous energies upon a multiplication of household cares which her ingenuity alone could have devised within a domain like a nut-shell. Such rubbing and polishing—such arranging and rearranging of useless nick-nacks, had never yet been known in these utilitarian regions. And, what seemed amusing enough, Mrs. Keene, whose time passed in laborious nothings, often reproved her lawful lord very sharply for wasting *his* precious hours upon birds and flowers, squirrels and guinea-pigs, to say nothing of the turkeys and the magnificent peacock, which screamed at least half of every night, so that his master was fain to lock him up in an outhouse, for fear the neighbours should kill him in revenge for the murder of their sleep. These forms of solace Mrs. Keene often condemned as "really ridic'lous," yet she cleaned the bird-cages with indefatigable punctuality, and seemed never happier than when polishing with anxious care the bars of the squirrel's tread-mill. But there was one never-dying subject of debate between this worthy couple,—the company and services of the fair Clarissa, who was equally the darling of both, and superlatively useful in every department which claimed the attention of either. How the maiden, light-footed as she was, ever contrived to satisfy both uncle and aunt, seemed really mysterious. It was, "Mr. Keene, don't keep Clary wasting her time there when I've *so much* to do!"—or, on the other hand, "My dear! do send Clary out to help *me* a little! I'm sure she's been stewing there long enough!" And Clary, though she could not perhaps be in two places at once, certainly accomplished as much as if she could.

On the morning of which we speak, the young lady, having risen very early, and brushed and polished to her aunt's content, was now busily engaged in performing the various behests of her uncle, a service much more to her taste. She was as completely at home among birds and flowers as a poet or a Peri; and not Ariel himself, (of whom I dare say she had never heard,) accomplished with more grace his gentle spiriting. After all was "perform'd to point,"—when no dahlia remained unsupported,—no cluster of many-hued asters without its neat hoop,—when no intrusive weed could be discerned, even through Mr. Keene's spectacles,—Clarissa took the opportunity to ask if she might take the pony for a ride.

"To see those poor Ashburns, uncle."

"They're a lazy, impudent set, Clary."

"But they are all sick, uncle; almost every one of the family down with ague. Do let me go and carry them something. I hear they are completely destitute of comforts."

"And so they ought to be, my dear," said Mr. Keene, who could not forget what he considered Ashburn's impertinence.

But his habitual kindness prevailed, and he concluded his remonstrance (after giving voice to some few remarks which would not have gratified the Ashburns particularly,) by saddling the pony himself, arranging Clarissa's riding-dress with all the assiduity of a gallant cavalier, and giving into her hand, with her neat silver-mounted whip, a little basket, well crammed by his wife's kind care with delicacies for the invalids. No wonder that he looked after her with pride as she rode off! There are few prettier girls than the bright-eyed Clarissa.

When the pony reached the log-causeway,—just where the thick copse of witch-hazel skirts Mr. Ashburn's moist domain,—some unexpected occurrence is said to have startled, not the sober pony, but his very sensitive rider; and it has been asserted that the pony stirred not from the said hazel screen for a longer time than it would take to count a hundred, very deliberately. What faith is to be attached to this rumour, the historian ventures not to determine. It may be relied on as a fact, however, that a strong arm led the pony over the slippery corduroy, but no further; for Clarissa Bensley cantered alone up the green slope which leads to Mr. Ashburn's door.

"How are you this morning, Mrs. Ashburn?" asked the young visitant as she entered the wretched den, her little basket on her arm, her sweet face all flushed, and her eyes more than half-suffused with tears,—the effect of the keen morning wind, we suppose.

"Law sakes alive!" was the reply, "I ain't no how. I'm clear tuckered out with these young 'uns. They've had the agur already this morning, and they're as cross as bear-cubs."

"Ma!" screamed one, as if in confirmation of the maternal remark, "I want some tea!"

"Tea! I ha'n't got no tea, and you know that well enough!"

"Well, give me a piece o' sweetcake then, and a pickle."

"The sweetcake was gone long ago, and I ha'n't nothing to make more—so shut your head!" And as Clarissa whispered to the poor pallid child that she would bring him some if he would be a good boy and not tease his mother, Mrs. Ashburn produced, from a barrel of similar delicacies, a yellow cucumber, something less than a foot long, "pickled" in whiskey and water—and this the child began devouring eagerly.

Miss Bensley now set out upon the table the varied contents of her basket. "This honey," she said, showing some as limpid as water, "was found a day or two ago in uncle's woods—wild honey—isn't it beautiful?"

Mrs. Ashburn fixed her eyes on it without speaking, but her husband, who just then came in, did not command himself so far. "Where did you say you got that honey?" he asked.

"In our woods," repeated Clarissa; "I never saw such quantities; and a good deal of it as clear and beautiful as this."

"I thought as much!" said Ashburn angrily; "and now, Clary Bensley," he added, "you'll just take that cursed honey back to your uncle, and tell him to keep it, and eat it, and I hope it will choke him! and if I live, I'll make him rue the day he ever touched it."

Miss Bensley gazed on him, lost in astonishment. She could think of nothing but that he must have gone suddenly mad, and this idea made her instinctively hasten her steps toward the pony.

"Well! if you won't take it, I'll send it after ye!" cried Ashburn, who had lashed himself into a rage; and he hurled the little jar, with all the force of his powerful arm, far down the path by which Clarissa was about to depart, while his poor wife tried to restrain him with a piteous "Oh, father! don't! don't!"

Then, recollecting himself a little,—for he is far from being habitually brutal,—he made an awkward apology to the frightened girl.

"I ha'n't nothing agin *you,* Miss Bensley; you've always been kind to me and mine; but that old devil of an uncle of yours, that can't bear to let a poor man live,—I'll larn him who he's got to deal with! Tell him to look out, for he'll have reason!"

He held the pony while Clarissa mounted, as if to atone for his rudeness to herself; but he ceased not to repeat his denunciations against Mr. Keene as long as she was within hearing. As she paced over the logs, Ashburn, his rage much cooled by this ebullition, stood looking after her.

"I swan!" he exclaimed; "if there ain't that very feller that went with us to the bee-tree, leading Clary Bensley's horse over the crossway!"

Clarissa felt obliged to repeat to her uncle the rude threats which had so much terrified her; and it needed but this to confirm Mr. Keene's suspicious dislike of Ashburn, whom he had already learned to regard as one of the worst specimens of western character that had yet crossed his path. He had often felt the vexations of his new position to be almost intolerable, and was disposed to imagine himself the predestined victim of all the ill-will and all the impositions of the neighbourhood. It unfortunately happened, about this particular time, that he had been more than usually visited with disasters which are too common in a new country to be much regarded by those who know what they mean. His fences had been thrown down, his corn-field robbed, and even the lodging-place of the peacock forcibly attempted. But from the moment he discovered that Ashburn had a grudge against him, he thought neither of unruly oxen, mischievous boys, nor exasperated neighbours, but concluded that the one unlucky house in the swamp was the ever-welling fountain of all this bitterness. He had not yet been long enough among us to discern how much our "bark is waur than our bite."

And, more unfortunate still, from the date of this unlucky morning call, (I have long considered morning calls particularly unlucky), the fair Clarissa seemed to have lost all her sprightliness. She shunned her usual haunts, or if she took a walk, or a short ride, she was sure to return sadder than she went. Her uncle noted the change imme-diately, but forbore to question her, though he pointed out the symp-toms to his more obtuse lady, with a request that she would "find out what Clary wanted." In the performance of this delicate duty, Mrs. Keene fortunately limited herself to the subjects of health and new clothes,—so that Clarissa, though at first a little fluttered, an-swered very satisfactorily without stretching her conscience.

"Perhaps it's young company, my dear," continued the good woman; "to be sure there's not much of that as yet; but you never seemed to care for it when we lived at L——. You used to sit as con-tented over your work or your book, in the long evenings, with nobody but your uncle and me, and Charles Darwin,—why can't you now?"

"So I can, dear aunt," said Clarissa; and she spoke the truth so warmly that her aunt was quite satisfied.

It was on a very raw and gusty evening, not long after the occur-rences we have noted, that Mr. Keene, with his handkerchief carefully wrapped round his chin, sallied forth after dark, on an expedition to the post-office. He was thinking how vexatious it was—how like every thing else in this disorganized, or rather unorganized new country, that the weekly mail should not be obliged to arrive at regu-lar hours, and those early enough to allow of one's getting one's letters before dark. As he proceeded he became aware of the approach of two persons, and though it was too dark to distinguish faces, he heard distinctly the dreaded tones of Silas Ashburn.

"No! I found you were right enough there! I couldn't get at him that way; but I'll pay him for it yet!"

He lost the reply of the other party in this iniquitous scheme, in the rushing of the wild wind which hurried him on his course; but he had heard enough! He made out to reach the office, and receiving his paper, and hastening desperately homeward, had scarcely spirits even to read the price-current, (though he did mechanically glance at that corner of the "Trumpet of Commerce,") before he retired to bed in meditative sadness; feeling quite unable to await the striking of nine on the kitchen clock, which, in all ordinary circumstances, "toll'd the hour for retiring."

It is really surprising the propensity which young people have for sitting up late! Here was Clarissa Bensley, who was so busy all day that one would have thought she might be glad to retire with the chickens,—here she was, sitting in her aunt's great rocking-chair by the remains of the kitchen fire, at almost ten o'clock at night! And such a night too! The very roaring of the wind was enough to have affrighted a stouter heart than hers, yet she scarcely seemed even to hear it! And how lonely she must have been! Mr. and Mrs. Keene had been gone an hour, and in all the range of bird-cages that lined the room, not a feather was stirring, unless it might have been the green eyebrow of an old parrot, who was slily watching the fireside with one optic, while the other pretended to be fast asleep. And what was old Poll watching? We shall be obliged to tell tales.

There was another chair besides the great rocking-chair,—a high-backed chair of the olden time; and this second chair was drawn up quite near the first, and on the back of the tall antiquity leaned a young gentleman. This must account for Clary's not being terrified, and for the shrewd old parrot's staring so knowingly.

"I will wait no longer," said the stranger, in a low, but very decided tone; (and as he speaks, we recognise the voice of the young hunter.) "You are too timid, Clarissa, and you don't do your uncle justice. To be sure he was most unreasonably angry when we parted, and I am ashamed to think that I was angry too. To-morrow I will see him and tell him so; and I shall tell him too, little trembler, that I have you on my side; and we shall see if together we cannot persuade him to forget and forgive."

This, and much more that we shall not betray, was said by the tall young gentleman, who, now that his cap was off, showed brow and eyes such as are apt to go a good way in convincing young ladies; while Miss Bensley seemed partly to acquiesce, and partly to cling to her previous fears of her uncle's resentment against his former protégé, which, first excited by some trifling offence, had been rendered serious by the pride of the young man and the pepperiness of the old one.

When the moment came which Clarissa insisted should be the very last of the stranger's stay, some difficulty occurred in unbolting the kitchen door, and Miss Bensley proceeded with her guest through an open passage-way to the front part of the house, when she undid the front door, and dismissed him with a strict charge to tie up the gate just as he found it, lest some unlucky chance should realize Mr. Keene's fears of nocturnal invasion. And we must leave our perplexed heroine standing, in meditative mood, candle in hand, in the very centre of the little parlour, which served both for entrance-hall and *salon*.

We have seen that Mr. Keene's nerves had received a terrible shock on this fated evening, and it is certain that for a man of sober imagination, his dreams were terrific. He saw Ashburn, covered from crown to sole with a buzzing shroud of bees, trampling on his flower-beds, tearing up his honey-suckles root and branch, and letting his canaries and Java sparrows out of their cages; and, as his eyes recoiled from this horrible scene, they encountered the shambling form of Joe, who, besides aiding and abetting in these enormities, was making awful strides, axe in hand, towards the sanctuary of the pea-fowls.

He awoke with a cry of horror, and found his bed-room full of smoke. Starting up in agonized alarm, he awoke Mrs. Keene, and half-dressed, by the red light which glimmered around them, they rushed together to Clarissa's chamber. It was empty. To find the stairs was the next thought, but at the very top they met the dreaded bee-finder armed with a prodigious club!

"Oh mercy! don't murder us!" shrieked Mrs. Keene, falling on her knees; while her husband, whose capsicum was completely roused, began pummelling Ashburn as high as he could reach, bestowing on him at the same time, in no very choice terms, his candid opinion as to the propriety of setting people's houses on fire, by way of revenge.

"Why, you're both as crazy as loons!" was Mr. Ashburn's polite exclamation, as he held off Mr. Keene at arm's length. "I was comin' up o' purpose to tell you that you needn't be frightened. It's only the ruff o' the shanty there,—the kitchen, as you call it."

"And what have you done with Clarissa?"—"Ay! where's my niece?" cried the distracted pair.

"Where is she? why, down stairs to be sure, takin' care o' the traps they throw'd out o' the shanty. I was out a 'coon-hunting, and see the light, but I was so far off that they'd got it pretty well down before I got here. That 'ere young spark o' Clary's worked like a beaver, I tell ye!"

It must not be supposed that one half of Ashburn's hasty explanation "penetrated the interior" of his hearers' heads. They took in the idea of Clary's safety, but as for the rest, they concluded it only an effort to mystify them as to the real cause of the disaster.

"You need not attempt," solemnly began Mr. Keene, "you need not think to make me believe, that you are not the man that set my house on fire. I know your revengeful temper; I have heard of your threats, and you shall answer for all, sir! before you're a day older!"

Ashburn seemed struck dumb, between his involuntary respect for Mr. Keene's age and character, and the contemptuous anger with which his accusations filled him. "Well! I swan!" said he after a pause; "but here comes Clary; *she's* got common sense; ask her how the fire happened."

"It's all over now, uncle," she exclaimed, almost breathless; "it has not done so *very* much damage."

"Damage!" said Mrs. Keene, dolefully; "we shall never get things clean again while the world stands!"

"And where are my birds?" inquired the old gentleman.

"All safe—quite safe; we moved them into the parlour."

"We! who, pray?"

"Oh! the neighbours came, you know, uncle; and—Mr. Ashburn—"

"Give the devil his due," interposed Ashburn; "you know very well that the whole concern would have gone if it hadn't been for that young feller."

"What young fellow? where?"

"Why here," said Silas, pulling forward our young stranger; "this here chap."

"Young man," began Mr. Keene,—but at the moment, up came somebody with a light, and while Clarissa retreated behind Mr. Ashburn, the stranger was recognised by her aunt and uncle as Charles Darwin.

"Charles! what on earth brought you here?"

"Ask Clary," said Ashburn, with grim jocoseness.

Mr. Keene turned mechanically to obey, but Clarissa had disappeared.

"Well! I guess I can tell you something about it, if nobody else won't," said Ashburn; "I'm something of a Yankee, and it's my notion that there was some sparkin' a goin' on in your kitchen, and that somehow or other the young folks managed to set it a-fire."

The old folks looked more puzzled than ever. *"Do* speak, Charles," said Mr. Keene; "what *does* it all mean? Did you set my house on fire?"

"I'm afraid I must have had some hand in it, sir," said Charles, whose self-possession seemed quite to have deserted him.

"You!" exclaimed Mr. Keene; "and I've been laying it to this man!"

"Yes! you know'd I owed you a spite, on account o' that plaguy bee-tree," said Ashburn; "a guilty conscience needs no accuser. But you was much mistaken if you thought I was sich a bloody-minded villain as to burn your gimcrackery for that! If I could have paid you for it, fair and even, I'd ha' done it with all my heart and soul. But I don't set men's houses a-fire when I get mad at 'em."

"But you threatened vengeance," said Mr. Keene.

"So I did, but that was when I expected to get it by law, though; and this here young man knows that, if he'd only speak."

Thus adjured, Charles did speak, and so much to the purpose that it did not take many minutes to convince Mr. Keene that Ashburn's evil-mindedness was bounded by the limits of the law, that precious privilege of the Wolverine. But there was still the mystery of Charles's apparition, and in order to its full unravelment, the blushing Clarissa had to be enticed from her hiding-place, and brought to confession. And then it was made clear that she, with all her innocent looks, was the moving cause of the mighty mischief. She it was who encouraged Charles to believe that her uncle's anger would not last for ever; and this had led Charles to venture into the neighbourhood; and it was while consulting together, (on this particular point, of course,) that they managed to set the kitchen curtain on fire, and then—the reader knows the rest.

These things occupied some time in explaining,—but they were at length, by the aid of words and more eloquent blushes, made so clear, that Mr. Keene concluded, not only to new roof the kitchen, but to add a very pretty wing to one side of the house. And at the present time, the steps of Charles Darwin, when he returns from a surveying tour, seek the little gate as naturally as if he had never lived any where else. And the sweet face of Clarissa is always there, ready to welcome him, though she still finds plenty of time to keep in order the complicated affairs of both uncle and aunt.

And how goes life with our friends the Ashburns? Mr. Keene has done his very best to atone for his injurious estimate of Wolverine honour, by giving constant employment to Ashburn and his sons, and owning himself always the obliged party, without which concession all he could do would avail nothing. And Mrs. Keene and Clarissa have been unwearied in their kind attentions to the family, supplying them with so many comforts that most of them have got rid of the ague, in spite of themselves. The house has assumed so cheerful an appearance that I could scarcely recognise it for the same squalid den it had often made my heart ache to look upon. As I was returning from my last visit there, I encountered Mr. Ashburn, and remarked to him how very comfortable they seemed.

"Yes," he replied; "I've had pretty good luck lately; but I'm a goin' to pull up stakes and move to Wisconsin. I think I can do better, further West."

HARRIET BEECHER STOWE

★ ★ ★

While living in Cincinnati and mingling with members of the James Hall local-color school, Harriet Beecher Stowe (1811-1896) looked backward to "the period when our own hard, rocky, sterile New England was a sort of half Hebrew theocracy, half ultra-democratic republic of little villages, . . . burning like live coals . . . with all the fervid activity of an intense, newly kindled, peculiar, and individual life." In *The Mayflower* (1843) she idealized the aristocracy, while in *Oldtown Folks* (1869) and *Sam Lawson's Oldtown Fireside Stories* (1871), with the village do-nothing as narrator, she penetrated into the marrow of everyday life. Mrs. Stowe generally wove a Biblical text and moral advice into her tales, much as she did in *Uncle Tom's Cabin* (1852). Her work is excellent in its quiet insight into the springs of personal conduct, in the apt handling of dialect, and in picturing rural folkways. Born in Litchfield, Connecticut, she taught four years in Cincinnati, and married Professor Calvin E. Stowe there. After 1850 they moved to Brunswick, Maine; later to Andover, and Hartford, with winters at Mandarin, Florida.

★ ★ ★

The Minister's Housekeeper

SCENE.—*The shady side of a blueberry-pasture.*—SAM LAWSON *with the boys, picking blueberries.*—SAM, *loq.*

"WAL, you see, boys, 'twas just here,—Parson Carryl's wife she died along in the forepart o' March: my cousin Huldy she undertook to keep house for him. The way on't was, that Huldy she went to take care o' Mis' Carryl in the fust on't, when she fust took sick. Huldy was a tailoress by trade; but then she was one o' these 'ere facultized persons that has a gift for most anything, and that was how Mis' Carryl come to set sech store by her, that, when she was sick, nothin' would do for her but she must have Huldy round all the time: and the minister he said he'd make it good to her all the same, and she shouldn't lose nothin' by it. And so Huldy she stayed with Mis' Carryl full three months afore she died, and got to seein' to everything pretty much round the place.

"Wal, arter Mis' Carryl died, Parson Carryl he'd got so kind o' used to hevin' on her round, takin' care o' things, that he wanted her to stay along a spell; and so Huldy she stayed along a spell, and poured out his tea, and mended his close, and made pies and cakes, and cooked and washed and ironed, and kep' everything as neat as a pin. Huldy was a drefful chipper sort o' gal; and work sort o' rolled off from her like water off a duck's back. There wa'n't no gal in Sherburne that could put sich a sight o' work through as Huldy; and yet, Sunday mornin', she always come out in the singers' seat like one o' these 'ere June roses, lookin' so fresh and smilin', and her voice was jest as clear and sweet as a meadow lark's—Lordy massy! I 'member how she used to sing some o' them 'ere places where the treble and counter used to go together: her voice kind o' trembled a little, and it sort o' went through and through a feller! tuck him right where he lived!"

Here Sam leaned contemplatively back with his head in a clump of sweet-fern, and refreshed himself with a chew of young wintergreen. "This 'ere young wintergreen, boys, is jest like a feller's thoughts o' things that happened when he was young: it comes up jest so fresh and tender every year, the longest time you hev to live; and you can't help chawin' on't though 'tis sort o' stingin'. I don't never get over likin' young wintergreen."

"But about Huldah, Sam?"

"Oh yes! about Huldy. Lordy Massy! when a feller is Indianin' round, these 'ere pleasant summer days, a feller's thoughts gits like a flock o' young partridges: they's up and down and everywhere; 'cause one place is jest about as good as another, when they's all so kind o' comfortable and nice. Wal, about Huldy,—as I was a-sayin'. She was jest as handsome a gal to look at as a feller could have; and I think a nice, well-behaved young gal in the singers' seat of a Sunday is a means o' grace: it's sort o' drawin' to the unregenerate, you know. Why, boys, in them days, I've walked ten miles over to Sherburne of a Sunday mornin', jest to play the bass-viol in the same singers' seat with Huldy. She was very much respected, Huldy was; and, when she went out to tailorin', she was allers bespoke six months ahead, and sent for in waggins up and down for ten miles round; for the young fellers was allers 'mazin' anxious to be sent after Huldy, and was quite free to offer to go for her. Wal, after Mis' Carryl died, Huldy got to be sort o' housekeeper at the minister's, and saw to every-thing, and did everything: so that there wa'n't a pin out o' the way.

"But you know how 'tis in parishes: there allers is women that thinks the minister's affairs belongs to them, and they ought to have the rulin' and guidin' of 'em; and, if a minister's wife dies, there's folks that allers has their eyes open on providences,—lookin' out who's to be the next one.

"Now, there was Mis' Amaziah Pipperidge, a widder with snappin' black eyes, and a hook nose,—kind o' like a hawk; and she was one o' them up-and-down commandin' sort o' women, that feel that they have a call to be seein' to everything that goes on in the parish, and 'specially to the minister.

"Folks did say that Mis' Pipperidge sort o' sot her eye on the Parson for herself: wal, now that 'ere might 'a' been, or it might not. Some folks thought it was a very suitable connection. You see, she hed a good property of her own, right nigh to the minister's lot, and was allers kind o' active and busy; so, takin' one thing with another, I shouldn't wonder if Mis' Pipperidge should 'a' thought that Provi-dence p'inted that way. At any rate, she went up to Deakin Blodgett's wife, and they two sort o' put their heads together a-mournin' and condolin' about the way things was likely to go on at the minister's now Mis' Carryl was dead. Ye see, the Parson's wife, she was one of them women who hed their eyes everywhere and on everything. She was a little thin woman, but tough as Inger rubber, and smart as a steel trap; and there wa'n't a hen laid an egg, or cackled, but Mis' Carryl was right there to see about it; and she hed the garden made in the spring, and the medders mowed in sum-mer, and the cider made, and the corn husked, and the apples got in the fall; and the doctor, he hedn't nothin' to do but jest sit stock-still a-meditatin' on Jerusalem and Jericho and them things that ministers think about. But Lordy massy! he didn't know nothin' about where anything he eat or drunk or wore come from or went to: his wife jest led him round in temporal things and took care on him like a baby.

"Wal, to be sure, Mis' Carryl looked up to him in spirituals, and thought all the world on him; for there wa'n't a smarter minister nowhere round. Why, when he preached on decrees and election, they used to come clear over from South Parish, and West Sherburne, and Oldtown to hear him; and there was sich a row o' waggins tied along by the meetin'-house that the stables was all full, and all the hitchin'-posts was full clean up to the tavern, so that folks said the doctor made the town look like a gineral trainin'-day a Sunday.

"He was gret on texts, the doctor was. When he hed a p'int to prove, he'd jest go through the Bible, and drive all the texts ahead o' him like a flock o' sheep; and then, if there was a text that seemed agin him, why, he'd come out with his Greek and Hebrew, and kind o' chase it round a spell, jest as ye see a feller chase a contrary bell-wether, and make him jump the fence arter the rest. I tell you, there wa'n't no text in the Bible that could stand agin the doctor when his blood was up. The year arter the doctor was app'inted to preach the 'lection sermon in Boston, he made such a figger that the Brattle Street Church sent a committee right down to see if they couldn't get him to Boston; and then the Sherburne folks, they up and raised his salary; ye see, there ain't nothin' wakes folks up like somebody else's wantin' what you've got. Wal, that fall they made him a Doctor o' Divinity at Cambridge College, and so they sot more by him than ever. Wal, you see, the doctor, of course he felt kind o' lonesome and afflicted when Mis' Carryl was gone; but railly and truly, Huldy was so up to everything about house, that the doctor didn't miss nothin' in a temporal way. His shirt-bosoms was pleated finer than they ever was, and them ruffles round his wrists was kep' like the driven snow; and there wa'n't a brack in his silk stockin's, and his shoe-buckles was kep' polished up, and his coats brushed, and then there wa'n't no bread and biscuit like Huldy's; and her butter was like solid lumps o' gold; and there weren't no pies to equal hers; and so the doctor never felt the loss o' Mis' Carryl at table. Then there was Huldy allers oppisite to him, with her blue eyes and her cheeks like two fresh peaches. She was kind o' pleasant to look at; and the more the doctor looked at her the better he liked her; and so things seemed to be goin' on quite quiet and comfortable ef it hadn't been that Mis' Pipperidge and Mis' Deakin Blodgett and Mis' Sawin got their heads together a-talkin' about things.

" 'Poor man,' says Mis' Pipperidge, 'what can that child that he's got there do towards takin' the care of all that place? It takes a mature woman,' she says, 'to tread in Mis' Carryl's shoes.'

" 'That it does,' said Mis' Blodgett; 'and, when things once get to runnin' downhill, there ain't no stoppin' on 'em,' says she.

"Then Mis' Sawin she took it up. (Ye see, Mis' Sawin used to go out to dressmakin', and was sort o' jealous, 'cause folks sot more by

Huldy than they did by her.) 'Well,' says she, 'Huldy Peters is well enough at her trade. I never denied that, though I do say I never did believe in her way o' makin' buttonholes; and I must say, if 'twas the dearest friend I hed, that I thought Huldy tryin' to fit Mis' Kittridge's plum-colored silk was a clear piece o' presumption; the silk was jist sp'iled, so 'twa'n't fit to come into the meetin'-house. I must say, Huldy's a gal that's always too venteresome about takin' 'sponsibilities she don't know nothin' about.'

" 'Of course she don't,' said Mis' Deakin Blodgett. 'What does she know about all the lookin' and seein' to that there ought to be in guidin' the minister's house. Huldy's well meanin', and she's good at her work, and good in the singers' seat; but Lordy massy! she hain't got no experience. Parson Carryl ought to have an experienced woman to keep house for him. There's the spring house-cleanin' and the fall house-cleanin' to be seen to, and the things to be put away from the moths; and then the gettin' ready for the Association and all the ministers' meetin's; and the makin' the soap and the candles, and settin' the hens and turkeys, watchin' the calves, and seein' after the hired men and the garden; and there that 'ere blessed man jist sets there at home as serene, and has nobody round but that 'ere gal, and don't even know how things must be a-runnin' to waste!'

"Wal, the upshot on't was, they fussed and fuzzled and wuzzled till they'd drinked up all the tea in the teapot; and then they went down and called on the Parson, and wuzzled him all up talkin' about this, that, and t'other that wanted lookin' to, and that it was no way to leave everything to a young chit like Huldy, and that he ought to be lookin' about for an experienced woman. The Parson he thanked 'em kindly, and said he believed their motives was good, but he didn't go no further. He didn't ask Mis' Pipperidge to come and stay there and help him, nor nothin' o' that kind; but he said he'd attend to matters himself. The fact was, the Parson had got such a likin' for havin' Huldy round, that he couldn't think o' such a thing as swappin' her off for the Widder Pipperidge.

"But he thought to himself, 'Huldy is a good girl; but I oughtn't to be a-leavin' everything to her,—it's too hard on her. I ought to be instructin' and guidin' and helpin' of her; 'cause 'tain't everybody could be expected to know and do what Mis' Carryl did'; and so at it he went; and Lordy massy! didn't Huldy hev a time on't when the minister began to come out of his study, and want to tew round and see to things? Huldy, you see, thought all the world of the minister, and she was 'most afraid to laugh; but she told me she couldn't, for the life of her, help it when his back was turned, for he wuzzled things up in the most singular way. But Huldy she'd jest say, 'Yes, sir,' and get him off into his study, and go on her own way.

"'Huldy,' says the minister one day, 'you ain't experienced outdoors; and, when you want to know anything, you must come to me.'

"'Yes, sir,' says Huldy.

"'Now, Huldy,' says the Parson, 'you must be sure to save the turkey-eggs, so that we can have a lot of turkeys for Thanksgiving.'

"'Yes, sir,' says Huldy; and she opened the pantry-door, and showed him a nice dishful she'd been a-savin' up. Wal, the very next day the Parson's hen-turkey was found killed up to old Jim Scroggs's barn. Folks said Scroggs killed it; though Scroggs he stood to it he didn't: at any rate, the Scroggses they made a meal on't; and Huldy she felt bad about it, 'cause she'd set her heart on raisin' the turkeys; and says she, 'Oh, dear! I don't know what I shall do. I was just ready to set her.'

"'Do, Huldy?' says the Parson. 'Why, there's the other turkey, out there by the door; and a fine bird, too, he is.'

"Sure enough, there was the old tom-turkey a-struttin' and a-sidlin' and a-quitterin', and a-floutin' his tail-feathers in the sun, like a lively young widower, all ready to begin life over ag'in.

"'But,' says Huldy, 'you know *he* can't set on eggs.'

"'He can't? I'd like to know why,' says the Parson. 'He shall set on eggs, and hatch 'em too.'

"'O doctor!' says Huldy, all in a tremble; 'cause, you know, she didn't want to contradict the minister, and she was afraid she should laugh,—'I never heard that a tom-turkey would set on eggs.'

"'Why, they ought to,' said the Parson, getting quite 'arnest; what else be they good for? you just bring out the eggs, now, and put 'em in the nest, and I'll make him set on 'em.'

"So Huldy she thought there weren't no way to convince him but to let him try: so she took the eggs out, and fixed 'em all nice in the nest; and then she come back and found old Tom a-skirmishin' with the Parson pretty lively, I tell ye. Ye see, old Tom he didn't take the idee at all; and he flopped and gobbled, and fit the Parson; and the Parson's wig got round so that his cue stuck straight out over his ear, but he'd got his blood up. Ye see, the old doctor was used to carryin' his p'ints o' doctrine; and he hadn't fit the Arminians and Socinians to be beat by a tom-turkey; so finally he made a dive, and ketched him by the neck in spite o' his floppin', and stroked him down, and put Huldy's apron round him.

" 'There, Huldy,' he says, quite red in the face, 'we've got him now'; and he traveled off to the barn with him as lively as a cricket.

"Huldy came behind jist chokin' with laugh, and afraid the minister would look round and see her.

" 'Now, Huldy, we'll crook his legs, and set him down,' says the Parson, when they got him to the nest; 'you see he is getting quiet, and he'll set there all right.'

"And the Parson he sot him down; and old Tom he sot there solemn enough, and held his head down all droopin', lookin' like a rail pious old cock, as long as the Parson sot by him.

" 'There! you see how still he sets,' says the Parson to Huldy.

"Huldy was 'most dyin' for fear she should laugh. 'I'm afraid he'll get up,' says she, 'when you do.'

" 'Oh no, he won't!' says the Parson, quite confident. 'There, there,' says he, layin' his hands on him, as if pronouncin' a blessin'. But when the Parson riz up, old Tom he riz up too, and began to march over the eggs.

" 'Stop, now!' says the Parson. 'I'll make him get down ag'in: hand me that corn-basket; we'll put that over him.'

"So he crooked old Tom's legs, and got him down ag'in; and they put the corn-basket over him, and then they both stood and waited.

" 'That'll do the thing, Huldy,' said the Parson.

" 'I don't know about it,' says Huldy.

" 'Oh yes, it will, child! I understand,' says he.

"Just as he spoke, the basket riz right up and stood, and they could see old Tom's long legs.

" 'I'll make him stay down, confound him,' says the Parson; for, ye see, parsons is men, like the rest on us, and the doctor had got his spunk up.

" 'You jist hold him a minute, and I'll get something that'll make him stay, I guess'; and out he went to the fence, and brought in a long, thin, flat stone, and laid it on old Tom's back.

"Old Tom he wilted down considerable under this, and looked railly as if he was goin' to give in. He stayed still there a good long spell, and the minister and Huldy left him there and come up to the house; but they hadn't more than got in the door before they see old Tom a-hippin' along, as high-steppin' as ever, sayin', 'Talk! talk! and quitter! quitter!' and struttin' and gobblin' as if he'd come through the Red Sea, and got the victory.

" 'Oh, my eggs!' says Huldy. 'I'm afraid he's smashed 'em!'

"And sure enough, there they was, smashed flat enough under the stone.

" 'I'll have him killed,' said the Parson: 'we won't have such a critter round.'

"But the Parson he slep' on't, and then didn't do it; he only
come out next Sunday with a tiptop sermon on the ' 'Riginal Cuss'
that was pronounced on things in gineral, when Adam fell, and
showed how everything was allowed to go contrary ever since. There
was pigweed, and pusley, and Canady thistles, cut-worms, and bag-
worms, and canker-worms, to say nothin' of rattlesnakes. The doctor
made it very impressive and sort o' improvin'; but Huldy she told
me, goin' home, that she hardly could keep from laughin' two or
three times in the sermon when she thought of old Tom a-standin'
up with the corn-basket on his back.

"Wal, next week Huldy she jist borrowed the minister's horse
and side-saddle, and rode over to South Parish to her Aunt Bascome's,—Widder Bascome's, you know, that lives there by the trout-
brook,—and got a lot o' turkey-eggs o' her, and come back and set
a hen on 'em, and said nothin'; and in good time there was as nice
a lot o' turkey-chicks as ever ye see.

"Huldy never said a word to the minister about his experiment,
and he never said a word to her; but he sort o' kep' more to his
books, and didn't take it on him to advise so much.

"But not long arter he took it into his head that Huldy ought
to have a pig to be a-fattin' with the buttermilk. Mis' Pipperidge
set him up to it; and jist then old Tim Bigelow, out to Juniper
Hill, told him if he'd call over he'd give him a little pig.

"So he sent for a man, and told him to build a pig-pen right out
by the well, and have it all ready when he came home with his pig.

"Huldy she said she wished he might put a curb round the well
out there, because in the dark, sometimes, a body might stumble
into it; and the Parson he told him he might do that.

"Wal, old Aikin, the carpenter, he didn't come till most the middle
of the arternoon; and then he sort o' idled, so that he didn't get up
the well-curb till sundown; and then he went off and said he'd
come and do the pig-pen next day.

"Wal, arter dark, Parson Carryl he driv into the yard, full chizel,
with his pig. He'd tied up his mouth to keep him from squealin'; and
he see what he thought was the pig-pen,—he was rather near-sighted,—
and so he ran and threw piggy over; and down he dropped into the
water, and the minister put out his horse and pranced off into the
house quite delighted.

" 'There, Huldy, I've got you a nice little pig.'

" 'Dear me!' says Huldy: 'where have you put him?'

" 'Why, out there in the pig-pen, to be sure.'

" 'Oh dear me!' says Huldy: 'that's the well-curb. There ain't no pig-pen built,' says she.

" 'Lordy massy!' says the Parson: 'then I've thrown the pig in the well!'

"Wal, Huldy she worked and worked, and finally she fished piggy out in the bucket, but he was dead as a doornail; and she got him out o' the way quietly, and didn't say much; and the Parson he took to a great Hebrew book in his study; and says he, 'Huldy, I ain't much in temporals,' says he. Huldy says she kind o' felt her heart go out to him, he was so sort o' meek and helpless and larned; and says she, 'Wal, Parson Carryl, don't trouble your head no more about it; I'll see to things'; and sure enough, a week arter there was a nice pen, all ship-shape, and two little white pigs that Huldy bought with the money for the butter she sold at the store.

" 'Wal, Huldy,' said the Parson, 'you are a most amazin' child: you don't say nothin', but you do more than most folks.'

"Arter that the Parson set sich store by Huldy that he come to her and asked her about everything, and it was amazin' how everything she put her hand to prospered. Huldy planted marigolds and larkspurs, pinks and carnations, all up and down the path to the front door, and trained up mornin'-glories and scarlet-runners round the windows. And she was always a-gettin' a root here, and a sprig there, and a seed from somebody else,—for Huldy was one o' them that has the gift, so that ef you jist give 'em the leastest sprig of anything they make a great bush out of it right away; so that in six months Huldy had roses and geraniums and lilies, sich as it would 'a took a gardener to raise. The Parson he took no notice at fust; but when the yard was all ablaze with flowers he used to come and stand in a kind o' maze at the front door, and say, 'Beautiful, beautiful! Why, Huldy, I never see anything like it.' And then when her work was done arternoons, Huldy would sit with her sewin' in the porch, and sing and trill away till she'd draw the meadow larks and the bobolinks and the orioles to answer her, and the great big elm-tree overhead would get perfectly rackety with the birds; and the Parson, settin' there in his study, would git to kind o' dreamin' about the angels, and golden harps, and the New Jerusalem; but he wouldn't speak a word, 'cause Huldy she was jist like them wood-thrushes, she never could sing so well when she thought folks was hearin'. Folks noticed, about this time, that the Parson's sermons got to be like Aaron's rod, that budded and blossomed; there was things in 'em about flowers and birds, and more 'special about the music o' heaven. And Huldy she noticed, that ef there was a hymn run in her head while she was round a-workin' the minister was sure to give it out next Sunday. You see, Huldy was jist like a bee: she always sung when she was workin', and you could hear her trillin', now down in the corn-patch, while she was pickin' the corn; and now in the buttery, while she was workin' the butter; and now she'd go singin' down cellar, and then she'd be singin' up overhead, so that she seemed to fill a house chock full o' music.

"Huldy was so sort o' chipper and fair-spoken that she got the hired men all under her thumb: they come to her and took her orders jist as meek as so many calves; and she traded at the store, and kep' the accounts, and she hed her eyes everywhere, and tied up all the ends so tight that there wa'n't no gettin' round her. She wouldn't let nobody put nothin' off on Parson Carryl, cause he was a minister. Huldy was allers up to anybody that wanted to make a hard bargain; and, afore he knew jist what he was about, she'd got the best end of it, and everybody said that Huldy was the most capable gal that they'd ever traded with.

"Wal, come to the meetin' of the Association, Mis' Deakin Blodgett and Mis' Pipperidge come callin' up to the Parson's, all in a stew, and offerin' their services to get the house ready; but the doctor he jist thanked 'em quite quiet, and turned 'em over to Huldy; and Huldy she told 'em that she'd got everything ready, and showed 'em her pantries, and her cakes and her pies and her puddin's, and took 'em all over the house; and they went peekin' and pokin', openin' cupboard doors, and lookin' into drawers; and they couldn't find so much as a thread out o' the way, from garret to cellar, and so they went off quite discontented. Arter that the women set a new trouble a-brewin'. Then they begun to talk that it was a year now since Mis' Carryl died; and it railly wasn't proper such a young gal to be stayin' there, who everybody could see was a-settin' her cap for the minister.

"Mis' Pipperidge said that, so long as she looked on Huldy as the hired gal, she hadn't thought much about it; but Huldy was railly takin' on airs as an equal, and appearin' as mistress o' the house in a way that would make talk if it went on. And Mis' Pipperidge she driv round up to Deakin Abner Snow's, and down to Mis' 'Lijah Perry's, and asked them if they wasn't afraid that the way the Parson and Huldy was a-goin' on might make talk. And they said they hadn't thought on't before, but now, come to think on't, they was sure it would; and they all went and talked with somebody else, and asked them if they didn't think it would make talk. So come Sun-

day, and Huldy saw folks a-noddin' and a winkin', and a-lookin'
arter her, and she begun to feel drefful sort o' disagreeable. Finally
Mis' Sawin she says to her, 'My dear, didn't you never think folks
would talk about you and the minister?'

" 'No: why should they?' says Huldy, quite innocent.

" 'Wal, dear,' says she, 'I think it's a shame; but they say you're
tryin' to catch him, and that it's so bold and improper for you to be
courtin' of him right in his own house,—you know folks will talk,
—I thought I'd tell you 'cause I think so much of you,' says she.

"Huldy was a gal of spirit, and she despised the talk, but it made
her drefful uncomfortable; and when she got home at night she sat
down in the mornin'-glory porch, quite quiet, and didn't sing a
word.

"The minister he had heard the same thing from one of his
deakins that day; and when he saw Huldy so kind o' silent, he says
to her, 'Why don't you sing, my child?'

"He hed a pleasant sort o' way with him, the minister had, and
Huldy had got to likin' to be with him, and it all come over her
that perhaps she ought to go away; and her throat kind o' filled up
so she couldn't hardly speak; and, says she, 'I can't sing tonight.'

"Says he, 'You don't know how much good your singin' has done
me, nor how much good you have done me in all ways, Huldy.
I wish I knew how to show my gratitude.'

" 'O sir!' says Huldy, 'is it improper for me to be here?'

" 'No, dear,' says the minister, 'but ill-natured folks will talk; but
there is one way we can stop it, Huldy—if you will marry me.
You'll make me very happy, and I'll do all I can to make *you* happy.
Will you?'

"Wal, Huldy never told me jist what she said to the minister,—
gals never does give you the particulars of them 'ere things jist as
you'd like 'em,—only I know the upshot and the hull on't was, that
Huldy she did a consid'able lot o' clear starchin' and ironin' the next
two days; and the Friday o' next week the minister and she rode
over together to Dr. Lothrop's in Oldtown; and the doctor, he jist
made 'em man and wife, 'spite of envy of the Jews,' as the hymn
says. Wal, you'd better believe there was a-starin' and a-wonderin'
next Sunday mornin' when the second bell was a-tollin', and the
minister walked up the broad aisle with Huldy, all in white, arm
in arm with him, and he opened the minister's pew, and handed
her in as if she was a princess; for, you see, Parson Carryl come of
a good family, and was a born gentleman, and had a sort o' grand
way o' bein' polite to women-folks. Wal, I guess there was a-rus'lin'

among the bunnets. Mis' Pipperidge gin a great bounce, like corn poppin' on a shovel, and her eyes glared through her glasses at Huldy as if they'd 'a' sot her afire; and everybody in the meetin'-house was a-starin', I tell yew. But they couldn't none of 'em say nothin' agin Huldy's looks; for there wa'n't a crimp nor a frill about her that wa'n't jis' so; and her frock was white as the driven snow, and she had her bunnet all trimmed up with white ribbins; and all the fellows said the old doctor had stole a march, and got the handsomest gal in the parish.

"Wal, arter meetin' they all come round the Parson and Huldy at the door, shakin' hands and laughin'; for by that time they was about agreed that they'd got to let putty well alone.

"'Why, Parson Carryl,' says Mis' Deakin Blodgett, 'how you've come it over us.'

"'Yes,' says the Parson, with a kind o' twinkle in his eye. 'I thought,' says he, 'as folks wanted to talk about Huldy and me, I'd give 'em somethin' wuth talkin' about.'"

ROSE TERRY COOKE

★ ★ ★

The monotonous routine of toilworn farmers' wives, of lonely unmarried women, and of inarticulate men wrestling with their souls' destiny, "the life that sent them to early graves, . . . the life that is so beautiful in the poet's numbers, so terrible in its stony reality," forms the basis of stories by Rose Terry Cooke (1827-1892). Yet she imparts to these spinsters and deacons a touch of kindliness, for stark reality is relieved with homely philosophy and humor emerging from their fortitude. As early as 1857, in "Uncle Josh," she broke from the prevailing sentimental tradition to analyze deep-seated traits developed in the granite soil of New England. Born near Hartford, Connecticut, Miss Terry married in 1873 and thereafter resided chiefly in the Connecticut that furnished the scenes for her stories. In its first year, 1857-1858, under the editorship of James Russell Lowell, *The Atlantic Monthly* accepted eight of her stories; these, with others, have been collected in *Somebody's Neighbors* (1881), *The Sphinx's Children* (1886), *Huckleberries Gathered from New England Hills* (1891).

★ ★ ★

Uncle Josh

JOSH CRANE was a Yankee born and bred, a farmer on Plainfield Hill, and a specimen. If some strange phrases were grafted on his New-England vernacular, it was because, for fifteen years of his youth, he had followed the sea; and the sea, to return the compliment, thereafter followed him.

His father, old Josh Crane, kept the Sanbury gristmill, and was a drunken, shiftless old creature, who ended his days in a tumble-down red house a mile below Plainfield Centre, being "took with the tremens," as black Peter said when he came for the doctor,—all too late; for the "tremens" had indeed taken him off.

Mrs. Crane, our Josh's mother, was one of those calm, meek, patient creatures, by some inscrutable mystery always linked to such men; "martyrs by the pang without the palm," of whom a noble army shall yet rise out of New England's desolate valleys and melancholy hills to take their honor from the Master's hand. For years this woman lived alone with her child in the shattered red house, spin-ning, knitting, washing, sewing, scrubbing, to earn bread and water, sometimes charity-fed, but never failing at morning and night, with one red and knotted hand upon her boy's white hair, and the other on her worn Bible, to pray, with an intensity that boy never forgot, for his well-being for ever and ever: for herself she never prayed aloud.

Then came the country's pestilence, consumption; and after long struggles, relapses, rallies,—all received in the same calm patience,—Hetty Crane died in a summer's night, her little boy asleep beside her, and a whippoorwill on the apple-tree by the door sounding on her flickering sense the last minor note of life.

When Josh woke up, and knew his mother was dead, he did not behave in the least like good little boys in books, but dressed himself without a tear or a sob, and ran for the nearest neighbor.

"Sakes alive!" said "Miss" Ranney. "I never did see sech a cretur as that are boy in all my days! He never said nothin' to me when he came to our folks's, only jest, 'Miss Ranney, I guess you'd better come cross lots to see mother: she don't seem to be alive.'—'Dew tell!' sez I. An' so I slipt on my Shaker bunnet jist as quick's I could; but he was off, spry's a cricket, an' when I got there he was a-settin' the rooms to rights. He'd spunked up a fire, and hung on the kittle: so I sed nothin', but stept along inter the bedroom, and turned down the kiver, and gin a little screech, I was so beat; for, sure enough, Hetty Crane was dead an' cold. Josh he heerd me, for he was clos't onto me; and he never spoke, but he come up to the bed, and he put his head down, and laid his cheek right along hers (and 'twan't no redder'n her'n), an' staid so 'bout a minnit; then he cleared out, and I never see him no more all day. But Miss Good'in she come in; and she said he'd stopped there, an' sent her over.

"Well, we laid out Hetty, and fixed up the house, and put up a curtain to her winder. And Miss Good'in she 'n' I calkerlated to set up all night; and we was jest puttin' a mess of tea to draw so's to keep lively, when in come Josh, drippin' wet; for the dews was dreadful heavy them August nights. And he said nothin' more'n jest to answer when he was spoke to. And Miss Good'in was a real feelin' woman: she guessed he'd better be let alone. So he drink't a cup of tea, and then he started off into the bedroom; and when she went in there, 'long towards midnight, there he was, fast asleep on the bed beside of the corpse, as straight as a pin, only holdin' on to one of its hands. Miss Good'in come back cryin'; and I thought I should 'a' boo-hooed right out. But I kinder strangled it down, and we set to work to figger out what was a-goin' to be done with the poor little chap. That house of their'n that old Josh had bought of Mr. Ranney hadn't never been paid for, only the interest-money whenever Miss Crane could scrape it up, so't that would go right back into husband's hands; an' they hadn't got no cow, nor no pig; and we agreed the s'lectmen would hev' to take him, and bind him out.

"I allers mistrusted that he'd waked up, and heerd what we said; for next morning, when we went to call him, he was gone, and his shirts an' go-to-meetin's too; and he never come back to the funeral, nor a good spell after.

"I know, after Hetty was buried, and we'd resolved to sell what things she had to get her a head-stone,—for Mr. Ranney wouldn't never put in for the rest of his interest money,—I took home her old Bible, and kep' it for Josh; and the next time I see him was five and twenty years after, when he come back from sea-farin', an' settled down to farmin' on't. And he sot by that Bible a dredful sight, I expect: for he gin our Sall the brightest red-an'-yeller bandanner you ever see; she used to keep it to take to meetin'."

"Miss" Ranney was certainly right in her "guess." Josh had heard in that miserable midnight the discussion of his future, and, having a well-founded dread of the selectmen's tender-mercies, had given a last caress to his dead mother, and run away to Boston, where he shipped for a whaling-voyage; was cast away on the Newfoundland shore after ten years of sea-life; and being at that time a stout youth of twenty, sick of his seamanship, he had hired himself to work in a stone-yard; and, by the time he was thirty-five, had laid up enough money to return a thrifty bachelor, and, buying a little farm on Plainfield Hill, settled down to his ideal of life, and become the amusement of part of the village, and the oracle of the rest.

We boys adored Uncle Josh; for he was always ready to rig our boats, spin us yarns a week long, and fill our pockets with apples red and russet as his own honest face. With the belles of the village

Uncle Josh had no such favor. He would wear a pigtail, in spite of scoff and remonstrance; he would smoke a cutty-pipe; and he did swear like a sailor, from mere habit and forgetfulness, for no man not professedly religious had a diviner instinct of reverence and worship than he. But it was as instinctive in him to swear as it was to breathe; and some of our boldly speculative and law-despising youngsters held that it was no harm in him, any more than "gosh" and "thunder" were in us, for really he meant no more.

However, Uncle Josh did not quite reciprocate the contempt of the sex. Before long he began to make Sunday-night visitations at Deacon Stone's, to "brush his hat o' mornings," to step spry, and wear a stiff collar and stock, instead of the open tie he had kept, with the pigtail, long after jacket and tarpaulin had been dismissed the service: so the village directly discovered that Josh Crane was courting the school-mistress, "Miss Eunice," who boarded at Deacon Stone's. What Miss Eunice's surname might be, I never knew; nor did it much matter. She was the most kindly, timid, and lovable creature that ever tried to reduce a district school into manners and arithmetic. She lives in my memory still,—a tall, slight figure, with tender brown eyes and a sad face, its broad, lovely forehead shaded with silky light hair, and her dress always dim-tinted,—faded perhaps,—but scrupulously neat and stable.

Everybody knew why Miss Eunice looked so meekly sad, and why she was still "Miss" Eunice: she had been "disapp'inted." She had loved a man better than he loved her, and therein, copying the sweet angels, made a fatal mistake, broke her girl's heart, and went to keeping school for a living.

All the young people pitied and patronized her; all the old women agreed that she was "a real clever little fool;" and men regarded her with a species of wonder and curiosity, first for having a breakable heart, and next for putting that member to fatal harm for one of their kind. But boys ranked Miss Eunice even above Uncle Josh; for there lives in boys a certain kind of chivalry, before the world has sneered it out of them, that regards a sad or injured woman as a creature claiming all their care and protection. And it was with a thrill of virtuous indignation that we heard of Josh Crane's intentions toward Miss Eunice; nor were we very pitiful of our old friend, when Mrs. Stone announced to old Mrs. Ranney (who was deaf as a post, and therefore very useful, passively, in spreading news confided to her, as this was in the church-porch), that "Miss Eunice wa'n't a-goin' to hev' Josh Crane, 'cause he wa'n't a professor; but she didn't want nobody to tell on't:" so everybody did.

It was, beside, true. Miss Eunice was a sincerely religious woman; and though Josh Crane's simple, fervent love-making had stirred a thrill within her she had thought quite impossible, still she did not think it was right to marry an irreligious man, and she told him so with a meek firmness that quite broke down poor Uncle Josh, and he went back to his farming with profounder respect than ever for Miss Eunice, and a miserable opinion of himself.

But he was a person without guile of any sort. He would have cut off his pigtail, sold his tobacco-keg, tried not to swear, for her sake; but he could not pretend to be pious, and he did not.

A year or two afterward, however, when both had quite got past the shyness of meeting, and set aside, if not forgotten, the past, there was a revival of religion in Plainfield; no great excitement, but a quiet springing-up of "good seed" sown in past generations, it may be; and among the softened hearts and moist eyes were those of Uncle Josh. His mother's prayers had slept in the leaves of his mother's Bible, and now they awoke to be answered.

It was strangely touching, even to old Parson Pitcher, long used to such interviews with the oddest of all people under excitement,— rugged New-Englanders,—to see the simple pathos that vivified Uncle Josh's story of his experience; and when, in the midst of a sentence about his dead mother, and her petitions for his safety, with tears dripping down both cheeks, he burst into a hallelujah metre tune, adapting the words,—

"Though seed lie buried long in dust," &c.,

and adding to the diversity of rhythm the discordance of his sea-cracked voice, it was a doubtful matter to Parson Pitcher whether he should laugh or cry; and he was forced to compromise with a hysterical snort, just as Josh brought out the last word of the verse on a powerful fugue,—

"Cro-o-o-o-op!"

So earnest and honest was he, that, for a whole week after he had been examined and approved by the church committee as a probationer, he never once thought of Miss Eunice; when suddenly, as he was reading his Bible, and came across the honorable mention of that name by the apostle, he recollected, with a sort of shamefaced delight, that now, perhaps, she would have him. So, with no further ceremony than reducing his gusty flax-colored hair to order by means of a pocket-comb, and washing his hands at the pump, away he strode to the schoolhouse, where it was Miss Eunice's custom to linger after school till her fire was burnt low enough to "rake up."

Josh looked in at the window as he "brought to" (in his own phrase) "alongside the school'us," and there sat the lady of his love knitting a blue stocking, with an empty chair most propitiously placed beside her in front of the fireplace. Josh's heart rose up mightily; but he knocked as little a knock as his great knuckles could effect, was bidden in, and sat himself down on the chair in a paroxysm of bashfulness, nowise helped by Miss Eunice's dropped eyes and persistent knitting. So he sat full fifteen minutes, every now and then clearing his throat in a vain attempt to introduce the point, till at length, desperate enough, he made a dash into the middle of things, and bubbled over with, "Miss Eunice, I've got religion! I'm sot out for to be a real pious man. Can't you feel to hev' me now?"

What Miss Eunice's little trembling lips answered, I cannot say; but I know it was satisfactory to Josh; for his first reverent impulse, after he gathered up her low words, was to clasp his hands, and say, "Amen," as if somebody had asked a blessing. Perhaps he felt he had received one in Miss Eunice.

When spring came they were married, and were happy, Yankee fashion, without comment or demonstration, but very happy. Uncle Josh united with the church, and was no disgrace to his profession save and except in one thing,—he would swear. Vainly did deacons, brethren, and pastor assail him with exhortation, remonstrance, and advice; vainly did his meek wife look at him with pleading eyes; vainly did he himself repent and strive and watch: "the stump of Dagon remained," and was not to be easily uprooted.

At length Parson Pitcher, being greatly scandalized at Josh's expletives, used unluckily in a somewhat excited meeting on church business (for in prayer-meetings he never answered any calls to rise, lest habit should get the better of him, and shock the very sinners he might exhort),—Parson Pitcher himself made a pastoral call at the farm, and found its master in the garden, hoeing corn manfully.

"Good-day, Mr. Crane!" said the old gentleman.

"Good-day, Parson Pitcher, good-day! d—— hot day, sir," answered the unconscious Josh.

"Not so hot as hell for swearers," sternly responded the parson, who, being of a family renowned in New England for noway mincing matters, sometimes verged upon profanity himself, though unawares. Josh threw down his hoe in despair.

"O Lord!" said he. "There it goes again, I swear! the d—— dogs take it! If I don't keep a-goin'! O Parson Pitcher! what shall I dew?

It swears of itself. I am clean beat tryin' to head it off. Con— No!
I mean confuse it all! I'm such an old hand at the wheel, sir!"

Luckily for Josh, the parson's risibles were hardly better in hand
than his own profanity; and it took him now a long time to pick
up his cane, which he had dropped in the currant-bushes, while Josh
stood among the corn-hills wiping the sweat off his brow, in an
abject state of penitence and humility; and, as the parson emerged like
a full moon from the leafy currants, he felt more charitably toward
Josh than he had done before. "It is a very bad thing, Mr. Crane,"
said he mildly,—"not merely for yourself; but it scandalizes the
church-members, and I think you should take severe measures to
break up the habit."

"What upon arth shall I do, sir?" piteously asked Josh: "it's the
d—dest plague! Oh! I swan to man I've done it agin!"

And here, with a long howl, Josh threw himself down in the weeds,
and kicked out like a half-broken colt, wishing in his soul the earth
would hide him, and trying to feel as bad as he ought to; for his
honest conscience sturdily refused to convict him in this matter, faithful as it was in much less-sounding sins.

I grieve to say that Parson Pitcher got behind an apple-tree, and
there—cried perhaps; for he was wiping his eyes, and shaking all
over, when he walked off; and Josh, getting up considerably in a
state of dust, if not ashes and sackcloth, looked sheepishly about for
his reprover, but he was gone.

Parson Pitcher convened the deacons and a few of the uneasy
brethren that night in his study, and expounded to them the duty
of charity for people who would sleep in meeting, had to drink
bitters for their stomachs' sake, never came to missionary meetings
for fear of the contribution-box, or swore without knowing it; and
as Deacon Stone did now and then snore under the pulpit, and
brother Eldridge had a "rheumatiz" that nothing but chokeberry-
rum would cure; and that is very apt to affect the head, and brother
Peters had so firm a conviction that money is the root of all evil,
that he kept his from spreading, they all agreed to have patience
with brother Crane's tongue-ill; and Parson Pitcher smiled as he shut
the door behind them, thinking of that first stone that no elder nor
ruler could throw.

Nevertheless, he paid another visit to Josh the next week, and found
him in a hopeful state.

"I've hit on't now, Parson Pitcher!" said he, without waiting for a
more usual salutation. "Miss Eunice she helped me; she's a master
cretur for inventions. I s-sugar! There, that's it. When I'm a-goin'

to speak quick, I catch up somethin' else that's got the same letter on the bows, and I tell yew, it goes, 'r else it's somethin'.—Hollo! I see them d-dipper sheep is in my corn. Git aout! git aout! you d-dandelions! Git aout!" Here he scrambled away after the stray sheep, just in time for the parson, who had quieted his face and walked in to see Mrs. Crane, when Josh came back dripping, and exclaiming, "Pepper-grass! them is the d-drowndedest sheep I ever see."

This new spell of "Miss Eunice's," as Josh always called his wife, worked well while it was new. But the unruly tongue relapsed; and meek Mrs. Crane had grown to look upon it—as she would upon a wooden leg, had that been Josh's infirmity—with pity and regret, the purest result of a charity which "endureth and hopeth all things," eminently her ruling trait.

Every thing else went on prosperously. The farm paid well, and Josh laid up money, but never for himself. They had no children, a sore disappointment to both their kindly hearts; but all the poor and orphan little ones in the town seemed to have a special claim on their care and help. Nobody ever went away hungry from Josh's door, or unconsoled from Miss Eunice's "keeping-room." Everybody loved them both, and in time people forgot that Josh swore; but he never did; a keen pain discomforted him whenever he saw a child look up astonished at his oath. He had grown so far toward "the full ear," that he understood what an offence his habit was; and it pained him very much that it could not be overcome, even in so long a trial. But soon other things drew on to change the current of Josh's penitent thoughts.

He had been married about ten years when Miss Eunice began to show signs of failing health. She was, after the Yankee custom, somewhat older than her husband, and of too delicate a make to endure the hard life Connecticut farmers' wives must or do lead. Josh was as fond of her as he could be; but he did not know how to demonstrate it. All sorts of comforts she had, as far as food and fire and clothing went, but no recreation. No public amusements ever visited Plainfield, a sparse and quiet village far off the track of any railroad. The farmers could not spend time to drive round the country with their wives, or to go visiting, except now and then on Sunday nights to a neighbor's; sometimes to a paring or husking bee, the very essence of which was work. Once a year a donation-party at the minister's, and a rare attendance upon the sewing-circle, distasteful to Josh, who must get and eat his supper alone in that case,—these were all the amusements Miss Eunice knew. Books she had none, except her Bible, "Boston's Fourfold State," a dictionary, and an arithmetic,—relics of her school; and, if ever she wished for more, she repressed the wish, because these ought to be enough. She did not know, or dared not be conscious, that humanity needs something for its lesser and trivial life; that "by all these things men live," as well as by the word and by bread.

So she drudged on uncomplainingly, and after ten years of patience and labor, took to her bed, and was pronounced by the Plainfield doctor to have successively "a spine in the back," a "rising of the lungs," and a "gittaral complaint of the lights." (Was it catarrhal?) Duly was she blistered, plastered, and fomented, dosed with Brandreth's pills, mullein-root in cider, tansy, burdock, bitter-sweet, catnip, and boneset teas, sow-bugs tickled into a ball, and swallowed alive, dried rattlesnakes' flesh, and the powder of a red squirrel, shut into a red-hot oven living, baked till powderable, and then put through that process in a mortar, and administered fasting.

Dearly beloved, I am not improvising. All these, and sundry other and filthier medicaments which I refrain from mentioning, did once, perhaps do still, abound in the inlands of this Yankeedom, and slay their thousands yearly, as with the jaw-bone of an ass.

Of course Miss Eunice pined and languished, not merely from the "simples" that she swallowed, but because the very fang that had set itself in the breast of Josh's gentle mother gnawed and rioted in hers. At length some idea of this kind occurred to Uncle Josh's mind. He tackled up Boker, the old horse, and set out for Sanbury, where there lived a doctor of some eminence, and returned in triumph, with Dr. Sawyer following in his own gig.

Miss Eunice was carefully examined by the physician, a pompous but kindly man, who saw at once there was no hope and no help for his fluttered and panting patient.

When the millennium comes, let us hope it will bring physicians of sufficient fortitude to forbear dosing in hopeless cases: it is vain to look for such in the present condition of things. And Dr. Sawyer was no better than his kind: he hemmed, hawed, screwed up one eye, felt Miss Eunice's pulse again, and uttered oracularly,—

"I think a portion of some sudorific febrifuge would probably allay Mrs. Crane's hectic."

"Well, I expect it would," confidently asserted Josh. "Can I get it to the store, doctor?"

"No, sir: it should be compounded in the family, Mr. Crane."

"Dew tell!" responded Josh, rather crestfallen, but brightening up as the doctor went on to describe, in all the polysyllables he could muster, the desirable fluid. At the end Josh burst out joyfully with,—

"I sw-swan! 'tain't nothin' but lemonade with gumarabac in't."

Dr. Sawyer gave him a look of contempt, and took his leave, Josh laboring under the profound and happy conviction that nothing ailed Miss Eunice, if lemonade was all that she needed; while the doctor called, on his way home, to see Parson Pitcher, and to him confided the mournful fact that Miss Eunice was getting ready for heaven fast, could scarcely linger another week by any mortal help. Parson Pitcher grieved truly; for he loved and respected Eunice, and held her as the sweetest and brightest example of unobtrusive religion in all his church: moreover, he knew how Josh would feel; and he dreaded the task of conveying to him this painful intelligence, resolving, nevertheless, to visit them next day with that intent, as it was now too near night to make it convenient.

But a more merciful and able shepherd than he preceded him, and spared Josh the lingering agony of an expectation that could do him no good. Miss Eunice had a restless night after Dr. Sawyer's visit; for, with the preternatural keenness of her disease, she read the truth in his eye and tone. Though she had long looked on to this end, and was ready to enter into rest, the nearness of that untried awe agitated her, and forbade her sleep; but faith, unfailing in bitter need, calmed her at length, and with peace written upon her face she slept till dawn. A sudden pang awoke her, and her start roused Josh. He lifted her on the pillow, where the red morning light showed her gasping and gray with death: he turned all cold.

"Good-by, Josh!" said her tender voice, fainting as it spoke, and, with one upward rapturous look of the soft brown eyes they closed forever, and her head fell back on Josh's shoulder, dead.

There the neighbor who "did chores" for her of late found the two when she came in. Josh had changed since his mother died; for the moment Mrs. Casey lifted his wife from his arm, and laid her patient, peaceful face back on its pillow, Josh flung himself down beside her, and cried aloud with the passion and carelessness of a child. Nobody could rouse him, nobody could move him, till Parson Pitcher came in, and, taking his hand, raised and led him into the keeping-room. There Josh brushed off the mist before his drenched eyes with the back of his rough hand, and looked straight at Parson Pitcher.

"O Lord! she's dead," said he, as if he alone of all the world knew it.

"Yes, my son, she is dead," solemnly replied the parson. "It is the will of God, and you must consent."

"I can't, I can't! I a'n't a-goin' to," sobbed Josh. " 'Ta'n't no use talkin'—if I'd only 'xpected somethin': it's that—doctor! O Lord! I've swore, and Miss Eunice is dead! Oh gracious goody! what be I a-goin' to do? Oh, dear, oh, dear! O Miss Eunice!"

Parson Pitcher could not even smile: the poor fellow's grief was too deep. What could he think of to console him, but that deepest comfort to the bereaved,—her better state? "My dear friend, be comforted. Eunice is with the blessed in heaven."

"I know it. I know it. She allers was nigh about fit to get there without dyin'. O Lordy! she's gone to heaven, and I ha'n't!"

No, there was no consoling Uncle Josh: that touch of nature showed it. He was alone, and refused to be comforted: so Parson Pitcher made a fervent prayer for the living, that unawares merged into a thanksgiving for the dead, and went his way, sorrowfully convicted that his holy office had in it no supernatural power or aid, that some things are too deep and too mighty for man.

Josh's grief raved itself into worn-out dejection, still too poignant to bear the gentlest touch: his groans and cries were heart-breaking at the funeral, and it seemed as if he would really die with agony while the despairing wretchedness of the funeral hymn, the wailing cadences of "China," poured round the dusty and cobwebbed meeting-house to which they carried his wife in her coffin, one sultry August Sunday, to utter prayers and hymns above her who now needed no prayer, and heard the hymns of heaven.

After this, Josh retired to his own house, and, according to Mrs. Casey's story, neither slept nor ate; but this was somewhat apocryphal: and, three days after the funeral, Parson Pitcher, betaking himself to the Crane farm, found Uncle Josh whittling out a set of clothes-pegs on his door-step, but looking very downcast and miserable.

"Good-morning, Mr. Crane!" said the good divine.

"Mornin', Parson Pitcher! Hev' a cheer?"

The parson sat down on the bench of the stoop, and wistfully surveyed Josh, wondering how best to introduce the subject of his loss; but the refractory widower gave no sign, and at length the parson spoke.

"I hope you begin to be resigned to the will of Providence, my dear Mr. Crane?"

"No, I don't, a speck!" honestly retorted Josh. Parson Pitcher was shocked.

"I hoped to find you in a better frame," said he.

"I can't help it!" exclaimed Josh, flinging down a finished peg emphatically. "I ain't resigned. I want Miss Eunice. I ain't willin' to have her dead: I can't and I ain't; and that's the hull on't! And I'd a —— sight ruther— Oh, goody! I've swore agin. Lord-a-massy! 'n' she ain't here to look at me when I do, and I'm goin' straight *to* the d——! Oh, land, there it goes! Oh, dear soul! can't a feller help himself nohow?"

And, with that, Josh burst into a passion of tears, and fled past Parson Pitcher into the barn, from whence he emerged no more till the minister's steps were heard crunching on the gravel-path toward the gate; when Josh, persistent as Galileo, thrust his head out of the barn-window, and repeated in a louder and more strenuous key, "I ain't willin', Parson Pitcher!" leaving the parson in a dubious state of mind, on which he ruminated for some weeks; finally concluding to leave Josh alone with his Bible till time should blunt the keen edge of his pain, and reduce him to reason. And he noticed with great satisfaction that Josh came regularly to church and conference-meetings, and at length resumed his work with a due amount of composure.

There was in the village of Plainfield a certain Miss Ranney, daughter of the aforesaid Mrs. Ranney, the greatest vixen in those parts, and of course an old maid. Her temper and tongue had kept off suitors in her youth, and had in nowise softened since. Her name was Sarah, familiarized into Sally; and as she grew up to middle age, that pleasant, kindly title being sadly out of keeping with her nature, everybody called her Sall Ran, and the third generation scarce knew she had another name.

Any uproar in the village always began with Sall Ran; and woe be to the unlucky boy who pilfered an apple under the overhanging trees of Mrs. Ranney's orchard by the road, or tilted the well-sweep of her stony-curbed well to get a drink. Sall was down upon the offender like a hail-storm; and cuffs and shrieks mingled in wild chorus with her shrill scolding, to the awe and consternation of every child within half a mile.

Judge, then, of Parson Pitcher's amazement, when, little more than a year after Miss Eunice's death, Josh was ushered into his study one evening, and, after stroking a new stovepipe hat for a long time, at length said he had "come to speak about bein' published." The parson drew a long breath, partly for the mutability of man, partly of pure wonder.

"Who are you going to marry, Mr. Crane?" said he, after a pause.

Another man might have softened the style of his wife to be: not Josh.

"Sall Ran," said he undauntedly. Parson Pitcher arose from his chair, and, with both hands in his pockets, advanced upon Josh like horse and foot together. But he stood his ground.

"What in the name of common sence and decency do you mean by marrying that woman, Joshu-way Crane?" thundered the parson.

"Well, ef you'll set down, Parson Pitcher, I'll tell ye the rights on't. You see, I'm dreadful pestered with this here swearin' way I've got. I kinder thought it would wear off, if Miss Eunice kep' a-lookin' at me; but she's died." Here Josh interpolated a great blubbering sob. "And I'm gettin' so d—— bad! There! you see, parson, I doo swear dreadful; and I ain't no more resigned to her dyin' than I used ter be, and I can't stan' it. So I set to figgerin' on it out, and I guess I've lived too easy, hain't had enough 'flictions and trials. So I concluded I hed oughter put myself to the wind'ard of some squalls, so's to learn navigation; and I couldn't tell how, till suddenly I brought to mind Sall Ran, who is the D—— and all. Oh, dear, I've nigh about swore agin! And I concluded she'd be the nearest to a cat-o'-nine-tails I could get to tewtor me. And then I reklected what old Cap'n Thomas used to say when I was a boy aboard of his whaler: 'Boys,' sez he, 'you're allers sot to hev' your own way, and you've got ter hev mine: so's it's pooty clear that I shall flog you to rope-yarns, or else you'll hev to make b'lieve my way's your'n, which'll suit all round.' So you see, Parson Pitcher, I wa'n't a-goin' to put myself in a way to quarrel with the Lord's will agin; and I don't expect you to hev' no such trouble with me twice, as you've hed sence Miss Eunice up an' died. I swan I'll give up reasonable next time, seein' it's Sall."

Hardly could Parson Pitcher stand this singular screed of doctrine, or the shrewd and self-satisfied yet honest expression of face with which Josh clinched his argument. Professing himself in great haste to study, he promised to publish as well as to marry Josh, and, when his odd parishioner was out of hearing, indulged himself with a long fit of laughter, almost inextinguishable, over Josh's patent Christianizer.

Great was the astonishment of the whole congregation on Sunday, when Josh's intentions were given out from the pulpit, and strangely mixed and hesitating the congratulations he received after his marriage, which took place in the following week. Parson Pitcher took a curious interest in the success of Josh's project, and had to acknowledge its beneficial effects, rather against his will.

Sall Ran was the best of housekeepers, as scolds are apt to be; or is it in reverse that the rule began? She kept the farmhouse Quakerly clean, and every garment of her husband's scrupulously mended and refreshed. But, if the smallest profanity escaped Uncle Josh's lips, he did indeed "hear thunder;" and, with the ascetic devotion of a Guyonist, he endured every objurgatory torrent to the end, though his soft and kindly heart would now and then cringe and quiver in the process.

It was all for his good, he often said; and, by the time Sall Ran had been in Miss Eunice's place for an equal term of years, Uncle Josh had become so mild-spoken, so kind, so meek, that surely his dead wife must have rejoiced over it in heaven, even as his brethren did on earth.

And now came the crowning honor of his life. Uncle Josh was made a deacon. Sall celebrated the event by a new black silk frock; and asked Parson Pitcher home to tea after the church-meeting, and to such a tea as is the great glory of a New-England housekeeper. Pies, preserves, cake, biscuit, bread, shortcake, cheese, honey, fruit, and cream, were pressed and pressed again upon the unlucky parson, till he was quite in the condition of Charles Lamb and the omnibus, and gladly saw the signal of retreat from the table; he withdrawing himself to the bench on the stoop, to breathe the odorous June air, and talk over matters and things with Deacon Josh, while "Miss Crane cleared off."

Long and piously the two worthies talked; and at length came a brief pause, broken by Josh. "Well, Parson Pitcher, that 'are calkerlation of mine about Sall did come out nigh onter right, didn't it?"

"Yes indeed, my good friend," returned the parson. "The trial she has been to you has been really blessed, and shows most strikingly the use of discipline in this life."

"Yes," said Josh. "If Miss Eunice had lived, I don't know but what I should 'a' ben a swearin' man to this day; but Sall she's rated it out o' me. And I'm gettin' real resigned too."

The meek complacency of the confession still gleamed in Uncle Josh's eyes as he went in to prayers; but Sall Ran looked redder than the crimson peonies on her posy-bed.

Parson Pitcher made an excellent prayer, particularly descanting on the use of trials; and when he came to an end, and arose to say good-night, Mrs. Crane had vanished: so he had to go home without taking leave of her. Strange to say, during the following year a rumor crept through the village that "Miss Deacon Crane" had not been heard to scold once for months; that she even held her tongue under provocation; this last fact being immediately put to the test by a few evil-minded and investigating boys, who proceeded to pull her fennel-bushes through the pickets, and nip the yellow heads; receiving for their audacious thieving no more than a mild request not to "do that," which actually shamed them into apologizing.

With this confirmation, even Parson Pitcher began to be credulous of report, and sent directly for Deacon Crane to visit him.

"How's your wife, Deacon?" said the parson, as soon as Josh was fairly seated in the study.

"Well, Parson Pitcher, she's most onsartainly changed. I don't believe she's got riled mor'n once, or gin it to me once, for six months."

"Very singular," said Parson Pitcher. "I am glad for both of you. But what seems to have wrought upon her?"

"Well," said Uncle Josh, with a queer glitter in his eye, "I expect she must 'a' ben to the winder that night you 'n' I sot a-talkin' on the stoop about 'flictions and her; for next day I stumbled, and spilt a lot o' new milk onto the kitchen-floor. That allers riled her: so I began to say, 'Oh, dear, I'm sorry, Sall!' when she ups right away, and sez, sez she, 'you hain't no need to be skeered, Josh Crane: you've done with 'flictions in this world. I sha'n't never scold you no more. I ain't a-goin' to be made a pack-horse to carry my husband to heaven.' And she never said no more to me, nor I to her; but she's ben nigh about as pretty-behaved as Miss Eunice ever since; and I hope I sha'n't take to swearin'. I guess I sha'n't; but I do feel kinder crawly about bein' resigned."

However, Uncle Josh's troubles were over. Sall Ran dropped her name for "Aunt Sally," and finally joined the church, and was as good in her strenuous way as her husband in his meekness; for there are "diversities of gifts." And when the Plainfield bell, one autumn day, tolled a long series of eighty strokes, and Deacon Crane was gathered to his rest in the daisy-sprinkled burying-yard beside Miss Eunice, the young minister who succeeded Parson Pitcher had almost as hard a task to console Aunt Sally as his predecessor had to instil resignation, on a like occasion, into Uncle Josh.

Grit

"Look a-here, Phoebe, I won't hev no such goin's-on here. That feller's got to make tracks. I don't want none o' Jake Potter's folks round, 'nd you may as well lay your account with it, 'nd fix accordin'."

Phoebe Fyler set her teeth together, and looked her father in the face with her steady gray eyes; but she said nothing, and the old man scrambled up into his rickety wagon and drove off.

"Fyler grit" was a proverb in Pasco, and old Reuben did credit to the family reputation. But his share of "grit" was not simply endurance, perseverance, dogged persistence, and courage, but a most unlimited obstinacy and full faith in his own wisdom. Phoebe was his own child, and when things came to an open struggle between them, it was hard to tell which would conquer.

There had been a long quarrel between the Fylers and Potters —such a quarrel as can only be found in little country villages, where people are thrown so near together and have so little to divert their minds that they become as belligerent as a company of passengers on a sailing vessel—fire easily and smoulder long. But Phoebe Fyler was a remarkably pretty girl, with great, clear gray eyes, a cheek like the wild rose, abundance of soft brown hair, and a sweet firm mouth and square cleft chin that told their own story of Fyler blood; and Tom Potter was a smart, energetic, fiery young fellow, ready to fight for his rights and then to shake hands with his enemy, whichever beat. There was no law to prevent his falling in love with Phoebe because their fathers had hated each other; indeed, that was rather an inducement. His honest, generous heart looked on the family feud with pity and regret. He would like to cancel it, especially if marrying Phoebe would do it.

And why should she hate him? Her father was an old tyrant in his family; and the feeble, pale mother, who had always trembled at his step since the girl could remember, had never taught her to love her father, because she did not love him herself. Obedience, indeed, was ground into Phoebe. It was obey or suffer in that family, and the rod hanging over the shelf was not in vain. But when she grew up, and left the childish instinct or habit behind her, and the Fyler grit developed, she had the sense to avoid an open conflict whenever she could, for her mother's sake.

This, however, was a matter of no small importance to Phoebe. She had met Tom Potter time after time at sewing societies, sleigh rides, huckleberryings, and other rustic amusements; they sat together in the singers' seat, they went to rehearsal; but Tom had never come home with her until lately, and then always parted at the doorsill. Now he had taken the decisive step; he had come Sunday evening to call, and every Pasco girl knew what that meant. It was a declaration. But while Phoebe's heart beat at his clear whistle outside, and stood still at his knock, she saw with dismay her father rise to open the door.

"Good-evening, Mr. Fyler."

"How de do? how de do?" was the sufficiently cordial reply; for the old man was half blind, and by the flicker of his tallow candle could noway discern who his visitor might be.

"I don't really make out who ye be," he went on, peering into the darkness.

"My name's Potter. Is Phoebe to home?"

"Jake Potter's son?"

"Yes, I be. Is Phoebe to home?"

An ominous flash from Tom's black eyes accentuated the question this time, but old Reuben was too blind to see it. He drew back the candle, and said, in a surly but decisive tone,—

" 'Tain't no matter to you ef she is or ef she ain't," and calmly shut the door in his face.

For a moment Tom Potter was furious. Decency forbade that he should take the door off its rackety hinges, like Samson at the gates of Gaza, but he felt a strong impulse to do so, and then an equally strong one to laugh, for the affair had its humorous side. The result was that neither humor nor anger prevailed; but as he strode away, a fixed purpose to woo and marry Phoebe, "whether or no," took possession of him.

"I'll see ef Potter faculty can't match Fyler grit," he muttered to himself; and not without reason, for the Potters had that trait which conquers the world far more surely and subtly than grit,—"faculty," *i.e.,* a clear head and a quick wit, and capacity of adaptation that wrests from circumstance its stringent sceptre, and is the talisman of what the world calls "luck."

In the mean time Phoebe, by the kitchen fire, sat burning with rage. Her father came back chuckling.

"I've sent that spark up chimney pretty everlastin' quick."

Phoebe's red lips parted for a rude answer, but her mother signaled to her from beyond the fire-place, and the sad pale face had its usual effect on her. She knew that sore heart would ache beyond any sleep if she and her father came to words; so she took up her candle to go to bed, but she did not escape.

"You've no need to be a-muggin' about that feller, Phoebe," cackled the old man after her. "He won't never darken my doors, nor your'n nuther; so ye jest stop a-hankerin' arter him, right off slap. The idee! a Potter a-comin' here arter you!"

Phoebe's eyes blazed. She stopped on the lower stair, and spoke sharply,—

"Mebbe you'll find there's more things can go out o' the chimney than sparks," and then hurried up, banging the door behind her in very womanish fashion, and burst into tears as soon as she reached her room.

It was Tuesday morning when old Fyler drove from his door, hurling the words at the beginning of our story at Phoebe, on the doorstep.

He had found out that Tom Potter had gone to Hartford the day before for a week's stay, and took the chance to drive sixteen miles down the river on some business, sure that in his day's absence Tom could not get back to Pasco, and Phoebe would be safe.

But man proposes in vain sometimes. Mr. Fyler did his errand at Taunton, ate his dinner at the dirty little tavern, and set out for home. As he was jogging quietly along, laying plans for the easy discomfiture of Tom and Phoebe, a loud roll of wheels roused him, a muffled roar like a heavy pulse beat, a shriek as of ten thousand hysterical females, and right in the face and eyes of old Jerry appeared a locomotive under full headway, coming round a curve of the track, which the old man had either forgotten, or not known, ran beside the highway for nearly half a mile. Jerry was old and sober and steady, but what man even could bear the sudden and unforeseen charge of a railway engine bearing down upon him face to face? The horse started, reared, jumped aside, and took to his heels for dear life; the wagon tilted up on a convenient stone, and threw the driver violently out; but in all the shock and terror the "Fyler grit" never failed. With horny hands he grasped the reins so powerfully that the horse could drag him but a few steps before he was stopped by the weight on the bit, and then, as Reuben tried to gather himself out of the dust and consider the situation, he found that one leg hung helpless from the knee, his cheek and forehead were well grazed, and his teeth—precious possession, over whose cost he had groaned and perspired as a necessary but dreadful expense—had disappeared entirely. This was the worst blow. Half blind, with a terrified horse and a broken leg, totally alone and seventy-seven years old, who else would have stopped to consider their false teeth? But he dragged himself over the ground, holding the reins with one hand, groping and fumbling in the dust, till fortunately the missing set was found, uninjured by wheel or stone, but considerably mixed up with kindred clay.

"Whoa, I tell ye! whoa!" shouted the old man to Jerry, who, with wild eyes and erect ears, stood quivering and eager to be off.

"Darn ye, stan' still!" and jerking the reins by way of comment, he crept and hitched himself toward the wagon. Jerry looked round, and seemed to understand the situation. He set down the pawing forefoot, lowered the pointed ears, and, though he trembled still, stood as a rock might, till, with pain and struggle, his master raised himself on one foot against the wheel, and, setting his lips tight, contrived to get into the wagon, and on to the seat. "Git up!" he said, and Jerry started with a spring that brought a dark flush of pain to the old man's cheek. But he did not stop nor stay for pain. "Git up, I tell ye! We've got to git as fur as Baxter, anyhow. Go 'long, Jerry." And on he drove, though the broken leg, beginning to swell and press on the stiff boot-leg, gave him exquisite pain. But a mile or two passed before he met any one, for it was just noon, and all the countryfolk were at their dinner. At last a man appeared in the distance, and Reuben drew up by the roadside, and shouted to him to stop. It proved to be an Irishman, on his way to a farm just below.

"Say, have ye got a jackknife?" was Reuben's salutation.

"Yis, surr, I have that; and a fuss-rate knoife as iver ye see. What's wantin'?"

"Will yer ole hoss stan' a spell?"

"Sure he'll stand still the day afther niver, av I'd let him. It's standin' he takes to far more than goin'."

"Then you git out, will ye, 'nd fetch yer knife over here 'nd cut my boot-leg down."

"What 'n the wurrld are ye afther havin' yer boot cut for?" queried the Irishman, clambering down to the ground.

"Well, I got spilt out a piece back. Hoss got skeert by one o' them pesky ingines, 'nd I expect I broke my leg. It's kinder useless, 'nd it's kep' a-swellin' ever sence, so's't it hurts like blazes, I tell ye."

"The divil an' all—broke yer leg, man alive? An' how did ye get back to the waggin?"

"Oh, I wriggled in somehow. Come, be quick! I want to git to Baxter right off."

"Why, is it mad ye are? Turn about, man. There's Kinney's farm just beyant a bit. Come in there. I'll fetch the docthor for yez."

"No, I won't stop. I must git to the tavern to Baxter fust; then I'll go home, if I can fix it."

"The Lord help ye, thin, ye poor old crathur!"

"You help me fust, and don't jaw no more."

And so snapped at, the astounded Irishman proceeded to cut the boot off—a slow and painful process, but of some relief when over; and Jerry soon heard the word of command to start forward. Three more hard uphill miles brought them to the tavern, just at the entrance of Baxter, and Jerry stopped at the backdoor.

"Hullo!" shouted the old man; and the man who kept the house rose from his armchair with a yawn and sauntered leisurely to the piazza. But his steps quickened as soon as he found out what was the matter, and with neighborly aid Mr. Fyler was soon carried upstairs and laid on a bed, and the doctor sent for. "Say, don't ye give Jerry no oats, now I tell ye. I won't pay for 'em. He's used to hay, 'nd he'll get a mess o' meal to-night arter we get home."

"Why, you can't get home to-night!" exclaimed the landlord.

"Can't I? I will, anyhow, ye'd better believe. I've got to be there whether or no. Where's that darned doctor? Brush the dirt off'n my coat, will ye? 'nd here, jest rence off them teeth," handing them out of his pocket. "I lost 'em out, 'nd hed to scrape round in the dirt quite a spell afore I found 'em."

"Well, I swan to man!" ejaculated the landlord. "Do you mean to say you hunted round after them 'ere things after you'd got a broke leg?"

"Sure's you live, sir. I hitched around just like a youngster a-learnin' to creep, 'nd drawed my leg along back side o' me; I'm kinder blind, ye see, or I should ha' found 'em quicker."

"By George! ef you hain't got the most grit!" And the landlord went off to tell his tale in the office.

"Take him up a drink o' rum, Joe," was the comment of a hearer. "I know him. He polishes his nose four time a week, you bet; rum's kinder nateral to him. His dad kep' a corner grocery. A drink 'll do him good. I'll stan' treat, fur he's all-fired close. He'd faint away afore he'd buy a drink, fur he 'stills his own cider-brandy. But flesh an' blood can't allers go it on grit, ef 'tis Fyler grit, 'nd he'll feel considerable mean afore the doctor gets here. Fetch him up a good stiff sling, 'nd chalk it down to me."

A kindly and timely tonic the sling seemed to be, and the old fellow took it with great ease.

"Taste kinder nateral?" inquired the interested landlord, with suspended spoon.

"It's reel refrashin'," was the long-delayed answer, as the empty tumbler went back to join the unoccupied spoon. "Now fetch on yer doctor." And without a groan or a word the old man bore the examination, which revealed the fact that both bones of the leg were fractured; or, as the landlord expressed it to a gaping and expectant crowd outside, "His leg's broke short off in two places." Without any more ado Reuben bore the setting and splinting of the crushed limb, and accepted meekly another dose of the "refrashin'" fluid from the bar-room. "Now, doctor, I want to be a-travelin' right off."

"Traveling! where to?" demanded the doctor, glaring at him over his spectacles.

"Where to! why, back to our folks's, to Pasco."

"You travel to the land of Nod, man. Go to sleep; you won't see Pasco to-day nor to-morrow."

"I'm a-goin', anyhow. I tell ye I've got ter. Important bizness. I wouldn't be kep' here for a thousand dollars."

The doctor saw a hot flush rise to his face, and an ominous glitter invade the dull eye. He knew his man, and he knew what determined opposition and helplessness might do for him. At seventy-seven, a broken leg is no trifle; but if fever sets in, matters become complicated.

"Well," he said, by way of humoring the refractory patient, "if you're bound to go, you must go to-night; to-morrow 'll be harder for you to move." And with a friendly nod he left the room, and the landlord followed him.

"Ye don't expect he's a-goin' to go, do ye, doctor?"

"Lord, man! he might as well stand on his head! Still, you don't know old Reub Fyler, perhaps. He's as clear grit as a grindstone, and if he is bound to go, he'll go; heaven nor earth won't stop him, nor men neither." And the doctor stepped into his sulky and drove off.

An hour afterward Reuben Fyler insisted on being sent home. A neighbor from Pasco, who had come down after grain with a long wagon, heard of the accident, and happened in.

"I'm bound to git home, John Barnes," said the old man. "I've got ter; I've got bizness. Well, I might as well tell ye, that darned Potter feller's a-snakin' 'nd a-sneakin' round arter Phoebe, 'nd ef I'm laid up here, he'll be hangin' round there as sure as guns. Fust I know they'll up 'nd git married. I'll see him hanged fust! I'm goin' hum to-night. I can keep her under my thumb ef I'm there; but ye know how 'tis: when the cat's away"—

"H'm!" said John Barnes—a man slow of speech, but perceptive. "Well, ef you're bound to go, you can have my waggin, 'nd I'll drive your'n up."

"But change hosses; I can't drive no hoss but Jerry."

"You drive!" exclaimed John, in unfeigned astonishment.

"My arms ain't broke, I tell ye, 'nd I ain't a-goin' to pay nobody for what I can do myself, you can jest swear to that."

And John Barnes retreated to hold council with the bar-room loungers. But remonstrance was in vain. About five o'clock the long wagon was brought up, the seat shoved quite back to the end, and an extempore bed made of flour bags, hay, and old buffalo-robes on the floor of the rickety vehicle; the old man was carried carefully down, packed in as well as the case allowed, his splinted and bandaged leg tied to the side to keep it steady, his head propped up with his overcoat rolled into a bundle, and an old carriage carpet thrown over him and tucked in. Then another "refrashin'" fluid was administered, and the reins being put into his hands, with a sharp chirrup to old Jerry, he started off at a quick trot, and before John Barnes could get into his wagon and follow, Fyler was round the corner, out of sight, speeded by the cheers and laughter of the spectators, and eulogized by the landlord, as he bit off the end of a fresh cigar, as "the darnedest piece of Fyler grit or any other grit I ever see!"

In the mean time Phoebe at home went about her daily work in a kind of sullen peace: peaceful, because her father was out of the way for one day at least; sullen, because she foresaw no end of trouble coming to her, but never for one moment had an idea of giving up Tom Potter, or of any way to achieve her freedom except by enduring obstinacy. Many another girl, quick-witted or well read in novels, would have enjoyed the situation with a certain zest, and already invented plenty of stratagems; but Phoebe had not been educated in modern style, and tact or cunning was not native to her; she could endure or resist to the death, but she could not elude or beguile, and her father knew it. Her mother was helpless to aid her; but, with the courage mothers have, she set herself out of the question, and having thought deeply all the morning, over the knitting-work, which was all she could do now, she surprised Phoebe in the midst of her potato-paring by suddenly saying:—

"Phoebe, I see what you're a-thinkin' of, and I want to say my say now, afore anybody comes in. I've heerd enough o' Tom Potter to know he's a reel likely young feller; he's stiddy, 'nd he's a professor besides, 'nd he's got a good trade; there ain't no reason on airth why you shouldn't keep company with him, ef you like him. It's clear senseless to hev your life spoiled because your folks 'nd his folks querreled, away back, about a water right."

Phoebe dropped the potatoes, and gave her mother a speechless hug, that brought the tears into those pale blue eyes.

"Softly, dear! I don't mean to set ye ag'inst your pa, noways; but I don't think man nor woman hes a right to say their gal sha'n't marry a man that ain't bad nor shiftless, jest 'cause they don't fancy him; 'nd I don't want to leave ye here when I go, to live my life over agin."

"Oh, mother," exclaimed Phoebe, almost dropping the pan again, "I think it would be awful mean of me to leave you here alone!"

" 'Twouldn't be no worse, Phoebe. I should miss ye, no doubt on 't; I should miss ye consider'ble, but then I shouldn't worry over your hard times here as I do, some, all the time."

Poor saint! she fought her battle there by the fireside, and nobody saw it but the "cloud of witnesses," who had hung over many a martyrdom before that was not illustrated by fire or sword.

Phoebe choked a little, and her clear eyes softened; she was only a girl, and she did not fully understand what her mother had suffered and renounced for her, but she loved her with all her warm heart.

"I can't help ye none, Phoebe," Mrs. Fyler went on, with a patient smile, "but I can comfort ye, mebbe, and, as fur as my consent goes, you hev it, ef you want to marry Tom; but oh! Phoebe, be sure, sure as death, you *do* want to: don't marry him to get away from home. I'd ruther see ye drowned in Long Pond."

Phoebe's cheek colored deeply and her bright eyes fell, for her mother's homely words were solemn in their meaning and tone.

"I *am* sure, mother," she said softly, and went away to fetch more wood for the fire; and neither of the women spoke again of the matter, but Phoebe's brow cleared of its trouble, and her mother lay back in her chair and prayed in her heart. Poor woman! she had mighty need of such a refuge.

So night came on, and after long delay they ate their supper, presuming that the head of the house was delayed by business, little thinking how he, strapped into John Barnes's wagon, was pursuing his homeward road in the gathering darkness and solitude; for though John caught up with him soon, after a mile or two some empty sacks fell out of the Barnes wagon, and no sooner did John miss them than he coolly turned back and left old Reuben to find his way alone. But the old man did not care; he had courage for anything; so he drove

along as cheerily as ever, though his dim sight was darkened further
by the darkening air, the overhanging trees, and the limit set to his
vision by the horse's head, which from his position was all he could
see before him.

About nine o'clock a benighted traveler driving toward Baxter from
Pasco way, with his wife, discerned dimly an approaching horse and
wagon, apparently without a driver. He reined his own horse and
covered buggy into the ditch, to give room, but the road was narrow, and the other horse kept in the middle.

"Turn out! turn out!" shouted the anxious man. "Are you asleep
or drunk? Turn out, I tell you!"

But old Fyler heard the echo only of the strenuous voice, and turned
out the wrong way, setting his own wheels right into the wheels of
the stranger's buggy.

"You drunken idiot! back, back, I say! you've run right into me"
—not without objurgations of a slightly profane character to emphasize
his remark. "Back, I say! The devil! can't you hear?"

By this time both horses were excited; the horse in the ditch began
to plunge, the other one to rear and back, till, what between the pull
of his master on the reins and his own terror, Jerry backed his load
down the steep bank at the roadside, and but for a tree that caught
the wheel, horse, driver, and wagon would have gone headlong into
a situation of fatal reverses, where even Fyler grit could not avail.

"Murder!" cried the old man. "I've broke my leg, 'nd I'm pitchin'
over th' edge! Lordy massy! stop the cretur! Who be ye? Ketch his
head, can't ye? Thunderation! I'm a-tippin', sure's ye live!"

"Let your horse alone, you old fool!" shouted the exasperated traveler, who was trying vainly to tie his own to some saplings by the
roadside, while his wife scrambled out as best she might over the
floundering wheels. But by the time the man succeeded, Fyler's horse
had been so demonstrative that the wagon wheels were twisted and
locked together, the wagon body tilted up to a dangerous degree, and
the old man rolled down to the other side and half out, where he
hung helpless, tied by the knee, sick with the pain of his wrenched
leg, and unable to stir; but still he yelled for help.

"Can you hold this plaguy horse's head, Anne?" said the traveler.
"I never can right the wheels while he plunges and rears like that."

"I'll try," was the quiet response; and being a woman of courage
and weight, she hung on to the bridle, though Jerry made frantic
efforts to lift her off the ground and stand on his hind-legs, till the
wagon was righted, the groaning old man replaced, his story told, and

he ready once more to shake the reins, which still were grasped in his hard hands.

"But you ain't going on alone in this dark?" asked the astonished traveler.

"Yes, I be, yes, I be—sartain. I shall git on well enough ef I don't meet nobody, 'nd I guess I sha'n't."

"But you met us."

"Well, it's a-growin' later 'nd later; there won't be many folks out to-night; they ginerly knows enough to stay to hum arter dark out our way." With which Parthian remark he chirruped to Jerry and trotted away, without a word of thanks or acknowledgment, aching and groaning, and muttering to himself, "Darned fool! what'd he want to be a-kitin' round in a narrer road this time o' night? Fixed me out, I guess; but I'll get hum, anyhow. Git up, Jerry!"

And Jerry got up to such a purpose that about twelve o'clock that night a loud shouting at the front door roused Phoebe and her mother, and they were forced to call in a couple of men from the next neighbor's, at least a quarter of a mile away, to get the old man into the house, undressed, and put to bed.

As might have been expected, fever set in; but he fought that with "Fyler grit." And though fever is a force of itself, there is a certain willful vitality and strength of will in some people that exert wonderful influence over physical maladies; and after a few days of pain and discomfort and anger with himself and everybody else, the old man grew more comfortable, and proceeded to rule his family as usual. By dint of questioning the daily visitors who always flock about the victim of an accident in a country village, he had kept himself posted as to Tom Potter's absence; but its limit was drawing to an end now, and he took alarm. He had not imagined that Tom might be as well informed on his part, and that more than one note had passed through the post-office already between the young couple. Nor did he know that the postmistress was a warm friend of Tom's; for he had rescued her only child from the threatening horns of his father's Ayrshire bull, when little Fanny had ventured to cross the pasture lot after strawberries, and her red shawl attracted that ill-conditioned quadruped's notice and aroused his wrath. Tom's correspondence was safe and secret in passing through aunty Leland's hands. But as soon as Reuben Fyler ceased to need doses from the drug store and ice from the tavern, Phoebe was kept within range of his eye and ear. Still, she knew Tom was at home now, and evening after evening his cheery whistle passed through the window as he sauntered by,— a signal to Phoebe to get outside if she could; but she never could.

However, "Potter faculty" was at work for her. When the county paper was sent over from the post-office by a small boy, he had directions from aunty Leland to give it at once into Phoebe's hand, "and nobody else's." So he waited about till Phoebe opened the kitchen door to sweep out the dust, and gave it to her with a significant wink—not that he knew what his wink signified at all, but, with the true *gamin* instinct, he gathered an idea from the widow Leland's special instructions that "somethin' wuz to pay," as he expressed it to himself.

And Phoebe, as she hastened in from the door to carry the paper to her father's bedside, perceived on the margin, in a well-known handwriting, these words, "Look out for lambs." As she hung up her broom, she tore off the inscription and tossed it into the fire; and then, while she patiently went through the gossip, politics, religion, and weekly story of the "Slabtown News," exercised herself mightily as to what that mystic sentence might mean; but not till the soft and fragrant darkness of the June evening set in did she find a clew to the mystery.

Old Fyler had a few pure-blood merino sheep on his farm that were the very apple of his eye. Not that he had ever bought such expensive commodities; but a wealthy farmer in the next town owned a small flock some years before, which the New England nuisance of dogs at last succeeded in slaying or scattering. In some panic of the sort, one had escaped to the woods, and, after long straying, been found by Fyler, with a new-born pair of lambs beside her, in a wood on the limit of Pasco township, where he was cutting his winter supply. Of course this windfall was too valuable to be neglected. The hay brought for Jerry's dinner was made into a soft bed, and, with the help of an Irishman, who was chopping also, the sheep and her family lifted into the wagon and taken home. Pasco was not infested with dogs; only two or three could be numbered in the village. And after the old sheep was wonted to her quarters a little, fed by hand, cosseted, and made at home, she was turned into a lot with the cows. And woe betide any dog that intruded among the beautiful Ayrshires! So the sheep increased year after year, carefully sheltered in cold weather, as became their high breeding, till now between thirty and forty ranged the sweet short pastures of the Fyler farm, and their fleeces were the wonder and admiration of all the town.

Late that night—late, I mean, for Pasco, for the old-fashioned nine-o'clock bell had but just rung, though Mrs. Fyler had gone to bed upstairs an hour ago, and Phoebe was just spreading an extempore bed on the lounge in the kitchen, to be where her father might call her in case of need—a piteous bleat, unmistakably the bleat of a lamb in some kind of distress, was heard outside. The old man started up from his pillow.

"What 'n thunder's that, Phoebe?"

"Sounds some like a lamb."

"Sounds like a lamb! Anybody 'd think you was a durn fool. 'Tis a lamb, I tell ye. One o' them leetle creturs hez strayed away out o' the paddock. I 'xpect boys hez ben in there a-foolin' round 'cause I'm laid up abed. Lordy! I wish to the land I could smash that 'ere ingine. Go 'long out, gal, 'nd see to 't. It'll stray a mile mebbe ef ye don't. You've got ter look out for lambs. They don't know nothin'."

Phoebe started as her father repeated the very phrase penciled on the edge of the paper; the lamb kept bleating, and the dimple in the girl's rosy cheek deepened while she found her bonnet, and, turning the key of the kitchen door, stepped out into the starlit night. That lamb was evidently behind the woodshed, but so was somebody else; for Phoebe had hardly discerned its curly back in the shadow before she was grasped in a stringent embrace, and Tom Potter actually kissed her.

"Go 'long!" she whispered indignantly. But Tom did not seem to mind her, and probably she became resigned to the infliction, for at least ten minutes elapsed before that go-between of a lamb was restored to its anxious mother in the paddock, and full half the time was wasted in a whispered dialogue—with punctuation marks.

Very rosy indeed Miss Phoebe looked as she returned to the house.

"Seems to me ye was everlastin' long 'bout ketchin' that lamb," growled old Reuben.

"Well, I had to put it back, 'nd fix up the little gate. One hinge was off on 't, 'nd 'twas kinder canted round, so's 't the lamb got out, 'nd was too simple to get back."

Oh, Phoebe! Well it was that no oath compelled the speaking of the whole truth—of who unhinged the gate, or who had the lamb safe by a long string, having previously captured it in the paddock for purposes of decoy, or how, indeed, a letter came to be in that calico pocket, making an alarming crackle whenever she moved, terribly loud to her, but silent to the sleepy old man in his bed.

Phoebe went about very thoughtful the next day. The letter contained an astounding proposition. It was an artful letter, too, for it began with a recital of all the difficulties that made the way of true love proverbially rugged, and convinced her of what she had unconsciously admitted before, that she could never marry her lover in the world with her father's consent and the pleasant observances of ordinary life. Then it went on to plead in tender and manly fashion the writer's own affection; his ability to give her a pleasant and happy home, for he had just bought out the Pasco blacksmith shop, the owner thereof having moved to Hartford, where Tom had spent that week settling up the matter, and the smithy was a good business, being the only one in a wide radius. And it wound up with a proposal that as soon as her father got so much better that her mother could care for him alone, Phoebe should slip out some fine night on to the roof, thence to the top of the henhouse, and so to the ground, and meet Tom and his sister, who would be with him, at Peter Green's wood, half a mile away, and just at the edge of the Fyler farm. Phoebe was to consider the matter fully and talk it over with her mother, and when she had made up her mind, to put a letter in the corner of the cow-shed, where she milked daily, under a stone, where she would also find an answer, and probably other epistles thereafter.

Phoebe was not a girl to take such a proposal lightly. She did, indeed, consider it long and in earnest. Day by day, as her father grew better, with a rapidity astonishing in so old a man,—for Reuben Fyler's adventures are literally true,—he became more and more ill-tempered and exasperating. The pain of the knitting bones, the bed-weariness, the constant fret over farm-work that was either neglected or hired out, worked on his naturally growling temper, and made life unpleasant to all around him as well as himself. Phoebe's mind was made up more by her father than even her own affection for Tom, or her mother's gentle encouragement. The old man vented his temper on Phoebe in the matter of Tom Potter more and more frequently; he reviled the Potter tribe, root and branch, in a radical and persistent way that would have done credit to an ancient Israelite cursing Canaan; he even taunted Phoebe with favoring such a chicken-hearted lover, scared with one slam of a door in his face; and Phoebe's inherited "grit" was taxed strongly to keep her tongue quiet lest she should betray her own secret; yet angry as she was, there was a glint of fun underlying her anger, to think how thoroughly Tom had countermined her father, which set the deep, lovely dimples in cheek and chin alight, and sparkled in each steady eye, almost belying the angry brow and set lips.

So it came about that she yielded to the inner pressure and the outer persuasion. Her father was able now to get about a little on crutches, and sit at the window overlooking the cow-shed; yet it was there, right under his suspicious eyes, that Phoebe took the time, while she was milking and her mother feeding a new-weaned calf, to unfold her plans.

"Mother," she began, with eyes fixed on her pail, "I can't stand it any longer; my mind's made up. I'm going to Tom, if you keep in the same mind you was."

"Yes, dear; I think it is the best for both of us. But don't tell me any more about it than you can help. Tell me what you want me to do for you, but"—

"Yes, I know," answered Phoebe. "I don't want you to do anything, mother; only you'll know if you miss me."

"Yes; and I want to tell you, Phoebe. Several years back I've kinder taken comfort a-fixin' for this time. I've hed a chance now 'nd then to sew a little, 'nd I've made ye a set o' things when you was off to school odd times, 'nd washed 'em up 'nd put 'em up chamber for ye in the old press drawers. Then I've laid up some little too, out of a dozen of eggs here, 'nd a little milk there, 'nd twenty gold dollars grandmother give me before she died. I guess there's nigh about fifty by this time; and the black silk dress aunt Sary sent me from York, arter her Sam spent that year here, never's ben cut. You better take that to Taunton to-morrer to be made."

"Oh, mother!"

"Well, dear, you're all I've got. Why shouldn't I? Oh, that pesky calf!" and just in time to divert sentiment into a safer channel, the calf threw up its head, knocked the good woman backward into the dirt, and with tail high in air, and its four feet apparently going four ways at once, began one of those wild canters about the yard which calves indulge in. Phoebe had to laugh, as her mother, indignant but unhurt, rose up from the ground, and old Fyler at the kitchen window grinned with amusement. So Phoebe transported her modest fitting-out little by little to Julia Potter, who was her only confidante in the matter, and could not even see Phoebe, but punctually went for the bundles, when Tom was notified that they would be left in the further barn, which opened on another road, for better convenience in haying. The black silk dress also was consigned to her care, with Phoebe's new bonnet, sent by express from Taunton along with the dress.

The day set for Phoebe's departure was the 3d of July, since the racket and wakefulness which pervade even country towns on this anniversary would make Tom's late drive less noticeable. In the afternoon of the sultry day ominous flashes of tempest began to play about the far horizon, whence all day long great "thunder-caps" had rolled their still and solemn heights of rounded pearl and shadow upward through the stainless blue of heaven. Phoebe gave her mother a stringent hug and kiss on the stairs as she went up, little knowing how that mother's heart sank in her breast, or how dim were the sad eyes that dared not let a tear fall to relieve them. By nine o'clock the house was still, except for low mutterings of the storm and distant wheels hurrying through the night, which made Phoebe's heart beat wildly. She made a small bundle of needful things, wrapped it in a little shawl, put on her hat, and, taking her shoes in her hand, slipped softly out of the window to the shed roof, and thence to the ground. She felt like a guilty thing enough as she stole over the hen-coop and roused the fluttering fowls, bringing out an untimely crow from one young rooster. But the thought of Tom and her father nerved her to action. Putting on her shoes hastily, she took a bee-line for Green's wood, where, at the corner of a certain fence, she was to find Tom and Julia. The storm was coming up now rapidly, but Phoebe did not feel any fear; the frequent flashes blinded her, but the road was plain after she had passed through the home lots and found the highway; and she met no one, as she had feared, for even those irrepressible patriots, the boys, had sought shelter from probable rain that would spoil their powder and wet their firecrackers. But when Phoebe arrived at the rendezvous, her heart beat thick with trouble or fear, for no one was there. She knew Tom had got her letter; he had left a rapturous answer in its place, but what had kept him?

She sat down among the sweet-fern bushes and tufts of long grass to quiet herself and think, and being a cool-headed, reasonable girl, composed herself to the idea that something had delayed her lover, and she must have patience; but as the minutes went on long and slow enough, the thunder pealing loud and louder, the lightning darting swift lances from heaven to earth, and a sharp rush of rain rattling on the stiff oak leaves above her, Phoebe determined to go home; not without a certain indignation in her heart at the careless-ness of the man who ought to have been not only ready, but wait-ing to receive her, but also a reserve of judgment, for she had a great trust in Tom. Drenched to the skin, and chilled by the cold wind that rose with the storm, she retraced her steps, and dragging a short ladder from the cow-shed, contrived to get back on the roof, wet and slippery as it was; but to her dismay and wonder the window of her room was not only shut, but tightly fastened, and the paper shade let down before it. Her father, waking with the noise of the heavy thunder, bethought himself of the lambs in the paddock, not being certain that Phoebe had remembered to fold them. He got up and hobbled to the stairs, calling her loudly, but with no reply. In vain his wife urged him to lie down while she called Phoebe; he wanted to scold her awake, and with pains and groans he drew himself up the stairs, only to find her bed untouched and her window open. At once the state of things flashed upon him; he did not swear, but setting his lips at their utmost vicious angle, shut and fastened the window, and let down the shade, fancying Phoebe had gone out to meet her lover, and would try to return.

"I've fixed the jade," was his first utterance, as he reëntered his own room. "She's gone 'nd slipped out o' the winder for to meet that darned Potter feller. See ef she'll git in agin. A good wettin' down 'll sarve her right."

"Oh, Reuben!" remonstrated his wife.

"You shet up. She's got to ketch it, I tell ye," he growled back; and his wife, consoled by the belief that her darling was by that time in kindly hands, lay down again and slept, to be roused an hour after by a loud knocking at the back door.

"What ye want?" demanded the old man, who had not slept, but waited for this result.

"It's me, father," said Phoebe's resolute voice. "Let me in; I'm out in the rain."

Mrs. Fyler sprang from her bed, but Reuben caught her arm and pulled her back.

"You lie still, I tell ye," he growled; and then went on, in a louder key, "Folks don't come into my door by night onless they've gone out on 't."

"Let me in, father; it's me,—Phoebe. I'm wet through."

The poor mother made one more effort to rise, but was held with vise-like grasp, as her lord and master retorted,—

"No wet folks wanted here. You could ha' staid in ef you'd ha' wanted to keep dry."

Phoebe's spirit rose at the taunt. Had she been let in, even to receive the expected indignation and scolding, there would have been no second exploit of the kind, for she was thoroughly disgusted with herself and partially with her lover; but when steel strikes steel, it is only to elicit sparks. Her "Fyler grit" took possession of her. Picking up her soaked bundle, she set out for the Potter farm, which lay two long miles away, on a hillside, and was approached by a wood road as well as the highway. But the wood road was the shortest and most lonely. She was sure to meet no one in that grassy track. So she struck into it at once.

A weary walk it proved. The storm went on with unabated fury.

Rain poured fiercely down. Her rough way was full of stones, of fallen boughs, and crossed by new-made brooks from the mountain springs, suddenly filled and overflowing. But, with stubborn courage, Phoebe kept on, though more than once she fell at length among the dripping weeds and grasses, and was sorely bruised by stones and jarred by the fall.

But it was a resolved and rosy face that presented itself when the kitchen door of the farm-house on Potter Hill opened to a firm, sharp knock. There were friendly lights in the windows, and Mrs. Potter's kind old countenance beamed with pity and surprise as she beheld Phoebe on the doorstep.

"Mercy's sakes alive, Phoebe! You be half drowned, child. Come in, come in, quick! Where's Tom and July?"

"Well," said Phoebe, with a little laugh, "that's just what I'd like to know."

"You don't mean to say they hain't fetched ye? Why, how under the canopy did ye get here?"

So Phoebe told her tale of woe, while her wet clothes were taken off by the old lady (who was watching for the party, and had sent the "help" and the younger part of the family to bed hours ago), and was told, in her turn, how Tom and his sister had set off at half past eight, and how they had been expected back "ever 'nd ever so long," so that Phoebe was supposed to have come with them when she appeared.

"I'll bet a cent that colt's run away. Tom would take the colt. He thought the old hoss was kinder feeble 'nd slow-goin'. But I'd ruther ha' took him—slow 'nd sure, ye know."

Here was food for anxiety; but it did not last long, for wheels rattled up from the highway side of the house, an angry "Whoa, whoa, I tell ye!" was heard outside, and in a moment Tom strode in half carrying his sister, wet with rain and crying.

"Take care o' Jule, mother; she's about dead. There ain't a cent's worth o' grit in her."

A low laugh stopped him very suddenly. He looked round, and there, by the little blaze in the chimney, which had been lit to warm her a cup of tea, sat Phoebe, rosy, smiling, and prettier than ever, in Julia's pink calico gown and a soft white shawl of his mother's.

"Tom! Tom! you'll get her all damp again!" screamed Mrs. Potter; from which it may be inferred what Tom was about.

However, Phoebe seemed to be used to dampness. Perhaps the night's experience had hardened her, for she made no effort to withdraw from this present second-hand shower, while Tom explained how the colt had been frightened, just as they drove by the post-office, at a giant cracker, and dashed off down the meadow road at full speed. This would not have mattered if a sudden jolt had not broken one side of the thills short off, whereupon the colt kicked and plunged till he broke the other, and with a sudden dash pulled Tom all but out of the wagon, tore the reins out of his hands, and set off at full speed, leaving them three miles from Green's wood, two from any house, with a broken wagon, no horse, and an approaching tempest. There was nothing to do but to walk back to the village, hire another "team," and through the pouring storm drive to Green's wood on the chance of seeing Phoebe.

Naturally they did not see her; and then Tom in despair drove round to Reuben Fyler's house, whistled under Phoebe's window, rattled pebbles against the pane, and at last knocked at the door, but with no sign or answer to reward him. Then Julia insisted on being taken home, and Tom was forced to yield, since he was at his wits' end, and there he found Phoebe.

"Tom, be still!" was the irrelevant remark uttered by Phoebe at the end of the recital, and she blushed more rosily than ever as she said it.

But Mrs. Potter, with motherly sense, served the hot supper that had been covered up in the chimney-corner so long, and when it had been done justice to in the most unsentimental manner, sent the whole party peremptorily to their rooms.

In the morning the runaway colt was brought home bright and early, and Tom put him into the borrowed wagon and drove off with Phoebe, Julia, and his mother to the minister's house, where Parson Russell gave him undeniable rights to run away with Phoebe hereafter as much as he liked.

The news came quickly to her father's ears, and, strange to say, the old man chuckled. Perhaps his comments will explain. "Stumped it all the way up there in the dark, did she? thunderin' an' lightnin' too. Well, now, I tell ye, there ain't another gal in Pasco darst to ha' done it. She's clear Fyler. Our folks ain't made o' all dust; they're three quarter grit, you kin swear to 't. The darned little cretur! she beats all. Well! well! well! Wife, ain't you heerd what aunt Nabby's a-sayin'?"

"Yes, I did."

"Law, Mr. Fyler," put in aunt Nabby, "I thought ye 'd be madder 'n a yaller hornet."

"So ye come to hear me buzz, did ye? 'Tain't safe to reckon on folks. Mis' Fyler, you fetch your bunnet; I'll tell Sam to harness up, 'nd you drive up to Potter's 'nd see the gal. She's a chip o' the old block. I guess I'll let her hev that 'ere brown 'nd white heifer for a settin' up. 'Tain't best, nuther, to fight with the blacksmith, when there ain't but one handy."

"Well, now, I am beat," muttered aunt Nabby. "I thought ye 'd ha' held out ugly to the day o' judgment, I've heern tell so much about Fyler grit."

"I think it's likely," was the composed reply. "It's bad ye 're dis-app'inted, ain't it? but didn't it never come to ye that it takes more grit to back down hill than to go 'long up it?"

"Mebbe it doos—mebbe it doos," said aunt Nabby, shaking her head with the wisdom of an owl.

RICHARD MALCOLM JOHNSTON

★ ★ ★

Richard Malcolm Johnston (1822-1898) sketched scenes and characters remembered from early days on a large plantation near Powelton, Georgia. Gathered in *Georgia Sketches* (1864), *Dukesborough Tales* (1871), and a dozen later volumes, these humorous stories mirror taciturn, slow, downright country people with a strong native sense of justice. After graduating from Mercer University, Johnston alternated teaching with the practice of law. From 1862 to 1867 he conducted a boys' school, which was closed partly because of the effects of the Reconstruction. On removing his school from Georgia to Baltimore, he was encouraged to write by Sidney Lanier. During his last years he worked in the Office of Education, Washington, D. C. This lifelong interest in education led to the writing of sketches about cruel schoolmasters, whose tactics had evoked his own code of kindly friendship between teacher and students.

★ ★ ★

How Mr. Bill Williams Took the Responsibility

"Our honor teacheth us
That we be bold in every enterprise."

CHAPTER I

WHEN Josiah Lorriby came into our neighborhood to keep a school I was too young to go to it alone. Having no older brother or sister to go along with me, my parents, although they were desirous for me to begin, were about to give it up, when fortunately it was ascertained that William Williams, a big fellow whose widowed mother resided near to us, intended to go for one term and complete his education preparatory to being better fitted for an object of vast ambition which he had in view. His way lay by our door, and as he was one of the most accommodating persons in the world, he proffered to take charge of me. Without hesitation and with much gratitude this was accepted, and I was delivered over into his keeping.

William Williams was so near being a man that the little boys used to call him Mr. Bill. I never can forget the stout homespun dress-coat which he used to wear, with the big pockets opening horizontally across the outer side of the skirts. Many a time, when I was fatigued by walking or the road was wet with rains, have I ridden upon his back, my hands resting upon his shoulders and my feet standing in those capacious pockets. Persons who have never tried that way of travelling have no just idea, I will venture to say, how sweet it is. Mr. Bill had promised to take care of me, and he kept his word.

On the first morning when the school was opened, we went together to it. About one mile and a half distant stood the school-house. Eighteen by twenty feet were its dimensions. It was built of logs and covered with clap-boards. It had one door, and opposite to that a hole in the wall two feet square, which was called the window. It stood in the corner of one of our fields (having formerly been used as a fodder-house), and on the brow of a hill, at the foot of which, over-shadowed by oak trees, was a noble spring of fresh water. Our way led us by this spring. Just as we reached it, Mr. Bill pointed to the summit and said:

"Yonder it is, Squire."

Mr. Bill frequently called me Squire, partly from mere facetious-ness, and partly from his respect for my father, who was a Justice of the Peace.

I did not answer. We ascended the hill, and Mr. Bill led me into the presence of the genius of the place.

Mr. Josiah Lorriby was a remarkable man, at least in appearance. He was below the middle height, but squarely built. His body was good enough, but his other parts were defective. He had a low flat head, with very short hair and very long ears. His arms were reason-ably long, but his hands and legs were disproportionately short. Many tales were told of his feet, on which he wore shoes with iron soles. He was sitting on a split-bottom chair, on one side of the fire-place. Under him, with his head peering out between the rounds, sitting on his hind legs and standing on his fore legs, was a small yellow dog, without tail or ears. This dog's name was Rum. On the side of the hearth, in another split-bottom, sat a tall raw-boned woman with the reddest eyes that I have ever seen. This was Mrs. Mehitable, Mr. Lorriby's wife. She had ridden to the school on a small aged mare, perfectly white and totally blind. Her name was Kate.

When I had surveyed these four personages,—this satyr of a man, this tailless dog, this red-eyed woman, and this blind old mare, a sense of fear and helplessness came over me, such as I had never felt before, and have never·felt since. I looked at Mr. Bill Williams, but he was observing somebody else, and did not notice me. The other pupils, eighteen or twenty in number, seemed to be in deep meditation. My eyes passed from one to another of the objects of my dread; but they became finally fastened upon the dog. His eyes also had wandered, but only with vague curiosity, around upon all the pupils, until they became fixed upon me. We gazed at each other several moments. Though he sat still, and I sat still, it seemed to me that we were drawing continually nearer to each other. Suddenly I lifted up my voice and screamed with all my might. It was so sudden and sharp that everybody except the woman jumped. She indifferently pointed to the dog. Her husband arose, came to me, and in soothing tones asked what was the matter.

"I am scared!" I answered, as loud as I could speak.

"Scared of what, my little man? of the dog?"

"I am scared of ALL of you!"

He laughed with good humor, bade me not be afraid, called up Rum, talked to us both, enjoined upon us to be friends, and prophesied that we would be such—the best that had ever been in the world. The little creature became cordial at once, reared his fore feet upon his master, took them down, reared them upon me, and in the absence of a tail to wag, twisted his whole hinder-parts in most violent assurance that if I should say the word we were friends already. Such kindness, and so unexpected, dissolved my apprehensions. I was in a condition to accept terms far less liberal. So I acceded, and went to laughing outright. Everybody laughed, and Rum, who could do nothing better in that line, ran about and barked as joyously as any dog with a tail could have done. In the afternoon when school was dismissed, I invited Rum to go home with me; but he, waiting as I supposed for a more intimate acquaintance, declined.

CHAPTER II

It was delightful to consider how auspicious a beginning I had made. Other little boys profited by it. Mr. Lorriby had no desire to lose any of his scholars, and we all were disposed to take as much advantage as possible of his apprehension, however unfounded, that on account of our excessive timidity our parents might remove us from the school. Besides, we knew that we were to lose nothing by being on friendly terms with Rum. The dread of the teacher's wife soon passed away. She had but little to say, and less to do. Nobody had any notion of any reason which she had for coming to the school. At first she occasionally heard a spelling-class recite. After a little time she began to come much less often, and in a few weeks her visits had decreased to one in several days. Mrs. Lorriby seemed a very proud woman; for she not only had little to say to anybody, but although she resided only a mile and a half from the school-house, she never walked, but invariably rode old Kate. These were small things, yet we noticed them.

Mr. Lorriby was not of the sort of schoolmasters whom men use to denominate by the title of *knock-down and drag out*. He was not such a man as Israel Meadows. But although he was good-hearted enough, he was somewhat politic also. Being a new-comer, and being poor, he determined to manage his business with due regard to the tastes, the wishes, and the prejudices of the community in which he labored. He decidedly preferred a mild reign; but it was said he could easily accommodate himself to those who required a more vigorous policy. He soon learned that the latter was the favorite here. People complained that there was little or no whipping. Some who had read the fable of the frogs who desired a sovereign, were heard to declare that Josiah Lorriby was no better than "Old King Log." One patron spoke of taking his children home, placing the boy at the plough and the girl at the spinning-wheel.

Persons in those days loved their children, doubtless, as well as now; but they had some strange ways of showing their love. The strangest of all was the evident gratification which the former felt when the latter were whipped at school. While they all had a notion that education was something which it was desirable to get, it was believed that the impartation of it needed to be conducted in most mysterious ways. The school-house of that day was, in a manner, a cave of Trophonius, into which urchins of both sexes entered amid certain incomprehensible ceremonies, and were everlastingly subject

and used to be whirled about, body and soul, in a vortex of confusion.
I might pursue the analogy and say that, like the votaries of Trophonius, they were not wont to smile until long after this violent and
rotatory indoctrination; but rather to weep and lament, unless they
were brave like Apollonius, or big like Allen Thigpen, and so could
bully the priest far enough to have the bodily rotation dispensed with.
According to these notions, the principles of the education of books
were not to be addressed to the mind and to the heart; but, if they
were expected to stick, they must be beaten with rods into the back.
Through this ordeal of painful ceremonies had the risen generation
gone, and through the same ordeal they honestly believed that the
present generation ought to go, and must go. No exception was made
in favor of genius. Its back was to be kept as sore as stupidity's;
for, being yoked with the latter, it must take the blows, the oaths, and
the imprecations. I can account for these things in no other way than
by supposing that the old set of persons had come out of the old system
with minds so bewildered as to be ever afterwards incapable of
thinking upon it in a reasonable manner. In one respect there is
a considerable likeness between mankind and some individuals of
the brute creation. The dog seems to love best that master who
beats him before giving him a bone. I have heard persons say (those
who had carefully studied the nature and habits of that animal) that
the mule is wont to evince a gratitude somewhat touching when a
bundle of fodder is thrown to him at the close of a day on which he
has been driven within an inch of his life. So with the good people
of former times. They had been beaten so constantly and so mysteriously at school, that they seemed to entertain a grateful affection for
it ever afterwards. It was, therefore, with feelings of benign satisfaction, sometimes not unmixed with an innocent gaiety of mind, that
they were wont to listen to their children when they complained of the
thrashings they daily received, some of which would be wholly unaccountable. Indeed the latter sort seemed to be considered, of all
others, the most salutary. When the punishment was graduated by
the offence, it was supporting too great a likeness to the affairs of
every-day life, and therefore wanting in solemn impressiveness. But
when a schoolmaster for no accountable reason whipped a boy, and
so set his mind in a state of utter bewilderment as to what could be
the matter, and the most vague speculations upon what was to become
of him in this world, to say nothing of the next, ah! then it was that
the experienced felt a happiness that was gently ecstatic. They re-
curred in their minds to their own school time, and they concluded
that, as these things had not killed them, they must have done them

good. So some of our good mothers in Israel, on occasions of great religious excitement, as they bend over a shrieking sinner, smile in serene happiness as they fan his throbbing temples, and fondly encourage him to shriek on; thinking of the pit from which they were digged, and of the rock upon which they now are standing, they shout, and sing, and fan, and fanning ever, continue to sing and shout.

CHAPTER III

When Mr. Lorriby had sounded the depths of public sentiment, he became a new man. One Monday morning he announced that he was going to turn over a new leaf, and he went straightway to turning it over. Before night several boys, from small to medium, had been flogged. He had not begun on the girls, except in one instance. In that I well remember the surprise I felt at the manner in which her case was disposed of. Her name was Susan Potter. She was about twelve years old, and well grown. When she was called up, inquiry was made by the master if any boy present was willing to take upon himself the punishment which must otherwise fall upon her. After a moment's silence, Seaborn Byne, a boy of fourteen, rose and presented himself. He was good-tempered and fat, and his pants and round jacket fitted him closely. He advanced with the air of a man who was going to do what was right, with no thought of consequences. Miss Potter unconcernedly went to her seat.

But Seaborn soon evinced that he was dissatisfied with a bargain that was so wholly without consideration. I believed then, and I believe to this day, that but for his being so good a mark he would have received fewer stripes. But his round fat body and legs stood so temptingly before the rod, and the latter fell upon good flesh so entirely through its whole length, that it was really hard to stop. He roared with pain so unexpectedly severe, and violently rubbed each spot of recent infliction. When it was over, he came to his seat and looked at Susan Potter. She seemed to feel like laughing. Seaborn got no sympathy, except from a source which he despised; that was his younger brother, Joel. Joel was weeping in secret.

"Shut up your mouth," whispered Seaborn, threateningly, and Joel shut up.

Then I distinctly heard Seaborn mutter the following words:

"Ef I ever takes another for her, or any of 'em, may I be dinged, and then dug up and dinged over again."

I have no doubt that he kept his oath, for I continued to know Seaborn Byne until he was an old man, and I never knew a person who persistently held that vicarious system of school punishment in deeper disgust. What his ideas were about being "dinged," and about that operation being repeated, I did not know; but I supposed it was something that, if possible, would better be avoided.

Such doings as these made a great change in the feelings of us little ones. Yet I continued to run the crying schedule. It failed at last, and I went under.

Mr. Lorriby laid it upon me remorselessly. I had never dreamed that he would give me such a flogging—I who considered myself, as everybody else considered me, a favorite. Now the charm was gone, the charm of security. It made me very sad. I lost my love for the teacher. I even grew cold towards Rum, and Rum in his turn grew cold towards me. Not that we got into open hostilities. For saving an occasional fretfulness, Rum was a good fellow and personally I had liked him. But then he was from principle a thorough Lorriby, and therefore our intimacy must stop, and did stop.

In a short time Mr. Lorriby had gone as nearly all round the school as it was prudent to go. Every boy but two had received his portion, some once, some several times. These two were Mr. Bill Williams, and another big boy named Jeremiah Hobbes. These were, of course, as secure against harm from Mr. Lorriby as they would have been had he been in Guinea. Every girl also had been flogged, or had had a boy flogged for her, except Betsy Ann Acry, the belle of the school. She was a light-haired, blue-eyed, plump, delicious-looking girl, fourteen years old. Now for Miss Betsy Ann Acry, as it was known to everybody about the school-house, Mr. Bill Williams had a partiality which, though not avowed, was decided. He had never courted her in set words, but he had observed her from day to day, and noticed her ripening into womanhood with constantly increasing admiration. He was scarcely a match for her even if they both had been in condition to marry. He knew this very well. But considerations of this sort seldom do a young man any good. More often than otherwise they make him worse. At least such was their effect upon Mr. Bill. The greater the distance between him and Miss Betsy Ann, the more he yearned across it. He sat in school where he could always see her, and oh, how he eyed her! Often, often have I noticed Mr. Bill, leaning the side of his head upon his arms, extended on the desk in front of him, and looking at her with a countenance which, it seemed to me, ought to make some impression. Betsy Ann received it all as if it was no more than she was entitled to, but showed no sign whether she set any value upon the possession or not. Mr. Bill hoped she did; the rest of us believed she did not.

Mr. Bill had another ambition, which was, if possible, even higher than the winning of Miss Acry. Having almost extravagant notions of the greatness of Dukesborough, and the distinction of being a resident within it, he had long desired to go there as a clerk in a store. He had made repeated applications to be taken in by Messrs. Bland & Jones, and it was in obedience to a hint from these gentlemen that he had determined to take a term of finishing off at the school of Mr. Lorriby. This project was never out of his mind, even in moments of his fondest imaginings about Miss Betsy Ann. It would have been not easy to say which he loved the best. The clerkship seemed to become nearer and nearer after each Saturday's visit to town, until at last he had a distinct offer of the place. The salary was small, but he waived that consideration in view of the exaltation of the office and the greatness of living in Dukesborough. He accepted, to enter upon his duties in four weeks, when the quarter session of the school would expire.

The dignified ways of Mr. Bill after this made considerable impression upon all the school. Even Betsy Ann condescended to turn her eyes oftener in the direction where he happened to be, and he was almost inclined to glory in the hope that the possession of one dear object would draw the other along with it. At least he felt that if he should lose the latter, the former would be the highest consolation which he could ask. The news of the distinguished honor that had been conferred upon him reached the heads of the school early on the Monday following the eventful Saturday when the business was done. I say heads, for of late Mrs. Mehitable and old Kate came almost every day. Mrs. Lorriby received the announcement without emotion. Mr. Lorriby, on the other hand, in spite of the prospect of losing a scholar, was almost extravagant in his congratulations.

"It was a honor to the whole school," he said. "I feels it myself. Sich it war under all the circumstances. It was obleeged to be, and sich it war, and as it war sich, I feels it myself."

Seaborn Byne heard this speech. Immediately afterwards he turned to me and whispered the following comment:

"He be dinged! the decateful old son-of-a-gun!"

CHAPTER IV

It was the unanimous opinion amongst Mr. Lorriby's pupils that he was grossly inconsistent with himself: that he ought to have begun with the rigid policy at first, or have held to the mild. Having once enjoyed the sweets of the latter, thoughts would occasionally rise and questions would be asked. Seaborn Byne was not exactly the head, but he was certainly the orator of a revolutionary party. Not on his own account; for he had never yet, except as the voluntary substitute of Miss Susan Potter, felt upon his own body the effects of the change of discipline. Nor did he seem to have any apprehensions on that score. He even went so far as to say to Mr. Bill Williams, who had playfully suggested the bare idea of such a thing, that "ef old Jo Lorriby raised his old pole on him, he would put his lizzard" (as Seaborn facetiously called his knife) "into his paunch." He always carried a very big knife, with which he would frequently stab imaginary Lorribys in the persons of saplings and pumpkins, and even the air itself. This threat had made his brother Joel extremely unhappy. His little heart was bowed down with the never-resting fear and belief that Seaborn was destined to commit the crime of murder upon the body of Mr. Lorriby. On the other hand Seaborn was constantly vexed by the sight of the scores of floggings which Joel received. Poor Joel had somehow in the beginning of his studies gotten upon the wrong road, and as nobody ever brought him back to the starting point, he was destined, it seemed, to wander about lost evermore. The more floggings he got, the more hopeless and wild were his efforts at extrication. It was unfortunate for him that his brother took any interest in his condition. Seaborn had great contempt for him, but yet he remembered that he was his brother, and his brother's heart would not allow itself to feel no concern. That concern manifested itself in endeavoring to teach Joel himself out of school, and in flogging him himself by way of preventing Joel's having to submit to that disgrace at the hands of old Joe. So eager was Seaborn in this brotherly design, and so indocile was Joel, that for every flogging which the latter received from the master he got from two to three from Seaborn.

However, the inflictions which Seaborn made, strictly speaking, could not be called floggings. Joel, among his other infirmities, had that of being unable to take care of his spelling-books. He had torn to pieces so many that his mother had obtained a paddle and pasted on both sides of it as many words as could be crowded there. Mrs. Byne, who was a woman of decision, had been heard to say that she meant to head him at this destructive business, and now she believed that she had done it. But this instrument was made to subserve a double purpose with Joel. It was at once the object, and in his brother's hands was the stimulus, of his little ambition. Among all these evils, floggings from Mr. Lorriby and paddlings from Seaborn, and the abiding apprehension that the former was destined to be murdered by the latter, Joel Byne's was a case to be pitied.

"It ar a disgrace," said Mr. Bill to me one morning as we were going to school, "and I wish Mr. Larrabee knowed it. Between him and Sebe, that little innocent individiel ar bent on bein' useded up bodaciously. Whippins from Mr. Larrabee and paddlins from Sebe! The case ar wusser than ef thar was two Larrabees. That ar the ontimeliest paddle that ever *I* seen. He have to try to larn his paddle, and when he can't larn it, Sebe, he take his paddle, fling down Joel, and paddle him *with* his paddle. In all my experence, I has not seed jest sich a case. It ar beyant hope."

Mr. Bill's sympathy made him serious, and indeed gloomy. The road on which the Bynes came to school met ours a few rods from the spring. We were now there, and Mr. Bill had scarcely finished this speech when we heard behind us the screams of a child.

"Thar it is agin," said Mr. Bill. "At it good and soon. It do beat everything in this blessed and ontimely world. Ef it don't, ding me!"

We looked behind us. Here came Joel at full speed, screaming with all his might, hatless, with his paddle in one hand and his dinner-bucket, without cover, hanging from the other. Twenty yards behind him ran Seaborn, who had been delayed by having to stop in order to pick up Joel's hat and the bucket-cover. Just before reaching the spring, the fugitive was overtaken and knocked down. Seaborn then getting upon him and fastening his arms with his own knees, seized the paddle and exclaimed:

"Now, you rascal! spell that word agin, sir. Ef you don't, I'll paddle you into a pancake. Spell *'Crucifix,'* sir."

Joel attempted to obey.

"*S* agin, you little devil! *S-i, si!* Ding my skin ef you shan't larn it, or I'll paddle you as long as thar's poplars to make paddles outen."

And he turned Joel over and made him ready.

"Look a here, Sebe!" interposed Mr. Bill; "fun's fun, but too much is too much."

Now what these words were intended to be preliminary to, there was no opportunity of ascertaining; for just then Mr. Josiah Lorriby, who had diverged from his own way in order to drink at the spring, presented himself.

"What air you about thar, Sebion Byne?"

Seaborn arose, and though he considered his conduct not only justifiable, but praiseworthy, he looked a little crest-fallen.

"Ah, indeed! You're the assistant teacher, air you? Interfering with *my* business, and *my* rights, and *my* duties, and *my*—hem! Let us all go to the school-house now. Mr. Byne will manage business hereafter. I—as for me, I aint nowhar now. Come, Mr. Byne, le's go to school."

Mr. Lorriby and Seaborn went on, side by side. Mr. Bill looked as if he were highly gratified. "Ef he don't get it now, he never will."

Alas for Joel! Delivered from Seaborn, he was yet more miserable than before, and he forgot his own griefs in his pity for the impending fate of Mr. Lorriby, and his apprehension for the ultimate consequence of this day's work to his brother. He pulled me a little behind Mr. Bill, and tremblingly whispered:

"Poor Mr. Larrabee! Do you reckon they will hang Seaby, Phil?"

"What for?" I asked.

"For killing Mr. Larrabee."

I answered that I hoped not.

"Oh, Phil! Seaby have sich a big knife! An' he have stob more saplins! and more punkins! and more watermillions! and more mushmillions! And he have even stob our old big yaller cat! And he have call every one of 'em Larrabee. And it's my pinion that ef it warn't for my paddle, he would a stob me befo' now. You see, Phil, paddlin me sorter cools and swages him down a leetle bit. Oh, Seaby ar a tremenduous boy, and he ar *goin* to stob Mr. Larrabee this blessed day."

As we neared the school-house we saw old Kate at the usual stand, and we knew that Mrs. Lorriby was at hand. She met her husband at the door, and they had some whispering together, of which the case of Seaborn was evidently the subject. Joel begged me to stay with him outside until the horrible thing was over. So we stopped and peeped in between the logs. We had not to wait long. Mr. Lorriby, his mate standing by his side, at once began to lay on, and Seaborn roared. The laying on and the roaring continued until the master was satisfied. When all was over, I looked into Joel's face. It was radiant with smiles. I never have seen greater happiness upon the countenance of childhood. Happy little fellow! Seaborn would not be hung. That illusion was gone forever. He actually hugged his paddle to his breast, and with a gait even approaching the triumphant, walked into the house.

CHAPTER V

Having broken the ice upon Seaborn, Mr. Lorriby went into the sport of flogging him whenever he felt like it. Seaborn's revolutionary sentiments grew deeper and stronger constantly. But he was now, of course, hopeless of accomplishing any results himself, and he knew that the only chance was to enlist Jeremiah Hobbes, or Mr. Bill

Williams, and make him the leader in the enterprise. Very soon, however, one of these chances was lost. Hobbes received and accepted an offer to become an overseer on a plantation, and Seaborn's hopes were now fixed upon Mr. Bill alone. That also was destined soon to be lost by the latter's prospective clerkship. Besides, Mr. Bill, being even-tempered, and never having received and being never likely to receive any provocation from Mr. Lorriby, the prospect of making anything out of him was gloomy enough. In vain Seaborn raised innuendoes concerning his pluck. In vain he tried every other expedient, even to secretly drawing on Mr. Bill's slate a picture of a very little man flogging a very big boy, and writing as well as he could the name of Mr. Lorriby near the former and that of Mr. Bill near the latter. Seaborn could not disguise himself; and Mr. Bill when he saw the pictures informed the artist that if he did not mind what he was about he would get a worse beating than ever Joe Larrabee gave him. Seaborn had but one hope left, but that involved some little delicacy, and could be managed only by its own circumstances. It might do, and it might not do. If Seaborn had been accustomed to asking special Divine interpositions, he would have prayed that if anything was to be made out of this, it might be made before Mr. Bill should leave. Sure enough it did come. Just one week before the quarter was out it came. But I must premise the narration of this great event with a few words.

Between Mrs. Lorriby and Miss Betsy Ann Acry the relations were not very agreeable. Among other things which were the cause of this were the unwarrantable liberties which Miss Acry sometimes took with Kate, Mrs. Lorriby's mare. Betsy Ann, in spite of all dangers (not the least of which was that of breaking her own neck), would treat herself to an occasional ride whenever circumstances allowed. One day at play-time, when Mrs. Lorriby was out upon one of her walks, which she sometimes took at that hour, Betsy Ann hopped upon the mare, and bantered me for a race to the spring and back. I accepted. We set out. I beat old Kate on the return, because she stumbled and fell. A great laugh was raised, and we were detected by Mrs. Lorriby. Passing me, she went up to Betsy Ann, and thus spoke:

"Betsy Ann Acree, libities is libities, and horses is horses, which is mars is mars. I have ast you not to ride this mar, which she was give to me by my parrent father, and which she have not been rid, no, not by Josiah Lorribee hisself, and which I have said I do not desires she shall be spilt in her gaits, and which I wants and desires you will not git upon the back of that mar nary nother time."

After this event these two ladies seemed to regard each other with even increased dislike.

Miss Betsy Ann Acry had heretofore escaped correction for any of her shortcomings, although they were not few. She was fond of mischief, and no more afraid of Mr. Lorriby than Mr. Bill Williams was. Indeed, Miss Betsy Ann considered herself to be a woman, and she had been heard to say that a whipping was something which she would take from nobody. Mr. Lorriby smiled at her mischievous tricks, but Mrs. Lorriby frowned. These ladies came to dislike each other more and more. The younger, when in her frolics, frequently noticed the elder give her husband a look which was expressive of much meaning. Seaborn had also noticed this, and the worse Miss Acry grew, the oftener Mrs. Lorriby came to the school. The truth is that Seaborn had pondered so much that he at last made a profound discovery. He had come to believe fully, and in this he was right, that the object which the female Lorriby had in coming at all was to protect the male. A bright thought! He communicated it to Miss Acry, and slyly hinted several times that he believed she was afraid of Old Red Eye, as he denominated the master's wife. Miss Acry indignantly repelled every such insinuation, and became only the bolder in what she said and what she did. Seaborn knew that the Lorribys were well aware of Mr. Bill's preference for the girl, and he intensely enjoyed her temerity. But it was hard to satisfy him that she was not afraid of Old Red Eye. If Old Red Eye had not been there, Betsy Ann would have done so and so. The reason why she did not do so and so, was because Old Red Eye was about. Alas for human nature!—male and female. Betsy Ann went on and on, until she was brought to a halt. The occasion was thus.

There was in the school a boy of about my own size, and a year or two older, whose name was Martin Granger. He was somewhat of a pitiful-looking creature—whined when he spoke, and was frequently in quarrels, not only with the boys, but with the girls. He was suspected of sometimes playing the part of spy and informer to the Lorribys, both of whom treated him with more consideration than any other pupil, except Mr. Bill Williams. Miss Betsy Ann cordially disliked him, and she honored myself by calling me her favorite in the whole school.

Now Martin and I got ourselves very unexpectedly into a fight. I had divided my molasses with him at dinner-time for weeks and weeks. A few of the pupils whose parents could afford to have that luxury, were accustomed to carry it to school in phials. I usually ate my part after boring a hole in my biscuit and then filling it up. I have

often wished since I have been grown that I could relish that preparation as I relished it when a boy. But as we grow older our tastes
change. Martin Granger relished the juice even more than I. In all
my observations I have never known a person of any description who
was as fond of molasses as he was. It did me good to see him eat it.
He never brought any himself, but he used to hint, in his whining
way, that the time was not distant when his father would have a
whole kegful, and when he should bring it to school in his mother's
big snuff-bottle, which was well known to us all. Although I was not
so sanguine of the realisation of this prospect as he seemed to be, yet
I had not on that account become tired of furnishing him. I only
grew tired of his presence while at my dinner, and I availed myself
of a trifling dispute one day to shut down upon him. I not only did
not invite him to partake of my molasses, but I rejected his spon-
taneous proposition to that effect. He had been dividing it with me
so long that I believe he thought my right to cut him off now was
estopped. He watched me as I bored my holes and poured in and
ate, and even wasted the precious fluid. I could not consume it all.
When I had finished eating, I poured water into the phial and made
what we called "beverage." I would drink a little, then shake it and
hold it up before me. The golden bubbles shone gloriously in the
sun-light. I had not said a word to Martin during these interesting
operations, nor even looked towards him. But I knew that his eyes
were upon me and the phial. Just as I swallowed the last drop, his full
heart could bear no more, and he uttered a cry of pain. I turned to
him and asked him what was the matter. The question seemed to be
considered as adding insult to injustice.

"Corn deternally trive your devilish hide," he answered, and gave
me the full benefit of his clenched fist upon my stomach. He was
afterwards heard to say that "thar was the place whar he wanted to
hit fust." We closed, scratched, pulled hair, and otherwise struggled
until we were separated. Martin went immediately to Mr. Lorriby,
gave his version of the brawl, and just as the school was to be dismissed for the day, I was called up and flogged without inquiry and
without explanation.

Miss Betsy Ann Acry had seen the fight. When I came to my seat,
crying bitterly, her indignation could not contain itself.

"Mr. Larribee," she said, her cheeks growing redder, "you have
whipped that boy for nothing."

Betsy Ann, with all her pluck, had never gone so far as this. Mr.
Lorriby turned pale and looked at his wife. Her red eyes fairly

glistened with fire. He understood it, and said to Betsy Ann in a hesitating tone,—

"You had better keep your advice to yourself."

"I did not give you any advice. I just said you whipped that boy for nothing, and I said the truth."

"Aint that advice, madam?"

"I am no madam, I thank you, sir; and if that's advice—"

"Shet up your mouth, Betsy Ann Acry."

"Yes, sir," said Betsy Ann, very loud, and she fastened her pretty pouting lips together, elevated her head, inclined a little to one side, and seemed amusedly awaiting further orders.

The female Lorriby here rose, went to her husband, and whispered earnestly to him. He hesitated, and then resolved.

"Come here to me, Betsy Ann Acry."

She went up as gaily as if she expected a present.

"I am going to whip Betsy Ann Acry. Ef any boy here wants to take it for her, he can now step forrards."

Betsy Ann patted her foot, and looked neither to the right nor to the left, nor yet behind her.

When a substitute was invited to appear, the house was still as a graveyard. I rubbed my legs apologetically, and looked up at Seaborn, who sat by me.

"No, sir; if I do may I be dinged, and then dug up and—" I did not listen to the remainder; and as no one else seemed disposed to volunteer, and as the difficulty was brought about upon my own account, and as Betsy Ann liked me and I liked Betsy Ann, I made a desperate resolution, and rose and presented myself. Betsy Ann appeared to be disgusted.

"I don't think I would whip that child any more to-day, if I was in your place, especially for other folk's doings."

"That's jest as you say."

"Well, I say go back to your seat, Phil."

I obeyed, and felt relieved and proud of myself. Mr. Lorriby began to straighten his switch. Then I and all the other pupils looked at Mr. Bill Williams.

CHAPTER VI

Oh! what an argument was going on in Mr. Bill's breast. Vain had been all efforts heretofore made to bring him in any way into collision with the Lorribys. He had even kept himself out of all combinations to get a little holiday by an innocent ducking, and useless had been all appeals heretofore to his sympathies; for he was like the rest who had been through the ordeal of the schools, and had grown to believe that it did more good than harm. If it had been anybody but Betsy Ann Acry, he would have been unmoved. But it *was* Betsy Ann Acry, and he had been often heard to say that if Betsy Ann Acry should have to be whipped, he should take upon himself the responsibility of seeing that that must not be done. And now that contingency had come. What ought to be done? How was this responsibility to be discharged? Mr. Bill wished that the female Lorriby had stayed away that day. He did not know exactly why he wished it, but he wished it. To add to his other difficulties, Miss Betsy Ann had never given any token of her reciprocation of his regard; for now that the novelty of the future clerkship had worn away, she had returned to her old habit of never seeming to notice that there was such a person as himself. But the idea of a switch falling upon her whose body from the crown of her head to the soles of her feet was so precious to him, outweighed every other consideration, and he made up his mind to be as good as his word, and *take the responsibility*. Just as the male Lorriby (the female by his side) was about to raise the switch—

"Stop a minute, Mr. Larrabee!" he exclaimed, advancing in a highly excited manner.

The teacher lowered his arm and retreated one step, looking a little irresolute. His wife advanced one step, and looking straight at Mr. Bill, her robust frame rose at least an inch higher.

"Mr. Larrabee! I—ah—don't exactly consider myself—ah—as a scholar here now; because—ah—I expect to move to Dukesborough in a few days, and keep store thar for Mr. Bland & Jones."

To his astonishment, this announcement, so impressive heretofore, failed of the slightest effect now, when, of all times, an effect was desired. Mr. Lorriby, in answer to a sign from his wife, had recovered his lost ground, and looked placidly upon him, but answered nothing.

"I say," repeated Mr. Bill distinctly, as if he supposed he had not been heard, "I say that I expect in a few days to move to Dukesborough; to live thar; to keep store thar for Mr. Bland & Jones."

"Well, William, I think I have heard that before. I want to hear you talk about it some time when it aint school time, and when we aint so busy as we air now at the present."

"Well, but—" persisted Mr. Bill.

"Well, but?" inquired Mr. Lorriby.

"Yes, sir," answered the former, insistingly.

"Well, but what? Is this case got anything to do with it? Is *she* got anything to do with it?"

"In cose it have not," answered Mr. Bill, sadly.

"Well, what makes you tell us of it now, at the present?" Oh! what a big word was that *us,* then, to Josiah Lorriby.

"Mr. Larrabee," urged Mr. Bill, in as persuasive accents as he could employ; "no, sir, Mr. Larrabee, it have not got anything to do with it; but yit—"

"Well, yit what, William?"

"Well, Mr. Larrabee, I thought as I *was* a-goin to quit school soon, and as I *was* a-goin to move to Dukesborough—as I *was* a-goin *right outen* your school intoo Dukesborough as it war, to keep store thar, may be you mout, as a favor, do me a favor before I left."

"Well! may I be dinged, and then dug up and dinged over agin!" This was said in a suppressed whisper by a person at my side. "Beggin! beggin! ding his white-livered hide—beg-gin!"

"Why, William," replied Mr. Lorriby, "ef it war convenant, and the favor war not too much, it mout be that I mout grant it."

"I thought you would, Mr. Larrabee. The favor aint a big one— leastways, it aint a big one to you. It would be a mighty—" But Mr. Bill thought he could hardly trust himself to say how big a one it would be to himself.

"Well, what is it, William?"

"Mr. Larrabee!—sir, Mr. Larrabee, I ax it as a favor of you, not to whip Betsy Ann—which is Miss Betsy Ann Acry."

"Thar now!" groaned Seaborn, and bowed his head in despair.

The male Lorriby looked upon the female. Her face had relaxed somewhat from its stern expression. She answered his glance by one which implied a conditional affirmative.

"Ef Betsy Ann Acry will behave herself, and keep her impudence to herself, I will let her off this time."

All eyes turned to Betsy Ann. I never saw her look so fine as she raised up her head, tossed her yellow ringlets back, and said in a tone increasing in loudness from beginning to end:

"But Betsy Ann Acry won't *do it.*"

"Hello agin thar!" whispered Seaborn, and raised his head. His dying hopes of a big row were revived. This was the last opportunity, and he was as eager as if the last dollar he ever expected to make had been pledged upon the event. I have never forgotten his appearance, as with his legs wide apart, his hands upon his knees, his lips apart, but his teeth firmly closed, he gazed upon that scene.

Lorriby, the male, was considerably disconcerted, and would have compromised; but Lorriby, the female, again in an instant resumed her hostile attitude, and this time her great eyes looked like two balls of fire. She concentrated their gaze upon Betsy Ann with a ferocity which was appalling. Betsy Ann tried to meet them, and did for one moment; but in another she found she could not hold out longer; so she buried her face in her hands and sobbed. Mr. Bill could endure no more. Both arms fairly flew out at full length.

"The fact ar," he cried, "that I am goin to *take the responsibility!* Conshequenches may be conshequenches, but I shall take the responsibility." His countenance was that of a man who had made up his mind. It had come at last, and we were perfectly happy.

The female Lorriby turned her eyes from Betsy Ann and fixed them steadily on Mr. Bill. She advanced a step forward, and raised her arms and placed them on her sides. The male Lorriby placed himself immediately behind his mate's right arm, while Rum, who seemed to understand what was going on, came up, and standing on his mistress's left, looked curiously up at Mr. Bill.

Seaborn Byne noticed this last movement. "Well, ef that don't beat creation! You in it too, is you?" he muttered through his teeth. "Well, never do you mind. Ef I don't fix you and put you whar you'll never know no more but what you've got a tail, may I be dinged, and then," etc.

It is true that Seaborn had been counted upon for a more important work than the neutralising of Rum's forces; still, I knew that Mr. Bill wanted and needed no assistance. We were all ready, however— that is, I should say, all but Martin. He had no griefs, and therefore no desires.

Such was the height of Mr. Bill's excitement that he did not even seem to notice the hostile demonstrations of these numerous and various foes. His mind was made up, and he was going right on to his purpose.

"Mr. Larrabee," he said firmly, "I am goin to take the responsibility. I axed you as a favor to do me a favor before I left. I aint much used to axin favors; but sich it war now. It seem as ef that favor cannot be grant. Yea, sich is the circumstances. But it must be so. Sense I have been here they aint been no difficulties betwixt you and me, nor betwixt me and Miss Larrabee; and no nothin of the sort, not even betwixt me and Rum. That dog have sometimes snap at my legs; but I have bore it for peace, and wanted no fuss. Sich, therefore, it was why I axed the favor *as* a favor. But it can't be hoped, and so I takes the responsibility. Mr. Larrabee, sir, and you, Miss Larrabee, I am goin from this school right into Dukesborough, straight into Mr. Bland's store, to clerk thar. Sich bein all the circumstances, I hates to do what I tells you I'm goin to do. But it can't be hoped, it seem, and I ar goin to do it."

Mr. Bill announced this conclusion in a very highly elevated tone.

"Oh, yes, ding your old hides of you!" I heard at my side.

"Mr. Larrabee, and you, Miss Larrabee," continued the speaker, "I does not desires that Betsy Ann Acry shall be whipped. I goes on to say that as sich it ar, and as sich the circumstances, Betsy Ann Acry can't be whipped whar I ar ef I can keep it from bein done."

"You heerd that, didn't you?" asked Seaborn, low, but cruelly triumphant; and Seaborn looked at Rum as if considering how he should begin the battle with him.

Mrs. Lorriby seldom spoke. Whenever she did, it was to the point.

"Yes, but Weelliam Weelliams, you can't keep it from bein done." And she straightened herself yet taller, and raising her hands yet higher upon her sides, changed the angle of elbows from obtuse to acute.

"Yes, but I kin," persisted Mr. Bill. "Mr. Larrabee! Mr. Larrabee!"

This gentleman had lowered his head, and was peering at Mr. Bill through the triangular opening formed by his mate's side and arm. The reason why Mr. Bill addressed him twice, was because he had missed him when he threw the first address over her shoulder. The last was sent through the triangle.

"Mr. Larrabee! I say it kin be done, and I'm goin to do it. Sir, little as I counted on sich a case, yit still it ar so. Let the conshequenches be what they be, both now and some futur day. Mr. Larrabee, sir, that whippin that you was a-goin to give to Betsy Ann Acry cannot fall upon her shoulders, and—that is, upon her shoulders, and before my face. Instid of sich, sir, you may jest—instid of whippin her, sir, you may—instid of her, give it, sir—notwithstandin and nevertheless—you may give it to ME."

CHAPTER VII

"Oh! what a fall was there, my countrymen!
Then you and I and all of us fell down!"

If the pupils of Josiah Lorriby's school had had the knowledge of all tongues; if they had been familiar with the histories of all the base men of all the ages, they could have found no words in which to characterise, and no person with whom to compare, Mr. Bill Williams. If they had known what it was to be a traitor, they might have admitted that he was more like this, the most despicable of all characters, than any other. But they would have argued that he was baser than all other traitors, because he had betrayed, not only others, but himself. Mr. Bill Williams, the big boy, the future resident of Dukesborough, the expectant clerk, the vindicator of persecuted girlhood in the person of the girl he loved, the pledge-taker of responsibilities,—that he should have taken the pains, just before he was going away, to degrade himself by proposing to take upon his own shoulders the rod that had never before descended but upon the backs and legs of children! Poor Seaborn Byne! If I ever saw expressed in a human being's countenance, disgust, anger and abject hopelessness, I saw them as I turned to look at him. He spoke not one word, not even in whispers, but he looked as if he could never more place confidence in mortal flesh.

When Mr. Bill had concluded his ultimatum, the female Lorriby's arms came down, and the male Lorriby's head went up. They sent each the other a smile. Both were smart enough to be satisfied. The latter was more than satisfied.

"I am proud this day of William Williams. It air so, and I can but say I air proud of him. William Williams were now in a position to stand up and shine in his new spere of action. If he went to Dukesborough to keep store thar, he mout now go sayin that as he had been a good scholar, so he mout expect to be a good clerk, and fit to be trusted, yea, with thousands upon thousands, ef sich mout be the case. But as it was so, and as he have been to us all as it war, and no difficulties, and no nothin of the sort, and he war goin, and it mout be soon, yea, it mout be to-morrow, from this school straight intoo a store, I cannot, nor I cannot. No, far be it. This were a skene too solemn and too lovely for sich. I cannot, nor I cannot. William Williams may now take his seat."

Mr. Bill obeyed. I was glad that he did not look at Betsy Ann as she turned to go to hers. But she looked at him. I saw her, and little as I was, I saw also that if he ever had had any chance of winning her, it was gone from him forever. It was now late in the afternoon, and we were dismissed. Without saying a word to any one, Mr. Bill took his arithmetic and slate (for ciphering, as it was called then, was his only study). We knew what it meant, for we felt, as well as he, that this was his last day at school. As my getting to school depended upon his continuance, I did not doubt that it was my last also.

On the way home, but not until separating from all the other boys, Mr. Bill showed some disposition to boast.

"You all little fellows was monstous badly skeerd this evening, Squire."

"Wasn't you scared too?" I asked.

"Skeerd? I'd like to see the schoolmaster that could skeer me. I skeerd of Joe Larrabee?"

"I did not think you were scared of him."

"Skeerd of who then? Miss Larrabee? Old Red Eye? She mout be redder-eyed than what she ar, and then not skeer me. Why look here, Squire, how would I look goin into Dukesborough, into Mr. Bland and Jones' store, right from bein skeerd of old Miss Larrabee; to be runnin right intoo Mr. Bland and Jones' store, and old Meheti-billy Larrabee right arter me, or old Joe nuther. It wur well for him that he never struck Betsy Ann Acry. Ef he had a struck her, Joe Larrabee's strikin days would be over."

"But wasn't you goin to take her whippin for her?"

"Lookee here, Squire, I didn't take it, did I?"

"No, but you said you was ready to take it."

"Poor little fellow!" he said, compassionately. "Squire, you are yit young in the ways of this sorrowful and ontimely world. Joe Larrabee knows me, and I knows Joe Larrabee, and as the feller said, that ar sufficient."

We were now at our gate. Mr. Bill bade me good evening, and passed on; and thus ended his pupilage and mine at the school of Josiah Lorriby.

BRET HARTE

★ ★ ★

The Argonauts of '49 faced the problem of moral laxity within their ranks by enforcing against undesirables an improvised code of frontier law. With rough justice the Vigilantes drove forth or executed miscreants. Bret Harte (1836-1902) first utilized this rich material; his stories reveal moral contrasts in isolated California mining communities: depraved women and unregenerate men in moments of stress demonstrate saintlike virtues. To the tall-tale humor devices of the frontier Harte added Dickens's tricks of sentiment and pathos. After the astonishing success of *The Luck of Roaring Camp* (1870), which popularized local-color technique, Harte continued to write volume after volume of stories constructed on the original pattern. Born in Albany, New York, but in youth taken west, Harte worked at many occupations before achieving fame as a writer. For almost a decade after 1878 he was a consul in Germany and Scotland; his last years were spent in England.

★ ★ ★

Tennessee's Partner

I DO not think that we ever knew his real name. Our ignorance of it certainly never gave us any social inconvenience, for at Sandy Bar in 1854 most men were christened anew. Sometimes these appellatives were derived from some distinctiveness of dress, as in the case of "Dungaree Jack;" or from some peculiarity of habit, as shown in "Saleratus Bill," so called from an undue proportion of that chemical in his daily bread; or from some unlucky slip, as exhibited in "The

Iron Pirate," a mild, inoffensive man, who earned that baleful title by his unfortunate mispronunciation of the term "iron pyrites." Perhaps this may have been the beginning of a rude heraldry; but I am constrained to think that it was because a man's real name in that day rested solely upon his own unsupported statement. "Call yourself Clifford, do you?" said Boston, addressing a timid new-comer with infinite scorn; "hell is full of such Cliffords!" He then introduced the unfortunate man, whose name happened to be really Clifford, as "Jaybird Charley,"—an unhallowed inspiration of the moment that clung to him ever after.

But to return to Tennessee's Partner, whom we never knew by any other than this relative title; that he had ever existed as a separate and distinct individuality we only learned later. It seems that in 1853 he left Poker Flat to go to San Francisco, ostensibly to procure a wife. He never got any farther than Stockton. At that place he was attracted by a young person who waited upon the table at the hotel where he took his meals. One morning he said something to her which caused her to smile not unkindly, to somewhat coquettishly break a plate of toast over his upturned, serious, simple face, and to retreat to the kitchen. He followed her, and emerged a few moments later, covered with more toast and victory. That day week they were married by a Justice of the Peace, and returned to Poker Flat. I am aware that something more might be made of this episode, but I prefer to tell it as it was current at Sandy Bar,—in the gulches and barrooms,—where all sentiment was modified by a strong sense of humor.

Of their married felicity but little is known, perhaps for the reason that Tennessee, then living with his partner, one day took occasion to say something to the bride on his own account, at which, it is said, she smiled not unkindly and chastely retreated,—this time as far as Marysville, where Tennessee followed her, and where they went to housekeeping without the aid of a Justice of the Peace. Tennessee's Partner took the loss of his wife simply and seriously, as was his fashion. But to everybody's surprise, when Tennessee one day returned from Marysville, without his partner's wife,—she having smiled and retreated with somebody else,—Tennessee's Partner was the first man to shake his hand and greet him with affection. The boys who had gathered in the cañon to see the shooting were naturally indignant. Their indignation might have found vent in sarcasm but for a certain look in Tennessee's Partner's eye that indicated a lack of humorous appreciation. In fact, he was a grave man, with a steady application to practical detail which was unpleasant in a difficulty.

Meanwhile a popular feeling against Tennessee had grown up on the Bar. He was known to be a gambler; he was suspected to be a thief. In these suspicions Tennessee's Partner was equally compromised; his continued intimacy with Tennessee after the affair above quoted could only be accounted for on the hypothesis of a copartnership of crime. At last Tennessee's guilt became flagrant. One day he overtook a stranger on his way to Red Dog. The stranger afterward related that Tennessee beguiled the time with interesting anecdote and reminiscence, but illogically concluded the interview in the following words: "And now, young man, I'll trouble you for your knife, your pistols, and your money. You see your weppings might get you into trouble at Red Dog, and your money's a temptation to the evilly disposed. I think you said your address was San Francisco. I shall endeavor to call." It may be stated here that Tennessee had a fine flow of humor, which no business preoccupation could wholly subdue.

This exploit was his last. Red Dog and Sandy Bar made common cause against the highwayman. Tennessee was hunted in very much the same fashion as his prototype, the grizzly. As the toils closed around him, he made a desperate dash through the Bar, emptying his revolver at the crowd before the Arcade Saloon, and so on up Grizzly Cañon; but at its farther extremity he was stopped by a small man on a gray horse. The men looked at each other a moment in silence. Both were fearless, both self-possessed and independent, and both types of a civilization that in the seventeenth century would have been called heroic, but in the nineteenth simply "reckless." "What have you got there?—I call," said Tennessee, quietly. "Two bowers and an ace," said the stranger, as quietly, showing two revolvers and a bowie-knife. "That takes me," returned Tennessee; and, with this gambler's epigram, he threw away his useless pistol, and rode back with his captor.

It was a warm night. The cool breeze which usually sprang up with the going down of the sun behind the *chaparral*-crested mountain was that evening withheld from Sandy Bar. The little cañon was stifling with heated resinous odors, and the decaying driftwood on the Bar sent forth faint, sickening exhalations. The feverishness of day and its fierce passions still filled the camp. Lights moved restlessly along the bank of the river, striking no answering reflection from its tawny current. Against the blackness of the pines the windows of the old loft above the express-office stood out staringly bright; and through their curtainless panes the loungers below could see the forms of those who were even then deciding the fate of Tennessee.

And above all this, etched on the dark firmament, rose the Sierra, remote and passionless, crowned with remoter passionless stars.

The trial of Tennessee was conducted as fairly as was consistent with a judge and jury who felt themselves to some extent obliged to justify, in their verdict, the previous irregularities of arrest and indictment. The law of Sandy Bar was implacable, but not vengeful. The excitement and personal feeling of the chase were over; with Tennessee safe in their hands they were ready to listen patiently to any defence, which they were already satisfied was insufficient. There being no doubt in their own minds, they were willing to give the prisoner the benefit of any that might exist. Secure in the hypothesis that he ought to be hanged, on general principles, they indulged him with more latitude of defence than his reckless hardihood seemed to ask. The Judge appeared to be more anxious than the prisoner, who, otherwise unconcerned, evidently took a grim pleasure in the responsibility he had created. "I don't take any hand in this yer game," had been his invariable but good-humored reply to all questions. The Judge—who was also his captor—for a moment vaguely regretted that he had not shot him "on sight," that morning, but presently dismissed this human weakness as unworthy of the judicial mind. Nevertheless, when there was a tap at the door, and it was said that Tennessee's Partner was there on behalf of the prisoner, he was admitted at once without question. Perhaps the younger members of the jury, to whom the proceedings were becoming irksomely thoughtful, hailed him as a relief.

For he was not, certainly, an imposing figure. Short and stout, with a square face, sunburned into a preternatural redness, clad in a loose duck "jumper" and trousers streaked and splashed with red soil, his aspect under any circumstances would have been quaint, and was now even ridiculous. As he stooped to deposit at his feet a heavy carpet-bag he was carrying, it became obvious, from partially developed legends and inscriptions, that the material with which his trousers had been patched had been originally intended for a less ambitious covering. Yet he advanced with great gravity, and after shaking the hand of each person in the room with labored cordiality, he wiped his serious, perplexed face on a red bandanna handkerchief, a shade lighter than his complexion, laid his powerful hand upon the table to steady himself, and thus addressed the Judge:—

"I was passin' by," he began, by way of apology, "and I thought I'd just step in and see how things was gittin' on with Tennessee thar, —my pardner. It's a hot night. I disremember any sich weather before on the Bar."

He paused a moment, but nobody volunteering any other meteorological recollection, he again had recourse to his pocket-handkerchief, and for some moments mopped his face diligently.

"Have you anything to say on behalf of the prisoner?" said the Judge, finally.

"Thet's it," said Tennessee's Partner, in a tone of relief. "I come yar as Tennessee's pardner,—knowing him nigh on four year, off and on, wet and dry, in luck and out o' luck. His ways ain't allers my ways, but thar ain't any p'ints in that young man, thar ain't any liveliness as he's been up to, as I don't know. And you sez to me, sez you,—confidential-like, and between man and man,—sez you, 'Do you know anything in his behalf?' and I sez to you, sez I,—confidential-like, as between man and man,—'What should a man know of his pardner?'"

"Is this all you have to say?" asked the Judge impatiently, feeling, perhaps, that a dangerous sympathy of humor was beginning to humanize the court.

"Thet's so," continued Tennessee's Partner. "It ain't for me to say anything agin' him. And now, what's the case? Here's Tennessee wants money, wants it bad, and doesn't like to ask it of his old pardner. Well, what does Tennessee do? He lays for a stranger, and he fetches that stranger; and you lays for *him,* and you fetches *him;* and the honors is easy. And I put it to you, bein' a far-minded man, and to you, gentlemen all, as far-minded men, ef this isn't so."

"Prisoner," said the Judge, interrupting, "have you any questions to ask this man?"

"No! no!" continued Tennessee's Partner hastily. "I play this yer hand alone. To come down to the bed-rock, it's just this: Tennessee, thar, has played it pretty rough and expensive-like on a stranger, and on this yer camp. And now, what's the fair thing? Some would say more; some would say less. Here's seventeen hundred dollars in coarse gold and a watch,—it's about all my pile,—and call it square!" And before a hand could be raised to prevent him, he had emptied the contents of the carpet-bag upon the table.

For a moment his life was in jeopardy. One or two men sprang to their feet, several hands groped for hidden weapons, and a suggestion to "throw him from the window" was only overridden by a gesture from the Judge. Tennessee laughed. And apparently oblivious of the excitement, Tennessee's Partner improved the opportunity to mop his face again with his handkerchief.

When order was restored, and the man was made to understand, by the use of forcible figures and rhetoric, that Tennessee's offence could not be condoned by money, his face took a more serious and sanguinary hue, and those who were nearest to him noticed that his rough hand trembled slightly on the table. He hesitated a moment as he slowly returned the gold to the carpet-bag, as if he had not yet entirely caught the elevated sense of justice which swayed the tribunal, and was perplexed with the belief that he had not offered enough. Then he turned to the Judge, and saying, "This yer is a lone hand, played alone, and without my pardner," he bowed to the jury and was about to withdraw, when the Judge called him back. "If you have anything to say to Tennessee, you had better say it now." For the first time that evening the eyes of the prisoner and his strange advocate met. Tennessee smiled, showed his white teeth, and saying, "Euchred, old man!" held out his hand. Tennessee's Partner took it in his own, and saying, "I just dropped in as I was passin' to see how things was gettin' on," let the hand passively fall, and adding that "it was a warm night," again mopped his face with his handkerchief, and without another word withdrew.

The two men never again met each other alive. For the unparalleled insult of a bribe offered to Judge Lynch—who, whether bigoted, weak, or narrow, was at least incorruptible—firmly fixed in the mind of that mythical personage any wavering determination of Tennessee's fate; and at the break of day he was marched, closely guarded, to meet it at the top of Marley's Hill.

How he met it, how cool he was, how he refused to say anything, how perfect were the arrangements of the committee, were all duly reported, with the addition of a warning moral and example to all future evildoers, in the Red Dog Clarion, by its editor, who was present, and to whose vigorous English I cheerfully refer the reader. But the beauty of that midsummer morning, the blessed amity of earth and air and sky, the awakened life of the free woods and hills, the joyous renewal and promise of Nature, and, above all, the infinite Serenity that thrilled through each, was not reported, as not being a part of the social lesson. And yet, when the weak and foolish deed was done, and a life, with its possibilities and responsibilities, had passed out of the misshapen thing that dangled between earth and sky, the birds sang, the flowers bloomed, the sun shone, as cheerily as before; and possibly the Red Dog Clarion was right.

Tennessee's Partner was not in the group that surrounded the ominous tree. But as they turned to disperse, attention was drawn to the singular appearance of a motionless donkey-cart halted at the side of the road. As they approached, they at once recognized the venerable Jenny and the two-wheeled cart as the property of Tennessee's Partner,—used by him in carrying dirt from his claim; and a few paces distant the owner of the equipage himself, sitting under a buckeye tree, wiping the perspiration from his glowing face. In answer to an inquiry, he said he had come for the body of the "diseased," "if it was all the same to the committee." He didn't wish to "hurry anything;" he could "wait." He was not working that day; and when the gentlemen were done with the "diseased" he would take him. "Ef thar is any present," he added, in his simple, serious way, "as would care to jine in the fun'l, they kin come." Perhaps it was from a sense of humor, which I have already intimated was a feature of Sandy Bar,—perhaps it was from something even better than that; but two thirds of the loungers accepted the invitation at once.

It was noon when the body of Tennessee was delivered into the hands of his partner. As the cart drew up to the fatal tree, we noticed that it contained a rough oblong box,—apparently made from a section of sluicing,—and half filled with bark and the tassels of pine. The cart was further decorated with slips of willow, and made fragrant with buckeye-blossoms. When the body was deposited in the box, Tennessee's Partner drew over it a piece of tarred canvas, and gravely mounting the narrow seat in front, with his feet upon the shafts, urged the little donkey forward. The equipage moved slowly on, at that decorous pace which was habitual with Jenny even under less solemn circumstances. The men—half curiously, half jestingly, but all good-humoredly—strolled along beside the cart; some in advance, some a little in the rear, of the homely catafalque. But, whether from the narrowing of the road or some present sense of decorum, as the cart passed on, the company fell to the rear in couples, keeping step, and otherwise assuming the external show of a formal procession. Jack Folinsbee, who had at the outset played a funeral march in dumb show upon an imaginary trombone, desisted, from a lack of sympathy and appreciation,—not having, perhaps, your true humorist's capacity to be content with the enjoyment of his own fun.

The way led through Grizzly Cañon, by this time clothed in funereal drapery and shadows. The redwoods, burying their moccasined feet in the red soil, stood in Indian-file along the track, trailing an uncouth benediction from their bending boughs upon the passing bier. A hare, surprised into helpless inactivity, sat upright and pulsating in the ferns by the roadside, as the *cortège* went by. Squirrels hastened to gain a secure outlook from higher boughs; and the blue-jays, spreading their wings, fluttered before them like outriders, until the outskirts of Sandy Bar were reached, and the solitary cabin of Tennessee's Partner.

Viewed under more favorable circumstances, it would not have been a cheerful place. The unpicturesque site, the rude and unlovely outlines, the unsavory details, which distinguish the nest-building of the California miner, were all here, with the dreariness of decay super-added. A few paces from the cabin there was a rough enclosure, which, in the brief days of Tennessee's Partner's matrimonial felicity, had been used as a garden, but was now overgrown with fern. As we approached it we were surprised to find that what we had taken for a recent attempt at cultivation was the broken soil about an open grave.

The cart was halted before the enclosure; and rejecting the offers of assistance with the same air of simple self-reliance he had displayed throughout, Tennessee's Partner lifted the rough coffin on his back, and deposited it unaided, within the shallow grave. He then nailed down the board which served as a lid, and mounting the little mound of earth beside it, took off his hat, and slowly mopped his face with his handkerchief. This the crowd felt was a preliminary to speech; and they disposed themselves variously on stumps and boulders, and sat expectant.

"When a man," began Tennessee's Partner slowly, "has been running free all day, what's the natural thing for him to do? Why, to come home. And if he ain't in a condition to go home, what can his best friend do? Why, bring him home! And here's Tennessee has been running free, and we brings him home from his wandering." He paused, and picked up a fragment of quartz, rubbed it thoughtfully on his sleeve, and went on: "It ain't the first time that I've packed him on my back, as you see'd me now. It ain't the first time that I brought him to this yer cabin when he couldn't help himself; it ain't the first time that I and Jinny have waited for him on yon hill, and picked him up and so fetched him home, when he couldn't speak, and didn't know me. And now that it's the last time, why"—he paused, and rubbed the quartz gently on his sleeve— "you see it's sort of rough on his pardner. And now, gentlemen," he added abruptly, picking up his long-handled shovel, "the fun'l's over; and my thanks, and Tennessee's thanks, to you for your trouble."

Resisting any proffers of assistance, he began to fill in the grave, turning his back upon the crowd, that after a few moments' hesitation gradually withdrew. As they crossed the little ridge that hid Sandy Bar from view, some, looking back, thought they could see Tennessee's Partner, his work done, sitting upon the grave, his shovel

between his knees, and his face buried in his red bandanna handkerchief. But it was argued by others that you couldn't tell his face from
his handkerchief at that distance; and this point remained undecided.

In the reaction that followed the feverish excitement of that day,
Tennessee's Partner was not forgotten. A secret investigation had
cleared him of any complicity in Tennessee's guilt, and left only a
suspicion of his general sanity. Sandy Bar made a point of calling
on him, and proffering various uncouth but well-meant kindnesses.
But from that day his rude health and great strength seemed visibly
to decline; and when the rainy season fairly set in, and the tiny
grass-blades were beginning to peep from the rocky mound above
Tennessee's grave, he took to his bed.

One night, when the pines beside the cabin were swaying in the
storm, and trailing their slender fingers over the roof, and the roar
and rush of the swollen river were heard below, Tennessee's Partner
lifted his head from the pillow, saying, "It is time to go for Tennessee; I must put Jinny in the cart;" and would have risen from his
bed but for the restraint of his attendant. Struggling, he still pursued his singular fancy: "There, now, steady, Jinny,—steady, old girl.
How dark it is! Look out for the ruts,—and look out for him, too,
old gal. Sometimes, you know, when he's blind drunk, he drops
down right in the trail. Keep on straight up to the pine on the top
of the hill. Thar! I told you so!—thar he is,—coming this way, too,
—all by himself, sober, and his face a-shining. Tennessee! Pardner!"

And so they met.

The Romance of Madroño Hollow

THE latch on the garden gate of the Folinsbee Ranch clicked twice.
The gate itself was so much in shadow, that lovely night, that
"old man Folinsbee," sitting on his porch, could distinguish nothing
but a tall white hat and beside it a few fluttering ribbons, under
the pines that marked the entrance. Whether because of this fact, or
that he considered a sufficient time had elapsed since the clicking of
the latch for more positive disclosure, I do not know; but after a
few moments' hesitation he quietly laid aside his pipe and walked
slowly down the winding path toward the gate. At the Ceanothus
hedge he stopped and listened.

There was not much to hear. The hat was saying to the ribbons that it was a fine night, and remarking generally upon the clear outline of the Sierras against the blue-black sky. The ribbons, it so appeared, had admired this all the way home, and asked the hat if it had ever seen anything half so lovely as the moonlight on the summit. The hat never had; it recalled some lovely nights in the South in Alabama ("in the South in Ahlabahm" was the way the old man heard it), but then there were other things that made this night seem so pleasant. The ribbons could not possibly conceive what the hat could be thinking about. At this point there was a pause, of which Mr. Folinsbee availed himself to walk very grimly and craunchingly down the gravel-walk toward the gate. Then the hat was lifted, and disappeared in the shadow, and Mr. Folinsbee confronted only the half-foolish, half-mischievous, but wholly pretty face of his daughter.

It was afterwards known to Madroño Hollow that sharp words passed between "Miss Jo" and the old man, and that the latter coupled the names of one Culpepper Starbottle and his uncle, Colonel Starbottle, with certain uncomplimentary epithets, and that Miss Jo retaliated sharply. "Her father's blood before her father's face boiled up and proved her truly of his race," quoted the blacksmith, who leaned toward the noble verse of Byron. "She saw the old man's bluff and raised him," was the directer comment of the college-bred Masters.

Meanwhile the subject of these animadversions proceeded slowly along the road to a point where the Folinsbee mansion came in view, —a long, narrow, white building, unpretentious, yet superior to its neighbors, and bearing some evidences of taste and refinement in the vines that clambered over its porch, in its French windows, and the white muslin curtains that kept out the fierce California sun by day, and were now touched with silver in the gracious moonlight. Culpepper leaned against the low fence, and gazed long and earnestly at the building. Then the moonlight vanished, ghostlike, from one of the windows, a material glow took its place, and a girlish figure, holding a candle, drew the white curtains together. To Culpepper it was a vestal virgin standing before a hallowed shrine; to the prosaic observer I fear it was only a dark-haired young woman, whose wicked black eyes still shone with unfilial warmth. Howbeit, when the figure had disappeared he stepped out briskly into the moonlight of the high-road. Here he took off his distinguishing hat to wipe his forehead, and the moon shone full upon his face.

It was not an unprepossessing one, albeit a trifle too thin and lank and bilious to be altogether pleasant. The cheek-bones were prominent, and the black eyes sunken in their orbits. Straight black hair fell slant-wise off a high but narrow forehead, and swept part of a hollow cheek. A long black mustache followed the perpendicular curves of his mouth. It was on the whole a serious, even Quixotic face, but at times it was relieved by a rare smile of such tender and even pathetic sweetness, that Miss Jo is reported to have said that, if it would only last through the ceremony, she would have married its possessor on the spot. "I once told him so," added that shameless young woman; "but the man instantly fell into a settled melancholy, and hasn't smiled since."

A half-mile below the Folinsbee Ranch the white road dipped and was crossed by a trail that ran through Madroño Hollow. Perhaps because it was a near cut-off to the settlement, perhaps from some less practical reason, Culpepper took this trail, and in a few moments stood among the rarely beautiful trees that gave their name to the valley. Even in that uncertain light the weird beauty of these harlequin masqueraders was apparent; their red trunks—a blush in the moonlight, a deep blood-stain in the shadow—stood out against the silvery green foliage. It was as if Nature in some gracious moment had here caught and crystallized the gypsy memories of the transplanted Spaniard, to cheer him in his lonely exile.

As Culpepper entered the grove, he heard loud voices. As he turned toward a clump of trees, a figure so *bizarre* and characteristic that it might have been a resident Daphne—a figure overdressed in crimson silk and lace, with bare brown arms and shoulders, and a wreath of honeysuckle—stepped out of the shadow. It was followed by a man. Culpepper started. To come to the point briefly, he recognized in the man the features of his respected uncle, Colonel Starbottle; in the female, a lady who may be briefly described as one possessing absolutely no claim to an introduction to the polite reader. To hurry over equally unpleasant details, both were evidently under the influence of liquor.

From the excited conversation that ensued, Culpepper gathered that some insult had been put upon the lady at a public ball which she had attended that evening; that the Colonel, her escort, had failed to resent it with the sanguinary completeness that she desired. I regret that, even in a liberal age, I may not record the exact and even picturesque language in which this was conveyed to her hearers. Enough that, at the close of a fiery peroration, with feminine inconsistency she flew at the gallant Colonel, and would have visited her delayed vengeance upon his luckless head, but for the prompt interference of Culpepper. Thwarted in this, she threw herself upon the ground, and then into unpicturesque hysterics. There was a fine moral lesson, not only in this grotesque performance of a sex which cannot afford to be grotesque, but in the ludicrous concern with which it inspired the two men. Culpepper, to whom woman was more or less angelic, was pained and sympathetic; the Colonel, to whom she was more or less improper, was exceedingly terrified and embarrassed. Howbeit the storm was soon over, and after Mistress Dolores had returned a little dagger to its sheath (her garter), she quietly took herself out of Madroño Hollow, and happily out of these pages forever. The two men, left to themselves, conversed in low tones. Dawn stole upon them before they separated: the Colonel quite sobered and in full possession of his usual jaunty self-assertion; Culpepper with a baleful glow in his hollow cheek, and in his dark eyes a rising fire.

The next morning the general ear of Madroño Hollow was filled with rumors of the Colonel's mishap. It was asserted that he had been invited to withdraw his female companion from the floor of the Assembly Ball at the Independence Hotel, and that, failing to do this, both were expelled. It is to be regretted that in 1854 public opinion was divided in regard to the propriety of this step, and that there was some discussion as to the comparative virtue of the ladies who were not expelled; but it was generally conceded that the real *casus belli* was political. "Is this a dashed Puritan meeting?" had asked the Colonel, savagely. "It's no Pike County shindig," had responded the floor-manager, cheerfully. "You're a Yank!" had screamed the Colonel, profanely qualifying the noun. "Get! you border ruffian," was the reply. Such at least was the substance of the reports. As, at that sincere epoch, expressions like the above were usually followed by prompt action, a fracas was confidently looked for.

Nothing, however, occurred. Colonel Starbottle made his appearance next day upon the streets with somewhat of his usual pomposity, a little restrained by the presence of his nephew, who accompanied him, and who, as a universal favorite, also exercised some restraint upon the curious and impertinent. But Culpepper's face wore a look of anxiety quite at variance with his usual grave repose. "The Don don't seem to take the old man's set-back kindly," observed the sympathizing blacksmith. "P'r'aps he was sweet on Dolores himself," suggested the skeptical expressman.

It was a bright morning, a week after this occurrence, that Miss Jo Folinsbee stepped from her garden into the road. This time the latch did not click as she cautiously closed the gate behind her. After a moment's irresolution, which would have been awkward but that it was charmingly employed, after the manner of her sex, in adjusting a bow under a dimpled but rather prominent chin, and in pulling down the fingers of a neatly fitting glove, she tripped toward the settlement. Small wonder that a passing teamster drove his six mules into the wayside ditch and imperilled his load, to keep the dust from her spotless garments; small wonder that the "Lightning Express" withheld its speed and flash to let her pass, and that the expressman, who had never been known to exchange more than rapid monosyllables with his fellow-man, gazed after her with breathless admiration. For she was certainly attractive. In a country where the ornamental sex followed the example of youthful Nature, and were prone to overdress and glaring efflorescence, Miss Jo's simple and tasteful raiment added much to the physical charm of, if it did not actually suggest a sentiment to, her presence. It is said that Euchre-deck Billy, working in the gulch at the crossing, never saw Miss Folinsbee pass but that he always remarked apologetically to his partner, that "he believed he *must* write a letter home." Even Bill Masters, who saw her in Paris presented to the favorable criticism of that most fastidious man, the late Emperor, said that she was stunning, but a big discount on what she was at Madroño Hollow.

It was still early morning, but the sun, with California extravagance, had already begun to beat hotly on the little chip hat and blue ribbons, and Miss Jo was obliged to seek the shade of a by-path. Here she received the timid advances of a vagabond yellow dog graciously, until, emboldened by his success, he insisted upon accompanying her, and, becoming slobberingly demonstrative, threatened her spotless skirt with his dusty paws, when she drove him from her with some slight acerbity, and a stone which haply fell within fifty feet of its destined mark. Having thus proved her ability to defend herself, with characteristic inconsistency she took a small panic, and, gathering her white skirts in one hand, and holding the brim of her hat over her eyes with the other, she ran swiftly at least a hundred yards before she stopped. Then she began picking some ferns and a few wildflowers still spared to the withered fields, and then a sudden distrust of her small ankles seized her, and she inspected them narrowly for those burrs and bugs and snakes which are supposed to lie in wait for helpless womanhood. Then she plucked some golden heads of wild oats, and with a sudden inspiration placed them in her black hair, and then came quite unconsciously upon the trail leading to Madroño Hollow.

Here she hesitated. Before her ran the little trail, vanishing at last into the bosky depths below. The sun was very hot. She must be very far from home. Why should she not rest awhile under the shade of a madroño?

She answered these questions by going there at once. After thoroughly exploring the grove, and satisfying herself that it contained no other living human creature, she sat down under one of the largest trees, with a satisfactory little sigh. Miss Jo loved the madroño. It was a cleanly tree; no dust ever lay upon its varnished leaves; its immaculate shade never was known to harbor grub or insect.

She looked up at the rosy arms interlocked and arched above her head. She looked down at the delicate ferns and cryptogams at her feet. Something glittered at the root of the tree. She picked it up; it was a bracelet. She examined it carefully for cipher or inscription; there was none. She could not resist a natural desire to clasp it on her arm, and to survey it from that advantageous view-point. This absorbed her attention for some moments; and when she looked up again she beheld at a little distance Culpepper Starbottle.

He was standing where he had halted, with instinctive delicacy, on first discovering her. Indeed, he had even deliberated whether he ought not to go away without disturbing her. But some fascination held him to the spot. Wonderful power of humanity! Far beyond jutted an outlying spur of the Sierra, vast, compact, and silent. Scarcely a hundred yards away, a league-long chasm dropped its sheer walls of granite a thousand feet. On every side rose up the serried ranks of pine-trees, in whose close-set files centuries of storm and change had wrought no breach. Yet all this seemed to Culpepper to have been planned by an all-wise Providence as the natural background to the figure of a pretty girl in a yellow dress.

Although Miss Jo had confidently expected to meet Culpepper somewhere in her ramble, now that he came upon her suddenly, she felt disappointed and embarrassed. His manner, too, was more than usually grave and serious, and more than ever seemed to jar upon that audacious levity which was this giddy girl's power and security in a society where all feeling was dangerous. As he approached her she rose to her feet, but almost before she knew it he had taken her hand and drawn her to a seat beside him. This was not what Miss Jo had expected, but nothing is so difficult to predicate as the exact preliminaries of a declaration of love.

What did Culpepper say? Nothing, I fear, that will add anything to the wisdom of the reader; nothing, I fear, that Miss Jo had not heard substantially from other lips before. But there was a certain conviction, fire-speed, and fury in the manner that was deliciously novel to the young lady. It was certainly something to be courted in the

nineteenth century with all the passion and extravagance of the sixteenth; it was something to hear, amid the slang of a frontier society,
the language of knight-errantry poured into her ear by this lantern-
jawed, dark-browed descendant of the Cavaliers.

I do not know that there was anything more in it. The facts, however, go to show that at a certain point Miss Jo dropped her glove,
and that in recovering it Culpepper possessed himself first of her
hand and then her lips. When they stood up to go, Culpepper had
his arm around her waist, and her black hair, with its sheaf of golden
oats, rested against the breast pocket of his coat. But even then I
do not think her fancy was entirely captive. She took a certain satisfaction in this demonstration of Culpepper's splendid height, and mentally compared it with a former flame, one Lieutenant McMirk, an
active, but under-sized Hector, who subsequently fell a victim to the
incautiously composed and monotonous beverages of a frontier garrison. Nor was she so much preoccupied but that her quick eyes,
even while absorbing Culpepper's glances, were yet able to detect,
at a distance, the figure of a man approaching. In an instant she
slipped out of Culpepper's arm, and, whipping her hands behind
her, said, "There's that horrid man!"

Culpepper looked up and beheld his respected uncle panting and
blowing over the hill. His brow contracted as he turned to Miss Jo:
"You don't like my uncle!"

"I hate him!" Miss Jo was recovering her ready tongue.

Culpepper blushed. He would have liked to enter upon some details of the Colonel's pedigree and exploits, but there was not time.
He only smiled sadly. The smile melted Miss Jo. She held out her
hand quickly, and said, with even more than her usual effrontery,
"Don't let that man get you into any trouble. Take care of yourself, dear, and don't let anything happen to you."

Miss Jo intended this speech to be pathetic; the tenure of life among
her lovers had hitherto been very uncertain. Culpepper turned toward her, but she had already vanished in the thicket.

The Colonel came up, panting. "I've looked all over town for you,
and be dashed to you, sir. Who was that with you?"

"A lady." (Culpepper never lied, but he was discreet.)

"D—n 'em all! Look yar, Culp, I've spotted the man who gave
the order to put me off the floor" ("flo" was what the Colonel said)
"the other night!"

"Who was it?" asked Culpepper, listlessly.

"Jack Folinsbee."

"Who?"

"Why, the son of that dashed nigger-worshipping, psalm-singing Puritan Yankee. What's the matter, now? Look yar, Culp, you ain't goin' back on your blood, ar' ye? You ain't goin' back on your word? Ye ain't going down at the feet of this trash, like a whipped hound?"

Culpepper was silent. He was very white. Presently he looked up, and said quietly, "No."

Culpepper Starbottle had challenged Jack Folinsbee, and the challenge was accepted. The cause alleged was the expelling of Culpepper's uncle from the floor of the Assembly Ball by the order of Folinsbee. This much Madroño Hollow knew, and could swear to; but there were other strange rumors afloat, of which the blacksmith was an able expounder. "You see, gentlemen," he said to the crowd gathered around his anvil, "I ain't got no theory of this affair; I only give a few facts as have come to my knowledge. Culpepper and Jack meets quite accidental like in Bob's saloon. Jack goes up to Culpepper and says, 'A word with you.' Culpepper bows and steps aside in this way, Jack standing about *here*." (The blacksmith demonstrates the position of the parties with two old horseshoes on the anvil.) "Jack pulls a bracelet from his pocket and says, 'Do you know that bracelet?' Culpepper says, 'I do not,' quite cool-like and easy. Jack says, 'You gave it to my sister.' Culpepper says, still cool as you please, 'I did not.' Jack says, 'You lie, G—d d—n you,' and draws his derringer. Culpepper jumps forward about here" (reference is made to the diagram) "and Jack fires. Nobody hit. It's a mighty cur'o's thing, gentlemen," continued the blacksmith, dropping suddenly into the abstract, and leaning meditatively on his anvil,—"it's a mighty cur'o's thing that nobody gets hit so often. You and me empties our revolvers sociably at each other over a little game, and the room full, and nobody gets hit! That's what gets me."

"Never mind, Thompson," chimed in Bill Masters, "there's another and a better world where we shall know all that, and—become better shots. Go on with your story."

"Well, some grabs Culpepper and some grabs Jack, and so separates them. Then Jack tells 'em as how he had seen his sister wear a bracelet which he knew was one that had been given to Dolores by Colonel Starbottle. That Miss Jo wouldn't say where she got it, but owned up to having seen Culpepper that day. Then the most cur'o's thing of it yet, what does Culpepper do but rise up and takes all back that he said, and allows that he *did* give her the bracelet. Now my opinion, gentlemen, is that he lied; it ain't like that man to give a gal that he respects anything off that piece, Dolores. But it's all the same now, and there's but one thing to be done."

The way this one thing was done belongs to the record of Madroño Hollow. The morning was bright and clear; the air was slightly chill, but that was from the mist which arose along the banks of the river. As early as six o'clock the designated ground—a little opening in the madroño grove—was occupied by Culpepper Starbottle, Colonel Starbottle, his second, and the surgeon. The Colonel was exalted and excited, albeit in a rather imposing, dignified way, and pointed out to the surgeon the excellence of the ground, which at that hour was wholly shaded from the sun, whose steady stare is more or less discomposing to your duellist. The surgeon threw himself on the grass and smoked his cigar. Culpepper, quiet and thoughtful, leaned against a tree and gazed up the river. There was a strange suggestion of a picnic about the group, which was heightened when the Colonel drew a bottle from his coat-tails, and, taking a preliminary draught, offered it to the others. "Cocktails, sir," he explained with dignified precision. "A gentleman, sir, should never go out without 'em. Keeps off the morning chill. I remember going out in '53 with Hank Boompointer. Good ged, sir, the man had to put on his overcoat, and was shot in it. Fact!"

But the noise of wheels drowned the Colonel's reminiscences, and a rapidly driven buggy, containing Jack Folinsbee, Calhoun Bungstarter, his second, and Bill Masters, drew up on the ground. Jack Folinsbee leaped out gayly. "I had the jolliest work to get away without the governor's hearing," he began, addressing the group before him with the greatest volubility. Calhoun Bungstarter touched his arm, and the young man blushed. It was his first duel.

"If you are ready, gentlemen," said Mr. Bungstarter, "we had better proceed to business. I believe it is understood that no apology will be offered or accepted. We may as well settle preliminaries at once, or I fear we shall be interrupted. There is a rumor in town that the Vigilance Committee are seeking our friends the Starbottles, and I believe, as their fellow-countryman, I have the honor to be included in their warrant."

At this probability of interruption, that gravity which had hitherto been wanting fell upon the group. The preliminaries were soon arranged and the principals placed in position. Then there was a silence.

To a spectator from the hill, impressed with the picnic suggestion, what might have been the popping of two champagne corks broke the stillness.

Culpepper had fired in the air. Colonel Starbottle uttered a low curse. John Folinsbee sulkily demanded another shot.

Again the parties stood opposed to each other. Again the word was given, and what seemed to be the simultaneous report of both pistols rose upon the air. But after an interval of a few seconds all were surprised to see Culpepper slowly raise his unexploded weapon and fire it harmlessly above his head. Then, throwing the pistol upon the ground, he walked to a tree and leaned silently against it.

Jack Folinsbee flew into a paroxysm of fury. Colonel Starbottle raved and swore. Mr. Bungstarter was properly shocked at their conduct. "Really, gentlemen, if Mr. Culpepper Starbottle declines another shot, I do not see how we can proceed."

But the Colonel's blood was up, and Jack Folinsbee was equally implacable. A hurried consultation ensued, which ended by Colonel Starbottle taking his nephew's place as principal, Bill Masters acting as second, *vice* Mr. Bungstarter, who declined all further connection with the affair.

Two distinct reports rang through the Hollow. Jack Folinsbee dropped his smoking pistol, took a step forward, and then dropped heavily upon his face.

In a moment the surgeon was at his side. The confusion was heightened by the trampling of hoofs, and the voice of the blacksmith bidding them flee for their lives before the coming storm. A moment more and the ground was cleared, and the surgeon, looking up, beheld only the white face of Culpepper bending over him.

"Can you save him?"

"I cannot say. Hold up his head a moment, while I run to the buggy."

Culpepper passed his arm tenderly around the neck of the insensible man. Presently the surgeon returned with some stimulants.

"There, that will do, Mr. Starbottle, thank you. Now my advice is to get away from here while you can. I'll look after Folinsbee. Do you hear?"

Culpepper's arm was still round the neck of his late foe, but his head had dropped and fallen on the wounded man's shoulder. The surgeon looked down, and, catching sight of his face, stooped and lifted him gently in his arms. He opened his coat and waistcoat. There was blood upon his shirt, and a bullet-hole in his breast. He had been shot unto death at the first fire.

The Iliad of Sandy Bar

Before nine o'clock it was pretty well known all along the river that the two partners of the "Amity Claim" had quarrelled and separated at daybreak. At that time the attention of their nearest neighbor had been attracted by the sounds of altercations and two consecutive pistol-shots. Running out, he had seen, dimly, in the gray mist that rose from the river, the tall form of Scott, one of the partners, descending the hill toward the *cañon;* a moment later, York, the other partner, had appeared from the cabin, and walked in an opposite direction toward the river, passing within a few feet of the curious watcher. Later it was discovered that a serious Chinaman, cutting wood before the cabin, had witnessed part of the quarrel. But John was stolid, indifferent, and reticent. "Me choppee wood, me no fightee," was his serene response to all anxious queries. "But what did they *say,* John?" John did not *sabe.* Colonel Starbottle deftly ran over the various popular epithets which a generous public sentiment might accept as reasonable provocation for an assault. But John did not recognize them. "And this yer's the cattle," said the Colonel, with some severity, "that some thinks oughter be allowed to testify ag'in' a White Man! Git—you heathen!"

Still the quarrel remained inexplicable. That two men, whose amiability and grave tact had earned for them the title of "The Peacemakers," in a community not greatly given to the passive virtues,— that these men, singularly devoted to each other, should suddenly and violently quarrel, might well excite the curiosity of the camp. A few of the more inquisitive visited the late scene of conflict, now deserted by its former occupants. There was no trace of disorder or confusion in the neat cabin. The rude table was arranged as if for breakfast; the pan of yellow biscuit still sat upon that hearth whose dead embers might have typified the evil passions that had raged there but an hour before. But Colonel Starbottle's eye—albeit somewhat bloodshot and rheumy—was more intent on practical details. On examination, a bullet-hole was found in the doorpost, and another, nearly opposite, in the casing of the window. The Colonel called attention to the fact that the one "agreed with" the bore of Scott's revolver, and the other with that of York's derringer. "They must hev stood about yer," said the Colonel, taking position; "not mor'n three feet apart, and—missed!" There was a fine touch of pathos in the falling inflection of the Colonel's voice, which was not without effect. A delicate perception of wasted opportunity thrilled his auditors.

But the Bar was destined to experience a greater disappointment. The two antagonists had not met since the quarrel, and it was vaguely rumored that, on the occasion of a second meeting, each had determined to kill the other "on sight." There was, consequently, some excitement—and, it is to be feared, no little gratification—when, at ten o'clock, York stepped from the Magnolia Saloon into the one long straggling street of the camp, at the same moment that Scott left the blacksmith's shop at the forks of the road. It was evident, at a glance, that a meeting could only be avoided by the actual retreat of one or the other.

In an instant the doors and windows of the adjacent saloons were filled with faces. Heads unaccountably appeared above the river-banks and from behind bowlders. An empty wagon at the cross-road was suddenly crowded with people, who seemed to have sprung from the earth. There was much running and confusion on the hillside. On the mountain-road, Mr. Jack Hamlin had reined up his horse, and was standing upright on the seat of his buggy. And the two objects of this absorbing attention approached each other.

"York's got the sun," "Scott'll line him on that tree," "He's waitin' to draw his fire," came from the cart; and then it was silent. But above this human breathlessness the river rushed and sang, and the wind rustled the tree-tops with an indifference that seemed obtrusive. Colonel Starbottle felt it, and in a moment of sublime preoccupation, without looking around, waved his cane behind him, warningly to all nature, and said, "Shu!"

The men were now within a few feet of each other. A hen ran across the road before one of them. A feathery seed-vessel, wafted from a wayside tree, fell at the feet of the other. And, unheeding this irony of nature, the two opponents came nearer, erect and rigid, looked in each other's eyes, and—passed!

Colonel Starbottle had to be lifted from the cart. "This yer camp is played out," he said, gloomily, as he affected to be supported into the Magnolia. With what further expression he might have indicated his feelings it was impossible to say, for at that moment Scott joined the group. "Did you speak to me?" he asked of the Colonel, dropping his hand, as if with accidental familiarity, on that gentleman's shoulder. The Colonel, recognizing some occult quality in the touch, and some unknown quantity in the glance of his questioner, contented himself by replying, "No, sir," with dignity. A few rods away, York's conduct was as characteristic and peculiar. "You had a mighty fine chance; why didn't you plump him?" said Jack Hamlin, as York drew near the buggy. "Because I hate him," was the reply, heard only by Jack. Contrary to popular belief, this reply was not hissed between the lips of the speaker, but was said in an ordinary tone. But Jack Hamlin, who was an observer of mankind, noticed that the speaker's hands were cold, and his lips dry, as he helped him into the buggy, and accepted the seeming paradox with a smile.

When Sandy Bar became convinced that the quarrel between York and Scott could not be settled after the usual local methods, it gave no further concern thereto. But presently it was rumored that the "Amity Claim" was in litigation, and that its possession would be expensively disputed by each of the partners. As it was well known that the claim in question was "worked out" and worthless, and that the partners, whom it had already enriched, had talked of abandoning it but a day or two before the quarrel, this proceeding could only be accounted for as gratuitous spite. Later, two San Francisco lawyers made their appearance in this guileless Arcadia, and were eventually taken into the saloons, and—what was pretty much the same thing— the confidences of the inhabitants. The results of this unhallowed intimacy were many subpœnas; and, indeed, when the "Amity Claim" came to trial, all of Sandy Bar that was not in compulsory attendance at the county seat came there from curiosity. The gulches and ditches for miles around were deserted. I do not propose to describe that already famous trial. Enough that, in the language of the plaintiff's counsel, "it was one of no ordinary significance, involving the inherent rights of that untiring industry which had developed the Pactolian resources of this golden land"; and, in the homelier phrase of Colonel Starbottle, "A fuss that gentlemen might hev settled in ten minutes over a social glass, ef they meant business; or in ten seconds with a revolver, ef they meant fun." Scott got a verdict, from which York instantly appealed. It was said that he had sworn to spend his last dollar in the struggle.

In this way Sandy Bar began to accept the enmity of the former partners as a lifelong feud, and the fact that they had ever been friends was forgotten. The few who expected to learn from the trial the origin of the quarrel were disappointed. Among the various conjectures, that which ascribed some occult feminine influence as the cause was naturally popular, in a camp given to dubious compliment of the sex. "My word for it, gentlemen," said Colonel Starbottle, who had been known in Sacramento as a Gentleman of the Old School, "there's some lovely creature at the bottom of this." The gallant Colonel then proceeded to illustrate his theory, by divers sprightly stories, such as Gentlemen of the Old School are in the habit of repeating, but which, from deference to the prejudices of gentlemen of a more recent school, I refrain from transcribing here. But it would appear that even the Colonel's theory was fallacious. The only woman who personally might have exercised any influence over the partners was the pretty daughter of "old man Folinsbee," of Poverty Flat, at whose hospitable house—which exhibited some comforts and refinements rare in that crude civilization—both York and Scott were frequent visitors. Yet into this charming retreat York strode one evening, a month after the quarrel, and, beholding Scott sitting there, turned to the fair hostess with the abrupt query, "Do you love this man?" The young woman thus addressed returned that answer—at once spirited and evasive—which would occur to most of my fair readers in such an exigency. Without another word, York left the house. "Miss Jo" heaved the least possible sigh as the door closed on York's curls and square shoulders, and then, like a good girl, turned to her insulted guest. "But would you believe it, dear?" she afterward related to an intimate friend, "the other creature, after glowering at me for a moment, got upon its hind legs, took its hat, and left, too; and that's the last I've seen of either."

The same hard disregard of all other interests or feelings in the gratification of their blind rancor characterized all their actions. When York purchased the land below Scott's new claim, and obliged the latter, at a great expense, to make a long détour to carry a "tail-race" around it, Scott retaliated by building a dam that overflowed York's claim on the river. It was Scott, who, in conjunction with Colonel Starbottle, first organized that active opposition to the Chinamen, which resulted in the driving off of York's Mongolian laborers; it was York who built the wagon-road and established the express which rendered Scott's mules and pack-trains obsolete; it was Scott who called into life the Vigilance Committee which expatriated York's friend, Jack Hamlin; it was York who created the "Sandy Bar Herald," which characterized the act as "a lawless outrage," and Scott as a "Border Ruffian"; it was Scott, at the head of twenty masked men, who, one moonlight night, threw the offending "forms" into the yellow river, and scattered the type in the dusty road. These proceedings were received in the distant and more civilized outlying towns as vague indications of progress and vitality. I have before me a copy of the "Poverty Flat Pioneer," for the week ending August 12, 1856, in which the editor, under the head of "County Improvements," says:

"The new Presbyterian Church on C Street, at Sandy Bar, is completed. It stands upon the lot formerly occupied by the Magnolia Saloon, which was so mysteriously burnt last month. The temple, which now rises like a Phœnix from the ashes of the Magnolia, is virtually the free gift of H. J. York, Esq., of Sandy Bar, who purchased the lot and donated the lumber. Other buildings are going up in the vicinity, but the most noticeable is the 'Sunny South Saloon,' erected by Captain Mat. Scott, nearly opposite the church. Captain Scott has spared no expense in the furnishing of this saloon, which promises to be one of the most agreeable places of resort in old Tuolumne. He has recently imported two new, first-class billiard-tables, with cork cushions. Our old friend, 'Mountain Jimmy,' will dispense liquors at the bar. We refer our readers to the advertisement in another column. Visitors to Sandy Bar cannot do better than give 'Jimmy' a call." Among the local items occurred the following: "H. J. York, Esq., of Sandy Bar, has offered a reward of $100 for the detection of the parties who hauled away the steps of the new Presbyterian Church, C Street, Sandy Bar, during divine service on Sabbath evening last. Captain Scott adds another hundred for the capture of the miscreants who broke the magnificent plate-glass windows of the new saloon on the following evening. There is some talk of reorganizing the old Vigilance Committee at Sandy Bar."

When, for many months of cloudless weather, the hard, unwinking sun of Sandy Bar had regularly gone down on the unpacified wrath of these men, there was some talk of mediation. In particular, the pastor of the church to which I have just referred—a sincere, fearless, but perhaps not fully enlightened man—seized gladly upon the occasion of York's liberality to attempt to reunite the former partners. He preached an earnest sermon on the abstract sinfulness of discord and rancor. But the excellent sermons of the Rev. Mr. Daws were directed to an ideal congregation that did not exist at Sandy Bar,—a congregation of beings of unmixed vices and virtues, of single impulses, and perfectly logical motives, of preternatural simplicity, of childlike faith, and grown-up responsibilities. As, unfortunately, the people who actually attended Mr. Daws's church were mainly very human, somewhat artful, more self-excusing than self-accusing, rather good-natured, and decidedly weak, they quietly shed that portion of the sermon which referred to themselves, and, accepting York and Scott—who were both in defiant attendance—as curious examples of those ideal beings above referred to, felt a certain satisfaction—which, I fear, was not altogether Christian-like—in their "raking-down." If Mr. Daws expected York and Scott to shake hands after the sermon, he was disappointed. But he did not relax his purpose. With that quiet fearlessness and determination which had won for him the respect of men who were too apt to regard piety as synonymous with effeminacy, he attacked Scott in his own house. What he said has not been recorded, but it is to be feared that it was part of his sermon. When he had concluded, Scott looked at him, not unkindly, over the glasses of his bar, and said, less irreverently than the words might convey, "Young man, I rather like your style; but when you know York and me as well as you do God Almighty, it'll be time to talk."

And so the feud progressed; and so, as in more illustrious examples, the private and personal enmity of two representative men led gradually to the evolution of some crude, half-expressed principle or belief. It was not long before it was made evident that those beliefs were identical with certain broad principles laid down by the founders of the American Constitution, as expounded by the statesmanlike A.; or were the fatal quicksands, on which the ship of state might be wrecked, warningly pointed out by the eloquent B. The practical result of all which was the nomination of York and Scott to represent the opposite factions of Sandy Bar in legislative councils.

For some weeks past, the voters of Sandy Bar and the adjacent camps had been called upon, in large type to "RALLY!" In vain the great pines at the cross-roads—whose trunks were compelled to bear this and other legends—moaned and protested from their windy watch-towers. But one day, with fife and drum, and flaming transparency, a procession filed into the triangular grove at the head of the gulch. The meeting was called to order by Colonel Starbottle, who, having once enjoyed legislative functions, and being vaguely known as a "war-horse," was considered to be a valuable partisan of York. He concluded an appeal for his friend, with an enunciation of principles, interspersed with one or two anecdotes so gratuitously coarse that the very pines might have been moved to pelt him with their cast-off cones, as he stood there. But he created a laugh, on which his candidate rode into popular notice; and when York rose to speak, he was greeted with cheers. But, to the general astonishment, the new speaker at once launched into bitter denunciation of his rival. He not only dwelt upon Scott's deeds and example, as known to Sandy Bar, but spoke of facts connected with his previous career, hitherto unknown to his auditors. To great precision of epithet and directness of statement, the speaker added the fascination of revelation and exposure. The crowd cheered, yelled, and were delighted, but when this astounding philippic was concluded, there was a unanimous call for "Scott!" Colonel Starbottle would have resisted this manifest impropriety, but in vain. Partly from a crude sense of justice, partly from a meaner craving for excitement, the assemblage was inflexible; and Scott was dragged, pushed, and pulled upon the platform.

As his frowsy head and unkempt beard appeared above the railing, it was evident that he was drunk. But it was also evident, before he opened his lips, that the orator of Sandy Bar—the one man who could touch their vagabond sympathies (perhaps because he was not above appealing to them)—stood before them. A consciousness of this power lent a certain dignity to his figure, and I am not sure but that his very physical condition impressed them as a kind of regal unbending and large condescension. Howbeit, when this unexpected Hector arose from the ditch, York's myrmidons trembled.

"There's naught, gentlemen," said Scott, leaning forward on the railing,—"there's naught as that man hez said as isn't true. I was run outer Cairo; I did belong to the Regulators; I did desert from the army; I did leave a wife in Kansas. But thar's one thing he didn't charge me with, and, maybe, he's forgotten. For three years, gentlemen, I was that man's pardner!—" Whether he intended to say more, I cannot tell; a burst of applause artistically rounded and enforced the climax, and virtually elected the speaker. That fall he went to Sacramento, York went abroad; and for the first time in many years, distance and a new atmosphere isolated the old antagonists.

With little of change in the green wood, gray rock, and yellow river, but with much shifting of human landmarks, and new faces in its habitations, three years passed over Sandy Bar. The two men, once so identified with its character, seemed to have been quite forgotten. "You will never return to Sandy Bar," said Miss Folinsbee, the "Lily of Poverty Flat," on meeting York in Paris, "for Sandy Bar is no more. They call it Riverside now; and the new town is built higher up on the river-bank. By the by, 'Jo' says that Scott has won his suit about the 'Amity Claim,' and that he lives in the old cabin, and is drunk half his time. O, I beg your pardon," added the lively lady, as a flush crossed York's sallow cheek; "but, bless me, I really thought that old grudge was made up. I'm sure it ought to be."

It was three months after this conversation, and a pleasant summer evening, that the Poverty Flat coach drew up before the veranda of the Union Hotel at Sandy Bar. Among its passengers was one, apparently a stranger, in the local distinction of well-fitting clothes and closely shaven face, who demanded a private room and retired early to rest. But before sunrise next morning he arose, and, drawing some clothes from his carpet-bag, proceeded to array himself in a pair of white duck trousers, a white duck overshirt, and straw hat. When his toilet was completed, he tied a red bandanna handkerchief in a loop and threw it loosely over his shoulders. The transformation was complete. As he crept softly down the stairs and stepped into the road, no one would have detected in him the elegant stranger of the previous night, and but few have recognized the face and figure of Henry York of Sandy Bar.

In the uncertain light of that early hour, and in the change that had come over the settlement, he had to pause for a moment to recall where he stood. The Sandy Bar of his recollection lay below him, nearer the river; the buildings around him were of later date and newer fashion. As he strode toward the river, he noticed here a schoolhouse and there a church. A little farther on, "The Sunny South" came in view, transformed into a restaurant, its gilding faded and its paint rubbed off. He now knew where he was; and, running briskly down a declivity, crossed a ditch, and stood upon the lower boundary of the Amity Claim.

The gray mist was rising slowly from the river, clinging to the tree-tops and drifting up the mountain-side, until it was caught among these rocky altars, and held a sacrifice to the ascending sun. At his feet the earth, cruelly gashed and scarred by his forgotten engines, had, since the old days, put on a show of greenness here and there, and now smiled forgivingly up at him, as if things were not so bad after all. A few birds were bathing in the ditch with a pleasant suggestion of its being a new and special provision of nature, and a hare ran into an inverted sluice-box, as he approached, as if it were put there for that purpose.

He had not yet dared to look in a certain direction. But the sun was now high enough to paint the little eminence on which the cabin stood. In spite of his self-control, his heart beat faster as he raised his eyes toward it. Its window and door were closed, no smoke came from its *adobe* chimney, but it was else unchanged. When within a few yards of it, he picked up a broken shovel, and, shouldering it with a smile, strode toward the door and knocked. There was no sound from within. The smile died upon his lips as he nervously pushed the door open.

A figure started up angrily and came toward him,—a figure whose bloodshot eyes suddenly fixed into a vacant stare, whose arms were at first outstretched and then thrown up in warning gesticulation,—a figure that suddenly gasped, choked, and then fell forward in a fit.

But before he touched the ground, York had him out into the open air and sunshine. In the struggle, both fell and rolled over on the ground. But the next moment York was sitting up, holding the convulsed frame of his former partner on his knee, and wiping the foam from his inarticulate lips. Gradually the tremor became less frequent, and then ceased; and the strong man lay unconscious in his arms.

For some moments York held him quietly thus, looking in his face. Afar, the stroke of a woodman's axe—a mere phantom of sound— was all that broke the stillness. High up the mountain, a wheeling hawk hung breathlessly above them. And then came voices, and two men joined them.

"A fight?" No, a fit; and would they help him bring the sick man to the hotel?

And there, for a week, the stricken partner lay, unconscious of aught but the visions wrought by disease and fear. On the eighth day, at sunrise, he rallied, and, opening his eyes, looked upon York, and pressed his hand; then he spoke:—

"And it's you. I thought it was only whiskey."

York replied by taking both of his hands, boyishly working them backward and forward, as his elbow rested on the bed, with a pleasant smile.

"And you've been abroad. How did you like Paris?"

"So, so. How did *you* like Sacramento?"

"Bully."

And that was all they could think to say. Presently Scott opened his eyes again.

"I'm mighty weak."

"You'll get better soon."

"Not much."

A long silence followed, in which they could hear the sounds of wood-chopping, and that Sandy Bar was already astir for the coming day. Then Scott slowly and with difficulty turned his face to York, and said,—

"I might hev killed you once."

"I wish you had."

They pressed each other's hands again, but Scott's grasp was evidently failing. He seemed to summon his energies for a special effort.

"Old man!"

"Old chap."

"Closer!"

York bent his head toward the slowly fading face.

"Do ye mind that morning?"

"Yes."

A gleam of fun slid into the corner of Scott's blue eye, as he whispered,—

"Old man, thar *was* too much saleratus in that bread!"

It is said that these were his last words. For when the sun, which had so often gone down upon the idle wrath of these foolish men, looked again upon them reunited, it saw the hand of Scott fall cold and irresponsive from the yearning clasp of his former partner, and it knew that the feud of Sandy Bar was at an end.

How Santa Claus Came to Simpson's Bar

I⊤ had been raining in the valley of the Sacramento. The North Fork had overflowed its banks, and Rattlesnake Creek was impassable. The few boulders that had marked the summer ford at Simpson's Crossing were obliterated by a vast sheet of water stretching to the foot-hills. The upstage was stopped at Granger's; the last mail had been abandoned in the *tules,* the rider swimming for his life. "An area," remarked the Sierra Avalanche, with pensive local pride, "as large as the State of Massachusetts is now under water."

Nor was the weather any better in the foot-hills. The mud lay deep on the mountain road; wagons that neither physical force nor moral objurgation could move from the evil ways into which they had fallen encumbered the track, and the way to Simpson's Bar was indicated by broken-down teams and hard swearing. And farther on, cut off and inaccessible, rained upon and bedraggled, smitten by high winds and threatened by high water, Simpson's Bar, on the eve of Christmas Day, 1862, clung like a swallow's nest to the rocky entablature and splintered capitals of Table Mountain, and shook in the blast.

As the night shut down on the settlement, a few lights gleamed through the mist from the windows of cabins on either side of the highway, now crossed and gullied by lawless streams and swept by marauding winds. Happily most of the population were gathered at Thompson's store, clustered around a red-hot stove, at which they silently spat in some accepted sense of social communion that perhaps rendered conversation unnecessary. Indeed, most methods of diversion had long since been exhausted on Simpson's Bar; high water had suspended the regular occupations on gulch and on river, and a consequent lack of money and whiskey had taken the zest from most illegitimate recreation. Even Mr. Hamlin was fain to leave the Bar with fifty dollars in his pocket—the only amount actually realized of the large sums won by him in the successful exercise of his arduous profession. "Ef I was asked," he remarked somewhat later,—"ef I was asked to pint out a purty little village where a retired sport as didn't care for money could exercise hisself, frequent and lively, I'd say Simpson's Bar; but for a young man with a large family depending on his exertions, it don't pay." As Mr. Hamlin's family consisted mainly of female adults, this remark is quoted rather to show the breadth of his humor than the exact extent of his responsibilities.

Howbeit, the unconscious objects of this satire sat that evening in the listless apathy begotten of idleness and lack of excitement. Even the sudden splashing of hoofs before the door did not arouse them. Dick Bullen alone paused in the act of scraping out his pipe, and lifted his head, but no other one of the group indicated any interest in, or recognition of, the man who entered.

It was a figure familiar enough to the company, and known in Simpson's Bar as "The Old Man." A man of perhaps fifty years; grizzled and scant of hair, but still fresh and youthful of complexion. A face full of ready but not very powerful sympathy, with a chameleon-like aptitude for taking on the shade and color of contiguous moods and feelings. He had evidently just left some hilarious companions, and did not at first notice the gravity of the group, but clapped the shoulder of the nearest man jocularly, and threw himself into a vacant chair.

"Jest heard the best thing out, boys! Ye know Smiley, over yar— Jim Smiley—funniest man in the Bar? Well, Jim was jest telling the richest yarn about"—

"Smiley's a —— fool!" interrupted a gloomy voice.

"A particular —— skunk!" added another in sepulchral accents.

A silence followed these positive statements. The Old Man glanced quickly around the group. Then his face slowly changed. "That's so," he said reflectively, after a pause, "certingly a sort of a skunk and suthin' of a fool. In course." He was silent for a moment as in painful contemplation of the unsavoriness and folly of the unpopular Smiley. "Dismal weather, ain't it?" he added, now fully embarked on the current of prevailing sentiment. "Mighty rough papers on the boys, and no show for money this season. And to-morrow's Christmas."

There was a movement among the men at this announcement, but whether of satisfaction or disgust was not plain. "Yes," continued the

Old Man in the lugubrious tone he had, within the last few moments, unconsciously adopted,—"yes, Christmas, and to-night's Christmas Eve. Ye see, boys, I kinder thought—that is, I sorter had an idee, jest passin' like, you know—that maybe ye'd all like to come over to my house to-night and have a sort of tear round. But I suppose, now, you wouldn't? Don't feel like it, maybe?" he added with anxious sympathy, peering into the faces of his companions.

"Well, I don't know," responded Tom Flynn with some cheerfulness. "P'r'aps we may. But how about your wife, Old Man? What does *she* say to it?"

The Old Man hesitated. His conjugal experience had not been a happy one, and the fact was known to Simpson's Bar. His first wife, a delicate, pretty little woman, had suffered keenly and secretly from the jealous suspicions of her husband, until one day he invited the whole Bar to his house to expose her infidelity. On arriving, the party found the shy, *petite* creature quietly engaged in her household duties, and retired abashed and discomfited. But the sensitive woman did not easily recover from the shock of this extraordinary outrage. It was with difficulty she regained her equanimity sufficiently to release her lover from the closet in which he was concealed, and escape with him. She left a boy of three years to comfort her bereaved husband. The Old Man's present wife had been his cook. She was large, loyal, and aggressive.

Before he could reply, Joe Dimmick suggested with great directness that it was the "Old Man's house," and that, invoking the Divine Power, if the case were his own, he would invite whom he pleased, even if in so doing he imperilled his salvation. The Powers of Evil, he further remarked, should contend against him vainly. All this delivered with a terseness and vigor lost in this necessary translation.

"In course. Certainly. Thet's it," said the Old Man, with a sympathetic frown. "Thar's no trouble about *thet*. It's my own house, built every stick on it myself. Don't you be afeard o' her, boys. She *may* cut up a trifle rough—ez wimmin do—but she'll come round." Secretly the Old Man trusted to the exaltation of liquor and the power of courageous example to sustain him in such an emergency.

As yet, Dick Bullen, the oracle and leader of Simpson's Bar, had not spoken. He now took his pipe from his lips. "Old Man, how's that yer Johnny gettin' on? Seems to me he didn't look so peart last time I seed him on the bluff heavin' rocks at Chinamen. Didn't seem to take much interest in it. Thar was a gang of 'em by yar yesterday,— drownded out up the river,—and I kinder thought o' Johnny, and how he'd miss 'em! Maybe now, we'd be in the way ef he wus sick?"

The father, evidently touched not only by this pathetic picture of Johnny's deprivation, but by the considerate delicacy of the speaker, hastened to assure him that Johnny was better and that a "little fun might 'liven him up." Whereupon Dick arose, shook himself, and saying, "I'm ready. Lead the way, Old Man: here goes," himself led the way with a leap, a characteristic howl, and darted out into the night. As he passed through the outer room he caught up a blazing brand from the hearth. The action was repeated by the rest of the party, closely following and elbowing each other, and before the astonished proprietor of Thompson's grocery was aware of the intention of his guests the room was deserted.

The night was pitchy dark. In the first gust of wind their temporary torches were extinguished, and only the red brands dancing and flitting in the gloom like drunken will-o'-the-wisps indicated their whereabouts. Their way led up Pine-Tree Cañon, at the head of which a broad, low, bark-thatched cabin burrowed in the mountain-side. It was the home of the Old Man, and the entrance to the tunnel in which he worked when he worked at all. Here the crowd paused for a moment, out of delicate deference to their host, who came up panting in the rear.

"P'r'aps ye'd better hold on a second out yer, whilst I go in and see that things is all right," said the Old Man, with an indifference he was far from feeling. The suggestion was graciously accepted, the door opened and closed on the host, and the crowd, leaning their backs against the wall and cowering under the eaves, waited and listened.

For a few moments there was no sound but the dripping of water from the eaves, and the stir and rustle of wrestling boughs above them. Then the men became uneasy, and whispered suggestion and suspicion passed from the one to the other. "Reckon she's caved in his head the first lick!" "Decoyed him inter the tunnel and barred him up, likely." "Got him down and sittin' on him." "Prob'ly biling suthin' to heave on us: stand clear the door, boys!" For just then the latch clicked, the door slowly opened, and a voice said, "Come in out o' the wet."

The voice was neither that of the Old Man nor of his wife. It was the voice of a small boy, its weak treble broken by that preternatural hoarseness which only vagabondage and the habit of premature self-assertion can give. It was the face of a small boy that looked up at theirs,—a face that might have been pretty, and even refined, but that it was darkened by evil knowledge from within, and dirt and hard experience from without. He had a blanket around his shoulders, and had evidently just risen from his bed. "Come in," he repeated, "and don't make no noise. The Old Man's in there talking to mar," he continued, pointing to an adjacent room which seemed to be a kitchen, from which the Old Man's voice came in deprecating accents. "Let me be," he added querulously to Dick Bullen, who had caught him up, blanket and all, and was affecting to toss him into the fire; "let go o' me, you d—d old fool, d' ye hear?"

Thus adjured, Dick Bullen lowered Johnny to the ground with a smothered laugh, while the men, entering quietly, ranged themselves around a long table of rough boards which occupied the centre of the room. Johnny then gravely proceeded to a cupboard and brought out several articles, which he deposited on the table. "Thar's whiskey. And crackers. And red herons. And cheese." He took a bite of the latter on his way to the table. "And sugar." He scooped up a mouthful *en route* with a small and very dirty hand. "And terbacker. Thar's dried appils too on the shelf, but I don't admire 'em. Appils is swellin'. Thar," he concluded, "now wade in, and don't be afeard. *I* don't mind the old woman. She don't b'long to *me*. S'long."

He had stepped to the threshold of a small room, scarcely larger than a closet, partitioned off from the main apartment, and holding in its dim recess a small bed. He stood there a moment looking at the company, his bare feet peeping from the blanket, and nodded.

"Hello, Johnny! You ain't goin' to turn in agin, are ye?" said Dick.

"Yes, I are," responded Johnny decidedly.

"Why, wot's up, old fellow?"

"I'm sick."

"How sick?"

"I've got a fevier. And childblains. And roomatiz," returned Johnny, and vanished within. After a moment's pause, he added in the dark, apparently from under the bed-clothes, "And biles!"

There was an embarrassing silence. The men looked at each other and at the fire. Even with the appetizing banquet before them, it seemed as if they might again fall into the despondency of Thompson's grocery, when the voice of the Old Man, incautiously lifted, came deprecatingly from the kitchen.

"Certainly! Thet's so. In course they is. A gang o' lazy, drunken loafers, and that ar Dick Bullen's the ornariest of all. Didn't hev no more *sabe* than to come round yar, with sickness in the house and no provision. Thet's what I said: 'Bullen,' sez I, 'it's crazy drunk you are, or a fool,' sez I, 'to think o' such a thing.' 'Staples,' I sez, 'be you a man, Staples, and 'spect to raise h—ll under my roof, and invalids lyin' round?' But they would come,—they would. Thet's wot you must 'spect o' such trash as lays round the Bar."

A burst of laughter from the men followed this unfortunate exposure. Whether it was overheard in the kitchen, or whether the Old Man's irate companion had just then exhausted all other modes of expressing her contemptuous indignation, I cannot say, but a back door was suddenly slammed with great violence. A moment later and the Old Man reappeared, haply unconscious of the cause of the late hilarious outbursts, and smiled blandly.

"The old woman thought she'd jest run over to Mrs. MacFadden's for a sociable call," he explained with jaunty indifference as he took a seat at the board.

Oddly enough it needed this untoward incident to relieve the embarrassment that was beginning to be felt by the party, and their natural audacity returned with their host. I do not propose to record the convivialities of that evening. The inquisitive reader will accept the statement that the conversation was characterized by the same intellectual exaltation, the same cautious reverence, the same fastidious delicacy, the same rhetorical precision, and the same logical and coherent discourse, somewhat later in the evening, which distinguish similar gatherings of the masculine sex in more civilized localities and under more favorable auspices. No glasses were broken in the absence of any; no liquor was uselessly spilt on the floor or table in the scarcity of that article.

It was nearly midnight when the festivities were interrupted. "Hush!" said Dick Bullen, holding up his hand. It was the querulous voice of Johnny from his adjacent closet: "Oh, dad!"

The Old Man arose hurriedly and disappeared in the closet. Presently he reappeared. "His rheumatiz is coming on agin bad," he explained, "and he wants rubbin'." He lifted the demijohn of whiskey from the table and shook it. It was empty. Dick Bullen put down his tin cup with an embarrassed laugh. So did the others. The Old Man examined their contents, and said hopefully, "I reckon that's enough; he don't need much. You hold on, all o' you, for a spell, and I'll be back;" and vanished in the closet with an old flannel shirt and the whiskey. The door closed but imperfectly, and the following dialogue was distinctly audible:—

"Now, sonny, whar does she ache worst?"

"Sometimes over yar and sometimes under yer; but it's most powerful from yer to yer. Rub yer, dad."

A silence seemed to indicate a brisk rubbing. Then Johnny:—

"Hevin' a good time out yar, dad?"

"Yes, sonny."

"To-morrer's Chrismiss,—ain't it?"

"Yes, sonny. How does she feel now?"

"Better. Rub a little furder down. Wot's Chrismiss, any way? Wot's it all about?"

"Oh, it's a day."

This exhaustive definition was apparently satisfactory, for there was a silent interval of rubbing. Presently Johnny again:—

"Mar sez that everywhere else but yer everybody gives things to everybody Chrismiss, and then she jist waded inter you. She sez thar's a man they call Sandy Claws, not a white man, you know, but a kind o' Chinemin, comes down the chimbley night afore Chrismiss and gives things to chillern,—boys like me. Puts 'em in their butes! Thet's what she tried to play upon me. Easy, now, pop, whar are you rubbin' to,—thet's a mile from the place. She jest made that up, didn't she, jest to aggrewate me and you? Don't rub thar. . . . Why, dad!"

In the great quiet that seemed to have fallen upon the house the sigh of the near pines and the drip of leaves without was very distinct. Johnny's voice, too, was lowered as he went on: "Don't you take on now, for I'm gettin' all right fast. Wot's the boys doin' out thar?"

The Old Man partly opened the door and peered through. His guests were sitting there sociably enough, and there were a few silver coins and a lean buckskin purse on the table. "Bettin' on suthin',— some little game or 'nother. They're all right," he replied to Johnny, and recommenced his rubbing.

"I'd like to take a hand and win some money," said Johnny reflectively, after a pause.

The Old Man glibly repeated what was evidently a familiar formula, that if Johnny would wait until he struck it rich in the tunnel, he'd have lots of money, etc., etc.

"Yes," said Johnny, "but you don't. And whether you strike it or I win it, it's about the same. It's all luck. But it's mighty cur'o's about Chrismiss,—ain't it? Why do they call it Chrismiss?"

Perhaps from some instinctive deference to the overhearing of his guests, or from some vague sense of incongruity, the Old Man's reply was so low as to be inaudible beyond the room.

"Yes," said Johnny, with some slight abatement of interest, "I've heerd o' *him* before. Thar, that'll do, dad. I don't ache near so bad as I did. Now wrap me tight in this yer blanket. So. Now," he added in a muffled whisper, "sit down yer by me till I go asleep." To assure himself of obedience, he disengaged one hand from the blanket, and, grasping his father's sleeve, again composed himself to rest.

For some moments the Old Man waited patiently. Then the unwonted stillness of the house excited his curiosity, and without moving from the bed he cautiously opened the door with his disengaged hand, and looked into the main room. To his infinite surprise it was dark and deserted. But even then a smouldering log on the hearth broke, and by the upspringing blaze he saw the figure of Dick Bullen sitting by the dying embers.

"Hello!"

Dick started, rose, and came somewhat unsteadily toward him.

"War's the boys?" said the Old Man.

"Gone up the cañon on a little *pasear*. They're coming back for me in a minit. I'm waitin' round for 'em. What are you starin' at, Old Man?" he added, with a forced laugh; "do you think I'm drunk?"

The Old Man might have been pardoned the supposition, for Dick's eyes were humid and his face flushed. He loitered and lounged back to the chimney, yawned, shook himself, buttoned up his coat and laughed. "Liquor ain't so plenty as that, Old Man. Now don't you git up," he continued, as the Old Man made a movement to release his sleeve from Johnny's hand. "Don't you mind manners. Sit jest whar you be; I'm goin' in a jiffy. Thar, that's them now."

There was a low tap at the door. Dick Bullen opened it quickly, nodded "Good-night" to his host, and disappeared. The Old Man would have followed him but for the hand that still unconsciously grasped his sleeve. He could have easily disengaged it; it was small, weak, and emaciated. But perhaps because it *was* small, weak, and emaciated he changed his mind, and, drawing his chair closer to the bed, rested his head upon it. In this defenceless attitude the potency of his earlier potations surprised him. The room flickered and faded before his eyes, reappeared, faded again, went out, and left him—asleep.

Meantime Dick Bullen, closing the door, confronted his companions. "Are you ready?" said Staples. "Ready," said Dick; "what's the time?" "Past twelve," was the reply; "can you make it?—it's nigh on fifty miles, the round trip hither and yon." "I reckon," returned Dick shortly. "Whar's the mare?" "Bill and Jack's holdin' her at the crossin'." "Let 'em hold on a minit longer," said Dick.

He turned and reëntered the house softly. By the light of the guttering candle and dying fire he saw that the door of the little room was open. He stepped toward it on tiptoe and looked in. The Old Man had fallen back in his chair, snoring, his helpless feet thrust out in a line with his collapsed shoulders, and his hat pulled over his eyes. Beside him, on a narrow wooden bedstead, lay Johnny, muffled tightly in a blanket that hid all save a strip of forehead and a few curls damp with perspiration. Dick Bullen made a step forward, hesitated, and glanced over his shoulder into the deserted room. Everything was quiet. With a sudden resolution he parted his huge mustaches with both hands, and stooped over the sleeping boy. But even as he did so a mischievous blast, lying in wait, swooped down the chimney, rekindled the hearth, and lit up the room with a shameless glow, from which Dick fled in bashful terror.

His companions were already waiting for him at the crossing. Two of them were struggling in the darkness with some strange misshapen bulk, which as Dick came nearer took the semblance of a great yellow horse.

It was the mare. She was not a pretty picture. From her Roman nose to her rising haunches, from her arched spine hidden by the stiff *machillas* of a Mexican saddle, to her thick, straight, bony legs, there was not a line of equine grace. In her half-blind but wholly vicious white eyes, in her protruding under-lip, in her monstrous color, there was nothing but ugliness and vice.

"Now, then," said Staples, "stand cl'ar of her heels, boy, and up with you. Don't miss your first holt of her mane, and mind ye get your off stirrup *quick*. Ready!"

There was a leap, a scrambling struggle, a bound, a wild retreat of the crowd, a circle of flying hoofs, two springless leaps that jarred the earth, a rapid play and jingle of spurs, a plunge, and then the voice of Dick somewhere in the darkness. "All right!"

"Don't take the lower road back onless you're hard pushed for time! Don't hold her in down hill. We'll be at the ford at five. G'lang! Hoopa! Mula! GO!"

A splash, a spark struck from the ledge in the road, a clatter in the rocky cut beyond, and Dick was gone.

.   .   .   .

Sing, O Muse, the ride of Richard Bullen! Sing, O Muse, of chivalrous men! the sacred quest, the doughty deeds, the battery of low churls, the fearsome ride and gruesome perils of the Flower of Simpson's Bar! Alack! she is dainty, this Muse! She will have none of this bucking brute and swaggering, ragged rider, and I must fain follow him in prose, afoot!

It was one o'clock, and yet he had only gained Rattlesnake Hill. For in that time Jovita had rehearsed to him all her imperfections and practised all her vices. Thrice had she stumbled. Twice had she thrown up her Roman nose in a straight line with the reins, and, resisting bit and spur, struck out madly across country. Twice had

she reared, and, rearing, fallen backward; and twice had the agile
Dick, unharmed, regained his seat before she found her vicious legs
again. And a mile beyond them, at the foot of a long hill, was Rattlesnake Creek. Dick knew that here was the crucial test of his ability
to perform his enterprise, set his teeth grimly, put his knees well into
her flanks, and changed his defensive tactics to brisk aggression.
Bullied and maddened, Jovita began the descent of the hill. Here
the artful Richard pretended to hold her in with ostentatious objurgation and well-feigned cries of alarm. It is unnecessary to add that
Jovita instantly ran away. Nor need I state the time made in the
descent; it is written in the chronicles of Simpson's Bar. Enough that
in another moment, as it seemed to Dick, she was splashing on the
overflowed banks of Rattlesnake Creek. As Dick expected, the mo-
mentum she had acquired carried her beyond the point of balking,
and, holding her well together for a mighty leap, they dashed into
the middle of the swiftly flowing current. A few moments of kicking,
wading, and swimming, and Dick drew a long breath on the opposite bank.

The road from Rattlesnake Creek to Red Mountain was tolerably
level. Either the plunge in Rattlesnake Creek had dampened her
baleful fire, or the art which led to it had shown her the superior
wickedness of her rider, for Jovita no longer wasted her surplus
energy in wanton conceits. Once she bucked, but it was from force
of habit; once she shied, but it was from a new, freshly-painted
meeting-house at the crossing of the county road. Hollows, ditches,
gravelly deposits, patches of freshly-springing grasses, flew from beneath her rattling hoofs. She began to smell unpleasantly, once or
twice she coughed slightly, but there was no abatement of her strength
or speed. By two o'clock he had passed Red Mountain and begun
the descent to the plain. Ten minutes later the driver of the fast
Pioneer coach was overtaken and passed by a "man on a Pinto hoss,"
—an event sufficiently notable for remark. At half past two Dick
rose in his stirrups with a great shout. Stars were glittering through
the rifted clouds, and beyond him, out of the plain, rose two spires,
a flagstaff, and a straggling line of black objects. Dick jingled his spurs
and swung his *riata,* Jovita bounded forward, and in another moment
they swept into Tuttleville, and drew up before the wooden piazza
of "The Hotel of All Nations."

What transpired that night at Tuttleville is not strictly a part of
this record. Briefly I may state, however, that after Jovita had been
handed over to a sleepy ostler, whom she at once kicked into unpleasant consciousness, Dick sallied out with the barkeeper for a

tour of the sleeping town. Lights still gleamed from a few saloons and gambling-houses; but, avoiding these, they stopped before several closed shops, and by persistent tapping and judicious outcry roused the proprietors from their beds, and made them unbar the doors of their magazines and expose their wares. Sometimes they were met by curses, but oftener by interest and some concern in their needs, and the interview was invariably concluded by a drink. It was three o'clock before this pleasantry was given over, and with a small waterproof bag of India rubber strapped on his shoulders Dick returned to the hotel. But here he was waylaid by Beauty,—Beauty opulent in charms, affluent in dress, persuasive in speech, and Spanish in accent! In vain she repeated the invitation in "Excelsior," happily scorned by all Alpine-climbing youth, and rejected by this child of the Sierras,— a rejection softened in this instance by a laugh and his last gold coin. And then he sprang to the saddle, and dashed down the lonely street and out into the lonelier plain, where presently the lights, the black line of houses, the spires, and the flagstaff sank into the earth behind him again and were lost in the distance.

The storm had cleared away, the air was brisk and cold, the outlines of adjacent landmarks were distinct, but it was half past four before Dick reached the meeting-house and the crossing of the county road. To avoid the rising grade he had taken a longer and more circuitous road, in whose viscid mud Jovita sank fetlock deep at every bound. It was a poor preparation for a steady ascent of five miles more; but Jovita, gathering her legs under her, took it with her usual blind, unreasoning fury, and a half hour later reached the long level that led to Rattlesnake Creek. Another half hour would bring him to the creek. He threw the reins lightly upon the neck of the mare, chirruped to her, and began to sing.

Suddenly Jovita shied with a bound that would have unseated a less practised rider. Hanging to her rein was a figure that had leaped from the bank, and at the same time from the road before her arose a shadowy horse and rider. "Throw up your hands," commanded the second apparition, with an oath.

Dick felt the mare tremble, quiver, and apparently sink under him. He knew what it meant, and was prepared.

"Stand aside, Jack Simpson. I know you, you d—d thief! Let me pass, or"—

He did not finish the sentence. Jovita rose straight in the air with a terrific bound, throwing the figure from her bit with a single shake of her vicious head, and charged with deadly malevolence down on the impediment before her. An oath, a pistol-shot, horse and highwayman rolled over in the road, and the next moment Jovita was a hundred yards away. But the good right arm of her rider, shattered by a bullet, dropped helplessly at his side.

Without slacking his speed he shifted the reins to his left hand. But a few moments later he was obliged to halt and tighten the saddle-girths that had slipped in the onset. This in his crippled condition took some time. He had no fear of pursuit, but, looking up, he saw that the eastern stars were already paling, and that the distant peaks had lost their ghostly whiteness, and now stood out blackly against a lighter sky. Day was upon him. Then completely absorbed in a single idea, he forgot the pain of his wound, and, mounting again, dashed on towards Rattlesnake Creek. But now Jovita's breath came broken by gasps, Dick reeled in his saddle, and brighter and brighter grew the sky.

Ride, Richard; run, Jovita; linger, O day!

For the last few rods there was a roaring in his ears. Was it exhaustion from a loss of blood, or what? He was dazed and giddy as he swept down the hill, and did not recognize his surroundings. Had he taken the wrong road, or was this Rattlesnake Creek?

It was. But the brawling creek he had swam a few hours before had risen, more than doubled its volume, and now rolled a swift and resistless river between him and Rattlesnake Hill. For the first time that night Richard's heart sank within him. The river, the mountain, the quickening east, swam before his eyes. He shut them to recover his self-control. In that brief interval, by some fantastic mental process, the little room at Simpson's Bar and the figures of the sleeping father and son rose upon him. He opened his eyes wildly, cast off his coat, pistol, boots, and saddle, bound his precious pack tightly to his shoulders, grasped the bare flanks of Jovita with his bared knees, and with a shout dashed into the yellow water. A cry rose from the opposite bank as the head of a man and horse struggled for a few moments against the battling current, and then were swept away amidst uprooted trees and whirling driftwood.

•　　　•　　　•　　　•　　　•　　　•　　　•

The Old Man started and woke. The fire on the hearth was dead, the candle in the outer room flickering in its socket, and somebody was rapping at the door. He opened it, but fell back with a cry before the dripping, half-naked figure that reeled against the doorpost.

"Dick?"

"Hush! Is he awake yet?"

"No; but, Dick"—

"Dry up, you old fool! Get me some whiskey, *quick!*" The Old Man flew, and returned with—an empty bottle! Dick would have sworn, but his strength was not equal to the occasion. He staggered, caught at the handle of the door, and motioned to the Old Man.

"Thar's suthin' in my pack yer for Johnny. Take it off. I can't."

The Old Man unstrapped the pack, and laid it before the exhausted man.

"Open it, quick."

He did so with trembling fingers. It contained only a few poor toys,—cheap and barbaric enough, goodness knows, but bright with paint and tinsel. One of them was broken; another, I fear, was irretrievably ruined by water; and on the third—ah me! there was a cruel spot.

"It don't look like much, that's a fact," said Dick ruefully. . . . "But it's the best we could do. . . . Take 'em, Old Man, and put 'em in his stocking, and tell him—tell him, you know—hold me, Old Man"— The Old Man caught at his sinking figure. "Tell him," said Dick, with a weak little laugh,—"tell him Sandy Claus has come."

And even so, bedraggled, ragged, unshaven and unshorn, with one arm hanging helplessly at his side, Santa Claus came to Simpson's Bar, and fell fainting on the first threshold. The Christmas dawn came slowly after, touching the remoter peaks with the rosy warmth of ineffable love. And it looked so tenderly on Simpson's Bar that the whole mountain, as if caught in a generous action, blushed to the skies.

PHILANDER DEMING

★ ★ ★

Transcribing court trials in legal records and actual incidents of Adirondack life in magazine sketches became, during the 1870's, the alternating activities of Philander Deming (1829-1915). His first stories, contributed as early as 1873 to *The Atlantic Monthly,* were as unadorned and uncolored as the matter he recorded in court; with awareness of New York mountaineers' responses to the vicissitudes of life, he recounted narratives of people, self-possessed and reticent, yet ready to follow their convictions to the limit. Born in Schoharie County, New York, Deming taught school before attending the University of Vermont and Albany Law School. Becoming a court stenographer, he demonstrated successfully a verbatim system of shorthand reporting and prepared a handbook, *The Court Stenographer* (1879). His tales were collected in *Adirondack Stories* (1880), containing "Lost," and in *Tompkins, and Other Folks* (1885). His reflective, shy, mellow qualities emerge from his autobiography, *The Story of a Pathfinder* (1907).

★ ★ ★

Lost

H E was lost in the edge of the Adirondack Wilderness. It must have been the sound of the flail. "Thud, thud, thud," came the beat of the dull, thumping strokes through the thick, opaque, gray fog. Willie was hardly four years old; and when once he was a few rods away from the barn, off on the plain of monotonous yellow stubble, he could not tell where he was, and could not detect the deceptive nature of the sound and its echo. He could see nothing: whichever way he looked, wherever he walked, there were the same reverberations; and the same narrow dome of watery gray was everywhere shutting close down around him. As he followed the muffled sound, in his efforts to get back to the barn, it seemed to retreat from him, and he ran faster to overtake it. He ran on and on, and so was lost.

That night and the next day a few neighbors, gathered from the adjoining farms, searched for Willie. They wandered about the fields and the margin of the woods, but found no trace of the lost child. It became apparent that a general search must be made.

The fog had cleared away on the second morning after Willie was lost, as about a hundred woodsmen and farmers and hunters, gathered from the farms and forest and settlement nearby, called Whiskey Hollow, stood and sat in grotesque groups around the little farmhouse and barn, waiting the grand organization into line, preparatory to sweeping the woods, and finding Willie.

During all the hours of the two previous nights the lanterns and torches had been flashing in and out behind the logs and brush of the fallows; and the patches of snow that lingered in spite of the April rains gave evidence that every foot of the adjacent clearing had been trampled over in the search. But the men were not yet satisfied that the search about the farm had been thorough. Standing by the house, they could see the field of the night's work,—the level stubble of the grain-lot, and the broad, irregular hollow used as pasture, and filled with stumps and logs and brush. Here and there could be seen men still busy poking sticks under the logs, and working around bog-holes in the low ground. "You see it stands to reason," said Jim, addressing a group by the house, "that a little chap less than four years old could not get out of this clearing into the woods."

A white-haired patriarch remarked, with great confidence and solemnity, "The boy is within half a mile of the house; and, if I can have command of six men, I will find him." The patriarch continued to press his suggestion until he secured his company and started off, feeling that he carried a great weight of responsibility. He joined the log-pokers and bog-explorers; but nothing came of his search.

The morning was wearing away; the men, gathered from a great distance, were impatient of the delay to organize the line.

Willie had been out nearly forty-eight hours. Could it be that he had passed beyond the stubble-field into the forest, nearly half a mile from the house? If he had managed to cross the brook at the edge of the woods, he had the vast Adirondack Wilderness before him. It was time to search thoroughly and upon a large scale, if the boy was to be found alive.

But a reason for delay was whispered around,—the fortune-woman was coming. Soon a rough farm-wagon came up the road and through the yard-gate, and stopped in front of the door of the farmhouse. There was a hush of voices, and a reverent look upon the part of some of the men, and a snicker and digging of their neighbors' ribs upon the part of others, as a large, coarse-featured woman was helped out of the wagon by the driver of the team.

This female was the famous fortune-woman. Some of these dwellers on the edge of the wilderness were no better than the classic Greek and noble Roman of ancient times; for they believed in divination.

The fortune-woman went into the house where the mother of Willie sat, crying. The men crowded the room and windows and door. Some of the men looked solemn; some jeered. Out at the door Josh explained apologetically to the unbelievers, that, "inasmuch as some thinks as how she can tell, and some thinks as how she can't, so it were thought better for to go and fetch her, so as that all might satisfactory themselves, and no fault found, and every thing done for the little boy."

After a brief *séance* with the teacup in the house, the fortune-woman, urged by the men, went "out of doors" and walked up along the hollow with her teacup, experimenting to find the child. About half of the men straggled after her. Jim declared to the group who lingered at the house that he would sell out and leave, if the entire crowd disgraced the town by following after that "old she-devil."

To a stranger coming upon the field at this time, the scene was curious and picturesque, and some of it unaccountable. In the background was a vast descending plain of evergreen forest, sloping away from the Adirondack highlands to the dim distance of the St. Lawrence Valley, where could be seen the white, thread-like line of the great river; and still beyond the Canada woods, melting away to a measureless distance of airy blue. In the foreground was a vulgar old woman waddling along, and snatching here and there a teacup-ful of water from the puddles formed by the melting snow; and fifty vigorous men in awe-struck attitudes were gazing at her, and, when she moved, they followed her.

Odd as this grotesque performance seemed, it had in it a touch of the old heathenish grandeur belonging to the ancient superstitions. The same strange light that through all time has shone from human faces as souls reach after the great infinite unknown shone from the faces of some of these men. There were fine visages among them. Burly Josh and a hunter with dark, poetic eyes would have been a match for handsome, pious Æneas or the heroes of Hellas, who watched the flight of birds, and believed in a fortune-woman at Delphos.

But the simple faith of these modern worshippers was not rewarded: after the Greek pattern, the oracle gave ambiguous responses. The old woman proclaimed, with her eyes snapping venomously, that there was "a big black baste a-standin' over the swate child." She announced, with a swing of her right arm extending around half a circle, that "the dear, innocent darlin' was somewhere about off that way from the house." She scolded the men sharply for their laziness, telling them they had not looked for the lost child, but were waiting around the house, "while the blessed baby starved, and the big black baste stood over him."

Dan caught at this, and declared that the "old hypocrite" was no fool. She knew enough to understand that "it was no way to find a lost boy to shell out a whole township of able-bodied men, and set them to chase an old woman around a lot."

The fortune-woman came back to the house, held a final grand *séance* with the teacup divinity, and declared that the "swate child" was within half a mile of the place, and if they would only look they would find him, and that, if they did not look, within two days "the big black baste would devour the poor, neglected darlin'." After this the fortune-woman was put into the wagon again, and Josh drove her home. It was fully in accordance with the known perversity of human nature, that the faith of the believers in her infallibility was not in the slightest degree shaken.

The company, having been increased by fresh arrivals to more than one hundred men, organized for the search. The colonel ranged the men in line about twenty feet apart, extending across the wide stubble-field and the pasture. The men were directed by the colonel to "dress to the left;" that is, as he explained it, for each to watch the man at the left, and keep twenty feet from him, and observe all the ground in marching.

The word was given, and the line, more than half a mile long, began to move sidewise or platoon fashion, sweeping from the road by the house across the clearing to the woods. It was a grand charge upon the great wilderness. The long platoon, under the instruction of their commander, swept the woods bordering the clearing, and then, doubling back, made semicircular curves, going deeper and deeper at each return into the primeval forest. The limit of their marching and counter-marching in one direction was a river too broad to be crossed by fallen trees: it was sure that Willie could not have crossed the river. The termination of the marches in the other direction was controlled by the judgment of the colonel. It was a magnificent tramp through the wild, wet woods, under the giant trees, each eye strained, and expectant of the lost boy. Here and there, in advance of the line as it progressed, a partridge, aroused by the voices of the men, would start from the undergrowth, and trip along a few steps with her sharp, coquettish *"quit, quit, quit,"* and then whir away to some adjacent hollow, to be soon again aroused by the advancing line.

The afternoon was wearing away. The woods had been thoroughly explored for about two miles from the clearing,—far beyond what it seemed possible for an infant less than four years old to penetrate.

The colonel said he could think of nothing more to be done. The men returned in struggling groups to the farmhouse, tired, sad, hungry, and dispirited. There were many speculations whether Willie could be still alive, and, if alive, whether he could get through another night. "You see," said Josh, "such a *little* feller, and three days and two nights a-wettin' and a-freezin' and a-thawin', and no grub: why, he couldn't, don't you see?"

It was never found out, not even in Whiskey Hollow, where the men unveiled all their iniquities, who the wretch was that first started the dark suggestion about the *murder* of little Willie. Dan became very angry when the men, fatigued and famished, straggling back to the farmhouse from the disorganized line, as above narrated, began to hint that "things was tremendous queer," and that "them as lost could find," and that John, Willie's father, was a perfect hyena when he was "mad."

Dan, for the only time that day, became profane as he denounced the sneak, whoever it might be, who had started such a suggestion. He expressed the conviction that the fortune-woman had her foot in it some way. Superstitious fools, he said, were likely to be suspicious.

But Dan's anathemas did not stay the rising tide. As the searchers came back, suspicious glances were turned upon the father, who sat with his afflicted family at the house. Some of the searchers stealthily examined under the barn, believing that Willie had been "knocked on the head" with a flail, and concealed under the floor.

But John the father was no coward, and he had neighbors and friends who believed in him. They told him of the suspicions arising against him. On the instant he called a meeting at the little hovel of a schoolhouse, a few rods down the road. The hundred searchers gathered there, and filled the room, sitting, lolling, and lying upon the benches. The father of the lost child, almost a stranger to most of the searchers, took his place at the teacher's desk, and confronted his accusers.

It was plain, direct work. Here were a hundred men who had exhausted all known means of finding the lost boy; and more than fifty of them had said in effect to the man before them, "We think you killed him." All were looking at John: he rose up, and, facing the crowd with a dauntless eye, he made a speech.

If this were a story told by Homer or Herodotus, I suppose John's speech would figure as a wonderful piece of eloquence; for a man never had a grander opportunity to try his strength in persuading others than John had. But in fact there was nothing grand about the matter, except that here was a straightforward man with nerves of steel, who had been "hard hit," as Dan said, by the loss of his boy, and was now repelling with courage, and almost scorn, a thrust that might have killed a weaker man.

His speech was grammatically correct, cool, deliberate, and dignified. He said he had no knowledge of the black-hearted man who had originated so cruel a suspicion at such a time, and he did not wish to know who he was. He asked his hearers to consider how entirely without support in the known facts of the case the accusations were that had been suggested against him. It was a purely gratuitous assumption, with not a particle of evidence of any kind to establish it. He had understood that he was supposed to have killed his child in anger, and then concealed the body. Such a thing could not have happened with him as killing his own child or any other child in that way; and, if it had so happened, he would not have concealed it. He only wished to brand this creation of some vile man, there present probably, as a lie. That was all he had to say upon that point.

In continuing his speech, when he alluded to what he had suffered in losing the boy he loved the best of any thing on earth, there was a twitching of the muscles of his face, which, however he instantly controlled as unworthy of him. He closed his speech by appealing to his friends, who had known him long and well, to come forward at this time, and testify to his integrity.

As he ceased, the men rose up from the benches, and conversed together freely of the probabilities about John. A group of three or four gathered around him, and, placing their hands upon his shoulders, told the crowd that they had known John for twenty years, and that he was incapable of murder, or perfidy, or deceit, and as honest a man as could be found in the county.

It was decided not to search any farther that day, as there was no prospect now that Willie would be found alive. The men went home, agreeing to come again after three days, by which time the sleet and light snow that had fallen would have melted, and search for the body might be successfully made.

John went to his house. As he met his afflicted family, and realized that little Willie was now gone, that the search was given up, and his child was dead, his Spartan firmness yielded, and he wept such tears as strong, proud men weep when broken on the wheel of life. The last cruel stab at his moral nature and integrity hurt hard. He was a pure, upright man, a church-member, and without reproach.

As the three days were passing away that were to elapse before the search for the body should begin, it became apparent in the community that John's Homeric speech had done no good. The wise heads of Whiskey Hollow declared, that at the next search there would be, first of all, a thorough overhauling about the immediate premises. Their suspicions found some favor in the community. Some were discussing indignantly and some with tolerance, the probability of John's guilt. Even good Deacon Beezman, a magistrate who "lived out on the main road," and who was supposed to carry in his own person at least half of the integrity and intelligence of his neighborhood, declared that he would not spend more of his precious time in searching for the boy. He made it the chief point in the case that John "acted guilty." He had noticed that this rustic Spartan sat in his house, and read his newspaper with apparent interest, as in ordinary times, on the day of the last search; and this indifference was evidence of his guilt. It was apparent that any color of proof, if there had been any such thing, might have served as a pretence for an arrest of the afflicted father.

The morning appointed as the time to seek for the body came. The excitement was high; and men came from great distances to join in the exploration.

Eight miles away, up across the river that flowed through the forest, dwelt Logan Bill, a hunter. At an early hour he left his cabin, and took his course down the stream toward the gathering-point. There was an April sun shining; but in the wilderness solitudes it was cold and dreary. He kept along the margin of the stream to avoid the tangle of brush and fallen trees.

At nine o'clock, Logan was still three miles from John's clearing. He was passing through a hollow where the black spruce and pine made the forest gloomy. He came upon a bundle of clothing; he turned it over: it was Willie!

And thus alone in the wilderness Logan solved the mystery. Through three miles of trackless forest, under the sombre, sighing trees of the great woods, through the fog and falling rain and snow, the child had struggled on, feeling its way in the night along the margin of the river, until it grew weak and sick, and fell and died.

There was a choking in Logan's throat as he lifted the cold little body, and carried it onward down the stream, and noted the places where the infant must have climbed and scrambled in its little battle for life. It was a strange two hours to him as he bore the pure, beautiful, frozen corpse toward the settlement.

At eleven o'clock he reached the clearing. He saw the scattered groups of men gathered about John's house and barn. Some of the men seemed to be searching the barn to find the body of the boy they believed to be murdered. Logan felt his frame tremble, and his temples throb, realizing as he did the weight of life and death wrapped in the burden that he bore. He spoke no word, and made no gesture, but, holding the dead child in his arms, marched directly past the barn to the door-yard, and up in front of the house. There he stopped, and stood and looked with agitated face at the farmhouse door.

The shock of Logan's sudden coming was so great that no one said, "The body is found;" but all the men stopped talking, and some, pale and agitated, gathered in a close huddle around Logan, and looked at the little, white, frosted face, and in hushed tones asked where Logan had found the body.

A blanket was brought, and spread upon a dry place in the yard, and Logan laid his little burden upon it.

John came out, and approached the spot where his little Willie was lying. There was a deeper hush as the crowd made way for the father; and the rough men, some of whom were now crying, looked hard at John "to see how he would take it." John stood and gazed, unmoved and lionlike: not a muscle of his strong face quivered as he saw his boy. He called in a tone of authority for his family to come, and said to his wife in a clear, calm voice, as she came trembling, weeping, fainting, "Mother, look upon your son."

He turned, and surveyed the crowd with the same dauntless eye he had shown in making his Homeric speech at the schoolhouse. To some of the company that eye was now a dagger.

John was cool, calm, and polite. He uttered no reproach, and was kind in his words to all. A half-hour passed. The crowd went away in groups, discussing the amazing wonder, "how ever it could be that such a little feller as Willie could have got so far away from the house."

The next day religious services were held, and in the afternoon little Willie was laid to rest upon a sunny knoll. John wept at the grave. A poisoned arrow was drawn from the strong man's heart, and a great grief was there in its stead.

CONSTANCE FENIMORE WOOLSON

★　★　★

A grandniece of James Fenimore Cooper, Constance Fenimore Woolson (1840-1894) followed first in the footsteps of the romancer and of Bret Harte, but, with ever-deepening insight into social problems, later adopted the technique of Henry James. Unlike the earlier local colorists Miss Woolson chose many areas for fictional representation: Tuscarawas County, Ohio; Mackinac Island, Michigan; the Appalachian Highlands of Tennessee and Western North Carolina; the rice lands of South Carolina; Florida; and Italy. To precise geographical descriptions she added romantic action, often concerning newcomers to the area, the natives serving as colorful background. Her work roughly corresponded to her place of residence. Born in New Hampshire, she grew up in Cleveland, summered at Mackinac Island, removed to the South, and after 1879 resided in Europe. Her best story collections are *Castle Nowhere: Lake-Country Sketches* (1875), *Rodman the Keeper: Southern Sketches* (1880), and *The Front Yard, and Other Italian Stories* (1895). Her best novels are *For the Major* (1883) and *East Angels* (1886).

★　★　★

Solomon

MIDWAY in the eastern part of Ohio lies the coal country; round-topped hills there begin to show themselves in the level plain, trending back from Lake Erie; afterwards rising higher and higher, they stretch away into Pennsylvania and are dignified by the name of Alleghany Mountains. But no names have they in their Ohio birthplace, and little do the people care for them, save as storehouses for fuel. The roads lie along the slow-moving streams, and the farmers ride slowly over them in their broad-wheeled wagons, now and then passing dark holes in the bank from whence come little carts into the sunshine, and men, like *silhouettes*, walking behind them, with glow-worm lamps fastened in their hat-bands. Neither farmers nor miners glance up towards the hill-tops; no doubt they consider them useless mounds, and, were it not for the coal, they would envy their neighbors of the grain-country, whose broad, level fields stretch unbroken through Central Ohio; as, however, the canal-boats go away full, and long lines of coal-cars go away full, and every man's coal-shed is full, and money comes back from the great iron-mills of Pittsburgh, Cincinnati, and Cleveland, the coal country, though unknown in a picturesque point of view, continues to grow rich and prosperous.

Yet picturesque it is, and no part more so than the valley where stands the village of the quaint German Community on the banks of the slow-moving Tuscarawas River. One October day we left the lake behind us and journeyed inland, following the water-courses and looking forward for the first glimpse of rising ground; blue are the waters of Erie on a summer day, red and golden are its autumn sunsets, but so level, so deadly level are its shores that, at times, there comes a longing for the sight of distant hills. Hence our journey. Night found us still in the "Western Reserve": Ohio has some queer names of her own for portions of her territory, the "Fire Lands," the "Donation Grant," the "Salt Section," the "Refugee's Tract," and the "Western Reserve" are names well known, although not found on the maps. Two days more and we came into the coal country; near by were the "Moravian Lands," and at the end of the last day's ride we crossed a yellow bridge over a stream called the "One-Leg Creek."

"I have tried in vain to discover the origin of this name," I said, as we leaned out of the carriage to watch the red leaves float down the slow tide.

"Create one, then. A one-legged soldier, a farmer's pretty daughter, an elopement in a flat-bottomed boat, and a home upon this stream which yields its stores of catfish for their support," suggested Erminia.

"The original legend would be better than that if we could only find it, for real life is always better than fiction," I answered.

"In real life we are all masked; but in fiction the author shows the faces as they are, Dora."

"I do not believe we are all masked, Erminia. I can read my friends like a printed page."

"O, the wonderful faith of youth!" said Erminia, retiring upon her seniority.

Presently the little church on the hill came into view through a vista in the trees. We passed the mill and its flowing race, the black-smith's shop, the great grass meadow, and drew up in front of the quaint hotel where the trustees allowed the world's people, if unin-quisitive and decorous, to remain in the Community for short periods of time, on the payment of three dollars per week for each person. This village was our favorite retreat, our little hiding-place in the hill-country; at that time it was almost as isolated as a solitary island, for the Community owned thousands of outlying acres and held no intercourse with the surrounding townships. Content with their own, unmindful of the rest of the world, these Germans grew steadily richer and richer, solving quietly the problem of co-operative labor, while the French and Americans worked at it in vain with news-papers, orators, and even cannon to aid them. The members of the Community were no ascetic anchorites; each tiled roof covered a home with a thrifty mother and train of grave little children, the girls in short-waisted gowns, kerchiefs, and frilled caps, and the boys in tailed coats, long-flapped vests, and trousers, as soon as they were able to totter. We liked them all, we liked the life; we liked the mountain-high beds, the coarse, snowy linen, and the remarkable counterpanes; we liked the cream-stewed chicken, the Käse-lab, and fresh butter but, best of all, the hot bretzels for breakfast. And let not the hasty city imagination turn to the hard, salty, sawdust cake in the shape of a broken-down figure eight which is served with lager-beer in saloons and gardens. The Community bretzel was of a deli-cate flaky white in the inside, shading away into a golden-brown crust of crisp involutions, light as a feather, and flanked by little pats of fresh, unsalted butter and a deep-blue cup wherein the coffee was hot, the cream yellow, and the sugar broken lumps from the old-fashioned loaf, now alas! obsolete.

We stayed among the simple people and played at shepherdesses and pastorellas; we adopted the hours of the birds, we went to church on Sunday and sang German chorals as old as Luther. We even played at work to the extent of helping gather apples, eating the best, and riding home on top of the loaded four-horse wains. But one day we heard of a new diversion, a sulphur-spring over the hills about two miles from the hotel on land belonging to the Com-munity; and, obeying the fascination which earth's native medicines exercise over all earth's children, we immediately started in search of the nauseous spring. The road wound over the hill, past one of the apple orchards, where the girls were gathering the red fruit, and then down a little declivity where the track branched off to the Community coal-mine; then a solitary stretch through the thick woods, a long hill with a curve, and at the foot a little dell with a patch of meadow, a brook, and a log-house with overhanging roof, a forlorn house unpainted and desolate. There was not even the blue door which enlivened many of the Community dwellings. "This looks like the huts of the Black Forest," said Erminia. "Who would have supposed that we should find such an antique in Ohio!"

"I am confident that it was built by the M.B.'s," I replied. "They tramped, you know, extensively through the State, burying axes and leaving every now and then a mastodon behind them."

"Well, if the Mound-Builders selected this site they showed good taste," said Erminia, refusing, in her afternoon indolence, the argumentum nonsensicum with which we were accustomed to enliven our conversation. It was, indeed, a lovely spot,—the little meadow, smooth and bright as green velvet, the brook chattering over the pebbles, and the hills, gay in red and yellow foliage, rising abruptly on all sides. After some labor we swung open the great gate and entered the yard, crossed the brook on a mossy plank, and followed the path through the grass towards the lonely house. An old shepherd-dog lay at the door of a dilapidated shed like a block-house which had once been a stable; he did not bark, but rising slowly, came along beside us,—a large gaunt animal that looked at us with such melancholy eyes that Erminia stooped to pat him. Erminia had a weakness for dogs; she herself owned a wild beast of the dog kind that went by the name of the "Emperor Trajan," and, accompanied by this dignitary, she was accustomed to stroll up the avenues of C——, lost in maiden meditations.

We drew near the house and stepped up on the sunken piazza, but no signs of life appeared. The little loophole windows were pasted over with paper, and the plank door had no latch or handle. I knocked, but no one came. "Apparently it is a haunted house, and that dog is the spectre," I said, stepping back.

"Knock three times," suggested Erminia; "that is what they always do in ghost-stories."

"Try it yourself. My knuckles are not cast-iron."

Erminia picked up a stone and began tapping on the door. "Open sesame," she said, and it opened.

Instantly the dog slunk away to his block-house and a woman

confronted us, her dull face lighting up as her eyes ran rapidly over our attire from head to foot. "Is there a sulphur-spring here?" I asked. "We would like to try the water."

"Yes, it's here fast enough in the back hall. Come in, ladies; I'm right proud to see you. From the city, I suppose?"

"From C——," I answered; "we are spending a few days in the Community."

Our hostess led the way through the little hall, and throwing open a back door pulled up a trap in the floor, and there we saw the spring,—a shallow well set in stones, with a jar of butter cooling in its white water. She brought a cup, and we drank. "Delicious," said Erminia. "The true, spoiled-egg flavor! Four cups is the minimum allowance, Dora."

"I reckon it's good for the insides," said the woman, standing with arms akimbo and staring at us. She was a singular creature, with large black eyes, Roman nose, and a mass of black hair tightly knotted on the top of her head, but thin, pinched, and gaunt; her yellow forehead was wrinkled with a fixed frown, and her thin lips drawn down in permanent discontent. Her dress was a shapeless linsey-woolsey gown, and home-made list slippers covered her long, lank feet. "Be that the fashion?" she asked, pointing to my short, closely-fitting walking-dress.

"Yes," I answered; "do you like it?"

"Well, it does for you, sis, because you're so little and peaked-like, but it wouldn't do for me. The other lady, now, don't wear nothing like that; is she even with the style, too?"

"There is such a thing as being above the style, madam," replied Erminia, bending to dip up glass number two.

"Our figgers is a good deal alike," pursued the woman; "I reckon that fashion 'ud suit me best."

Willowy Erminia glanced at the stick-like hostess. "You do me honor," she said suavely. "I shall consider myself fortunate, madam, if you will allow me to send you patterns from C——. What are we if not well dressed?"

"You have a fine dog," I began hastily, fearing lest the great, black eyes should penetrate the sarcasm; "what is his name?"

"A stupid beast! He's none of mine; belongs to my man."

"Your husband?"

"Yes, my man. He works in the coal-mine over the hill."

"You have no children?"

"Not a brat. Glad of it, too."

"You must be lonely," I said, glancing around the desolate house.

To my surprise, suddenly the woman burst into a flood of tears, and sinking down on the floor she rocked from side to side, sobbing, and covering her face with her bony hands.

"What can be the matter with her?" I said in alarm, and, in my agitation, I dipped up some sulphur-water and held it to her lips.

"Take away the smelling stuff,—I hate it!" she cried, pushing the cup angrily from her.

Erminia looked on in silence for a moment or two, then she took off her neck-tie, a bright-colored Roman scarf, and threw it across the trap into the woman's lap. "Do me the favor to accept that trifle, madam," she said, in her soft voice.

The woman's sobs ceased as she saw the ribbon; she fingered it with one hand in silent admiration, wiped her wet face with the skirt of her gown, and then suddenly disappeared into an adjoining room, closing the door behind her.

"Do you think she is crazy?" I whispered.

"O, no; merely pensive."

"Nonsense, Erminia! But why did you give her that ribbon?"

"To develop her aesthetic taste," replied my cousin, finishing her last glass, and beginning to draw on her delicate gloves.

Immediately I began gulping down my neglected dose; but so vile was the odor that some time was required for the operation, and in the midst of my struggles our hostess reappeared. She had thrown on an old dress of plaid delaine, a faded red ribbon was tied over her head, and around her sinewed throat reposed the Roman scarf pinned with a glass brooch.

"Really, madam, you honor us," said Erminia gravely.

"Thankee, marm. It's so long since I've had on anything but that old bag, and so long since I've seen anything but them Dutch girls over to the Community, with their wooden shapes and wooden shoes, that it sorter come over me all 't oncet what a miserable life I've had. You see, I ain't what I looked like; now I've dressed up a bit I feel more like telling you that I come of good Ohio stock, without a drop of Dutch blood. My father, he kep' a store in Sandy, and I had everything I wanted until I must needs get crazy over painting Sol at the Community. Father, he wouldn't hear to it, and so I ran away; Sol, he turned out good for nothing to work, and so here I am, yer see, in spite of all his pictures making me out the Queen of Sheby."

"Is your husband an artist?" I asked.

"No, miss. He's a coal-miner, he is. But he used to like to paint me all sorts of ways. Wait, I'll show yer." Going up the rough stairs that led into the attic, the woman came back after a moment with a number of sheets of drawing-paper which she hung up along the walls with pins for our inspection. They were all portraits of the same face, with brick-red cheeks, enormous black eyes, and a profusion of shining black hair hanging over plump white shoulders; the costumes were various, but the faces were the same. I gazed in silence, seeing no likeness to anything earthly. Erminia took out her glasses and scanned the pictures slowly.

"Yourself, madam, I perceive," she said, much to my surprise.

"Yes, 'm, that's me," replied our hostess, complacently. "I never was like those yellow-haired girls over to the Community. Sol allers said my face was real rental."

"Rental?" I repeated, inquiringly.

"Oriental, of course," said Erminia. "Mr.—Mr. Solomon is quite right. May I ask the names of these characters, madam?"

"Queen of Sheby, Judy, Ruth, Esthy, Po-co-hon-tus, Goddessaliberty, Sunset, and eight Octobers, them with the grapes. Sunset's the one with the red paint behind it like clouds."

"Truly, a remarkable collection," said Erminia. "Does Mr. Solomon devote much time to his art?"

"No, not now. He couldn't make a cent out of it, so he's took to digging coal. He painted all them when we was first married, and he went a journey all the way to Cincinnati to sell 'em. First, he was going to buy me a silk dress and some ear-rings, and, after that, a farm. But pretty soon, home he come on a canal-boat, without a shilling, and a bringing all the pictures back with him! Well, then he tried most everything, but he never could keep to any one trade, for he'd just as lief quit work in the middle of the forenoon and go to painting; no boss 'll stand that, you know. We kep' a going down, and I had to sell the few things my father give me when he found I was married whether or no,—my chany, my feather-beds, and my nice clothes, piece by piece. I held on to the big looking-glass for four years, but at last it had to go, and then I just gave up and put on a linsey-woolsey gown. When a girl's spirit's once broke, she don't care for nothing, you know; so, when the Community offered to take Sol back as coal-digger, I just said, 'Go,' and we come." Here she tried to smear the tears away with her bony hands, and gave a low groan.

"Groaning probably relieves you," observed Erminia.

"Yes, 'm. It's kinder company like, when I'm all alone. But you see it's hard on the prettiest girl in Sandy to have to live in this lone lorn place. Why, ladies, you mightn't believe it, but I had open-work stockings, and feathers in my winter bunnets before I was married!" and the tears broke forth afresh.

"Accept my handkerchief," said Erminia; "it will serve your purpose better than fingers."

The woman took the dainty cambric and surveyed it curiously, held at arm's length. "Reg'lar thistle-down, now, ain't it?" she said; "and smells like a locust-tree blossom."

"Mr. Solomon, then, belonged to the Community?" I asked, trying to gather up the threads of the story.

"No, he didn't either; he's no Dutchman I reckon, he's a Lake County man, born near Painesville, he is."

"I thought you spoke as though he had been in the Community."

"So he had; he didn't belong, but he worked for 'em since he was a boy, did middling well, in spite of the painting, until one day, when he come over to Sandy on a load of wood and seen me standing at the door. That was the end of him," continued the woman, with an air of girlish pride; "he couldn't work no more for thinking of me."

"*Où la vanité va-t-elle se nicher?*" murmured Erminia, rising. "Come, Dora; it is time to return."

As I hastily finished my last cup of sulphur-water, our hostess followed Erminia towards the door. "Will you have your handkercher back, marm?" she said, holding it out reluctantly.

"It was a free gift, madam," replied my cousin; "I wish you a good afternoon."

"Say, will yer be coming again to-morrow?" asked the woman as I took my departure.

"Very likely; good-by."

The door closed, and then, but not till then, the melancholy dog joined us and stalked behind until we had crossed the meadow and reached the gate. We passed out and turned up the hill, but looking back we saw the outline of the woman's head at the upper window, and the dog's head at the bars, both watching us out of sight.

In the evening there came a cold wind down from the north, and the parlor, with its primitive ventilators, square openings in the side of the house, grew chilly. So a great fire of soft coal was built in the broad Franklin stove, and before its blaze we made good cheer, nor needed the one candle which flickered on the table behind us. Cider fresh from the mill, carded gingerbread, and new cheese crowned the scene, and during the evening came a band of singers, the young people of the Community, and sang for us the song of the Lorelei, accompanied by home-made violins and flageolets. At length we were left alone, the candle had burned out, the house door was barred, and the peaceful Community was asleep; still we two sat together with our feet upon the hearth, looking down into the glowing coals.

> "Ich weisz nicht was soll es bedeuten
> Dasz ich so traurig bin,"

I said, repeating the opening lines of the Lorelei; "I feel absolutely blue tonight."

"The memory of the sulphur-woman," suggested Erminia.

"Sulphur-woman! What a name!"

"Entirely appropriate, in my opinion."

"Poor thing! How she longed with a great longing for the finery of her youth in Sandy."

"I suppose from those barbarous pictures that she was originally in the flesh," mused Erminia; "at present she is but a bony outline."

"Such as she is, however, she has had her romance," I answered. "She is quite sure that there was one to love her; then let come what may, she has had her day."

"Misquoting Tennyson on such a subject!" said Erminia, with disdain.

"A man's a man for all that, and a woman's a woman too," I retorted. "You are blind, cousin, blinded with pride. That woman has had her tragedy, as real and bitter as any that can come to us."

"What have you to say for the poor man, then?" exclaimed Erminia, rousing to the contest. "If there is a tragedy at the sulphur-house, it belongs to the sulphur-man, not the sulphur-woman."

"He is not a sulphur-man, he is a coal-man; keep to your bearings, Erminia."

"I tell you," pursued my cousin earnestly, "that I pitied that unknown man with inward tears all the while I sat by that trap-door. Depend upon it, he had his dream, his ideal; and this country girl with her great eyes and wealth of hair represented the beautiful to his hungry soul. He gave his whole life and hope into her hands, and woke to find his goddess a common wooden image."

"Waste sympathy upon a coal-miner!" I said, imitating my cousin's former tone.

"If any one is blind, it is you," she answered, with gleaming eyes. "That man's whole history stood revealed in the selfish complainings of that creature. He had been in the Community from boyhood, therefore of course he had no chance to learn life, to see its art-treasures. He has been ship-wrecked, poor soul, hopelessly ship-wrecked."

"She too, Erminia."

"She!"

"Yes. If he loved pictures, she loved her chany and her feather-beds, not to speak of the big looking-glass. No doubt she had other lovers, and might have lived in a redbrick farm-house with ten un-opened front windows and a blistered door. The wives of men of genius are always to be pitied; they do not soar into the crowd of feminine admirers who circle round the husbands, and they are therefore called 'grubs,' 'worms of the earth,' 'drudges,' and other sweet titles."

"Nonsense," said Erminia, tumbling the arched coals into chaos with the poker; "it's after midnight, let us go up stairs." I knew very well that my beautiful cousin enjoyed the society of several poets, painters, musicians, and others of that ilk, without concerning her-self about their stay-at-home wives.

The next day the winds were out in battle array, howling over the Strasburg hills, raging up and down the river, and whirling the colored leaves wildly along the lovely road to the One-Leg Creek. Evidently there could be no rambling in the painted woods that day, so we went over to old Fritz's shop, played on his home-made piano, inspected the woolly horse who turned his crank patiently in an un-derground den, and set in motion all the curious little images which the carpenter's deft fingers had wrought. Fritz belonged to the Com-munity, and knew nothing of the outside world; he had a taste for mechanism, which showed itself in many labor-saving devices, and with it all he was the roundest, kindest little man, with bright eyes like a canary-bird.

"Do you know Solomon, the coal-miner?" asked Erminia, in her correct, well-learned German.

"Sol Bangs? Yes, I know him," replied Fritz, in his Württemberg dialect.

"What kind of a man is he?"

"Good for nothing," replied Fritz placidly.

"Why?"

"Wrong here"; tapping his forehead.

"Do you know his wife?" I asked.

"Yes."

"What kind of a woman is she?"

"Too much tongue. Women must not talk much."

"Old Fritz touched us both there," I said, as we ran back laugh-ing to the hotel through the blustering wind. "In his opinion, I sup-pose, we have the popular verdict of the township upon our two *protégés,* the sulphur-woman and her husband."

The next day opened calm, hazy, and warm, the perfection of Indian summer; the breezy hill was outlined in purple, and the trees glowed in rich colors. In the afternoon we started for the sulphur-spring without shawls or wraps, for the heat was almost oppressive; we loitered on the way through the still woods, gathering the tinted leaves, and wondering why no poet has yet arisen to celebrate in fit words the glories of the American autumn. At last we reached the turn whence the lonely house came into view, and at the bars we saw the dog awaiting us.

"Evidently the sulphur-woman does not like that melancholy animal," I said, as we applied our united strength to the gate.

"Did you ever know a woman of limited mind who liked a large dog?" replied Erminia. "Occasionally such a woman will fancy a small cur; but to appreciate a large, noble dog requires a large, noble mind."

"Nonsense with your dogs and minds," I said, laughing. "Wonderful! There is a curtain."

It was true. The paper had been removed from one of the windows, and in its place hung some white drapery, probably part of a sheet rigged as a curtain.

Before we reached the piazza the door opened, and our hostess appeared. "Glad to see yer, ladies," she said. "Walk right in this way to the keeping-room."

The dog went away to his block-house, and we followed the woman into a room on the right of the hall; there were three rooms, beside the attic above. An Old-World German stove of brick-work occupied a large portion of the space, and over it hung a few tins, and a clock whose pendulum swung outside; a table, a settle, and some stools completed the furniture; but on the plastered walls were two rude brackets, one holding a cup and saucer of figured china, and the other surmounted by a large bunch of autumn leaves, so beautiful in themselves and so exquisitely arranged that we crossed the room to admire them.

"Sol fixed 'em, he did," said the sulphur-woman; "he seen me setting things to rights, and he would do it. I told him they was trash, but he made me promise to leave 'em alone in case you should call again."

"Madam Bangs, they would adorn a palace," said Erminia severely.

"The cup is pretty too," I observed, seeing the woman's eyes turn that way.

"It's the last of my chany," she answered, with pathos in her voice,— "the very last piece."

As we took our places on the settle we noticed the brave attire of our hostess. The delaine was there; but how altered! Flounces it had, skimped, but still flounces, and at the top was a collar of crochet cotton reaching nearly to the shoulders; the hair too was braided in imitation of Erminia's sunny coronet, and the Roman scarf did duty as a belt around the large flat waist.

"You see she tries to improve," I whispered, as Mrs. Bangs went into the hall to get some sulphur-water for us.

"Vanity," answered Erminia.

We drank our dose slowly, and our hostess talked on and on. Even I, her champion, began to weary of her complainings. "How dark it is!" said Erminia at last, rising and drawing aside the curtain. "See, Dora, a storm is close upon us."

We hurried to the door, but one look at the black cloud was enough to convince us that we should not reach the Community hotel before it would break, and somewhat drearily we returned to the keeping-room, which grew darker and darker, until our hostess was obliged to light a candle. "Reckon you'll have to stay all night; I'd like to have you, ladies," she said. "The Community ain't got nothing covered to send after you, except the old king's coach, and I misdoubt they won't let that out in such a storm, steps and all. When it begins to rain in this valley, it do rain, I can tell you; and from the way it's begun, 'twon't stop 'fore morning. You just let me send the Roarer over to the mine, he'll tell Sol; Sol can tell the Community folks, so they'll know where you be."

I looked somewhat aghast at this proposal, but Erminia listened to the rain upon the roof a moment, and then quietly accepted; she remembered the long hills of tenacious red clay, and her kid boots were dear to her.

"The Roarer, I presume, is some faithful kobold who bears your message to and from the mine," she said, making herself as comfortable as the wooden settle would allow.

The sulphur-woman stared. "Roarer's Sol's old dog," she answered, opening the door; "perhaps one of you will write a bit of a note for him to carry in his basket.—Roarer, Roarer!"

The melancholy dog came slowly in, and stood still while she tied a small covered basket around his neck.

Erminia took a leaf from her tablets and wrote a line or two with the gold pencil attached to her watch-chain.

"Well now, you do have everything handy, I do declare," said the woman, admiringly.

I glanced at the paper.

"MR. SOLOMON BANGS:—My cousin Theodora Wentworth and myself have accepted the hospitality of your house for the night. Will you be so good as to send tidings of our safety to the Community, and oblige,

"ERMINIA STUART."

The Roarer started obediently out into the rain-storm with his little basket; he did not run, but walked slowly, as if the storm was nothing compared to his settled melancholy.

"What a note to send to a coal-miner!" I said, during a momentary absence of our hostess.

"Never fear; it will be appreciated," replied Erminia.

"What is this king's carriage of which you spoke?" I asked, during the next hour's conversation.

"O, when they first come over from Germany, they had a sort of a king; he knew more than the rest, and he lived in that big brick house with dormel-windows and a cuperler, that stands next the garden. The carriage was hisn, and it had steps to let down, and curtains and all; they don't use it much now he's dead. They're a queer set anyhow! The women look like meal-sacks. After Sol seen me, he couldn't abide to look at 'em."

Soon after six we heard the great gate creak.

"That's Sol," said the woman, "and now of course Roarer'll come in and track all over my floor." The hall door opened and a shadow passed into the opposite room, two shadows,—a man and a dog.

"He's going to wash himself now," continued the wife; "he's always washing himself, just like a horse."

"New fact in natural history, Dora love," observed Erminia.

After some moments the miner appeared,—a tall, stooping figure with high forehead, large blue eyes, and long, thin, yellow hair; there was a singularly lifeless expression in his face, and a far-off look in his eyes. He gazed about the room in an absent way, as though he scarcely saw us. Behind him stalked the Roarer, wagging his tail slowly from side to side.

"Now then, don't yer see the ladies, Sol? Where's yer manners?" said his wife sharply.

"Ah,—yes,—good evening," he said vaguely. Then his wandering eyes fell upon Erminia's beautiful face, and fixed themselves there with strange intentness.

"You received my note, Mr. Bangs," said my cousin in her soft voice.

"Yes, surely. You are Erminia," replied the man, still standing in the centre of the room with fixed eyes. The Roarer laid himself down behind his master, and his tail, still wagging, sounded upon the floor with a regular tap.

"Now then, Sol, since you've come home, perhaps you'll entertain the ladies while I get supper," quoth Mrs. Bangs; and forthwith began a clatter of pans.

The man passed his long hand abstractedly over his forehead. "Eh," he said with long-drawn utterance,—"eh-h? Yes, my rose of Sharon, certainly, certainly."

"Then why·don't you do it?" said the woman, lighting the fire in the brick-stove.

"And what will the ladies please to do?" he answered, his eyes going back to Erminia.

"We will look over your pictures, sir," said my cousin, rising; "they are in the upper room, I believe."

A great flush rose in the painter's thin cheeks. "Will you," he said eagerly,—"will you? Come!"

"It's a broken-down old hole, ladies; Sol will never let me sweep it out. Reckon you'll be more comfortable here," said Mrs. Bangs, with her arms in the flour.

"No, no, my lily of the valley. The ladies will come with me; they will not scorn the poor room."

"A studio is always interesting," said Erminia, sweeping up the rough stairs behind Solomon's candle. The dog followed us, and laid himself down on an old mat, as though well accustomed to the place. "Eh-h, boy, you came bravely through the storm with the lady's note," said his master, beginning to light candle after candle. "See him laugh!"

"Can a dog laugh?" I asked.

"Certainly; look at him now. What is that but a grin of happy contentment? Don't the Bible say, 'grin like a dog'?"

"You seem much attached to the Roarer!"

"Tuscarora, lady, Tuscarora. Yes, I love him well. He has been with me through all, and he has watched the making of all my pictures; he always lies there when I paint."

By this time a dozen candles were burning on shelves and brackets, and we could see all parts of the attic studio. It was but a poor place, unfloored in the corners where the roof slanted down, and having no ceiling but the dark beams and thatch; hung upon the walls were the pictures we had seen, and many others, all crude and highly colored, and all representing the same face,—the sulphur-woman in her youth, the poor artist's only ideal. He showed us these one by one, handling them tenderly, and telling us, in his quaint language, all they symbolized. "This is Ruth, and denoteth the power of hope," he said. "Behold Judith, the queen of revenge. And this dear one is Rachel, for whom Jacob served seven years, and it seemed unto him but a day, so well he loved her." The light shone on his pale face, and we noticed the far-off look in his eyes, and the long, tapering fingers coming out from the hard-worked, broad palm. To me it was a melancholy scene, the poor artist with his daubs and the dreary attic.

But Erminia seemed eagerly interested; she looked at the staring pictures, listened to the explanations, and at last she said gently, "Let me show you something of perspective, and the part that shadows play in a pictured face. Have you any crayons?"

No; the man had only his coarse paints and lumps of charcoal; taking a piece of coal in her delicate hand my cousin began to work upon a sheet of drawing-paper attached to the rough easel. Solomon watched her intently, as she explained and demonstrated some of the rules of drawing, the lights and shades, and the manner of representing the different features and curves. All his pictures were full faces, flat and unshaded; Erminia showed him the power of the profile and the three-quarter view. I grew weary of watching them, and pressing my face against the little window gazed out into the night; steadily the rain came down and the hills shut us in like a well. I thought of our home in C——, and its bright lights, warmth, company, and life. Why should we come masquerading out among the Ohio hills at this late season? And then I remembered that it was because Erminia would come; she liked such expeditions, and from childhood I had always followed her lead. *"Dux nascitur,* etc., etc." Turning away from the gloomy night, I looked towards the easel again; Solomon's cheeks were deeply flushed, and his eyes shone like stars. The lesson went on, the merely mechanical hand explaining its art to the ignorant fingers of genius. Erminia had taken lessons all her life, but she had never produced an original picture, only copies.

At last the lesson was interrupted by a voice from below, "Sol, Sol, supper's ready!" No one stirred until, feeling some sympathy for the amount of work which my ears told me had been going on below, I woke up the two enthusiasts and took them away from the easel down stairs into the keeping-room, where a loaded table and a scarlet hostess bore witness to the truth of my surmise. Strange things we ate that night, dishes unheard of in towns, but not unpalatable. Erminia had the one china cup for her corn-coffee: her grand air always secured her such favors. Tuscarora was there and ate of the best, now and then laying his shaggy head on the table, and, as his master said, "smiling at us"; evidently the evening was his gala time. It was nearly nine when the feast was ended, and I immediately proposed retiring to bed, for, having but little art enthusiasm, I dreaded a vigil in that dreary attic. Solomon looked disappointed, but I ruthlessly carried off Erminia to the opposite room, which we afterwards suspected was the apartment of our hosts, freshened and set in order in our honor. The sound of the rain on the piazza roof lulled us soon to sleep, in spite of the strange surroundings; but more than once I woke and wondered where I was, suddenly remembering the lonely house in its lonely valley with a shiver of discomfort. The next morning we woke at our usual hour, but some time after the miner's departure; breakfast was awaiting us in the keeping-room, and our hostess said that an ox-team from the Community would come for us before nine. She seemed sorry to part with us, and refused any remuneration for our stay; but none the less did we promise ourselves to send some dresses and even ornaments from C——, to feed that poor, starving love of finery. As we rode away in the ox-cart, the Roarer looked wistfully after us through the bars; but his melancholy mood was upon him again, and he had not the heart even to wag his tail.

As we were sitting in the hotel parlor, in front of our soft coal fire in the evening of the following day, and discussing whether or no we should return to the city within the week, the old landlord entered without his broad-brimmed hat,—an unusual attention, since he was a trustee and a man of note in the Community, and removed his hat for no one nor nothing; we even suspected that he slept in it.

"You know Zolomon Barngs," he said slowly.

"Yes," we answered.

"Well, he's dead. Kilt in de mine." And putting on the hat, removed, we now saw, in respect for death, he left the room as suddenly as he had entered it. As it happened, we had been discussing the couple, I, as usual, contending for the wife, and Erminia, as usual, advocating the cause of the husband.

"Let us go out there immediately to see her, poor woman!" I said, rising.

"Yes, poor man, we will go to him!" said Erminia.

"But the man is dead, cousin."

"Then he shall at least have one kind, friendly glance before he is carried to his grave," answered Erminia quietly.

In a short time we set out in the darkness, and dearly did we have to pay for the night ride; no one could understand the motive of our going, but money was money, and we could pay for all peculiarities. It was a dark night, and the ride seemed endless as the oxen moved slowly on through the red clay mire. At last we reached the turn and saw the little lonely house with its upper room brightly lighted.

"He is in the studio," said Erminia; and so it proved. He was not dead, but dying; not maimed, but poisoned by the gas of the mine, and rescued too late for recovery. They had placed him upon the floor on a couch of blankets, and the dull-eyed Community doctor stood at his side. "No good, no good," he said; "he must die." And then, hearing of the returning cart, he left us, and we could hear the tramp of the oxen over the little bridge, on their way back to the village.

The dying man's head lay upon his wife's breast, and her arms supported him; she did not speak, but gazed at us with a dumb agony in her large eyes. Erminia knelt down and took the lifeless hand streaked with coal-dust in both her own. "Solomon," she said, in her soft, clear voice, "do you know me?"

The closed eyes opened slowly, and fixed themselves upon her face a moment; then they turned towards the window, as if seeking something.

"It's the picter he means," said the wife. "He sat up most all last night a doing it."

I lighted all the candles, and Erminia brought forward the easel; upon it stood a sketch in charcoal wonderful to behold,—the same face, the face of the faded wife, but so noble in its idealized beauty that it might have been a portrait of her glorified face in Paradise. It was a profile, with the eyes upturned,—a mere outline, but grand in conception and expression. I gazed in silent astonishment.

Erminia said, "Yes, I knew you could do it, Solomon. It is perfect of its kind." The shadow of a smile stole over the pallid face, and then the husband's fading gaze turned upward to meet the wild, dark eyes of the wife.

"It's you, Dorcas," he murmured; "that's how you looked to me, but I never could get it right before." She bent over him, and silently we watched the coming of the shadow of death; he spoke only once, "My rose of Sharon,"—and then in a moment he was gone, the poor artist was dead.

Wild, wild was the grief of the ungoverned heart left behind; she was like a mad-woman, and our united strength was needed to keep her from injuring herself in her frenzy. I was frightened, but Erminia's strong little hands and lithe arms kept her down until, exhausted, she lay motionless near her dead husband. Then we carried her down stairs and I watched by the bedside, while my cousin went back to the studio. She was absent some time, and then she came back to keep the vigil with me through the long, still night. At dawn the woman woke, and her face looked aged in the gray light. She was quiet, and took without a word the food we had prepared, awkwardly enough, in the keeping-room.

"I must go to him, I must go to him," she murmured, as we led her back.

"Yes," said Erminia, "but first, let me make you tidy. He loved to see you neat." And with deft, gentle touch she dressed the poor creature, arranging the heavy hair so artistically that, for the first time, I saw what she might have been, and understood the husband's dream.

"What is that?" I said, as a peculiar sound startled us.

"It's Roarer. He was tied up last night, but I suppose he's gnawed the rope," said the woman. I opened the hall door, and in stalked the great dog, smelling his way directly up the stairs.

"O, he must not go!" I exclaimed.

"Yes, let him go, he loved his master," said Erminia; "we will go too." So silently we all went up into the chamber of death.

The pictures had been taken down from the walls, but the wonderful sketch remained on the easel, which had been moved to the head of the couch where Solomon lay. His long, light hair was smooth, his face peacefully quiet, and on his breast lay the beautiful bunch of autumn leaves which he had arranged in our honor. It was a striking picture,—the noble face of the sketch above, and the dead face of the artist below. It brought to my mind a design I had once seen, where Fame with her laurels came at last to the door of the poor artist and gently knocked; but he had died the night before!

The dog lay at his master's feet, nor stirred until Solomon was carried out to his grave.

The Community buried the miner in one corner of the lonely little meadow. No service had they and no mound was raised to mark the spot, for such was their custom; but in the early spring we went down again into the valley, and placed a block of granite over the grave. It bore the inscription:—

SOLOMON.

He will finish his work in Heaven.

Strange as it may seem, the wife pined for her artist husband. We found her in the Community trying to work, but so aged and bent that we hardly knew her. Her large eyes had lost their peevish discontent, and a great sadness had taken the place.

"Seems like I couldn't get on without Sol," she said, sitting with us in the hotel parlor after work hours. "I kinder miss his voice, and all them names he used to call me; he got 'em out of the Bible, so they must have been good, you know. He always thought everything I did was right, and he thought no end of my good looks, too; I suppose I've lost 'em all now. He was mighty fond of me; nobody in all the world cares a straw for me now. Even Roarer wouldn't stay with me, for all I petted him; he kep' a going out to that meader and a lying by Sol, until, one day, we found him there dead. He just died of sheer loneliness, I reckon. I sha'n't have to stop long I know, because I keep a dreaming of Sol, and he always looks at me like he did when I first knew him. He was a beautiful boy when I first saw him on that load of wood coming into Sandy. Well, ladies, I must go. Thank you kindly for all you've done for me. And say, Miss Stuart, when I die you shall have that coal picter; no one else 'ud vally it so much."

Three months after, while we were at the sea-shore, Erminia received a long tin case, directed in a peculiar handwriting; it had been forwarded from C——, and contained the sketch and a note from the Community.

"E. STUART:—The woman Dorcas Bangs died this day. She will be put away by the side of her husband, Solomon Bangs. She left the enclosed picture, which we hereby send, and which please acknowledge by return of mail.
                                        "JACOB BOLL, *Trustee.*"

I unfolded the wrappings and looked at the sketch. "It is indeed striking," I said. "She must have been beautiful once, poor woman!"

"Let us hope that at least she is beautiful now, for her husband's sake, poor man!" replied Erminia.

Even then we could not give up our preferences.

Peter, the Parson

IN November, 1850, a little mining settlement stood forlornly on the shore of Lake Superior. A log dock ran out into the dark water; a roughly-built furnace threw a glare against the dark sky; several stamping mills kept up their monotonous tramping day and night;

and evil-minded saloons beset the steps on all sides. Back into the pine forest ran the white sand road leading to the mine, and on the right were clustered the houses, which were scarcely better than shanties, although adorned with sidling porches and sham-windowed fronts. Winter begins early in these high latitudes. Navigation was still open, for a scow with patched sails was coming slowly up the bay, but the air was cold, and the light snow of the preceding night clung unmelted on the north side of the trees. The pine forest had been burned away to make room for the village; blackened stumps rose everywhere in the weedy streets, and, on the outskirts of the clearing, grew into tall skeletons, bleached white without, but black and charred within—a desolate framing for a desolate picture. Everything was bare, jagged and unfinished; each poor house showed hasty makeshifts—no doors latched, no windows fitted. Pigs were the principal pedestrians. At four o'clock this cold November afternoon, the saloons, with their pine fires and red curtains, were by far the most cheerful spots in the landscape, and their ruddy invitations to perdition were not counterbalanced by a single opposing gleam, until the Reverend Herman Peters prepared his chapel for vespers.

Herman Warriner Peters was a slender little man, whose blue eyes, fair hair and unbearded face misled the observer into the idea of extreme youth. There was a boyishness in his air, or, rather, lack of air, and a nervous timidity in his manner, which stamped him as a person of no importance—one of those men who, not of sufficient consequence to be disliked, are simply ignored by a well-bred world, which pardons anything rather than insignificance. And if ignored by a well-bred world, what by an ill-bred? Society at Algonquin was worse than ill-bred, inasmuch as it had never been bred at all. Like all mining settlements, it esteemed physical strength the highest good, and next to that an undaunted demeanor and flowing vocabulary, designated admiringly as "powerful sassy." Accordingly it made unlimited fun of the Reverend Herman Warriner Peters, and derived much enjoyment from calling him "Peter," pretending to think it was his real name, and solemnly persisting in the mistake in spite of all the painstaking corrections of the unsuspecting little man.

The Reverend Herman wrapped himself in his thin old cloak and twisted a comforter around his little throat, as the clock warned him of the hour. He was not leaving much comfort behind him; the room was dreary and bare, without carpet, fire, or easy chair. A cot-bed, which sagged hopelessly, a wash-bowl set on a dry-goods box, flanked by a piece of bar-soap and a crash towel, a few pegs on the cracked wall, one wooden chair and his own little trunk completed the furniture. The Reverend Herman boarded with Mrs. Malone, and ate her streaked biscuit and fried meat without complaint. The woman could rise to yeast and a gridiron when the surveyors visited Algonquin, or when the directors of the iron company came up in the summer; but the streaked biscuit and fried steak were "good enough for the little parson, bless him!"

There were some things in the room, however, other than furniture, namely, a shelf full of religious books, a large and appalling picture of the crucifixion, and a cross six feet in height, roughly made of pine saplings, and fixed to the floor in a wooden block. There was also a small colored picture, with the words "Santa Margarita" inscribed beneath. The picture stood on a bracket fashioned of shingles, and below it hung a poor little vase filled with the last colored leaves.

"Ye only want the Howly Vargin now, to be all right, yer riverence," said Mrs. Malone, who was, in name at least, a Roman Catholic.

"All honor and affection are, no doubt, due to the Holy Mary," answered the Reverend Herman, nervously; "but the Anglican Church does not—at present—allow her claim to—to adoration." And he sighed.

"Why don't yer jest come right out now, and be a rale Catholic," said Mrs. Malone, with a touch of sympathy. "You're next door to it, and it's aisy to see yer aint happy in yer mind. If yer was a rale praste, now, with the coat and all, 'stead of being a make-believe, the boys 'ud respect yer more, and wouldn't notice yer soize so much. Or yer might go back to the cities (for I don't deny they do loike a big fist up here), and loikely enough yer could find aisy work there that 'ud suit yer."

"I like hard work, Mrs. Malone," said the little parson.

"But you're not fit for it, sir. You'll niver get on here if yer stay till judgment day. Why, yer aint got ten people, all told, belongin' to yer chapel, and you're here a year already!"

The Reverend Herman sighed again, but made no answer. He sighed now as he left his cold room and stepped out into the cold street. The wind blew as he made his way along between the stumps, carefully going round the pigs, who had selected the best places for their siestas. He held down his comforter with one bare hand; the other clutched the end of a row of books, which filled his thin arm from the shoulder down. He limped as he walked. An ankle had been cruelly injured some months previously; the wound had healed, but he was left permanently and awkwardly lame. At the time, the dastardly injury had roused a deep bitterness in the parson's heart, for grace and activity had been his one poor little bodily gift, his one small pride. The activity had returned, not the grace. But he had learned to limp bravely along, and the bitterness had passed away.

Lights shone comfortably from the Pine-Cone Saloon as he passed.

"Hallo! Here's Peter the Parson," sang out a miner, standing at the door; and forth streamed all the loungers to look at him.

"Say, Peter, come in and have a drop to warm yer," said one.

"Look at his poor little ribs, will yer?" said another, as his cloak blew out like a sail.

"Let him alone! He's going to have his preaching all to himself, as usual," said a third. "Them books is all the congregation *he* can get, poor little chap!"

The parson's sensitive ears heard every word. He quickened his steps, and, with his usual nervous awkwardness, stumbled and fell, dropping all the books, amid the jeering applause of the bystanders. Silently he rose and began collecting his load, the wind every now and then blowing his cloak over his head as he stooped, and his difficulties increased by the occasional gift of a potato full in the breast, and a flood of witty commentaries from the laughing group at the saloon door. As he picked up the last volume and turned away, a missile, deftly aimed, took off his hat, and sent it over a fence into a neighboring field. The parson hesitated, but as a small boy had already given chase, not to bring it back, but to send it further away, he abandoned the hat,—his only one,—and walked on among the stumps bare-headed, his thin hair blown about by the raw wind, and his blue eyes reddened with cold and grief.

The Episcopal Church of St. John and St. James was a rough little building, with recess-chancel, ill-set Gothic windows, and a half-finished tower. It owed its existence to the zeal of a director's wife, who herself embroidered its altar-cloth and book-marks, and sent thither the artificial flowers and candles which she dared not suggest at home; the poor Indians, at least, should not be deprived of them! The director's wife died, but left by will a pittance of two hundred dollars per annum towards the rector's salary. In her fancy she saw Algonquin, a thriving town, whose inhabitants believed in the Anglican succession, and sent their children to Sunday-school. In reality, Algonquin remained a lawless mining settlement, whose inhabitants believed in nothing, and whose children hardly knew what Sunday meant, unless it was more whisky than usual. The two hundred dollars and the chapel, however, remained fixed facts, and the Eastern directors, therefore, ordered a picturesque church to be delineated on their circulars, and themselves constituted a non-resident vestry. One or two young missionaries had already tried the field, failed, and gone away, but the present incumbent, who had equally tried and equally failed, remained.

On this occasion he unlocked the door and entered the little sanctuary. It was cold and dark, but he made no fire, for there was neither stove nor hearth. Lighting two candles,—one for the congregation and one for himself,—he distributed the books among the benches and the chancel, and dusted carefully the little altar, with its faded embroideries and flowers. Then he retired into the shed which served as a vestry-room, and in a few minutes issued forth, clad in his robes of office, and knelt at the chancel rail. There was no bell to summon the congregation, and no congregation to summon; but still he began in his clear voice, "Dearly beloved brethren," and continued on unwavering through the confession, the absolution, and the psalms, leaving a silence for the corresponding responses, and devoutly beginning the first lesson. In the midst of "Zephaniah" there was a slight noise at the door and a step sounded over the rough floor. The solitary reader did not raise his eyes, and, the lesson over, he bravely lifted up his mild tenor in the chant, "It is a good thing to give thanks unto the Lord, and to sing praises unto Thy name, O Most Highest." A girl's voice took up the air; the mild tenor dropped into its own part, and the two continued the service in a duet, spoken and sung, to its close. Then the minister retired, with his candle, to the shed, and, hanging up his surplice, patiently waited, pacing to and fro in the cold. Patiently waited; and for what? For the going away of the only friend he had in Algonquin.

The congregation lingered; its shawl must be refastened; indeed, it must be entirely refolded. Its hat must be retied, and the ribbons carefully smoothed. Still there was no sound from the vestry-room. It collected all the prayer-books, and piled them near the candle, making a separate journey for each little volume. Still no one. At last, with lingering step and backward glance, slowly it departed and carried its disappointed face homeward. Then Peter the Parson issued forth, lifted the careful pile of books with tender hand, and extinguishing the lights, went out bareheaded into the darkness. The vesper service of St. John and St. James was over.

After a hot, unwholesome supper the minister returned to his room and tried to read; but the candle flickered, the cold seemed to blur the book, and he found himself gazing at the words without taking in their sense. Then he began to read aloud, slowly walking up and down, and carrying the candle to light the page; but through all the learned sentences there still crept to the surface the miserable consciousness of bodily cold. "And mental, too, Heaven help me!" he thought. "But I cannot afford a fire at this season, and, indeed, it ought not to be necessary. This delicacy must be subdued; I will go out and walk." Putting on his cloak and comforter (O deceitful name!) he remembered that he had no hat. Would his slender store of money allow a new one? Unlocking his trunk, he drew out a thin purse hidden away among his few carefully folded clothes,—the poor trunk was but half full,—and counted its contents. The sum was pitifully small, and it must yet last many weeks. But a hat was necessary, whereas a fire was a mere luxury. "I must harden myself," thought the little parson sternly, as he caught himself shuddering with the cold; "this evil tendency to self-indulgence must and shall be crushed."

He went down towards the dock where stood the one store of Algonquin—stealing along in the darkness to hide his uncovered condition. Buying a hat, the poorest one there, from the Jew proprietor, he lingered a moment near the stove to warm his chilled hands. Mr. Marx, rendered good-natured by the bold cheat he had perpetrated, affably began a conversation.

"Sorry to see yer still limp bad. But it aint so hard as it would be if yer was a larger man. Yer see there aint much of yer to limp; that's one comfort. Hope business is good at yer chapel, and that Mrs. Malone gives yer enough to eat; yer don't look like it, though. The winter has sot in early, and times is hard." And did the parson know that "Brother Saul has come in from the mine, and is a-holding forth in the school-house this very minit?"

No; the parson did not know it. But he put on his new hat, whose moth-holes had been skillfully blackened over with ink, and turned towards the door.

"It's nothing to me, of course," continued Mr. Marx, with a liberal wave of his dirty hand; "all your religions are alike to me, I'm free to say. But I wonder yer and Saul don't work together, parson. Yer might do a heap of good if yer was to pull at the same oar, now."

The words echoed in the parson's ears as he walked down to the beach, the only promenade in Algonquin free from stumps. Could he do a "heap of good," by working with that ignorant, coarse, roaring brother, whose blatant pride, dirty shirt, and irreverent familiarity with all things sacred were alike distasteful, nay, horrible to his sensitive mind. Pondering, he paced the narrow strip of sand under the low bluff; but all his efforts did not suffice to quicken or warm his chilled blood. Nevertheless he expanded his sunken chest and drew in long breaths of the cold night air, and beat his little hands vigorously together, and ran to and fro. "Aha!" he said to himself, "this is glorious exercise." And then he went home, colder than ever; it was his way thus to make a reality of what ought to be.

Passing through one of the so-called streets, he saw a ruddy glow in front of the school-house; it was a pine-knot fire whose flaring summons had not been unheeded. The parson stopped a moment and warmed himself, glancing meanwhile furtively within where Brother Saul was holding forth in clarion tones to a crowded congregation; his words reached the listener's ear, and verified the old proverb. "There's brimstone and a fiery furnace for them as doubts the truth, I tell you. Prayin' out of a book—and flowers—and candles—and night-gownds 'stead of decent coats—for it's night-gownds they look like though they may call them surpluses," (applause from the miners,)—"won't do no good. Sech nonsense will never save souls. You've jest got to fall down on your knees and pray hard—hard— with groaning and roaring of the spirit—until you're as weak as a rag. Nothing else will do; nothing,—nothing."

The parson hurried away, shrinking (though unseen) from the rough finger pointed at him. Before he was out of hearing, a hymn sounded forth on the night breeze—one of those nondescript songs that belong to the border, a favorite with the Algonquin miners because of a swinging chorus wherein they roared out their wish to "die a-shouting," in company with all the kings and prophets of Israel, each one fraternally mentioned by name.

Reaching his room, the parson hung up his cloak and hat, and sat down quietly with folded hands. Clad in dressing gown and slippers, in an easy chair, before a bright fire, a reverie, thus, is the natural ending for a young man's day. But here the chair was hard and straight-backed, there was no fire, and the candle burned with a feeble, blue flame; the small figure in its limp black clothes, with its little gaitered feet pressed close together on the cold floor as if for warmth, its clasped hands, its pale face and blue eyes fixed on the blank expanse of the plastered wall, was pathetic in its patient discomfort. After a while a tear fell on the clasped hands and startled their coldness with its warmth. The parson brushed the token of weakness hastily away, and rising, threw himself at the foot of the large wooden cross with his arms clasping its base. In silence for many moments he lay thus prostrate; then, extinguishing the candle, he sought his poor couch. But later in the night, when all Algonquin slept, a crash of something falling was heard in the dark room followed by the sound of a scourge mercilessly used, and murmured Latin prayers, the old cries of penitence that rose during night-vigils from the monasteries of the Middle Ages. And why not English words? Was there not something of affectation in the use of these medieval phrases? Maybe so; but at least there was nothing affected in the stripes made by the scourge. The next morning all was as usual in the little room save that the picture of Santa Margarita was torn in twain, and the bracket and vase shattered to fragments on the floor below.

At dawn the parson rose, and after a conscientious bath in the tub of icy water brought in by his own hands the previous evening, he started out with his load of prayer-books, his face looking haggard and blue in the cold morning light. Again he entered the chapel, and having arranged the books and dusted the altar, he attired himself in his robes and began the service at half-past six precisely. "From the rising of the sun even unto the going down of the same," he read, and in truth the sun was just rising. As the evening prayer was "vespers," so this was "matins" in the parson's mind. He had his "vestments" too, of various ritualistic styles, and washed them himself, ironing them out afterwards with fear and difficulty in Mrs. Malone's disorderly kitchen, poor little man! No hand turned the latch, no step came across the floor this morning; the parson had the service all to himself, and, as it was Friday, he went through the Litany, omitting nothing, and closing with a hymn. Then, gathering up his books, he went home to breakfast.

"How peaked yer do look, sir," exclaimed ruddy Mrs. Malone, as she handed him a cup of muddy coffee. "What, no steak? Do, now; for I aint got nothin' else. Well, if yer won't—but there's nothin' but the biscuit, then. Why, even Father O'Brien himself 'lows meat for the sickly, Friday or no Friday."

"I am not sickly, Mrs. Malone," replied the little parson with dignity.

A young man with the figure of an athlete sat at the lower end of the table, tearing the tough steak voraciously with his strong teeth, chewing audibly, and drinking with a gulping noise. He paused as the parson spoke, and regarded him with wonder, not unmixed with contempt.

"You aint sickly?" he repeated. "Well, if you aint, then I'd like to know who is, that's all."

"Now, you jest eat your breakfast, Steve, and let the parson alone," interposed Mrs. Malone. "Sorry to see that little picture all tore, sir," she continued, turning the conversation in her blundering good-nature. "It was a moighty pretty picture, and looked uncommonly like Rosie Ray."

"It was a copy of an Italian painting, Mrs. Malone," the parson hastened to reply; "Santa Margarita."

"Oh, I dare say; but it looked iver so much like Rosie for all that."

A deep flush had crossed the parson's pale face. The athlete saw it, and muttered to himself angrily, casting surly sidelong glances up the table, and breathing hard; the previous evening he had happened to pass the Chapel of Saint John and Saint James as its congregation of one was going in the door.

After two hours spent in study, the parson went out to visit the poor and sick of the parish; all were poor, and one was sick, the child of an Englishwoman, a miner's wife. The mother, with a memory of her English training, dusted a chair for the minister, and dropped a courtesy, as he seated himself by the little bed; but she seemed embarrassed, and talked volubly of anything and everything save the child. The parson listened to the unbroken stream of words while he stroked the boy's soft cheek, and held the wasted little hand in his. At length he took a small bottle from his pocket, and looked around for a spoon; it was a pure and delicate cordial which he had often given to the sick child to sustain its waning strength.

"Oh, if you please, sir,—indeed, I don't feel sure that it does Harry any good. Thank you for offering it so free—but—but, if you'd just as lieve—I—I'd rather not, sir, if you please, sir."

The parson looked up in astonishment; the costly cordial had robbed him of many a fire.

"Why don't you tell the minister the truth," called out a voice from the inner room, the harsh voice of the husband. "Why don't you say right out that Brother Saul was here last night, and prayed over the child, and give it some of his own medicine, and telled you not to touch the parson's stuff; he said it was pizen, he did."

The parson rose, cut to the heart. He had shared his few dimes with this woman, and had hoped much from her on account of her early church-training. On Sunday she had been one of the few who came to the chapel, and when, during the summer, she was smitten with fever, he had read over her the prayers from "the Visitation of the Sick;" he had baptized this child now fading away, and had loved the little fellow tenderly, taking pleasure in fashioning toys for his baby hands, and saving for him the few cakes of Mrs. Malone's table.

"I didn't mean to have Saul—I didn't indeed, sir," said the mother, putting her apron to her eyes. "But Harry he was so bad last night, and the neighbors sort o' persuaded me into it. Brother Saul does pray so powerful strong, sir, that it seems as though it must do some good some way; and he's a very comfortable talker too, there's no denying that. Still I didn't mean it, sir; and I hope you'll forgive me."

"There is nothing to forgive," replied the parson gently; and, leaving his accustomed coin on the table, he went away.

Wandering at random through the pine forest, unable to overcome the dull depression at his heart, he came suddenly upon a large bull-dog; the creature, one of the ugliest of its kind, eyed him quietly, with a slow wrinkling of the sullen upper lip.

The parson visibly trembled.

" 'Fraid, are ye?" called out a voice, and the athlete of the break-fast-table showed himself.

"Call off your dog, please, Mr. Long."

"He aint doin' nothin', parson. But you're at liberty to kick him, if you like," said the man, laughing as the dog snuffed stealthily around the parson's gaiters. The parson shifted his position; the dog followed. He stepped aside; so did the dog. He turned and walked away with a determined effort at self-control; the dog went closely behind, brushing his ankles with his ugly muzzle. He hurried; so did the dog. At last, overcome with the nervous physical timidity which belonged to his constitution, he broke into a run, and fled as if for life, hearing the dog close behind and gaining with every step. The jeering laugh of the athlete followed him through the pine tree aisles, but he heeded it not, and when at last he spied a log-house on one side he took refuge within like a hunted hare, breathless and trembling. An old woman smoking a pipe was its only occupant. "What's the matter?" she said. "Oh, the dog?" And, taking a stick of wood, she drove the animal from the door, and sent him fleeing back to his master. The parson sat down by the hearth to recover his composure.

"Why, you're most frightened to death, aint yer?" said the old woman, as she brushed against him to make up the fire. "You're all of a tremble. I wouldn't stray so far from home if I was you, child."

Her vision was imperfect, and she took the small, cowering figure for a boy.

The minister went home.

After dinner, which he did not eat, as the greasy dishes offended his palate, he shut himself up in his room to prepare his sermon for the coming Sunday. It made no difference whether there would be any one to hear it or not, the sermon was always carefully written, and carefully delivered, albeit short, according to the ritualistic usage, which esteems the service all, the sermon nothing. His theme on this occasion was "The General Councils of the Church," and the sermon, an admirable production of its kind, would have been esteemed, no doubt, in English Oxford, or in the General Theological Seminary of New York City. He wrote earnestly and ardently, deriving a keen enjoyment from the work; the mechanical part also was exquisitely finished, the clear sentences standing out like the work of a sculptor. Then came vespers; and the congregation this time was composed of two, or, rather, three persons; the girl, the owner of the dog, and the dog himself. The man entered during service with a noisy step, managing to throw over a bench, coughing, humming, and talking to his dog; half of the congregation was evidently determined upon mischief. But the other half rose with the air of a little queen, crossed the intervening space with an open prayer-book, gave it to the man, and, seating herself near by, fairly awed him into good behavior. Rose Ray was beautiful; and the lion lay at her feet. As for the dog, with a wave of her hand she ordered him out, and the beast humbly withdrew. It was noticeable that the parson's voice gained strength as the dog disappeared.

"I aint going to stand by and see it, Rosie," said the man, as, the service over, he followed the girl into the street. "That puny little chap!"

"He cares nothing for me," answered the girl quickly.

"He shan't have a chance to care, if I know myself. You're free to say 'no' to me, Rosie, but you aint free to say 'yes' to him. A regular coward! That's what he is. Why, he ran away from my dog this very afternoon—ran like he was scared to death!"

"You set the dog on him, Steve."

"Well, what if I did? He needn't have run; any other man would have sent the beast flying."

"Now, Steve, do promise me that you won't tease him any more," said the girl, laying her hand upon the man's arm as he walked by her side. His face softened.

"If he had any spirit he'd be ashamed to have a girl beggin' for him not to be teased. But never mind that; I'll let him alone fast enough, Rosie, if you will too."

"If I will," repeated the girl, drawing back, as he drew closer to her side; "what can you mean?"

"Oh, come now! You know very well you're always after him— a-goin' to his chapel where no one else goes hardly—a-listenin' to his preachin'—and a-havin' your picture hung up in his room."

It was a random shaft, sent carelessly, more to finish the sentence with a strong point than from any real belief in the athlete's mind.

"What!"

"Leastways so Mrs. Malone said. I took breakfast there this morning."

The girl was thrown off her guard, her whole face flushed with joy, she could not for the moment hide her agitation. "My picture!" she murmured, and clasped her hands. The light from the Pine-Cone crossed her face, and revealed the whole secret; Steven Long saw it, and fell into a rage. After all, then, she did love the puny parson!

"Let him look out for himself, that's all," he muttered with a fierce gesture, as he turned towards the saloon door. (He felt a sudden thirst for vengeance, and for whisky.) "I'll be even with him, and I won't be long about it neither. You'll never have the little parson alive, Rose Ray! He'll be found missin' some fine mornin', and nobody will be to blame but you either." He disappeared, and the girl stood watching the spot where his dark, angry face had been. After a time she went slowly homeward, troubled at heart; there was neither law nor order at Algonquin, and not without good cause did she fear.

The next morning, as the parson was coming from his solitary matin-service through thick-falling snow, this girl met him, slipped a note into his hand, and disappeared like a vision. The parson went homeward, carrying the folded paper under his cloak pressed close to his heart; "I am only keeping it dry," he murmured to himself. This was the note:

"Respected Sir:

"I must see you, you air in danger. Please come to the Grotter this afternoon at three and I remain yours respectful,

"Rose Ray."

The Reverend Herman Warriner Peters read these words over and over; then he went to breakfast, but ate nothing, and, coming back to his room, he remained the whole morning motionless in his chair. At first the red flamed in his cheek, but gradually it faded, and gave place to a pinched pallor; he bowed his head upon his hands, communed with his own heart, and was still. As the dinner-bell rang he knelt down on the cold hearth, made a little funeral pyre of the note torn into fragments, watched it slowly consume, and then, carefully collecting the ashes, he laid them at the base of the large cross.

At two o'clock he set out for the Grotto, a cave two miles from the village along the shore, used by the fishermen as a camp during the summer. The snow had continued falling, and now lay deep on the even ground; the pines were loaded with it, and everything was white save the waters of the bay, heaving sullenly, dark and leaden, as though they knew the icy fetters were nearly ready for them. The parson walked rapidly along in his awkward, halting gait; overshoes he had none, and his cloak was but a sorry substitute for the blankets and skins worn by the miners. But he did not feel cold when he opened the door of the little cabin which had been built out in front of the cave, and found himself face to face with the beautiful girl who had summoned him there. She had lighted a fire of pine knots on the hearth, and set the fishermen's rough furniture in order; she had cushioned a chair-back with her shawl and heated a flat stone for a foot-warmer.

"Take this seat, sir," she said, leading him thither.

The parson sank into the chair and placed his old, soaked gaiters on the warm stone; but he said not one word.

"I thought perhaps you'd be tired after your long walk, sir," continued the girl, "and so I took the liberty of bringing something with me." As she spoke she drew into view a basket, and took from it delicate bread, chicken, cakes, preserved strawberries and a little tin coffee-pot which, set on the coals, straightway emitted a delicious fragrance; nothing was forgotten—cream, sugar, nor even snowy napkins.

The parson spoke not a word.

But the girl talked for both, as with flushed cheeks and starry eyes she prepared the tempting meal, using many pretty arts and graceful motions, using in short every power she possessed to charm the silent guest. The table was spread, the viands arranged, the coffee poured into the cup; but still the parson spoke not, and his blue eyes were almost stern as he glanced at the tempting array. He touched nothing.

"I thought you would have liked it all," said the girl at last, when she saw her little offerings despised. "I brought them all out myself— and I was so glad thinking you'd like them—and now—," her voice broke, and the tears flowed from her pretty, soft eyes. A great tenderness came over the parson's face.

"Do not weep," he said quickly. "See, I am eating. See, I am enjoying everything. It is all good, nay, delicious." And in his haste he partook of each dish, and lifted the coffee-cup to his lips. The girl's face grew joyous again, and the parson struggled bravely against his own enjoyment; in truth, what with the warm fire, the easy-chair, the delicate food, the fragrant coffee, and the eager, beautiful face before him, a sense of happiness came over him in long surges, and for the moment his soul drifted with the warm tide.

"You *do* like it, don't you?" said the girl with delight, as he slowly drank the fragrant coffee, his starved lips lingering over the delicious brown drops. Something in her voice jarred on the trained nerves and roused them to action again.

"Yes, I do like it—only too well," he answered; but the tone of his voice had altered. He pushed back his chair, rose, and began pacing to and fro in the shadow beyond the glow of the fire.

"Thou glutton body!" he murmured. "But thou shalt go empty for this." Then, after a pause, he said in a quiet, even tone, "You had something to tell me, Miss Ray."

The girl's face had altered; but rallying, she told her story earnestly —of Steven Long, his fierce temper, his utter lawlessness, and his threats.

"And why should Steven Long threaten me?" said the parson. "But you need not answer," he continued in an agitated voice. "Say to Steven Long—say to him," he repeated in louder tones, "that I shall never marry. I have consecrated my life to my holy calling."

There was a long silence; the words fell with crushing weight on both listener and speaker. We do not realize even our own deter-minations, sometimes, until we have told them to another. The girl rallied first; for she still hoped.

"Mr. Peters," she said, taking all her courage in her hands and coming towards him, "is it wrong to marry?"

"For me—it is."

"Why?"

"Because I am a priest."

"Are you a Catholic, then?"

"I am a Catholic, although not in the sense you mean. Mine is the true Catholic faith which the Anglican Church has kept pure from the errors of Rome, and mine it is to make my life accord with the high office I hold."

"Is it part of your high office to be cold—and hungry—and wretched?"

"I am not wretched."

"You are;—now, and at all times. You are killing yourself."

"No; else I had died long, long ago."

"Well, then, of what use is your poor life as you now live it, either to yourself or any one else? Do you succeed among the miners? How many have you brought into the church?"

"Not one."

"And yourself? Have you succeeded, so far, in making yourself a saint?"

"God knows I have not," replied the parson, covering his face with his hands as the questions probed his sore, sad heart. "I have failed in my work, I have failed in myself, I am of all men most miserable! —most miserable!"

The girl sprang forward and caught his arm, her eyes full of love's pity. "You know you love me," she murmured; "why fight against it? For I—I love you!"

What did the parson do?

He fell upon his knees, but not to her, and uttered a Latin prayer, short but fervid.

"All the kingdoms of the world and the glory of them," he murmured, "would not be to me so much as this!" Then he rose.

"Child," he said, "you know not what you do." And, opening the door, he went away into the snowy forest. But the girl's weeping voice called after him, "Herman, Herman." He turned; she had sunk upon the threshold. He came back and lifted her for a moment in his arms.

"Be comforted, Rosamond," he said tenderly. "It is but a fancy, you will soon forget me. You do not really love me—such a one as I," he continued, bringing forward, poor heart! his own greatest sorrow with unpitying hand. "But thank you, dear, for the gentle fancy." He stood a moment, silent; then touched her dark hair with his quivering lips and disappeared.

Sunday morning the sun rose unclouded, the snow lay deep on the ground, the first ice covered the bay; winter had come. At ten o'clock the customary service began in the Chapel of Saint John and Saint James, and the little congregation shivered, and whispered that it must really try to raise money enough for a stove. The parson did not feel the cold, although he looked almost bloodless in his white surplice. The Englishwoman was there, repentant—the sick child had not rallied under the new ministration; Mrs. Malone was there from sheer good nature, and several of the villagers and two or three miners had strolled in because they had nothing else to do, Brother Saul having returned to the mine. Rose Ray was not there. She was no saint, so she stayed at home and wept like a sinner.

The congregation, which had sat silent through the service, fell entirely asleep during the sermon on the "General Councils." Suddenly, in the midst of a sentence, there came a noise that stopped the parson and woke the sleepers. Two or three miners rushed into the chapel and spoke to the few men present. "Come out," they cried, "come out to the mine. The thief's caught at last, and who do you think it is? Saul, Brother Saul himself, the hypocrite! They tracked him to his den, and there they found the barrels, and sacks, and kegs, but the stuff he's made away with, most of it. He took it all, every crumb, and us a starving!"

"We've run in to tell the town," said another. "We've got him fast, and we're going to make a 'sample of him. Come out and see the fun."

"Yes," echoed a third, who lifted a ruffianly face from his short squat figure, "and we'll take our own time, too. He's made us suffer, and now he shall suffer a bit, if I know myself."

The women shuddered as, with an ominous growl, all the men went out together.

"I misdoubt they'll hang him," said Mrs. Malone, shaking her head as she looked after them.

"Or worse," said the miner's wife.

Then the two departed, and the parson was left alone. Did he cut off the service? No. Deliberately he finished every word of the sermon, sang a hymn, and spoke the final prayer; then, after putting everything in order, he too left the little sanctuary, but he did not go homeward, he took the road to the mine.

"Don't—ee go, sir, don't!" pleaded the Englishwoman, standing in her doorway as he passed. "You won't do no good, sir."

"Maybe not," answered the parson, gently, "but at least I must try."

He entered the forest, the air was still and cold, the snow crackled under his feet, and the pine-trees stretched away in long white aisles. He looked like a pigmy as he hastened on among the forest giants, his step more languid than usual from sternest vigil and fasting.

"Thou proud, evil body, I have conquered thee!" he had said in the cold dawning. And he had; at least, the body answered not again.

The mine was several miles away, and to lighten the journey the little man sang a hymn, his voice sounding through the forest in singular melody. It was an ancient hymn that he sang, written long ago by some cowled monk, and it told in quaint language of the joys of "Paradise! Oh Paradise!" He did not feel the cold as he sang of the pearly gates.

In the late afternoon his halting feet approached the mine; as he drew near the clearing he heard a sound of many voices shouting together, followed by a single cry, and a momentary silence more fearful than the clamor. The tormentors were at work. The parson ran forward and, passing the log huts which lay between, came out upon the scene. A circle of men stood there around a stake. Fastened by a long rope, crouched the wretched prisoner, his face turned to the color of dough, his coarse features drawn apart like an animal in terror, and his hoarse voice never ceasing its piteous cry, "Have mercy, good gentlemen! Dear gentlemen, have mercy!"

At a little distance a fire of logs was burning, and from the brands scattered around it was evident that the man had served as a target for the fiery missiles; in addition he bore the marks of blows, and his clothes were torn and covered with mud as though he had been dragged roughly over the ground. The lurid light of the fire cast a glow over the faces of the miners, behind rose the Iron Mountain, dark in shadow, and on each side stretched out the ranks of the white pine-trees like ghosts assembled as silent witnesses against the cruelty of man. The parson rushed forward, broke through the circle, and threw his arms around the prisoner at the stake, protecting him with his slender body.

"If ye kill him, ye must kill me also," he cried, in a ringing voice.

On the border, the greatest crime is robbery. A thief is worse than a murderer; a life does not count so much as life's supplies. It was not for the murderer that the Lynch law was made, but for the thief. For months these Algonquin miners had suffered loss; their goods, their provisions, their clothes, and their precious whisky had been stolen, day after day, and all search had proved vain; exasperated, several times actually suffering from want, they had heaped up a great store of fury for the thief, fury increased tenfold when, caught at last, he proved to be no other than Brother Saul, the one man whom they had trusted, the one man whom they had clothed and fed before themselves, the one man from whom they had expected better things. An honest, bloodthirsty wolf in his own skin was an animal they respected; indeed, they were themselves little better. But a wolf in sheep's clothing was utterly abhorrent to their peculiar sense of honor. So they gathered around their prey, and esteemed it rightfully theirs; whisky had sharpened their enjoyment.

To this savage band, enter the little parson. "What! Are ye men?" he cried. "Shame, shame, ye murderers!"

The miners stared at the small figure that defied them, and for the moment their anger gave way before a rough sense of the ludicrous.

"Hear the little man," they cried. "Hurrah, Peter! Go ahead!"

But they soon wearied of his appeal and began to answer back.

"What are clothes or provisions to a life?" said the minister.

"Life aint worth much without 'em, parson," replied a miner. "He took all we had, and we've gone cold and hungry 'long of him, and he knowed it. And all the time we was a-giving him of the best, and a-believing his praying and his preaching."

"If he is guilty, let him be tried by the legal authorities."

"We're our own legal 'thorities, Parson."

"The country will call you to account."

"The country won't do nothing of the kind. Much the country cares for us poor miners frozen up here in the woods! Stand back, Parson. Why should you bother about Saul? You always hated him."

"Never! Never!" answered the parson earnestly.

"You did too, and he knowed it. 'Twas because he was dirty and couldn't mince his words as you do."

The parson turned to the crouching figure at his side. "Friend," he said, "if this is true,—and the heart is darkly deceitful and hides from man his own worst sins,—I humbly ask your forgiveness."

"O come! None of your gammon," said another miner impatiently. "Saul didn't care whether you liked him or not, for he knowed you was only a coward."

"'Fraid of a dog! 'Fraid of a dog!" shouted half a dozen voices, and a frozen twig struck the parson's cheek, and drew blood.

"Why, he's got blood!" said one. "I never thought he had any."

"Come, Parson," said a friendly miner, advancing from the circle, "we don't want to hurt *you,* but you might as well understand that we're the masters here."

"And if ye are the masters, then be just. Give the criminal to me; I will myself take him to the nearest judge, the nearest jail, and deliver him up."

"He'll be more likely to deliver *you* up, I reckon, Parson."

"Well, then, send a committee of your own men with me—"

"We've got other things to do besides taking long journeys over the ice to 'commodate thieves, Parson. Leave the man to us."

"And to torture? Men, men, ye would not treat a beast so!"

"A beast don't steal our food and whisky," sang out a miner.

"Stand back, stand back," shouted several voices. "You're too little to fight, Parson."

"But not too little to die," answered the minister, throwing up his arms towards the sky.

For an instant his words held the men in check; they looked at each other, then at him.

"Think of yourselves," continued the minister. "Are ye without fault? If ye murder this man ye are worse than he is."

But here the minister went astray in his appeal, and ran against the views of the border.

"Worse! Worse than a sneaking thief! Worse than a praying hypocrite who robs the very men that feed him! Look here, we won't stand that! Sheer off, or take the consequences." And a burning brand struck the parson's coat, and fell on the head of the crouching figure at his side, setting fire to its hair. Instantly the parson extinguished the light flame, and drew the burly form closer within his arms, so that the two stood as one. "Not one, but both of us," he cried.

A new voice spoke next, the voice of the oldest miner, the most hardened reprobate there. "Let go that rascal, Parson. He's the fellow that lamed you last spring. He set the trap himself; I seen him a-doing it."

Involuntarily, for a moment, Herman Peters drew back; the trap set at the chapel door, the deliberate, cruel intention, the painful injury, and its life-long result, brought the angry color to his pale face. The memory was full of the old bitterness.

But Saul, feeling himself deserted, dragged his miserable body forward, and clasped the parson's knees. With desperate hands he clung, and he was not repulsed. Without a word the parson drew him closer, and again faced the crowd.

"Why, the man's a downright fool!" said the old miner. "That Saul lamed him for life, and all for nothing, and still he stands by him. The man's mad!"

"I am not mad," answered the parson, and his voice rang out clear and sweet. "But I am a minister of the great God who has said to men, 'Thou shalt do no murder.' O men! O brothers! look back into your own lives. Have ye no crimes, no sins to be forgiven? Can ye expect mercy when ye give none? Let this poor creature go, and it shall be counted unto you for goodness. Ye, too, must sometime die; and when the hour comes, as it often comes in lives like yours with sudden horror, ye will have this good deed to remember. For charity, —which is mercy,—shall cover a multitude of sins."

He ceased, and there was a momentary pause. Then a stern voice answered, "Facts won't alter, Parson. The man is a thief, and must be punished. Your talk may do for women-folks, not for us."

"Women-folks!" repeated the ruffian-faced man who had made the women shudder at the chapel. "He's a sly fox, this parson! He didn't go out to meet Rosie Ray at the Grotter yesterday, oh, no!"

"Liar!" shouted a man, who had been standing in the shadow on the outskirts of the crowd, taking, so far, no part in the scene. He forced himself to the front; it was Steven Long, his face dark with passion.

"No liar at all, Steve," answered the first. "I seen 'em there with my own eyes; they had things to eat and everything. Just ask the parson."

"Yes, ask the parson," echoed the others, and with the shifting humor of the border, they stopped to laugh over the idea. "Ask the parson."

Steven Long stepped forward and confronted the little minister. His strong hands were clenched, his blood was on fire with jealousy. The bull-dog followed his master, and smelled around the parson's gaiters—the same poor old shoes, his only pair, now wet with melted snow. The parson glanced down apprehensively.

"'Fraid of a dog! 'Fraid of a dog!" shouted the miners again, laughing uproariously. The fun was better than they had anticipated.

"Is it true?" demanded Steven Long, in a hoarse voice. "Did you meet that girl at the Grotter yesterday?"

"I did meet Rosamond Ray at the Grotto yesterday," answered the parson; "but—"

He never finished the sentence. A fragment of iron ore struck him on the temple. He fell, and died, his small body lying across the thief, whom he still protected, even in death.

The murder was not avenged; Steven Long was left to go his own way. But as the thief was also allowed to depart unmolested, the principles of border justice were held to have been amply satisfied.

The miners attended the funeral in a body, and even deputed one of their number to read the Episcopal burial service over the rough pine coffin, since there was no one else to do it. They brought out the chapel prayer-books, found the places, and followed as well as they could; for "he thought a deal of them books. Don't you remember how he was always carrying 'em backward and forward, poor little chap!"

The Chapel of Saint John and Saint James was closed for the season. In the summer a new missionary arrived; he was not Ritualistic, and before the year was out he married Rosamond Ray.

King David

THE scholars were dismissed. Out they trooped,—big boys, little boys, and full-grown men. Then what antics, what linked lines of scuffling, what double shuffles, leaps, and somersaults, what rolling laughter, interspersed with short yelps, and guttural cries, as wild and free as the sounds the mustangs make, gamboling on the plains! For King David's scholars were black,—black as the ace of spades. He did not say that; he knew very little about the ace. He said simply that his scholars were "colored"; and sometimes he called them "the Children of Ham." But so many mistakes were made over this title, in spite of his careful explanations (the Children having an undoubted taste for bacon), that he finally abandoned it, and fell back upon the national name of "freedmen," a title both good and true. He even tried to make it noble, speaking to them often of their wonderful lot as the emancipated teachers and helpers of their race; laying before them their mission in the future, which was to go over to Africa, and wake out of their long sloth and slumber the thousands of souls there. But Cassius and Pompey had only a mythic idea of Africa; they looked at the globe as it was turned around, they saw it there on the other side, and then their attention wandered off to an adventurous ant, who was making the tour of Soudan, and crossing the mountains of Kong, as though they were nothing.

Lessons over, the scholars went home. The school-master went home too, wiping his forehead as he went. He was a grave young man, tall and thin, somewhat narrow-chested, with the diffident air of a country student. And yet this country student was here, far down in the South, hundreds of miles away from the New Hampshire village where he had thought to spend his life as teacher of the district school. Extreme near-sightedness, and an inherited delicacy of constitution which he bore silently, had kept him out of the field during the days of the war. "I should be only an encumbrance," he thought. But when the war was over, the fire which had burnt within burst forth in the thought, "the Freedmen!" There was work fitted to his hand; that one thing he could do. "My turn has come at last," he said. "I feel the call to go." Nobody cared much because he was leaving. "Going down to teach the blacks?" said the farmers. "I don't see as you're called, David. We've paid dear enough to set 'em free, goodness knows, and now they ought to look out for themselves."

"But they must first be taught," said the school-master. "Our responsibility is great; our task is only just begun."

"Stuff!" said the farmers. What with the graves down in the South, and the taxes up in the North, they were not prepared to hear any talk about beginning. Beginning, indeed! They called it ending. The slaves were freed; and it was right they should be freed. But Ethan and Abner were gone, and their households were left unto them desolate. Let the blacks take care of themselves.

So, all alone, down came David King, with such aid and instruction as the Freedman's Bureau could give him, to this little settlement among the pines, where the freedmen had built some cabins in a careless way, and then seated themselves to wait for fortune. Freedmen! Yes; a glorious idea! But how will it work its way out into practical life? What are you going to do with tens of thousands of ignorant, childish, irresponsible souls thrown suddenly upon your hands,—souls that will not long stay childish, and that have in them also all the capacities for evil that you yourselves have,—you with your safeguards of generations of conscious responsibility and self-government, and yet—so many lapses! This is what David King thought. He did not see his way exactly; no, nor the nation's way. But he said to himself, "I can at least begin; if I am wrong I shall find it out in time. But now it seems to me that our first duty is to educate them." So he began at "a, b and c;" "you must not steal;" "you must not fight;" "you must wash your faces;" which may be called, I think, the first working-out of the emancipation problem.

Jubilee-town was the name of the settlement; and when the schoolmaster announced his own, David King, the title struck the imitative minds of the scholars, and, turning it around, they made "King David" of it, and kept it so. Delighted with the novelty, the Jubilee freedmen came to school in such numbers that the master was obliged to classify them; boys and men in the mornings and afternoons; the old people in the evenings; the young women and girls by themselves for an hour in the early morning. "I cannot do full justice to all," he thought, "and in the men lies the danger, in the boys the hope; the women cannot vote. Would to God the men could not either, until they have learned to read and to write, and to maintain themselves respectably!" For, abolitionist as he was, David King would have given years of his life for the power to restrict the suffrage. Not having this power, however, he worked at the problem in the only way left open: "Take two apples from four apples, Julius,—how many will be left?" "What is this I hear, Caesar, about stolen bacon?"

On this day the master went home, tired and dispirited; the novelty was over on both sides. He had been five months at Jubilee, and his scholars were more of a puzzle to him than ever. They learned, some of them, readily; but they forgot as readily. They had a vast capacity for parrot-like repetition, and caught his long words so quickly, and repeated them so volubly, with but slight comprehension of their meaning, that his sensitive conscience shrank from using them, and he was forced back upon a rude plainness of speech which was a pain to his pedagogic ears. Where he had once said "demean your-selves with sobriety," he now said "don't get drunk." He would have fared better if he had learned to say "uncle" and "aunty," or "maumer," in the familiar Southern fashion. But he had no knowl-edge of the customs;—how could he have? He could only blunder on in his slow Northern way.

His cabin stood in the pine forest, at a little distance from the settle-ment; he had allowed himself that grace. There was a garden around it, where Northern flowers came up after a while,—a little pale, per-haps, like English ladies in India, but doubly beautiful and dear to exiled eyes. The school-master had cherished from the first a wish for a cotton-field,—a cotton-field of his own. To him a cotton-field represented the South,—a cotton-field in the hot sunshine, with a gang of slaves toiling under the lash of an overseer. This might have been a fancy picture; and it might not. At any rate it was real to him. There was, however, no overseer now, and no lash; no slaves and very little toil. The Negroes would work only when they pleased; and that was generally not at all. There was no doubt but that they were almost hopelessly improvident and lazy. "Entirely so," said the planters. "Not quite," said the Northern school-master. And therein lay the difference between them.

David lighted his fire of pitch-pine, spread his little table, and began to cook his supper carefully. When it was nearly ready, he heard a knock at his gate. Two representative specimens of his scholars were waiting without,—Jim, a field-hand, and a woman named Esther, who had been a house-servant in a planter's family. Jim had come "to borry an ax," and Esther to ask for medicine for a sick child.

"Where is your own ax, Jim?" said the school-master.

"Somehow et's rusty, sah. Dey gets rusty mighty quick."

"Of course, because you always leave them out in the rain. When will you learn to take care of your axes?"

"Don' know, mars."

"I have told you not to call me master," said David. "I am not your master."

"You's school-mars, I reckon," answered Jim, grinning at his repartee.

"Well, Jim," said the school-master, relaxing into a smile, "you have the best of it this time; but you know quite well what I mean. You can take the ax; but bring it back to-night. And you must see about getting a new one immediately; there is something to begin with. Now, Esther, what is it? Your boy sick? Probably it is because you let him drink the water out of that swampy pool. I warned you."

"Yes, sah," said the woman impassively.

She was a slow, dull-witted creature, who had executed her tasks marvelously well in the planter's family, never varying by a hair's breadth either in time or method during long years. Freed, she was lost at once; if she had not been swept along by her companions she would have sat down dumbly by the way-side, and died. The school-master offered supper to both of his guests. Jim took a seat at the table at once, nothing loth, and ate and drank, talking all the time with occasional flashes of wit, and an unconscious suggestion of ferocity in the way he hacked and tore the meat with his clasp-knife, and his strong white teeth. Esther stood; nothing could induce her to sit in the master's presence. She ate and drank quietly, and dropped a courtesy whenever he spoke to her, not from any especial respect or gratitude, however, but from habit. "I may possibly teach the man something," thought the school-master; "but what a terrible creature to turn loose in the world, with power in his hand! Hundreds of these men will die, nay, must die violent deaths before their people can learn what freedom means, and what it does not mean. As for the woman, it is hopeless; she cannot learn. But her child can. In truth, our hope is in the children."

And then he threw away every atom of the food, washed his dishes, made up the fire, and went back to the beginning again and cooked a second supper. For he still shrank from personal contact with the other race. A Southerner would have found it impossible to comprehend the fortitude it required for the New Englander to go through his daily rounds among them. He did his best; but it was duty, not liking. Supper over, he went to the school-house again; in the evenings, he taught the old people. It was an odd sight to note them as they followed the letters with a big crooked forefinger, slowly spelling out words of three letters. They spelled with their whole bodies, stooping over the books which lay before them until their old grizzled heads and gay turbans looked as if they were set on the table by the chins in a long row. Patiently the master taught them; they had gone no farther than "cat" in five long months. He made the letters for them on the black-board again and again, but the treat of the evening was the making of these letters on the board by the different scholars in turn. "Now, Dinah—B." And old Dinah would hobble up proudly, and, with much screwing of her mouth and tongue and many long hesitations, produce something which looked like a figure eight gone mad. Joe had his turn next, and he would make, perhaps, an H for a D. The master would go back and explain to him carefully the difference, only to find at the end of ten minutes that the whole class was hopelessly confused; Joe's mistake had routed them all. There was one pair of spectacles among the old people; these were passed from hand to hand as the turn came, not from necessity always, but as an adjunct to the dignity of reading.

"Never mind the glasses, Tom. Surely you can spell 'bag' without them."

"Dey helps, Mars King David," replied old Tom with solemn importance. He then adorned himself with the spectacles, and spelled it—"g, a, b."

But the old people enjoyed their lesson immensely; no laughter, no joking broke the solemnity of the scene, and they never failed to make an especial toilet,—much shirt-collar for the old men, and clean turbans for the old women. They seemed to be generally half-crippled, poor old creatures; slow in their movements as tortoises, and often unwieldy; their shoes were curiosities of patches, rags, strings, and carpeting. But sometimes a fine old black face was lifted from the slow-moving bulk, and from under wrinkled eyelids keen sharp eyes met the master's, as intelligent as his own.

There was no church proper in Jubilee; on Sundays, the people, who were generally Baptists, assembled in the school-room, where services were conducted by a brother who had "de gif' ob preachin'" and who poured forth a flood of Scripture phrases with a volubility, incoherence and earnestness alike extraordinary. Presbyterian David attended these services, not only for the sake of example, but also because he steadfastly believed in "the public assembling of ourselves together for the worship of Almighty God."

"Perhaps they understand him," he thought, noting the rapt black faces, "and I, at least, have no right to judge them,—I, who with all the lights I have had, still find myself unable to grasp the great doctrine of Election." For David had been bred in Calvinism, and many a night when younger and more hopeful of arriving at finalities, had he wrestled with its problems. He was not so sure, now, of arriving at finalities, either in belief or in daily life; but he thought the fault lay with himself, and deplored it.

The Yankee school-master was, of course, debarred from intercourse with those of his own color in the neighborhood. There were no "poor whites" there; he was spared the sight of their long, clay-colored faces, lank yellow hair, and half open mouths; he was not brought into contact with the ignorance and dense self-conceit of this singular class. The whites of the neighborhood were planters, and they regarded the school-master as an interloper, a fanatic, a knave or a fool, according to their various degrees of bitterness. The phantom of a cotton-field still haunted the master, and he often walked by the abandoned fields of these planters, and noted them carefully. In addition to his fancy, there was now another motive. Things were not going well at Jubilee, and he was anxious to try whether the men would not work for good wages, paid regularly, and for their Northern teacher and friend. Thus it happened that Harnett Ammerton, retired planter, perceived, one afternoon, a stranger walking up the avenue that led to his dilapidated mansion; and as he was near-sighted, and as any visitor was, besides, a welcome interruption in his dull day, he went out upon the piazza to meet him, and, not until he had offered a chair, did he recognize his guest. He said nothing; for he was in his own house. But a gentleman can freeze the atmosphere around him even in his own house, and this he did. The school-master stated his errand simply; he wished to rent one of the abandoned cotton-fields for a year. The planter could have answered with satisfaction that his fields might lie forever untilled before Yankee hands should touch them. But he was a poor man now, and money was money. He endured his visitor, and he rented his field; and, with the perplexed feelings of his class, he asked himself how it was, how it could be, that a man like that—yes, like that— had money, while he himself had none! David had but little money, —a mere handful to throw away in a day, the planter would have thought in the lavish old times; but David had the New England thrift.

"I am hoping that the unemployed hands over at Jubilee will cultivate this field for me," he said; "for fair wages, of course. I know nothing of cotton myself."

"You will be disappointed," said the planter.

"But they must live; they must lay up something for the winter."

"They do not know enough to live. They might exist, perhaps, in Africa as the rest of their race exists, but here, in this colder climate, they must be taken care of, worked, and fed, as we work and feed our horses—precisely in the same way."

"I cannot agree with you," replied David, a color rising in his thin face. "They are idle and shiftless, I acknowledge that; but is it not the natural result of generations of servitude and ignorance?"

"They have not capacity for anything save ignorance."

"You do not know then, perhaps, that I—that I am trying to educate those who are over at Jubilee," said David. There was no aggressive confidence in his voice; he knew that he had accomplished little as yet. He looked wistfully at his host as he spoke.

Harnett Ammerton was a born patrician; poor, homely, awkward David felt this in every nerve as he sat there. For he loved beauty in spite of himself, and in spite of his belief that it was a tendency of the old Adam. (Old Adam has such nice things to bother his descendants with; almost a monopoly, if we are to believe some creeds.) So now David tried not to be influenced by the fine face before him, and steadfastly went on to sow a little seed, if possible, even upon this prejudiced ground.

"I have a school over there," he said.

"I have heard something of the kind, I believe," replied the old planter, as though Jubilee town were a thousand miles away instead of a blot upon his own border.

"May I ask how you are succeeding?"

There was a fine irony in the question. David felt it, but replied courageously that success, he hoped, would come in time.

"And I, young man, hope that it will never come! The Negro with power in his hand, which you have given him, with a little smattering of knowledge in his shallow, crafty brain,—a knowledge which you and your kind are now striving to give him,—will become an element of more danger in this land than it has ever known before. You Northerners do not understand the blacks. They are an inferior race by nature; God made them so. And God forgive those (although I never can) who have placed them over us,—yes, virtually over us, their former masters,—poor ignorant creatures!"

At this instant an old Negro came up the steps, with an armful of wood, and the eye of the Northerner noted (was forced to note) the contrast: there sat the planter, his head crowned with silver hair, his finely chiseled face glowing with the warmth of his indignant words; and there passed the old slave bent and black, his low forehead and broad animal features seeming to typify scarcely more intelligence than that of the dog that followed him. The planter spoke to the servant in his kindly way as he passed, and the old black face lighted with pleasure. This, too, the school-master's sensitive mind noted; none of his pupils looked at him with anything like that affection. "But it *is* right they should be freed, it *is* right," he said to himself as he walked back to Jubilee, "and to that belief will I cling as long as I have my being. It *is* right." And then he came into Jubilee, and found three of his freedmen drunk, and quarreling in the street.

Heretofore the settlement, poor and forlorn as it was, had escaped the curse of drunkenness. No liquor was sold in the vicinity, and David had succeeded in keeping his scholars from wandering aimlessly about the country from place to place,—often the first use the blacks made of their freedom. Jubilee did not go to the liquor. But, at last, the liquor had come to Jubilee. Shall they not have all rights and privileges, these new-born citizens of ours? The bringer of these doctrines, and of the fluids to moisten them, was a white man, one of that class which has gone down on the page of American history, knighted with the initials C. B. "The captain" the Negroes called him,—and he was highly popular already, three hours of the captain being worth three weeks of David, as far as familiarity went. The man was a glib-tongued, smartly dressed fellow, well supplied with money, and his errand was, of course, to influence the votes at the next election. David, meanwhile, had so carefully kept all talk of politics from his scholars, that they hardly knew that an election was near. It became, now, a contest between the two higher intelligences. If the school-master had but won the easily-won and strong affections of his pupils! But, in all those months, he had gained only a dutiful attention. They did not even respect him as they had respected their old masters, and the cause (poor David!) was that very thrift and industry which he relied upon as an example.

"Ole Mars Ammerton would nebber wash his dishes ef dey was nebber washed," confided Maum June to Elsy, as they caught sight of David's shining pans.

The school-master could have had a retinue of servants for small price, or no price at all; but to tell a truth (which he never told), he could not endure them about him.

"I must have one spot to myself," he said feverishly, after he had labored all day among them, teaching, correcting untidy ways, administering simple medicines, or binding up a bruised foot. But he never dreamed that this very isolation of his personality, this very thrift, were daily robbing him of the influence which he so earnestly longed to possess. In New England, every man's house was his castle; and every man's hands were thrifty. He forgot the easy familiarity, the lordly ways, the crowded households, and the royal carelessness, to which the slaves had always been accustomed in their old masters' homes.

At first the captain attempted intimacy.

"No reason why you and me shouldn't work together," he said with a confidential wink. "This thing's being done all over the South, and easy done, too. Now's the time for smart chaps like us,—

'transition,' you know. The old Southerners are mad, and won't come forward, so we'll just sail in and have a few years of it. When they're ready to come back,—why, we'll give 'em up the place again, of course, if our pockets are well lined. Come now, just acknowledge that the Negroes have got to have somebody to lead 'em."

"It shall not be such as you," said David indignantly. "See those two men quarreling; that is the work of the liquor you have given them!"

"They've as good a right to their liquor as other men have," replied the captain, carelessly, "and that's what I tell 'em; they ain't slaves now,—they're free. Well, boss,—sorry you don't like my idees, but can't help it; must go ahead. Remember, I offered you a chance, and you would not take it. Morning."

The five months had grown into six and seven, and Jubilee-town was known far and wide as a dangerous and disorderly neighborhood. The old people and the children still came to school, but the young men and boys had deserted in a body. The school-master's cotton-field was neglected; he did a little there himself every day, but the work was novel, and his attempts awkward and slow. One afternoon, Harnett Ammerton rode by on horseback; the road passed near the angle of the field where the school-master was at work.

"How is your experiment succeeding?" said the planter, with a little smile of amused scorn as he saw the lonely figure.

"Not very well," replied David.

He paused and looked up earnestly into the planter's face. Here was a man who had lived among the blacks all his life, and knew them; if he would but give honest advice! The school-master was sorely troubled that afternoon. Should he speak? He would at least try.

"Mr. Ammerton," he said, "do you intend to vote at the approaching election?"

"No," replied the planter; "nor any person of my acquaintance."

"Then incompetent, and, I fear, evil-minded men will be put into office."

"Of course; the certain result of Negro voting."

"But if you, sir, and the class to which you belong, would exert yourselves, I am inclined to think much might be done. The breach will only grow broader every year; act now, while you have still influence left."

"Then you think that we have influence," said the planter.

He was curious concerning the ideas of this man, who, although not like the typical Yankee exactly, was yet plainly a fanatic; while as to dress and air—why, Zip, his old valet, had more polish.

"I know at least that I have none," said David. Then he came a step nearer. "Do you think, sir," he began slowly, "that I have gone to work in the wrong way? Would it have been wiser to have obtained some post of authority over them,—the office of justice of the peace, for instance, with power of arrest?"

"I know nothing about it," said the planter curtly, touching his horse with his whip and riding on. He had no intention of stopping to discuss ways and means with an abolition school-master!

Things grew from bad to worse at Jubilee. Most of the men had been field-hands, there was but little intelligence among them; the few bright minds among David's pupils caught the specious arguments of the captain, and repeated them to the others. The captain explained how much power they held; the captain laid before them glittering plans; the captain said that by good rights each family ought to have a plantation to repay them for their years of enforced labor; the captain promised them a four-story brick college for their boys, which was more than King David had ever promised, teacher though he was. They found out that they were tired of King David and his narrow talk; and they went over to Hildore Corners, where a new store had been opened, which contained, among other novelties, a bar. This was one of the captain's benefactions. "If you pay your money for it, you've as good a right to your liquor as any one, I guess;" he observed. "Not that it's anything to me, of course; but I allow I like to see fair play!"

It was something to him, however; the new store had a silent partner. And this was but one of many small and silent enterprises in which he was engaged throughout the neighborhood.

The women of Jubilee, more faithful than the men, still sent their children to school; but they did it with discouraged hearts, poor things! Often now, they were seen with bandaged heads and bruised bodies, the result of drunken blows from husband or brother; and, left alone, they were obliged to labor all day to get the poor food they ate, and to keep clothes on their children. Patient by nature, they lived along as best they could, and toiled in their small fields like horses; but the little prides, the vague grotesque aspirations and hopes that had come to them with their freedom, gradually faded away. "A blue-painted front do';" "a black silk apron with red ribbons;" "to make a minister of little Job;" and "a real crock'ry pitcher," were wishes unspoken now. The thing was only how to live from day to day, and keep the patched clothes together. In the meanwhile, trashy finery was sold at the new store, and the younger girls wore gilt ear-rings.

The master, toiling on at his vain task, was at his wit's end. "They will not work, before long they must steal," he said. He brooded and thought, and at last one morning he came to a decision. The same day in the afternoon he set out for Hildore Corners. He had thought of a plan. As he was walking rapidly through the pine woods, Harnett Ammerton on horseback passed him. This time the Northerner had no questions to ask; nay, he almost hung his head, so ashamed was he of the reputation that had attached itself to the field of his labors. But the planter reined in his horse when he saw who it was; he was the questioner now.

"School-master," he began, "in the name of all the white families about here, I really must ask if you can do nothing to keep in order those miserable, drinking, ruffianly Negroes of yours over at Jubilee? Why,—we shall all be murdered in our beds before long! Are you aware of the dangerous spirit they have manifested lately?"

"Only too well," said David.

"What are you going to do? How will it end?"

"God knows."

"God knows. Is that all you have to say? Of course He knows; but the question is, do you know? You have brought the whole trouble down upon our heads by your confounded insurrectionary school! Just as I told you, your Negroes, with the little smattering of knowledge you have given them, are now the most dangerous, riotous, thieving, murdering rascals in the district."

"They are bad; but it is not the work of the school, I hope."

"Yes, it is," said the planter angrily.

"They have been led astray lately, Mr. Ammerton; a person has come among them—"

"Another Northerner."

"Yes," said David, a flush rising in his cheek; "but not all Northerners are like this man, I trust."

"Pretty much all we see are; look at the State."

"Yes, I know it; I suppose time alone can help matters," said the troubled teacher.

"Give up your school, and come and join us," said the planter abruptly; "you, at least, are honest in your mistakes. We are going to form an association for our own protection; join with us. You can teach my grandsons if you like, provided you do not put any of your—your fanaticism into them."

This was an enormous concession for Harnett Ammerton to make; something in the school-master's worn face had drawn it out.

"Thank you," said David slowly; "it is kindly meant, sir. But I cannot give up my work. I came down to help the freedmen, and—"

"Then stay with them," said the planter, doubly angry for the very kindness of the moment before. "I thought you were a decent-living white man, according to your fashion, but I see I was mistaken. Dark days are coming, and you turn your back upon those of your own color and side with the slaves! Go and herd with your Negroes,—but, look you, sir, we are prepared. We will shoot down any one found upon our premises after dark,—shoot him down like a dog. It has come to that, and, by Heaven! we shall protect ourselves."

He rode on. David sat down on a fallen tree for a moment, and leaned his head upon his hand. Dark days were coming, as the planter had said; nay, were already there. Was he in any way responsible for them? He tried to think. "I know not," he said at last; "but I must still go on and do the best I can. I must carry out my plan." He rose and went forward to the Corners.

A number of Jubilee men were lounging near the new store, and one of them was reading aloud from a newspaper which the captain had given him; he had been David's brightest scholar and he could read readily; but what he read was inflammable matter of the worst kind, a speech which had been written for just such purposes, and which was now being circulated through the district. Mephistopheles in the form of Harnett Ammerton seemed to whisper in the school-master's ears, "Do you take pride to yourself that you taught that man to read?"

The reader stopped; he had discovered the new auditor; the men stared; they had never seen the master at the Corners before. They drew together and waited; he approached them, and paused a moment; then he began to speak.

"I have come, friends," he said, "to make a proposition to you. You, on your side, have nothing laid up for the winter, and I, on my side, am anxious to have your work. I have a field, you know, a cotton-field; what do you say to going to work there, all of you, for a month? I will agree to pay you more than any man about here pays, and you shall have the cash every Monday morning regularly. We will hold a meeting over at Jubilee, and you shall choose your own overseer; for I am very ignorant about cotton-fields; I must trust to you. What do you say?"

The men looked at each other, but no one spoke.

"Think of your little children without clothes."

Still silence.

"I have not succeeded among you," continued the teacher, "as well as I hoped to succeed. You do not come to school any more, and I suppose it is because you do not like me."

Something like a murmur of dissent came from the group. The voice went on:

"I have thought of something I can do, however; I can write to the North for another teacher to take my place, and he shall be a man of your own race; one who is educated, and, if possible, also a clergyman of your own faith. You can have a little church, then, and Sabbath services. As soon as he comes, I will yield my place to him; but, in the meantime, will you not cultivate that field for me? I ask it as a favor. It will be but for a little while, for, when the new teacher comes, I shall go, unless, indeed," he added, looking around with a smile that was almost pathetic in its appeal, "you should wish me to stay."

There was no answer. He had thrown out this last little test question suddenly. It had failed.

"I am sorry I have not succeeded better at Jubilee," he said after a short pause,—and his voice had altered in spite of his self-control,— "but at least you will believe, I hope, that I have tried."

"Dat's so;" "dat's de trouf," said one or two; the rest stood irresolute. But at this moment a new speaker came forward; it was the captain, who had been listening in ambush.

"All gammon, boys, all gammon," he began, seating himself familiarly among them on the fence-rail. "The season for planting's over, and your work would be thrown away in that field of his. He knows it, too; he only wants to see you marching around to his whistling. And he pays you double wages, does he? Double wages for perfectly useless work! Doesn't that show, clear as daylight, what he's up to? If he hankers so after your future,—your next winter, and all that,—why don't he give yer the money right out, if he's so flush? But no; he wants to put you to work, and that's all there is of it. He can't deny a word I've said, either."

"I do not deny that I wish you to work, friends," began David—

"There! he tells yer so himself," said the captain; "he wants yer back in yer old places again. *I* seen him talking to old Ammerton the other day. Give 'em a chance, them two classes, and they'll have you slaves a second time before you know it."

"Never!" cried David. "Friends, it is not possible that you can believe this man! We have given our lives to make you free," he added passionately, "we came down among you, bearing your freedom in our hands—"

"Come now,—I'm a Northerner too, ain't I?" interrupted the captain; "there's two kinds of Northerners, boys. *I* was in the army, and that's more than he can say. Much freedom *he* brought down in *his* hands, safe at home in his narrer-minded, penny-scraping village! He wasn't in the army at all, boys, and he can't tell you he was."

This was true; the school-master could not. Neither could he tell them what was also true, namely, that the captain had been an attaché of a sutler's tent, and nothing more. But the sharp-witted captain had the whole history of his opponent at his fingers' ends.

"Come along, boys," said this jovial leader; "we'll have suthin' to drink the health of this tremenjous soldier in,—this fellow as fought so hard for you and for your freedom. I always thought he looked like a fighting man, with them fine broad shoulders of his!" He laughed loudly, and the men trooped into the store after him. The school-master, alone outside, knew that his chance was gone. He turned away and took the homeward road. One of his plans had failed; there remained now nothing save to carry out the other.

Prompt as usual, he wrote his letter as soon as he reached his cabin, asking that another teacher, a colored man if possible, should be sent down to take his place.

"I fear I am not fitted for the work," he wrote; "I take shame to myself that this is so. Yet, being so, I must not hinder by any disappointed strivings the progress of the great mission. I will go back among my own kind; it may be that some whom I shall teach may yet succeed where I have failed." The letter could not go until the next morning. He went out and walked up and down in the forest. A sudden impulse came to him; he crossed over to the school-house and rang the little tinkling belfry-bell. His evening class had disbanded some time before; the poor old aunties and uncles crept off to bed very early now, in order to be safely out of the way when their disorderly sons and grandsons came home. But something moved the master to see them all together once more. They came across the green, wondering, and entered the school-room; some of the younger wives came too, and the children. The master waited, letter in hand. When they were all seated,

"Friends," he said, "I have called you together to speak to you of a matter which lies very near my own heart. Things are not going on well at Jubilee. The men drink; the children go in rags. Is this true?"

Groans, and slow assenting nods answered him. One old woman

shrieked out shrilly, "It is de Lord's will," and rocked her body to and fro.

"No, it is not the Lord's will," answered the school-master gently; "you must not think so. You must strive to reclaim those who have gone astray; you must endeavor to inspire them with renewed aspirations toward a higher plane of life; you must—I mean," he said, correcting himself, "you must try to keep the men from going over to the Corners and getting drunk."

"But dey will do it, sah; what can we do?" said Uncle Scipio, who sat leaning his chin upon his crutch and peering at the teacher with sharp intelligence in his old eyes. "If dey won't stay fo' you, sah, will dey stay fo' us?"

"That is what I was coming to," said the master. (They had opened the subject even before he could get to it! They saw it too, then,—his utter lack of influence.) "I have not succeeded here as I hoped to succeed, friends; I have not the influence I ought to have." Then he paused. "Perhaps the best thing I can do will be to go away," he added, looking quickly from face to face to catch the expression. But there was nothing visible. The children stared stolidly back, and the old people sat unmoved; he even fancied that he could detect relief in the eyes of one or two, quickly suppressed, however, by the innate politeness of the race. A sudden mist came over his eyes; he had thought that perhaps some of them would care a little. He hurried on: "I have written to the North for a new teacher for you, a man of your own people, who will not only teach you, but also, as a minister, hold services on the Sabbath; you can have a little church of your own then. Such a man will do better for you than I have done, and I hope you will like him,"—he was going to say, "better than you have liked me," but putting down all thought of self, he added, "and that his work among you will be abundantly blessed."

"Glory! glory!" cried an old aunty. "A color'd preacher ob our own,—glory! glory!"

Then Uncle Scipio rose slowly, with aid of his crutches, and, as orator of the occasion, addressed the master.

"You see, sah, how it is; you see, Mars King David," he said, waving his hand apologetically, "a color'd man will unnerstan us, 'specially ef he hab libed at de Souf; we don't want no Nordern free niggahs hyar. But a 'spectable color'd preacher, now, would be de makin' ob Jubilee, fo' dis worl' an' de nex'."

"Fo' dis worl' and de nex'," echoed the old woman.

"Our service to you, sah, all de same," continued Scipio, with a grand bow of ceremony; "but you hab nebber *quite* unnerstan us, sah, nebber quite; an' you can nebber do much fo' us, sah, on 'count ob dat fack,—ef you'll scuse my saying so. But it is de trouf. We give you our t'anks and our congratturrurlations, an' we hopes you'll go j'yful back to your own people, an' be a shining light to 'em forebber more."

"A shinin' light forebber more," echoed the rest. One old woman, inspired apparently by the similarity of words, began a hymn about "the shining shore," and the whole assembly, thinking no doubt that it was an appropriate and complimentary termination to the proceedings, joined in with all their might, and sang the whole six verses through with fervor.

"I should like to shake hands with you all as you go out," said the master, when at last the song was ended, "and,—and I wish, my friends, that you would all remember me in your prayers to-night before you sleep."

What a sight was that when the pale Caucasian, with the intelligence of generations on his brow, asked for the prayers of these sons of Africa, and gently, nay, almost humbly, received the pressure of their black toil-hardened hands as they passed out! They had taught him a great lesson, the lesson of a failure.

The school-master went home, and sat far into the night, with his head bowed upon his hands. "Poor worm!" he thought, "poor worm! who even went so far as to dream of saying, 'Here am I, Lord, and these brethren whom Thou hast given me!'"

The day came for him to go; he shouldered his bag and started away. At a turn in the road, some one was waiting for him; it was dull-faced Esther with a bunch of flowers, the common flowers of her small garden-bed. "Good-bye, Esther," said the master, touched almost to tears by the sight of the solitary little offering.

"Good-bye, mars," said Esther. But she was not moved; she had come out into the woods from a sort of instinct, as a dog follows a little way down the road, to look after a departing carriage.

"David King has come back home again, and taken the district school," said one village gossip to another.

"Has he, now? Didn't find the blacks what he expected, I guess."

GEORGE WASHINGTON CABLE

★ ★ ★

Out of musty archives George Washington Cable (1844-1925) extracted vivid, melodramatic incidents with which to illuminate the unique features of the early nineteenth-century Creole civilization of Louisiana, the colorful society of New Orleans, and the luxuriant wildness of swamps and bayous. The Creoles, white descendants of French or Spanish pioneers in Louisiana or the French West Indies, did not fully approve of Cable's characterizations. A native of New Orleans, Cable at fourteen became the family breadwinner. After service in the Confederate Army, he entered the cotton business. Feeling the challenge to utilize wasted local romance materials, he wrote the stories now collected in *Old Creole Days* (1879). Other Creole stories followed: *The Grandissimes* (1880), *Madame Delphine* (1881), and *Strange True Stories of Louisiana* (1889). When in 1885 Cable moved to Northampton, Massachusetts, he engaged in polemic writing and lost much of his original force.

★ ★ ★

'Tite Poulette

KRISTIAN KOPPIG was a rosy-faced, beardless young Dutchman. He was one of that army of gentlemen who, after the purchase of Louisiana, swarmed from all parts of the commercial world, over the mountains of Franco-Spanish exclusiveness, like the Goths over the Pyrenees, and settled down in New Orleans to pick up their fortunes, with the diligence of hungry pigeons. He may have been a German; the distinction was too fine for Creole haste and disrelish.

He made his home in a room with one dormer window looking out, and somewhat down, upon a building opposite, which still stands, flush with the street, a century old. Its big, round-arched windows in a long, second-story row, are walled up, and two or three from time to time have had smaller windows let into them again, with odd little latticed peep-holes in their batten shutters. This had already been done when Kristian Koppig first began to look at them from his solitary dormer window.

All the features of the building lead me to guess that it is a remnant of the old Spanish Barracks, whose extensive structure fell by government sale into private hands a long time ago. At the end toward the swamp a great, oriental-looking passage is left, with an arched entrance, and a pair of ponderous wooden doors. You look at it, and almost see Count O'Reilly's artillery come bumping and trundling out, and dash around into the ancient Plaza to bang away at King St. Charles's birthday.

I do not know who lives there now. You might stand about on the opposite *banquette* for weeks and never find out. I suppose it is a residence, for it does not look like one. That is the rule in that region.

In the good old times of duels, and bagatelle-clubs, and theatre-balls, and Cayetano's circus, Kristian Koppig rooming as described, there lived in the portion of this house, partly overhanging the archway, a palish handsome woman, by the name—or going by the name—of Madame John. You would hardly have thought of her being "colored." Though fading, she was still of very attractive countenance, fine, rather severe features, nearly straight hair carefully kept, and that vivid black eye so peculiar to her kind. Her smile, which came and went with her talk, was sweet and exceedingly intelligent; and something told you, as you looked at her, that she was one who had had to learn a great deal in this troublesome life.

"But!"—the Creole lads in the street would say—"her daughter!" and there would be lifting of arms, wringing of fingers, rolling of eyes, rounding of mouths, gaspings and clasping of hands. "So beautiful, beautiful, beautiful! White?—white like a water lily! White—like a magnolia!"

Applause would follow, and invocation of all the saints to witness. And she could sing.

"Sing?" (disdainfully)—"if a mocking-bird can *sing!* Ha!"

They could not tell just how old she was; they "would give her about seventeen."

Mother and daughter were very fond. The neighbors could hear them call each other pet names, and see them sitting together, sewing, talking happily to each other in the unceasing French way, and see them go out and come in together on their little tasks and errands. " 'Tite Poulette," the daughter was called; she never went out alone.

And who was this Madame John?

"Why, you know!—she was"—said the wig-maker at the corner to Kristian Koppig—"I'll tell you. You know?—she was"—and the rest atomized off in a rasping whisper. She was the best yellow-fever nurse in a thousand yards round; but that is not what the wig-maker said.

A block nearer the river stands a house altogether different from the remnant of old barracks. It is of frame, with a deep front gallery over which the roof extends. It has become a den of Italians, who sell fuel by daylight, and by night are up to no telling what extent of deviltry. This was once the home of a gay gentleman, whose first name happened to be John. He was a member of the Good Children Social Club. As his parents lived with him, his wife would, according to custom, have been called Madame John; but he had no wife. His father died, then his mother; last of all, himself. As he is about to be off, in comes Madame John, with 'Tite Poulette, then an infant, on her arm.

"Zalli," said he, "I am going."

She bowed her head, and wept.

"You have been very faithful to me, Zalli."

She wept on.

"Nobody to take care of you now, Zalli."

Zalli only went on weeping.

"I want to give you this house, Zalli; it is for you and the little one."

An hour after, amid the sobs of Madame John, she and the "little one" inherited the house, such as it was. With the fatal caution which characterizes ignorance, she sold the property and placed the proceeds in a bank, which made haste to fail. She put on widow's weeds, and wore them still when 'Tite Poulette "had seventeen," as the frantic lads would say.

How they did chatter over her. Quiet Kristian Koppig had never seen the like. He wrote to his mother, and told her so. A pretty fellow at the corner would suddenly double himself up with beckoning to a knot of chums; these would hasten up; recruits would come in from two or three other directions; as they reached the corner their countenances would quickly assume a genteel severity, and presently, with her mother, 'Tite Poulette would pass—tall, straight, lithe, her great black eyes made tender by their sweeping lashes, the faintest tint of color in her Southern cheek, her form all grace, her carriage a wonder of simple dignity.

The instant she was gone every tongue was let slip on the marvel of her beauty; but, though theirs were only the loose New Orleans morals of over fifty years ago, their unleashed tongues never had attempted any greater liberty than to take up the pet name, 'Tite Poulette. And yet the mother was soon to be, as we shall discover, a paid dancer at the Salle de Condé.

To Zalli, of course, as to all "quadroon ladies," the festivities of the Conde-street ball-room were familiar of old. There, in the happy days when dear Monsieur John was young, and the eighteenth century old, she had often repaired under guard of her mother—dead now, alas!—and Monsieur John would slip away from the dull play and dry society of Théâtre d'Orléans, and come around with his crowd of elegant friends; and through the long sweet hours of the ball she had danced, and laughed, and coquetted under her satin mask, even to the baffling and tormenting of that prince of gentlemen, dear Monsieur John himself. No man of questionable blood dare set his foot within the door. Many noble gentlemen were pleased to dance with her. Colonel De —— and General La ——: city councilmen and officers from the Government House. There were no paid dancers then. Every thing was decorously conducted indeed! Every girl's mother was there, and the more discreet always left before there was too much drinking. Yes, it was gay, gay!—but sometimes dangerous. Ha! more times than a few had Monsieur John knocked down some long-haired and long-knifed rowdy, and kicked the breath out of him for looking saucily at her; but that was like him, he was so brave and kind;—and he is gone!

There was no room for widow's weeds there. So when she put these on, her glittering eyes never again looked through her pink and white mask, and she was glad of it; for never, never in her life had they so looked for anybody but her dear Monsieur John, and now he was in heaven—so the priest said—and she was a sick-nurse.

Living was hard work; and, as Madame John had been brought up tenderly, and had done what she could to rear her daughter in the same mistaken way, with, of course, no more education than the ladies in society got, they knew nothing beyond a little music and embroidery. They struggled as they could, faintly; now giving a few private dancing lessons, now dressing hair, but ever beat back by the steady detestation of their imperious patronesses; and, by and by, for want of that priceless worldly grace known among the flippant as "money-sense," these two poor children, born of misfortune and the complacent badness of the times, began to be in want.

Kristian Koppig noticed from his dormer window one day a man standing at the big archway opposite, and clanking the brass knocker on the wicket that was in one of the doors. He was a smooth man, with his hair parted in the middle, and his cigarette poised on a tiny gold holder. He waited a moment, politely cursed the dust, knocked again, threw his slender sword-cane under his arm, and wiped the inside of his hat with his handkerchief.

Madame John held a parley with him at the wicket. 'Tite Poulette was nowhere seen. He stood at the gate while Madame John went upstairs. Kristian Koppig knew him. He knew him as one knows a snake. He was the manager of the *Salle de Condé.* Presently Madame John returned with a little bundle, and they hurried off together.

And now what did this mean? Why, by any one of ordinary acuteness the matter was easily understood, but, to tell the truth, Kristian Koppig was a trifle dull, and got the idea at once that some damage was being planned against 'Tite Poulette. It made the gentle Dutchman miserable not to be minding his own business, and yet—

"But the woman certainly will not attempt"—said he to himself—"no, no! she cannot." Not being able to guess what he meant, I cannot say whether she could or not. I know that next day Kristian Koppig, glancing eagerly over the *"Ami des Lois,"* read an advertisement which he had always before skipped with a frown. It was headed, *"Salle de Condé,"* and, being interpreted, signified that a new dance was to be introduced, the *Danse de Chinois,* and that *a young lady* would follow it with the famous *"Danse du Shawl."*

It was the Sabbath. The young man watched the opposite window steadily and painfully from early in the afternoon until the moon shone bright; and from the time the moon shone bright until Madame John!—joy!—Madame John! and not 'Tite Poulette, stepped through the wicket, much dressed and well muffled, and hurried off toward the *Rue Condé.* Madame John was the "young lady;" and the young man's mind, glad to return to its own unimpassioned affairs, relapsed into quietude.

Madame John danced beautifully. It had to be done. It brought some pay, and pay was bread; and every Sunday evening, with a touch here and there of paint and powder, the mother danced the dance of the shawl, the daughter remaining at home alone.

Kristian Koppig, simple, slow-thinking young Dutchman, never noticing that he stayed at home with his window darkened for the very purpose, would see her come to her window and look out with a little wild, alarmed look in her magnificent eyes, and go and come again, and again, until the mother, like a storm-driven bird, came panting home.

Two or three months went by.

One night, on the mother's return, Kristian Koppig coming to his room nearly at the same moment, there was much earnest conversation, which he could see, but not hear.

" 'Tite Poulette," said Madame John, "you are seventeen."

"True, Maman."

"Ah! My child, I see not how you are to meet the future." The voice trembled plaintively.

"But how, Maman?"

"Ah! you are not like others; no fortune, no pleasure, no friend."

"Maman!"

"No, no;—I thank God for it; I am glad you are not; but you will be lonely, lonely, all your poor life long. There is nò place in this world for us poor women. I wish that we were either white or black!"—and the tears, two "shining ones," stood in the poor quadroon's eyes.

The daughter stood up, her eyes flashing.

"God made us, Maman," she said with a gentle, but stately smile.

"Ha!" said the mother, her keen glance darting through her tears, "Sin made *me, yes."

"No," said 'Tite Poulette, "God made us. He made us just as we are; not more white, not more black."

"He made you, truly!" said Zalli. "You are so beautiful; I believe it well." She reached and drew the fair form to a kneeling posture. "My sweet, white daughter!"

Now the tears were in the girl's eyes. "And could I be whiter than I am?" she asked.

"Oh, no, no! 'Tite Poulette," cried the other; "but if we were only *real white!*—both of us; so that some gentleman might come to see me and say 'Madame John, I want your pretty little chick. She is so beautiful. I want to take her home. She is so good—I want her to be my wife.' Oh, my child, my child, to see that I would give my life—I would give my soul! Only you should take me along to be your servant. I walked behind two young men to-night; they were coming home from their office; presently they began to talk about you."

'Tite Poulette's eyes flashed fire.

"No, my child, they spoke only the best things. One laughed a little at times and kept saying 'Beware!' but the other—I prayed the Virgin to bless him, he spoke such kind and noble words. Such gentle pity; such a holy heart! 'May God defend her,' he said, *chérie;* he said, 'May God defend her, for I see no help for her.' The other one laughed and left him. He stopped in the door right across the street. Ah, my child, do you blush? Is that something to bring the rose to your cheek? Many fine gentlemen at the ball ask me often, 'How is your daughter, Madame John?'"

The daughter's face was thrown into the mother's lap, not so well satisfied, now, with God's handiwork. Ah, how she wept! Sob, sob, sob; gasps and sighs and stifled ejaculations, her small right hand clinched and beating on her mother's knee; and the mother weeping over her.

Kristian Koppig shut his window. Nothing but a generous heart and a Dutchman's phlegm could have done so at that moment. And even thou, Kristian Koppig!——for the window closed very slowly.

He wrote to his mother, thus:

"In this wicked city, I see none so fair as the poor girl who lives opposite me, and who, alas! though so fair, is one of those whom the taint of caste has cursed. She lives a lonely, innocent life in the midst of corruption, like the lilies I find here in the marshes, and I have great pity for her. 'God defend her,' I said to-night to a fellow-clerk, 'I see no help for her.' I know there is a natural, and I think proper, horror of mixed blood (excuse the mention, sweet mother), and I feel it, too; and yet if she were in Holland to-day, not one of a hundred suitors would detect the hidden blemish."

In such strain this young man wrote on trying to demonstrate the utter impossibility of his ever loving the lovable unfortunate, until the midnight tolling of the cathedral clock sent him to bed.

About the same hour Zalli and 'Tite Poulette were kissing good-night.

"'Tite Poulette, I want you to promise me one thing."

"Well, Maman?"

"If any gentleman should ever love you and ask you to marry,—not knowing, you know,—promise me you will not tell him you are not white."

"It can never be," said 'Tite Poulette.

"But if it should," said Madame John pleadingly.

"And break the law?" asked 'Tite Poulette, impatiently.

"But the law is unjust," said the mother.

"But it is the law!"

"But you will not, dearie, will you?"

"I would surely tell him!" said the daughter.

When Zalli, for some cause, went next morning to the window, she started.

" 'Tite Poulette!"—she called softly without moving. The daughter came. The young man, whose idea of propriety had actuated him to this display, was sitting in the dormer window, reading. Mother and daughter bent a steady gaze at each other. It meant in French, "If he saw us last night!"—

"Ah! dear," said the mother, her face beaming with fun—

"What can it be, Maman?"

"He speaks—oh! ha, ha!—he speaks—such miserable French!"

It came to pass one morning at early dawn that Zalli and 'Tite Poulette, going to mass, passed a café, just as—who should be coming out but Monsieur, the manager of the *Salle de Condé*. He had not yet gone to bed. Monsieur was astonished. He had a Frenchman's eye for the beautiful, and certainly there the beautiful was. He had heard of Madame John's daughter, and had hoped once to see her, but did not; but could this be she?

They disappeared within the cathedral. A sudden pang of piety moved him. He followed. 'Tite Poulette was already kneeling in the aisle. Zalli, still in the vestibule, was just taking her hand from the font of holy-water.

"Madame John," whispered the manager.

She courtesied.

"Madame John, that young lady—is she your daughter?"

"She—she—is my daughter," said Zalli, with somewhat of alarm in her face, which the manager misinterpreted.

"I think not, Madame John." He shook his head, smiling, as one too wise to be fooled.

"Yes, Monsieur, she is my daughter."

"O no, Madame John, it is only make-believe, I think."

"I swear she is, Monsieur de la Rue."

"Is that possible?" pretending to waver, but convinced in his heart of hearts, by Zalli's alarm, that she was lying. "But how? Why does she not come to our ball-room with you?"

Zalli, trying to get away from him, shrugged and smiled. "Each to his taste, Monsieur; it pleases her not."

She was escaping, but he followed one step more. "I shall come to see you, Madame John."

She whirled and attacked him with her eyes. "Monsieur must not give himself the trouble!" she said, the eyes at the same time adding, "Dare to come!" She turned again, and knelt to her devotions. The manager dipped in the font, crossed himself, and departed.

Several weeks went by, and M. de la Rue had not accepted the fierce challenge of Madame John's eyes. One or two Sunday nights she had succeeded in avoiding him, though fulfilling her engagement in the *Salle;* but by and by pay-day,—a Saturday,—came round, and though the pay was ready, she was loath to go up to Monsieur's little office.

It was an afternoon in May. Madame John came to her own room, and, with a sigh, sank into a chair. Her eyes were wet.

"Did you go to his office, dear mother?" asked 'Tite Poulette.

"I could not," she answered, dropping her face in her hands.

"Maman, he has seen me at the window!"

"While I was gone?" cried the mother.

"He passed on the other side of the street. He looked up purposely, and saw me." The speaker's cheeks were burning red.

Zalli wrung her hands.

"It is nothing, mother; do not go near him."

"But the pay, my child."

"The pay matters not."

"But he will bring it here; he wants the chance."

That was the trouble, sure enough.

About this time Kristian Koppig lost his position in the German importing house where, he had fondly told his mother, he was indispensable.

"Summer was coming on," the senior said, "and you see our young men are almost idle. Yes, our engagement *was* for a year, but ah —we could not foresee"—etc., etc., "besides" (attempting a parting flattery), "your father is a rich gentleman, and you can afford to take the summer easy. If we can ever be of any service to you," etc., etc.

So the young Dutchman spent the afternoons at his dormer window reading and glancing down at the little casement opposite, where a small, rude shelf had lately been put out, holding a row of cigar-boxes with wretched little botanical specimens in them trying to die. 'Tite Poulette was their gardener; and it was odd to see,— dry weather or wet,—how many waterings per day those plants could take. She never looked up from her task; but I know she performed it with that unacknowledged pleasure which all girls love and deny, that of being looked upon by noble eyes.

On this particular Saturday afternoon in May, Kristian Koppig had been witness of the distressful scene over the way. It occurred to 'Tite Poulette that such might be the case, and she stepped to the casement to shut it. As she did so, the marvellous delicacy of Kristian Koppig moved him to draw in one of his shutters. Both young heads came out at one moment, while at the same instant—

"Rap, rap, rap, rap, rap!" clanked the knocker on the wicket. The black eyes of the maiden and the blue over the way, from looking into each other for the first time in life, glanced down to the arched doorway upon Monsieur the manager. Then the black eyes disappeared within, and Kristian Koppig thought again, and re-opening his shutter, stood up at the window prepared to become a bold spectator of what might follow.

But for a moment nothing followed.

"Trouble over there," thought the rosy Dutchman, and waited. The manager waited too, rubbing his hat and brushing his clothes with the tips of his kidded fingers.

"They do not wish to see him," slowly concluded the spectator.

"Rap, rap, rap, rap, rap!" quoth the knocker, and M. de la Rue looked up around at the windows opposite and noticed the handsome young Dutchman looking at him.

"Dutch!" said the manager, softly, between his teeth.

"He is staring at me," said Kristian Koppig to himself;—"but then I am staring at him, which accounts for it."

A long pause, and then another long rapping.

"They want him to go away," thought Koppig.

"Knock hard!" suggested a street youngster, standing by.

"Rap, rap"— The manager had no sooner recommenced than several neighbors looked out of doors and windows.

"Very bad," thought our Dutchman; "somebody should make him go off. I wonder what they will do."

The manager stepped into the street, looked up at the closed window, returned to the knocker, and stood with it in his hand.

"They are all gone out, Monsieur," said the street-youngster.

"You lie!" said the cynosure of neighboring eyes.

"Ah!" thought Kristian Koppig; "I will go down and ask him"— Here his thoughts lost outline; he was only convinced that he had somewhat to say to him, and turned to go down stairs. In going he became a little vexed with himself because he could not help hurrying. He noticed, too, that his arm holding the stair-rail trembled in

a silly way, whereas he was perfectly calm. Precisely as he reached the
street-door the manager raised the knocker; but the latch clicked
and the wicket was drawn slightly ajar.

Inside could just be descried Madame John. The manager bowed,
smiled, talked, talked on, held money in his hand, bowed, smiled,
talked on, flourished the money, smiled, bowed, talked on and plainly
persisted in some intention to which Madame John was steadfastly
opposed.

The window above, too,—it was Kristian Koppig who noticed that,
—opened a wee bit, like the shell of a terrapin. Presently the manager
lifted his foot and put forward an arm, as though he would enter
the gate by pushing, but as quick as gunpowder it clapped—in his
face!

You could hear the fleeing feet of Zalli pounding up the staircase.

As the panting mother re-entered her room, "See, Maman," said
'Tite Poulette, peeping at the window, "the young gentleman from
over the way has crossed!"

"Holy Mary bless him!" said the mother.

"I will go over," thought Kristian Koppig, "and ask him kindly if
he is not making a mistake."

"What are they doing, dear?" asked the mother, with clasped
hands.

"They are talking; the young man is tranquil, but 'Sieur de la Rue
is very angry," whispered the daughter; and just then—pang! came
a sharp, keen sound rattling up the walls on either side of the narrow way, and "Aha!" and laughter and clapping of female hands
from two or three windows.

"Oh! what a slap!" cried the girl, half in fright, half in glee, jerking herself back from the casement simultaneously with the report.
But the "ahas" and laughter, and clapping of feminine hands, which
still continued, came from another cause. 'Tite Poulette's rapid action
had struck the slender cord that held up an end of her hanging
garden, and the whole rank of cigar-boxes slid from their place,
turned gracefully over as they shot through the air, and emptied
themselves plump upon the head of the slapped manager. Breathless,
dirty, pale as whitewash, he gasped a threat to be heard from again,
and, getting round the corner as quick as he could walk, left Kristian
Koppig, standing motionless, the most astonished man in that street.

"Kristian Koppig, Kristian Koppig," said Greatheart to himself,
slowly dragging up-stairs, "what a mischief you have done. One
poor woman certainly to be robbed of her bitter wages, and another

—so lovely!—put to the burning shame of being the subject of a street brawl! What will this silly neighborhood say? 'Has the gentleman a heart as well as a hand?' 'Is it jealousy?'" There he paused, afraid himself to answer the supposed query; and then—"Oh! Kristian Koppig, you have been such a dunce!" "And I cannot apologize to them. Who in this street would carry my note, and not wink and grin over it with low surmises? I cannot even make restitution. Money? They would not dare receive it. Oh! Kristian Koppig, why *did* you not mind your own business? Is she any thing to you? Do you love her? *Of course not!* Oh!—such a dunce!"

The reader will eagerly admit that however faulty this young man's course of reasoning, his conclusion was correct. For mark what he did.

He went to his room, which was already growing dark, shut his window, lighted his big Dutch lamp, and sat down to write. "Something *must* be done," said he aloud, taking up his pen; "I will be calm and cool; I will be distant and brief; but—I shall have to be kind or I may offend. Ah! I shall have to write in French; I forgot that; I write it so poorly, dunce that I am, when all my brothers and sisters speak it so well." He got out his French dictionary. Two hours slipped by. He made a new pen, washed and re-filled his inkstand, mended his "abominable!" chair, and after two hours more made another attempt, and another failure. "My head aches," said he, and lay down on his couch, the better to frame his phrases.

He was awakened by the Sabbath sunlight. The bells of the Cathedral and the Ursulines' chapel were ringing for high mass, and a mocking-bird, perching on a chimney-top above Madame John's rooms, was carolling, whistling, mewing, chirping, screaming, and trilling with the ecstasy of a whole May in his throat. "Oh! sleepy Kristian Koppig," was the young man's first thought, "—such a dunce!"

Madame John and daughter did not go to mass. The morning wore away, and their casement remained closed. "They are offended," said Kristian Koppig, leaving the house, and wandering up to the little Protestant affair known as Christ Church.

"No, possibly they are not," he said, returning and finding the shutters thrown back.

By a sad accident, which mortified him extremely, he happened to see, late in the afternoon,—hardly conscious that he was looking across the street,—that Madame John was—dressing. Could it be that she was going to the *Salle de Condé?* He rushed to his table and began to write.

He had guessed aright. The wages were too precious to be lost. The manager had written her a note. He begged to assure her that he was a gentleman of the clearest cut. If he had made a mistake the previous afternoon, he was glad no unfortunate result had followed except his having been assaulted by a ruffian; that the *Danse du Shawl* was promised in his advertisement, and he hoped Madame John (whose wages were in hand waiting for her) would not fail to assist as usual. Lastly, and delicately put, he expressed his conviction that Mademoiselle was wise and discreet in declining to entertain gentlemen at her home.

So, against much beseeching on the part of 'Tite Poulette, Madame John was going to the ball-room. "Maybe I can discover what 'Sieur de la Rue is planning against Monsieur over the way," she said, knowing certainly the slap would not be forgiven; and the daughter, though tremblingly, at once withdrew her objections.

The heavy young Dutchman, now thoroughly electrified, was writing like mad. He wrote and tore up, wrote and tore up, lighted his lamp, started again, and at last signed his name. A letter by a Dutchman in French!—what can be made of it in English? We will see:

"Madame and Mademoiselle:

"A stranger, seeking not to be acquainted, but seeing and admiring all days the goodness and high honor, begs to be pardoned of them for the mistakes, alas! of yesterday, and to make reparation and satisfaction in destroying the ornaments of the window, as well as the loss of compensation from Monsieur the manager, with the enclosed bill of the *Banque de la Louisiane* for fifty dollars ($50). And, hoping they will seeing what he is meaning, remains, respectfully,   "Kristian Koppig.

"P.S.—Madame must not go to the ball."

He must bear the missive himself. He must speak in French. What should the words be? A moment of study—he has it, and is off down the long three-story stairway. At the same moment Madame John stepped from the wicket, and glided off to the *Salle de Condé,* a trifle late.

"I shall see Madame John, of course," thought the young man, crushing a hope, and rattled the knocker. 'Tite Poulette sprang up from praying for her mother's safety. "What has she forgotten?" she asked herself, and hastened down. The wicket opened. The two innocents were stunned.

"Aw—aw"—said the pretty Dutchman, "aw,"—blurted out something in virgin Dutch, . . . handed her the letter, and hurried down street.

"Alas! what have I done?" said the poor girl, bending over her candle, and bursting into tears that fell on the unopened letter. "And what shall I do? It may be wrong to open it—and worse not to." Like her sex, she took the benefit of the doubt, and intensified her perplexity and misery by reading and misconstruing the all but unintelligible contents. What then? Not only sobs and sighs, but moaning and beating of little fists together, and outcries of soul-felt agony stifled against the bedside, and temples pressed into knitted palms, because of one who "sought *not to be* acquainted," but offered money —money!—in pity to a poor—shame on her for saying that!—a poor *nigresse*.

And now our self-confessed dolt turned back from a half-hour's walk, concluding there might be an answer to his note. "Surely Madame John will appear this time." He knocked. The shutter stirred above, and something white came fluttering wildly down like a shot dove. It was his own letter containing the fifty-dollar bill. He bounded to the wicket, and softly but eagerly knocked again.

"Go away," said a trembling voice from above.

"Madame John?" said he; but the window closed, and he heard a step, the same step on the stair. Step, step, every step one step deeper into his heart. 'Tite Poulette came to the closed door.

"What will you?" said the voice within.

"I—I—don't wish to see you. I wish to see Madame John."

"I must pray Monsieur to go away. My mother is at the *Salle de Condé.*"

"At the ball!" Kristian Koppig strayed off, repeating the words for want of definite thought. All at once it occurred to him that at the ball he could make Madame John's acquaintance with impunity. "Was it courting sin to go?" By no means; he should, most likely, save a woman from trouble, and help the poor in their distress.

Behold Kristian Koppig standing on the floor of the *Salle de Condé.* A large hall, a blaze of lamps, a bewildering flutter of fans and floating robes, strains of music, columns of gay promenaders, a long row of turbaned mothers lining either wall, gentlemen of the portlier sort filling the recesses of the windows, whirling waltzers gliding here and there—smiles and grace, smiles and grace; all fair, orderly, elegant, bewitching. A young Creole's laugh mayhap a little loud, and— truly there were many sword-canes. But neither grace nor foulness satisfied the eye of the zealous young Dutchman.

Suddenly a muffled woman passed him, leaning on a gentleman's arm. It looked like—it must be, Madame John. Speak quick, Kristian Koppig; do not stop to notice the man!

"Madame John"—bowing—"I am your neighbor, Kristian Koppig."

Madame John bows low, and smiles—a ball-room smile, but is frightened, and her escort,—the manager,—drops her hand and slips away.

"Ah, Monsieur," she whispers excitedly, "you will be killed if you stay here a moment. Are you armed? No. Take this." She tried to slip a dirk into his hands, but he would not have it.

"Oh, my dear young man, go! Go quickly!" she pleaded, glancing furtively down the hall.

"I wish you not to dance," said the young man.

"I have danced already; I am going home. Come; be quick! we will go together. She thrust her arm through his, and they hastened into the street. When a square had been passed there came a sound of men running behind them.

"Run, Monsieur, run!" she cried, trying to drag him; but Monsieur Dutchman would not.

"*Run*, Monsieur! Oh, my God! it is 'Sieur"—

"*That* for yesterday!" cried the manager, striking fiercely with his cane. Kristian Koppig's fist rolled him in the dirt.

"*That* for 'Tite Poulette!" cried another man dealing the Dutchman a terrible blow from behind.

"And *that* for me!" hissed a third, thrusting at him with something bright.

"*That* for yesterday!" screamed the manager, bounding like a tiger; "That!" "THAT!" "Ha!"

Then Kristian Koppig knew that he was stabbed.

"That!" and "That!" and "That!" and the poor Dutchman struck wildly here and there, grasped the air, shut his eyes, staggered, reeled, fell, rose half up, fell again for good, and they were kicking him and jumping on him. All at once they scampered. Zalli had found the night-watch.

"Buz-z-z-z!" went a rattle. "Buz-z-z-z!" went another.

"Pick him up."

"Is he alive?"

"Can't tell; hold him steady; lead the way, misses."

"He's bleeding all over my breeches."

"This way—here—around this corner."

"This way now—only two squares more."

"Here we are."

"Rap-rap-rap!" on the old brass knocker. Curses on the narrow wicket, more on the dark archway, more still on the twisting stairs.

Up at last and into the room.

"Easy, easy, push this under his head! never mind his boots!"

So he lies—on 'Tite Poulette's own bed.

The watch are gone. They pause under the corner lamp to count profits;—a single bill—*Banque de la Louisiane,* fifty dollars. Providence is kind—tolerably so. Break it at the "Guillaume Tell." "But did you ever hear any one scream like that girl did?"

And there lies the young Dutch neighbor. His money will not flutter back to him this time; nor will any voice behind a gate "beg Monsieur to go away." O, Woman!—that knows no enemy so terrible as man! Come nigh, poor Woman, you have nothing to fear. Lay your strange electric touch upon the chilly flesh; it strikes no eager mischief along the fainting veins. Look your sweet looks upon the grimy face, and tenderly lay back the locks from the congested brows; no wicked misinterpretation lurks to bite your kindness. Be motherly, be sisterly, fear nought. Go, watch him by night; you may sleep at his feet and he will not stir. Yet he lives, and shall live —may live to forget you, who knows? But for all that, be gentle and watchful; be womanlike, we ask no more; and God reward you!

Even while it was taking all the two women's strength to hold the door against Death, the sick man himself laid a grief upon them.

"Mother," he said to Madame John, quite a master of French in his delirium, "dear mother, fear not; trust your boy; fear nothing. I will not marry 'Tite Poulette; I cannot. She is fair, dear mother, but ah! she is not—don't you know, mother? don't you know? The race! the race! Don't you know that she is jet black. Isn't it?"

The poor nurse nodded "Yes," and gave a sleeping draught; but before the patient quite slept he started once and stared.

"Take her away,"—waving his hand—"take your beauty away. She is jet white. Who could take a jet white wife? O, no, no, no, no!"

Next morning his brain was right.

"Madame," he weakly whispered, "I was delirious last night?"

Zalli shrugged. "Only a very, very, wee, wee trifle of a bit."

"And did I say something wrong or—foolish?"

"O, no, no," she replied; "you only clasped your hands, so, and prayed, prayed all the time to the dear Virgin."

"To the Virgin?" asked the Dutchman, smiling incredulously.

"And St. Joseph—yes, indeed," she insisted; "you may strike me dead."

And so, for politeness' sake, he tried to credit the invention, but grew suspicious instead.

Hard was the battle against death. Nurses are sometimes amazons, and such were these. Through the long, enervating summer, the contest lasted; but when at last the cool airs of October came stealing in at the bedside like long-banished little children, Kristian Koppig rose upon his elbow and smiled them a welcome.

The physician, blessed man, was kind beyond measure; but said some inexplicable things, which Zalli tried in vain to make him speak in an undertone. "If I knew Monsieur John?" he said, "certainly! Why, we were chums at school. And he left you so much as that, Madame John? Ah! my old friend John, always noble! And you had it all in that naughty bank? Ah, well, Madame John, it matters little. No, I shall not tell 'Tite Poulette. Adieu."

And another time:—"If I will let you tell me something? With pleasure, Madame John. No, and not tell anybody, Madame John. No, Madame, not even 'Tite Poulette. What?"—a long whistle—"is that pos-si-ble?—and Monsieur John knew it?—encouraged it?—eh, well, eh, well!—But—can I believe you, Madame John? Oh! you have Monsieur John's sworn statement. Ah! very good, truly, but—you *say* you have it; but where is it? Ah! to-morrow!" a sceptical shrug. "Pardon me, Madame John, I think perhaps, *perhaps* you are telling the truth.

"If I think you did right? Certainly! What nature keeps back, accident sometimes gives, Madame John; either is God's will. Don't cry. 'Stealing from the dead?' No! It was giving, yes! They are thanking you in heaven, Madame John."

Kristian Koppig, lying awake, but motionless and with closed eyes, hears in part, and, fancying he understands, rejoices with silent intensity. When the doctor is gone he calls Zalli.

"I give you a great deal of trouble, eh, Madame John?"

"No, no; you are no trouble at all. Had you the yellow fever—ah! then!"

She rolled her eyes to signify the superlative character of the tribulations attending yellow fever.

"I had a lady and gentleman once—a Spanish lady and gentleman, just off the ship; both sick at once with the fever—delirious—could not tell their names. Nobody to help me but sometimes Monsieur John! I never had such a time,—never before, never since,—as that time. Four days and nights this head touched not a pillow."

"And they died!" said Kristian Koppig.

"The third night the gentleman went. Poor Señor! 'Sicur John,—he did not know the harm,—gave him some coffee and toast! The fourth night it rained and turned cool, and just before day the poor lady"—

"Died!" said Koppig.

Zalli dropped her arms listlessly into her lap and her eyes ran brimful.

"And left an infant!" said the Dutchman, ready to shout with exultation.

"Ah! no, Monsieur," said Zalli.

The invalid's heart sank like a stone.

"Madame John,"—his voice was all in a tremor,—"tell me the truth. Is 'Tite Poulette your own child?"

"Ah-h-h, ha! ha! what foolishness! Of course she is my child!" And Madame gave vent to a true Frenchwoman's laugh.

It was too much for the sick man. In the pitiful weakness of his shattered nerves he turned his face into his pillow and wept like a child. Zalli passed into the next room to hide her emotion.

"Maman, dear Maman," said 'Tite Poulette, who had overheard nothing, but only saw the tears.

"Ah! my child, my child, my task—my task is too great—too great for me. Let me go now—another time. Go and watch at his bedside."

"But, Maman,"—for 'Tite Poulette was frightened,—"he needs no care now."

"Nay, but go, my child; I wish to be alone."

The maiden stole in with averted eyes and tiptoed to the window—*that window*. The patient, already a man again, gazed at her till she could feel the gaze. He turned his eyes from her a moment to gather resolution. And now, stout heart, farewell; a word or two friendly parting—nothing more.

" 'Tite Poulette."

The slender figure at the window turned and came to the bedside.

"I believe I owe my life to you," he said.

She looked down meekly, the color rising in her cheek.

"I must arrange to be moved across the street, to-morrow, on a litter."

She did not stir or speak.

"And I must now thank you, sweet nurse, for your care. Sweet nurse! Sweet nurse!"

She shook her head in protestation.

"Heaven bless you, 'Tite Poulette!"

Her face sank lower.

"God has made you very beautiful, 'Tite Poulette!"

She stirred not. He reached, and gently took her little hand, and as he drew her one step nearer, a tear fell from her long lashes. From the next room, Zalli, with a face of agonized suspense, gazed upon the pair, undiscovered. The young man lifted the hand to lay it upon his lips, when, with a mild, firm force, it was drawn away, yet still rested in his own upon the bedside, like some weak thing snared, that could only not get free.

"Thou wilt not have my love, 'Tite Poulette?"

No answer.

"Thou wilt not, beautiful?"

"Cannot!" was all that she could utter, and upon their clasped hands the tears ran down.

"Thou wrong'st me, 'Tite Poulette. Thou dost not trust me; thou fearest the kiss may loosen the hands. But I tell thee nay. I have struggled hard, even to this hour, against Love, but I yield me now; I yield; I am his unconditioned prisoner forever. God forbid that I ask aught but that you will be my wife."

Still the maiden moved not, looked not up, only rained down tears.

"Shall it not be, 'Tite Poulette?" He tried in vain to draw her.

" 'Tite Poulette?" So tenderly he called! And then she spoke.

"It is against the law."

"It is not!" cried Zalli, seizing her round the waist and dragging her forward. "Take her! she is thine. I have robbed God long enough. Here are the sworn papers—here! Take her; she is as white as snow—so! Take her, kiss her; Mary be praised! I never had a child—she is the Spaniard's daughter!"

Belles Demoiselles Plantation

THE original grantee was Count ——, assume the name to be De Charleu; the old Creoles never forgive a public mention. He was the French king's commissary. One day, called to France to explain the lucky accident of the commissariat having burned down with his account-books inside, he left his wife, a Choctaw Comptesse, behind.

Arrived at court, his excuses were accepted, and that tract granted him where afterwards stood Belles Demoiselles Plantation. A man cannot remember everything! In a fit of forgetfulness he married a French gentlewoman, rich and beautiful, and "brought her out." However, "All's well that ends well"; a famine had been in the colony, and the Choctaw Comptesse had starved, leaving nought but a half-caste orphan family lurking on the edge of the settlement, bearing our French gentlewoman's own new name, and being mentioned in Monsieur's will.

And the new Comptesse—she tarried but a twelve-month, left Monsieur a lovely son, and departed, led out of this vain world by the swamp-fever.

From this son sprang the proud Creole family of De Charleu. It rose straight up, up, up, generation after generation, tall, branchless, slender, palm-like; and finally, in the time of which I am to tell, flowered with all the rare beauty of a century-plant, in Artemise, Innocente, Felicité, the twins Marie and Martha, Leontine and little Septima: the seven beautiful daughters for whom their home had been fitly named Belles Demoiselles.

The Count's grant had once been a long point, round which the Mississippi used to whirl, and seethe, and foam, that it was horrid to behold. Big whirlpools would open and wheel about in the savage eddies under the low bank, and close up again, and others open, and spin, and disappear. Great circles of muddy surface would boil up from hundreds of feet below, and gloss over, and seem to float away, —sink, come back again under water, and with only a soft hiss surge up again, and again drift off, and vanish. Every few minutes the loamy bank would tip down a great load of earth upon its besieger, and fall back a foot,—sometimes a yard,—and the writhing river would press after, until at last the Pointe was quite swallowed up, and the great river glided by in a majestic curve, and asked no more; the bank stood fast, the "caving" became a forgotten misfortune, and the diminished grant was a long, sweeping, willowy bend, rustling with miles of sugar-cane.

Coming up the Mississippi in the sailing craft of those early days, about the time one first could descry the white spires of the old St. Louis Cathedral, you would be pretty sure to spy, just over to your right under the levee, Belles Demoiselles Mansion, with its broad veranda and red painted cypress roof, peering over the embankment, like a bird in the nest, half hid by the avenue of willows which one of the departed De Charleus,—he that married a Marot,—had planted on the levee's crown.

The house stood unusually near the river, facing eastward, and standing four-square, with an immense veranda about its sides, and a flight of steps in front spreading broadly downward, as we open arms to a child. From the veranda nine miles of river were seen; and in their compass, near at hand, the shady garden full of rare and beautiful flowers; farther away broad fields of cane and rice, and the distant quarters of the slaves, and on the horizon everywhere a dark belt of cypress forest.

The master was old Colonel De Charleu,—Jean Albert Henri Joseph De Charleu-Marot, and "Colonel" by the grace of the first American governor. Monsieur,—he would not speak to any one who called him "Colonel,"—was a hoary-headed patriarch. His step was firm, his form erect, his intellect strong and clear, his countenance classic, serene, dignified, commanding, his manners courtly, his voice musical,—fascinating. He had had his vices,—all his life; but had borne them, as his race does, with a serenity of conscience and a cleanness of mouth that left no outward blemish on the surface of the gentleman. He had gambled in Royal Street, drank hard in Orleans Street, run his adversary through in the duelling-ground at Slaughter-house Point, and danced and quarreled at the St. Philippe street-theater quadroon balls. Even now, with all his courtesy and bounty, and a hospitality which seemed to be entertaining angels, he was bitter-proud and penurious, and deep down in his hard-finished heart loved nothing but himself, his name, and his motherless children. But these!—their ravishing beauty was all but excuse enough for the unbounded idolatry of their father. Against these seven goddesses he never rebelled. Had they even required him to defraud old De Carlos—

I can hardly say.

Old De Carlos was his extremely distant relative on the Choctaw side. With this single exception, the narrow thread-like line of descent from the Indian wife, diminished to a mere strand by injudicious alliances, and deaths in the gutters of old New Orleans, was extinct. The name, by Spanish contact, had become De Carlos; but this one surviving bearer of it was known to all, and known only, as Injin Charlie.

One thing I never knew a Creole to do. He will not utterly go back on the ties of blood, no matter what sort of knots those ties may be. For one reason, he is never ashamed of his or his father's sins; and for another,—he will tell you—he is "all heart"!

So the different heirs of the De Charleu estate had always strictly regarded the rights and interests of the De Carloses, especially their ownership of a block of dilapidated buildings in a part of the city, which had once been very poor propery, but was beginning to be valuable. This block had much more than maintained the last De Carlos through a long and lazy lifetime, and, as his household consisted only of himself, and an aged and crippled negress, the inference was irresistible that he "had money." Old Charlie, though by *alias* an "Injin," was plainly a dark white man, about as old as Colonel De Charleu, sunk in the bliss of deep ignorance, shrewd, deaf, and, by repute at least, unmerciful.

The Colonel and he always conversed in English. This rare accomplishment, which the former had learned from his Scotch wife,—the latter from up-river traders,—they found an admirable medium of communication, answering, better than French could, a similar purpose to that of the stick which we fasten to the bit of one horse and breast-gear of another, whereby each keeps his distance. Once in a while, too, by way of jest, English found its way among the ladies of Belles Demoiselles, always signifying that their sire was about to have business with old Charlie.

Now a long-standing wish to buy out Charlie troubled the Colonel. He had no desire to oust him unfairly; he was proud of being always fair; yet he did long to engross the whole estate under one title. Out of his luxurious idleness he had conceived this desire, and thought little of so slight an obstacle as being already somewhat in debt to old Charlie for money borrowed, and for which Belles Demoiselles was, of course, good, ten times over. Lots, buildings, rents, all, might as well be his, he thought, to give, keep, or destroy. "Had he but the old man's heritage. Ah! he might bring that into existence which his *belles demoiselles* had been begging for, 'since many years;' a home,—and such a home,—in the gay city. Here he should tear down this row of cottages, and make his garden wall; there that long rope-walk should give place to vine-covered arbors; the bakery yonder should make way for a costly conservatory; that wine warehouse should come down, and the mansion go up. It should be the finest in the State. Men should never pass it, but they should say—'the palace of the De Charleus; a family of grand descent, a people of elegance and bounty, a line as old as France, a fine old man, and seven daughters as beautiful as happy; whoever dare attempt to marry there must leave his own name behind him!'

"The house should be of stones fitly set, brought down in ships from the land of '*les Yankees,*' and it should have an airy belvedere, with a gilded image tiptoeing and shining on its peak, and from it you should see, far across the gleaming folds of the river, the red roof of Belles Demoiselles, the country-seat. At the big stone gate there should be a porter's lodge, and it should be a privilege even to see the ground."

Truly they were a family fine enough, and fancy-free enough to have fine wishes, yet happy enough where they were, to have had no wish but to live there always.

To those, who, by whatever fortune, wandered into the garden of Belles Demoiselles some summer afternoon as the sky was reddening towards evening, it was lovely to see the family gathered out upon the tiled pavement at the foot of the broad front steps, gayly chatting and jesting, with that ripple of laughter that comes so pleasingly from a bevy of girls. The father would be found seated in their midst, the center of attention and compliment, witness, arbiter, umpire, critic, by his beautiful children's unanimous appointment, but the single vassal, too, of seven absolute sovereigns.

Now they would draw their chairs near together in eager discussion of some new step in the dance, or the adjustment of some rich adornment. Now they would start about him with excited comments to see the eldest fix a bunch of violets in his buttonhole. Now the twins would move down a walk after some unusual flower, and be greeted on their return with the high-pitched notes of delighted feminine surprise.

As evening came on they would draw more quietly about their paternal center. Often their chairs were forsaken, and they grouped themselves on the lower steps, one above another, and surrendered themselves to the tender influences of the approaching night. At such an hour the passer on the river, already attracted by the dark figures of the broad-roofed mansion, and its woody garden standing against the glowing sunset, would hear the voices of the hidden group rise from the spot in the soft harmonies of an evening song; swelling clearer and clearer as the thrill of music warmed them into feeling, and presently joined by the deeper tones of the father's voice; then, as the daylight passed quite away, all would be still, and he would know that the beautiful home had gathered its nestlings under its wings.

And yet, for mere vagary, it pleased them not to be pleased.

"Arti!" called one sister to another in the broad hall, one morning,—mock amazement in her distended eyes,—"something is goin' to took place!"

"Comm-e-n-t?"—long-drawn perplexity.

"Papa is goin' to town!"

The news passed up stairs.

"Inno!"—one to another meeting in a doorway,—"something is goin' to took place!"

"Qu'est-ce que c'est!" vain attempt at gruffness.

"Papa is goin' to town!"

The unusual tidings were true. It was afternoon of the same day that the Colonel tossed his horse's bridle to his groom, and stepped up to old Charlie, who was sitting on his bench under a China-tree, his head, as was his fashion, bound in a Madras handkerchief. The "old man" was plainly under the effect of spirits, and smiled a deferential salutation without trusting himself to his feet.

"Eh, well Charlie!"—the Colonel raised his voice to suit his kinsman's deafness,—"how is those times with my friend Charlie?"

"Eh?" said Charlie, distractedly.

"Is that goin' well with my friend Charlie?"

"In de house,—call her,"—making a pretense of rising.

"Non, non! I don't want,"—the speaker paused to breathe—" 'ow is collection?"

"Oh!" said Charlie, "every day he make me more poorer!"

"What do you hask for it?" asked the planter indifferently, designating the house by a wave of his whip.

"Ask for w'at?" said Injin Charlie.

"De *house!* What you ask for it?"

"I don't believe," said Charlie.

"What you would *take* for it!" cried the planter.

"Wait for w'at?"

"What you would *take* for the whole block?"

"I don't want to sell him!"

"I'll give you *ten thousand dollah* for it."

"Ten t'ousand dollah for dis house? Oh, no, dat is no price. He is blame good old house,—dat old house." (Old Charlie and the Colonel never swore in the presence of each other.) "Forty years dat old house didn't had to be paint! I easy can get fifty t'ousand dollah for dat old house."

"Fifty thousand picayunes; yes," said the Colonel.

"She's a good house. Can make plenty money," pursued the deaf man.

"That's what make you so rich, eh, Charlie?"

"Non, I don't make nothing. Too blame clever, me, dat's de troub'. She's a good house,—make money fast like a steamboat,—make a barrel full in a week! Me, I lose money all de days. Too blame clever."

"Charlie!"

"Eh?"

"Tell me what you'll take."

"Make? I don't make *nothing*. Too blame clever."

"What will you *take?*"

"Oh! I got enough already,—half drunk now."

"What will you take for the 'ouse?"

"You want to buy her?"

"I don't know,"—(shrug),—"may*be,*—if you sell it cheap."

"She's a bully old house."

There was a long silence. By and by old Charlie commenced—

"Old Injin Charlie is a low-down dog."

"*C'est vrai, oui!*" retorted the Colonel in an undertone.

"He's got Injin blood in him."

The Colonel nodded assent.

"But he's got some blame good blood, too, ain't it?"

The Colonel nodded impatiently.

"*Bien!* Old Charlie's Injin blood says, 'sell de house, Charlie, you blame old fool!' *Mais,* old Charlie's good blood says, 'Charlie! if you sell dat old house, Charlie, you low-down old dog, Charlie, what de Compte De Charleu make for you grace-gran-muzzer, de dev' can eat you, Charlie, I don't care.'"

"But you'll sell it anyhow, won't you, old man?"

"No!" And the *no* rumbled off in muttered oaths like thunder out on the Gulf. The incensed old Colonel wheeled and started off.

"Curl!" (Colonel) said Charlie, standing up unsteadily.

The planter turned with an inquiring frown.

"I'll trade with you!" said Charlie.

The Colonel was tempted. "'Ow'll you trade?" he asked.

"My house for yours!"

The old Colonel turned pale with anger. He walked very quickly back, and came close up to his kinsman.

"Charlie!" he said.

"Injin Charlie,"—with a tipsy nod.

But by this time self-control was returning. "Sell Belles Demoiselles to you?" he said in a high key, and then laughed "Ho, ho, ho!" and rode away.

A cloud, but not a dark one, overshadowed the spirits of Belles Demoiselles' plantation. The old master, whose beaming presence had always made him a shining Saturn, spinning and sparkling within the bright circle of his daughters, fell into musing fits, started out of frowning reveries, walked often by himself, and heard business from his overseer fretfully.

No wonder. The daughters knew his closeness in trade, and attributed to it his failure to negotiate for the Old Charlie buildings,—so to call them. They began to depreciate Belles Demoiselles. If a north wind blew, it was too cold to ride. If a shower had fallen, it was too muddy to drive. In the morning the garden was wet. In the evening the grasshopper was a burden. Ennui was turned into capital; every headache was interpreted a premonition of ague; and when the native exuberance of a flock of ladies without a want or a care burst out in laughter in the father's face, they spread their French eyes, rolled up their little hands, and with rigid wrists and mock vehemence vowed and vowed again that they only laughed at their misery, and should pine to death unless they could move to the sweet city. "Oh! the theater! Oh! Orleans Street! Oh, the masquerade! the Place d'Armes! the ball!" and they would call upon Heaven with French irreverence, and fall into each other's arms, and whirl down the hall singing a waltz, end with a grand collision and fall, and, their eyes streaming merriment, lay the blame on the slippery floor, that would some day be the death of the whole seven.

Three times more the fond father, thus goaded, managed, by accident,—business accident,—to see old Charlie and increase his offer; but in vain. He finally went to him formally.

"Eh?" said the deaf and distant relative. "For what you want him, eh? Why you don't stay where you halways be 'appy? Dis is a blame old rat-hole,—good for old Injin Charlie,—tha's all. Why you don't stay where you be halways 'appy? Why you don't buy somewheres else?"

"That's none of your business," snapped the planter. Truth was, his reasons were unsatisfactory even to himself.

A sullen silence followed. Then Charlie spoke:

"Well, now, look here; I sell you old Charlie's house."

"*Bien!* and the whole block," said the Colonel.

"Hold on," said Charlie. "I sell you de 'ouse and de block. Den I go and git drunk, and go to sleep; de dev' comes along and says, 'Charlie! old Charlie, you blame low-down old dog, wake up! What you doin' here? Where's de 'ouse what Monsieur le Compte give your grace-gran-muzzer? Don't you see dat fine gentyman, De Charleu, done gone and tore him down and make him over new, you blame old fool, Charlie, you low-down old Injin dog!'"

"I'll give you forty thousand dollars," said the Colonel.

"For de 'ouse?"

"For all."

The deaf man shook his head.

"Forty-five!" said the Colonel.

"What a lie? For what you tell me 'What a lie?' I don't tell you no lie."

"Non, non! I give you *forty-five!"* shouted the Colonel.

Charlie shook his head again.

"Fifty."

He shook it again.

The figures rose and rose to—

"Seventy-five!"

The answer was an invitation to go away and let the owner alone, as he was, in certain specified respects, the vilest of living creatures, and no company for a fine gentyman.

The "fine gentyman" longed to blaspheme,—but before old Charlie! —in the name of pride, how could he? He mounted and started away.

"Tell you what I'll make wid you," said Charlie.

The other, guessing aright, turned back without dismounting, smiling.

"How much Belles Demoiselles hoes me now?" asked the deaf one.

"One hundred and eighty thousand dollars," said the Colonel, firmly.

"Yass," said Charlie. "I don't want Belles Demoiselles."

The old Colonel's quiet laugh intimated it made no difference either way.

"But me," continued Charlie, "me,—I'm got le Compte De Charleu's blood in me, any'ow,—a litt' bit, any'ow, ain't it?"

The Colonel nodded that it was.

"Bien! If I go out of dis place and don't go to Belles Demoiselles, de peoples will say,—day will say, 'Old Charlie he been all doze time tell a blame *lie!* He ain't no kin to his old grace-gran-muzzer, not a blame bit! He don't got nary drop of De Charleu blood to save his blame low-down old Injin soul! No, sare! What I want wid money, den? No, sare! My place for yours!"

He turned to go into the house, just too soon to see the Colonel make an ugly whisk at him with his riding-whip. Then the Colonel, too, moved off.

Two or three times over, as he ambled homeward, laughter broke through his annoyance, as he recalled old Charlie's family pride and the presumption of his offer. Yet each time he could but think better of—not the offer to swap, but the preposterous ancestral loyalty. It was so much better than he could have expected from his "low-down" relative, and not unlike his own whim withal—the proposition which went with it was forgiven.

This last defeat bore so harshly on the master of Belles Demoiselles, that the daughters, reading chagrin in his face, began to repent. They loved their father as daughters can, and when they saw their pretended dejection harassing him seriously they restrained their complaints, displayed more than ordinary tenderness, and heroically and ostentatiously concluded there was no place like Belles Demoiselles. But the new mood touched him more than the old, and only refined his discontent. Here was a man, rich without the care of riches, free from any real trouble, happiness as native to his house as perfume to his garden, deliberately, as it were with premeditated malice, taking joy by the shoulder and bidding her be gone to town, whither he might easily have followed, only that the very same ancestral nonsense that kept Injin Charlie from selling the old place for twice its value prevented him from choosing any other spot for a city home.

Heaven sometimes pities such rich men and sends them trouble.

But by and by the charm of nature and the merry hearts around prevailed; the fit of exalted sulks passed off, and after a while the year flared up at Christmas, flickered, and went out.

New Year came and passed; the beautiful garden of Belles Demoiselles put on its spring attire; the seven fair sisters moved from rose to rose; the cloud of discontent had warmed into invisible vapor in the rich sunlight of family affection, and on the common memory the only scar of last year's wound was old Charlie's sheer impertinence in crossing the caprice of the De Charleus. The cup of gladness seemed to fill with the filling of the river.

How high that river was! Its tremendous current rolled and tumbled and spun along, hustling the long funeral flotillas of drift,—and how near shore it came! Men were out day and night, watching the levee. On windy nights even the old Colonel took part, and grew light-hearted with occupation and excitement, as every minute the river threw a white arm over the levee's top, as though it would vault over. But all held fast, and, as the summer drifted in, the water sunk down into its banks and looked quite incapable of harm.

On a summer afternoon of uncommon mildness, old Colonel Jean Albert Henry Joseph de Charleu-Marot, being in a mood for reverie, slipped the custody of his feminine rulers and sought the crown of the levee, where it was his wont to promenade. Presently he sat upon a stone bench,—a favorite seat. Before him lay his broad-spread fields; near by, his lordly mansion; and being still,—perhaps by female contact,—somewhat sentimental, he fell to musing on his past. It was hardly worthy to be proud of. All its morning was reddened with mad frolic, and far toward the meridian it was marred with elegant rioting. Pride had kept him well-nigh useless, and despised the honors won by valor; gaming had dimmed prosperity; death had taken his heavenly wife; voluptuous ease had mortgaged his lands; and yet his house still stood, his sweet-smelling fields were still fruitful, his name was fame enough; and yonder and yonder, among the trees and flowers, like angels walking in Eden, were the seven goddesses of his only worship.

Just then a slight sound behind him brought him to his feet. He cast his eyes anxiously to the outer edge of the little strip of bank between the levee's base and the river. There was nothing visible. He paused, with his ear toward the water, his face full of frightened expectation. Ha! There came a single plashing sound, like some great beast slipping into the river, and little waves in a wide semicircle came out from under the bank and spread over the water.

"My God!"

He plunged down the levee and bounded through the low weeds to the edge of the bank. It was sheer, and the water about four feet below. He did not stand quite on the edge, but fell upon his knees a couple of yards away, wringing his hands, moaning and weeping, and staring through his watery eyes at a fine, long crevice just discernible under the matted grass, and curving outward on either hand toward the water.

"My God!" he sobbed aloud; "my God!" and even while he called, his God answered: the tough Bermuda grass stretched and snapped, the crevice slowly became a gape, and softly, gradually, with no sound but the closing of the water at last, a ton or more of earth settled into the boiling eddy and disappeared.

At the same instant a pulse of the breeze brought from the garden behind, the joyous, thoughtless laughter of the fair mistresses of Belles Demoiselles.

The old Colonel sprang up and clambered over the levee. Then forcing himself to a more composed movement he hastened into the house and ordered his horse.

"Tell my children to make merry while I am gone," he left word. "I shall be back to-night," and the horse's hoofs clattered down a by-road leading to the city.

"Charlie," said the planter, riding up to a window, from which the old man's nightcap was thrust out, "what you say, Charlie,—my house for yours, eh, Charlie—what you say?"

" 'Ello!" said Charlie; "from where you come from dis time of to-night?"

"I come from the Exchange." (A small fraction of the truth.)

"What you want?" said matter-of-fact Charlie.

"I come to trade."

The low-down relative drew the worsted off his ears. "Oh! yass," he said with an uncertain air.

"Well, old man Charlie, what you say; my house for yours,—like you said,—eh, Charlie?"

"I dunno," said Charlie; "it's nearly mine now. Why you don't stay dare youse'f?"

"Because I don't want!" said the Colonel savagely; "is dat reason enough for you? you better take me in de notion, old man, I tell you,—yes!"

Charlie never winced; but how his answer delighted the Colonel! Quoth Charlie:

"I don't care—I take him!—*mais,* possession give right off."

"Not the whole plantation, Charlie; only—"

"I don't care," said Charlie; "we easy can fix dat. *Mais,* what for you don't want to keep him? I don't want him. You better keep him."

"Don' you try to make no fool of me, old man," cried the planter.

"Oh, no!" said the other. "Oh, no! but you make a fool of your-self, ain't it?"

The dumbfounded Colonel stared; Charlie went on:

"Yass! Belles Demoiselles is more wort' dan tree block like dis one. I pass by dare since two weeks. Oh, pritty Belles Demoiselles! De cane was wave in de wind, de garden smell like a bouquet, de white-cap was jump up and down on de river; seven *belles demoiselles* was ridin' on horses. 'Pritty, pritty, pritty!' says old Charlie; ah! *Monsieur le père,* 'ow 'appy, 'appy, 'appy!"

"Yass!" he continued—the Colonel still staring—"le Compte De Charleu have two familie. One was low-down Choctaw, one was high-up *noblesse.* He gave the low-down Choctaw dis old rat-hole; he give Belles Demoiselles to you gran-fozzer; and now you don't be *satisfait.* What I'll do wid Belles Demoiselles? She'll break me in two years, yass. And what you'll do wid old Charlie's house; eh? You'll tear her down and make you'se'f a blame old fool. I rather wouldn't trade!"

The planter caught a big breathful of anger, but Charlie went straight on:

"I rather wouldn't, *mais* I will do it for you;—just the same, like Monsieur le Compte would say, 'Charlie, you old fool, I want to shange houses wid you.'"

So long as the Colonel suspected irony he was angry, but as Charlie seemed, after all, to be certainly in earnest, he began to feel conscience-stricken. He was by no means a tender man, but his lately-discovered misfortune had unhinged him, and this strange, unde-served, disinterested family fealty on the part of Charlie touched his heart. And should he still try to lead him into the pitfall he had dug? He hesitated;—no, he would show him the place by broad daylight, and if he chose to overlook the "caving bank," it would be his own fault;—a trade's a trade.

"Come," said the planter, "come at my house to-night; to-morrow we look at the place before breakfast, and finish the trade."

"For what?" said Charlie.

"Oh, because I got to come in town in the morning."

"I don't want," said Charlie. "How I'm goin' to come dere?"

"I git you a horse at the liberty stable."

"Well—anyhow—I don't care—I'll go." And they went.

When they had ridden a long time, and were on the road darkened by hedges of Cherokee rose, the Colonel called behind him to the "low-down" scion:

"Keep the road, old man."

"Eh?"

"Keep the road."

"Oh, yes; all right; I keep my word; we don't goin' to play no tricks, eh?"

But the Colonel seemed not to hear. His ungenerous design was beginning to be hateful to him. Not only old Charlie's unprovoked goodness was prevailing; the eulogy on Belles Demoiselles had stirred the depths of an intense love for his beautiful home. True, if he held to it, the caving of the bank, at its present fearful speed, would let the house into the river within three months; but were it not better to lose it so, than sell his birthright? Again,—coming back to the first thought,—to betray his own blood! It was only Injin Charlie; but had not the De Charleu blood just spoken out in him? Un-consciously he groaned.

After a time they struck a path approaching the plantation in the rear, and a little after, passing from behind a clump of live-oaks, they came in sight of the villa. It looked so like a gem, shining through its dark grove, so like a great glow-worm in the dense foliage, so significant of luxury and gayety, that the poor master, from an overflowing heart, groaned again.

"What?" asked Charlie.

The Colonel only drew his rein, and, dismounting mechanically, contemplated the sight before him. The high, arched doors and windows were thrown wide to the summer air; from every opening the bright light of numerous candelabra darted out upon the sparkling foliage of magnolia and bay, and here and there in the spacious verandas a colored lantern swayed in the gentle breeze. A sound of revel fell on the ear, the music of harps; and across one window, brighter than the rest, flitted, once or twice, the shadows of dancers. But oh! the shadows flitting across the heart of the fair mansion's master!

"Old Charlie," said he, gazing fondly at his house, "you and me is both old, eh?"

"Yass," said the stolid Charlie.

"And we has both been bad enough in our time, eh, Charlie?"

Charlie, surprised at the tender tone, repeated "Yass."

"And you and me is mighty close?"

"Blame close, yass."

"But you never know me to cheat, old man!"

"No,"—impassively.

"And do you think I would cheat you now?"

"I dunno," said Charlie. "I don't believe."

"Well, old man, old man,"—his voice began to quiver,—"I shan't cheat you now. My God!—old man, I tell you—you better not make the trade!"

"Because for what?" asked Charlie in plain anger; but both looked quickly toward the house! The Colonel tossed his hands wildly in the air, rushed forward a step or two, and giving one fearful scream of agony and fright, fell forward on his face in the path. Old Charlie stood transfixed with horror. Belles Demoiselles, the realm of maiden beauty, the home of merriment, the house of dancing, all in the tremor and glow of pleasure, suddenly sunk, with one short, wild wail of terror—sunk, sunk, down, down, down, into the merciless, unfathomable flood of the Mississippi.

Twelve long months were midnight to the mind of the childless father; when they were only half gone, he took his bed; and every day, and every night, old Charlie, the "low-down," the "fool," watched him tenderly, tended him lovingly, for the sake of his name, his

misfortunes and his broken heart. No woman's step crossed the floor
of the sick-chamber, whose western dormer-windows overpeered the
dingy architecture of old Charlie's block; Charlie and a skilled physician, the one all interest, the other all gentleness, hope, and patience
—these only entered by the door; but by the window came in a
sweet-scented evergreen vine, transplanted from the caving bank of
Belles Demoiselles. It caught the rays of sunset in its flowery net
and let them softly in upon the sick man's bed; gathered the glancing beams of the moon at midnight, and often wakened the sleeper
to look, with his mindless eyes, upon their pretty silver fragments
strewn upon the floor.

By and by there seemed—there was—a twinkling dawn of returning reason. Slowly, peacefully, with an increase unseen from day
to day, the light of reason came into the eyes, and speech became
coherent; but withal there came a failing of the wrecked body, and
the doctor said that monsieur was both better and worse.

One evening, as Charlie sat by the vine-clad window with his
fireless pipe in his hand, the old Colonel's eyes fell full upon his own,
and rested there.

"Charl—," he said with an effort, and his delighted nurse hastened
to the bedside and bowed his best ear. There was an unsuccessful
effort or two, and then he whispered, smiling with sweet sadness,—

"We didn't trade."

The truth, in this case, was a secondary matter to Charlie; the
main point was to give a pleasing answer. So he nodded his head
decidedly, as who should say—"Oh yes, we did, it was a bona-fide
swap!" but when he saw the smile vanish, he tried the other expedient and shook his head with still more vigor, to signify that
they had not so much as approached a bargain; and the smile returned.

Charlie wanted to see the vine recognized. He stepped backward
to the window with a broad smile, shook the foliage, nodded and
looked smart.

"I know," said the Colonel, with beaming eyes, "—many weeks."
The next day—
"Charl—"
The best ear went down.
"Send for a priest."
The priest came, and was alone with him a whole afternoon.
When he left, the patient was very haggard and exhausted, but
smiled and would not suffer the crucifix to be removed from his
breast.

One more morning came. Just before dawn Charlie, lying on a pallet in the room, thought he was called, and came to the bed-side.

"Old man," whispered the failing invalid, "is it caving yet?"

Charlie nodded.

"It won't pay you out."

"Oh, dat makes not'in," said Charlie.

Two big tears rolled down his brown face.

"Dat makes not'in."

The Colonel whispered once more:

"*Mes belles demoiselles!* in paradise:—in the garden—I shall be with them at sunrise"; and so he was.

Jean-ah Poquelin

I N the first decade of the present century, when the newly established American Government was the most hateful thing in Louisiana—when the Creoles were still kicking at such vile innovations as
the trial by jury, American dances, anti-smuggling laws, and the
printing of the Governor's proclamation in English—when the Anglo-
American flood that was presently to burst in a crevasse of immigration upon the delta had thus far been felt only as slippery seepage
which made the Creole tremble for his footing—there stood, a short
distance above what is now Canal Street, and considerably back from
the line of villas which fringed the river-bank on Tchoupitoulas Road,
an old colonial plantation-house half in ruin.

It stood aloof from civilization, the tracts that had once been its
indigo fields given over to their first noxious wildness, and grown up
into one of the horridest marshes within a circuit of fifty miles.

The house was of heavy cypress, lifted up on pillars, grim, solid,
and spiritless, its massive build a strong reminder of days still earlier,
when every man had been his own peace officer and the insurrection
of the blacks a daily contingency. Its dark, weather-beaten roof and
sides were hoisted up above the jungly plain in a distracted way, like
a gigantic ammunition-wagon stuck in the mud and abandoned by
some retreating army. Around it was a dense growth of low water
willows, with half a hundred sorts of thorny or fetid bushes, savage
strangers alike to the "language of flowers" and to the botanist's
Greek. They were hung with countless strands of discolored and

prickly smilax, and the impassable mud below bristled with *chevaux de frise* of the dwarf palmetto. Two lone forest-trees, dead cypresses, stood in the centre of the marsh, dotted with roosting vultures. The shallow strips of water were hid by myriads of aquatic plants, under whose coarse and spiritless flowers, could one have seen it, was a harbor of reptiles, great and small, to make one shudder to the end of his days.

The house was on a slightly raised spot, the levee of a draining canal. The waters of this canal did not run; they crawled, and were full of big, ravening fish and alligators, that held it against all comers.

Such was the home of old Jean Marie Poquelin, once an opulent indigo planter, standing high in the esteem of his small, proud circle of exclusively male acquaintances in the old city; now a hermit, alike shunned by and shunning all who had ever known him. "The last of his line," said the gossips. His father lies under the floor of the St. Louis Cathedral, with the wife of his youth on one side, and the wife of his old age on the other. Old Jean visits the spot daily. His half-brother—alas! there was a mystery; no one knew what had become of the gentle, young half-brother, more than thirty years his junior, whom once he seemed so fondly to love, but who, seven years ago, had disappeared suddenly, once for all, and left no clew of his fate.

They had seemed to live so happily in each other's love. No father, mother, wife to either, no kindred upon earth. The elder a bold, frank, impetuous, chivalric adventurer; the younger a gentle, studious, book-loving recluse; they lived upon the ancestral estate like mated birds, one always on the wing, the other always in the nest.

There was no trait in Jean Marie Poquelin, said the old gossips, for which he was so well known among his few friends as his apparent fondness for his "little brother." "Jacques said this," and "Jacques said that;" he "would leave this or that, or any thing to Jacques," for Jacques was a scholar, and "Jacques was good," or "wise," or "just," or "far-sighted," as the nature of the case required; and "he should ask Jacques as soon as he got home," since Jacques was never elsewhere to be seen.

It was between the roving character of the one brother, and the bookishness of the other, that the estate fell into decay. Jean Marie, generous gentleman, gambled the slaves away one by one, until none was left, man or woman, but one old African mute.

The indigo-fields and vats of Louisiana had been generally abandoned as unremunerative. Certain enterprising men had substituted the culture of sugar; but while the recluse was too apathetic to take so active a course, the other saw larger, and, at that time, equally respectable profits, first in smuggling, and later in the African slave-trade. What harm could he see in it? The whole people said it was vitally necessary, and to minister to a vital public necessity,—good enough, certainly, and so he laid up many a doubloon, that made him none the worse in the public regard.

One day old Jean Marie was about to start upon a voyage that was to be longer, much longer, than any that he had yet made. Jacques had begged him hard for many days not to go, but he laughed him off, and finally said, kissing him:

"*Adieu, 'tit frère.*"

"No," said Jacques, "I shall go with you."

They left the old hulk of a house in the sole care of the African mute, and went away to the Guinea coast together.

Two years after, old Poquelin came home without his vessel. He must have arrived at his house by night. No one saw him come. No one saw "his little brother;" rumor whispered that he, too, had returned, but he had never been seen again.

A dark suspicion fell upon the old slave-trader. No matter that the few kept the many reminded of the tenderness that had ever marked his bearing to the missing man. The many shook their heads. "You know he has a quick and fearful temper;" and "why does he cover his loss with mystery?" "Grief would out with the truth."

"But," said the charitable few, "look in his face; see that expression of true humanity." The many did look in his face, and, as he looked in theirs, he read the silent question: "Where is thy brother Abel?" The few were silenced, his former friends died off, and the name of Jean Marie Poquelin became a symbol of witchery, devilish crime, and hideous nursery fictions.

The man and his house were alike shunned. The snipe and duck hunters forsook the marsh, and the wood-cutters abandoned the canal. Sometimes the hardier boys who ventured out there snake-shooting heard a low thumping of oar-locks on the canal. They would look at each other for a moment half in consternation, half in glee, then rush from their sport in wanton haste to assail with their gibes the unoffending, withered old man, who, in rusty attire, sat in the stern of a skiff, rowed homeward by his white-headed African mute.

"O Jean-ah Poquelin! O Jean-ah! Jean-ah Poquelin!"

It was not neccessary to utter more than that. No hint of wickedness, deformity, or any physical or moral demerit; merely the name and tone of mockery: "Oh, Jean-ah Poquelin!" and while they tumbled one over another in their needless haste to fly, he would rise carefully from his seat, while the aged mute, with downcast face, went on rowing, and rolling up his brown fist and extending it toward the urchins, would pour forth such an unholy broadside of French imprecation and invective as would all but craze them with delight.

Among both blacks and whites the house was the object of a thousand superstitions. Every midnight, they affirmed, the *feu follet* came out of the marsh and ran in and out of the rooms, flashing from window to window. The story of some lads, whose word in ordinary statements was worthless, was generally credited, that the night they camped in the woods, rather than pass the place after dark, they saw, about sunset, every window blood-red, and on each of the four chimneys an owl sitting, which turned his head three times round, and moaned and laughed with a human voice. There was a bottomless well, everybody professed to know, beneath the sill of the big front door under the rotten veranda; whoever set his foot upon that threshold disappeared forever in the depth below.

What wonder the marsh grew as wild as Africa! Take all the Faubourg Ste. Marie, and half the ancient city, you would not find one graceless dare-devil reckless enough to pass within a hundred yards of the house after nightfall.

The alien races pouring into old New Orleans began to find the few streets named for the Bourbon princes too strait for them. The wheel of fortune, beginning to whirl, threw them off beyond the ancient corporation lines, and sowed civilization and even trade upon the lands of the Graviers and Girods. Fields became roads, roads streets. Everywhere the leveller was peering through his glass, rodsmen were whacking their way through willow-brakes and rose-hedges, and the sweating Irishmen tossed the blue clay up with their long-handled shovels.

"Ha! that is all very well," quoth the Jean-Baptistes, feeling the reproach of an enterprise that asked neither co-operation nor advice of them, "but wait till they come yonder to Jean Poquelin's marsh; ha! ha! ha!" The supposed predicament so delighted them, that they put on a mock terror and whirled about in an assumed stampede, then caught their clasped hands between their knees in excess of mirth, and laughed till the tears ran; for whether the street-makers mired in the marsh, or contrived to cut through old "Jean-ah's" property, either event would be joyful. Meantime a line of tiny rods, with bits of white paper in their split tops, gradually extended its way

straight through the haunted ground, and across the canal diago-
nally.

"We shall fill that ditch," said the men in mud-boots, and brushed
close along the chained and padlocked gate of the haunted mansion.
Ah, Jean-ah Poquelin, those were not Creole boys, to be stampeded
with a little hard swearing.

He went to the Governor. That official scanned the odd figure with
no slight interest. Jean Poquelin was of short, broad frame, with a
bronzed leonine face. His brow was ample and deeply furrowed. His
eye, large and black, was bold and open like that of a war-horse, and
his jaws shut together with the firmness of iron. He was dressed in a
suit of Attakapas cottonade, and his shirt unbuttoned and thrown
back from the throat and bosom, sailor-wise, showed a herculean
breast, hard and grizzled. There was no fierceness or defiance in his
look, no harsh ungentleness, no symptom of his unlawful life or
violent temper; but rather a peaceful and peaceable fearlessness.
Across the whole face, not marked in one or another feature, but as
it were laid softly upon the countenance like an almost imperceptible
veil, was the imprint of some great grief. A careless eye might easily
overlook it, but, once seen, there it hung—faint, but unmistakable.

The Governor bowed.

"*Parlez-vous français?*" asked the figure.

"I would rather talk English, if you can do so," said the Governor.

"My name, Jean Poquelin."

"How can I serve you, Mr. Poquelin?"

"My 'ouse is yond'; *dans le marais là-bas.*"

The Governor bowed.

"Dat *marais* billong to me."

"Yes, sir."

"To me; Jean Poquelin; I hown 'im meself."

"Well, sir?"

"He don't billong to you; I get him from me father."

"That is perfectly true, Mr. Poquelin, as far as I am aware."

"You want to make strit pass yond'?"

"I do not know, sir; it is quite probable; but the city will indemnify
you for any loss you may suffer—you will get paid, you understand."

"Strit can't pass dare."

"You will have to see the municipal authorities about that, Mr.
Poquelin."

A bitter smile came upon the old man's face.

"*Pardon, Monsieur,* you is not *le Gouverneur?*"

"Yes."

"*Mais,* yes. You har *le Gouverneur*—yes. Veh-well. I come to you. I tell you, strit can't pass at me 'ouse."

"But you will have to see"—

"I come to you. You is *le Gouverneur.* I know not the new laws. I ham a Fr-r-rench-a-man! Fr-rench-a-man have something *aller au contraire*—he come at his *Gouverneur.* I come at you. If me not had been bought from me king like *bossals* in the hold time, ze king gof—France would-a-show *Monsieur le Gouverneur* to take care his men to make strit in right places. *Mais,* I know; we billong to *Monsieur le Président.* I want you do somesin for me, eh?"

"What is it?" asked the patient Governor.

"I want you tell *Monsieur le Président,* strit—can't—pass—at—me—'ouse."

"Have a chair, Mr. Poquelin;" but the old man did not stir. The Governor took a quill and wrote a line to a city official, introducing Mr. Poquelin, and asking for him every possible courtesy. He handed it to him, instructing him where to present it.

"Mr. Poquelin," he said, with a conciliatory smile, "tell me, is it your house that our Creole citizens tell such odd stories about?"

The old man glared sternly upon the speaker, and with immovable features said:

"You don't see me trade some Guinea nigga'?"

"Oh, no."

"You don't see me make some smugglin'?"

"No, sir; not at all."

"But, I am Jean Marie Poquelin. I mine me hown bizniss. Dat all right? Adieu."

He put his hat on and withdrew. By and by he stood, letter in hand, before the person to whom it was addressed. This person employed an interpreter.

"He says," said the interpreter to the officer, "he come to make you the fair warning how you muz not make the street pas' at his 'ouse."

The officer remarked that "such impudence was refreshing;" but the experienced interpreter translated freely.

"He says: 'Why you don't want?' " said the interpreter.

The old slave-trader answered at some length.

"He says," said the interpreter, again turning to the officer, "the marass is a too unhealth' for peopl' to live."

"But we expect to drain his old marsh; it's not going to be a marsh."

"*Il dit*"—The interpreter explained in French.

The old man answered tersely.

"He says the canal is a private," said the interpreter.

"Oh! *that* old ditch; that's to be filled up. Tell the old man we're going to fix him up nicely."

Translation being duly made, the man in power was amused to see a thunder-cloud gathering on the old man's face.

"Tell him," he added, "by the time we finish, there'll not be a ghost left in his shanty."

The interpreter began to translate, but—

"*J' comprends, J' comprends,*" said the old man, with an impatient gesture, and burst forth, pouring curses upon the United States, the President, the Territory of Orleans, Congress, the Governor and all his subordinates, striding out of the apartment as he cursed, while the object of his maledictions roared with merriment and rammed the floor with his foot.

"Why, it will make his old place worth ten dollars to one," said the official to the interpreter.

" 'Tis not for de worse of de property," said the interpreter.

"I should guess not," said the other, whittling his chair,—"seems to me as if some of these old Creoles would liever live in a crawfish hole than to have a neighbor."

"You know what make old Jean Poquelin make like that? I will tell you. You know"—

The interpreter was rolling a cigarette, and paused to light his tinder; then, as the smoke poured in a thick double stream from his nostrils, he said, in a solemn whisper:

"He is a witch."

"Ho, ho, ho!" laughed the other.

"You don't believe it? What you want to bet?" cried the interpreter, jerking himself half up and thrusting out one arm while he bared it of its coat-sleeve with the hand of the other. "What you want to bet?"

"How do you know?" asked the official.

"Dass what I goin' to tell you. You know, one evening I was shooting some *grosbec*. I killed three; but I had trouble to find them, it was becoming so dark. When I have them I start' to come home; then I got to pas' at Jean Poquelin's house."

"Ho, ho, ho!" laughed the other, throwing his leg over the arm of his chair.

"Wait," said the interpreter. "I come along slow, not making some noises; still, still"—

"And scared," said the smiling one.

"*Mais,* wait. I get all pas' the 'ouse. 'Ah!' I say; 'all right!' Then I see two thing' before! Hah! I get as cold and humide, and shake like a leaf. You think it was nothing? There I see, so plain as can be (though it was making nearly dark), I see Jean—Marie—Po-que-lin walkin' right in front, and right there beside of him was something like a man—but not a man—white like paint!—I dropp' on the grass from scared—they pass'; so sure as I live 'twas the ghos' of Jacques Poquelin, his brother!"

"Pooh!" said the listener.

"I'll put my han' in the fire," said the interpreter.

"But did you never think," asked the other, "that that might be Jack Poquelin, as you call him, alive and well, and for some cause hid away by his brother?"

"But there har' no cause!" said the other, and the entrance of third parties changed the subject.

Some months passed and the street was opened. A canal was first dug through the marsh, the small one which passed so close to Jean Poquelin's house was filled, and the street, or rather a sunny road, just touched a corner of the old mansion's dooryard. The morass ran dry. Its venomous denizens slipped away through the bulrushes; the cattle roaming freely upon its hardened surface trampled the superabundant undergrowth. The bellowing frogs croaked to westward. Lilies and the flower-de-luce sprang up in the place of reeds; smilax and poison-oak gave way to the purple-plumed iron-weed and pink spiderwort; the bindweeds ran everywhere blooming as they ran, and on one of the dead cypresses a giant creeper hung its green burden of foliage and lifted its scarlet trumpets. Sparrows and redbirds flitted through the bushes, and dewberries grew ripe beneath. Over all these came a sweet, dry smell of salubrity which the place had not known since the sediments of the Mississippi first lifted it from the sea.

But its owner did not build. Over the willow-brakes, and down the vista of the open street, bright new houses, some singly, some by ranks, were prying in upon the old man's privacy. They even settled down toward his southern side. First a wood-cutter's hut or two, then a market gardener's shanty, then a painted cottage, and all at once the faubourg had flanked and half surrounded him and his dried-up marsh.

Ah! then the common people began to hate him. "The old tyrant!" "You don't mean an old *tyrant?*" "Well, then, why don't he build when the public need demands it? What does he live in that un-neighborly way for?" "The old pirate!" "The old kidnapper!" How easily even the most ultra Louisianians put on the imported virtues of the North when they could be brought to bear against the hermit. "There he goes, with the boys after him! Ah! ha! ha! Jean-ah Poquelin! Ah! Jean-ah! Aha! aha! Jean-ah Marie! Jean-ah Poquelin! The old villain!" How merrily the swarming Américains echo the spirit of persecution! "The old fraud," they say—"pretends to live in a haunted house, does he? We'll tar and feather him some day. Guess we can fix him."

He cannot be rowed home along the old canal now; he walks. He has broken sadly of late, and the street urchins are ever at his heels. It is like the days when they cried: "Go up, thou bald-head," and the old man now and then turns and delivers ineffectual curses.

To the Creoles—to the incoming lower class of superstitious Germans, Irish, Sicilians, and others—he became an omen and embodiment of public and private ill-fortune. Upon him all the vagaries of their superstitions gathered and grew. If a house caught fire, it was imputed to his machinations. Did a woman go off in a fit, he had bewitched her. Did a child stray off for an hour, the mother shivered with the apprehension that Jean Poquelin had offered him to strange gods. The house was the subject of every bad boy's invention who loved to contrive ghostly lies. "As long as that house stands we shall have bad luck. Do you not see our pease and beans dying, our cabbages and lettuce going to seed and our gardens turning to dust, while every day you can see it raining in the woods? The rain will never pass old Poquelin's house. He keeps a fetich. He has conjured the whole Faubourg St. Marie. And why, the old wretch? Simply because our playful and innocent children call after him as he passes."

A "Building and Improvement Company," which had not yet got its charter, "but was going to," and which had not, indeed, any tangible capital yet, but "was going to have some," joined the "Jean-ah Poquelin" war. The haunted property would be such a capital site for a market-house! They sent a deputation to the old mansion to ask its occupant to sell. The deputation never got beyond the chained gate and a very barren interview with the African mute. The President of the Board was then empowered (for he had studied French in Pennsylvania and was considered qualified) to call and persuade M. Poquelin to subscribe to the company's stock; but—

"Fact is, gentlemen," he said at the next meeting, "it would take us at least twelve months to make Mr. Pokaleen understand the rather original features of our system, and he wouldn't subscribe when we'd done; besides, the only way to see him is to stop him on the street."

There was a great laugh from the Board; they couldn't help it. "Better meet a bear robbed of her whelps," said one.

"You're mistaken as to that," said the President. "I did meet him, and stopped him, and found him quite polite. But I could get no satisfaction from him; the fellow wouldn't talk in French, and when I spoke in English he hoisted his old shoulders up, and gave the same answer to every thing I said."

"And that was—?" asked one or two, impatient of the pause.

"That it 'don't worse w'ile?' "

One of the Board said: "Mr. President, this market-house project, as I take it, is not altogether a selfish one; the community is to be benefited by it. We may feel that we are working in the public interest [the Board smiled knowingly], if we employ all possible means to oust this old nuisance from among us. You may know that at the time the street was cut through, this old Poquelann did all he could to prevent it. It was owing to a certain connection which I had with that affair that I heard a ghost story [smiles, followed by a sudden dignified check]—ghost story, which, of course, I am not going to relate; but I *may* say that my profound conviction, arising from a prolonged study of that story, is, that this old villain, John Poquelann, has his brother locked up in that old house. Now, if this is so, and we can fix it on him, I merely *suggest* that we can make the matter highly useful. I don't know," he added, beginning to sit down, "but that it is an action we owe to the community—hem!"

"How do you propose to handle the subject?" asked the President.

"I was thinking," said the speaker, "that, as a Board of Directors, it would be unadvisable for us to authorize any action involving trespass; but if you, for instance, Mr. President, should, as it were, for mere curiosity, *request* some one, as, for instance, our excellent Secretary, simply as a personal favor, to look into the matter—this is merely a suggestion."

The Secretary smiled sufficiently to be understood that, while he certainly did not consider such preposterous service a part of his duties as secretary, he might, notwithstanding, accede to the President's request; and the Board adjourned.

Little White, as the Secretary was called, was a mild, kind-hearted little man, who, nevertheless, had no fear of any thing, unless it was the fear of being unkind.

"I tell you frankly," he privately said to the President, "I go into this purely for reasons of my own."

The next day, a little after nightfall, one might have descried this little man slipping along the rear fence of the Poquelin place; preparatory to vaulting over into the rank, grass-grown yard, and bearing himself altogether more after the manner of a collector of rare chickens than according to the usage of secretaries.

The picture presented to his eye was not calculated to enliven his mind. The old mansion stood out against the western sky, black and silent. One long, lurid pencil-stroke along a sky of slate was all that was left of daylight. No sign of life was apparent; no light at any window, unless it might have been on the side of the house hidden from view. No owls were on the chimneys, no dogs were in the yard.

He entered the place, and ventured up behind a small cabin which stood apart from the house. Through one of its many crannies he easily detected the African mute crouched before a flickering pine-knot, his head on his knees, fast asleep.

He concluded to enter the mansion, and, with that view, stood and scanned it. The broad rear steps of the veranda would not serve him; he might meet some one midway. He was measuring, with his eye, the proportions of one of the pillars which supported it, and estimating the practicability of climbing it, when he heard a foot-step. Some one dragged a chair out toward the railing, then seemed to change his mind and began to pace the veranda, his footfalls re-sounding on the dry boards with singular loudness. Little White drew a step backward, got the figure between himself and the sky, and at once recognized the short, broad-shouldered form of old Jean Poquelin.

He sat down upon a billet of wood, and, to escape the stings of a whining cloud of mosquitoes, shrouded his face and neck in his hand-kerchief, leaving his eyes uncovered.

He had sat there but a moment when he noticed a strange, sicken-ing odor, faint, as if coming from a distance, but loathsome and horrid.

Whence could it come? Not from the cabin; not from the marsh, for it was as dry as powder. It was not in the air; it seemed to come from the ground.

Rising up, he noticed, for the first time, a few steps before him a narrow footpath leading toward the house. He glanced down it—ha! right there was some one coming—ghostly white!

Quick as thought, and as noiselessly, he lay down at full length against the cabin. It was bold strategy, and yet, there was no denying it, little White felt that he was frightened. "It is not a ghost," he said to himself. "I *know* it cannot be a ghost;" but the perspiration burst out at every pore, and the air seemed to thicken with heat. "It is a living man," he said in his thoughts. "I hear his footstep, and I hear old Poquelin's footsteps, too, separately, over on the veranda. I am not discovered; the thing has passed; there is that odor again; what a smell of death! Is it coming back? Yes. It stops at the door of the cabin. Is it peering in at the sleeping mute? It moves away. It is in the path again. Now it is gone." He shuddered. "Now, if I dare venture, the mystery is solved." He rose cautiously, close against the cabin, and peered along the path.

The figure of a man, a presence if not a body—but whether clad in some white stuff or naked, the darkness would not allow him to determine—had turned, and now, with a seeming painful gait, moved slowly from him. "Great Heaven! can it be that the dead do walk?" He withdrew again the hands which had gone to his eyes. The dreadful object passed between two pillars and under the house. He listened. There was a faint sound as of feet upon a staircase; then all was still except the measured tread of Jean Poquelin walking on the veranda, and the heavy respirations of the mute slumbering in the cabin.

The little Secretary was about to retreat; but as he looked once more toward the haunted house a dim light appeared in the crack of a closed window, and presently old Jean Poquelin came, dragging his chair, and sat down close against the shining cranny. He spoke in a low, tender tone in the French tongue, making some inquiry. An answer came from within. Was it the voice of a human? So unnatural was it —so hollow, so discordant, so unearthly—that the stealthy listener shuddered again from head to foot; and when something stirred in some bushes near by—though it may have been nothing more than a rat—and came scuttling through the grass, the little Secretary actually turned and fled. As he left the enclosure he moved with bolder leisure through the bushes; yet now and then he spoke aloud: "Oh, oh! I see, I understand!" and shut his eyes in his hands.

How strange that henceforth little White was the champion of Jean Poquelin! In season and out of season—wherever a word was uttered against him—the Secretary, with a quiet, aggressive force that instantly arrested gossip, demanded upon what authority the statement or conjecture was made; but as he did not condescend to explain his own remarkable attitude, it was not long before the disrelish and suspicion which had followed Jean Poquelin so many years fell also upon him.

It was only the next evening but one after his adventure that he made himself a source of sullen amazement to one hundred and fifty boys, by ordering them to desist from their wanton hallooing. Old Jean Poquelin, standing and shaking his cane, rolling out his long-drawn maledictions, paused and stared, then gave the Secretary a courteous bow and started on. The boys, save one, from pure astonishment, ceased; but a ruffianly little Irish lad, more daring than any had yet been, threw a big hurtling clod, that struck old Poquelin between the shoulders and burst like a shell. The enraged old man wheeled with uplifted staff to give chase to the scampering vagabond; and— he may have tripped, or he may not, but he fell full length. Little White hastened to help him up, but he waved him off with a fierce imprecation and staggering to his feet resumed his way homeward. His lips were reddened with blood.

Little White was on his way to the meeting of the Board. He would have given all he dared spend to have staid away, for he felt both too fierce and too tremulous to brook the criticisms that were likely to be made.

"I can't help it, gentlemen; I can't help you to make a case against the old man, and I'm not going to."

"We did not expect this disappointment, Mr. White."

"I can't help that, sir. No, sir; you had better not appoint any more investigations. Somebody'll investigate himself into trouble. No, sir; it isn't a threat, it is only my advice, but I warn you that whoever takes the task in hand will rue it to his dying day—which may be hastened, too."

The President expressed himself surprised.

"I don't care a rush," answered little White, wildly and foolishly. "I don't care a rush if you are, sir. No, my nerves are not disordered; my head's as clear as a bell. No, I'm *not* excited."

A Director remarked that the Secretary looked as though he had waked from a nightmare.

"Well, sir, if you want to know the fact, I have; and if you choose to cultivate old Poquelin's society you can have one, too."

"White," called a facetious member, but White did not notice. "White," he called again.

"What?" demanded White, with a scowl.

"Did you see the ghost?"

"Yes, sir; I did," cried White, hitting the table, and handing the President a paper which brought the Board to other business.

The story got among the gossips that somebody (they were afraid to say little White) had been to the Poquelin mansion by night and beheld something appalling. The rumor was but a shadow of the truth, magnified and distorted as is the manner of shadows. He had seen skeletons walking, and had barely escaped the clutches of one by making the sign of the cross.

Some madcap boys with an appetite for the horrible plucked up courage to venture through the dried marsh by the cattle-path, and come before the house at a spectral hour when the air was full of bats. Something which they but half saw—half a sight was enough—sent them tearing back through the willow-brakes and acacia bushes to their homes, where they fairly dropped down, and cried:

"Was it white?" "No—yes—nearly so—we can't tell—but we saw it." And one could hardly doubt, to look at their ashen faces, that they had, whatever it was.

"If that old rascal lived in the country we come from," said certain Américains, "he'd have been tarred and feathered before now, wouldn't he, Sanders?"

"Well, now he just would."

"And we'd have rid him on a rail, wouldn't we?"

"That's what I allow."

"Tell you what you *could* do." They were talking to some rollicking Creoles who had assumed an absolute necessity for doing *something*. "What is it you call this thing where an old man marries a young girl, and you come out with horns and"—

"Charivari?" asked the Creoles.

"Yes, that's it. Why don't you shivaree him?" Felicitous suggestion.

Little White, with his wife beside him, was sitting on their doorsteps on the sidewalk, as Creole custom had taught them, looking toward the sunset. They had moved into the lately-opened street. The view was not attractive on the score of beauty. The houses were small and scattered, and across the flat commons, spite of the lofty tangle of weeds and bushes, and spite of the thickets of acacia, they needs must see the dismal old Poquelin mansion, tilted awry and shutting out the declining sun. The moon, white and slender, was hanging the tip of its horn over one of the chimneys.

"And you say," said the Secretary, "the old black man has been going by here alone? Patty, suppose old Poquelin should be concocting some mischief; he don't lack provocation; the way that clod hit him the other day was enough to have killed him. Why, Patty, he dropped as quick as *that!* No wonder you haven't seen him. I wonder if they haven't heard something about him up at the drug-store. Suppose I go and see."

"Do," said his wife.

She sat alone for half an hour, watching that sudden going out of the day peculiar to the latitude.

"That moon is ghost enough for one house," she said, as her husband returned. "It has gone right down the chimney."

"Patty," said little White, "the drug-clerk says the boys are going to shivaree old Poquelin tonight. I'm going to try to stop it."

"Why, White," said his wife, "you'd better not. You'll get hurt."

"No, I'll not."

"Yes, you will."

"I'm going to sit out here until they come along. They're compelled to pass right by here."

"Why, White, it may be midnight before they start; you're not going to sit out here till then."

"Yes, I am."

"Well, you're very foolish," said Mrs. White in an undertone, looking anxious, and tapping one of the steps with her foot.

They sat a very long time talking over little family matters.

"What's that?" at last said Mrs. White.

"That's the nine-o'clock gun," said White, and they relapsed into a long-sustained, drowsy silence.

"Patty, you'd better go in and go to bed," said he at last.

"I'm not sleepy."

"Well, you're very foolish," quietly remarked little White, and again silence fell upon them.

"Patty, suppose I walk out to the old house and see if I can find out any thing."

"Suppose," said she, "you don't do any such—listen!"

Down the street arose a great hubbub. Dogs and boys were howling and barking; men were laughing, shouting, groaning, and blowing horns, whooping, and clanking cow-bells, whinnying, and howling, and rattling pots and pans.

"They are coming this way," said little White. "You had better go into the house, Patty."

"So had you."

"No. I'm going to see if I can't stop them."

"Why, White!"

"I'll be back in a minute," said White, and went toward the noise.

In a few moments the little Secretary met the mob. The pen hesitates on the word, for there is a respectable difference, measurable only on the scale of the half century, between a mob and a *charivari*. Little White lifted his ineffectual voice. He faced the head of the disorderly column, and cast himself about as if he were made of wood and moved by the jerk of a string. He rushed to one who seemed, from the size and clatter of his tin pan, to be a leader. *"Stop these fellows, Bienvenu, stop them just a minute, till I tell them something."* Bienvenu turned and brandished his instruments of discord in an imploring way to the crowd. They slackened their pace, two or three hushed their horns and joined the prayer of little White and Bienvenu for silence. The throng halted. The hush was delicious.

"Bienvenu," said little White, "don't shivaree old Poquelin to-night; he's"—

"My fwang," said the swaying Bienvenu, "who tail you I goin' to chahivahi somebody, eh? You sink bickause I make a little playfool wiz zis tin pan zat I am *dhonk?*"

"Oh, no, Bienvenu, old fellow, you're all right. I was afraid you might not know that old Poquelin was sick, you know, but you're not going there, are you?"

"My fwang, I vay soy to tail you zat you ah dhonk as de dev'. I am *shem* of you. I ham ze servan' of ze *publique*. Zese *citoyens* goin' to wickwest Jean Poquelin to give to the Ursuline' two hondred fifty dolla' "—

"*Hé quoi!*" cried a listener, "*Cinq cent piastres, oui!*"

"*Oui!*" said Bienvenu, "and if he wiffuse we make him some lit' *musique;* ta-ra-ta!" He hoisted a merry hand and foot, then frowning, added: "Old Poquelin got no bizniz dhink s'much w'isky."

"But, gentlemen," said little White, around whom a circle had gathered, "the old man is very sick."

"My faith!" cried a tiny Creole, "we did not make him to be sick. W'en we have say we going make *le charivari,* do you want that we hall tell a lie? My faith! 'sfools!"

"But you can shivaree somebody else," said desperate little White.

"*Oui!*" cried Bienvenu, "*et chahivahi* Jean-ah Poquelin tomo'w!"

"Let us go to Madame Schneider!" cried two or three, and amid huzzas and confused cries, among which was heard a stentorian Celtic call for drinks, the crowd again began to move.

"*Cent piastres pour l'hôpital de charité!*"

"Hurrah!"

"One hongred dolla' for Charity Hospital!"

"Hurrah!"

"Whang!" went a tin pan, the crowd yelled, and Pandemonium gaped again. They were off at a right angle.

Nodding, Mrs. White looked at the mantel-clock.

"Well, if it isn't away after midnight."

The hideous noise down street was passing beyond earshot. She raised a sash and listened. For a moment there was silence. Some one came to the door.

"Is that you, White?"

"Yes." He entered. "I succeeded, Patty."

"Did you?" said Patty, joyfully.

"Yes. They've gone down to shivaree the old Dutchwoman who married her step-daughter's sweetheart. They say she has got to pay a hundred dollars to the hospital before they stop."

The couple retired, and Mrs. White slumbered. She was awakened by her husband snapping the lid of his watch.

"What time?" she asked.

"Half-past three. Patty, I haven't slept a wink. Those fellows are out yet. Don't you hear them?"

"Why, White, they're coming this way!"

"I know they are," said White, sliding out of bed and drawing on his clothes, "and they're coming fast. You'd better go away from that window, Patty! My! what a clatter!"

"Here they are," said Mrs. White, but her husband was gone. Two or three hundred men and boys pass the place at a rapid walk straight down the broad, new street, toward the hated house of ghosts. The din was terrific. She saw little White at the head of the rabble brandishing his arms and trying in vain to make himself heard; but they only shook their heads, laughing and hooting the louder, and so passed, bearing him on before them.

Swiftly they pass out from among the houses, away from the dim oil lamps of the street, out into the broad starlit commons, and enter the willowy jungles of the haunted ground. Some hearts fail and their owners lag behind and turn back, suddenly remembering how near morning it is. But the most part push on, tearing the air with their clamor.

Down ahead of them in the long, thicket-darkened way there is—singularly enough—a faint, dancing light. It must be very near the old house; it is. It has stopped now. It is a lantern, and is under a well-known sapling which has grown up on the wayside since the canal was filled. Now it swings mysteriously to and fro. A goodly number of the more ghost-fearing give up the sport; but a full hundred move forward at a run, doubling their devilish howling and banging.

Yes; it is a lantern, and there are two persons under the tree. The crowd draws near—drops into a walk; one of the two is the old African mute; he lifts the lantern up so that it shines on the other; the crowd recoils; there is a hush of all clangor, and all at once, with a cry of mingled fright and horror from every throat, the whole throng rushes back, dropping every thing, sweeping past little White and hurrying on, never stopping until the jungle is left behind, and then to find that not one in ten has seen the cause of the stampede, and not one of the tenth is certain what it was.

There is one huge fellow among them who looks capable of any villany. He finds something to mount on, and, in the Creole *patois,* calls a general halt. Bienvenu sinks down, and, vainly trying to recline gracefully, resigns the leadership. The herd gather round the speaker; he assures them that they have been outraged. Their right peaceably to traverse the public streets has been trampled upon. Shall such encroachments be endured? It is now daybreak. Let them go now by the open light of day and force a free passage of the public highway!

A scattering consent was the response, and the crowd, thinned now and drowsy, straggled quietly down toward the old house. Some drifted ahead, others sauntered behind, but every one, as he again neared the tree, came to a stand-still. Little White sat upon a bank of turf on the opposite side of the way looking very stern and sad. To each newcomer he put the same question:

"Did you come here to go to old Poquelin's?"

"Yes."

"He's dead." And if the shocked hearer started away he would say: "Don't go away."

"Why not?"

"I want you to go to the funeral presently."

If some Louisianian, too loyal to dear France or Spain to understand English, looked bewildered, some one would interpret for him; and presently they went. Little White led the van, the crowd trooping after him down the middle of the way. The gate, that had never been seen before unchained, was open. Stern little White stopped a short distance from it; the rabble stopped behind him. Something was moving out from under the veranda. The many whisperers stretched upward to see. The African mute came very slowly toward the gate, leading by a cord in the nose a small brown bull, which was harnessed to a rude cart. On the flat body of the cart, under a black cloth, were seen the outlines of a long box.

"Hats off, gentlemen," said little White, as the box came in view, and the crowd silently uncovered.

"Gentlemen," said little White, "here come the last remains of Jean Marie Poquelin, a better man, I'm afraid, with all his sins,—yes a better—a kinder man to his blood—a man of more self-forgetful goodness—than all of you put together will ever dare to be."

There was a profound hush as the vehicle came creaking through the gate; but when it turned away from them toward the forest, those in front started suddenly. There was a backward rush, then all stood still again staring one way; for there, behind the bier, with eyes cast down and labored step, walked the living remains—all

that was left—of little Jacques Poquelin, the long-hidden brother—
a leper, as white as snow.

Dumb with horror, the cringing crowd gazed upon the walking
death. They watched, in silent awe, the slow *cortège* creep down the
long, straight road and lessen on the view, until by and by it stopped
where a wild, unfrequented path branched off into the undergrowth toward the rear of the ancient city.

"They are going to the *Terre aux Lépreux*," said one in the crowd.
The rest watched them in silence.

The little bull was set free; the mute, with the strength of an ape,
lifted the long box to his shoulder. For a moment more the mute
and the leper stood in sight, while the former adjusted his heavy
burden; then, without one backward glance upon the unkind human
world, turning their faces toward the ridge in the depths of the
swamp known as the Leper's Land, they stepped into the jungle, disappeared, and were never seen again.

MARY NOAILLES MURFREE

★ ★ ★

In the Tennessee mountains, which deform and cast a "spell" upon their primitive, superstitious people, Mary Noailles Murfree (1850-1922) placed the setting of stories with an underlying refrain, tediously repeated, of despair, stolidity, and repression. The epic grandeur of the highlands intensifies the poverty-stricken cleanliness of the inhabitants; their dialect, as well as derogatory epithets, sometimes cruelly caricatures these people by contrast with the author's polished nature descriptions. Miss Murfree, born near Murfreesboro, suffered paralysis in childhood, spent her summers in the Cumberland mountains, and at the close of the Civil War moved to St. Louis, whence she sent to *The Atlantic Monthly* her first stories under the pseudonym, "Charles Egbert Craddock." Discovery of her identity made a best seller of *In the Tennessee Mountains* (1884), in which the second of the following stories appeared.

★ ★ ★

Taking the Blue Ribbon at the County Fair

JENKS HOLLIS sat on the fence. He slowly turned the quid of tobacco in his cheek, and lifting up his voice spoke with an oracular drawl:—

"Ef he kin take the certif'cate it's the mos' ez he kin do. He ain't never a-goin' ter git no premi-*um* in this life, sure's ye air a born sinner."

And he relapsed into silence. His long legs dangled dejectedly among the roadside weeds; his brown jeans trousers, that had despaired of ever reaching his ankles, were ornamented here and there with ill-adjusted patches, and his loose-fitting coat was out at the elbows. An old white wool hat drooped over his eyes, which were fixed absently on certain distant blue mountain ranges, that melted tenderly into the blue of the noonday sky, and framed an exquisite mosaic of poly-tinted fields in the valley, far, far below the grim gray crag on which his little home was perched.

Despite his long legs he was a light weight, or he would not have chosen as his favorite seat so rickety a fence. His interlocutor, a heavier man, apparently had some doubts, for he leaned only slightly against one of the projecting rails as he whittled a pine stick, and with his every movement the frail structure trembled. The log cabin seemed as rickety as the fence. The little front porch had lost a puncheon here and there in the flooring—perhaps on some cold winter night when Hollis's energy was not sufficiently exuberant to convey him to the woodpile; the slender posts that upheld its roof seemed hardly strong enough to withstand the weight of the luxuriant vines with their wealth of golden gourds which had clambered far over the moss-grown clapboards; the windows had fewer panes of glass than rags; and the chimney, built of clay and sticks, leaned portentously away from the house. The open door displayed a rough, uncovered floor; a few old rush-bottomed chairs; a bedstead with a patch-work calico quilt, the mattress swagging in the centre and showing the badly arranged cords below; strings of bright red pepper hanging from the dark rafters; a group of tow-headed, grave-faced, barefooted children; and, occupying almost one side of the room, a broad, deep, old-fashioned fireplace, where winter and summer a lazy fire burned under a lazy pot.

Notwithstanding the poverty of the aspect of the place and the evident sloth of its master, it was characterized by a scrupulous cleanliness strangely at variance with its forlorn deficiencies. The rough floor was not only swept but scoured; the dark rafters, whence depended the flaming banners of the red pepper, harbored no cobwebs; the grave faces of the white-haired children bore no more dirt than was consistent with their recent occupation of making mud-pies; and the sedate, bald-headed baby, lying silent but wide-awake in an uncouth wooden cradle, was as clean as clear spring water and yellow soap could make it. Mrs. Hollis herself, seen through the vista of opposite open doors, energetically rubbing the coarse wet clothes upon the resonant washboard, seemed neat enough in her blue-and-white checked homespun dress, and with her scanty hair drawn smoothly back from her brow into a tidy little knot on the top of her head.

Spare and gaunt she was, and with many lines in her prematurely old face. Perhaps they told of the hard fight her brave spirit waged against the stern ordering of her life; of the struggles with squalor, —inevitable concomitant of poverty,—and to keep together the souls and bodies of those numerous children, with no more efficient assistance than could be wrung from her reluctant husband in the short intervals when he did not sit on the fence. She managed as well as she could; there was an abundance of fine fruit in that low line of foliage behind the house—but everybody on Old Bear Mountain had fine fruit. Something rarer, she had good vegetables—the planting and hoeing being her own work and her eldest daughter's; an occasional shallow furrow representing the contribution of her husband's plough. The althea-bushes and the branches of the laurel sheltered a goodly number of roosting hens in these September nights; and to the pond, which had been formed by damming the waters of the spring branch in the hollow across the road, was moving even now a stately procession of geese in single file. These simple belongings were the trophies of a gallant battle against unalterable conditions and the dragging, dispiriting clog of her husband's inertia.

His inner life—does it seem hard to realize that in that uncouth personality concentred the complex, incomprehensible, ever-shifting emotions of that inner life which, after all, is so much stronger, and deeper, and broader than the material? Here, too, beat the hot heart of humanity—beat with no measured throb. He had his hopes, his pleasure, his pain, like those of a higher culture, differing only in object, and something perhaps in degree. His disappointments were bitter and lasting; his triumphs, few and sordid; his single aspiration—to take the premium offered by the directors of the Kildeer County Fair for the best equestrian.

This incongruous and unpromising ambition had sprung up in this wise: Between the country people of Kildeer County and the citizens of the village of Colbury, the county-seat, existed a bitter and deeply rooted animosity manifesting itself at conventions, elections for the legislature, etc., the rural population voting as a unit against the town's candidate. On all occasions of public meetings there was a struggle to crush any invidious distinction against the "country boys," especially at the annual fair. Here to the rustics of Kildeer County came the tug of war. The population of the outlying districts was more numerous, and, when it could be used as a suffrage-engine, all-powerful; but the region immediately adjacent to the town was far more fertile. On those fine meadows grazed the graceful Jersey; there gamboled sundry long-tailed colts with long-tailed pedigrees;

there greedy Berkshires fattened themselves to abnormal proportions; and the merinos could hardly walk, for the weight of their own rich wardrobes. The well-to-do farmers of this section were hand-in-glove with the town's people; they drove their trotters in every day or so to get their mail, to chat with their cronies, to attend to their affairs in court, to sell or to buy—their pleasures centred in the town, and they turned the cold shoulder upon the country, which supported them, and gave their influence to Colbury, accounting themselves an integrant part of it. Thus, at the fairs the town claimed the honor and glory. The blue ribbon decorated cattle and horses bred within ten miles of the flaunting flag on the judges' stand, and the foaming mountain-torrents and the placid stream in the valley beheld no cerulean hues save those of the sky which they reflected.

The premium offered this year for the best rider was, as it happened, a new feature, and excited especial interest. The country's blood was up. Here was something for which it could fairly compete, with none of the disadvantages of the false position in which it was placed. Hence a prosperous landed proprietor, the leader of the rural faction, dwelling midway between the town and the range of mountains that bounded the county on the north and east, bethought himself one day of Jenkins Hollis, whose famous riding had been the feature of a certain dashing cavalry charge—once famous, too—forgotten now by all but the men who, for the first and only time in their existence, penetrated in those war days the blue mountains fencing in their county from the outer world, and looked upon the alien life beyond that wooded barrier. The experience of those four years, submerged in the whirling rush of events elsewhere, survives in these eventless regions in a dreamy, dispassionate sort of longevity. And Jenkins Hollis's feat of riding stolidly—one could hardly say bravely—up an almost sheer precipice to a flame-belching battery came suddenly into the landed magnate's recollection with the gentle vapors and soothing aroma of a meditative after-dinner pipe. Quivering with party spirit, Squire Goodlet sent for Hollis and offered to lend him the best horse on the place, and a saddle and bridle, if he would go down to Colbury and beat those town fellows out on their own ground.

No misgivings had Hollis. The inordinate personal pride characteristic of the mountaineer precluded his feeling a shrinking pain at the prospect of being presented, a sorry contrast, among the well-clad, well-to-do town's people, to compete in a public contest. He did not appreciate the difference—he thought himself as good as the best.

And to-day, complacent enough, he sat upon the rickety fence at home, oracularly disparaging the equestrian accomplishments of the town's noted champion.

"I dunno—I dunno," said his young companion doubtfully. "Hackett sets mighty firm onto his saddle. He's ez straight ez any shingle, an' ez tough ez a pine-knot. He come up hyar las' summer—war it las' summer, now? No, 'twar summer afore las'—with some o' them other Colbury folks, a-fox-huntin', an' a-deer-huntin', an' one thing an' 'nother. I seen 'em a time or two in the woods. An' he kin ride jes' ez good 'mongst the gullies and boulders like ez ef he had been born in the hills. He ain't a-goin' ter be beat easy."

"It don't make no differ," retorted Jenks Hollis. "He'll never git no premi-*um*. The certif'cate's good a-plenty fur what ridin' he kin do."

Doubt was still expressed in the face of the young man, but he said no more, and, after a short silence, Mr. Hollis, perhaps not relishing his visitor's want of appreciation, dismounted, so to speak, from the fence, and slouched off slowly up the road.

Jacob Brice still stood leaning against the rails and whittling his pine stick, in no wise angered or dismayed by his host's unceremonious departure, for social etiquette is not very rigid on Old Bear Mountain. He was a tall athletic fellow, clad in a suit of brown jeans, which displayed, besides the ornaments of patches, sundry deep grass stains about the knees. Not that piety induced Brice to spend much time in the lowly attitude of prayer, unless, indeed, Diana might be accounted the goddess of his worship. The green juice was pressed out when kneeling, hidden in some leafy, grassy nook, he heard the infrequent cry of the wild turkey, or his large, intent blue eyes caught a glimpse of the stately head of an antlered buck, moving majestically in the alternate sheen of the sunlight and shadow of the overhanging crags; or while with his deft hunter's hands he dragged himself by slow, noiseless degrees through the ferns and tufts of rank weeds to the water's edge, that he might catch a shot at the feeding wild duck. A leather belt around his waist supported his powder-horn and shot-pouch,—for his accoutrements were exactly such as might have been borne a hundred years ago by a hunter of Old Bear Mountain,—and his gun leaned against the trunk of a chestnut-oak.

Although he still stood outside the fence, aimlessly lounging, there was a look on his face of a half-suppressed expectancy, which rendered the features less statuesque than was their wont—an expectancy that showed itself in the furtive lifting of his eyelids now and then, enabling him to survey the doorway without turning his head. Suddenly his face reassumed its habitual, inexpressive mask of immobility, and the furtive eyes were persistently downcast.

A flare of color, and Cynthia Hollis was standing in the doorway, leaning against its frame. She was robed, like September, in brilliant yellow. The material and make were of the meanest, but there was a certain appropriateness in the color with her slumberous dark eyes and the curling tendrils of brown hair which fell upon her forehead and were clustered together at the back of her neck. No cuffs and no collar could this costume boast, but she had shown the inclination to finery characteristic of her age and sex by wearing around her throat, where the yellow hue of her dress met the creamy tint of her skin, a row of large black beads, threaded upon a shoe-string in default of an elastic, the brass ends flaunting brazenly enough among them. She held in her hand a string of red pepper, to which she was adding some newly gathered pods. A slow job Cynthia seemed to make of it.

She took no more notice of the man under the tree than he accorded to her. There they stood, within twelve feet of each other, in utter silence, and, to all appearance, each entirely unconscious of the other's existence: he whittling his pine stick; she, slowly, slowly stringing the pods of red pepper.

There was something almost portentous in the gravity and sobriety of demeanor of this girl of seventeen; she manifested less interest in the young man than her own grandmother might have shown.

He was constrained to speak first. "Cynthy"—he said at length, without raising his eyes or turning his head. She did not answer; but he knew without looking that she had fixed those slumberous brown eyes upon him, waiting for him to go on. "Cynthy"—he said again, with a hesitating, uneasy manner. Then, with an awkward attempt at raillery, "Ain't ye never a-thinkin' 'bout a-gittin' married?"

He cast a laughing glance toward her, and looked down quickly at his clasp-knife and the stick he was whittling. It was growing very slender now.

Cynthia's serious face relaxed its gravity. "Ye air foolish, Jacob," she said, laughing. After stringing on another pepper-pod with great deliberation, she continued: "Ef I war a-studyin' 'bout a-gittin' married, thar ain't nobody round 'bout hyar ez I'd hev." And she added another pod to the flaming red string, so bright against the yellow of her dress.

That stick could not long escape annihilation. The clasp-knife moved vigorously through its fibres, and accented certain arbitrary clauses in its owner's retort. "Ye talk like," he said, his face as monotonous in its expression as if every line were cut in marble—"ye talk like—ye thought ez how I—war a-goin' ter ax ye—ter marry me. I ain't though, nuther."

The stick was a shaving. It fell among the weeds. The young hunter shut his clasp-knife with a snap, shouldered his gun, and without a word of adieu on either side the conference terminated, and he walked off down the sandy road.

Cynthia stood watching him until the laurel-bushes hid him from sight; then sliding from the door-frame to the step, she sat motionless, a bright-hued mass of yellow draperies and red peppers, her slumberous deep eyes resting on the leaves that had closed upon him.

She was the central figure of a still landscape. The mid-day sunshine fell in broad effulgence upon it; the homely, dun-colored shadows had been running away all the morning, as if shirking the contrast with the splendors of the golden light, until nothing was left of them except a dark circle beneath the wide-spreading trees. No breath of wind stirred the leaves, or rippled the surface of the little pond. The lethargy of the hour had descended even upon the towering pine-trees, growing on the precipitous slope of the mountain, and showing their topmost plumes just above the frowning, gray crag— their melancholy song was hushed. The silent masses of dazzling white clouds were poised motionless in the ambient air, high above the valley and the misty expanse of the distant, wooded ranges.

A lazy, lazy day, and very, very warm. The birds had much ado to find sheltering shady nooks where they might escape the glare and the heat; their gay carols were out of season, and they blinked and nodded under their leafy umbrellas, and fanned themselves with their wings, and twittered disapproval of the weather. "Hot, hot, red-hot!" said the birds—"broiling hot!"

Now and then an acorn fell from among the serrated chestnut leaves, striking upon the fence with a sounding thwack, and rebounding in the weeds. Those chestnut-oaks always seem to unaccustomed eyes the creation of Nature in a fit of mental aberration—useful freak! the mountain swine fatten on the plenteous mast, and the bark is highly esteemed at the tan-yard.

A large cat was lying at full length on the floor of the little porch, watching with drowsy, half-closed eyes the assembled birds in the tree. But she seemed to have relinquished the pleasures of the chase until the mercury should fall.

Close in to the muddiest side of the pond over there, which was all silver and blue with the reflection of the great masses of white clouds, and the deep azure sky, a fleet of shining, snowy geese was moored, perfectly motionless too. No circumnavigation for them this hot day.

And Cynthia's dark brown eyes, fixed upon the leafy vista of the road, were as slumberous as the noontide sunshine.

"Cynthy! whar *is* the gal?" said poor Mrs. Hollis, as she came around the house to hang out the ragged clothes on the althea-bushes and the rickety fence. "Cynthy, air ye a-goin' ter sit thar in the door all day, an' that thar pot a-bilin' all the stren'th out'n that thar cabbige an' roas'in'-ears? Dish up dinner, child, an' don't be so slow an' slack-twisted like yer dad."

Great merriment there was, to be sure, at the Kildeer Fair grounds, situated on the outskirts of Colbury, when it became known to the convulsed town faction that the gawky Jenks Hollis intended to compete for the premium to be awarded to the best and most graceful rider. The contests of the week had as usual resulted in Colbury's favor; this was the last day of the fair, and the defeated country population anxiously but still hopefully awaited its notable event.

A warm sun shone; a brisk autumnal breeze waved the flag flying from the judges' stand; a brass band in the upper story of that structure thrilled the air with the vibrations of popular waltzes and marches, somewhat marred now and then by mysteriously discordant bass tones; the judges, portly, red-faced, middle-aged gentlemen, sat below in cane-botton chairs critically a-tilt on the hind legs. The rough wooden amphitheatre, a bold satire on the stately Roman edifice, was filled with the denizens of Colbury and the rosy rural faces of the country people of Kildeer County; and within the charmed arena the competitors for the blue ribbon and the saddle and bridle to be awarded to the best rider were just now entering, ready mounted, from a door beneath the tiers of seats, and were slowly making the tour of the circle around the judges' stand. One by one they came, with a certain nonchalant pride of demeanor, conscious of an effort to display themselves and their horses to the greatest advantage, and yet a little ashamed of the consciousness. For the most part they were young men, prosperous-looking, and clad according to the requirements of fashion which prevailed in this little town. Shut in though it was from the pomps and vanities of the world by the encircling chains of blue ranges and the bending sky which rested upon their summits, the frivolity of the mode, though somewhat belated, found its way and ruled with imperative rigor. Good riders they were undoubtedly, accustomed to the saddle almost from infancy, and well mounted. A certain air of gallantry, always characteristic of an athletic horseman, commended these equestrian figures to the eye as they slowly circled about. Still they came—eight—nine—ten—the eleventh, the long, lank frame of Jenkins Hollis mounted on Squire Goodlet's "John Barleycorn."

The horsemen received this ungainly addition to their party with polite composure, and the genteel element of the spectators remained silent too from the force of good breeding and good feeling; but the "roughs," always critically a-loose in a crowd, shouted and screamed with derisive hilarity. What they were laughing at Jenks Hollis never knew. Grave and stolid, but as complacent as the best, he too made the usual circuit with his ill-fitting jeans suit, his slouching old wool hat, and his long, gaunt figure. But he sat the spirited "John Barleycorn" as if he were a part of the steed, and held up his head with unwonted dignity, inspired perhaps by the stately attitudes of the horse, which were the result of no training nor compelling reins, but the instinct transmitted through a long line of high-headed ancestry. Of a fine old family was "John Barleycorn."

A deeper sensation was in store for the spectators. Before Jenkins Hollis's appearance most of them had heard of his intention to compete, but the feeling was one of unmixed astonishment when entry No. 12 rode into the arena, and, on the part of the country people, this surprise was supplemented by an intense indignation. The twelfth man was Jacob Brice. As he was a "mounting boy," one would imagine that, if victory should crown his efforts, the rural faction ought to feel the elation of success, but the prevailing sentiment toward him was that which every well-conducted mind must entertain concerning the individual who runs against the nominee. Notwithstanding the fact that Brice was a notable rider, too, and well calculated to try the mettle of the town's champion, there arose from the excited countrymen a keen, bitter, and outraged cry of "Take him out!" So strongly does the partisan heart pulsate to the interests of the nominee! This frantic petition had no effect on the interloper. A man who has inherited half a dozen violent quarrels, any one of which may at any moment burst into a vendetta,—inheriting little else,—is not easily dismayed by the disapprobation of either friend or foe. His statuesque features, shaded by the drooping brim of his old black hat were as calm as ever, and his slow blue eyes did not, for one moment, rest upon the excited scene about him, so unspeakably new to his scanty experience. His fine figure showed to great advantage on horseback, despite his uncouth, coarse garb; he was mounted upon a sturdy, brown mare of obscure origin, but good-looking, clean-built, sure-footed, and with the blended charm of spirit and docility; she represented his whole estate, except his gun and his lean, old hound, that had accompanied him to the fair, and was even now improving the shining hour by quarreling over a bone outside the grounds with other people's handsomer dogs.

The judges were exacting. The riders were ordered to gallop to the right—and around they went. To the left—and there was again the spectacle of the swiftly circling equestrian figures. They were required to draw up in a line, and to dismount; then to mount, and again to alight. Those whom these manœuvres proved inferior were dismissed at once, and the circle was reduced to eight. An exchange of horses was commanded; and once more the riding, fast and slow, left and right, the mounting and dismounting were repeated. The proficiency of the remaining candidates rendered them worthy of more difficult ordeals. They were required to snatch a hat from the ground while riding at full gallop. Pistols loaded with blank cartridges were fired behind the horses, and subsequently close to their quivering and snorting nostrils, in order that the relative capacity of the riders to manage a frightened and unruly steed might be compared, and the criticism of the judges mowed the number down to four.

Free speech is conceded by all right-thinking people to be a blessing. It is often a balm. Outside of the building and of earshot the defeated aspirants took what comfort they could in consigning, with great fervor and volubility, all the judicial magnates to that torrid region unknown to polite geographical works.

Of the four horsemen remaining in the ring, two were Jenkins Hollis and Jacob Brice. Short turns at full gallop were prescribed. The horses were required to go backward at various gaits. Bars were brought in and the crowd enjoyed the exhibition of the standing-leap, at an ever-increasing height and then the flying-leap—a tumultuous confused impression of thundering hoofs and tossing mane and grim defiant faces of horse and rider, in the lightning-like moment of passing. Obstructions were piled on the track for the "long jumps," and in one of the wildest leaps a good rider was unhorsed and rolled on the ground while his recreant steed that had balked at the last moment scampered around and around the arena in a wild effort to find the door beneath the tiers of seats to escape so fierce a competition. This accident reduced the number of candidiates to the two mountaineers and Tip Hackett, the man whom Jacob had pronounced a formidable rival. The circling about, the mounting and dismounting, the exchange of horses were several times repeated without any apparent result, and excitement rose to fever heat.

The premium and certificate lay between the three men. The town faction trembled at the thought that the substantial award of the saddle and bridle, with the decoration of the blue ribbon, and the intangible but still precious secondary glory of the certificate and the red ribbon might be given to the two mountaineers, leaving the crack rider of Colbury in an ignominious lurch; while the country party feared Hollis's defeat by Hackett rather less than that Jenks would be required to relinquish the premium to the interloper Brice, for the young hunter's riding had stricken a pang of prophetic terror to more than one partisan rustic's heart. In the midst of the perplexing doubt, which tried the judges' minds, came the hour for dinner, and the decision was postponed until after that meal.

The competitors left the arena, and the spectators transferred their attention to unburdening hampers, or to jostling one another in the dining-hall.

Everybody was feasting but Cynthia Hollis. The intense excitement of the day, the novel sights and sounds utterly undreamed of in her former life, the abruptly struck chords of new emotions suddenly set vibrating within her, had dulled her relish for the midday meal; and while the other members of the family repaired to the shade of a tree outside the grounds to enjoy that refection, she wandered about the "floral hall," gazing at the splendors of bloom thronging there, all so different from the shy grace, the fragility of poise, the delicacy of texture of the flowers of her ken,—the rhododendron, the azalea, the Chilhowee lily,—yet vastly imposing in their massed exuberance and scarlet pride, for somehow they all seemed high colored.

She went more than once to note with a kind of aghast dismay those trophies of feminine industry, the quilts; some were of the "log cabin" and "rising sun" variety, but others were of geometric intricacy of form and were kaleidoscopic of color with an amazing labyrinth of stitchings and embroideries—it seemed a species of effrontery to dub one gorgeous poly-tinted silken banner a quilt. But already it bore a blue ribbon, and its owner was the richer by the prize of a glass bowl and the envy of a score of deft-handed competitors. She gazed upon the glittering jellies and preserves, upon the biscuits and cheeses, the hair-work and wax flowers, and paintings. These latter treated for the most part of castles and seas rather than of the surrounding altitudes, but Cynthia came to a pause of blank surprise in front of a shadow rather than a picture which represented a spring of still brown water in a mossy cleft of a rock where the fronds of a fern seemed to stir in the foreground. "I hev viewed the like o' that a many a time," she said disparagingly. To her it hardly seemed rare enough for the blue ribbon on the frame.

In the next room she dawdled through great piles of prize fruits and vegetables—water-melons unduly vast of bulk, peaches and pears and pumpkins of proportions never seen before out of a nightmare, stalks of Indian corn eighteen feet high with seven ears each,—all apparently attesting what they could do when they would, and that all the enterprise of Kildeer County was not exclusively of the feminine persuasion.

Finally Cynthia came out from the midst of them and stood leaning against one of the large pillars which supported the roof of the amphitheatre, still gazing about the half-deserted building, with the smouldering fires of her slumberous eyes newly kindled.

To other eyes and ears it might not have seemed a scene of tumultuous metropolitan life, with the murmuring trees close at hand dappling the floor with sycamore shadows, the fields of Indian corn across the road, the exuberant rush of the stream down the slope just beyond, the few hundred spectators who had intently watched the events of the day; but to Cynthia Hollis the excitement of the crowd and movement and noise could no further go.

By the natural force of gravitation Jacob Brice presently was walking slowly and apparently aimlessly around to where she was standing. He said nothing, however, when he was beside her, and she seemed entirely unconscious of his presence. Her yellow dress was as stiff as a board, and as clean as her strong, young arms could make it; at her throat were the shining black beads; on her head she wore a limp, yellow calico sunbonnet, which hung down over her eyes, and almost obscured her countenance. To this article she perhaps owed the singular purity and transparency of her complexion, as much as to the mountain air, and the chiefly vegetable fare of her father's table. She wore it constantly, although it operated almost as a mask, rendering her more easily recognizable to their few neighbors by her flaring attire than by her features, and obstructing from her own view all surrounding scenery, so that she could hardly see the cow, which so much of her time she was slowly poking after.

She spoke unexpectedly, and without any other symptom that she knew of the young hunter's proximity. "I never thought, Jacob, ez how ye would hev come down hyar, all the way from the mountings, to ride agin my dad, an' beat him out'n that thar saddle an' bridle."

"Ye won't hev nothin' ter say ter me," retorted Jacob sourly.

A long silence ensued.

Then he resumed didactically, but with some irrelevancy, "I tole ye t'other day ez how ye war old enough ter be a-studyin' 'bout gittin' married."

"They don't think nothin' of ye ter our house, Jacob. Dad's always a-jowin' at ye." Cynthia's candor certainly could not be called in question.

The young hunter replied with some natural irritation: "He hed better not let me hear him, ef he wants to keep whole bones inside his skin. He better not tell me, nuther."

"He don't keer enough 'bout ye, Jacob, ter tell ye. He don't think nothin' of ye."

Love is popularly supposed to dull the mental faculties. It developed in Jacob Brice sudden strategic abilities.

"Thar is them ez does," he said diplomatically.

Cynthia spoke promptly with more vivacity than usual, but in her customary drawl and apparently utterly irrelevantly:—

"I never in all my days see no sech red-headed gal ez that thar Becky Stiles. She's the red-headedest gal ever I see." And Cynthia once more was silent.

Jacob resumed, also irrelevantly:—

"When I goes a-huntin' up yander ter Pine Lick, they is mighty perlite ter me. They ain't never done nothin' agin me, ez I knows on." Then, after a pause of deep cogitation, he added, "Nor hev they said nothin' agin me, nuther."

Cynthia took up her side of the dialogue, if dialogue it could be called, with wonted irrelevancy: "That thar Becky Stiles, she's got the freckledest face—ez freckled ez any turkey-aig" (with an indescribable drawl on the last word).

"They ain't done nothin' agin me," reiterated Jacob astutely, "nor said nothin' nuther—none of 'em."

Cynthia looked hard across the amphitheatre at the distant Great Smoky Mountains shimmering in the hazy September sunlight—so ineffably beautiful, so delicately blue, that they might have seemed the ideal scenery of some impossibly lovely ideal world. Perhaps she was wondering what the unconscious Becky Stiles, far away in those dark woods about Pine Lick, had secured in this life besides her freckled face. Was this the sylvan deity of the young hunter's adoration?

Cynthia took off her sunbonnet to use it for a fan. Perhaps it was well for her that she did so at this moment; it had so entirely concealed her head that her hair might have been the color of Becky Stiles's, and no one the wiser. The dark brown tendrils curled delicately on her creamy forehead; the excitement of the day had flushed

her pale cheeks with an unwonted glow; her eyes were alight with
their newly kindled fires; the clinging curtain of her bonnet had concealed the sloping curves of her shoulders—altogether she was attractive enough, despite the flare of her yellow dress, and especially attractive to the untutored eyes of Jacob Brice. He relented suddenly, and
lost all the advantages of his tact and diplomacy.

"I likes ye better nor I does Becky Stiles," he said moderately. Then
with more fervor, "I likes ye better nor any gal I ever see."

The usual long pause ensued.

"Ye hev got a mighty cur'ous way o' showin' it," Cynthia replied.

"I dunno what ye're talkin' 'bout, Cynthy."

"Ye hev got a mighty cur'ous way o' showin' it," she reiterated,
with renewed animation—"a-comin' all the way down hyar from the
mountings ter beat my dad out'n that thar saddle an' bridle, what
he's done sot his heart onto. Mighty cur'ous way."

"Look hyar, Cynthy." The young hunter broke off suddenly, and
did not speak again for several minutes. A great perplexity was surg-
ing this way and that in his slow brains—a great struggle was waging
in his heart. He was to choose between love and ambition—nay,
avarice too was ranged beside his aspiration. He felt himself an assured
victor in the competition, and he had seen that saddle and bridle.
They were on exhibition to-day, and to him their material and work-
manship seemed beyond expression wonderful, and elegant, and substantial. He could never hope otherwise to own such accoutrements.
His eyes would never again even rest upon such resplendent objects,
unless indeed in Hollis's possession. Any one who has ever loved a
horse can appreciate a horseman's dear desire that beauty should go
beautifully caparisoned. And then, there was his pride in his own
riding, and his anxiety to have his pre-eminence in that accomplishment acknowledged and recognized by his friends, and, dearer
triumph still, by his enemies. A terrible pang before he spoke again.

"Look hyar, Cynthy," he said at last; "ef ye will marry me, I won't
go back in yander no more. I'll leave the premi-*um* ter them ez kin
git it."

"Ye're foolish, Jacob," she replied, still fanning with the yellow
calico sunbonnet. "Ain't I done tole ye, ez how they don't think
nothin' of ye ter our house? I don't want all of 'em a-jowin' at me,
too."

"Ye talk like ye ain't got good sense, Cynthy," said Jacob irritably.
"What's ter hender me from hitchin' up my mare ter my uncle's
wagon an' ye an' me a-drivin' up hyar to the Cross-Roads, fifteen
mile, and git Pa'son Jones ter marry us? We'll get the license down

hyar ter the Court House afore we start. An' while they'll all be
a-foolin' away thar time a-ridin' round that thar ring, ye an' me
will be a-gittin' married." Ten minutes ago Jacob Brice did not think
riding around that ring was such a reprehensible waste of time.
"What's ter hender? It don't make no differ how they jow then."

"I done tole ye, Jacob," said the sedate Cynthia, still fanning with
the sunbonnet.

With a sudden return of his inspiration, Jacob retorted, affecting
an air of stolid indifference: "Jes' ez *ye* choose. I won't hev ter ax
Becky Stiles twict."

And he turned to go.

"I never said no, Jacob," said Cynthia precipitately. "I never said
ez how I wouldn't hev ye."

"Waal, then, jes' come along with me right now while I hitch up
the mare. I ain't a-goin' ter leave yer a-standin' hyar. Ye're too skittish.
Time I come back ye'd hev done run away I dunno whar." A moment's pause and he added: "Is ye a-goin' ter stand thar all day,
Cynthy Hollis, a-lookin' up an' around, and a-turnin' yer neck fust
this way and then t'other, an' a-lookin' fur all the worl' like a wild
turkey in a trap, or one o' them thar skeery young deer, or sech
senseless critters? What ails the gal?"

"Thar'll be nobody ter help along the work ter our house," said
Cynthia, the weight of the home difficulties bearing heavily on her
conscience.

"What's ter hender ye from a-goin' down thar an' lendin' a hand
every wunst in a while? But ef ye're a-goin' ter stand thar like ye
hedn't no more action than a—a-dunno-what,—jes' like yer dad, I
ain't. I'll jes' leave ye a-growed ter that thar post, an' I'll jes' light
out stiddier, an' afore the cows git ter Pine Lick, I'll be thar too. Jes'
ez ye choose. Come along ef ye wants ter come. I ain't a-goin' ter ax
ye no more."

"I'm a-comin'," said Cynthia.

There was great though illogical rejoicing on the part of the country
faction when the crowds were again seated, tier above tier, in the
amphitheatre, and the riders were once more summoned into the
arena, to discover from Jacob Brice's unaccounted-for absence that he
had withdrawn and left the nominee to his chances.

In the ensuing competition it became very evident to the not altogether impartially disposed judges that they could not, without in-
curring the suspicions alike of friend and foe, award the premium
to their fellow-townsman. Straight as a shingle though he might be,

more prepossessing to the eye, the ex-cavalryman of fifty battles was far better trained in all the arts of horsemanship.

A wild shout of joy burst from the rural party when the most portly and rubicund of the portly and red-faced judges advanced into the ring and decorated Jenkins Hollis with the blue ribbon. A frantic antistrophe rent the air. "Take it off!" vociferated the bitter town faction—"take it off!"

A diversion was produced by the refusal of the Colbury champion to receive the empty honor of the red ribbon and the certificate. Thus did he except to the ruling of the judges. In high dudgeon he faced about and left the arena, followed shortly by the decorated Jenks, bearing the precious saddle and bridle, and going with a wooden face to receive the congratulations of his friends.

The entries for the slow mule race had been withdrawn at the last moment; and the spectators, balked of that unique sport, and the fair being virtually over, were rising from their seats and making their noisy preparations for departure. Before Jenks had cleared the fair-building, being somewhat impeded by the moving mass of humanity, he encountered one of his neighbors, a listless mountaineer, who spoke on this wise:—

"Does ye know that thar gal o' yourn—that thar Cynthy?"

Mr. Hollis nodded his expressionless head—presumably he did know Cynthia.

"Waal," continued his leisurely interlocutor, still interrogative, "does ye know Jacob Brice?"

Ill-starred association of ideas! There was a look of apprehension on Jenkins Hollis's wooden face.

"They hev done got a license down hyar ter the Court House an' gone a-kitin' out on the Old B'ar road."

This was explicit.

"Whar's my horse?" exclaimed Jenks, appropriating "John Barley-corn" in his haste. Great as was his hurry, it was not too imperative to prevent him from strapping upon the horse the premium saddle, and inserting in his mouth the new bit and bridle. And in less than ten minutes a goodly number of recruits from the crowd assembled in Colbury were also "a-kitin'" out on the road to Old Bear, delighted with a new excitement, and bent on running down the eloping couple with no more appreciation of the sentimental phase of the question and the tender illusions of love's young dream than if Jacob and Cynthia were two mountain foxes.

Down the red-clay slopes of the outskirts of the town "John Barley-corn" thunders with a train of horsemen at his heels. Splash into the clear fair stream whose translucent depths tell of its birthplace among the mountain springs—how the silver spray showers about as the pursuers surge through the ford leaving behind them a foamy wake!— and now they are pressing hard up the steep ascent of the opposite bank, and galloping furiously along a level stretch of road, with the fences and trees whirling by, and the September landscape flying on the wings of the wind. The chase leads past fields of tasseled Indian corn, with yellowing thickly swathed ears, leaning heavily from the stalk; past wheat-lands, the crops harvested and the crab-grass having its day at last; past "woods-lots" and their black shadows, and out again into the September sunshine; past rickety little homes, not unlike Hollis's own, with tow-headed children, exactly like his, standing with wide eyes, looking at the rush and hurry of the pursuit—sometimes in the ill-kept yards a wood-fire is burning under the boiling sorghum kettle, or beneath the branches of the orchard near at hand a cider-mill is crushing the juice out of the red and yellow, ripe and luscious apples. Homeward-bound prize cattle are overtaken—a Durham bull, reluctantly permitting himself to be led into a fence corner that the hunt may sweep by unobstructed, and turning his proud blue-ribboned head angrily toward the riders as if indignant that anything except him should absorb attention; a gallant horse, with another floating blue streamer, bearing himself as becometh a king's son; the chase comes near to crushing sundry grunting porkers impervious to pride and glory in any worldly distinctions of cerulean decorations, and at last is fain to draw up and wait until a flock of silly overdressed sheep, running in frantic fear every way but the right way, can be gathered together and guided to a place of safety.

And once more, forward; past white frame houses with porches, and vine-grown verandas, and well-tended gardens, and groves of oak and beech and hickory trees—"John Barleycorn" makes an ineffectual but gallant struggle to get in at the large white gate of one of these comfortable places, Squire Goodlet's home, but he is urged back into the road, and again the pursuit sweeps on. Those blue mountains, the long parallel ranges of Old Bear and his brothers, seem no more a misty, uncertain mirage against the delicious indefinable tints of the horizon. Sharply outlined they are now, with dark, irregular shadows upon their precipitous slopes which tell of wild ravines, and rock-lined gorges, and swirling mountain torrents, and great, beetling, gray crags. A breath of balsams comes on the freshening wind—the lungs expand to meet it. There is a new aspect in the scene; a revivifying current thrills through the blood; a sudden ideal beauty descends on prosaic creation.

" 'Pears like I can't git my breath good in them flat countries," says Jenkins Hollis to himself, as "John Barleycorn" improves his speed under the exhilarating influence of the wind. "I'm nigh on to siffli-cated every time I goes down yander ter Colbury" (with a jerk of his wooden head in the direction of the village).

Long stretches of woods are on either side of the road now, with no sign of the changing season in the foliage save the slender, pointed, scarlet leaves and creamy plumes of the sourwood, gleaming here and there; and presently another panorama of open country unrolls to the view. Two or three frame houses appear with gardens and orchards, a number of humble log cabins, and a dingy little store, and the Cross-Roads are reached. And here the conclusive intelligence meets the party that Jacob and Cynthia were married by Parson Jones an hour ago, and were still "a-kitin'," at last accounts, out on the road to Old Bear.

The pursuit stayed its ardor. On the auspicious day when Jenkins Hollis took the blue ribbon at the County Fair and won the saddle and bridle he lost his daughter.

They saw Cynthia no more until late in the autumn when she came, without a word of self-justification or apology for her conduct, to lend her mother a helping hand in spinning and weaving her little brothers' and sisters' clothes. And gradually the *éclat* attendant upon her nuptials was forgotten, except that Mrs. Hollis now and then remarks that she "dunno how we could hev bore up agin Cynthy's a-runnin' away like she done, ef it hedn't a-been fur that thar saddle an' bridle an' takin' the blue ribbon at the County Fair."

Over on the T'other Mounting

STRETCHING out laterally from a long oblique line of the Southern Alleghanies are two parallel ranges, following the same course through several leagues, and separated by a narrow strip of valley hardly half a mile in width. As they fare along arm in arm, so to speak, sundry differences between the close companions are distinctly apparent. One is much the higher, and leads the way; it strikes out all the bold curves and angles of the course, meekly attended by the lesser ridge; its shadowy coves and sharp ravines are repeated in miniature as its comrade falls into the line of march; it seems to have its companion in charge, and to conduct it away from the majestic procession of mountains that traverses the State.

But, despite its more imposing appearance, all the tangible advantages are possessed by its humble neighbor. When Old Rocky-Top, as the lower range is called, is fresh and green with the tender verdure of spring, the snow still lies on the summit of the T'other Mounting, and drifts deep into treacherous rifts and chasms, and muffles the voice of the singing pines; and all the crags are hung with gigantic glittering icicles, and the woods are gloomy and bleak. When the sun shines bright on Old Rocky-Top, clouds often hover about the loftier mountain, and storms brew in that higher atmosphere: the all-pervading winter winds surge wildly among the groaning forests, and wrench the limbs from the trees, and dash huge fragments of cliffs down deep gorges, and spend their fury before they reach the sheltered lower spur. When the kindly shades of evening slip softly down on drowsy Rocky-Top, and the work is laid by in the rough little houses, and the simple home-folks draw around the hearth, day still lingers in a weird, paralytic life among the tree-tops of the T'other Mounting; and the only remnant of the world visible is that stark black line of its summit, stiff and hard against the faint green and saffron tints of the sky. Before the birds are well awake on Old Rocky-Top, and while the shadows are still thick, the T'other Mounting has been called up to a new day. Lonely dawns these: the pale gleam strikes along the October woods, bringing first into uncertain twilight the dead yellow and red of the foliage, presently heightened into royal gold and crimson by the first ray of sunshine; it rouses the timid wild-fowl; it drives home the plundering fox; it meets, perhaps, some lumbering bear or skulking mountain wolf; it flecks with light and shade the deer, all gray and antlered; it falls upon no human habitation, for the few settlers of the region have a persistent predilection for Old Rocky-Top. Somehow, the T'other Mounting is vaguely in ill repute among its neighbors,—it has a bad name.

"It's the onluckiest place ennywhar nigh about," said Nathan White, as he sat one afternoon upon the porch of his log-cabin, on the summit of Old Rocky-Top, and gazed up at the heights of the T'other Mounting across the narrow valley. "I hev hearn tell all my days ez how, ef ye go up thar on the T'other Mounting, suthin' will happen ter ye afore ye kin git away. An' I knows myself ez how—'twar ten year ago an' better—I went up thar, one Jan'ry day, a-lookin' fur my cow, ez hed strayed off through not hevin' enny calf ter our house; an' I fund the cow, but jes' tuk an' slipped on a icy rock,

an' bruk my ankle-bone. 'Twar sech a job a-gittin' off 'n that thar
T'other Mounting an' back over hyar, it hev l'arned me ter stay away
from thar."

"Thar war a man," piped out a shrill, quavering voice from within
the door,—the voice of Nathan White's father, the oldest inhabitant
of Rocky-Top,—"thar war a man hyar, nigh on ter fifty year ago,—
he war mightily gin ter thievin' horses; an' one time, while he war
a-runnin' away with Pete Dilks's dapple-gray mare,—they called her
Luce, five year old she war,—Pete, he war a-ridin' a-hint him on his
old sorrel mare,—*her* name 'twar Jane, an'—the Jeemes boys, they
war a-ridin' arter the horse-thief too. Thar, now! I clar forgits what
horses them Jeemes boys war a-ridin' of." He paused for an instant
in anxious reflection. "Waal, sir! it do beat all that I can't remember
them Jeemes boys' horses! Anyways, they got ter that thar tricky
ford through Wild-Duck River, thar on the side o' the T'other
Mounting, an' the horse-thief war ahead, an' he hed ter take it fust.
An' that thar river,—it rises yander in them pines, nigh about," pointing with a shaking fore-finger,—"an' that thar river jes' spun him out
'n the saddle like a top, an' he warn't seen no more till he hed floated
nigh ter Colbury, ez dead ez a door-nail, nor Pete's dapple-gray mare
nuther; she bruk her knees agin them high stone banks. But he war
a good swimmer, an' he war drowned. He war witched with the
place, ez sure ez ye air born."

A long silence ensued. Then Nathan White raised his pondering
eyes with a look of slow curiosity. "What did Tony Britt say he war
a-doin' of, when ye kem on him suddint in the woods on the T'other
Mounting?" he asked, addressing his son, a stalwart youth, who was
sitting upon the step, his hat on the back of his head, and his hands
in the pockets of his jeans trousers.

"He said he war a-huntin', but he hedn't hed no sort 'n luck. It
'pears ter me ez all the game thar is witched somehow, an' ye can't
git no good shot at nuthin'. Tony tole me to-day that he got up three
deer, an' hed toler'ble aim; an' he missed two, an' the t'other jes'
trotted off with a rifle-ball in his flank, ez onconsarned ez ef he hed
hit him with an acorn."

"I hev always hearn ez everything that belongs on that thar T'other
Mounting air witched, an' ef ye brings away so much ez a leaf, or a
stone, or a stick, ye fotches a curse with it," chimed in the old man,
" 'kase thar hev been sech a many folks killed on the T'other Mounting."

"I tole Tony Britt that thar word," said the young fellow, "an'
'lowed ter him ez how he hed tuk a mighty bad spot ter go a-huntin'."

"What did he say?" demanded Nathan White.

"He say he never knowed ez thar war murders commit on T'other Mounting, an' ef thar war he 'spects 'twar nuthin' but Injuns, long time ago. But he 'lowed the place war powerful onlucky, an' he believed the mounting war witched."

"Ef Tony Britt's arter enny harm," said the octogenarian, "he'll never come off 'n that thar T'other Mounting. It's a mighty place for bad folks ter make thar eend. Thar's that thar horse thief I war a-tellin' 'bout, an' that dapple-gray mare,—her name 'twar Luce. An' folks ez is a-runnin' from the sheriff jes' takes ter the T'other Mounting ez nateral ez if it war home; an' ef they don't git cotched, they is never hearn on no more." He paused impressively. "The rocks falls on 'em, an' kills 'em; an' I'll tell ye jes' how I knows," he resumed, oracularly. " 'Twar sixty year ago, nigh about, an' me an' them Jeemes boys war a-burnin' of lime tergether over on the T'other Mounting. We hed a lime-kiln over thar, jes' under Piney Notch, an' never hed no luck, but jes' stuck ter it like fools, till Hiram Jeemes got one of his eyes put out. So we quit burnin' of lime on the T'other Mounting, 'count of the place bein' witched, an' kem over hyar ter Old Rocky-Top, an' got along toler'ble well, cornsiderin'. But one day, whilst we war a-workin' on the T'other Mounting, what d'ye think I fund in the rock? The print of a bare foot in the solid stone, ez plain an' ez nateral ez ef the track hed been lef' in the clay yestiddy. Waal, I knowed it war the track o' Jeremiah Stubbs, what shot his step-brother, an' gin the sheriff the slip, an' war las' seen on the T'other Mounting, 'kase his old shoe jes' fit the track, fur we tried it. An' a good while arterward I fund on that same T'other Mounting—in the solid stone, mind ye—a fish, what he had done br'iled fur supper, jes' turned ter a stone."

"So thar's the Bible made true," said an elderly woman, who had come to the door to hear this reminiscence, and stood mechanically stirring a hoe-cake batter in a shallow wooden bowl. "Ax fur a fish, an' ye'll git a stone."

The secret history of the hills among which they lived was indeed as a sealed book to these simple mountaineers.

"The las' time I war ter Colbury," said Nathan White, "I hearn the sheriff a-talkin' 'bout how them evil-doers an' sech runs for the T'other Mounting fust thing; though he 'lowed ez it war powerful foxy in 'em ter try ter hide thar, 'kase he said, ef they wunst reaches it, he mought ez well look fur a needle in a hay-stack. He 'lowed ef he hed a posse a thousand men strong he couldn't git 'em out."

"He can't find 'em, 'kase the rocks falls on 'em, or swallers 'em in," said the old man. "Ef Tony Britt is up ter mischief he'll never come back no more. He'll git into worser trouble than ever he see afore."

"He hev done seen a powerful lot of trouble, fust one way an' another, 'thout foolin' round the T'other Mounting," said Nathan White. "They tells me ez he got hisself indicted, I believes they calls it, or suthin', down yander ter the court at Colbury,—that war year afore las',—an' he hed ter pay twenty dollars fine; 'kase when he war over-seer of the road he jes' war constant in lettin' his friends, an' folks ginerally, off 'thout hevin' 'em fined, when they didn't come an' work on the road,—though that air the way ez the overseers hev always done, without nobody a-tellin' on 'em an' sech. But them ez warn't Tony Britt's friends seen a mighty differ. He war dead sure ter fine Caleb Hoxie seventy-five cents, 'cordin' ter the law, fur every day that he war summonsed ter work an' never come; 'kase Tony an' Caleb hed some sort 'n grudge agin one another 'count of a spavined horse what Caleb sold ter Tony, makin' him out to be a sound critter,—though Caleb swears he never knowed the horse war spavined when he sold him ter Tony, no more 'n nuthin'. Caleb war mightily worked up 'bout this hyar finin' business, an' him an' Tony hed a tussle 'bout it every time they kem tergether. But Caleb war always sure ter git the worst of it, 'kase Tony, though he air toler'ble spindling sort o' build, he air somehow or other sorter stringy an' tough, an' makes a right smart show in a reg'lar knock-down an' drag-out fight. So Caleb he war beat every time, an' fined too. An' he tried wunst ter shoot Tony Britt, but he missed his aim. An' when he war a-layin' off how ter fix Tony, fur treatin' him that way, he war a-stoppin', one day, at Jacob Green's blacksmith's shop, yander, a mile down the valley, an' he war a-talkin' 'bout it ter a passel o' folks thar. An' Lawyer Rood from Colbury war thar, an' Jacob war a-shoein' of his mare; an' he hearn the tale, an' axed Caleb whyn't he report Tony ter the court, an' git him fined fur neglect of his duty, bein' overseer of the road. An' Caleb never knowed before that it war the law that everybody what war summonsed an' didn't come must be fined, or the overseer must be fined hisself; but he knowed that Tony hed been a-lettin' of his friends off, an' folks ginerally, an' he jes' 'greed fur Lawyer Rood ter stir up trouble fur Tony. An' he done it. An' the court fined Tony twenty dollars fur them ways o' his'n. An' it kept him so busy a-scufflin' ter raise the twenty dollars that he never hed a chance ter give Caleb Hoxie more'n one or two beatin's the whole time he war a-scrapin' up the money."

This story was by no means unknown to the little circle, nor did its narrator labor under the delusion that he was telling a new thing.

It was merely a verbal act of recollection, and an attentive silence reigned as he related the familiar facts. To people who live in lonely regions this habit of retrospection (especially noticeable in them) and an enduring interest in the past may be something of a compensation for the scanty happenings of the present. When the recital was concluded, the hush for a time was unbroken, save by the rush of the winds, bringing upon their breath the fragrant woodland odors of balsams and pungent herbs, and a fresh and exhilarating suggestion of sweeping over a volume of falling water. They stirred the fringed shadow of a great pine that stood, like a sentinel, before Nathan White's door and threw its colorless simulacrum, a boastful lie twice its size, far down the sunset road. Now and then the faint clangor of a cowbell came from out the tangled woods about the little hut, and the low of homeward-bound cattle sounded upon the air, mellowed and softened by the distance. The haze that rested above the long, narrow valley was hardly visible, save in the illusive beauty with which it invested the scene,—the tender azure of the far-away ranges; the exquisite tones of the gray and purple shadows that hovered about the darkening coves and along the deep lines marking the gorges; the burnished brilliance of the sunlight, which, despite its splendor, seemed lonely enough, lying motionless upon the lonely landscape and on the still figures clustered about the porch. Their eyes were turned toward the opposite steeps, gorgeous with scarlet oak and sumac, all in autumnal array, and their thoughts were busy with the hunter on the T'other Mounting and vague speculations concerning his evil intent.

"It 'pears ter me powerful strange ez Tony goes a-foolin' round that thar T'other Mounting, cornsiderin' what happened yander in its shadow," said the woman, coming again to the door, and leaning idly against the frame; the bread was baking over the coals. "That thar wife o' his'n, afore she died, war always frettin' 'kase way down thar on the backbone, whar her house war, the shadow o' the T'other Mounting laid on it fur an hour an' better every day of the worl'. She 'lowed ez it always put her in mind o' the shadow o' death. An' I thought 'bout that thar sayin' o' hern the day when I see her a-lyin' stiff an' cold on the bed, an' the shadow of the T'other Mounting drappin' in at the open door, an' a-creepin' an' a-creepin' over her face. An' I war plumb glad when they got that woman under ground, whar, ef the sunshine can't git ter her, neither kin the shadow. Ef ever thar war a murdered woman, she war one. Arter all that hed come an' gone with Caleb Hoxie, fur Tony Britt ter go arter him, 'kase he war a yerb-doctor, ter git him ter physic

his wife, who war nigh about dead with the lung fever, an' gin up
by old Dr. Marsh!—it looks ter me like he war plumb crazy,—though
him an' Caleb hed sorter made friends 'bout the spavined horse an'
sech afore then. Jes' ez soon ez she drunk the stuff that Caleb fixed
fur her she laid her head back an' shet her eyes, an' never opened
'em no more in this worl'. She war a murdered woman, an' Caleb
Hoxie done it through the yerbs he fixed fur her."

A subtile amethystine mist had gradually overlaid the slopes of the
T'other Mounting, mellowing the brilliant tints of the variegated
foliage to a delicious hazy sheen of mosaics; but about the base the
air seemed dun-colored, though transparent; seen through it, even
the red of the crowded trees was but a sombre sort of magnificence,
and the great masses of gray rocks, jutting out among them here and
there, wore a darkly frowning aspect. Along the summit there was
a blaze of scarlet and gold in the full glory of the sunshine; the top-
most cliffs caught its rays, and gave them back in unexpected gleams
of green or grayish-yellow, as of mosses, or vines, or huckleberry
bushes, nourished in the heart of the deep fissures.

"Waal," said Nathan White, "I never did believe ez Caleb gin
her ennythink ter hurt,—though I knows thar is them ez does. Caleb
is the bes' yerb-doctor I ever see. The rheumatiz would nigh on ter
hev killed me, ef it warn't fur him, that spell I hed las' winter. An'
Dr. Marsh, what they hed up afore the gran' jury, swore that the
yerbs what Caleb gin her war nuthin' to hurt; *he* said, though, they
couldn't holp nor hender. An' but fur Dr. Marsh they would hev
jailed Caleb ter stand his trial, like Tony wanted 'em ter do. But Dr.
Marsh said she died with the consumption, jes' the same, an' Caleb's
yerbs war wholesome, though they warn't no 'count at all."

"I knows I ain't a-goin' never ter tech nuthin' he fixes fur me
no more," said his wife, "an' I'll be bound nobody else in these hyar
mountings will, nuther."

"Waal," drawled her son, "I knows fur true ez he air tendin' now
on old Gideon Croft, what lives over yander in the valley on the
t'other side of the T'other Mounting, an' is down with the fever. He
went over thar yestiddy evening, late; I met him when he war goin',
an' he tole me."

"He hed better look out how he comes across Tony Britt," said
Nathan White; "fur I hearn, the las' time I war ter the Settlemint,
how Tony hev swore ter kill him the nex' time he sees him, fur
a-givin' of pizenous yerbs ter his wife. Tony air mightily outdone
'kase the gran' jury let him off. Caleb hed better be sorter keerful
how he goes a-foolin' round these hyar dark woods."

The sun had sunk, and the night, long held in abeyance, was coming fast. The glooms gathered in the valley; a soft gray shadow hung over the landscape, making familiar things strange. The T'other Mounting was all a dusky, sad purple under the faintly pulsating stars, save that high along the horizontal line of its summit gleamed the strange red radiance of the dead and gone sunset. The outline of the foliage was clearly drawn against the pure lapis lazuli tint of the sky behind it; here and there the uncanny light streamed through the bare limbs of an early leafless tree, which looked in the distance like some bony hand beckoning, or warning, or raised in horror.

"*Anythink* mought happen thar!" said the woman, as she stood on night-wrapped Rocky-Top and gazed up at the alien light, so red in the midst of the dark landscape. When she turned back to the door of the little hut, the meagre comforts within seemed almost luxury, in their cordial contrast to the desolate, dreary mountain yonder and the thought of the forlorn, wandering hunter. A genial glow from the hearth diffused itself over the puncheon floor; the savory odor of broiling venison filled the room as a tall, slim girl knelt before the fire and placed the meat upon the gridiron, her pale cheeks flushing with the heat; there was a happy suggestion of peace and unity when the four generations trooped in to their supper, grandfather on his grandson's arm, and a sedate two-year-old bringing up the rear. Nathan White's wife paused behind the others to bar the door, and once more, as she looked up at the T'other Mounting, the thought of the lonely wanderer smote her heart. The red sunset light had died out at last, but a golden aureola heralded the moon-rise, and a gleaming thread edged the masses of foliage; there was no faint suggestion now of mist in the valley, and myriads of stars filled a cloudless sky. "He hev done gone home by this time," she said to her daughter-in-law, as she closed the door, "an' ef he ain't, he'll hev a moon ter light him."

"Air ye a-studyin' 'bout Tony Britt yit?" asked Nathan White. "He hev done gone home a good hour by sun, I'll be bound. Jes' ketch Tony Britt a-huntin' till sundown, will ye! He air a mighty pore hand ter work. 'Stonishes me ter hear he air even a-huntin' on the T'other Mounting."

"I don't believe he's up ter enny harm," said the woman; "he hev jes' tuk ter the woods with grief."

"'Pears ter me," said the daughter-in-law, rising from her kneeling posture before the fire, and glancing reproachfully at her husband, —"'pears ter me ez ye mought hev brought him hyar ter eat his supper along of we-uns, stiddier a-leavin' him a-grievin' over his dead wife in them witched woods on the T'other Mounting."

The young fellow looked a trifle abashed at this suggestion. "I never wunst thought of it," he said. "Tony never stopped ter talk more'n a minit, nohow."

The evening wore away; the octogenarian and the sedate two-year-old fell asleep in their chairs shortly after supper; Nathan White and his son smoked their cob-pipes, and talked fitfully of the few incidents of the day; the women sat in the firelight with their knitting, silent and absorbed, except that now and then the elder, breaking from her reverie, declared, "I can't git Tony Britt out'n my head nohow in the worl'."

The moon had come grandly up over the T'other Mounting, casting long silver lights and deep black shadows through all the tangled recesses and yawning chasms of the woods and rocks. In the vast wilderness the bright rays met only one human creature, the belated hunter making his way homeward through the dense forest with an experienced woodman's craft. For no evil intent had brought Tony Britt to the T'other Mounting; he had spent the day in hunting, urged by the strong necessity without which the mountaineer seldom makes any exertion. Dr. Marsh's unavailing skill had cost him dear; his only cow was sold to make up the twenty dollars fine which his revenge on Caleb Hoxie had entailed upon him; without even so much as a spavined horse tillage was impossible, and the bounteous harvest left him empty-handed, for he had no crops to gather. The hardships of extreme poverty had reinforced the sorrows that came upon him in battalions, and had driven him far through long aisles of the woods, where the night fell upon him unaware. The foliage was all embossed with exquisite silver designs that seemed to stand out some little distance from the dark masses of leaves; now and then there came to his eyes that emerald gleam never seen upon verdure in the daytime,—only shown by some artificial light, or the moon's sweet uncertainty. The wind was strong and fresh, but not cold; here and there was a glimmer of dew. Once, and once only, he thought of the wild traditions which peopled the T'other Mounting with evil spirits. He paused with a sudden chill; he glanced nervously over his shoulder down the illimitable avenues of the lonely woods. The grape-vines, hanging in festoons from tree to tree, were slowly swinging back and forth, stirred by the wind. There was a dizzy dance of shadows whirling on every open space where the light lay on the ground. The roar and fret of Wild-Duck River, hidden there somewhere in the pines, came on the breeze like a strange, weird, fitful voice, crying out amid the haunted solitudes of the T'other Mounting. He turned abruptly, with his gun on his shoulder, and pursued his way through the trackless desert in the direction of his home. He had been absorbed in his quest and his gloomy thoughts, and did not realize the distance he had traversed until it lay before him to be retraced; but his superstitious terror urged him to renewed exertions. "Ef ever I gits off'n this hyar witched mounting," he said to himself, as he tore away the vines and brambles that beset his course, "I'll never come back agin while I lives." He grew calmer when he paused on a huge projecting crag, and looked across the narrow valley at the great black mass opposite, which he knew was Old Rocky-Top; its very presence gave him a sense of companionship and blunted his fear, and he sat down to rest for a few minutes, gazing at the outline of the range he knew so well, so unfamiliar from a new stand-point. How low it seemed from the heights of the T'other Mounting! Could that faint gleam be the light in Nathan White's house? Tony Britt glanced further down the indistinct slope, where he knew his own desolate, deserted hut was crouched. "Jes' whar the shadow o' the T'other Mounting can reach it," he thought, with a new infusion of bitterness. He averted his eyes; he would look no longer; he threw himself at full length among the ragged clumps of grass and fragments of rock, and turned his face to the stars. It all came back to him then. Sometimes, in his sordid cares and struggles for his scanty existence, his past troubles were dwarfed by the present. But here on the lonely cliff, with the infinite spaces above him and the boundless forest below, he felt anew his isolation. No light on earth save the far gleam from another man's home, and in heaven only the drowning face of the moon, drifting slowly through the blue floods of the skies. He was only twenty-five; he had youth and health and strength, but he felt that he had lived his life; it seemed long, marked as it was by cares and privation and persistent failure. Little as he knew of life, he knew how hard his had been, even meted by those of the poverty-stricken wretches among whom his lot was cast. "An' sech luck!" he said, as his sad eyes followed the drifting dead face of the moon. "Along o' that thar step-mother o' mine till I war growed; an' then when I war married, an' we hed got the house put up, an' war beginnin' ter git along like other folks kin, an' Car'line's mother gin her that thar calf what growed ter a cow, an' through pinchin' an' savin' we made out ter buy that thar horse from Caleb Hoxie, jes' ez we war a-startin' ter work a crap he lays down an' dies; an' that cussed twenty dollars ez I hed ter pay ter the court; an' Car'line jes' a-gittin' sick, an' a-wastin' an' a-wastin' away, till

I, like a fool, brung Caleb thar, an' he pizens her with his yerbs—God A'mighty! ef I could jes' lay my hands wunst on that scoundrel I wouldn't leave a mite of him, ef he war pertected by a hundred lyin', thievin' gran' juries! But he can't stay a-hidin' forevermo'. He's got ter 'count ter me, ef he ain't ter the law; an' he'll see a mighty differ atwixt us. I swear he'll never draw another breath!"

He rose with a set, stern face, and struck a huge bowlder beside him with his hard clenched hand as he spoke. He had not even an ignorant idea of an impressive dramatic pose; but if the great gaunt cliff had been the stage of a theatre his attitude and manner at that instant would have won him applause. He was all alone with his poverty and his anguished memories, as men with such burdens are apt to be.

The bowlder on which, in his rude fashion, he had registered his oath was harder than his hard hand, and the vehemence of the blow brought blood; but he had scarcely time to think of it. His absorbed reverie was broken by a rustling other than that of the eddying wind. He raised his head and looked about him, half expecting to see the antlers of a deer. Then there came to his ears the echo of the tread of man. His eyes mechanically followed the sound. Forty feet down the face of the crag a broad ledge jutted out, and upon it ran a narrow path, made by stray cattle, or the feet of their searching owners; it was visible from the summit for a distance of a hundred yards or so, and the white glamour of the moonbeams fell full upon it. Before a speculation had suggested itself, a man walked slowly into view along the path, and with starting eyes the hunter recognized his dearest foe. Britt's hand lay upon the bowlder; his oath was in his mind; his unconscious enemy had come within his power. Swifter than a flash the temptation was presented. He remembered the warnings of his lawyer at Colbury last week, when the grand jury failed to find a true bill against Caleb Hoxie,—that he was an innocent man, and must go unscathed, that any revenge for fancied wrongs would be dearly rued; he remembered, too, the mountain traditions of the falling rocks burying evil-doers in the heart of the hills. Here was his opportunity. He would have a life for a life, and there would be one more legend of the very stones conspiring to punish malefactors escaped from men added to the terrible "sayin's" of the T'other Mounting. A strong belief in the supernatural influences of the place was rife within him; he knew nothing of Gideon Croft's fever and the errand that had brought the herb-doctor through the "witched mounting;" had he not been transported thither by some invisible agency, that the rocks might fall upon him and crush him?

The temptation and the resolve were simultaneous. With his hand upon the bowlder, his hot heart beating fast, his distended eyes burning upon the approaching figure, he waited for the moment to come. There lay the long, low, black mountain opposite, with only the moon beams upon it, for the lights in Nathan White's house were extinguished; there was the deep, dark gulf of the valley; there, forty feet below him, was the narrow, moon-flooded path on the ledge, and the man advancing carelessly. The bowlder fell with a frightful crash, the echoes rang with a scream of terror, and the two men—one fleeing from the dreadful danger he had barely escaped, the other from the hideous deed he thought he had done—ran wildly in opposite directions through the tangled autumnal woods.

Was every leaf of the forest endowed with a woful voice, that the echo of that shriek might never die from Tony Britt's ears? Did the storied, retributive rocks still vibrate with this new victim's frenzied cry? And what was this horror in his heart! Now,—so late,—was coming a terrible conviction of his enemy's innocence, and with it a fathomless remorse.

All through the interminable night he fled frantically along the mountain's summit, scarcely knowing whither, and caring for nothing except to multiply the miles between him and the frightful object that he believed lay under the bowlder which he had dashed down the precipice. The moon sank beneath the horizon; the fantastic shadows were merged in the darkest hour of the night; the winds died, and there was no voice in all the woods, save the wail of Wild-Duck River and the forever-resounding screams in the flying wretch's ears. Sometimes he answered them in a wild, hoarse, inarticulate cry; sometimes he flung his hands above his head and wrung them in his agony; never once did he pause in his flight. Panting, breathless, exhausted, he eagerly sped through the darkness; tearing his face upon the brambles; plunging now and then into gullies and unseen quagmires; sometimes falling heavily, but recovering himself in an instant, and once more struggling on; striving to elude the pursuing voices, and to distance forever his conscience and his memory.

And then came that terrible early daylight that was wont to dawn upon the T'other Mounting when all the world besides was lost in slumber; the wan, melancholy light showed dimly the solemn trees and dense undergrowth; the precarious pitfalls about his path; the long deep gorges; the great crags and chasms; the cascades, steely gray, and white; the huge mass, all hung about with shadows, which he knew was Old Rocky-Top, rising from the impenetrably dark val-

ley below. It seemed wonderful to him, somehow, that a new day
should break at all. If, in a revulsion of nature, that utter blackness
had continued forever and ever it would not have been strange, after
what had happened. He could have borne it better than the sight of
the familiar world gradually growing into day, all unconscious of his
secret. He had begun the descent of the T'other Mounting, and he
seemed to carry that pale dawn with him; day was breaking when
he reached the foot of Old Rocky-Top, and as he climbed up to his
own deserted, empty little shanty, it too stood plainly defined in the
morning light. He dragged himself to the door, and impelled by some
morbid fascination he glanced over his shoulder at the T'other
Mounting. There it was, unchanged, with the golden largess of a
gracious season blazing upon every autumnal leaf. He shuddered, and
went into the fireless, comfortless house. And then he made an appalling discovery. As he mechanically divested himself of his shot-
pouch and powder-horn he was stricken by a sudden consciousness
that he did not have his gun! One doubtful moment, and he remembered that he had laid it upon the crag when he had thrown himself down to rest. Beyond question, it was there yet. His conscience
was still now,—his remorse had fled. It was only a matter of time
when his crime would be known. He recollected his meeting with
young White while he was hunting, and then Britt cursed the gun
which he had left on the cliff. The discovery of the weapon there
would be strong evidence against him, taken in connection with all
the other circumstances. True, he could even yet go back and recover
it, but he was mastered by the fear of meeting some one on the unfrequented road, or even in the loneliness of the T'other Mounting,
and strengthening the chain of evidence against him by the fact of
being once more seen in the fateful neighborhood. He resolved that
he would wait until night-fall, and then he would retrace his way,
secure his gun, and all might yet be well with him. As to the bowlder,
—were men never before buried under the falling rocks of the T'other
Mounting?

Without food, without rest, without sleep, his limbs rigid with the
strong tension of his nerves, his eyes bloodshot, haggard, and eager,
his brain on fire, he sat through the long morning hours absently
gazing across the narrow valley at the solemn, majestic mountain
opposite, and that sinister jutting crag with the indistinctly defined
ledges of its rugged surface.

After a time, the scene began to grow dim; the sun was still shining, but through a haze becoming momently more dense. The bril-
liantly tinted foliage upon the T'other Mounting was fading; the

cliffs showed strangely distorted faces through the semi-transparent blue vapor, and presently they seemed to recede altogether; the valley disappeared, and all the country was filled with the smoke of distant burning woods. He was gasping when he first became sensible of the smoke-laden haze, for he had seen nothing of the changing aspect of the landscape. Before his vision was the changeless picture of a night of mingled moonlight and shadow, the ill-defined black mass where Old Rocky-Top rose into the air, the impenetrable gloom of the valley, the ledge of the crag, and the unconscious figure slowly coming within the power of his murderous hand. His eyes would look on no other scene, no other face, so long as he should live.

He had a momentary sensation of stifling, and then a great weight was lifted. For he had begun to doubt whether the unlucky locality would account satisfactorily for the fall of that bowlder and the horrible object beneath it; a more reasonable conclusion might be deduced from the fact that he had been seen in the neighborhood, and the circumstance of the deadly feud. But what wonder would there be if the dry leaves on the T'other Mounting should be ignited and the woods burned! What explanations might not such a catastrophe suggest!—a frantic flight from the flames toward the cliff and an accidental fall. And so he waited throughout the long day, that was hardly day at all, but an opaque twilight, through which could be discerned only the stony path leading down the slope from his door, only the blurred outlines of the bushes close at hand, only the great gaunt limbs of a lightning-scathed tree, seeming entirely severed from the unseen trunk, and swinging in the air sixty feet above the earth.

Toward night-fall the wind rose and the smoke-curtain lifted, once more revealing to the settlers upon Old Rocky-Top the sombre T'other Mounting, with the belated evening light still lurid upon the trees, —only a strange, faint resemblance of the sunset radiance, rather the ghost of a dead day. And presently this apparition was gone, and the deep purple line of the witched mountain's summit grew darker against the opaline skies, till it was merged in a dusky black, and the shades of the night fell thick on the landscape.

The scenic effects of the drama, that serve to widen the mental vision and cultivate the imagination of even the poor in cities, were denied these primitive, simple people; but that magnificent pageant of the four seasons, wherein was forever presented the imposing splendor of the T'other Mounting in an ever-changing grandeur of aspect, was a gracious recompense for the spectacular privileges of civilization. And this evening the humble family party on Nathan White's porch beheld a scene of unique impressiveness.

The moon had not yet risen; the winds were awhirl; the darkness draped the earth as with a pall. Out from the impenetrable gloom of the woods on the T'other Mounting there started, suddenly, a scarlet globe of fire; one long moment it was motionless, but near it the spectral outline of a hand appeared beckoning, or warning, or raised in horror,—only a leafless tree, catching in the distance a semblance of humanity. Then from the still ball of fire there streamed upward a long, slender plume of golden light, waving back and forth against the pale horizon. Across the dark slope of the mountain below, flashes of lightning were shooting in zigzag lines, and wherever they gleamed were seen those frantic skeleton hands raised and wrung in anguish. It was cruel sport for the cruel winds; they maddened over gorge and cliff and along the wooded steeps, carrying far upon their wings the sparks of desolation. From the summit, myriads of jets of flame reached up to the placid stars; about the base of the mountain lurked a lake of liquid fire, with wreaths of blue smoke hovering over it; ever and anon, athwart the slope darted the sudden lightning, widening into sheets of flame as it conquered new ground.

The astonishment on the faces grouped about Nathan White's door was succeeded by a startled anxiety. After the first incoherent exclamations of surprise came the pertinent inquiry from his wife, "Ef Old Rocky-Top war ter ketch too, whar would we-uns run ter?"

Nathan White's countenance had in its expression more of astounded excitement than of bodily fear. "Why, bless my soul!" he said at length, "the woods away over yander, what hev been burnin' all day, ain't nigh enough ter the T'other Mounting ter ketch it,—nuthin' like it."

"The T'other Mounting would burn, though, ef fire war put ter it," said his son. The two men exchanged a glance of deep significance.

"Do ye mean ter say," exclaimed Mrs. White, her fire-lit face agitated by a sudden superstitious terror, "that that thar T'other Mounting is fired by witches an' sech?"

"Don't talk so loud, Matildy," said her husband. "Them knows best ez done it."

"Thar's one thing sure," quavered the old man: "that thar fire will never tech a leaf on Old Rocky-Top. Thar's a church on this hyar mounting,—bless the Lord fur it!—an' we lives in the fear o' God."

There was a pause, all watching with distended eyes the progress of the flames.

"It looks like it mought hev been kindled in torment," said the young daughter-in-law.

"It looks down thar," said her husband, pointing to the lake of fire, "like the pit itself."

The apathetic inhabitants of Old Rocky-Top were stirred into an activity very incongruous with their habits and the hour. During the conflagration they traversed long distances to reach each other's houses and confer concerning the danger and the questions of supernatural agency provoked by the mysterious firing of the woods. Nathan White had few neighbors, but above the crackling of the timber and the roar of the flames there rose the quick beat of running footsteps; the undergrowth of the forest near at hand was in strange commotion; and at last, the figure of a man burst forth, the light of the fire showing the startling pallor of his face as he staggered to the little porch and sank, exhausted, into a chair.

"Waal, Caleb Hoxie!" exclaimed Nathan White, in good-natured raillery; "ye're skeered, fur true! What ails ye, ter think Old Rocky-Top air a-goin' ter ketch too? 'Tain't nigh dry enough, I'm a-thinkin'."

"Fire kindled that thar way can't tech a leaf on Old Rocky-Top," sleepily piped out the old man, nodding in his chair, the glare of the flames which rioted over the T'other Mounting gilding his long white hair and peaceful, slumberous face. "Thar's a church on Old Rocky-Top,—bless the"— The sentence drifted away with his dreams.

"Does ye believe—them—them"—Caleb Hoxie's trembling white lips could not frame the word—"them—done it?"

"Like ez not," said Nathan White. "But that ain't a-troublin' of ye an' me. I ain't never hearn o' them witches a-tormentin' of honest folks what ain't done nuthin' hurtful ter nobody," he added, in cordial reassurance.

His son was half hidden behind one of the rough cedar posts, that his mirth at the guest's display of cowardice might not be observed. But the women, always quick to suspect, glanced meaningly at each other with widening eyes, as they stood together in the door-way.

"I dunno,—I dunno," Caleb Hoxie declared huskily. "I ain't never done nuthin' ter nobody, an' what do ye s'pose them witches an' sech done ter me las' night, on that T'other Mounting? I war a-goin' over yander to Gideon Croft's fur ter physic him, ez he air mortal low with the fever; an' ez I war a-comin' alongside o' that thar high bluff"—it was very distinct, with the flames wreathing fantastically about its gray, rigid features—"they throwed a bowlder ez big ez this hyar porch down on ter me. It jes' grazed me, an' knocked me down, an' kivered me with dirt. An' I run home a-hollerin'; an' it seemed

ter me ter-day ez I war a-goin' ter screech an' screech all my life, like
some onsettled crazy critter. It 'peared like 'twould take a bar'l o' hop
tea ter git me quiet. An' now look yander!" and he pointed tremulously to the blazing mountain.

There was an expression of conviction on the women's faces. All
their lives afterward it was there whenever Caleb Hoxie's name was
mentioned; no more to be moved or changed than the stern, set faces
of the crags among the fiery woods.

"Thar's a church on this hyar mounting," said the old man feebly,
waking for a moment, and falling asleep the next.

Nathan White was perplexed and doubtful, and a superstitious awe
had checked the laughing youngster behind the cedar post.

A great cloud of flame came rolling through the sky toward them,
golden, pellucid, spangled through and through with fiery red stars;
poising itself for one moment high above the valley, then breaking
into myriads of sparks, and showering down upon the dark abysses
below.

"Look-a-hyar!" said the elder woman in a frightened under-tone
to her daughter-in-law; "this hyar wicked critter air too onlucky ter
be a-sittin' 'longside of us; we'll all be burnt up afore he gits hisself
away from hyar. An' who is that a-comin' yander?" For from the
encompassing woods another dark figure had emerged, and was slowly
approaching the porch. The wary eyes near Caleb Hoxie saw that
he fell to trembling, and that he clutched at a post for support. But
the hand pointing at him was shaken as with a palsy, and the voice
hardly seemed Tony Britt's as it cried out, in an agony of terror,
"What air ye a-doin' hyar, a-sittin' 'longside o' livin' folks? Yer bones
air under a bowlder on the T'other Mounting, an' ye air a dead man!"

They said ever afterward that Tony Britt had lost his mind "through
goin' a-huntin' jes' one time on the T'other Mounting. His spirit air
all broke, an' he's a mighty tame critter nowadays." Through his persistent endeavor he and Caleb Hoxie became quite friendly, and he
was even reported to "'low that he war sati'fied that Caleb never
gin his wife nuthin' ter hurt." "Though," said the gossips of Old
Rocky-Top, "them women up ter White's will hev it no other way
but that Caleb pizened her, an' they wouldn't take no yerbs from him
no more'n he war a rattlesnake. But Caleb always 'pears sorter skittish when he an' Tony air tergether, like he didn't know when Tony
war a-goin' ter fotch him a lick. But law! Tony air that changed that
ye can't make him mad 'thout ye mind him o' the time he called
Caleb a ghost."

A dark, gloomy, deserted place was the charred T'other Mounting through all the long winter. And when spring came, and Old Rocky-Top was green with delicate fresh verdure, and melodious with singing birds and chorusing breezes, and bedecked as for some great festival with violets and azaleas and laurel-blooms, the T'other Mounting was stark and wintry and black with its desolate, leafless trees. But after a while the spring came for it, too: the buds swelled and burst; flowering vines festooned the grim gray crags; and the dainty freshness of the vernal season reigned upon its summit, while all the world below was growing into heat and dust. The circuit-rider said it reminded him of a tardy change in a sinner's heart: though it come at the eleventh hour, the glorious summer is before it, and a full fruition; though it work but an hour in the Lord's vineyard, it receives the same reward as those who labored through all the day.

"An' it always did 'pear ter me ez thar war mighty little jestice in that," was Mrs. White's comment.

But at the meeting when that sermon was preached Tony Britt told his "experience." It seemed a confession, for according to the gossips he " 'lowed that he hed flung that bowlder down on Caleb Hoxie, —what the witches flung, ye know,—'kase he believed then that Caleb hed killed his wife with pizenous yerbs; an' he went back the nex' night an' fired the woods, ter make folks think when they fund Caleb's bones that he war a-runnin' from the blaze an' fell off'n the bluff." And everybody on Old Rocky-Top said incredulously, "Pore Tony Britt! He hev los' his mind through goin' a-huntin' jes' one time on the T'other Mounting."

SARAH ORNE JEWETT

★ ★ ★

Quiet, gentler aspects of Maine life are pictured with artful simplicity by Sarah Orne Jewett (1849-1909). Anxious only to portray her people's grand simplicity arising from worthy old traditions and noble memories, she never argued a thesis or attempted to solve social problems. Even in "The Gray Mills of Farley," with its ready-made opportunity for a discussion of capitalist enterprise, she studiously emphasized the influence of environment upon character. No turbulence or melodramatic action intrudes into the peace of her sketches; common, everyday activities acquire a romantic beauty. Born in South Berwick, Maine, Miss Jewett accompanied her father on his rounds as a physician and unconsciously acquired literary materials. Her masterpiece is *The Country of the Pointed Firs* (1896), but from 1877 to 1904 she produced over a hundred additional tales, of which certainly no fewer than thirty-two are memorable. "Miss Debby's Neighbors" and "A White Heron" are reprinted by permission of Houghton Mifflin Company.

★ ★ ★

A Lost Lover

For a great many years it had been understood in Longfield that Miss Horatia Dane once had a lover, and that he had been lost at sea. By little and little, in one way and another, her acquaintances had found out or made up the whole story, and Miss Dane stood in the position, not of an unmarried woman exactly, but rather of having spent most of her life in a long and lonely widowhood. She looked like a person with a history, strangers often said (as if we each did not have a history), and her own unbroken reserve about this romance of hers gave everybody the more respect for it.

The Longfield people paid willing deference to Miss Dane: her family had always been one that could be liked and respected, and she was the last that was left in the old home of which she was so fond. This was a high, square house, with a row of pointed windows in its roof, a peaked porch in front, with some lilac-bushes around it, and down by the road was a long, orderly procession of poplars, like a row of sentinels standing guard. She had lived here alone since her father's death, twenty years before. She was a kind, just woman, whose pleasures were of a stately and sober sort, and she seemed not unhappy in her loneliness, though she sometimes said gravely that she was the last of her family, as if the fact had a great sadness for her.

She had some middle-aged and elderly cousins living at a distance, and they came occasionally to see her; but there had been no young people staying in the house for many years until this summer, when the daughter of her youngest cousin had written to ask if she might come to make a visit. She was a motherless girl of twenty, both older and younger than her years. Her father and brother, who were civil engineers, had taken some work upon the line of a railway in the far Western country. Nelly had made many long journeys with them before and since she had left school, and she had meant to follow them now after she had spent a fortnight with the old cousin whom she had not seen since her childhood. Her father had laughed at the visit as a freak, and had warned her of the dullness and primness of Longfield; but the result was that the girl found herself very happy in the comfortable home. She was still her own free, unfettered, lucky, and sunshiny self, and the old house was so much pleasanter for the girlish face and life that Miss Horatia had, at first timidly and then most heartily, begged her to stay for the whole summer, or even the autumn, until her father was ready to come East. The name of Dane was very dear to Miss Horatia, and she grew fonder of her guest: when the village people saw her glance at the girl affectionately, as they sat together in the family pew of a Sunday, or saw them walking together after tea, they said it was a good thing for Miss Horatia; how bright she looked! and no doubt she would leave all her money to Nelly Dane, if she played her cards well.

But we will do Nelly justice and say that she was not mercenary; she would have scorned such a thought. She had grown to have a great love for her cousin Horatia, and she liked to please her. She idealized her, I have no doubt; and her repression, her grave courtesy and rare words of approval had a great fascination for a girl who had just been used to people who chattered, and were upon most intimate terms with you directly, and could forget you with equal ease. And Nelly liked having so admiring and easily pleased an audience as Miss Dane and her old servant Melissa. She liked to be queen of her company; she had so many gay, bright stories of what had happened to herself and her friends; beside, she was clever with her needle, and had all those practical gifts which elderly women approve so heartily in girls. They liked her pretty clothes; she was sensible and economical and busy; they praised her to each other and to the world; even stubborn old Andrew, the man to whom even Miss Horatia spoke with deference, would do anything she asked. Nelly would by no means choose so dull a life as this for the rest of her days, but she enjoyed it immensely for the time being. She instinctively avoided all that would shock the grave dignity and old-school ideas of Miss Dane; and somehow she never had felt happier or better satisfied with life. I think it was because she was her best and most lady-like self. It was not long before she knew the village people almost as well as Miss Dane did, and she became a very great favorite, as a girl so easily can who is good-natured and pretty, and well versed in city fashions; who has that tact and cleverness that come to such a nature from going about the world and knowing many people.

She had not been in Longfield many weeks before she heard something of Miss Dane's love story; for one of her new friends said, in a confidential moment, "Does your cousin ever speak to you about the young man to whom she was engaged to be married?" and Nelly answered no, with great wonder, and not without regret at her own ignorance. After this she kept her eyes and ears open for whatever news of this lover's existence might be found.

At last it happened one day that she had a good chance for a friendly talk with Melissa,—for who should know about the family affairs better than she? Miss Horatia had taken her second-best parasol, with the deep fringe, and had gone majestically down the street to do some morning errands which she could trust to no one. Melissa was shelling peas at the shady backdoor-step, and Nelly came strolling round from the garden, along the clean-swept flag-stones, and sat down to help her. Melissa moved along, with a grim smile, to make room for her. "You needn't bother yourself," said she. "I've nothing else to do; you'll green your fingers all over;" but she was evidently pleased to have company.

"My fingers will wash," said Nelly, "and I've nothing else to do, either; please push the basket this way a little, or I shall scatter the pods, and then you will scold." She went to work busily, while she tried to think of the best way to find out the story she wished to hear.

"There!" said Melissa, "I never told Miss H'ratia to get some citron, and I settled yesterday to make some pound-cake this forenoon, after I got dinner along a piece. She's most out o' mustard, too; she's set about having mustard to eat with her beef, just as the old colonel was before her. I never saw any other folks eat mustard with their roast beef; but every family has their own tricks. I tied a thread round my left-hand little finger purpose to remember that citron, before she came down this morning. I hope I ain't losing my fac'lties." It was seldom that Melissa was so talkative as this at first. She was clearly in a talkative mood.

"Melissa," asked Nelly, with great bravery, after a minute or two of silence, "who was it that my cousin Horatia was going to marry? It's odd that I shouldn't know; but I don't remember father's ever speaking of it, and I shouldn't think of asking her."

"I s'pose it'll seem strange to you," said Melissa, beginning to shell the peas a great deal faster, "but as many years as I have lived in this house with her,—her mother, the old lady, fetched me up,—I never knew Miss H'ratia to say a word about him. But there! she knows I know, and we've got an understanding on many things we never talk over as some folks would. I've heard about it from other folks. She was visiting her great-aunt in Salem when she met with him. His name was Carrick, and it was presumed they were going to be married when he came home from the voyage he was lost on. He had the promise of going out master of a new ship. They didn't keep company long; it was made up of a sudden, and folks here didn't get hold of the story till some time after. I've heard some that ought to know say it was only talk, and they never were engaged to be married no more than I am."

"You say he was lost at sea?" asked Nelly.

"The ship never was heard from; they supposed she was run down in the night out in the South Seas, somewhere. It was a good while before they gave up expecting news, but none ever come. I think she set everything by him, and took it very hard losing of him. But there, she'd never say a word; you're the freest-spoken Dane I ever saw, but you may take it from your mother's folks. I know he gave her that whale's tooth with the ship drawn on it that's on the mantel-piece in her room; she may have a sight of other keepsakes, for all I know, but it ain't likely;" and here there was a pause, in which Nelly grew sorrowful as she thought of the long waiting for tidings of the missing ship, and of her cousin's solitary life. It was so odd to think of prim Miss Horatia's being in love with a sailor; there was a young lieutenant in the navy whom Nelly herself liked dearly, and he had gone away on a long voyage. "Perhaps she's been just as well off," said Melissa. "She's dreadful set, y'r cousin H'ratia is, and sailors is high-tempered men. I've heard it hinted that he was a fast fellow, and if a woman's got a good home like this, and's able to do for herself, she'd better stay there. I ain't going to give up a certainty for an uncertainty,—that's what *I* always tell 'em," added Melissa, with great decision, as if she were besieged by lovers; but Nelly smiled inwardly as she thought of the courage it would take to support any one who wished to offer her companion his heart and hand. It would need desperate energy to scale the walls of that garrison.

The green peas were all shelled presently, and Melissa said, gravely, that she should have to be lazy now until it was time to put in the meat. She wasn't used to being helped unless there was extra work, and she calculated to have one piece of work join on to another. However, it was no account, and she was obliged for the company; and Nelly laughed merrily as she stood washing her hands in the shining old copper basin at the sink. The sun would not be round that side of the house for a long time yet, and the pink and blue morning-glories were still in their full bloom and freshness. They grew over the window, twined on strings exactly the same distance apart. There was a box crowded full of green houseleeks down at the side of the door; they were straying over the edge, and Melissa stooped stiffly down with an air of disapproval at their untidiness. "They straggle all over everything," said she, "and they're no kind of use, only Miss's mother she set everything by 'em. She fetched 'em from home with her when she was married; her mother kep' a box, and they came from England. Folks used to say they was good for bee stings." Then she went into the inner kitchen, and Nelly went slowly away along the flag-stones to the garden from whence she had come. The garden-gate opened with a tired creak and shut with a clack, and she noticed how smooth and shiny the wood was where the touch of so many hands had worn it. There was a great pleasure to this girl in finding herself among such old and well-worn things. She had been for a long time in cities or at the West, and among the old fashions and ancient possessions of Longfield it seemed to her that everything had its story, and she liked the quietness and unchangeableness with which life seemed to go on from year to year. She had seen many a dainty or gorgeous garden, but never one that she had liked so well as this, with its herb bed and its broken rows of currant bushes, its tall stalks of white lilies and its wandering rose-bushes and honeysuckles, that had bloomed beside the straight paths for so many more summers than she herself had lived. She picked a little nosegay of late red roses, and carried it into the house to put on the parlor table. The wide hall door was standing open, with its green outer blinds closed, and the old hall was dim and cool. Miss Horatia did not like a glare of sunlight, and she abhorred flies with her whole heart. Nelly could hardly see her way through the rooms, it had been so bright out of doors; but she brought the tall champagne glass of water from the dining-room and put the flowers in their place. Then she looked at two silhouettes which stood on the mantel in carved ebony frames. They were portraits of an uncle of Miss Dane and his wife. Miss Dane had thought Nelly looked like this uncle the evening before. She could not see the likeness herself, but the pictures suggested something else, and she turned suddenly and went hurrying up the stairs to Miss Horatia's own room, where she remembered to have seen a group of silhouettes fastened to the wall. There were seven or eight, and she looked at the young men among them most carefully, but they were all marked with the name of Dane: they were Miss Horatia's brothers, and our friend hung them on their little brass hooks again with a feeling of disappointment. Perhaps her cousin had a quaint miniature of the lover, painted on ivory and shut in a worn red morocco case; she hoped she should get a sight of it some day. This story of the lost sailor had a wonderful charm for the girl. Miss Horatia had never been so interesting to her before. How she must have mourned for the lover, and missed him, and hoped there would yet be news from the ship! Nelly thought she would tell her her own little love story some day, though there was not much to tell yet, in spite of there being so much to think about. She built a little castle in Spain, as she sat in the front window-seat of the upper hall, and dreamed pleasant stories for herself until the sharp noise of the front-gate latch waked her, and she looked out through the blind to see her cousin coming up the walk.

Miss Horatia looked hot and tired, and her thoughts were not of any fashion of romance. "It is going to be very warm," said she. "I have been worrying ever since I have been gone because I forgot to ask Andrew to pick those white currants for the minister's wife. I promised that she should have them early this morning. Would you go out to the kitchen and ask Melissa to step in for a moment, my dear?"

Melissa was picking over red currants to make a pie, and rose from her chair with a little unwillingness. "I guess they could wait until afternoon," said she, as she came back. "Miss H'ratia's in a fret because she forgot about sending some white currants to the minister's. I told her that Andrew had gone to have the horses shod and wouldn't be back till near noon. I don't see why part of the folks in the world should kill themselves trying to suit the rest. As long as I haven't got any citron for the cake, I suppose I might go out and pick 'em," added Melissa, ungraciously. "I'll get some to set away for tea, anyhow."

Miss Dane had a letter to write after she had rested from her walk, and Nelly soon left her in the dark parlor and went back to the sunshiny garden to help Melissa, who seemed to be taking life with more than her usual disapproval. She was sheltered by an enormous gingham sun-bonnet.

"I set out to free my mind to your cousin H'ratia, this morning," said she, as Nelly crouched down at the opposite side of the bush where she was picking; "but we can't agree on that p'int, and it's no use. I don't say nothing; you might 's well ask the moon to face about and travel the other way as to try to change Miss H'ratia's mind. I ain't going to argue it with her, it ain't my place; I know that as well as anybody. She'd run her feet off for the minister's folks any day, and though I do say he's a fair preacher, they haven't got a speck o' consideration nor fac'lty; they think the world was made for them, but I think likely they'll find out it wasn't; most folks do. When he first was settled here I had a fit o' sickness, and he come to see me when I was getting over the worst of it. He did the best he could; I always took it very kind of him; but he made a prayer, and he kep' sayin' 'this aged handmaid,' I should think a dozen times. Aged handmaid!" said Melissa, scornfully, "I don't call myself aged yet, and that was more than ten years ago; I never made pretensions to being younger than I am, but you'd 'a' thought I was a topplin' old creatur' going on a hundred."

Nelly laughed; Melissa looked cross and moved on to the next currant bush. "So that's why you don't like the minister?" But the question did not seem to please.

"I hope I never should be set against a preacher by such as that," and Nelly hastened to change the subject, but there was to be a last word. "I like to see a minister that's solid minister right straight through, not one of these veneered folks. But old parson Croden spoilt me for setting under any other preaching."

"I wonder," said Nelly, after a little, "if cousin Horatia has any picture of that Captain Carrick?"

"He wasn't captain," said Melissa. "I never heard that it was any more than they talked of giving him a ship next voyage."

"And you never saw him? he never came here to see her?"

"Bless you, no! She met with him at Salem, where she was spending the winter, and he went right away to sea. I've heard a good deal more about it of late years than I ever did at the time. I suppose the Salem folks talked about it enough. All I know is, there was other good matches that offered to her since and couldn't get her, and I suppose it was on account of her heart's being buried in the deep with *him;*" and this unexpected bit of sentiment, spoken in Melissa's grummest tone, seemed so funny to her young companion that she bent very low to pick from a currant twig close to the ground, and could not ask any more questions for some time.

"I have seen her a sight o' times when I knew she was thinking about him," Melissa went on, pleasantly, this time with a tenderness in her voice that touched Nelly's heart. "She's been dreadful lonesome. She and the old colonel, her father, wasn't much company to each other, and she always kep' everything to herself. The only time she ever said a word to me was one night six or seven years ago this Christmas; they got up a Christmas-tree in the vestry, and she went, and I did, too; I guess everybody in the whole church and parish that could crawl turned out to go. The children they made a dreadful racket. I'd ha' got my ears took off if I had been so forth-putting when I was little. I was looking round for Miss H'ratia 'long at the last of the evening, and somebody said they'd seen her go home. I hurried, and I couldn't see any light in the house, and I was afraid she was sick or something. She come and let me in, and I see she had been a-cryin'. I says, 'Have you heard any bad news?' but she said no, and began to cry again, real pitiful. 'I never felt so lonesome in my life,' said she, 'as I did down there; it's a dreadful thing to be left all alone in the world.' I did feel for her, but I couldn't seem to say a word. I put some pine chips I had handy for morning on the kitchen fire, and I made her up a cup o' good hot tea quick 's I could, and took it to her, and I guess she felt better; she never went to bed till three o'clock that night. I couldn't shut my eyes till I heard her come up-stairs. There, I set everything by Miss H'ratia. I haven't got no folks, either; I was left an orphan over to Deerfield, where Miss's mother come from, and she took me out o' the town farm to bring up. I remember when I come here I was so small I had a box to stand up on when I helped wash the dishes. There's nothing I ain't had to make me comfortable, and I do just as I'm a mind to, and call in extra help every day of the week if I give the word; but I've had my lonesome times, and I guess Miss H'ratia knew."

Nelly was very much touched by this bit of a story; it was a new idea to her that Melissa should have so much affection and be so sympathetic. People never will get over being surprised that chestnut burs are not as rough inside as they are outside, and the girl's heart warmed toward the old woman who had spoken with such unlooked-for sentiment and pathos. Melissa went to the house with her basket, and Nelly also went in, but only to put on another hat and see if it were straight, in a minute spent before the old mirror, and then she hurried down the long elm-shaded street to buy a pound of citron for the cake. She left it on the kitchen table when she came back, and nobody ever said anything about it, only there were two delicious pound-cakes—a heart and a round—on a little blue china plate beside Nelly's plate at tea.

After tea Nelly and Miss Dane sat in the front door-way, the elder woman in a high-backed arm-chair and the younger on the door-step. The tree-toads and crickets were tuning up heartily, the stars showed a little through the trees, and the elms looked heavy and black against the sky. The fragrance of the white lilies in the garden blew through the hall. Miss Horatia was tapping the ends of her fingers together. Probably she was not thinking of anything in particular; she had had a very peaceful day, with the exception of the currants, and they had, after all, gone to the parsonage some time before noon. Beside this, the minister had sent word that the delay made no trouble, for his wife had unexpectedly gone to Downton to pass the day and night. Miss Horatia had received the business letter for which she had been looking for several days; so there was nothing to regret deeply for that day, and there seemed to be nothing for one to dread on the morrow.

"Cousin Horatia," asked Nelly, "are you sure you like having me here? are you sure I don't trouble you?"

"Of course not," said Miss Dane, without a bit of sentiment in her tone; "I find it very pleasant having young company, though I am used to being alone; and I don't mind it so much as I suppose you would."

"I should mind it very much," said the girl, softly.

"You would get used to it, as I have," said Miss Dane. "Yes, dear, I like having you here better and better; I hate to think of your going away;" and she smoothed Nelly's hair as if she thought she might have spoken coldly at first, and wished to make up for it. This rare caress was not without its effect.

"I don't miss father and Rob so very much," owned Nelly, frankly, "because I have grown used to their coming and going; but sometimes I miss people—Cousin Horatia, did I ever say anything to you about George Forest?"

"I think I remember the name," answered Miss Dane.

"He is in the navy, and he has gone a long voyage, and—I think everything of him; I missed him awfully, but it is almost time to get a letter from him."

"Does your father approve of him?" asked Miss Dane, with great propriety. "You are very young yet, and you must not think of such a thing carelessly. I should be so much grieved if you threw away your happiness."

"Oh, we are not really engaged," said Nelly, who felt a little chilled. "I suppose we are, too, only nobody knows yet. Yes, father knows him as well as I do, and he is very fond of him. Of course I should not keep it from father, but he guessed at it himself. Only it's such a long cruise, Cousin Horatia,—three years, I suppose, away off in China and Japan."

"I have known longer voyages than that," said Miss Dane, with a quiver in her voice; and she rose suddenly and walked away, this grave, reserved woman, who seemed so contented and so comfortable. But when she came back she asked Nelly a great deal about her lover, and learned more of the girl's life than she ever had before. And they talked together in the pleasantest way about this pleasant subject, which was so close to Nelly's heart, until Melissa brought the candles at ten o'clock, that being the hour of Miss Dane's bed-time.

But that night Miss Dane did not go to bed at ten; she sat by the window in her room, thinking. The moon rose late, and after a little while she blew out her candles, which were burning low. I suppose that the years which had come and gone since the young sailor had sailed away on that last voyage of his had each added to her affection for him. She was a person who clung the more fondly to youth as she left it the further behind.

This is such a natural thing: the great sorrows of our youth sometimes become the amusements of our later years; we can only remember them with a smile. We find that our lives look fairer to us, and we forget what used to trouble us so much, when we look back. Miss Dane certainly had come nearer to truly loving the sailor than she had any one else, and the more she had thought of it the more it became the romance of her life. She no longer asked herself, as she often had done in middle life, whether if he had lived and had come home she would have loved and married him. She had minded less and less year by year, knowing that her friends and neighbors thought her faithful to the love of her youth. Poor, gay, handsome Joe Carrick! how fond he had been of her, and how he had looked at her that day he sailed away out of Salem harbor on the ship *Chevalier!* If she had only known that she never should have seen him again, poor fellow!

But, as usual, her thoughts changed their current a little at the end of her reverie. Perhaps, after all, loneliness was not so hard to bear as other sorrows; she had had a pleasant life; God had been very good to her, and had spared her many trials and granted her many blessings. She would try and serve him better. "I am an old woman now," she said to herself. "Things are better as they are; God knows best, and I never should have liked to be interfered with."

Then she shut out the moonlight and lighted her candles again, with an almost guilty feeling. "What should I think if Nelly sat up till nearly midnight looking out at the moon?" thought she. "It is very silly, but it is such a beautiful night. I should like to have her see the moon shining through the tops of the trees;" but Nelly was sleeping the sleep of the just and sensible in her own room.

Next morning at breakfast Nelly was a little conscious of there having been uncommon confidences the night before, but Miss Dane was her usual calm and somewhat formal self, and proposed their making a few calls after dinner, if the weather were not too hot. Nelly at once wondered what she had better wear. There was a certain black grenadine which Miss Horatia had noticed with approval, and she remembered that the lower ruffle needed hemming, and made up her mind that she would devote most of the time before dinner to that and to some other repairs. So after breakfast was over she brought the dress down-stairs, with her work-box, and settled herself in the dining-room. Miss Dane usually sat there in the morning; it was a pleasant room, and she could keep an unsuspected watch over the kitchen and Melissa, who did not need watching in the least. I dare say it was for the sake of being within the sound of a voice.

Miss Dane marched in and out that morning: she went up-stairs and came down again, and she was busy for a while in the parlor. Nelly was sewing steadily by a window where one of the blinds was a little way open and tethered in its place by a string. She hummed a tune to herself over and over:—

> "What will you do, love, when I am going,
>   With white sails flowing, the seas beyond?"

and old Melissa, going to and fro at her work in the kitchen, grumbled out bits of an ancient psalm-tune, at intervals. There seemed to be some connection between these fragments in her mind; it was like a ledge of rock in a pasture, that sometimes runs under the ground and then crops out again. I think it was the tune of Windham.

Nelly found there was a good deal to be done to the grenadine dress when she looked it over critically, and she was very diligent. It was quiet in and about the house for a long time, until suddenly she heard the sound of heavy footsteps coming in from the road. The side-door was in a little entry between the room where Nelly sat and the kitchen; and the new-comer knocked loudly. "A tramp," said Nelly to herself, while Melissa came to open the door, wiping her hands hurriedly on her apron.

"I wonder if you couldn't give me something to eat," said the man.

"I suppose I could," answered Melissa. "Will you step in?" Beggars were very few in Longfield, and Miss Dane never wished anybody to go away hungry from her house. It was off the grand highway of tramps, but they were by no means unknown.

Melissa searched among her stores, and Nelly heard her putting one plate after another on the kitchen table, and thought that the breakfast promised to be a good one if it was late.

"Don't put yourself out," said the man, as he moved his chair nearer. "I put up at an old barn three or four miles above here, last night, and there didn't seem to be very good board there."

"Going far?" inquired Melissa concisely.

"Boston," said the man. "I'm a little too old to travel afoot. Now if I could go by water it would seem nearer. I'm more used to the water. This is a royal good piece o' beef. I suppose you couldn't put your hand on a mug of cider?" This was said humbly, but the tone failed to touch Melissa's heart.

"No, I couldn't," said she, decisively; so there was an end of that, and the conversation seemed to flag for a time.

Presently, Melissa came to speak to Miss Dane, who had just come down-stairs. "Could you stay in the kitchen a few minutes?" she whispered. "There's an old creatur' there that looks foreign: he came to the door for something to eat, and I gave it to him; but he's miser'ble-looking, and I don't like to leave him alone. I'm just in the midst o' dressing the chickens. He'll be through pretty quick, according to the way he's eating now."

Miss Dane followed her without a word, and the man half rose and said, "Good morning, madam," with unusual courtesy, and when

Melissa was out of hearing he spoke again: "I suppose you haven't any cider?" to which his hostess answered, "I couldn't give you any this morning," in a tone that left no room for argument. He looked as if he had had a great deal too much to drink already.

"How far do you call it from here to Boston?" he asked, and was told that it was eighty miles. "I'm a slow traveler," said he; "sailors don't take much to walking." Miss Dane asked him if he had been a sailor. "Nothing else," replied the man, who seemed much inclined to talk; he had been eating like a hungry dog, as if he were half starved,—a slouching, red-faced, untidy-looking old man, with some traces of former good looks still to be discovered in his face. "Nothing else. I ran away to sea when I was a boy, and I followed it until I got so old they wouldn't ship me even for cook." There was something in his feeling for once so comfortable, perhaps it was being with a lady like Miss Dane, who pitied him, that lifted his thoughts a little from their usual low level. "It's drink that's been the ruin of me," said he. "I ought to have been somebody. I was nobody's fool when I was young. I got to be mate of a first-rate ship, and there was some talk o' my being captain before long. She was lost that voyage, and three of us were all that was saved; we got picked up by a Chinese junk. She had the plague aboard of her, and my mates died of it and I was sick; it was a hell of a place to be in. When I got ashore I shipped on an old bark that pretended to be coming round the Cape, and she turned out to be a pirate. I just went to the dogs. I've been from bad to worse ever since."

"It's never too late to mend," said Melissa, who came into the kitchen just then for a string to tie the chickens.

"Lord help me, yes, it is," said the sailor. "It's easy for you to say that; I'm too old. I ain't been master of this craft for a good while," and he laughed at his melancholy joke.

"Don't say that," said Miss Dane.

"Well, now, what could an old wreck like me do to earn a living, and who'd want me if I could? You wouldn't. I don't know when I've been treated so decent as this before. I'm all broke down;" but his tone was no longer sincere; he had fallen back on his profession of beggar.

"Couldn't you get into some asylum or—there's the Sailors' Snug Harbor; isn't that for men like you? It seems such a pity for a man of your years to be homeless and a wanderer. Haven't you any friends at all?" and here, suddenly, Miss Dane's face altered, and she grew very white; something startled her. She looked as one might who saw a fearful ghost.

"No," said the man; "but my folks used to be some of the best in Salem. I haven't shown my head there this good while. I was an orphan. My grandmother brought me up. Why, I didn't come back to the States for thirty or forty years. Along at the first of it I used to see men in port that I used to know, but I always dodged 'em, and I was way off in outlandish places. I've got an awful sight to answer for. I used to have a good wife when I was in Australia. I don't know where I haven't been, first and last. I was always a hard fellow. I've spent as much as a couple o' fortunes, and here I am. Devil take it!"

Nelly was still sewing in the dining-room, but soon after Miss Dane had gone out to the kitchen one of the doors between had slowly closed itself with a plaintive whine. The round stone that Melissa used to keep it open had been pushed away. Nelly was a little annoyed; she liked to hear what was going on, but she was just then holding her work with great care in a place that was hard to sew, so she did not move. She heard the murmur of voices, and thought after a while that the old vagabond ought to go away by this time. What could be making her cousin Horatia talk so long with him? It was not like her, at all. He would beg for money, of course, and she hoped Miss Horatia would not give him a single cent.

It was some time before the kitchen door opened, and the man came out with clumsy, stumbling steps. "I'm much obliged to you," he said, "and I don't know but it is the last time I'll get treated as if I was a gentleman. Is there anything I could do for you round the place?" he asked hesitatingly, and as if he hoped that his offer would not be accepted.

"No," answered Miss Dane. "No, thank you. Good-by," and he went away.

I said he had been lifted a little above his low life; he fell back again directly, before he was out of the gate. "I'm blessed if she didn't give me a ten-dollar bill!" said he. "She must have thought it was a one. I'll get out o' call as quick as I can; hope she won't find it out and send anybody after me." Visions of unlimited drinks and other things in which the old sailor found pleasure flitted through his stupid mind. "How the old lady stared at me once!" he thought. "Wonder if she was anybody I used to know? 'Downton?' I don't know as I ever heard of the place;" and he scuffed along the dusty road, and that night he was very drunk, and the next day he went wandering on, God only knows where!

But Nelly and Melissa both had heard a strange noise in the kitchen, as if some one had fallen, and had found that Miss Horatia had fainted dead away. It was partly the heat, she said, when she saw their anxious faces as she came to herself; she had had a little headache all the morning; it was very hot and close in the kitchen, and the faintness had come upon her suddenly. They helped her walk into the cool parlor presently, and Melissa brought her a glass of wine; and Nelly sat beside her on a footstool, as she lay on the sofa, and fanned her. Once she held her cheek against Miss Horatia's hand for a minute, and she will never know as long as she lives what a comfort she was that day.

Every one but Miss Dane forgot the old sailor-tramp in this excitement that followed his visit. Do you guess already who he was? But the certainty could not come to you with the chill and horror it did to Miss Dane. There had been something familiar in his look and voice from the first, and then she had suddenly known him, her lost lover. It was an awful change that the years had made in him; he had truly called himself a wreck. He was like some dreary wreck, in its decay and utter ruin, its miserable ugliness and worthlessness, falling to pieces in the slow tides of a lifeless southern sea.

And he had once been her lover, Miss Dane thought many times in the days that came after. Not that there was ever anything asked or promised between them, but they had liked each other dearly, and had parted with deep sorrow. She had thought of him all these years so tenderly; she had believed always that his love had been greater than her own, and never once had doubted that the missing ship *Chevalier* had carried with it down into the sea a heart that was true to her.

By little and little this all grew familiar, and she accustomed herself to the knowledge of her new secret. She shuddered at the thought of the misery of a life with him, and she thanked God for sparing her such shame and despair. The distance between them seemed immense. She had been a person of so much consequence among her friends, and so dutiful and irreproachable a woman. She had not begun to understand what dishonor is in the world; her life had been shut in by safe and orderly surroundings. It was a strange chance that had brought this wanderer to her door. She remembered his wretched untidiness. She would not have liked even to touch him. She had never imagined him grown old; he had always been young to her. It was a great mercy he had not known her; it would have been a most miserable position for them both; and yet she thought, with sad surprise, that she had not known she had changed so entirely. She thought of the different ways their roads in life had gone;

she pitied him; she cried about him more than once, and she wished that she could know he was dead. He might have been such a brave, good man, with his strong will and resolute courage. God forgive him for the wickedness which his strength had been made to serve. "God forgive him!" said Miss Horatia to herself, sadly, over and over again. She wondered if she ought to have let him go away and so have lost sight of him; but she could not do anything else. She suffered terribly on his account; she had a pity such as God's pity must be for even his willful sins.

So her romance was all over with; yet the town's-people still whispered it to strangers, and even Melissa and Nelly never knew how she had lost her lover in so strange and sad a way in her latest years. Nobody observed much change; but Melissa noticed that the whale's tooth had disappeared from its place in Miss Horatia's room, and her old friends said to each other that she began to show her age a great deal; she seemed really like an old woman now; she was not the woman she had been a year ago.

This is all of the story; but I so often wish when a story comes to an end that I knew what became of the people afterward. Shall I tell you that Miss Horatia clings more and more fondly to her young cousin Nelly; and that Nelly will stay with her a great deal before she marries, and sometimes afterward, when the lieutenant goes away to sea? Shall I say that Miss Dane seems as well satisfied and comfortable as ever, though she acknowledges she is not so young as she used to be, and somehow misses something out of her life? It is the contentment of winter rather than that of summer; the flowers are out of bloom now for her, and under the snow. And Melissa, will not she always be the same, with a quaintness and freshness and toughness like a cedar-tree, to the end of her days? Let us hope they will live on together and be untroubled this long time yet, the two good women; and let us wish Nelly much pleasure, and a sweet soberness and fearlessness as she grows older and finds life a harder thing to understand and a graver thing to know.

Miss Debby's Neighbors

THERE is a class of elderly New England women which is fast dying out:—those good souls who have sprung from a soil full of the true New England instincts; who were used to the old-fashioned ways, and whose minds were stored with quaint country lore and tradition. The fashions of the newer generations do not reach them; they are quite unconscious of the western spirit and enterprise, and belong to the old days, and to a fast-disappearing order of things.

But a shrewder person does not exist than the spokeswoman of the following reminiscences, whose simple history can be quickly told, since she spent her early life on a lonely farm, leaving it only once for any length of time,—one winter when she learned her trade of tailoress. She afterward sewed for her neighbors, and enjoyed a famous reputation for her skill; but year by year, as she grew older, there was less to do, and at last, to use her own expression, "Everybody got into the way of buying cheap, ready-made-up clothes, just to save 'em a little trouble," and she found herself out of business, or nearly so. After her mother's death, and that of her favorite brother Jonas, she left the farm and came to a little house in the village, where she lived most comfortably the rest of her life, having a small property which she used most sensibly. She was always ready to render any special service with her needle, and was a most welcome guest in any household, and a most efficient helper. To be in the same room with her for a while was sure to be profitable, and as she grew older she was delighted to recall the people and events of her earlier life, always filling her descriptions with wise reflections and much quaint humor. She always insisted, not without truth, that the railroads were making everybody look and act of a piece, and that the young folks were more alike than people of her own day. It is impossible to give the delightfulness of her talk in any written words, as well as many of its peculiarities, for her way of going round Robin Hood's barn between the beginning of her story and its end can hardly be followed at all, and certainly not in her own dear loitering footsteps.

On an idle day her most devoted listener thought there was nothing better worth doing than to watch this good soul at work. A book was held open for the looks of the thing, but presently it was allowed to flutter its leaves and close, for Miss Debby began without any apparent provocation:—

"They may say whatever they have a mind to, but they can't persuade me that there's no such thing as special providences," and she twitched her strong linen thread so angrily through the carpet she was sewing, that it snapped and the big needle flew into the air. It had to be found before any further remarks could be made, and the listener also knelt down to search for it. After a while it was discovered clinging to Miss Debby's own dress, and after reharnessing it she went to work again at her long seam. It was always significant

of a succession of Miss Debby's opinions when she quoted and be-
rated certain imaginary persons whom she designated as "They," who
stood for the opposite side of the question, and who merited usually
her deepest scorn and fullest antagonism. Her remarks to these offending parties were always prefaced with "I tell 'em," and to the
listener's mind "they" always stood rebuked, but not convinced, in
spiritual form it may be, but most intense reality; a little group as
solemn as Miss Debby herself. Once the listener ventured to ask who
"they" were, in her early childhood, but she was only answered by a
frown. Miss Debby knew as well as any one the difference between
figurative language and a lie. Sometimes they said what was right
and proper, and were treated accordingly; but very seldom, and on
this occasion it seemed that they had ventured to trifle with sacred
things.

"I suppose you're too young to remember John Ashby's grandmother? A good woman she was, and she had a dreadful time with
her family. They never could keep the peace, and there was always as
many as two of them who didn't speak with each other. It seems to
come down from generation to generation like a—*curse!*" And Miss
Debby spoke the last word as if she had meant it partly for her thread,
which had again knotted and caught, and she snatched the offered
scissors without a word, but said peaceably, after a minute or two,
that the thread wasn't what it used to be. The next needleful proved
more successful, and the listener asked if the Ashbys were getting on
comfortably at present.

"They always behave as if they thought they needed nothing," was
the response. "Not that I mean that they are any ways contented,
but they never will give in that other folks holds a candle to 'em.
There's one kind of pride that I do hate,—when folks is satisfied
with their selves and don't see no need of improvement. I believe
in self-respect, but I believe in respecting other folks's rights as much
as your own; but it takes an Ashby to ride right over you. I tell 'em
it's the spirit of the tyrants of old, and it's the kind of pride that
goes before a fall. John Ashby's grandmother was a clever little woman
as ever stepped. She came ,from over Hardwick way, and I think she
kep' 'em kind of decent-behaved as long as she was round; but she
got wore out a doin' of it, an' went down to her grave in a quick
consumption. My mother set up with her the night she died. It was in
May, towards the latter part, and an awful rainy night. It was the
storm that always comes in apple-blossom time. I remember well
that mother come crying home in the morning and told us Mis' Ashby
was dead. She brought Marilly with her, that was about my own age,

and was taken away within six months afterwards. She pined herself to death for her mother, and when she caught the scarlet fever she went as quick as cherry-bloom when it's just ready to fall and a wind strikes it. She wa'n't like the rest of 'em. She took after her mother's folks altogether.

"You know our farm was right next to theirs,—the one Asa Hopper owns now, but he's let it all run out,—and so, as we lived some ways from the stores, we had to be neighborly, for we depended on each other for a good many things. Families in lonesome places get out of one supply and another, and have to borrow until they get a chance to send to the village; or sometimes in a busy season some of the folks would have to leave work and be gone half a day. Land, you don't know nothing about old times, and the life that used to go on about here. You can't step into a house anywheres now that there ain't the county map and they don't fetch out the photograph book; and in every district you'll find all the folks has got the same chromo picture hung up, and all sorts of luxuries and makeshifts o' splendor that would have made the folks I was fetched up by stare their eyes out o' their heads. It was all we could do to keep along then; and if anybody was called rich, it was only because he had a great sight of land,—and then it was drudge, drudge the harder to pay the taxes. There was hardly any ready money; and I recollect well that old Tommy Simms was reputed wealthy, and it was told over fifty times a year that he'd got a solid four thousand dollars in the bank. He strutted round like a turkey-cock, and thought he ought to have his first say about everything that was going.

"I was talking about the Ashbys, wasn't I? I do' know's I ever told you about the fight they had after their father died about the old house. Joseph was married to a girl he met in camp-meeting time, who had a little property—two or three hundred dollars—from an old great uncle that she'd been keeping house for; and I don't know what other plans she may have had for spending of her means, but she laid most of it out in a husband; for Joseph never cared any great about her that I could see, though he always treated her well enough. She was a poor ignorant sort of thing, seven years older than he was; but she had a pleasant kind of a face, and seemed like an overgrown girl of six or eight years old. I remember just after they was married Joseph was taken down with a quinsy sore throat, —being always subject to them,—and mother was over in the forenoon, and she was one that was always giving right hand and left, and she told Susan Ellen—that was his wife—to step over in the afternoon and she would give her some blackberry preserve for him;

she had some that was nice and it was very healing. So long about half-past one o'clock, just as we had got the kitchen cleared, and mother and I had got out the big wheels to spin a few rolls,—we always liked to spin together, and mother was always good company;—my brother Jonas—that was the youngest of us—looked out of the window, and says he: 'Here comes Joe Ashby's wife with a six-quart pail.'

"Mother she began to shake all over with a laugh she tried to swallow down, but I didn't know what it was all about, and in come poor Susan Ellen and lit on the edge of the first chair and set the pail down beside of her. We tried to make her feel welcome, and spoke about everything we could contrive, seein' as it was the first time she'd been over; and she seemed grateful and did the best she could, and lost her strangeness with mother right away, for mother was the best hand to make folks feel to home with her that I ever come across. There ain't many like her now, nor never was, I tell 'em. But there wa'n't nothing said about the six-quart pail, and there it set on the floor, until Susan Ellen said she must be going and mentioned that there was something said about a remedy for Joseph's throat. 'Oh, yes,' says mother, and she brought out the little stone jar she kept the preserve in, and there wa'n't more than the half of it full. Susan Ellen took up the cover off the pail, and I walked off into the bedroom, for I thought I should laugh, certain. Mother put in a big spoonful, and another, and I heard 'em drop, and she went on with one or two more, and then she give up. 'I'd give you the jar and welcome,' she says, 'but I ain't very well off for preserves, and I was kind of counting on this for tea in case my brother's folks are over.' Susan Ellen thanked her, and said Joseph would be obliged, and back she went acrost the pasture. I can see that big tin pail now a-shining in the sun.

"The old man was alive then, and he took a great spite against poor Susan Ellen, though he never would if he hadn't been set on by John; and whether he was mad because Joseph had stepped in to so much good money or what, I don't know,—but he twitted him about her, and at last he and the old man between 'em was too much to bear, and Joe fitted up a couple o' rooms for himself in a building he'd put up for a kind of work-shop. He used to carpenter by spells, and he clapboarded it and made it as comfortable as he could, and he ordered John out of it for good and all; but he and Susan Ellen both treated the old sir the best they knew how, and Joseph kept right on with his farm work same as ever, and meant to lay up a little money to join with his wife's, and push off as soon as he could for the sake of peace, though if there was anybody set by the farm it was Joseph. He was to blame for some things,—I never saw an Ashby that wasn't,—and I dare say he was aggravating. They were clearing a piece of woodland that winter, and the old man was laid up in the house with the rheumatism, off and on, and that made him fractious, and he and John connived together, till one day Joseph and Susan Ellen had taken the sleigh and gone to Freeport Four Corners to get some flour and one thing and another, and to have the horse shod beside, so they was likely to be gone two or three hours. John Jacobs was going by with his oxen, and John Ashby and the old man hailed him, and said they'd give him a dollar if he'd help 'em, and they hitched the two yoke, his and their'n, to Joseph's house. There wa'n't any foundation to speak of, the sills set right on the ground, and he'd banked it up with a few old boards and some pine spills and sand and stuff, just to keep the cold out. There wa'n't but a little snow, and the roads was smooth and icy, and they slipped it along as if it had been a hand-sled, and got it down the road a half a mile or so to the fork of the roads, and left it settin' there right on the heater-piece. Jacobs told afterward that he kind of disliked to do it, but he thought as long as their minds were set, he might as well have the dollar as anybody. He said when the house give a slew on a sideling piece in the road, he heard some of the crockery-ware smash down, and a branch of an oak they passed by caught hold of the stove-pipe that come out through one of the walls, and give that a wrench, but he guessed there wa'n't no great damage. Joseph may have given 'em some provocation before he went away in the morning,—I don't know *but* he did, and I don't know *as* he did,—but at any rate when he was coming home late in the afternoon he caught sight of his house (some of our folks was right behind, and they saw him), and he stood right up in the sleigh and shook his fist, he was so mad; but afterwards he bu'st out laughin'. It did look kind of curi's; it wa'n't bigger than a front entry, and it set up so pert right there on the heater-piece, as if he was calc'latin' to farm it. The folks said Susan Ellen covered up her face in her shawl and begun to cry. I s'pose the pore thing was discouraged. Joseph was awful mad,—he was kind of laughing and cryin' together. Our folks stopped and asked him if there was anything they could do, and he said no; but Susan Ellen went in to view how things were, and they made up a fire, and then Joe took the horse home, and I guess they had it hot and heavy. Nobody supposed they'd ever make up 'less there was a funeral in the family to bring 'em together, the fight had gone so far,—but 'long in the winter old Mr. Ashby, the boys' father, was taken down with a spell o' sickness, and there wa'n't anybody they could get to come and look after the house. The doctor hunted, and they all hunted, but there didn't seem to be anybody—'twa'n't so thick settled as now, and there was no spare help—so John had to eat humble pie, and go and ask Susan Ellen if she wouldn't come back and let by-gones be by-gones. She was as good-natured a creatur' as ever stepped, and did the best she knew, and she spoke up as pleasant as could be, and said she'd go right off that afternoon and help 'em through.

"The old Ashby had been a hard drinker in his day and he was all broke down. Nobody ever saw him that he couldn't walk straight, but he got a crooked disposition out of it, if nothing else. I s'pose there never was a man loved sperit better. They said one year he was over to Cyrus Parker's to help with the haying, and there was a jug o' New England rum over by the spring with some ginger-bread and cheese and stuff; and he went over about every half an hour to take something, and along about half-past ten he got the jug middling low, so he went to fill it up with a little water, and lost holt of it and it sunk, and they said he drunk the spring dry three times!

"Joe and Susan Ellen stayed there at the old place well into the summer, and then after planting they moved down to the Four Corners where they had bought a nice little place. Joe did well there, —he carried on the carpenter trade, and got smoothed down consider-able, being amongst folks. John he married a Pecker girl, and got his match too; she was the only living soul he ever was afraid of. They lived on there a spell and—why, they must have lived there all of fifteen or twenty years, now I come to think of it, for the time they moved was after the railroad was built. 'Twas along in the winter and his wife she got a notion to buy a place down to the Falls below the Corners after the mills got started and have John work in the spinning-room while she took boarders. She said 'twa'n't no use staying on the farm, they couldn't make a living off from it now they'd cut the growth. Joe's folks and she never could get along, and they said she was dreadfully riled up hearing how much Joe was getting in the machine shop.

"They needn't tell me about special providences being all moon-shine," said Miss Debby for the second time, "if here wa'n't a plain one, I'll never say one word more about it. You see, that very time Joe Ashby got a splinter in his eye and they were afraid he was going to lose his sight, and he got a notion that he wanted to go back to farming. He always set everything by the old place, and he had a boy growing up that neither took to his book nor to mill work, and he wanted to farm it too. So Joe got hold of John one day when he come in with some wood, and asked him why he wouldn't take his place for a year or two, if he wanted to get to the village, and let him go out to the old place. My brother Jonas was standin' right by and heard 'em and said he never heard nobody speak civiller. But John swore and said he wa'n't going to be caught in no such a trap as that. His father left him the place and he was going to do as he'd a mind to. There'd be'n trouble about the property, for old Mr. Ashby had given Joe some money he had in the bank. Joe had got to be well off, he could have bought most any farm about here, but he wanted the old place 'count of his attachment. He set everything by his mother, spite of her being dead so long. John hadn't done very well spite of his being so sharp, but he let out the best of the farm on shares, and bought a mis'able sham-built little house down close by the mills,—and then some idea or other got into his head to fit that up to let and move it to one side of the lot, and haul down the old house from the farm to live in themselves. There wa'n't no time to lose, else the snow would be gone; so he got a gang o' men up there and put shoes underneath the sills, and then they assembled all the oxen they could call in, and started. Mother was living then, though she'd got to be very feeble, and when they come for our yoke she wouldn't have Jonas let 'em go. She said the old house ought to stay in its place. Everybody had been telling John Ashby that the road was too hilly, and besides the house was too old to move, they'd rack it all to pieces dragging it so fur; but he wouldn't listen to no reason.

"I never saw mother so stirred up as she was that day, and when she see the old thing a moving she burst right out crying. We could see one end of it looking over the slope of the hill in the pasture between it and our house. There was two windows that looked our way, and I know Mis' Ashby used to hang a piece o' something white out o' one of 'em when she wanted mother to step over for anything. They set a good deal by each other, and Mis' Ashby was a lame woman. I shouldn't ha' thought John would had 'em haul the house right over the little gardin she thought so much of, and broke down the laylocks and flowering currant she set everything by. I remember when she died I wasn't more'n seven or eight year old, it was all in full bloom and mother she broke off a branch and laid into the coffin. I do' know as I've ever seen any since or set in a room and had the sweetness of it blow in at the windows without remembering that day,—'twas the first funeral I ever went to, and that may be some reason. Well, the old house started off and mother watched it as long as she could see it. She was sort o' feeble herself then, as I said, and we went on with the work,—'twas a Saturday, and we was baking and churning and getting things to rights generally. Jonas had been over in the swamp getting out some wood he'd cut earlier in the winter—and along in the afternoon he come in and said he s'posed I wouldn't want to ride down to the Corners so late, and I said I did feel just like it, so we started off. We went the Birch Ridge road, because he wanted to see somebody over that way,—and when we was going home by the straight road, Jonas laughed and said we hadn't seen anything of John Ashby's moving, and he guessed he'd got stuck somewhere. He was glad he hadn't nothing to do with it. We drove along pretty quick, for we were some belated, and we didn't like to leave mother all alone after it come dark. All of a sudden Jonas stood up in the sleigh, and says he, 'I don't believe but the cars is off the track;' and I looked and there did seem to be something the matter with 'em. They hadn't been running more than a couple o' years then, and we was prepared for anything.

"Jonas he whipped up the horse and we got there pretty quick, and I'll be bound if the Ashby house hadn't got stuck fast right on the track, and stir it one way or another they couldn't. They'd been there since quarter-past one, pulling and hauling,—and the men was all hoarse with yelling, and the cars had come from both ways and met there,—one each side of the crossing,—and the passengers was walking about, scolding and swearing,—and somebody'd gone and lit up a gre't bonfire. You never see such a sight in all your life! I happened to look up at the old house, and there were them two top windows that used to look over to our place, and they had caught the shine of the firelight, and made the poor old thing look as if it was scared to death. The men was banging at it with axes and crowbars, and it was dreadful distressing. You pitied it as if it was a live creatur'. It come from such a quiet place, and always looked kind of comfortable, though so much war had gone on amongst the Ashbys. I tell you it was a judgment on John, for they got it shoved back after a while, and then wouldn't touch it again,—not one of the men,—nor let their oxen. The plastering was all stove, and the outside walls all wrenched apart,—and John never did anything more about it; but let it set there all summer, till it burnt down, and there was an end, one night in September. They supposed some traveling folks slept in it and set it afire, or else some boys did it for fun. I was glad it was out of the way. One day, I know, I was

coming by with mother, and she said it made her feel bad to see
the little strips of leather by the fore door, where Mis' Ashby had
nailed up a rosebush once. There! there ain't an Ashby alive now of
the old stock, except young John. Joe's son went off to sea, and I
believe he was lost somewhere in the China seas, or else he died of
a fever; I seem to forget. He was called a smart boy, but he never
could seem to settle down to anything. Sometimes I wonder folks
is as good as they be, when I consider what comes to 'em from their
folks before 'em, and how they're misshaped by nature. Them Ashbys
never was like other folk, and yet some good streak or other there
was in every one of 'em. You can't expect much from such hindered
creatur's,—it's just like beratin' a black and white cat for being a
poor mouser. It ain't her fault that the mice see her quicker than
they can a gray one. If you get one of them masterful dispositions
put with a good strong will towards the right, that's what makes
the best of men; but all them Ashbys cared about was to grasp and
get, and be cap'ns. They liked to see other folks put down, just as
if it was going to set them up. And they didn't know nothing.
They make me think of some o' them old marauders that used to
hive up into their castles, in old times, and then go out a-over-setting
and plundering. And I tell you that same sperit was in 'em. They
was born a couple o' hundred years too late. Kind of left-over folks,
as it were." And Miss Debby indulged in a quiet chuckle as she
bent over her work. "John he got captured by his wife,—she carried too many guns for him. I believe he died very poor and her
own son wouldn't support her, so she died over in Freeport poorhouse. And Joe got along better; his wife was clever but rather slack,
and it took her a good while to see through things. She married
again pretty quick after he died. She had as much as seven or eight
thousand dollars, and she was taken just as she stood by a roving
preacher that was holding meetings here in the winter time. He sold
out her place here, and they went up country somewheres that he
come from. Her boy was lost before that, so there was nothing to
hinder her. There, don't you think I'm always a-fault-finding! When
I get hold of the real thing in folks, I stick to 'em,—but there's an
awful sight of poor material walking about that ain't worth the
ground it steps on. But when I look back a little ways, I can't blame
some of 'em; though it does often seem as if people might do better if they only set to work and tried. I must say I always do feel
pleased when I think how mad John was,—this John's father,—when
he couldn't do just as he'd a mind to with the pore old house. I
couldn't help thinking of Joe's mansion, that he and his father hauled

down to the heater-piece in the fork of the roads. Sometimes I wonder where them Ashbys all went to. They'd mistake one place for
the other in the next world, for 'twould make heaven out o' hell,
because they could be disagreeing with somebody, and—well, I don't
know,—I'm sure they kep' a good row going while they was in this
world. Only with mother;—somehow she could get along with anybody, and not always give 'em their way either."

A White Heron

I

THE woods were already filled with shadows one June evening,
just before eight o'clock, though a bright sunset still glimmered
faintly among the trunks of the trees. A little girl was driving home
her cow, a plodding, dilatory, provoking creature in her behavior, but
a valued companion for all that. They were going away from whatever light there was, and striking deep into the woods, but their
feet were familiar with the path, and it was no matter whether their
eyes could see it or not.

There was hardly a night the summer through when the old cow
could be found waiting at the pasture bars; on the contrary, it was
her greatest pleasure to hide herself away among the huckleberry
bushes, and though she wore a loud bell she had made the discovery
that if one stood perfectly still it would not ring. So Sylvia had to
hunt for her until she found her, and call Co'! Co'! with never an
answering Moo, until her childish patience was quite spent. If the
creature had not given good milk and plenty of it, the case would
have seemed very different to her owners. Besides, Sylvia had all the
time there was, and very little use to make of it. Sometimes in pleasant
weather it was a consolation to look upon the cow's pranks as an
intelligent attempt to play hide and seek, and as the child had no
playmates she lent herself to this amusement with a good deal of zest.
Though this chase had been so long that the wary animal herself
had given an unusual signal of her whereabouts, Sylvia had only
laughed when she came upon Mistress Moolly at the swampside,
and urged her affectionately homeward with a twig of birch leaves.
The old cow was not inclined to wander farther, she even turned
in the right direction for once as they left the pasture, and stepped

along the road at a good pace. She was quite ready to be milked now, and seldom stopped to browse. Sylvia wondered what her grandmother would say because they were so late. It was a great while since she had left home at half-past five o'clock, but everybody knew the difficulty of making this errand a short one. Mrs. Tilley had chased the hornéd torment too many summer evenings herself to blame any one else for lingering, and was only thankful as she waited that she had Sylvia, nowadays, to give such valuable assistance. The good woman suspected that Sylvia loitered occasionally on her own account; there never was such a child for straying about out-of-doors since the world was made! Everybody said that it was a good change for a little maid who had tried to grow for eight years in a crowded manufacturing town, but, as for Sylvia herself, it seemed as if she never had been alive at all before she came to live at the farm. She thought often with wistful compassion of a wretched geranium that belonged to a town neighbor.

"'Afraid of folks,'" old Mrs. Tilley said to herself, with a smile, after she had made the unlikely choice of Sylvia from her daughter's houseful of children, and was returning to the farm. "'Afraid of folks,' they said! I guess she won't be troubled no great with 'em up to the old place!" When they reached the door of the lonely house and stopped to unlock it, and the cat came to purr loudly, and rub against them, a deserted pussy, indeed, but fat with young robins, Sylvia whispered that this was a beautiful place to live in, and she never should wish to go home.

The companions followed the shady wood-road, the cow taking slow steps and the child very fast ones. The cow stopped long at the brook to drink, as if the pasture were not half a swamp, and Sylvia stood still and waited, letting her bare feet cool themselves in the shoal water, while the great twilight moths struck softly against her. She waded on through the brook as the cow moved away, and listened to the thrushes with a heart that beat fast with pleasure. There was a stirring in the great boughs overhead. They were full of little birds and beasts that seemed to be wide awake, and going about their world, or else saying good-night to each other in sleepy twitters. Sylvia herself felt sleepy as she walked along. However, it was not much farther to the house, and the air was soft and sweet. She was not often in the woods so late as this, and it made her feel as if she were a part of the gray shadows and the moving leaves. She was just thinking how long it seemed since she first came to the farm a year ago, and wondering if everything went on in the noisy town just the same as when she was there; the thought of the great red-faced boy who used to chase and frighten her made her hurry along the path to escape from the shadow of the trees.

Suddenly this little woods-girl is horror-stricken to hear a clear whistle not very far away. Not a bird's-whistle, which would have a sort of friendliness, but a boy's whistle, determined, and somewhat aggressive. Sylvia left the cow to whatever sad fate might await her, and stepped discreetly aside into the bushes, but she was just too late. The enemy had discovered her, and called out in a very cheerful and persuasive tone, "Halloa, little girl, how far is it to the road?" and trembling Sylvia answered almost inaudibly, "A good ways."

She did not dare to look boldly at the tall young man, who carried a gun over his shoulder, but she came out of her bush and again followed the cow, while he walked alongside.

"I have been hunting for some birds," the stranger said kindly, "and I have lost my way, and need a friend very much. Don't be afraid," he added gallantly. "Speak up and tell me what your name is, and whether you think I can spend the night at your house, and go out gunning early in the morning."

Sylvia was more alarmed than before. Would not her grandmother consider her much to blame? But who could have foreseen such an accident as this? It did not seem to be her fault, and she hung her head as if the stem of it were broken, but managed to answer "Sylvy," with much effort when her companion again asked her name.

Mrs. Tilley was standing in the doorway when the trio came into view. The cow gave a loud moo by way of explanation.

"Yes, you'd better speak up for yourself, you old trial! Where'd she tucked herself away this time, Sylvy?" But Sylvia kept an awed silence; she knew by instinct that her grandmother did not comprehend the gravity of the situation. She must be mistaking the stranger for one of the farmer-lads of the region.

The young man stood his gun beside the door, and dropped a lumpy game-bag beside it; then he bade Mrs. Tilley good-evening, and repeated his wayfarer's story, and asked if he could have a night's lodging.

"Put me anywhere you like," he said. "I must be off early in the morning, before day; but I am very hungry, indeed. You can give me some milk at any rate, that's plain."

"Dear sakes, yes," responded the hostess, whose long slumbering hospitality seemed to be easily awakened. "You might fare better if you went out to the main road a mile or so, but you're welcome to what we've got. I'll milk right off, and you make yourself at home. You can sleep on husks or feathers," she proffered graciously. "I raised them all myself. There's good pasturing for geese just below here towards the ma'sh. Now step round and set a plate for the gentleman, Sylvy!" And Sylvia promptly stepped. She was glad to have something to do, and she was hungry herself.

It was a surprise to find so clean and comfortable a little dwelling in this New England wilderness. The young man had known the horrors of its most primitive housekeeping, and the dreary squalor of that level of society which does not rebel at the companionship of hens. This was the best thrift of an old-fashioned farmstead, though on such a small scale that it seemed like a hermitage. He listened eagerly to the old woman's quaint talk, he watched Sylvia's pale face and shining gray eyes with ever growing enthusiasm, and insisted that this was the best supper he had eaten for a month, and afterward the new-made friends sat down in the door-way together while the moon came up.

Soon it would be berry-time, and Sylvia was a great help at picking. The cow was a good milker, though a plaguy thing to keep track of, the hostess gossiped frankly, adding presently that she had buried four children, so Sylvia's mother, and a son (who might be dead) in California were all the children she had left. "Dan, my boy, was a great hand to go gunning," she explained sadly. "I never wanted for pa'tridges or gray squer'ls while he was to home. He's been a great wand'rer, I expect, and he's no hand to write letters. There, I don't blame him, I'd ha' seen the world myself if it had been so I could."

"Sylvy takes after him," the grandmother continued affectionately, after a minute's pause. "There ain't a foot o' ground she don't know her way over, and the wild creaturs counts her one o' themselves. Squer'ls she'll tame to come an' feed right out o' her hands, and all sorts o' birds. Last winter she got the jay-birds to bangeing here, and I believe she'd 'a' scanted herself of her own meals to have plenty to throw out amongst 'em, if I hadn't kep' watch. Anything but crows, I tell her, I'm willin' to help support—though Dan he had a tamed one o' them that did seem to have reason same as folks. It was round here a good spell after he went away. Dan an' his father they didn't hitch,—but he never held up his head ag'in after Dan had dared him an' gone off."

The guest did not notice this hint of family sorrows in his eager interest in something else.

"So Sylvy knows all about birds, does she?" he exclaimed, as he looked round at the little girl who sat, very demure but increasingly sleepy, in the moonlight. "I am making a collection of birds myself. I have been at it ever since I was a boy." (Mrs. Tilley smiled.) "There are two or three very rare ones I have been hunting for these five years. I mean to get them on my own ground if they can be found."

"Do you cage 'em up?" asked Mrs. Tilley doubtfully, in response to this enthusiastic announcement.

"Oh no, they're stuffed and preserved, dozens and dozens of them," said the ornithologist, "and I have shot or snared every one myself. I caught a glimpse of a white heron a few miles from here on Saturday, and I have followed it in this direction. They have never been found in this district at all. The little white heron, it is," and he turned again to look at Sylvia with the hope of discovering that the rare bird was one of her acquaintances.

But Sylvia was watching a hop-toad in the narrow footpath.

"You would know the heron if you saw it," the stranger continued eagerly. "A queer tall white bird with soft feathers and long thin legs. And it would have a nest perhaps in the top of a high tree, made of sticks, something like a hawk's nest."

Sylvia's heart gave a wild beat; she knew that strange white bird, and had once stolen softly near where it stood in some bright green swamp grass, away over at the other side of the woods. There was an open place where the sunshine always seemed strangely yellow and hot, where tall, nodding rushes grew, and her grandmother had warned her that she might sink in the soft black mud underneath and never be heard of more. Not far beyond were the salt marshes just this side the sea itself, which Sylvia wondered and dreamed much about, but never had seen, whose great voice could sometimes be heard above the noise of the woods on stormy nights.

"I can't think of anything I should like so much as to find that heron's nest," the handsome stranger was saying. "I would give ten dollars to anybody who could show it to me," he added desperately, "and I mean to spend my whole vacation hunting for it if need be. Perhaps it was only migrating, or had been chased out of its own region by some bird of prey."

Mrs. Tilley gave amazed attention to all this, but Sylvia still watched the toad, not divining, as she might have done at some calmer time, that the creature wished to get to its hole under the door-step, and was much hindered by the unusual spectators at that hour of the evening. No amount of thought, that night, could decide how many wished-for treasures the ten dollars, so lightly spoken of, would buy.

The next day the young sportsman hovered about the woods, and Sylvia kept him company, having lost her first fear of the friendly lad, who proved to be most kind and sympathetic. He told her many things about the birds and what they knew and where they lived and what they did with themselves. And he gave her a jack-knife, which she thought as great a treasure as if she were a desert-islander. All day long he did not once make her troubled or afraid except when he brought down some unsuspecting singing creature from its bough. Sylvia would have liked him vastly better without his gun; she could not understand why he killed the very birds he seemed to like so much. But as the day waned, Sylvia still watched the young man with loving admiration. She had never seen anybody so charming and delightful; the woman's heart, asleep in the child, was vaguely thrilled by a dream of love. Some premonition of that great power stirred and swayed these young creatures who traversed the solemn woodlands with soft-footed silent care. They stopped to listen to a bird's song; they pressed forward again eagerly, parting the branches—speaking to each other rarely and in whispers; the young man going first and Sylvia following, fascinated, a few steps behind, with her gray eyes dark with excitement.

She grieved because the longed-for white heron was elusive, but she did not lead the guest, she only followed, and there was no such thing as speaking first. The sound of her own unquestioned voice would have terrified her—it was hard enough to answer yes or no when there was need of that. At last evening began to fall, and they drove the cow home together, and Sylvia smiled with pleasure when they came to the place where she heard the whistle and was afraid only the night before.

II

Half a mile from home, at the farther edge of the woods, where the land was highest, a great pine-tree stood, the last of its generation. Whether it was left for a boundary mark, or for what reason, no one could say; the wood choppers who had felled its mates were dead and gone long ago, and a whole forest of sturdy trees, pines and oaks and maples, had grown again. But the stately head of this old pine towered above them all and made a landmark for sea and shore miles and miles away. Sylvia knew it well. She had always believed that whoever climbed to the top of it could see the ocean; and the little girl had often laid her hand on the great rough trunk and looked up wistfully at those dark boughs that the wind always stirred, no matter how hot and still the air might be below. Now she thought of the tree with a new excitement, for why, if one climbed it at break of day could not one see all the world, and easily discover from whence the white heron flew, and mark the place, and find the hidden nest?

What a spirit of adventure, what wild ambition! What fancied triumph and delight and glory for the later morning when she could make known the secret! It was almost too real and too great for the childish heart to bear.

All night the door of the little house stood open and the whippoor-wills came and sang upon the very step. The young sportsman and his old hostess were sound asleep, but Sylvia's great design kept her broad awake and watching. She forgot to think of sleep. The short summer night seemed as long as the winter darkness, and at last when the whippoorwills ceased, and she was afraid the morning would after all come too soon, she stole out of the house and followed the pasture path through the woods, hastening toward the open ground beyond, listening with a sense of comfort and companion-ship to the drowsy twitter of a half-awakened bird, whose perch she had jarred in passing. Alas, if the great wave of human interest which flooded for the first time this dull little life should sweep away the satisfactions of an existence heart to heart with nature and the dumb life of the forest!

There was the huge tree asleep yet in the paling moonlight, and small and silly Sylvia began with utmost bravery to mount to the top of it, with tingling, eager blood coursing the channels of her whole frame, with her bare feet and fingers, that pinched and held like bird's claws to the monstrous ladder reaching up, up, almost to the sky itself. First she must mount the white oak tree that grew alongside, where she was almost lost among the dark branches and the green leaves heavy and wet with dew; a bird fluttered off its nest, and a red squirrel ran to and fro and scolded pettishly at the harmless housebreaker. Sylvia felt her way easily. She had often climbed there, and knew that higher still one of the oak's upper branches chafed against the pine trunk, just where its lower boughs were set close together. There, when she made the dangerous pass from one tree to the other, the great enterprise would really begin.

She crept out along the swaying oak limb at last, and took the daring step across into the old pine-tree. The way was harder than she thought; she must reach far and hold fast, the sharp dry twigs caught and held her and scratched her like angry talons, the pitch made her thin little fingers clumsy and stiff as she went round and round the tree's great stem, higher and higher upward. The sparrows and robins in the woods below were beginning to wake and twitter to the dawn, yet it seemed much lighter there aloft in the pine-tree, and the child knew she must hurry if her project were to be of any use.

The tree seemed to lengthen itself out as she went up, and to reach farther and farther upward. It was like a great main-mast to the voyaging earth; it must truly have been amazed that morning through all its ponderous frame as it felt this determined spark of human spirit wending its way from higher branch to branch. Who knows how steadily the least twigs held themselves to advantage this light, weak creature on her way! The old pine must have loved his new dependent. More than all the hawks, and bats, and moths, and even the sweet-voiced thrushes, was the brave, beating heart of the solitary gray-eyed child. And the tree stood still and frowned away the winds that June morning while the dawn grew bright in the east.

Sylvia's face was like a pale star, if one had seen it from the ground, when the last thorny bough was past, and she stood trembling and tired but wholly triumphant, high in the tree-top. Yes, there was the sea with the dawning sun making a golden dazzle over it, and toward that glorious east flew two hawks with slow-moving pinions. How low they looked in the air from that height when one had only seen them before far up, and dark against the blue sky. Their gray feathers were as soft as moths; they seemed only a little way from the tree, and Sylvia felt as if she too could go flying away among the clouds. Westward, the woodlands and farms reached miles and miles into the distance; here and there were church steeples, and white villages, truly it was a vast and awesome world!

The birds sang louder and louder. At last the sun came up bewilderingly bright. Sylvia could see the white sails of ships out at sea, and the clouds that were purple and rose-colored and yellow at first began to fade away. Where was the white heron's nest in the sea of green branches, and was this wonderful sight and pageant of the world the only reward for having climbed to such a giddy height? Now look down again, Sylvia, where the green marsh is set among the shining birches and dark hemlocks; there where you saw the white heron once you will see him again; look, look! a white spot of him like a single floating feather comes up from the dead hemlock and grows larger, and rises, and comes close at last, and goes by the landmark pine with steady sweep of wing and outstretched slender neck and crested head. And wait! wait! do not move a foot

or a finger, little girl, do not send an arrow of light and consciousness from your two eager eyes, for the heron has perched on a pine
bough not far beyond yours, and cries back to his mate on the nest
and plumes his feathers for the new day!

The child gives a long sigh a minute later when a company of
shouting cat-birds comes also to the tree, and vexed by their fluttering
and lawlessness the solemn heron goes away. She knows his secret
now, the wild, light, slender bird that floats and wavers, and goes
back like an arrow presently to his home in the green world beneath.
Then Sylvia, well satisfied, makes her perilous way down again, not
daring to look far below the branch she stands on, ready to cry
sometimes because her fingers ache and her lamed feet slip. Wondering over and over again what the stranger would say to her, and
what he would think when she told him how to find his way straight
to the heron's nest.

"Sylvy, Sylvy!" called the busy old grandmother again and again,
but nobody answered, and the small husk bed was empty and Sylvia
had disappeared.

The guest waked from a dream, and remembering his day's pleasure
hurried to dress himself that it might sooner begin. He was sure
from the way the shy little girl looked once or twice yesterday that
she had at least seen the white heron, and now she must really be
made to tell. Here she comes now, paler than ever, and her worn
old frock is torn and tattered, and smeared with pine pitch. The
grandmother and the sportsman stand in the door together and question her, and the splendid moment has come to speak of the dead
hemlock-tree by the green marsh.

But Sylvia does not speak after all, though the old grandmother
fretfully rebukes her, and the young man's kind, appealing eyes are
looking straight in her own. He can make them rich with money;
he has promised it, and they are poor now. He is so well worth
making happy, and he waits to hear the story she can tell.

No, she must keep silence! What is it that suddenly forbids her
and makes her dumb? Has she been nine years growing and now,
when the great world for the first time puts out a hand to her, must
she thrust it aside for a bird's sake? The murmur of the pine's green
branches is in her ears, she remembers how the white heron came
flying through the golden air and how they watched the sea and
the morning together, and Sylvia cannot speak; she cannot tell the
heron's secret and give its life away.

Dear loyalty, that suffered a sharp pang as the guest went away disappointed later in the day, that could have served and followed him and loved him as a dog loves! Many a night Sylvia heard the echo of his whistle haunting the pasture path as she came home with the loitering cow. She forgot even her sorrow at the sharp report of his gun and the sight of thrushes and sparrows dropping silent to the ground, their songs hushed and their pretty feathers stained and wet with blood. Were the birds better friends than their hunter might have been,—who can tell? Whatever treasures were lost to her, woodlands and summer-time, remember! Bring your gifts and graces and tell your secrets to this lonely country child!

The Gray Mills of Farley

THE mills of Farley were close together by the river, and the gray houses that belonged to them stood, tall and bare, alongside. They had no room for gardens or even for little green side-yards where one might spend a summer evening. The Corporation, as this compact village was called by those who lived in it, was small but solid; you fancied yourself in the heart of a large town when you stood midway of one of its short streets, but from the street's end you faced a wide green farming country. On spring and summer Sundays, groups of the young folks of the Corporation would stray out along the country roads, but it was very seldom that any of the older people went. On the whole, it seemed as if the closer you lived to the mill-yard gate, the better. You had more time to loiter on a summer morning, and there was less distance to plod through the winter snows and rains. The last stroke of the bell saw almost everybody within the mill doors.

There were always fluffs of cotton in the air like great white bees drifting down out of the picker chimney. They lodged in the cramped and dingy elms and horse-chestnuts which a former agent had planted along the streets, and the English sparrows squabbled over them in eaves-corners and made warm, untidy great nests that would have contented an Arctic explorer. Somehow the Corporation homes looked like make-believe houses or huge stage-properties, they had so little individuality or likeness to the old-fashioned buildings that made homes for people out on the farms. There was more homelikeness in the sparrows' nests, or even the toylike railroad station at the end of the main street, for that was warmed by steam, and the station-master's wife, thriftily taking advantage of the steady heat, brought her house-plants there and kept them all winter on the broad window-sills.

The Corporation had followed the usual fortunes of New England manufacturing villages. Its operatives were at first eager young men and women from the farms near by, these being joined quickly by pale English weavers and spinners, with their hearty-looking wives and rosy children; then came the flock of Irish families, poorer and simpler than the others but learning the work sooner, and gayer-hearted; now the Canadian-French contingent furnished all the new help, and stood in long rows before the noisy looms and chattered in their odd, excited fashion. They were quicker-fingered, and were willing to work cheaper than any other workpeople yet.

There were remnants of each of these human tides to be found as one looked about the mills. Old Henry Dow, the overseer of the cloth-hall, was a Lancashire man and some of his grandchildren had risen to wealth and prominence in another part of the country, while he kept steadily on with his familiar work and authority. A good many elderly Irishmen and women still kept their places; everybody knew the two old sweepers, Mary Cassidy and Mrs. Kilpatrick, who were looked upon as pillars of the Corporation. They and their compatriots always held loyally together and openly resented the incoming of so many French.

You would never have thought that the French were for a moment conscious of being in the least unwelcome. They came gaily into church and crowded the old parishioners of St. Michael's out of their pews, as on week-days they took their places at the looms. Hardly one of the old parishioners had not taken occasion to speak of such aggressions to Father Daley, the priest, but Father Daley continued to look upon them all as souls to be saved and took continual pains to rub up the rusty French which he had nearly forgotten, in order to preach a special sermon every other Sunday. This caused old Mary Cassidy to shake her head gravely.

"Mis' Kilpatrick, ma'am," she said one morning. "Faix, they ain't folks at all, 'tis but a pack of images they do be, with all their chatter like birds in a hedge."

"Sure then, the holy Saint Francis himself was after saying that the little birds was his sisters," answered Mrs. Kilpatrick, a godly old woman who made the stations every morning, and was often seen reading a much-handled book of devotions. She was moreover always ready with a friendly joke.

"They ain't the same at all was in them innocent times, when there was plinty saints living in the world," insisted Mary Cassidy. "Look at them thrash, now!"

The old sweeping-women were going downstairs with their brooms. It was almost twelve o'clock, and like the old drayhorse in the mill yard they slackened work in good season for the noonday bell. Three gay young French girls ran downstairs past them; they were let out for the afternoon and were hurrying home to dress and catch the 12:40 train to the next large town.

"That little one is Meshell's daughter; she's a nice child too, very quiet, and has got more Christian tark than most," said Mrs. Kilpatrick. "They live overhead o' me. There's nine o' themselves in the two rooms; two does be boarders."

"Those upper rooms bees very large entirely at Fitzgibbon's," said Mary Cassidy with unusual indulgence.

" 'Tis all the company cares about is to get a good rent out of the pay. They're asked every little while by honest folks 'on't they build a trifle o' small houses beyond the church up there, but no, they'd rather the money and kape us like bees in them old hives. Sure in winter we're better for having the more fires, but summer is the pinance!"

"They all says 'why don't folks build their own houses'; they does always be talking about Mike Callahan and how well he saved up and owns a pritty place for himself convanient to his work. You might tell them he'd money left him by a brother in California till you'd be black in the face, they'd stick to it 'twas in the picker he earnt it from themselves," grumbled Mary Cassidy.

"Them French spinds all their money on their backs, don't they?" suggested Mrs. Kilpatrick, as if to divert the conversation from dangerous channels. "Look at them three girls now, off to Spincer with their fortnight's pay in their pocket!"

"A couple o' onions and a bag o' crackers is all they want and a pinch o' lard to their butter," pronounced Mary Cassidy with scorn. "The whole town of 'em 'on't be the worse of a dollar for steak the week round. They all go back and buy land in Canada, they spend no money here. See how well they forget their pocketbooks every Sunday for the collection. They do be very light too, they've more laugh than ourselves. 'Tis myself's getting old anyway, I don't laugh much now."

"I like to see a pritty girl look fine," said Mrs. Kilpatrick. "No, they don't be young but once——"

The mill bell rang, and there was a moment's hush of the jarring, racketing machinery and a sudden noise of many feet trampling across the dry, hard pine floors. First came an early flight of boys bursting out of the different doors, and chasing one another down the winding stairs two steps at a time. The old sweepers, who had not quite reached the bottom, stood back against the wall for safety's sake until all these had passed, then they kept on their careful way, the crowd passing them by as if they were caught in an eddy of the stream. Last of all they kept sober company with two or three lame persons and a cheerful delayed little group of new doffers, the children who minded bobbins in the weave-room and who were young enough to be tired and even timid. One of these doffers, a pale, pleasant-looking child, was all fluffy with cotton that had clung to her little dark plaid dress. When Mrs. Kilpatrick spoke to her she answered in a hoarse voice that appealed to one's sympathy. You felt that the hot room and dry cotton were to blame for such hoarseness; it had nothing to do with the weather.

"Where are you living now, Maggie, dear?" the old woman asked.

"I'm in Callahan's yet, but they won't keep me after to-day," said the child. "There's a man wants to get board there, they're changing round in the rooms and they've no place for me. Mis' Callahan couldn't keep me 'less I'd get my pay raised."

Mrs. Kilpatrick gave a quick glance at Mary Cassidy. "Come home with me then, till yez get a bite o' dinner, and we'll talk about it," she said kindly to the child. "I'd a wish for company the day."

The two old companions had locked their brooms into a three-cornered closet at the stair-foot and were crossing the mill yard together. They were so much slower than the rest that they could only see the very last of the crowd of mill people disappearing along the streets and into the boarding-house doors. It was late autumn, the elms were bare, one could see the whole village of Farley, all its poverty and lack of beauty, at one glance. The large houses looked as if they belonged to a toy village, and had been carefully put in rows by a childish hand; it was easy to lose all sense of size in looking at them. A cold wind was blowing bits of waste and paper high into the air; now and then a snowflake went swiftly by like a courier of winter. Mary Cassidy and Mrs. Kilpatrick hugged their old woolen shawls closer about their round shoulders, and the little girl followed with short steps alongside.

II

The agent of the mills was a single man, keen and business-like, but quietly kind to the people under his charge. Sometimes, in times of peace, when one looks among one's neighbors wondering who would make the great soldiers and leaders if there came a sudden call to war, one knows with a flash of recognition the presence of military genius in such a man as he. The agent spent his days in following what seemed to many observers to be only a dull routine, but all his steadiness of purpose, all his simple intentness, all his gifts of strategy and powers of foresight, and of turning an interruption into an opportunity, were brought to bear upon this dull routine with a keen pleasure. A man in his place must know not only how to lead men, but how to make the combination of their force with the machinery take its place as a factor in the business of manufacturing. To master workmen and keep the mills in running order and to sell the goods successfully in open market is as easy to do badly as it is difficult to do well.

The agent's father and mother, young people who lived for a short time in the village, had both died when he was only three years old, and between that time and his ninth year he had learned almost everything that poverty could teach, being left like Maggie to the mercy of his neighbors. He remembered with a grateful heart those who were good to him, and told him of his mother, who had married for love but unwisely. Mrs. Kilpatrick was one of these old friends, who said that his mother was a lady, but even Mrs. Kilpatrick, who was a walking history of the Corporation, had never known his mother's maiden name, much less the place of her birth. The first great revelation of life had come when the nine-year-old boy had money in his hand to pay his board. He was conscious of being looked at with a difference; the very woman who had been hardest to him and let him mind her babies all the morning when he, careful little soul, was hardly more than a baby himself, and then pushed him out into the hungry street at dinner time, was the first one who beckoned him now, willing to make the most of his dollar and a quarter a week. It seemed easy enough to rise from uttermost poverty and dependence to where one could set his mind upon the highest honor in sight, that of being agent of the mills, or to work one's way steadily to where such an honor was grasped at thirty-two. Every year the horizon had set its bounds wider and wider, until the mills of Farley held but a small place in the manufacturing world. There were offers enough of more salary and higher position from those who came to know the agent, but he was part of Farley itself, and had come to care deeply about his neighbors, while a larger mill and salary were not exactly the things that could tempt his ambition. It was but a lonely life for a man in the old agent's quarters where one of the widows of the Corporation, a woman who had been brought up in a gentleman's house in the old country, kept house for him with a certain show of propriety. Ever since he was a boy his room was never without its late evening light, and books and hard study made his chief companionship.

As Mrs. Kilpatrick went home holding little Maggie by the hand that windy noon, the agent was sitting in the company's counting-room with one of the directors and largest stockholders, and they were just ending a long talk about the mill affairs. The agent was about forty years old now and looked fifty. He had a pleasant smile, but one saw it rarely enough, and just now he looked more serious than usual.

"I am very glad to have had this long talk with you," said the old director. "You do not think of any other recommendations to be made at the meeting next week?"

The agent grew a trifle paler and glanced behind him to be sure that the clerks had gone to dinner.

"Not in regard to details," he answered gravely. "There is one thing which I see to be very important. You have seen the books, and are clear that nine per cent. dividend can easily be declared?"

"Very creditable, very creditable," agreed the director; he had recognized the agent's ability from the first and always upheld him generously. "I mean to propose a special vote of thanks for your management. There isn't a minor corporation in New England that stands so well to-day."

The agent listened. "We had some advantages, partly by accident and partly by lucky foresight," he acknowledged. "I am going to ask your backing in something that seems to me not only just but important. I hope that you will not declare above a six per cent. dividend at that directors' meeting; at the most, seven per cent.," he said.

"What! What!" exclaimed the listener. "No, sir!"

The agent left his desk-chair and stood before the old director as if he were pleading for himself. A look of protest and disappointment changed the elder man's face and hardened it a little, and the agent saw it.

"You know the general condition of the people here," he explained humbly. "I have taken great pains to keep hold of the best that have come here; we can depend upon them now and upon the quality of their work. They made no resistance when we had to cut down wages two years ago; on the contrary, they were surprisingly reasonable, and you know that we shut down for several weeks at the time of the alterations. We have never put their wages back as we might easily have done, and I happen to know that a good many families have been able to save little or nothing. Some of them have been working here for three generations. They know as well as you and I and the books do when the mills are making money. Now I wish that we could give them the ten per cent. back again, but in view of the general depression perhaps we can't do that except in the way I mean. I think that next year we're going to have a very hard pull to get along, but if we can keep back three per cent., or even two, of this dividend we can not only manage to get on without a shut-down or touching our surplus, which is quite small enough, but I can have some painting and repairing done in the tenements. They've needed it for a long time——"

The old director sprang to his feet. "Aren't the stockholders going to have any rights then?" he demanded. "Within fifteen years we have had three years when we have passed our dividends, but the operatives never can lose a single day's pay!"

"That was before my time," said the agent, quietly. "We have averaged nearly six and a half per cent. a year taking the last twenty years together, and if you go back farther the average is even larger. This has always been a paying property; we've got our new machinery now, and everything in the mills themselves is just where we want it. I look for far better times after this next year, but the market is glutted with goods of our kind, and nothing is going to be gained by cut-downs and forcing lower-cost goods into it. Still, I can keep things going one way and another, making yarn and so on," he said pleadingly. "I should like to feel that we had this extra surplus. I believe that we owe it to our operatives."

The director had walked heavily to the window and put his hands deep into his side-pockets. He had an angry sense that the agent's hands were in his pockets too.

"I've got some pride about that nine per cent., sir," he said loftily to the agent.

"So have I," said the agent, and the two men looked each other in the face.

"I acknowledge my duty to the stockholders," said the younger man presently. "I have tried to remember that duty ever since I took the mills eight years ago, but we've got an excellent body of operatives, and we ought to keep them. I want to show them this next year that we value their help. If times aren't as bad as we fear we shall still have the money——"

"Nonsense. They think they own the mills now," said the director, but he was uncomfortable, in spite of believing he was right. "Where's my hat? I must have my luncheon now, and afterward there'll hardly be time to go down and look at the new power-house with you—I must be off on the quarter-to-two train."

The agent sighed and led the way. There was no use in saying anything more and he knew it. As they walked along they met old Mrs. Kilpatrick returning from her brief noonday meal with little Maggie, whose childish face was radiant. The old woman recognized one of the directors and dropped him a decent curtsey as she had been taught to salute the gentry sixty years before.

The director returned the salutation with much politeness. This was really a pleasant incident, and he took a silver half dollar from his pocket and gave it to the little girl before he went on.

"Kape it safe, darlin'," said the old woman; "you'll need it yet. Don't be spending all your money in sweeties; 'tis a very cold world to them that haves no pince in their pocket."

The child looked up at Mrs. Kilpatrick apprehensively; then the sunshine of hope broke out again through the cloud.

"I am going to save fine till I buy a house, and you and me'll live there together, Mrs. Kilpatrick, and have a lovely coal fire all the time."

"Faix, Maggie, I have always thought some day I'd kape a pig and live pritty in me own house," said Mrs. Kilpatrick. "But I'm the old sweeper yet in Number Two. 'Tis a world where some has and more wants," she added with a sigh. "I got the manes for a good buryin', the Lord be praised, and a bitteen more beside. I wouldn't have that if Father Daley was as croping as some."

"Mis' Mullin does always be scolding 'bout Father Daley having all the collections," ventured Maggie, somewhat adrift in so great a subject.

"She's no right then!" exclaimed the old woman angrily; "she'll get no luck to be grudging her pince that way. 'Tis hard work anny priest would have to kape the likes of hersilf from being haythens altogether."

There was a nine per cent. annual dividend declared at the directors' meeting the next week, with considerable applause from the board and sincere congratulations to the agent. He looked thinner and more sober than usual, and several persons present, whose aid he had asked in private, knew very well the reason. After the meeting was over the senior director, and largest stockholder, shook hands with him warmly.

"About that matter you suggested to me the other day," he said, and the agent looked up eagerly. "I consulted several of our board in regard to the propriety of it before we came down, but they all agreed with me that it was no use to cross a bridge until you come to it. Times look a little better, and the operatives will share in the accession of credit to a mill that declares nine per cent. this year. I hope that we shall be able to run the mills with at worst only a moderate cut-down, and they may think themselves very fortunate when so many hands are being turned off everywhere."

The agent's face grew dark. "I hope that times will take a better turn," he managed to say.

"Yes, yes," answered the director. "Good-bye to you, Mr. Agent! I am not sure of seeing you again for some time," he added with unusual kindliness. "I am an old man now to be hurrying round to board meetings and having anything to do with responsibilities like these. My sons must take their turn."

There was an eager protest from the listeners, and presently the busy group of men disappeared on their way to the train. A nine per cent. dividend naturally made the Farley Manufacturing Company's stock go up a good many points, and word came presently that the largest stockholder and one or two other men had sold out. Then the stock ceased to rise, and winter came on apace, and the hard times which the agent had foreseen came also.

III

One noon in early March there were groups of men and women gathering in the Farley streets. For a wonder, nobody was hurrying toward home and dinner was growing cold on some of the long boarding-house tables.

"They might have carried us through the cold weather; there's but a month more of it," said one middle-aged man sorrowfully.

"They'll be talking to us about economy now, some o' them big thinkers; they'll say we ought to learn how to save; they always begin about that quick as work stops," said a youngish woman angrily. She was better dressed than most of the group about her and had the keen, impatient look of a leader. "They'll say that manufacturing is going to the dogs, and capital's in worse distress than labor——"

"How is it those big railroads get along? They can't shut down, there's none o' them stops; they cut down sometimes when they have to, but they don't turn off their help this way," complained somebody else.

"Faith then! they don't know what justice is. They talk about their justice all so fine," said a pale-faced young Irishman—"justice is nine per cent. last year for the men that had the money and no rise at all for the men that did the work."

"They say the shut-down's going to last all summer anyway. I'm going to pack my kit to-night," said a young fellow who had just married and undertaken with unusual pride and ambition to keep house. "The likes of me can't be idle. But where to look for any work for a mule spinner, the Lord only knows!"

Even the French were sobered for once and talked eagerly among themselves. Halfway down the street, in front of the French grocery, a man was haranguing his compatriots from the top of a packing-box. Everybody was anxious and excited by the sudden news. No work after a week from to-morrow until times were better. There had already been a cut-down, the mills had not been earning anything all winter. The agent had hoped to keep on for at least two months longer, and then to make some scheme about running at half time in the summer, setting aside the present work for simple yarn-making. He knew well enough that the large families were scattered through the mill rooms and that any pay would be a help. Some of the young men could be put to other work for the company; there was a huge tract of woodland farther back among the hills where some timber could be got ready for shipping. His mind was full of plans and anxieties and the telegram that morning struck him like a blow. He had asked that he might keep the card-room prices up to where the best men could make at least six dollars and a half a week and was hoping for a straight answer, but the words on the yellow paper seemed to dance about and make him dizzy. "Shut down Saturday 9th until times are better!" he repeated to himself. "Shut down until times are worse here in Farley!"

The agent stood at the counting-room window looking out at the piteous, defenseless groups that passed by. He wished bitterly that his own pay stopped with the rest; it did not seem fair that he was not thrown out upon the world too.

"I don't know what they're going to do. They shall have the last cent I've saved before anybody suffers," he said in his heart. But there were tears in his eyes when he saw Mrs. Kilpatrick go limping out of the gate. She waited a moment for her constant companion, poor little Maggie the doffer, and they went away up the street toward their

poor lodging holding each other fast by the hand. Maggie's father and
grandfather and great-grandfather had all worked in the Farley mills;
they had left no heritage behind them but work for this orphan child;
they had never been able to save so much that a long illness, a prolonged old age, could not waste their slender hoards away.

IV

It would have been difficult for an outsider to understand the sudden plunge from decent comfort to actual poverty in this small mill
town. Strange to say, it was upon the smaller families that the strain
fell the worst in Farley, and upon men and women who had nobody
to look to but themselves. Where a man had a large household of
children and several of these were old enough to be at work, and to
put aside their wages or pay for their board; where such a man was
of a thrifty and saving turn and a ruler of his household like old
James Dow in the cloth-hall, he might feel sure of a comfortable
hoard and be fearless of a rainy day. But with a young man who
worked single-handed for his wife and a little flock, or one who had
an invalid to work for, that heaviest of burdens to the poor, the door
seemed to be shut and barred against prosperity, and life became a
test of one's power of endurance.

The agent went home late that noon from the counting-room. The
street was nearly empty, but he had no friendly look or word for
anyone whom he passed. Those who knew him well only pitied him,
but it seemed to the tired man as if every eye must look at him with
reproach. The long mill buildings of gray stone with their rows of
deep-set windows wore a repellent look of strength and solidity. More
than one man felt bitterly his own personal weakness as he turned to
look at them. The ocean of fate seemed to be dashing him against
their gray walls—what use was it to fight against the Corporation?
Two great forces were in opposition now, and happiness could come
only from their serving each other in harmony.

The stronger force of capital had withdrawn from the league; the
weaker one, labor, was turned into an utter helplessness of idleness.
There was nothing to be done; you cannot rebel against a shut-down,
you can only submit.

A week later the great wheel stopped early on the last day of work.
Almost everyone left his special charge of machinery in good order,
oiled and cleaned and slackened with a kind of affectionate lingering
care, for one person loves his machine as another loves his horse.

Even little Maggie pushed her bobbin-box into a safe place near the overseer's desk and tipped it up and dusted it out with a handful of waste. At the foot of the long winding stairs Mrs. Kilpatrick was putting away her broom, and she sighed as she locked the closet door; she had known hard times before. "They'll be wanting me with odd jobs; we'll be after getting along some way," she said with satisfaction.

"March is a long month, so it is—there'll be plinty time for change before the ind of it," said Mary Cassidy hopefully. "The agent will be thinking whatever can he do; sure he's very ingenious. Look at him how well he persuaded the directors to l'ave off wit' making cotton cloth like everybody else, and catch a chance wit' all these new linings and things! He's done very well, too. There bees no sinse in a shut-down anny way, the looms and cards all suffers and the bands all slacks if they don't get stiff. I'd sooner pay folks to tind their work whatever it cost."

" 'Tis true for you," agreed Mrs. Kilpatrick.

"What'll ye do wit' the shild, now she's no chance of pay, any more?" asked Mary relentlessly, and poor Maggie's eyes grew dark with fright as the conversation abruptly pointed her way. She sometimes waked up in misery in Mrs. Kilpatrick's warm bed, crying for fear that she was going to be sent back to the poorhouse.

"Maggie an' me's going to kape together awhile yet," said the good old woman fondly. "She's very handy for me, so she is. We 'on't part with 'ach other whativer befalls, so we 'on't," and Maggie looked up with a wistful smile, only half reassured. To her the shut-down seemed like the end of the world.

Some of the French people took time by the forelock and boarded the midnight train that very Saturday with all their possessions. A little later two or three families departed by the same train, under cover of the darkness between two days, without stopping to pay even their house rent. These mysterious flittings, like that of the famous Tartar tribe, roused a suspicion against their fellow countrymen, but after a succession of such departures almost everybody else thought it far cheaper to stay among friends. It seemed as if at any moment the great mill wheels might begin to turn, and the bell begin to ring, but day after day the little town was still and the bell tolled the hours one after another as if it were Sunday. The mild spring weather came on and the women sat mending or knitting on the doorsteps. More people moved away; there were but few men and girls left now in the quiet boarding-houses, and the spare tables were stacked one upon another at the end of the rooms. When planting-

time came, word was passed about the Corporation that the agent
was going to portion out a field that belonged to him a little way out
of town on the South road, and let every man who had a family take
a good-sized piece to plant. He also offered seed potatoes and garden
seeds free to anyone who would come and ask for them at his house.
The poor are very generous to each other, as a rule, and there was
much borrowing and lending from house to house, and it was wonderful how long the people seemed to continue their usual fashions
of life without distress. Almost everybody had saved a little bit of
money and some had saved more; if one could no longer buy beefsteak he could still buy flour and potatoes, and a bit of pork lent a
pleasing flavor, to content an idle man who had nothing to do but
to stroll about town.

V

One night the agent was sitting alone in his large, half-furnished
house. Mary Moynahan, his housekeeper, had gone up to the church.
There was a timid knock at the door.

There were two persons waiting, a short, thick-set man and a pale
woman with dark, bright eyes who was nearly a head taller than her
companion.

"Come in, Ellen; I'm glad to see you," said the agent. "Have you
got your wheelbarrow, Mike?" Almost all the would-be planters of
the field had come under cover of darkness and contrived if possible
to avoid each other.

" 'Tisn't the potatoes we're after asking, sir," said Ellen. She was
always spokes-woman, for Mike had an impediment in his speech.
"The childher come up yisterday and got them while you'd be down
at the counting-room. 'Twas Mary Moynahan saw to them. We do be
very thankful to you, sir, for your kindness."

"Come in," said the agent, seeing there was something of consequence to be said. Ellen Carroll and he had worked side by side many
a long day when they were young. She had been a noble wife to Mike,
whose poor fortunes she had gladly shared for sake of his good heart,
though Mike now and then paid too much respect to his often infirmities. There was a slight flavor of whisky now on the evening air, but
it was a serious thing to put on your Sunday coat and go up with
your wife to see the agent.

"We've come wanting to talk about any chances there might be
with the mill," ventured Ellen timidly, as she stood in the lighted
room; then she looked at Mike for reassurance. "We're very bad off,
you see," she went on. "Yes, sir, I got them potaties, but I had to bake

a little of them for supper and more again the day, for our breakfast. I don't know whatever we'll do whin they're gone. The poor children does be entreating me for them, Dan!"

The mother's eyes were full of tears. It was very seldom now that anybody called the agent by his Christian name; there was a natural reserve and dignity about him, and there had come a definite separation between him and most of his old friends in the two years while he had managed to go to the School of Technology in Boston.

"Why didn't you let me know it was bad as that?" he asked. "I don't mean that anybody here should suffer while I've got a cent."

"The folks don't like to be begging, sir," said Ellen sorrowfully, "but there's lots of them does be in trouble. They'd ought to go away when the mills shut down, but for nobody knows where to go. Farley ain't like them big towns where a man'd pick up something else to do. I says to Mike: 'Come, Mike, let's go up after dark and tark to Dan; he'll help us out if he can,' says I——"

"Sit down, Ellen," said the agent kindly, as the poor woman began to cry. He made her take the armchair which the weave-room girls had given him at Christmas two years before. She sat there covering her face with her hands, and trying to keep back her sobs and go quietly on with what she had to say. Mike was sitting across the room with his back to the wall anxiously twirling his hat round and round. "Yis, we're very bad off," he contrived to say after much futile stammering. "All the folks in the Corporation, but Mr. Dow, has got great bills run up now at the stores, and thim that had money saved has lint to thim that hadn't—'twill be long enough before anybody's free. Whin the mills start up we'll have to spind for everything at once. The children is very hard on their clothes and they're all dropping to pieces. I thought I'd have everything new for them this spring, they do be growing so. I minds them and patches them the best I can." And again Ellen was overcome by tears. "Mike an' me's always been conthrivin' how would we get something laid up, so if anny one would die or be long sick we'd be equal to it, but we've had great pride to see the little gerrls go looking as well as anny, and we've worked very steady, but there's so manny of us we've had to pay rint for a large tenement and we'd only seventeen dollars and a little more when the shut-down was. Sure the likes of us has a right to earn more than our living, ourselves being so willing-hearted. 'Tis a long time now that Mike's been steady. We always had the pride to hope we'd own a house ourselves, and a pieceen o' land, but I'm thankful now—'tis as well for us; we've no chances to pay taxes now."

Mike made a desperate effort to speak as his wife faltered and began to cry again, and seeing his distress forgot her own, and supplied the halting words. "He wants to know if there's any work he could get, some place else than Farley. Himself's been sixteen years now in the picker, first he was one of six and now he is one of the four since you got the new machines, yourself knows it well."

The agent knew about Mike; he looked compassionate as he shook his head. "Stay where you are, for a while at any rate. Things may look a little better, it seems to me. We will start up as soon as anyone does. I'll allow you twenty dollars a month after this; here are ten to start with. No, no, I've got no one depending on me and my pay is going on. I'm glad to share it with my friends. Tell the folks to come up and see me, Ahern and Sullivan and Michel and your brother Con; tell anybody you know who is really in distress. You've all stood by me!"

" 'Tis all the lazy ones 'ould be coming if we told on the poor boy," said Ellen gratefully, as they hurried home. "Ain't he got the good heart? We'd ought to be very discrate, Mike!" and Mike agreed by a most impatient gesture, but by the time summer had begun to wane the agent was a far poorer man than when it had begun. Mike and Ellen Carroll were only the leaders of a sorrowful procession that sought his door evening after evening. Some asked for help who might have done without it, but others were saved from actual want. There were a few men who got work among the farms, but there was little steady work. The agent made the most of odd jobs about the mill yards and contrived somehow or other to give almost every household a lift. The village looked more and more dull and forlorn, but in August, when a traveling show ventured to give a performance in Farley, the Corporation hall was filled as it seldom was filled in prosperous times. This made the agent wonder, until he followed the crowd of workless, sadly idle men and women into the place of entertainment and looked at them with a sudden comprehension that they were spending their last cent for a little cheerfulness.

VI

The agent was going into the counting-room one day when he met old Father Daley and they stopped for a bit of friendly talk.

"Could you come in for a few minutes, sir?" asked the younger man. "There's nobody in the counting-room."

The busy priest looked up at the weather-beaten clock in the mill tower.

"I can," he said. " 'Tis not so late as I thought. We'll soon be having the mail."

The agent led the way and brought one of the directors' comfortable chairs from their committee-room. Then he spun his own chair face-about from before his desk and they sat down. It was a warm day in the middle of September. The windows were wide open on the side toward the river and there was a flicker of light on the ceiling from the sunny water. The noise of the fall was loud and incessant in the room. Somehow one never noticed it very much when the mills were running.

"How are the Duffys?" asked the agent.

"Very bad," answered the old priest gravely. "The doctor sent for me—he couldn't get them to take any medicine. He says that it isn't typhoid; only a low fever among them from bad food and want of care. That tenement is very old and bad, the drains from the upper tenement have leaked and spoiled the whole west side of the building. I suppose they never told you of it?"

"I did the best I could about it last spring," said the agent. "They were afraid of being turned out and they hid it for that reason. The company allowed me something for repairs as usual and I tried to get more; you see I spent it all before I knew what a summer was before us. Whatever I have done since I have paid for, except what they call legitimate work and care of property. Last year I put all Maple Street into first-rate order—and meant to go right through the Corporation. I've done the best I could," he protested with a bright spot of color in his cheeks. "Some of the men have tinkered up their tenements and I have counted it toward the rent, but they don't all know how to drive a nail."

" 'Tis true for you; you have done the best you could," said the priest heartily, and both the men were silent, while the river, which was older than they and had seen a whole race of men disappear before they came—the river took this opportunity to speak louder than ever.

"I think that manufacturing prospects look a little brighter," said the agent, wishing to be cheerful. "There are some good orders out, but of course the buyers can take advantage of our condition. The treasurer writes me that we must be firm about not starting up until we are sure of business on a good paying margin."

"Like last year's?" asked the priest, who was resting himself in the armchair. There was a friendly twinkle in his eyes.

"Like last year's," said the agent. "I worked like two men, and I pushed the mills hard to make that large profit. I saw there was

trouble coming, and I told the directors and asked for a special surplus, but I had no idea of anything like this."

"Nine per cent. in these times was too good a prize," said Father
Daley, but the twinkle in his eyes had suddenly disappeared.

"You won't get your new church for a long time yet," said the
agent.

"No, no," said the old man impatiently. "I have kept the foundations going as well as I could, and the talk, for their own sakes. It
gives them something to think about. I took the money they gave
me in collections and let them have it back again for work. 'Tis
well to lead their minds," and he gave a quick glance at the agent.
" 'Tis no pride of mine for church-building and no good credit with
the bishop I'm after. Young men can be satisfied with those things,
not an old priest like me that prays to be a father to his people."

Father Daley spoke as man speaks to man, straight out of an honest
heart.

"I see many things now that I used to be blind about long ago,"
he said. "You may take a man who comes over, him and his wife.
They fall upon good wages and their heads are turned with joy.
They've been hungry for generations back and they've always seen
those above them who dressed fine and lived soft, and they want a
taste of luxury too; they're bound to satisfy themselves. So they'll
spend and spend and have beefsteak for dinner every day just because
they never had enough before, but they'd turn into wild beasts of
selfishness, most of 'em, if they had no check. 'Tis there the church
steps in. 'Remember your Maker and do Him honor in His house
of prayer,' says she. 'Be self-denying, be thinking of eternity and of
what's sure to come!' And you will join with me in believing that
it's never those who have given most to the church who come first
to the ground in a hard time like this. Show me a good church and
I'll show you a thrifty people." Father Daley looked eagerly at the
agent for sympathy.

"You speak the truth, sir," said the agent. "Those that give most
are always the last to hold out with honest independence and the
first to do for others."

"Some priests may have plundered their parishes for pride's sake;
there's no saying what is in poor human nature," repeated Father
Daley earnestly. "God forgive us all for unprofitable servants of Him
and His church. I believe in saying more about prayer and right
living, and less about collections, in God's house, but it's the giving
hand that's the rich hand all the world over."

"I don't think Ireland has ever sent us over many misers; Saint Patrick must have banished them all with the snakes," suggested the agent with a grim smile. The priest shook his head and laughed a little and then both men were silent again in the counting-room.

The mail train whistled noisily up the road and came into the station at the end of the empty street, then it rang its loud bell and puffed and whistled away again.

"I'll bring your mail over, sir," said the agent, presently. "Sit here and rest yourself until I come back and we'll walk home together."

The leather mail-bag looked thin and flat and the leisurely post-master had nearly distributed its contents by the time the agent had crossed the street and reached the office. His clerks were both off on a long holiday; they were brothers and were glad of the chance to take their vacations together. They had been on lower pay; there was little to do in the counting-room—hardly anybody's time to keep or even a letter to write.

Two or three loiterers stopped the agent to ask him the usual question if there were any signs of starting up; an old farmer who sat in his long wagon before the post-office asked for news too, and touched his hat with an awkward sort of military salute.

"Come out to our place and stop a few days," he said kindly. "You look kind of pinched up and bleached out, Mr. Agent; you can't be needed much here."

"I wish I could come," said the agent, stopping again and looking up at the old man with a boyish, expectant face. Nobody had happened to think about him in just that way, and he was far from thinking about himself. "I've got to keep an eye on the people that are left here; you see they've had a pretty hard summer."

"Not so hard as you have!" said the old man, as the agent went along the street. "You've never had a day of rest more than once or twice since you were born!"

There were two letters and a pamphlet for Father Daley and a thin handful of circulars for the company. In busy times there was often all the mail matter that a clerk could bring. The agent sat down at his desk in the counting-room and the priest opened a thick foreign letter with evident pleasure. " 'Tis from an old friend of mine; he's in a monastery in France," he said. "I only hear from him once a year," and Father Daley settled himself in his armchair to read the close-written pages. As for the agent of the mills, he had quickly opened a letter from the treasurer and was not listening to anything that was said.

Suddenly he whirled round in his desk chair and held out the letter to the priest. His hand shook and his face was as pale as ashes.

"What is it? What's the matter?" cried the startled old man, who had hardly followed the first pious salutations of his own letter to their end. "Read it to me yourself, Dan. Is there any trouble?"

"Orders—I've got orders to start up; we're going to start—I wrote them last week——"

But the agent had to spring up from his chair and go to the window next the river before he could steady his voice to speak. He thought it was the look of the moving water that made him dizzy. "We're going to start up the mills as soon as I can get things ready." He turned to look up at the thermometer as if it were the most important thing in the world; then the color rushed to his face and he leaned a moment against the wall.

"Thank God!" said the old priest devoutly. "Here, come and sit down, my boy. Faith, but it's good news, and I'm the first to get it from you."

They shook hands and were cheerful together; the foreign letter was crammed into Father Daley's pocket, and he reached for his big cane.

"Tell everybody as you go up the street, sir," said Dan. "I've got a hurricane of things to see to; I must go the other way down to the storehouses. Tell them to pass the good news about town as fast as they can; 'twill hearten up the women." All the anxious look had gone as if by magic from the agent's face.

Two weeks from that time the old mill bell stopped tolling for the slow hours of idleness and rang out loud and clear for the housekeepers to get up, and rang for breakfast, and later still for all the people to go in to work. Some of the old hands were gone for good and new ones must be broken in in their places, but there were many familiar faces to pass the counting-room windows into the mill yard. There were French families which had reappeared with surprising promptness, Michel and his pretty daughter were there, and a household of cousins who had come to the next tenement. The agent stood with his hands in his pockets and nodded soberly to one group after another. It seemed to him that he had never felt so happy in his life.

"Jolly-looking set this morning," said one of the clerks whose desk was close beside the window; he was a son of one of the directors, who had sent him to the agent to learn something about manufacturing.

"They've had a bitter hard summer that you know nothing about," said the agent slowly.

Just then Mrs. Kilpatrick and old Mary Cassidy came along, and little Maggie was with them. She had got back her old chance at doffing and the hard times were over. They all smiled with such blissful satisfaction that the agent smiled too, and even waved his hand.

MARY HARTWELL CATHERWOOD

★ ★ ★

Primarily a romancer in the tradition of Sir Walter Scott and
Francis Parkman, Mary Hartwell Catherwood (1847-1902) wrote
interesting narratives concerning the French occupation of the
New World and the daring exploits of soldiers of fortune over-
coming treacherous Indians in wild forests bordering the upper
Great Lakes and the St. Lawrence River. Yet Mrs. Catherwood
also could portray realistically the experiences of early inhabitants
of Ohio, where she was born and educated; of Indiana, where
she first resided after marriage; and of Illinois, where, at Hoopes-
ton and Chicago, she spent her last years. "The Stirring-Off,"
from *The Queen of the Swamp* (1899), pictures the familiar activity of making maple sugar in Ohio, while "Pontiac's Lookout," localized at Mackinac Island, describes incidents in the days
of *coureurs de bois* and fur company agents. Other picturesque
narratives are found in *Mackinac and Lake Stories* (1899) and in
The Spirit of an Illinois Town (1897). "Pontiac's Lookout" is
reprinted from *The Chase of Saint-Castin* (1894) by permission
of Houghton Mifflin Company.

★ ★ ★

The Stirring-Off

Time, 1850

DAVIS's boys said to all the young men at singing-school, "Come
over to 'r sugar-camp Saturday night; we're goin' to stir off."
The young men, sitting on the fence to which horses were tied in
dusky rows, playfully imitated the preacher when he gave out ap-

pointments, and replied they would be there, no preventing Providence, at early candle-lighting.

Jane Davis, attended by her cousin, also circulated among the girls in the school-house during that interval in singing-school called recess, and invited them to the stirring-off.

The Davises, though by no means the richest, were the most hospitable family in the Swamp. They came from Virginia. Their stable swarmed with fine horses, each son and daughter owning a colt; and the steeds of visiting neighbors often crowded the stalls until these looked like a horse-fair.

The Davises entertained every day in the year. Their house was unpretending even for those times, being of unpainted wood, with a bedroom at each side of the porch, a sitting-room where guns and powder-horns hung over the fireplace, a kitchen, and a loft. Yet here sojourned relations from other counties, and even from over the mountains. Here on Christmas and New Year's days were made great turkey-roasts. Out of it issued Jane Davis to the dances and parties where she was a belle, and her brothers, ruddy, huge-limbed, black-eyed, and dignified as any young men in Fairfield County.

They kept bees, and raised what were called noble turnips. Their farm appeared to produce solely for the use of guests. In watermelon season they kept what might be termed open field. Their cookery was celebrated, and their cordiality as free as sunshine. No unwelcome guest could alight at Davis's. The head of the family, Uncle Davis was a "general," and this title carried as much social weight as that of judge. About their premises hung an atmosphere of unending good times. On Sunday afternoons late in November all the raw young men of the neighborhood drew in a circle to Davis's fireplace, scraping turnips or apples. Now the steel knives moved in concert, and now they jarred; the hollow wall of a turnip protested against the scrape, and Aunt Davis passed the heaping pan again. Or cracked walnuts and hickory nuts were the offerings. Then every youth sat with an overflowing handkerchief on his lap, and the small blade of his knife busy with the kernels,—backlog and forestick being bombarded with shells which burned in blue and crimson.

So when the Davises were ready to stir off in their sugar-camp, it was the most natural thing in the world for them to invite their neighbors to come and eat the sugar, and for their neighbors to come and do so.

The camp threw its shine far among leafless trees. Three or four iron kettles steamed on a pole over the fire. In a bark lodge near by, Aunt Davis had put a lunch of pies and cakes before she went home, to be handed around at the stirring-off. It was a clear starry night, the withered sod crisp underfoot with the stiffness of ice. Any group approaching silently could hear the tapped maples dripping a liquid nocturne into trough or pan.

But scarcely any groups approached silently. They were heard chatting in the open places, and their calls raised echoes.

John and Eck Davis had collected logs and chunks and spread robes and blankets until the seating capacity of the camp was nearly equal to that of George's Chapel. Some of the girls took off their wraps and hung them in the bark house. One couple carried away a bucket for more sugar-water to cool a kettle, and other couples sauntered after them. There were races on the spongy dead leaves, and sudden squalls of remonstrance.

Jane Davis stood in the midst of her company, moving a long wooden stirrer in the kettle about to sugar-off. Though her beauty was neither brown nor white, nor, in fact, positive beauty of any kind, it cajoled everybody. Her hair was folded close to her cheeks. There was innocent audacity in the curving line of every motion she made. The young men were so taken by the spell of her grace that she was accused of being unrighteously engaged to three at once, and about to add her cousin Tom Randall to the list.

Tom Randall was a Virginian, spending the winter in Ohio. He was handsome, merry as Mercutio, and so easy in his manners that the Swamp youths watched him with varying emotions. He brought his songs over the mountains: one celebrated the swiftness of the electric telegraph in flashing news from Baltimore to Wheeling; another was about a Quaker courtship, and set all the Swamp girls to rattling the lady's brisk response,—

> "What care I for your rings or money,—
> Faddle-a-ding, a-ding, a-day;
> I want a man that will call me honey,—
> Faddle-a-ding, a-ding, a-day!"

Tom Randall sat close to the fire, hanging his delicate hands, which had never done a day's chopping, over his knees. He looked much of a gentleman, Nora Waddell remarked aside to Philip Welchammer. To all the girls he was a central figure, as Jane was a central figure to the young men.

But Philip claimed that Virginians were no nearer perfection than out-and-out Swamp fellows.

"I didn't say he was a perfect gentleman," said Nora, with cautious moderation, "for I wouldn't say so of any man."

"He ain't proud," admitted Philip. "He's free to talk with everybody."

"Humph!" remarked Mary Thompson, sitting at the other side of Philip; "he ought to be. Folks in Georger Chapel neighborhood is just as good as anybody."

"Well, anyhow, I know he ain't a prettier dancer than Jane," sighed Nora, whose folks would not allow her to indulge in the godless motion which the music of a fiddle inspires. While Jane stirred and chatted, she was swaying and taking dance-steps, as if unable to refrain from spinning away through the trees. In this great woods drawing-room, where so many were gathered, it was impossible for her to hear any comment that went on.

"Jane makes a good appearance on the floor," responded Philip, who, being male, could withstand the general denunciations of the preacher and his mother's praying at him in meeting. "I like to lead her out to dance."

"Uncle and Aunt Davis are just as easy with Jane as if they wasn't perfessors of religion," sighed Nora Waddell.

"And their boys thinks so much of her," added Mary Thompson. "John can't go anywhere unless she ties his neck-han'ketcher for him. I've knowed him, when Jane was sick, to come and lean over her to get it fixed."

"If she's to leave them," said Philip, "I wonder how they'd do without her?"

"She's goin' to marry Cousin Jimmy Thompson, that I know," said Mary.

"She's engaged to Dr. Miller in Lancaster," insisted Nora. "I've saw voluntines he's sent her."

"Dick Hanks thinks he's goin' to get her," laughed Philip. "He told me she's as good as promised him. And Dick's a good feller, if he wasn't such a coward."

"I don't believe Jane wants anybody," said Nora Waddell. "She's light-minded, and likes to enjoy herself."

Dick Hanks stood by Jane and insisted on helping her to move the stirrer. His hair inclosed his head in the shape of a thatch, leaving but narrow eaves of forehead above his eyebrows, though his expression was open and amiable. He looked like one of Bewick's cuts of an English carter. The Hankses, however, were a rich family, and, in spite of their eccentricities, a power in the county. Old Jimmy Hanks so dreaded the grave that he had a marble vault hewed, watching its progress for years, and getting himself ready to occupy it a few weeks after its completion. Lest he should be buried alive, his will decreed that the vault should be unlocked and the coffin examined at intervals. The sight of a face floating in alcohol and spotted with drops from the metal casket not proving grateful to his heirs, the key was soon conveniently lost.

His son Dick, hearty in love and friendship and noble in brawn, so feared the dark that he would not go into an unlighted room. When left by himself at the parting of roads after a night's frolic, he galloped his horse through brush and mire, and it was told that he had more than once reached home without a whole stitch to his back.

But in spite of the powers of darkness, Dick was anxious to take Jane Davis under his protection. The fire and the noisy company kept him from lifting his eyes to the treetops swaying slowly overhead, and the lonesome stars. All through the woods winter-night sounds and sudden twig cracklings could be heard. Dick, however, meant to take Jane Davis home, whether he could persuade one of the Davis boys to go home with him afterward or not.

In those days neighborhoods were intensely local. The people knew what historians have not yet learned about the value of isolated bits of human life. These young folks in the sugar-camp knew nothing of the events and complications of the great world, but they all felt more or less interested in the politics of Jane Davis's entanglements.

Her brother kept dipping a long spoon into the kettle she stirred, and dropping the liquid into a tin cup of cold sugar-water. As long as the hot stuff twined about in ropy arms, it was syrup; but as soon as it settled to the bottom in a clear mass, it was wax, and the change from wax to the grain of sugar is a sudden one.

When Eck Davis announced, "It's waxed," the kettle was slung off in haste, and everybody left the tree which had propped his back, or the robe on which he had leaned, and the graining sugar was served in saucers and handed around. It could be eaten with spoons or "worked" into crackling ropes. Davis's boys took off the syrup kettles and covered them up in the bark lodge. They would be emptied into stone jars when the more important business of entertaining company was over. The fire now shone redder. Jane was cutting up pies and cakes in the bark house, all this warm light focused on her lowered eyelids, when more of her suitors arrived.

"I knowed the entire posse would be out," said Philip Welchammer in a laughing undertone to the girls sitting beside him. "Davises never misses invitin' anybody."

"You're too late, Jimmy Thompson," called Jane's elder brother before he noticed the preacher was in the party. "Your sheer's e't."

When, however, Dr. Miller from Lancaster also came forward, John stood up stiffly and put on his company grandeur. He held the town-man in some awe, and was bound to be constrained by the preacher.

Jimmy Thompson, having met Jane with awkward heartiness, said he would make the young folks acquainted with Brother Gurley. They all knew Brother Gurley; but Jimmy was a wild young man, and his audacity in "brother"-ing the preacher was more delicious than home-made sugar. He afterward explained that the preacher had been turned onto the old folks for Sunday, and he asked him along to the frolic without suspicionin' he'd come, but the preacher, he took a-holt as if that was the understandin'.

Jane met Brother Gurley and Dr. Miller with equal ease. A hush fell upon the company, and they ate and watched her serve the new-comers and appear to balance such formidable individuals in her hands. Affectation was in that region the deadliest sin a girl could commit against her own popularity, and Jane's manner was always beautifully simple.

The preacher had a clean-shaven, large face, huge blue eyes, and laughing white teeth, and a sprinkling of fine, indefinitely tinted hair. His figure was vigorous, and well made to bear the hardships of a Methodist circuit-rider. His presence had the grasp of good-fellowship and power, and rather dwarfed Dr. Miller, whom all the girls thought a very pretty man. Dr. Miller wore side-whiskers, and a Lancaster suit of clothes finished by a fine round cloak hooked under his chin. When he took off his hat to bow, two curls fell over his forehead. The woman who would not take Dr. Miller if he wanted her must expect to have the pick of creation, and maybe she would miss it after all. He talked to Jane and ate maple sugar with the greatest of Lancaster ease, telling her he had put up with his cousin in Millersport and borrowed a horse to ride to camp. John Davis at once said the folks at home expected him to put up with them over Sunday, and the other young men resented the doctor's prompt acceptance of Davis's hospitality.

The preacher, holding his saucer of sugar in his left hand, was going around and giving the right hand of fellowship to every young person in camp. This was the proper and customary thing for him to do. A preacher who went into company anywhere on the circuit without shaking hands and pushing and strengthening his acquaint-ance would be a worse stumbling-block than a backslider given up to superfluous clothing and all kinds of sinful levity, or a new con-vert with artificials in her bonnet. But there was a tingling quality in Brother Gurley's grasp which stirred the blood; and his heavy voice was as prevailing in its ordinary tones as in the thunders of the pulpit.

"Did you bring your wife with you, Brother Gurley?" simpered Tabitha Gill, a dwarfish, dark old maid, devout in church and esteemed for her ability to make a good prayer.

Mary Thompson whispered behind her back, "Tabitha Gill's always for findin' out whether a preacher's married or not before anybody else does."

"Not this time," replied Brother Gurley, warming Sister Gill's heart with a broad, class-meeting smile. "But I expect to bring her with me when I come around again."

"Do," said Tabitha; "and stop at our house."

"I'm obliged to you, Sister Gill," replied the preacher. "You have a fine community of young people here."

"But they ain't none of 'em converted. There's a good deal of levity in Georger Chapel neighborhood. Now, Jane, now,—Jane Davis, —she's a girl nobody can help likin', but many's the night that she's danced away in sinful amusement. I wish you'd do somethin' for her soul, Brother Gurley."

"I'll try," responded the preacher heartily. He looked with a tender and indulgent eye at Jane, who was dividing her company into two parts, to play one innocent play before the camp broke up.

"Come away from here," whispered Philip Welchammer to the girl beside him, seceding from the preacher's group and adding himself to Jane's. "Tabitha Gill will be haulin' us all up to the mourners' bench pretty soon."

They played "clap-out," the girls sitting in their wraps all ready to depart, and the young men turning up their collars and tying on their comforters while waiting a summons. Jane was leader, and with much tittering and secrecy each young lady imparted to Jane the name of the youth she wished to have sit beside her. Dick Hanks was called first, and he stood looking at the array from which he could take but one choice, his lips dropping apart and his expression like that he used to display under the dunce-cap at Gum College. During this interval of silence the drip of sugar-water into troughs played a musical phrase or two, and the stirring and whinnying of the horses could be heard where they were tied to saplings. No rural Ohioan ever walked a quarter of a mile if he had any kind of beast or conveyance to carry him.

Then Dick of course sat down by the wrong girl, and was clapped out, and Dr. Miller was called. Dr. Miller made a pleasing impression by hesitating all along the line, and when he sat down by Mary

Thompson her murmur of assent was a tribute to his sagacity. Cousin Tom Randall was summoned, and sung two or three lines of the "Quaker's Courtship" before throwing himself on the mercy of Nora Waddell. He was clapped out, and said he always expected it. West of the Alleghanies was no place for him; they were even goin' to clap him out up at uncle's. Then the preacher came smiling joyfully, and placed himself by Tabitha Gill, where he was tittered over and allowed to remain; and one by one the seats were filled, the less fortunate men making a second trial with more success when their range was narrowed.

Everybody rose up to go home. But a great many "good-nights," and reproaches for social neglect, and promises of future devotion to each other, had first to be exchanged. Then Jimmy Thompson, who had driven in his buggy expressly to take Jane Davis home, and was wondering what he should do with the preacher, saw with astonishment that Brother Gurley had Jane upon his own arm and was tucking her shawl close to her chin. Her black eyes sparkled within a scarlet hood. She turned about with Brother Gurley, facing all the young associates of her life, and said, "We want you all to come to our house after preachin' to-morrow. The presidin' elder will be there."

"I don't care nothin' about the presidin' elder," muttered Jimmy Thompson.

"Goin' to be a weddin', you know," explained John Davis, turning from assisting his brother Eck to empty the syrup kettles, and beaming warmly over such a general occasion. "The folks at meeting will all be invited, but Jane said she wanted to ask the young people separate to-night."

"And next time I come around the circuit," said Brother Gurley, gathering Jane's hand in his before the company, "I'll bring my wife with me."

They walked away from the campfire, Jane turning her head once or twice to call "Good-night, all," as if she still clung to every companionable hand. The party watched her an instant in silence. Perhaps some were fanciful enough to see her walking away from the high estate of a doctor's wife in Lancaster, from the Hanks money, and Jimmy Thompson's thrift, into the constant change and unfailing hardships of Methodist itinerancy. The dancing motion would disappear from her gait, and she who had tittered irreverently at her good mother's labors with backsliders at the mourners' bench would come to feel an interest in such sinners herself.

"Dog'd if I thought Jane Davis would ever marry a preacher!" burst out Jimmy Thompson, in sudden and hot disapproval.

"Don't it beat all!" murmured Tabitha Gill. "And her an unconverted woman in the error of her ways! Jane's too young for a preacher's wife."

"Jane's fooled us all," owned Philip Welchammer heartily. To keep intended nuptials a family secret until a day or a few hours before the appointed time was as much a custom of the country as was prying into and spying out such affairs. Surprising her friends by her wedding was, therefore, adding to Jane's social successes; but only Dr. Miller could perceive her true reason for assembling her suitors at the last moment. While discarding them all, her hospitable nature clung to their friendship; she wished to tell them in a group the change she contemplated, so that no one could accuse her of superior kindness to another. Her very cruelties were intended mercies.

"That's the way the pretty girls go," sighed Cousin Tom Randall, seizing hold of Jane's younger brother: "the preachers get 'em. Come on, Eck; I have to be helped home."

"I don't see when he courted her," breathed Dick Hanks, closing his lips after many efforts.

"Preachers is chain-lightnin'," laughed Jimmy Thompson. "He's been around often enough, and always stoppin' there."

"To-morrow after preachin'," said John impressively, as he came forward after hastily covering the jars. "We're goin' to have a turkey-dinner, and we want you all to be sure to come. And next time Brother Gurley and Jane makes the circuit, we'll have the infair at our house, too."

"That's just like Davises," exclaimed one of the dispersing group in the midst of their eager promises; "they wouldn't be satisfied unless they give the weddin' and the infair both, and invited all quarterly meetin' to set down to the table. I thought there was doin's over at their house; but then they're always bakin' and fussin'."

They could all picture a turkey-roast at Davis's: the crisp, brown turkeys rising from their own dripping, squares of pone as yellow as buttercups, and biscuits calculated to melt whitely with honey from glass dishes of sweet-smelling combs. There would be every kind of vegetable grown in the Swamp, and game from the banks of the Feeder and Reservoir, pies and cakes and coffee, and at least eight kinds of preserves. Jane Davis and the preacher would stand up in front of the fireplace, and after the ceremony there would be a constant rattle of jokes from the presiding elder and his assistants. And over the whole house would hang that happy atmosphere which makes one think of corn ripening on a sunny hillside in still September weather. A dozen times the long tables would be replenished and supplied with plates, all the usual features of a turkey-roast at Davis's being exaggerated by the importance of the occasion; and Aunt Davis would now and then forget to urge a guest while she hurriedly wiped her eyes and replied to some expression of neighborly sympathy, that they had to lose Jane some time, and it was a good thing for a girl to get a religious man. Then about dusk the preachers and their congregation would start again to chapel, and Jane, in Millersport clothes, would shine on the front seats as a bride, certain of an ovation when the after-meeting handshaking came. It would be a spite if she sat where tallow candles could drip on her from one of the wooden chandeliers, but she would enjoy hearing her bridegroom exhort, and he would feel like exhorting with all his might.

"Well, Doc," said John Davis, turning from the deserted camp and sinking fire to place himself by the bridle of the young man from Lancaster.

"No," answered Dr. Miller, "I'm obliged to you, John; but I'll ride back to Millersport tonight."

"You don't feel put out?" urged John, conscious of a pang because all the good fellows who courted Jane could not become his brothers-in-law.

"No; oh, no," protested Dr. Miller with chagrin. "She'd a right to suit herself. I'll be around some other day."

"We'd take it hard if you didn't," said John.

"But just now," concluded the doctor, "I feel what a body might call—stirred-off."

Dick Hanks was riding up close to Jimmy Thompson, while Jimmy unblanketed his mare and prepared for a deliberate departure.

"John, now," remarked Jimmy,—"he brothered the preacher right up, didn't he? They'll be makin' a class-leader o' John yet, if they can git him to quit racin' horses."

"Which way you goin' home, Jimmy?" inquired Dick Hanks anxiously.

"The long way, round by Georger Chapel, where I can look at the tombstones for company. Want to go along? We can talk over the weddin', and you're only two mile from home at our woods' gate."

"I guess I'll take the short cut through the brush," said Dick.

Jimmy drove through the clearing and fence-gap, where John Davis was waiting to lay up the rails again.

"What's that?" said John, and they both paused to listen.

It was a sound of crashing and scampering, of smothered exclamation and the rasping and tearing of garments. Dick Hanks was whipping his steed through the woods, against trees, logs, and branches, as if George's Chapel graveyard, containing the ghastly vault of his father, and George's Chapel preacher, waving Jane Davis in one victorious hand, were both in merciless pursuit of him.

Pontiac's Lookout

JENIEVE LALOTTE came out of the back door of her little house on Mackinac beach. The front door did not open upon either street of the village; and other domiciles were scattered with it along the strand, each little homestead having a front inclosure palisaded with oaken posts. Wooded heights sent a growth of bushes and young trees down to the pebble rim of the lake.

It had been raining, and the island was fresh as if new made. Boats and bateaux, drawn up in a great semicircle about the crescent bay, had also been washed; but they kept the marks of their long voyages to the Illinois Territory, or the Lake Superior region, or Canada. The very last of the winterers were in with their bales of furs, and some of these men were now roaring along the upper street in new clothes, exhilarated by spending on good cheer in one month the money it took them eleven months to earn. While in "hyvernements," or winter quarters, and on the long forest marches, the allowance of food per day, for a winterer, was one quart of corn and two ounces of tallow. On this fare the hardiest voyageurs ever known threaded a pathless continent and made a great traffic possible. But when they returned to the front of the world,—that distributing point in the straits,—they were fiercely importunate for what they considered the best the world afforded.

A segment of rainbow showed over one end of Round Island. The sky was dull rose, and a ship on the eastern horizon turned to a ship of fire, clean-cut and poised, a glistening object on a black bar of water. The lake was still, with blackness in its depths. The American flag on the fort rippled, a thing of living light, the stripes transparent. High pink clouds were riding down from the north, their flush dying as they piled aloft. There were shadings of peacock colors in the shoal water. Jenieve enjoyed this sunset beauty of the island, as she ran over the rolling pebbles, carrying some leather shoes by their leather strings. Her face was eager. She lifted the shoes to show them to three little boys playing on the edge of the lake.

"Come here. See what I have for you."

"What is it?" inquired the eldest, gazing betwixt the hairs scattered on his face; he stood with his back to the wind. His bare shins reddened in the wash of the lake, standing beyond its rim of shining gravel.

"Shoes," answered Jenieve, in a note triumphant over fate.

"What's shoes?" asked the smallest half-breed, tucking up his smock around his middle.

"They are things to wear on your feet," explained Jenieve; and her red-skinned half-brothers heard her with incredulity. She had told their mother, in their presence, that she intended to buy the children some shoes when she got pay for her spinning; and they thought it meant fashions from the Fur Company's store to wear to mass, but never suspected she had set her mind on dark-looking clamps for the feet.

"You must try them on," said Jenieve, and they all stepped experimentally from the water, reluctant to submit. But Jenieve was mistress in the house. There is no appeal from a sister who is a father to you, and even a substitute for your living mother.

"You sit down first, François, and wipe your feet with this cloth."

The absurdity of wiping his feet before he turned in for the night tickled François, though he was of a strongly aboriginal cast, and he let himself grin. Jenieve helped him struggle to encompass his lithe feet with the clumsy brogans.

"You boys are living like Indians."

"We are Indians," asserted François.

"But you are French, too. You are my brothers. I want you to go to mass looking as well as anybody."

Hitherto their object in life had been to escape mass. They objected to increasing their chances of church-going. Moccasins were the natural wear of human beings, and nobody but women needed even moccasins until cold weather. The proud look of an Iroquois taking spoils disappeared from the face of the youngest, giving way to uneasy anguish. The three boys sat down to tug, Jenieve going encouragingly from one to another. François lay on his back and pushed his heels skyward. Contempt and rebellion grew also in the faces of Gabriel and Toussaint. They were the true children of François Iroquois, her mother's second husband, who had been wont to lounge about Mackinac village in dirty buckskins and a calico shirt having one red and one blue sleeve. He had also bought a tall silk hat at the Fur

Company's store, and he wore the hat under his blanket when it rained. If tobacco failed him, he scraped and dried willow peelings, and called them kinnickinnick. This worthy relation had worked no increase in Jenieve's home except an increase of children. He frequently yelled around the crescent bay, brandishing his silk hat in the exaltation of rum. And when he finally fell off the wharf into deep water, and was picked out to make another mound in the Indian burying-ground, Jenieve was so fiercely elated that she was afraid to confess it to the priest. Strange matches were made on the frontier, and Indian wives were commoner than any other kind; but through the whole mortifying existence of this Indian husband Jenieve avoided the sight of him, and called her mother steadily Mama Lalotte. The girl had remained with her grandmother, while François Iroquois carried off his wife to the Indian village on a western height of the island. Her grandmother had died, and Jenieve continued to keep house on the beach, having always with her one or more of the half-breed babies, until the plunge of François Iroquois allowed her to bring them all home with their mother. There was but one farm on the island, and Jenieve had all the spinning which the sheep afforded. She was the finest spinner in that region. Her grandmother had taught her to spin with a little wheel, as they still do about Quebec. Her pay was small. There was not much money then in the country, but bills of credit on the Fur Company's store were the same as cash, and she managed to feed her mother and the Indian's family. Fish were to be had for the catching, and she could get corn-meal and vegetables for her soup pot in partial exchange for her labor. The luxuries of life on the island were air and water, and the glories of evening and morning. People who could buy them got such gorgeous clothes as were brought by the Company. But usually Jenieve felt happy enough when she put on her best red homespun bodice and petticoat for mass or to go to dances. She did wish for shoes. The ladies at the fort had shoes, with heels which clicked when they danced. Jenieve could dance better, but she always felt their eyes on her moccasins, and came to regard shoes as the chief article of one's attire.

Though the joy of shoeing her brothers was not to be put off, she had not intended to let them keep on these precious brogans of civilization while they played beside the water. But she suddenly saw Mama Lalotte walking along the street near the lake with old Michel Pensonneau. Beyond these moving figures were many others, of engagés and Indians, swarming in front of the Fur Company's great warehouse. Some were talking and laughing; others were in a line, bearing bales of furs from bateaux just arrived at the log-and-stone wharf stretched from the centre of the bay. But all of them, and curious women peeping from their houses on the beach, particularly Jean Bati' McClure's wife, could see that Michel Pensonneau was walking with Mama Lalotte.

This sight struck cold down Jenieve's spine. Mama Lalotte was really the heaviest charge she had. Not twenty minutes before had that flighty creature been set to watch the supper pot, and here she was, mincing along, and fixing her pale blue laughing eyes on Michel Pensonneau, and bobbing her curly flaxen head at every word he spoke. A daughter who has a marrying mother on her hands may become morbidly anxious; Jenieve felt she should have no peace of mind during the month the coureurs-de-bois remained on the island. Whether they arrived early or late, they had soon to be off to the winter hunting-grounds; yet here was an emergency.

"Mama Lalotte!" called Jenieve. Her strong young fingers beckoned with authority. "Come here to me. I want you."

The giddy parent, startled and conscious, turned a conciliating smile that way. "Yes, Jenieve," she answered obediently, "I come." But she continued to pace by the side of Michel Pensonneau.

Jenieve desired to grasp her by the shoulder and walk her into the house; but when the world, especially Jean Bati' McClure's wife, is watching to see how you manage an unruly mother, it is necessary to use some adroitness.

"Will you please come here, dear Mama Lalotte? Toussaint wants you."

"No, I don't!" shouted Toussaint. "It is Michel Pensonneau I want, to make me some boats."

The girl did not hesitate. She intercepted the couple, and took her mother's arm in hers. The desperation of her act appeared to her while she was walking Mama Lalotte home; still, if nothing but force will restrain a parent, you must use force.

Michel Pensonneau stood squarely in his moccasins, turning redder and redder at the laugh of his cronies before the warehouse. He was dressed in new buckskins, and their tawny brightness made his florid cheeks more evident. Michel Pensonneau had been brought up by the Cadottes of Sault Ste. Marie, and he had rich relations at Cahokia, in the Illinois Territory. If he was not as good as the family of François Iroquois, he wanted to know the reason why. It is true, he was past forty and a bachelor. To be a bachelor, in that region, where Indian wives were so plenty and so easily got rid of, might bring some reproach on a man. Michel had begun to see that it did. He was an easy, gormandizing, good fellow, shapelessly fat, and he never had stirred himself during his month of freedom to do any courting. But Frenchmen of his class considered fifty the limit of an active life. It behooved him now to begin looking around; to prepare a fireside for himself. Michel was a good clerk to his employers. Cumbrous though his body might be, when he was in the woods he never shirked any hardship to secure a specially fine bale of furs.

Mama Lalotte, propelled against her will, sat down, trembling, in the house. Jenieve, trembling also, took the wooden bowls and spoons from a shelf and ladled out soup for the evening meal. Mama Lalotte was always willing to have the work done without trouble to herself, and she sat on a three-legged stool, like a guest. The supper pot boiled in the centre of the house, hanging on the crane which was fastened to a beam overhead. Smoke from the clear fire passed that · richly darkened transverse of timber as it ascended, and escaped through a hole in the bark roof. The Fur Company had a great building with chimneys; but poor folks were glad to have a cedar hut of one room, covered with bark all around and on top. A fire-pit, or earthen hearth, was left in the centre, and the nearer the floor could be brought to this hole, without danger, the better the house was. On winter nights, fat French and half-breed children sat with heels to this sunken altar, and heard tales of massacre or privation which made the family bunks along the wall seem couches of luxury. It was the aboriginal hut patterned after his Indian brother's by the Frenchman; and the succession of British and American powers had not yet improved it. To Jenieve herself, the crisis before her, so insignificant against the background of that historic island, was more important than massacre or conquest.

"Mama,"—she spoke tremulously,—"I was obliged to bring you in. It is not proper to be seen on the street with an engagé. The town is now full of these bush-lopers."

"Bush-lopers, mademoiselle!" The little flaxen-haired woman had a shrill voice. "What was your own father?"

"He was a clerk, madame," maintained the girl's softer treble, "and always kept good credit for his family at the Company's store."

"I see no difference. They are all the same."

"François Iroquois was not the same." As the girl said this she felt a powder-like flash from her own eyes.

Mama Lalotte was herself a little ashamed of the François Iroquois alliance, but she answered, "He let me walk outside the house, at least. You allow me no amusement at all. I cannot even talk over the fence to Jean Bati' McClure's wife."

"Mama, you do not understand the danger of all these things, and I do. Jean Bati' McClure's wife will be certain to get you into trouble. She is not a proper woman for you to associate with. Her mind runs on nothing but match-making."

"Speak to her, then, for yourself. I wish you would get married."

"I never shall," declared Jenieve. "I have seen the folly of it."

"You never have been young," complained Mama Lalotte. "You don't know how a young person feels."

"I let you go to the dances," argued Jenieve. "You have as good a time as any woman on the island. But old Michel Pensonneau," she added sternly, "is not settling down to smoke his pipe for the remainder of his life on this doorstep."

"Monsieur Pensonneau is not old."

"Do you take up for him, Mama Lalotte, in spite of me?" In the girl's rich brunette face the scarlet of the cheeks deepened. "Am I not more to you than Michel Pensonneau or any other engagé? He is old; he is past forty. Would I call him old if he were no more than twenty?"

"Every one cannot be only twenty and a young agent," retorted her elder; and Jenieve's ears and throat reddened, also.

"Have I not done my best for you and the boys? Do you think it does not hurt me to be severe with you?"

Mama Lalotte flounced around on her stool, but made no reply. She saw peeping and smiling at the edge of the door a neighbor's face, that encouraged her insubordinations. Its broad, good-natured upper lip thinly veiled with hairs, its fleshy eyelids and thick brows, expressed a strength which she had not, yet would gladly imitate.

"Jenieve Lalotte," spoke the neighbor, "before you finish whipping your mother you had better run and whip the boys. They are throwing their shoes in the lake."

"Their shoes!" Jenieve cried, and she scarcely looked at Jean Bati' McClure's wife, but darted outdoors along the beach.

"Oh, children, have you lost your shoes?"

"No," answered Toussaint, looking up with a countenance full of enjoyment.

"Where are they?"

"In the lake."

"You didn't throw your new shoes in the lake?"

"We took them for boats," said Gabriel freely. "But they are not even fit for boats."

"I threw mine as far as I could," observed François. "You can't make anything float in them."

She could see one of them stranded on the lake bottom, loaded with stones, its strings playing back and forth in the clear water. The others were gone out to the straits. Jenieve remembered all her toil for them, and her denial of her own wants that she might give to these half-savage boys, who considered nothing lost that they threw into the lake.

She turned around to run to the house. But there stood Jean Bati' McClure's wife, talking through the door, and encouraging her mother to walk with coureurs-de-bois. The girl's heart broke. She took to the bushes to hide her weeping, and ran through them towards the path she had followed so many times when her only living kindred were at the Indian village. The pine woods received her into their ascending heights, and she mounted towards sunset.

Panting from her long walk, Jenieve came out of the woods upon a grassy open cliff, called by the islanders Pontiac's Lookout, because the great war chief used to stand on that spot, forty years before, and gaze southward, as if he never could give up his hope of the union of his people. Jenieve knew the story. She had built playhouses here, when a child, without being afraid of the old chief's lingering influence; for she seemed to understand his trouble, and this night she was more in sympathy with Pontiac than ever before in her life. She sat down on the grass, wiping the tears from her hot cheeks, her dark eyes brooding on the lovely straits. There might be more beautiful sights in the world, but Jenieve doubted it; and a white gull drifted across her vision like a moving star.

Pontiac's Lookout had been the spot from which she watched her father's bateau disappear behind Round Island. He used to go by way of Detroit to the Canadian woods. Here she wept out her first grief for his death; and here she stopped, coming and going between her mother and grandmother. The cliff down to the beach was clothed with a thick growth which took away the terror of falling, and many a time Jenieve had thrust her bare legs over the edge to sit and enjoy the outlook.

There were old women on the island who could remember seeing Pontiac. Her grandmother had told her how he looked. She had heard that, though his bones had been buried forty years beside the Mississippi, he yet came back to the Lookout every night during that summer month when all the tribes assembled at the island to receive money from a new government. He could not lie still while they took a little metal and ammunition in their hands in exchange for their country. As for the tribes, they enjoyed it. Jenieve could see their night fires begin to twinkle on Round Island and Bois Blanc, and the rising hubbub of their carnival came to her like echoes across the strait. There was one growing star on the long hooked reef which reached out from Round Island, and figures of Indians were silhouetted against the lake, running back and forth along that high stone ridge. Evening coolness stole up to Jenieve, for the whole water world was purpling; and sweet pine and cedar breaths, humid and invisible, were all around her. Her trouble grew small, laid against the granite breast of the island, and the woods darkened and sighed behind her. Jenieve could hear the shout of some Indian boy at the distant village. She was not afraid, but her shoulders contracted with a shiver. The place began to smell rankly of sweetbrier. There was no sweetbrier on the cliff or in the woods, though many bushes grew on alluvial slopes around the bay. Jenieve loved the plant, and often stuck a piece of it in her bosom. But this was a cold smell, striking chill to the bones. Her flesh and hair and clothes absorbed the scent, and it cooled her nostrils with its strange ether, the breath of sweetbrier, which always before seemed tinctured by the sun. She had a sensation of moving sidewise out of her own person; and then she saw the chief Pontiac standing on the edge of the cliff. Jenieve knew his back, and the feathers in his hair which the wind did not move. His head turned on a pivot, sweeping the horizon from St. Ignace, where the white man first set foot, to Round Island, where the shameful fires burned. His hard, set features were silver color rather than copper, as she saw his profile against the sky. His arms were folded in his blanket. Jenieve was as sure that she saw Pontiac as she was sure of the rock on which she sat. She poked one finger through the sward to the hardness underneath. The rock was below her, and Pontiac stood before her. He turned his head back from Round Island to St. Ignace. The wind blew against him, and the brier odor, sickening sweet, poured over Jenieve.

She heard the dogs bark in Mackinac village, and leaves moving behind her, and the wash of water at the base of the island which always sounded like a small rain. Instead of feeling afraid, she was in a nightmare of sorrow. Pontiac had loved the French almost as well as he loved his own people. She breathed the sweetbrier scent, her neck stretched forward and her dark eyes fixed on him; and as his head turned back from St. Ignace his whole body moved with it, and he looked at Jenieve.

His eyes were like a cat's in the purple darkness, or like that heatless fire which shines on rotting bark. The hoar-frosted countenance was noble even in its most brutal lines. Jenieve, without knowing she was saying a word, spoke out:—

"Monsieur the chief Pontiac, what ails the French and Indians?"

"Malatat," answered Pontiac. The word came at her with force.

"Monsieur the chief Pontiac," repeated Jenieve, struggling to understand, "I say, what ails the French and Indians?"

"Malatat!" His guttural cry rang through the bushes. Jenieve was so startled that she sprung back, catching herself on her hands. But without the least motion of walking he was far westward, showing like a phosphorescent bar through the trees, and still moving on, until the pallor was lost from sight.

Jenieve at once began to cross herself. She had forgotten to do it before. The rankness of sweetbrier followed her some distance down the path, and she said prayers all the way home.

You cannot talk with great spirits and continue to chafe about little things. The boys' shoes and Mama Lalotte's lightness were the same as forgotten. Jenieve entered her house with dew in her hair, and an unterrified freshness of body for whatever might happen. She was certain she had seen Pontiac, but she would never tell anybody to have it laughed at. There was no candle burning, and the fire had almost died under the supper pot. She put a couple of sticks on the coals, more for their blaze than to heat her food. But the Mackinac night was chill, and it was pleasant to see the interior of her little home flickering to view. Candles were lighted in many houses along the beach, and amongst them Mama Lalotte was probably roaming,—for she had left the door open towards the lake,—and the boys' voices could be heard with others in the direction of the log wharf.

Jenieve took her supper bowl and sat down on the doorstep. The light cloud of smoke, drawn up to the roof-hole, ascended behind her, forming an azure gray curtain against which her figure showed, round-wristed and full-throated. The starlike camp fires on Round Island were before her, and the incessant wash of the water on its pebbles was company to her. Somebody knocked on the front door.

"It is that insolent Michel Pensonneau," thought Jenieve. "When he is tired he will go away." Yet she was not greatly surprised when the visitor ceased knocking and came around the palisades.

"Good-evening, Monsieur Crooks," said Jenieve.

"Good-evening, mademoiselle," responded Monsieur Crooks, and he leaned against the hut side, cap in hand, where he could look at her. He had never yet been asked to enter the house. Jenieve continued to eat her supper.

"I hope monsieur your uncle is well?"

"My uncle is well. It isn't necessary for me to inquire about madame your mother, for I have just seen her sitting on McClure's doorstep."

"Oh," said Jenieve.

The young man shook his cap in a restless hand. Though he spoke French easily, he was not dressed like an engagé, and he showed through the dark the white skin of the Saxon.

"Mademoiselle Jenieve,"—he spoke suddenly,—"you know my uncle is well established as agent of the Fur Company, and as his assistant I expect to stay here."

"Yes, monsieur. Did you take in some fine bales of furs to-day?"

"That is not what I was going to say."

"Monsieur Crooks, you speak all languages, don't you?"

"Not all. A few. I know a little of nearly every one of our Indian dialects."

"Monsieur, what does 'malatat' mean?"

"'Malatat'? That's a Chippewa word. You will often hear that. It means 'good for nothing.'"

"But I have heard that the chief Pontiac was an Ottawa."

The young man was not interested in Pontiac.

"A chief would know a great many dialects," he replied. "Chippewa was the tongue of this island. But what I wanted to say is that I have had a serious talk with the agent. He is entirely willing to have me settle down. And he says, what is the truth, that you are the best and prettiest girl at the straits. I have spoken my mind often enough. Why shouldn't we get married right away?"

Jenieve set her bowl and spoon inside the house, and folded her arms.

"Monsieur, have I not told you many times? I cannot marry. I have a family already."

The young agent struck his cap impatiently against the bark weather-boarding. "You are the most offish girl I ever saw. A man cannot get near enough to you to talk reason."

"It would be better if you did not come down here at all, Monsieur Crooks," said Jenieve. "The neighbors will be saying I am setting a bad example to my mother."

"Bring your mother up to the Fur Company's quarters with you, and the neighbors will no longer have a chance to put mischief into her head."

Jenieve took him seriously, though she had often suspected, from what she could see at the fort, that Americans had not the custom of marrying an entire family.

"It is really too fine a place for us."

Young Crooks laughed. Squaws had lived in the Fur Company's quarters, but he would not mention this fact to the girl.

His eyes dwelt fondly on her in the darkness, for though the fire behind her had again sunk to embers, it cast up a little glow; and he stood entirely in the star-embossed outside world. It is not safe to talk in the dark: you tell too much. The primitive instinct of truth-speaking revives in force, and the restraints of another's presence are gone. You speak from the unseen to the unseen over leveled barriers of reserve. Young Crooks had scarcely said that place was nothing, and he would rather live in that little house with Jenieve than in the Fur Company's quarters without her, when she exclaimed openly, "And have old Michel Pensonneau put over you!"

The idea of Michel Pensonneau taking precedence of him as master of the cedar hut was delicious to the American, as he recalled the engagé's respectful slouch while receiving the usual bill of credit.

"One may laugh, monsieur. I laugh myself; it is better than crying. But it is the truth that Mama Lalotte is more care to me than all the boys. I have no peace except when she is asleep in bed."

"There is no harm in Madame Lalotte."

"You are right, monsieur. Jean Bati' McClure's wife puts all the mischief in her head. She would even learn to spin, if that woman would let her alone."

"And I never heard any harm of Michel Pensonneau. He is a good enough fellow, and he has more to his credit on the Company's books than any other engagé now on the island."

"I suppose you would like to have him sit and smoke his pipe the rest of his days on your doorstep?"

"No, I wouldn't," confessed the young agent. "Michel is a saving man, and he uses very mean tobacco, the cheapest in the house."

"You see how I am situated, monsieur. It is no use to talk to me."

"But Michel Pensonneau is not going to trouble you long. He has relations at Cahokia, in the Illinois Territory, and he is fitting himself out to go there to settle."

"Are you sure of this, monsieur?"

"Certainly I am, for we have already made him a bill of credit to our correspondent at Cahokia. He wants very few goods to carry across the Chicago portage."

"Monsieur, how soon does he intend to go?"

"On the first schooner that sails to the head of the lake; so he may set out any day. Michel is anxious to try life on the Mississippi, and his three years' engagement with the Company is just ended."

"I also am anxious to have him try life on the Mississippi," said Jenieve, and she drew a deep breath of relief. "Why did you not tell me this before?"

"How could I know you were interested in him?"

"He is not a bad man," she admitted kindly. "I can see that he means very well. If the McClures would go to the Illinois Territory with him— But, Monsieur Crooks," Jenieve asked sharply, "do people sometimes make sudden marriages?"

"In my case they have not," sighed the young man. "But I think well of sudden marriages myself. The priest comes to the island this week."

"Yes, and I must take the children to confession."

"What are you going to do with me, Jenieve?"

"I am going to say good-night to you, and shut my door." She stepped into the house.

"Not yet. It is only a little while since they fired the sunset gun at the fort. You are not kind to shut me out the moment I come."

She gave him her hand, as she always did when she said good-night, and he prolonged his hold of it.

"You are full of sweetbrier. I didn't know it grew down here on the beach."

"It never did grow here, Monsieur Crooks."

"You shall have plenty of it in your garden, when you come home with me."

"Oh, go away, and let me shut my door, monsieur. It seems no use to tell you I cannot come."

"No use at all. Until you come, then, good-night."

Seldom are two days alike on the island. Before sunrise the lost dews of paradise always sweeten those scented woods, and the birds begin to remind you of something you heard in another life, but have forgotten. Jenieve loved to open her door and surprise the east. She stepped out the next morning to fill her pail. There was a lake of translucent cloud beyond the water lake: the first unruffled, and the second wind-stirred. The sun pushed up, a flattened red ball, from the lake of steel ripples to the lake of calm clouds. Nearer, a schooner with its sails down stood black as ebony between two bars of light drawn across the water, which lay dull and bleak towards the shore. The addition of a schooner to the scattered fleet of sail-boats, bateaux, and birch canoes made Jenieve laugh. It must have arrived from Sault Ste. Marie in the night. She had hopes of getting rid of Michel Pensonneau that very day. Since he was going to Cahokia, she felt stinging regret for the way she had treated him before the whole village; yet her mother could not be sacrificed to politeness. Except his capacity for marrying, there was really no harm in the old fellow, as Monsieur Crooks had said.

The humid blockhouse and walls of the fort high above the bay began to glisten in emerging sunlight, and Jenieve determined not to be hard on Mama Lalotte that day. If Michel came to say good-by, she would shake his hand herself. It was not agreeable for a woman so fond of company to sit in the house with nobody but her daughter. Mama Lalotte did not love the pine woods, or any place where she would be alone. But Jenieve could sit and spin in solitude all day, and think of that chill silver face she had seen at Pontiac's Lookout, and the floating away of the figure, a phosphorescent bar through the trees, and of that spoken word which had denounced the French and Indians as good for nothing. She decided to tell the priest, even if he rebuked her. It did not seem any stranger to Jenieve than many things which were called natural, such as the morning miracles in the eastern sky, and the growth of the boys, her dear torments. To Jenieve's serious eyes, trained by her grandmother, it was not as strange as the sight of Mama Lalotte, a child in maturity, always craving amusement, and easily led by any chance hand.

The priest had come to Mackinac in the schooner during the night. He combined this parish with others more or less distant, and he opened the chapel and began his duties as soon as he arrived. Mama Lalotte herself offered to dress the boys for confession. She put their best clothes on them, and then she took out all her own finery. Jenieve had no suspicion while the little figure preened and burnished itself, making up for the lack of a mirror by curves of the neck to look itself well over. Mama Lalotte thought a great deal about what she wore. She was pleased, and her flaxen curls danced. She kissed Jenieve on both cheeks, as if there had been no quarrel, though unpleasant things never lingered in her memory. And she made the boys kiss Jenieve; and while they were saddened by clothes, she also made them say they were sorry about the shoes.

By sunset, the schooner, which had sat in the straits all day, hoisted its sails and rounded the hooked point of the opposite island. The gun at the fort was like a parting salute, and a shout was raised by coureurs-de-bois thronging the log wharf. They trooped up to the fur warehouse, and the sound of a fiddle and the thump of soft-shod feet were soon heard; for the French were ready to celebrate any occasion with dancing. Laughter and the high excited voices

of women also came from the little ball-room, which was only the
office of the Fur Company.

Here the engagés felt at home. The fiddler sat on the top of the
desk, and men lounging on a row of benches around the walls
sprang to their feet and began to caper at the violin's first invitation.
Such maids and wives as were nearest the building were haled in,
laughing, by their relations; and in the absence of the agents, and of
that awe which goes with making your cross-mark on a paper, a
quick carnival was held on the spot where so many solemn contracts
had been signed. An odor of furs came from the packing-rooms
around, mixed with gums and incense-like whiffs. Added to this was
the breath of the general store kept by the agency. Tobacco and
snuff, rum, chocolate, calico, blankets, wood and iron utensils, fire-
arms, West India sugar and rice,—all sifted their invisible essences
on the air. Unceiled joists showed heavy and brown overhead. But
there was no fireplace, for when the straits stood locked in ice and
the island was deep in snow, no engagé claimed admission here.
He would be a thousand miles away, toiling on snowshoes with his
pack of furs through the trees, or bargaining with trappers for his
contribution to this month of enormous traffic.

Clean buckskin legs and brand-new belted hunting-shirts whirled
on the floor, brightened by sashes of crimson or kerchiefs of orange.
Indians from the reservation on Round Island, who happened to be
standing, like statues, in front of the building, turned and looked
with lenient eye on the performance of their French brothers. The
fiddler was a nervous little Frenchman with eyes like a weasel, and
he detected Jenieve Lalotte putting her head into the room. She
glanced from figure to figure of the dancers, searching through the
twilight for what she could not find; but before he could call her
she was off. None of the men, except a few Scotch-French, were
very tall, but they were a handsome, muscular race, fierce in enjoyment, yet with a languor which prolonged it, and gave grace to
every picturesque pose. Not one of them wanted to pain Lalotte's
girl, but, as they danced, a joyful fellow would here and there spring
high above the floor and shout, "Good voyage to Michel Pensonneau
and his new family!" They had forgotten the one who amused
them yesterday, and remembered only the one who amused them
to-day.

Jenieve struck on Jean Bati' McClure's door, and faced his wife,
speechless, pointing to the schooner ploughing southward.

"Yes, she's gone," said Jean Bati' McClure's wife, "and the boys
with her."

The confidante came out on the step, and tried to lay her hand on Jenieve's shoulder, but the girl moved backward from her.

"Now let me tell you, it is a good thing for you, Jenieve Lalotte. You can make a fine match of your own to-morrow. It is not natural for a girl to live as you have lived. You are better off without them."

"But my mother has left me!"

"Well, I am sorry for you; but you were hard on her."

"I blame you, madame!"

"You might as well blame the priest, who thought it best not to let them go unmarried. And she has taken a much worse man than Michel Pensonneau in her time."

"My mother and my brothers have left me here alone," repeated Jenieve; and she wrung her hands and put them over her face. The trouble was so overwhelming that it broke her down before her enemy.

"Oh, don't take it to heart," said Jean Bati' McClure's wife, with ready interest in the person nearest at hand. "Come and eat supper with my man and me to-night, and sleep in our house if you are afraid."

Jenieve leaned her forehead against the hut, and made no reply to these neighborly overtures.

"Did she say nothing at all about me, madame?"

"Yes; she was afraid you would come at the last minute and take her by the arm and walk her home. You were too strict with her, and that is the truth. She was glad to get away to Cahokia. They say it is fine in the Illinois Territory. You know she is fond of seeing the world."

The young supple creature trying to restrain her shivers and sobs of anguish against the bark house side was really a moving sight; and Jean Bati' McClure's wife, flattening a masculine upper lip with resolution, said promptly,—

"I am going this moment to the Fur Company's quarters to send young Monsieur Crooks after you."

At that Jenieve fled along the beach and took to the bushes. As she ran, weeping aloud like a child, she watched the lessening schooner; and it seemed a monstrous thing, out of nature, that her mother was on that little ship, fleeing from her, with a thoughtless face set smiling towards a new world. She climbed on, to keep the schooner in sight, and made for Pontiac's Lookout, reckless of what she had seen there.

The distant canvas became one leaning sail, and then a speck, and then nothing. There was an afterglow on the water which turned it to a wavering pavement of yellow-pink sheen. In that clear, high atmosphere, mainland shores and islands seemed to throw out the evening purples from themselves, and thus to slowly reach for one another and form darkness. Jenieve had lain on the grass, crying, "O Mama—François—Toussaint—Gabriel!" But she sat up at last, with her dejected head on her breast, submitting to the pettiness and treachery of what she loved. Bats flew across the open place. A sudden rankness of sweetbrier, taking her breath away by its icy puff, reminded her of other things, and she tried to get up and run. Instead of running she seemed to move sidewise out of herself, and saw Pontiac standing on the edge of the cliff. His head turned from St. Ignace to the reviving fires on Round Island, and slowly back again from Round Island to St. Ignace. Jenieve felt as if she were choking, but again she asked out of her heart to his,—

"Monsieur the chief Pontiac, what ails the French and Indians?"

He floated around to face her, the high ridges of his bleached features catching light; but this time he showed only dim dead eyes. His head sunk on his breast, and Jenieve could see the fronds of the feathers he wore traced indistinctly against the sky. The dead eyes searched for her and could not see her; he whispered hoarsely to himself, "Malatat!"

The voice of the living world calling her name sounded directly afterwards in the woods, and Jenieve leaped as if she were shot. She had the instinct that her lover must not see this thing, for there were reasons of race and religion against it. But she need not have feared that Pontiac would show himself, or his long and savage mourning for the destruction of the red man, to any descendant of the English. As the bushes closed behind her she looked back: the phosphoric blur was already so far in the west that she could hardly be sure she saw it again. And the young agent of the Fur Company, breaking his way among leaves, met her with both hands; saying gayly, to save her the shock of talking about her mother:—

"Come home, come home, my sweetbrier maid. No wonder you smell of sweetbrier. I am rank with it myself, rubbing against the dewy bushes."

JOEL CHANDLER HARRIS

★ ★ ★

In 1862 a rural newspaper owner encouraged Joel Chandler Harris (1848-1908), then a printer's apprentice, to read extensively and to study Georgia Negro life. From this training eventually grew the Uncle Remus animal fables, containing a subtle characterization of the Old Negro raconteur against a plantation background, and accurately presenting Negro folklore, habits, and dialect. Quite different in mood are the seven collections of realistic short stories about plantation servants and owners, and emotionally primitive Georgia mountaineers who cling tenaciously to their ancient freedom. Although these stories won less fame than the fables, they are localized as folklore rarely is, and they reveal Harris's awareness of Georgia social conditions and deep love for the mountain countryside. A practicing journalist throughout life, Harris was associated a quarter century with the *Atlanta Constitution*. "Trouble on Lost Mountain" is reprinted from *Free Joe* (1887) by permission of Charles Scribner's Sons, and "Ananias" from *Balaam and His Master* (1891) by permission of Houghton Mifflin Company.

★ ★ ★

Trouble on Lost Mountain

THERE is no doubt that when Miss Babe Hightower stepped out on the porch, just after sunrise one fine morning in the spring of 1876, she had the opportunity of enjoying a scene as beautiful as any that nature offers to the human eye. She was poised, so to speak, on the shoulder of Lost Mountain, a spot made cheerful and hospitable by her father's industry, and by her own inspiring presence. The scene, indeed, was almost portentous in its beauty. Away above her the summer of the mountain was bathed in sunlight, while in the valley below the shadows of dawn were still hovering—a slow-moving sea of transparent gray, touched here and there with silvery reflections of light. Across the face of the mountain that lifted itself to the skies, a belated cloud trailed its wet skirts, revealing, as it fled westward, a panorama of exquisite loveliness. The fresh, tender foliage of the young pines, massed here and there against the mountain side, moved and swayed in the morning breeze until it seemed to be a part of the atmosphere, a pale-green mist that would presently mount into the upper air and melt away. On a dead pine a quarter of a mile away, a turkey-buzzard sat with wings outspread to catch the warmth of the sun; while far above him, poised in the illimitable blue, serene, almost motionless, as though swung in the centre of space, his mate overlooked the world. The wild honeysuckles clambered from bush to bush, and from tree to tree, mingling their faint, sweet perfume with the delicious odors that seemed to rise from the valley, and float down from the mountain to meet in a little whirlpool of fragrance in the porch where Miss Babe Hightower stood. The flowers and the trees could speak for themselves; the slightest breeze gave them motion: but the majesty of the mountain was voiceless; its beauty was forever motionless. Its silence seemed more suggestive than the lapse of time, more profound than a prophet's vision of eternity, more mysterious than any problem of the human mind.

It is fair to say, however, that Miss Babe Hightower did not survey the panorama that lay spread out below her, around her, and above her, with any peculiar emotions. She was not without sentiment, for she was a young girl just budding into womanhood, but all the scenery that the mountain or the valley could show was as familiar to her as the fox-hounds that lay curled up in the fence-corners, or the fowls that crowed and clucked and cackled in the yard. She had discovered, indeed, that the individuality of the mountain was impressive, for she was always lonely and melancholy when away from it; but she viewed it, not as a picturesque affair to wonder at, but as a companion with whom she might hold communion. The mountain was something more than a mountain to her. Hundreds of times, when a little child, she had told it her small troubles, and it had seemed to her that the spirit of comfort dwelt somewhere near the precipitous summit. As she grew older the mountain played a less important part in her imagination, but she continued to regard it with a feeling of fellowship which she never troubled herself to explain or define.

Nevertheless, she did not step out on the porch to worship at the shrine of the mountain, or to enjoy the marvelous picture that nature presented to the eye. She went out in obedience to the shrilly uttered command of her mother:

"Run, Babe, run! That plegged old cat's a-tryin' to drink out'n the water-bucket. Fling a cheer at 'er! Sick the dogs on 'er."

The cat, understanding the situation, promptly disappeared when it saw Babe, and the latter had nothing to do but make such demonstrations as are natural to youth, if not to beauty. She seized one of the many curious crystal formations which she had picked up on the mountain, and employed for various purposes of ornamentation, and sent it flying after the cat. She threw with great strength and accuracy, but the cat was gone. The crystal went zooning into the fence-corner where one of the hounds lay; and this sensitive creature, taking it for granted that he had been made the special object of attack, set up a series of loud yells by way of protest. This aroused the rest of the dogs, and in a moment that particular part of the mountain was in an uproar. Just at that instant a stalwart man came around the corner of the house. He was bareheaded, and wore neither coat nor vest. He was tall and well made, though rather too massive to be supple. His beard, which was full and flowing, was plentifully streaked with gray. His appearance would have been strikingly ferocious but for his eyes, which showed a nature at once simple and humorous—and certainly the strongly molded, square-set jaws, and the firm lips needed some such pleasant corrective.

"Great Jerusalem, Babe!" cried this mild-eyed giant. "What could 'a' possessed you to be a-chunkin' ole Blue that away? Ag'in bullaces is ripe you'll git your heart sot on 'possum, an' whar' is the 'possum comin' from ef ole Blue's laid up? Blame my hide ef you ain't a-cuttin' up some mighty quare capers fer a young gal."

"Why, Pap!" exclaimed Babe, as soon as she could control her laughter, "that rock didn't tetch ole Blue. He's sech a make-believe, I'm a great mind to hit him a clip jest to show you how he can go on."

"Now, don't do that, honey," said her father. "Ef you want to chunk anybody, chunk me. I kin holler lots purtier'n ole Blue. An' ef you don't want to chunk me, chunk your mammy fer ole acquaintance' sake. She's big an' fat."

"Oh, Lordy!" exclaimed Mrs. Hightower from the inside of the house. "Don't set her atter me, Abe—don't, fer mercy's sake. Get her in the notion, an' she'll be a-yerkin' me aroun' thereckly like I wuz a rag-baby. I'm a-gittin' too ole fer ter be romped aroun' by a great big double-j'inted gal like Babe. Projick wi' 'er yourself, but make 'er let me alone."

Abe turned and went around the house again, leaving his daughter standing on the porch, her cheeks glowing, and her black eyes sparkling with laughter. Babe loitered on the porch a moment, looking into the valley. The gray mists had lifted themselves into the upper air, and the atmosphere was so clear that the road leading to the mountain could be followed by the eye, save where it ran under the masses of foliage; and it seemed to be a most devious and versatile road, turning back on itself at one moment only to plunge boldly forward the next. Nor was it lacking in color. On the levels it was of dazzling whiteness, shining like a pool of water; but at points where it made a visible descent it was alternately red and gray. Something or other on this variegated road attracted Miss Babe's attention, for she shaded her eyes with her hand, and leaned forward. Presently she cried out:

"Pap!—oh, pap! there's a man a-ridin' up Peevy's Ridge."

This information was repeated by Babe's mother; and in a few moments the porch, which was none too commodious, though it was very substantial, was occupied by the entire Hightower family, which included Grandsir Hightower, a white-haired old man, whose serenity seemed to be borrowed from another world. Mrs. Hightower herself was a stout, motherly-looking woman, whose whole appearance betokened contentment, if not happiness. Abe shaded his eyes with his broad hand, and looked toward Peevy's Ridge.

"I reckon maybe it's Tuck Peevy hisse'f," Mrs. Hightower remarked.

"That's who I 'lowed hit wiz," said Grandsir Hightower, in the tone of one who had previously made up his mind.

"Well, I reckon I ought to know Tuck Peevy," exclaimed Babe.

"That's so," said Grandsir Hightower. "Babe oughter know Tuck. She oughter know him certain an' shore; bekaze he's bin a-floppin' in an' out er this house ever' Sunday fer mighty nigh two year'. Some sez he likes Babe, an' some sez he likes Susan's fried chicken. Now, in my day and time—"

"He's in the dreen now," said Babe, interrupting her loquacious grandparent, who threatened to make some embarrassing remark. "He's a-ridin' a gray."

"He's a mighty early bird," said Abe, "less'n he's a-headin' fer the furder side. Maybe he's a revenue man," he continued. "They say they're a-gwine to heat the hills mighty hot from this on."

"You hain't got nothing gwine on down on the branch, is you, Abe?" inquired Grandsir Hightower, with pardonable solicitude.

"Well," said Abe evasively, "I hain't kindled no fires yit, but you better b'lieve I'm a-gwine to keep my beer from sp'ilin'. The way I do my countin', one tub of beer is natchally wuth two revenue chaps."

By this time the horseman who had attracted Babe's attention came into view again. Abe studied him a moment, and remarked:

"That hoss steps right along, an' the chap a-straddle of him is got on store-clo'es. Fetch me my rifle, Babe. I'll meet that feller half-way an' make some inquirements about his famerly, an' maybe I'll fetch a squir'l back."

With this Abe called to his dogs, and started off.

"Better keep your eye open, Pap," cried Sis. "Maybe it's the sheriff."

Abe paused a moment, and then pretended to be hunting a stone with which to demolish his daughter, whereupon Babe ran laughing into the house. The allusion to the sheriff was a stock joke in the Hightower household, though none of them made such free use of it as Babe, who was something more than a privileged character, so far as her father was concerned. On one occasion shortly after the war, Abe had gone to the little county town on business, and had been vexed into laying rough hands on one of the prominent citizens who was a trifle under the influence of liquor. A warrant was issued, and Dave McLendon, the sheriff of the county, a stumpy little man, whose boldness and prudence made him the terror of criminals, was sent to serve it. Abe, who was on the lookout for some such visitation, saw him coming, and prepared himself. He stood in the doorway, with his rifle flung carelessly across his left arm.

"Hold on thar, Dave!" he cried, as the latter came up. The sheriff, knowing his man, halted.

"I hate to fling away my manners, Dave," he went on, "but folks is gittin' to be mighty funny these days. A man's obleeged to s'arch his best frien's 'fore he kin find out the'r which aways. Dave, what sort of a dockyment is you got ag'in' me?"

"I got a warrant, Abe," said the sheriff, pleasantly.

"Well, Dave, hit won't fetch me," said Abe.

"Oh, yes!" said the sheriff. "Yes, it will, Abe. I bin a-usin' these kind er warrants a mighty long time, an' they fetches a feller every whack."

"Now, I'll tell you what, Dave," said Abe, patting his rifle, "I got a dockyment here that'll fetch you a blame sight quicker'n your dockyment'll fetch me; an' I tell you right now, plain an' flat, I hain't a-gwine to be drug aroun' an' slapped in jail."

The sheriff leaned carelessly against the rail fence in the attitude of a man who is willing to argue an interesting question.

"Well, I tell you how I feel about it, Abe," said the sheriff, speaking very slowly. "You kin shoot me, but you can't shoot the law. Bang away at me, an' thar's another warrant atter you. This yer one what I'm already got don't amount to shucks, so you better fling on your coat, saddle your horse, an' go right along wi' me thes es neighborly ez you please."

"Dave," said Abe, "if you come in at that gate you er a goner."

"Well, Abe," the sheriff replied, "I 'lowed you'd kick; I know what human natur' on these hills is, an' so I thes axed some er the boys to come along. They er right down thar in the holler. They ain't got no mo' idea what I come fer'n the man in the moon; yit they'd make a mighty peart posse. Tooby shore, a great big man like you ain't afeard fer ter face a little bit er law."

Abe Hightower hesitated a moment, and then went into the house. In a few minutes he issued forth and went out to the gate where the sheriff was. The faces of the two men were a study. Neither betrayed any emotion nor alluded to the warrant. The sheriff asked after the "crap"; and Abe told him it was "middlin' peart," and asked him to go into the house and make himself at home until the horse could be saddled. After a while the two rode away. Once during the ride Abe said:

"I'm mighty glad it wa'n't that feller what run ag'in' you last fall, Dave."

"Why?" asked the sheriff.

"Bekaze I'd 'a' plugged him, certain an' shore," said Abe.

"Well," said the sheriff, laughing, "I wuz a-wishin' mighty hard thes about that time that the t'other feller had got 'lected."

The warrant amounted to nothing, and Abe was soon at home with his family; but it suited his high-spirited daughter to twit him occasionally because of his tame surrender to the sheriff, and it suited Dave to treat the matter good-humoredly.

Abe Hightower took his way down the mountain; and about two miles from his house, as the road ran, he met the stranger who had attracted Babe's attention. He was a handsome young fellow, and he was riding a handsome horse—a gray, that was evidently used to sleeping in a stable where there was plenty of feed in the trough.

The rider also had a well-fed appearance. He sat his horse somewhat jauntily, and there was a jocund expression in his features very pleasing to behold. He drew rein as he saw Abe, and gave a military salute in a careless, offhand way that was in strict keeping with his appearance.

"Good morning, sir," he said.

"Howdy?" said Abe.

"Fine day this."

"Well, what little I've saw of it is purty tollerbul."

The young fellow laughed, and his laughter was worth hearing. It had the ring of youth in it.

"Do you chance to know a Mr. Hightower?" he asked, throwing a leg over the pommel of the saddle.

"Do he live anywheres aroun' in these parts?" Abe inquired.

"So I'm told."

"Well, the reason I ast," said Abe, leaning his rifle against a tree, "is bekaze they mought be more'n one Hightower runnin' loose."

"You don't know him, then?"

"I know one on 'em. Any business wi' him?"

"Well, yes—a little. I was told he lived on this road. How far is his house?"

"Well, I'll tell you"—Abe took off his hat and scratched his head—"some folks mought take a notion hit wuz a long ways off, an' then, ag'in, yuther folks mought take a notion that hit wuz lots nigher. Hit's accordin' to the way you look at it."

"Is Mr. Hightower at home?" inquired the stranger, regarding Abe with some curiosity.

"Well," said Abe cautiously, "I don't reckon he's right slam bang at home, but I lay he ain't fur off."

"If you happen to see him, pray tell him there's a gentleman at his house who would like very much to see him."

"Well, I tell you what, mister," said Abe, speaking very slowly. "You're a mighty nice young feller—anybody kin shet the'r eyes and see that—but folks 'roun' here is mighty kuse; they is that away. Ef I was you, I'd thes turn right 'roun' in my tracks 'n' let that ar Mister Hightower alone. I wouldn't pester wi' 'im. He hain't no fitten company fer you."

"Oh, but I must see him," said the stranger. "I have business with him. Why, they told me down in the valley that Hightower, in many respects, is the best man in the county."

Abe smiled for the first time. It was the ghost of a smile.

"Shoo!" he exclaimed. "They don't know him down thar nigh as good as he's know'd up here. An' that hain't all. Thish yer Mister

Hightower you er talkin' about is got a mighty bad case of measles at his house. You'd be ableedze to ketch 'em ef you went thar."

"I've had the measles," said the stranger.

"But these here measles," persisted Abe, half shutting his eyes and gazing at the young man steadily, "kin be cotched twicet. Thayer wuss 'n the smallpox—lots wuss."

"My dear sir, what do you mean?" the young man inquired, observing the significant emphasis of the mountaineer's language.

"Hit's thes like I tell you," said Abe. "Looks like folks has mighty bad luck when they go a-rippitin' hether an' yan on the mounting. It hain't been sech a monst'us long time sense one er them revenue fellers come a-paradin' up thish yer same road, a-makin' inquirements fer Hightower. *He* cotch the measles; bless you, he took an' cotch 'em by the time he got in hailin' distance of Hightower's, an' he had to be toted down. I disremember his name, but he wuz a mighty nice-lookin' young feller, peart an' soople, an' thes about your size an' weight."

"It was no doubt a great pity about the revenue chap," said the young man sarcastically.

"Lor', yes!" exclaimed Abe seriously; "lots er nice folks must 'a' cried about that man!"

"Well," said the other, smiling, "I must see Hightower. I guess he's a nicer man than his neighbors think he is."

"Shoo!" said Abe, "he hain't a bit nicer'n what I am, an' I lay he hain't no purtier. What mought be your name, mister?"

"My name is Chichester, and I'm buying land for some Boston people. I want to buy some land right on this mountain if I can get it cheap enough."

"Jesso," said Abe, "but wharbouts in thar do Hightower come in?"

"Oh, he knows all about the mountain, and I want to ask his advice and get his opinions," said Chichester.

Something about Mr. Chichester seemed to attract Abe Hightower. Perhaps it was the young fellow's fresh, handsome appearance; perhaps it was his free-and-easy attitude, suggestive of the commercial tourist, that met the approbation of the mountaineer. At any rate, Abe smiled upon the young man in a fatherly way and said: " 'Twixt you an' me an' yon pine, you hain't got no furder to go fer to strike up wi' Hightower. I'm the man you er atter."

Chichester regarded him with some degree of amazement.

"My dear sir," he exclaimed, "why should you desire to play the sphinx?"

"Spinks?" said Abe, with something like a grimace; "the Spinks famerly lived furder up the mounting, but they er done bin weeded out by the revenue men too long ago to talk about. The ole man's in jail in Atlanty er some'rs else, the boys is done run'd off, an' the gal's a trollop. No Spinks in mine, cap', *ef* you please!"

Chichester laughed at the other's earnestness. He mistook it for drollery.

"I let you know, cap'," Abe went on, "you can't be boss er your own doin's an' give ever' passin' man your name."

"Well, I'm very glad to meet you," said Chichester heartily; "I'll have a good deal of business in this neighborhood first and last, and I'm told there isn't anything worth knowing about the mountain that you don't know."

"That kind er talk," Abe replied, "kin be run in the groun', yit I hain't a-denyin' but what I've got a kind er speakin' acquaintance wi' the neighborhood whar I'm a-livin' at. Ef you er huntin' my house, thes drive right on. I'll be thar ag'in you git thar."

Chichester found a very cordial welcome awaiting him when he arrived at Hightower's house. Even the dogs were friendly, and the big cat came out from its hiding-place to rub against his legs as he sat on the little porch.

"By the time you rest your face an' han's," said Abe, "I reckon breakfast'll be ready."

Chichester, who was anxious to give no trouble, explained that he had had a cup of coffee at Peevy's before starting up the mountain. He said, moreover, that the mountain was so bracing that he felt as if he could fast a week and still fatten.

"Well, sir," Abe remarked, "hit's mighty little we er got to offer, an' that little's mighty common, but, sech as 'tis, you er more'n welcome. Hit's diffunt wi' me when the mornin' air blows at me. Hit makes me wanter nibble at somepin'. I dunner whar you come from, an' I ain't makin' no inquirements, but down in these parts you can't spat a man harder betwixt the eyes than to set back an' not break bread wi' 'im."

Mr. Chichester had been warned not to wound the hospitality of the simple people among whom he was going, and he was quick to perceive that his refusal to "break bread" with the Hightowers would be taken too seriously. Whereupon, he made a most substantial apology—an apology that took the shape of a ravenous appetite, and did more than justice to Mrs. Hightower's fried chicken, crisp biscuits, and genuine coffee. Mr. Chichester also made himself as agreeable as he knew how, and he was so pleased with the impression he made that he, on his side, admitted to himself that the

Hightowers were charmingly quaint, especially the shy girl of whom he caught a brief glimpse now and then as she handed her mother fresh supplies of chicken and biscuits.

There was nothing mysterious connected with the visit of Mr. Chichester to Lost Mountain. He was the agent of a company of Boston capitalists who were anxious to invest money in Georgia marble quarries, and Chichester was on Lost Mountain for the purpose of discovering the marble beds that had been said by some to exist there. He had the versatility of a modern young man, being something of a civil engineer and something of a geologist; in fine, he was one of the many "general utility" men that improved methods enable the high schools and colleges to turn out. He was in the habit of making himself agreeable wherever he went, but behind his levity and general good-humor there was a good deal of seriousness and firmness of purpose.

He talked with great freedom to the Hightowers, giving a sort of commercial coloring, so to speak, to the plans of his company with respect to land investments on Lost Mountain; but he said nothing about his quest for marble.

"The Lord send they won't be atter fetchin' the railroad kyars among us," said Grandsir Hightower fervently.

"Well, sir," said Chichester, "there isn't much danger."

"Now, I dunno 'bout that," said the old man querulously, "I dunno 'bout that. They're gittin' so these days they'll whirl in an' do e'enamost anything what you don't want 'em to do. I kin stan' out thar in the hoss-lot any cle'r day an' see the smoke er their ingines, an' sometimes hit looks like I kin hear 'em snort an' cough. They er plenty nigh enough. The Lord send they won't fetch 'em no nigher. Fum Giner'l Jackson's time plump tell now, they ere bin a-fetchin' destruction to the country. You'll see it. I mayn't see it myself, but you'll see it. Fust hit was Giner'l Jackson an' the bank, an' now hit's the railroad kyars. You'll see it!"

"And yet," said Chichester, turning toward the old man, as Hope might beam benignantly on the Past, "everybody and everything seems to be getting along very well. I think the only thing necessary now is to invent something or other to keep the cinders out of a man's eyes when he rides on the railroads."

"Don't let 'em fool you," said the old man earnestly. "Ever'thing's in a tangle, an' ther hain't no Whig party for to ontangle it. Giner'l Jackson an' the cussid bank is what done it."

Just then Miss Babe came out on the little porch, and seated herself on the bench that ran across one end. "Cap'," said Abe, with some show of embarrassment, as if not knowing how to get through a necessary ceremony, "this is my gal, Babe. She's the oldest and the youngest. I'm name' Abe an' she's name' Babe, sort er rimin' like."

The unaffected shyness of the young girl was pleasant to behold, and if it did not heighten her beauty, it certainly did not detract from it. It was a shyness in which there was not an awkward element, for Babe had the grace of youth and beauty, and conscious independence animated all her movements.

" 'Ceppin' me an' the ole 'oman," said Abe, "Babe is the best-lookin' one er the famerly."

The girl reddened a little, and laughed lightly with the air of one who is accustomed to give and take jokes, but said nothing.

"I heard of Miss Babe last night," said Chichester, "and I've got a message for her."

"Wait!" exclaimed Abe triumphantly; "I'll bet a hoss I kin call the name 'thout movin' out'n my cheer. Hold on!" he continued. "I'll bet another hoss I kin relate the message word for word."

Babe blushed violently, but laughed good-humoredly. Chichester adjusted himself at once to this unexpected informality, and allowed himself to become involved in it.

"Come, now!" he cried, "I'll take the bet."

"I declare!" said Mrs. Hightower, laughing, "you all oughtn' to pester Babe that way."

"Wait!" said Abe. "The name er the man what sont the word is Tuck Peevy, an' when he know'd you was a-comin' here, he sort er sidled up an' ast you for to please be so good as to tell Miss Babe he'd drap in nex' Sunday, an' see what her mammy is a-gwine ter have for dinner."

"Well, I have won the bet," said Chichester. "Mr. Peevy simply asked me to tell Miss Babe that there would be a singing at Philadelphia camp-ground Sunday. I hardly know what to do with two horses."

"Maybe you'll feel better," said Abe, "when somebody tells you that my hoss is a mule. Well, well, well!" he went on. "Tuck didn't say he was comin', but I be boun' he comes, an' more'n that, I be boun' a whole passel er gals an' boys'll foller Babe home."

"In giner'lly," said Grandsir Hightower, "I hate for to make remarks 'bout folks when they hain't settin' whar they kin hear me, but that ar Tuck Peevy is got a mighty bad eye. I hearn 'im a-quollin' wi' one er them Simmons boys las' Sunday gone wuz a week, an' I tell you he's got the Ole Boy in 'im. An' his appetite's wuss'n his eye."

"Well," said Mrs. Hightower, "nobody 'roun' here don't begrudge him his vittles, I reckon."

"Oh, by no means—by no manner er means," said the old man, suddenly remembering the presence of Chichester. "Yit they oughter be reason in all things; that's what I say—reason in all things, espeshually when hit comes to gormandizin'."

The evident seriousness of the old man was very comical. He seemed to be possessed by the unreasonable economy that not infrequently seizes on old age.

"They hain't no begrudgin' 'roun' here," he went on. "Lord! ef I'd 'a' bin a-begrudgin' I'd 'a' thes natchally bin e't up wi' begrudges. What wer' the word the poor creetur sent to Babe?"

Chichester repeated the brief and apparently uninteresting message, and Grandsir Hightower groaned dismally.

"I dunner what sot him so ag'in' Tuck Peevy," said Abe, laughing. "Tuck's e'en about the peartest chap in the settlement, an' a mighty handy man, put him whar you will."

"Why, Aberham!" exclaimed the old man, "you go on like a man what's done gone an' took leave of his sev'm senses. You dunner what sot me ag'in' the poor creetur? Why, time an' time ag'in I've tol' you it's his ongodly hankerin' atter the flesh-pots. The Bible's ag'in' it, an' I'm ag'in' it. Wharbouts is it put down that a man is ever foun' grace in the cubberd?"

"Well, I lay a man that works is boun' ter eat," said Abe.

"Oh, I hain't no 'count—I can't work," said the old man, his wrath, which had been wrought to a high pitch, suddenly taking the shape of plaintive humility. "Yit 'tain't for long. I'll soon be out'n the way, Aberham."

"Shoo!" said Abe, placing his hand affectionately on the old man's shoulder. "You er mighty nigh as spry as a kitten. Babe, honey, fill your grandsir's pipe. He's a-missin' his mornin' smoke."

Soothed by his pipe, the old man seemed to forget the existence of Tuck Peevy, and his name came up for discussion no more.

But Chichester, being a man of quick perceptions, gathered from the animosity of the old man, and the rather uneasy attitude of Miss Babe, that the discussion of Peevy's appetite had its origin in the lover-like attentions which he had been paying to the girl. Certainly Peevy was excusable, and if his attentions had been favorably received, he was to be congratulated, Chichester thought; for in all that region it would have been difficult to find a lovelier specimen of

budding womanhood than the young girl who had striven so un-
successfully to hide her embarrassment as her grandfather proceeded,
with the merciless recklessness of age, to criticize Peevy's strength
and weakness as a trencherman.

As Chichester had occasion to discover afterward, Peevy had his
peculiarities; but he did not seem to be greatly different from other
young men to be found in that region. One of his peculiarities was
that he never argued about anything. He had opinions on a great
many subjects, but his reasons for holding his opinions he kept to
himself. The arguments of those who held contrary views he would
listen to with great patience, even with interest; but his only reply
would be a slow, irritating smile and a shake of the head. Peevy
was homely, but there was nothing repulsive about his homeliness.
He was tall and somewhat angular; he was sallow; he had high cheek-
bones, and small eyes that seemed to be as alert and as watchful
as those of a ferret; and he was slow and deliberate in all his movements, taking time to digest and consider his thoughts before replying to the simplest question, and even then his reply was apt
to be evasive. But he was good-humored and obliging, and, consequently, was well thought of by his neighbors and acquaintances.

There was one subject in regard to which he made no concealment, and that was his admiration for Miss Babe Hightower. So
far as Peevy was concerned, she was the one woman in the world.
His love for her was a passion at once patient, hopeful, and innocent. He displayed his devotion less in words than in his attitude;
and so successful had he been that it was generally understood that
by camp-meeting time Miss Babe Hightower would be Mrs. Tuck
Peevy. That is to say, it was understood by all except Grandsir Hightower, who was apt to chuckle sarcastically when the subject was
broached.

"They hain't arry livin' man," he would say, "what's ever seed
anybody wi' them kind er eyes settled down an' married. No, sirs!
Hit's the vittles Tuck Peevy's atter. Why, bless your soul an' body!
he thes natchally dribbles at the mouth when he gits a whiff from the
dinner-pot."

Certainly no one would have supposed that Tuck Peevy ever had
a sentimental emotion or a romantic notion, but Grandsir Hightower did him great injustice. Behind his careless serenity he was
exceedingly sensitive. It is true he was a man difficult to arouse;
but he was what his friends called "a mighty tetchy man" on some
subjects, and one of these subjects was Babe. Another was the
revenue men. It was generally supposed by Peevy's acquaintances on

Lost Mountain that he had a moonshine apparatus over on Sweet-water; but this supposition was the result, doubtless, of his well-known prejudice against the deputies sent out to enforce the revenue laws.

It had been the intention of Chichester to remain only a few days in that neighborhood; but the Hightowers were so hospitably inclined, and the outcroppings of minerals so interesting, that his stay was somewhat prolonged. Naturally, he saw a good deal of Peevy, who knew all about the mountain, and who was frequently able to go with him on his little excursions when Abe Hightower was otherwise engaged. Naturally enough, too, Chichester saw a great deal of Babe. He was interested in her because she was young and beautiful, and because of her quaint individuality. She was not only unconventional, but charmingly so. Her crudeness and her ig-norance seemed to be merely phases of originality.

Chichester's interest in Babe was that of a studiously courteous and deferent observer, but it was jealously noted and resented by Tuck Peevy. The result of this was not at first apparent. For a time Peevy kept his jealous suggestions to himself, but he found it impossible to conceal their effect. Gradually, he held himself aloof, and finally made it a point to avoid Chichester altogether. For a time Babe made the most of her lover's jealousy. After the manner of her sex, she was secretly delighted to discover that he was furious at the thought that she might inadvertently have cast a little bit of a smile at Mr. Chichester; and on several occasions she heartily enjoyed Peevy's angry suspicions. But after a while she grew tired of such inconsistent and foolish manifestations. They made her unhappy, and she was too vigorous and too practical to submit to unhappiness with that degree of humility which her more cultivated sisters sometimes exhibit. One Sunday afternoon, knowing Chicester to be away, Tuck Peevy saun-tered carelessly into Hightower's yard, and seated himself on the steps of the little porch. It was his first visit for several days, and Babe received him with an air of subdued coolness and indifference that did credit to her sex.

"Wharbouts is your fine gent this mornin'?" inquired Peevy, after a while.

"Wharbouts is who?"

"Your fine gent wi' the sto'-clo'es on."

"I reckon you mean Cap'n Chichester, don't you?" inquired Babe innocently.

"Oh, yes!" exclaimed Peevy; "he's the chap I'm a-making my in-quirements atter."

"He's over on Sweetwater, I reckon. Leastways thar's whar he started to go."

"On Sweetwater. Oh, yes!" Peevy paused and ran his long slim fingers through his thin straight hair. "I'm mighty much afeard," he went on after a pause, "that that fine gent o' yourn is a-gwine ter turn out for to be a snake. That's what I'm afeard un."

"Well," said Babe, with irritating coolness, "he don't do any of his sneakin' aroun' here. Ef he sneaks, he goes some'ers else to sneak. He don't hang aroun' an' watch his chance to drap in an' pay his calls. I reckon he'd walk right in at the gate thar ef he know'd the Gov'ner er the State wuz a-settin' here. I'm mighty glad I hain't saw none er his sneakin'."

Peevy writhed under this comment on his own actions, but said nothing in reply.

"You don't come to see folks like you useter," said Babe, softening a little. "I reckon you er mighty busy down thar wi' your craps."

Peevy smiled until he showed his yellow teeth. It was not intended to be a pleasant smile.

"I reckon I come lots more'n I'm wanted," he replied. "I hain't got much sense," he went on, "but I got a leetle bit, an' I know when my room's wuth more'n my comp'ny."

"Your hints has got more wings'n stings," said Babe. "But ef I had in my min' what you er got in yourn—"

"Don't say the word, Babe!" exclaimed Peevy, for the first time fixing his restless eyes on her face. "Don't!"

"Yes, I'll say it," said Babe solemnly. "I oughter 'a' said it a long time ago when you wuz a-cuttin' up your capers bekaze Phli Varnadoe wuz a-comin' here to see Pap. I oughter 'a' said it then, but I'll say it now, right pine-blank. Ef I had in my min' what you er got in yourn, I wouldn't never darken this door no more."

Peevy rose, and walked up and down the porch. He was deeply moved, but his face showed his emotion only by a slight increase of sallowness. Finally he paused, looking at Babe.

"I lay you'd be mighty glad ef I didn't come no more," he said, with a half smile. "I reckon it kinder rankles you for to see old Tuck Peevy a-hangin' roun' when the t'other feller's in sight." Babe's only reply was a scornful toss of the head.

"Oh, yes!" Peevy went on, "hit rankles you might'ly; yit I lay it won't rankle you so much atter your daddy is took an' jerked off to Atlanty. I tell you, Babe, that ar man is one er the revenues—they hain't no two ways about that."

Babe regarded her angry lover seriously.

"Hit ain't no wonder you make up your min' ag'in' him when you er done made it up ag'in' me. I know in reason they must be somep'n 'nother wrong when a great big grown man kin work hisself up to holdin' spite. Goodness knows, I wish you wuz like you useter be when I fust know'd you."

Peevy's sallow face flushed a little at the remembrance of those pleasant, peaceful days; but, somehow, the memory of them had the effect of intensifying his jealous mood.

" 'Tain't me that's changed aroun'," he exclaimed passionately, "an' 'tain't the days nuther. Hit's you—you! An' that fine gent that's a-hanging roun' here is the 'casion of it. Ever'whar I go, hit's the talk. Babe, you know you er lovin' that man!"

Peevy was wide of the mark, but the accusation was so suddenly and so bluntly made that it brought the blood to Babe's face—a tremulous flush that made her fairly radiant for a moment. Undoubtedly Mr. Chichester had played a very pleasing part in her youthful imagination, but never for an instant had he superseded the homely figure of Tuck Peevy. The knowledge that she was blushing gave Babe an excuse for indignation that women are quick to take advantage of. She was so angry, indeed, that she made another mistake.

"Why, Tuck Peevy!" she cried, "you shorely must be crazy. He wouldn't wipe his feet on sech as me!"

"No," said Peevy, "I 'lowed he wouldn't, an' I 'lowed as how you wouldn't wipe your feet on me." He paused a moment, still smiling his peculiar smile. "Hit's a long ways down to Peevy, ain't it?"

"You er doin' all the belittlin'," said Babe.

"Oh, no, Babe! Ever'thing's changed. Why, even them dogs barks atter me. Ever'thing's turned wrong-sud-outerds. An' you er changed wuss'n all."

"Well, you don't reckon I'm a-gwine ter run out'n the gate thar an' fling myself at you, do you?" exclaimed Babe.

"No, I don't. I've thes come to-day for to git a cle'r understan'in'." He hesitated a moment and then went on: "Babe, will you marry me to-morrow?" He asked the question with more eagerness than he had yet displayed.

"No, I won't!" exclaimed Babe, "ner the nex' day nuther. The man I marry'll have a lots better opinion of me than what you er got."

Babe was very indignant, but she paused to see what effect her words would have. Peevy rubbed his hands nervously together, but he made no response. His serenity was more puzzling than that of the mountain. He still smiled vaguely, but it was not a pleasing smile. He looked hard at Babe for a moment, and then down at his clumsy feet. His agitation was manifest, but it did not take the shape of words. In the trees overhead two jays were quarreling with a catbird, and in the upper air a bee-martin was fiercely pursuing a sparrow-hawk.

"Well," he said, after a while, "I reckon I better be gwine."

"Wait till your hurry's over," said Babe, in a gentler tone.

Peevy made no reply, but passed out into the road and disappeared down the mountain. Babe followed him to the gate, and stood looking after him; but he turned his head neither to the right nor to the left, and in a little while she went into the house with her head bent upon her bosom. She was weeping. Grandsir Hightower, who had shuffled out on the porch to sun himself, stared at the girl with amazement.

"Why, honey!" he exclaimed, "what upon the top side er the yeth ails you?"

"Tuck has gone home mad, an' he won't never come back no more," she cried.

"What's the matter wi' 'im?"

"Oh, he's thes mad along er me."

"Well, well, well!" exclaimed the old man, fumbling feebly in his pockets for his red bandanna handkerchief, "what kind of a come-off is this? Did you ast him to stay to dinner, honey?"

"No—no; he didn't gimme a chance."

"I 'lowed you didn't," exclaimed Grandsir Hightower triumphantly. "I thes natchally 'lowed you didn't. That's what riled 'im. An' now he'll go off an' vilify you. Well, well, well! he's missed his dinner! The fust time in many's the long day. Watch 'im, Babe! Watch 'im, honey! The Ole Boy's in 'im. I know 'im; I've kep' my two eyes on 'im. For a mess er turnip-greens an' dumperlin's that man 'u'd do murder." The old man paused and looked all around, as if by that means to dissipate a suspicion that he was dreaming. "An' so Tuck missed his dinner! Tooby shore—tooby shore!"

"Oh, hit ain't that," cried Babe; "he's jealous of Cap'n Chichester."

"Why, the good Lord, honey! what makes you run on that way?"

"He tol' me so," said Babe.

"Jealous!" exclaimed Grandsir Hightower, "jealous er that young feller! Merciful powers, honey! he's a-begrudgin' 'im the vittles what he eats. I know'd it the minnit I seed 'im come a-sa'nterin' in the yard. Lord, Lord! I wish in my soul the poor creetur could git a chance at one er them ar big Whig barbecues what they useter have."

But there was small consolation in all this for Babe; and she went into the house, where her forlorn appearance attracted the attention of her mother. "Why, Babe! what in the worl'!" exclaimed this practical woman, dropping her work in amazement. "What in the name er sense ails you?" Babe had no hesitation in telling her mother the facts.

"Well, my goodness!" was Mrs. Hightower's comment, "I wouldn't go aroun' whinin' about it, ef I wuz you—that I wouldn't. Nobody never ketched me whinin' 'roun' atter your pappy 'fore we wuz married, an' he wuz lots purtier than what Tuck Peevy is. When your pappy got tetchy, I thes says to myself, s'I: 'Ef I'm wuth havin', I'm wuth scramblin' atter;' an' ef your pappy hadn't 'a' scrambled an' scuffled 'roun' he wouldn't 'a' got me nuther, ef I do up an' say it myself. I'd a heap druther see you fillin' them slays an' a-fixin' up for to weave your pappy some shirts, than to see you a-whinin' 'roun' atter any chap on the top side er the yeth, let 'lone Tuck Peevy."

There was little consolation even in this, but Babe went about her simple duties with some show of spirit; and when her father and Chichester returned from their trip on Sweetwater, it would have required a sharp eye to discover that Babe regarded herself as "wearing the green willow." For a few days she avoided Chichester, as if to prove her loyalty to Peevy; but as Peevy was not present to approve her conduct or to take advantage of it, she soon grew tired of playing an unnecessary part. Peevy persisted in staying away; and the result was that Babe's anger—a healthy quality in a young girl —got the better of her grief. Then wonder took the place of anger; but behind it all was the hope that before many days Peevy would saunter into the house, armed with his inscrutable smile, and inquire, as he had done a hundred times before, how long before dinner would be ready. This theory was held by Grandsir Hightower, but, as it was a very plausible one, Babe adopted it as her own.

Meanwhile, it is not to be supposed that two lovers, one sulking and the other sighing, had any influence on the season. The spring had made some delay in the valley before taking complete possession of the mountain, but this delay was not significant. Even on the mountain, the days began to suggest the ardor of summer. The air was alternately warm and hazy, and crisp and clear. One day Kenesaw would cast aside its asmospheric trappings, and appear to lie within speaking distance of Hightower's door; the next, it would withdraw behind its blue veil, and seem far enough away to belong to another world. On Hightower's farm the corn was high enough to whet its green sabres against the wind. One evening Chichester, Hightower, and Babe sat on the little porch with their faces turned toward Kenesaw. They had been watching a line of blue smoke on the mountain in the distance; and, as the twilight deepened into dusk, they saw that the summit of Kenesaw was crowned by a thin fringe of fire. As the darkness gathered, the bright belt of flame projected against the vast expanse of night seemed to belong to the vision of St. John.

"It looks like a picture out of the Bible," suggested Chichester somewhat vaguely.

"It's wuss'n that, I reckon," said Abe. "Some un's a-losin' a mighty sight of fencin'; an' timber's timber these days, lemme tell you."

"Maybe some un's a-burnin' bresh," said Babe.

"Bless you! they don't pile bresh in a streak a mile long," said Abe.

The thin line of fire crept along slowly, and the people on the little porch sat and watched it. Occasionally it would crawl to the top of a dead pine, and leave a fiery signal flaming in the air.

"What is the matter with Peevy?" asked Chichester. "I met him on the mountain the other day, and he seemed not to know me."

"He don't know anybody aroun' here," said Babe with a sigh.

"Hit's thes some er his an' Babe's capers," Hightower remarked with a laugh. "They er bin a-cuttin' up this away now gwine on two year'. I reckon ag'in' camp-meetin' time Tuck'll drap in an' make hisself know'd. Gals and boys is mighty funny wi' the'r gwines-on."

After a little, Abe went into the house, and left the young people to watch the fiery procession on Kenesaw.

"The next time I see Peevy," said Chichester gallantly, "I'll take him by the sleeve, and show him the road to Beauty's bower."

"Well, you nee'nter pester wi' 'im on account of me," said Babe. Chichester laughed. The fact that so handsome a girl as Babe should deliberately fall in love with so lank and ungainly a person as Tuck Peevy seemed to him to be one of the problems that philosophers ought to concern themselves with; but, from his point of view, the fact that Babe had not gradually faded away, according to the approved rules of romance, was entirely creditable to human nature on the mountain. A candle, burning in the room that Chichester occupied, shone through the window faintly, and fell on Babe, while Chichester sat in the shadow. As they were talking, a mocking-bird in the apple trees awoke, and poured into the ear of night a flood of delicious melody. Hearing this, Babe seized Chichester's hat, and placed it on her head.

"There must be some omen in that," said Chichester.

"They say," said Babe, laughing merrily, "that ef a gal puts on a man's hat when she hears a mocker sing at night, she'll get married that year an' do well."

"Well, I'm sorry I haven't got a bonnet to put on," exclaimed Chichester.

"Oh, it don't work that away!" cried Babe.

The mocking-bird continued to sing, and finally brought its concert to a close by giving a most marvelous imitation of the liquid, silvery chimes of the wood-thrush.

There was a silence for one brief moment. Then there was a red flash under the apple trees followed by the sharp crack of a rifle. There was another brief moment of silence, and then the young girl sighed softly, leaned forward, and fell from her chair.

"What's this?" cried Abe, coming to the door.

"The Lord only knows!" exclaimed Chichester. "Look at your daughter!"

Abe stepped forward, and touched the girl on the shoulder. Then he shook her gently, as he had a thousand times when rousing her from sleep.

"Babe! git up! Git up, honey, an' go in the house. You ought to 'a' been abed long ago. Git up, honey." Chichester stood like one paralyzed. For the moment he was incapable of either speech or action.

"I know what she's atter," said Abe tenderly. "You wouldn't believe it skacely, but this yer great big chunk of a gal wants her ole pappy to pick her up an' tote her thes like he useter when she was er little bit of a scrap."

"I think she has been shot," said Chichester. To his own ears his voice seemed to be the voice of some other man.

"Shot!" exclaimed Abe. "Why, who's a-gwine to shoot Babe? Lord, Cap'n! you dunner nothin' 'tall 'bout Babe ef you talk that away.— Come on, honey." With that Abe lifted his child in his arms, and carried her into the house. Chichester followed. All his faculties were benumbed, and he seemed to be walking in a dream. It seemed that no such horrible confusion as that by which he was surrounded could have the remotest relation to reality.

Nevertheless, it did not add to his surprise and consternation to find, when Abe had placed the girl on her bed, that she was dead.

A little red spot on her forehead, half-hidden by the glossy curling hair, showed that whoever held the rifle aimed it well.

"Why, honey," said Abe, wiping away the slight blood-stain that showed itself, "you struck your head a'in' a nail. Git up! you oughtn't to be a-gwine on this away before comp'ny."

"I tell you she is dead!" cried Chichester. "She has been murdered!" The girl's mother had already realized this fact, and her tearless grief was something pitiful to behold. The gray-haired grandfather had also realized it.

"I'd druther see her a-lyin' thar dead," he exclaimed, raising his weak and trembling hands heavenward, "than to see her Tuck Peevy's wife."

"Why, gentermen!" exclaimed Abe, "how *kin* she be dead? I oughter know my own gal, I reckon. Many's an' many's the time she's worried me, a-playin' 'possum, an' many's an' many's the time has I sot by her waitin' tell she let on to wake up. Don't you all pester wi' her. She'll wake up therreckly."

At this juncture Tuck Peevy walked into the room. There was a strange glitter in his eyes, a new energy in his movements. Chichester sprang at him, seized him by the throat, and dragged him to the bedside.

"You cowardly, skulking murderer!" he exclaimed, "see what you have done!"

Peevy's sallow face grew ashen. He seemed to shrink and collapse under Chichester's hand. His breath came thick and short. His long, bony fingers clutched nervously at his clothes.

"I aimed at the hat!" he exclaimed huskily.

He would have leaned over the girl, but Chichester flung him away from the bedside, and he sank down in a corner, moaning and shaking. Abe took no notice of Peevy's entrance, and paid no attention to the crouching figure mumbling in the corner, except, perhaps, so far as he seemed to recognize in Chichester's attack on Peevy a somewhat vigorous protest against his own theory; for, when there was comparative quiet in the room, Hightower raised himself, and exclaimed, in a tone that showed both impatience and excitement:

"Why, great God A'mighty, gentermen, don't go on that way! They hain't no harm done. Thes let us alone. Me an' Babe's all right. She's bin a-playin' this away ev'ry sence she wuz a little bit of a gal. Don't less make her mad, gentermen, bekaze ef we do she'll take plum tell day atter to-morrer for to come 'roun' right."

Looking closely at Hightower, Chichester could see that his face was colorless. His eyes were sunken, but shone with a peculiar brilliancy, and great beads of perspiration stood on his forehead. His whole appearance was that of a man distraught. Here was another tragedy!

Seeking a momentary escape from the confusion and perplexity into which he had been plunged by the horrible events of the night, Chichester passed out into the yard, and stood bareheaded in the cool wind that was faintly stirring among the trees. The stars shone remote and tranquil, and the serenity of the mountain, the awful silence that seemed to be, not the absence of sound, but the presence of some spiritual entity, gave assurance of peace. Out there, in the cold air, or in the wide skies, or in the vast gulf of night, there was nothing to suggest either pity or compassion—only the mysterious tranquillity of nature.

This was the end, so far as Chichester knew. He never entered the Hightower house again. Something prompted him to saddle his horse and ride down the mountain. The tragedy and its attendant troubles were never reported in the newspapers. The peace of the mountain remained undisturbed, its silence unbroken.

But should Chichester, who at last accounts was surveying a line of railway in Mexico, ever return to Lost Mountain, he would find Tuck Peevy a gaunt and shrunken creature, working on the Hightower farm, and managing such of its small affairs as call for management. Sometimes, when the day's work is over, and Peevy sits at the fireside saying nothing, Abe Hightower will raise a paralytic hand, and cry out as loud as he can that it's almost time for Babe to quit playing 'possum. At such times we may be sure that, so far as Peevy is concerned, there is still trouble on Lost Mountain.

Ananias

I

MIDDLE GEORGIA, after Sherman passed through on his famous march to the sea, was full of the direst confusion and despair, and there were many sad sights to be seen. A wide strip of country with desolate plantations, and here and there a lonely chimney standing sentinel over a pile of blackened and smouldering ruins, bore melancholy testimony to the fact that war is a very serious matter. All this is changed now, of course. The section through which the grim commander pushed his way to the sea smiles under the applica-

tion of new and fresher energies. We have discovered that war, horrible as it is, sometimes drags at its bloody tumbril wheel certain
fructifying and fertilizing forces. If this were not so, the contest in
which the South suffered the humiliation of defeat, and more, would
have been a very desperate affair indeed. The troubles of that unhappy time—its doubts, its difficulties, and its swift calamities—will
never be known to posterity, for they have never been adequately
described.

It was during this awful period—that is to say, in January, 1866—
that Lawyer Terrell, of Macon, made the acquaintance of his friend
Ananias. In the midst of the desolation to be seen on every hand, this
Negro was the forlornest spectacle of all. Lawyer Terrell overtook
him on the public highway between Macon and Rockville. The Negro
wore a ragged blue army overcoat, a pair of patched and muddy blue
breeches, and had on the remnants of what was once a military
cap. He was leading a lame and broken-down horse through the mud,
and was making his way toward Rockville at what appeared to be
a slow and painful gait. Curiosity impelled Lawyer Terrell to draw
rein as he came up with the Negro.

"Howdy, boss?" he said, taking off his tattered cap. Responding
to his salutation, the lawyer inquired his name. "I'm name' Ananias,
suh," he replied.

The name seemed to fit him exactly. A meaner-looking Negro
Lawyer Terrell had never seen. There was not the shadow of a smile
on his face, and seriousness ill became him. He had what is called a
hang-dog look. A professional overseer in the old days would have
regarded him as a Negro to be watched, and a speculator would have
put him in chains the moment he bought him. With a good deal
of experience with Negroes, Lawyer Terrell had never seen one whose
countenance and manner were more repulsive.

"Well," said the lawyer, still keeping along with him in the muddy
road, "Ananias is a good name."

"Yasser," he replied; "dat w'at mammy say. Mammy done dead
now, but she say dat dey wuz two Ananiases. Dey wuz ole Ananias
en young Ananias. One un um wuz de Liar, en de udder wuz de
Poffit. Dat w'at mammy say. I'm name' atter de Poffit."

Lawyer Terrell laughed, and continued his cross-examination.

"Where are you going?"

"Who? Me? I'm gwine back ter Marster, suh."

"What is your master's name?"

"Cunnel Benjamime Flewellen, suh."

"Colonel Benjamin Flewellen; yes; I know the colonel well. What are you going back there for?"

"Who? Me? Dat my home, suh. I bin brung up right dar, suh— right 'longside er Marster en my young mistiss, suh."

"Miss Ellen Flewellen," said Lawyer Terrell, reflectively. At this remark the Negro showed a slight interest in the conversation; but his interest did not improve his appearance.

"Yasser, dat her name, sho; but we-all call her Miss Nelly."

"A very pretty name, Ananias," remarked Lawyer Terrell.

"Lord! yasser."

The Negro looked up at this, but Lawyer Terrell had his eyes fixed on the muddy road ahead of him. The lawyer was somewhat youngish himself, but his face had a hard, firm expression common to those who are in the habit of having their own way in the court-house and elsewhere.

"Where have you been, Ananias?" said the lawyer presently.

"Who? Me? I bin 'long wid Sherman army, suh."

"Then you are quite a soldier by this time."

"Lord! yasser! I bin wid um fum de time dey come in dese parts plumb tell dey got ter Sander'ville. You ain't never is bin ter Sander'-ville, is you, boss?"

"Not to say right in the town, Ananias, but I've been by there a great many times." Lawyer Terrell humored the conversation, as was his habit.

"Well, suh," said Ananias, "don't you never go dar; special don't you go dar wid no army, kaze hit's de longes' en de nasties' road fum dar ter yer w'en you er comin' back dat I ever is lay my two eyes on."

"Why did you come back, Ananias?"

"Who? Me? Well, suh, w'en de army come 'long by home dar, look like eve'ybody got der eye sot on me. Go whar I would, look alike all de folks wuz a-watchin' me. 'Bout time de army wuz a-pilin' in on us, Marse Wash Jones, w'ich I never is done 'im no harm dat I knows un, he went ter Marster, he did, en he 'low dat ef dey don't keep mighty close watch on Ananias dey'd all be massycreed in deir beds. I know Marse Wash tol' Marster dat, kaze Ma'y Ann, w'ich she wait on de table, she come right outer de house en tol' me so. Right den, suh, I 'gun ter feel sorter skittish. Marster had done got me ter hide all de stock out in de swamp, en I 'low ter myse'f, I did, dat I'd des go over dar en stay wid um. I ain't bin dar so mighty long, suh, w'en yer come de Yankees, en wid um wuz George, de carriage-driver, de nigger w'at Marster think mo' uv dan he do all de balance er his niggers. En now, den, dar wuz George a-fetchin' de Yankees right whar he know de stock wuz hid at."

"George was a very handy Negro to have around," said Lawyer Terrell.

"Yasser. Marster thunk de worl' en all er dat nigger, en dar he wuz showin' de Yankees whar de mules en hosses wuz hid at. Well, suh, soon ez he see me, George he put out, en I staid dar wid de hosses. I try ter git dem folks not ter kyar um off, I beg um en I plead wid um, but dey des laugh at me, suh. I follered 'long atter um, en dey driv dem hosses en mules right by de house. Marster wuz stannin' out in de front porch, en w'en he see de Yankees got de stock, en me 'long wid um, suh, he des raise up his han's—so—en drap um down by his side, en den he tuck 'n tu'n roun' en go in de house. I run ter de do', I did, but Marster done fassen it, en den I run roun' de back way, but de back do' wuz done fassen too. I know'd dey didn't like me," Ananias went on, picking his way carefully through the mud, "en I wuz mos' out'n my head, kaze I ain't know w'at ter do. 'Tain't wid niggers like it is wid white folks, suh. White folks know w'at ter do, kaze dey in de habits er doin' like dey wanter, but niggers, suh—niggers, dey er diffunt. Dey dunner w'at ter do."

"Well, what did you do?" asked Lawyer Terrell.

"Who? Me? Well, suh, I des crope off ter my cabin, en I draw'd up a cheer front er de fier, en stirred up de embers, en sot dar. I ain't sot dar long 'fo' Marster come ter de do'. He open it, he did, en he come in. He 'low, 'You in dar, Ananias?' I say, 'Yasser.' Den he come in. He stood dar, he did, en look at me. I ain't raise my eyes, suh; I des look in de embers. Bime-by he say, 'Ain't I allers treat you well, Ananias?' I 'low, 'Yasser.' Den he say, 'Ain't I raise you up fum a little baby, w'en you got no daddy?' I 'low, 'Yasser.' He say, 'How come you treat me dis a-way, Ananias? W'at make you show dem Yankees whar my hosses en mules is?'"

Ananias paused as he picked his way through the mud, leading his broken-down horse.

"What did you tell him?" said Lawyer Terrell, somewhat curtly.

"Well, suh, I dunner w'at de name er God come 'cross me. I wuz dat full up dat I can't talk. I tried ter tell Marster des zactly how it wuz, but look like I wuz all choke up. White folks kin talk right straight 'long, but niggers is diffunt. Marster stood dar, he did, en look at me right hard, en I know by de way he look dat his feelin's wuz hurted, en dis make me wuss. Eve'y time I try ter talk, suh, sumpin' ne'r kotch me in de neck, en 'fo' I kin come ter myse'f, suh,

Marster wuz done gone. I got up en tried ter holler at 'im, but dat ketch wuz dar in my neck, suh, en mo' special wuz it dar, suh, w'en I see dat he wuz gwine 'long wid his head down; en dey mighty few folks, suh, dat ever is see my Marster dat a-way. He kyar his head high, suh, ef I do say it myse'f."

"Why didn't you follow after him and tell him about it?" inquired Lawyer Terrell, drawing his lap robe closer about his knee.

"Dat des zactly w'at I oughter done, suh; but right den en dar I ain't know w'at ter do. I know'd dat nigger like me ain't got no business foolin' 'roun' much, en dat wuz all I did know. I sot down, I did, en I make up my min' dat ef Marster got de idee dat I had his stock run'd off, I better git out fum dar; en den I went ter work, suh, en I pack up w'at little duds I got, en I put out wid de army. I march wid um, suh, plum tell dey got ter Sander'ville, en dar I ax um w'at dey gwine pay me fer gwine wid um. Well, suh, you mayn't b'lieve me, but dem w'ite mens dey des laugh at me. All dis time I bin runnin' over in my min' 'bout Marster en Miss Nelly, en w'en I fin' out dat dey wa'n't no pay fer niggers gwine wid de army I des up en say ter myse'f dat dat kind er business ain't gwine do fer me."

"If they had paid you anything," said Lawyer Terrell, "I suppose you would have gone on with the army?"

"Who? Me? Dat I wouldn't," replied Ananias, emphatically—"dat I wouldn't. I'd 'a got my money, en I'd 'a come back home, kaze I boun' you I wa'n't a-gwine ter let Marster drap off en die widout knowin' who run'd dem stock off. No, suh. I wuz des 'bleege ter come back."

"Ananias," said Lawyer Terrell, "you are a good man."

"Thanky, suh!—thanky, Marster!" exclaimed Ananias, taking off his weather-beaten cap. "You er de fus white man dat ever tol' me dat sence I bin born'd inter de worl'. Thanky, suh!"

"Good-by," said Lawyer Terrell, touching his horse lightly with the whip.

"Good-by, Marster!" said Ananias, with unction. "Good-by, Marster, en thanky!"

Lawyer Terrell passed out of sight in the direction of Rockville. Ananias went in the same direction, but he made his way over the road with a lighter heart.

II

It is to be presumed that Ananias's explanation was satisfactory to Colonel Benjamin Flewellen, for he settled down on his former master's place, and proceeded to make his presence felt on the farm as it had never been felt before. Himself and his army-worn horse were decided accessions, for the horse turned out to be an excellent animal. Ananias made no contract with his former master, and asked for no wages. He simply took possession of his old quarters, and began anew the life he had led in slavery times—with this difference: in the old days he had been compelled to work, but now he was working of his own free-will and to please himself. The result was that he worked much harder.

It may be said here that though Colonel Benjamin Flewellen was a noted planter, he was not much of a farmer. Before and during the war he had intrusted his plantation and his planting interests to the care of an overseer. For three hundred dollars a year—which was not much of a sum in slavery times—he could be relieved of all the cares and anxieties incident to the management of a large plantation. His father before him had conducted the plantation by proxy, and Colonel Benjamin Flewellen was not slow to avail himself of a long-estab-lished custom that had been justified by experience. Moreover, Colonel Flewellen had a taste for literature. His father had gathered together a large collection of books, and Colonel Flewellen had added to this until he was the owner of one of the largest private libraries in a State where large private libraries were by no means rare. He wrote verse on occasion, and essays in defence of slavery. There are yet living men who believed that his "Reply" to Charles Sumner's attack on the South was so crushing in its argument and its invective—particu-larly its invective—that it would go far toward putting an end to the abolition movement. Colonel Flewellen's "Reply" filled a page of the New York *Day-Book,* and there is no doubt that he made the most of the limited space placed at his disposal.

With his taste and training it is not surprising that Colonel Benja-min Flewellen should leave his plantation interests to the care of Mr. Washington Jones, his overseer, and devote himself to the liberal arts. He not only wrote and published the deservedly famous "Reply" to Charles Sumner, which was afterward reprinted in pamphlet form for the benefit of his friends and admirers, but he collected his fugi-tive verses in a volume, which was published by an enterprising New York firm "for the author"; and in addition to this he became the proprietor and editor of the Rockville *Vade-Mecum,* a weekly paper devoted to "literature, science, politics, and the news."

When, therefore, the collapse came, the colonel found himself prac-tically stranded. He was not only land-poor, but he had no experience in the management of his plantation. Ananias, when he returned from his jaunt with the army, was of some help, but not much. He knew how the plantation ought to be managed, but he stood in awe of the colonel, and he was somewhat backward in giving his advice. In fact, he had nothing to say unless his opinion was asked, and this was not often, for Colonel Flewellen had come to entertain the general opinion about Ananias, which was, in effect, that he was a sneaking, hypocritical rascal who was not to be depended on; a good enough worker, to be sure, but not a Negro in whom one could repose confidence.

The truth is, Ananias's appearance was against him. He was ugly and mean-looking, and he had a habit of slipping around and keeping out of the way of white people—a habit which, in that day and time, gave everybody reason enough to distrust him. As a result of this, Ananias got the credit of every mean act that could not be traced to any responsible source. If a smoke-house was broken open in the night, Ananias was the thief. The finger of suspicion was pointed at him on every possible occasion. He was thought to be the head and front of the Union League, a political organization set in motion by the shifty carpet-baggers for the purpose of consolidating the Negro vote against the whites. In this way prejudice deepened against him all the while, until he finally became something of an Ishmaelite, holding no intercourse with any white people but Colonel Flewellen and Miss Nelly.

Meanwhile, as may be supposed, Colonel Flewellen was not making much of a success in managing his plantation. Beginning without money, he had as much as he could do to make "buckle and tongue meet," as the phrase goes. In fact he did not make them meet. He farmed on the old lavish plan. He borrowed money, and he bought provisions, mules, and fertilizers on credit, paying as much as two hundred per cent. interest on his debts.

Strange to say, his chief creditor was Mr. Washington Jones, his former overseer. Somehow or other Mr. Jones had thrived. He had saved money as an overseer, being a man of simple tastes and habits, and when the crash came he was comparatively a rich man. When affairs settled down somewhat, Mr. Jones blossomed out as a commission merchant, and he soon established a large and profitable business. He sold provisions and commercial fertilizers, he bought cotton, and he was not above any transaction, however small, that promised to bring him a dime where he had invested a thrip. He was a very thrifty man indeed. In addition to his other business he shaved notes and bought mortgages, and in this way the fact came to be recognized, as early as 1868, that he was what is known as "a leading citizen." He did not hesitate to grind a man when he had him in his clutches, and on this account he made enemies; but as his worldly possessions grew and assumed tangible proportions, it is not to be denied that he had more friends than enemies.

For a while Mr. Washington Jones's most prominent patron was Colonel Benjamin Flewellen. The colonel, it should be said, was not only a patron of Jones, but he patronized him. He made his purchases, chiefly on credit, in a lordly, superior way, as became a gentleman whose hireling Jones had been. When the colonel had money he was glad to pay cash for his supplies, but it happened somehow that he rarely had money. Jones, it must be confessed, was very accommodating. He was anxious to sell to the colonel on the easiest terms, so far as payment was concerned, and he often, in a sly way, flattered the colonel into making larger bills than he otherwise would have made.

There could be but one result, and though that result was inevitable, everybody about Rockville seemed to be surprised. The colonel had disposed of his newspaper long before, and one day there appeared in the columns which he had once edited with such care a legal notice to the effect that he had applied to the ordinary of the county, in proper form, to set aside a homestead and personalty. This meant that the colonel, with his old-fashioned ways and methods, had succumbed to the inevitable. He had a house and lot in town, and this was set apart as his homestead by the judge of ordinary. Mr. Washington Jones, you may be sure, lost no time in foreclosing his mortgages, and the fact soon came to be known that he was now the proprietor of the Flewellen Place.

Just at this point the colonel first began to face the real problems of life, and he found them to be very knotty ones. He must live— but how? He knew no law, and was acquainted with no business. He was a gentleman and a scholar; but these accomplishments would not serve him; indeed, they stood in his way. He had been brought up to no business, and it was a little late in life—the colonel was fifty or more—to begin to learn. He might have entered upon a political career, and this would have been greatly to his taste, but all the local offices were filled by competent men, and just at that time a Southerner to the manner born had little chance to gain admission to Congress. The Republican "reconstructionists," headed by Thaddeus Stevens, barred the way. The outlook was gloomy indeed.

Nelly Flewellen, who had grown to be a beautiful woman, and who was as accomplished as she was beautiful, gave music lessons; but in Rockville at that time there was not much to be made by teaching music. It is due to the colonel to say that he was bitterly opposed to this project, and he was glad when his daughter gave it up in despair. Then she took in sewing surreptitiously, and did other things that a girl of tact and common sense would be likely to do when put to the test.

The colonel and his daughter managed to get along somehow, but it was a miserable existence compared to their former estate of luxury. Just how they managed, only one person in the wide world knew, and that person was Ananias. Everybody around Rockville said it was very queer how the colonel, with no money and little credit, could afford to keep a servant, and a man-servant at that. But there was nothing queer about it. Ananias received no wages of any sort; he asked for none; he expected none. A child of misfortune himself, he was glad to share the misfortunes of his former master. He washed, he ironed, he cooked, he milked, and he did more. He found time to do little odd jobs around town, and with the money thus earned he was able to supply things that would otherwise have been missing from Colonel Flewellen's table. He was as ugly and as mean-looking as ever, and as unpopular. Even the colonel mistrusted him, but he managed to tolerate him. The daughter often had words of praise for the shabby and forlorn-looking Negro, and these, if anything, served to lighten his tasks.

But in spite of everything that his daughter or Ananias could do, the colonel continued to grow poorer. To all appearances—and he managed to keep up appearances to the last—he was richer than many of his neighbors, for he had a comfortable house, and he still had credit in the town. Among the shopkeepers there were few that did not respect and admire the colonel for what he had been. But the colonel, since his experience with Mr. Washington Jones, looked with suspicion on the credit business. The result was that he and his daughter and Ananias lived in the midst of the ghastliest poverty.

As for Ananias, he could stand it well enough; so, perhaps, could the colonel, he being a man, and a pretty stout one; but how about the young lady? This was the question that Ananias was continually asking himself, and circumstances finally drove him to answering it in his own way. There was this much to be said about Ananias; when he made up his mind, nothing could turn him, humble as he was; and then came a period in the career of the family to which he had attached himself when he was compelled to make up his mind or see them starve.

III

At this late day there is no particular reason for concealing the facts. Ananias took the responsibility on his shoulders, and thereafter the colonel's larder was always comparatively full. At night Ananias would sit and nod before a fire in the kitchen, and after everybody else had gone to bed he would sneak out into the darkness, and be gone for many hours; but whether the hours of his absence were many or few, he never returned empty-handed. Sometimes he would bring a "turn" of wood, sometimes a bag of meal or potatoes, sometimes a side of meat or a ham, and sometimes he would be compelled to stop, while yet some distance from the house, to choke a chicken that betrayed a tendency to squall in the small still hours between midnight and morning. The colonel and his daughter never knew whence their supplies came. They only knew that Ananias suddenly developed into a wonderfully good cook, for it is a very good cook indeed that can go on month after month providing excellent meals without calling for new supplies.

But Ananias had always been peculiar, and if he grew a trifle more uncommunicative than usual, neither the colonel nor the colonel's daughter was expected to take notice of the fact. Ananias was a sullen Negro at best, but his sullenness was not at all important, and nobody cared whether his demeanor was grave or gay, lively or severe. Indeed, except that he was an object of distrust and suspicion, nobody cared anything at all about Ananias. For his part, Ananias seemed to care nothing for people's opinions, good, bad, or indifferent. If the citizens of Rockville thought ill of him, that was their affair altogether. Ananias went sneaking around, attending to what he conceived to be his own business, and there is no doubt that, in some way, he managed to keep Colonel Flewellen's larder well supplied with provisions.

About this time Mr. Washington Jones, who had hired a clerk for his store, and who was mainly devoting his time to managing, as proprietor, the Flewellen Place, which he had formerly managed as overseer, began to discover that he was the victim of a series of mysterious robberies and burglaries. Nobody suffered but Mr. Jones, and everybody said that it was not only very unjust, but very provoking also, that this enterprising citizen should be systematically robbed, while all his neighbors should escape. These mysterious robberies soon became the talk of the whole county. Some people sympathized with Jones, while others laughed at him. Certainly the mystery was a very funny mystery, for when Jones watched his potato hill, his smoke-house was sure to be entered. If he watched his smoke-house, his potato hill would suffer. If he divided his time watching both of these, his storehouse would be robbed. There was no regularity about this; but it was generally conceded that the more Jones watched, the more he was robbed, and it finally came to be believed in the county that Jones, to express it in the vernacular, "hollered too loud to be hurt much."

At last one day it was announced that Jones had discovered the thief who had been robbing him. He had not caught him, but he had seen him plainly enough to identify him. The next thing that Rockville knew, a warrant had been issued for Ananias, and he was arrested. He had no commitment trial. He was lodged in jail to await trial in the Superior Court. Colonel Flewellen was sorry for the Negro, as well he might be, but he was afraid to go on his bond. Faithful as Ananias had been, he was a Negro, after all, the colonel argued, and if he was released on bond he would not hesitate to run away, if such an idea should occur to him.

Fortunately for Ananias he was not permitted to languish in jail. The Superior Court met the week after he was arrested, and his case was among the first called. It seemed to be a case, indeed, that needed very little trying. But a very curious incident happened in the court-room.

Among the lawyers present was Mr. Terrell, of Macon. Mr. Terrell was by all odds the greatest lawyer practising in that circuit. He was so great, indeed, that he was not called "major," or "colonel," or "judge." He ranked with Stephens and Hill, and like these distinguished men his title was plain "Mr." Mr. Terrell practised in all the judicial circuits of the State, and had important cases in all of them. He was in Rockville for the purpose of arguing a case to be tried at that term, and which he knew would be carried to the Supreme Court of the State, no matter what the verdict of the lower court might be. He was arranging and verifying his authorities anew, and he was very busy when the sheriff came into the court-house bringing Ananias. The judge on the bench thought he had never seen a more rascally-looking prisoner; but even rascally-looking prisoners have their rights, and so, when Ananias's case was called, the judge asked him in a friendly way if he had counsel—if he had engaged a lawyer to defend him.

Ananias did not understand at first, but when the matter was made plain to him he said he could get a lawyer. Whereupon he walked over to where Mr. Terrell sat immersed in his big books, and touched him on the shoulder. The lawyer looked up.

"I'm name' Ananias, suh," said the Negro.

"I remember you," said Mr. Terrell. "What are you doing here?"

"Dey got me up fer my trial, suh, en I 'ain't got nobody fer ter speak de word fer me, suh, en I 'low'd maybe—"

Ananias paused. He knew not what else to say. He had no sort of claim on this man. He saw everybody around him laughing. The great lawyer himself smiled as he twirled his eye-glasses on his fingers. Ananias was embarrassed.

"You want me to speak the word?" said Mr. Terrell.

"Yes, suh, if you please, suh."

"You need not trouble yourself, Mr. Terrell," said the judge, affably. "I was about to appoint counsel."

"May it please your honor," said Mr. Terrell, rising, "I will defend this boy. I know nothing whatever of the case, but I happen to know something of the Negro."

There was quite a little stir in the court-room at this announcement. The loafers outside the railings of the bar, who had seen Ananias every day for a good many years, leaned forward to take another look at him. The lawyers inside the bar also seemed to be interested in the matter. Some thought that the great lawyer had taken the Negro's case by way of a joke, and they promised themselves a good deal of enjoyment, for it is not every day that a prominent man is seen at play. Others knew not what to think, so that between those who regarded it as a practical joke and those who thought that Mr. Terrell might be in a serious mood, the affair caused quite a sensation.

"May it please the court," said Mr. Terrell, his firm voice penetrating to every part of the large room, "I know nothing of this case; therefore I will ask half an hour's delay to look over the papers and to consult with my client."

"Certainly," said the judge, pleasantly. "Mr. Sheriff, take the prisoner to the Grand Jury room, so that he may consult with his counsel."

The sheriff locked the prisoner and the lawyer in the Grand Jury room, and left his deputy there to open the door when Mr. Terrell announced that the conference was over. In the mean time the court proceeded with other business. Cases were settled, dismissed, or postponed. A couple of young lawyers fell into a tumultuous wrangle over an immaterial point, which the judge disposed of with a wave of his hand.

In the Grand Jury room Ananias was telling his volunteer counsel a strange tale.

IV

"And do you mean to tell me that you really stole these things from Jones?" said Mr. Terrell, after he had talked a little with his client.

"Well, suh," replied Ananias, unabashed, "I didn't zackly steal um, suh, but I tuck um; I des tuck um, suh."

"What call had you to steal from Jones? Weren't you working for Colonel Flewellen? Didn't he feed you?" inquired the lawyer. Ananias shifted about from one foot to the other, and whipped his legs with his shabby hat, which he held in his hand. Lawyer Terrell, seated in a comfortable chair, and thoroughly at his ease, regarded the Negro curiously. There appeared to be a pathetic element even in Ananias's manner.

"Well, suh," he said, after a while, seeing that he could not escape from the confession, "ef I hadn't a-tuck dem things fum Marse Wash Jones, my Marster en my young mistiss would 'a sot dar en bodaciously starve deyse'f ter deff. I done seed dat, suh. Dey wuz too proud ter tell folks dey wuz dat bad off, suh, en dey'd 'a sot dar, en des bodaciously starve deyse'f ter deff, suh. All dey lifetime, suh, dey bin use ter havin' deir vittles put right on de table whar dey kin git it, en w'en de farmin' days done gone, suh, dey wa'n't nobody but Ananias fer put de vittles dar; en I des hatter scuffle 'roun' en git it de bes' way I kin. I speck, suh," Ananias went on, his countenance brightening up a little, "dat ef de wuss had a-come ter de wuss, I'd 'a stole de vittles; but I 'ain't had ter steal it, suh; I des went en tuck it fum Marse Wash Jones, kaze it come off'n Marster's lan', suh."

"Why, the land belongs to Jones," said Lawyer Terrell.

"Dat w'at dey say, suh; but eve'y foot er dat lan' b'longded ter de Flewellen fambly long 'fo' Marse Wash Jones' deddy sot up a hat-shop in de neighborhoods. I dunner how Marse Wash git dat lan', suh; I know it b'longded in de Flewellen fambly sence 'way back, en dey got deir graveyard dar yit."

Lawyer Terrell's unusually stern face softened a little. He saw that Ananias was in earnest, and his sympathies were aroused. He had some further conversation with the Negro, questioning him in regard to a great many things that assumed importance in the trial.

When Lawyer Terrell and his client returned to the court-room they found it filled with spectators. Somehow it became generally known that the great advocate was to defend Ananias, and a large crowd of people had assembled to watch developments. In some way

the progress of Ananias and the deputy-sheriff through the crowd
that filled all the aisles and doorways had been delayed; but when
the Negro, forlorn and wretched-looking, made his appearance in the
bar for the purpose of taking a seat by his counsel, there was a general
laugh. Instantly Lawyer Terrell was upon his feet.

"May it please your honor, what *is* the duty of the sheriff of this
county if it is not to keep order in this court-room?"

The ponderous staff of the sheriff came down on the floor with a
thump; but it was unnecessary. Silence had fallen on the spectators
with the first words of the lawyer. The crowd knew that he was a
game man, and they admired him for it. His whole attitude, as he
gazed at the people around him, showed that he was full of fight.
His heavy blond hair, swept back from his high forehead, looked
like the mane of a lion, and his steel-gray eyes glittered under his
shaggy and frowning brows.

The case of the State *versus* Ananias Flewellen, *alias* Ananias
Harper—a name he had taken since freedom—was called in due form.
It was observed that Lawyer Terrell was very particular to strike
certain names from the jury list, but this gave no cue to the line
of his defence. The first witness was Mr. Washington Jones, who
detailed the circumstances of the various robberies of which he had
been the victim as well as he knew how. He had suspected Ananias,
but had not made his suspicions known until he was sure—until he
had caught him stealing sweet-potatoes.

The cross-examination of the witness by Ananias's counsel was
severe. The fact was gradually developed that Mr. Jones caught the
Negro stealing potatoes at night; that the night was dark and cloudy;
that he did not actually catch the Negro, but saw him; that he did
not really see the Negro clearly, but knew "in reason" that it must
be Ananias.

The fact was also developed that Mr. Jones was not alone when he
saw Ananias, but was accompanied by Mr. Miles Cottingham, a small
farmer in the neighborhood, who was well known all over the county
as a man of undoubted veracity and of the strictest integrity.

At this point Lawyer Terrell, who had been facing Mr. Jones with
severity painted on his countenance, seemed suddenly to recover his
temper. He turned to the listening crowd, and said, in his blandest
tones, "Is Mr. Miles Cottingham in the room?"

There was a pause, and then a small boy perched in one of the
windows, through which the sun was streaming, cried out, "He's
a-standin' out yander by the horse-rack."

Whereupon a subpœna was promptly made out by the clerk of the court, and the deputy-sheriff, putting his head out of a window, cried:

"Miles G. Cottingham! Miles G. Cottingham! Miles G. Cottingham! Come into court."

Mr. Cottingham was fat, rosy, and cheerful. He came into court with such a dubious smile on his face that his friends in the room were disposed to laugh, but they remembered that Lawyer Terrell was somewhat intolerant of these manifestations of good-humor. As for Mr. Cottingham himself, he was greatly puzzled. When the voice of the court crier reached his ears he was in the act of taking a dram, and, as he said afterward, he "come mighty nigh drappin' the tumbeler." But he was not subjected to any such mortification. He tossed off his dram in fine style, and went to the court-house, where, as soon as he had pushed his way to the front, he was met by Lawyer Terrell, who shook him heartily by the hand, and told him his testimony was needed in order that justice might be done.

Then Mr. Cottingham was put on the stand as a witness for the defence

"How old are you, Mr. Cottingham?" said Lawyer Terrell.

"Ef I make no mistakes, I'm a-gwine on sixty-nine," replied the witness.

"Are your eyes good?"

"Well, sir, they er about ez good ez the common run; not so good ez they mought be, en yit good enough fer me."

"Did you ever see that Negro before?" The lawyer pointed to Ananias.

"Which nigger? That un over there? Why, that's thish yer God-forsakin' Ananias. Ef it had a-bin any yuther nigger but Ananias I wouldn't 'a bin so certain and shore; bekaze sence the war they er all so mighty nigh alike I can't tell one from t'other sca'cely. All eckceppin' of Ananias; I'd know Ananias ef I met 'im in kingdom come wi' his hair all swinjed off."

The jury betrayed symptoms of enjoying this testimony; seeing which, the State's attorney rose to his feet to protest.

"May it please the court—"

"One moment, your honor!" exclaimed Lawyer Terrell. Then, turning to the witness: "Mr. Cottingham, were you with Mr. Jones when he was watching to catch a thief who had been stealing from him?"

"Well, sir," replied Mr. Cottingham, "I sot up wi' him one night, but I disremember in pertickler what night it wuz."

"Did you see the thief?"

"Well, sir," said Mr. Cottingham, in his deliberate way, looking around over the court-room with a more judicial air than the judge on the bench, "ef you push me close I'll tell you. The' wuz a consid'-able flutterment in the neighborhoods er whar we sot, an' me an' Wash done some mighty sly slippin' up en surrounderin'; but ez ter seein' anybody, we didn't see 'im. We heerd 'im a-scuttlin' an' a-run-nin', but we didn't ketch a glimpse un 'im, nuther har ner hide."

"Did Mr. Jones see him?"

"No more'n I did. I wuz right at Wash's elbow. We heerd the villyun a-runn', but we never seed 'im. Atterwards, when we got back ter the house, Wash he 'lowed it must 'a bin that nigger Ananias thar, an' I 'lowed it jess mought ez well be Ananias ez any yuther nigger, bekaze you know yourself—"

"That will do, Mr. Cottingham," said Lawyer Terrell, blandly. The State's attorney undertook to cross-examine Mr. Cottingham, but he was a blundering man, and the result of his cross-examination was simply a stronger and more impressive repetition of Mr. Cotting-ham's testimony.

After this the solicitor was willing to submit the case to the jury without argument, but Mr. Terrell said that if it pleased the Court he had a few words to say to the jury in behalf of his client. The speech made by the State's attorney was flat and stale. He was not interested in the case; but Lawyer Terrell's appeal to the jury is still remembered in Rockville. It was not only powerful, but inimitable; it was humorous, pathetic, and eloquent. When he concluded, the jury, which was composed mostly of middle-aged men, was in tears. The feelings of the spectators were also wrought up to a very high pitch, and when the jury found a verdict of "not guilty," without retiring, the people in the court-room made the old house ring again with applause.

And then something else occurred. Pressing forward through the crowd came Colonel Benjamin Flewellen. His clothes were a trifle shabby, but he had the air of a prince of the blood. His long white hair fell on his shoulders, and his movements were as precise as those of a grenadier. The spectators made way for him. Those nearest noticed that his eyes were moist, and that his nether lip was a-tremble, but no one made any remark. Colonel Flewellen pressed forward until he reached Ananias, who, scarcely comprehending the situation, was sitting with his hands folded and his head bent down. The colonel placed his hand on the Negro's shoulder.

"Come, boy," he said, "let's go home."

"Me, Marster?" said the Negro, looking up with a dazed expres-sion. It was the tone, and not the words, that Ananias heard.

"Yes, old fellow, your Miss Nelly will be waiting for us."

"Name er God!" exclaimed Ananias, and then he arose and followed his old master out of the court-room. Those who watched him as he went saw that the tears were streaming down his face, but there was no rude laughter when he made a futile attempt to wipe them off with his coat tail. This display of feeling on the part of the Negro was somewhat surprising to those who witnessed it, but nobody was surprised when Ananias appeared on the streets a few days after with head erect and happiness in his face.

THOMAS NELSON PAGE

★　★　★

Negro slaves report in dialect the romantic activities of their aristocratic Virginia owners in the stories of Thomas Nelson Page (1853-1922). Thoroughbreds all, the men are tall, proud, punctilious, chivalrous; the women, amiable and noble. The daughters exist to love and be loved, while the young men are unhappy until they have overcome seemingly insuperable obstacles to win beautiful brides. The Negroes, since the narrators are almost exclusively house servants, live only to serve the white people near them. Page, born in Hanover County, Virginia, studied at the University of Virginia Law School and rose to eminence as an attorney in Richmond. After 1893 he lived in Washington, D. C. From 1913 to 1919 he was ambassador to Italy. "Polly," from Page's first and best collection of stories, *In Ole Virginia* (1887), and "P'laski's Tunaments" from *Elsket* (1891) are reprinted by permission of Charles Scribner's Sons.

★　★　★

Polly: A Christmas Recollection

IT was Christmas Eve. I remember it just as if it was yesterday. The Colonel had been pretending not to notice it, but when Drinkwater Torm * knocked over both the great candlesticks, and in his attempt to pick them up lurched over himself and fell sprawling on the floor, he yelled at him. Torm pulled himself together, and began an explanation, in which the point was that he had not "teched

---

* This spelling is used because he was called "Torm" until it became his name. [*Page's note.*]

447

a drap in Gord knows how long," but the Colonel cut him short.
"Get out of the room, you drunken vagabond!" he roared.

Torm was deeply offended. He made a low, grand bow, and with
as much dignity as his unsteady condition would admit, marched
very statelily from the room, and passing out through the dining-
room, where he stopped to abstract only one more drink from the
long, heavy, cut-glass decanter on the sideboard, meandered to his
house in the back-yard, where he proceeded to talk religion to
Charity, his wife, as he always did when he was particularly drunk.
He was expounding the vision of the golden candlestick, and the
bowl and seven lamps and two olive-trees, when he fell asleep.

The roarer, as has been said, was the Colonel; the meanderer was
Drinkwater Torm. The Colonel gave him the name, "because," he
said, "if he were to drink water once he would die."

As Drinkwater closed the door, the Colonel continued, fiercely:

"Damme, Polly, I will! I'll sell him to-morrow morning; and if I
can't sell him I'll give him away."

Polly, with troubled great dark eyes, was wheedling him vigorously.

"No; I tell you, I'll sell him.—'Misery in his back!' the mischief!
he's a drunken, trifling, good-for-nothing nigger! and I have sworn
to sell him a thousand—yes, ten thousand times; and now I'll have
to do it to keep my word."

This was true. The Colonel swore this a dozen times a day—every
time Torm got drunk, and as that had occurred very frequently for
many years before Polly was born, he was not outside of the limit.
Polly, however, was the only one this threat ever troubled. The
Colonel knew he could no more have gotten on without Torm than
his old open-faced watch, which looked for all the world like a model
of himself, could have run without the mainspring. From tying his
shoes and getting his shaving-water to making his juleps and lighting
his candles, which was all he had to do, Drinkwater Torm was necessary to him. (I think he used to make the threat just to prove to
himself that Torm did not own him; if so, he failed in his purpose—
Torm did own him.) Torm knew it as well as he, or better; and
while Charity, for private and wifely reasons, occasionally held the
threat over him when his expoundings passed even her endurance,
she know it also.

Thus, Polly was the only one it deceived or frightened. It always
deceived her, and she never rested until she had obtained Torm's
reprieve "for just one more time." So on this occasion, before she got
down from the Colonel's knees, she had given him in bargain "just

one more squeeze," and received in return Torm's conditional pardon, "only till next time."

Everybody in the county knew the Colonel, and everybody knew Drinkwater Torm, and everybody who had been to the Colonel's for several years past (and that was nearly everybody in the county, for the Colonel kept open house) knew Polly. She had been placed in her chair by the Colonel's side at the club dinner on her first birthday after her arrival, and had been afterward placed on the table and allowed to crawl around among and in the dishes to entertain the gentlemen, which she did to the applause of every one, and of herself most of all; and from that time she had exercised in her kingdom the functions of both Vashti and Esther, and whatever Polly ordered was done. If the old inlaid piano in the parlor had been robbed of strings, it was all right, for Polly had taken them. Bob had cut them out for her, without a word of protest from any one but Charity. The Colonel would have given her his heartstrings if Polly had required them.

She had owned him body and soul from the second he first laid eyes on her, when, on the instant he entered the room, she had stretched out her little chubby hands to him, and on his taking her had, after a few infantile caresses, curled up and, with her finger in her mouth, gone to sleep in his arms like a little white kitten.

Bob used to wonder in a vague, boyish way where the child got her beauty, for the Colonel weighed two hundred and fifty pounds, and was as ugly as a red head and thirty or forty years of Torm's mint-juleps piled on a somewhat reckless college career could make him; but one day, when the Colonel was away from home, Charity showed him a daguerreotype of a lady, which she got out of the top drawer of the Colonel's big secretary with the brass lions on it, and it looked exactly like Polly. It had the same great big dark eyes and the same soft white look, though Polly was stouter; for she was a great tomboy, and used to run wild over the place with Bob, climbing cherry-trees, fishing in the creek, and looking as blooming as a rose, with her hair all tangled over her pretty head, until she grew quite large, and the Colonel got her a tutor. He thought of sending her to a boarding-school, but the night he broached the subject he raised such a storm, and Polly was in such a tempest of tears, that he gave up the matter at once. It was well he did so, for Polly and Charity cried all night and Torm was so overcome that even next morning he could not bring the Colonel his shaving-water, and he had to shave with cold water for the first time in twenty years. He therefore employed a tutor. Most people said the child ought to have had a

governess, and one or two single ladies of forgotten age in the neighborhood delicately hinted that they would gladly teach her; but the
Colonel swore that he would have no women around him, and he
would be eternally condemned if any should interfere with Polly; so
he engaged Mr. Cranmer, and invited Bob to come over and go to
school to him also, which he did; for his mother, who had up to
that time taught him herself, was very poor, and was unable to send
him to school, her husband, who was the Colonel's fourth cousin,
having died largely indebted, and all of his property, except a small
farm adjoining the Colonel's, and a few Negroes, having gone into
the General Court.

Bob had always been a great favorite with the Colonel, and ever
since he was a small boy he had been used to coming over and
staying with him.

He could gaff a chicken as well as Drinkwater Torm, which was a
great accomplishment in the Colonel's eyes; for he had the best
game-chickens in the county, and used to fight them, too, matching
them against those of one or two of his neighbors who were similarly
inclined, until Polly grew up and made him stop. He could tame a
colt quicker than anybody on the plantation. Moreover he could shoot
more partridges in a day than the Colonel, and could beat him shooting with a pistol as well, though the Colonel laid the fault of the
former on his being so fat, and that of the latter on his spectacles.
They used to practice with the Colonel's old pistols that hung in
their holsters over the tester of his bed, and about which Drinkwater
used to tell so many lies; for although they were kept loaded, and
their brass-mounted butts peeping out of their leathern covers used
to look ferocious enough to give some apparent ground for Torm's
story of how "he and the Colonel had shot Judge Cabell spang
through the heart," the Colonel always said that Cabell behaved very
handsomely, and that the matter was arranged on the field without
a shot. Even at that time some people said that Bob's mother was
trying to catch the Colonel, and that if the Colonel did not look out
she would yet be the mistress of his big plantation. And all agreed
that the boy would come in for something handsome at the Colonel's
death; for Bob was his cousin and his nearest male relative, if Polly
was his niece, and he would hardly leave her all his property, especially as she was so much like her mother, with whom, as everybody
knew, the Colonel had been desperately in love, but who had treated
him badly, and, notwithstanding his big plantation and many Negroes,
had run away with his younger brother, and both of them had died
in the South of yellow fever, leaving of all their children only this

little Polly; and the Colonel had taken Drinkwater and Charity, and had travelled in his carriage all the way to Mississippi, to get and bring Polly back.

It was Christmas Eve when they reached home, and the Colonel had sent Drinkwater on a day ahead to have the fires made and the house aired for the baby; and when the carriage drove up that night you would have thought a queen was coming, sure enough.

Every hand on the plantation was up at the great house waiting for them, and every room in the house had a fire in it. (Torm had told the overseer so many lies that he had had the men cutting wood all day, although the regular supply was already cut.) And when Charity stepped out of the carriage, with the baby all bundled up in her arms, making a great show about keeping it wrapped up, and walked up the steps as slowly as if it were made of gold, you could have heard a pin drop; even the Colonel fell back, and spoke in a whisper. The great chamber was given up to the baby, the Colonel going to the wing room, where he always stayed after that. He spoke of sitting up all night to watch the child, but Charity assured him that she was not going to take her eyes off of her during the night, and with a promise to come in every hour and look after them, the Colonel went to his room, where he snored until nine o'clock the next morning.

But I was telling what people said about Bob's mother.

When the report reached the Colonel about the widow's designs, he took Polly on his knees and told her all about it, and then both laughed until the tears ran down the Colonel's face and dropped on his big flowered vest and on Polly's little blue frock; and he sent the widow next day a fine short-horned heifer to show his contempt of the gossip.

And now Bob was the better shot of the two; and they taught Polly to shoot also, and to load and unload the pistols, at which the Colonel was as proud as if one of his young stags had whipped an old rooster.

But they never could induce her to shoot at anything except a mark. She was the tenderest-hearted little thing in the world.

If her taste had been consulted she would have selected a cross-bow, for it did not make such a noise, and she could shoot it without shutting her eyes; besides that, she could shoot it in the house, which, indeed, she did, until she had shot the eyes out of nearly all the be-wigged gentlemen and bare-necked, long-fingered ladies on the walls. Once she came very near shooting Torm's eye out also; but this was an accident, though Drinkwater declared it was not, and tried to make out that Bob had put her up to it. "Dat's de mischievouses' boy Gord uver made," he said, complainingly, to Charity. Fortunately, his eye got well, and it gave him an excuse for staying half drunk for nearly a week; and afterward, like a dog that has once been lame in his hind-leg, whenever he saw Polly, and did not forget it, he squinted up that eye and tried to look miserable. Polly was quite a large girl then, and was carrying the keys (except when she lost them), though she could not have been more than twelve years old; for it was just after this that the birthday came when the Colonel gave her her first real silk dress. It was blue silk, and came from Richmond, and it was hard to tell which was the proudest, Polly, or Charity, or Drinkwater, or the Colonel. Torm got drunk before the dinner was over, "drinking de healthsh to de young mistis in de sky-blue robes what stands befo' de throne, you know," he explained to Charity, after the Colonel had ordered him from the dining-room, with promises of prompt sale on the morrow.

Bob was there, and it was the last time Polly ever sucked her thumb. She had almost gotten out of the habit anyhow, and it was in a moment of forgetfulness that she let Bob see her do it. He was a great tease, and when she was smaller had often worried her about it until she would fly at him and try to bite him with her little white teeth. On this occasion, however, she stood everything until he said that about a girl who wore a blue silk dress sucking her thumb; then she boxed his jaws. The fire flew from his eyes, but hers were even more sparkling. He paused for a minute, and then caught her in his arms and kissed her violently. She never sucked her thumb after that.

This happened out in front of her mammy's house, within which Torm was delivering a powerful exhortation on temperance; and, strange to say, Charity took Bob's side, while Torm espoused Polly's, and afterward said she ought to have "tooken a stick and knocked Marse Bob's head spang off." This, fortunately, Polly did not do (and when Bob went to the university afterward he was said to have the best head in his class). She just turned around and ran into the house, with her face very red. But she never slapped Bob after that. Not long after this he went off to college; for Mr. Cranmer, the tutor, said he already knew more than most college graduates did, and that it would be a shame for him not to have a university education. When the question of ways and means was mooted, the Colonel, who was always ready to lend money if he had it, and to borrow it if he did not, swore he would give him all the money he wanted; but, to his astonishment, Bob refused to accept it, and although the

Colonel abused him for it, and asked Polly if she did not think he was a fool (which Polly did, for she was always ready to take and spend all the money he or any one else gave her), yet he did not like him the less for it, and he finally persuaded Bob to take it as a loan, and Bob gave him his bond.

The day before he left home he was over at the Colonel's, where they had a great dinner for him, and Polly presided in her newest silk dress (she had three then); and when Bob said good-by she slipped something into his hand, and ran away to her room, and when he looked at it, it was her ten-dollar gold piece, and he took it.

He was at college not quite three years, for his mother was taken sick, and he had to come home and nurse her; but he had stood first in most of his classes, and not lower than third in any; and he had thrashed the carpenter on Vinegar Hill, who was the bully of the town. So that although he did not take his degree, he had gotten the start which enabled him to complete his studies during the time he was taking care of his mother, which he did until her death, so that as soon as he was admitted to the bar he made his mark. It was his splendid defence of the man who shot the deputy-sheriff at the court-house on election day that brought him out as the Democratic candidate for the Constitutional Convention, where he made such a reputation as a speaker that the *Enquirer* declared him the rising man of the State; and even the *Whig* admitted that perhaps the Loco-foco party might find a leader to redeem it. Polly was just fifteen when she began to take an interest in politics; and although she read the papers diligently, especially the *Enquirer,* which her uncle never failed to abuse, yet she never could exactly satisfy herself which side was right; for the Colonel was a stanch Whig, while most people must have been Democrats, as Bob was elected by a big majority. She wanted to be on the Colonel's side, and made him explain everything to her, which he did to his own entire satisfaction, and to hers too, she tried to think; but when Bob came over to tea, which he very frequently did, and the Colonel and he got into a discussion, her uncle always seemed to her to get the worst of the argument; at any rate, he generally got very hot. This, however, might have been because Bob was so cool, while the Colonel was so hot-tempered.

Bob had grown up very handsome. His mouth was strong and firm, and his eyes were splendid. He was about six feet, and his shoulders were as broad as the Colonel's. She did not see him now as often as she did when he was a boy, but it was because he was kept so busy by his practice. (He used to get cases in three or four counties now, and big ones at that.) She knew, however, that she was just as good a friend of his as ever; indeed, she took the trouble to tell herself so. A compliment to him used to give her the greatest happiness, and would bring deeper roses into her cheeks. He was the greatest favorite with everybody. Torm thought that there was no one in the world like him. He had long ago forgiven him his many pranks, and said "he was the grettest gent'man in the county skusin him [Torm] and the Colonel," and that "he al'ays handled heself to he raisin'," by which Torm made indirect reference to regular donations made to him by the aforesaid "gent'man," and particularly to an especially large benefaction then lately conferred. It happened one evening at the Colonel's, after dinner, when several guests, including Bob, were commenting on the perfections of various ladies who were visiting in the neighborhood that summer. The praises were, to Torm's mind, somewhat too liberally bestowed, and he had attempted to console himself by several visits to the pantry; but when all the list was disposed of, and Polly's name had not been mentioned, endurance could stand it no longer, and he suddenly broke in with his judgment that they "didn't none on 'em hol' a candle to his young mistis, whar wuz de ve'y pink an' flow'r on 'em all."

The Colonel, immensely pleased, ordered him out, with a promise of immediate sale on the morrow. But that evening, as he got on his horse, Bob slipped into his hand a five-dollar gold piece, and he told Polly that if the Colonel really intended to sell Torm, just to send him over to his house; he wanted the benefit of his judgment.

Polly, of course, did not understand his allusion, though the Colonel had told her of Torm's speech; but Bob had a rose on his coat when he came out of the window, and the long pin in Polly's bodice was not fastened very securely, for it slipped, and she lost all her other roses, and he had to stoop and pick them up for her. Perhaps, though, Bob was simply referring to his having saved some money, for shortly afterward he came over one morning, and, to the Colonel's disgust, paid him down in full the amount of his bond. He attempted a somewhat formal speech of thanks, but broke down in it so lamentably that two juleps were ordered out by the Colonel to reinstate easy relations between them—an effect which apparently was not immediately produced—and the Colonel confided to Polly next day that since the fellow had been taken up so by those Loco-focos he was not altogether as he used to be.

"Why, he don't even drink his juleps clear," the old man asserted, as if he were charging him with, at the least, misprision of treason. "However," he added, softening as the excuse presented itself to his mind, "that may be because his mother was always so opposed to it.

You know mint never would grow there," he pursued to Polly, who had heard him make the same observation, with the same astonishment, a hundred times. "Strangest thing I ever knew. But he's a confoundedly clever fellow, though, Polly," he continued, with a sudden reviving of the old-time affection. "Damme! I like him." And, as Polly's face turned a sweet carmine, added: "Oh, I forgot, Polly; didn't mean to swear; damme! if I did. It just slipped out. Now I haven't sworn before for a week; you know I haven't; yes, of course, I mean except *then*." For Polly, with softly fading color, was reading him the severest of lectures on his besetting sin, and citing an ebullition over Torm's failing of the day before. "Come and sit down on your uncle's knee and kiss him once as a token of forgiveness. Just one more squeeze," as the fair girlish arms were twined about his neck, and the sweetest of faces was pressed against his own rough cheek. "Polly, do you remember," asked the old man, holding her off from him and gazing at the girlish face fondly—"do you remember how, when you were a little scrap, you used to climb up on my knee and squeeze me, 'just once more,' to save that rascal Drinkwater, and how you used to say you were 'going to marry Bob' and me when you were grown up?"

Polly's memory, apparently, was not very good. That evening, however, it seemed much better, when, dressed all in soft white, and with cheeks reflecting the faint tints of the sunset clouds, she was strolling through the old flower-garden with a tall young fellow whose hat sat on his head with a jaunty air, and who was so very careful to hold aside the long branches of the rose-bushes. They had somehow gotten to recalling each in turn some incident of the old boy-and-girl days. Bob knew the main facts as well as she, but Polly remembered the little details and circumstances of each incident best, except those about the time they were playing "knucks" together. Then, singularly, Bob recollected most. He was positive that when she cried because he shot so hard, he had kissed her to make it well. Curiously, Polly's recollection failed again, and was only distinct about very modern matters. She remembered with remarkable suddenness that it was tea-time.

They were away down at the end of the garden, and her lapse of memory had a singular effect on Bob; for he turned quite pale, and insisted that she did remember it; and then said something about having wanted to see the Colonel, and having waited, and did so strangely that if that rose-bush had not caught her dress, he might have done something else. But the rose-bush caught her dress, and Polly, who looked really scared at it or at something, ran away just as the Colonel's voice was heard calling them to tea.

Bob was very silent at the table, and when he left, the Colonel was quite anxious about him. He asked Polly if she had not noticed his depression. Polly had not.

"That's just the way with you women," said the Colonel, testily. "A man might die under your very eyes, and you would not notice it. *I* noticed it, and I tell you the fellow's sick. I say he's sick!" he reiterated, with a little habit he had acquired since he had begun to grow slightly deaf. "I shall advise him to go away and have a little fling somewhere. He works too hard, sticks too close at home. He never goes anywhere except here, and he don't come here as he used to do. He ought to get married. Advise him to get married. Why don't he set up to Sally Brent or Malviny Pegram? He's a likely fellow, and they'd both take him—fools if they didn't;—I say they are fools if they didn't. What say?"

"I didn't say anything," said Polly, quietly going to the piano.

Her music often soothed the Colonel to sleep.

The next morning but one Bob rode over, and instead of hooking his horse to the fence as he usually did, he rode on around toward the stables. He greeted Torm, who was in the backyard, and after extracting some preliminary observations from him respecting the "misery in his back," he elicited the further facts that Miss Polly was going down the road to dine at the Pegrams', of which he had some intimation before, and that the Colonel was down on the river farm, but would be back about two o'clock. He rode on.

At two o'clock promptly Bob returned. The Colonel had not yet gotten home. He, however, dismounted, and, tying his horse, went in. He must have been tired of sitting down, for he now walked up and down the portico without once taking a seat.

"Marse Bob'll walk heself to death," observed Charity to Torm, from her door.

Presently the Colonel came in, bluff, warm, and hearty. He ordered dinner from the front gate as he dismounted, and juleps from the middle of the walk, greeted Bob with a cheeriness which that gentleman in vain tried to imitate, and was plumped down in his great split-bottomed chair, wiping his red head with his still redder bandana handkerchief, and abusing the weather, the crops, the newspapers, and his overseer before Bob could get breath to make a single remark. When he did, he pitched in on the weather.

That is a safe topic at all times. It was astonishing how much comfort Bob got out of it this afternoon. He talked about it until dinner began to come in across the yard, the blue china dishes gleaming in the hands of Phœbe and her numerous corps of ebon and mahogany assistants, and Torm brought out the juleps, with the mint looking as if it were growing in the great silver cans, with frosted work all over the sides.

Dinner was rather a failure, so far as Bob was concerned. Perhaps he missed something that usually graced the table; perhaps only his body was there, while he himself was down at Miss Malviny Pegram's; perhaps he had gone back and was unfastening an impertinent rose-bush from a filmy white dress in the summer twilight; perhaps—; but anyhow he was so silent and abstracted that the Colonel rallied him good-humoredly, which did not help matters.

They had adjourned to the porch, and had been there for some time, when Bob broached the subject of his visit.

"Colonel," he said, suddenly, and wholly irrelevant to everything that had gone before, "there is a matter I want to speak to you about —a—ah—we—a little matter of great importance to—ah—myself." He was getting very red and confused, and the Colonel instantly divining the matter, and secretly flattering himself, and determining to crow over Polly, said, to help him out:

"Aha, you rogue, I knew it. Come up to the scratch, sir. So you are caught at last. Ah, you sly fox! It's the very thing you ought to do. Why, I know half a dozen girls who'd jump at you. I knew it. I said so the other night. Polly—"

Bob was utterly off his feet by this time. "I want to ask your consent to marry Polly," he blurted out desperately; "I love her."

"The devil you do!" exclaimed the Colonel. He could say no more; he simply sat still, in speechless, helpless, blank amazement. To him Polly was still a little girl climbing his knees, and an emperor might not aspire to her.

"Yes, sir, I do," said Bob, calm enough now—growing cool as the Colonel became excited. "I love her, and I want her."

"Well, sir, you can't have her!" roared the Colonel, pulling himself up from his seat in the violence of his refusal. He looked like a tawny lion whose lair had been invaded.

Bob's face paled, and a look came on it that the Colonel recalled afterward, and which he did not remember ever to have seen on it before, except once, when, years ago, some one shot one of his dogs—a look made up of anger and of dogged resolution. "I will!" he said, throwing up his head and looking the Colonel straight in the eyes, his voice perfectly calm, but his eyes blazing, the mouth drawn close, and the lines of his face as if they had been carved in granite.

"I'll be —— if you shall!" stormed the Colonel: "the King of England should not have her!" and, turning, he stamped into the house and slammed the door behind him.

Bob walked slowly down the steps and around to the stables, where he ordered his horse. He rode home across the fields without a word, except, as he jumped his horse over the line fence, "I will have her," he repeated, between his fast-set teeth.

That evening Polly came home all unsuspecting anything ot the kind; the Colonel waited until she had taken off her things and come down in her fresh muslin dress. She surpassed in loveliness the rose-buds that lay on her bosom, and the impertinence that could dare aspire to her broke over the old man in a fresh wave. He had nursed his wrath all the evening.

"Polly!" he blurted out, suddenly rising with a jerk from his arm-chair, and unconsciously striking an attitude before the astonished girl, "do you want to marry Bob?"

"Why, no," cried Polly, utterly shaken out of her composure by the suddenness and vehemence of the attack.

"I *knew it!*" declared the Colonel, triumphantly. "It was a piece of cursed impertinence!" and he worked himself up to such a pitch of fury, and grew so red in the face, that poor Polly, who had to steer between two dangers, was compelled to employ all her arts to soothe the old man and keep him out of a fit of apoplexy. She learned the truth, however, and she learned something which, until that time, she had never known; and though, as she kissed her uncle "good-night," she made no answer to his final shot of, "Well, I'm glad we are not going to have any nonsense about the fellow; I have made up my mind, and we'll treat his impudence as it deserves," she locked her door carefully when she was within her own room, and the next morning she said she had a headache.

Bob did not come that day.

If the Colonel had not been so hot-headed—that is, if he had not been a man—things would doubtless have straightened themselves out in some of those mysterious ways in which the hardest knots into which two young peoples' affairs contrive to get untangle themselves; but being a man, he must needs, man-like, undertake to manage according to his own plan, which is always the wrong one.

When, therefore, he announced to Polly at the breakfast-table that morning that she would have no further annoyance from that fellow's impertinence; for he had written him a note apologizing for leaving him abruptly in his own house the day before, but forbidding him, in both their names, to continue his addresses, or, indeed, to put his foot on the place again; he fully expected to see Polly's face brighten, and to receive her approbation and thanks. What, then, was his disappointment to see her face grow distinctly white. All she said was, "Oh, uncle!"

It was unfortunate that the day was Sunday, and that the Colonel went with her to church (which she insisted on attending, notwithstanding her headache), and was by when she met Bob. They came on each other suddenly. Bob took off his hat and stood like a soldier on review, erect, expectant, and a little pale. The Colonel, who had almost forgotten his "impertinence," and was about to shake hands with him as usual, suddenly remembered it, and drawing himself up, stepped to the other side of Polly, and handed her by the younger gentleman as if he were protecting her from a mob. Polly, who had been looking anxiously everywhere but in the right place, meaning to give Bob a smile which would set things straight, caught his eye only at that second, and felt rather than saw the change in his attitude and manner. She tried to throw him the smile, but it died in her eyes, and even after her back was turned she was sensible of his defiance. She went into church, and dropped down on her knees in the far end of her pew, with her little heart needing all the consolations of her religion.

The man she prayed hardest for did not come into church that day.

Things went very badly after that, and the knots got tighter and tighter. An attempt which Bob made to loosen them failed disastrously, and the Colonel, who was the best-hearted man in the world, but whose prejudices were made of wrought iron, took it into his head that Bob had insulted him, and Polly's indirect efforts at pacification aroused him to such an extent that for the first time in his life he was almost hard with her. He conceived the absurd idea that she was sacrificing herself for Bob on account of her friendship for him, and that it was his duty to protect her against herself, which, man-like, he proceeded to do in his own fashion, to poor Polly's great distress.

She was devoted to her uncle, and knew the strength of his affection for her. On the other hand, Bob and she had been friends so long. She never could remember the time when she did not have Bob. But he had never said a word of love to her in his life. To be sure, on that evening in the garden she had known it just as well as if he had fallen on his knees at her feet. She knew his silence was just because he had owed her uncle the money; and oh! if she just hadn't gotten frightened; and oh! if her uncle just hadn't done it; and oh! she was so unhappy! The poor little thing, in her own dainty, white-curtained room, where were the books and things he had given her, and the letters he had written her, used to—but that is a secret. Anyhow, it was not because he was gone. She knew that was not the reason—indeed, she very often said so to herself; it was because he had been treated so unjustly, and suffered so, and she had done it all. And she used to introduce many new petitions into her prayers, in which, if there was not any name expressed, she felt that it would be understood, and the blessings would reach him just the same.

The summer had gone, and the Indian summer had come in its place, hazy, dreamy, and sad. It always made Polly melancholy, and this year, although the weather was perfect, she was affected, she said, by the heat, and did not go out of doors much. So presently her cheeks were not as blooming as they had been, and even her great dark eyes lost some of their lustre; at least, Charity thought so, and said so too, not only to Polly, but to her master, whom she scared half to death; and who, notwithstanding that Dr. Stopper was coming over every other day to see a patient on the plantation, and that the next day was the time for his regular visit, put a boy on a horse that night and sent him with a note urging him to come the next morning to breakfast.

The doctor came, and spent the day: examined Polly's lungs and heart, prescribed out-door exercise, and left something less than a bushel-basketful of medicines for her to take.

Polly was, at the time of his visit, in a very excited state, for the Colonel had, with a view of soothing her, the night before delivered a violent philippic against marriage in general, and in particular against marriage with "impudent young puppies who did not know their places;" and he had proposed an extensive tour, embracing all the United States and Canada, and intended to cover the entire winter and spring following. Polly, who had stood as much as she could stand, finally rebelled, and had with flashing eyes and mantling cheeks espoused Bob's cause with a courage and dash which had almost routed the old Colonel. "Not that he was anything to her except a friend," she was most careful to explain; but she was tired of hearing her "friend" assailed, and she thought that it was the highest compliment a man could pay a woman, etc., etc., for all of which she did a great deal of blushing in her own room afterwards.

Thus it happened, that she was both excited and penitent the next day, and thinking to make some atonement, and at the same time to take the prescribed exercise, which would excuse her from taking the medicines, she filled a little basket with goodies to take old Aunt Betty at the Far Quarters; and thus it happened, that, as she was coming back along the path which ran down the meadow on the other side of the creek which was the dividing line between the two plantations, and was almost at the foot-bridge that Somebody had made for her so carefully with logs cut out of his own woods, and the long shadows of the willows made it gloomy, and everything was so still that she had grown very lonely and unhappy—thus it happened, that just as she was thinking how kind he had been about making the bridge and hand-rail so strong, and about everything, and how cruel he must think her, and how she would never see him any more as she used to do, she turned the clump of willows to step up on the log, and there he was standing on the bridge just before her, looking down into her eyes! She tried to get by him —she remembered that afterwards; but he was so mean. It was always a little confused in her memory, and she could never recall exactly how it was. She was sure, however, that it was because he was so pale that she said it, and that she did not begin to cry until afterwards, and that it was because he would not listen to her explanation; and that she didn't let him do it, she could not help it, and she did not know her head was on his shoulder.

Anyhow, when she got home that evening her improvement was so apparent that the Colonel called Charity in to note it, and declared that Virginia country doctors were the finest in the world, and that Stopper was the greatest doctor in the State. The change was wonderful, indeed; and the old gilt mirror with its gauze-covered frame would never have known for the sad-eyed Polly of the day before the bright, happy maiden that stood before it now and smiled at the beaming face which dimpled at its own content.

Old Betty's was a protracted pleurisy, and the good things Polly carried her daily did not tend to shorten the sickness. Ever afterwards she "blessed the Lord for dat chile" whenever Polly's name was mentioned. She would doubtless have included Bob in her benison had she known how sympathetic he was during this period.

But although he was inspecting that bridge every afternoon regularly, notwithstanding Polly's oft-reiterated wish and express orders as regularly declared, no one knew a word of all this. And it was a bow drawn at a venture when, on the evening that Polly had tried to carry out her engagement to bring her uncle around, the old man had said, "Why, hoity-toity! the young rascal's cause seems to be thriving." She had been so confident of her success that she was not prepared for failure, and it struck her like a fresh blow; and though she did not cry until she got into her own room, when she got there she threw herself on the bed and cried herself to sleep. "It was so cruel in him," she said to herself, "to desire me never to speak to him again! and, oh! if he should really catch him on the place and shoot him!" The pronouns in our language were probably invented by young women.

The headache Polly had the next morning was not invented. Poor little thing! her last hope was gone. She determined to bid Bob good-by, and never see him again. She had made up her mind to this on her knees, so she knew she was right. The pain it cost her satisfied her that she was.

She was firmly resolved when she set out that afternoon to see old Betty, who was in everybody's judgment except her own quite convalescent, and whom Dr. Stopper pronounced entirely well. She wavered a little in her resolution when, descending the path along the willows, which were leafless now, she caught sight of a tall figure loitering easily up the meadow, and she abandoned—that is, she forgot it altogether when, having doubtfully suggested it, she was suddenly enfolded in a pair of strong arms, and two gray eyes, lighting a handsome face strong with the self-confidence which women love, looked down into hers.

Then he proposed it!

Her heart almost stood still at his boldness. But he was so strong, so firm, so reasonable, so self-reliant, and yet so gentle, she could not but listen to him. Still she refused—and she never did consent; she forbade him ever to think of it again. Then she begged him never to come there again, and told him of her uncle's threats, and of her fears for him; and then, when he laughed at them, she begged him never, never, under any circumstances, to take any notice of what her uncle might do or say, but rather to stand still and be shot dead; and then, when Bob promised this, she burst into tears, and he had to hold her and comfort her like a little girl.

It was pretty bad after that, and but for Polly's out-door exercise she would undoubtedly have succumbed. It seemed as if something had come between her and her uncle. She no longer went about singing like a bird. She suffered under the sense of being misunderstood, and it was so lonely! He too was oppressed by it. Even Torm shared in it, and his expositions assumed a cast terrific in the last degree.

It was now December.

One evening it culminated. The weather had been too bad for Polly to go out, and she was sick. Finally Stopper was sent for. Polly, who, to use Charity's expression, was "pestered till she was fractious," rebelled flatly, and refused to keep her bed or to take the medicines prescribed. Charity backed her. Torm got drunk. The Colonel was in a fume, and declared his intention to sell Torm next morning, as usual, and to take Charity and Polly and go to Europe. This was well enough; but to Polly's consternation, when she came to breakfast next morning, she found that the old man's plans had ripened into a scheme to set out on the very next day for Louisiana and New Orleans, where he proposed to spend the winter looking after some plantations she had, and showing her something of the world. Polly remonstrated, rebelled, cajoled. It was all in vain. Stopper had seriously frightened the old man about her health, and he was adamant. Preparations were set on foot; the brown hair trunks, with their lines of staring brass tacks, were raked out and dusted; the Colonel got into a fever, ordered up all the Negroes in the yard, and gave instructions from the front door, like a major-general reviewing his troops; got Torm, Charity, and all the others into a wild flutter; attempted to superintend Polly's matters; made her promises of fabulous gifts; became reminiscent, and told marvelous stories of his old days, which Torm corroborated; and so excited Polly and the plantation generally, that from old Betty, who came from the Far Quarters for the purpose of taking it in, down to the blackest little dot on the place, there was not one who did not get into a wild whirl, and talk as if they were all going to New Orleans the next morning, with Joe Rattler on the boot.

Polly had, after a stout resistance, surrendered to her fate, and packed her modest trunk with very mingled feelings. Under other circumstances she would have enjoyed the trip immensely; but she felt now as if it were parting from Bob forever. Her heart was in her throat all day, and even the excitement of packing could not drive away the feeling. She knew she would never see him again. She tried to work out what the end would be. Would he die, or would he marry Malviny Pegram? Every one said she would just suit him, and she'd certainly marry him if he asked her.

The sun was shining over the western woods. Bob rode down that way in the afternoon, even when it was raining; he had told her so. He would think it cruel of her to go away thus, and never even let him know. She would at least go and tell him good-by. So she did.

Bob's face paled suddenly when she told him all, and that look which she had not seen often before settled on it. Then he took her hand and began to explain everything to her. He told her that he had

loved her all her life; showed her how she had inspired him to
work for and win every success that he had achieved; how it had been
her work even more than his. Then he laid before her the life plans
he had formed, and proved how they were all for her, and for her
only. He made it all so clear, and his voice was so confident, and
his face so earnest, as he pleaded and proved it step by step, that she
felt, as she leaned against him and he clasped her closely, that he was
right, and that she could not part from him.

That evening Polly was unusually silent; but the Colonel thought
she had never been so sweet. She petted him until he swore that
no man on earth was worthy of her, and that none should ever have
her.

After tea she went to his room to look over his clothes (her especial
work), and would let no one, not even her mammy, help her; and
when the Colonel insisted on coming in to tell her some more concerning the glories of New Orleans in his day, she finally put him
out and locked the door on him.

She was very strange all the evening. As they were to start the
next morning, the Colonel was for retiring early; but Polly would
not go; she loitered around, hung about the old fellow, petted him,
sat on his knee and kissed him, until he was forced to insist on her
going to bed. Then she said good-night, and astonished the Colonel
by throwing herself into his arms and bursting out crying.

The old man soothed her with caresses and baby talk, such as he
used to comfort her with when she was a little girl, and when she
became calm he handed her to her door as if she had been a duchess.

The house was soon quiet, except that once the Colonel heard
Polly walking in her room, and mentally determined to chide her
for sitting up so late. He, however, drifted off from the subject when
he heard some of his young mules galloping around the yard, and
he made a sleepy resolve to sell them all, or to dismiss his overseer
next day for letting them out of the lot. Before he had quite determined which he should do, he dropped off to sleep again.

It was possibly about this time that a young man lifted into her
saddle a dark-habited little figure, whose face shone very white in
the starlight, and whose tremulous voice would have suggested a refusal had it not been drowned in the deep, earnest tone of her lover.
Although she declared that she could not think of doing it, she had
on her hat and furs and riding-habit when Bob came. She did, indeed, really beg him to go away; but a few minutes later a pair of
horses cantered down the avenue toward the lawn gate, which shut
with a bang that so frightened the little lady on the bay mare that

the young man found it necessary to lean over and throw a steadying arm around her.

For the first time in her life Polly saw the sun rise in North Carolina, and a few hours later a gentle-voiced young clergyman, whose sweet-faced wife was wholly carried away by Polly's beauty, received under protest Bob's only gold piece, a coin which he twisted from his watch-chain with the promise to quadruple it if he would preserve it until he could redeem it.

When Charity told the Colonel next morning that Polly was gone, the old man for the first time in fifty years turned perfectly white. Then he fell into a consuming rage, and swore until Charity would not have been much surprised to see the devil appear in visible shape and claim him on the spot. He cursed Bob, cursed himself, cursed Torm, Charity, and the entire female sex individually and collectively, and then, seized by a new idea, he ordered his horse, that he might pursue the runaways, threatened an immediate sale of his whole plantation, and the instantaneous death of Bob, and did in fact get down his great brass-mounted pistols, and lay them by him as he made Torm, Charity, and a half-dozen younger house-servants dress him.

Dressing and shaving occupied him about an hour—he always averred that a gentleman could not dress like a gentleman in less time—and, still breathing out threatenings and slaughter, he marched out of his room, making Torm and Charity follow him, each with a pistol. Something prompted him to stop and inspect them in the hall. Taking first one and then the other, he examined them curiously.

"Well, I'll be——!" he said, dryly, and flung both of them crashing through the window. Turning, he ordered waffles and hoe-cakes for breakfast, and called for the books to have prayers.

Polly had utilized the knowledge she had gained as a girl, and had unloaded both pistols the night before, and rammed the balls down again without powder, so as to render them harmless.

By breakfast time Torm was in a state of such advanced intoxication that he was unable to walk through the back yard gate, and the Colonel was forced to content himself with sending by Charity a message that he would get rid of him early the next morning. He straitly enjoined Charity to tell him, and she as solemnly promised to do so. "Yes, suh, *I* gwi' tell him," she replied, with a faint tone of being wounded at his distrust; and she did.

She needed an outlet.

Things got worse. The Colonel called up the overseer and gave new orders, as if he proposed to change everything. He forbade any mention of Polly's name, and vowed that he would send for Mr. Steep, his lawyer, and change his will to spite all creation. This humor, instead of wearing off, seemed to grow worse as the time stretched on, and Torm actually grew sober in the shadow that had fallen on the plantation. The Colonel had Polly's room nailed up and shut himself up in the house.

The Negroes discussed the condition of affairs in awed undertones, and watched him furtively whenever he passed. Various opinions by turns prevailed. Aunt Betty, who was regarded with veneration, owing partly to the interest the lost Polly had taken in her illness, and partly to her great age (to which she annually added three years) prophesied that he was going to die "in torments," just like some old uncle of his whom no one else had ever heard of until now, but who was raked up by her to serve as a special example. The chief resemblance seemed to be a certain "rankness in cussin'."

Things were certainly going badly, and day by day they grew worse. The Colonel became more and more morose.

"He don' even quoil no mo'," Torm complained pathetically to Charity. "He jes set still and study. I 'feard he gwine 'stracted."

It was, indeed, lamentable. It was accepted on the plantation that Miss Polly had gone for good—some said down to Louisiana—and would never come back any more. The prevailing impression was that, if she did, the Colonel would certainly kill Bob. Torm had not a doubt of it.

Thus matters stood three days before Christmas. The whole plantation was plunged in gloom. It would be the first time since Miss Polly was a baby that they had not had "a big Christmas."

Torm's lugubrious countenance one morning seemed to shock the Colonel out of his lethargy. He asked how many days there would be before Christmas, and learning that there were but three, he ordered preparations to be made for a great feast and a big time generally. He had the woodpile replenished as usual, got up his presents, and superintended the Christmas operations himself, as Polly used to do. But it was sad work, and when Torm and Charity retired Christmas Eve night, although Torm had imbibed plentifully, and the tables were all spread for the great dinner for the servants next day, there was no peace in Torm's discourse; it was all of wrath and judgment to come.

He had just gone to sleep when there was a knock at the door.

"Who dat out dyah?" called Charity. "You niggers better go 'long to bed."

The knock was repeated.

"Who dat out dyah, I say?" queried Charity, testily. "Whyn't you go 'long 'way from dat do'? Torm, Torm, dee's somebody at de do'," she said, as the knocking was renewed.

Torm was hard to wake, but at length he got up and moved slowly to the door, grumbling to himself all the time.

When finally he undid the latch, Charity, who was in bed, heard him exclaim, "Well, name o' Gord! good Gord A'mighty!" and burst into a wild explosion of laughter.

In a second she too was outside of the door, and had Polly in her arms, laughing, jumping, hugging, and kissing her while Torm executed a series of caracoles around them.

"Whar Marse Bob?" asked both Negroes, finally, in a breath.

"Hello, Torm! How are you, Mam' Charity?" called that gentleman, cheerily, coming up from where he had been fastening the horses; and Charity, suddenly mindful of her peculiar appearance and of the frosty air, "scuttled" into the house, conveying her young mistress with her.

Presently she came out dressed, and invited Bob in too. She insisted on giving them something to eat; but they had been to supper, and Polly was much too excited hearing about her uncle to eat anything. She cried a little at Charity's description of him, which she tried to keep Bob from seeing, but he saw it, and had to—however, when they got ready to go home, Polly insisted on going to the yard and up on the porch, and when there, she actually kissed the window-blind of the room whence issued a muffled snore suggestive at least of some degree of forgetfulness. She wanted Bob to kiss it too, but that gentleman apparently found something else more to his taste, and her entreaty was drowned in another sound.

Before they remounted their horses Polly carried Bob to the greenhouse, where she groped around in the darkness for something, to Bob's complete mystification. "Doesn't it smell sweet in here?" she asked.

"I don't smell anything but that mint bed you've been walking on," he laughed.

As they rode off, leaving Torm and Charity standing in the road, the last thing Polly said was, "Now be sure you tell him—nine o'clock."

"Umm! I know he gwi' sell me den sho 'nough," said Torm, in a tone of conviction, as the horses cantered away in the frosty night.

Once or twice, as they galloped along, Bob made some allusion to the mint bed on which Polly had stepped, to which she made no reply.

But as he helped her down at her own door, he asked, "What in the world have you got there?"

"Mint," said she, with a little low, pleased laugh.

By light next morning it was known all over the plantation that Miss Polly had returned. The rejoicing, however, was clouded by the fear that nothing would come of it.

In Charity's house it was decided that Torm should break the news. Torm was doubtful on the point as the time drew near, but Charity's mind never wavered. Finally he went in with his master's shaving-water, having first tried to establish his courage by sundry pulls at a black bottle. He essayed three times to deliver the message, but each time his courage failed, and he hastened out under pretence of the water having gotten cold. The last time he attracted Charity's attention.

"Name o' Gord, Torm, you gwine to scawl hawgs?" she asked, sarcastically.

The next time he entered the Colonel was in a fume of impatience, so he had to fix the water. He set down the can, and bustled about with hypocritical industry. The Colonel, at last, was almost through; Torm retreated to the door. As his master finished, he put his hand on the knob, and turning it, said, "Miss Polly come home larse night; sh' say she breakfast at nine o'clock."

Slapbang! came the shaving-can, smashing against the door, just as he dodged out, and the roar of the Colonel followed him across the hall.

When finally their master appeared on the portico, Torm and Charity were watching in some doubt whether he would not carry out on the spot his long-threatened purpose. He strode up and down the long porch, evidently in great excitement.

"He's turrible dis mornin'," said Torm; "he th'owed de whole kittle o' b'ilin' water at me."

"Pity he didn' scawl you to death," said his wife, sympathizingly. She thought Torm's awkwardness had destroyed Polly's last chance. Torm resorted to his black bottle, and proceeded to talk about the lake of brimstone and fire.

Up and down the portico strode the old Colonel. His horse was at the rack, where he was always brought before breakfast. (For twenty years he had probably never missed a morning.) Finally he walked down, and looked at the saddle; of course, it was all wrong. He fixed it, and, mounting, rode off in the opposite direction to that whence his invitation had come. Charity, looking out of her door, inserted into her diatribe against "all wuthless, drunken, fool niggers" a pathetic parenthesis to the effect that "Ef Marster meet Marse Bob dis mornin', de don' be a hide nor hyah left o'nyah one on 'em; an' dat lamb over dyah maybe got oystchers waitin' for him too."

Torm was so much impressed that he left Charity and went out of doors.

The Colonel rode down the plantation, his great gray horse quivering with life in the bright winter sunlight. He gave him the rein, and he turned down a cross-road which led out of the plantation into the main highway. Mechanically he opened the gate and rode out. Before he knew where he was he was through the wood, and his horse had stopped at the next gate. It was the gate of Bob's place. The house stood out bright and plain among the yard trees; lines of blue smoke curled up almost straight from the chimneys; and he could see two or three Negroes running backward and forward between the kitchen and the house. The sunlight glistened on something in the hand of one of them, and sent a ray of dazzling light all the way to the old man. He knew it was a plate or a dish. He took out his watch and glanced at it; it was five minutes to nine o'clock. He started to turn around to go home. As he did so, the memory of all the past swept over him, and of the wrong that had been done him. He would go in and show them his contempt for them by riding in and straight out again; and he actually unlatched the gate and went in. As he rode across the field he recalled all that Polly had been to him from the time when she had first stretched out her arms to him; all the little ways by which she had brought back his youth, and had made his house home, and his heart soft again. Every scene came before him as if to mock him. He felt once more the touch of her little hand; heard again the sound of her voice as it used to ring through the old house and about the grounds; saw her and Bob as children romping about his feet, and he gave a great gulp as he thought how desolate the house was now. He sat up in his saddle stiffer than ever. D—— him! he would enter his very house, and there to his face and hers denounce him for his baseness; he pushed his horse to a trot. Up to the yard gate he rode, and, dismounting, hitched his horse to the fence, and slamming the gate fiercely behind him, stalked up the walk with his heavy whip clutched fast in his hand. Up the walk and up the steps, without a pause, his face set as grim as rock, and purple with suppressed emotion; for a deluge of memories was overwhelming him.

The door was shut; they had locked it on him; but he would burst it in, and— Ah! what was that?

The door flew suddenly open; there was a cry, a spring, a vision of something swam before his eyes, and two arms were clasped about his neck, while he was being smothered with kisses from the sweetest mouth in the world, and a face made up of light and laughter, yet tearful, too, like a dew-bathed flower, was pressed to his, and before the Colonel knew it he had, amid laughter and sobs and caresses, been borne into the house, and pressed down at the daintiest little breakfast-table eyes ever saw, set for three persons, and loaded with steaming dishes, and with a great fresh julep by the side of his plate, and Torm standing behind his chair, whilst Bob was helping him to "oystchers," and Polly, with dimpling face, was attempting the exploit of pouring out his coffee without moving her arm from around his neck.

The first thing he said after he recovered his breath was, "Where did you get this mint?"

Polly broke into a peal of rippling, delicious laughter, and tightened the arm about his neck.

"Just one more squeeze," said the Colonel; and as she gave it he said, with the light of it all breaking on him, "Damme if I don't sell you! or, if I can't sell you, I'll give you away—that is, if he'll come over and live with us."

That evening, after the great dinner, at which Polly had sat in her old place at the head of the table, and Bob at the foot, because the Colonel insisted on sitting where Polly could give him one more squeeze, the whole plantation was ablaze with "Christmas," and Drinkwater Torm, steadying himself against the sideboard, delivered a discourse on peace on earth and good-will to men so powerful and so eloquent that the Colonel, delighted, rose and drank his health, and said, "Damme if I ever sell him again!"

P'laski's Tunaments

I HAD the good fortune to come from "the old county of Hanover," as that particular division of the State of Virginia is affectionately called by nearly all who are so lucky as to have first seen the light amid its broom-straw fields and ragged forests; and to this happy circumstance I owe the honor of a special visit from one of its most loyal citizens. Indeed, the glories of his native county were so embalmed in his memory and were so generously and continuously imparted to all his acquaintances that he was universally known after

an absence of forty years as "Old Hanover." I had not been long in
F—— when I was informed that I might, in right of the good fortune respecting my birthplace to which I have referred, expect a visit
from my distinguished fellow-countyman, and thus I was not surprised when one afternoon a message was brought in that "Ole
Hanover was in the yard, and had called to pay his bes' bespecks to
de gent'man what hed de honor to come f'om de ole county."

I immediately went out, followed by my host, to find that the visit
was attended with a formality which raised it almost to the dignity of
a ceremonial. "Old Hanover" was accompanied by his wife, and was
attended by quite a number of other Negroes, who had followed him
either out of curiosity excited by the importance he had attached to the
visit, or else in the desire to shine in reflected glory as his friends. "Old
Hanover" himself stood well out in front of the rest, like an old
African chief in state with his followers behind him about to receive
an embassy. He was arrayed with great care, in a style which I thought
at first glance was indicative of the clerical calling, but which I
soon discovered was intended to be merely symbolical of approxima-
tion to the dignity which was supposed to pertain to that profession.
He wore a very long and baggy coat which had once been black,
but was now tanned by exposure to a reddish brown, a vest which
looked as if it had been velvet before the years had eaten the nap
from it and changed it into a fabric not unlike leather. His shirt
was obviously newly washed for the occasion, and his high clean collar
fell over an ample and somewhat bulging white cloth which partook of the qualities of both stock and necktie. His skin was of that
lustrous black which shines as if freshly oiled, and his face was
closely shaved except for two tufts of short white hair, one on each
side, which shone like snow against his black cheeks. He wore an
old and very quaint beaver, and a pair of large, old-fashioned, silver-
rimmed spectacles, which gave him an air of portentous dignity.

When I first caught sight of him he was leaning on a long hickory
stick, which might have been his staff of state, and his face was set
in an expression of superlative importance. As I appeared, however,
he at once removed his hat, and taking a long step forward, made
me a profound bow. I was so much impressed by him that I failed
to catch the whole of the grandiloquent speech with which he greeted
me. I had evidently secured his approval; for he boldly declared that
he "would 'a' recognized me for one of de rail quality ef he had
foun' me in a cuppen." I was immediately conscious of the effect
which his endorsement produced on his companions. They regarded

me with new interest, if any expression so bovine deserved to be thus characterized.

"I tell dese folks up heah dee don' know nuthin' 'bout rail quality," he asserted, with a contemptuous wave of his arm, which was manifestly intended to embrace the entire section in its comprehensive sweep. "Dee 'ain' nuver had no 'quaintance wid it," he explained, condescendingly. His friends accepted this criticism with proper submissiveness.

"De Maconses, de Berkeleyses, de Carterses, de Bassettses, de Wickhames, de Nelsonses, an' dem!"—(the final ending was plainly supposed to give additional dignity)—"now *dee* is sho' 'nough quality. I know all 'bout 'em." He paused long enough to permit this to sink in. "I b'longst to Doc' Macon. *You* know what *he* wuz?"

His emphasis compelled me to acknowledge his exalted position or abandon forever all hope of retaining my own; so I immediately assented, and inquired how long he had been in "this country," as he designated his adopted region. He turned with some severity to one of his companions, a stout and slatternly woman, very black, and many years his junior.

"How long is I been heah, Lucindy?"

The woman addressed, by way of answer, turned half away and gave a little nervous laugh. "I don' know how long you been heah, you been heah so long; mos' forty years, I reckon." This sally called from her companions a little ripple of amusement.

"Dat's my wife, suh," the old gentleman explained, apologetically. "She's de one I got now; she come f'om up heah in dis kentry." His voice expressed all that the words were intended to convey. Lucindy, who appeared accustomed to such contemptuous reference, merely gave another little explosion which shook her fat shoulders.

As I was, however, expected to endorse all his views, I changed the embarrassing subject by inquiring how he had happened to leave the old county.

"Ole marster gi' me to Miss Fanny when she ma'yed Marse William Fitzhugh," he explained. "I wuz ma'yed den to Marth' Ann; she wuz Miss Fanny's maid, an' when she come up heah wid Miss Fanny, I recompany her." He would not admit that his removal was a permanent one. "I al'ays layin' out to go back home, but I 'ain' been yit. Dee's mos' all daid b'fo' dis, suh?"

He spoke as if this were a fact, but there was a faint inquiry in his eyes if not in his tone. I was sorry not to be able to inform him differently, and, to change the subject, I started to ask him a question. "Martha Ann—" I began, and then paused, irresolute.

"She's daid too," he said, simply.

"How many children have you?" I asked.

"I 'ain' got but one now, suh, ef I got dat one," he replied; "dat's P'laski."

"How many have you had?"

"Well, suh, dat's a partic'lar thing to tell," he said, with a whimsical look on his face. "De Scripturs says you is to multiply an' replanish de uth; but I s'pecks I's had some several mo'n my relowance; dar's Jeems, an' Peter, an' Jeremiah, an' Hezekiah, an' Zekyel, Ananias an' Malachi, Matthew an' Saint Luke, besides de gals. Dee's all gone; an' now I 'ain' got but jes dat P'laski. He's de wuthlisses one o' de whole gang. He tecks after his mammy."

The reference to Pulaski appeared to occasion some amusement among his friends, and I innocently inquired if he was Martha Ann's son.

"Nor, *suh, dat* he warn'!" was the vehement and indignant answer. "Ef he hed 'a' been, he nuver would 'a' got me into all dat trouble. Dat wuz de mortification o' my life, suh. He got all dat meanness f'om his mammy. Dat ooman dyah is his mammy." He indicated the plump Lucindy with his long stick, which he poked at her contemptuously. "Dat's what I git for mar'yin' one o' dese heah up-kentry niggers!" The "up-kentry" spouse was apparently quite accustomed to this characterization, for she simply looked away, rather in embarrassment at my gaze being directed to her than under any stronger emotion. Her liege continued: "Lucindy warn' quality like me an' Marth' Ann, an' her son tooken after her. What's in de myah will come out in de colt; an' he is de meanes' chile I uver had. I name de urrs f'om de Scriptur', but he come o' a diff'ent stock, an' I name him arter Mr. P'laski Greener, whar Lucindy use' to b'longst to, an' I reckon maybe dat's de reason he so natchally evil. I had mo' trouble by recount o' dat boy 'n I hed when I los' Marth' Ann."

The old fellow threw back his head and gave a loud "Whew!" actually removing his large spectacles in his desperation at Pulaski's wickedness. Again there was a suppressed chuckle from his friends; so, seeing that some mystery attached to the matter, I put a question which started him.

"Well, I'll tell you, suh," he began. "Hit all growed out of a tunament, suh. You an' I knows all discerning tunaments, 'cuz we come f'om de ole county o' Hanover whar dee *raise* tunaments"—(he referred to them as if they had been a species of vegetable)—"but we 'ain' nuver hearn de modification of a *nigger* ridin' in a tunament?"

I admitted this, and, after first laying his hat carefully on the ground, he proceeded:

"Well, you know, suh, dat P'laski got de notionment in he haid dat he wuz to ride in a tunament. He got dat f'om dat ooman." He turned and pointed a trembling finger at his uncomplaining spouse; and then slowly declared, "Lord! I wuz outdone dat day."

I suggested that possibly he had not followed Solomon's injunction as rigidly as Pulaski's peculiar traits of character had demanded; but he said, promptly:

"Yes, suh, I did. I whupped him faithful; but he took whuppin' like a ole steer. Hickory didn' 'pear to have no 'feck on him. He didn' had no memory; he like a ole steer, got a thick skin an' a short memory; he wuz what I call one o' dese disorde'ly boys."

He paused long enough to permit this term, taken from the police court reports, to make a lodgement, and then proceeded:

"He wuz so wuthless at home, I hired him out to ole Mis' Twine for fo' dollars an' a half a mont'—an' mo'n he wuth too!—to see ef white ooman kin git any wuck out'n him. A po' white ooman kin git wuck out a nigger ef anybody kin, an' 'twuz down dyah dat he got had foolishness lodgicated in he haid. You see, ole Mis' Twine warn' so fur f'om Wash'n'n. Nigger think ef he kin git to Wash'n'n, he done got in heaven. Well, I hires him to ole Mis' Twine, 'cuz I think she'll keep P'laski straight, an' ef I don' git but one fo' dollars an' a half f'om him, hit's dat much; but 'pear like he got to runnin' an' consortin' wid some o' dem urr free-issue niggers roun' dyah an' dee larne him mo' foolishness 'n I think dee able; 'cuz a full hawg cyarn drink no mo'.'"

The old fellow launched out into diatribes against the "free issues," who, he declared, expected to be "better than white folks, like white folks ain' been free sense de wull begin." He, however, shortly returned to his theme.

"Well, fust thing I knowed, one Sunday I wuz settin' down in my house, an' heah come P'laski all done fixed up wid a high collar on, mos' high as ole master's, an' wid a better breeches on 'n I uver war in my *life,* an' wid a creevat! an' a cane! an' wid a seegar! He come in de do', an' hol' he seegar in he han', sort o' so" (illustrating), "an' he teck off he hat kine of flourishy 'whur,' an' say, 'Good mornin', pa an' ma.' He mammy—*dat* she—monsus pleaged wid dem manners; she ain' know no better; but I 'ain' nuver like nobody to gobble roun' *me,* an' I say, 'Look heah, boy, don' fool wid me; I ain' feelin' well today, an' ef you fool wid me, when I git done wid you, you oon feel well you'self.' Den he kine o' let he feathers down; an' presney he say he warn me to len' him three dollars an' a half. I ax him what he warn do wid it, 'cuz I know I ain' gwine len' to him— jes well len' money to a mus'-rat hole—an' he say he warn it for a tunament. 'Hi!' I say, 'P'laski, what air a tunament?' I mecked out, you see, like I 'ain' recognizated what he meck correspondence to; an' he start to say, 'A tunament, pa—' but I retch for a barrel hoop whar layin' by kine o' aimable like, an' he stop, like young mule whar see mud-puddle in de road, an' say, 'a tunament—a tunament is whar you gits 'pon a hoss wid a pole, an' rides hard as you kin, an' pokes de pole at a ring, an'—' When he gits right dyah, I interrup's him, an' I say, 'P'laski,' says I, 'I's raised wid de fust o' folks, 'cuz I's raised wid de Maconses at Doc' Macon's in Hanover, an' I's spectated fish fries, an' festibals, an' bobbycues; but I 'ain' nuver witness nuttin' like dat— a nigger ridin' 'pon a hoss hard as he kin stave, an' nominatin' of it a tunament,' I says. 'You's talkin' 'bout a hoss-race,' I says, ' 'cuz dat's de on'yes' thing,' I says, 'a nigger rides in.' You know, suh," he broke in, suddenly, "you an' I's seen many a hoss-race, 'cuz we come f'om hoss-kentry, right down dyah f'om whar Marse Torm Doswell live, an' we done see hoss-races whar wuz hoss-races sho' 'nough, at de ole Fyarfiel' race-co'se, whar hosses use' to run could beat buds flyin', an' so I tole him. I tole him I nuver heah nobody but a po' white folks' nigger call a hoss-race a tunament; an' I tole him I reckon de pole he talkin' 'bout wuz de hick'ry dee use to tune de boys' backs wid recasionally when dee did'n ride right. Dat cut him down might'ly, 'cuz dat ermine him o' de hick'ries I done wyah out 'pon him; but he say, 'Nor; 'tis a long pole whar you punch th'oo a ring, an' de one whar punch de moes, he crown de queen.' I tole him dat de on'yes queen I uver heah 'bout wuz a cow ole master had, whar teck de fust prize at de State fyah in Richmond one year; but he presist dat dis wuz a tunament queen, and he warn three dollars an' a half to git him a new shut an' to pay he part ov de supper. Den I tole him ef he think I gwine give him three dollars an' a half for dat foolishness he mus' think I big a fool as he wuz. Wid dat he begin to act kine o' aggervated, which I teck for impidence, 'cuz I nuver could abeah chillern ner women to be sullen roun' me; an' I gi' him de notification dat ef I cotch him foolin' wid any tunament I gwine ride him tell he oon know wherr he ain't a mule hisself; an' I gwine have hick'ry pole dyah too. Den I tolt him he better go 'long back to ole Mis' Twine, whar I done hire him to; an' when he see me pick up de barrel hoop an' start to roll up my sleeve, he went; an' I heah he jine dat Jim Sinkfiel', an' dat's what git me into all dat tribilation."

"What got you in?" I inquired, in some doubt as to his meaning.

"Dat tunament, suh. P'laski rid it. An', what's mo', suh, he won de queen—one o' ole man Bob Sibly's impident gals—an' when he come to crown her, he crown her wid old Mis' Twine's weddin'-ring!"

There was a subdued murmur of amusement in the group behind him, and I could not but inquire how he came to perform so extraordinary a ceremony.

"Dat I don' know, suh; but so 'twair. Fust information I had on it wuz when I went down to ole Mis' Twine's to git he mont's weges. I receive de ontelligence on de way dat he had done lef' dyah, an' dat ole Mis' Twine gol' ring had lef' by de same road at de same time. Dat correspondence mortify me might'ly, 'cuz I hadn' raise P'laski no sich a ways as dat. He wuz dat ooman son, to be sho, an' I knowed he wuz wuthless, but still I hadn' respect him to steal ole Mis' Twine weddin'-ring, whar she wyah on her finger ev'y day, an' whar wuz gol' too. I want de infimation 'bout de fo' dollars an' a half, so I went 'long; but soon as ole Mis' Twine see me she began to quoil. I tell her I jes come to git de reasonment o' de matter, an' I 'ain' got nuthin' 'tall to say 'bout P'laski. Dat jes like bresh on fire; she wuss'n befo'. She so savigrous I tolt her I 'ain' nuver had nobody to prevaricate nuttin' 'bout me; dat I b'longst to Doc' Macon, o' Hanover, an' I ax her ef she knowed de Maconses. She say, nor, she 'ain' know 'em, nor she ain' nuver hearn on 'em, an' she wish she hadn' nuver hearn on me an' my thievin' boy—dat's P'laski. Well, tell den I mighty consarned 'bout P'laski; but when she say she 'ain' nuver hearn on de Maconses, I ain' altogether b'lieve P'laski done teck her ring, cause I ain' know whether she got any ring; though I know sense de tunament he mean enough for anything; an' I tolt her so, an' I tolt her I wuz raise wid quality—sence she ain' know de Maconses, I ain' tolt her no mo' 'bout dem, 'cuz de Bible say you is not to cast pearls befo' hawgs—an' dat I had tote de corn-house keys many a time, an' Marth' Ann used to go in ole mistis' trunks same as ole mistis herself. Right dyah she mought 'a' cotch me ef she had knowed dat P'laski warn' Marth' Ann son; but she ain' know de Maconses, an' in cose she ain' 'quainted wid de servants, so she don' know it. Well, suh, she rar an' she pitch. Yo' nuver heah a ooman talk so befo' in yo' life; an' fust thing I knew she gone in de house, she say she gwine git a gun an' run me off dat lan'. But I ain' wait for dat: don' nobody have to git gun to run me off dee lan'. I jes' teck my foot in my han' an' come 'long 'way by myself, 'cuz I think maybe a ooman 'at could cuss like a man mout shoot like a man too."

"Where did you go and what did you do next?" I asked the old fellow as he paused, with a whimsical little nod of satisfaction at his wisdom.

"I went home, suh," he said. "I heah on de way dat P'laski had sho 'nough done crownt Bob Sibly's gal Lizzy Susan wid de ring, an' dat he wuz gwine to Wash'n'n, but wuz done come home to git some things befo' he went; so I come straight 'long behinst him jes swift' as my foot could teck me. I didn' was'e much time," he said, with some pride, "'cuz he had done mighty nigh come gittin' me shot. I jes stop long enough to cut me a bunch o' right keen hick'ries, an' I jes come 'long shakin' my foot. When I got to my house I ain' fine nobody dyah but Lucindy—dat ve'y ooman dyah"—pointing his long stick at her—"an' I lay my hick'ries on de bed, an' ax her is she see P'laski. Fust she meck out dat she ain' heah me, she so induschus; I nuver see her so induschus; but when I meck 'quiration agin she 'bleeged to answer me, an' she 'spon' dat she 'ain' see him; 'cuz she see dat my blood wuz up, an' she know dee wuz trouble 'pendin' for P'laski. Dat worry me might'ly, an' I say, 'Lucindy, ef you is don' meck dat boy resent hisself f'om heah, you is done act like a po' white folks' nigger,' I say, 'an' you's got to beah de depravity o' his trans-gression.' When I tolt her dat she nuver got mad, 'cuz she know she air not quality like me an' Marth' Ann; but she 'pear right smartly disturbed, an' she 'clar' she 'ain' lay her eyes on P'laski. She done 'clar' so partic'lar I 'mos' incline' to b'lieve her; but all on a suddent I heah some 'n' sneeze, 'Quechew!' De soun' come f'om onder de bed, an' I jes retch over an' gether in my bunch o' hick'ries, an' I say, 'Come out!' Lucindy say, 'Dat's a cat'; an' I say, 'Yes,' I say, 'hit's a cat I gwine skin, too.'

"I jes stoop down, an' peep onder de bed, an', sho 'nough, dyah wuz P'laski squinch up onder dyah, cane an' seegar, an' all, jes like a ole hyah in a trap. I ketch him by de leg an' juck him out, an' don' you know, suh, dat ooman had done put *my* shut on dat boy, an' wuz gittin' ready to precipitate him in flight! I tolt her hit wuz p'intedly oudacious for her an' her son, after he had done stolt ole Mis' Twine weddin'-ring, to come to my own house an' rob me jes like I wuz a hen-roos'!"

"What reply did she make to that?" I asked, to facilitate his narra-tive.

"She 'ain' possessed no reply to dat indictment," he said, pompously. "She glad by dat time to remit me to terminate my excitement on P'laski, an' so I did. He hollered tell dee say you could heah him two miles; he fyahly lumbered." The old fellow gave a chuckle of satisfaction at the reminiscence, and began to draw figures in the sand with his long stick. Suddenly, however, he looked up. "Ef I had a-intimated how much tribilation dat lumberin' wuz gwine to get me in, he nuver would 'a' hollered. Dat come o' dat chicken-stealin' nigger Jim Sinkfiel'; he cyahed him off."

He again became reflective, so I asked, "Haven't you seen him since?"

"Oh, yes, suh, I seen him since," he answered. "I seen him after I come out o' jail; but 'twuz a right close thing. I thought I wuz gone."

"Gone! for whipping him?"

"Nor, suh; 'bout de murder."

"Murder?"

"Yes, suh; murder o' him—o' P'laski."

"But you did not murder him?"

"Nor, suh; an' dat wuz whar de trouble presisted. Ef I had a-murdered him I'd 'a' knowed whar he wuz when dee wanted him; but, as 'twair, when de time arrove, I wair unable to perduce him; an' I come mighty nigh forfeitin' my life."

My exclamation of astonishment manifestly pleased him, and he proceeded with increased gravity and carefulness of diction:

"You see, suh, 'twair dis way." He laid his stick carefully down, and spreading open the yellowish palm of one hand, laid the index finger of the other on it, as if it had been a map. "When I waked up nex' mornin' an' called P'laski, he did not rappear. He had departured; an' so had my shut! Ef 't hadn' been for de garment I wouldn' 'a' keered so much, for I knowed I'd git my han's on him sometime: hawgs mos'ly comes up when de acorns all gone, an' I know hick'ries ain' gwine stop growin'; but I wuz cawnsiderably tossified decernin' my garment, an' I gin Lucindy a little direction 'bout dat. But I jes went on gittin' my sumac, an' whenever I come 'cross a right straight hick'ry, I gethered dat too, an' laid it by, 'cuz hick'ries grow mighty fine in ole fiel's whar growin' up like. An' one day I wuz down in de bushes, an' Mr. 'Lias Lumpkins, de constable, come ridin' down dyah whar I wuz, an' ax me whar P'laski is. Hit come in my mine torectly dat he warn P'laski 'bout de ring, an' I tell him I air not aware whar P'laski is; an' den he tell me he got warrant for me, an' I mus' come on wid him. I still reposed, in co'se, 'twuz 'bout de ring, an' I say I ain' had nuttin' to do wid it. An' he say, 'Wid what?' An' I say, 'Wid de ring.' Den he say, 'Oh!' an' he say, ' 'Tain' nuttin' 'bout de ring; 'tis for murder.' Well, I know I ain' murder nobody, an' I ax him who dee say I done murder;

an' he ax me agin, 'Whar air P'laski?' I tell him I don' know whar P'laski air; I know I ain' murder him! Well, suh, hit subsequently repeared dat dis wuz de wuss thing I could 'a' said, 'cuz when de trial come on, Major Torm Woods made mo' o' dat 'n anything else at all; an' hit 'pears like ef you's skused o' murder er stealin', you mus'n' say you ain' do it, 'cuz dat's dangersomer 'n allowin' you *is* do it.

"Well, I went 'long wid him. I ax him to le' me go by my house; but he say, nor, he 'ain' got time, dat he done been dyah. An' he teck me 'long to de cote-house, an' *lock me up in de jail!* an' lef' me dyah in de dark on de rock flo'! An' dyah I rejourned all night long. An' I might 'a' been dyah now, ef 't hadn' been dat de co'te come on. Nex' mornin' Mr. Landy Wilde come in dyah an' ax me how I gittin' on, an' ef I warn anything. I tell him I gittin' on toler'ble, an' I ain' warn nuttin' but a little tobacco. I warn git out, but I knew I cyarn do dat, 'cuz 'twuz de ambitiouses smellin' place I ever smelt in my life. I tell you, suh, I is done smell all de smells o' mink an' mus' an' puffume, but I 'ain' nuver smell nuttin' like dat jail. Mr. Landy Wilde had to hole he nose while he in dyah; an' he say he'll git de ole jedge to come an' ac' as my council. I tell him, 'Nor; Gord put me in dyah, an' I reckon He'll git me out when He ready.' I tell you, suh, I wair p'intedly ashame for de ole jedge, whar wuz a gent'man, to come in sich a scand'lous smellin' place as dat. But de ole jedge come; an' he say hit wuz a —— shame to put a humin in sich place, an' he'd git me bail; which I mus' say— even ef he is a church member—might be ixcused ef you jes consider dat smell. But when de cote meet, dee wouldn' gi' me no bail, 'cuz dee say I had done commit murder; an' I heah Jim Sinkfiel' an' Mr. Lumpkins an' ole Mis' Twine went in an' tole de gran' jury I sutney had murder P'laski, an' bury him down in de sumac bushes; an' dee had de gre't bundle o' switches dee fine in my house, an' dee redite me, an' say ef I 'ain' murder him, why'n't I go 'long an' preduce him. Dat's a curisome thing, suh; dee tell you to go 'long an' fine anybody, an' den lock you up in jail a insec' couldn' git out."

I agreed with him as to the apparent inconsistency of this, and he proceeded:

"Well, suh, at las' de trial come on; 'twuz April cote, an' dee had me in de cote-house, an' set me down in de cheer, wid de jury right in front o' me, an' de jedge settin' up in he pulpit, lookin' mighty aggeravated. Dat wuz de fus' time I 'gin to feel maybe I sort o' forgittin' things. I had done been thinkin' so much lately in jail 'bout de ole doctor—dat's ole master—an' Marth' Ann, an' all de ole times in Hanover, I wuz sort o' misty as I wuz settin' dyah in de cheer, an' I jes heah sort o' buzzin' roun' me, an' I warn' altogether certified dat I warn' back in ole Hanover. Den I heah 'em say dat de ole jedge wuz tooken down an' wuz ixpected to die, an' dee ax me don' I warn a continuance. I don' know what dat mean, 'sep dee say I'd have to go back to jail, an' sense I smell de fresh air I don' warn do dat no mo'; so I tell 'em, 'Nor; I ready to die.' An' den dee made me stan' up; an' dee read dat long paper to me 'bout how I done murder P'laski; dee say I had done whup him to death, an' had done shoot him, an' knock him in de haid, an' kill him mo' ways 'n 'twould 'a' teck to kill him ef he had been a cat. Lucindy wuz dyah. I had done had her gwine 'bout right smart meckin' quiration for P'laski. At least she *say* she had," he said, with a sudden reservation, and a glance of some suspicion toward his spouse. "An' dee wuz a whole parecel o' niggers stan'in' roun' dyah; black as buzzards roun' a ole hoss whar dyin'. An' don' you know, dat Jim Sinkfiel' say he sutney hope dee would hang me, an' all jes 'cuz he owe' me two dollars an' seventy-three cents, whar he ain' warn pay me!"

"Did not you have counsel?" I inquired.

"Council?"

"Yes—a lawyer."

"Oh, nor, suh; dat is, I had council, but not a la'yar, edzactly," he replied, with careful discrimination. "I had a some sort of a la'yer, but not much of a one. I had ixpected ole Jedge Thomas to git me off; 'cuz he knowed me; he wuz a gent'man, like we is; but when he wuz tooken sick so providential I wouldn' had not urrs; I lef' it to Gord. De jedge ax me at de trial didn' I had no la'yer, and I tell him nor, not dyah; an' he ax me didn' I had no money to git one; an' I erspon', 'Nor, I didn' had none,' although I had at dat time forty-three dollars an' sixty-eight cents in a ole rag in my waistcoat linin', whar I had wid me down in de sumac bushes, an' whar I thought I better hole on to, an' 'ain' made no mention on. So den de jedge ax me wouldn' I had a young man dyah—a right tall young man; an' I enform him: 'Yes, suh. I didn' reckon 'twould hu't none.' So den he say he wuz my council."

There was such a suggestion of contempt in his tone that I inquired if he had not done very well.

"Oh, yes, suh," he drawled, slowly, "he done toler'ble well—considerin'. He do de bes' he kin, I reckon. He holler an' mix me up some right smart; but dee wuz too strong for him; he warn' no mo' to 'em 'n wurrm is to woodpecker. Major Torm Woods, de common wealph's attorney, is a powerful la'yer; he holler so you kin heah him *three* mile. An' ole Mis' Twine wuz dyah, whar tell all 'bout de ring, an' how impident I wuz to her dat day, an' skeer her to death. An' dat Jim Sinkfiel', he wuz dyah, an' tolt 'bout how I beat P'laski, an' how he heah him 'way out in main road, hollerin' 'murder.' An' dee had de gre't bundle o' hick'ries dyah, whar dee done fine in my house, an' dee had so much evi*dence* dat presney I 'mos' begin to think maybe I had done kilt P'laski sho 'nough, an' had disermembered it. An' I thought 'bout Marth' Ann an' all de urr chil'ern, an' I wondered ef dee wuz to hang me ef I wouldn' fine her; an' I got so I 'mos' hoped dee would sen' me. An' den de jury went out, and stay some time, an' come back an' say I wuz guilty, an' sen' me to de Pen'tentiy for six years."

I had followed him so closely, and been so satisfied of his innocence, that I was surprised into an exclamation of astonishment, at which he was evidently much pleased.

"What did your counsel do?" I asked.

He put his head on one side. "He? He jes lean over an' ax did I warn to repeal. I tell him I didn' know. Den he ax me is I got any money at all. I tell him, nor; ef I had I would 'a' got me a la'yer."

"What happened then?" I inquired, laughing at his discomfiting reply.

"Well, den de jedge tole me to stan' up, an' ax me has I got anything to say. Well, I know dat my las' chance, an' I tell him, 'yes, suh.' An' he inform me to precede wid de relation, an' so I did. I preceded, an' I tolt 'em dyah in de cote-house ev'y wud jes like I have explanificated it heah. I tolt 'em all 'bout Marth' Ann an' de chillern I hed had; I reformed 'em all decernin' de Maconses; an' I notified 'em how P'laski wuz dat urr ooman's son, not Marth' Ann's, an' 'bout de tunament, an' how I had demonstrated wid him not to ride dyah, an' how he had repudicated my admonition, an' had crown de queen wid ole Mis' Twine weddin'-ring, whar he come nigh gittin' me shot fur; an' how I had presented him de hick'ry, an' 'bout how he had departed de premises while I was 'sleep, an' had purloined my garment, an' how I wuz waitin' for him, an' getherin' de hick'ry crap an' all. An' dee wuz all laughin', 'cuz dee know I wuz relatin' de gospel truth, an' jes den I heah some o' de niggers back behine call out, 'Hi! heah he now!' an' I look roun', an', ef you b'lieve me, suh, dyah wuz P'laski, jes repeared, all fixed up, wid he cane an' seegar an' all, jes like I had drawed he resemblance. He had done been to Wash'n'n, an' had done come back to see de hangin'.'"

The old fellow broke into such a laugh at the reminiscence that I asked him, "Well, what was the result?"

"De result, suh, wuz de jury teck back all dee had say, an' ax me to go down to de tavern an' have much whiskey as I could stan' up to, an' dee'd pay for it; an' de jedge distructed 'em to tu'n me loose. P'laski, he wuz sort o' bothered; he ain' know wherr to be disapp'inted 'bout de hangin' or pleased wid bein' set up so as de centre of distraction, tell ole Mis' Twine begin to talk 'bout 'restin' of him. Dat set him back; but I ax 'em, b'fo' dee 'rest him, couldn' I have jurisdictionment on him for a leetle while. Dee grant my beques', 'cuz dee know I gwine to erward him accordin' to his becessities, an' I jes nod my head to him an' went out. When we got roun' 'hine de jail, I invite him to per*ject* his coat. He nex' garment wuz my own shut, an' I tolt him to remove dat too; dat I had to git nigh to he backbone, an' I couldn' 'ford to weah out dat shut no mor'n he had done already weah it. Somebody had done fetch de bunch o' hick'ries whar dee had done fine in my house, an' hit look jes like Prov*idence*. I lay 'em by me while I put him on de altar. I jes made him wrop he arms roun' a little locus'-tree, an' I fasten he wris'es wid he gallowses, 'cuz I didn' warn was'e dem hick'ries; an' all de time I bindin' him I tellin' him 'bout he sins. Den, when I had him ready, I begin, an' I rehearse de motter wid him f'om de time he had ax me 'bout de tunament tell he come to see me hang, an' wid ev'y wud I gin him admonition, tell when I got thoo wid him he wouldn' 'a' tetch a ring ef he had been in 'em up to he neck; an' as to shuts, he would 'a' gone stark naked b'fo' he'd 'a' put one on. He back gin out b'fo' my hick'ries did; but I didn' wholly lors 'em. I receive' de valyation o' dem too, 'cuz when I let up on P'laski, fust man I see wuz dat Jim Sinkfiel', whar had warn me hang 'cuz he didn' warn pay me two dollars an' seventy-three cents. He wuz standin' dyah lookin' on, 'joyin' hiself. I jes walk up to him an' I tolt him dat he could pay it right den, or recommodate me to teck de res' o' de hick'ries. He try to blunder out o' it, but all de folks know 'bout it an' dee wuz wid me, an' b'fo' he knowed it some on 'em had he coat off, an' had stretch him roun' de tree, an' tolt me to perceed. An' I perceeded.

"I hadn' quite wo' out one hick'ry when he holler dat he'd borry de money an' pay it; but I tolt him, nor; hick'ries had riz; dat I had three mo', an' I warn show him a man kin meck a boy holler 'murder' an' yit not kill him. An' dat I did, too; b'fo' I wuz done he hollered 'murder' jes natchel as P'laski."

The old fellow's countenance beamed with satisfaction at the recollection of his revenge, and I rewarded his narrative with a donation which he evidently considered liberal; for he not only was profuse in his thanks, but he assured me that the county of Hanover had produced four people of whom he was duly proud—Henry Clay, Doctor Macon, myself, and himself.

ALICE FRENCH

★ ★ ★

Although vitally interested in sociology and economics, interests acquired from her father, a railroad president and iron manufacturer, Alice French (1850-1934), who wrote under the pen name of "Octave Thanet," achieved fame, not for serious works on social problems, but for local-color stories about Canada, Iowa, and Arkansas. Best, possibly, are the narratives in *Knitters in the Sun* (1887) and in *Otto the Knight, and Other Trans-Mississippi Stories* (1891), descriptive of social conditions near her winter home at Clover Bend, Arkansas. Despite discernment of character traits and sureness of touch, she tended to sentimentalize problems, particularly those of the relations between capital and labor and between the races, and to indulge in special pleading in behalf of her own solutions. Yet her work illustrates the belief that "the short story mirrors our multitudinous American life." The following stories are reprinted by permission of Francis Henry French.

★ ★ ★

The Mortgage on Jeffy

THERE are few more beautiful sights than an Arkansas forest in late February; I mean a forest in the river-bottoms, where every hollow is a cypress brake. Prickly joints of bamboo-brier make a kind of green hatching, like shadows in an etching, for a little space above the wet ground between the great trees. Utterly bare are the tree-branches, save for a few rusty shreds clinging to the cypress-tops, a few bunches of mistletoe on the sycamores, or a gleam of holly-leaves in the thicket; but scarlet berries flicker on purple limbs, the cane grows a fresher green, and, in February, red shoots will be decking the maple-twigs, there will be ribbons of weeds which glitter like jewels, floating under the pools of water and ferns waving above, while the moss paints the silvery bark of sycamores, white-oaks, and gum-trees on the north side as high as the branches, and higher, with an incomparable soft and vivid green. The white trunks show the brighter for their gray tops and for that background everywhere of innumerable shades of gray and purple and shell-red which the blurred lines of twigs and branches make against the horizon. Such a forest is in my mind now. What an effect of fantastic and dainty magnificence the moss and the water and the shining trees produce! The dead trunks are dazzling white, the others have the lustrous haze of silver; it is not a real forest, it is a picture in an old missal, illuminated in silver and green. Yet beautiful as it is, there is something weird and dreary in its beauty—in those shadowy pools of water, masked by the tangle of brier and cane; in those tall trees that grow so thickly, and grow, I know, just as thickly for uncounted miles; in the shadows and mists which are instead of foliage; in the red streaks on the blunt edges of the cypress-roots and the stains on the girdled gum-trees, as if every blow of the axe had drawn blood—there is a touch of the sinister, even, and it would not be hard to conjure up a mediæval devil or two behind such monstrous growths as those cypress "knees."

Through this forest winds a rude road, winding because of the river, for these red smears to the right are willow-branches which mark the course of the Black River. On the February day that I recall, a one-armed man was driving a pair of stout horses to an open spring-wagon, the kind of wagon called in Arkansas "a hack." The wagon was new, and the harness had none of the ropes, odd chains, or old straps apt to garnish harness on a plantation. The driver, also, though wearing nothing better than a faded gray-flannel shirt, jean overalls, and rubber boots, was clean and even tidy in his appearance. His broad shoulders and long back promised a frame of unusual height, should he straighten himself up, instead of slouching forward until his hat-rim and its fringe of black curls made a semicircle between his shoulders. The reins were about his neck, and he guided his horses with his one hand. For all his empty sleeve, Jeff Griffin was the best driver "in the bottom." At the same time his elbow steadied the object on his knees. This was carefully wrapped in a piece of that bagging which is used for cotton-bales. Presently he checked his horses, to very gently remove the wrappings, bending over them a plain, kind, tear-stained face. He was looking at a little coffin. It was simply made, yet in a workmanlike fashion, too, and was painted white, with silver nails and handles.

"Ain't it beaucherful!" he murmured; "it mought rouse 'er!"

"Howdy, Mist' Griffin," called a voice from the roadside, with those mellow intonations which are as much the property of a black throat as the color of its skin. "Kin ye gimme lift fur's de twurn?"

Griffin perceived that he was abreast of an old Negro, on foot, carrying a bag of meal on his shoulder. He knew him, Uncle Nate, who worked on the Widow Brand's farm. It was inevitable, according to the customs of the country, that Jeff should let the old man climb into the wagon.

"Ben down ter de Bend," said he, settling himself comfortably on the back seat; "my ole woman ben r'arin' an' chargin' fur mo' meal. Cudn't cotch dat fool mewl; hed tu gether de bag on my wethers an' walk. Whut ye got dar', Mist' Griffin? Looks like—fo' de Lawd, hit's a coffin!"

"Hit's fur—fur little Bulah," said Griffin, choking.

"Not Cap'n Bulah's baby! My Lawd, ain't dat too bad? W'y, I seen de *Eller* a-layin' at de landin' dis ev'nin' w'en I come by. An' Cap'n Bulah, don' she be takin' on turrible?"

"She kep' walkin' the floor with it all las' night, long's it lived. Never made a lisp er complaint. Done anything the doctor commanded, an' all her word was, 'Doctor, don' let 'er suffer!' but w'en she seen doctor war doin' his bestmost, she never said nary nuther word. Looked like she wudn't hinder 'im a-frettin'. She are mighty fair-minded, Cap'n Bulah, Nate."

"Is so," agreed Nate, sympathetically; "but whut a sight er trubbel she done hab, fust de cap'n, an' now de onlies' chile she got dyin' off. Was hit sick long, sah?"

"On'y two days. 'T hed crowp."

"Dey all b'en stoppin' ter yo' house sence de boat tied up fur ter hab de b'iler fixed?"

"Yes. The baby b'en sorter weakly-like all winter. Bulah, she war mighty timid of her—but didn't do no good."

"Looks like," said Uncle Nate; "sut'nly de ways er de Lawd is dark, an' we uns cayn't get round 'em, nohow. Now, dar's dat ar baby de mudder leff ter de sto' las' Chewsday; ye heerd on't?" Griffin shook his head. "By gum, ain't dat cuse! W'y, 'twar dat ar Headlights, 's dey calls 'er, kase of dem big feery eyes er her'n. Tall woman; ye knowed 'er, picked cotton for dey all at de Bend. 'Peared ter set a heap er store by de little trick,* too; but she taken up with a mover, an' he p'intedly swore dat w'en he got married he didn't want no boot. So Headlights, she putt de baby unner de counter an' lit out; an' dey bofe done gone. Mist' Frank, he clerks ter de sto' now, an' he fotched de baby home ter his maw fur ter keep twell somebuddy'd want hit. An' dar dat baby is, eatin' hearty, dat his own mudder don' keer ter keep; an' dar's Cap'n Bulah a-mournin' an' refuzin' ter be comfurted, like dat woman in de Scripter—I disremembers her name. Dat's what tries de fait'; mo' ye studies on hit, mo' you' tried. Darfur, O Lawd, 'lighten we all's unnerstandin's; fur we's up peart like de grass, an' en de mawnin' we's p'intedly cut down." Here the stream of Uncle Nate's consolations meandered into the safe channel of his prayers (Uncle Nate had a gift) and flowed placidly on for a while, Griffin not hearing a word.

The latter's thoughts took their own dreary way, in vagrant, unuttered sentences: "She's rockin'; in the little red rocker, 'sides the bed. She done hilt Bulah en her arms ever sence she dressed of her. She are a-holdin' 'er now. She ain't cried, nur wept, nur spoke; jes' sets thar a-rockin' her baby an' lookin' at its face. Oh, Bulah, won' you let nobuddy holp ye? Hits pore little han's a-hangin' down— my Lord, how cole 'tis! Oh, pore little Bulah! pore little Bulah! but ye don' never need suffer no more, baby. Bulah, won' ye lemme cyar the baby a spell?"—his thoughts had gone back to the horrible night just past; he was pleading with the poor mother again. "Ye'll shore drop; ye cayn't keep up that-away! Lemme take 'er; I kin make out 'ith one arm. I done cyared 'er a heap. 'Tain't no good talkin'—she don' hear me. Oh, Bulah, she don' have no more pain; the Lord taken 'er outen it now. Let S'leeny take 'er; you lay down. Don' cry so, S'leeny, mabbe it frets 'er ter hear us; we kin cry, out-doors."

Now it was the doctor's voice speaking: "You must rouse her somehow; she'll die or go crazy if you don't."

"Rouse her? Lord God! how kin I, w'en I cayn't make her hear me? I wish't it b'en me stiddier the baby, Bulah; I b'en prayin' all night ter the Lord ter take me stiddier her. Won' ye jes' lift you' head, Bulah, an' try ter listin? It's Jeff talkin' ter ye! Ye know how Jeff allus thought a heap er ye—naw, naw, ye never kin know what I thought er ye! Never ye min' what I say, honey, I cayn't b'ar to see ye settin' that-away, an' I say quar things. *Do* ye hear me, Bulah?

* Trick, in Arkansas speech, means a number of things: a child, an article, a stratagem, a machine; in fact, it is as hard-worked a word as "thing." [*Miss French's note.*]

Oh, Lord God!" He remembered so vividly just how useless his efforts were that he groaned aloud.

Uncle Nate stopped short.

"I wuz forgittin' everythin' but my trubbel, Nate," said Griffin; "wuz ye sayin' suthin'?"

"I wuz jes' speakin' 'bout dat ar baby, sah; sayin' 'twar a year 'n' haff ole, jest."

"Yes—the baby—jes' seventeen months," said Griffin, in a dazed way; then, with quite a new expression, he turned his head on the black man. "Ye mean Headlights's baby; what like is hit? Is hit pretty?"

"Iz t' dat," said Uncle Nate, judicially, "I ain't no jedge. Looks right puny an' ga'nted,* but I lay it git over dat at we uns'. Yeah's de twurn, Mist' Griffin! I wish't ye well, sah!"

The "twurn" meant the fork of the road. One of the bifurcations goes on deeper into the swamp, the other deflects toward a clearing wherein, back of cotton-fields and garden, stands a comfortable battened house, the widow Brand's house. A certain trig look about land and buildings may be due to the fact—always kept well to the fore—that the widow came from Georgia. Jeff could see her tall figure on the porch, now; she was caressing a baby. His heart gave a kind of leap in his breast, and he turned white and grabbed at Nate's bag.

"Nate," said he, almost in a whisper, "I wanter see that ar chile! Is't a boy ur a gyurl?"

"Thar 'tis," replied Nate; "li'le boy. Won' ye come by, sah?"

The widow came out to meet them, the baby in her arms. She always wore her hair looped smoothly over her ears and fastened behind with a "tuckin' comb." It was black hair, having a shine to it like her eyes. Spare and tanned as her features were, they were not uncomely, and their expression of shrewd alertness softened wonderfully when she recognized her visitors. The boy certainly was thin, —pale, too,—still, a pretty, bright little fellow, who ruffled the widow's sleek hair and slapped her cheeks, in the gayest humor. Griffin could not understand why he felt a curious pang of relief, seeing how unlike the little castaway was to the dead child. He saluted the widow.

"Oh, we're all stirrin'," she replied. "Aunt Fanny b'en over 'n' tole me 'bout you all's 'fliction. They jes' puttin' the gears on the mewls."

"Won' ye come long er me, Mis' Brand, now!" interrupted Jeff,

---

* Thin; puny is always used for sickly; pert always means lively, well. [*Miss French's note.*]

eagerly; "an' cayn't ye fotch 'long the baby? Ye heerd 'bout Bulah? I'm turrible skeered up 'bout 'er, an' I sorter 'lowed mabbe the little trick mought rouse 'er—being leff so lonesome like; ye know Bulah's powerful good-hearted."

"We kin try," said the widow, musingly; "ye got good sense fur a man person, Jeff."

She was very soon in the wagon, on the seat behind Griffin, watching him as they drove silently through the swamp. She thought that his had been a lonesome kind of life. Jeff Griffin had come back from the wars with an arm the less, to support his bedridden mother, his widowed sister and her family, and a forlorn little cousin with no nearer kindred than they—Bulah Norman. "Old Man Griffin" and the "big boys" had been killed long before. Jeff himself was seventeen, but he had been a soldier for two years. The Griffins originally came from Tennessee. They bought a little farm on the outskirts of a large plantation on the Black River. They were all of them honest, hard-working people, and Jeff had a natural turn for business, though he could not write his name. Those days, there was money in cotton; those halcyon days when we burned our cottonseed for fuel, yet could get more for the cotton alone than we can get for them both now. Jeff toiled early and late. As the widow from Georgia told her son Frank (a good fellow, clever, too, but a bit touched by the climate), Jeff Griffin's one arm did more than any other man's two. He prospered; he bought more land, he built a house for his mother,—just the year before she died, poor soul,—and generously started his nieces and nephews in life. One by one they drifted out into the world until only their mother and Bulah Norman, now grown into quite a pretty lass of eighteen, remained in the house with Jeff. Bulah was eleven years younger than Jeff. He had always been devoted to her. When she was a child he never tired of her prattle; he gave her a calf, a colt, a saddle, a riding-whip, while every other girl in the settlement was content with a pawpaw switch; he could not do enough for her. If he was too busy to go to school himself, he was never too busy to drive "the little tricks" over to the schoolhouse, and every evening, Bulah, "the least little trick of all," used to teach him what she had learned. Bulah was very fond of Jeff, in a filial way; but Jeff loved Bulah with all his heart and soul and strength. He was such a dry, quiet, matter-of-fact fellow that nobody ever dreamed of such a thing; that is, nobody but the widow. How do women manage to discover a reticent man's passion? Jeff had never confided in the widow; but one day she remarked to him, with the calm bluntness of the backwoods,

"Look a yere, Jeff, ef you don' make haste an' court Bulah she'll be takin' up with that thar triflin', biggity Sam Eller that she met up with down to Newport w'ilst she's stoppin' with S'leeny's gyurl. She will so."

"Po' Jeff!" the widow was saying to herself, now, "I come too late. He done got her prommus then. Jeff looked like he was jes' gittin' up by a spell er sickness, them days—p'int blank gashly; but he never let on, jes' talked natchell to Bulah, an', law me, what a sight er truck he guv 'er! An' thar she leff that nice house that he done fixed up so lady-fine fur her, an' her room, all papered, gran' 's Mrs. Francis's,—roses all over the walls, and the ceilin' painted blew like the sky,—t' go and live with Sam Eller in a boat! I reckon she found out right quick that thar warn't nuthin' t' *him* 'cept good looks an' brags! an' ye cayn't eat neither. Wonder how long 'fore he begun borryin' money er Jeff. He wuż no force, nohow. Say he war blin' drunk w'en he tumbled outen the pilot-house, spang on the deck, an' mashed 'is shin, and never got up by it. Lived a whole year ayfter, too. Bulah war mighty long-sufferin' with him, tendin' on him night 'n' day, an' runnin' the boat, too; an', in course, the baby mus' come in the thick of it! An' 't made me mad, seein' him so ill * with her. I don' guess a man person kin holp r'arin' on ye, *some,* w'en he's sick, kase he wants out so bad, r'iles 'im all up; but *he* wuz a-cussin' and sw'arin' the plum' w'ile, an' steamboat cap'ns natchelly kin cuss wusser'n anybody else; 'clare, I don' see how she cud b'ar 't sich a patient way. What wud she 'a' done 'outen Jeff? Keepin' the cap'n under, an' lendin' money, and lettin' S'leeny go an' stay on the boat by spells to holp 'er an' cherkin' 'er up—law me, I never seen a man person like Jeff Griffin! An' now that the Lord done took the cap'n, an' she kin have her time an' her pleasure, she won' go home long er Jeff; naw, she mus' run the boat twell she kin pay off the money—jes' biggity, *she* is! How come she don' marry Jeff? That ar'd pay him best. Nex' thing, he mus' coax S'leeny to go long er Bulah, an' leave him 'lone with jes' Aunt Fanny ter 'tend ter 'im. I know *her* cookin'; ye cud build chimbleys outen her light bread. An' now, this have ter come on 'em—po' Bulah!"

She bit off her sigh, lest it should disturb Jeff, for they had come to their journey's end, and the horses were standing. There were the brown cotton-rows and the whitish-brown stalks strewn over them; there, under the elm-trees, was Aunt Fanny's cabin, and there was

* Cross. [*Miss French's note.*]

the house, long, low, with its black roof and white-washed walls. The open gallery in the centre had been decorated with bunches of sweet herbs and strings of red pepper. Two or three saddles and a gun are expected to hang in an Arkansas "gallery;" they were a little brighter than common here.

The new-comers stepped softly through the gallery into a large room. Bulah was sitting, precisely as Jeff's imagination had pictured her, rocking her dead baby. An elderly woman had her back to them, leaning over the hearth, and the turkey-wing in her hand, with which she was brushing the bricks, moved by jerks as if the hand were nervous.

Bulah did not look up; her head was bent over the waxen face on her arm. The dead calm of her own face was more ghastly and pitiful to see than any anguish. All the while, she was rocking very gently, never ceasing, or in the least varying the motion. Her chair made the merest creak; yet, all at once, the other woman hurled the turkey-wing aside to wring her hands, sobbing: "Bulah, I cayn't enjure t' hear ye! For the Lord's sake putt her down! 'Tain't Christian-like. Oh, dear! oh, dear! she don' hear a word."

She did not seem to hear. To her, in that awful mystery of grief, where her soul was with her dead child and her dead hopes, all this outside jar and fret vibrated so faintly, that before she could comprehend their presence they had ceased. Nor did she seem to notice Jeff when he showed her the coffin, begging her, weeping, to look at it.

The widow, with the child in her arms, stepped across the floor on tiptoe. "Bulah," said she, solemnly, "the Lord taken you' baby, an' this yere baby's mother have desarted him, an' he's all alone on earth. Cayn't ye find it in you' heart t' have pity on him?"

She put the child down, close to the strange-looking, silent woman, and, naturally enough, he began to cry.

At the first whimper, Bulah's eyes were lifted; with an indescribably wild and agonizing inquiry, she stared at the small creature, now quite terrified, and wailing, "Mammy! mammy!"

"Ye ain't got no mother, baby," said she; then, with her dreadful composure, "nur I ain't got no baby." She would have loosened one arm to touch the little fellow, but the action seemed to recall something; for, screaming "How could she! how could she!" she burst into a passion of tears, and while she wept, the widow gently took the dead child out of her clasp.

Little Bulah's grave had been green for months, and it was on an autumn day that Jeff Griffin stood on the platform of the plantation store, waiting for the *Samuel Eller* to round the Bend. Being Saturday afternoon, there was a pretty bustle about the settlement —a hum from the mill where the cotton-wagons were unloading, a continual ring of the hammer from the smithy, and a far-away song floating up from the cotton-fields filled with pickers. At least thirty horses were tied to the fence-rail on the left, and a score of booted legs dangled over either platform. Occasionally, a sunbonnet might appear in the doorway, but it was likely to go straightway about its business, having possibly more business than belonged to the boots. All about this wee hubbub of human life was the forest; maples and hackberry-trees kept up their autumn revelries in scarlet and gold, and their gay leaves, fluttering amid the sad-colored foliage of the cypress, looked like courtiers dancing with Puritans. To the right, the woods on either side the river-bank seemed to converge; that was "the Bend."

"Yon she comes!" cried Jeff, spying a cork-screw of smoke above the tree-tops. He spoke to the widow from Georgia, who had just emerged from the store, in a very clean and stiff print gown, and was prudently testing some new snuff before carrying it away.

"Cap'n Bulah never misses," she answered; "ain't it amazin' how well she done! Say she done passed her examination, an' got a license reg'lar. The mate says they ain't many like 'er. Expect S'leeny stayed down t' Black Rock 'ith her son. How are you all's little trick?"

"Oh, he's right peart," said Jeff, his plain face quite beaming; "gittin' on smart. Talks a heap. Follers me roun' everywhar, laffin', an' grabbin' at my pants—sorter good them little fingers feel, don't they? Put him on ole Nig, las' week. I wish't you'd a seen 'im; fust, he looked mighty jubious; then he begins to laff. He'll git likened to ridin' mighty briefly."

"Yo' mos' petted on him 's Bulah, ain't ye? How come ye don' keep him an' her both with ye, allus? Actchelly, Jeff, my bones is wearin' out waitin' t' dance at yo' weddin'!"

The reply to such jocularity ought to have been a sheepish grin, but Jeff looked very downcast. "Ye won't never dance at *my* weddin'," said he, "an' iz t' Bulah, she have laid by t' stay single."

"Wal, I didn't aim t' drag * ye, Jeff, but—law me!" The caustic twitch of the widow's lips disappeared in a gurgle of dismay; she will never be nearer swallowing her snuff-stick. On the landing in front

---

* Tease. [*Miss French's note.*]

of her was a tall woman, whose wild beauty could not be obscured
by her wretched dress—a draggled brown-stuff skirt, ragged blue
jacket, and towsled red handkerchief, knotted awry. A mass of glossy
black hair was straggling out of its coil over the red triangle behind;
her battered hat shaded a bold profile, cut cleanly, like the head
on a Roman coin. The sun, which plays havoc with dainty beauties,
had only deepened the rich tints of her skin, and brightened the untamed fire in her eyes. She was as graceful and unconscious as a
panther.

"Headlights!" muttered Mrs. Brand, under her breath.

Jeff had not even seen her; all his eyes were for the boat. Yes,
that was Bulah on the upper deck, and there was the dear little
white head against her skirts. Other people might see merely a slip
of a woman, with plenty of freckles on her fair skin, a firm little
mouth, and pathetic blue eyes. What Jeff saw—but how can I picture the radiant being as the lover sees her?

Now the plank is down, and Jeff, with his one arm and his Southern gallantry, is helping the widow across, who doesn't need helping
one whit, but accepts it as the duty of a "man person." In a minute they are on the deck, and Jeff has little Jeffy on his shoulders
and can look at Bulah. But why have Tom Bracelin, the deputy-
sheriff, and his two men come on board, and does that shabby woman
mean to take passage on the *Samuel Eller?* She pushed the under-
lings aside with an imperious elbow, and got close to Jeff and the
little fellow.

"That's him!" she shouted, "that's my chile! Take him 'way,
boss!"

"Oh!" exclaimed Bulah, and flung herself upon Jeffy's small legs,
the only portion of him within reaching distance.

"What ye seekin'?" demanded Jeff, sternly.

"I are seekin' my own chile, thet I leff unner the store-counter,"
Headlights answered, "an' you uns taken him."

"Ye wicked critter! do ye reckon we all will guv him up t' ye?"

"I reckon ye'll have ter," said Headlights, composedly; "they's a
right smart er folkses kin sw'ar hit's my chile. You all ain't 'dopted
of 'im, nur nuthin'!"

"Look a yere, you Mis' Headlights, or whutsomever 's yo' name,"
said Mrs. Brand, "ain't ye got no natchell motherlike feelin's 'bout
the po' little trick's own intrusts? Look at him bein' raised so good,
gwine ev'ry Sunday t' school or t' preachin', an' gittin' washed hisseff
ever' mawnin', an' good cloze, and his knees patched beaucherful, an'
look a' them copper toes,"—shaking poor Jeffy's foot at her,—"an'

you cayn't so much as guv him proper victuals; I seen ye, myseff, feedin' up that innercent chile on gouber peas and hog's melts! My word, I wonder he got any insides leff—he hadn't orter have."

Headlights listened quite unmoved to this homily, and equally unmoved she heard the threats of the boat people and the remonstrances of Mr. Francis, who had come aboard. The owner of the plantation was no more to her than the deck-hands. There is a depth of poverty as arrogant as riches, and social distinctions count for nothing in that grave.

"Ye kin r'ar all ye like," said she, tossing her black mane, "I'm gwine cyar off my boy. Yere, baby, come to mammy, mammy got candy."

But Jeffy gripped Jeff's neck all the harder, whimpering "Jeffy 'faid! 'Way, lady! 'Way, lady!" and, with a very black frown, Headlights beckoned the officer to help her.

He advanced, looking desperately ill at ease. "I'm right sorry, ma'am," said he, "but she's got the law on her side, and I have to do my juty."

Jeff and the mate of the boat exchanged glances; they had the simple Southern plan of dumping the officers overboard and steaming off down the river; they were willing, however, that Mrs. Brand should try her device first.

"Wal, Tom Bracelin," said she, as it were clearing the decks for action by throwing away her snuff-stick, "I never did 'low t' see *you* draggin' off a po' harmless little chile int' perdition—fur ye know 'tain't no better 'mongst them cotton-pickers—you with you' own six little tricks t' home, too! How'd ye enj'y hevin' them two least ones tolled off by a gang er cotton-pickers? Cap'n Bulah sets 's much store by thet ar baby iz you kin by yourn; and mo' too, kase it's all she's got. Nur wud I of b'lieved it er *you*, Lafayette Sands,"— wheeling round upon one of the deputies, who tried, ineffectually, to blow his nose to hide his confusion,—"them evenin's you an' Bulah Norman wud come home from school tergether an' be projickin' roun' my kitchin for light bread an' smear. Naw, sir, I didn't guess them days ye wud do Bulah meaner'n a murderer! Iz fur *you*, sir," —the second deputy jumped,—"I ain't got no acquaintance with ye, but you' a pretty man, an' I jedge ye to be a clever man,"—the second deputy rubbed off a smirk with a very big hand,—"an' I don't guess ye aim ter hurt that ar pretty chile, ef *'tis* the law! Onyhow, gentlemen," concluded the widow, in the most unexpected way, "ye won't let 'er cyar that chile 'way th'out payin' Cap'n Bulah board."

"Board!" screamed Headlights, "who ever heerd er payin' board fur a baby?"

"Board war guv that baby," retorted the undaunted Georgian; "good board, too. An' feedin' a chile ain't like sloppin' a pig, neither. Ye cayn't devil them little stummicks with leavin's; they has t' have good victuals that cost money. That chile b'en boarded frum last er Feberary to last er October—makes eight months. Call it two dollars a month; that's p'int blank cheap; twicet eight's sixteen. Then the cloze; Cap'n Bulah done spent most er nine dollars fur truck fur that ar chile, ain't she, Mr. Francis?"

"More," replied Mr. Francis, with a twinkle in his eye—he saw the widow's drift; "she must have eleven dollars charged on the petty ledger, now."

"I'm blamed my skin," the cotton-picker struck in, "if I ever spent dollar 'n' haff on the chile. Quit yo' funnin', I won't pay board!"

"Reckon some folkses wud count in the boat-fares gwine back'ards and for'ards on the river," continued the widow, "but we uns ain't graspin'. Twicet eight's sixteen, an' eleven is twenty-seven. Thar ar's ciphered right, ain't it?"

Headlights burst into a fierce sort of laughter, crying, "I ain't got twenty-seven cents!"

"Oh, we uns air content t' take a morgige on the chile," replied the widow, calmly, "for six months; an' we'll keep the chile twell then, an' ef ye don't pay then we'll keep the chile furever mo'. Mr. Francis is a squire; he'll draw up the papers. Do you all 'gree to that?"

Bulah released her hold on Jeffy to look around; her pallid features and entreating eyes said more than her voice: "Oh, gentlemen, be merciful, look how he loves me; he ain't nuthin' to *her;* don't part us! He's always b'en puny; he'll die off in the swamps, like she'll take him."

The men whispered together. They were indeed glad of a loophole of escape; and the upshot of the matter was the production by Mr. Francis (after an interval in the cabin) of a document duly drawn up and reading as follows: "I, Sabrina Mathews, alias Headlights, do promise to pay to Mrs. Bulah Eller, of Lawrence County, Arkansas, the sum of twenty-seven dollars on or before the fifteenth day of April, 18—; and if I do not pay the aforesaid sum of twenty-seven dollars by or before the fifteenth day of April, 18—, I hereby promise to give and bequeath and resign to the said Mrs. Bulah Eller my child, now known as Jefferson Griffin Eller, to keep for her child;

and I do hereby promise to renounce any and all my claims to the aforesaid Jefferson Griffin Eller."

It was only when Headlights was convinced that the sheriff and his men would do no more for her that she consented to make her mark to this paper. She insisted upon her right to pay before the six months, and Mr. Francis did not venture to refuse. "Oh, let 'er have it her way," said the widow; then, in an undertone to Bulah, "Git shet of 'er now, an' we kin gether the chile an' light out, don' ye see?"

So Headlights had her way, and signed; and every man on the boat who could write his name witnessed, with a dim idea that he was helping Cap'n Bulah.

Having made her mark, Headlights strode up to Jeff, who was still holding the boy. Bulah would have stepped between them.

"I ain't aimin' t' hurt him," said the cotton-picker. "Ye won't stop me kissin' of him oncet, will ye?"

The two women glared at each other, probably with as venomous feelings as those two historic dames who puzzled King Solomon. But Jeff had said truly that Bulah was a fair-minded woman. "Ye got the right to," said she.

Headlights bent over the baby with surprising gentleness. She was so tall that it was easy for her to reach his hair and his little averted cheek as he clung to Jeff's neck. She whispered something, of which Jeff only caught the words "sorry" and "hurt ye," and immediately ran off the boat so swiftly and recklessly that she nearly fell into the water.

"Well, that critter!" said the deputy, "she come to me yesterday. She's got out with the fellow she ran off with. Lum Shinault was telling me *he* heard he gave 'er the hickory, an' she drawed a knife on him. Now, she's back with the rest of the Missouri folks, terrible anxious to git her baby; she'd orter b'en anxious a spell back, *I* take it."

After that day the *Samuel Eller* made her regular trips round the Bend; but no one ever saw the little white curls dancing over the deck. A good many people believed that Jeffy really was on board; if so, he never came out of hiding. Headlights did not go away. She stayed on, picking cotton, until the ragged white streamers were all stripped off the brown stalks. Two or three times Jeff caught a glimpse of her prowling about his own fields. He never attempted to speak to her, and she gave him nothing more than a scowl. He was watching her secretly. He was sure that she must be saving money; for she was sober on Christmas Day, when the rest of the cotton-pickers were a howling mob, and, for that matter, there were very few steady legs left on the plantation. One day, visiting Bulah and S'leeny on the boat (good-by, now, to the happy times when Jeff could watch Bulah, with Jeffy on her knees, on the other side of his own fireplace), he observed that Bulah seemed troubled. Finally, she brought out a little package, and told him that while the boat was unloading at Newport, Jeffy had been allowed to walk in the street with S'leeny ("for the chile's gitting right puny cooped up so, and I had to see to the loadin'"), and a woman had spoken to him and given him the package. "S'leeny don't know her by sight, but she suspicioned 'twas *her,* an' she called her to stop and take the things back, but she run too quick. See, Jeff!"

She displayed a flimsy red silk handkerchief and a child's harp.

"Yes, hit war Headlights," said Jeff, gravely; "she bought 'em at the store. Frank Brand tole me. I 'lowed then she got 'em for Jeffy—Law me, Bulah, what ye doin'?"

He caught Bulah's hand just in time to prevent harp and handkerchief going into the Black River.

"Lemme 'lone, Jeff," cried she, with flashing eyes; "Jeffy's b'en talkin' of the critter ever sence."

"Oh, hush, honey," said Jeff, soothingly; " 'tis rilin', but don' throw the critter's pore little truck overboard. She got sorter feelin's, I expeck, too."

"I *hate* her," said Bulah; "I'd like to *kill* her!"

But she dropped the bundle on the deck instead of in the water.

All this made Jeff feverishly anxious, for he was positive that if Headlights did not go away Bulah would sell the boat and hide herself somewhere with the child; besides, he had a dread of some collision between the two women. "An' ef Bulah mixes with Headlights she'll shore git killed up!" thought Jeff. Therefore it was a mighty relief to him, one day, to see the whole troop of the cotton-pickers, Headlights in their midst, ploughing through the mud on the road to the railway station, six miles away. He rode the whole muddy way after them, to see them safely on the train bound for Missouri. Then he rode home, singing. Possibly he was jubilant too soon, since Headlights got out at the next village.

Jeff went straight to the landing. He heard the refrain of the "roustabouts'" aimless song,

"Four o'clock done come at las'!"

and he could see the cotton-bales bounding along the plank; down among them he ran, light as a boy.

"She's gone!" cried Bulah; "I see it in yo' face! Oh, Jeff, take us home, Jeffy's plum' sick. Simmons can take the boat to Black Rock."

Of course she went; and, late as it was then, Jeff rode ten miles for the doctor. The next morning he rode again to the railway station, to telegraph to a larger town for some medicines. He must wait for the train to bring them, so that it was after noon before he could start homeward. The road is the worst in the country-side, and just then, to use the phrase of the bottom, " 'twud mire a snipe." He was crawling along, two thirds of the way home, when his mule shied, with a great splash, and nearly reared off the roadway. "Dad gum ye!" cried Jeff, irritably, "whut—by grabs, hit's a human critter!"

The cause of the beast's fright lay athwart some logs, her skirts trailing in the mud. No sooner had Jeff lifted her head than he uttered a loud cry: "My Lord, it's Headlights!"

There was no response; the head lay on his arm like a stone; evidently she had sat down to rest, and swooned. Jeff heartily wished that she were dead instead; but he could not leave her thus. He glanced disconsolately about him—at his mule improving the unexpected leisure to munch cane-leaves; at the brilliant, desolate sweep of swamp, silver-trees, green moss, gray pools of water, and the rotten corduroy raised a little out of the ooze. "Wal, the Lord's mussiful," groaned Jeff, "they's a right smart er water 'roun', onyhow."

He got Headlights's head in a more comfortable position, and splashed water on her face until a gasp arrested his hand and she looked dizzily up at him, murmuring, "Then I done got thar. How's baby?"

"Git whar? You' in the swamp, gyurl. Wake up!"

Headlights did sit up, and moaned.

"I cudn't make out," she muttered. "Lemme 'lone, Jeff Griffin; how come ye done slopped me all over? I'll shore be chillin' ter-morrer."

"Ye'll shore be chillin' ef ye don' git up outen this yere slosh."

"How's my baby?—least ye mought tell me that much."

"Wal, he are plum' bad, then," answered Jeff, gloomily—angrily, too, since he saw nothing for him to do but to put Headlights on his mule and walk himself; it would be like murder to leave her in the swamp, and the mule could not carry two through such mud. Yet he felt a twinge of pity as he saw the tears rolling down Headlights's cheeks at his words. "Ye mus' git on my mule," said he, more kindly; "ye cayn't walk, an' ye mus' git outen the swamp."

She struggled to her feet and let him help her into the saddle, saying, "I'll ride a spell, then I kin walk." Had she attempted to ride in the usual feminine posture, she would certainly have fallen off the mule, being nearly unconscious; luckily, neither Jeff nor she thought of such a thing. By and by she began to shiver violently.

"Thar 'tis, wust sorter chill, an' we uns' house the nighest by two miles!" At the idea he groaned aloud, for the relentless hospitality of the bottom left him no alternative.

"Mist' Griffin," spoke Headlights, feebly, "I'll get down, ef you' tired. I kin make out. On'y won't ye tell me more 'bout my baby, fust?"

"Wal, Headlights, he come down yistiddy, an' his fever ain't cooled, an' doctor, he's skeered er pneumony; but he says he are a heap apter ter git up by it fur havin' of such good 'tendance like his—like Bulah's and S'leeny's. Don't ye go fur to cry, Headlights; ye shake all over, an' I cayn't hole ye!"

Headlights somehow choked her sobs. Jeff went on: "Now, Headlights, I'm goin' cyar ye home with me, case ye ain't fit t' walk. Now be ye goin' t' devil us, onyhow? try fur t' toll Jeffy way an'"—

"Naw, naw, I ain't no short; * I fight fair. I wudn't do ye sicher way."

"Wal," muttered Jeff to himself, "I expeck S'leeny'll be r'arin' on me, an' Bulah—but Bulah's fair-minded. Onyhow, cayn't be holped, an' they'll git over it, some way."

With this reflection, which has eked out many a man's courage on the brink of a tussle with his womankind, Jeff waded along. A good deal of the time he had to hold Headlights on the mule or she would have slipped off through sheer weakness, and all the while she appeared to be in a kind of stupor. Once he asked her how she happened to hear of Jeffy's illness; how she came to be at the station. She said: "I came ter git Jeffy; I knowed ye'd have him back by ye, quick's ye 'lowed I done lit out. I heerd the men t' the deppo a-talkin' 'bout ye. I walked from Hoxie on the track; started afore sun up." He thought that her mind must be wandering.

It was a dismal journey, tedious to the last degree, but at last the mule turned in at his own gate, and S'leeny, hearing the hounds' chorus of welcome, ran out to meet him. She lifted up her hands in horror when she recognized his companion. "My, my, my, Jeff Griffin! are ye clean bereft?"

"You hush!" whispered Jeff. "I didn't ax 'er. I run up with 'er in

* No cheat. [*Miss French's note.*]

the woods. She war layin' on a log dead's * a hammer. I cudn't leave 'er that-away, cud I?"

"Guv me the med'cines, an' you cyar 'er straight t' Mis' Brand's."

"I cayn't. Look at 'er: she are chillin', this minnit."

Headlights had staggered into the gallery; now she would have fallen, had not both brother and sister caught her. "Ye *see!*" said Jeff.

"What'll Bulah say?" groaned S'leeny; "law me, ain't she got 'nuff trubbels an' triberlations 'thouten *you* a-pilin' more onto her?"

But this was only the futile last stroke of a vanquished fighter, the natural impulse of the woman to find the man to blame; S'leeny had her own conscience, and Jeff knew that she would make no more objections. In fact, she helped him to get Headlights to the fire, and got the quinine and whiskey before she went to Bulah. Headlights had revived a little and was sitting in the armchair, when Bulah softly opened the door and came in. Jeff ventured one furtive glance, and began to poke the fire.

"Don't take on, Bulah," begged he, with that artless freedom from tact which is the right of his sex; "onyhow, she's Jeffy's mother"—

"I wanter know 'bout my baby," interrupted Headlights.

Bulah's chin went up a little: "I expect you mean my Jeffy; he's mighty bad"—

"Kin I look on him—jest oncet—jes' fur a minnit?"

"He'd most like be scared up to see a stranger," said Bulah, coldly.

"Law me," cried the helpless man between the two women, "Bulah, how *kin* ye be so cruel?"

It was the first word of reproach that he had ever spoken to her, and it must have gone straight to her heart, for she put both hands there quickly, with a sort of gasp, like a person stabbed; a little flicker of color came into her cheeks and went out, leaving her extremely pale. Jeff was already in an agony of remorse, crying, "Naw, naw, ye ain't! It's me that's cruel."

"Yes, I am; yes, I was," said Bulah. "Come, Headlights, ye cayn't walk; lean on me. Ye mus' jes' look at him an' come out!"

"I kin walk," answered Headlights, shortly. Walk she did, though unsteadily, across the gallery into the other room. It was the pretty room, with the roses on the wall-paper and the sky-blue ceiling. S'leeny could have fainted when she beheld that tall shape, all wet and muddy, and the wild face and burning eyes. Headlights, not venturing to advance, for fear of awakening the little sleeper, stood on the

---

* They have a peculiar use of the word "dead" for "senseless." "He knocked him dead," they will say, or, "She was plum' dead for an hour." [*Miss French's note.*]

threshold, where she could see the bed, and gazed with an agony of longing at the flaxen curls and flushed cheek on the pillow. After a moment, she bent down very carefully, and began to remove her miserable shoes. S'leeny almost screamed to see Bulah kneel and take off those dreadful, mud-soaked shoes herself.

"Though, to be shore," reflected S'leeny, "they'd of p'intedly tracked the floor. Mabbe that's how come she done it." So little do the ones nearest us know of the strange and complex emotions which war in our motives. But Jeff understood. His wet eyes met Bulah's, and afterward she remembered his look; though then her own feelings were swept away by the spectacle of the overpowering feeling before her. Headlights crept up to the bed. She bent over the sleeper; and the desperate misery in her face touched even S'leeny. Her breath came in gasps, with the fierce pain which she would not show. At that moment, Bulah, living over again her own desolation, felt a horrible kinship with this mother, suffering as she had suffered; yet all the while her heart seemed to stand still with fear and impatience, lest Jeffy should wake and be frightened. After all, Headlights only kissed a stray lock of hair. Then she stole out of the room, and, before they could stop her, ran out of the house, just as she was.

Jeff and Bulah found her in the cow-shed, crouched on a pile of hay. Jeff tried to say something comforting, but he stopped as soon as she turned her face.

Headlights spoke: "Yes, I know he'll git well. 'Tain't that. I seen 'im. 'Tain't no good me hopin' fur ter take him 'way. I cud never have thin's fixed up so good fur 'im when he's sick. He's puny. He'd die up, shore." She drew in her breath and said, with a mighty effort, "Ye kin hev him fur good. I won't pester ye no more."

"Oh, my Lord!" said Bulah. The tears blinded her, and they were tears for Headlights; she was disarmed by her adversary's surrender. "Come, ye poor thing," said she, gently; "come in an' get rested, an' then ye can help me tend him."

In her turn, she had made the greatest concession in her power. Headlights rose submissively to follow her, but before she took a step she touched Bulah's arm, saying, "They's one thing more—you uns 'll be gittin' married."

"Me!" Bulah said huskily, and choked.

"Ye got you' mind mighty sot on 'er, ain't ye?" said Headlights to Jeff.

Surely it was his good angel that prompted his answer: "It b'en sot on 'er all the days I knowed her, Headlights. They ain't nobuddy on earth like 'er, to my mind."

"An' ye jes' done got 'er," said Headlights. "Wal, I don' keer, all I want's fur ye ter prommus ter be allus good ter my boy, whatsumever"—

"We will," said Bulah, solemnly. "Now, come on in."

Bulah led her into the house. She was burning with fever. Bulah put her to bed, where, almost instantly, she fell asleep. But it was the widow from Georgia and S'leeny who entered presently, bearing each a stick, and, as it were, fished the outcast's clothes from the chair, with countenances on which were vividly painted the sensations natural to two such notable housewives, and bore them out into the yard, and hung them on the line to air.

"An' ef it do come on to rain," remarked the widow, complacently, "it'll holp t' clean 'em all the mo'!"

Bulah had gone back to Jeffy. Jeff whispered to her that he was sure that the boy was better—his breathing was easier, he was sleeping quietly. "An' look," said Jeff, "them little curls er his'n is plum' wet: the fever's cooled; he won' git pneumony ayfter all!" Bulah looked. She sank down on her knees, and Jeff knew what she was doing; his own heart swelled with gratitude, not the less fervent because confused and dumb.

Headlights was fated to keep her word. Her chill developed into pneumonia, and as Mrs. Brand (who came over to nurse her) observed truly, "Cotton-pickers never had no ruggedness, an' she cudn't pear ter git up by it." She added: "Headlights warn't a bit ill; jes' iz easy, patient critter like ye ever seen; didn't know nuthin' most er the time."

Once, just before the end, she seemed conscious. Jeffy had been brought in to see her—polite little Jeffy, who had been well drilled in his lesson beforehand. "Po' lady, so sick," said Jeffy; "Jeffy sorry. Make it aw well;" and, giving her the only remedy his babyish mind knew, he took her face between his little soft hands, and kissed it.

The sleeper stirred in her sleep. "Yes, yes, baby," she murmured drowsily, "mammy knows. 'Tis cole in the cotton. Mammy cyar 'im home. Have a fire." Then she opened her eyes wide and saw them all. The spark in her dim eyes seemed to glow again, but no longer in anger or pain; she looked at Bulah, steadily, with the strange, peaceful, solemn gaze of the dying.

"Yes, I will," said Bulah, as though she had been asked a question; indeed, it seemed to Bulah that she had.

Headlights fumbled at her throat, with an old shoestring that was around it; when Bulah drew out a leather bag, she smiled. "Fur— him," she murmured, and her hand groped for the child. Almost before it touched him, she was away from him and all earthly troubles, in the merciful shadows; and so gently did those waters of oblivion submerge her soul that no ripple was left to mark when it finally sank forever.

"An' I 'clare," avowed Mrs. Brand to S'leeny, "I are plum' surprised by myseff, I b'en cryin' fur that ar critter like she war my own kin. But she war so sorter bidable an' decent, an' done the little trick so decent, ayfter all! I sw'ar some folkses don' git no fair show in this world!"

"Bulah been cryin' too," said S'leeny. "Wal, I don' see no call fur grievin'. All I wisht are that she'd of leff some money fur the buryin'. Bulah, she will have Mr. Dake make one er his fust-rate coffins, though I say his second-bes' is plenty good nuff. Jeff done gone fur 't now."

"She guv a little bag t' Bulah; whar's it at, Bulah?"

"It's Jeffy's," said Bulah, showing it, "but I don't guess there's any harm in lookin' "—

"My word, *no!*" cried the widow, with her fingers inside. The contents of the bag were a roll of bank-bills and a folded paper. The roll contained twenty-seven dollars. The paper was a copy of the mortgage on Jeffy. The widow from Georgia dropped into a chair, alternately shook her head and waved her hands, and finished by wiping her eyes, without saying a word.

"My, my, my!" cried S'leeny, "ain't it a main mussy the critter died; she cud of taken Jeffy 'way!"

But Bulah, who had grown very pale, said, "S'leeny, ye don't know. That woman trusted me. I'm a-goin' to tell Jeffy all 'bout 'er when I give him this. Headlights, can ye hear me? You paid the mortgage, an' he b'longs to *you,* too!"

The Loaf of Peace

IF the kitchen-door stand open—and the door of an Arkansas kitchen is likely to stand open on a late February day—you can look from the kettles of the big stove to the bend of the Black River, to the steep bank where red willow twigs top the velvet down which will be grass, and across the gray waters to willows and sycamores and canebrakes and a few cabins in the clearings. Should you step to the door, you can see the plantation-store and mill, and a score of gambrel-roofed white houses. In the fields, the whitish-brown cotton-stalks lie on the dun-colored earth. The birds are singing in the cypress forest, and a red-bird flutters his gorgeous wings on a stray stalk that has escaped the cutter.

Aunt Callie, one day in February, saw the fields and the bird, and also a little girl whose flannel cape was the color of the bird's wing, and whose thick hair had a gleam of the same tint.

"Humph," said Aunt Callie, "reckon by her favor, dat ar's Haskett's gell comin' by."

"Haskett's gell," otherwise Mizzie Haskett, came awkwardly and shyly down the walk, and balanced herself on the kitchen steps. She wore her holiday attire, a blue-and-white cotton frock, red flannel cape, and a large bonnet (evidently made for a much older head) decked with red roses. Her hair was tied with a bright new green ribbon; and round a soft and snowy little neck was a large white frill in which glittered an imitation-gold pin. Certainly her pretty skin did not need it, but she was powdered (or, to be accurate, floured) profusely; this last Southern touch of art being added, injudiciously, after the putting on of the red cape. She was, moreover, consumed with embarrassment, which sent a flood of blushes through the flour layer, over her skin, from the roots of her hair to the nape of her neck.

"Ye seekin' ary pusson, Sissy?" said Aunt Callie, frigidly. She had cooked for "the quality" twenty years, and she knew her own dignity.

"I be'n seekin' Miss Dora, please," the little girl answered meekly, in a very sweet voice.

Miss Caroll, overhearing both question and answer, hastened to invite the child to come in, which she did after a long interval of scraping her shoes outside.

Once in the kitchen, seated, and her feet twisted behind the rungs of a kitchen chair, Mizzie gasped twice, then said, "Paw sent me. It dropped through."

"What do you mean?" said Miss Caroll.

"It was sorter sad-lookin'," continued Mizzie, on the verge of tears. "Paw made out to eat it, but I knowed 'twasn't right."

"Eat what? I really don't understand."

"The brown bread, ma'am," sobbed Mizzie, big tears rolling down her cheeks, but persistently gasping her way through her sentences. "I put it in the steamer, like—you all—tole me; but—it dropped through an' spread out. Didn't raise up high like you all's."

"You unfortunate child!" said Dora, "do you mean that you poured your brown bread into the steamer—without any tin?"

This, it appeared, was precisely what Mizzie had done.

" 'Cause Mis' Caroll didn't say nuthin' 'cept 'Put it into the steamer.' "

"Paw and me made it together," said she, taking out a square of cotton to wipe her eyes; "an' when it come out so sad an' curis-lookin' he said for me to come here to-day, 'cause you all wud be makin' of you' bread, an' mabbe wudn't mind me lookin' on. Tole me to shore wipe my feet dry. Paw'd hate terrible for me to pester ye."

Aunt Callie visibly softened under this humility. "Dar, sot still an' watch me, den," said she.

"I'll tell you," said Dora; "I taught Aunt Callie our New England bread."

She could not have asked a more attentive scholar, Mizzie watching every motion of the great wooden spoon with the eyes of a hawk, and her lips moving at intervals as do those of a child who inaudibly repeats a lesson to himself.

Presently, the brown batter being safely in the tin mould, and the mould in the steamer, the small maid asked:—

"Please, ma'am, cud we all buy a tin trick like that at the store?" Being informed that she could, she sighed with relief, extricated her feet from the chair, and "made her manners."

"I'm much obliged to you all, ma'am, an' I wish ye well."

Hereupon she would have gone, had not Dora detained her to slip a slice of cake and some apples into her hand.

They saw her stop, a little distance from the house, and carefully wrap the cake in a piece of paper.

"She'll never tech a bite o' dat ar," said Aunt Callie,—"jes' tote it home to de young uns. She do dem chil'en good as a mudder. Dey ain't got any mudder, ye un'erstan'. She keep de 'ouse alone ebber sence her maw died. Dar's her paw; and Sal' Jane, dat's goin' on ten; and de baby, dat's two; an' her, dat's mabbe fo'teen. De cookin' an' scrubbin' an' makin' de cloze, she an' her paw, dey do it all. When he makin' a crop, den *she* do it all. But in winter he makes out to sen' 'er ter school mos' days 'cept washin' day. He guv 'er dat pin, but mos' times she lends it ter Sal' Jane. Sal' Jane's all fur havin' 'er time an' 'er pleasure; but Mizpah, she's studdy."

Certainly she looked steady, too steady for her years, as she picked her way through the mud. She had stopped at the store, and the "tin trick" glittered under the crook of her elbow. Passing through the "settlement," she went over the brow of the tiny hill, down into the cypress brake. She hastened her pace, tripping along the dim forest ways. Beautiful ways they are in February, with the white bark shining like silver, and the velvet moss coating the north side of the cypresses and sycamores, and the glitter of red berries on the blue-black twigs of the hackberry-trees, and the ferns waving in the damp places, and the little "bluets" which deck the ground, first of all the brave company of spring flowers; but none of these did brisk little Mizzie see, because she was too busy planning for the two younger children and for "Paw."

"We cud make out right well, ef 'twasn't fur that thar cotton," she said to herself. "Well, I wudn't keer 'bout losin' the cotton, either, ef 'twasn't fur such a sight of bad feelin's. I jes' take the all-overs * every time I see paw getherin' his gun to go out. An' it used to be so nice!"

Mizzie sighed heavily. By this time she had come out upon a clearing and cotton-fields. On the edge of the cotton-fields stood a bright blue house. Evidently it was a new house; not only was its color a surprise to the eye accustomed to the universal whitewash of plantation taste, but its snug architecture and straight chimneys proclaimed its recent building. A little girl sat on the porch beside a lank Arkansas hound. The hound rushed across the fields with joyful yelps. Mizzie hushed him as best she could.

"Down, Jeru! Down, charge! You'll fotch him out, shore."

The little girl had followed the dog. She was about Mizzie's age, and her black curls streamed out behind her as she ran.

"My, how long you was!" she exclaimed. "Did she tell ye?"

Mizzie nodded.

"Yes. You be thar, this evening," replied she, solemnly; and she added, "I reckon I'd best fetch 'long the baby. Sal' Jane has had 'im all the mornin'. You mustn't ax too much of them little folks."

"All right. I'll fetch 'long my doll."

The little girl looked about her with a hurried and stealthy air, then pushed her pretty face through the fence rails to kiss Mizzie, saying:—

"You' right good to fix it for me so nice! An' I do love you better 'n any gell in this worl' "—

"O Doshy!" cried Mizzie, "I see him comin'. Oh, fly!"

Instantly she herself darted across the road and plunged into the brake. Doshy ran swiftly toward the house. A voice commanded her to stop; she had been seen. She turned and went back to her father. He was a short, dark man, who snapped an ox-goad against his boot-legs in an unpleasant manner.

"Ain't that gell Dock Haskett's?" he inquired. "Warn't that her here yisterday, too?"

* Shivers. [*Miss French's note.*]

"Yes, sir," said Doshy.

"Didn't I tole ye I didn't want ye to have no more talk with Haskett's folks?"

Then Doshy plucked up heart to answer. "Paw, I cayn't help it. She's so good. An' I like her better 'n any little gell in school."

"Good!" repeated the father, with strong derision. "Good! Ain't she a Haskett? Ain't she got a red head like his'n? Aw, them red heads kin talk an' git 'roun' decent folks, but they'll do ye a meanness whenever ye trust 'em. Look at me! Kin I walk right yit? Confound him, I'll tote that ar bullet er his'n 'roun', long's I live! An' my gell a-wantin' ter run with his gell! I ain't got patience to enjure hit. Go 'long!"

The child made no answer, but, stifling a sob, flew into the house.

Sullenly the father limped about his work. He was not at all a harsh father, and that unusual look of fright and hurt that his girl had worn smote his heart.

"Now I made the little trick feel bad. Blame it all!" he muttered, while he saddled his horse; and he felt all the more bitter toward Haskett, the cause of his ill-temper.

Everybody on the plantation knew that there was open war, a strong and bitter feud, between Luther Morrow and Dock Haskett. Yet, not six months before, they had been warm friends. The quarrel began over a trifle—a dispute as to which of the hunters was the better shot. There was a match which decided nothing, and a hog-hunt in which each shot the same number of wild hogs, and both claimed the last boar. The two men's tempers waxed warmer, and, by consequence, their friendship cooled, and foolish friends made the matter worse. And, finally, Jerusalem Jones, Luther's pet hound, must needs choose this season of wrath to steal a ham from the Haskett gallery. Dock Haskett, unhappily, snatched up his gun and shot at the beast. He missed Jerusalem Jones, but he hit Jerusalem's master, who was on his way to the Hasketts', bent on conciliation, owing to his wife's entreaties. (He even had it in mind to tell Dock that he was in no hurry for the payment of a certain note that would fall due in February. In their friendly days, Luther had lent Dock money.) Enraged at such a reception, Luther brought his own gun to his shoulder, and there was a very pretty fusilade before Mizzie and the neighbors could reach the place from the cotton-fields. Dock had a shot in the shoulder, and Luther was on the ground with that shot in the leg, which was not yet healed.

To-day, for the first time, Luther was able to ride to the store. He went on no pacific mission. Dock was saving his last bales of cotton for the higher spring-prices. They were at the gin, near the store. Luther's business was to have them attached for his debt. The very first person whom he met, after he had concluded this business, was a tall man, lean and awkward, with a kindly freckled face and red hair—in short, Dock Haskett.

He had heard about the cotton. He rode straight up to Luther. "This yere ain't no place for talkin'," said he. "If ye reckon I done ye any wrong, I am ready to have it out with ye any time an' place ye like; but I promised my gell to fotch her some flour, and I got ter git it back to her fust."

Before the two men separated, they had agreed to meet "an' talk 'bout things" that afternoon, at a lonely spot in the cypress brake, midway between their houses.

Then they rode home, carrying no very good appetite to their dinners.

Dock found the new brown bread over the fire when he entered the room at home which was the Hasketts' kitchen, dining-room, and bed-chamber all in one.

The baby toddled to meet him, babbling an inarticulate welcome which Mizzie interpreted at length—the baby was sixteen months old, and more fluent than intelligible of speech.

An apple and a piece of cake had been saved for the father.

"Ye all had some?" said he. Sal' Jane assured him they had, "all 'cept Mizzie, an' *she* fotched 'em."

"Mizzie an' me'll go shares," said Dock. "Ye are allers good to the little tricks. Reckon I kin trust 'em with ye."

He sighed in a curious way, Mizzie thought, as he spoke, and as he kissed her. While she was laying the table for dinner, he helped her, as usual, but more than once he caught himself standing still, dish in hand, staring around the room. To a mere stranger, it might have seemed bare and comfortless. The bricks on the hearth and in the great black throat of the fireplace were uneven and broken. It was a meagre array of tin and delft that was ranged on the shelf above. The walls were unplastered, and their sole ornaments were two colored cards,—one, presented with a box of soap, representing a very chubby infant washing himself; the other, the gift of a stray insurance agent, a red and black sketch of a burning house. The floor was in waves, and the only piece of carpet was before the bed. Dock himself had chopped the rude bedstead out of white-oak timbers, and Mizzie had stuffed the pillows and the mattress with cotton. The great cracks in the walls where the clapboards were warped or broken had been plastered with mud. There were barely two panes of glass in the single window of the room. But Dock looked fondly at the red cushions covering the broken seats of the cane-bottomed chairs, at the figured brown oilcloth on the table, and the bright tin spoons which shone in the blue glass jug bought by Mizzie's cotton-money, and the lamp filled with real coal oil, and it seemed to him a truly luxurious and beautiful apartment, only he used no such fine words.

"Don't it look good!" thought Dock, sorrowfully. "Ye feelin' puny * to-day, paw?" said Mizzie, with an anxious look.

"Naw, honey, I war jes' studyin'." In a minute he added, in a serious tone, "Mizzie, do ye set's much store by Doshy Morrow now'days ez ye use ter?"

Mizzie came up closer to him and leaned her head against his arm, while she answered, "Yes, paw. *She* ain't hurted you, ye know." She twisted the cloth of his sleeve, and went on, "Paw, wud ye—wud ye mind my learnin' Doshy to make this 'ere bread?"

"In co'se not, honey. I ain't no ill-will ter the little trick, nur to her maw neether. She war powerful kind to us all, onct." He muttered under his breath, "May be she'd be kind ag'in, if"—

Instead of completing the sentence, he kissed the anxious little face.

Mizzie thought that he was even kinder than usual that day. After their simple dinner, she saw him chopping wood. He chopped a great pile, enough to last a long while, in the mild weather of February and March. Then he brought the sack of meal into the gallery from the shed. "Handier fur ye," he muttered; and he cut up the half a pig which hung in the shed, so that it was ready for cooking.

By this time, the hour was near three by the wheezy old clock on the shelf. Dock returned to the house.

Sal' Jane was poking the fire, at that moment, with an important air which was explained by her first speech.

"Mizzie's gone with the baby, an' I'm to keep the water b'ilin', so the bread won't spile."

"That's right, honey," said her father. He kissed her and went out again.

She thought nothing of his having his gun over his shoulder.

About the same time, Luther Morrow, also carrying a gun, was shutting his gate. He looked grimly and sadly at the cotton-fields and the house, but he forced a smile when his wife nodded to him from the doorway; and after he had walked a little distance he turned to wave his hand.

* Ill. [*Miss French's note.*]

"Mendoshy's alluz b'en a good wife ter me," he thought; "mabbe she'd like fer ter 'member that 'ar, ef anythin' happens."

The place of meeting was marked by a blasted cypress growing on the edge of a ravine or "slash." A tangle of thorn-trees, papaws, and trumpet-vines made a rude hedge above the bank on the road-side. Luther's first glance showed him Dock's tall figure in blue jeans, outlined against the chalk-white of the cypress. At the same moment, Dock perceived his enemy, and both men advanced, frowning. Half-way they stopped as abruptly as if shot, with a curious embarrassed, shamefaced look. Yet that which had stopped them was but a child's laugh. Immediately it was answered by another childish laugh.

"They're down thar in the slash, I reckon," said Dock. "Say, warn't that yo' gell's voice?"

"Yes; warn't t'other un *your'n?*" said Luther. He was seized with an absurd and incongruous curiosity.

"Cayn't we get nearer to see?" said he.

Dock jerked his thumb over his shoulder, saying, "Thar's a opener place a piece back."

"All right," said Luther.

Neither man caring to walk ahead of the other, the two marched peaceably side by side.

Just so,—the abrupt remembering it and the sting of it made Dock wince,—just so they had walked over that very road a year before; then they carried a coffin between them, and the coffin was that of Dock's wife. She was buried out in the woods, as she had wished. The spot was not twenty rods away. Luther had been Dock's good friend and neighbor then, and it was Mrs. Morrow who brought the bunch of holly and red berries that was lying on the coffin. "And how comes it we b'en walkin' yere to-day, seekin' each other's blood?" thought Dock.

Luther's reflections were of another nature.

"Thar! if that ar bad little trick are runnin' with Haskett's gell agin, ayfter my tellin' her—I jes' *will* guv 'er the bud*—leastways, I'll skeer 'er up, a-promisin' it to her!"

Dock soon halted where the underbrush was less dense.

Each of the men eyed the other sharply before getting on his hands and knees to crawl through. Luther, half-way, met with a mishap, catching on a thorn-tree. A smothered exclamation from him attracted Dock's notice.

* Switch. [*Miss French's note.*]

"My foot got cotched in the elbow-brush," he groaned, "and that ar blamed thorn-tree's got hold er my breeches; I cayn't reach it with my han's, nur I cayn't kick it 'way with my foot. Say, kin ye cut the ornery branch off?"

"Waal, ye *be* helt fas', ain't ye?" Dock answered, hastening to his aid, without a sign of levity. He solemnly cut away the limb of the thorn-tree.

"Thank 'e," said Luther, in a surly voice.

They both crawled to the edge. In some way they both felt a disposition to postpone their quarrel. They looked over the hedge of "elbow-brush" and thorn-tree and leafless trumpet-vine. Down below, in the hollow, a fire had been built against a log. Three sticks, crossed above, supported a kettle on which rested a covered tin vessel. A savory steam arose from this, crisping in the air, delicious to the nostrils and beautiful to the eye. Close to the fire, Mizzie and Doshy sat together. The baby sat on a blanket beside Mizzie, hilariously playing with Doshy's new doll. On the outskirts of the group, the dog, Jerusalem Jones, was chasing a pig.

"Whut they monkeyin' with onyhow?" said Luther.

"Hush! Hark to 'em!" said Dock.

Doshy was explaining something to Mizzie: "An' he loves brown bread a turrible sight. He eat some to Mis' Caroll's, an' he b'en talkin' 'bout it ever since. An' I'll have this yere fur supper, an' he'll eat it, an' he'll say, 'Who made it?' an' I'll say, 'Me;' an' I'll say *you* learned me, an' then he'll 'low you' a real nice little girl."

"I'm 'fraid he won't," said Mizzie; "my paw don't mind a bit my likin' you; but you' paw'd like for to set the dog on me."

"Naw, he wudn't neether," cried Doshy. "He jes' lets on ter be cross; he's *real* good, inside. Don' ye mind how he gethered them pecans fur we-all afore they had the trouble? He's real kind; he never whips none o' us. Jes' *sez* he will—but he *don't*."

"Blame it all, the pesky littly trick! She b'en 'cute nuff ter fin' that out," cried Luther, while Dock stifled a chuckle.

"My paw's good, too," said Mizzie. "He chopped a right smart er wood fur me to-day. I never have to chop wood."

"Neither does maw," said Doshy, proudly. "My paw always does hit, an' he done a heap to-day, too."

The two fathers exchanged glances; without a word each read what the other's forebodings had been, by what he remembered of his own. And each felt, in a vague and dubious way, complimented by the other's dread of being killed.

A loud scream from one of the little girls turned their eyes back to the fire. Jerusalem Jones had worked mischief. He thought it was an unprotected orphan of a pig that he was harassing; so, barking and jumping, he had chased the wretched little beast into the brake. But, in a second, he came back faster than he went, and pursued by three wild hogs. These wild hogs are hideous creatures, long, muscular, with great black heads, and tusks like scimiters curling upward out of their jaws. They would have ended Jerusalem Jones's ill-doing in short order, had they caught him. Jerusalem, howling with fright, bounded up to the girls, the wild hogs at his heels, uttering the strange, fierce sound which these beasts make when they rally to face the hunter. It is the note of danger. The girls turned pale. They leaped to their feet. Mizzie snatched up the baby. With a single bound and a mighty swing of her strong little arms, she dropped the astonished infant in the midst of a thicket of thorn-trees. Then, snatching a brand from the fire, she stood at bay.

"Fight 'em with the fire, Doshy!" she said; "don' let 'em git our bread!"

Doshy had bravely caught a stick, but seeing the baby safe, she had flown to the rescue of Jerusalem Jones. The dog was rolling on the ground in desperate conflict with the smallest hog. In his agony, Jerusalem wrenched himself free and made a flying leap through the fire, thereby overturning the gypsy kettle and sending the brown bread tin headlong at the hogs. Doshy uttered a piteous scream:—

"Oh, my bread! my nice bread!"

Mizzie was on the other side nearer the brown-bread. Before the huge black noses could touch the tin, she kicked over the log.

"Gether the bread an' run!" she screamed.

The two hogs turned on Mizzie. Doshy was running to her playmate's aid; but she was too far away. Horrified, she saw one infuriated boar strike the burning stick out of the brave little hand. "Jeru! Jeru!" she cried in her despair, while she threw her stick at the hog.

Let it be told to his credit, Jerusalem responded; though he had run on his own account, though he was bleeding in half a dozen places, the dog leaped back into the fray, drove his teeth through the big boar's ear, and hung there. The boar had caught Mizzie's skirt; he flung up his wicked head now. But, meanwhile, the other boar, with his teeth clashing, his eyes like red coals—

"Oh, Lord, Luther!" gasped Dock, "cayn't ye git a sight at it? My pore little gell's square in front o' *me!*"

He shut his eyes for one intolerable second; the next, the ping of a bullet made him crash his way through the brush, and slip recklessly down the bank. As an apple falls when hit by a stone, the boar tumbled to the ground. Then Dock's bullet laid the other hog beside him.

The sagacious Jerusalem had loosened his hold when he saw the gun-barrel. Now he capered over the body with yells of triumph. But he ceased his dance and looked in amazement at his master, who was actually hugging Haskett's girl.

"Please, Mister Morrow," she said, "look a' the baby. I put 'im in, but I cayn't git 'im out."

The baby, however, was already in his father's arms. Doshy was mourning over her brown bread.

"Put it back in the steamer," commanded Mizzie, adding: "Oh, please, Mister Morrow, 'tain't Doshy's fault, bein' with me; I coaxed her fur ter learn ter make the bread!"

"Honey," her father answered tenderly, "it's the bes' bread ever was baked!—an' Haskett 'n' me'll eat it together. Won't we, Dock?"

"We will so," said Dock, rubbing the tears from his eyes, "an' I guv in, now, 'bout the shootin'. *I* cudn't hev made that shot jest un'er the child's elbow! Why, ye got a han' o' iron"—

"An' *I* guv in 'bout that ar ornery, triflin', no-'count dog," answered Luther; "ye was right for ter shoot 'im, Dock. Ye kin kill him off, this minnit, ef yer wan' ter." .

"Naw, sir. Not ayfter his tacklin' that hoeg ez he did," cried Dock; "but ye know, Luther,—I meant that shot, six months ago, fer him, not fer *you;* an' I are turrible sorry I done hit"—

"Shet up!" said Luther, impulsively. "I've done ez mean by you ez you've done by me. Blamed if I know how it come we-uns was fightin', onyhow. Say, let's take the brown bread ter my house an' eat it—an' tell Mendoshy."

Thus it happened that the man who passed the Morrow house that evening had a most extraordinary tale to relate at the store.

"I tell ye, they was all roun' the table, Dock Haskett an' his baby, an' his two gells an' all the Morrowses. An' Luther he kissed Haskett's gell spang on the forehead, an' he war a-cuttin' her a hunk o' brown bread. An' Dock, he says, 'She didn't do no better nor *yore* gell;' an' then Luther he guvs his gell a buss, too, an' they all were a-laffin', an' Mis' Morrow she laffed till she cried."

Aunt Callie's comment was, "Waal, good cookin' 's never wasted, an' them gells ain't likely to fergit how to make brown bread. I ain't sorry I l'arned 'er, though, ez a gineral thing, I ain't no 'pinion er folkses romancin' 'roun' my kitchen."

MARY E. WILKINS FREEMAN

★ ★ ★

Inflexible integrity to traditions of frugality and piety marks the conduct of many grim, humble New Englanders in the stories of Mary E. Wilkins Freeman (1852-1930). Yet a quiet, often unconscious, humor softens the asperities of these formally religious, intensely loyal people, clinging to their ideals amidst the depressing drudgery of rural, seaside, or factory life, and finding some compensation in daily routine. The dominant theme of Mrs. Freeman's stories is the power of the individual to rise above limitations. An astonishing range of character, incident, and mood is reflected in her many books; concerned chiefly with humanity, she seldom enlarged upon nature backgrounds. Born in Randolph, Massachusetts, Mrs. Freeman grew up in Brattleboro, Vermont, and studied one year at Mt. Holyoke College. In 1902 she married Dr. Charles M. Freeman and made her residence thereafter in Metuchen, New Jersey. "Gentian," from *A Humble Romance* (1887), and "A New England Nun" and "A Village Singer," from *A New England Nun* (1891), are reprinted by permission of Harper and Brothers, publishers.

★ ★ ★

Gentian

It had been raining hard all night; when the morning dawned clear everything looked vivid and unnatural. The wet leaves on the trees and hedges seemed to emit a real green light of their own; the tree trunks were black and dank, and the spots of moss on them stood out distinctly.

A tall old woman was coming quickly up the street. She had on a stiffly starched calico gown, which sprang and rattled as she walked. She kept smoothing it anxiously. "Gittin' every mite of the stiff'nin' out," she muttered to herself.

She stopped at a long cottage house, whose unpainted walls, with white window-facings, and wide sweep of shingled roof, looked dark and startling through being sodden with rain.

There was a low stone wall by way of fence, with a gap in it for a gate.

She had just passed through this gap when the house door opened, and a woman put out her head.

"Is that you, Hannah?" said she.

"Yes, it's me." She laid a hard emphasis on the last word; then she sighed heavily.

"Hadn't you better hold your dress up comin' through that wet grass, Hannah? You'll git it all bedraggled."

"I know it. I'm a-gittin' every mite of the stiff'nin' out on't. I worked half the forenoon ironin' on't yesterday, too. Well, I thought I'd got to git over here an' fetch a few of these fried cakes. I thought mebbe Alferd would relish 'em fur his breakfast; an' he'd got to have 'em while they was hot; they ain't good fur nothin' cold; an' I didn't hev a soul to send—never do. How is Alferd this mornin', Lucy?"

" 'Bout the same, I guess."

" 'Ain't had the doctor yit?"

"No." She had a little, patient, pleasant smile on her face, looking up at her questioner.

The women were sisters. Hannah was Hannah Orton, unmarried. Lucy was Mrs. Tollet. Alfred was her sick husband.

Hannah's long, sallow face was deeply wrinkled. Her wide mouth twisted emphatically as she talked.

"Well, I know one thing; ef he was my husband he'd *hev* a doctor."

Mrs. Tollet's voice was old, but there was a childish tone in it, a sweet, uncertain pipe.

"No; you couldn't make him, Hannah; you couldn't, no more'n me. Alferd was allers jest so. He ain't never thought nothin' of doctors, nor doctors' stuff."

"Well, I'd make him take somethin'. In my opinion he needs somethin' bitter." She screwed her mouth as if the bitter morsel were on her own tongue.

"Lor'! he wouldn't take it, you know, Hannah."

"He'd hev to. Gentian would be good fur him."

"He wouldn't tech it."

"I'd make him, ef I put it in his tea unbeknownst to him."

"Oh, I wouldn't dare to."

"Land! I guess I'd dare to. Ef folks don't know enough to take what's good fur 'em, they'd orter be made to by hook or crook. I don't believe in deceivin' generally, but I don't believe the Lord would hev let folks hed the faculty fur deceivin' in 'em ef it wa'n't to be used fur good sometimes. It's my opinion Alferd won't last long ef he don't hev somethin' pretty soon to strengthen of him up an' give him a start. Well, it ain't no use talkin'. I've got to git home an' put this dress in the wash-tub agin, I s'pose. I never see such a sight— jest look at that! You'd better give Alferd those cakes afore they git cold."

"I shouldn't wonder ef he relished 'em. You was real good to think of it, Hannah."

"Well, I'm a-goin'. Every mite of the stiff'nin's out. Sometimes it seems as ef thar wa'n't no end to the work. I didn't know how to git out this mornin', anyway."

When Mrs. Tollet entered the house she found her husband in a wooden rocking-chair with a calico cushion, by the kitchen window. He was a short, large-framed old man, but he was very thin. There were great hollows in his yellow cheeks.

"What you got thar, Lucy?"

"Some griddle-cakes Hannah brought."

"Griddle-cakes!"

"They're real nice-lookin' ones. Don't you think you'd relish one or two, Alferd?"

"Ef you an' Hannah want griddle-cakes, you kin hev griddle-cakes."

"Then you don't want to hev one, with some maple merlasses on it? They've kept hot; she hed 'em kivered up."

"Take 'em away!"

She set them meekly on the pantry shelf; then she came back and stood before her husband, gentle deprecation in her soft old face and in the whole poise of her little slender body.

"What *will* you hev fur breakfast, Alferd?"

"I don' know. Well, you might as well fry a little slice of bacon, an' git a cup of tea."

"Ain't you 'most afeard of—bacon, Alferd?"

"No, I ain't. Ef anybody's sick, they kin tell what they want themselves 'bout as well's anybody kin tell 'em. They don't hev any hankerin' arter anythin' unless it's good for 'em. When they need anythin', natur gives 'em a longin' arter it. I wish you'd hurry up an' cook that bacon, Lucy. I'm awful faint at my stomach."

She cooked the bacon and made the tea with no more words. Indeed, it was seldom that she used as many as she had now. Alfred Tollet, ever since she had married him, had been the sole autocrat of all her little Russias; her very thoughts had followed after him, like sheep.

After breakfast she went about putting her house in order for the day. When that was done, and she was ready to sit down with her sewing, she found that her husband had fallen asleep in his chair. She stood over him a minute, looking at his pale old face with the sincerest love and reverence. Then she sat down by the window and sewed, but not long. She got her bonnet and shawl stealthily, and stole out of the house. She sped quickly down the village street. She was light-footed for an old woman. She slackened her pace when she reached the village store, and crept hesitatingly into the great lumbering, rank-smelling room, with its dark, newly-sprinkled floor. She bought a bar of soap; then she stood irresolute.

"Anything else this mornin', Mis' Tollet?" The proprietor himself, a narrow-shouldered, irritable man, was waiting on her. His tone was impatient. Mrs. Tollet was too absorbed to notice it. She stood hesitating.

"*Is* there anything else you want?"

"Well—I don' know; but—p'rhaps I'd better—hev—ten cents' wuth of gentian." Her very lips were white; she had an expression of frightened, guilty resolution. If she had asked for strychnine, with a view to her own bodily destruction, she would not have had a different look.

The man mistook it, and his conscience smote him. He thought his manner had frightened her, but she had never noticed it.

"Goin' to give your husband some bitters?" he asked, affably, as he handed her the package.

She started and blushed. "No—I—thought some would be good fur—me."

"Well, gentian is a first-rate bitter. Good-morning, Mis' Tollet."

"Good-morning, Mr. Gill."

She was trembling all over when she reached her house door. There is a subtle, easily raised wind which blows spirits about like leaves, and she had come into it with her little paper of gentian. She had hidden the parcel in her pocket before she entered the kitchen. Her husband was awake. He turned his wondering, half-resentful eyes towards her without moving his head.

"Where hev you been, Lucy?"

"I—jest went down to the store a minit, Alferd, while you was asleep."

"What fur?"

"A bar of soap."

Alfred Tollet had always been a very healthy man until this spring. Some people thought that his illness was alarming now, more from its unwontedness and consequent effect on his mind, than from anything serious in its nature. However that may have been, he had complained of great depression and languor all the spring, and had not attempted to do any work.

It was the beginning of May now.

"Ef Alferd kin only git up May hill," Mrs. Tollet's sister had said to her, "he'll git along all right through the summer. It's a dretful tryin' time."

So up May hill, under the white apple and plum boughs, over the dandelions and the young grass, Alfred Tollet climbed, pushed and led faithfully by his loving old wife. At last he stood triumphantly on the summit of that fair hill, with its sweet, wearisome ascent. When the first of June came, people said, "Alfred Tollet's a good deal better."

He began to plant a little and bestir himself.

"Alferd's out workin' in the garden," Mrs. Tollet told her sister one afternoon. She had strolled over to her house with her knitting after dinner.

"You don't say so! Well, I thought when I see him Sunday that he was lookin' better. He's got through May, an' I guess he'll pull through. I did feel kinder worried 'bout him one spell— Why, Lucy, what's the matter?"

"Nothin'. Why?"

"You looked at me dretful kind of queer an' distressed, I thought."

"I guess you must hev imagined it, Hannah. Thar ain't nothin' the matter." She tried to look unconcernedly at her sister, but her lips were trembling.

"Well, I don't know 'bout it. You look kinder queer now. I guess you walked too fast comin' over here. You allers did race."

"Mebbe I did."

"For the land's sake, jest see that dust you tracked in! I've got to git the dust-pan an' brush now, an' sweep it up."

"I'll do it."

"No; set still. I'd rather see to it myself."

As the summer went on Alfred Tollet continued to improve. He was as hearty as ever by September. But his wife seemed to lose as he gained. She grew thin, and her small face had a solemn, anxious look. She went out very little. She did not go to church at all, and she had been a devout church-goer. Occasionally she went over to her sister's, that was all. Hannah watched her shrewdly. She was a woman who arrived at conclusions slowly; but she never turned aside from the road to them.

"Look a-here, Lucy," she said one day, "I know what's the matter with you; thar's somethin' on your mind; an' I think you'd better out with it."

The words seemed propelled like bullets by her vehemence. Lucy shrank down and away from them, her pitiful eyes turned up towards her sister.

"Oh, Hannah, you scare me; I don't know what you mean."

"Yes, you do. Do you s'pose I'm blind? You're worrying yourself to death, an' I want to know the reason why. Is it anything 'bout Alferd?"

"Yes—don't, Hannah."

"Well, I'll go over an' give him a piece of my mind! I'll see—"

"Oh, Hannah, don't! It ain't him. It's me—it's me."

"What on airth hev you done?"

Mrs. Tollet began to sob.

"For the land sake, stop cryin' an' tell me."

"Oh, I—give him—gentian."

"Lucy Ann Tollet, air you crazy? What ef you did give him gentian? I don't see nothin' to take on so about."

"I—deceived him, an' it's been 'most killin' me to think on't ever since."

"What do you mean?"

"I put it in his tea, the way you said."

"An' he never knew it?"

"He kinder complained 'bout its tastin' bitter, an' I told him 'twas his mouth. He asked me ef it didn't taste bitter to me, an' I said, 'No.' I don' know nothin' what's goin' to become of me. Then I had to be so keerful 'bout putting too much on't in his tea, that I was afraid he wouldn't get enough. So I put little sprinklin's on't in the bread an' pies an' everythin' I cooked. An' when he'd say nothin' tasted right nowadays, an' somehow everything was kinder bitterish, I'd tell him it must be his mouth."

"Look here, Lucy, you didn't eat everythin' with gentian in it yourself?"

"Course I did."

"Fur the land sake!"

"I s'pose the stuff must hev done him good; he's picked right up ever since he begun takin' it. But I can't git over my deceivin' of him so. I've 'bout made up my mind to tell him."

"Well, all I've got to say is you're a big fool if you do. I declare, Lucy Ann Tollet, I never saw sech a woman! The idee of your worryin' over such a thing as that, when it's done Alferd good, too! P'rhaps you'd ruther he'd died?"

"Sometimes I think I hed 'most ruther."

"Well!"

In the course of a few days Mrs. Tollet did tell her husband. He received her disclosure in precisely the way she had known that he would. Her nerves received just the shock which they were braced to meet.

They had come home from meeting on a Sunday night. Mrs. Tollet stood before him; she had not even taken off her shawl and little black bonnet.

"Alferd," said she, "I've got somethin' to tell you; it's been on my mind a long time. I meant it all fur the best; but I've been doin' somethin' wrong. I've been deceivin' of you. I give you gentian last spring when you was so poorly. I put little sprinklin's on't into everything you ate. An' I didn't tell the truth when I said 'twas your mouth, an' it didn't taste bitter to me."

The old man half closed his eyes, and looked at her intently; his mouth widened out rigidly. "You put a little gentian into everything I ate unbeknownst to me, did you?" said he. "H'm!"

"Oh, Alferd, don't look at me so! I meant it all fur the best. I was afeard you wouldn't git well without you hed it, Alferd. I was dretful worried about you; you didn't know nothin' about it, but I was. I laid awake nights a-worryin' an' prayin'. I know I did wrong; it wa'n't right to deceive you, but it was all along of my worryin' an' my thinkin' so much of you, Alferd. I was afeard you'd die an' leave me all alone; an'—it 'most killed me to think on't."

Mr. Tollet pulled off his boots, then pattered heavily about the house, locking the doors and making preparations for retiring. He would not speak another word to his wife about the matter, though she kept on with her piteous little protestations.

Next morning, while she was getting breakfast, he went down to the store. The meal, a nice one—she had taken unusual pains with it—was on the table when he returned; but he never glanced at it. His hands were full of bundles, which he opened with painstaking deliberation. His wife watched apprehensively. There was a new tea-pot, a pound of tea, and some bread and cheese, also a salt mackerel.

Mrs. Tollet's eyes shone round and big; her lips were white. Her husband put a pinch of tea in the new teapot, and filled it with boiling water from the kettle.

"What air you a-doin' on, Alferd?" she asked, feebly.

"I'm jest a-goin' to make sure I hev some tea, an' somethin' to eat without any gentian in it."

"Oh, Alferd, I made these corn-cakes on purpose, an' they air real light. They 'ain't got no gentian on 'em, Alferd."

He sliced his bread and cheese clumsily, and sat down to eat them in stubborn silence.

Mrs. Tollet, motionless at her end of the table, stared at him with an appalled look. She never thought of eating anything herself.

After breakfast, when her husband started out to work, he pointed at the mackerel. "Don't you tech that," said he.

"But, Alferd—"

"I ain't got nothin' more to say. Don't you tech it."

Never a morning had passed before but Lucy Tollet had set her house in order; to-day she remained there at the kitchen-table till noon, and did not put away the breakfast dishes.

Alfred came home, kindled up the fire, cooked and ate his salt mackerel imperturbably; and she did not move or speak till he was about to go away again. Then she said, in a voice which seemed to shrink of itself, "Alferd!"

He did not turn his head.

"Alferd, you must answer me; I'm in airnest. Don't you want me to do nothin' fur you any more? Don't you never want me to cook anything fur you agin?"

"No; I'm afeard of gittin' things that's bitter."

"I won't never put any gentian in anything agin, Alferd. Won't you let me git supper?"

"No, I won't. I don't want to talk no more about it. In futur I'm a-goin' to cook my vittles myself, an' that's all thar is about it."

"Alferd, if you don't want me to do nothin' fur you, mebbe— you'll think I ain't airnin' my own vittles; mebbe—you'd rather I go over to Hannah's—"

She sobbed aloud when she said that. He looked startled, and eyed her sharply for a minute. The other performer in the little melodrama which this thwarted, arbitrary old man had arranged was adopting a *rôle* that he had not anticipated, but he was still going to abide by his own.

"Mebbe 'twould be jest as well," said he. Then he went out of the door.

Hannah Orton was in her kitchen sewing when her sister entered.

"Fur the land sake, Lucy, what is the matter?"

"I've left him—I've left Alferd! Oh! oh!"

Lucy Tollet gasped for breath; she sank into a chair, and leaned her head against the wall. Hannah got some water.

"Don't, Lucy—there, there! Drink this, poor lamb!"

She did not quite faint. She could speak in a few minutes. "He bought him a new tea-pot this mornin', Hannah, an' some bread an' cheese and salt mackerel. He's goin' to do his own cookin'; he don't want me to do nothin' more fur him; he's afeard I'll put gentian in it. I've left him! I've come to stay with you!"

"You told him, then?"

"I hed to; I couldn't go on so no longer. He wouldn't let me tech that mackerel, an' it orter hev been soaked. It was salt enough to kill him."

"Serve him right ef it did."

"Hannah Orton, I ain't a-goin' to hev a thing said agin Alferd."

"Well, ef you want to stan' up fur Alferd Tollet, you kin. You allers would stan' up fur him agin your own folks. Ef you want to keep on carin' fur sech a miserable, set, unfeelin'—"

"Don't you say another word, Hannah—not another one; I won't hear it."

"I ain't a-goin' to say nothin'; thar ain't any need of your bein' so fierce. Now don't cry so, Lucy. We shell git along real nice here together. You'll get used to it arter a little while, an' you'll see you air a good deal better off without him; you've been nothin' but jest a slave ever since you was married. Don't you s'pose I've seen it? I've pitied you so, I didn't know what to do. I've seen the time when I'd like to ha' shook Alferd."

"Don't, Hannah."

"I ain't a-goin' to say nothin' more. You jest stop cryin', an' try an' be calm, or you'll be sick. Hev you hed any dinnei?"

"I don't want none."

"You've got to eat somethin', Lucy Ann Tollet. Thar ain't no sense in your givin' up so. I've got a nice little piece of lamb, an' some pease an' string-beans, left over, an' I'm a-goin' to get 'em. You've got to eat 'em, an' then you'll feel better. Look-a here, I want to know ef Alferd drove you out of the house 'cause you give him gentian? I ain't got it through my head yet."

"I asked him ef he'd ruther hev me go, an' he said mebbe 'twould be jest as well. I thought I shouldn't hev no right to stay ef I couldn't git his meals for him."

"Right to stay! Lucy Ann Tollet, ef it wa'n't fur the grace of the Lord, I believe you'd be a simpleton. I don't understand no sech goodness; I allers thought it would run into foolishness some time, an' I believe it has with you. Well, don't worry no more about it; set up an' eat your dinner. Jest smooth out that mat under your feet a little; you've got it all scrolled up."

No bitter herb could have added anything to the bitterness of that first dinner which poor Lucy Tollet ate after she had left her own home. Time and custom lessened, but not much, the bitterness of the subsequent ones. Hannah had sewed for her living all her narrow, single life; Lucy shared her work now. They had to live frugally; still they had enough. Hannah owned the little house in which she lived.

Lucy Tollet lived with her through the fall and winter. Her leaving her husband started a great whirlpool of excitement in this little village. Hannah's custom doubled: people came ostensibly for work, but really for information. They quizzed her about her sister, but Hannah could be taciturn. She did their work and divulged nothing, except occasionally when she was surprised. Then she would let fall a few little hints, which were not at Lucy's expense.

They never saw Mrs. Tollet; she always ran when she heard any one coming. She never went out to church nor on the street. She grew to have a morbid dread of meeting her husband or seeing him. She would never sit at the window, lest he might go past. Hannah could not understand this; neither could Lucy herself.

Hannah thought she was suffering less, and was becoming weaned from her affection, because she did so. But in reality she was suffering more, and her faithful love for her imperious old husband was strengthening.

All the autumn and winter she stayed and worked quietly; in the spring she grew restless, though not perceptibly. She had never bewailed herself much after the first; she dreaded her sister's attacks on Alfred. Silence as to her own grief was her best way of defending him.

Towards spring she often let her work fall in her lap, and thought. Then she would glance timidly at Hannah, as if she could know what her thoughts were; but Hannah was no mind-reader. Hannah, when she set out for meeting one evening in May, had no conception whatever of the plan which was all matured in her sister's mind.

Lucy watched her out of sight; then she got herself ready quickly. She smoothed her hair, put on her bonnet and shawl, and started up the road towards her old home.

There was no moon, but it was clear and starry. The blooming trees stood beside the road like sweet, white, spring angels; there was a whippoorwill calling somewhere over across the fields. Lucy Tollet saw neither stars nor blooming trees; she did not hear the whippoor-will. That hard, whimsical old man in the little weather-beaten house ahead towered up like a grand giant between the white trees and this one living old woman; his voice in her ears drowned out all the sweet notes of the spring birds.

When she came in sight of the house there was a light in the kitchen window. She crept up to it softly and looked in. Alfred was standing there with his hat on. He was looking straight at the window, and he saw her the minute her little pale face came up above the sill.

He opened the door quickly and came out. "Lucy, is that you?"

"Oh, Alferd, let me come home! I'll never deceive you agin!"

"You jest go straight back to Hannah's this minute."

She caught hold of his coat. "Oh, Alferd, don't—don't drive me away agin! It'll kill me this time; it will! it will!"

"You go right back."

She sank right down at his feet then, and clung to them. "Alferd, I won't go; I won't! I won't! You sha'n't drive me away agin. Oh, Alferd, don't drive me away from home! I've lived here with you for fifty year a'most. Let me come home an' cook fur you, an' do fur you agin. Oh, Alferd, Alferd!"

"See here, Lucy—git up; stop takin' on so. I want to tell you some-thin'. You jest go right back to Hannah's, an' don't you worry. You set down an' wait a minute. Thar!"

Lucy looked at him. "What do you mean, Alferd?"

"Never you mind; you jist go right along."

Lucy Tollet sped back along the road to Hannah's, hardly know-ing what she was about. It is doubtful if she realized anything but a blind obedience to her husband's will, and a hope of something roused by a new tone in his voice. She sat down on the door-step and waited, she did not know for what. In a few minutes she heard the creak of heavy boots, and her husband came in sight. He walked straight up to her.

"I've come to ask you to come home, Lucy. I'm a-feelin' kinder poorly this spring, an'—I want you ter stew me up a little gentian. That you give me afore did me a sight of good."

"Oh, Alferd!"

"That's what I'd got ¹aid out to do when I see you at the winder, Lucy, an' I was a-goin' to do it."

A New England Nun

IT was late in the afternoon, and the light was waning. There was a difference in the look of the tree shadows out in the yard. Somewhere in the distance cows were lowing and a little bell was tinkling; now and then a farm-wagon tilted by, and the dust flew; some blue-shirted laborers with shovels over their shoulders plodded past; little swarms of flies were dancing up and down before the peoples' faces in the soft air. There seemed to be a gentle stir arising over everything for the mere sake of subsidence—a very premonition of rest and hush and night.

This soft diurnal commotion was over Louisa Ellis also. She had been peacefully sewing at her sitting-room window all the afternoon. Now she quilted her needle carefully into her work, which she folded precisely, and laid in a basket with her thimble and thread and scissors. Louisa Ellis could not remember that ever in her life she had mislaid one of these little feminine appurtenances, which had become, from long use and constant association, a very part of her personality.

Louisa tied a green apron round her waist, and got out a flat straw hat with a green ribbon. Then she went into the garden with a little blue crockery bowl, to pick some currants for her tea. After the currants were picked she sat on the back door-step and stemmed them, collecting the stems carefully in her apron, and afterwards throwing them into the hen-coop. She looked sharply at the grass beside the step to see if any had fallen there.

Louisa was slow and still in her movements; it took her a long time to prepare her tea; but when ready it was set forth with as much grace as if she had been a veritable guest to her own self. The little square table stood exactly in the centre of the kitchen, and was covered with a starched linen cloth whose border pattern of flowers glistened. Louisa had a damask napkin on her tea-tray, where were arranged a cut-glass tumbler full of teaspoons, a silver cream-pitcher, a china sugar-bowl, and one pink china cup and saucer. Louisa used china every day—something which none of her neighbors did. They whispered about it among themselves. Their daily tables were laid with common crockery, their sets of best china stayed in the parlor closet, and Louisa Ellis was no richer nor better bred than they. Still she would use the china. She had for her supper a glass dish full of sugared currants, a plate of little cakes, and one of light white biscuits. Also a leaf or two of lettuce, which she cut up daintily. Louisa was very fond of lettuce, which she raised to perfection in her little garden. She ate quite heartily, though in a delicate, pecking way; it seemed almost surprising that any considerable bulk of the food should vanish.

After tea she filled a plate with nicely baked thin corn-cakes, and carried them out into the back-yard.

"Cæsar!" she called. "Cæsar! Cæsar!"

There was a little rush, and the clank of a chain, and a large yellow-and-white dog appeared at the door of his tiny hut, which was half hidden among the tall grasses and flowers. Louisa patted him and gave him the corn-cakes. Then she returned to the house and washed the tea-things, polishing the china carefully. The twilight had deepened; the chorus of the frogs floated in at the open window wonderfully loud and shrill, and once in a while a long sharp drone from a tree-toad pierced it. Louisa took off her green gingham apron, disclosing a shorter one of pink and white print. She lighted her lamp, and sat down again with her sewing.

In about half an hour Joe Dagget came. She heard his heavy step on the walk, and rose and took off her pink-and-white apron. Under that was still another—white linen with a little cambric edging on the bottom; that was Louisa's company apron. She never wore it without her calico sewing apron over it unless she had a guest. She had barely folded the pink and white one with methodical haste and laid it in a table-drawer when the door opened and Joe Dagget entered.

He seemed to fill up the whole room. A little yellow canary that had been asleep in his green cage at the south window woke up and fluttered wildly, beating his little yellow wings against the wires. He always did so when Joe Dagget came into the room.

"Good-evening," said Louisa. She extended her hand with a kind of solemn cordiality.

"Good-evening, Louisa," returned the man, in a loud voice.

She placed a chair for him, and they sat facing each other, with the table between them. He sat bolt-upright, toeing out his heavy feet squarely, glancing with a good-humored uneasiness around the room.

She sat gently erect, folding her slender hands in her white-linen lap.

"Been a pleasant day," remarked Dagget.

"Real pleasant," Louisa assented, softly. "Have you been haying?" she asked, after a little while.

"Yes, I've been haying all day, down in the ten-acre lot. Pretty hot work."

"It must be."

"Yes, it's pretty hot work in the sun."

"Is your mother well to-day?"

"Yes, mother's pretty well."

"I suppose Lily Dyer's with her now?"

Dagget colored. "Yes, she's with her," he answered, slowly.

He was not very young, but there was a boyish look about his large face. Louisa was not quite as old as he, her face was fairer and smoother, but she gave people the impression of being older.

"I suppose she's a good deal of help to your mother," she said, further.

"I guess she is; I don't know how mother'd get along without her," said Dagget, with a sort of embarrassed warmth.

"She looks like a real capable girl. She's pretty-looking too," remarked Louisa.

"Yes, she is pretty fair-looking."

Presently Dagget began fingering the books on the table. There was a square red autograph album, and a Young Lady's Gift-Book which had belonged to Louisa's mother. He took them up one after the other and opened them; then laid them down again, the album on the Gift-Book.

Louisa kept eying them with mild uneasiness. Finally she rose and changed the position of the books, putting the album underneath. That was the way they had been arranged in the first place.

Dagget gave an awkward little laugh. "Now what difference did it make which book was on top?" said he.

Louisa looked at him with a deprecating smile. "I always keep them that way," murmured she.

"You do beat everything," said Dagget, trying to laugh again. His large face was flushed.

He remained about an hour longer, then rose to take leave. Going out, he stumbled over a rug, and trying to recover himself, hit Louisa's work-basket on the table, and knocked it on the floor.

He looked at Louisa, then at the rolling spools; he ducked himself awkwardly toward them, but she stopped him. "Never mind," said she; "I'll pick them up after you're gone."

She spoke with a mild stiffness. Either she was a little disturbed, or his nervousness affected her, and made her seem constrained in her effort to reassure him.

When Joe Dagget was outside he drew in the sweet evening air with a sigh, and felt much as an innocent and perfectly well-intentioned bear might after his exit from a china shop.

Louisa, on her part, felt much as the kind-hearted, long-suffering owner of the china shop might have done after the exit of the bear.

She tied on the pink, then the green apron, picked up all the scattered treasures and replaced them in her work-basket, and straightened the rug. Then she set the lamp on the floor, and began sharply examining the carpet. She even rubbed her fingers over it, and looked at them.

"He's tracked in a good deal of dust," she murmured. "I thought he must have."

Louisa got a dust-pan and brush, and swept Joe Dagget's track carefully.

If he could have known it, it would have increased his perplexity and uneasiness, although it would not have disturbed his loyalty in the least. He came twice a week to see Louisa Ellis, and every time, sitting there in her delicately sweet room, he felt as if surrounded by a hedge of lace. He was afraid to stir lest he should put a clumsy foot or hand through the fairy web, and he had always the consciousness that Louisa was watching fearfully lest he should.

Still the lace and Louisa commanded perforce his perfect respect and patience and loyalty. They were to be married in a month, after a singular courtship which had lasted for a matter of fifteen years. For fourteen out of the fifteen years the two had not once seen each other, and they had seldom exchanged letters. Joe had been all those years in Australia, where he had gone to make his fortune, and where he had stayed until he made it. He would have stayed fifty years if it had taken so long, and come home feeble and tottering, or never come home at all, to marry Louisa.

But the fortune had been made in the fourteen years, and he had come home now to marry the woman who had been patiently and unquestioningly waiting for him all that time.

Shortly after they were engaged he had announced to Louisa his determination to strike out into new fields, and secure a competency before they should be married. She had listened and assented with the sweet serenity which never failed her, not even when her lover set forth on that long and uncertain journey. Joe, buoyed up as he was by his sturdy determination, broke down a little at the last, but Louisa kissed him with a mild blush, and said good-by.

"It won't be for long," poor Joe had said, huskily; but it was for fourteen years.

In that length of time much had happened. Louisa's mother and brother had died, and she was all alone in the world. But greatest happening of all—a subtle happening which both were too simple to understand—Louisa's feet had turned into a path, smooth maybe under a calm, serene sky, but so straight and unswerving that it could only meet a check at her grave, and so narrow that there was no room for any one at her side.

Louisa's first emotion when Joe Dagget came home (he had not apprised her of his coming) was consternation, although she would not admit it to herself, and he never dreamed of it. Fifteen years ago she had been in love with him—at least she considered herself to be. Just at that time, gently acquiescing with and falling into the natural drift of girlhood, she had seen marriage ahead as a reasonable feature and a probable desirability of life. She had listened with calm docility to her mother's views upon the subject. Her mother was remarkable for her cool sense and sweet, even temperament. She talked wisely to her daughter when Joe Dagget presented himself, and Louisa accepted him with no hesitation. He was the first lover she had ever had.

She had been faithful to him all these years. She had never dreamed of the possibility of marrying any one else. Her life, especially for the last seven years, had been full of a pleasant peace; she had never felt discontented nor impatient over her lover's absence; still she had always looked forward to his return and their marriage as the inevitable conclusion of things. However, she had fallen into a way of placing it so far in the future that it was almost equal to placing it over the boundaries of another life.

When Joe came she had been expecting him, and expecting to be married for fourteen years, but she was as much surprised and taken aback as if she had never thought of it.

Joe's consternation came later. He eyed Louisa with an instant confirmation of his old admiration. She had changed but little. She still kept her pretty manner and soft grace, and was, he considered, every whit as attractive as ever. As for himself, his stent was done; he had turned his face away from fortune-seeking, and the old winds of romance whistled as loud and sweet as ever through his ears. All the song which he had been wont to hear in them was Louisa; he had for a long time a loyal belief that he heard it still, but finally it seemed to him that although the winds sang always that one song, it had another name. But for Louisa the wind had never more than murmured; now it had gone down, and everything was still. She listened for a little while with half-wistful attention; then she turned quietly away and went to work on her wedding clothes.

Joe had made some extensive and quite magnificent alterations in his house. It was the old homestead; the newly-married couple would live there, for Joe could not desert his mother, who refused to leave her old home. So Louisa must leave hers. Every morning, rising and going about among her neat maidenly possessions, she felt as one looking her last upon the faces of dear friends. It was true that in a measure she could take them with her, but, robbed of their old environments, they would appear in such new guises that they would almost cease to be themselves. Then there were some peculiar features of her happy solitary life which she would probably be obliged to relinquish altogether. Sterner tasks than these graceful but half-needless ones would probably devolve upon her. There would be a large house to care for; there would be company to entertain; there would be Joe's rigorous and feeble old mother to wait upon; and it would be contrary to all thrifty village traditions for her to keep more than one servant. Louisa had a little still, and she used to occupy herself pleasantly in summer weather with distilling the sweet and aromatic essences from roses and peppermint and spearmint. By-and-by her still must be laid away. Her store of essences was already considerable, and there would be no time for her to distil for the mere pleasure of it. Then Joe's mother would think it foolishness; she had already hinted her opinion in the matter. Louisa dearly loved to sew a linen seam, not always for use, but for the simple, mild pleasure which she took in it. She would have been loath to confess how more than once she had ripped a seam for the mere delight of sewing it together again. Sitting at her window during long sweet afternoons, drawing her needle gently through the dainty fabric, she was peace itself. But there was small chance of such foolish comfort in the future. Joe's mother, domineering, shrewd old matron that she was even in her old age, and very likely even Joe himself, with his honest masculine rudeness, would laugh and frown down all these pretty but senseless old maiden ways.

Louisa had almost the enthusiasm of an artist over the mere order and cleanliness of her solitary home. She had throbs of genuine triumph at the sight of the window-panes which she had polished until they shone like jewels. She gloated gently over her orderly bureau-drawers, with their exquisitely folded contents redolent with lavender and sweet clover and very purity. Could she be sure of the endurance of even this? She had visions, so startling that she half repudiated them as indelicate, of coarse masculine belongings strewn about in endless litter; of dust and disorder arising necessarily from a coarse masculine presence in the midst of all this delicate harmony.

Among her forebodings of disturbance, not the least was with regard to Cæsar. Cæsar was a veritable hermit of a dog. For the greater part of his life he had dwelt in his secluded hut, shut out from the society of his kind and all innocent canine joys. Never had Cæsar since his early youth watched at a woodchuck's hole; never had he known the delights of a stray bone at a neighbor's kitchen door. And it was all on account of a sin committed when hardly out of his puppyhood. No one knew the possible depth of remorse of which this mild-visaged, altogether innocent-looking old dog might be capable; but whether or not he had encountered remorse, he had encountered a full measure of righteous retribution. Old Cæsar seldom lifted up his voice in a growl or a bark; he was fat and sleepy; there were yellow rings which looked like spectacles around his dim old eyes; but there was a neighbor who bore on his hand the imprint of several of Cæsar's sharp white youthful teeth, and for that he had lived at the end of a chain, all alone in a little hut, for fourteen years. The neighbor, who was choleric and smarting with the pain of his wound, had demanded either Cæsar's death or complete ostracism. So Louisa's brother, to whom the dog had belonged, had built him his little kennel and tied him up. It was now fourteen years since, in a flood of youthful spirits, he had inflicted that memorable bite, and with the exception of short excursions, always at the end of the chain, under the strict guardianship of his master or Louisa, the old dog had remained a close prisoner. It is doubtful if, with his limited ambition, he took much pride in the fact, but it is certain that he was possessed of considerable cheap fame. He was regarded by all the children in the village and by many adults as a very monster of ferocity. St. George's dragon could hardly have surpassed in evil repute Louisa Ellis's old yellow dog. Mothers charged their children with solemn emphasis not to go too near to him, and the children listened and believed greedily, with a fascinated appetite for terror, and ran by Louisa's house stealthily, with many sidelong and backward glances at the terrible dog. If perchance he sounded a hoarse bark, there was a panic. Wayfarers chancing into Louisa's yard eyed him with respect, and inquired if the chain were stout. Cæsar at large might have seemed a very ordinary dog and excited no comment whatever; chained, his reputation overshadowed him, so that he lost his own proper outlines and looked darkly vague and enormous. Joe Dagget, however, with his good-humored sense and shrewdness, saw him as he was. He strode valiantly up to him and patted him on the head, in spite of Louisa's soft clamor of warning, and even attempted to set him loose. Louisa grew so alarmed that he desisted, but kept announcing his opinion in the matter quite forcibly at intervals. "There ain't a better-natured dog in town," he would say, "and it's downright cruel to keep him tied up there. Some day I'm going to take him out."

Louisa had very little hope that he would not, one of these days, when their interests and possessions should be more completely fused in one. She pictured to herself Cæsar on the rampage through the quiet and unguarded village. She saw innocent children bleeding in his path. She was herself very fond of the old dog, because he had belonged to her dead brother, and he was always very gentle with her; still she had great faith in his ferocity. She always warned people not to go too near him. She fed him on ascetic fare of corn-mush and cakes, and never fired his dangerous temper with heating and sanguinary diet of flesh and bones. Louisa looked at the old dog munching his simple fare, and thought of her approaching marriage and trembled. Still no anticipation of disorder and confusion in lieu of sweet peace and harmony, no forebodings of Cæsar on the rampage, no wild fluttering of her little yellow canary, were sufficient to turn her a hair's-breadth. Joe Dagget had been fond of her and working for her all these years. It was not for her, whatever came to pass, to prove untrue and break his heart. She put the exquisite little stitches into her wedding-garments, and the time went on until it was only a week before her wedding-day. It was a Tuesday evening, and the wedding was to be a week from Wednesday.

There was a full moon that night. About nine o'clock Louisa strolled down the road a little way. There were harvest-fields on either hand, bordered by low stone walls. Luxuriant clumps of bushes grew beside the wall, and trees—wild cherry and old apple-trees—at intervals. Presently Louisa sat down on the wall and looked about her with mildly sorrowful reflectiveness. Tall shrubs of blueberry and meadow-sweet, all woven together and tangled with blackberry vines and horsebriers, shut her in on either side. She had a little clear space between them. Opposite her, on the other side of the road, was a spreading tree; the moon shone between its boughs, and the leaves twinkled like silver. The road was bespread with a beautiful shifting dapple of silver and shadow; the air was full of a mysterious sweetness. "I wonder if it's wild grapes?" murmured Louisa. She sat there some time. She was just thinking of rising, when she heard footsteps and low voices, and remained quiet. It was a lonely place, and she felt a little timid. She thought she would keep still in the shadow and let the persons, whoever they might be, pass her.

But just before they reached her the voices ceased, and the footsteps. She understood that their owners had also found seats upon the stone wall. She was wondering if she could not steal away unobserved, when the voice broke the stillness. It was Joe Dagget's. She sat still and listened.

The voice was announced by a loud sigh, which was as familiar as itself. "Well," said Dagget, "you've made up your mind, then, I suppose?"

"Yes," returned another voice; "I'm going day after to-morrow."

"That's Lily Dyer," thought Louisa to herself. The voice embodied itself in her mind. She saw a girl tall and full-figured, with a firm, fair face, looking fairer and firmer in the moonlight, her strong yellow hair braided in a close knot. A girl full of a calm rustic strength and bloom, with a masterful way which might have beseemed a princess. Lily Dyer was a favorite with the village folk; she had just the qualities to arouse the admiration. She was good and handsome and smart. Louisa had often heard her praises sounded.

"Well," said Joe Dagget, "I ain't got a word to say."

"I don't know what you could say," returned Lily Dyer.

"Not a word to say," repeated Joe, drawing out the words heavily. Then there was a silence. "I ain't sorry," he began at last, "that that happened yesterday—that we kind of let on how we felt to each other. I guess it's just as well we knew. Of course I can't do anything any different. I'm going right on an' get married next week. I ain't going back on a woman that's waited for me fourteen years, an' break her heart."

"If you should jilt her to-morrow, I wouldn't have you," spoke up the girl, with sudden vehemence.

"Well, I ain't going to give you the chance," said he; "but I don't believe you would, either."

"You'd see I wouldn't. Honor's honor, an' right's right. An' I'd never think anything of any man that went against 'em for me or any other girl; you'd find that out, Joe Dagget."

"Well, you'll find out fast enough that I ain't going against 'em for you or any other girl," returned he. Their voices sounded almost as if they were angry with each other. Louisa was listening eagerly.

"I'm sorry you feel as if you must go away," said Joe, "but I don't know but it's best."

"Of course it's best. I hope you and I have got common-sense."

"Well, I suppose you're right." Suddenly Joe's voice got an undertone of tenderness. "Say, Lily," said he, "I'll get along well enough myself, but I can't bear to think— You don't suppose you're going to fret much over it?"

"I guess you'll find out I sha'n't fret much over a married man."

"Well, I hope you won't—I hope you won't, Lily. God knows I do. And—I hope—one of these days—you'll—come across somebody else—"

"I don't see any reason why I shouldn't." Suddenly her tone changed. She spoke in a sweet, clear voice, so loud that she could have been heard across the street. "No, Joe Dagget," said she, "I'll never marry any other man as long as I live. I've got good sense, an' I ain't going to break my heart nor make a fool of myself; but I'm never going to be married, you can be sure of that. I ain't that sort of a girl to feel this way twice."

Louisa heard an exclamation and a soft commotion behind the bushes; then Lily spoke again—the voice sounded as if she had risen. "This must be put a stop to," said she. "We've stayed here long enough. I'm going home."

Louisa sat there in a daze, listening to their retreating steps. After a while she got up and slunk softly home herself. The next day she did her housework methodically; that was as much a matter of course as breathing; but she did not sew on her wedding-clothes. She sat at her window and meditated. In the evening Joe came. Louisa Ellis had never known that she had any diplomacy in her, but when she came to look for it that night she found it, although meek of its kind, among her little feminine weapons. Even now she could hardly believe that she had heard aright, and that she would not do Joe a terrible injury should she break her troth-plight. She wanted to sound him without betraying too soon her own inclinations in the matter. She did it successfully, and they finally came to an understanding; but it was a difficult thing, for he was as afraid of betraying himself as she.

She never mentioned Lily Dyer. She simply said that while she had no cause of complaint against him, she had lived so long in one way that she shrank from making a change.

"Well, I never shrank, Louisa," said Dagget. "I'm going to be honest enough to say that I think maybe it's better this way; but if you'd wanted to keep on, I'd have stuck to you till my dying day. I hope you know that."

"Yes, I do," said she.

That night she and Joe parted more tenderly than they had done for a long time. Standing in the door, holding each other's hands, a last great wave of regretful memory swept over them.

"Well, this ain't the way we've thought it was all going to end, is it, Louisa?" said Joe.

She shook her head. There was a little quiver on her placid face.

"You let me know if there's ever anything I can do for you," said he. "I ain't ever going to forget you, Louisa." Then he kissed her, and went down the path.

Louisa, all alone by herself that night, wept a little, she hardly knew why; but the next morning, on waking, she felt like a queen who, after fearing lest her domain be wrested away from her, sees it firmly insured in her possession.

Now the tall weeds and grasses might cluster around Cæsar's little hermit hut, the snow might fall on its roof year in and year out, but he never would go on a rampage through the unguarded village. Now the little canary might turn itself into a peaceful yellow ball night after night, and have no need to wake and flutter with wild terror against its bars. Louisa could sew linen seams, and distil roses, and dust and polish and fold away in lavender, as long as she listed. That afternoon she sat with her needle-work at the window, and felt fairly steeped in peace. Lily Dyer, tall and erect and blooming, went past; but she felt no qualm. If Louisa Ellis had sold her birthright she did not know it, the taste of the pottage was so delicious, and had been her sole satisfaction for so long. Serenity and placid narrowness had become to her as the birthright itself. She gazed ahead through a long reach of future days strung together like pearls in a rosary, every one like the others, and all smooth and flawless and innocent, and her heart went up in thankfulness. Outside was the fervid summer afternoon; the air was filled with the sounds of the busy harvest of men and birds and bees; there were halloos, metallic clatterings, sweet calls, and long hummings. Louisa sat, prayerfully numbering her days, like an uncloistered nun.

A Village Singer

THE trees were in full leaf, a heavy south wind was blowing, and there was a loud murmur among the new leaves. The people noticed it, for it was the first time that year that the trees had so murmured in the wind. The spring had come with a rush during the last few days.

The murmur of the trees sounded loud in the village church, where the people sat waiting for the service to begin. The windows were open; it was a very warm Sunday for May.

The church was already filled with this soft sylvan music—the tender harmony of the leaves and the south wind, and the sweet, desultory whistles of birds—when the choir arose and began to sing.

In the centre of the row of women singers stood Alma Way. All the people stared at her, and turned their ears critically. She was the new leading soprano. Candace Whitcomb, the old one, who had sung in the choir for forty years, had lately been given her dismissal. The audience considered that her voice had grown too cracked and uncertain on the upper notes. There had been much complaint, and after long deliberation the church-officers had made known their decision as mildly as possible to the old singer. She had sung for the last time the Sunday before, and Alma Way had been engaged to take her place. With the exception of the organist, the leading soprano was the only paid musician in the large choir. The salary was very modest, still the village people considered it large for a young woman. Alma was from the adjoining village of East Derby; she had quite a local reputation as a singer.

Now she fixed her large solemn blue eyes; her long, delicate face, which had been pretty, turned paler; the blue flowers on her bonnet trembled; her little thin gloved hands, clutching the singing-book, shook perceptibly; but she sang out bravely. That most formidable mountain-height of the world, self-distrust and timidity, arose before her, but her nerves were braced for its ascent. In the midst of the hymn she had a solo; her voice rang out piercingly sweet; the people nodded admiringly at each other; but suddenly there was a stir; all the faces turned toward the windows on the south side of the church. Above the din of the wind and the birds, above Alma Way's sweetly straining tones, arose another female voice, singing another hymn to another tune.

"It's her," the women whispered to each other; they were half aghast, half smiling.

Candace Whitcomb's cottage stood close to the south side of the church. She was playing on her parlor organ, and singing, to drown out the voice of her rival.

Alma caught her breath; she almost stopped; the hymn-book waved like a fan; then she went on. But the long husky drone of the parlor organ and the shrill clamor of the other voice seemed louder than anything else.

When the hymn was finished, Alma sat down. She felt faint; the woman next her slipped a peppermint into her hand. "It ain't worth minding," she whispered, vigorously. Alma tried to smile; down in the audience a young man was watching her with a kind of fierce pity.

In the last hymn Alma had another solo. Again the parlor organ droned above the carefully delicate accompaniment of the church organ, and again Candace Whitcomb's voice clamored forth in another tune.

After the benediction, the other singers pressed around Alma. She did not say much in return for their expressions of indignation and sympathy. She wiped her eyes furtively once or twice, and tried to smile. William Emmons, the choir leader, elderly, stout, and smooth-faced, stood over her, and raised his voice. He was the old musical dignitary of the village, the leader of the choral club and the singing-schools. "A most outrageous proceeding," he said. People had coupled his name with Candace Whitcomb's. The old bachelor tenor and old maiden soprano had been wont to walk together to her home next door after the Saturday night rehearsals, and they had sung duets to the parlor organ. People had watched sharply her old face, on which the blushes of youth sat pitifully, when William Emmons entered the singing-seats. They wondered if he would ever ask her to marry him.

And now he said further to Alma Way that Candace Whitcomb's voice had failed utterly of late, that she sang shockingly, and ought to have had sense enough to know it.

When Alma went down into the audience-room, in the midst of the chattering singers, who seemed to have descended, like birds, from song flights to chirps, the minister approached her. He had been waiting to speak to her. He was a steady-faced, fleshy old man, who had preached from that one pulpit over forty years. He told Alma, in his slow way, how much he regretted the annoyance to which she had been subjected, and intimated that he would endeavor to prevent a recurrence of it. "Miss Whitcomb—must be—reasoned with," said he; he had a slight hesitation of speech, not an impediment. It was as if his thoughts did not slide readily into his words, although both were present. He walked down the aisle with Alma, and bade her good-morning when he saw Wilson Ford waiting for her in the doorway. Everybody knew that Wilson Ford and Alma were lovers; they had been for the last ten years.

Alma colored softly, and made a little imperceptible motion with her head; her silk dress and the lace on her mantle fluttered, but she did not speak. Neither did Wilson, although they had not met before that day. They did not look at each other's faces—they seemed to see each other without that—and they walked along side by side.

They reached the gate before Candace Whitcomb's little house. Wilson looked past the front yard, full of pink and white spikes on flowering bushes, at the lace-curtained windows; a thin white profile, stiffly inclined, apparently over a book, was visible at one of them. Wilson gave his head a shake. He was a stout man, with features so strong that they overcame his flesh. "I'm going up home with you, Alma," said he; "and then—I'm just coming back, to give Aunt Candace one blowing up."

"Oh, don't, Wilson."

"Yes, I shall. If you want to stand this kind of a thing you may; I sha'n't."

"There's no need of your talking to her. Mr. Pollard's going to."

"Did he say he was?"

"Yes. I think he's going in before the afternoon meeting, from what he said."

"Well, there's one thing about it, if she does that thing again this afternoon, I'll go in there and break that old organ up into kindling-wood." Wilson set his mouth hard, and shook his head again.

Alma gave little side glances up at him, her tone was deprecatory, but her face was full of soft smiles. "I suppose she does feel dreadfully about it," said she. "I can't help feeling kind of guilty, taking her place."

"I don't see how you're to blame. It's outrageous, her acting so."

"The choir gave her a photograph album last week, didn't they?"

"Yes. They went there last Thursday night, and gave her an album and a surprise-party. She ought to behave herself."

"Well, she's sung there so long, I suppose it must be dreadful hard for her to give it up."

Other people going home from church were very near Wilson and Alma. She spoke softly that they might not hear; he did not lower his voice in the least. Presently Alma stopped before a gate.

"What are you stopping here for?" asked Wilson.

"Minnie Lansing wanted me to come and stay with her this noon."

"You're going home with me."

"I'm afraid I'll put your mother out."

"Put mother out! I told her you were coming, this morning. She's got all ready for you. Come along; don't stand here."

He did not tell Alma of the pugnacious spirit with which his mother had received the announcement of her coming, and how she had stayed at home to prepare the dinner, and make a parade of her hard work and her injury.

Wilson's mother was the reason why he did not marry Alma. He would not take his wife home to live with her, and was unable to support separate establishments. Alma was willing enough to be married and put up with Wilson's mother, but she did not complain of his decision. Her delicate blond features grew sharper, and her blue eyes more hollow. She had had a certain fine prettiness, but now she was losing it, and beginning to look old, and there was a prim, angular, old maiden carriage about her narrow shoulders.

Wilson never noticed it, and never thought of Alma as not possessed of eternal youth, or capable of losing or regretting it.

"Come along, Alma," said he; and she followed meekly after him down the street.

Soon after they passed Candace Whitcomb's house, the minister went up the front walk and rang the bell. The pale profile at the window had never stirred as he opened the gate and came up the walk. However, the door was promptly opened, in response to his ring. "Good-morning, Miss Whitcomb," said the minister.

"*Good*-morning." Candace gave a sweeping toss of her head as she spoke. There was a fierce upward curl to her thin nostrils and her lips, as if she scented an adversary. Her black eyes had two tiny cold sparks of fury in them, like an enraged bird's. She did not ask the minister to enter, but he stepped lumberingly into the entry, and she retreated rather than led the way into her little parlor. He settled into the great rocking-chair and wiped his face. Candace sat down again in her old place by the window. She was a tall woman, but very slender and full of pliable motions, like a blade of grass.

"It's a—very pleasant day," said the minister.

Candace made no reply. She sat still, with her head drooping. The wind stirred the looped lace-curtains; a tall rose-tree outside the window waved; soft shadows floated through the room. Candace's parlor organ stood in front of an open window that faced the church; on the corner was a pitcher with a bunch of white lilacs. The whole room was scented with them. Presently the minister looked over at them and sniffed pleasantly.

"You have—some beautiful—lilacs there."

Candace did not speak. Every line of her slender figure looked flexible, but it was a flexibility more resistant than rigor.

The minister looked at her. He filled up the great rocking-chair; his arms in his shiny black coat-sleeves rested squarely and comfortably upon the hair-cloth arms of the chair.

"Well, Miss Whitcomb, I suppose I—may as well come to—the point. There was—a little—matter I wished to speak to you about. I don't suppose you were—at least I can't suppose you were—aware of it, but—this morning, during the singing by the choir, you played and—sung a little too—loud. That is, with—the windows open. It—disturbed us—a little. I hope you won't feel hurt—my dear Miss Candace, but I knew you would rather I would speak of it, for I knew—you would be more disturbed than anybody else at the idea of such a thing."

Candace did not raise her eyes; she looked as if his words might sway her through the window. "I ain't disturbed at it," said she. "I did it on purpose; I meant to."

The minister looked at her.

"You needn't look at me. I know jest what I'm about. I sung the way I did on purpose, an' I'm goin' to do it again, an' I'd like to see you stop me. I guess I've got a right to set down to my own organ, an' sing a psalm tune on a Sabbath day, 'f I want to; an' there ain't no amount of talkin' an' palaverin' a-goin' to stop me. See there!" Candace swung aside her skirts a little. "Look at thàt!"

The minister looked. Candace's feet were resting on a large red-plush photograph album.

"Makes a nice footstool, don't it?" said she.

The minister looked at the album, then at her; there was a slowly gathering alarm in his face; he began to think she was losing her reason.

Candace had her eyes full upon him now, and her head up. She laughed, and her laugh was almost a snarl. "Yes; I thought it would make a beautiful footstool," said she. "I've been wantin' one for some time." Her tone was full of vicious irony.

"Why, miss—" began the minister; but she interrupted him:

"I know what you're a-goin' to say, Mr. Pollard, an' now I'm goin' to have my say; I'm a-goin' to speak. I want to know what you think of folks that pretend to be Christians treatin' anybody the way they've treated me? Here I've sung in those singin'-seats forty year. I 'ain't never missed a Sunday, except when I've been sick, an' I've gone an' sung a good many times when I'd better been in bed, an' now I'm turned out without a word of warnin'. My voice is jest as good as ever 'twas; there can't anybody say it ain't. It wa'n't ever quite so high-pitched as that Way girl's, mebbe; but she flats the whole durin' time. My voice is as good an' high to-day as it was twenty year ago; an' if it wa'n't, I'd like to know where the Christianity comes in. I'd like to know if it wouldn't be more to the credit of folks in a church to keep an old singer an' an old minister, if they didn't sing an' hold forth quite so smart as they used to, ruther than turn 'em off an' hurt their feelin's. I guess it would be full as much to the glory of God. S'pose the singin' an' the preachin' wa'n't quite so good, what difference would it make? Salvation don't hang on anybody's hittin' a high note, that I ever heard of. Folks are gettin' as high-steppin' an' fussy in a meetin'-house as they are in a tavern, nowadays. S'pose they should turn you off, Mr. Pollard, come an' give you a photograph album, an' tell you to clear out, how'd you like it? I ain't findin' any fault with your preachin'; it was always good enough to suit me; but it don't stand to reason folks'll be as took up with your sermons as when you was a young man. You can't expect it. S'pose they should turn you out in your old age, an' call in some young bob squirt, how'd you feel? There's William Emmons, too; he's three years older'n I am, if he does lead the choir an' run all the singin' in town. If my voice has gi'en out, it stan's to reason his has. It ain't, though. William Emmons sings jest as well as he ever did. Why don't they turn him out the way they have me, an' give him a photograph album? I dun know but it would be a good idea to send everybody, as soon as they get a little old an' gone by, an' young folks begin to push, onto some desert island, an' give 'em each a photograph album. Then they can sit down an' look at pictures the rest of their days. Mebbe government'll take it up.

"There they come here last week Thursday, all the choir, jest about eight o'clock in the evenin', an' pretended they'd come to give me a nice little surprise. Surprise! h'm! Brought cake an' oranges, an' was jest as nice as they could be, an' I was real tickled. I never had a surprise-party before in my life. Jenny Carr she played, an' they wanted me to sing alone, an' I never suspected a thing. I've been mad ever since to think what a fool I was, an' how they must have laughed in their sleeves.

"When they'd gone I found this photograph album on the table, all done up as nice as you please, an' directed to Miss Candace Whitcomb from her many friends, an' I opened it, an' there was the letter inside givin' me notice to quit.

"If they'd gone about it any decent way, told me right out honest that they'd got tired of me, an' wanted Alma Way to sing instead of me, I wouldn't minded so much; I should have been hurt 'nough, for I'd felt as if some that had pretended to be my friends wa'n't; but it wouldn't have been as bad as this. They said in the letter that they'd always set great value on my services, an' it wa'n't from any lack of appreciation that they turned me off, but they thought the duty was gettin' a little too arduous for me. H'm! I hadn't complained. If they'd turned me right out fair an' square, showed me the door, an' said, 'Here, you get out,' but to go an' spill molasses, as it were, all over the threshold, tryin' to make me think it's all nice an' sweet—

"I'd sent that photograph album back quick's I could pack it, but I didn't know who started it, so I've used it for a footstool. It's all it's good for, 'cordin' to my way of thinkin'. An' I ain't been particular to get the dust off my shoes before I used it neither."

Mr. Pollard, the minister, sat staring. He did not look at Candace; his eyes were fastened upon a point straight ahead. He had a look of helpless solidity, like a block of granite. This country minister, with his steady, even temperament, treading with heavy precision his one track for over forty years, having nothing new in his life except the new sameness of the seasons, and desiring nothing new, was incapable of understanding a woman like this, who had lived as quietly as he, and all the time held within herself the elements of revolution. He could not account for such violence, such extremes, except in a loss of reason. He had a conviction that Candace was getting beyond herself. He himself was not a typical New-Englander; the national elements of character were not pronounced in him. He was aghast and bewildered at this outbreak, which was tropical, and more than tropical, for a New England nature has a floodgate, and the power which it releases is an accumulation. Candace Whitcomb had been a quiet woman, so delicately resolute that the quality had been scarcely noticed in her, and her ambition had been unsuspected. Now the resolution and the ambition appeared raging over her whole self.

She began to talk again. "I've made up my mind that I'm goin' to sing Sundays the way I did this mornin', an' I don't care what folks say," said she. "I've made up my mind that I'm goin' to take matters into my own hands. I'm goin' to let folks see that I ain't trod down quite flat, that there's a little rise left in me. I ain't goin' to give up beat yet a while; an' I'd like to see anybody stop me. If I ain't got a right to play a psalm tune on my organ an' sing, I'd like to know. If you don't like it, you can move the meetin'-house."

Candace had had an inborn reverence for clergymen. She had always treated Mr. Pollard with the utmost deference. Indeed, her manner toward all men had been marked by a certain delicate stiffness and dignity. Now she was talking to the old minister with the homely freedom with which she might have addressed a female gossip over the back fence. He could not say much in return. He did not feel competent to make headway against any such tide of passion; all he could do was to let it beat against him. He made a few expostulations, which increased Candace's vehemence; he expressed his regret over the whole affair, and suggested that they should kneel and ask the guidance of the Lord in the matter, that she might be led to see it all in a different light.

Candace refused flatly. "I don't see any use prayin' about it," said she. "I don't think the Lord's got much to do with it, anyhow."

It was almost time for the afternoon service when the minister left. He had missed his comfortable noontide rest, through this encounter with his revolutionary parishioner. After the minister had gone, Candace sat by the window and waited. The bell rang, and she watched the people file past. When her nephew Wilson Ford with Alma appeared, she grunted to herself. "She's thin as a rail," said she; "guess there won't be much left of her by the time Wilson gets her. Little soft-spoken nippin' thing, she wouldn't make him no kind of a wife, anyway. Guess it's jest as well."

When the bell had stopped tolling, and all the people entered the church, Candace went over to her organ and seated herself. She arranged a singing-book before her, and sat still, waiting. Her thin, colorless neck and temples were full of beating pulses; her black eyes were bright and eager; she leaned stiffly over toward the music-rack, to hear better. When the church organ sounded out she straightened herself; her long skinny fingers pressed her own organ-keys with nervous energy. She worked the pedals with all her strength; all her slender body was in motion. When the first notes of Alma's solo began, Candace sang. She had really possessed a fine voice, and it was wonderful how little she had lost it. Straining her throat with jealous fury, her notes were still for the main part true. Her voice filled the whole room; she sang with wonderful fire and expression. That, at least, mild little Alma Way could never emulate. She was full of steadfastness and unquestioning constancy, but there were in her no smouldering fires of ambition and resolution. Music was not to her what it had been to her older rival. To this obscure woman, kept relentlessly by circumstances in a narrow track, singing in the village choir had been as much as Italy was to Napoleon—and now on her island of exile she was still showing fight.

After the church service was done, Candace left the organ and went over to her old chair by the window. Her knees felt weak, and shook under her. She sat down, and leaned back her head. There were red spots on her cheeks. Pretty soon she heard a quick slam of her gate, and an impetuous tread on the gravel-walk. She looked up, and there was her nephew Wilson Ford hurrying up to the door. She cringed a little, then she settled herself more firmly in her chair.

Wilson came into the room with a rush. He left the door open, and the wind slammed it to after him.

"Aunt Candace, where are you?" he called out, in a loud voice.

She made no reply. He looked around fiercely, and his eyes seemed to pounce upon her.

"Look here, Aunt Candace," said he, "are you crazy?" Candace said nothing. "Aunt Candace!" She did not seem to see him. "If you don't answer me," said Wilson, "I'll just go over there and pitch that old organ out of the window!"

"Wilson Ford!" said Candace, in a voice that was almost a scream.

"Well, what say! What have you got to say for yourself, acting the way you have? I tell you what 'tis, Aunt Candace, I won't stand it."

"I'd like to see you help yourself."

"I will help myself. I'll pitch that old organ out of the window, and then I'll board up the window on that side of your house. Then we'll see."

"It ain't your house, and it won't never be."

"Who said it was my house? You're my aunt, and I've got a little lookout for the credit of the family. Aunt Candace, what are you doing this way for?"

"It don't make no odds what I'm doin' so for. I ain't bound to give my reasons to a young fellar like you, if you do act so mighty toppin'. But I'll tell you one thing, Wilson Ford, after the way you've spoke to-day, you sha'n't never have one cent of my money, an' you can't never marry that Way girl if you don't have it. You can't never take her home to live with your mother, an' this house would have been mighty nice an' convenient for you some day. Now you won't get it. I'm goin' to make another will. I'd made one, if you did but know it. Now you won't get a cent of my money, you nor your mother neither. An' I ain't goin' to live a dreadful while longer, neither. Now I wish you'd go home; I want to lay down. I'm 'bout sick."

Wilson could not get another word from his aunt. His indignation had not in the least cooled. Her threat of disinheriting him did not cow him at all; he had too much rough independence, and indeed his aunt Candace's house had always been too much of an air-castle for him to contemplate seriously. Wilson, with his burly frame and his headlong common-sense, could have little to do with air-castles, had he been hard enough to build them over graves. Still, he had not admitted that he never could marry Alma. All his hopes were based upon a rise in his own fortunes, not by some sudden convulsion, but by his own long and steady labor. Some time, he thought, he should have saved enough for the two homes.

He went out of his aunt's house still storming. She arose after the door had shut behind him, and got out into the kitchen. She thought that she would start a fire and make a cup of tea. She had not eaten anything all day. She put some kindling-wood into the stove and touched a match to it; then she went back to the sitting-room, and settled down again into the chair by the window. The fire in the kitchen-stove roared, and the light wood was soon burned out. She thought no more about it. She had not put on the teakettle. Her head ached, and once in a while she shivered. She sat at the window while the afternoon waned and the dusk came on. At seven o'clock the meeting bell rang again, and the people flocked by. This time she did not stir. She had shut her parlor organ. She did not need to out-sing her rival this evening; there was only congregational singing at the Sunday-night prayer-meeting.

She sat still until it was nearly time for meeting to be done; her head ached harder and harder, and she shivered more. Finally she arose. "Guess I'll go to bed," she muttered. She went about the house, bent over and shaking, to lock the doors. She stood a minute in the back door, looking over the fields to the woods. There was a red light over there. "The woods are on fire," said Candace. She watched with a dull interest the flames roll up, withering and destroying the tender green spring foliage. The air was full of smoke, although the fire was half a mile away.

Candace locked the door and went in. The trees with their delicate garlands of new leaves, with the new nests of song birds, might fall, she was in the roar of an intenser fire; the growths of all her springs and the delicate wontedness of her whole life were going down in it. Candace went to bed in her little room off the parlor, but she could not sleep. She lay awake all night. In the morning she crawled to the door and hailed a little boy who was passing. She bade him go for the doctor as quickly as he could, then to Mrs. Ford's, and ask her to come over. She held on to the door while she was talking. The boy stood staring wonderingly at her. The spring wind fanned her face. She had drawn on a dress skirt and put her shawl over her shoulders, and her gray hair was blowing over her red cheeks.

She shut the door and went back to her bed. She never arose from it again. The doctor and Mrs. Ford came and looked after her, and she lived a week. Nobody but herself thought until the very last that she would die; the doctor called her illness merely a light run of fever; she had her senses fully.

But Candace gave up at the first. "It's my last sickness," she said to Mrs. Ford that morning when she first entered; and Mrs. Ford had laughed at the notion; but the sick woman held to it. She did not seem to suffer much physical pain; she only grew weaker and weaker, but she was distressed mentally. She did not talk much, but her eyes followed everybody with an agonized expression.

On Wednesday William Emmons came to inquire for her. Candace heard him out in the parlor. She tried to raise herself on one elbow that she might listen better to his voice.

"William Emmons come in to ask how you was," Mrs. Ford said, after he was gone.

"I—heard him," replied Candace. Presently she spoke again. "Nancy," said she, "where's that photograph album?"

"On the table," replied her sister, hesitatingly.

"Mebbe—you'd better—brush it up a little."

"Well."

Sunday morning Candace wished that the minister should be asked to come in at the noon intermission. She had refused to see him before. He came and prayed with her, and she asked his forgiveness for the way she had spoken the Sunday before. "I—hadn't ought to—spoke so," said she. "I was—dreadful wrought up."

"Perhaps it was your sickness coming on," said the minister, soothingly.

Candace shook her head. "No—it wa'n't. I hope the Lord will—forgive me."

After the minister had gone, Candace still appeared unhappy. Her pitiful eyes followed her sister everywhere with the mechanical persistency of a portrait.

"What is it you want, Candace?" Mrs. Ford said at last. She had nursed her sister faithfully, but once in a while her impatience showed itself.

"Nancy!"

"What say?"

"I wish—you'd go out when—meetin's done, an'—head off Alma an' Wilson, an'—ask 'em to come in. I feel as if—I'd like to—hear her sing."

Mrs. Ford stared. "Well," said she.

The meeting was now in session. The windows were all open, for it was another warm Sunday. Candace lay listening to the music when it began, and a look of peace came over her face. Her sister had smoothed her hair back, and put on a clean cap. The white curtain in the bedroom window waved in the wind like a white sail. Candace almost felt as if she were better, but the thought of death seemed easy.

Mrs. Ford at the parlor window watched for the meeting to be out. When the people appeared, she ran down the walk and waited for Alma and Wilson. When they came she told them what Candace wanted, and they all went in together.

"Here's Alma an' Wilson, Candace," said Mrs. Ford, leading them to the bedroom door.

Candace smiled. "Come in," she said, feebly. And Alma and Wilson entered and stood beside the bed. Candace continued to look at them, the smile straining her lips.

"Wilson!"

"What is it, Aunt Candace?"

"I ain't altered that—will. You an' Alma can—come here an'—live— when I'm—gone. Your mother won't mind livin' alone. Alma can have—all—my things."

"Don't, Aunt Candace." Tears were running over Wilson's cheeks, and Alma's delicate face was all of a quiver.

"I thought—maybe—Alma'd be willin' to—sing for me," said Candace.

"What do you want me to sing?" Alma asked, in a trembling voice.

" 'Jesus, lover of my soul.' "

Alma, standing there beside Wilson, began to sing. At first she could hardly control her voice, then she sang sweetly and clearly.

Candace lay and listened. Her face had a holy and radiant expression. When Alma stopped singing it did not disappear, but she looked up and spoke, and it was like a secondary glimpse of the old shape of a forest tree through the smoke and flame of the transfiguring fire the instant before it falls. "You flatted a little on—soul," said Candace.

JAMES LANE ALLEN

★　★　★

The tragic pain of man's life emerges from stories localized in the Bluegrass region of Kentucky by James Lane Allen (1849-1925). Not unlike Thoreau, Allen portrayed in poetic phrases and with scientific accuracy the beauty of landscape, of birds, and of growing things; although the description frequently seems intrusive, the nature background serves to interpret human experiences and to enforce lessons drawn from the warping effects of sin. Allen, born near Lexington, attended Transylvania University, became a teacher, and wrote critical essays before attempting fiction. In addition to his first collection of stories, *Flute and Violin* (1891), his important books are *A Kentucky Cardinal* (1894), *Aftermath* (1895), *The Choir Invisible* (1897), and *The Reign of Law* (1900). "Two Gentleman of Kentucky" is reprinted from *Flute and Violin* by permission of The Macmillan Company.

★　★　★

Two Gentlemen of Kentucky

"The woods are hushed, their music is no more:
The leaf is dead, the yearning passed away:
New leaf, new life—the days of frost are o'er:
New life, new love, to suit the newer day."

THE WOODS ARE HUSHED

IT was near the middle of the afternoon of an autumnal day, on the wide, grassy plateau of Central Kentucky.

The Eternal Power seemed to have quitted the universe and left all nature folded in the calm of the Eternal Peace. Around the pale-

blue dome of the heavens a few pearl-colored clouds hung motionless, as though the wind had been withdrawn to other skies. Not a
crimson leaf floated downward through the soft, silvery light that
filled the atmosphere and created the sense of lonely, unimaginable
spaces. This light overhung the far-rolling landscape of field and
meadow and wood, crowning with faint radiance the remoter low-
swelling hill-tops and deepening into dreamy half-shadows on their
eastern slopes. Nearer, it fell in a white flake on an unstirred sheet
of water which lay along the edge of a mass of sombre-hued woodland, and nearer still it touched to spring-like brilliancy a level, green
meadow on the hither edge of the water, where a group of Durham
cattle stood with reversed flanks near the gleaming trunks of some
leafless sycamores. Still nearer, it caught the top of the brown foliage
of a little bent oak-tree and burned it into a silvery flame. It lit on
the back and the wings of a crow flying heavily in the path of its
rays, and made his blackness as white as the breast of a swan. In
the immediate foreground, it sparkled in minute gleams along the
stalks of the coarse, dead weeds that fell away from the legs and
the flanks of a white horse, and slanted across the face of the rider
and through the ends of his gray hair, which straggled from beneath
his soft black hat.

The horse, old and patient and gentle, stood with low-stretched
neck and closed eyes half asleep in the faint glow of the waning heat;
and the rider, the sole human presence in all the field, sat looking
across the silent autumnal landscape, sunk in reverie. Both horse
and rider seemed but harmonious elements in the panorama of still-
life, and completed the picture of a closing scene.

To the man it was a closing scene. From the rank, fallow field
through which he had been riding he was now surveying, for the
last time, the many features of a landscape that had been familiar
to him from the beginning of memory. In the afternoon and the
autumn of his age he was about to rend the last ties that bound
him to his former life, and, like one who had survived his own destiny,
turn his face towards a future that was void of everything he held
significant or dear.

The Civil War had only the year before reached its ever-memorable
close. From where he sat there was not a home in sight, as there
was not one beyond the reach of his vision, but had felt its influence. Some of his neighbors had come home from its camps and
prisons, aged or altered as though by half a lifetime of years. The
bones of some lay whitening on its battlefields. Families, reassembled

around their hearth-stones, spoke in low tones unceasingly of defeat and victory, heroism and death. Suspicion and distrust and estrangement prevailed. Former friends met each other on the turnpikes without speaking; brothers avoided each other in the streets of the neighboring town. The rich had grown poor; the poor had become rich. Many of the latter were preparing to move West. The Negroes were drifting blindly hither and thither, deserting the country and flocking to the towns. Even the once united church of his neighborhood was jarred by the unstrung and discordant spirit of the times. At affecting passages in the sermons men grew pale and set their teeth fiercely; women suddenly lowered their black veils and rocked to and fro in their pews; for it is always at the bar of Conscience and before the very altar of God that the human heart is most wrung by a sense of its losses and the memory of its wrongs. The war had divided the people of Kentucky as the false mother would have severed the child.

It had not left the old man unscathed. His younger brother had fallen early in the conflict, borne to the end of his brief warfare by his impetuous valor; his aged mother had sunk under the tidings of the death of her latest-born; his sister was estranged from him by his political differences with her husband; his old family servants, men and women, had left him, and grass and weeds had already grown over the door-steps of the shut, noiseless cabins. Nay, the whole vast social system of the old régime had fallen, and he was henceforth but a useless fragment of the ruins.

All at once his mind turned from the cracked and smoky mirror of the times and dwelt fondly upon the scenes of the past. The silent fields around him seemed again alive with the Negroes, singing as they followed the ploughs down the corn-rows or swung the cradles through the bearded wheat. Again, in a frenzy of merriment, the strains of the old fiddles issued from crevices of cabin-doors to the rhythmic beat of hands and feet that shook the rafters and the roof. Now he was sitting on his porch, and one little Negro was blacking his shoes, another leading his saddle-horse to the stiles, a third bringing his hat, and a fourth handing him a glass of ice-cold sangaree; or now he lay under the locust-trees in his yard, falling asleep in the drowsy heat of the summer afternoon, while one waved over him a bough of pungent walnut leaves, until he lost consciousness and by-and-by awoke to find that they both had fallen asleep side by side on the grass and that the abandoned fly-brush lay full across his face.

From where he sat also were seen slopes on which picnics were danced under the broad shade of maples and elms in June by those whom death and war had scattered like the transitory leaves that once had sheltered them. In this direction lay the district school-house where on Friday evenings there were wont to be speeches and debates; in that, lay the blacksmith's shop where of old he and his neighbors had met on horseback of Saturday afternoons to hear the news, get the mails, discuss elections, and pitch quoits. In the val-ley beyond stood the church at which all had assembled on calm Sun-day mornings like the members of one united family. Along with these scenes went many a chastened reminiscence of bridal and funeral and simpler events that had made up the annals of his country life.

The reader will have a clearer insight into the character and past career of Colonel Romulus Fields by remembering that he repre-sented a fair type of that social order which had existed in rank perfection over the blue-grass plains of Kentucky during the final decades of the old régime. Perhaps of all agriculturists in the United States the inhabitants of that region had spent the most nearly idyllic life, on account of the beauty of the climate, the richness of the land, the spacious comfort of their homes, the efficiency of their Negroes, and the characteristic contentedness of their dispositions. Thus nature and history combined to make them a peculiar class, a cross between the aristocratic and the bucolic, being as simple as shepherds and as proud as kings, and not seldom exhibiting among both men and women types of character which were as remarkable for pure, ten-der, noble states of feeling as they were commonplace in powers and cultivation of mind.

It was upon this luxurious social growth that the war naturally fell as a killing frost, and upon no single specimen with more blight-ing power than upon Colonel Fields. For destiny had quarried and chiselled him, to serve as an ornament in the barbaric temple of hu-man bondage. There *were* ornaments in that temple, and he was one. A slave-holder with Southern sympathies, a man educated not beyond the ideas of his generation, convinced that slavery was an evil, yet seeing no present way of removing it, he had of all things been a model master. As such he had gone on record in Kentucky, and no doubt in a Higher Court; and as such his efforts had been put forth to secure the passage of many of those milder laws for which his State was distinguished. Often, in those dark days, his face, anxious and sad, was to be seen amid the throng that surrounded the blocks on which slaves were sold at auction; and more than one poor wretch he had bought to save him from separation from his family or from being sold into the Southern plantations—afterwards riding far and near to find him a home on one of the neighboring farms.

But all those days were over. He had but to place the whole picture of the present beside the whole picture of the past to realize what the contrast meant for him.

At length he gathered the bridle reins from the neck of his old horse and turned his head homeward. As he rode slowly on, every spot gave up its memories. He dismounted when he came to the cattle and walked among them, stroking their soft flanks and feeling in the palm of his hand the rasp of their salt-loving tongues; on his sideboard at home was many a silver cup which told of premiums on cattle at the great fairs. It was in this very pond that as a boy he had learned to swim on a cherry rail. When he entered the woods, the sight of the walnut-trees and the hickory-nut trees, loaded on the topmost branches, gave him a sudden pang.

Beyond the woods he came upon the garden, which he had kept as his mother had left it—an old-fashioned garden with an arbor in the centre, covered with Isabella grape-vines on one side and Catawba on the other; with walks branching thence in four directions, and along them beds of jump-up-johnnies, sweet-williams, daffodils, sweet-peas, larkspur, and thyme, flags and the sensitive-plant, celestial and maiden's-blush roses. He stopped and looked over the fence at the very spot where he had found his mother on the day when the news of the battle came.

She had been kneeling, trowel in hand, driving away vigorously at the loamy earth, and, as she saw him coming, had risen and turned towards him her face with the ancient pink bloom on her clear cheeks and the light of a pure, strong soul in her gentle eyes. Overcome by his emotions, he had blindly faltered out the words, "Mother, John was among the killed!" For a moment she had looked at him as though stunned by a blow. Then a violent flush had overspread her features, and then an ashen pallor; after which, with a sudden proud dilating of her form as though with joy, she had sunk down like the tenderest of her lily-stalks, cut from its root.

Beyond the garden he came to the empty cabin and the great wood-pile. At this hour it used to be a scene of hilarious activity—the little Negroes sitting perched in chattering groups on the top-most logs or playing leap-frog in the dust, while some picked up baskets of chips or dragged a back-log into the cabins.

At last he drew near the wooden stiles and saw the large house of which he was the solitary occupant. What darkened rooms and noiseless halls! What beds, all ready, that nobody now came to sleep in, and cushioned old chairs that nobody rocked! The house and the contents of its attic, presses, and drawers could have told much of the history of Kentucky from almost its beginning; for its foundations had been laid by his father near the beginning of the century, and through its doors had passed a long train of forms, from the veterans of the Revolution to the soldiers of the Civil War. Old coats hung up in closets; old dresses folded away in drawers; saddle-bags and buckskin-leggins; hunting-jackets, powder-horns, and militiamen hats; looms and knitting-needles; snuffboxes and reticules—what a treasure-house of the past it was! And now the only thing that had the springs of life within its bosom was the great, sweet-voiced clock, whose faithful face had kept unchanged amid all the swift pageantry of changes.

He dismounted at the stiles and handed the reins to a gray-haired Negro, who had hobbled up to receive them with a smile and a gesture of the deepest respect.

"Peter," he said, very simply, "I am going to sell the place and move to town. I can't live here any longer."

With these words he passed through the yard-gate, walked slowly up the broad pavement, and entered the house.

MUSIC NO MORE

On the disappearing form of the colonel was fixed an ancient pair of eyes that looked out at him from behind a still more ancient pair of silver-rimmed spectacles with an expression of indescribable solicitude and love.

These eyes were set in the head of an old gentleman—for such he was—named Peter Cotton, who was the only one of the colonel's former slaves that had remained inseparable from his person and his altered fortunes. In early manhood Peter had been a wood-chopper; but he had one day had his leg broken by the limb of a falling tree, and afterwards, out of consideration for his limp, had been made supervisor of the wood-pile, gardener, and a sort of nondescript servitor of his master's luxurious needs.

Nay, in larger and deeper characters must his history be writ, he having been, in days gone by, one of those ministers of the gospel whom conscientious Kentucky masters often urged to the exercise of spiritual functions in behalf of their benighted people. In course of preparation for this august work, Peter had learned to read and had come to possess a well-chosen library of three several volumes—*Webster's Spelling-Book, The Pilgrim's Progress,* and the Bible. But even these unusual acquisitions he deemed not enough; for being touched with a spark of poetic fire from heaven, and fired by the African's fondness for all that is conspicuous in dress, he had conceived for himself the creation of a unique garment which should symbolize in perfection the claims and consolations of his apostolic office. This was nothing less than a sacred blue-jeans coat that he had had his old mistress make him, with very long and spacious tails, whereon, at his further direction, she embroidered sundry texts of Scripture which it pleased him to regard as the fit visible annunciations of his holy calling. And inasmuch as his mistress, who had had the coat woven on her own looms from the wool of her finest sheep, was, like other gentlewomen of her time, rarely skilled in the accomplishments of the needle, and was moreover in full sympathy with the piety of his intent, she wrought of these passages a border enriched with such intricate curves, marvellous flourishes, and harmonious letterings, that Solomon never reflected the glory in which Peter was arrayed whenever he put it on. For after much prayer that the Almighty wisdom would aid his reason in the difficult task of selecting the most appropriate texts, Peter had chosen seven—one for each day in the week—with such tact, and no doubt heavenly guidance, that when braided together they did truly constitute an eloquent epitome of Christian duty, hope, and pleading.

From first to last they were as follows: "Woe is unto me if I preach not the gospel;" "Servants, be obedient to them that are your masters according to the flesh;" "Come unto me, all ye that labour and are heavy laden;" "Consider the lilies of the field, how they grow; they toil not, neither do they spin;" "Now abideth faith, hope, and charity, these three; but the greatest of these is charity;" "I would not have you to be ignorant, brethren, concerning them which are asleep;" "For as in Adam all die, even so in Christ shall all be made alive." This concatenation of texts Peter wished to have duly solemnized, and therefore, when the work was finished, he further requested his mistress to close the entire chain with the word "Amen," introduced in some suitable place.

But the only spot now left vacant was one of a few square inches, located just where the coat-tails hung over the end of Peter's spine; so that when any one stood full in Peter's rear, he could but marvel at the sight of so solemn a word emblazoned in so unusual a locality.

Panoplied in this robe of righteousness, and with a worn leathern Bible in his hand, Peter used to go around of Sundays, and during the week, by night, preaching from cabin to cabin the gospel of his heavenly Master.

The angriest lightnings of the sultriest skies often played amid the

darkness upon those sacred coat-tails and around that girdle of everlasting texts, as though the evil spirits of the air would fain have
burned them and scattered their ashes on the roaring winds. The
slow-sifting snows of winter whitened them as though to chill their
spiritual fires; but winter and summer, year after year, in weariness
of body, often in sore distress of mind, for miles along this lonely
road and for miles across that rugged way, Peter trudged on and on,
withal perhaps as meek a spirit as ever grew foot-sore in the paths
of its Master. Many a poor over-burdened slave took fresh heart and
strength from the sight of that celestial raiment; many a stubborn,
rebellious spirit, whose flesh but lately quivered under the lash, was
brought low by its humble teaching; many a worn-out old frame,
racked with pain in its last illness, pressed a fevered lip to its hopeful
hem; and many a dying eye closed in death peacefully fixed on its
immortal pledges.

When Peter started abroad, if a storm threatened, he carried an
old cotton umbrella of immense size; and as the storm burst, he
gathered the tails of his coat carefully up under his armpits that they
might be kept dry. Or if caught by a tempest without his umbrella,
he would take his coat off and roll it up inside out, leaving his body
exposed to the fury of the elements. No care, however, could keep
it from growing old and worn and faded; and when the slaves were
set free and he was called upon by the interposition of Providence
to lay it finally aside, it was covered by many a patch and stain as
proofs of its devoted usage.

One after another the colonel's old servants, gathering their children
about them, had left him, to begin their new life. He bade them all
a kind good-bye, and into the palm of each silently pressed some gift
that he knew would soon be needed. But no inducement could make
Peter or Phillis, his wife, budge from their cabin. "Go, Peter! Go,
Phillis!" the colonel had said time and again. "No one is happier that
you are free than I am; and you can call on me for what you need to
set you up in business." But Peter and Phillis asked to stay with him.
Then suddenly, several months before the time at which this sketch
opens, Phillis had died, leaving the colonel and Peter as the only relics
of that populous life which had once filled the house and the cabins.
The colonel had succeeded in hiring a woman to do Phillis's work;
but her presence was a strange note of discord in the old domestic
harmony, and only saddened the recollections of its vanished peace.

Peter had a short, stout figure, dark-brown skin, smooth-shaven
face, eyes round, deep-set and wide apart, and a short, stub nose
which dipped suddenly into his head, making it easy for him to wear

the silver-rimmed spectacles left him by his old mistress. A peculiar conformation of the muscles between the eyes and the nose gave him the quizzical expression of one who is about to sneeze, and this was heightened by a twinkle in the eyes which seemed caught from the shining of an inner sun upon his tranquil heart.

Sometimes, however, his face grew sad enough. It was sad on this afternoon while he watched the colonel walk slowly up the pavement, well overgrown with weeds, and enter the house, which the setting sun touched with the last radiance of the finished day.

NEW LIFE

About two years after the close of the war, therefore, the colonel and Peter were to be found in Lexington, ready to turn over a new leaf in the volumes of their lives, which already had an old-fashioned binding, a somewhat musty odor, and but few unwritten leaves remaining.

After a long, dry summer you may have seen two gnarled old apple-trees, that stood with interlocked arms on the western slope of some quiet hill-side, make a melancholy show of blooming out again in the autumn of the year and dallying with the idle buds that mock their sapless branches. Much the same was the belated, fruitless efflorescence of the colonel and Peter.

The colonel had no business habits, 'no political ambition, no wish to grow richer. He was too old for society, and without near family ties. For some time he wandered through the streets like one lost—sick with yearning for the fields and woods, for his cattle, for familiar faces. He haunted Cheapside and the court-house square, where the farmers always assembled when they came to town; and if his eye lighted on one, he would button-hole him on the street-corner and lead him into a grocery and sit down for a quiet chat. Sometimes he would meet an aimless, melancholy wanderer like himself, and the two would go off and discuss over and over again their departed days; and several times he came unexpectedly upon some of his old servants who had fallen into bitter want, and who more than repaid him for the help he gave by contrasting the hardships of a life of freedom with the ease of their shackled years.

In the course of time, he could but observe that human life in the town was reshaping itself slowly and painfully, but with resolute energy. The colossal structure of slavery had fallen, scattering its ruins far and wide over the State; but out of the very débris was being taken the material to lay the deeper foundations of the new social edifice. Men and women as old as he were beginning life over and trying to fit themselves for it by changing the whole attitude and habit of their minds—by taking on a new heart and spirit. But when a great building falls, there is always some rubbish, and the colonel and others like him were part of this. Henceforth they possessed only an antiquarian sort of interest, like the stamped bricks of Nebuchadnezzar.

Nevertheless he made a show of doing something, and in a year or two opened on Cheapside a store for the sale of hardware and agricultural implements. He knew more about the latter than anything else; and, furthermore, he secretly felt that a business of this kind would enable him to establish in town a kind of headquarters for the farmers. His account-books were to be kept on a system of twelve months' credit; and he resolved that if one of his customers couldn't pay then, it would make no difference.

Business began slowly. The farmers dropped in and found a good lounging-place. On county-court days, which were great market-days for the sale of sheep, horses, mules, and cattle in front of the colonel's door, they swarmed in from the hot sun and sat around on the counter and the ploughs and machines till the entrance was blocked to other customers.

When a customer did come in, the colonel, who was probably talking with some old acquaintance, would tell him just to look around and pick out what he wanted and the price would be all right. If one of those acquaintances asked for a pound of nails, the colonel would scoop up some ten pounds and say, "I reckon that's about a pound, Tom." He had never seen a pound of nails in his life; and if one had been weighed on his scales, he would have said the scales were wrong.

He had no great idea of commercial despatch. One morning a lady came in for some carpet-tacks, an article that he had forgotten to lay in. But he at once sent off an order for enough to have tacked a carpet pretty well all over Kentucky; and when they came, two weeks later, he told Peter to take her up a dozen papers with his compliments. He had laid in, however, an ample and especially fine assortment of pocket-knives, for that instrument had always been to him one of gracious and very winning qualities. Then when a friend dropped in he would say, "General, don't you need a new pocket-knife?" and, taking out one, would open all the blades and commend the metal and the handle. The "general" would inquire the price, and the colonel, having shut the blades, would hand it to him, saying in a careless, fond way, "I reckon I won't charge you anything for that." His mind could not come down to the low level of such ignoble barter, and he gave away the whole case of knives.

These were the pleasanter aspects of his business life, which did not lack as well its tedium and crosses. Thus there were many dark stormy days when no one he cared to see came in; and he then became rather a pathetic figure, wandering absently around amid the symbols of his past activity, and stroking the ploughs, like dumb companions. Or he would stand at the door and look across at the old court-house, where he had seen many a slave sold and had listened to the great Kentucky orators.

But what hurt him most was the talk of the new farming and the abuse of the old which he was forced to hear; and he generally refused to handle the improved implements and mechanical devices by which labor and waste were to be saved.

Altogether he grew tired of "the thing," and sold out at the end of the year with a loss of over a thousand dollars, though he insisted he had done a good business.

As he was then seen much on the streets again and several times heard to make remarks in regard to the sidewalks, gutters, and crossings, when they happened to be in bad condition, the *Daily Press* one morning published a card stating that if Colonel Romulus Fields would consent to make the race for mayor he would receive the support of many Democrats, adding a tribute to his virtues and his influential past. It touched the colonel, and he walked down-town with a rather commanding figure the next morning. But it pained him to see how many of his acquaintances returned his salutations very coldly; and just as he was passing the Northern Bank he met the young opposition candidate—a little red-haired fellow, walking between two ladies, with a rose-bud in his button-hole—who refused to speak at all, but made the ladies laugh by some remark he uttered as the colonel passed. The card had been inserted humorously, but he took it seriously; and when his friends found this out, they rallied round him. The day of election drew near. They told him he must buy votes. He said he wouldn't buy a vote to be mayor of the New Jerusalem. They told him he must "mix" and "treat." He refused. Foreseeing he had no chance, they besought him to withdraw. He said he would not. They told him he wouldn't poll twenty votes. He replied that *one* would satisfy him, provided it was neither begged nor bought. When his defeat was announced, he accepted it as another evidence that he had no part in the present—no chance of redeeming his idleness.

A sense of this weighed heavily on him at times; but it is not likely that he realized how pitifully he was undergoing a moral shrinkage in consequence of mere disuse. Actually, extinction had set in with him long prior to dissolution, and he was dead years before his heart ceased beating. The very basic virtues on which had rested his once spacious and stately character were now but the mouldy corner-stones of a crumbling ruin.

It was a subtle evidence of deterioration in manliness that he had taken to dress. When he had lived in the country, he had never dressed up unless he came to town. When he had moved to town, he thought he must remain dressed up all the time; and this fact first fixed his attention on a matter which afterwards began to be loved for its own sake. Usually he wore a Derby hat, a black diagonal coat, gray trousers, and a white necktie. But the article of attire in which he took chief pleasure was hose; and the better to show the gay colors of these, he wore low-cut shoes of the finest calf-skin, turned up at the toes. Thus his feet kept pace with the present, however far his head may have lagged in the past; and it may be that this stream of fresh fashions, flowing perennially over his lower extremities like water about the roots of a tree, kept him from drying up altogether.

Peter always polished his shoes with too much blacking, perhaps thinking that the more the blacking the greater the proof of love. He wore his clothes about a season and a half—having several suits— and then passed them on to Peter, who, foreseeing the joy of such an inheritance, bought no new ones. In the act of transferring them the colonel made no comment until he came to the hose, from which he seemed unable to part without a final tribute of esteem, as: "These are fine, Peter;" or, "Peter, these are nearly as good as new." Thus Peter, too, was dragged through the whims of fashion. To have seen the colonel walking about his grounds and garden followed by Peter, just a year and a half behind in dress and a yard and a half behind in space, one might well have taken the rear figure for the colonel's double, slightly the worse for wear, somewhat shrunken, and cast into a heavy shadow.

Time hung so heavily on his hands at night that with a happy inspiration he added a dress suit to his wardrobe, and accepted the first invitation to an evening party.

He grew excited as the hour approached, and dressed in a great fidget for fear he should be too late.

"How do I look, Peter?" he inquired at length, surprised at his own appearance.

"Splendid, Marse Rom," replied Peter, bringing in the shoes with more blacking on them than ever before.

"I think," said the colonel, apologetically—"I think I'd look better if I'd put a little powder on. I don't know what makes me so red in the face."

But his heart began to sink before he reached his hostess's, and he had a fearful sense of being the observed of all observers as he slipped through the hall and passed rapidly up to the gentlemen's room. He stayed there after the others had gone down, bewildered and lonely, dreading to go down himself. By-and-by the musicians struck up a waltz, and with a little cracked laugh at his own performance he cut a few shines of an unremembered pattern; but his ankles snapped audibly, and he suddenly stopped with the thought of what Peter would say if he should catch him at these antics. Then he boldly went down-stairs.

He had touched the new human life around him at various points: as he now stretched out his arms towards its society, for the first time he completely realized how far removed it was from him. Here he saw a younger generation—the flowers of the new social order—sprung from the very soil of fraternal battlefields, but blooming together as the emblems of oblivious peace. He saw fathers, who had fought madly on opposite sides, talking quietly in corners as they watched their children dancing, or heard them toasting their old generals and their campaigns over their champagne in the supper-room. He was glad of it; but it made him feel, at the same time, that, instead of treading the velvety floors, he ought to step up and take his place among the canvases of old-time portraits that looked down from the walls.

The dancing he had done had been not under the blinding glare of gaslight, but by the glimmer of tallow-dips and star-candles and the ruddy glow of cavernous firesides—not to the accompaniment of an orchestra of wind-instruments and strings, but to a chorus of girls' sweet voices, as they trod simpler measures, or to the maddening sway of a gray-haired Negro fiddler standing on a chair in the chimney-corner. Still, it is significant to note that his saddest thought, long after leaving, was that his shirt bosom had not lain down smooth, but stuck out like a huge cracked egg-shell; and that when, in imitation of the others, he had laid his white silk handkerchief across his bosom inside his vest, it had slipped out during the evening, and had been found by him, on confronting a mirror, flapping over his stomach like a little white masonic apron.

"Did you have a nice time, Marse Rom?" inquired Peter, as they drove home through the darkness.

"Splendid time, Peter, splendid time," replied the colonel, nervously.

"Did you dance any, Marse Rom?"

"I didn't *dance*. Oh, I *could* have danced if I'd *wanted* to; but I didn't."

Peter helped the colonel out of the carriage with pitying gentleness when they reached home. It was the first and only party.

Peter also had been finding out that his occupation was gone.

Soon after moving to town, he had tendered his pastoral services to one of the fashionable churches of the city—not because it was fashionable, but because it was made up of his brethren. In reply he was invited to preach a trial sermon, which he did with gracious unction.

It was a strange scene, as one calm Sunday morning he stood on the edge of the pulpit, dressed in a suit of the colonel's old clothes, with one hand in his trousers-pocket, and his lame leg set a little forward at an agle familiar to those who know the statues of Henry Clay.

How self-possessed he seemed, yet with what a rush of memories did he pass his eyes slowly over that vast assemblage of his emancipated people! With what feelings must he have contrasted those silk hats, and walking-canes, and broadcloths; those gloves and satins, laces and feathers, jewelry and fans—that whole many-colored panorama of life—with the weary, sad, and sullen audiences that had often heard him of old under the forest trees or by the banks of some turbulent stream!

In a voice husky, but heard beyond the flirtation of the uttermost pew, he took his text: "Consider the lilies of the field, how they grow; they toil not, neither do they spin." From this he tried to preach a new sermon, suited to the newer day. But several times the thoughts of the past were too much for him, and he broke down with emotion.

The next day a grave committee waited on him and reported that the sense of the congregation was to call a colored gentleman from Louisville. Private objections to Peter were that he had a broken leg, wore Colonel Fields's second-hand clothes, which were too big for him, preached in the old-fashioned way, and lacked self-control and repose of manner.

Peter accepted his rebuff as sweetly as Socrates might have done. Humming the burden of an old hymn, he took his righteous coat from a nail in the wall and folded it away in a little brass-nailed deer-skin trunk, laying over it the spelling-book and *The Pilgrim's Progress,* which he had ceased to read. Thenceforth his relations to his people were never intimate, and even from the other servants of the

colonel's household he stood apart. But the colonel took Peter's rejection greatly to heart, and the next morning gave him the new silk
socks he had worn at the party. In paying his servants the colonel
would sometimes say, "Peter, I reckon I'd better begin to pay you a
salary; that's the style now." But Peter would turn off, saying he
didn't "have no use fur no salary."

Thus both of them dropped more and more out of life, but as they
did so drew more and more closely to each other. The colonel had
bought a home on the edge of the town, with some ten acres of
beautiful ground surrounding. A high osage-orange hedge shut it in,
and forest trees, chiefly maples and elms, gave to the lawn and house
abundant shade. Wild-grape vines, the Virginia-creeper, and the
climbing-oak swung their long festoons from summit to summit,
while honeysuckles, clematis, and the Mexican-vine clambered over
arbors and trellises, or along the chipped stone of the low, old-
fashioned house. Just outside the door of the colonel's bedroom slept
an ancient, broken sundial.

The place seemed always in half-shadow, with hedge-rows of box,
clumps of dark holly, darker firs half a century old, and aged, crape-
like cedars.

It was in the seclusion of this retreat, which looked almost like a
wild bit of country set down on the edge of the town, that the colonel
and Peter spent more of their time as they fell farther in the rear
of onward events. There were no such flower-gardens in the city,
and pretty much the whole town went thither for its flowers, pre-
ferring them to those that were to be had for a price at the nurseries.

There was, perhaps, a suggestion of pathetic humor in the fact that
it should have called on the colonel and Peter, themselves so nearly
defunct, to furnish the flowers for so many funerals; but, it is certain,
almost weekly the two old gentlemen received this chastening admonition of their all-but-spent mortality. The colonel cultivated the rarest
fruits also, and had under glass varieties that were not friendly to
the climate; so that by means of the fruits and flowers there was
established a pleasant social bond with many who otherwise would
never have sought them out.

But others came for better reasons. To a few deep-seeing eyes the
colonel and Peter were ruined landmarks on a fading historic landscape, and their devoted friendship was the last steady burning-down
of that pure flame of love which can never again shine out in the
future of the two races. Hence a softened charm invested the drowsy
quietude of that shadowy paradise in which the old master without
a slave and the old slave without a master still kept up a brave

pantomime of their obsolete relations. No one ever saw in their intercourse ought but the finest courtesy, the most delicate consideration. The very tones of their voices in addressing each other were as good as sermons on gentleness, their antiquated playfulness as melodious as the babble of distant water. To be near them was to be exorcised of evil passions.

The sun of their day had indeed long since set; but like twin clouds lifted high and motionless into some far quarter of the gray twilight skies, they were still radiant with the glow of the invisible orb.

Henceforth the colonel's appearances in public were few and regular. He went to church on Sundays, where he sat on the edge of the choir in the centre of the building, and sang an ancient bass of his own improvisation to the older hymns, and glanced furtively around to see whether any one noticed that he could not sing the new ones. At the Sunday-school picnics the committee of arrangements allowed him to carve the mutton, and after dinner to swing the smallest children gently beneath the trees. He was seen on Commencement Day at Morrison Chapel, where he always gave his bouquet to the valedictorian. It was the speech of that young gentleman that always touched him, consisting as it did of farewells.

In the autumn he might sometimes be noticed sitting high up in the amphitheatre at the fair, a little blue around the nose, and looking absently over into the ring where the judges were grouped around the music-stand. Once he had strutted around as a judge himself, with a blue ribbon in his button-hole, while the band played "Sweet Alice, Ben Bolt," and "Gentle Annie." The ring seemed full of young men now, and no one even thought of offering him the privileges of the grounds. In his day the great feature of the exhibition had been cattle; now everything was turned into a horse-show. He was always glad to get home again to Peter, his true yoke-fellow. For just as two old oxen—one white and one black—that have long toiled under the same yoke will, when turned out to graze at last in the widest pasture, come and put themselves horn to horn and flank to flank, so the colonel and Peter were never so happy as when ruminating side by side.

NEW LOVE

In their eventless life the slightest incident acquired the importance of a history. Thus, one day in June, Peter discovered a young couple love-making in the shrubbery, and with the deepest agitation reported the fact to the colonel.

Never before, probably, had the fluttering of the dear god's wings brought more dismay than to these ancient involuntary guardsmen of his hiding-place. The colonel was at first for breaking up what he considered a piece of underhand proceedings, but Peter reasoned stoutly that if the pair were driven out they would simply go to some other retreat; and without getting the approval of his conscience to this view, the colonel contented himself with merely repeating that they ought to go straight and tell the girl's parents. Those parents lived just across the street outside his grounds. The young lady he knew very well himself, having a few years before given her the privilege of making herself at home among his flowers. It certainly looked hard to drive her out now, just when she was making the best possible use of his kindness and her opportunity. Moreover, Peter walked down street and ascertained that the young fellow was an energetic farmer living a few miles from town, and son of one of the colonel's former friends; on both of which accounts the latter's heart went out to him. So when, a few days later, the colonel, followed by Peter, crept up breathlessly and peeped through the bushes at the pair strolling along the shady perfumed walks, and so plainly happy in that happiness which comes but once in a lifetime, they not only abandoned the idea of betraying the secret, but afterwards kept away from that part of the grounds, lest they should be an interruption.

"Peter," stammered the colonel, who had been trying to get the words out for three days, "do you suppose he has already—*asked* her?"

"Some's pow'ful quick on de trigger, en some's mighty slow," replied Peter, neutrally. "En some," he added, exhaustively, "don't use de trigger 't all!"

"I always thought there had to be asking done by *somebody*," remarked the colonel, a little vaguely.

"I nuver axed Phillis!" exclaimed Peter, with a certain air of triumph.

"Did Phillis ask *you*, Peter?" inquired the colonel, blushing and confidential.

"No, no, Marse Rom! I couldn't er stood dat from no 'oman!" replied Peter, laughing and shaking his head.

The colonel was sitting on the stone steps in front of the house, and Peter stood below, leaning against a Corinthian column, hat in hand, as he went on to tell his love-story.

"Hit all happ'n dis way, Marse Rom. We wuz gwine have pra'r-meetin', en I 'lowed to walk home wid Phillis en ax 'er on de road. I been 'lowin' to ax 'er heap o' times befo', but I ain' jes nuver done so. So I says to myse'f, says I, 'I jes mek my sermon to-night kiner lead up to whut I gwine tell Phillis on de road home.' So I tuk my tex' from de *lef'* tail o' my coat: 'De greates' o' dese is charity;' caze I knowed charity wuz same ez love. En all de time I wuz preachin' an' glorifyin' charity en identifyin' charity wid love, I couldn' he'p thinkin' 'bout what I gwine say to Phillis on de road home. Dat mek me feel better; en de better I *feel*, de better I *preach,* so hit boun' to mek my *heahehs* feel better likewise—Phillis 'mong um. So Phillis she jes sot dah listenin' en listenin' en lookin' like we wuz a'ready on de road home, till I got so wuked up in my feelin's I jes knowed de time wuz come. By-en-by, I had n' mo' 'n done preachin' en wuz lookin' roun' to git my Bible en my hat, 'fo' up popped dat big Charity Green, who been settin' 'longside o' Phillis en tekin' ev'ylas' thing I said to *her*se'f. En she tuk hole o' my han' en squeeze it, en say she felt mos' like shoutin'. En 'fo' I knowed it, I jes see Phillis wrap 'er shawl roun' 'er head en tu'n 'er nose up at me right quick en flip out de dooh. De dogs howl mighty mou'nful when I walk home by myse'f *dat* night," added Peter, laughing to himself, "en I ain' preach dat sermon no mo' tell atter me en Phillis wuz married.

"Hit wuz long time," he continued, " 'fo' Phillis come to heah me preach any mo'. But 'long 'bout de nex' fall we had big meetin', en heap mo' um j'ined. But Phillis, she ain't nuver j'ined yit. I preached mighty nigh all roun' my coat-tails till I say to myse'f, D' ain't but one tex' lef', en I jes got to fetch 'er wid dat! De tex' wuz on de *right* tail o' my coat: 'Come unto me, all ye dat labor en is heavy laden.' Hit wuz a ve'y momentous sermon, en all 'long I jes see Phillis wras'lin' wid 'erse'f, en I say, 'She *got* to come *dis* night, de Lohd he'pin' me.' En I had n' mo' 'n said de word, 'fo' she jes walked down en guv me 'er han'.

"Den we had de baptizin' in Elkhorn Creek, en de watter wuz deep en de curren' tol'ble swif'. Hit look to me like dere wuz five hundred uv um on de creek side. By-en-by I stood on de edge o' de watter, en Phillis she come down to let me baptize 'er. En me en 'er j'ined han's en waded out in the creek, mighty slow, caze Phillis didn' have no shot roun' de bottom uv 'er dress, en it kep' bobbin' on top de watter till I pushed it down. But by-en-by we got 'way out in de creek, en bof uv us wuz tremblin'. En I says to 'er ve'y kin'ly, 'When I put you un'er de watter, Phillis, you mus' try en hole yo'se'f stiff, so I can lif' you up easy.' But I hadn't mo' 'n jes got 'er laid back over de watter ready to souze 'er un'er when 'er feet flew up off de bottom uv de creek, en when I retched out to fetch 'er up, I stepped in a hole; en 'fo' I knowed it, we wuz flounderin' roun' in de watter, en de hymn dey was singin' on de bank sounded mighty confused-like. En Phillis she swallowed some watter, en all 't oncet she jes grap me right tight roun' de neck, en say mighty quick, says she, 'I gwine marry whoever gits me out'n dis yere watter!'

"En by-en-by, when me en 'er wuz walkin' up de bank o' de creek, drippin' all over, I says to 'er, says I:

"'Does you 'member what you said back yon'er in de watter, Phillis?'

"'I ain' out'n no watter yit,' says she, ve'y contemptuous.

"'When does you consider yo'se'f out'n de watter?' says I, ve'y humble.

"'When I git dese soakin' clo'es off'n my back,' says she.

"Hit wuz good dark when we got home, en atter a while I crope up to de dooh o' Phillis's cabin en put my eye down to de key-hole, en see Phillis jes settin' 'fo' dem blazin' walnut logs dressed up in 'er new red linsey dress, en 'er eyes shinin'. En I shuk so I 'mos' faint. Den I tap easy on de dooh, en say in a mighty tremblin' tone, says I:

"'Is you out'n de watter yit, Phillis?'

"'I got on dry dress,' says she.

"'Does you 'member what you said back yon'er in de watter, Phillis?' says I.

"'De latch-string on de outside de dooh,' says she, mighty sof'.

"En I walked in."

As Peter drew near the end of this reminiscence, his voice sank to a key of inimitable tenderness; and when it was ended he stood a few minutes, scraping the gravel with the toe of his boot, his head dropped forward. Then he added, huskily:

"Phillis been dead heap o' years now;" and turned away.

This recalling of the scenes of a time long gone by may have awakened in the breast of the colonel some gentle memory; for after Peter was gone he continued to sit a while in silent musing. Then getting up, he walked in the falling twilight across the yard and through the gardens until he came to a secluded spot in the most distant corner. There he stooped or rather knelt down and passed his hands, as though with mute benediction, over a little bed of old-fashioned China pinks. When he had moved in from the country he had brought nothing away from his mother's garden but these, and in all the years since no one had ever pulled them, as Peter well knew; for one day the colonel had said, with his face turned away:

"Let them have all the flowers they want; but leave the pinks."

He continued kneeling over them now, touching them softly with his fingers, as though they were the fragrant, never-changing symbols of voiceless communion with his past. Still it may have been only the early dew of the evening that glistened on them when he rose and slowly walked away, leaving the pale moonbeams to haunt the spot.

Certainly after this day he showed increasing concern in the young lovers who were holding clandestine meetings in his grounds.

"Peter," he would say, "why, if they love each other, don't they get married? Something may happen."

"I been spectin' some'n' to happ'n fur some time, ez dey been quar'lin' right smart lately," replied Peter, laughing.

Whether or not he was justified in this prediction, before the end of another week the colonel read a notice of their elopement and marriage; and several days later he came up from down-town and told Peter that everything had been forgiven the young pair, who had gone to house-keeping in the country. It gave him pleasure to think he had helped to perpetuate the race of blue-grass farmers.

THE YEARNING PASSED AWAY

It was in the twilight of a late autumn day in the same year that nature gave the colonel the first direct intimation to prepare for the last summons. They had been passing along the garden walks, where a few pale flowers were trying to flourish up to the very winter's edge, and where the dry leaves had gathered unswept and rustled beneath their feet. All at once the colonel turned to Peter, who was a yard and a half behind, as usual, and said:

"Give me your arm, Peter, I feel tired;" and thus the two, for the first time in all their lifetime walking abreast, passed slowly on.

"Peter," said the colonel, gravely, a minute or two later, "we are like two dried-up stalks of fodder. I wonder the Lord lets us live any longer."

"I reck'n He's managin' to use us *some* way, or we wouldn' be heah," said Peter.

"Well, all I have to say is, that if He's using me, He can't be in much of a hurry for his work," replied the colonel.

"He uses snails, en I *know* we ain' ez slow ez *dem,*" argued Peter, composedly.

"I don't know. I think a snail must have made more progress since the war than I have."

The idea of his uselessness seemed to weigh on him, for a little later he remarked, with a sort of mortified smile:

"Do you think, Peter, that we would pass for what they call representative men of the New South?"

"We done *had* ou' day, Marse Rom," replied Peter. "We got to pass fur what we *wuz*. Mebbe de *Lohd's* got mo' use fur us yit 'n *people* has," he added, after a pause.

From this time on the colonel's strength gradually failed him; but it was not until the following spring that the end came.

A night or two before his death his mind wandered backward, after the familiar manner of the dying, and his delirious dreams showed the shifting, faded pictures that renewed themselves for the last time on his wasting memory. It must have been that he was once more amid the scenes of his active farm life, for his broken snatches of talk ran thus:

"Come, boys, get your cradles! Look where the sun is! You are late getting to work this morning. That is the finest field of wheat in the county. Be careful about the bundles! Make them the same size and tie them tight. That swath is too wide, and you don't hold your cradle right, Tom. . . .

"Sell *Peter! Sell Peter Cotton!* No, sir! You might buy *me* some day and work *me* in your cotton-field; but as long as he's mine, you can't buy Peter, and you can't buy any of *my* Negroes. . . .

"Boys! boys! If you don't work faster, you won't finish this field to-day. . . . You'd better go in the shade and rest now. The sun's very hot. Don't drink too much ice-water. There's a jug of whisky in the fence-corner. Give them a good dram around, and tell them to work slow till the sun gets lower." . . .

Once during the night a sweet smile played over his features as he repeated a few words that were part of an old rustic song and dance. Arranged, not as they came broken and incoherent from his lips, but as he once had sung them, they were as follows:

> "O Sister Phœbe! How merry were we
> When we sat under the juniper-tree,
>   The juniper-tree, heigho!
> Put this hat on your head! Keep your head warm;
> Take a sweet kiss! It will do you no harm,
>   Do you no harm, I know!"

After this he sank into a quieter sleep, but soon stirred with a look of intense pain.

"Helen! Helen!" he murmured. "Will you break your promise? Have you changed in your feelings towards me? I have brought you the pinks. Won't you take the pinks, Helen?"

Then he sighed as he added, "It wasn't her fault. If she had only known—"

Who was the Helen of that far-away time? Was this the colonel's love-story?

But during all the night, whithersoever his mind wandered, at intervals it returned to the burden of a single strain—the harvesting. Towards daybreak he took it up again for the last time:

"O boys, boys, *boys!* If you don't work faster you won't finish the field to-day. Look how low the sun is! . . . I am going to the house. They can't finish the field to-day. Let them do what they can, but don't let them work late. I want Peter to go to the house with me. Tell him to come on." . . .

In the faint gray of the morning, Peter, who had been watching by the bedside all night, stole out of the room, and going into the garden pulled a handful of pinks—a thing he had never done before— and, re-entering the colonel's bedroom, put them in a vase near his sleeping face. Soon afterwards the colonel opened his eyes and looked around him. At the foot of the bed stood Peter, and on one side sat the physician and a friend. The night-lamp burned low, and through the folds of the curtains came the white light of early day.

"Put out the lamp and open the curtains," he said, feebly. "It's day." When they had drawn the curtains aside, his eyes fell on the pinks, sweet and fresh with the dew on them. He stretched out his hand and touched them caressingly, and his eyes sought Peter's with a look of grateful understanding.

"I want to be alone with Peter for a while," he said, turning his face towards the others.

When they were left alone, it was some minutes before anything was said. Peter, not knowing what he did, but knowing what was coming, had gone to the window and hid himself behind the curtains, drawing them tightly around his form as though to shroud himself from sorrow.

At length the colonel said, "Come here!"

Peter, almost staggering forward, fell at the foot of the bed, and, clasping the colonel's feet with one arm, pressed his cheek against them.

"Come closer!"

Peter crept on his knees and buried his head on the colonel's thigh.

"Come up here—*closer;*" and putting one arm around Peter's neck he laid the other hand softly on his head, and looked long and tenderly into his eyes. "I've got to leave you, Peter. Don't you feel sorry for me?"

"Oh, Marse Rom!" cried Peter, hiding his face, his whole form shaken by sobs.

"Peter," added the colonel with ineffable gentleness, "if I had served my Master as faithfully as you have served yours, I should not feel ashamed to stand in his presence."

"If my Marseter is ez mussiful to me ez you have been—"

"I have fixed things so that you will be comfortable after I am gone. When your time comes, I should like you to be laid close to me. We can take the long sleep together. Are you willing?"

"That's whar I want to be laid."

The colonel stretched out his hand to the vase, and taking the bunch of pinks, said very calmly:

"Leave these in my hand; I'll carry them with me." A moment more, and he added:

"If I shouldn't wake up any more, good-bye, Peter!"

"Good-bye, Marse Rom!"

And they shook hands a long time. After this the colonel lay back on the pillows. His soft, silvery hair contrasted strongly with his child-like, unspoiled, open face. To the day of his death, as is apt to be true of those who have lived pure lives but never married, he had a boyish strain in him—a softness of nature, showing itself even now in the gentle expression of his mouth. His brown eyes had in them the same boyish look when, just as he was falling asleep, he scarcely opened them to say:

"Pray, Peter."

Peter, on his knees, and looking across the colonel's face towards the open door, through which the rays of the rising sun streamed in upon his hoary head, prayed, while the colonel fell asleep, adding a few words for himself now left alone.

Several hours later, memory led the colonel back again through the dim gate-way of the past, and out of that gate-way his spirit finally took flight into the future.

Peter lingered a year. The place went to the colonel's sister, but he was allowed to remain in his quarters. With much thinking of the past, his mind fell into a lightness and a weakness. Sometimes he would be heard crooning the burden of old hymns, or sometimes seen sitting beside the old brass-nailed trunk, fumbling with the spelling-book and *The Pilgrim's Progress*. Often, too, he walked out to the cemetery on the edge of the town, and each time could hardly find the colonel's grave amid the multitude of the dead.

One gusty day in spring, the Scotch sexton, busy with the blades of blue-grass springing from the animated mould, saw his familiar figure standing motionless beside the colonel's resting-place. He had taken off his hat—one of the colonel's last bequests—and laid it on the colonel's head-stone. On his body he wore a strange coat of faded blue, patched and weather-stained, and so moth-eaten that parts of the curious tails had dropped entirely away. In one hand he held an open Bible, and on a much-soiled page he was pointing with his finger to the following words:

"I would not have you ignorant, brethren, concerning them which are asleep."

It would seem that, impelled by love and faith, and guided by his wandering reason, he had come forth to preach his last sermon on the immortality of the soul over the dust of his dead master.

The sexton led him home, and soon afterwards a friend, who had loved them both, laid him beside the colonel.

It was perhaps fitting that his winding-sheet should be the vestment in which, years agone, he had preached to his fellow-slaves in bondage; for if it so be that the dead of this planet shall come forth from their graves clad in the trappings of mortality, then Peter should arise on the Resurrection Day wearing his old jeans coat.

F. HOPKINSON SMITH

★ ★ ★

While preparing letterpress to accompany water color sketches, Francis Hopkinson Smith (1838-1915), an artist and engineer, discovered a talent for descriptive writing. *Col. Carter of Cartersville* (1891), his first work of fiction, grew out of a decision to put his most successful after-dinner stories into print. Smith's mastery of anecdote, local color, and characterization gave rise to many books of travel, tales, and novels. Always sympathetic with the underprivileged, as in *The Other Fellow* (1899) and *The Under Dog* (1903), he looked into secret places of the mind for "tenderness hiding beneath suspected cruelty, refinement under assumed coarseness, the joy of giving forcing its way through thick crusts of pretended avarice." Born in Baltimore, Smith rose from shipping clerk to the presidency of a nationally known engineering concern. "Six Hours in Squantico" from *A Day at Laguerre's* (1892) is reprinted by permission of Houghton Mifflin Company.

★ ★ ★

Six Hours in Squantico

SQUANTICO was not my destination. I confess to hearing from my berth in the Pullman, when the train stopped in the depot, all the customary sounds—the bumpings and couplings of the cars, the relieved "Whuff!" of the locomotive catching its breath after the night's run, the shouts of the hackmen, and the rumbling of the baggage trucks. I remember also the "Dust you off, sir," of the suddenly attentive porter levying blackmail with his brush, the glare of the lanterns, and blinding flash of the headlight.

All this came to me as I lay half awake in my section, but it did not suggest Squantico. On the contrary, it meant prospective peace and comfort, and another hour's nap, when I would be finally side-tracked outside the station in Washington. So I turned over and enjoyed it.

Experience teaches me that the going astray of the best-laid plans is not wholly confined to men and mice; it includes Pullmans.

My first intimation came from the expectant blackmailer.

"Eight o'clock, sir; last berth occupied."

More positive data proceeded from the conductor, who clicked a punch under my nose and blurted out, "Tickets!"

I fumbled mechanically under my pillow, and remembering, said sleepily, "Gave them to you last night."

"Not to me. Want your tickets for Richmond."

I sat up. Whole rows of people up and dressed for all day were quietly and contentedly occupying their seats. Every berth was swept away. My curtains alone dangled from the continuous brass rod, every eye in the car being fastened on my traveling bedroom.

"I am not going to Richmond. I get off at Washington."

"Wrong car, sir. Left Washington two hours ago."

"Stop at the next station," I gasped, grabbing my coat.

The conductor peered through the car window, pulled the bell-rope, and called out, "All out for Squantico!" and the next moment I was shivering in a pool of snow and water, my bag bottom side up, the rear of the retreating train filling a distant cut.

A man in a fur hat and blue overcoat regarded me a moment, picked up a mail-pouch from a half-melted snow-bank, and preceded me up a muddy road flanked by a worm-fence. I overtook him, and added my bag to his load.

"When can I get back to Washington?"

"Ten minutes past two."

I made a hurried calculation. Six hours! What could a man do with six hours in a hole like this? Before I had turned the road I had learned all that could possibly interest me: the hotel was closed; Colonel Jarvis kept a store third house from the corner; and Mrs. Jarvis could get me a breakfast.

It was not a cheery morning to land anywhere. January thaw mornings never are. A drizzling rain saturated everything. A steaming fog hung over the low country, drifted out over the river, and made ghosts of the piles of an unfinished dock. The mud was inches deep under the snow, which lay sprawling out in patches covering the ground like a wornout coat. A dozen of cheaply constructed houses and stores built of wood fronted on one side of a broad road. Opposite the group was a great barn of a building, with its doors and lower windows boarded up. This was the hotel.

The man with the pouch exchanged my bag for a dime, pointed to a collection of empty drygoods boxes ranged along the sidewalk ahead, and disappeared within a door bearing a swinging tin sign marked "Post-Office." I rounded the largest box, climbed the steps, and entered the typical country store.

"Is Colonel Jarvis in?"

Four men hugging a cast-iron stove pushed back their chairs. One —a lank, chin-bearded Virginian—straightened himself out and came forward. He wore a black slouch hat, a low-cut velvet vest with glass buttons—all gone but two—a shoestring necktie, and a pair of carpet slippers very much run down at the heel.

"I'm Kurnal Jarvis, zur. What kin I do for you?"

"I am adrift here, and cannot return for some hours. The mail man said perhaps Mrs. Jarvis would get me a cup of coffee."

The colonel replied that he did not keep a hotel, or, in fact, a house of entertainment of any kind; but that since the closing—he should say the collapse—of the Ocomoke Hotel he had prevailed upon Mrs. Jarvis to spread a humble table for the comfort and restoration of the wayfarer and stranger. If I would do him the honor of preceding him through the folding-doors to the right, he would conduct me to Mrs. Jarvis, a chop, and a cup of coffee.

The breakfast was fairly good, although the vivid imagination of the colonel was not realized, Mrs. Jarvis—a soft-voiced, gentle, sweet-spoken little woman—apologizing for the condition of her larder, and substituting corn-bread and a sliver of bacon for the chop, and a weak decoction of toasted sweet-potato skins and chicory for the divine essence of old mocha.

While she served me I, with no better motive than the mere killing of time until the 2:10 train should rescue me from what promised to be a most forlorn experience, drew from her not only her own history but that of her unfortunate neighbors.

It seems that some years back a capitalist from New York, uniting with other money-bags from Richmond, had settled upon the town of Squantico as presenting, by reason of its location, extraordinary advantages for river and rail transportation; that, in pursuance of this scheme, they had bought up all the land in and around the village, had staked out avenues and town lots, erected an imposing hotel surmounted by a cupola, and had started an immense pile dock trampling out into the river; that they had surveyed and partly graded a certain railroad, described as a "sixty-pound steel-rail and iron-bridge road," having one terminus on the wandering dock and the other in a network of arteries connecting with the "heart of the whole Southern system"; that, in addition to these local and contiguous improvements, such small trifles as a courthouse of granite, a public school of brick with stone trimmings, extensive waterworks, and ridiculously cheap gas were to be immediately erected and introduced. All these enlargements, improvements, and benefits were duly set forth in a large circular, or handbill, with headlines in red ink, a flyspecked copy of which could still be found tacked up behind the colonel's bar. In addition to these gratuities, large discounts were offered to the earliest settlers purchasing town lots and erecting structures thereon, the terms being within reach of the poorest—one-fourth cash, and the balance in three yearly installments of an equal amount.

Beguiled by these conditions and prospects, the colonel had sold his farm—that is, his wife's—on the James River, had moved their household effects to Squantico, paid the first installment, and erected the store and dwelling. This had absorbed their means.

All went well for the first year, or until the hotel was finished. Then came the collapse. One morning all work ceased on the dock and railroad, and it transpired that another capitalist of pointedly opposite views from the original group of projectors had gobbled up the roadbed of the projected railway, and had carried its terminus far out of reach of Squantico, and miles down the river. This had occurred three years back.

Since that date a complicated sort of melancholy had settled down over Squantico; the proprietors of the hotel had closed its doors from sheer starvation—not so much from want of something to eat as for want of somebody to eat it—the unfinished dock had gone to decay and the town to ruin. Squantico had shriveled up like a gourd in a September frost.

Nor was this all. Since the collapse no one had been able to meet the second and third payments on the land; the original capitalists wanted their pound of flesh; foreclosure proceedings had already been begun, and the act of dispossession was to be taken at the next spring term of the county court. Everybody in the village besides themselves was in the same plight.

I paid for my breakfast, sympathized deeply with the gentle, sad lady, and started out into the store.

The colonel widened the circle around the stove, turned to the three other chair holders, and introduced me as "My friend Major—" and paused for my name. As I did not supply it, he glanced toward my bag for relief, caught sight of a baggage label pasted across one end, marked "B., Room ——, N. Y.," and went straight on, as serene as an auctioneer with a fictitious bid:

"Broom—Major Broom—gentlemen, from New York."

The occupants stood erect for an instant, and immediately sank into their chairs again.

If the title was a surprise to me, I being a plain landscape-painter, without any capitals of any kind before or after my patronymic, the effrontery of displacing it by an express company's check simply took my breath away. But I did not correct him. It was not worth the while. He thanked me with his eye for my forbearance, and placed a chair at my disposal.

The colonel's eye, by-the-way, was not the least interesting feature of his countenance. It was a moist, watery eye, suggestive of a system of accounts kept mostly in chalk on a set of books covering half the swinging doors in the county. From between these watery spots protruded a sharp, beaklike nose.

The colonel connected the two features by placing his forefinger longitudinally along his nose until the nail closed the left optic, and remarked, in a dry, husky voice, that it was about his time, and would I join him? Instantly three pair of legs dropped from the stove rail, an equal number of chairs were emptied, and their occupants filed through a green door. I excused myself on the ground of a late breakfast, and while they were absent made an inventory of the interior. It consisted of one long room, on each side of which ran a pine counter. This was littered up with scraps of wrapping paper, a moldy cheese covered by a wire fly screen, some cracker boxes, and a case with a glass top containing small piles of plug tobacco and some jars of stick candy. Behind these counters were ranged pine shelves, holding the usual assortment of hardware, dry-goods, canned vegetables, and groceries. On the bottom shelf lay a grillage of bar soap, left out to dry. All the top shelves were packed with empty boxes—labels outside—indicating to the unpractised eye certain commercial resources.

Outside, the rain fell in a drizzle, and the fog settled in wavy wreaths.

Along the road staggered a single team—horse and mule tandem —harnessed or rather tied up in clothes-lines, and drawing a cart as large as a shoe box, loaded with cord-wood, the whole followed by a Negro in cowhide boots, an old army coat, and a straw hat. The movement was slow, but sure enough to convince one that they had not all died in their tracks overnight.

I followed this team with my eye until the fog swallowed it up; watched a flock of geese pick their way across the road, the leader's nose high in the air, as if disgusted with the day; went over in my mind the delay of preparing the breakfast, the time lost in its disposal, the long talk with Mrs. Jarvis, and my many experiences since, and concluded that it must be high noon. I looked at my watch, and a chill crept down my spine. It was but a quarter past nine!

Five hours more!

Disheartened but not wholly cast down, I rummaged over a lot of wrapping paper, borrowed a pencil, and made outline sketches of some pigeons drying their feathers under the eaves of the stable roof; interviewed the boy feeding the pigs; listened enviously to their contented grunts; and at last, in sheer desperation, returned to the store and sat down. The hours were leaden. Would I never get away? I began to have murderous intentions toward the porter. I remembered his exact expression when he promised the night before to wake me at eight o'clock. I could have sworn, on thinking it over, that he knew I was in the wrong car, and had concealed the fact, tempted by the opulence expressed in my new London bag. I felt that it had all been a devilish scheme to rob me of a double quarter, and throw me out into the mud in this thawstricken town.

In my broodings I began to take in the colonel, following his movements around the store, wondering whether he was not in the conspiracy, and had set the clock back to insure my missing the train. A moment's reflection convinced me of the absurdity of all my misgivings, and I resolved to rise to the occasion. Mark Tapley would have made a gala-day of it. I decided to study the citizens.

The colonel was waiting on a customer—the only real one I had seen—a mulatto girl with a jug.

"Misser Jarvis, Miss 'Manthy sez dat thimble w'at you sent her las' week wuz ur i'on thimble, an' she want ur steel one. An' she sez ef yer ain't got no steel one she want ur squart o' molasses."

"Where's the thimble?" said the colonel.

"I drap it in de snow-bank out yer—'deed an' double I did—an' I 'most froze lookin' fur't."

The colonel sighed.

While he was filling the jug an old man in an overcoat made from a gray army blanket, and dragging a long Kentucky rifle by the muzzle, straggled in, and asked for a box of percussion-caps and half a pound of powder. Then resting his shooting-iron against the counter, and pushing his long, skinny, cramped hands through his coat sleeves, he opened his thin fingers out before the stove, and ventured the remark that it was "right smart chilly."

"Any game, uncle?" I inquired.

"Mostly turkeys, zur; but they's gittin' miz'ble sca'ce lately. 'Fo' de wah 'twarn't nuthin' to git a passel of turkeys 'fore breakfas'. But you can't git 'em now. Dese yer scand'l'us-back ducks is mo' plenty than they wuz; but there ain't no gret shucks on 'em nary way."

The colonel handed the old man his ammunition, replaced a cracker box, threw his legs over the counter, and took the chair next me, his heels on the rail.

"Here on business, major?"

"No; pleasure," I replied wearily.

"Sorry the weather is so bad, zur; Squantico is not looking its best. Had you been here some few years ago, it would have looked dif'rent to you, zur."

"You mean before the scheme started?"

"Scheme or swindle, either way, zur. Perhaps you know Mr. Isaac Hoyle?"

I expressed my ignorance.

"Or have heard of the Squantico Land and Improvement Company?"

I was equally at fault, except what I had learned through Mrs. Jarvis.

"Then, zur, you are in no way connected with the gang of scoundrels who would rob us of our homes?"

I assured him that he had hit it exactly.

"Allow me to shake you by the han', zur, and offer you an apology. We took you for a lawyer, zur, from New York, come down about these fo'closure proceedin's. Will you join me?" Again all the legs came down simultaneously with a bang, but my firmness prevailed, and they were slowly elevated once more.

"What are you going to do about the matter?" I asked.

"What can we do, zur? We are bound hand and foot. We are prostrate, zur—prostrate."

"Do?" said I, a ray of hope lighting up my spirits. "Would you have built this house if Hoyle had not agreed to build his railroad?"

"Of co'se not," said the colonel.

"Did he build?"

"Not a foot."

"Did you?"

"Certainly."

"Well, then, colonel, sue Hoyle."

The colonel rose from his chair, and fixed upon me his drier eye. The loungers straightened up and formed a circle.

"Are there any waterworks, granite schoolhouses, city halls, and other such metropolitan luxuries around?" I continued.

The colonel shook his head.

"Had these been erected, and had the program as marked out in that bespattered circular behind your door been carried out, would you be as poor as you are, or would you not now have a warehouse across the road to hold your surplus stock, and three wagons constantly back up before your door to serve your customers? I tell you, sue Isaac Hoyle."

"Keurnal," said Jarvis—I did not correct the promotion—"would you have any objection to elucidate your views before some of our leadin' citizens? They indicate a grasp of this subject, zur, which is giantlike—yez, zur, giantlike! Jedge Drummond and Gen'ral Lownes are at this moment in the post-office, two ver' remarkable men, zur, quite our fo'most citizens. Might I send for them?"

"I would be delighted to meet the gentlemen." It might consume an hour. "Send for them, my dear sir; nothing would give me greater pleasure."

"Here, Joe," said the colonel, calling a Negro who had lounged in from the road, and was now hovering on the outside of the circle; "g'w'up to the post-office, and tell Jedge Drummond and Gen'ral Lownes to come yer quick." The boy shuffled out, and Jarvis laid his hand on my shoulder. "It's a pleasure, keurnel, a gen-u-ine pleasure, zur, to meet a man of yo' caliber. Allow me to grasp yo' han', and ask you before the arrival of my friends to—"

There was a slight movement toward the green door, but I checked it before the sentence was complete.

"No! Well, zur, we will make it later. By the way, keurnal, before I forget it"—the colonel locked his arm through mine and led me aside—"do not offer Mrs. Jarvis any compensation for yo' breakfast. She comes of a very high family, zur, and has a very sensitive nature. Of course, if you insist, I—" and my trade dollar dropped without a sound into his desolate pocket. "Here, boy! Did you fin' the gentlemen?"

"De gin'ral done gone duckin', sah, 'fore daylight, but the jedge say he is comin' right away scat."

The judge was on the boy's heels. As he entered, his eye wandered restlessly toward the green door. He had evidently misunderstood the message. I arose to greet him, the ring of listeners widening out to do justice to the impending ceremony. While the colonel squared himself for the opening address, I took in the general outline of the judge. He was the exact opposite of my host—a short, fat, shad-shaped man of some fifty years or more, whose later life had been spent in a ceaseless effort to keep his clothes up snug around the waist, his failures above being recorded in the wrinkles of his almost buttonless coat, and his successes below in the bagging of his trousers at the knee. He wore low shoes that did not match, and white cotton stockings a week old. A round, good-natured face, ornamented by a mustache dyed brown and a stump of a cigar, surmounted the whole.

"Jedge Drummond," began the colonel, "I sent my servant for you, zur, to introduce to you my ve'y particular friend General Broom, of the metropolis, zur, who is visiting the South, and who dropped in upon us this morning to breakfast. General Broom, zur, is one of the most remark'ble men of the day, and, although a soldier like ourselves, has devoted himself since the wah to the practise of the law, and now stands at the zenith, the ve'y zenith, zur, of his p'o-fession."

The judge expressed himself as overwhelmed, extended three fin-gers, and corrugated his vest pattern into wrinkles in the effort to squeeze himself between the arms of a chair. Jarvis then continued:

"Gen'l Broom is deeply interested in the misfortunes which have overtaken Squantico, and has given expression to some ideas lookin' to'ards our vested rights which are startlin', zur. Broom, will you kindly repeat yo' views to the jedge?"

I did so briefly. To my mind it was simply a matter of contract. A land company had staked out a comparative wilderness, and as an inducement to investors and settlers had made certain promises, which, under the circumstances, were binding agreements. These agreements covered the erection of certain municipal buildings, public conveniences, and improvements, together with a hotel, a dock, and a railroad. Only a fraction of these had been carried out. I would remind them, furthermore, that these agreements were distributed broadcast, and if not in writing were in print, which in this case was the same thing. Relying on these documents certain capitalists, like my friend Colonel Jarvis, had invested a very large portion of their surplus in erecting structures suitable only for a city of considerable commercial importance. The result was a matter of history.

Judge Drummond nodded, shifted his cigar, and remarked that the argument "was a sledge-hammer." He was delighted at the oppor-tunity of knowing a man with so colossal a grasp.

The store began filling up—the hurried exit of the boy and the instantaneous return of the judge having had its effect on the several

citizens who had witnessed the occurrence. With each new arrival I
was obliged to make a fresh statement, the colonel enlarging upon
my abilities and rank until I began to shudder lest he should land
me either in the White House or upon the Supreme Bench.

I was beginning afresh on the last arrival—a weazened-faced old
fellow with one tooth—when a fog-choked whistle sounded down
the river, and every man except Jarvis and the judge filed out, crossed
the road, and waited on the end of the unfinished dock until a
wheezy side-wheel boat landed a Negro woman and a yellow-painted
trunk. This, I learned, occurred every day; nothing else did. As soon
as order was restored, Jarvis executed a peculiar sign with his left
eye; three citizens, including the judge, understood it, followed him
into a corner, consulted for a moment, and returned, the colonel
leading.

"Gen'ral Broom," said he, "yo' masterly anal'sis of our rights in this
fo'closure matter convinces us that, if we are to be protected at all,
we must place ourselves in yo' han's. We know that your duties are
overwhelmin', and yo' time precious; but if you would consent to
accept a retainer, and appear for these cases at the spring meeting
of the county co't in April, we shall consider them settled. What
amount would you fix?"

The idea appalled me, but I was in for it. "Gentlemen," I said,
"your confidence, stranger as I am to most of you, is embarrassing.
As my main purpose would be to wrest from this grasping monopoly
property which, if not yours, should be, I would be willing to accept
only a small portion of the amount I might recover as my fee"—
at this point Jarvis had great difficulty in restraining the outburst—
"together with a trifling cash payment"—the noise moderated—
"which could be placed in the hands of Colonel Jarvis, to be used
for preliminary expenses."

A dead silence ensued. My selection for stakeholder had evidently
cast a chill over the room. This hardened into a frigid disapproval
when the judge, voicing the assemblage, remarked that the "colonel
would take good care of all the cash he would get." Had not Mrs.
Jarvis announced dinner, the situation would have become oppressive.
The colonel punctured the stillness by instantly subscribing for his
proportion, and asked the judge what amount he would contribute.
That legal luminary rose slowly, picked up a crumb of cheese that
had escaped the fly screen, and remarked that he would look over
the list of his real estate and see. An audible smile permeated the
crowd, the old sportsman's share widening into a grin, with an aside

all to himself: "Real 'state? Golly! Reckon he kearries mos' of it on his shoes."

"My dear," said the colonel, as we followed his wife into the dining-room, "you of co'se understan' that today the gen'ral is our guest."

That gentle lady only replied with her eyes. I detailed another coin of the realm to alleviate the loneliness of my contribution of the morning, and took up my line of march to the station with just ten minutes to spare, the colonel carrying my bag, and about all the male population of Squantico serving as escort except the judge, who excused himself on the ground that he had "left his rubbers in his office."

When I go South now, I pass Squantico in the night.

MARY HALLOCK FOOTE

★　★　★

To truthful pictures of the Snake, Bear, and Grand River country and of numerous mining communities, Mary Hallock Foote (1847-1938) has added stories of men and women concerned with the fundamental problems of conduct or adjustment to new conditions in the unweeded life of the frontier. Famous as an illustrator, she turned to writing, she says, when "I found the West and its absorbing material too much for my pencil." Born in Milton, New York, she studied art in New York City. After her marriage in 1876 to a mining engineer, she lived in California, Colorado, and Idaho where she found the irrigation-ditches, the mines, engineering camps and army posts, the storms and chinooks that afforded material for her writings and drawings. Her books include *The Led-Horse Claim* (1883), *In Exile and Other Stories* (1894), *Cœur d'Alène* (1894). "Maverick" is reprinted from *The Cup of Trembling, and Other Stories* (1895) by permission of Houghton Mifflin Company.

★　★　★

Maverick

TRAVELING BUTTES is a lone stage-station on the road, largely speaking, from Blackfoot to Boise. I do not know whether the stages take that road now, but ten years ago they did, and the man who kept the stage-house was a person of primitive habits and corresponding appearances named Gilroy.

The stage-house is perhaps half a mile from the foot of the largest butte, one of three that loom on the horizon, and appear to "travel"

from you, as you approach them from the plains. A day's ride with
the Buttes as a landmark is like a stern chase, in that you seem never
to gain upon them.

From the stage-house the plain slopes up to the foot of the Big
Butte, which rises suddenly in the form of an enormous tepee, as if
Gitchie Manito, the mighty, had here descended and pitched his
tent for a council of the nations.

The country is destitute of water. To say that it is "thirsty" is to
mock with vain imagery that dead and mummied land on the borders
of the Black Lava. The people at the stage-house had located a
precious spring, four miles up, in a cleft near the top of the Big
Butte; they piped the water down to the house and they sold it to
travelers on that Jericho road at so much per horse. The man was
thrown in, but the man usually drank whisky.

Our guide commented unfavorably on this species of husbandry,
which is common enough in the arid West, and as legitimate as
selling oats or hay; but he chose to resent it in the case of Gilroy,
and to look upon it as an instance of individual and exceptional
meanness.

"Any man that will jump God's water in a place like this, and sell
it the same as drinks—he'd sell water to his own father in hell!"

This was our guide's opinion of Gilroy. He was equally frank, and
much more explicit, in regard to Gilroy's sons. "But," he concluded,
with a philosopher's acceptance of existing facts, "it ain't likely that
any of that outfit will ever git into trouble, so long as Maverick is
sheriff of Lemhi County."

We were about to ask why, when we drove up to the stage-house,
and Maverick himself stepped out and took our horses.

"What the—infernal has happened to the man?" my companion,
Ferris, exclaimed; and our guide answered indifferently, as if he were
speaking of the weather,—

"Some Injuns caught him alone in an out-o'-the-way ranch, when
he was a kid, and took a notion to play with him. This is what was
left when they got through. I never see but one worse-looking man,"
he added, speaking low, as Maverick passed us with the team: "him
a bear wiped over the head with its paw. 'Twas quicker over with,
I expect, but he lived, and *he* looked worse than Maverick."

"Then I hope to the Lord I may never see him!" Ferris ejaculated;
and I noticed that he left his dinner untasted, though he had boasted
of a hunter's appetite.

We were two college friends on a hunting trip, but we had not got into the country of game. In two days more we expected to make Jackson's Hole, and I may mention that "hole," in this region, signifies any small, deep valley, well hidden amidst high mountains, where moisture is perennial, and grass abounds. In these pockets of plenty, herds of elk gather and feed as tame as park pets; and other hunted creatures, as wild but less innocent, often find sanctuary here, and cache their stolen stock and other spoil of the road and the range.

We did not forget to put our question concerning Maverick, that unhappy man, in his character of legalized protector of the Gilroy gang. What did our free-spoken guide mean by that insinuation?

We were told that Gilroy, in his rough-handed way, had been as a father to the lad, after the savages wreaked their pleasure on him: and his people being dead or scattered, Maverick had made himself useful in various humble capacities at the stage-house, and had finally become a sort of factotum there and a member of the family. And though perfectly square himself, and much respected on account of his personal courage and singular misfortunes, he could never see the old man's crookedness, nor the more than crookedness of his sons. He was like a son of the house, himself; but most persons agreed that it was not as a brother he felt toward Rose Gilroy. And a tough lookout it was for the girl; for Maverick was one whom no man would lightly cross, and in her case he was acting as "general dog around the place," as our guide called it. The young fellows were shy of the house, notwithstanding the attraction it held. It was likely to be Maverick or nobody for Rose.

We did not see Rose Gilroy, but we heard her step in the stage-house kitchen, and her voice, as clear as a lark's, giving orders to the tall, stooping, fair young Swede, who waited on us at table, and did other work of a menial character in that singular establishment.

"How is it the watch-dog allows such a pretty sprig as that around the place?" Ferris questioned, eyeing our knight of the trencher, who blushed to feel himself remarked.

"He won't stay," our guide pronounced; "they don't none of 'em stay when they're good-lookin'. The old man he's failin' considerable these days,—gettin' kind o' silly,—and the boys are away the heft of the time. Maverick pretty much runs the place. I don't justly blame the critter. He's watched that little Rose grow up from a baby. How's he goin' to quit being fond of her now she's a woman? I dare say he'd a heap sooner she'd stayed a little girl. And these yere boys around here they're a triflin' set, not half so able to take care of her as Maverick. He's got the sense and he's got the sand; but there's that awful head on him! I don't blame him much, lookin' the way he does, and feelin' the same as any other man."

We left Traveling Buttes and its cruel little love-story, but we had not gone a mile when a horseman overtook us with a message for Ferris from his new foreman at the ranch, a summons which called him back for a day at the least. Ferris was exceedingly annoyed: a day at the ranch meant four days on the road; but the business was imperative. We held a brief council, and decided that, with Ferris returning, our guide should push on with the animals and camp out-fit into a country of grass, and look up a good camping-spot (which might not be the first place he struck) this side of Jackson's Hole. It remained for me to choose between going with the stuff, or staying for a longer look at the phenomenal Black Lava fields at Arco; Arco being another name for desolation on the very edge of that weird stone sea. This was my ostensible reason for choosing to remain at Arco; but I will not say the reflection did not cross me that Arco is only sixteen miles from Traveling Buttes—not an insurmountable distance between geology and a pretty girl, when one is five and twenty, and has not seen a pretty face for a month of Sundays.

Arco, at that time, consisted of the stage-house, a store, and one or two cabins—a poor little seed of civilization dropped by the wayside, between the Black Lava and the hills where Lost River comes down and "sinks" on the edge of the lava. The station is somewhat back from the road, with its face—a very grimy, unwashed countenance— to the lava. Quaking asps and mountain birches follow the water, pausing a little way up the gulch behind the house, but the eager grass tracks it all the way till it vanishes; and the dry bed of the stream goes on and spreads in a mass of coarse sand and gravel, beaten flat, flailed by the feet of countless driven sheep that have gathered here. For this road is on the great overland sheep-trail from Oregon eastward—the march of the million mouths, and what the mouths do not devour the feet tramp down.

The staple topic of conversation at Arco was one very common in the Far West, when a tenderfoot is of the company. The poorest place can boast of some distinction, and Arco, though hardly on the high-road of fashion and commerce, had frequently been named in print in connection with crime of a highly sensational and picturesque character. Scarcely another fifty miles of stage-road could boast of so many and such successful road-jobs; and although these affairs were of almost monthly occurrence, and might be looked for to come off always within that noted danger-limit, yet it was a fact that the law had never yet laid finger on a man of the gang, nor gained the smallest clew to their hide-out. It was a difficult country around Arco, one that lent itself to secrecy. The road-agents came, and took, and vanished as if the hills were copartners as well as the receivers of their goods. As for the lava, which was its front dooryard, so to speak, for a hundred miles, the man did not live who could say he had crossed it. What it held or was capable of hiding, in life or in death, no man knew.

The day after Ferris left me I rode out upon that arrested tide—those silent breakers which for ages have threatened, but never reached, the shore. I tried to fancy it as it must once have been, a sluggish, vitreous flood, filling the great valley, and stiffening as it slowly pushed toward the bases of the hills. It climbed and spread, as dough rises and crawls over the edge of the pan. The Black Lava is always called a sea—that image is inevitable; yet its movement had never in the least the character of water. "This is where hell pops," an old plainsman feelingly described it, and the suggestion is perfect. The colors of the rock are those produced by fire: its texture is that of slag from a furnace. One sees how the lava hardened into a crust, which cracked and sank in places, mingling its tumbled edges with the creeping flood not cooled beneath. After all movement had ceased and the mass was still, time began upon its tortured configurations, crumbled and wore and broke, and sifted a little earth here and there, and sealed the burnt rock with fairy print of lichens, serpent-green and orange and rust-red. The spring rains left shallow pools which the summer dried. Across it, a few dim trails wander a little way and give out, like the water.

For a hundred miles to the Snake River this Plutonian gulf obliterates the land—holds it against occupation or travel. The shoes of a marching army would be cut from their feet before they had gone a dozen miles across it; horses would have no feet left; and water would have to be packed as on an ocean, or a desert, cruise.

I rode over places where the rock rang beneath my horse's hoofs like the iron cover of a manhole. I followed the hollow ridges that mounted often forty feet above my head, but always with that gruesome effect of thickening movement—that sluggish, atomic crawl; and I thought how one man pursuing another into this frozen hell might lose himself, but never find the object of his quest. If he took the wrong furrow, he could not cross from one blind gut into another, nor hope to meet the fugitive at any future turning.

I don't know why the fancy of a flight and pursuit so have haunted me, in connection with the Black Lava; probably the desperate and lawless character of our conversation at the stage-house gave rise to it.

I had fallen completely under the spell of that skeleton flood. I watched the sun sink, as it sinks at sea, beyond its utmost ragged ridges; I sat on the borders of it, and stared across it in the gray moonlight; I rode out upon it when the Buttes, in their delusive nearness, were as blue as the gates of amethyst, and the morning was as fair as one great pearl; but no peace or radiance of heaven or earth could change its aspect more than that of a mound of skulls. When I began to dream about it, I thought I must be getting morbid. This is worse than Gilroy's, I said; and I promised myself I would ride up there next day and see if by chance one might get a peep at the Rose that all were praising, but none dared put forth a hand to pluck. Was it indeed so hard a case for the Rose? There are women who can love a man for the perils he has passed. Alas, Maverick! could any one get used to a face like that?

Here, surely, was the story of Beauty and her poor Beast humbly awaiting, in the mask of a brutish deformity, the recognition of Love pure enough to divine the soul beneath, and unselfish enough to deliver it. Was there such love as that at Gilroy's? However, I did not make that ride.

It was the fourth night of clear, desert moonlight since Ferris had left me: I was sleepless, and so I heard the first faint throb of a horse's feet approaching from the east, coming on at a great pace, and making the turn to the stage-house. I looked out, and on the trodden space in front I saw Maverick dismounting from a badly blown horse.

"Halloo! what's up?" I called from the open window of my bedroom on the ground-floor.

"Did two men pass here on horseback since dark?"

"Yes," I said; "about twelve o'clock: a tall man and a little short fellow."

"Did they stop to water?"

"No, they did not; and they seemed in such a tearing hurry that I watched them down the road—"

"I am after those men, and I want a fresh horse," he cut in. "Call up somebody quick!"

"Shall you take one of the boys along?" I inquired, with half an eye to myself, after I had obeyed his command.

He shook his head. "Only one horse here that's good for anything: I want that myself."

"There is my horse," I suggested; "but I'd rather be the one who rides her. She belongs to a friend."

"Take her, and come on, then, but understand—this ain't a Sunday-school picnic."

"I'm with you, if you'll have me."

"I'd sooner have your horse," he remarked, shifting the quid of tobacco in his cheek.

"You can't have her without me, unless you steal her," I said.

"Git your gun, then, and shove some grub into your pockets: I can't wait for nobody."

He swung himself into the saddle.

"What road do you take?"

"There ain't but one," he shouted, and pointed straight ahead.

I overtook him easily within the hour; he was saving his horse, for this was his last chance to change until Champagne Station, fifty miles away.

He gave me rather a cynical smile of recognition as I ranged alongside, as if to say, "You'll probably get enough of this before we are through." The horses settled down to their work, and they "humped theirselves," as Maverick put it, in the cool hours before sunrise.

At daybreak his awful face struck me all afresh, as inscrutable in its strange distortion as some stone god in the desert, from whose graven hideousness a thousand years of mornings have silently drawn the veil.

"What do you want those fellows for?" I asked, as we rode. I had taken for granted that we were hunting suspects of the road-agent persuasion.

"I want 'em on general principles," he answered shortly.

"Do you think you know them?"

"I think they'll know me. All depends on how they act when we get within range. If they don't pay no attention to us, we'll send a shot across their bows. But more likely they'll speak first."

He was very gloomy, and would keep silence for an hour at a time. Once he turned on me as with a sudden misgiving.

"See here, don't you git excited; and whatever happens, don't you meddle with the little one. If the big fellow cuts up rough, he'll take his chances, but you leave the little one to me. I want him—I want him for State's evidence," he finished hoarsely.

"The little one must be the Benjamin of the family," I thought— "one of the bad young Gilroys, whose time has come at last; and Sheriff Maverick finds his duty hard."

I could not say whether I really wished the men to be overtaken, but the spirit of the chase had undoubtedly entered into my blood. I felt as most men do, who are not saints or cowards, when such work as this is to be done. But I knew I had no business to be along.

It was one thing for Maverick, but the part of an amateur in a man-hunt is not one to boast of.

The sun was now high, and the fresh tracks ahead of us were plain in the dust. Once they left the road and strayed off into the lava, incomprehensibly to me; but Maverick understood, and pressed forward. "We'll strike them again further on. D—— fool!" he muttered, and I observed that he alluded but to one, "huntin' waterholes in the lava in the tail end of August!"

They could not have found water, for at Belgian Flat they had stopped and dug for it in the gravel, where a little stream in freshet time comes down the gulch from the snow-fields higher up, and sinks, as at Arco, on the lip of the lava. They had dug, and found it, and saved us the trouble, as Maverick remarked.

Considerable water had gathered since the flight had paused here and lost precious time. We drank our fill, refreshed our horses, and shifted the saddle-girths; and I managed to stow away my lunch during the next mile or so, after offering to share it with Maverick, who refused it as if the notion of food made him sick. He had considerable whisky aboard, but he was, I judged, one of those men on whom drink has little effect; else some counter-flame of excitement was fighting it in his blood.

I looked for the development of the personal complication whenever we should come up with the chase, for the man's eye burned, and had his branded countenance been capable of any expression that was not cruelly travestied, he would have looked the impersonation of wild justice.

It was now high noon, and our horses were beginning to feel the steady work; yet we had not ridden as they brought the good news from Ghent: that is the pace of a great lyric; but it's not the pace at which justice, or even vengeance, travels in the Far West. Even the furies take it coolly when they pursue a man over these roads, and on these poor brutes of horses, in fifty-mile stages, with drought thrown in.

Maverick had had no mercy on the pony that brought him sixteen miles; but this piece of horse-flesh he now bestrode must last him through at least to Champagne Station, should we not overhaul our men before. He knew well when to press and when to spare the pace, a species of purely practical consideration which seemed habitual with him; he rode like an automaton, his baleful face borne straight before him—the Gorgon's head.

Beyond Belgian Flat—how far beyond I do not remember, for I was beginning to feel the work, too, and the country looked all alike to me as we made it, mile by mile—the road follows close along by the lava, but the hills recede, and a little trail cuts across, meeting the road again at Deadman's Flat. Here we could not trust to the track, which from the nature of the ground was indistinct. So we divided our forces, Maverick taking the trail,—which I was quite willing he should do, for it had a look of most sinister invitation,— while I continued by the longer road. Our little discussion, or some atmospheric change,—some breath of coolness from the hills,—had brought me up out of my stupor of weariness. I began to feel both alert and nervous; my heart was beating fast. The still sunshine lay all around us, but where Maverick's white horse was climbing, the shadows were turning eastward, and the deep gulches, with their patches of aspen, were purple instead of brown. The aspens were left shaking where he broke through them and passed out of sight.

I kept on at a good pace, and about three o'clock I, being then as much as half a mile away, saw the spot which I knew must be Deadman's Flat; and there were our men, the tall one and his boyish mate, standing quietly by their horses in broad sunlight, as if there were no one within a hundred miles. Their horses had drunk, and were cropping the thin grass, which had set its tooth in the gravel where, as at the other places, a living stream had perished. I spurred forward, with my heart thumping, but before they saw me I saw Maverick coming down the little gulch; and from the way he came I knew that he had seen them.

The scene was awful in its treacherous peacefulness. Their shadows slept on the broad bed of sunlight, and the gulch was as cool and still as a lady's chamber. The great dead desert received the silence like a secret.

Tenderfoot as I was, I knew quite well what must happen now; yet I was not prepared—could not realize it—even when the tall one put his hand quickly behind him and stepped ahead of his horse. There was the flash of his pistol, and the loud crack echoing in the hill, a second shot, and then Maverick replied deliberately, and the tall one was down, with his face in the grass.

I heard a scream that sounded strangely like a woman's; but there were only the three, the little one, acting wildly, and Maverick bending over him who lay with his face in the grass. I saw him turn the body over, and the little fellow seemed to protest, and to try to push him away. I thought it strange he made no more of a fight, but I was not near enough to hear what those two said to each other.

Still, the tragedy did not come home to me. It was all like a scene, and I was without feeling in it except for that nervous trembling which I could not control.

Maverick stood up at length, and came slowly toward me, wiping his face. He kept his hat in his hand, and, looking down at it, said huskily:—

"I gave that man his life when I found him last spring runnin' loose like a wild thing in the mountains, and now I've took it; and God above knows I had no grudge ag'in' him, if he had stayed in his place. But he would have it so."

"Maverick, I saw it all, and I can swear it was self-defense."

His face drew into the tortured grimace which was his smile. "This here will never come before a jury," he said. "It's a family affair. Did ye see how he acted? Steppin' up to me like he was a first-class shot, or else a fool. He ain't nary one; he's a poor silly tool, the whip-hand of a girl that's boltin' from her friends like they was her mortal enemies. Go and take a look at him; then maybe you'll understand."

He paused, and uttered the name of Jesus Christ, but not as such men often use it, with an inconsequence dreadful to hear: he was not idly swearing, but calling that name to witness solemnly in a case that would never come before a jury.

I began to understand.

"Is it—is the girl—"

"Yes; it's our poor little Rose—that's the little one, in the gray hat. She'll give herself away if I don't. She don't care for nothin' nor nobody. She was runnin' away with that fellow—that dish-washin' Swede what I found in the mountings eatin' roots like a ground-hog, with the ends of his feet froze off. Now you know all I know—and more than she knows, for she thinks she was fond of him. She wa'n't, never—for I watched 'em, and I know. She was crazy to git away, and she took him for the chance."

His excitement passed, and we sat apart and watched the pair at a distance. She—the little one—sat as passively by her dead as Maverick pondering his cruel deed; but with both it was a hopeless quiet.

"Come," he said at length, "I've got to bury him. You look after her, and keep her with you till I git through. I'm givin' you the hardest part," he added wistfully, as if he fully realized how he had cut himself off from all such duties, henceforth, to the girl he was consigning to a stranger's care.

I told him I thought that the funeral had more need of me than the mourner, and I shrank from intruding myself.

"I dassent leave her by herself—see? I don't know what notion she may take next, and she won't let me come within a rope's len'th of her."

I will not go over again that miserable hour in the willows, where I made her stay with me, out of sight of what Maverick was doing. Ours were the tender mercies of the wicked, I fear; but she must have felt that sympathy at least was near her, if not help. I will not say that her youth and distressful loveliness did not sharpen my perception of a sweet life wasted, gone utterly astray, which might have brought God's blessing into some man's home—perhaps Maverick's, had he not been so hardly dealt with. She was not of that great disposition of heart which can love best that which has sorest need of love; but she was all woman, and helpless and distraught with her tangle of grief and despair, the nature of which I could only half comprehend.

We sat there by the sunken stream, on the hot gravel where the sun had lain, the willows sifting their inconstant shadows over us; and I thought how other things as precious as "God's water" go astray on the Jericho road, or are captured and sold for a price, while dry hearts ache with the thirst that asks a "draught divine."

The man's felt hat she wore, pulled down over her face, was pinned to her coil of braids which had slipped from the crown of her head. The hat was no longer even a protection; she cast it off, and the blonde braids, that had not been smoothed for a day and night, fell like ropes down her back. The sun had burned her cheeks and neck to a clear crimson; her blue eyes were as wild with weeping as a child's. She was a rose, but a rose that had been trampled in the dust; and her prayer was to be left there, rather than that we should take her home.

I suppose I must have had some influence over her, for she allowed me to help her to arrange her forlorn disguise, and put her on her horse, which was more than could have been expected from the way she had received me. And so, about four o'clock, we started back.

There was a scene when we headed the horses west; she protesting with wild sobs that she would not, could not, go home, that she would rather die, that we should never get her back alive, and so on. Maverick stood aside bitterly, and left her to me, and I was aware of a grotesque touch of jealousy—which, after all, was perhaps natural—in his dour face whenever he looked back at us. He kept some distance ahead, and waited for us when we fell too far in the rear.

This would happen when from time to time her situation seemed to overpower her, and she would stop in the road, and wring her hands, and try to throw herself out of the saddle, and pray me to let her go.

"Go where?" I would ask. "Where do you wish to go? Have you any plan, or suggestion, that I could help you to carry out?" But I said it only to show her how hopeless her resistance was. This she would own piteously, and say: "Nobody can help me. There ain't nowhere for me to go. But I can't go back. You won't let him make me, will you?"

"Why cannot you go back to your father and your brothers?"

This would usually silence her, and, setting her teeth upon her trouble, she would ride on, while I reproached myself, I knew not why.

After one of these struggles—when she had given in to the force of circumstances, but still unconsenting and rebellious—Maverick fell back, and ranged his horse by her other side.

"I know partly what's troubling you, and I'd rid you of that part quick enough," he said, with a kind of dogged patience in his hard voice; "but you can't get on there without me. You know that, don't you? You don't blame me for staying?"

"I don't blame you for anything but what you've done to-day. You've broke my heart, and ruined me, and took away my last chance, and I don't care what becomes of me, so I don't have to go back."

"You don't have to any more than you have to live. Dyin' is a good deal easier, but we can't always die when we want to. Suppose I found a little lost child on the road, and it cried to go home, and I didn't know where 'home' was, would I leave it there just because it cried and hung back? I'd take you to a better home if I knew of one; but I don't. And there's the old man. I suppose we could get some doctor to certify that he's out of his mind, and get him sent up to Blackfoot; but I guess we'd have to buy the doctor first."

"Oh, hush, do, and leave me alone," she said.

Maverick dug his spurs into his horse, and plunged ahead.

"There," she cried, "now you know part of it; but it's the least part—the least, the least! Poor father, he's awful queer. He don't more than half the time know who I am," she whispered. "But it ain't him I'm running away from. It's myself—my own life."

"What is it—can't you tell me?"

She shook her head, but she kept on telling, as if she were talking to herself.

"Father he's like I told you, and the boys—oh, that's worse! I can't get a decent woman to come there and live, and the women at Arco won't speak to me because I'm livin' there alone. They say—they think I ought to get married—to Maverick or somebody. I'll die first. I *will* die, if there's any way to, before I'll marry him!"

This may not sound like tragedy as I tell it, but I think it was tragedy to her. I tried to persuade her that it must be her imagination about the women at Arco; or, if some of them did talk,—as indeed I myself had heard, to my shame and disgust,—I told her I had never known that place where there was not one woman, at least, who could understand and help another in her trouble.

"*I* don't know of any," she said simply.

There was no more to do, but ride on, feeling like her executioner; but

> "Ride hooly, ride hooly, now, gentlemen,
> Ride hooly now wi' me,"

came into my mind; and no man ever kept beside a "wearier burd" on a sadder journey.

At dusk we came to Belgian Flat, and here Maverick, dismounting, mixed a little whisky in his flask with water which he dipped from the pool. She must have recalled who dug the well, and with whom she had drunk in the morning. He held it to her lips. She rejected it with a strong shudder of disgust.

"Drink it!" he commanded. "You'll kill yourself, carryin' on like this." He pressed it on her, but she turned away her face like a sick and rebellious child.

"Maybe she'll drink it for you," said Maverick, with bitter patience, handing me the cup.

"Will you?" I asked her gently. She shook her head, but at the same time she let me take her hand, and put it down from her face, and I held the cup to her lips. She drank it, every drop. It made her deathly sick, and I took her off her horse, and made a pillow of my coat, so that she could lie down. In ten minutes she was asleep. Maverick covered her with his coat after she was no longer conscious.

We built a fire on the edge of the lava, for we were both chilled and both miserable, each for his own part in that day's work.

The flat is a little cup-shaped valley formed by high hills, like dark walls, shutting it in. The lava creeps up to it in front.

We hovered over the fire, and Maverick fed it, savagely, in silence. He did not recognize my presence by a word—not so much as if I had been a strange dog. I relieved him of it after a while, and went out a little way on the lava. At first all was blackness after the strong glare of the fire; but gradually the desolation took shape, and I stumbled about in it, with my shadow mocking me in derisive beckonings, or crouching close at my heels, as the red flames towered or fell. I stayed out there till I was chilled to the bone, and then went back defiantly. Maverick sat as if he had not moved, his elbows on his knees, his face in his hands. I wondered if he were thinking of that other sleeper under the birches of Deadman's Gulch, victim of an unhappy girl's revolt. Had she loved him? Had she deceived him as well as herself? It seemed to me they were all like children who had lost their way home.

By midnight the moon had risen high enough to look at us coldly over the tops of the great hills. Their shadows crept forth upon the lava. The fire had died down. Maverick rose, and scattered the winking brands with his boot-heel.

"We must pull out," he said. "I'll saddle up, if you will—" The hoarseness in his voice choked him, and he nodded toward the sleeper.

I dreaded to waken the poor Rose. She was very meek and quiet after the brief respite sleep had given her. She sat quite still, and watched me while I shook the sand from my coat, put it on, and buttoned it to the chin, and drew my hat down more firmly. There was a kind of magnetism in her gaze; I felt it creep over me like the touch of a soft hand.

When her horse was ready, Maverick brought it, and left it standing near, and went back to his own, without looking toward us.

"Come, you poor, tired little girl," I said, holding out my hand. She could not find her way at first in the uncertain light, and she seemed half asleep still, so I kept her hand in mine, and guided her to her horse. "Now, once more up," I encouraged her; and suddenly she was clinging to me, and whispering passionately.

"Can't you take me somewhere? Where are those women that you know?" she cried, shaking from head to foot.

"Dear little soul, all the women I know are two thousand miles away," I answered.

"But can't you take me *somewhere?* There must be some place. I know you would be good to me; and you could go away afterward, and I wouldn't trouble you any more."

"My child, there is not a place under the heavens where I could take you. You must go on like a brave girl, and trust to your friends. Keep up your heart, and the way will open. God will not forget you," I said, and may He forgive me for talking cant to that poor soul in her bitter extremity.

She stood perfectly still one moment while I held her by the hands. I think she could have heard my heart beat; but there was nothing I could do. Even now I wake in the night, and wonder if there was any other way—but one; the way that for one wild moment I was half tempted to take.

"Yes; the way will open," she said very low. She cast off my hands, and in a second she was in the saddle, and off up the road, riding for her life. And we two men knew no better than to follow her.

I knew better, or I think, now, that I did. I told Maverick we had pushed her far enough. I begged him to hold up and at least not to let her see us on her track. He never answered a word, but kept straight on, as if possessed. I don't think he knew what he was doing. At least there was only one thing *he* was capable of doing—following that girl till he dropped.

Two miles beyond the Flat there is another turn, where the shoulder of a hill comes down and crowds the road, which passes out of sight. She saw us hard upon her, as she reached this bend. Maverick was ahead. Her horse was doing all he could, but it was plain he could not do much more. She looked back, and flung out her hand in the man's sleeve that half covered it. She gave a little whimpering cry, the most dreadful sound I ever heard from any hunted thing.

We made the turn after her; and there lay the road white in the moonlight, and as bare as my hand. She had escaped us.

We pulled up the horses, and listened. Not a sound came from the hills or the dark gulches, where the wind was stirring the quaking asps; the lonesome hush-sh made the silence deeper. But we heard a horse's step go clink, clinking—a loose, uncertain step wandering away in the lava.

"Look! Look there! My God!" groaned Maverick.

There was her horse limping along one of the hollow ridges, but the saddle was empty.

"She has taken to the lava!"

I had no need to be told what that meant; but if I had needed, I learned what it meant before the night was through. I think that if I were a poet, I could add another "dolorous circle" to the wailing-place for lost souls.

But she had found a way. Somewhere in that stony-hearted wilderness she is at rest. We shall see her again when the sea—the stupid, cruel sea that crawls upon the land—gives up its dead.

HAMLIN GARLAND

★ ★ ★

Crusader for local color in his *Crumbling Idols* (1893), Hamlin Garland (1860-1940) also battled for social justice in his pictures of the financial plight and harsh toil of the prairie farmers in two collections of short stories, *Main-Travelled Roads* (1891) and *Prairie Folks* (1893). After two political novels and two novels partly descriptive of the hardships of farm women, Garland wrote for popular magazines several spirited romances of the Far West. *A Son of the Middle Border* (1917), the best of eight books of autobiography and reminiscences, describes his family's land hunger, their incessant struggle, and his early years as a writer. Born in Wisconsin, he moved with his family to Iowa, to Dakota, and back to Wisconsin. To perfect himself as a teacher, he studied in Boston, but a visit to his parents in 1887 fired his ambition to write realistic fiction of farm life. The following stories are reprinted by permission of the author.

★ ★ ★

The Return of a Private

THE nearer the train drew toward La Crosse, the soberer the little group of "vets" became. On the long way from New Orleans they had beguiled tedium with jokes and friendly chaff; or with planning with elaborate detail what they were going to do now, after the war. A long journey, slowly, irregularly, yet persistently pushing northward. When they entered on Wisconsin territory they gave a cheer, and another when they reached Madison, but after that they sank into a dumb expectancy. Comrades dropped off at one

598

or two points beyond, until there were only four or five left who were bound for La Crosse County.

Three of them were gaunt and brown, the fourth was gaunt and pale, with signs of fever and ague upon him. One had a great scar down his temple, one limped, and they all had unnaturally large, bright eyes, showing emaciation. There were no bands greeting them at the station, no banks of gayly dressed ladies waving handkerchiefs and shouting "Bravo!" as they came in on the caboose of a freight train into the towns that had cheered and blared at them on their way to war. As they looked out or stepped upon the platform for a moment, while the train stood at the station, the loafers looked at them indifferently. Their blue coats, dusty and grimy, were too familiar now to excite notice, much less a friendly word. They were the last of the army to return, and the loafers were surfeited with such sights.

The train jogged forward so slowly that it seemed likely to be midnight before they should reach La Crosse. The little squad grumbled and swore, but it was no use; the train would not hurry, and, as a matter of fact, it was nearly two o'clock when the engine whistled "down brakes."

All of the group were farmers, living in districts several miles out of the town, and all were poor.

"Now, boys," said Private Smith, he of the fever and ague, "we are landed in La Crosse in the night. We've got to stay somewhere till mornin'. Now I ain't got no two dollars to waste on a hotel. I've got a wife and children, so I'm goin' to roost on a bench and take the cost of a bed out of my hide."

"Same here," put in one of the other men. "Hide'll grow on again, dollars'll come hard. It's goin' to be mighty hot skirmishin' to find a dollar these days."

"Don't think they'll be a deputation of citizens waitin' to 'scort us to a hotel, eh?" said another. His sarcasm was too obvious to require an answer.

Smith went on, "Then at daybreak we'll start for home—at least, I will."

"Well, I'll be dummed if I'll take two dollars out o' *my* hide," one of the younger men said. "I'm goin' to a hotel, ef I don't never lay up a cent."

"That'll do f'r you," said Smith; "but if you had a wife an' three young uns dependin' on yeh—"

"Which I ain't, thank the Lord! and don't intend havin' while the court knows itself."

The station was deserted, chill, and dark, as they came into it at exactly a quarter to two in the morning. Lit by the oil lamps that flared a dull red light over the dingy benches, the waiting room was not an inviting place. The younger man went off to look up a hotel, while the rest remained and prepared to camp down on the floor and benches. Smith was attended to tenderly by the other men, who spread their blankets on the bench for him, and, by robbing themselves, made quite a comfortable bed, though the narrowness of the bench made his sleeping precarious.

It was chill, though August, and the two men, sitting with bowed heads, grew stiff with cold and weariness, and were forced to rise now and again and walk about to warm their stiffened limbs. It did not occur to them, probably, to contrast their coming home with their going forth, or with the coming home of the generals, colonels, or even captains—but to Private Smith, at any rate, there came a sickness at heart almost deadly as he lay there on his hard bed and went over his situation.

In the deep of the night, lying on a board in the town where he had enlisted three years ago, all elation and enthusiasm gone out of him, he faced the fact that with the joy of home-coming was already mingled the bitter juice of care. He saw himself sick, worn out, taking up the work on his half-cleared farm, the inevitable mortgage standing ready with open jaw to swallow half his earnings. He had given three years of his life for a mere pittance of pay, and now!—

Morning dawned at last, slowly, with a pale yellow dome of light rising silently above the bluffs, which stand like some huge storm-devastated castle, just east of the city. Out to the left the great river swept on its massive yet silent way to the south. Bluejays called across the water from hillside to hillside through the clear, beautiful air, and hawks begin to skim the tops of the hills. The older men were astir early, but Private Smith had fallen at last into a sleep, and they went out without waking him. He lay on his knapsack, his gaunt face turned toward the ceiling, his hands clasped on his breast, with a curious pathetic effect of weakness and appeal.

An engine switching near woke him at last, and he slowly sat up and stared about. He looked out of the window and saw that the sun was lightening the hills across the river. He rose and brushed his hair as well as he could, folded his blankets up, and went out to find his companions. They stood gazing silently at the river and at the hills.

"Looks natcher'l, don't it?" they said, as he came out.

"That's what it does," he replied. "An' it looks good. D' yeh see that peak?" He pointed at a beautiful symmetrical peak, rising like a slightly truncated cone, so high that it seemed the very highest of them all. It was touched by the morning sun and it glowed like a beacon, and a light scarf of gray morning fog was rolling up its shadowed side.

"My farm's just beyond that. Now, if I can only ketch a ride, we'll be home by dinner-time."

"I'm talkin' about breakfast," said one of the others.

"I guess it's one more meal o' hardtack f'r me," said Smith.

They foraged around, and finally found a restaurant with a sleepy old German behind the counter, and procured some coffee, which they drank to wash down their hardtack.

"Time'll come," said Smith, holding up a piece by the corner, "when this'll be a curiosity."

"I hope to God it will! I bet I've chawed hardtack enough to shingle every house in the coolly. I've chawed it when my lampers was down, and when they wasn't. I've took it dry, soaked, and mashed. I've had it wormy, musty, sour, and blue-mouldy. I've had it in little bits and big bits; 'fore coffee an' after coffee. I'm ready f'r a change. I'd like t' git holt jest about now o' some of the hot biscuits my wife c'n make when she lays herself out f'r company."

"Well, if you set there gabblin', you'll never *see* yer wife."

"Come on," said Private Smith. "Wait a moment, boys; less take suthin'. It's on me." He led them to the rusty tin dipper which hung on a nail beside the wooden water-pail, and they grinned and drank. Then shouldering their blankets and muskets, which they were "takin' home to the boys," they struck out on their last march.

"They called that coffee Jayvy," grumbled one of them, but it never went by the road where government Jayvy resides. I reckon I know coffee from peas."

They kept together on the road along the turnpike, and up the winding road by the river, which they followed for some miles. The river was very lovely, curving down along its sandy beds, pausing now and then under broad basswood trees, or running in dark, swift, silent currents under tangles of wild grapevines, and drooping alders, and haw trees. At one of these lovely spots the three vets sat down on the thick green sward to rest, "on Smith's account." The leaves of the trees were as fresh and green as in June, the jays called cheery greetings to them, and kingfishers darted to and fro with swooping, noiseless flight.

"I tell yeh, boys, this knocks the swamps of Loueesiana into kingdom come."

"You bet. All they c'n raise down there is snakes, niggers, and p'rticler hell."

"An' fightin' men," put in the older man.

"An' fightin' men. If I had a good hook an' line I'd sneak a pick'rel out o' that pond. Say, remember that time I shot that alligator—"

"I guess we'd better be crawlin' along," interrupted Smith, rising and shouldering his knapsack, with considerable effort, which he tried to hide.

"Say, Smith, lemme give you a lift on that."

"I guess I c'n manage," said Smith, grimly.

"Course. But, yo' see, I may not have a chance right off to pay yeh back for the times you've carried my gun and hull caboodle. Say, now, gimme that gun, anyway."

"All right, if yeh feel like it, Jim," Smith replied, and they trudged along doggedly in the sun, which was getting higher and hotter each half-mile.

"Ain't it queer there ain't no teams comin' along," said Smith, after a long silence.

"Well, no, seein's it's Sunday."

"By jinks, that's a fact. It *is* Sunday. I'll git home in time f'r dinner, sure!" he exulted. "She don't hev dinner usially till about *one* on Sundays." And he fell into a muse, in which he smiled.

"Well, I'll git home jest about six o'clock, jest about when the boys are milkin' the cows," said old Jim Cranby. "I'll step into the barn, an' then I'll say: 'He*ah*! why ain't this milkin' done before this time o' day?' An' then won't they yell!" he added, slapping his thigh in great glee.

Smith went on. "I'll jest go up the path. Old Rover'll come down the road to meet me. He won't bark; he'll know me, an' he'll come down waggin' his tail an' showin' his teeth. That's his way of laughin'. An' so I'll walk up to the kitchen door, an' I'll say, '*Dinner* f'r a hungry man!' An' then she'll jump up, an'—"

He couldn't go on. His voice choked at the thought of it. Saunders, the third man, hardly uttered a word, but walked silently behind the others. He had lost his wife the first year he was in the army. She died of pneumonia, caught in the autumn rains while working in the fields in his place.

They plodded along till at last they came to a parting of the ways. To the right the road continued up the main valley; to the left it went over the big ridge.

"Well, boys," began Smith, as they grounded their muskets and looked away up the valley, "here's where we shake hands. We've marched together a good many miles, an' now I s'pose we're done."

"Yes, I don't think we'll do any more of it f'r a while. I don't want to, I know."

"I hope I'll see yeh once in a while, boys, to talk over old times."

"Of course," said Saunders, whose voice trembled a little, too. "It ain't *exactly* like dyin'." They all found it hard to look at each other.

"But we'd ought'r go home with you," said Cranby. "You'll never climb that ridge with all them things on yer back."

"Oh, I'm all right! Don't worry about me. Every step takes me nearer home, yeh see. Well, good-by, boys."

They shook hands. "Good-by. Good luck!"

"Same to you. Lemme know how you find things at home."

"Good-by."

"Good-by."

He turned once before they passed out of sight, and waved his cap, and they did the same, and all yelled. Then all marched away with their long, steady, loping, veteran step. The solitary climber in blue walked on for a time, with his mind filled with the kindness of his comrades, and musing upon the many wonderful days they had had together in camp and field.

He thought of his chum, Billy Tripp. Poor Billy! A "minie" ball fell into his breast one day, fell wailing like a cat, and tore a great ragged hole in his heart. He looked forward to a sad scene with Billy's mother and sweetheart. They would want to know all about it. He tried to recall all that Billy had said, and the particulars of it, but there was little to remember, just that wild wailing sound high in the air, a dull slap, a short, quick, expulsive groan, and the boy lay with his face in the dirt in the ploughed field they were marching across.

That was all. But all the scenes he had since been through had not dimmed the horror, the terror of that moment, when his boy comrade fell, with only a breath between a laugh and a death-groan. Poor handsome Billy! Worth millions of dollars was his young life.

These sombre recollections gave way at length to more cheerful feelings as he began to approach his home coolly. The fields and houses grew familiar, and in one or two he was greeted by people seated in the doorways. But he was in no mood to talk, and pushed on steadily, though he stopped and accepted a drink of milk once at the well-side of a neighbor.

The sun was burning hot on that slope, and his step grew slower, in spite of his iron resolution. He sat down several times to rest. Slowly he crawled up the rough, reddish-brown road, which wound along the hillside, under great trees, through dense groves of jack oaks, with tree-tops far below him on his left hand, and the hills far above him on his right. He crawled along like some minute, wingless variety of fly.

He ate some hardtack, sauced with wild berries, when he reached the summit of the ridge, and sat there for some time, looking down into his home coolly.

Sombre, pathetic figure! His wide, round, gray eyes gazing down into the beautiful valley, seeing and not seeing, the splendid cloud-shadows sweeping over the western hills and across the green and yellow wheat far below. His head drooped forward on his palm, his shoulders took on a tired stoop, his cheek-bones showed painfully. An observer might have said, "He is looking down upon his own grave."

II

Sunday comes in a Western wheat harvest with such sweet and sudden relaxation to man and beast that it would be holy for that reason, if for no other, and Sundays are usually fair in harvest-time. As one goes out into the field in the hot morning sunshine, with no sound abroad save the crickets and the indescribably pleasant silken rustling of the ripened grain, the reaper and the very sheaves in the stubble seem to be resting, dreaming.

Around the house, in the shade of the trees, the men sit, smoking, dozing, or reading the papers, while the women, never resting, move about at the housework. The men eat on Sundays about the same as on other days, and breakfast is no sooner over and out of the way than dinner begins.

But at the Smith farm there were no men dozing or reading. Mrs. Smith was alone with her three children, Mary, nine, Tommy, six, and little Ted, just past four. Her farm, rented to a neighbor, lay at the head of a coolly or narrow gully, made at some far-off post-glacial period by the vast and angry floods of water which gullied these tremendous furrows in the level prairie—furrows so deep that undisturbed portions of the original level rose like hills on either side, rose to quite considerable mountains.

The chickens wakened her as usual that Sabbath morning from dreams of her absent husband, from whom she had not heard for weeks. The shadows drifted over the hills, down the slopes, across the wheat, and up the opposite wall in leisurely way, as if, being Sunday, they could take it easy also. The fowls clustered about the housewife as she went out into the yard. Fuzzy little chickens swarmed out from the coops, where their clucking and perpetually disgruntled mothers tramped about, petulantly thrusting their heads through the spaces between the slats.

A cow called in a deep, musical bass, and a calf answered from a little pen near by, and a pig scurried guiltily out of the cabbages. Seeing all this, seeing the pig in the cabbages, the tangle of grass in the garden, the broken fence which she had mended again and again—the little woman, hardly more than a girl, sat down and cried. The bright Sabbath morning was only a mockery without him!

A few years ago they had bought this farm, paying part, mortgaging the rest in the usual way. Edward Smith was a man of terrible energy. He worked "nights and Sundays," as the saying goes, to clear the farm of its brush and of its insatiate mortgage! In the midst of his Herculean struggle came the call for volunteers, and with the grim and unselfish devotion to his country which made the Eagle Brigade able to "whip its weight in wild-cats," he threw down his scythe and grub-axe, turned his cattle loose, and became a blue-coated cog in a vast machine for killing men, and not thistles. While the millionaire sent his money to England for safe-keeping, this man, with his girl-wife and three babies, left them on a mortgaged farm, and went away to fight for an idea. It was foolish, but it was sublime for all that.

That was three years before, and the young wife, sitting on the well-curb on this bright Sabbath harvest morning, was righteously rebellious. It seemed to her that she had borne her share of the country's sorrow. Two brothers had been killed, the renter in whose hands her husband had left the farm had proved a villain; one year the farm had been without crops, and now the overripe grain was waiting the tardy hand of the neighbor who had rented it, and who was cutting his own grain first.

About six weeks before, she had received a letter saying, "We'll be discharged in a little while." But no other word had come from him. She had seen by the papers that his army was being discharged, and from day to day other soldiers slowly percolated in blue streams back into the State and county, but still *her* hero did not return.

Each week she had told the children that he was coming, and she had watched the road so long that it had become unconscious; and as she stood at the well, or by the kitchen door, her eyes were fixed unthinkingly on the road that wound down the coolly.

Nothing wears on the human soul like waiting. If the stranded mariner, searching the sun-bright seas, could once give up hope of a ship, that horrible grinding on his brain would cease. It was this waiting, hoping, on the edge of despair, that gave Emma Smith no rest.

Neighbors said, with kind intentions: "He's sick, maybe, an' can't start north just yet. He'll come along one o' these days."

"Why don't he write?" was her question, which silenced them all. This Sunday morning it seemed to her as if she could not stand it longer. The house seemed intolerably lonely. So she dressed the little ones in their best calico dresses and home-made jackets, and, closing up the house, set off down the coolly to old Mother Gray's.

"Old Widder Gray" lived at the "mouth of the coolly." She was a widow woman with a large family of stalwart boys and laughing girls. She was the visible incarnation of hospitality and optimistic poverty. With Western open-heartedness she fed every mouth that asked food of her, and worked herself to death as cheerfully as her girls danced in the neighborhood harvest dances.

She waddled down the path to meet Mrs. Smith with a broad smile on her face.

"Oh, you little dears! Come right to your granny. Gimme me a kiss! Come right in, Mis' Smith. How are yeh, anyway? Nice mornin', ain't it? Come in an' set down. Everything's in a clutter, but that won't scare you any."

She led the way into the best room, a sunny, square room, carpeted with a faded and patched rag carpet, and papered with white-and-green-striped wall-paper, where a few faded effigies of dead members of the family hung in variously sized oval walnut frames. The house resounded with singing, laughter, whistling, tramping of heavy boots, and riotous scufflings. Half-grown boys came to the door and crooked their fingers at the children, who ran out, and were soon heard in the midst of the fun.

"Don't s'pose you've heard from Ed?" Mrs. Smith shook her head. "He'll turn up some day, when you ain't lookin' for 'm." The good old soul had said that so many times that poor Mrs. Smith derived no comfort from it any longer.

"Liz heard from Al the other day. He's comin' some day this week. Anyhow, they expect him."

"Did he say anything of—"

"No, he didn't," Mrs. Gray admitted. "But then it was only a short letter, anyhow. Al ain't much for writin', anyhow.—But come out and see my new cheese. I tell yeh, I don't believe I ever had better luck in my life. If Ed should come, I want you should take him up a piece of this cheese."

It was beyond human nature to resist the influence of that noisy, hearty, loving household, and in the midst of the singing and laughing the wife forgot her anxiety, for the time at least, and laughed and sang with the rest.

About eleven o'clock a wagon-load more drove up to the door, and Bill Gray, the widow's oldest son, and his whole family, from Sand Lake Coolly, piled out amid a good-natured uproar. Every one talked at once, except Bill, who sat in the wagon with his wrists on his knees, a straw in his mouth, and an amused twinkle in his blue eyes.

"Ain't heard nothin' o' Ed, I s'pose?" he asked in a kind of bellow. Mrs. Smith shook her head. Bill, with a delicacy very striking in such a great giant, rolled his quid in his mouth, and said:

"Didn't know but you had. I hear two or three of the Sand Lake boys are comin'. Left New Orleenes some time this week. Didn't write nothin' about Ed, but no news is good news in such cases, mother always says."

"Well, go put out yer team," said Mrs. Gray, "an' go 'n bring me in some taters, an', Sim, you go see if you c'n find some corn. Sadie, you put on the water to bile. Come now, hustle yer boots, all o' yeh. If I feed this yer crowd, we've got to have some raw materials. If y' think I'm goin' to feed yeh on pie—you're jest mightily mistaken."

The children went off into the fields, the girls put dinner on to boil, and then went to change their dresses and fix their hair. "Somebody might come," they said.

"Land sakes, I hope not! I don't know where in time I'd set 'em, 'less they'd eat at the second table," Mrs. Gray laughed, in pretended dismay.

The two older boys, who had served their time in the army, lay out on the grass before the house, and whittled and talked desultorily about the war and the crops, and planned buying a threshing-machine. The older girls and Mrs. Smith helped enlarge the table and put on the dishes, talking all the time in that cheery, incoherent, and meaningful way a group of such women have,—a conversation to be taken for its spirit rather than for its letter, though Mrs. Gray at last got the ear of them all and dissertated at length on girls.

"Girls in love ain't no use in the whole blessed week," she said. "Sundays they're a-lookin' down the road, expectin' he'll come. Sunday afternoons they can't think o' nothin' else, 'cause he's here. Monday mornin's they're sleepy and kind o' dreamy and slimpsy, and good f'r nothin' on Tuesday and Wednesday. Thursday they git absent-minded, an' begin to look off toward Sunday agin, an' mope aroun' and let the dishwater git cold, right under their noses. Friday they break dishes, an' go off in the best room an' snivel, an' look

out o' the winder. Saturdays they have queer spurts o' workin' like all
p'ssessed, an' spurts o' frizzin' their hair. An' Sunday they begin it all
over agin."

The girls giggled and blushed, all through this tirade from their
mother, their broad faces and powerful frames anything but suggestive of lackadaisical sentiment. But Mrs. Smith said:

"Now, Mrs. Gray, I hadn't ought to stay to dinner. You've got—"

"Now you set right down! If any of them girls' beaus comes, they'll
have to take what's left, that's all. They ain't s'posed to have much
appetite, nohow. No, you're goin' to stay if they starve, an' they ain't
no danger o' that."

At one o'clock the long table was piled with boiled potatoes, cords
of boiled corn on the cob, squash and pumpkin pies, hot biscuit,
sweet pickles, bread and butter, and honey. Then one of the girls
took down a conch-shell from a nail, and going to the door, blew a
long, fine, free blast, that showed there was no weakness of lungs
in her ample chest.

Then the children came out of the forest of corn, out of the creek,
out of the loft of the barn, and out of the garden.

"They come to their feed f'r all the world jest like the pigs when
y' holler 'poo-ee!' See 'em scoot!" laughed Mrs. Gray, every wrinkle
on her face shining with delight.

The men shut up their jack-knives, and surrounded the horse-
trough to souse their faces in the cold, hard water, and in a few
moments the table was filled with a merry crowd, and a row of
wistful-eyed youngsters circled the kitchen wall, where they stood
first on one leg and then on the other, in impatient hunger.

"Now pitch in, Mrs. Smith," said Mrs. Gray, presiding over the
table. "You know these men critters. They'll eat every grain of it,
if yeh give 'em a chance. I swan, they're made o' India-rubber, their
stomachs is, I know it."

"Haf to eat to work," said Bill, gnawing a cob with a swift, circular
motion that rivalled a corn-sheller in results.

"More like workin' to eat," put in one of the girls, with a giggle.
"More eat 'n work with you."

"*You* needn't say anything, Net. Any one that'll eat seven ears—"

"I didn't, no such thing. You piled your cobs on my plate."

"That'll do to tell Ed Varney. It won't go down here where we
know yeh."

"Good land! Eat all yeh want! They's plenty more in the fiel's,
but I can't afford to give you young uns tea. The tea is for us women-

folks, and 'specially f'r Mis' Smith an' Bill's wife. We're a-goin' to tell fortunes by it."

One by one the men filled up and shoved back, and one by one the children slipped into their places, and by two o'clock the women alone remained around the débris-covered table, sipping their tea and telling fortunes.

As they got well down to the grounds in the cup, they shook them with a circular motion in the hand, and then turned them bottom-side-up quickly in the saucer, then twirled them three or four times one way, and three or four times the other, during a breathless pause. Then Mrs. Gray lifted the cup, and, gazing into it with profound gravity, pronounced the impending fate.

It must be admitted that, to a critical observer, she had abundant preparation for hitting close to the mark, as when she told the girls that "somebody was comin'." "It's a man," she went on gravely. "He is cross-eyed—"

"Oh, you hush!" cried Nettie.

"He has red hair, and is death on b'iled corn and hot biscuit."

The others shrieked with delight.

"But he's goin' to get the mitten, that red-headed feller is, for I see another feller comin' up behind him."

"Oh, lemme see, lemme see!" cried Nettie.

"Keep off," said the priestess, with a lofty gesture. "His hair is black. He don't eat so much, and he works more."

The girls exploded in a shriek of laughter, and pounded their sister on the back.

At last came Mrs. Smith's turn, and she was trembling with excitement as Mrs. Gray again composed her jolly face to what she considered a proper solemnity of expression.

"Somebody is comin' to *you*," she said, after a long pause. "He's got a musket on his back. He's a soldier. He's almost here. See?"

She pointed at two little tea-stems, which really formed a faint suggestion of a man with a musket on his back. He had climbed nearly to the edge of the cup. Mrs. Smith grew pale with excitement. She trembled so she could hardly hold the cup in her hand as she gazed into it.

"It's Ed," cried the old woman. "He's on the way home. Heavens an' earth! There he is now!" She turned and waved her hand out toward the road. They rushed to the door to look where she pointed.

A man in a blue coat, with a musket on his back, was toiling slowly up the hill on the sun-bright, dusty road, toiling slowly, with bent head half hidden by a heavy knapsack. So tired it seemed that walking was indeed a process of falling. So eager to get home he would not stop, would not look aside, but plodded on, amid the cries of the locusts, the welcome of the crickets, and the rustle of the yellow wheat. Getting back to God's country, and his wife and babies!

Laughing, crying, trying to call him and the children at the same time, the little wife, almost hysterical, snatched her hat and ran out into the yard. But the soldier had disappeared over the hill into the hollow beyond, and, by the time she had found the children, he was too far away for her voice to reach him. And, besides, she was not sure it was her husband, for he had not turned his head at their shouts. This seemed so strange. Why didn't he stop to rest at his old neighbor's house? Tortured by hope and doubt, she hurried up the coolly as fast as she could push the baby wagon, the blue-coated figure just ahead pushing steadily, silently forward up the coolly.

When the excited, panting little group came in sight of the gate they saw the blue-coated figure standing, leaning upon the rough rail fence, his chin on his palms, gazing at the empty house. His knapsack, canteen, blankets, and musket lay upon the dusty grass at his feet.

He was like a man lost in a dream. His wide, hungry eyes devoured the scene. The rough lawn, the little unpainted house, the field of clear yellow wheat behind it, down across which streamed the sun, now almost ready to touch the high hill to the west, the crickets crying merrily, a cat on the fence near by, dreaming, unmindful of the stranger in blue—

How peaceful it all was. O God! How far removed from all camps, hospitals, battle lines. A little cabin in a Wisconsin coolly, but it was majestic in its peace. How did he ever leave it for those years of tramping, thirsting, killing?

Trembling, weak with emotion, her eyes on the silent figure, Mrs. Smith hurried up to the fence. Her feet made no noise in the dust and grass, and they were close upon him before he knew of them. The oldest boy ran a little ahead. He will never forget that figure, that face. It will always remain as something epic, that return of the private. He fixed his eyes on the pale face covered with a ragged beard.

"Who *are* you, sir?" asked the wife, or, rather, started to ask, for he turned, stood a moment, and then cried:

"Emma!"

"Edward!"

The children stood in a curious row to see their mother kiss this bearded, strange man, the elder girl sobbing sympathetically with her mother. Illness had left the soldier partly deaf, and this added to the strangeness of his manner.

But the youngest child stood away, even after the girl had recognized her father and kissed him. The man turned then to the baby, and said in a curiously unpaternal tone:

"Come here, my little man; don't you know me?" But the baby backed away under the fence and stood peering at him critically.

"My little man!" What meaning in those words! This baby seemed like some other woman's child, and not the infant he had left in his wife's arms. The war had come between him and his baby—he was only a strange man to him, with big eyes; a soldier, with mother hanging to his arm, and talking in a loud voice.

"And this is Tom," the private said, drawing the oldest boy to him. *"He'll* come and see me. *He* knows his poor old pap when he comes home from the war."

The mother heard the pain and reproach in his voice and hastened to apologize.

"You've changed so, Ed. He can't know yeh. This is papa, Teddy; come and kiss him—Tom and Mary do. Come, won't you?" But Teddy still peered through the fence with solemn eyes, well out of reach. He resembled a half-wild kitten that hesitates, studying the tones of one's voice.

"I'll fix him," said the soldier, and sat down to undo his knapsack, out of which he drew three enormous and very red apples. After giving one to each of the older children, he said:

"Now I guess he'll come. Eh, my little man? Now come see your pap."

Teddy crept slowly under the fence, assisted by the overzealous Tommy, and a moment later was kicking and squalling in his father's arms. Then they entered the house, into the sitting room, poor, bare, art-forsaken little room, too, with its rag carpet, its square clock, and its two or three chromos and pictures from *Harper's Weekly* pinned about.

"Emma, I'm all tired out," said Private Smith, as he flung himself down on the carpet as he used to do, while his wife brought a pillow to put under his head, and the children stood about munching their apples.

"Tommy, you run and get me a pan of chips, and Mary, you get the tea-kettle on, and I'll go and make some biscuit."

And the soldier talked. Question after question he poured forth about the crops, the cattle, the renter, the neighbors. He slipped his heavy government brogan shoes off his poor, tired, blistered feet, and lay out with utter, sweet relaxation. He was a free man again, no longer a soldier under command. At supper he stopped once, listened and smiled. "That's old Spot. I know her voice. I s'pose that's her calf out there in the pen. I can't milk her to-night, though. I'm too tired. But I tell you, I'd like a drink o' her milk. What's become of old Rove?"

"He died last winter. Poisoned, I guess." There was a moment of sadness for them all. It was some time before the husband spoke again, in a voice that trembled a little.

"Poor old feller! He'd 'a' known me half a mile away. I expected him to come down the hill to meet me. It 'ud 'a' been more like comin' home if I could 'a' seen him comin' down the road an' waggin' his tail, an' laughin' that way he has. I tell yeh, it kind o' took hold o' me to see the blinds down an' the house shut up."

"But, yeh see, we—we expected you'd write again 'fore you started. And then we thought we'd see you if you *did* come," she hastened to explain.

"Well, I ain't worth a cent on writin'. Besides, it's just as well yeh didn't know when I was comin'. I tell you, it sounds good to hear them chickens out there, an' turkeys, an' the crickets. Do you know they don't have just the same kind o' crickets down South? Who's Sam hired t' help cut yer grain?"

"The Ramsey boys."

"Looks like a good crop; but I'm afraid I won't do much gettin' it cut. This cussed fever an' ague has got me down pretty low. I don't know when I'll get rid of it. I'll bet I've took twenty-five pounds of quinine if I've taken a bit. Gimme another biscuit. I tell yeh, they taste good, Emma. I ain't had anything like it— Say, if you'd 'a' hear'd me braggin' to th' boys about your butter 'n' biscuits I'll bet your ears 'ud 'a' burnt."

The private's wife colored with pleasure. "Oh, you're always a-braggin' about your things. Everybody makes good butter."

"Yes; old lady Snyder, for instance."

"Oh, well, she ain't to be mentioned. She's Dutch."

"Or old Mis' Snively. One more cup o' tea, Mary. That's my girl! I'm feeling better already. I just b'lieve the matter with me is, I'm *starved*."

This was a delicious hour, one long to be remembered. They were like lovers again. But their tenderness, like that of a typical American family, found utterance in tones, rather than in words. He was praising her when praising her biscuit, and she knew it. They grew soberer when he showed where he had been struck, one ball burning the back of his hand, one cutting away a lock of hair from his temple, and one passing through the calf of his leg. The wife shuddered to think how near she had come to being a soldier's widow. Her waiting no longer seemed hard. This sweet, glorious hour effaced it all.

Then they rose, and all went out into the garden and down to the barn. He stood beside her while she milked old Spot. They began to plan fields and crops for next year.

His farm was weedy and encumbered, a rascally renter had run away with his machinery (departing between two days), his children needed clothing, the years were coming upon him, he was sick and emaciated, but his heroic soul did not quail. With the same courage with which he had faced his Southern march he entered upon a still more hazardous future.

Oh, that mystic hour! The pale man with big eyes standing there by the well, with his young wife by his side. The vast moon swinging above the eastern peaks, the cattle winding down the pasture slopes with jangling bells, the crickets singing, the stars blooming out sweet and far and serene; the katydids rhythmically calling, the little turkeys crying querulously, as they settled to roost in the poplar tree near the open gate. The voices at the well drop lower, the little ones nestle in their father's arms at last, and Teddy falls asleep there.

The common soldier of the American volunteer army had returned. His war with the South was over, and his fight, his daily running fight with nature and against the injustice of his fellow-men, was begun again.

Lucretia Burns

I

LUCRETIA BURNS had never been handsome, even in her days of early girlhood, and now she was middle-aged, distorted with work and child-bearing, and looking faded and worn as one of the boulders that lay beside the pasture fence near where she sat milking a large white cow.

She had no shawl or hat and no shoes, for it was still muddy in the little yard, where the cattle stood patiently fighting the flies and mosquitoes swarming into their skins, already wet with blood. The evening was oppressive with its heat, and a ring of just-seen thunderheads gave premonitions of an approaching storm.

She rose from the cow's side at last, and, taking her pails of foaming milk, staggered toward the gate. The two pails hung from her lean arms, her bare feet slipped on the filthy ground, her greasy and faded calico dress showed her tired and swollen ankles, and the mosquitoes swarmed mercilessly on her neck and bedded themselves in her colorless hair.

The children were quarrelling at the well, and the sound of blows could be heard. Calves were querulously calling for their milk, and little turkeys, lost in a tangle of grass, were piping plaintively.

The sun just setting struck through a long, low rift, like a boy peeping beneath the eaves of a huge roof. Its light brought out Lucretia's face as she leaned her sallow forehead on the top bar of the gate and looked toward the west.

It was a pitifully worn, almost tragic face—long, thin, sallow, hollow-eyed. The mouth had long since lost the power to shape itself into a kiss, and had a droop at the corners which seemed to announce a breaking-down at any moment into a despairing wail. The collarless neck and sharp shoulders showed painfully.

She felt vaguely that the night was beautiful. The setting sun, the noise of frogs, the nocturnal insects beginning to pipe—all in some way called her girlhood back to her, though there was little in her girlhood to give her pleasure. Her large gray eyes grew round, deep, and wistful as she saw the illimitable craggy clouds grow crimson, roll slowly up, and fire at the top. A childish scream recalled her.

"Oh, my soul!" she half groaned, half swore, as she lifted her milk and hurried to the well. Arriving there, she cuffed the children right and left with all her remaining strength, saying in justification:—

"My soul! can't you—you young 'uns, give me a minute's peace? Land knows, I'm almost gone up; washin', an' milkin' six cows, and tendin' you, and cookin' f'r *him,* ought 'o be enough f'r one day! Sadie, you let him drink now 'r I'll slap your head off, you hateful thing! Why can't you behave, when you know I'm jest about dead?" She was weeping now, with nervous weakness. "Where's y'r pa?" she asked after a moment, wiping her eyes with her apron.

One of the group, the one cuffed last, sniffed out, in rage and grief:—

"He's in the corn-field; where'd ye s'pose he was?"

"Good land! why don't the man work all night? Sile, you put that dipper in that milk agin, an' I'll whack you till your head'll swim! Sadie, le' go Pet, an' go 'n get them turkeys out of the grass 'fore it gits dark! Bob, you go tell y'r dad if he wants the rest o' them cows

milked he's got 'o do it himself. I jest can't, and what's more, I
won't," she ended, rebelliously.

Having strained the milk and fed the children, she took some
skimmed milk from the cans and started to feed the calves bawling
strenuously behind the barn. The eager and unruly brutes pushed
and struggled to get into the pails all at once, and in consequence
spilt nearly all of the milk on the ground. This was the last trial;
the woman fell down on the damp grass and moaned and sobbed
like a crazed thing. The children came to seek her and stood around
like little partridges, looking at her in scared silence, till at last the
little one began to wail. Then the mother rose wearily to her feet,
and walked slowly back toward the house.

She heard Burns threshing his team at the well, with the sound
of oaths. He was tired, hungry, and ill-tempered, but she was too
desperate to care. His poor, overworked team did not move quickly
enough for him, and his extra long turn in the corn had made him
dangerous. His eyes gleamed wrathfully from his dust-laid face.

"Supper ready?" he growled.

"Yes, two hours ago."

"Well, I can't help it!" he said, understanding her reproach. "That
devilish corn is gettin' too tall to plough again, and I've got 'o go
through it to-morrow or not at all. Cows milked?"

"Part of 'em."

"How many left?"

"Three."

"Hell! Which three?"

"Spot, and Brin, and Cherry."

"*Of* course, left the three worst ones. I'll be damned if I milk a
cow to-night. I don't see why you play out jest the nights I need
ye most." Here he kicked a child out of the way. "Git out o' that!
Hain't you got no sense? I'll learn ye—"

"Stop that, Sim Burns," cried the woman, snatching up the child.
"You're a reg'lar ol' hyeny,—that's what you are," she added defiantly,
roused at last from her lethargy.

"You're a—beauty, that's what *you* are," he said, pitilessly. "Keep
your brats out f'um under my feet." And he strode off to the barn
after his team, leaving her with a fierce hate in her heart. She heard
him yelling at his team in their stalls: "Git around there, damn
yeh."

The children had had their supper; so she took them to bed. She
was unusually tender to them, for she wanted to make up in some
way for her previous harshness. The ferocity of her husband had

shown up her own petulant temper hideously, and she sat and sobbed in the darkness a long time beside the cradle where little Pet slept.

She heard Burns come growling in and tramp about, but she did not rise. The supper was on the table; he could wait on himself. There was an awful feeling at her heart as she sat there and the house grew quiet. She thought of suicide in a vague way; of somehow taking her children in her arms and sinking into a lake somewhere, where she would never more be troubled, where she could sleep forever, without toil or hunger.

Then she thought of the little turkeys wandering in the grass, of the children sleeping at last, of the quiet, wonderful stars. Then she thought of the cows left unmilked, and listened to them stirring uneasily in the yard. She rose, at last, and stole forth. She could not rid herself of the thought that they would suffer. She knew what the dull ache in the full breasts of a mother was, and she could not let them stand at the bars all night moaning for relief.

The mosquitoes had gone, but the frogs and katydids still sang, while over in the west Venus shone. She was a long time milking the cows; her hands were so tired she had often to stop and rest them, while the tears fell unheeded into the pail. She saw and felt little of the external as she sat there. She thought in vague retrospect of how sweet it seemed the first time Sim came to see her; of the many rides to town with him when he was an accepted lover; of the few things he had given her—a coral breastpin and a ring.

She felt no shame at her present miserable appearance; she was past personal pride. She hardly felt as if the tall, strong girl, attractive with health and hope, could be the same soul as the woman who now sat in utter despair listening to the heavy breathing of the happy cows, grateful for the relief from their burden of milk.

She contrasted her lot with that of two or three women that she knew (not a very high standard), who kept hired help, and who had fine houses of four or five rooms. Even the neighbors were better off than she, for they didn't have such quarrels. But she wasn't to blame—Sim didn't— Then her mind changed to a dull resentment against "things." Everything seemed against her.

She rose at last and carried her second load of milk to the well, strained it, washed out the pails, and, after bathing her tired feet in a tub that stood there, she put on a pair of horrible shoes, without stockings, and crept stealthily into the house. Sim did not hear her as she slipped up the stairs to the little low unfinished chamber beside her oldest children. She could not bear to sleep near *him* that night,—she wanted a chance to sob herself to quiet.

As for Sim, he was a little disturbed, but would as soon have cut off his head as acknowledged himself in the wrong. As he went to bed, and found her still away, he yelled up the stairway:—

"Say, old woman, ain't ye comin' to bed?" Upon receiving no answer he rolled his aching body into the creaking bed. "Do as y' damn please about it. If y' want to sulk y' can." And in such wise the family grew quiet in sleep, while the moist, warm air pulsed with the ceaseless chime of the crickets.

II

When Sim Burns woke the next morning he felt a sharper twinge of remorse. It was not a broad or well-defined feeling—just a sense that he had been unduly irritable, not that on the whole he was not in the right. Little Pet lay with the warm June sunshine filling his baby eyes, curiously content in striking at flies that buzzed around his little mouth.

The man thrust his dirty, naked feet into his huge boots, and, without washing his face or combing his hair, went out to the barn to do his chores.

He was a type of the average prairie farmer, and his whole surrounding was typical of the time. He had a quarter-section of fine level land, bought with incredible toil, but his house was a little box-like structure, costing, perhaps, five hundred dollars. It had three rooms and the ever-present summer kitchen at the back. It was unpainted and had no touch of beauty,—a mere box.

His stable was built of slabs and banked and covered with straw. It looked like a den, was low and long, and had but one door in the end. The cow-yard held ten or fifteen cattle of various kinds, while a few calves were bawling from a pen near by. Behind the barn, on the west and north, was a fringe of willows forming a "wind-break." A few broken and discouraged fruit trees, standing here and there among the weeds, formed the garden. In short, he was spoken of by his neighbors as "a hard-working cuss, and tol'ably well fixed."

No grace had come or ever could come into his life. Back of him were generations of men like himself, whose main business had been to work hard, live miserably, and beget children to take their places when they died.

His courtship had been delayed so long on account of poverty that it brought little of humanizing emotion into his life. He never mentioned his love-life now, or if he did, it was only to sneer obscenely at it. He had long since ceased to kiss his wife or even speak kindly to her. There was no longer any sanctity to life or love. He chewed tobacco and toiled on from year to year without any very clearly defined idea of the future. His life was mainly regulated from without.

He was tall, dark, and strong, in a flat-chested, slouching sort of way, and had grown neglectful of even decency in his dress. He wore the American farmer's customary outfit of rough brown pants, hickory shirt, and greasy wool hat. It differed from his neighbors' mainly in being a little dirtier and more ragged. His grimy hands were broad and strong as the clutch of a bear, and he was a "terrible feller to turn off work," as Councill said. "I'd ruther have Sim Burns work for me one day than some men three. He's a linger." He worked with unusual speed this morning, and ended by milking all the cows himself as a sort of savage penance for his misdeeds the previous evening, muttering in self-defence:—

"Seems 's if ever' cussid thing piles on to me at once. That corn, the road-tax, and hayin' comin' on, and now *she* gits her back up—"

When he went back to the well he sloshed himself thoroughly in the horse-trough and went to the house. He found breakfast ready, but his wife was not in sight. The older children were clamoring around the uninviting breakfast table, spread with cheap ware and with boiled potatoes and fried salt pork as the principal dishes.

"Where's y'r ma?" he asked, with a threatening note in his voice, as he sat down by the table.

"She's in the bedroom."

He rose and pushed open the door. The mother sat with the babe in her lap, looking out of the window down across the superb field of timothy, moving like a lake of purple water. She did not look around. She only grew rigid. Her thin neck throbbed with the pulsing of blood to her head.

"What's got into you *now*?" he said, brutally. "Don't be a fool. Come out and eat breakfast with me, an' take care o' y'r young ones."

She neither moved nor made a sound. With an oath he turned on his heel and went out to the table. Eating his breakfast in his usual wolfish fashion, he went out into the hot sun with his team and riding-plough, not a little disturbed by this new phase of his wife's "cantankerousness." He ploughed steadily and sullenly all the forenoon, in the terrific heat and dust. The air was full of tempestuous threats, still and sultry, one of those days when work is a punishment. When he came in at noon he found things the same—dinner on the table, but his wife out in the garden with the youngest child.

"I c'n stand it as long as *she* can," he said to himself, in the hearing of the children, as he pushed back from the table and went back to work.

When he had finished the field of corn it was after sundown, and he came up to the house, hot, dusty, his shirt wringing wet with sweat, and his neck aching with the work of looking down all day at the corn-rows. His mood was still stern. The multitudinous lift, and stir, and sheen of the wide, green field had been lost upon him.

"I wonder if she's milked them cows," he muttered to himself. He gave a sigh of relief to find she had. But she had done so not for his sake, but for the sake of the poor, patient dumb brutes.

When he went to the bedroom after supper, he found that the cradle and his wife's few little boxes and parcels—poor, pathetic properties!—had been removed to the garret, which they called a chamber, and he knew he was to sleep alone again.

"She'll git over it, I guess." He was very tired, but he didn't feel quite comfortable enough to sleep. The air was oppressive. His shirt, wet in places, and stiff with dust in other places, oppressed him more than usual; so he rose and removed it, getting a clean one out of a drawer. This was an unusual thing for him, for he usually slept in the same shirt which he wore in his day's work; but it was Saturday night, and he felt justified in the extravagance.

In the meanwhile poor Lucretia was brooding over her life in a most dangerous fashion. All she had done and suffered for Simeon Burns came back to her till she wondered how she had endured it all. All day long in the midst of the glorious summer landscape she brooded.

"I hate him," she thought, with a fierce blazing up through the murk of her musing. "I hate t' live. But they ain't no hope. I'm tied down. I can't leave the children, and I ain't got no money. I couldn't make a living out in the world. I ain't never seen anything an' don't know anything."

She was too simple and too unknowing to speculate on the loss of her beauty, which would have brought her competency once—if sold in the right market. As she lay in her little attic bed, she was still sullenly thinking, wearily thinking of her life. She thought of a poor old horse which Sim had bought once, years before, and put to the plough when it was too old and weak to work. She could see her again as in a vision, that poor old mare, with sad head drooping, toiling, toiling, till at last she could no longer move, and lying

down under the harness in the furrow, groaned under the whip,—
and died.

Then she wondered if her own numbness and despair meant death,
and she held her breath to think harder upon it. She concluded at
last, grimly, that she didn't care—only for the children.

The air was frightfully close in the little attic, and she heard the
low mutter of the rising storm in the west. She forgot her troubles
a little, listening to the far-off gigantic footsteps of the tempest.

Boom, boom, boom, it broke nearer and nearer, as if a vast cordon
of cannon was being drawn around the horizon. Yet she was conscious only of pleasure. She had no fear. At last came the sweep of
cool, fragrant storm-wind, a short and sudden dash of rain, and
then in the cool, sweet hush which followed, the worn and weary
woman fell into a deep sleep.

III

When she woke the younger children were playing about on the
floor in their night-clothes, and little Pet was sitting in a square of
sunshine, intent on one of his shoes. He was too young to know how
poor and squalid his surroundings were,—the patch of sunshine flung
on the floor glorified it all. He—little animal—was happy.

The poor of the Western prairies lie almost as unhealthily close
together as do the poor of the city tenements. In the small hut of
the peasant there is as little chance to escape close and tainting contact as in the coops and dens of the North End of proud Boston. In
the midst of oceans of land, floods of sunshine and gulfs of verdure,
the farmer lives in two or three small rooms. Poverty's eternal cordon
is ever round the poor.

"Ma, why didn't you sleep with Pap last night?" asked Bob, the
seven-year-old, when he saw she was awake at last. She flushed a dull
red.

"You hush, will yeh? Because—I—it was too warm—and there was
a storm comin'. You never mind askin' such questions. Is he gone
out?"

"Yup. I heerd him callin' the pigs. It's Sunday, ain't it, ma?"

The fact seemed to startle her.

"Why, yes, so it is! Wal! Now, Sadie, you jump up an' dress
quick 's y' can, an' Bob an' Sile, you run down an' bring s'm' water,"
she commanded, in nervous haste, beginning to dress. In the middle
of the room there was scarce space to stand beneath the rafters.

When Sim came in for his breakfast he found it on the table, but his wife was absent.

"Where's y'r ma?" he asked, with a little less of the growl in his voice.

"She's upstairs with Pet."

The man ate his breakfast in dead silence, till at last Bob ventured to say:—

"What makes ma ac' so?"

"Shut up!" was the brutal reply. The children began to take sides with the mother—all but the oldest girl, who was ten years old. To her the father turned now for certain things to be done, treating her in his rough fashion as a housekeeper, and the girl felt flattered and docile accordingly.

They were pitiably clad; like many farm-children, indeed, they could hardly be said to be clad at all. Sadie had on but two garments, a sort of undershirt of cotton and a faded calico dress, out of which her bare, yellow little legs protruded, lamentably dirty and covered with scratches.

The boys also had two garments, a hickory shirt and a pair of pants like their father's, made out of brown denim by the mother's never-resting hands—hands that in sleep still sewed, and skimmed, and baked, and churned. The boys had gone to bed without washing their feet, which now looked like toads, calloused, brown, and chapped.

Part of this the mother saw with her dull eyes as she came down, after seeing the departure of Sim up the road with the cows. It was a beautiful Sunday morning, and the woman might have sung like a bird if men had been as kind to her as Nature. But she looked dully out upon the seas of ripe grasses, tangled and flashing with dew, out of which the bobolinks and larks sprang. The glorious winds brought her no melody, no perfume, no respite from toil and care.

She thought of the children she saw in the town,—children of the merchant and banker, clean as little dolls, the boys in knickerbocker suits, the girls in dainty white dresses,—and a vengeful bitterness sprang up in her heart. She soon put the dishes away, but felt too tired and listless to do more.

"Taw-bay-wies! Pet want ta-aw-bay-wies!" cried the little one, tugging at her dress.

Listlessly, mechanically she took him in her arms, and went out into the garden, which was fragrant and sweet with dew and sun. After picking some berries for him, she sat down on the grass under the row of cottonwoods, and sank into a kind of lethargy. A kingbird chattered and shrieked overhead, the grasshoppers buzzed in the grasses, strange insects with ventriloquistic voices sang all about her —she could not tell where.

"Ma, can't I put on my clean dress?" insisted Sadie.

"I don't care," said the brooding woman, darkly. "Leave me alone."

Oh, if she could only lie here forever, escaping all pain and weariness! The wind sang in her ears; the great clouds, beautiful as heavenly ships, floated far above in the vast, dazzling deeps of blue sky; the birds rustled and chirped around her; leaping insects buzzed and clattered in the grass and in the vines and bushes. The goodness and glory of God was in the very air, the bitterness and oppression of man in every line of her face.

But her quiet was broken by Sadie, who came leaping like a fawn down through the grass.

"Oh, ma, Aunt Maria and Uncle William are coming. They've jest turned in."

"I don't care if they be!" she answered in the same dully irritated way. "What're they comin' here to-day for, I wan' to know." She stayed there immovably, till Mrs. Councill came down to see her, piloted by two or three of the children. Mrs. Councill, a jolly, large-framed woman, smiled brightly, and greeted her in a loud, jovial voice. She made the mistake of taking the whole matter lightly; her tone amounted to ridicule.

"Sim says you've been having a tantrum, Creeshy. Don't know what for, he says."

"He don't," said the wife, with a sullen flash in her eyes. "*He* don't know why! Well, then, you just tell him what I say. I've lived in hell long enough. I'm done. I've slaved here day in and day out f'r twelve years without pay,—not even a decent word. I've worked like no nigger ever worked 'r could work and live. I've given him all I had, 'r ever expect to have. I'm wore out. My strength is gone, my patience is gone. I'm done with it,—that's a *part* of what's the matter."

"My sakes, Lucreeshy! You mustn't talk that way."

"But I *will*," said the woman, as she supported herself on one palm and raised the other. "I've *got* to talk that way." She was ripe for an explosion like this. She seized upon it with eagerness. "They ain't no use o' livin' this way, anyway. I'd take poison if it wa'n't f'r the young ones."

"Lucreeshy Burns!"

"Oh, I mean it."

"Land sakes alive, I b'lieve you're goin' crazy!"

"I shouldn't wonder if I was. I've had enough t' drive an Indian crazy. Now you jest go off an' leave me 'lone. I ain't no mind to visit,—they ain't no way out of it, and I'm tired o' trying to *find* a way. Go off an' let me be."

Her tone was so bitterly hopeless that the great, jolly face of Mrs. Councill stiffened into a look of horror such as she had not known for years. The children, in two separate groups, could be heard rioting. Bees were humming around the clover in the grass, and the kingbird chattered ceaselessly from the Lombardy poplar tip. Both women felt all this peace and beauty of the morning dimly, and it disturbed Mrs. Councill because the other was so impassive under it all. At last, after a long and thoughtful pause, Mrs. Councill asked a question whose answer she knew would decide it all—asked it very kindly and softly:—

"Creeshy, are you comin' in?"

"No," was the short and sullenly decisive answer. Mrs. Councill knew that was the end, and so rose with a sigh, and went away.

"Wal, good-by," she said, simply.

Looking back, she saw Lucretia lying at length, with closed eyes and hollow cheeks. She seemed to be sleeping, half buried in the grass. She did not look up nor reply to her sister-in-law, whose life was one of toil and trouble also, but not so hard and helpless as Lucretia's. By contrast with most of her neighbors, she seemed comfortable.

"Sim Burns, what you ben doin' to that woman?" she burst out, as she waddled up to where the two men were sitting under a cottonwood tree, talking and whittling after the manner of farmers.

"Nawthin' 's fur 's I know," answered Burns, not quite honestly, and looking uneasy.

"You needn't try t' git out of it like that, Sim Burns," replied his sister. "That woman never got into that fit f'r *nawthin'*."

"Wal, if you know more about it than I do, whadgy ask *me* fur?" he replied, angrily.

"Tut, tut!" put in Councill, "hold y'r horses! Don't git on y'r ear, children! Keep cool, and don't spile y'r shirts. Most likely you're all t' blame. Keep cool an' swear less."

"Wal, I'll bet Sim's more to blame than she is. Why, they ain't a harder-workin' woman in the hull State of Ioway than she is—"

"Except Marm Councill."

"Except nobody. Look at her, jest skin and bones."

Councill chuckled in his vast way. "That's so, mother; measured in that way, she leads over you. You git fat on it."

She smiled a little, her indignation oozing away. She never *"could stay mad,"* her children were accustomed to tell her. Burns refused to talk any more about the matter, and the visitors gave it up, and got out their team and started for home, Mrs. Councill firing this parting shot:—

"The best thing you can do to-day is t' let her alone. Mebbe the children 'll bring her round ag'in. If she does come round, you see 't you treat her a little more 's y' did when you was a-courtin' her."

"This way," roared Councill, putting his arm around his wife's waist. She boxed his ears, while he guffawed and clucked at his team.

Burns took a measure of salt and went out into the pasture to salt the cows. On the sunlit slope of the field, where the cattle came running and bawling to meet him, he threw down the salt in handfuls, and then lay down to watch them as they eagerly licked it up, even gnawing a bare spot in the sod in their eagerness to get it all.

Burns was not a drinking man; he was hard-working, frugal; in fact, he had no extravagances except his tobacco. His clothes he wore until they all but dropped from him; and he worked in rain and mud, as well as dust and sun. It was this suffering and toiling all to no purpose that made him sour and irritable. He didn't see why he should have so little after so much hard work.

He was puzzled to account for it all. His mind—the average mind —was weary with trying to solve an insoluble problem. His neighbors, who had got along a little better than himself, were free with advice and suggestion as to the cause of his persistent poverty.

Old man Bacon, the hardest-working man in the county, laid it to Burns's lack of management. Jim Butler, who owned a dozen farms (which he had taken on mortgages), and who had got rich by buying land at government price and holding for a rise, laid all such cases as Burns's to "lack of enterprise, foresight."

But the larger number, feeling themselves in the same boat with Burns, said:—

"I d' know. Seems as if things get worse an' worse. Corn an' wheat gittin' cheaper 'n' cheaper. Machinery eatin' up profits—got to *have* machinery to harvest the cheap grain, an' then the machinery eats up profits. Taxes goin' up. Devil to pay all round; I d' know what in thunder *is* the matter."

The Democrats said protection was killing the farmers; the Republicans said no. The Grangers growled about the middle-men; the Greenbackers said there wasn't circulating medium enough, and, in the midst of it all, hard-working, discouraged farmers, like Simeon Burns, worked on, unable to find out what really was the matter.

And there, on this beautiful Sabbath morning, Sim sat and thought and thought, till he rose with an oath and gave it up.

IV

It was hot and brilliant again the next morning as Douglas Radbourn drove up the road with Lily Graham, the teacher of the school in the little white schoolhouse. It was blazing hot, even though not yet nine o'clock, and the young farmers ploughing beside the fence looked longingly and somewhat bitterly at Radbourn seated in a fine top-buggy beside a beautiful creature in lace and cambric.

Very beautiful the town-bred "schoolma'am" looked to those grimy, sweaty fellows, superb fellows too, physically, with bare red arms and leather-colored faces. She was as if builded of the pink and white clouds soaring far up there in the morning sky. So cool, and sweet, and dainty.

As she came in sight, their dusty and sweaty shirts grew biting as the poisoned shirt of the Norse myth, their bare feet in the brown dirt grew distressingly flat and hoof-like, and their huge, dirty, brown, chapped and swollen hands grew so repulsive that the mere remote possibility of some time in the far future standing a chance of having an introduction to her, caused them to wipe their palms on their trousers' legs stealthily.

Lycurgus Banks swore when he saw Radbourn: "That cuss thinks he's ol' hell this morning. He don't earn his living. But he's just the kind of cuss to get holt of all the purty girls."

Others gazed with simple, sad wistfulness upon the slender figure, pale, sweet face, and dark eyes of the young girl, feeling that to have talk with such a fairylike creature was a happiness too great to ever be their lot. And when she had passed they went back to work with a sigh and feeling of loss.

As for Lily, she felt a pang of pity for these people. She looked at this peculiar form of poverty and hardship much as the fragile, tender girl of the city looks upon the men laying a gas-main in the streets. She felt, sympathetically, the heat and grime, and, though but the faintest idea of what it meant to wear such clothing came to her, she shuddered. Her eyes had been opened to these things by Radbourn, a classmate at the Seminary.

The young fellow knew that Lily was in love with him, and made distinct effort to keep the talk upon impersonal subjects. He liked her very much, probably because she listened so well.

"Poor fellows," sighed Lily, almost unconsciously, "I hate to see them working there in the dirt and hot sun. It seems a hopeless sort of life, doesn't it?"

"Oh, but this is the most beautiful part of the year," said Radbourn. "Think of them in the mud, in the sleet; think of them husking corn in the snow, a bitter wind blowing; think of them a month later in the harvest; think of them imprisoned here in winter!"

"Yes, it's dreadful! But I never felt it so keenly before. You have opened my eyes to it. Of course, I've been on a farm, but not to live there."

"Writers and orators have lied so long about 'the idyllic' in farm life, and said so much about the 'independent American farmer,' that he himself has remained blind to the fact that he's one of the hardest-working and poorest-paid men in America. See the houses they live in,—hovels."

"Yes, yes, I know," said Lily; a look of deeper pain swept over her face. "And the fate of the poor women; oh, the fate of the women!"

"Yes, it's a matter of statistics," went on Radbourn, pitilessly, "that the wives of the American farmers fill our insane asylums. See what a life they lead, most of them; no music, no books. Seventeen hours a day in a couple of small rooms—dens. Now there is Sim Burns! What a travesty of a home! Yet there are a dozen just as bad in sight. He works like a fiend—so does his wife—and what is their reward? Simply a hole to hibernate in and to sleep and eat in in summer. A dreary present and a well-nigh hopeless future. No, they have a future, if they knew it, and we must tell them."

"I know Mrs. Burns," Lily said, after a pause; "she sends several children to my school. Poor, pathetic little things, half-clad and wistful-eyed. They make my heart ache; they are so hungry for love, and so quick to learn."

As they passed the Burns farm, they looked for the wife, but she was not to be seen. The children had evidently gone up to the little white schoolhouse at the head of the lane. Radbourn let the reins fall slack as he talked on. He did not look at the girl; his eyebrows were drawn into a look of gloomy pain.

"It isn't so much the grime that I abhor, nor the labor that crooks their backs and makes their hands bludgeons. It's the horrible waste of life involved in it all. I don't believe God intended a man to be bent to plough-handles like that, but that isn't the worst of it. The worst of it is, these people live lives approaching automata. They become machines to serve others more lucky or more unscrupulous than themselves. What is the world of art, of music, of literature, to these poor devils,—to Sim Burns and his wife there, for example? Or even to the best of these farmers?"

The girl looked away over the shimmering lake of yellow-green corn. A choking came into her throat. Her gloved hand trembled.

"What is such a life worth? It's all very comfortable for us to say, 'They don't feel it.' How do we know what they feel? What do we know of their capacity for enjoyment of art and music? They never have leisure or opportunity. The master is very glad to be taught by preacher, and lawyer, and novelist, that his slaves are contented and never feel any longings for a higher life. These people live lives but little higher than their cattle—are *forced* to live so. Their hopes and aspirations are crushed out, their souls are twisted and deformed just as toil twists and deforms their bodies. They are on the same level as the city laborer. The very religion they hear is a soporific. They are taught to be content here that they may be happy hereafter. Suppose there isn't any hereafter?"

"Oh, don't say that, please!" Lily cried.

"But I don't *know* that there is," he went on remorselessly, "and I do know that these people are being robbed of something more than money, of all that makes life worth living. The promise of milk and honey in Canaan is all very well, but I prefer to have mine here; then I'm sure of it."

"What can we do?" murmured the girl.

"Do? Rouse these people for one thing; preach *discontent,* a noble discontent."

"It will only make them unhappy."

"No, it won't; not if you show them the way out. If it does, it's better to be unhappy striving for higher things, like a man, than to be content in a wallow like swine."

"But what *is* the way out?"

This was sufficient to set Radbourn upon his hobby-horse. He outlined his plan of action: the abolition of all indirect taxes, the State control of all privileges the private ownership of which interfered with the equal rights of all. He would utterly destroy speculative holdings of the earth. He would have land everywhere brought to its best use, by appropriating all ground rents to the use of the state, etc., etc., to which the girl listened with eager interest, but with only partial comprehension.

As they neared the little schoolhouse, a swarm of midgets in pink dresses, pink sun-bonnets, and brown legs, came rushing to meet their teacher, with that peculiar devotion the children in the country develop for a refined teacher.

Radbourn helped Lily out into the midst of the eager little scholars, who swarmed upon her like bees on a lump of sugar, till even Radbourn's gravity gave way, and he smiled into her lifted eyes,—an unusual smile, that strangely enough stopped the smile on her own lips, filling her face with a wistful shadow, and her breath came hard for a moment, and she trembled.

She loved that cold, stern face, oh, so much! and to have him smile was a pleasure that made her heart leap till she suffered a smothering pain. She turned to him to say:—

"I am very thankful, Mr. Radbourn, for another pleasant ride," adding in a lower tone, "it was a very great pleasure; you always give me so much. I feel stronger and more hopeful."

"I'm glad you feel so. I was afraid I was prosy with my land doctrine."

"Oh, no! Indeed no! You have given me a new hope; I am exalted with the thought; I shall try to think it all out and apply it."

And so they parted, the children looking on and slyly whispering among themselves. Radbourn looked back after a while, but the bare white hive had absorbed its little group, and was standing bleak as a tombstone and hot as a furnace on the naked plain in the blazing sun.

"America's pitiful boast!" said the young radical, looking back at it. "Only a miserable hint of what it might be."

All that forenoon, as Lily faced her noisy group of barefooted children, she was thinking of Radbourn, of his almost fierce sympathy for these poor, supine farmers, hopeless and in some cases content in their narrow lives. The children almost worshipped the beautiful girl who came to them as a revelation of exquisite neatness and taste,—whose very voice and intonation awed them.

They noted, unconsciously of course, every detail. Snowy linen, touches of soft color, graceful lines of bust and side, the slender fingers that could almost speak, so beautifully flexile were they. Lily herself sometimes, when she shook the calloused, knotted, stiffened hands of the women, shuddered with sympathetic pain to think that the crowning wonder and beauty of God's world should be so maimed and distorted from its true purpose.

Even in the children before her she could see the inherited results of fruitless labor, and, more pitiful yet, in the bent shoulders of the older ones she could see the beginnings of deformity that would soon be permanent; and as these thoughts came to her, she clasped the wondering children to her side, with a convulsive wish to make life a little brighter for them.

"How is your mother to-day?" she asked of Sadie Burns, as she was eating her luncheon on the drab-colored table near the open window.

"Purty well," said Sadie, in a hesitating way.

Lily was looking out, and listening to the gophers whistling as they raced to and fro. She could see Bob Burns lying at length on the grass in the pasture over the fence, his heels waving in the air, his hands holding a string which formed a snare. It was like fishing to young Izaak Walton.

It was very still and hot, and the cheep and trill of the gophers and the chatter of the kingbirds alone broke the silence. A cloud of butterflies were fluttering about a pool near; a couple of big flies buzzed and mumbled on the pane.

"What ails your mother?" Lily asked, recovering herself and looking at Sadie, who was distinctly ill at ease.

"Oh, I dunno," Sadie replied, putting one bare foot across the other.

Lily insisted.

"She 'n' pa's had an awful row—"

"Sadie!" said the teacher, warningly, "what language!"

"I mean they quarrelled, an' she don't speak to him any more."

"Why, how dreadful!"

"An' pa, he's awful cross; and she won't eat when he does, an' I haf to wait on table."

"I believe I'll go down and see her this noon," said Lily to herself, as she divined a little of the state of affairs in the Burns family.

V

Sim was mending the pasture fence as Lily came down the road toward him. He had delayed going to dinner to finish his task, and was just about ready to go when Lily spoke to him.

"Good morning, Mr. Burns. I am just going down to see Mrs. Burns. It must be time to go to dinner,—aren't you ready to go? I want to talk with you."

Ordinarily he would have been delighted with the idea of walk-

ing down the road with the schoolma'am, but there was something
in her look which seemed to tell him that she knew all about his
trouble, and, besides, he was not in good humor.

"Yes, in a minnit—soon's I fix up this hole. Them shotes, I b'lieve,
would go through a keyhole, if they could once get their snoots in."

He expanded on this idea as he nailed away, anxious to gain time.
He foresaw trouble for himself. He couldn't be rude to this sweet
and fragile girl. If a *man* had dared to attack him on his domestic
shortcomings, he could have fought. The girl stood waiting for him,
her large, steady eyes full of thought, gazing down at him from the
shadow of her broad-brimmed hat.

"The world is so full of misery anyway, that we ought to do the
best we can to make it less," she said at last, in a musing tone, as
if her thoughts had unconsciously taken on speech. She had always
appealed to him strongly, and never more so than in this softly uttered abstraction—that it was an abstraction added to its power with
him.

He could find no words for reply, but picked up his hammer and
nail-box, and slouched along the road by her side, listening without
a word to her talk.

"Christ was patient, and bore with his enemies. Surely we ought
to bear with our—friends," she went on, adapting her steps to his.
He took off his torn straw hat and wiped his face on his sleeve, being
much embarrassed and ashamed. Not knowing how to meet such
argument, he kept silent.

"How *is* Mrs. Burns!" said Lily at length, determined to make
him speak. The delicate meaning in the emphasis laid on *is* did not
escape him.

"Oh, she's all right—I mean she's done her work jest the same as
ever. I don't see her much—"

"I didn't know—I was afraid she was sick. Sadie said she was acting strangely."

"No, she's well enough—but—"

"But what is the trouble? Won't you let me help you, *won't* you?"
she pleaded.

"Can't anybody help us. We've got 'o fight it out, I s'pose," he replied, a gloomy note of resentment creeping into his voice. "She's
ben in a devil of a temper f'r a week."

"Haven't you been in the same kind of a temper too?" demanded
Lily, firmly but kindly. "I think most troubles of this kind come from
bad temper on both sides. Don't you? Have you done your share at
being kind and patient?"

They had reached the gate now, and she laid her hand on his arm to stop him. He looked down at the slender gloved hand on his arm, feeling as if a giant had grasped him; then he raised his eyes to her face, flushing a purplish red as he remembered his grossness. It seemed monstrous in the presence of this girl-advocate. Her face was like silver; her eyes seemed pools of tears.

"I don't s'pose I have," he said at last, pushing by her. He could not have faced her glance another moment. His whole air conveyed the impression of destructive admission. Lily did not comprehend the extent of her advantage or she would have pursued it further. As it was she felt a little hurt as she entered the house. The table was set, but Mrs. Burns was nowhere to be seen. Calling her softly, the young girl passed through the shabby little living-room to the oven-like bedroom which opened off it, but no one was about. She stood for a moment shuddering at the wretchedness of the room.

Going back to the kitchen, she found Sim about beginning on his dinner. Little Pet was with him; the rest of the children were at the schoolhouse.

"Where is she?"

"I d' know. Out in the garden, I expect. She don't eat with me now. I never see her. She don't come near *me*. I ain't seen her since Saturday."

Lily was shocked inexpressibly and began to see more clearly the magnitude of the task she had set herself to do. But it must be done; she felt that a tragedy was not far off. It must be averted.

"Mr. Burns, what have you done? What *have* you done?" she asked in terror and horror.

"Don't lay it all to *me!* She hain't done nawthin' but complain f'r ten years. I couldn't do nothin' to suit her. She was always naggin' me."

"I don't think Lucretia Burns would nag anybody. I don't say you're *all* to blame, but I'm afraid you haven't acknowledged you were *any* to blame. I'm afraid you've not been patient with her. I'm going out to bring her in. If she comes, will you *say* you were *part* to blame? You needn't beg her pardon—just say you'll try to be better. Will you do it? Think how much she has done for you! Will you?"

He remained silent, and looked discouragingly rude. His sweaty, dirty shirt was open at the neck, his arms were bare, his scraggly teeth were yellow with tobacco, and his uncombed hair lay tumbled about on his high, narrow head. His clumsy, unsteady hands played with the dishes on the table. His pride was struggling with his sense of justice; he knew he ought to consent, and yet it was so hard to acknowledge himself to blame. The girl went on in a voice piercingly sweet, trembling with pity and pleading.

"What word can I carry to her from you? I'm going to go and see her. If I could take a word from *you*, I know she would come back to the table. Shall I tell her you feel to blame?"

The answer was a long time coming; at last the man nodded an assent, the sweat pouring from his purple face. She had set him thinking; her victory was sure.

Lily almost ran out into the garden and to the strawberry patch, where she found Lucretia in her familiar, colorless, shapeless dress, picking berries in the hot sun, the mosquitoes biting her neck and hands.

"Poor, pathetic, dumb sufferer!" the girl thought as she ran up to her.

She dropped her dish as she heard Lily coming, and gazed up into the tender, pitying face. Not a word was spoken, but something she saw there made her eyes fill with tears, and her throat swell. It was pure sympathy. She put her arms around the girl's neck and sobbed for the first time since Friday night. Then they sat down on the grass under the hedge, and she told her story, interspersed with Lily's horrified comments.

When it was all told, the girl still sat listening. She heard Radbourn's calm, slow voice again. It helped her not to hate Burns; it helped her to pity and understand him.

"You must remember that such toil brutalizes a man; it makes him callous, selfish, unfeeling, necessarily. A fine nature must either adapt itself to its hard surroundings or die. Men who toil terribly in filthy garments day after day and year after year cannot easily keep gentle; the frost and grime, the heat and cold, will soon or late enter into their souls. The case is not all in favor of the suffering wives and against the brutal husbands. If the farmer's wife is dulled and crazed by her routine, the farmer himself is degraded and brutalized."

As well as she could Lily explained all this to the woman, who lay with her face buried in the girl's lap. Lily's arms were about her thin shoulders in an agony of pity.

"It's hard, Lucretia, I know,—more than you can bear,—but you mustn't forget what Sim endures too. He goes out in the storms and in the heat and dust. His boots are hard, and see how his hands are all bruised and broken by his work! He was tired and hungry when he said that—he didn't really mean it."

The wife remained silent.

"Mr. Radbourn says work, as things go now, *does* degrade a man in spite of himself. He says men get coarse and violent in spite of themselves, just as women do when everything goes wrong in the house,—when the flies are thick, and the fire won't burn, and the irons stick to the clothes. You see, you both suffer. Don't lay up this fit of temper against Sim—will you?"

The wife lifted her head and looked away. Her face was full of hopeless weariness.

"It ain't this once. It ain't that 't all. It's having no let-up. Just goin' the same thing right over 'n' over—no hope of anything better."

"If you had hope of another world—"

"Don't talk that. I don't want that kind o' comfort. I want a decent chance here. I want 'o rest an' be happy *now*." Lily's big eyes were streaming with tears. What should she say to the desperate woman? "What's the use? We might jest as well die—all of us."

The woman's livid face appalled the girl. She was gaunt, heavy-eyed, nerveless. Her faded dress settled down over her limbs, showing the swollen knees and thin calves; her hands, with distorted joints, protruded painfully from her sleeves. All about her was the ever recurring wealth and cheer of nature that knows no favor,—the bees and flies buzzing in the sun, the jay and the kingbird in the poplars, the smell of strawberries, the motion of lush grass, the shimmer of corn-blades tossed gayly as banners in a conquering army.

Like a flash of keener light, a sentence shot across the girl's mind: "Nature knows no title-deed. The bounty of her mighty hands falls as the sunlight falls, copious, impartial; her seas carry all ships; her air is for all lips, her lands for all feet."

"Poverty and suffering such as yours will not last." There was something in the girl's voice that roused the woman. She turned her dull eyes upon the youthful face.

Lily took her hand in both hers as if by a caress she could impart her own faith.

"Look up, dear. When nature is so good and generous, man must come to be better, surely. Come, go in the house again. Sim is there; he expects you; he told me to tell you he was sorry." Lucretia's face face twitched a little at that, but her head was bent. "Come; you can't live this way. There isn't any other place to go to."

No, that was the bitterest truth. Where on this wide earth, with its forth-shooting fruits and grains, its fragrant lands and shining seas, could this dwarfed, bent, broken, middle-aged woman go? Nobody wanted her, nobody cared for her. But the wind kissed her drawn lips as readily as those of the girl, and the blooms of clover nodded to her as if to a queen.

Lily had said all she could. Her heart ached with unspeakable pity and a sort of terror.

"Don't give up, Lucretia. This may be the worst hour of your life. Live and bear with it all for Christ's sake,—for your children's sake. Sim told me to tell you he was to blame. If you will only see that you are both to blame and yet neither to blame, then you can rise above it. Try, dear!"

Something that was in the girl imparted itself to the wife, electrically. She pulled herself together, rose silently, and started toward the house. Her face was rigid, but no longer sullen. Lily followed her slowly, wonderingly.

As she neared the kitchen door, she saw Sim still sitting at the table; his face was unusually grave and soft. She saw him start and shove back his chair, saw Lucretia go to the stove and lift the tea-pot, and heard her say, as she took her seat beside the baby:—

"Want some more tea?"

She had become a wife and mother again, but in what spirit the puzzled girl could not say.

GRACE ELIZABETH KING

* * *

Impelled through pride to correct George Washington Cable's allegedly false views of Creole character, Grace Elizabeth King (1851-1932) re-created through plotless narratives the traditions and manners of aristocratic society in New Orleans. Possessing some Creole blood, mixed with English, Scotch, and Irish, and spending virtually her whole life in New Orleans, she spoke authoritatively of its cultural life and social patterns. Her forte was the presentation of minute character studies in a romantic atmosphere; through her pages moves a succession of Creole ladies: Bonne Maman, Madame Josephine, Marie Modeste, Pupasse, and Mimi. Concern with locality led to historical work: for a quarter century she was secretary of the Louisiana Historical Society. Her later literary endeavors were social or historical studies of Florida, New Orleans, Louisiana, and Mt. Vernon. The following sketches from *Balcony Stories* (1893) are reprinted through the courtesy of Miss Nina Ausley King.

* * *

A Drama of Three

It was a regular dramatic performance every first of the month in the little cottage of the old General and Madame B——.

It began with the waking up of the General by his wife, standing at the bedside with a cup of black coffee.

"Hé! Ah! Oh, Honorine! Yes; the first of the month, and affairs —to be transacted."

On those mornings when affairs were to be transacted there was not much leisure for the household; and it was Honorine who constituted the household. Not the old dressing-gown and slippers, the old, old trousers, and the antediluvian neck-foulard of other days! Far from it. It was a case of warm water (with even a fling of cologne in it), of the trimming of beard and mustache by Honorine, and the black broadcloth suit, and the brown satin stock, and that *je ne sais quoi de dégagé* which no one could possess or assume like the old General. Whether he possessed or assumed it is an uncertainty which hung over the fine manners of all the gentlemen of his day, who were kept through their youth in Paris to cultivate *bon ton* and an education.

It was also something of a gala-day for Madame la Générale too, as it must be a gala-day for all old wives to see their husbands pranked in the manners and graces that had conquered their maidenhood, and exhaling once more that ambrosial fragrance which once so well incensed their compelling presence.

Ah, to the end a woman loves to celebrate her conquest! It is the last touch of misfortune with her to lose in the old, the ugly, and the commonplace her youthful lord and master. If one could look under the gray hairs and wrinkles with which time thatches old women, one would be surprised to see the flutterings, the quiverings, the thrills, the emotions, the coals of the heart-fires which death alone extinguishes, when he commands the tenant to vacate.

Honorine's hands chilled with the ice of sixteen as she approached scissors to the white mustache and beard. When her finger-tips brushed those lips, still well formed and roseate, she felt it, strange to say, on her lips. When she asperged the warm water with cologne, —it was her secret delight and greatest effort of economy to buy this cologne,—she always had one little moment of what she called faintness—that faintness which had veiled her eyes, and chained her hands, and stilled her throbbing bosom, when as a bride she came from the church with him. It was then she noticed the faint fragrance of the cologne bath. Her lips would open as they did then, and she would stand for a moment and think thoughts to which, it must be confessed, she looked forward from month to month. What a man he had been! In truth he belonged to a period that would accept nothing less from Nature than physical beauty; and Nature is ever subservient to the period. If it is to-day all small men, and to-morrow gnomes and dwarfs, we may know that the period is demanding them from Nature.

When the General had completed—let it be called no less than the ceremony of—his toilet, he took his chocolate and his *pain de*

Paris. Honorine could not imagine him breakfasting on anything but *pain de Paris*. Then he sat himself in his large armchair before his escritoire, and began transacting his affairs with the usual—

"But where is that idiot, that dolt, that sluggard, that snail, with my mail?"

Honorine, busy in the breakfast-room:

"In a moment, husband. In a moment."

"But he should be here now. It is the first of the month, it is nine o'clock, I am ready; he should be here."

"It is not yet nine o'clock, husband."

"Not yet nine! Not yet nine! Am I not up? Am I not dressed? Have I not breakfasted before nine?"

"That is so, husband. That is so."

Honorine's voice, prompt in cheerful acquiescence, came from the next room, where she was washing his cup, saucer, and spoon.

"It is getting worse and worse every day. I tell you, Honorine, Pompey must be discharged. He is worthless. He is trifling. Discharge him! Discharge him! Do not have him about! Chase him out of the yard! Chase him as soon as he makes his appearance! Do you hear, Honorine?"

"You must have a little patience, husband."

It was perhaps the only reproach one could make to Madame Honorine, that she never learned by experience.

"Patience! Patience! Patience is the invention of dullards and sluggards. In a well-regulated world there should be no need of such a thing as patience. Patience should be punished as a crime, or at least as a breach of the peace. Wherever patience is found police investigation should be made as for smallpox. Patience! Patience! I never heard the word—I assure you, I never heard the word in Paris. What do you think would be said there to the messenger who craved patience of you? Oh, they know too well in Paris—a rataplan from the walking-stick on his back, that would be the answer; and a, 'My good fellow, we are not hiring professors of patience, but legs.'"

"But husband, you must remember we do not hire Pompey. He only does it to oblige us, out of his kindness."

"Oblige us! Oblige me! Kindness! A Negro oblige me! Kind to me! That is it; that is it. That is the way to talk under the new régime. It is favor, and oblige, and education, and monsieur, and madame, now. What child's play to call this a country—a government! I would not be surprised"—jumping to his next position on this ever-recurring first of the month theme—"I would not be surprised if Pompey had failed to find the letter in the box. How do I know that the mail has not been tampered with? From day to day I expect to hear it. What is to prevent? Who is to interpose? The honesty of the officials? Honesty of the officials—that is good! What a farce—honesty of officials! That is evidently what has happened. The thought has not occurred to me in vain. Pompey has gone. He has not found the letter, and—well; that is the end."

But the General had still another theory to account for the delay in the appearance of his mail which he always posed abruptly after the exhaustion of the arraignment of the postoffice.

"And why not Journel?" Journel was their landlord, a fellow of means, but no extraction, and a favorite aversion of the old gentleman's. "Journel himself? You think he is above it, hé? You think Journel would not do such a thing? Ha! your simplicity, Honorine—your simplicity is incredible. It is miraculous. I tell you, I have known the Journels, from father to son, for—yes, for seventy-five years. Was not his grandfather the overseer on my father's plantation? I was not five years old when I began to know the Journels. And this fellow, I know him better than he knows himself. I know him as well as God knows him. I have made up my mind. I have made it up carefully that the first time that letter fails on the first of the month I shall have Journel arrested as a thief. I shall land him in the penitentiary. What! You think I shall submit to have my mail tampered with by a Journel? Their contents appropriated? What! You think there was no coincidence in Journel's offering me his postoffice box just the month—just the month, before those letters began to arrive? You think he did not have some inkling of them? Mark my words, Honorine, he did—by some of his subterranean methods. And all these five years he has been arranging his plans—that is all. He was arranging theft, which no doubt has been consummated to-day. Oh, I have regretted it—I assure you I have regretted it, that I did not promptly reject his proposition, that, in fact, I ever had anything to do with the fellow."

It was almost invariably, so regularly do events run in this world,—it was almost invariably that the Negro messenger made his appearance at this point. For five years the General had perhaps not been interrupted as many times, either above or below the last sentence. The mail, or rather the letter, was opened, and the usual amount—three ten-dollar bills—was carefully extracted and counted. And as if he scented the bills, even as the General said he did, within ten minutes after their delivery, Journel made his appearance to collect the rent.

It could only have been in Paris, among that old retired nobility, who counted their names back, as they expressed it, *"au de çà de déluge,"* that could have been acquired the proper manner of treating a *"roturier"* landlord: to measure him with the eyes from head to foot; to hand the rent—the ten-dollar bill—with the tips of the fingers; to scorn a look at the humbly tendered receipt; to say: "The cistern needs repairing, the roof leaks; I must warn you that unless such notifications meet with more prompt attention than in the past, you must look for another tenant," etc., in the monotonous tone of supremacy, and in the French, not of Journel's dictionary, nor the dictionary of any such as he, but in the French of Racine and Corneille; in the French of the above suggested circle, which inclosed the General's memory, if it had not inclosed—as he never tired of recounting—his starlike personality.

A sheet of paper always infolded the banknotes. It always bore, in fine but sexless tracery, "From one who owes you much."

There, that was it, that sentence, which, like a locomotive, bore the General and his wife far on these firsts of the month to two opposite points of the horizon, in fact, one from the other—"From one who owes you much."

The old gentleman would toss the paper aside with the bill receipt. In the man to whom the bright New Orleans itself almost owed its brightness, it was a paltry act to search and pick for a debtor. Friends had betrayed and deserted him; relatives had forgotten him; merchants had failed with his money; bank presidents had stooped to deceive him; for he was an old man, and had about run the gamut of human disappointments—a gamut that had begun with a C major of trust, hope, happiness, and money.

His political party had thrown him aside. Neither for ambassador, plenipotentiary, senator, congressman, not even for a clerkship, could he be nominated by it. Certes! "From one who owed him much." He had fitted the cap to a new head, the first of every month, for five years, and still the list was not exhausted. Indeed, it would have been hard for the General to look anywhere and not see some one whose obligations to him far exceeded this thirty dollars a month. Could he avoid being happy with such eyes?

But poor Madame Honorine! She who always gathered up the receipts, and the "From one who owes you much"; who could at an instant's warning produce the particular ones for any month of the past half-decade. She kept them filed, not only in her armoire, but the scrawled papers—skewered, as it were, somewhere else— where women from time immemorial have skewered such unsigned papers. She was not original in her thoughts—no more, for the matter of that, than the General was. Tapped at any time on the first of the month, when she would pause in her drudgery to reimpale her heart by a sight of the written characters on the scrap of paper, her thoughts would have been found flowing thus, "One can give everything, and yet be sure of nothing."

When Madame Honorine said "everything," she did not, as women in such cases often do, exaggerate. When she married the General, she in reality gave the youth of sixteen, the beauty (ah, do not trust the denial of those wrinkles, the thin hair, the faded eyes!) of an angel, the dot of an heiress. Alas! It was too little at the time. Had she in her own person united all the youth, all the beauty, all the wealth, sprinkled parsimoniously so far and wide over all the women in this land, would she at that time have done aught else with this than immolate it on the burning pyre of the General's affection? "And yet be sure of nothing."

It is not necessary, perhaps, to explain that last clause. It is very little consolation for wives that their husbands have forgotten, when some one else remembers. Some one else! Ah! there could be so many some one elses in the General's life, for in truth he had been irresistible to excess. But this was one particular some one else who had been faithful for five years. Which one?

When Madame Honorine solves that enigma, she has made up her mind how to act.

As for Journel, it amused him more and more. He would go away from the little cottage rubbing his hands with pleasure (he never saw Madame Honorine, by the way, only the General). He would have given far more than thirty dollars a month for this drama; for he was not only rich, but a great *farceur*.

La Grande Demoiselle

THAT was what she was called by everybody as soon as she was seen or described. Her name, besides baptismal titles, was Idalie Sainte Foy Mortemart des Islets. When she came into society, in the brilliant little world of New Orleans, it was the event of the season, and after she came in, whatever she did became also events. Whether she went, or did not go; what she said, or did not say; what she wore, and did not wear—all these became important matters of discussion, quoted as much or more than what the president said, or the governor thought. And in those days, the days of '59, New Orleans was not, as it is now, a one-heiress place, but it may be said that one could find heiresses then as one finds typewriting girls now.

Mademoiselle Idalie received her birth, and what education she had, on her parents' plantation, the famed old Reine Sainte Foy place, and it is no secret that, like the ancient kings of France, her birth exceeded her education.

It was a plantation, the Reine Sainte Foy, the richness and luxury of which are really well described in those perfervid pictures of tropical life, at one time the passion of philanthropic imaginations, excited and exciting over the horrors of slavery. Although these pictures were then often accused of being purposely exaggerated, they seem now to fall short of, instead of surpassing, the truth. Stately walls, acres of roses, miles of oranges, unmeasured fields of cane, colossal sugar-house—they were all there, and all the rest of it, with the slaves, slaves, slaves everywhere, whole villages of Negro cabins. And there were also, most noticeable to the natural, as well as to the visionary, eye—there were the ease, idleness, extravagance, self-indulgence, pomp, pride, arrogance, in short the whole enumeration, the moral *sine qua non,* as some people considered it, of the wealthy slaveholder of aristocratic descent and tastes.

What Mademoiselle Idalie cared to learn she studied, what she did not she ignored; and she followed the same simple rule untrammeled in her eating, drinking, dressing, and comportment generally; and whatever discipline may have been exercised on the place, either in fact or fiction, most assuredly none of it, even so much as in a threat, ever attained her sacred person. When she was just turned sixteen, Mademoiselle Idalie made up her mind to go into society. Whether she was beautiful or not, it is hard to say. It is almost impossible to appreciate properly the beauty of the rich, the very rich. The unfettered development, the limitless choice of accessories, the confidence, the self-esteem, the sureness of expression, the simplicity of purpose, the ease of execution—all these produce a certain effect of beauty behind which one really cannot get to measure length of nose, or brilliancy of eye. This much can be said: there was nothing in her that positively contradicted any assumption of beauty on her part, or credit of it on the part of others. She was very tall and very thin with small head, long neck, black eyes, and abundant straight black hair,—for which her hair-dresser deserved more praise than she,—good teeth, of course, and a mouth that, even in prayer, talked nothing but commands; that is about all she had *en fait*

d'ornements, as the modistes say. It may be added that she walked
as if the Reine Sainte Foy plantation extended over the whole earth,
and the soil of it were too vile for her tread. Of course she did not
buy her toilets in New Orleans. Everything was ordered from Paris,
and came as regularly through the customhouse as the modes and
robes to the milliners. She was furnished by a certain house there,
just as one of a royal family would be at the present day. As this
had lasted from her layette up to her sixteenth year, it may be imagined what took place when she determined to make her début. Then
it was literally, not metaphorically, *carte blanche,* at least so it got
to the ears of society. She took a sheet of notepaper, wrote the date
at the top, added, "I make my début in November," signed her name
at the extreme end of the sheet, addressed it to her dressmaker in
Paris, and sent it.

It was said that in her dresses the very handsomest silks were used
for linings, and that real lace was used where others put imitation,
—around the bottoms of the skirts, for instance,—and silk ribbons of
the best quality served the purposes of ordinary tapes; and sometimes the buttons were of real gold and silver, sometimes set with
precious stones. Not that she ordered these particulars, but the dress-
makers, when given *carte blanche* by those who do not condescend
to details, so soon exhaust the outside limits of garments that perforce
they take to plastering them inside with gold, so to speak, and, when
the bill goes in, they depend upon the furnishings to carry out a
certain amount of the contract in justifying the price. And it was
said that these costly dresses, after being worn once or twice, were
cast aside, thrown upon the floor, given to the Negroes—anything to
get them out of sight. Not an inch of the real lace, not one of the
jeweled buttons, not a scrap of ribbon, was ripped off to save. And
it was said that if she wanted to romp with her dogs in all her
finery, she did it; she was known to have ridden horseback, one
moonlight night, all around the plantation in a white silk dinner-dress
flounced with Alençon. And at night, when she came from the balls,
tired, tired to death as only balls can render one, she would throw
herself down upon her bed in her tulle skirts,—on top, or not, of
the exquisite flowers, she did not care,—and make her maid undress
her in that position; often having her bodices cut off her, because
she was too tired to turn over and have them unlaced.

That she was admired, raved about, loved even, goes without saying.
After the first month she held the refusal of half the beaux of New
Orleans. Men did absurd, undignified, preposterous things for her;
and she? Love? Marry? The idea never occurred to her. She treated

the most exquisite of her pretenders no better than she treated her Paris gowns, for the matter of that. She could not even bring herself to listen to a proposal patiently; whistling to her dogs, in the middle of the most ardent protestations, or jumping up and walking away with a shrug of the shoulders, and a "Bah!"

Well! Every one knows what happened after '59. There is no need to repeat. The history of one is the history of all. But there was this difference—for there is every shade of difference in misfortune, as there is every shade of resemblance in happiness. Mortemart des Islets went off to fight. That was natural; his family had been doing that, he thought, or said, ever since Charlemagne. Just as naturally he was killed in the first engagement. They, his family, were always among the first killed; so much so that it began to be considered assassination to fight a duel with any of them. All that was in the ordinary course of events. One difference in their misfortunes lay in that after the city was captured, their plantation, so near, convenient, and rich in all kinds of provisions, was selected to receive a contingent of troops—a colored company. If it had been a colored company raised in Louisiana it might have been different; and these Negroes mixed with the Negroes in the neighborhood,—and Negroes are no better than whites, for the proportion of good and bad among them,—and the officers were always off duty when they should have been on, and on when they should have been off.

One night the dwelling caught fire. There was an immediate rush to save the ladies. Oh, there was no hesitation about that! They were seized in their beds, and carried out in the very arms of their enemies; carried away off to the sugar-house, and deposited there. No danger of their doing anything but keep very quiet and still in their *chemises de nuit,* and their one sheet apiece, which was about all that was saved from the conflagration—that is, for them. But it must be remembered that this is all hearsay. When one has not been present, one knows nothing of one's own knowledge; one can only repeat. It has been repeated, however, that although the house was burned to the ground, and everything in it destroyed, wherever, for a year afterward, a man of that company or of that neighborhood was found, there could have been found also, without search-warrant, property that had belonged to the Des Islets. That is the story; and it is believed or not, exactly according to prejudice.

How the ladies ever got out of the sugar-house, history does not relate; nor what they did. It was not a time for sociability, either personal or epistolary. At one offensive word your letter, and you, very likely, examined; and Ship Island for a hotel, with soldiers for hostesses! Madame Des Islets died very soon after the accident—of rage, they say; and that was about all the public knew.

Indeed, at that time the society of New Orleans had other things to think about than the fate of the Des Islets. As for *la grande demoiselle,* she had prepared for her own oblivion in the hearts of her female friends. And the gentlemen,—her *preux chevaliers,*—they were burning with other passions than those which had driven them to her knees, encountering a little more serious response than "bahs" and shrugs. And, after all, a woman seems the quickest thing forgotten when once the important affairs of life come to men for consideration.

It might have been ten years according to some calculations, or ten eternities,—the heart and the almanac never agree about time,— but one morning old Champigny (they used to call him Champignon) was walking along his levee front, calculating how soon the water would come over, and drown him out, as the Louisianians say. It was before a seven-o'clock breakfast, cold, wet, rainy, and discouraging. The road was knee-deep in mud, and so broken up with hauling that it was like walking upon waves to get over it. A shower poured down. Old Champigny was hurrying in when he saw a figure approaching. He had to stop to look at it, for it was worth while. The head was hidden by a green *barège* veil, which the showers had plentifully besprinkled with dew; a tall, thin figure. Figure! No; not even could it be called a figure: straight up and down, like a finger or a post; high-shouldered, and a step—a step like a plow-man's. No umbrella; no—nothing more, in fact. It does not sound so peculiar as when first related—something must be forgotten. The feet—oh, yes, the feet—they were like waffle-irons, or frying-pans, or anything of that shape.

Old Champigny did not care for women—he never had; they simply did not exist for him in the order of nature. He had been married once, it is true, about a half century before; but that was not reckoned against the existence of his prejudice, because he was *célibataire* to his finger-tips, as any one could see a mile away. But that woman intrigued him.

He had no servant to inquire from. He performed all of his own domestic work in the wretched little cabin that replaced his old home. For Champigny also belonged to the great majority of the *nouveaux pauvres.* He went out into the rice-field, where were one or two hands that worked on shares with him, and he asked them. They knew immediately; there is nothing connected with the parish that a field-hand does not know at once. She was the teacher of the colored public school some three or four miles away. "Ah," thought Champigny, "some Northern lady on a mission." He watched to see her return in the evening, which she did, of course; in a blinding rain. Imagine the green *barège* veil then; for it remained always down over her face.

Old Champigny could not get over it that he had never seen her before. But he must have seen her, and, with his abstraction and old age, not have noticed her, for he found out from the Negroes that she had been teaching four or five years there. And he found out also—how, is not important—that she was Idalie Sainte Foy Mortemart des Islets. *La grande demoiselle!* He had never known her in the old days, owing to his uncomplimentary attitude toward women, but he knew of her, of course, and of her family. It should have been said that his plantation was about fifty miles higher up the river, and on the opposite bank to Reine Sainte Foy. It seemed terrible. The old gentleman had had reverses of his own, which would bear the telling, but nothing was more shocking to him than this—that Idalie Sainte Foy Mortemart des Islets should be teaching a public colored school for—it makes one blush to name it—seven dollars and a half a month. For seven dollars and a half a month to teach a set of—well! He found out where she lived, a little cabin—not so much worse than his own, for that matter—in the corner of a field; no companion, no servant, nothing but food and shelter. Her clothes have been described.

Only the good God himself knows what passed in Champigny's mind on the subject. We know only the results. He went and married *la grande demoiselle.* How? Only the good God knows that too. Every first of the month, when he goes to the city to buy provisions, he takes her with him—in fact, he takes her everywhere with him.

Passengers on the railroad know them well, and they always have a chance to see her face. When she passes her old plantation *la grande demoiselle* always lifts her veil for one instant—the inevitable green *barège* veil. What a face! Thin, long, sallow, petrified! And the neck! If she would only tie something around the neck! And her plain, coarse cottonade gown! The Negro women about her were better dressed than she.

Poor old Champignon! It was not an act of charity to himself, no doubt cross and disagreeable, besides being ugly. And as for love, gratitude!

KATE CHOPIN

*   *   *

Striking incidents in the emotional life of Red River Creoles and their Negro neighbors are dramatically presented in brilliant stories by Kate O'Flaherty Chopin (1851-1904). The character portraiture of these descendants of Grand Pré Acadians, vitalized by accuracy of dialect and faithfulness to proud traditions, constitutes the basic appeal in her work. Born in St. Louis of a Celtic father and a Creole mother, she spent her married years in New Orleans and Natchitoches Parish. Later in St. Louis she wrote *At Fault* (1890), a novel, and three collections of stories, two of which were published in book form. The morbid realism of *The Awakening* (1899), her second novel, evoked hostile criticism and for a time discouraged further writing. "Désirée's Baby," from *Bayou Folk* (1894), one of America's finest short stories, progresses steadily to the culminating sentence with an inevitability deriving from sheer genius. This and "A Gentleman of Bayou Têche" are reprinted by permission of Houghton Mifflin Company, and "Nég Créol" through the courtesy of Felix and George F. Chopin.

*   *   *

Désirée's Baby

As the day was pleasant, Madame Valmondé drove over to L'Abri to see Désirée and the baby.

It made her laugh to think of Désirée with a baby. Why, it seemed but yesterday that Désirée was but little more than a baby herself; when Monsieur in riding through the gateway of Valmondé had found her lying asleep in the shadow of the big stone pillar.

The little one awoke in his arms and began to cry for "Dada." That was as much as she could do or say. Some people thought that she might have strayed there of her own accord, for she was of the toddling age. The prevailing belief was that she had been purposely left by a party of Texans, whose canvas-covered wagon, late in the day, had crossed the ferry that Cotton Maïs kept, just below the plantation. In time Madame Valmondé abandoned every speculation but the one that Désirée had been sent her by a beneficent Providence to be the child of her affection, seeing that she was without child of flesh. For the girl grew to be beautiful and gentle, affectionate and sincere—the idol of Valmondé.

It was no wonder, when she stood one day against the stone pillar in whose shadow she had lain asleep, eighteen years before, that Armand Aubigny riding by and seeing her there, had fallen in love with her. This was the way all the Aubignys fell in love, as if struck by a pistol shot. The wonder was that he had not loved her before; for he had known her since his father brought him home from Paris, a boy of eight, after his mother died there. The passion that awoke in him that day, when he saw her at the gate, swept along like an avalanche, or a prairie fire, or like anything that drives headlong over all obstacles.

Monsieur Valmondé grew practical and wanted things well considered: that is, the girl's obscure origin. Armand looked into her eyes and did not care. He was reminded that she was nameless. What did it matter about a name when he could give her one of the oldest and proudest in Louisiana? He ordered the *corbeille* from Paris, and contained himself with what patience he could until it arrived.

Madame Valmondé had not seen Désirée and the baby for four weeks. When she reached L'Abri, she shuddered at first sight of it, as she always did. It was a sad-looking place, which for many years had not known the gentle presence of a mistress, old Monsieur Aubigny having married and buried his wife in France, and she having loved her own land too well ever to leave it. The roof came down steep and black like a cowl, reaching out beyond the wide galleries that encircled the yellow stuccoed house. Big, solemn oaks grew close to it, and their thick-leaved, far-reaching branches shadowed it like a pall. Young Aubigny's rule was a strict one, too, and under it his Negroes had forgotten how to be gay, as they had been during the old master's easy-going and indulgent lifetime.

The young mother was recovering slowly, and lay full length, in her soft white muslins and laces, upon a couch. The baby was beside her, upon her arm, where he had fallen asleep, at her breast. The yellow nurse woman sat beside a window fanning herself.

Madame Valmondé bent her portly figure over Désirée and kissed her, holding her an instant tenderly in her arms. Then she turned to the child.

"This is not the baby!" she exclaimed in startled tones. French was the language spoken at Valmondé in those days.

"I knew you would be astonished," laughed Désirée, "at the way he has grown. The little *cochon de lait!* Look at his legs, mama, and his hands and finger-nails—real finger-nails. Zandrine had to cut them this morning. Isn't it true, Zandrine?"

The woman bowed her turbaned head majestically, *"Mais si, Madame."*

"And the way he cries," went on Désirée, "is deafening. Armand heard him the other day as far away as La Blanche's cabin."

Madame Valmondé had never removed her eyes from the child. She lifted it and walked with it to the window that was lightest. She scanned the baby narrowly, then looked searchingly at Zandrine, whose face was turned to gaze across the fields.

"Yes, the child has grown, has changed," said Madame Valmondé, slowly, as she replaced it beside its mother. "What does Armand say?"

Désirée's face became suffused with a glow that was happiness itself.

"Oh, Armand is the proudest father in the parish, I believe, chiefly because it is a boy, to bear his name; though he says not—that he would have loved a girl as well. But I know it isn't true. I know he says that to please me. And mama," she added, drawing Madame Valmondé's head down to her, and speaking in a whisper, "he hasn't punished one of them—not one of them—since baby is born. Even Négrillon, who pretended to have burnt his leg that he might rest from work—he only laughed, and said Négrillon was a great scamp. Oh, mama, I'm so happy; it frightens me."

What Désirée said was true. Marriage, and later the birth of his son, had softened Armand Aubigny's imperious and exacting nature greatly. This was what made the gentle Désirée so happy, for she loved him desperately. When he frowned she trembled, but loved him. When he smiled, she asked no greater blessing of God. But Armand's dark, handsome face had not been disfigured by frowns since the day he fell in love with her.

When the baby was about three months old, Désirée awoke one day to the conviction that there was something in the air menacing her peace. It was at first too subtle to grasp. It had only been a

disquieting suggestion; an air of mystery among the blacks; unexpected visits from far-off neighbors who could hardly account for
their coming. Then a strange, an awful change in her husband's manner, which she dared not ask him to explain. When he spoke to her,
it was with averted eyes, from which the old love-light seemed to
have gone out. He absented himself from home; and when there,
avoided her presence and that of her child, without excuse. And
the very spirit of Satan seemed suddenly to take hold of him in his
dealings with the slaves. Désirée was miserable enough to die.

She sat in her room, one hot afternoon, in her *peignoir,* listlessly
drawing through her fingers the strands of her long, silky brown hair
that hung about her shoulders. The baby, half naked, lay asleep upon
her own great mahogany bed, that was like a sumptuous throne,
with its satin-lined half-canopy. One of La Blanche's little quadroon
boys—half naked too—stood fanning the child slowly with a fan of
peacock feathers. Désirée's eyes had been fixed absently and sadly
upon the baby, while she was striving to penetrate the threatening mist
that she felt was closing about her. She looked from her child to
the boy who stood beside him, and back again; over and over. "Ah!"
It was a cry that she could not help; which she was not conscious
of having uttered. The blood turned like ice in her veins, and a
clammy moisture gathered upon her face.

She tried to speak to the little quadroon boy; but no sound would
come, at first. When he heard his name uttered, he looked up, and
his mistress was pointing to the door. He laid aside the great, soft
fan, and obediently stole away over the polished floor, on his bare
tiptoes.

She stayed motionless, with gaze riveted upon her child, and her
face the picture of fright.

Presently her husband entered the room, and without noticing her,
went to a table and began to search among some papers which covered it.

"Armand," she called to him, in a voice which must have stabbed
him, if he was human. But he did not notice. "Armand," she said
again. Then she rose and tottered towards him. "Armand," she panted
once more, "look at our child. What does it mean? Tell me."

He coldly but gently loosened her fingers from about his arm and
thrust her hand away from him. "Tell me what it means!" she cried
despairingly.

"It means," he answered lightly, "that the child is not white; it
means that you are not white."

A quick conception of all that this accusation meant for her nerved her with unwonted courage to deny it. "It is a lie; it is not true, I am white! Look at my hair, it is brown; and my eyes are grey, Armand, you know they are grey. And my skin is fair," seizing his wrist. "Look at my hand; whiter than yours, Armand," she laughed hysterically.

"As white as La Blanche's," he returned cruelly; and went away leaving her alone with their child.

When she could hold a pen in her hand, she sent a despairing letter to Madame Valmondé.

"My mother, they tell me I am not white. Armand has told me that I am not white. For God's sake tell them it is not true. You must know it is not true. I shall die. I must die. I cannot be so unhappy, and live."

The answer that came was brief:

"My own Désirée: Come home to Valmondé; back to your mother who loves you. Come with your child."

When the letter reached Désirée, she went with it to her husband's study, and laid it open upon the desk before which he sat. She was like a stone image: silent, white, motionless after she placed it there.

In silence he ran his cold eyes over the written words. He said nothing. "Shall I go, Armand?" she asked in tones sharp with agonized suspense.

"Yes, go."

"Do you want me to go?"

"Yes, I want you to go."

He thought Almighty God had dealt cruelly and unjustly with him, and felt, somehow, that he was paying Him back in kind when he stabbed thus into his wife's soul. Moreover, he no longer loved her, because of the unconscious injury she had brought upon his home and name.

She turned away like one stunned by a blow, and walked slowly towards the door, hoping he would call her back.

"Good-by, Armand," she moaned.

He did not answer her. That was his last blow at fate.

Désirée went in search of her child. Zandrine was pacing the sombre gallery with it. She took the little one from the nurse's arms with no word of explanation, and descending the steps, walked away, under the live-oak branches.

It was an October afternoon; the sun was just sinking. Out in the still fields the Negroes were picking cotton.

Désirée had not changed the thin white garment nor the slippers which she wore. Her hair was uncovered and the sun's rays brought a golden gleam from its brown meshes. She did not take the broad, beaten road which led to the far-off plantation of Valmondé. She walked across a deserted field, where the stubble bruised her tender feet, so delicately shod, and tore her thin gown to shreds.

She disappeared among the reeds and willows that grew thick along the banks of the deep, sluggish bayou; and she did not come back again.

. . . .

Some weeks later there was a curious scene enacted at L'Abri. In the center of the smoothly swept back yard was a great bonfire. Armand Aubigny sat in the wide hallway that commanded a view of the spectacle; and it was he who dealt out to half a dozen Negroes the material which kept this fire ablaze.

A graceful cradle of willow, with all its dainty furbishings, was laid upon the pyre, which had already been fed with the richness of a priceless *layette*. Then there were silk gowns, and velvet and satin ones added to these; laces, too, and embroideries; bonnets and gloves; for the *corbeille* had been of rare quality.

The last thing to go was a tiny bundle of letters; innocent little scribblings that Désirée had sent to him during the days of their espousal. There was the remnant of one back in the drawer from which he took them. But it was not Désirée's; it was part of an old letter from his mother to his father. He read it. She was thanking God for the blessing of her husband's love:

"But, above all," she wrote, "night and day, I thank the good God for having so arranged our lives that our dear Armand will never know that his mother, who adores him, belongs to the race that is cursed with the brand of slavery."

A Gentleman of Bayou Têche

IT was no wonder Mr. Sublet, who was staying at the Hallet plantation, wanted to make a picture of Evariste. The 'Cadian was rather a picturesque subject in his way, and a tempting one to an artist looking for bits of "local color" along the Têche.

Mr. Sublet had seen the man on the back gallery just as he came out of the swamp, trying to sell a wild turkey to the housekeeper. He spoke to him at once, and in the course of conversation engaged him to return to the house the following morning and have his picture drawn. He handed Evariste a couple of silver dollars to show that his intentions were fair, and that he expected the 'Cadian to keep faith with him.

"He tell' me he want' put my picture in one fine '*Mag*'zine,' " said Evariste to his daughter, Martinette, when the two were talking the matter over in the afternoon. "W'at fo' you reckon he want' do dat?" They sat within the low, homely cabin of two rooms, that was not quite so comfortable as Mr. Hallet's Negro quarters.

Martinette pursed her red lips that had little sensitive curves to them, and her black eyes took on a reflective expression.

"Mebbe he yeard 'bout that big fish w'at you ketch las' winta in Carancro lake. You know it was all wrote about in the 'Suga Bowl.' " Her father set aside the suggestion with a deprecatory wave of the hand.

"Well, anyway, you got to fix yo'se'f up," declared Martinette, dismissing further speculation; "put on yo' otha pant'loon' an' yo' good coat; an' you betta ax Mr. Léonce to cut yo' hair, an' yo' w'sker' a li'le bit."

"It's w'at I say," chimed in Evariste. "I tell dat gent'man I'm goin' make myse'f fine. He say', 'No, no,' like he ent please'. He want' me like I come out de swamp. So much betta if my pant'loon' an' coat is tore, he say, an' color' like de mud." They could not understand these eccentric wishes on the part of the strange gentleman, and made no effort to do so.

An hour later Martinette, who was quite puffed up over the affair, trotted across to Aunt Dicey's cabin to communicate the news to her. The Negress was ironing; her irons stood in a long row before the fire of logs that burned on the hearth. Martinette seated herself in the chimney corner and held her feet up to the blaze; it was damp and a little chilly out of doors. The girl's shoes were considerably worn and her garments were a little too thin and scant for the winter season. Her father had given her the two dollars he had received from the artist, and Martinette was on her way to the store to invest them as judiciously as she knew how.

"You know, Aunt Dicey," she began a little complacently after listening awhile to Aunt Dicey's unqualified abuse of her own son, Wilkins, who was dining-room boy at Mr. Hallet's, "you know that stranger gentleman up to Mr. Hallet's? he want' to make my popa's picture; an' he say' he goin' put it in one fine *Mag*'zine yonda."

Aunt Dicey spat upon her iron to test its heat. Then she began to snicker. She kept on laughing inwardly, making her whole fat body shake, and saying nothing.

"W'at you laughin' 'bout, Aunt Dice?" inquired Martinette mistrustfully.

"I is n' laughin', chile!"

"Yas, you' laughin'."

"Oh, don't pay no 'tention to me. I jis studyin' how simple you an' yo' pa is. You is bof de simplest somebody I eva come 'crost."

"You got to say plumb out w'at you mean, Aunt Dice," insisted the girl doggedly, suspicious and alert now.

"Well, dat w'y I say you is simple," proclaimed the woman, slamming down her iron on an inverted, battered pie pan, "jis like you says, dey gwine put yo' pa's picture yonda in de picture paper. An' you know w'at readin' dey gwine sot down on'neaf dat picture?" Martinette was intensely attentive. "Dey gwine sot down on'neaf: 'Dis heah is one dem low-down 'Cajuns o' Bayeh Têche!'"

The blood flowed from Martinette's face, leaving it deathly pale; in another instant it came beating back in a quick flood, and her eyes smarted with pain as if the tears that filled them had been fiery hot.

"I knows dem kine o' folks," continued Aunt Dicey, resuming her interrupted ironing. "Dat stranger he got a li'le boy w'at ain't none too big to spank. Dat li'le imp he come a hoppin' in heah yistiddy wid a kine o' box on'neaf his arm. He say, 'Good mo'nin', madam. Will you be so kine an' stan' jis like you is dah at yo' i'onin', an' lef me take yo' picture?' I 'lowed I gwine make a picture outen him wid dis heah flati'on, ef he don' clar hisse'f quick. An' he say he baig my pardon fo' his intrudement. All dat kine o' talk to a ole nigga 'oman! Dat plainly sho' he don' know his place."

"W'at you want 'im to say, Aunt Dice?" asked Martinette, with an effort to conceal her distress.

"I wants 'im to come in heah an' say: 'Howdy, Aunt Dicey! will you be so kine and go put on yo' noo calker dress an' yo' bonnit w'at you w'ars to meetin', an' stan' 'side f'om dat i'onin'-boa'd w'ilse I gwine take yo' photygraph.' Dat de way fo' a boy to talk w'at had good raisin'."

Martinette had arisen, and began to take slow leave of the woman. She turned at the cabin door to observe tentatively: "I reckon it's Wilkins tells you how the folks they talk, yonda up to Mr. Hallet's."

She did not go to the store as she had intended, but walked with a dragging step back to her home. The silver dollars clicked in her pocket as she walked. She felt like flinging them across the field; they seemed to her somehow the price of shame.

The sun had sunk, and twilight was settling like a silver beam upon the bayou and enveloping the fields in a gray mist. Evariste, slim and slouchy, was waiting for his daughter in the cabin door. He had lighted a fire of sticks and branches, and placed the kettle before it to boil. He met the girl with his slow, serious, questioning eyes, astonished to see her empty-handed.

"How come you didn' bring nuttin' f'om de sto', Martinette?"

She entered and flung her gingham sun-bonnet upon a chair. "No, I didn' go yonda;" and with sudden exasperation: "You got to go take back that money; you mus'n' git no picture took."

"But, Martinette," her father mildly interposed, "I promise' 'im; an' he's goin' give me some mo' money w'en he finish."

"If he give you a ba'el o' money, you mus'n' git no picture took. You know w'at he want to put un'neath that picture, fo' ev'body to read?" She could not tell him the whole hideous truth as she had heard it distorted from Aunt Dicey's lips; she would not hurt him that much. "He's goin' to write: 'This is one *'Cajun* o' the Bayou Têche.'" Evariste winced.

"How you know?" he asked.

"I yeard so. I know it's true."

The water in the kettle was boiling. He went and poured a small quantity upon the coffee which he had set there to drip. Then he said to her: "I reckon you jus' as well go care dat two dolla' back, tomo' mo'nin'; me, I'll go yonda ketch a mess o' fish in Carancro lake."

Mr. Hallet and a few masculine companions were assembled at a rather late breakfast the following morning. The dining-room was a big, bare one, enlivened by a cheerful fire of logs that blazed in the wide chimney on massive andirons. There were guns, fishing tackle, and other implements of sport lying about. A couple of fine dogs strayed unceremoniously in and out behind Wilkins, the Negro boy who waited upon the table. The chair beside Mr. Sublet, usually occupied by his little son, was vacant, as the child had gone for an early morning outing and had not yet returned.

When breakfast was about half over, Mr. Hallet noticed Martinette standing outside upon the gallery. The dining-room door had stood open more than half the time.

"Isn't that Martinette out there, Wilkins?" inquired the jovial-faced young planter.

"Dat's who, suh," returned Wilkins. "She ben standin' dah sence mos' sun-up; look like she studyin' to take root to de gall'ry."

"What in the name of goodness does she want? Ask her what she wants. Tell her to come in to the fire."

Martinette walked into the room with much hesitancy. Her small, brown face could hardly be seen in the depths of the gingham sunbonnet. Her blue cottonade skirt scarcely reached the thin ankles that it should have covered.

"Bonjou'," she murmured, with a little comprehensive nod that took in the entire company. Her eyes searched the table for the "stranger gentleman," and she knew him at once, because his hair was parted in the middle and he wore a pointed beard. She went and laid the two silver dollars beside his plate and motioned to retire without a word of explanation.

"Hold on, Martinette!" called out the planter, "what's all this pantomime business? Speak out, little one."

"My popa don't want any picture took," she offered, a little timorously. On her way to the door she had looked back to say this. In that fleeting glance she detected a smile of intelligence pass from one to the other of the group. She turned quickly, facing them all, and spoke out, excitement making her voice bold and shrill: "My popa ent one low-down 'Cajun. He ent goin' to stan' to have that kine o' writin' put down un'neath his picture!"

She almost ran from the room, half blinded by the emotion that had helped her to make so daring a speech.

Descending the gallery steps she ran full against her father who was ascending, bearing in his arms the little boy, Archie Sublet. The child was most grotesquely attired in garments far too large for his diminutive person—the rough jeans clothing of some Negro boy. Evariste himself had evidently been taking a bath without the preliminary ceremony of removing his clothes, that were now half dried upon his person by the wind and sun.

"Yere you' li'le boy," he announced, stumbling into the room. "You ought not lef dat li'le chile go by hisse'f *comme ça* in de pirogue." Mr. Sublet darted from his chair, the others following suit almost as hastily. In an instant, quivering with apprehension, he had his little son in his arms. The child was quite unharmed, only somewhat pale and nervous, as the consequence of a recent very serious ducking.

Evariste related in his uncertain, broken English how he had been fishing for an hour or more in Carancro lake, when he noticed the boy paddling over the deep, black water in a shell-like pirogue. Nearing a clump of cypress-trees that rose from the lake, the pirogue became entangled in the heavy moss that hung from the tree limbs and trailed upon the water. The next thing he knew, the boat had over-turned, he heard the child scream, and saw him disappear beneath the still, black surface of the lake.

"W'en I done swim to de sho' wid 'im," continued Evariste, "I hurry yonda to Jake Baptiste's cabin, an' we rub 'im an' warm 'im up, an' dress 'im up dry like you see. He all right now, M'sieur; but you mus'n lef 'im go no mo' by hisse'f in one pirogue."

Martinette had followed into the room behind her father. She was feeling and tapping his wet garments solicitously, and begging him in French to come home. Mr. Hallet at once ordered hot coffee and a warm breakfast for the two; and they sat down at the corner of the table, making no manner of objection in their perfect simplicity. It was with visible reluctance and ill-disguised contempt that Wilkins served them.

When Mr. Sublet had arranged his son comfortably, with tender care, upon the sofa, and had satisfied himself that the child was quite uninjured, he attempted to find words with which to thank Evariste for this service which no treasure of words or gold could pay for. These warm and heartfelt expressions seemed to Evariste to exag-gerate the importance of his action, and they intimidated him. He at-tempted shyly to hide his face as well as he could in the depths of his bowl of coffee.

"You will let me make your picture now, I hope, Evariste," begged Mr. Sublet, laying his hand upon the 'Cadian's shoulder. "I want to place it among things I hold most dear, and shall call it 'A hero of Bayou Têche.'" This assurance seemed to distress Evariste greatly.

"No, no," he protested, "it's nuttin' hero' to take a li'le boy out de water. I jus' as easy do dat like I stoop down an' pick up a li'le chile w'at fall down in de road. I ent goin' to 'low dat, me. I don't git no picture took, va!"

Mr. Hallet, who now discerned his friend's eagerness in the mat-ter, came to his aid.

"I tell you, Evariste, let Mr. Sublet draw your picture, and you yourself may call it whatever you want. I'm sure he'll let you."

"Most willingly," agreed the artist.

Evariste glanced up at him with shy and child-like pleasure. "It's a bargain?" he asked.

"A bargain," affirmed Mr. Sublet.

"Popa," whispered Martinette, "you betta come home an' put on yo' otha pant'loon an' yo' good coat."

"And now, what shall we call the much-talked-of picture?" cheerily inquired the planter, standing with his back to the blaze.

Evariste in a business-like manner began carefully to trace on the tablecloth imaginary characters with an imaginary pen; he could not have written the real characters with a real pen—he did not know how.

"You will put on'neat' de picture," he said, deliberately, " 'Dis is one picture of Mista Evariste Anatole Bonamour, a gent'man of Bayou Têche.' "

Nég Créol

A T the remote period of his birth he had been named César François Xavier, but no one ever thought of calling him anything but Chicot, or Nég, or Maringouin. Down at the French market, where he worked among the fishmongers, they called him Chicot, when they were not calling him names that are written less freely than they are spoken. But one felt privileged to call him almost anything, he was so black, lean, lame, and shriveled. He wore a headkerchief, and whatever other rags the fishermen and their wives chose to bestow upon him. Throughout one whole winter he wore a woman's discarded jacket with puffed sleeves.

Among some startling beliefs entertained by Chicot was one that "Michié St. Pierre et Michié St. Paul" had created him. Of "Michié bon Dieu" he held his own private opinion, and a not too flattering one at that. This fantastic notion concerning the origin of his being he owed to the early teaching of his young master, a lax believer, and a great *farceur* in his day. Chicot had once been thrashed by a robust young Irish priest for expressing his religious views, and another time knifed by a Sicilian. So he had come to hold his peace upon that subject.

Upon another theme he talked freely and harped continuously. For years he had tried to convince his associates that his master had left a progeny, rich, cultured, powerful, and numerous beyond belief. This prosperous race of beings inhabited the most imposing mansions in the city of New Orleans. Men of note and position, whose names were familiar to the public, he swore were grandchildren, great-grandchildren, or, less frequently, distant relatives of his master, long deceased. Ladies who came to the market in carriages, or whose elegance of attire attracted the attention and admiration of the fishwomen, were all *des 'tites cousines* to his former master, Jean Boisduré. He never looked for recognition from any of these superior beings, but delighted to discourse by the hour upon their dignity and pride of birth and wealth.

Chicot always carried an old gunny-sack, and into this went his earnings. He cleaned stalls at the market, scaled fish, and did many odd offices for the itinerant merchants, who usually paid in trade for his service. Occasionally he saw the color of silver and got his clutch upon a coin, but he accepted anything, and seldom made terms. He was glad to get a handkerchief from the Hebrew, and grateful if the Choctaws would trade him a bottle of filé for it. The butcher flung him a soup-bone, and the fishmonger a few crabs or a paper bag of shrimps. It was the big *mulatresse, vendeuse de café,* who cared for his inner man.

Once Chicot was accused by a shoevender of attempting to steal a pair of ladies' shoes. He declared he was only examining them. The clamor raised in the market was terrific. Young Dagoes assembled and squealed like rats; a couple of Gascon butchers bellowed like bulls. Matteo's wife shook her fist in the accuser's face and called him incomprehensible names. The Choctaw women, where they squatted, turned their slow eyes in the direction of the fray, taking no further notice; while a policeman jerked Chicot around by the puffed sleeve and brandished a club. It was a narrow escape.

Nobody knew where Chicot lived. A man—even a nég créol— who lives among the reeds and willows of Bayou St. John, in a deserted chicken-coop constructed chiefly of tarred paper, is not going to boast of his habitation or to invite attention to his domestic appointments. When, after market hours, he vanished in the direction of St. Philip Street, limping, seemingly bent under the weight of his gunny-bag, it was like the disappearance from the stage of some petty actor whom the audience does not follow in imagination beyond the wings, or think of till his return in another scene.

There was one to whom Chicot's coming or going meant more than this. In *la maison grise* they called her La Chouette, for no earthly reason unless that she perched high under the roof of the old rookery and scolded in shrill sudden outbursts. Forty or fifty years before, when for a little while she acted minor parts with a company of French players (an escapade that had brought her grandmother to the grave), she was known as Mademoiselle de Montallaine. Seventy-five years before she had been christened Aglaé Boisduré.

No matter at what hour the old Negro appeared at her threshold. Mamzelle Aglaé always kept him waiting till she finished her prayers She opened the door for him and silently motioned him to a seat, re· turning to prostrate herself upon her knees before a crucifix and a shell filled with holy water that stood on a small table; it represented in her imagination an altar. Chicot knew that she did it to aggravate him; he was convinced that she timed her devotions to begin when she heard his footsteps on the stairs. He would sit with sullen eyes contemplating her long, spare, poorly clad figure as she knelt and read from her book or finished her prayers. Bitter was the religious warfare that had raged for years between them, and Mamzelle Aglaé had grown, on her side, as intolerant as Chicot. She had come to hold St. Peter and St. Paul in such utter detestation that she had cut their pictures out of her prayer-book.

Then Mamzelle Aglaé pretended not to care what Chicot had in his bag. He drew forth a small hunk of beef and laid it in her basket that stood on the bare floor. She looked from the corner of her eye, and went on dusting the table. He brought out a handful of potatoes, some pieces of sliced fish, a few herbs, a yard of calico, and a small pat of butter wrapped in lettuce leaves. He was proud of the butter, and wanted her to notice it. He held it out and asked her for something to put it in. She handed him a saucer, and looked indifferent and resigned, with lifted eyebrows.

"Pas d' sucre, Nég?"

Chicot shook his head and scratched it, and looked like a black picture of distress and mortification. No sugar! But to-morrow he would get a pinch here and a pinch there, and would bring as much as a cupful.

Mamzelle Aglaé then sat down, and talked to Chicot uninterruptedly and confidentially. She complained bitterly, and it was all about a pain that lodged in her leg; that crept and acted like a live, stinging serpent, twining about her waist and up her spine, and coiling round the shoulder-blade. And then *les rhumatismes* in her fingers! He could see for himself how they were knotted. She could not bend them; she could hold nothing in her hands, and had let a saucer fall that morning and broken it in pieces. And if she were to tell him that she had slept a wink through the night, she would be a liar, deserving of perdition. She had sat at the window *la nuit blanche*, hearing the hours strike and the market-wagons rumble. Chicot nodded, and kept up a running fire of sympathetic comment and suggestive remedies for rheumatism and insomnia: herbs, or *tisanes*, or *grigris*, or all three. As if he knew! There was Purgatory Mary, a perambulating soul whose office in life was to pray for the shades in purgatory,—she had brought Mamzelle Aglaé a bottle of *eau de Lourdes*, but so little of it! She might have kept her water of Lourdes, for all the good it did,—a drop! Not so much as would cure a fly or a mosquito! Mamzelle Aglaé was going to show Purgatory Mary the door when she came again, not only because of her avarice with the Lourdes water, but, beside that, she brought in on her feet dirt that could only be removed with a shovel after she left.

And Mamzelle Aglaé wanted to inform Chicot that there would be slaughter and bloodshed in la maison grise if the people below stairs did not mend their ways. She was convinced that they lived for no other purpose than to torture and molest her. The woman kept a bucket of dirty water constantly on the landing with the hope of Mamzelle Aglaé falling over it or into it. And she knew that the children were instructed to gather in the hall and on the stairway, and scream and make a noise and jump up and down like galloping horses, with the intention of driving her to suicide. Chicot should notify the policeman on the beat, and have them arrested, if possible, and thrust into the parish prison, where they belonged.

Chicot would have been extremely alarmed if he had ever chanced to find Mamzelle Aglaé in an uncomplaining mood. It never occurred to him that she might be otherwise. He felt that she had a right to quarrel with fate, if ever mortal had. Her poverty was a disgrace, and he hung his head before it and felt ashamed.

One day he found Mamzelle Aglaé stretched on the bed, with her head tied up in a handkerchief. Her sole complaint that day was, "Aïe—aïe—aïe! Aïe—aïe—aïe!" uttered with every breath. He had seen her so before, especially when the weather was damp.

"Vous pas bézouin tisane, Mamzelle Aglaé? Vous pas veux mo cri gagni docteur?"

She desired nothing. "Aïe—aïe—aïe!"

He emptied his bag very quietly, so as not to disturb her; and he wanted to stay there with her and lie down on the floor in case she needed him, but the woman from below had come up. She was an Irishwoman with rolled sleeves.

"It's a shtout shtick I'm afther giving her, Nég, and she do but knock on the flure it's me or Janie or wan of us that'll be hearing her."

"You too good, Brigitte. Aïe—aïe—aïe! Une goutte d'eau sucré, Nég! That Purg'tory Marie,—you see hair, ma bonne Brigitte, you tell hair go say li'le prayer là-bas au Cathédral. Aïe—aïe—aïe!"

Nég could hear her lamentation as he descended the stairs. It followed him as he limped his way through the city streets, and seemed part of the city's noise; he could hear it in the rumble of wheels and jangle of car-bells, and in the voices of those passing by.

He stopped at Mimotte the Voudou's shanty and bought a grigri,—a cheap one for fifteen cents. Mimotte held her charms at all prices.

This he intended to introduce next day into Mamzelle Aglaé's room, —somewhere about the altar,—to the confusion and discomfort of "Michié bon Dieu," who persistently declined to concern himself with the welfare of a Boisduré.

At night, among the reeds on the bayou, Chicot could still hear the woman's wail, mingled now with the croaking of the frogs. If he could have been convinced that giving up his life down there in the water would in any way have bettered her condition, he would not have hesitated to sacrifice the remnant of his existence that was wholly devoted to her. He lived but to serve her. He did not know it himself; but Chicot knew so little, and that little in such a distorted way! He could scarcely have been expected, even in his most lucid moments, to give himself over to self-analysis.

Chicot gathered an uncommon amount of dainties at market the following day. He had to work hard, and scheme and whine a little; but he got hold of an orange and a lump of ice and a *chou-fleur*. He did not drink his cup of *café au lait,* but asked Mimi Lambeau to put it in the little new tin pail that the Hebrew notion-vender had just given him in exchange for a mess of shrimps. This time, however, Chicot had his trouble for nothing. When he reached the upper room of la maison grise, it was to find that Mamzelle Aglaé had died during the night. He set his bag down in the middle of the floor, and stood shaking, and whined low like a dog in pain.

Everything had been done. The Irishwoman had gone for the doctor, and Purgatory Mary had summoned a priest. Furthermore, the woman had arranged Mamzelle Aglaé decently. She had covered the table with a white cloth, and had placed it at the head of the bed, with the crucifix and two lighted candles in silver candlesticks upon it: the little bit of ornamentation brightened and embellished the poor room. Purgatory Mary, dressed in shabby black, fat and breathing hard, sat reading half audibly from a prayer-book. She was watching the dead and the silver candlesticks, which she had borrowed from a benevolent society, and for which she held herself responsible. A young man was just leaving,—a reporter snuffing the air for items, who had scented one up there in the top room of la maison grise.

All the morning Janie had been escorting a procession of street Arabs up and down the stairs to view the remains. One of them— a little girl, who had had her face washed and had made a species of toilet for the occasion—refused to be dragged away. She stayed seated as if at an entertainment, fascinated alternately by the long, still figure of Mamzelle Aglaé, the mumbling lips of Purgatory Mary, and the silver candlesticks.

"Will ye get down on yer knees, man, and say a prayer for the dead!" commanded the woman.

But Chicot only shook his head, and refused to obey. He approached the bed, and laid a little black paw for a moment on the stiffened body of Mamzelle Aglaé. There was nothing for him to do here. He picked up his old ragged hat and his bag and went away.

"The black h'athen!" the woman muttered. "Shut the dure, child."

The little girl slid down from her chair, and went on tiptoe to shut the door which Chicot had left open. Having resumed her seat, she fastened her eyes upon Purgatory Mary's heaving chest.

"You, Chicot!" cried Matteo's wife the next morning. "My man, he read in paper 'bout woman name' Boisduré, use' b'long to big-a famny. She die roun' on St. Philip—po', same-a like church rat. It's any them Boisdurés you alla talk 'bout?"

Chicot shook his head in slow but emphatic denial. No, indeed, the woman was not of kin to his Boisdurés. He surely had told Matteo's wife often enough—how many times did he have to repeat it!—of their wealth, their social standing. It was doubtless some Boisduré of *les Attakapas;* it was none of his.

The next day there was a small funeral procession passing a little distance away,—a hearse and a carriage or two. There was the priest who had attended Mamzelle Aglaé, and a benevolent Creole gentleman whose father had known the Boisdurés in his youth. There were a couple of player-folk, who, having got wind of the story, had thrust their hands into their pockets.

"Look, Chicot!" cried Matteo's wife. "Yonda go the fune'al. Mus-a be that-a Boisduré woman we talken 'bout yesaday."

But Chicot paid no heed. What was to him the funeral of a woman who had died in St. Philip Street? He did not even turn his head in the direction of the moving procession. He went on scaling his red-snapper.

Suzette

MA'ME ZIDORE thrust her head in at the window to tell Suzette that Michel Jardeau was dead.

"Ah, bon Dieu!" cried the girl, clasping her hands, "c' pauv' Michel!"

Ma'me Zidore had heard the news from one of Chartrand's "hands" who was passing with his wagon through the cut-off when she was gathering wood. Her old back was at that moment bent beneath the fagots. She spoke loud and noisily in shrill outbursts. With her unsteady, claw-like fingers she kept brushing aside the wisp of wiry gray hair that fell across her withered cheek.

She knew the story from beginning to end. Michel had boarded the Grand Ecore flat that very morning at daybreak. Jules Bat, the ferry man, had found him waiting on the bank to cross when he carried the doctor over to see Racell's sick child. He could not say whether Michel were drunk or not; he was gruff and ill-humored and seemed to be half asleep. Ma'me Zidore thought it highly probable that the young man had been carousing all night and was still under the influence of liquor when he lost his balance and fell into the water. A half dozen times Jules Bat had called out to him, warning him of his danger, for he persisted in standing at the open end of the boat. Then all in one miserable second over he went like a log. The water was high and turbid as a boiling caldron. Jules Bat saw no more of him than if he had been so many pounds of lead dropped into Red River.

A few people had assembled at their gates across the way, having gathered from snatches of the old woman's penetrating tones that something of interest had happened. She left Suzette standing at the window and crossed the road slant-wise, her whole gaunt frame revealing itself through her scanty, worn garments as the soft, swift breeze struck her old body.

"Michel Jardeau est mort!" she croaked, telling her news so suddenly that the women all cried out in dismay, and little Pavie Ombre, who was just reviving from a spell of sickness, uttered not a sound, but swayed to and fro and sank gently down on her knees in a white, dead faint.

Suzette retired into the room and approaching the tiny mirror that hung above the chest of drawers proceeded to finish her toilet, in which task she had been interrupted by Ma'me Zidore's abrupt announcement of Michel Jardeau's death.

The girl every little while muttered under her breath:

"C' pauv' Michel." Yet her eyes were quite dry; they gleamed, but not with tears. Regret over the loss of "poor Michel" was in nowise distracting her attention from the careful arrangement of a bunch of carnations in the coils of her lustrous brown hair.

Yet she was thinking of him and wondering why she did not care.

A year ago—not so long as that—she had loved him desperately.

It began that day at the barbecue when, seized with sudden infatuation, he stayed beside her the whole day long; turning her head with his tones, his glances, and soft touches. Before that day he had seemed to care for little Pavie Ombre who had come out of her faint and was now wailing and sobbing across the way, indifferent to those who might hear her in passing along the road. But after that day he cared no longer for Pavie Ombre or any woman on earth besides Suzette. What a weariness that love had finally become to her, only herself knew.

Why did he persist? why could he not have understood? His attentions had fretted her beyond measure; it was torture to feel him there every Sunday at Mass with his eyes fastened upon her during the entire service. It was not her fault that he had grown desperate —that he was dead.

She turned her head this way and that way before the small glass noting the effect of the carnations in her hair. She gave light touches to the trimmings about her neck and waist, and adjusted the puffed sleeves of her white gown. She moved about the small room with a certain suppressed agitation, returning often to the mirror, and sometimes straying to the window.

Suzette was standing there when a sound arrested her attention —the distant tramp of an advancing herd of cattle. It was what she had been waiting for; what she had been listening for. Yet she trembled through her whole supple frame when she heard it, and the color began to mount into her cheeks. She stayed there at the window looking like a painted picture in its frame.

The house was small and low and stood a little back, with no inclosing fence about the grass plot that reached from the window quite to the edge of the road.

All was still, save for the tramp of the advancing herd. There was no dust, for it had rained during the morning; and Suzette could see them now, approaching with slow, swinging motion and tossing of long horns. Mothers had run out, gathering and snatching their little ones from the road. Baptiste, one of the drivers, shouted hoarsely, cracking his long whip, while a couple of dogs tore madly around snapping and barking.

The other driver, a straight-backed young fellow, sat his horse with familiar ease and carelessness. He wore a white flannel shirt, coarse trousers and leggings and a broad-brimmed gray felt. From the moment his figure appeared in sight, Suzette did not remove her eyes from him. The glow in her cheeks was resplendent now.

She was feeling in anticipation the penetration of his glance, the

warmth of his smile when he should see her. He would ride up to
the window, no doubt, to say good-bye, and she would give him
the carnations as a remembrance to keep till he came back.

But what did he mean? She turned a little chill with apprehension.
Why, at that precious moment should he bother about the unruly
beast that seemed bent upon making trouble? And there was that
idiot, that pig of a Baptiste pulling up on the other side of him—
talking to him, holding his attention. Mère de Dieu! how she hated
and could have killed the fool!

With a single impulse there was a sudden quickened movement
of the herd—a dash forward. Then they went! with lowered, tossing heads, rounding the bend that sloped down to the ford.

He had passed! He had not looked at her! He had not thought of
her! He would be gone three weeks—three eternities! and every hour
freighted with the one bitter remembrance of his indifference!

Suzette turned from the window—her face gray and pinched, with
all the warmth and color gone out of it. She flung herself upon the
bed and there she cried and moaned with wrenching sobs between.

The carnations drooped from their fastening and lay like a blood-
stain upon her white neck.

CHARLES W. CHESNUTT

★ ★ ★

The first American Negro with a firm sense of art in fiction was Charles Waddell Chesnutt (1858-1932) who, in *The Conjure Woman* (1899), created a worthy companion of Uncle Remus in the storytelling Uncle Julius. In these tales of North Carolina Negroes, Chesnutt pictures the traditions and superstitions of his race, particularly those associated with conjuring. In his novels, *The House Behind the Cedars* (1900), *The Marrow of Tradition* (1901), and *The Colonel's Dream* (1905), he investigated with propagandistic zeal every social problem of the Negro. Although born in Cleveland, Ohio, he was taken to North Carolina while still young, and there, in 1874, became a teacher at Fayetteville. Nine years later he entered journalism in New York City. Returning to his birthplace, he was admitted to the bar as a practicing attorney. "Sis' Becky's Pickaninny" is reprinted from *The Conjure Woman* by permission of Houghton Mifflin Company.

★ ★ · ★

Sis' Becky's Pickaninny

WE had not lived in North Carolina very long before I was able to note a marked improvement in my wife's health. The ozone-laden air of the surrounding piney woods, the mild and equable climate, the peaceful leisure of country life, had brought about in hopeful measure the cure we had anticipated. Toward the end of our second year, however, her ailment took an unexpected turn for the worse. She became the victim of a settled melancholy, attended with vague forebodings of impending misfortune.

"You must keep up her spirits," said our physician, the best in the neighboring town. "This melancholy lowers her tone too much, tends to lessen her strength, and, if it continue too long, may be fraught with grave consequences."

I tried various expedients to cheer her up. I read novels to her. I had the hands on the place come up in the evening and serenade her with plantation songs. Friends came in sometimes and talked, and frequent letters from the North kept her in touch with her former home. But nothing seemed to rouse her from the depression into which she had fallen.

One pleasant afternoon in spring, I placed an armchair in a shaded portion of the front piazza, and filling it with pillows led my wife out of the house and seated her where she would have the pleasantest view of a somewhat monotonous scenery. She was scarcely placed when old Julius came through the yard, and, taking off his tattered straw hat, inquired, somewhat anxiously:—

"How is you feelin' dis atternoon, ma'am?"

"She is not very cheerful, Julius," I said. My wife was apparently without energy enough to speak for herself.

The old man did not seem inclined to go away, so I asked him to sit down. I had noticed, as he came up, that he held some small object in his hand. When he had taken his seat on the top step, he kept fingering this object,—what it was I could not quite make out.

"What is that you have there, Julius?" I asked, with mild curiosity.

"Dis is my rabbit foot, suh."

This was at a time before this curious superstition had attained its present jocular popularity among white people, and while I had heard of it before, it had not yet outgrown the charm of novelty.

"What do you do with it?"

"I kyars it wid me fer luck, suh."

"Julius," I observed, half to him and half to my wife, "your people will never rise in the world until they throw off these childish superstitions and learn to live by the light of reason and common sense. How absurd to imagine that the fore-foot of a poor dead rabbit, with which he timorously felt his way along through a life surrounded by snares and pitfalls, beset by enemies on every hand, can promote happiness or success, or ward off failure or misfortune!"

"It is ridiculous," assented my wife, with faint interest.

"Dat's w'at I tells dese niggers roun' heah," said Julius. "De fo'-foot ain' got no power. It has ter be de hin'-foot, suh—de lef' hin'-foot er a grabe-ya'd rabbit, killt by a cross-eyed nigger on a da'k night in de full er de moon."

"They must be very rare and valuable," I said.

"Dey is kinder ska'ce, suh, en dey ain' no 'mount er money could buy mine, suh. I mought len' it ter anybody I sot sto' by, but I would n' sell it, no indeed, suh, I would n'."

"How do you know it brings good luck?" I asked.

" 'Ca'se I ain' had no bad luck sence I had it, suh, en I's had dis rabbit foot fer fo'ty yeahs. I had a good marster befo' de wah, en I wa'n't sol' erway, en I wuz sot free; en dat 'uz all good luck."

"But that doesn't prove anything," I rejoined. "Many other people have gone through a similar experience, and probably more than one of them had no rabbit's foot."

"Law, suh! you doan hafter prove 'bout de rabbit foot! Eve'ybody knows dat; leas'ways eve'ybody roun' heah knows it. But ef it has ter be prove' ter folks w'at wa'n't bawn en raise' in dis naberhood, dey is a' easy way ter prove it. Is I eber tol' you de tale er Sis' Becky en her pickaninny?"

"No," I said, "let us hear it." I thought perhaps the story might interest my wife as much or more than the novel I had meant to read from.

"Dis yer Becky," Julius began, "useter b'long ter ole Kunnel Pen'leton, who owned a plantation down on de Wim'l'ton Road, 'bout ten miles fum heah, des befo' you gits ter Black Swamp. Dis yer Becky wuz a fiel'-han', en a monst'us good 'un. She had a husban' oncet, a nigger w'at b'longed on de nex' plantation, but de man w'at owned her husban' died, en his lan' en his niggers had ter be sol' fer ter pay his debts. Kunnel Pen'leton 'lowed he'd 'a' bought dis nigger, but he had be'n bettin' on hoss races, en did n' hab no money, en so Becky's husban' wuz sol' erway ter Fuhginny.

"Co'se Becky went on some 'bout losin' her man, but she could n' he'p herse'f; en 'sides dat, she had her pickaninny fer ter comfo't her. Dis yer little Mose wuz de cutes', blackes', shiny-eyedes' little nigger you eber laid eyes on, en he wuz ez fon' er his mammy ez his mammy wuz er him. Co'se Becky had ter wuk en did n' hab much time ter was'e wid her baby. Ole Aun' Nancy, de plantation nuss down at de qua'ters, useter take keer er little Mose in de day-time, en atter de niggers come in fum de cotton-fiel' Becky 'ud git her chile en kiss 'im en nuss 'im, en keep 'im 'tel mawnin'; en on Sundays she'd hab 'im in her cabin wid her all day long.

"Sis' Becky had got sorter useter gittin' 'long widout her husban', w'en one day Kunnel Pen'leton went ter de races. Co'se w'en he went ter de races, he tuk his hosses, en co'se he bet on 'is own hosses, en co'se he los' his money; fer Kunnel Pen'leton did n' nebber hab no luck wid his hosses, ef he did keep hisse'f po' projeckin' wid 'em. But dis time dey wuz a hoss nam' Lightnin' Bub, w'at b'longed ter ernudder man, en dis hoss won de sweep-stakes; en Kunnel Pen'leton tuk a lackin' ter dat hoss, en ax' his owner w'at he wuz willin' ter take fer 'im.

"'I'll take a thousan' dollahs fer dat hoss,' sez dis yer man, who had a big plantation down to'ds Wim'l'ton, whar he rais' hosses fer ter race en ter sell.

"Well, Kunnel Pen'leton scratch' 'is head, en wonder whar he wuz gwine ter raise a thousan' dollahs; en he did n' see des how he could do it, fer he owed ez much ez he could borry a'ready on de skyo'ity he could gib. But he wuz des boun' ter hab dat hoss, so sezee:—

"'I'll gib you my note fer 'leven hund'ed dollahs fer dat hoss.'

"De yother man shuck 'is head, en sezee:—

"'Yo' note, suh, is better'n gol', I doan doubt; but I is made it a rule in my bizness not ter take no notes fum nobody. Howsomeber, suh, ef you is kinder sho't er fun's, mos' lackly we kin make some kin' er bahg'in. En w'iles we is talkin', I mought 's well say dat I needs ernudder good nigger down on my place. Ef you is got a good one ter spar', I mought trade wid you.'

"Now, Kunnel Pen'leton did n' r'ally hab no niggers fer ter spar', but he 'lowed ter hisse'f he wuz des bleedzd ter hab dat hoss, en so he sez, sezee:—

"'Well, I doan lack ter, but I reckon I'll haf ter. You come out ter my plantation ter-morrow en look ober my niggers, en pick out de one you wants.'

"So sho' 'nuff nex' day dis yer man come out ter Kunnel Pen'leton's place en rid roun' de plantation en glanshed at de niggers, en who sh'd he pick out fum 'em all but Sis' Becky.

"'I needs a noo nigger 'oman down ter my place,' sezee, 'fer ter cook en wash, en so on; en dat young 'oman 'll des fill de bill. You gimme her, en you kin hab Lightnin' Bug.'

"Now, Kunnel Pen'leton didn' lack ter trade Sis' Becky, ca'se she wuz nigh 'bout de bes' fiel'-han' he had; en 'sides, Mars Kunnel didn' keer ter take de mammies 'way fum dey chillun w'iles de chillun wuz little. But dis man say he want Becky, er e'se Kunnel Pen'leton could n' hab de race hoss.

"'Well,' sez de kunnel, 'you kin hab de 'oman. But I doan lack ter sen' her 'way fum her baby. W'at 'll you gimme fer dat nigger baby?'

" 'I doan want de baby,' sez de yuther man. 'I ain' got no use fer de baby.'

" 'I tell yer w'at I'll do,' 'lows Kunnel Pen'leton, 'I'll th'ow dat pickaninny in fer good measure.'

"But de yuther man shuck his head. 'No,' sezee, 'I's much erbleedzd, but I doan raise niggers; I raises hosses, en I doan wanter be both'rin' wid no nigger babies. Nemmine de baby. I'll keep dat 'oman so busy she'll fergit de baby; fer niggers is made ter wuk, en dey ain' got no time fer no sich foolis'ness ez babies.'

"Kunnel Pen'leton did n' wanter hu't Becky's feelin's,—fer Kunnel Pen'leton wuz a kin'-hea'ted man, en nebber lack' ter make no trouble fer nobody,—en so he tol' Becky he wuz gwine sen' her down ter Robeson County fer a day er so, ter he'p out his son-in-law in his wuk; en bein' ez dis yuther man wuz gwine dat way, he had ax' 'im ter take her 'long in his buggy.

" 'Kin I kyar little Mose wid me, marster?' ax' Sis' Becky.

" 'N-o,' sez de kunnel ez ef he wuz studyin' whuther ter let her take 'im er no; 'I reckon you better let Aun' Nancy look atter yo' baby fer de day or two you'll be gone, en she'll see dat he gits ernuff ter eat 'tel you gits back.'

"So Sis' Becky hug' en kiss' little Mose, en tol' 'im ter be a good little pickaninny, en take keer er hisse'f, en not fergit his mammy w'iles she wuz gone. En little Mose put his arms roun' his mammy en lafft en crowed des lack it wuz monst'us fine fun fer his mammy ter go 'way en leabe 'im.

"Well, dis yer hoss trader sta'ted out wid Becky, en bimeby, atter dey'd gone down de Lumbe'ton Road fer a few miles er so, dis man tu'nt roun' in a diffe'nt d'rection, en kep' goin' dat erway, 'tel bimeby Sis' Becky up 'n ax' 'im ef he wuz gwine ter Robeson County by a noo road.

" 'No, nigger,' sezee, 'I ain' gwine ter Robeson County at all. I's gwine ter Bladen County, whar my plantation is, en whar I raises all my hosses.'

" 'But how is I gwine ter git ter Mis' Laura's plantation down in Robeson County?' sez Becky, wid her hea't in her mouf, fer she 'mence' ter git skeered all er a sudden.

" 'You ain' gwine ter git dere at all,' sez de man. 'You b'longs ter me now, fer I done traded my bes' race hoss fer you, wid yo' ole marster. Ef you is a good gal, I'll treat you right, en ef you doan behabe yo'se'f,—w'y, w'at e'se happens 'll be yo' own fault.'

"Co'se Sis' Becky cried en went on 'bout her pickaninny, but co'se it did n' do no good, en bimeby dey got down ter dis yer man's place, en he put Sis' Becky ter wuk, en fergot all 'bout her habin' a pickaninny.

"Meanw'iles, w'en ebenin' come, de day Sis' Becky wuz tuk 'way, little Mose 'mence' ter got res'less, en bimeby, w'en his mammy did n' come, he sta'ted ter cry fer 'er. Aun' Nancy fed 'im en rocked 'im, en fin'lly he des cried en cried 'tel he cried hisse'f ter sleep.

"De nex' day he did n' 'pear ter be as peart ez yushal, en w'en night come he fretted en went on wuss'n he did de night befo'. De nex' day his little eyes 'mence' ter lose dey shine, en he would n' eat nuffin, en he 'mence' ter look so peaked dat Aun' Nancy tuk'n kyared 'im up ter de big house, en showed 'im ter her ole missis, en her ole missis gun her some med'cine fer 'im, en 'lowed ef he did n' git no better she sh'd fetch 'im up ter de big house ag'in, en dey'd hab a doctor, en nuss little Mose up dere. Fer Aun' Nancy's ole missis 'lowed he wuz a lackly little nigger en wu'th raisin'.

"But Aun' Nancy had l'arn' ter lack little Mose, en she did n' wanter hab 'im tuk up ter de big house. En so w'en he did n' git no better, she gethered a mess er green peas, and tuk de peas en de baby, en went ter see ole Aun' Peggy, de cunjuh 'oman down by de Wim'l'ton Road. She gun Aun' Peggy de mess er peas, en tol' her all 'bout Sis' Becky en little Mose.

"'Dat is a monst'us small mess er peas you is fotch' me,' sez Aun' Peggy, sez she.

"'Yas, I knows,' 'lowed Aun' Nancy, 'but dis yere is a monst'us small pickaninny.'

"'You'll hafter fetch me sump'n mo',' sez Aun' Peggy, 'fer you can't 'spec' me ter was'e my time diggin' roots en wukkin' cunj'ation fer nuffin.'

"'All right,' sez Aun' Nancy, 'I'll fetch you sumpin' mo' nex' time.'

"'You bettah,' sez Aun' Peggy, 'er e'se dey'll be trouble. W'at dis yer little pickaninny needs is ter see his mammy. You leabe 'im heah 'tel ebenin' en I'll show 'im his mammy.'

"So w'en Aun' Nancy had gone 'way, Aun' Peggy tuk 'n wukked her roots, en tu'nt little Mose ter a hummin'-bird, en sont 'im off ter fin' his mammy.

"So little Mose flewed, en flewed, en flewed away, 'tel bimeby he got ter de place whar Sis' Becky b'longed. He seed his mammy wuk-kin' roun' de ya'd, en he could tell fum lookin' at her dat she wuz trouble' in her min' 'bout sump'n, en feelin' kin' er po'ly. Sis' Becky heared sump'n hummin' roun' en roun' her, sweet en low. Fus' she 'lowed it wuz a hummin'-bird; den she thought it sounded lack her little Mose croonin' on her breas' way back yander on de ole planta-tion. En she des 'magine' it wuz her little Mose, en it made her feel bettah, en she went on 'bout her wuk pearter 'n she'd done sence she'd be'n down dere. Little Mose stayed roun' 'tel late in de ebenin', en den flewed back ez hard ez he could ter Aun' Peggy. Ez fer Sis' Becky, she dremp all dat night dat she wuz holdin' her pickaninny in her arms, en kissin' him, en nussin' him, des lack she useter do back on de ole plantation whar he wuz bawn. En fer th'ee er fo' days Sis' Becky went 'bout her wuk wid mo' sperrit dan she'd showed sence she'd be'n down dere ter dis man's plantation.

"De nex' day atter he come back, little Mose wuz mo' pearter en better 'n he had be'n fer a long time. But to'ds de een' er de week he 'mence' ter git res'less ag'in, en stop eatin', en Aun' Nancy kyared 'im down ter Aun' Peggy once mo', en she tu'nt 'im ter a mawkin'-bird dis time, en sont 'im off ter see his mammy ag'in.

"It did n' take him long fer ter git dere, en w'en he did, he seed his mammy standin' in de kitchen, lookin' back in de d'rection little Mose wuz comin' fum. En dey wuz tears in her eyes, en she look' mo' po'ly en peaked 'n she had w'en he wuz down dere befo'. So little Mose sot on a tree in de ya'd en sung, en sung, en sung, des fittin' ter split his th'oat. Fus' Sis' Becky did n' notice 'im much, but dis mawkin'-bird kep' stayin' roun' de house all day, en bimeby Sis' Becky des 'magine' dat mawkin'-bird wuz her little Mose crowin' en crowin', des lack he useter do w'en his mammy would come home at night fum de cotton-fiel'. De mawkin'-bird stayed roun' dere mos' all day, en w'en Sis' Becky went out in de ya'd one time, dis yer mawkin'-bird lit on her shoulder en peck' at de piece er bread she wuz eatin', en fluttered his wings so dey rub' up agin de side er her head. En w'en he flewed away 'long late in de ebenin', des 'fo' sun-down, Sis' Becky felt mo' better 'n she had sence she had heared dat hummin'-bird a week er so pas'. En dat night she dremp 'bout ole times ag'in, des lack she did befo'.

"But dis yer totin' little Mose down ter ol Aun' Peggy, en dis yer gittin' things fer ter pay de cunjuh 'oman, use' up a lot er Aun' Nancy's time, en she begun ter git kinder ti'ed. 'Sides dat, w'en Sis' Becky had be'n on de plantation, she had useter he'p Aun' Nancy wid de young uns ebenin's en Sundays; en Aun' Nancy 'mence' ter miss 'er monst'us, 'speshly sence she got a tech er de rheumatiz herse'f, en so she 'lows ter ole Aun' Peggy one day:—

"'Aun' Peggy, ain' dey no way you kin fetch Sis' Becky back home?'

"'Huh!' sez Aun' Peggy, 'I dunno 'bout dat. I'll hafter wuk my

roots en fin' out whuther I kin er no. But it'll take a monst'us heap
er wuk, en I can't was'e my time fer nuffin. Ef you'll fetch me sump'n
ter pay me fer my trouble, I reckon we kin fix it.'

"So nex' day Aun' Nancy went down ter see Aun' Peggy ag'in.

" 'Aun' Peggy,' sez she, 'I is fotch' you my bes' Sunday head-hankercher. Will dat do?'

"Aun' Peggy look' at de head-hankercher, en run her han' ober it,
en sez she:—

" 'Yas, dat'll do fus'-rate. I's be'n wukkin' my roots sence you be'n
gone, en I 'lows mos' lackly I kin git Sis' Becky back, but it's gwine
take fig'rin' en studyin' ez well ez cunj'in'. De fus' thing ter do'll be
ter stop fetchin' dat pickaninny down heah, en not sen' 'im ter see
his mammy no mo'. Ef he gits too po'ly, you lemme know, en I'll
gib you some kin' er mixtry fer ter make 'im fergit Sis' Becky fer a
week er so. So 'less'n you comes fer dat, you neenter come back ter
see me no mo' 'tel I sen's fer you.'

"So Aun' Peggy sont Aun' Nancy erway, en de fus' thing she done
wuz ter call a hawnet fum a nes' unner her eaves.

" 'You go up ter Kunnel Pen'leton's stable, hawnet,' sez she, 'en
sting de knees er de race hoss name' Lightnin' Bug. Be sho' en git
de right one.'

"So de hawnet flewed up ter Kunnel Pen'leton's stable en stung
Lightnin' Bug roun' de laigs, en de nex' mawnin' Lightnin' Bug's
knees wuz all swoll' up, twice't ez big ez dey oughter be. W'en
Kunnel Pen'leton went out ter de stable en see de hoss's laigs, hit
would 'a' des made you trimble lack a leaf fer ter heah him cuss dat
hoss trader. Howsomeber, he cool' off bimeby en tol' de stable boy
fer ter rub Lightnin' Bug's laigs wid some linimum. De boy done
ez his marster tol' 'im, en by de nex' day de swellin' had gone down
consid'able. Aun' Peggy had sont a sparrer, w'at had a nes' in one er
de trees close ter her cabin, fer ter watch w'at wuz gwine on 'roun'
de big house, en w'en dis yer sparrer tol' 'er de hoss wuz gittin'
ober de swellin', she sont de hawnet back fer ter sting 'is knees some
mo', en de nex' mawnin' Lightnin' Bug's laigs wuz swoll' up wuss'n
befo'.

"Well, dis time Kunnel Pen'leton wuz mad th'oo en th'oo, en all
de way 'roun', en he cusst dat hoss trader up en down, fum *A* ter
Izzard. He cusst so ha'd dat de stable boy got mos' skeered ter def,
en went off en hid hisse'f in de hay.

"Ez fer Kunnel Pen'leton, he went right up ter de house en got
out his pen en ink, en tuk off his coat en roll' up his sleeves, en writ
a letter ter dis yer hoss trader, en sezee:—

" 'You is sol' me a hoss w'at is got a ringbone er a spavin' er sump'n, en w'at I paid you fer wuz a soun' hoss. I wants you ter sen' my nigger 'oman back en take yo' ole hoss, er e'se I'll sue you, sho's you bawn.'

"But dis yer man wa'n't skeered a bit, en he writ back ter Kunnel Pen'leton dat a bahg'in wuz a bahg'in; dat Lightnin' Bug wuz soun' w'en he sol' 'im, en ef Kunnel Pen'leton did n' knowed ernuff 'bout hosses ter take keer er a fine racer, dat wuz his own fune'al. En he say Kunnel Pen'leton kin sue en be cusst fer all he keer, but he ain' gwine ter gib up de nigger he bought en paid fer.

"W'en Kunnel Pen'leton got dis letter he wuz madder'n he wuz befo', 'speshly 'ca'se dis man 'lowed he did n' know how ter take keer er fine hosses. But he could n' do nuffin but fetch a lawsuit, en he knowed, by his own 'spe'ience, dat lawsuits wuz slow ez de seben-yeah eetch en cos' mo' d'n dey come ter, en he 'lowed he better go slow en wait awhile.

"Aun' Peggy knowed w'at wuz gwine on all dis time, en she fix' up a little bag wid some roots en one thing en ernudder in it, en gun it ter dis sparrer er her'n, en tol' 'im ter take it 'way down yander whar Sis' Becky wuz, en drap it right befo' de do' er her cabin, so she'd be sho' en fin' it de fus' time she come out'n de do'.

"One night Sis' Becky dremp' her pickaninny wuz dead, en de nex' day she wuz mo'nin' en groanin' all day. She dremp' de same dream th'ee nights runnin', en den, de nex' mawnin' atter de las' night, she foun' dis yer little bag de sparrer had drap' in front her do'; en she 'lowed she'd be'n conju'd, en wuz gwine ter die, en ez long ez her pickaninny wuz dead dey wa'n't no use tryin' ter do nuffin no-how. En so she tuk'n went ter bed, en tol' her marster she'd be'n cunju'd en wuz gwine ter die.

"Her marster lafft at her, en argyed wid her, en tried ter 'suade her out'n dis yer fool notion, ez he called it,—fer he wuz one er dese yer w'ite folks w'at purten' dey doan b'liebe in cunj'in',—but hit wa'n't no use. Sis' Becky kep' gittin' wusser en wusser, 'tel fin'lly dis yer man 'lowed Sis' Becky wuz gwine ter die, sho' nuff. En ez he knowed dey had n' be'n nuffin de matter wid Lightnin' Bug w'en he traded 'im, he 'lowed mebbe he could kyo' 'im en fetch 'im roun' all right, leas'ways good 'nuff ter sell ag'in. En anyhow, a lame hoss wuz bet-ter'n a dead nigger. So he sot down en writ Kunnel Pen'leton a let-ter.

" 'My conscience,' sezee, 'has be'n troublin' me 'bout dat ringbone' hoss I sol' you. Some folks 'lows a hoss trader ain' got no conscience, but dey doan know me, fer dat is my weak spot, en de reason I ain' made no mo' money hoss tradin'. Fac' is,' sezee, 'I is got so I can't sleep nights fum studyin' 'bout dat spavin' hoss; en I is made up my min' dat, w'iles a bahg'in is a bahg'in, en you seed Lightnin' Bug befo' you traded fer 'im, principle is wuth mo' d'n money er hosses er niggers. So ef you'll sen' Lightnin' Bug down heah, I'll sen' yo' nigger 'oman back, en we'll call de trade off, en be ez good frien's ez we eber wuz, en no ha'd feelin's.'

"So sho' 'nuff, Kunnel Pen'leton sont de hoss back. En w'en de man w'at come ter bring Lightnin' Bug tol' Sis' Becky her pickaninny wa'n't dead, Sis' Becky wuz so glad dat she 'lowed she wuz gwine ter try ter lib 'tel she got back whar she could see little Mose once mo'. En w'en she retch' de ole plantation en seed her baby kickin' en crowin' en holdin' out his little arms to'ds her, she wush' she wuz n' cunju'd en did n' hafter die. En w'en Aun' Nancy tol' 'er all 'bout Aun' Peggy, Sis' Becky went down ter see de cunjuh 'oman, en Aun' Peggy tol' her she had cunju'd her. En den Aun' Peggy tuk de goopher off'n her, en she got well, en stayed on de plantation, en raise' her pickaninny. En w'en little Mose growed up, he could sing en whistle des lack a mawkin'-bird, so dat de w'it folks useter hab 'im come up ter de big house at night, en whistle en sing fer 'em, en dey useter gib 'im money en vittles en one thing er ernudder, w'ich he alluz tuk home ter his mammy; fer he knowed all 'bout w'at she had gone th'oo. He tu'nt out ter be a sma't man, en l'arnt de blacksmif trade; en Kunnel Pen'leton let 'im hire his time. En bimeby he bought his mammy en sot her free, en den he bought hisse'f, en tuk keer er Sis' Becky ez long ez dey bofe libbed."

My wife had listened to this story with greater interest than she had manifested in any subject for several days. I had watched her furtively from time to time during the recital, and had observed the play of her countenance. It had expressed in turn sympathy, indignation, pity, and at the end lively satisfaction.

"That is a very ingenious fairy tale, Julius," I said, "and we are much obliged to you."

"Why, John!" said my wife severely, "the story bears the stamp of truth, if ever a story did."

"Yes," I replied, "especially the humming-bird episode, and the mocking-bird digression, to say nothing of the doings of the hornet and the sparrow."

"Oh, well, I don't care," she rejoined, with delightful animation; "those are mere ornamental details and not at all essential. The story is true to nature, and might have happened half a hundred times, and no doubt did happen, in those horrid days before the war."

"By the way, Julius," I remarked, "your story doesn't establish what you started out to prove,—that a rabbit's foot brings good luck."

"Hit's plain 'nuff ter me, suh," replied Julius. "I bet young missis dere kin 'splain it herse'f."

"I rather suspect," replied my wife promptly, "that Sis' Becky had no rabbit's foot."

"You is hit de bull's-eye de fus' fire, ma'am," assented Julius. "Ef Sis' Becky had had a rabbit foot, she nebber would 'a' went th'oo all dis trouble."

I went into the house for some purpose, and left Julius talking to my wife. When I came back a moment later, he was gone.

My wife's condition took a turn for the better from this very day, and she was soon on the way to ultimate recovery. Several weeks later, after she had resumed her afternoon drives, which had been interrupted by her illness, Julius brought the rockaway round to the front door one day, and I assisted my wife into the carriage.

"John," she said, before I had taken my seat, "I wish you would look in my room, and bring me my handkerchief. You will find it in the pocket of my blue dress."

I went to execute the commission. When I pulled the handkerchief out of her pocket, something else came with it and fell on the floor. I picked up the object and looked at it. It was Julius's rabbit's foot.

MARGARET DELAND

★ ★ ★

Social and ethical problems form the basis of the stories and novels by Margaretta Wade Campbell Deland (1857-   ), yet through superior skill in characterization, in the management of incident to bring the problem concretely to focus, and in deftly satiric or humorous commentary, she gives dramatic surge to narratives otherwise likely to droop from the characters' oppressive concern with their sins. Her best collections of short stories, *Old Chester Tales* (1898) and *Dr. Lavendar's People* (1903), have their setting in Western Pennsylvania. The chief character, the Rev. Dr. Edward Lavendar, possesses all the attributes of a wise, kindly, tolerant parson. Mrs. Deland, born in Allegheny, now Pittsburgh, Pennsylvania, studied in New York, taught in Hunter College, and in 1880 married Lorin Deland. Her novels include *John Ward, Preacher* (1888), *The Awakening of Helena Richie* (1906), and *The Iron Woman* (1911). "The Child's Mother" is reprinted from *Old Chester Tales* by permission of Harper and ·Brothers, publishers.

★ ★ ★

The Child's Mother

I

THE winter of the "long frost" has never been forgotten in Old Chester. The river was frozen over solidly from the frightfully cold Sunday, just after Christmas, when Dr. Lavendar stayed at home and Sam Wright read the service, until the February thaw. Not that the thermometer was unreasonable; once in a while, to be sure, it did drop below zero, but for the greater part of the time there was only a dark, persistent cold, with high bleak winds; it was too cold for the soft silencing of snowstorms, though the flakes came sometimes, reluctantly, in little hard pellets, which were blown from the frozen ruts of the roads in whirls of icy dust. It was a deadly sort of cold that got into the bones, the old people said. Anyhow it got on to the nerves; certainly there never was a winter in Old Chester when so many things went wrong. There were happenings among his people that bowed Dr. Lavendar's heart down with sorrow and pain. Brave, high-minded, quick-tempered old James Shields died. The Todds quarrelled violently while that black cold held; and the eldest Miss Ferris was very, very ill. It was that spring that the "real Smiths'" eldest son brought disgrace upon their honest name; and that Miss Jane Jay, to the scandal and grief of her sisters, made up her mind not to go to church any more. And in the midst of all this perplexity and pain Mrs. Drayton, a little foolish hypochondriac with a bad temper, became so anxious about her spiritual condition that she felt it necessary to see her clergyman several times a week. To be sure, her solicitude for her soul was checked by Dr. Lavendar's calling her "woman," and telling her that it was more important to be amiable in her family than to make her peace with God.

"He has no spirituality," Mrs. Drayton said, weeping angrily; and did not send for him again for a fortnight.

It was early in December that old Mrs. King died, and though that meant that her daughter Rachel might draw a free breath after years of most wearing attendance, it meant also the grief of the poor daughter, whose occupation was gone.

Yes, it was a hard, dreary winter, and the old minister's heart was often heavy in his breast; and when one day there came to him a sorrow and a sin that did not concern any of his own people, he had a curious sense of relief in dealing with it.

"It doesn't touch any of 'em, thank the Lord!" he said to himself. Yet there was a puzzle in it that was to grow until it did touch—and very near home, too. But Dr. Lavendar did not see that at the beginning, fortunately.

It was one Monday. Dr. Lavendar never had "blue Mondays"— perhaps because he preached old sermons; perhaps because he was so dogmatically sure that the earth was the Lord's, and so were all the perplexities in it, and all the sorrows, too. On this particular Monday, just after dinner, he sat down by the fire (he had been out all the morning in the sleet and snow, so he felt he had earned a rest);

he put on his preposterous old flowered cashmere dressing-gown, and sat down by the fire, and lighted his pipe, and began to read *Robinson Crusoe*. Dr. Lavendar had long since lost count of the number of times he had read this immortal book, but that never interfered with his enjoyment of it; he had lost count of the number of times he had smoked his pipe, if one comes to counting things up. He had a way of sniffing and chuckling as he read, and he was oblivious to everything about him—even to the fire going out sometimes, or his little grizzly dog climbing up into the chair beside him, or the door opening and shutting. The door opened and shut now, and he never heard it; only, after a while he felt an uncomfortable sense of being watched, and looked up with a start that made Danny squeak and scramble down to the floor. A girl was sitting opposite him, her heavy eyes fixed on his face.

"Why—when did you come in?" he said, sharply. "Who are you?"

"I'm Mary Dean, sir. I come in a few minutes ago. I didn't want to disturb you, sir." She said it all heavily, with her miserable eyes looking past him, out of the window into the falling sleet. It was plain what was her trouble, poor child! The old man looked at her keenly, in silence; then he said, cheerfully:

"Come, come, we must have a better fire than this. You are cold, my dear. Suppose you drink a cup of tea, and then we will talk."

"I don't want no tea, sir, thank you," she answered. "I thought you might help me. I come from Upper Chester," she went on, vaguely. She looked about her as she spoke, and a little interest crept into her flat, impersonal voice. "Why are them swords hangin' over the mantel?" she asked; and then added, sighing, "I'm in trouble."

"How did you come down from the upper village in such weather?" Dr. Lavendar asked her, gently, after a minute's pause.

"I walked, sir."

He exclaimed, looking at her anxiously. "You must have dry clothing on, my child," he said, "and some food, before you say another word!"

The girl protested, weakly: "I ain't cold; I ain't hungry. I only thought you'd tell me what to do."

But of course she had to be taken care of. If his Mary had not had thirty years' experience of his "perfectly obsolete methods," as the new people expressed it, she might have been surprised to find herself waiting on this poor fallen creature, while Dr. Lavendar urged her to eat and drink, and showed her how Danny begged for bread with one paw on his nose and one outstretched. Afterwards, when, fed and clothed, the girl was comforted enough to cry, the old man listened to her story. It was not a new one. When one hears it, one knows the heads under which it divides itself: vanity first; love (so called) next; weakness in the end. It is so pitiful and foolish that to call it by the awful name of sin is almost to dignify it. The girl, as she told it, brightened up; she began to enjoy what was to her a dramatic situation; she told him that she "had always been real respectable, but she had been deceived"; that she hadn't a friend in the world—"nobody to take no interest in her," as she put it—for her father and mother were dead; and, oh, she was that unhappy! "I 'ain't slept a wink for 'most a month. I cry all night," she burst out. "I just do nothing at all but cry, and cry!"

"Well, I guess it's the best thing you can do," he answered, quietly.

Mary looked disappointed, and tossed her head a little. Then she said that of course she hadn't let on to anybody in Upper Chester what was wrong with her, because all her lady and gentlemen friends had always respected her. "That's why I come down here; I didn't want anybody at home to know," she explained, rocking back and forth miserably.

And then, perhaps because his face was so grave, she said, with a little resentment, that, anyway, it was her first misstep; "there's lots of girls worse than me;—and he's a *gentleman*," she added, lifting her head airily. Her glimmer of pride was like the sparkle of a scrap of tinsel in an ash heap. He would have married her, she went on, defending herself, only he was married already; so he really couldn't, she supposed.

Dr. Lavendar did not ask her the man's name, nor suggest any appeal to him for money; he had certain old-fashioned ideas about minding his own business in regard to the first matter, and certain other ideas concerning the injury to any lingering self-respect in the woman if the man bought his way out of his responsibility. He let her wander on in her vague, shallow talk. It was hard to see what was romance and what was truth. She had so far recovered herself as to laugh a little, foolishly, and say once more she "had made a mistake, of course," but if Dr. Lavendar would just help her, it should never happen again. "This time I'll keep my promise," she said, beginning to cry.

"*This* time?" said Dr. Lavendar to himself. "Ho!"

"But what am I going to do?" she said. "If my mother was to hear it, I suppose she'd kill me—"

"Your mother?" he repeated. "You said—"

But she did not notice her slip.

"Oh, dear! I don't know what's going to become of me, anyhow. And I haven't but ten cents to my name!"

With shaking fingers she opened her flat, thin pocketbook, and disclosed a few cents. This, at least, seemed to be true. "I'd die before any of my friends should know about it!" she sobbed.

Dr. Lavendar let her cry. He looked at her once or twice gravely, but he did not speak; he was wondering what woman in the parish he could call upon to help him. He was not stern with her, and he was not repelled or shocked by her depravity, as a younger man might have been in his place. He was old, and he was acquainted with grief, and he knew that this poor creature's wretchedness had in it, as yet, no understanding of sin; she was only inconvenienced by the consequences of wrongdoing. But the old man believed that the whip of shame and pain could drive her, as the Lord means it shall, into an appreciation of the expediency of morality—that first low step up to the full realization of the beauty of holiness. Being old, he knew all this, and was patient and tender with the poor fool, and did not look for anything so high, so awful, so deep, as what is called repentance. And then, beside the knowledge of life, which of itself makes the intellect patient, the situation was one which appealed profoundly to this old man who had never known the deep experience of paternity. The woman—so inextricably deep in the mire, the soul of her killed, almost before it had been born, the chances of her moral nature torn out of helpless, childless hands that did not know enough to protect them—a kitten drowned before its eyes were open! And the child—the baby, unborn, undesired, weighted with what an inheritance! There was no baseness in this poor, cheap, flimsy creature that could arouse a trace of scorn in him. He let her cry for a while, and then he said, mildly:

"Where is your other child?" She started, and looked over her shoulder in a half-frightened way:

"Why! how did you know? Oh, well, my soul! I won't deceive you: I—I left it in Albany with my sister. She's supporting it."

Dr. Lavendar sighed. "It's a pity you can't be truthful, Mary. I could help you better, you know. However, I won't ask you to tell the truth. I'll only ask you not to tell me any lies. That's easier, I guess. Come, now, promise me you won't tell me any more lies, and then I will know how to help you."

Of course she promised, sobbing a little, and fingering her poor empty pocketbook. After all, that was the important thing. How was he going to help her? She had no money, and she could not get any work; and if this minister wouldn't look after her, she would have to go to the workhouse.

But he was going to look after her: that was Dr. Lavendar's way. For, it must be admitted, Dr. Lavendar did not understand many things; he was only a little, feeble, behind-the-times old clergyman. Out of his scanty salary he was half supporting one shiftless woman with an enormous family, and a paralytic old man, and a consumptive girl. He did not stop to reflect that he was inviting mothers to burden society with their offspring, and encouraging old men to become paralytics, and offering a premium to consumption. No; he fed the hungry and clothed the naked, and never turned his face from the face of any poor man. He was not scientific; he was only human. He hoped and he believed that salvation was possible for every one— and so for this poor fallen woman with the empty pocketbook, whom he was going to look after. But he had to think about it a little while; so he bade her wait, while he went and fumbled among his papers and memoranda, and found the address of a worthy woman in Upper Chester who would take her to board and give her the care and attendance that she was going to need. Then he made a little calculation in his own mind that had reference to a certain old book upon Historical Sapphires, that he had long desired to own; then thrust out his lip and said, "Foolishness, foolishness!" under his breath; and brought a little roll of money and put it into her hand.

"You can go back on the stage to Upper Chester, and then you are to go to this street and number, and give this note to the kind woman who lives there. She will take you in, my child, and I will come and see you in a few days."

II

If Susan Carr had been in Old Chester that winter, Dr. Lavendar would have handed Mary Dean over to her, but she was paying a long visit in Mercer, and there seemed to be nobody to take care of the young woman but himself. Certainly he could not ask Miss Maria Welwood; she would have been most anxiously, tremulously kind, but her consciousness of the impropriety of the situation would have made her useless. Mrs. Dale was too stern; Mrs. Wright's large family took up all her time; Rose Knight was too young to know about such matters; and so was Sally Smith. Rachel King—well, yes, there was Rachel King. But her mother had just died, and Rachel needed a little time to breathe without any duty.

"Bless her heart!" he said to himself, "she sha'n't have any more work to do for a while, anyhow."

There was nothing for it but to look after the girl himself. So he put her into Mrs. Wiley's charge at Upper Chester, and took the long stage ride twice a week to visit her, and paid her board, and begged baby clothing for her, and watched over her in his queer, kind, dogmatic way.

"He's awful fond of fussin'," the girl said, wearily.

Mrs. Wiley had always a string of complaints ready for him: Mary was such a dreadful liar! She was that ungrateful, Mrs. Wiley had never seen the like of it! She hadn't any decent feelings, anyhow, for she made eyes at the baker's boy till Mrs. Wiley said she'd put her out on the sidewalk if she didn't behave!

"Wait; wait," he would say. "She'll love the child, and she'll be a better girl."

"It don't follow," said Mrs. Wiley, with a significant toss of her head. "She allows she left her first child in New York with an aunt, and I can't see as it reformed her any."

However, neither Mrs. Wiley's deductions nor the conflict in poor Mary's stories prevented Dr. Lavendar from hoping. After the baby was born, he was eager to see the mother, peering into her face with anxious eyes, as though he thought that the benediction of a baby's hand must have blotted out shiftiness and sensuality and meanness. But Mary only came out of the experience of birth with her smooth, shallow face prettier than ever. Then Dr. Lavendar bade Mrs. Wiley wait yet a little longer. "Wait until she begins to love it, and then we'll see!" he said.

"Oh, she loves it enough," Mrs. Wiley conceded, grudgingly. "I don't deny she loves it. When I take it up, she looks at me just like our old cat does when I touch her kittens. Yes, she loves it fast enough; but she's a bad girl, that's what she is, Dr. Lavendar!"

As for Dr. Lavendar himself, he was immensely entertained by the baby, though somewhat afraid of it. He used to hold it cautiously on his knee, chuckling to himself at its little, pink, clawlike hands, which grasped vaguely at him, and at its funny, nodding, bald head, and its tiny, bubbling lips. Mary would watch him languidly, and would laugh too, as though it was all an excellent joke.

"If it was a boy, I'd name it after you," she said, with coy facetiousness. At which Dr. Lavendar came out of his sunny mood, and said "Ho!" gruffly, and put the baby down. The girl was so utterly devoid of any understanding of the situation that, in spite of his hopefulness, she shocked him again and again. However, he kept on "looking after her."

The child was baptized Anna, though Mary had suggested Evelina. "Mary," Dr. Lavendar said, solemnly, "was your mother a good woman?"

"My mother?" the girl said, wincing. "She's—dead. She *was* good. My land! if she'd lived I wouldn't 'a' been here!" For once the easy tears had not risen; she looked at him sullenly, as though she hated him for some glaring contrast that came into her thoughts. "That's honest," she added, simply.

"Then we will name the baby after her, because she was good," he said; and "Anna," was accordingly "grafted into the body of Christ's church."

As soon as she was strong enough, he found a place for Mary to work, where she might have the baby with her. "The child and good honest work will save her," he would say to himself; but he used to shake his head over her when he sat smoking his pipe and thinking about his little world. "And that poor baby!" he would say, looking, perhaps, at his wrinkled forefinger, and thinking how the baby had clutched it.

Once he told Rachel King about it all, and how pretty the child was—that was when it was five months old, and the red and clawing stage was past, and the small bald head was covered with shining, silken rings of hair, and its eyes, no longer hid in creases of soft baby flesh, were blue and smiling, and its little mouth cooed for kisses.

"Oh," cried Rachel King, "to think that such a creature should have it!"

Not that Rachel King was hard, or that she had the shrinking that good Miss Maria Welwood would have had; but her whole heart rose at the mention of a baby. "The little darling," she said; and the color came up into her face, and her eyes gleamed. "I don't believe she loves it a bit."

"Oh yes, she does," said Dr. Lavendar, with a sigh; "yes, she does— in her way. And, Rachel, the baby may save her, you know. Yes, I believe she loves it."

"I don't," said Rachel King, stoutly; "not if this last story of her 'keeping company' with somebody is true. Why doesn't she devote herself to the baby?"

Rachel was sitting out in the garden with Dr. Lavendar; he had been smoking and watching the bees, and she had dropped in to gossip awhile. She was a large, maternal-looking woman of thirty-five. Silent and placid, with soft, light-brown hair parted in the middle and drawn smoothly down and back from a wide forehead, under which shone mild and brooding gray eyes—the eyes of a woman who was essentially, and always, and deeply, a mother; that look that can only come from experience.

But what had she mothered in the last nineteen years!

When Rachel was sixteen years old, Mrs. King fell ill; it was one of those illnesses from which we turn away our eyes, shuddering and humbled. Oh, our poor human nature! the pity of it, the shame of it, yet the helplessness and innocence of it! Rachel's mother gradually but swiftly came to be a child—in everything but years. She had lost a baby, and the grief had shaken the foundations of life. They first suspected how things were with the poor mind by the way she pored over the little clothes the dead child had worn, folding them and unfolding them, and talking to them, with little foolish laughter. It was then that some one whispered to some one else that Ellen King was not herself. So it went on, little by little—at first knowing, and rebelling with horror and with disgust; then, after a while, passively, she sank down into the bog of the merely animal. When Rachel was eighteen the last glimmer of the woman died out; there was left an eating, breathing, whimpering thing. She had her doll by that time, and Rachel used to tuck a bib under the poor shaking chin and feed her, and push down the naughty hands that tried to grasp the spoon, and wipe the milky lips, and kiss her, and—honor her. This was her baby, her duty, her passionately tender occupation—but it was her *mother;* and Rachel King's days ought to be long in the land! When she was about twenty-one a lover appeared, but she sent him away. "I can't leave mother. Father can't take care of her, you know, and Oscar is away; and Willy will be getting married some day. But it wouldn't be right that you should have to live with her," she said, wistfully. The lover protested; but she heard the weak note behind the affectionate words, and after that she was quite firm. "No; it can't be. I see that it couldn't possibly be." When he had gone, she went up to her mother's room and put her arms around her, and hid her eyes on her breast. "Oh, mother, mother!" she said, "can't you speak to me—just once?"

Mrs. King stroked the soft straight hair for a moment, and then plucked at it angrily, and cried and screamed, and said she wanted her dolly. . . . That had been Rachel's life for nineteen years; for Mrs. King had lived, and lived, and lived. All around her in the anxious, heavy-laden world sweet and buoyant and vital souls were sucked down into death; but the imbecile old woman went on living. Mr. King died in the early part of his wife's illness; and about eight years before the end came, William, the only son who lived at home, married, and went to a house of his own. He married a Mercer girl, who commended herself to him by her great good sense. Old Chester was not quite pleased that Willy should leave his mother and Rachel all alone, though it said, approvingly, that Martha Hayes would make the doctor a good wife. But what could the young man do? The sensible Mercer girl said, frankly, that she was very fond of Willy, but she simply *would not* live in the same house with his mother. Indeed, such was her Mercer sense (it certainly was not of Old Chester) that she said, during the latter part of her engagement, that she did not think it was quite prudent for a young married lady to live in the same house with such a frightful old creature!

So Rachel was left all alone with her child. It was a busy life, in its constant attendance; yet somehow it is the busy people who can always do a little more. If there was sickness in a neighbor's family, Rachel King took possession in a tranquil, sensible way; when there was death, her large, gentle hands were ready with those sacred touches that are so often left to hirelings; when there was sorrow, her soft breast was a most comforting pillow. So year by year went by, until the final flicker of her mother's life dropped into mere breathing—into silence—into death. And year by year the lines of maternity deepened in the daughter's face, until she was all mother.

Then, she was childless.

Oh, after such shame, how humanity raises itself in glorious death! Even Rachel, mourning and bewildered by the loss of occupation, felt it dumbly—the dignity, the mercy, the graciousness, of death! And to the poor soul, fettered in gross flesh, stumbling, stifling, struggling, what must it have been to emerge into the clean spaces of the stars!

After that, of course, Rachel could live her own life. But there was no question of a lover now; he had a wife and five children in another State. She could not go and live with Willy; her sensible sister-in-law (against this day) had for years been saying how foolish it was to live in other people's families; and Rachel had taken the hint. There were no nephews and nieces to love—nobody, indeed, to whom she was a necessity. Of all the bitter and heavy things in this sorry old world, the not being necessary is the bitterest and heaviest. With a deep, simple nature, a nature of brooding love, Rachel King had nothing in her life but the crumbs that fell from richer tables: the friendly acceptance of those services she was so happy to give. But she had nothing of her very own.

"To think that that creature has a baby!" she said.

"Well, well; we'll hope it will save her," Dr. Lavendar repeated.

"But think of the baby," Rachel insisted. "What kind of a bringing-up will it have?" She sighed as she spoke, not knowing that the necessity of her own empty arms and wide lap and deep soft bosom dictated the words.

"Well, Rachel, if we took the infants away from all the unworthy mothers, we'd have a pretty large orphan-asylum," Dr. Lavendar said, chuckling, "and it wouldn't be only the Mary Deans who would have to give 'em up, either. No, no; I believe the Lord understands this matter better than we do. The baby will make a woman of Mary yet!"

"Suppose she teaches it to tell lies?" Rachel King suggested.

"Ho! Suppose it teaches her to tell the truth?" he demanded. "No, Rachel. That baby is a missionary; a 'domestic missionary,' as you might say. I've great hopes for Mary—great hopes."

III

But Dr. Lavendar's hopes were greatly tried. In spite of the saving grace of a baby, bad reports came from the family for whom Mary Dean worked—she was an inveterate liar; she was untidy, and coarse in mind and body; she was dishonest—not in any large way, but rather in small meannesses.

"The only good thing about her is she *is* fond of that blessed baby," her exasperated mistress said once. "She kisses it sometimes as if she were possessed. But then, again, she'll slap it real hard if it slops its dress, or, maybe, pulls her hair when it's playing. It's a great baby to play," the good woman said, softening as she spoke.

However, Dr. Lavendar kept on hoping. Then came a time when he could hope no longer. It was one night in August—his Mary's night out, as it chanced. Dr. Lavendar came home from Wednesday evening lecture, plodding along in the darkness, a lantern swinging in one hand and his stick in the other. He was humming over to himself, with husky clearings of his voice at the end of each line, the last hymn:

> "The spa—cious fir—mament o-on hi-gh,
> And a-all the blue—ethereal sky—"

Then he fumbled for his latchkey and came up to his own doorstep, where was lying a little heap that moved and said, "Goo—oo—oo."

Dr. Lavendar stood still for a moment, and felt very cold. Then he stooped down and held the lantern over the baby's face. At that there was an unmistakable wail of fright—that sharp *"A-a-ach!"* that pierces the unaccustomed ear with such curious dismay. Fathers and mothers bear this cry with equanimity, and even seem to find it a cause for pride, but to the unbabied adult it is so piercing and so unpleasant that it almost seems as though there was something to be said for Herod. Not that Dr. Lavendar had any such inhuman thoughts; he lifted the baby up and carried it into the study, where he put it down in his armchair, and stumbled about for matches to light the lamp. In his anxiety he did not even take off his flapping felt hat, which encircled his face like a black nimbus. Holding the lamp in his hand, he came and stood over the bundle in his chair; the baby stopped crying and sucked in its lower lip, and returned his gaze. It was Mary's child. He recognized it at once, and did not need the dirty scrap of paper pinned on its breast:

"Mr. Lavendar i cant do for baby no longer it cries nights and do keep me awake and i got to do my work next day all the same and i cant stand it no longer and i cant do for it no longer i am sorrie i pittie poor baby to be left alone and i love my baby just as much as if i was married but i have to put it away i will never come back any more so get it a home and please excuse no more at present from your friend Miss Mary Dean   PS   i have decided to name it Evelina."

He read it, and then he looked at the baby blinking at the lamplight, in his armchair. "If you'll just wait a minute," he said, in an agitated voice, "I'll—I'll get a woman!"

The baby yawned; he saw the roof of its small pink mouth, like a kitten's. "I'll return immediately," he assured it; and hurried, almost running, out to the kitchen. But his maidservant was not there. "What shall I do?" he said. "Very likely it ought to be fed, or something. Perhaps it wants to be held. I'll get Rachel."

It was easy to get Rachel King, as she lived but a stone's-throw away; she was locking her front door when, halfway down the street, he called her and waved his lantern; and Rachel, in her placid mind, foresaw a sudden illness somewhere, and a night's watching before her. His breathless explanation sent her hurrying, faster than he could walk, back to the parsonage. When he got there she had the baby on her knee, and was taking off the faded shawl that the mother had wrapped around it, and mumbling her lips over the little dimpled arm.

"There's a pin somewhere that has scratched her," she said. "There, you little darling. Oh, dear me, Dr. Lavendar, that shawl is so dirty!

And look at this scratch on her little hand. There—there—there. Why, her little feet are as cold as stones!" She gathered the small feet into her hand, and cuddled the child up against her breast. "I feel her shiver!" she said, angrily. "I believe that wretched girl has given her her death of cold leaving her on that stone step. There, dear; there— there. Dear baby, bless your little heart! She says she 'was frightened all alone in the dark; frightened 'most to death,' she says. Yes, darling, yes. 'I was scared,' she says, 'and I was drefful cold.' There, now, are your little feet warm?"

Dr. Lavendar stood looking down at her, greatly relieved.

"But what am I going to do with it tonight?" he said, anxiously.

"Oh, I am going to take her home, sir. Dr. Lavendar, *give her to me?*"

"Oh, well, Rachel, I hope the mother will come back, you know. And, in fact, I suppose our first duty is to get hold of her and make her take it."

"What!" she interrupted, "when she deserted her? Give a child back to such a mother? No! she doesn't deserve her!"

"But, perhaps," he ventured, "the work really was too hard? There's her letter. You see what she says. I certainly ought to try to get a different kind of place for her, where she won't have so much to do. It is hard to be kept awake at night and then have to work, you know. We must try to make it possible for her to keep her child, poor girl."

"Dr. Lavendar, any woman who could write such a letter ought not to be allowed to have a child," Rachel said. "But I don't believe we'll ever hear from her again. Anyhow, I'm going to take this precious baby home with me! Little darling! do you want to come home and have some hot milk, and go sleepy? Well, you shall!— there, there, there!"

"I wish you would take her home, my dear, I wish you would," Dr. Lavendar said, "and tomorrow we can decide what we ought to do."

Rachel smiled, her eyes narrowing a little, but she said nothing. She wrapped the child up in her skirt, "I won't have that shawl touch her," she said, decidedly.

"Won't it cry if you take it out in the dark?" Dr. Lavendar inquired, meekly.

Rachel laughed.

" 'It'!" she said. *"She* won't cry in my arms."

That night was a wonderful one to Rachel King. The washing of the soft, uncared-for baby flesh; the feeding of the warmed and com-

forted little body; then the putting the child to sleep, sitting in a
low chair, and rocking slowly back and forth, back and forth, crooning, crooning, crooning, her shadow dipping and rising across the
ceiling of the faintly lighted room. When the baby was asleep Rachel
looked over the rough, grimy clothing, shaking her head, and touching the little petticoats with disgusted fingers.

"Ach—dirty!" she said. "They sha'n't touch her again; she's as
clean as a flower now."

And then she took her lamp and went up through the silent house
to the garret. Whenever Rachel came up here under the rafters of
the old house, she thought what a place it would be for children to
play on rainy days. Well, now, perhaps a little child should play here;
a little girl might use that old doll-house set back against the big
brick chimney. Rachel's breath quickened as this thought leaped up
in her heart. She put the lamp down on a chest, and, from under
the eaves, pulled out an old horsehair trunk; when she opened it a
scent of dried roses and sweet clover came from the clean old baby
linen that had been lying there some twenty years. Poor Mrs. King,
staggering from reason to imbecility, had put the little clothes away;
and every spring, for her sake, Rachel took them out, and aired them,
and put them back again.

On top of the baby clothes lay a battered old doll; when she lifted
it Rachel drew in her breath as though something hurt her. Then she
began to sort out the things she needed for the little rosy child of
dishonor and sin. The lamp flickered in the draught from the open
door, and cast her great shadow across the ceiling as, gently, she took
up one little garment after another. As she shook out the knitted
shirts and brushed some rose leaves from the folds of the yellowing
slips, a sense of providing for her own came warmly to her breast.
Her baby! She took her lamp and went downstairs again, the pile
of clothing on her arm.

The baby slept, warm and quiet, on Rachel's bed; she bent over it
to feel its soft breath on her cheek; then she gathered its feet into her
hand to be sure that they were warm, and lifted the arm which was
thrown up over its head and put it under the cover. It seemed as
though she could not take her eyes away from the child, even that
she might undress and lie down beside it. And when she did it was
not to sleep; a dozen times she raised herself on her elbow to look
down at the little figure beside her and listen for its breathing, and
lift its small relaxed hand to her lips. Sometimes she thought of the
woman who had deserted it: but never as if any of her shame were

connected with the child's personality. Only with indignation—and thankfulness!

It was a night of birth to this childless woman.

In those first days she did not ask Dr. Lavendar whether he was taking any steps to find the baby's mother, but she lived breathlessly. "I'll *buy* her, if that creature comes back," she said to herself, over and over. But the creature did not come back, though Dr. Lavendar tried his best to find some trace of her, to urge upon her the duty of caring for her child. And after a while Rachel's plan and plea seemed to the old minister the only way out of the matter: Rachel wanted the baby; and its own mother evidently did not; so it had best remain with Rachel. Certainly for the child there could be no question as to which lot in life was best for it.

But it was several months before Rachel King felt assured possession. "The mother may come back for it," Dr. Lavendar reminded her many times, "so don't let's be in a hurry." But in the end it was settled as Rachel wished. The mother drifted off into the world; and the little waif, which had drifted into a home, grew into a flowerlike child, pretty and happy and good.

IV

It was a most peaceable Old Chester childhood that came to little Anna, for Rachel preserved the traditions of the town in bringing her up—and that meant love and obedience, and the sweet, attendant grace of reverence, of which, alas, childhood is so often robbed in these emancipated days. In Old Chester the bringing up of their children occupied the women in a way at once religious and intellectual. Practically they had no other interest; individualism and the sense of social responsibility, those two characteristics of the modern woman, were not even guessed at—indeed, they would have been thought exceedingly unladylike. But the care of the individual child and the sense of responsibility for its morals made the interest and excitement and occupation of the mothers' lives. The great fear was that children might be "spoiled"; hence it was a subject for prayer that no sinful human instinct, no mere maternal feeling, should be allowed to interfere with discipline. Infants were punished, children were trained, youth was admonished, with religious devotion. It was a matter of pious pride to Old Chester that Mrs. Dale's first baby had cried himself into a spasm on being forced to drink the skin on scalded milk. It was perhaps unfortunate that Mrs. Dale should have tried to make the child take the crinkling scum in the first place;

but having tried, having called in several serious mothers to advise
and wrestle with the ten months' baby, having forced teaspoons
between small, wet lips, and held little fighting, struggling hands,
it was imperative that she should succeed. She succeeded. To be sure,
later on, young Eben Dale quarrelled with his mother and sowed
enough wild oats to feed the Augean stables; but he reformed in
time to die at thirty in the odor of sanctity—his conversion being,
Mrs. Dale believed, due to that rigid discipline of his youth (and
the mercy of God). Old Chester children were prayed for, and
agonized over, and sent supperless to bed, with a chapter in the Bible
to be committed to memory by the light of one uncertain candle
shining through their hungry tears. And most of them are grateful for it now.

As for Rachel King, she observed these traditions in the way in
which she cared for Anna; but it was always with tenderness. And
Anna was a dear and happy little child. She never knew that her
aunt, as she called Rachel, thought, and planned, and fairly lived
in her life. It would have been contrary to Rachel's principles to
allow the child to feel herself important; but nothing escaped the
kind eyes, the farseeing love, that punished and praised with that
calm justice which children so keenly appreciate. The little girl's
physical well-being was of absorbing interest to Rachel, but her spiritual well-being was a religion to the quiet, matter-of-fact woman,
who did not look any more capable of spiritual passion than did
some gentle, ruminative cow lying under a big tree in a sunny
meadow. Anna's possible inheritance was a horror to Rachel, and
when the child told her first lie her foster-mother was nearly sick with
dismay and anxiety. It was only one of the romancing lies as common to childhood as playing. Anna recited a long tale of how she
went to Dr. Lavendar's and rung the bell, and then tried to reach
up to the knocker, and tumbled down, and saw a large toad looking at her from beside the front steps, and how she was so frightened she ran every step of the way home. Rachel, when she found
this was pure invention, nearly broke her heart. Alarmed and stern,
she carried the story to Dr. Lavendar, who chuckled over it, and
blinked his eyes, and said:

"And she never left the yard, you say, the whole afternoon? Well,
well! what an imagination!"

"But, Dr. Lavendar, it was a lie," Rachel said, staring at him with
dismay.

"My dear, you can't say a child of four is a liar. Did you mean
to punish her?"

Rachel nodded, and sighed.

"Don't you do it! Laugh at her. That's all she needs. Tell her it's foolish to say things happened that didn't happen. Time enough to punish her when she does it to gain an end. Don't you see it was a tale to the child?"

"But her—the woman who deserted her lied so!"

"Her mother?"

Rachel winced. "Yes, that—that woman."

"That's true; poor Mary didn't seem able to tell the truth. Well, I suppose it's natural for you, Rachel, to be afraid of the inheritance from her earthly mother; but mind you don't forget her inheritance from her Heavenly Father, my dear."

Rachel bent her head, solemnly, listening and comforted.

"Dear me, dear me!" Dr. Lavendar ruminated. "How He has provided for one of the least of His little ones: the deserted child of a woman who was a sinner! Rachel, I wonder where she is. Suppose she were to come back?"

Rachel King had gotten up to go, comforted and smiling, though the tears were near the surface; her face hardened instantly. "She won't come back; if she did, it would be nothing to me."

"She might want to know about the child—where she is, and all that."

"You wouldn't tell her?" Rachel said, with a gasp.

Dr. Lavendar put his pipe down, and stuck out his lips in a way he had when he was puzzled. "I've never spoken of it to you, Rachel, but I've wondered about it. Not that I think we'll ever hear from her, poor creature—"

"'Poor' creature?" Rachel interrupted, violently. "Lost creature! wretch! fiend!" It was like the sudden show of teeth and claws the way in which the face of this slow, mild woman flamed with rage. "I hope she's dead!"

Dr. Lavendar looked up at her, open-mouthed.

"Well, now, Rachel, aren't you a little—harsh, maybe? As for Anna, she is that poor sinner's child—"

"No, no!" Rachel King broke in. "No, Dr. Lavendar, I can't hear you say that; I *can't!* She is my child."

"Now, my dear, you know that is really foolish," he said, shaking his head. "That girl who gave her birth is her mother; ye can't get around that, Rachel."

"That—woman, is only the mother of—of her body," Rachel King said, in a low voice. "I am her mother, Dr. Lavendar. Anna is mine. No; that—creature will never come back; but if she did, it would make no difference; it would make no more difference to me than it would to Mrs. Wright and her Lydia, or—or any mother. My child is *mine*."

"I wonder what the law would say?" Dr. Lavendar ventured, meekly.

"The law?" Rachel said. "What do I care for the law? That's man's word. God gave me that child, and only God shall take her from me!"

"But, Rachel," he protested, "a mother has a natural right; if she wanted her child (supposing she could feed it and take proper care of it), I think anybody would agree that she ought to have it."

Rachel King turned on him, panting; her hands were trembling, and her large face a dull, angry red. "Is food the only thing she needs, Dr. Lavendar? I would rather Anna was dead, I would sooner kill her with my own hands, than have her go to that—creature!" Without another word she turned and walked away from him.

As for Dr. Lavendar, he sat still, perfectly confounded by her violence.

"How people do surprise you!" he said to himself at last. "Well, it appears Solomon knew what he was talking about. It was the real mother who said, 'in no wise slay it.' Curious how nature can always be relied on to tell the truth. But how Rachel did surprise me!"

However, Rachel did not surprise him in this way again; indeed, though she came to see him on this matter or on that, things were not quite the same between them. A deep resentment and distrust grew up in her mind. Dr. Lavendar had, to her way of thinking, showed an unfriendly and unfeeling disposition which she had never suspected in him. She did not speak of this resentment, of course; but it burned and smouldered, and never quite went out. The anger of slow, mild, loving people has a lasting quality that mere bad-tempered folk cannot understand. Rachel used to reproach herself for the hardness of her heart, and say that she must remember that Dr. Lavendar was getting old, and could not understand things—"or else he would know that God gave Anna to me," she would say, over and over; her simple creed permitting the idea that her Creator had made a depraved mother commit the sin of abandoning her child so that another woman might have a child to love and care for. But she never again let the maternal passion burst out in such fierce words of possession.

Dr. Lavendar, however, pondered those words in his heart. He used to sit blinking at the fire, and rubbing Danny's ears, and thinking about it: after all, to whom did Anna really belong? Over and over he discussed it with himself, but only as an abstract proposition that interested him as any philosophical, impersonal question might. The first mother was gone, having resigned the baby to the chance of kindness; the second mother, so to speak, had taken her empty place, and was doing her neglected duty; thanks to her, little Anna was being brought up as a member of Christ, the child of God, and an inheritor of the Kingdom of Heaven. But to whom did she really belong?

He pottered about over this question with the same mild intellectual enjoyment with which in his salad days he had discussed (and disposed of) the errors of the Socinians and the Pelagians. And by-and-by he made up his mind, and decided, in his dogmatic way, that "there was no question about it": By the inalienable claim of nature Anna belonged to the woman who had brought her into the world.

So little Anna grew into a pleasant child. She was looked after a little more strictly than other children, and perhaps punished more; but it seemed as though she were loved more too. She had a very happy childhood: sewing on a hassock at Rachel's feet, her hair parted smoothly over her round, pure forehead, and her bright eyes eager as any other child's to be through with her task and get out to play; romping in the garden with other little girls; playing with her doll —an old doll given her by Rachel, whose eyes, when she put it into Anna's hands, were wet, and who stroked the dolly's head as if she loved it; learning to read at Rachel's knee out of a brown book with two fat gilt cherubs on the cover, called *Reading Without Tears*. However, Anna's childhood had its tears, fortunately. Rachel's love was not of that poor fibre that spares the wholesome salt of tears in the bread of life. So little Anna laughed and cried and played, and grew into a dear, good child.

And when she was ten years old, all this was weighed in the balance against the "inalienable claim of nature."

V

It was on Saturday, and the children were straggling up the street to the rectory for their catechism and collect class. Dr. Lavendar had had this class for forty years; the preceding generation had sat on the little hard benches in the dining-room, and learned that a collect was divided into three parts, the invocation, the petition, and the conclusion, just as this generation was learning it. Fathers and mothers, thirty years before, had recited in concert that their sponsors in baptism had renounced for them the devil and all his works, the pomps and vanities of this wicked world, and all the sinful lusts of the flesh; and now they were permitting their children to be reminded, once a week, that a like futile renunciation had been made for them.

On this particular Saturday it was raining, and was cold and blustery. But Old Chester children were brought up to believe that they were neither sugar nor salt; and so, when it was time to start, they trudged along through the rain and mud to the rectory. They were a sturdy, rosy set, very shy, quite clumsy, and stupidly, stolidly silent—except when they were alone; then they chattered like sparrows. The class met in the dining-room, the table being pushed over into one corner, and some benches placed in two rows in front of a blackboard. There was always a dish of apples on a side-table (or jumbles, if it was summer); and the five or six boys and seven or eight girls kept an eye on it, to cheer them through the half-hour of the old minister's talk. Dear me! how that dish kept up a sinking heart when its owner was asked (no one ever knew where the lightning was going to strike, so there was no such thing as cramming beforehand), *"What is thy duty towards thy neighbor?"* When collect class was over, the apples or jumbles were handed around, and each child took one, and said, "Thank you, sir." And then Danny was brought in and put through his tricks; and sometimes, if everything had gone very well, and "what desirest thou of God in this prayer?" and "What is thy duty to thy neighbor?" had been answered without a mistake, and Dr. Lavendar was especially good-natured, they were taken into the study and shown the lathe, and the little boxes of garnets and topazes and amethysts; and perhaps—oh, *very* rarely, maybe three times a year—one boy and one girl were chosen, turn about, to put a foot upon the treadle and start the lathe. And then how the collect class stood about, gaping with interest and awe!

This class met at two, and was such an institution of Old Chester that nobody ever thought of calling, or getting married, or being buried, at two o'clock of a Saturday afternoon. But on this rainy January Saturday, a little before two, a carriage drove up to the rectory gate, and a fat, sleepy-looking man helped a very pretty young woman to alight. He held an umbrella over her in a stupid, uncertain way as they walked up the garden path, and she scolded him sharply, and told him to look out, the water was dripping on her hat!

"What's the odds?" he said, good-naturedly. "I'll get you all the hats you want, Mamie."

"Here's the house," the young woman said. "Now, Gus, you sit out in the hall, and I'll talk to the old man."

"Why can't I come in too?"

"Oh, well, I'd rather see him alone," she said.

"All right," he responded, with a foolish grin.

Dr. Lavendar was in the dining-room, fussing over the arrangement of the little low benches, and printing the collect on the blackboard. The "**O Lord**" and the "**Amen**" were always written in very large letters, and the question, "What does Amen mean?" was always asked of the youngest Todd child, who was, poor boy, "wanting," and could only remember that one answer, which he recited as *"Sobeet."*

"There's a man and woman to see you, sir," Mary said. "I believe they're strangers. I guess they want to be married."

"Ho! What do they mean by coming at this hour?" said Dr. Lavendar.

"I told 'em you had the children coming," Mary defended herself —Mary was always defending herself; it is a characteristic of her class —"but they allowed they had to get back to Mercer to get a train for Australia, and they couldn't wait."

"If they go by rail to Australia they'll do well," said Dr. Lavendar. "Well, I guess I can marry 'em in ten minutes. Just be ready to come in, Mary, will you?"

Then he went shuffling out into the hall, where the man was sitting, holding his hat on his knees.

"No, sir; it's not me; it's my wife wants to see you. She's in beyont."

So they didn't want to get married. Dr. Lavendar saw Neddy Todd coming, rolling and stumbling and grinning, along the street, and made haste to go into his study.

Of course, as soon as he entered the room, Dr. Lavendar knew the woman. She had grown a little heavier; she was very well dressed, and was perhaps prettier than ten years before. It was the same face —mean and shallow and simpering; but there was a hungry look in it that he did not understand.

"I don't know as you recognize me," she began, airily. "I was—"

"I recognize you. You are Mary Dean."

"Well, I *was*. I'm Mrs. Gus Larkin now. I'm married." She laughed a little as she spoke, with a coquettish toss of her head. "That's him out in the hall. We're going to live in Australia. We sail on Tuesday. He's a mechanical engineer, and he gets real good wages. Well, he says I can take baby. So I come to get her." Her face, as she spoke, changed and grew anxious, and her breath came quickly. "She's well?" she said. "She's—alive? Why don't you say something?" she ended, shrilly. "My baby ain't—dead, is she?"

"No; oh no; no," he said, feebly. Then he sat down and looked at her. Two umbrellas, bobbing against each other, came up the path. Two more children. He wondered who they were.

Mary was instantly relieved and happy. "Of course it's a long time since I've seen her," she began; "but there! there hasn't been a day I 'ain't thought of her. Is she pretty? Well, about two months ago he married me, and as soon as I got a home of my own I just thought I'd have baby. That was my first thought, though of course I was real glad to be respectable. But I'll have baby, I says to myself. Well, he's real kind; I'll say that for him. And he said I could have her. So I've come to get her. We're going back to Mercer tonight, because we've got to start tomorrow morning. And Tuesday we get on the ship. Baby—well, there! She ain't a baby now; I suppose she's grown a big girl? She'll be real interested in seein' a ship. I am myself. I never seen a ship—or an ocean. Oh, well, sir, you don't know what it is to me to get my baby back again!"

Her face moved suddenly, with tears, but she smiled. Dr. Lavendar felt a curious faintness; the suddenness of the thing—an abstraction violently materialized, so to speak—gave him a physical as well as a moral shock. The real mother, a married woman, "respectable," as she said, was asking, naturally, simply, for her child. And of course she must have it.

"I do not think," he said, slowly, his voice deep and trembling, "that you really love your child: ten years of indifference to her fate does not show much love!" He began to get his breath, and sat up straight in his chair, glowering at her under stern brows.

"Well," she defended herself, "of course I see how it looks to you. But—there! I couldn't have her with me. Why, how could I? and me—the way I was? Why, I *wouldn't*. I loved her, though, all the time. I don't know as you'll believe me?"

Dr. Lavendar said to himself that he did not believe her; but deep down in his heart, in a frightened way, he knew that she was speaking the truth. "How long have you been married?" he said. She told him; and added that "he" was perfectly respectable.

"What do you call respectable?" Dr. Lavendar said; and even in his alarm and confusion he knew, with shame, that there was contempt in his voice—"what do *you* call respectable?"

"Well, Gus never was took up, and he never kept company with them that was took up," she said, proudly; "and he gets good wages. Before we broke up to go to his place in Australia we had a Brussels carpet on our parlor floor, and a piano—(we were getting it on instalments, but then it's all the same; it was standing right in our bow-window). Baby'll have a good home. He had twenty-two dollars a week, and he's going to have forty dollars in Melbourne. I'll dress her pretty, I can tell you!"

Respectability: "not to have been arrested!" Well! well! Anna, ten years old, trained in every sweet old-fashioned delicacy of thought and speech, in the nurture and admonition of the Lord, was to be thrown into such "respectability!"

"Mary," he said, clearing his throat, but speaking huskily and with a shaking voice, "you gave your child away. Why do you want her now? She is in a good home, and has good friends. Why don't you leave her there?"

She listened to him in amazement, and then burst out laughing. "Leave her? Well, I guess I won't! I'm willing to pay the folks for her board, if they ask it. But a child don't eat much, and I guess they've made her work; a bound-out child works her passage every time. Still, I'll pay. As for leavin' her—why, I married him more to get her a good home than anything else!"

The room darkened with a splash of rain against the window. Some more children came up through the garden, their umbrellas huddled together, and their little feet crunching the wet gravel of the path. He could hear the murmur of their chatter, and caught Theophilus Bell's shrill inquiry, "Say, Lydia, 'what is required of persons to be baptised?'" They came clattering into the hall; and then the house was silent again, except that the man waiting outside coughed, and moved about restlessly.

"I never signed papers to adopt her out—did I? Well, then, the law 'd give her to me. I'm her mother."

Her mother! Sacred and invincible word! There came keenly to his mind a phrase Rachel had used—*only the mother of her body.* Of course Rachel was wrong; but why hadn't she adopted Anna? for in the security of years, foolishly enough, the question of legal adoption had not been raised.

"Mary," he said, "think—think what you are doing!—to take her away from a good home. I—I hope you won't do it?"

She shook her head violently. "You needn't talk to me about good homes; I've got a good home for her. And I'm respectable."

"Oh, do give it up, Mary," he said, his voice shaking with agitation—"do consider her welfare! Mary, let me put it to your husband.

He is kind, as you say, to be willing to take her; but let me tell him—"

"No." She went and stood in front of the door, with a frightened look. "No!"

"Let me tell him how it is," he insisted. He had it in mind to offer these people money.

Mary caught him by the wrist. "No, you—you mustn't. He—I told him it was my sister's child. He—don't know."

Dr. Lavendar fell back, but his face cleared. "A lie!" he said. "Mary, you're not worthy of her. What do I care if you gave her birth? You are nothing but her mother! She shall stay where she is!"

Mary turned white; then she dropped down at his feet. "Give me my baby," she said. "Oh, Mr. Lavendar, give me my baby!" She put her arms about his knees and looked up at him, her voice hoarse and whispering. "I must have her—I must have her!" She dropped her face on the floor, moaning like an animal. He looked down at her, the difficult tears of age standing in his eyes.

"Mary," he said, trying to lift her, "stop—stop and think of An— of the child's best good. And, besides, you have another child; why not get it?"

"Dead," she said, brokenly; "dead."

"I believe," he said, solemnly, "it is better dead than with you. Alas that I must say so! And as for this child, that you deserted ten years ago, when I say she must stay where she is, I am not thinking of—of the people she is living with, who would be heartbroken to part with her; I'm thinking of her future—"

"Well, but," she interrupted, passionately, "what about me? Haven't I any future? You've got to give her to me!"

But he knew from her confession that her husband was ignorant of her past, and that he held the situation in his hand: she could not force him to give Anna up unless she betrayed herself; and that, it was plain, she would not do.

"I tell you," she insisted, "I'll give her as good a home as anybody. Oh, my little, little baby! I want my baby! Oh, you haven't a heart in you, to kill me like this! My baby—" Again she broke off, gasping and sobbing. It was horrible and heartbreaking. A timid knock at the door came like a crash into their ears.

"Mamie!"

Mary leaped to her feet, brushing her hand over her eyes, and panting, but holding herself rigid.

("Don't tell him," she said, rapidly;) and then laughed, in a silly, breathless way. "Go 'way, Gus; I ain't through yet."

"I thought I heard you takin' on," he said, peering suspiciously into the room.

"Oh, get out with you!" she answered. "No; I was just talking. Go back, I'll be out in a minute." The man withdrew, meekly.

Dr. Lavendar stood looking at her; he had no doubts now. "Not that which is natural but that which is spiritual," he thought to himself. He wondered if the children had all come; he wondered if Anna was sitting on one of the little hard benches, saying her catechism over to some other child. Mary talked on, passionately, but in a low voice. She urged every conceivable reason for the custody of her child, ending by saying, in sudden anger—for Dr. Lavendar only answered her by a slow, silent shake of the head—

"Well, I shouldn't think, if I'm so bad I can't have her, that the folks that has her would want a child with such bad blood in her!" She was trembling again, and ready for another wild burst of tears.

But as she spoke, Gus knocked once more. "Say, Mame: we've *got* to go; we'll miss the train."

"Shut the door," she said. Then looked full into Dr. Lavendar's face. *"Will you give me my child?"*

"No," he said, pityingly.

She stared at him a moment, her eyes narrowing, hate and fear and misery in her face. "Then—I'll go to hell!" she said; and turned and left him, shutting the door behind her softly.

"Come on," she told the meek husband.

Gus followed her out into the rain.

"Are you goin' after the young one now?" he said.

"No. He won't let me get her. He says she'd ought to stay with the folks that took her when my sister died."

Gus opened the carriage door for her, and chuckled. "Well, now, Mame, it would be quite a change for her. We're strangers to her, and she might be homesick. I didn't let on to you, but I thought of that. I don't know but what the old gentleman is right. And, you know, maybe—" He whispered something, looking at her out of his stupid, kindly eyes, his loose, weak mouth dropping into its meaningless smile.

Dr. Lavendar went to a little closet in the chimney breast, and took out a chunky black bottle and a glass. His hands shook so that the bottle and tumbler clinked together. He had to sit down a few minutes and get his breath and strength; the struggle had profoundly exhausted him; he looked very old as he sat there and swallowed his thimbleful of brandy.

"Solomon didn't know everything," he said to himself; "but may God forgive me if I've done wrong!"

In the dining-room the children were yawning and squabbling and hearing each other repeat the Collect and "your duty to your neighbor." It was nearly three. Theophilus Bell had instituted a game of "settlers escaping from Indians," which involved diving under the table, and leaping over the benches; but the girls felt that such levity was sacrilegious.

"There's prayer-books here," Anna King said, "so it's just the same as church."

"A prayer-book," returned Theophilus, scornfully, "isn't anything but a book; it's the prayers out of it that makes the church, and—" But his voice trailed off into quick subsidence as Dr. Lavendar came in.

"Well, children," he said, "you had to wait. I'm sorry. I think, though, as it's so late, we won't have any lesson—"

("Bully!" said Theophilus, under his breath.)

"—but we'll repeat the Collect, all together, and then you may go home."

"Aren't we going to have our apples?" remonstrated Theophilus.

"Oh, dear me, yes. Yes, yes. Come, Anna, my child, and kneel down here beside me. Children, let us pray:

"O Lord, we beseech Thee mercifully to receive the prayers of Thy people who call upon Thee; and grant that they may both perceive and know what things they ought to do, and also may have grace and power faithfully to fulfil the same; through Jesus Christ our Lord.

"Amen!" said Dr. Lavendar.

THOMAS ALLIBONE JANVIER

★ ★ ★

Lover of the strange and exotic, of areas and modes of existence old and highly colorful, Thomas Allibone Janvier (1849-1913) traveled much in Mexico, Colorado, and the Southwest, and made several prolonged visits abroad, especially to London and Southern France. Localities which won his affection, whether near or afar, he portrayed with charming freshness in stories, romances, and travel-guides. *Color Studies* (1885) contained sympathetic tales of Bohemian artist existence in 1881 near Washington Square, New York City. From 1882 to 1884 he lived in the Southwest and Mexico; these experiences were utilized in *Stories of Old New Spain* (1891) and *Santa Fe's Partner* (1907), stories splashed with local color and written with lightness, warmth, humor, and smoothness of diction. His life in New York City was productive of such volumes as *In Old New York* (1891), *The Uncle of an Angel* (1891), and *At the Casa Napoleon* (1914). Ten other full-length volumes and at least three dozen uncollected stories sustained his reputation among local colorists as one occupying a place of importance if not of high distinction.

★ ★ ★

The Lost Mine

IN the upper valley of the Rio Grande for a hundred years the Christian Spaniards had wrought evil in Christ's name. From their stronghold in the town of the Holy Faith their cruel power had spread out over all the valley-lands, constraining the Pueblo Indians, in the fear of death, to grievous toil in the mines, and to a yet more grievous service in the worship of the Spanish gods. And the Pueblos, in whose breasts hope scarce longer had a home, almost had ceased to beg from their own god deliverance. That was a most cruel and wicked time.

And it was in that time that marvelous treasure flowed from a certain mine up in the Sangre de Cristo mountains that was called, because it belonged to the Fathers whose monastery was at Santa Clara, *la mina de los Padres.* Of all the many rich mines in this silver-strewn range, the Mine of the Fathers was incomparably the richest. From it came wealth so great that even the avarice of those who fattened upon its kingly revenue was almost sated. And yet, as its shafts sank deeper, and as its galleries penetrated yet further into the bowels of the mountain, richer and richer grew its yield. So over all the realm of New Spain, and thence across seas even to the old Spanish country, the fame of *la mina de los Padres* went abroad.

But, with the story of its wondrous product of glittering silver, never a word was told of the bitter misery of those who toiled in its dark depths,—driven more harshly than ever beasts were driven, crushed down by toil to cruel and painful death, that the treasure might be wrung from the rock and brought within the reach of man. Nor was there any sign in the triumphant tidings sent homeward of the thousands of converts to the Christian faith at what cost of death to hundreds these thousands, through terror of death, had been won to the service of the Christian God; at what cost of rigid, ruthless mastership this service was maintained.

So at last, in that direful summer of the year 1680, the wind that the Spaniards had sown for a century came up a whirlwind of flame and blood, sweeping over and devastating all the land. Out from a clear sky came the storm. In a moment was upon them, in its terrible might and majesty, the pursuing wrath of God. Almost to a man the dwellers in the outpost towns—Taos, Santa Clara, San Ildefonso, Santa Cruz—were slain. At last even Santa Fe itself was abandoned, and the conquered masters fled pitifully southward for refuge from their conquering slaves. So was a great wrong punished; so at last was justice done to the Pueblos: when the God who is God of both pagan and Christian in his pity gave them his strength.

Long years passed by before the Spaniards again made good their hold upon the land; and when at last their strength in possession was restored, and the new dwellers in the monastery at Santa Clara sought to reopen the Mine of the Fathers, out of which those before them had drawn so great a revenue, no trace of the mine could they anywhere find! That the maps and plans of it which had been in the monastery should be gone was no surprising matter; but strange it was that the very mine itself should have vanished from the earth! Seeking it diligently, but finding it not, they came to know that the Pueblos, remembering the horror of their toil in former times, had destroyed the trail leading up to it among the mountains; with infinite labor had filled in the great main shaft, and had taken away all traces of the workings from around about the shaft's mouth. And knowing this, they sought to wrest the secret from them. Some were put to the torture, some were slain outright, that the living might be driven by dread of a like fate to tell where the mine was hid. But neither biting pain nor fear of death sufficed to shake their stern resolve. Bravely, grimly, in painful life and in dying agony, they held the secret locked within their breasts.

So the years drifted by and were marshaled into centuries; the power of the Spaniards waned to a shadow and vanished; a new race came in and possessed what, in times of old, had been their possessions; and while, through these fleeting years and slow-moving centuries, through all this wreck and change, the fame of *la mina de los Padres* lived on as a legend, the mine itself never was known of men.

In the legend of it that survived, 'twas said that upon him who should find it again would fall the curse of the Pueblos' god.

There is no more beautiful sight in all the fair land that once was the realm of New Spain than the view at sunset from Santa Clara looking westward, down the valley of the Rio Grande. The town—a score or so of brown adobe houses, clustered around the old church and the now partly ruined monastery—stands upon a little promontory, the last low wave of the foothills of the Sangre de Cristo range. The mountain ramparts which tower on each side of the valley go down in grand perspective toward the west, their peaks standing out blue-gray against the brighter blue-gray of the evening sky. And off toward the dying sun the sky takes a violent tint, and then a rose, and then a soft, rich red, and then a glowing crimson that is flecked and spangled with a great glory of flaming gold. Yet is the setting sun not seen, for, cutting off sight of it completely, the great castellated mountain of San Ildefonso raises the level lines of its broad battlements darkly, sharply against the dazzle of light and color beyond. Leading downward, as though it were a glittering highway to this lordly castle's gates, the Rio Grande flows smoothly between its low banks: the red and golden gleamings of the evening sky reflected on its rapid current. Each night there is fresh joy in beholding anew this magnificent resplendency, this perfect picture fresh from the hand of God.

Techita, sitting in a nook in the bluff below the walls of the old monastery, loved greatly to look upon this God-given picture; to watch its glory grow as the sun dropped down beyond the mountain of San Ildefonso and thence sent up rich colorings over all the western sky; to watch its glory wane as the sun sank yet lower behind the far mountains beyond, and the color-music slowly died away. And then, when the edge of night was come, and gray darkness was shutting in the west, and in the east only faint, soft colorings remained, it was her wont to go gently into the dusky church, and there, before the old picture of the sweet Santa Clara, make her pure offering of thankfulness in prayer.

Nor would Techita's thankfulness be lessened, as she walked slowly away from the church in the twilight, by catching sight of Juan standing by the doorway of his little home in a corner of the old monastery, and by seeing, even in the half darkness, the love-light shining in his eyes. Yet with her gladness that Juan loved her would come troublous doubts into Techita's heart. For, down in this old Mexican town, these two were living over the story that is as old as human life itself, and that ever is sorrowfully new—the story of a hopeless love.

A stranger coming to Santa Clara—at least a stranger from the barbarous northern country—would have perceived no outward difference in the estates of old Pablo, Techita's father, and of Techita's lover, Juan. Such a stranger, supposing that he had taken the trouble to think anything about them at all, would have "sized them up," after the abrupt, uncivil manner of *Americanos* generally, simply as a pair of poverty-stricken Mexicans; and he might have gone a step further, and wondered how on earth they managed to keep body and soul together, anyway. But so far as old Pablo was concerned, this estimate would have been very far astray. In point of fact, old Pablo was a rich man. Half a mile of the best land along the river was his; his also was the great flock of goats that every night at milking-time came trooping homeward to the corral; his also was the great herd of cattle that pastured on the *mesa negra,* half a dozen leagues away to the north; and in his granaries was a vast store of barley and beans and corn.

But Juan had neither flocks nor herds nor lands! All his earthly possessions were the few household things in the little home that the Padre, pitying him, had suffered him to make for himself in a corner of the old monastery. All his wealth was his strong young body and stout heart and ready hands.

Of a truth, this handsome Juan had been born into the world under an unlucky star. While he was yet a boy, the dreadful *viruelas* had swept down upon Santa Clara, and in a month's time his father and his mother, together with half the little town, were huddled into hastily dug graves. And he was still a boy when the old aunt who had cared for him died also, and left him to make his fight for life alone. Then it was that the good Padre had found for him a home in an odd corner of the old monastery, long since deserted of its old-time tenants and falling slowly into complete decay. Here, for a dozen years and more, he had made shift to live, helping the Padre in the offices of the church, herding goats, in the fallow season working in the fields. The Padre, whose heart was tender, greatly loved the lonely boy; and by the Padre's care he had become a prodigy of learning. Actually, he could read! And, still more wonderful, he could sign his name! and make about it, too, as brave a maze of flourishes as any Mexican in all the land. But for all his headful of knowledge, Juan was the poorest of the poor.

No wonder, then, that his love for Techita was hopeless. Pablo was a shrewd old fellow, with a keen eye—for all his look of sleepiness—for money-holding; and that his daughter (who also was his only child for Pablito and Pablito's mother had died together in a single day in that dismal smallpox time) should marry a rich man was the dearest purpose of his heart. During the past year or two, since Techita had begun to blossom into womanhood, the gossips of the little town had affirmed that the solemn old Don José, who owned the great *hacienda* at Abiqui, was the husband for Techita whom old Pablo had in mind. But there were those who said—saying it beneath the breath, for Señor Don Pablo was one whom it was not well to offend—that to put such a fate upon Techita would be a crime. And others, still bolder, declared that Juan and Techita, the handsomest couple in all the valley's length, were sent thus together into the world by the good God that they might be man and wife. But these whisperings never came to old Pablo's ears; and had they come, he would have laughed at them as old women's foolishness, so right it seemed to him that his daughter should wed her wealth with greater wealth; so absurd would have seemed to him the suggestion that she should wed with such a one as this goat-herding, field-working Juan.

Therefore it was that Techita, knowing well and dreading much her father's will concerning her, felt her heart troubled within her by knowing of the love that Juan had for her; by knowing that her own love was given to Juan in return. And often, as she knelt in the church as the daylight passed away, she prayed that the gentle Santa

Clara would soften her father's heart, so that happiness might come to her and to her lover. But the time went on, and no change came to open the way whereon she longed to go; and each passing month now, as she grew rapidly into womanhood, made the time more near for her to be the wife of Don José.

Thus matters stood when all the valley was filled with wonder by the sudden incoming of the *Americanos* from the North—not as an army waging war, as they had come three and thirty years before, but as an army building a railroad. What a railroad was, these people— whose only notions of locomotion were their own legs and the legs of *burros* and heavy wooden carts—did not at all know; but as it was an invention of the *Americanos* there could be no doubt that it was something devilish. Presently, as their fields were laid waste, and their cherished watercourses broken, all possible doubts of the absolute devilishness of the railroad were removed. It was a thing to be abhorred. And when, the railroad being builded, all manner of evil *Americanos*—cutthroats, desperadoes, the advance-guard of rascality that pours into each newly opened region of the West—came down upon them, destroying the pleasant peacefulness of their quiet land, their hatred of their old-time enemies grew yet more bitter and intense; the more intense because, instinctively, they knew their own powerlessness to stay the incoming stream.

The wave that surged down upon them was a mighty one; for, now that the railroad had opened the way to it, the ancient fame of the treasure-laden Sangre de Cristo was remembered, and everywhere the mountains were dotted with prospectors' camps. Once more the legend of the Mine of the Fathers was revived, and in many a camp hearts beat quicker and breath came shorter as the story of its marvelous riches was told anew. Again it was sought for, with not less eagerness and with more skill than it had been sought for two hundred years before; and again was the search fruitless and in vain. One after another they who sought for it gave up their search as hopeless, or were satisfied with making lesser strikes, until only one man remained to carry the search on. But this man stuck grimly to the purpose that had brought him southward from the States.

Dick Irving was a person who did what he made up his mind to do. Up in Pueblo—the Colorado town in the Arkansas Valley—he had come across a trooper of Price's old command, who had fought his way down from Taos to Santa Fe in 1847; and who, the fighting ended, had married a Mexican wife and had settled himself for life in the land that he had helped to win. There are not a few of these bits of army drift scattered over the country north of Santa Fe. And

this old soldier told so glowing a story of *la mina de los Padres* that
Irving forthwith sold out his interest in the "Rattling Meg," up at
Leadville, and in a week's time was down in the Sangre de Cristo
with his prospecting outfit, and at work.

"I'll find that mine or I'll die for it!" he told his Leadville partner
before he left for the south; and he added, his hand resting easily on
the handle of his forty-four:

"If any man is ahead of me, by ——, I'll shoot him and jump his
claim!"

In matters of this nature Dick Irving was a man who kept his word.

Techita sat in her nook under the edge of the bluff and watched
the sun go down, and very, very heavy was her heart. At last the
stroke that she had dreaded for so long had fallen: her father had told
her that the time had come when she must be the wife of Don José.
Nor would he so much as listen to her entreaties that this might not
be. Breaking in upon her words, he had said, "It is my will"—and
so had left her, desolate of hope.

That night there was no beauty for her in the sunset; and when
the glory was gone out of the sky, and she went slowly through the
dimness of twilight into the darkness of the church, bitter sorrow was
upon her and her eyes were weary with their weight of tears. She
knelt before the picture of the saint, as was her habit, but from her
lips there came no prayer. What was the good of praying? she
thought. Had she not prayed again and again with all the faith and
strength that was in her that she might be spared that which now
had come? The saint was far away in heaven—too far to heed the
pleadings of a poor, lonely child on earth. Ah! would that she were
safe in heaven, too!

And then, still kneeling upon the clay floor before the picture of the
saint, she fell into a dreary reverie, thinking of the lifetime of happiness for which she had hoped, of the lifetime of sorrow that now she
must endure. Yet, while she knelt thus, looking the while sadly, steadfastly upon the saint's sweet face, shining out from the surrounding
darkness as a gleam from the sunset's afterglow struck full upon it
through the little window beneath the roof, she seemed to see a look
of loving pity come into the gentle eyes, to see upon the tender lips a
pitying smile; and the hope came to her that the saint, forgiving her
for doubting her saintly power to comfort and to aid, even yet through
the saving strength of heavenly grace would turn her mourning into
joy. So there came into her troubled soul a little thrill of happiness.

"Techa!"

A quiver went over her, and for a moment her heart stopped beating, as the thought fell upon her that, in very truth, the saint had spoken—and then she knew that the voice sounding low in the darkness was the voice of Juan.

"Techa, art thou here? I must speak with thee. I have to tell thee of a great joy."

She made a little sound in answer, while rushing in upon her came the glad hope that the promise given her by the saint's pitying glance and smile was coming true.

"My Techa, listen! The good God has had pity for our sorrow, and the bar between us is broken down. A great wonder has happened, that has made me richer than thy father by a thousand fold. By God's grace I have found again the wonderful mine in the mountains that belonged to the Fathers back in the long-past time. I am rich, rich even beyond thought; and richer than all, because now thou also wilt be mine."

Then Juan told the story of the good fortune that had come to him. One corner of his dwelling-place in the old monastery—the corner in which was the little triangular fireplace—long had been in a ruinous state that promised at any time a fall. That day the fall had come, and from the broken wall had dropped out a roll of tough hide, in which were wrapped securely the lost plans of the ancient mine. Thus had they been hidden, by hands soon still in death, on that August day, two hundred years before, when the Pueblos rose in revolt against their Spanish taskmasters: the visible agents of the avenging wrath of God.

Yellow with age were the plans, pale the once black drafting, but still the plotting was distinct and clear: showing the site of the monastery; showing the long-lost trail leading up beyond the *arroyo* of San Pedro into the mountains; showing the mine itself, a league or more away, at the trail's end. To one knowing the country well, as Juan did, everything was clear. Over the mountainside, high up above the cañon wherein the mine was sunk, he had driven his goats a hundred times. There was no uncertainty about his discovery: *la mina de los Padres* was found, and was his!

With a quickly beating heart Techita listened to this wonderful story of good fortune; and as she listened a great gladness filled her soul. It was only the wealth of Don José, she knew, that had made him seem pleasant in her father's eyes; Juan, with his incomparably greater wealth, need have no fears now that his suit would be rejected. Happiness enveloped her, for now at last her happiness was sure. In perfect thankfulness she knelt again before the sweet Santa

Clara's picture, drawing Juan also on his knees beside her; and there, with grateful thoughts, for their hearts were all too full for words, they gave praise silently for the great goodness which, through Santa Clara's intercession, had come to them from the merciful and loving God.

Yet, even as she thus knelt, fear and misgiving came into Techita's soul. Mingled with her Spanish blood was the blood of the Pueblo race, of the pagans whom her Christian ancestors had treated so cruelly in the time of old; and together with her Christian faith was, if not faith, at least a fearful reverence for the Pueblos' god. In dread she remembered now, in the undercurrent of thought below her thoughts of thankfulness and praise, the direful prophecy that upon whomsoever should find again the Mine of the Fathers the curse of the Pueblos' god would fall.

Standing outside the door of the church, the young moon, just risen over the mountains in the east, shining faintly down upon them, Techita falteringly told her fears; and Juan, full of gladness now that his long sorrow was at an end, laughed lightly and bade her fear no more.

"We are good Christians, my Techa," he said, "and our valiant God and his brave saints watch over us. What need we fear from this false god, who for ages has been dead and gone?"

But as thus irreverently he spoke, there fell upon him also a strange sense of dread; for he also had Pueblo faith deep down in his heart, because of the Pueblo blood which flowed in his veins. By an effort he stirred himself and drove the dread away. In the faint light Techita did not mark the change that for a moment came over his face as he ceased to speak, and so had comfort from his cheerful words. It was indeed true, she thought, that the blessed saints were brave defenders against all evil powers; and she was well assured now that one of the saints at least—this gracious Santa Clara—had promised to them her potent aid. Therefore had she a firm foundation whereon to rest her faith and hope. Yet, as she walked slowly homeward, vague forebodings of coming sorrow forced themselves upon her; nor could she, with all her faith in Santa Clara's helpfulness, with all her bright hopes of the happiness that was to come, wholly drive these dark thoughts away.

Dick Irving was puzzled. He believed, and with good reason, that what he did not know about prospecting was not worth the finding out. And yet it was a point in prospecting that was puzzling him now, and, to use his own words, puzzling him "the worst kind."

The knotty question that was too much for him was where a piece of "float" came from that he had found in the *arroyo* of San Pedro. When he had found that particular piece of loose rock, it had made his heart jump and his mouth water. In the course of his extended experience in prospecting, he never had come across anything that for richness came anywhere near it; it was richer than the best of the Leadville carbonates, richer than the best of the ruby silver down in the Gunnison. On a rough calculation, he concluded that the vein where it came from would mill-run not less than a thousand ounces. If the vein had any body to it, that meant more millions than he could think of at once without shivering.

But the trouble was that the beginning of his prodigious find was also the end of it. The bit of float was like the footprint on Robinson Crusoe's island; there it was, solitary—not a sign to tell whence it came and what it belonged to. He was certain that there was not any more of it, for he had spent nearly a month in the *arroyo* turning over carefully every stone, and running his knowing eyes jealously along every crevice in its rocky walls. And now his mad was getting up. His reputation as a prospector was at stake. And more than this, he knew that close at hand, on the flanks of one of the two mountains which towered above him, was a mine which to find was to make his everlasting fortune; which to miss was to miss the great chance of his life—and the pleasing conviction was growing upon him more strongly every day that he was going to miss it.

He knew, of course, that almost his only chance was to follow up the float; and that was the reason why he had put in such thorough work upon the *arroyo*. When this failed him he took to the mountains themselves. It was a desperate chance, but it was the only chance left to him. He put in another barren month in this fashion, and then he was about ready to own himself beaten; to own that for once he had walked all around and all over the mine that he was looking for without being able to make even a good guess as to where it was. Once, indeed, for a moment, he had felt hopeful. In a little cañon, hard to enter because of a great wall formed across its mouth by jagged masses of rock which had fallen from the cliffs above, he came upon some surface rock that was identical with the bit of float that he had found. The ledge was oddly broken about its middle by a heap of gray, weather-worn fragments of stone. He never had come upon a formation like this, and had he been a geologist he would have found a good deal in it to interest him. Being simply a prospector, he examined the ledge purely with an eye to business; and from this point of view it was eminently unsatisfactory. There were, to be sure, traces of mineral, but not the least suggestion of the in-exhaustible wealth that he knew must be in the rock to which his specimen belonged. Therefore he kicked the ledge contemptuously, swore at his own ill luck and stupidity with the mellow fluency that can be acquired only by long residence in mining camps, and so turned sullenly away.

It would have strengthened Dick Irving's fast-lessening faith in his own instinct as a prospector, however, had he known that it was the art of man and not a freak of nature that was leading him astray; had he known that at the very moment when he was cursing his own stupidity *la mina de los Padres* was beneath his feet! Had he but tossed aside the piece of rock whereon he stood, he would have found —wasted by rust, but still recognizable—an old hammer-head from which the handle long since had moldered away; and so, to his quick intelligence, would have had proof enough that he had found the rich prize that he had sworn to find when he came down into the South.

On the evening of the day after that on which Juan had told Techita of his great discovery, he came to her again in the church to tell her that all had gone well with him in his search in the mountains, and that in very truth he had found the long-lost mine. In glad proof of his words he showed her a rusty hammer-head that he had pulled out from beneath a rock in the mouth of the filled-in shaft—the very ham-mer-head that Dick Irving, for all his cleverness, had failed to find.

"God has been very good to us, my Techa," he said, as they stood again beneath the picture of the gentle Santa Clara in the soft dark-ness that was stealing down upon the dying day. "His mercy has come to us in our sorrow, and through the entreaty of the dear saint, He has given us comfort in hope. All is well with us now. Thy father would indeed have refused thee to the goatherd Juan, but to Señor Don Juan, the owner of the Mine of the Fathers, he will not say no. I shall have thee for my very own, my Techita; and for all our lives long, in our love and happiness, we will praise thankfully and worship reverently this sweet saint who has taken from us our sorrow, and given us in its stead great joy.

"And see, my little one," he added, lightly, after they had stood for a little space with hands clasped closely and eyes turned gratefully upon the saint's face—"see! I have found the mine, and yet the curse has not fallen! There was only folly in thy fears, my little heart. The blessed saints are strong to stay and to save them who have faith in their holy goodness; strong to drive back the evil power of this false god, whom long ago they conquered and threw down."

And again, as he spoke these daring words, Juan felt a shudder of dread go through him. For all the bravery of his manliness the thought would come: What if, in defiance of the power for good of the blessed saints, the power for evil of the Pueblos' god even yet lived on?

Upon Techita's heart lay heavily this same dread; nor was it greatly lightened by Juan's cheerfulness. Almost was she persuaded by her great love for him to bid him give up the treasure that he had found; to suffer herself, a sacrifice for her love's sake, to be wed in accordance with her father's will. Better even this great misery, she thought, than that harm should come to her lover.

Thinking these doubting thoughts, she stood irresolute, her eyes turned questioningly upon Santa Clara's face; and again, in the soft, faint light that shone upon it, the sweet face seemed to smile upon her a promise of protection that bade her trust and hope. Therefore she hushed the doubts which were in her heart, and listened welcomingly to Juan's glad promises of the joy which was to be. And in making these promises Juan also forgot the fears which had beset him, and felt only a brave elation in the certainty of the happiness that had come to them from the good God. So, in the pale moonlight, they parted again, having in the brightness of their future a full and joyous faith.

Yet, in despite of this faith, through the long darkness of the night Techita, waking, was oppressed by dread; and in her sleep there came to her fearful dreams. And in waking and in sleeping the thought that possessed her was that out of the very fullness of her happiness a desolating, irremediable sorrow was to come.

Nor did the brightness of the sunshine, when at last day came again, chase away her dark forebodings. A great heaviness lay upon her soul; a dreary belief weighed upon her that the sorrow which was surely coming was very near at hand. Nor could she doubt that whatever this sorrow was to be, it must come to her through Juan. As she knew, Juan had gone once more into the mountains, along the way that he had told her of, to the old mine. Had he been in the village, or working in the near-by fields, she would have braved her father's displeasure and gone to him—so keen was her deep consciousness that a malignant power was loosed to do him harm.

Slowly the day wore on, each hour in passing adding to her restlessness and nervous dread. And at last, when the still time of noon was come, and all the town was hushed in sleep, she no longer could restrain the impulse that was upon her to go to him; to brave with him whatever was the danger; to defend him living; to lie down and die beside him should he be dead. Out from the silent house, out from the sleeping village, up the rock-strewn *arroyo* of San Pedro, Techita walked firmly; in her heart a great daring born of her greater love.

That day also Dick Irving went up into the mountains. He acknowledged to himself savagely that he had about got to the end of his rope, and this would be the last day of his foolery. For once he would have to own up that he had tackled a job that was too big for him; and he was the more ugly over it because the piece of float that he had in his pocket made him believe absolutely that all that was told of *la mina de los Padres* was true. He *knew* that the mine was somewhere up beyond the *arroyo* of San Pedro; and knowing this, and knowing how all his skillful search for it had ended in failure, he gritted his teeth together in sullen rage.

He thought himself more than half a fool for making this last expedition, for his faith that it would end in anything but another failure was very weak indeed. But he was a conscientious man,—as a prospector, that is,—and he was not quite satisfied to go north again without having one more look at the ledge of rocks in the little cañon. This was the one place in the mountains where he had struck rock identical with his specimen; and while he had convinced himself by his first exploration that there was no mineral in the ledge at all comparable with that in the float, his absolute failure in all other directions made him desirous of having yet another look here. Moreover, his careful study of the locality had shown him that, all things considered, the cañon was the most likely place from which the bit of float could have come. But for the mass of rocks in the cañon's mouth, he would have been quite certain that it was from there that his specimen had started. And this wall of rocks across the mouth of the cañon bothered him. In all the years that he had been prospecting he never had seen anything like it. If such a thing had not been impossible upon its face, he would have believed that the rocks had been broken loose deliberately and thrown down from the cliffs above, not by nature, but by man. The more that his mind had dwelt upon the oddity of this barrier, and upon the equal oddity of the mass of broken rocks in the line of the ledge, the more was his interest aroused. There was something queer about the place that attracted him, and he was determined to see it again. Of course, as he said to himself, with a good deal of hard swearing at his general brainlessness, there was nothing to be found there, and he only was going on a fool's errand again. But, all the same, with the dogged perseverance that was characteristic of him, he pulled himself together for the tough tramp up the *arroyo* and the mountainside beyond.

It was a tough tramp, and no mistake; and as he had not any heart worth speaking of in what he was doing, he went slowly and made many halts. This was not his usual way of working, but he was low in his mind and was thinking gloomy thoughts, which quite took the customary spring out of his toes and heels. There is but little satisfaction to a man in knowing that he has had his hand very nearly on great good fortune for two months and more, and yet is losing it after all. Dick Irving, whose nature was not a gentle one, was in a state of glowing rage as he reflected that this was just about where he was—rage at his luck, at himself, at all the world. About the one thing that could have given him any comfort just then would have been a fight. He was fairly aching to balance his own misfortunes by taking them out on somebody else's hide.

Suddenly he was aroused, by the deepening shadows in the *arroyo,* to the fact that the end of the day was not far off. As he had intended camping for the night in the cañon, this fact did not disconcert him, but it made him very considerably quicken his steps. Yet, for all his haste, the sun was near setting when he climbed the mass of stones lying in a great ridge across the cañon's mouth. Fortunately for his purposes, the cañon faced westward, and all within it was a blaze of mellow light from the level rays of the setting sun.

As he climbed the barrier he heard a clicking noise that made him start as though he had received a blow; and as he cautiously peered over the barrier's crest he saw a sight that sent the blood with a rush to his heart, and then fiercely tingling through all his veins. For the sound that he heard was the click of a pick against rock, and the sight that he saw was a man, not a hundred yards away from him, at work on the very ledge itself! If here truly was the lost mine, then was he too late; another set of stakes was in ahead of his!

Luckily, the other man had not heard him scrambling over the rocks, and so, for the present, at least, he was master of the situation. Getting into a good position for observation, and crouching so that he could see, yet could not be seen, he carefully studied the ground. Evidently the man had been at work for many hours, and had worked hard. The loose rocks which had lain in the break in the ledge were rolled away in all directions,—Dick could not but feel instinctive respect for the set of muscles that had dealt successfully with the tough lifting and hauling that this piece of work involved,—and the earth that had washed in between the stones had been carefully shoveled away. This was about all that had been accomplished. But it was enough. For there, clearly defined in the line of the ledge, was the square-cut mouth of the old shaft. *La mina de los Padres,* lost for two hundred years, again was found!

As Dick Irving realized the situation, the rage that had been upon him all day culminated. He was in a white heat of passion—and as tranquil as a morning in June. There was just one thing to be done, and he meant to do it.

"Only a Greaser, anyway," he muttered. "The idea," he added, disdainfully, "of a d——d Greaser owning the Mine of the Fathers!" In the excess of contemptuous disgust that this thought caused him he spat upon the ground.

Over the sights of his revolver he measured the distance carefully with his eye, and with commendable coolness decided that it was too great for certainty. As the business had to be done, he did not want to make a mess of it; moreover, as he prudently reflected, around the shoulder of the cañon there might be another man. With these judicious thoughts in mind, he worked his way softly across the wall of rocks—keeping well in the shelter of the great fragments—and down on its inner side. Once within the cañon, there was no difficulty in slipping from rock to rock, until he stopped at last behind two great boulders, and through the rift between them covered his man at a distance of less than a dozen yards.

Juan had stopped in his work, and stood leaning on the handle of his pick. Over him and around him shone a blaze of rich red light, the last rays of the setting sun. His face had a weary look and his strained muscles were relaxed; but stronger than his look of weariness was his look of joy, and even the pose of his tired body was elate. For the great triumph of his life was won: at last he knew himself a victor over Fate. In his happiness he spoke his thought aloud: "My Techa! the joy-time of our life has come!"

And even as he spoke these words the sharp crack of Dick Irving's revolver rattled and pealed and roared between the rocky walls of the cañon—and Juan sank down across the newly opened shaft of the Mine of the Fathers with a bullet through his heart. At that instant the sun dropped below the level of the wall of rocks, and all the lower portion of the cañon was left in dusk; duskier because in the upper portion the light still shone full and clear.

Through the cañon, mingling with the echoes of the pistol-shot, yet rising above them, shrilly, wailingly sounded a cry of mortal agony; a cry despairing, desolate, charged with the burden of a lifetime of bitter woe; a cry that made Dick Irving's weather-hardened face turn pale, and that sent a chill into the very depths of his tough heart; and while he wondered doubtingly, tremblingly, whence came this woful sound, Techita had sprung down from the crest of the ridge of rocks and was standing by her dead lover's side.

Her figure, seen in the gloom of the cañon and through the powder smoke that lingered in the rift between the boulders, loomed tall and indistinct against the darkness of the rocks beyond. He could not see her form; he could not see her face—wrenched with the agony that comes when love dies suddenly before despair. Raising her hand heavenward, like a prophetess of old, her voice hushed to the deep, solemn tone of one who stands upon the very border of Time, and sees out clearly into the awful mysteries of Eternity, she spoke: "The curse has fallen—the curse of the Pueblos' god!"

Dick Irving was satisfied with the good stroke of business that he had done, and his finer feelings rebelled against doing any more business of that sort just then. On the other hand, his sturdy common sense told him that there was only one course that he could rationally pursue; that he had gone too far for drawing back to be possible.

"As nasty a job as ever I got into," he said to himself, standing beside the shaft, as he drew two fresh cartridges from his belt, and dropped them into the emptied chambers of his revolver. Then, presently, in a burst of righteous indignation: "Confound her! It ain't my fault, anyway. Why couldn't she have had the sense to say she was a woman?" And then, as his nerves grew steadier, he added more cheerfully: "Well, after all, it's nothing but a pair of Greasers—lucky whack it was for me that I got here today, and in time to save the mine!"

Slowly the glory of the sunset spread across the west. Rising against the red and golden splendor, the battlements of San Ildefonso stood sharply lined; high into the gray-blue sky shot red and golden rays; over the broad waters of the Rio Grande played red and golden lights: all heaven and all the earth beneath seemed blended in a red and golden symphony. Then, slowly, all this splendor passed away, until nothing was left of it save, in the far east, over the distant mountains, a little rosy cloud.

In the still church, where hung the picture of the sweet Santa Clara, was loneliness; in the still cañon, high up on the mountain, was death. Over all the earth, darkening the silent church, darkening the silent cañon, had come gray night.

The Lucky Whack Mining Company, as Dick Irving himself declares,—and he ought to know, for he is president of it, and lives East
in a style that proves that he has lots of pay dirt somewhere,—is a
rattling success. Daily output, two thousand ounces—and millions in
sight.

FRANK NORRIS

★ ★ ★

Like Presley, one of his fictional characters, Frank Norris (1870-1902) struggled to write a great work which "should embrace in itself a whole epoch, a complete era, the voice of an entire people." That aim was partially fulfilled in his Epic of the Wheat —*The Octopus* (1901), *The Pit* (1903), and the unwritten *The Wolf,* novels undertaken in the spirit of the new deterministic sociology and developed in imitation of Zola's naturalistic technique. Fundamentally Norris was interested in the novel; yet his early Kiplingesque stories of California life have made his place secure as a regional author in the local-color tradition. Though born in Chicago and for some years an art student in Paris, Norris lived longest in California and is popularly associated with the city of his first literary success, San Francisco. From 1893 to 1897 he contributed stories and sketches to California magazines. His experiences as a correspondent in South Africa and as a war correspondent in Cuba were unfortunate; he contracted severe cases of fever which hastened his death. "The Third Circle," which was first published in 1895 in *The Wave,* is reprinted with the kind permission of Janet Black.

★ ★ ★

The Third Circle

THERE are more things in San Francisco's Chinatown than are dreamed of in Heaven and earth. In reality there are three parts of Chinatown—the part the guides show you, the part the guides don't show you, and the part that no one ever hears of. It is with the latter part that this story has to do. There are a good many stories that might be written about this third circle of Chinatown, but believe me, they never will be written—at any rate not until the "town" has been, as it were, drained off from the city, as one might drain a noisome swamp, and we shall be able to see the strange, dreadful life that wallows down there in the lowest ooze of the place—wallows and grovels there in the mud and in the dark. If you don't think this is true, ask some of the Chinese detectives (the regular squad are not to be relied on), ask them to tell you the story of the Lee On Ting affair, or ask them what was done to old Wong Sam, who thought he could break up the trade in slave girls, or why Mr. Clarence Lowney (he was a clergyman from Minnesota who believed in direct methods) is now a "dangerous" inmate of the State Asylum—ask them to tell you why Matsokura, the Japanese dentist, went back to his home lacking a face—ask them to tell you why the murderers of Little Pete will never be found, and ask them to tell you about the little slave girl, Sing Yee, or—no, on the second thought, don't ask for that story.

The tale I am to tell you now began some twenty years ago in a See Yup restaurant on Waverly Place—long since torn down—where it will end I do not know. I think it is still going on. It began when young Hillegas and Miss Ten Eyck (they were from the East, and engaged to be married) found their way into the restaurant of the Seventy Moons, late in the evening of a day in March. (It was the year after the downfall of Kearney and the discomfiture of the sand-lotters.) "What a dear, quaint, curious old place!" exclaimed Miss Ten Eyck.

She sat down on an ebony stool with its marble seat, and let her gloved hands fall into her lap, looking about her at the huge hanging lanterns, the gilded carven screens, the lacquer work, the inlay work, the colored glass, the dwarf oak trees growing in Satsuma pots, the marquetry, the painted matting, the incense jar of brass, high as a man's head, and all the grotesque jim-crackery of the Orient. The restaurant was deserted at that hour. Young Hillegas pulled up a stool opposite her and leaned his elbows on the table, pushing back his hat and fumbling for a cigarette.

"Might just as well be in China itself," he commented.

"Might?" she retorted; "we are in China, Tom—a little bit of China dug out and transplanted here. Fancy all America and the Nineteenth Century just around the corner! Look! You can even see the Palace Hotel from the window. See out yonder, over the roof of that temple—

the Ming Yen, isn't it?—and I can actually make out Aunt Harriett's rooms."

"I say, Harry" (Miss Ten Eyck's first name was Harriett), "let's have some tea."

"Tom, you're a genius! Won't it be fun! Of course we must have some tea. What a lark! And you can smoke if you want to."

"This is the way one ought to see places," said Hillegas, as he lit a cigarette; "just nose around by yourself and discover things. Now, the guides never brought us here."

"No, they never did. I wonder why? Why, we just found it out by ourselves. It's ours, isn't it, Tom, dear, by right of discovery?"

At that moment Hillegas was sure that Miss Ten Eyck was quite the most beautiful girl he ever remembered to have seen. There was a daintiness about her—a certain chic trimness in her smart tailor gown, and the least perceptible tilt of her crisp hat that gave her the last charm. Pretty she certainly was—the fresh, vigorous, healthful prettiness only seen in certain types of unmixed American stock. All at once Hillegas reached across the table, and, taking her hand, kissed the little crumpled round of flesh that showed where her glove buttoned.

The China boy appeared to take their order, and while waiting for their tea, dried almonds, candied fruit, and watermelon rinds, the pair wandered out upon the overhanging balcony and looked down into the darkening streets.

"There's that fortuneteller again," observed Hillegas, presently. "See—down there on the steps of the joss house?"

"Where? Oh, yes, I see."

"Let's have him up. Shall we? We'll have him tell our fortunes while we're waiting."

Hillegas called and beckoned, and at last got the fellow up into the restaurant.

"Hoh! You're no Chinaman," said he, as the fortuneteller came into the circle of the lantern-light. The other showed his brown teeth.

"Part Chinaman, part Kanaka."

"Kanaka?"

"All same Honolulu. Sabe? Mother Kanaka lady—washum clothes for sailor peoples down Kaui way," and he laughed as though it were a huge joke.

"Well, say, Jim," said Hillegas; "we want you to tell our fortunes. You sabe? Tell the lady's fortune. Who she going to marry, for instance."

"No fortune—tattoo."

"Tattoo?"

"Um. All same tattoo—three, four, seven, planty lil birds on lady's arm. Hey? You want tattoo?"

He drew a tattooing needle from his sleeve and motioned towards Miss Ten Eyck's arm.

"Tattoo my arm? What an idea! But wouldn't it be funny, Tom? Aunt Hattie's sister came back from Honolulu with the prettiest little butterfly tattooed on her finger. I've half a mind to try. And it would be so awfully queer and original."

"Let him do it on your finger, then. You never could wear evening dress if it was on your arm."

"Of course. He can tattoo something as though it was a ring, and my marquise can hide it."

The Kanaka-Chinaman drew a tiny fantastic-looking butterfly on a bit of paper with a blue pencil, licked the drawing a couple of times, and wrapped it about Miss Ten Eyck's little finger—the little finger of her left hand. The removal of the wet paper left an imprint of the drawing. Then he mixed his ink in a small sea-shell, dipped his needle, and in ten minutes had finished the tattooing of a grotesque little insect, as much butterfly as anything else.

"There," said Hillegas, when the work was done and the fortune-teller had gone his way; "there you are, and it will never come out. It won't do for you now to plan a little burglary, or forge a little check, or slay a little baby for the coral round its neck, 'cause you can always be identified by that butterfly upon the little finger of your left hand."

"I'm almost sorry now I had it done. Won't it ever come out? Pshaw! Anyhow I think it's very chic," said Harriett Ten Eyck.

"I say, though!" exclaimed Hillegas, jumping up; "where's our tea and cakes and things? It's getting late. We can't wait here all evening. I'll go out and jolly that chap along."

The Chinaman to whom he had given the order was not to be found on that floor of the restaurant. Hillegas descended the stairs to the kitchen. The place seemed empty of life. On the ground floor, however, where tea and raw silk were sold, Hillegas found a China-man figuring up accounts by means of little balls that slid to and fro upon rods. The Chinaman was a very gorgeous-looking chap in round horn spectacles and a costume that looked like a man's night-gown, of quilted blue satin.

"I say, John," said Hillegas to this one, "I want some tea. You sabe? —up stairs—restaurant. Give China boy order—he no come. Get plenty much move on. Hey?"

The merchant turned and looked at Hillegas over his spectacles.

"Ah," he said, calmly, "I regret that you have been detained. You will, no doubt, be attended to presently. You are a stranger in Chinatown?"

"Ahem!—well, yes—I—we are."

"Without doubt—without doubt!" murmured the other.

"I suppose you are the proprietor?" ventured Hillegas.

"I? Oh, no! My agents have a silk house here. I believe they sublet the upper floors to the See Yups. By the way, we have just received a consignment of India silk shawls you may be pleased to see."

He spread a pile upon the counter, and selected one that was particularly beautiful.

"Permit me," he remarked gravely, "to offer you this as a present to your good lady."

Hillegas's interest in this extraordinary Oriental was aroused. Here was a side of the Chinese life he had not seen, nor even suspected. He stayed for some little while talking to this man, whose bearing might have been that of Cicero before the Senate assembled, and left him with the understanding to call upon him the next day at the Consulate. He returned to the restaurant to find Miss Ten Eyck gone. He never saw her again. No white man ever did.

There is a certain friend of mine in San Francisco who calls himself Manning. He is a Plaza bum—that is, he sleeps all day in the old Plaza (that shoal where so much human jetsom has been stranded), and during the night follows his own devices in Chinatown, one block above. Manning was at one time a deep-sea pearl diver in Oahu, and, having burst his eardrums in the business, can now blow smoke out of either ear. This accomplishment first endeared him to me, and latterly I found out that he knew more of Chinatown than is meet and right for a man to know. The other day I found Manning in the shade of the Stevenson ship, just rousing from the effects of a jag on undiluted gin, and told him, or rather recalled to him, the story of Harriett Ten Eyck.

"I remember," he said, resting on an elbow and chewing grass. "It made a big noise at the time, but nothing ever came of it—nothing except a long row and the cutting down of one of Mr. Hillegas's Chinese detectives in Gambler's Alley. The See Yups brought a chap over from Peking just to do the business."

"Hatchet-man?" said I.

"No," answered Manning, spitting green; "he was a two-knife Kai-Gingh."

"As how?"

"Two knives—one in each hand—cross your arms and then draw 'em together, right and left scissor-fashion—damn near slashed his arm in two. He got five thousand for it. After that the detectives said they couldn't find much of a clue."

"And Miss Ten Eyck was not so much as heard from again?"

"No," answered Manning, biting his fingernails. "They took her to China, I guess, or may be up to Oregon. That sort of thing was new twenty years ago, and that's why they raised such a row, I suppose. But there are plenty of women living with Chinamen now, and nobody thinks anything about it, and they are Canton Chinamen, too—lowest kind of coolies. There's one of them up in St. Louis Place, just back of the Chinese theatre, and she's a Sheeny. There's a queer team for you—the Hebrew and the Mongolian—and they've got a kid with red, crinkly hair, who's a rubber in a Hamman bath. Yes, it's a queer team, and there's three more white women in a slave joint under Ah Yee's tan room. There's where I get my opium. They can talk a little English even yet. Funny thing—one of 'em's dumb, but if you get her drunk enough she'll talk a little English to you. It's a fact! I've seen 'em do it with her often—actually get her so drunk that she can talk. Tell you what," added Manning, struggling to his feet, "I'm going up there now to get some dope. You can come along, and we'll get Sadie (Sadie's her name)—we'll get Sadie full, and ask her if she ever heard about Miss Ten Eyck. They do a big business," said Manning, as we went along. "There's Ah Yee and these three women and a policeman named Yank. They get all the yen shee—that's the cleanings of the opium pipes, you know, and make it into pills and smuggle it into the cons over at San Quentin prison by means of the trusties. Why, they'll make five dollars' worth of dope sell for thirty by the time it gets into the yard over at the Pen. When I was over there, I saw a chap knifed behind a jute mill for a pill as big as a pea. Ah Yee gets the stuff, the three women roll it into pills, and the policeman, Yank, gets it over to the trusties somehow. Ah Yee is independent rich by now, and the policeman's got a bank account."

"And the women?"

"Lord! they're slaves—Ah Yee's slaves! They get the swift kick most generally."

Manning and I found Sadie and her two companions four floors underneath the tan room, sitting cross-legged in a room about as big as a big trunk. I was sure they were Chinese women at first, until my eyes got accustomed to the darkness of the place. They were dressed in Chinese fashions, but I noted soon that their hair was brown and the bridge of each one's nose was high. They were rolling pills from a jar of yen shee that stood in the middle of the floor, their fingers twinkling with a rapidity that was somehow horrible to see.

Manning spoke to them briefly in Chinese while he lit a pipe, and two of them answered with the true Canton singsong—all vowels and no consonants.

"That one's Sadie," said Manning, pointing to the third one, who remained silent the while. I turned to her. She was smoking a cigar, and from time to time spat through her teeth man-fashion. She was a dreadful-looking beast of a woman, wrinkled like a shriveled apple, her teeth quite black from nicotine, her hands bony and prehensile, like a hawk's claws—but a white woman beyond all doubt. At first Sadie refused to drink, but the smell of Manning's can of gin removed her objections, and in half an hour she was hopelessly loquacious. What effect the alcohol had upon the paralyzed organs of her speech I cannot say. Sober, she was tongue-tied—drunk, she could emit a series of faint bird-like twitterings that sounded like a voice heard from the bottom of a well.

"Sadie," said Manning, blowing smoke out of his ears, "what makes you live with Chinamen? You're a white girl. You got people somewhere. Why don't you get back to them?"

Sadie shook her head.

"Like um China boy better," she said in a voice so faint we had to stoop to listen. "Ah Yee's pretty good to us—plenty to eat, plenty to smoke, and as much yen shee as we can stand. Oh, I don't complain."

"You know you can get out of this whenever you want. Why don't you make a run for it some day when you're out? Cut for the Mission House on Sacramento street—they'll be good to you there."

"Oh!" said Sadie, listlessly, rolling a pill between her stained palms, "I been here so long I guess I'm kind of used to it. I've about got out of white people's ways by now. They wouldn't let me have my yen shee and my cigar, and that's about all I want nowadays. You can't eat yen shee long and care for much else, you know. Pass that gin along, will you? I'm going to faint in a minute."

"Wait a minute," said I, my hand on Manning's arm. "How long have you been living with Chinamen, Sadie?"

"Oh, I don't know. All my life, I guess. I can't remember back very far—only spots here and there. Where's that gin you promised me?"

"Only in spots?" said I; "here a little and there a little—is that it? Can you remember how you came to take up with this kind of life?"

"Sometimes I can and sometimes I can't," answered Sadie. Suddenly her head rolled upon her shoulder, her eyes closing. Manning shook her roughly.

"Let be! let be!" she exclaimed, rousing up; "I'm dead sleepy. Can't you see?"

"Wake up, and keep awake, if you can," said Manning; "this gentleman wants to ask you something."

"Ah Yee bought her from a sailor on a junk in the Pei Ho river," put in one of the other women.

"How about that, Sadie?" I asked. "Were you ever on a junk in a China river? Hey? Try and think?"

"I don't know," she said. "Sometimes I think I was. There's lots of things I can't explain, but it's because I can't remember far enough back."

"Did you ever hear of a girl named Ten Eyck—Harriett Ten Eyck —who was stolen by Chinamen here in San Francisco a long time ago?"

There was a long silence. Sadie looked straight before her, wide-eyed, the other women rolled pills industriously, Manning looked over my shoulder at the scene, still blowing smoke through his ears; then Sadie's eyes began to close and her head to loll sideways.

"My cigar's gone out," she muttered. "You said you'd have gin for me. Ten Eyck! Ten Eyck! No, I don't remember anybody named that." Her voice failed her suddenly, then she whispered:

"Say, how did I get that on me?"

She thrust out her left hand, and I saw a butterfly tattooed on the little finger.

WILLIAM ALLEN WHITE

★ ★ ★

Like the sunflower, William Allen White (1868-   ) belongs
to and is typical of Kansas; no other state has had a journalist
and writer of fiction more completely identified with the whole
life of the state, with its politics, religion, education, and social
activity. With forthright honesty he has appraised the virtues and
faults of his area; his stories are notable for their accuracy of
record. As editor of *The Emporia Gazette* he has been for upwards
of half a century the acknowledged spokesman of the Middle-
Western point of view. Born on February 10, 1868, he first won
national interest in 1896 by an editorial, "What's the Matter with
Kansas?" In this year he also published his first volume of short
stories, *The Real Issue,* tales of small towns, politics, and small
boys, the three themes of his later fiction. Representative narratives from his pen include *The Court of Boyville* (1899), *Stratagems and Spoils* (1901), *In Our Town* (1906), *A Certain Rich
Man* (1909), and *In the Heart of a Fool* (1918). "Conditions in
Western Kansas," says Mr. White, "have changed greatly since
1893," when "The Story of Aqua Pura" was written. This story
is reprinted from *The Real Issue* by permission of the author
and The Macmillan Company, publishers.

★ ★ ★

The Story of Aqua Pura

PEOPLE who write about Kansas, as a rule, write ignorantly, and
speak of the state as a finished product. Kansas, like Gaul of old,
is divided into three parts, differing as widely, each from the other, as
any three countries in the same latitude upon the globe. It would be
as untrue to classify together the Egyptian, the Indian and the Central

728

American, as to speak of the Kansas man without distinguishing between the Eastern Kansan, the Central Kansan, and the Western Kansan. Eastern Kansas is a finished community like New York or Pennsylvania. Central Kansas is finished, but not quite paid for; and the Western Kansas, the only place where there is any suffering from drouth or crop failures, is a new country—old only in a pluck which is slowly conquering the desert.

Aqua Pura was a western Kansas town, set high up, far out on the prairie. It was founded nine years ago, at the beginning of the boom, not by cowboys and ruffians, but by honest, ambitious men and women. Of the six men who staked out the townsite, two—Johnson and Barringer—were Harvard men; one, Nickols, was from Princeton; and the other three—Bemis, Bradley, and Hicks—had come from inland state universities. When their wives came west there was a Vassar reunion, and the first mail that arrived after the postoffice had been established brought the New York magazines. The town was like dozens of others that sprang up far out in the treacherous wilderness in that fresh, green spring of 1886.

They called it Aqua Pura, choosing a Latin name to proclaim to the world that it was not a rowdy town. The new yellow pine of the little village gleamed in the clear sunlight. It could be seen for miles on a clear, warm day, as it stood upon a rise of ground; and over in Maize, six miles away, the electric lights of Aqua Pura, which flashed out in the evening before the town was six months old, could be seen distinctly. A schoolhouse that cost twenty thousand dollars was built before the town had seen its first winter; and the first Christmas ball in Aqua Pura was held in an opera house that cost ten thousand. Money was plentiful; two- and three-story buildings rose on each side of the main street of the little place. The farmers who had taken homesteads in the country around the town had prospered. The sod had yielded handsomely from the first breaking. Those who had come too late to put in crops found it easy to borrow money. There was an epidemic of hope in the air. Everyone breathed the contagion. The public library association raised a thousand dollars for books during the winter, and in the spring a syndicate was formed to erect a library building. Aqua Pura could not afford to be behind other towns, and the railroad train that passed the place threw off packages of the newest books as fast as mails could come from New York. The sheet-iron tower of the Aqua Pura waterworks rose early in the spring of '87, and far out in the high grass the hydrants were scattered. Living water came bountifully from the wells that were sunk from fifty to one hundred feet in the ground.

Barringer was elected mayor at the municipal election in the spring of '87, and he platted out Barringer's Addition, and built a house there with borrowed money in June. There were two thousand people in Aqua Pura then. Hacks rolled prosperously over the smooth, hard, prairie streets; two banks opened; and the newspaper, which was printed the day the town was laid off, became a daily. Society grew gay, and people from all corners of the globe met in the booming village.

There was no lawless element. There was not a saloon in the town. A billiard hall and a dark room, wherein cards might be played surreptitiously, were the only institutions which made the people of Aqua Pura blush, when they took the innumerable "eastern capitalists," who visited Western Kansas that year, over the town. These "capitalists" were entertained at a three-story brick hotel, equipped with electricity and modern plumbing in order to excel Maize, where the hotel was an indifferent frame affair. There were throngs of well-dressed people on the streets, and sleek fat horses were hitched in front of the stores wherein the farmers traded.

This is the story of the rise. Barringer told it a thousand times. Barringer believed in the town to the last. When the terrible drouth of 1887, with its furnace-like breath, singed the town and the farms in Fountain County, Barringer led the majority which proudly claimed that the country was all right; and as chairman of the board of county commissioners, he sent a scathing message to the Governor, refusing aid. Barringer's own bank loaned money on land, whereon the crop had failed, to tide the farmers over the winter. Barringer's signature guaranteed loans from the east upon everything negotiable, and Aqua Pura thrived for a time upon promises. Here and there, in the spring of 1888, there was an empty building. One room of the opera house block was vacant. Barringer started a man in business, selling notions, who occupied the room. Barringer went east and pleaded with the men who had invested in the town to be easy on their debtors. Then came the hot winds of July, blowing out of the southwest, scorching the grass, shrivelling the grain, and drying up the streams that had filled in the spring. During the fall of that year the hotel, which had been open only in the lower story, closed. The opera house began to be used for "aid" meetings, and when the winter wind blew dust-blackened snow through the desolate streets of the little town, it rattled a hundred windows in vacant houses, and sometimes blew sun-warped boards from the high sidewalk that led across the gully to the big red grade of the unfinished "Chicago Air Line."

Barringer did not go east that year. He could not. But he wrote—

wrote regularly and bravely to the eastern capitalists who were concerned in his bank and loan company; and they grew colder and
colder as the winter deepened and the interest on defaulted loans
came not. Barringer's failure was announced in the spring of '89.
Nickols had left. Johnson had left. The other founders of Aqua Pura
had died in '87-'88, and their families had gone, and with them went
the culture and the ambition of the town. But Barringer held on and
lived, rent free, in the two front rooms of the barn of a hotel. His
daughter, Mary, frail, tanned, hollow-eyed, and withered by the
drouths, lived with him.

In 1890 the hot winds came again in the summer, and long and
steadily they blew, blighting everything. There were only five hundred people in Fountain County that year, and they lived on the taxes
from the railroad that crossed the county. Families were put on the
poor list without disgrace—it was almost a mark of political distinction—and in the little town many devices were in vogue to distribute
the county funds during the winter.

There was no rain that winter and the snow was hard and dry.
Cattle on the range suffered for water and died by the thousands. A
procession from the little town started eastward early in the spring.
White-canopied wagons, and wagons covered with oil tablecloths of
various hues, or clad in patchwork quilts, sought the rising sun.

Barringer grew thin, unkempt and gray. Every evening, when the
wind rattled in the deserted rooms of the old hotel, and made the
faded signs up and down the dreary street creak, the old man and his
daughter went over their books, balancing, accounting interest, figuring on mythical problems that the world had long since forgotten.

Christmas eve, 1891, the entire village, fifteen souls in all, assembled
at Barringer's house. He was hopeful, even cheerful, and talked
blithely of what "one good crop" would do for the country; although
there were no farmers left to plant it, even if nature had been harbor-
ing a smile for the dreary land. The year that followed that Christmas
promised much. There were spring rains, and in May, the brown grass
and the scattered patches of wheat grew green and fair to see. Barringer freshened up perceptibly. He sent an account of his indebted-
ness—on home-ruled Manilla paper—to his creditors in the east, and
faithfully assured them that he would remit all he owed in the fall.
A few wanderers straggled into Fountain County, lured by the green
fields and running brooks. The gray prairie wolf gave up the dugout
to human occupants. Lights in the prairie cabins twinkled back hope
to the stars. Before June there were a thousand people in Fountain
County. Aqua Pura's business-houses seemed to liven up. There was

a Fourth-of-July celebration in town. But the rain that spoiled the advertised "fireworks in the evening" was the last that fell until winter. A carload of aid from Central Kansas saved a hundred lives in Fountain County that year.

When the spring of 1893 opened, Barringer looked ten years older than he looked the spring before. The grass on the range was sere, and great cracks were in the earth. The winter had been dry. The spring opened dry, with high winds blowing through May. There were but five people on the townsite that summer: Barringer, his daughter, and the postmaster's family. Supplies came overland from Maize. A bloody county-seat war had given the rival town the prize in 1890. Barringer had plenty of money to buy food, for the county commissioners distributed the taxes which the railroad paid.

It was his habit to sit on the front porch of the deserted hotel and look across the prairies to the southwest and watch the breaking clouds scatter into the blue of the twilight. He could see the empty water tower silhouetted against the sky. The frame buildings that rose in the boom days had all been moved away, the line of the horizon was guarded at regular intervals by the iron hydrants far out on the prairie, that stood like sentinels hemming in the past. The dying wind seethed through the short, brown grass. Heat lightning winked devilishly in the distance, and the dissolving clouds that gathered every afternoon laughed in derisive thunder at the hopes of the worn old man sitting on the warped boards of the hotel porch. Night after night he sat there, waiting, with his daughter by his side. There had been a time when he was too proud to go to the east, where his name was a byword. Now he was too poor in purse and in spirit. So he sat and waited, hoping fondly for the realization of a dream which he feared could never come true.

There were days when the postmaster's four-year-old child sat with him. The old man and the child sat thus one evening when the old man sighed: "If it would only rain, there would be half a crop yet! If it would only rain!" The child heard him and sighed imitatively: "Yes, if it would only rain—what is rain, Mr. Barringer?" He looked at the child blankly and sat for a long time in silence. When he arose he did not even have a pretence of hope. He grew despondent from that hour, and a sort of hypochondria seized him. It was his fancy to exaggerate the phenomena of the drouth.

That fall when the winds piled the sand in the railroad "cuts" and the prairie was as hard and barren as the ground around a cabin door, Barringer's daughter died of fever. The old man seemed little moved by sorrow. But as he rode back from the bleak graveyard, through the sand cloud, in the carriage with the dry, rattling spokes, he could only mutter to the sympathizing friends who had come from Maize to mourn with him, "And we laid her in the hot and dusty tomb." He recalled an old song which fitted these words, and for days kept crooning: "Oh, we laid her in the hot and dusty tomb."

That winter the postmaster left. The office was discontinued. The county commissioners tried to get Barringer to leave. He would not be persuaded to go. The county commissioners were not insistent. It gave one of them an excuse for drawing four dollars a day from the county treasury; he rode from Maize to Aqua Pura every day with supplies for Barringer.

The old man cooked, ate, and slept in the office of the hotel. Day after day he put on his overcoat in the winter and made the rounds of the vacant store buildings. He walked up and down in the little paths through the brown weeds in the deserted streets, all day long, talking to himself. At night, when the prairie wind rattled through the empty building, blowing snow and sand down the halls, and in little drifts upon the broken stairs, the old man's lamp was seen by straggling travelers burning far into the night. He told his daily visitor that he was keeping his books.

Thus the winter passed. The grass came with the light mists of March. By May it had lost its color. By June it was brown, and the hot winds came again in August, curving the warped boards a little deeper on the floor of the hotel porch. Herders and travelers, straggling back to the green country, saw him sitting there at twilight, looking toward the southwest,—a grizzled, unkempt old man, with a shifting light in his eye. To such as spoke to him he always made the same speech: "Yes, it looks like rain, but it can't rain. The rain has gone dry out here. They say it rained at Hutchinson,—maybe so, I doubt it. There is no God west of Newton. He dried up in '90. They talk irrigation. That's an old story in hell. Where's Johnson? Not here! Where's Nickols? Not here! Bemis? Not here! Bradley? Not here! Hicks? Not here! Where's handsome Dick Barringer, Hon. Richard Barringer? Here! Here he is, holding down a hot brick in a cooling room of hell! Yes, it does look like rain, doesn't it?"

Then he would go over it all again, and finally cross the trembling threshold of the hotel, slamming the crooked, sun-steamed door behind him. There he stayed, summer and winter, looking out across the burned horizon, peering at the long, low, black line of clouds in the southwest, longing for the never-coming rain.

Cattle roamed the streets in the early spring, but the stumbling of the animals upon the broken walks did not disturb him, and the winds and the drouth soon drove them away. The messenger with provisions came every morning. The summer, with its awful heat, began to glow. The lightning and the thunder joked insolently in the distance at noon; and the stars in the deep, dry blue looked down and mocked the old man's prayers as he sat, at night, on his rickety sentry box. He tottered through the deserted stores calling his roll. Night after night he walked to the red clay grade of the uncompleted "Air Line" and looked over the dead level stretches of prairie. He would have gone away, but something held him to the town. Here he had risked all. Here, perhaps, in his warped fancy, he hoped to regain all. He had written so often, "Times will be better in the spring," that it was part of his confession of faith—that and "One good crop will bring the country around all right." This was written with red clay in the old man's nervous hand on the side of the hotel, on the faded signs, on the deserted inner walls of the store,—in fact, everywhere in Aqua Pura.

The wind told on him; it withered him, sapped his energy, and hobbled his feet.

One morning he awoke and a strange sound greeted his ears. There was a gentle tapping in the building and a roar that was not the guf-faw of the wind. He rushed for the door. He saw the rain, and bare-headed he ran to the middle of the streets where it was pouring down. The messenger from Maize with the day's supplies found him stand-ing there, vacantly, almost thoughtfully, looking up, the rain dripping from his grizzled head, and rivulets of water trickling about his shoes.

"Hello, Uncle Dick," said the messenger. "Enjoying the prospect? River's risin'; better come back with me."

But the old man only answered, "Johnson? Not here! Nickols? Not here! Bemis? Not here! Bradley? Not here! Hicks? Not here! And Barringer? Here! And now God's moved the rain belt west. Moved it so far west that there's hope for Lazarus to get irrigation from Abra-ham."

And with this the old man went into the house. There, when the five days' rain had ceased, and when the great river that flooded the barren plain had shrunk, the rescuing party, coming from Maize, found him. Beside his bed were his balanced books and his legal papers. In his dead eyes were a thousand dreams.

RUTH McENERY STUART

★   ★   ★

For twenty years an active writer of short stories, Ruth McEnery Stuart (1849-1917) treated consistently the material of her own native background in Louisiana, especially Avoyelles Parish and New Orleans, and Southern Arkansas, whither she removed in 1879 after her marriage to a planter. Her first volume, *A Golden Wedding* (1893), set the pattern and tone for subsequent stories that showed no flagging of energy or letdown in skillful plot construction. Until 1911 she averaged almost a volume a year; most distinctive are *Carlotta's Intended* (1894), *In Simkinsville* (1896), *Moriah's Mourning* (1898), *The Second Wooing of Salina Sue* (1905), and *Aunt Amity's Silver Wedding* (1908). Naturalness, kindliness, and humor mark her stories; there is no striving after effect, no brilliancy of mere technique; but there is charm in the use of dialect, and the stories convey the spirit of the post-Civil War South. Her Italians of New Orleans are enveloped in a vivid waterfront atmosphere; her Negroes of Upper Louisiana and Arkansas retain something of the plantation manner; her Simkinsville stories are adequately descriptive of Southern villages of a former day.

★   ★   ★

Aunt Delphi's Dilemma

OLD "Aunt Delphi," a superannuated crone of two hundred avoirdupois or thereabouts, was a privileged character on Honeyfield plantation.

A pensioner upon the bounty of her former owners, she had not an earthly responsibility excepting the self-assumed care of a thriving vegetable garden and poultry-yard, the proceeds of which, sold to her benefactors, supplied her with pocket-money.

Aunt Delphi had been a belle in colored society in her day and generation, and, if the whole truth must be told, the history of her matrimonial alliances is rather a tangled skein.

She was now a widow as truly as she had ever been a wife, excepting on a first occasion, when the legal bond had proven all too brittle for her playful handling. Since old age with its withering processes had overtaken her, Aunt Delphi had surrendered all her waning vitalities to religion, thus springing at a single bound from the position of a warning to that of a Christian example on the plantation. So, again, is the angle of reflection equal to the angle of incidence. The woman so recently notorious as a fisher of men for the mere sport of the angling had become a quoter of Scripture, a spiritual exhorter, even a visitor among the sick and dying, a closer of the eyes of the dead.

Since her conversion, her new peace had, as was befitting it should, seemed to permeate all her human relations, and she regarded the whole world benignly, both upward and downward. She carried counsel and delicacies to the humble cabins of the distressed or ailing with the same serene, beaming face that she bore when she wended her way to the great house with a nest of empty tin cans upon her arm, ostensibly to seek the advice of "Ole Miss" upon some trivial subject.

The advice was given or withheld according to the indications, but the cans were always taken from her to the pantry, filled, and returned.

These visits were generally paid just before dinner, and after her conference with "the white folks" the old woman would repair to the kitchen "to he'p thoo de dish-washin'," though she always consented with becoming hesitation to remain for a social meal with her chum, the cook.

As the usual interval between these social overtures was a week or ten days, Mrs. Stanley was somewhat surprised one summer morning to see Delphi trudging up the front walk three days after a former visit; and as she approached, a most mournful expression of face declared that she was in great distress of mind. Her ample lips were puckered into a royal purple flower set upon the most doleful of faces. She carried no petition in the shape of can or basket, and as she laboriously seated herself on the inverted top of the sewing-machine beside her mistress, the purple blossom declared her to be in great tribulation.

"Look lak I can't see my way straight dis mornin', mistus. Won't you please, ma'am, gimme a little drap o' some'h'n' 'nother ter raise my cour'ge tell I talks ter yer?"

The servant was called to bring some water, whereupon, with an indescribable play of features that resembled nothing so much as summer lightning, Aunt Delphi turned upon her mistress a look half reproach, half protest.

"What I wants wid water, mistus?" she pleaded. "You knows yo'se'f, ef you po's water in anything hit weakens it down. I's weakened down too much now. My *cour'ge* needs strenkenin', mistus, an' you knows dey ain't no cour'ge in water."

The "courage" being duly supplied from a bottle labelled "Blackberry Cordial," Aunt Delphi proceeded with her story. "You knows jestice an' 'ligion, Ole Miss," she resumed, "an' I wants ter insult you 'bout how I gwine ac' in dis heah trouble what's come ter me. How far down do a step-mammy's juties corndescend?"

The young ladies of the family had by this time drawn their chairs near, and the old woman had looked from one face to another as she put her question. As no one in the least understood her meaning, she proceeded to explain.

"Well, yer see, babies, I got a letter f'om the pos'-orfice las' night, an' Yaller Steve he read it out ter me, an' hit's f'om my stepson, Wash. I ain't heerd tell o' Wash sence 'fo' de wah; but he done written ter tell me dat he done got married, an' he got two sets o' twin babies, an' now he's wife she up an' dies, an' he got de unmotherless twins on 'is han's. An' Wash he say, bein' as I allus tole 'im I'd be a good mother ter 'im ef he'd commit me—he say he gwine trus' me ter raise dem sets o' twins."

Fumbling in her pocket, she presently produced a yellow envelope.

"You say there are four children?" said her mistress, by way of filling a pause.

"Yas, mistus, two full sets o' twins, 'cordin' ter what he say. Wash allus was a double-dealin' boy."

It was hard to repress a rising smile, but the old woman's disturbance of soul was so genuine that her mistress remarked, sympathetically,

"But Wash is only your stepson, if I remember rightly, Delphi?"

"Oh, yas, 'm. He's my fus' husban's boy. He's pa's a-livin' down in de Ozan bottom now. He an' me we been parted too long ter talk about, an' you know, mistus, I been married an' unmarried, off 'n' on, sence den. But, in co'se, all deze circumstancial go-betweens dey don't meck Wash ain't my stepson. Yer see, mistus, *I stood up in de chu'ch wid his daddy,* an' I wants ter do my juty by Wash, mo' in-special caze I done put 'im out'n de house on de 'count o' 'im a-raisin' his han' ter me, an' I ain't nuver is laid eyes on 'im sence. An' sence I foun' peace in 'ligion I ain't done nothin' but pray Gord ter lemme meck up wid Wash, an' now seem lak de answer done come; but hit's come loaded up purty heavy." She sighed, even wiped her eyes, as she continued: "I ain't see de way I kin raise dem fo' twins—no, I ain't."

"How old are they?" asked several at once.

"He ain't sign dey ages down by no special figgur, but, de way de letter run, I knows dey's des 'bout runnin' roun' an' cryin' size. Dat's des whar de trouble come in. Yer see I got nigh onter two honderd fryin'-size chickens in my little yard, an' ef I has ter turn fo' cryin'-size chillen in 'mongst 'em, hit'll be tur'ble. 'Caze I ain't nuver is seed a cryin'-size yit wha' ain't love ter chase de fryin'-size. Tell me, chillen, an' Ole Miss—you knows 'ligion an' jestice—how fur down do de step-mammy's juties corndescend?"

The question seemed so absurd that it was with difficulty that Mrs. Stanley, by assuming her look of greatest severity, forbade even an exchange of glances between her daughters. The old woman, in the meantime, had presented the letter to one of the young ladies to read. It proved to be in substance as she had quoted, and was signed "Yore Truely Son, Gorge Washington Brown."

"Dat soun' mighty sweet—'your truly son,'" said the old woman, as she heard the words read—"dat soun' mighty sweet—an' yit—an' yit I 'sputes de jestice. I wants ter be cancelized wid Wash, an' yit when he come ter me, fo'-in-han' like, an' offer me de whole load—tell de trufe, I don' know. Seem like we mought 'vide up de 'sponserbility some way, an' I'd even gin 'im he's ch'ice o' sets. Den agin, look lak dat ain't riverind jestice nuther, bein' as I ain't nothin' but he's step-mammy, an' ain't in no way 'sponserble fo' dem twins. Ef I was he's reel nachel mammy, in co'se I'd be, as yer mought say, back-handedly 'sponserble fur 'em. But as I is, I don't see it—no, I don't—less'n me a puttin' 'im out'n de house in a manner aggervated 'im ter it. I ain't done nothin' but walk de flo' all de endurin' night an' pray, an' I 'ain't see no light yit."

"I'll attend to this whole matter for you, Delphi," said her old mistress, taking advantage of a first real pause. "Let me write to Wash for you, telling him that you will take one of the older children, but that as you are getting old, you cannot do more."

The smile of relief and gratitude that spread over the old woman's face was really touching as she answered: "Thank Gord, Ole Miss! I b'lieve myse'f dat's de full jestice. I sho' do. I tries ter squander my shubshance on righteous livin', good as I kin, des lak de preacher say. An' you write de letter, mistus, an' tell 'im I say seek de Lord while it's day." And with profuse expression of gratitude, Aunt Delphi proceeded homeward with a lighter step and a cleared brow.

"This arrangement will be just the thing," said her mistress, as she moved away. "I have been trying to secure a child to live with the old woman and wait on her, but the mothers on the place scorn to have their children serve one of their own color. If old Delphi is at once appeasing her conscience and securing needed service, I shall congratulate myself upon helping her in the matter."

The letter was duly written.

It was about two weeks later when one morning after breakfast Aunt Delphi presented herself again at the front steps of the great house.

Hesitating here and casting upward to the group of ladies who sat within the hall door the most woe-begone of faces, she groaned aloud. Then, in a voice actually sepulchral in its deep intensity, she exclaimed:

"Why'n't yer ax me some'h'n', chillen? Quizzify me. Put de questioms. Ax me whar is I trapped deze heah black rabbits."

With this she lifted into view four little black children, starting them up the steps before her, while she followed, actually groaning aloud.

"Why'n't yer talk, chillen?" she continued, addressing the ladies, still keeping the children ahead of her. "Why'n't yer ax me is I see double, ur is you see double, ur is Wash behave 'isse'f double?" And throwing herself into a chair, Aunt Delphi fell to actual weeping.

The little girls, absurdly alike even as to size, though their ages were about four and five years respectively, stood in a row, each sucking her thumb, and in no wise embarrassed by the presence of strangers; and yet when in a moment one of them began slowly to back from the company, they all followed, until, touching the wall, they sat down in a row.

"Are these Wash's children?" asked her mistress, as soon as she could command her voice.

"Yas, Lord," she moaned, swaying her body to and fro.

"And so he brought them all. Where is he? When did they come?"

"Hol' on, mistus," she exclaimed, waving her hand to command silence. "Hol' on an' lemme start straight. In de searchin' hour o' midnight las' night, when eve'y hones' pusson was buried in Christian sleep, heah come 'a-rap-a-tap-tap!' on my kyabin do', des easy lak an' sof', lak some h'n' sperityal; an' I retched up an' stricken a match, an' open de do' an' listen, an' I ain't heerd no soun' but 'cep' one o' deze heah onsleepless morkin'-birds chantin' out secon'-han' music, an' all de time my eyes was turned high, an' I nuver 'spicioned nothin', tell right onder my foots deze heah fo' p'intedly matched babies come a-walkin' in, des lak you see 'em now, ev'y one a-suckin' 'er fis'."

"But where did they come from? Did Wash bring them?"

"What ails you, chillen, dat you don't heah me what I say. I don't know no mo'n dey say, an' dey ain't showed speech yit."

"And you haven't seen Wash?"

"Ain't I talkin' straight, baby? I say I 'ain't seed nothin', neither heerd nothin'. Tell de trufe, 'cep'n fur de co'n-brade dey done et, I'd look fur dem babies ter vanige out'n my sight des lak dey come. Co'se I done set 'em down ter Wash, bein' as he done 'nounced 'isse'f in de twins trade. But eh, Lord! What I gwine do wid 'em? An' de las' one o' 'em cryin'-sizes!"

The ladies called the children to them, and by dint of coaxing learned that they "comed wid daddy—to find mammy," and that they answered to the endearing names of Shug, Pud, Hun, and Babe. The conventional list of names had apparently not been taxed for their designation.

It was evidently a deeply laid scheme. Wash's letter was only a ruse to ascertain whether the old woman Delphi still lived or not, and he had cast his children upon her.

Poor old Delphi, chafing under the imposition, and overcome with the weight of so heavy a responsibility, sat softly weeping, while the ladies assured her that she should be relieved.

Wash, the poltroon, had covered his tracks well. No one on the place had seen or heard him, and the wheels whose tracks approached the fence had soon returned to the old ruts, and left no trace of their course.

Delphi's cabin was the same in which Wash had lived as a child. This fact Mrs. Stanley had unwittingly betrayed in her letter, in which she pleaded its single room as added excuse for her not taking more than one child.

During the two weeks following this, letters of inquiry concerning his lordship, the delectable sire George Washington Brown, were sent to leading persons in the town from whence his letter had been posted; but though several citizens of color bore this identical distinguished if not distinguishing name, no trace of the father of the twins was found.

A party of Negroes en route for Kansas had recently passed within five miles of Honeyfield plantation. Presumably Wash had been of this number. Starting out to begin life afresh, he had no doubt made good his proposal to his stepmother to "let by-gones be by-gones."

A month passed, and no news had come of the recreant father, neither had the sensation caused by Aunt Delphi's sudden acquisition of family begun to abate. The children, through whom she had been an object of interest far and near, and whose presence had brought generous gifts from all directions to the little cabin, were still there awaiting developments, and pending a decision as to the best disposition to be made of them.

Feeling that the matter had better be arranged and the old woman relieved, Mrs. Stanley decided one morning to call at the little cabin herself to talk the matter over. She had found good homes ready to welcome two of the children, and would take a third herself until she could be permanently provided for.

She found Aunt Delphi sitting on the doorstep, holding one of the four on either knee, while the other two sat on the ground at her feet. All were munching huge chunks of corn-bread and chattering like magpies. At sight of her mistress the old woman slipped the children to the ground, and, with elaborate apologies for the state of her cabin, which was indeed strewn with trash, improvised rag babies, and pallets, she proceeded to wipe off a chair with her apron before presenting it.

"Have you decided which one of the little girls you are going to keep?" Mrs. Stanley asked, after the usual interchange of civilities.

The old woman had seated herself opposite her mistress, and at the question she rolled her eyes mysteriously a moment before answering. Finally she said: "I b'lieve you's a min'-reader, mistus, I sho does, caze you done read out de subjec' dat's been on my min' all day; but yer ain't read it straight, Ole Miss—no, yer ain't." Turning, she looked fondly upon the children and chuckled. "Des look how happy dey is!" she said. "Dey des as happy as a nes' o' kittens, dat dey is! Why, mistus, I been overrun wid cats all my life, des caze I couldn't say de drownin' ur pizenin' word ter air kitten what look ter me in weakness. I done let a chicken-devourin' rat out'n a trap des caze I ketched a prayer in 'is eye. De way a cockroach run fur 'is life meck me draw back my brogan an' let 'im go. How is I gwine part wid any o' dem human babies?"

"What do you mean, Delphi? You surely cannot wish to keep four children to bring up at your time of life. It would be absurd."

"Hol' on, mistus, hol' on—don't go so fas'! Dem chillen done preached a heap o' sermons ter me, an' dey all got de same tex'; an' dat tex' hit splains out a new set o' argimints ev'y time. How yer reckon I feels, mistus, when I looks at dem babies an' see how p'intedly dey favors dey gramper? Lookin' at 'em ev'y day tecks my min' way back ter my co'tin' days, when love soun' in my ears lak a music chune picked on a banjer. An' when I looks back on my life I see how I loved de endurin' soun' so much I ain't keer who play de music. So de by-gone pictur's come back ter me one by one; but de one dat stay wid me is de one wha' show me my fus' husban', Dan; an' I see how I done trifled wid 'im, an' de quar'l we had, when I sassed back an' go one better'n him ev'y time ('caze we was bofe high-temprate). An' den I 'member de fight he fit wid Abum Saunders, 'caze Abum's love chune please my hearin'. Den come back a yether pictur'—*ole Dan* de way my min' see 'im now, 'cripit an' gray, maybe, an' lonesome an' failin', an' me his lawful wedded wife, an' all o' deze heah peart little gran'babies o' his'n right heah—next do' ter 'im, de way Gord reckon space. Dat's de way de sermon read, an' deze onconscious infams dey preaches it at me, inbeknowinst, ter meck up wid dey gramper, *an' I ain't gwine zist de sperit no mo'.* I gwine meck de movement ter be cancelized wid Dan; an' ef he's sick, I gwine nuss 'im; an' ef he's cranky an' fussy, I gwine shet my mouf an' say nothin': *but I gwine back ter 'im—dat is, ef he'll teck me!* An' ef you got a argimint agin it, mistus, don't spressify it in my hearin', please, ma'am, *'caze my min' made up.*"

Mrs. Stanley realized it would be somewhat inconsistent with her own professions to oppose a reconciliation between husband and wife, and as soon as she could recover from her surprise at the unexpected turn the affair was taking she wished the old woman all possible success and happiness in the step she had resolved to take. Indeed, before she had left the cabin she had herself written at her dictation the letter the old wife sent the next day to the husband from whom she had been estranged for thirty years or more.

A few days afterward there was an important arrival at Delphi's cabin. The letter had brought the old husband back to the feet of his early love.

A week later the departure took place. A capacious plantation wagon was piled high with bedding, boxes, and sundry household belongings, laid upon a foundation of chicken-coops, out of which curious feathered heads gazed in alternate-eyed wonder at the unusual proceeding. On the summit of the edifice sat the old couple in a veritable rose garden of little bobbing pink sunbonnets.

They were going to the old man's home. Delphi had made her formal adieux at the house, and wept her parting tears, but through them the sun of a new happiness was shining.

As the wagon moved out the gate the ladies waved good-bye from the gallery of the great house, and the old man, perceiving them, lifted his hat, bowing his body in a manner that was distinctly courtly.

Aunt Delphi up to this moment had been absorbed in her maternal task of safely seating the children, but now realizing that the supreme moment of last leave-taking was come, she threw one arm around her old husband, waving the other high in air as she began to sing. The wagon moved slowly down the road, and as the early sun coming through the pines covered it at intervals, it gleamed in the light, a bright bouquet of color. An occasional gust of wind brought snatches of her song even while the wagon was but a speck of color in the vista, and the effect was much heightened by the sound of a second voice, a wiry high tenor, playing all around the wind-wafted words—

". . . to part no mo'—no mo'."

CHARLES F. LUMMIS

★ ★ ★

Journalist, editor, traveler, storyteller, ethnologist, poet, musician, historian, antiquarian, philologist, organizer, campaigner, Charles F. Lummis (1859-1928) had a changing career, as varied and expansive as the West he lovingly celebrated. Born in Massachusetts, he contributed to *The Atlantic Monthly* at sixteen, and by the sale of *Birch Bark* (1879), poems printed on bark, earned his way through Harvard. Two years later he made the walking trip to California recounted in *A Tramp Across the Continent* (1892). Paralysis induced by overwork on a Los Angeles newspaper invalided him to New Mexico, where residence with Mexican shepherds and Pueblo Indians afforded substance for *A New Mexico David* (1891), *The King of the Broncos* (1897), *The Enchanted Burro* (1897), *Mesa, Cañon, and Pueblo* (1925), and other historical and fictional volumes. Although an explorer on horseback of Bolivia, Peru, Guatemala, and Mexico, he lived longest in the great Southwest and illustrated adequately the famous phrase he originated, "See America First." Lummis was successful in creating picturesque, vivid scenes instinct with wonder. "Bogged Down," from *The King of the Broncos,* is reprinted by permission of Charles Scribner's Sons, publishers.

★ ★ ★

Bogged Down

THAT always *was* a treacherous hole in the Agua Azul—that prettiest shallow in all the bluish brook whose source is the great spring that pours from under the edge of the fifty-mile lava-bed, and with its lower course half lost amid the thirsty sands of western New

744

Mexico—reappearing only now and then in disconnected but living pools. This particular spot was a few miles west from the Toltec Cattle Company's "home ranch"—headquarters of the score of cowboys who "rode the range" of a hundred thousand acres. There was a long, shallow arroyo down the middle of the valley, and in it a series of pools connected by a thin trickle of water. To each pool a deep, narrow trail in the turf had been worn by the daily processions of cattle trudging twenty miles to water.

The middle and largest pool was broad, shallow, clear, with a foot of limpid water lying mirror-like upon its bed of pretty, yellow sand. It was the most innocent-looking shallow in the world; such a place as would tempt children to wading if there had been children within twenty miles—as luckily there were not. One wading would have been the last; for that sunny pool was a smiling grave that had swallowed up more victims than there were inches in its circumference!

The whole brook was troublesome to the cattlemen, for in its marshy edges the stock was continually miring. One thick-chested cowboy on a heavy horse had no other duty than to "ride the creek" for twenty miles, to watch for cattle that had "bogged down," and help them out before they perished. Now the animals seemed to have learned that that particular pool was to be shunned; and there were seldom hoofprints along its border. But it had been costly learning. Within a week after the company took the ranch and turned in cattle, a huge black bull, the most valuable animal in the great herd, tried to cross there, and midway of the pool suddenly slumped shoulder-deep. In five minutes he had gone, and the clear water rippled innocently as ever over its yellow bed. In the eight years since, several scores of cattle, of all grades and sizes, had been similarly engulfed in this strange, automatic graveyard. Every one about the ranch knew "the Cow Trap"; and in crossing the creek of dark nights all were very careful to avoid that pool.

At the close of March the snow still lay in patches among the northern cedars of the Ventana. There was yet no green blade at that high altitude. The thin cattle, much the worse for wear by a New Mexican winter, looked in sorry trim. For six months they had wandered at will, unchecked by fences or rivers. Some had strayed off into Arizona, and some, drifting south before the fierce storms, were down in the Black Range. In a few weeks the cowboys would start on the annual roundup.

" 'Pears like them cattle's thet thin yo' kin see the brand through from the fur side!" grumbled Baby Bones to himself, as he loped easily past a tired bunch of recumbent cattle on his shaggy bronco.

"Et'll shore be a job to round 'em up, 'thout we ketch a bit o' new grass 'fore then." And in ruffled humor at the thought the young cowboy loped away on the dim trail to Cebollita, forty miles to the south.

Baby Bones was by no means a baby, either in mind or body; and Bones was a name which certainly did not figure in the record-pages of the old family Bible away back on the lonely Texas ranch. But when this tall, ungainly, dangling youth had first shambled into the T C C ranch-house in search of a job, wrinkled Jim had shouted, "Wal, baby, w'ere'd yo' git them bones?"—and "Baby Bones" he had been ever since. It is doubtful if any one on the ranch knew his true name. He was plain Baby Bones on the pay-roll, and in conversation, and to his face. There was a ludicrous aptness in the title, too—as there usually is with cowboy nicknames. His head was very small; and his thin, freckled face, with its insignificant pug nose, small mouth, little blue eyes without visible brows or lashes, and a general mildness of expression—all gave him a very childish look indeed. He was nearly six feet tall, with a long, thin neck, narrow, sloping shoulders, huge wrists and fists, and a general build, as old Jim said, "like a two-futted brandin' iron." But Baby Bones was very good-natured, and took with entire complacency the numerous rough jokes upon his appearance. He was aware he "warn't purty, but he knowed cows and bronks from away back." There was no better rider or roper in that company of experts; and as for deeper qualities, "the boys" had generally come to the conclusion that "thet Baby hed a heap o' sand, an' lots of savvy."

It was partly because of these qualities that the foreman had selected Baby Bones to make the rough ride to Cebollita, where there was ticklish work to be done. There were rumors from the friendly Pueblos that a band of Mexican "rustlers" were hiding in the caves at that end of the great lava-bed with the presumed intention of raiding the herds of the T C C.

One man could best spy out the matter. If he confirmed the reports, a strong squad of cowboys would take the field at once against the stock thieves.

The dangers of his mission did not seem to weigh upon the young vaquero. He was not more than eighteen years of age; but all those years had been on the frontier, and they had taught him a great many rough lessons. Of course if the rustlers discovered him, they would bushwhack him and hide his body in some gully; but he intended to keep out of sight—to "Injun on 'em a little," as he would have said.

If it *did* come to a fight—why, there was the Winchester slung along the saddle and the heavy six-shooter on his hip.

So he rode up the valley toward Cebollita, keeping a sharp eye to the great, black, contorted swell of lava on his right, and to the cedar-dotted slope from the mesa cliffs on his left. But there was nothing suspicious to be seen. Now and then a cottontail scurried into the fissures of the lava; or a coyote, with drooping brush, trotted leisurely out of gunshot. After the first few miles from the creek there were not even these; and the cowboy grew suspicious at seeing *nothing*.

"Wot's up?" he puzzled. "The cattle *allus* uses in here, fur the grass thet sticks along the *malpáis;* an' I cain't see wot's got 'em thet the' hain't nary head yere today— Oho!" He suddenly bent over from the saddle to glance at a faint print on a moist spot in the trail. In another instant he was off Tex's back, kneeling beside the telltale marks. Baby Bones had learned trailing from the Comanches; and, despite his youth, was noted for skill in that difficult science.

"So!" he muttered, as he rose. "Thet horse shore never was shod in these yere parts. Et's Chihuahua work, or I never want to see the back o' my neck! An' he was bein' rode tol'able hard, too, an' them tracks is today's!"

As he remounted, he pulled his six-shooter and turned the chambers watchfully, to be sure that no grit had got into the bearings, wiped it on the sleeve of his buckskin coat, and then saw to it that the rifle in its scabbard was in equally trustworthy trim.

Tex had kept up his tireless lope all the afternoon, but now the rein checked him to a slow trot, and frequently stopped him altogether as the rider looked and listened. At last Baby turned into a brown, grassy "bay" in the lava. Riding around a point, he staked Tex on the smooth turf, and hid the saddle and other trappings in a crevice of the rocks. Here the horse was out of sight from the trail, and here might safely be left. The sun was just setting. The south end of the lava-flow was not more than three miles away, and there were the caves which were supposed to shelter the robbers.

Baby Bones pulled from a capacious pocket a crushed lunch of frying-pan bread and boiled beef, and devoured it hastily. Then he mounted the lava-ridge and began to walk cautiously across it. On that fearful, cutting surface the heaviest boots would not outlast a few miles; but he knew that here the flow was narrow, and not more than a mile across. It was best to approach the camp of the "rustlers" from the west, since they would look for no danger from the pathless wilderness behind them.

He stumbled along in the thickening night, now crawling around narrow fissures of unknown depth, now falling over broken lava-blocks, now resuming his course with a long, ungainly stride.

As he reached the farther edge of the lava, he paused to listen. There was a feeling in him that he heard something. He laid his ear to the rocky floor to listen again, but could make out nothing.

After a moment, he straightened up, dissatisfied, clambered from the lava-swell to the ground, and hurried quietly southward, hugging the strange black wall that loomed above him in the darkness. But even yet he could not rid himself of the impression that there was something in the air—something too tiny for the ears to find, grope as they would, but still *something*—and at last he climbed again to the top of the *malpáis,* and stood listening. At first there was nothing; but presently he seemed to *feel,* rather than to hear, a faint far-off murmur like bees in swarming-time. Then there came a faint whisper of breeze from the southeast; and on it was a strange, low roll, as of surf on a distant shore.

So! There was only one thing in the world that could make that sound there—it was the roll of many hurrying hoofs over the dry sward.

"*Con-*SARN 'em!" he groaned under his breath. "Ef they hain't gi'n me the sack to hold! They shore hev rustled up a big bunch o' cattle, an' are goin' to run 'em acrost the range tonight an' up to Utah. An' me a-ketched up over yer, acrost the *malpáis* frum them an' Tex!"

He ran back across the ugly swell, tearing his boots, cutting his feet cruelly on the jagged points, but never thinking of the pain in his anger at being outwitted and his anxiety to thwart the robbers— just how, he had now no clear idea. The muffled tattoo of hoofs was nearer and louder now, and he could even hear occasional calls in Spanish. The thieves were running the cattle up the trail by which he had come, and running them hard. Soon they had passed, and the trampling roar began to sink and sink as the herd drew off into the distance.

"Good land!" the cowboy groaned. "I 'llow the' mus' be two hundred head! An' ef the' ain't hosses in the bunch, too, yo' can call my ears a fool. I'll bet they done raided the cavyyard [horse herd] up at Agua Fria; an' ef they did, the' mus' be a gang of 'em!"

He stumbled on with renewed vigor. But just as he discerned against the dark sky the cliff which walled the valley on the east, he gave a wild howl, and went tumbling into a ragged fissure.

Luckily, it was not one of the deeper ones that abound in that wild flow, or there would have been an end to the story of Baby

Bones. As it was, he fell full twenty feet, and lay stunned and bleeding, wedged between the narrow jaws of the lava-crack. It was a long time before he began to recollect himself and what had happened—perhaps an hour. But as his senses came back by degrees, and the sharp pain from many cuts and bruises stung him to clearer thought, he did remember; and at once the strong instinct of the chase filled his mind. It was hard work to drag himself out from that rocky pinch; but at last he did it, and with many groans tried to climb out of his fissure-prison. But the ragged walls were perpendicular—a monkey could not have scaled them. After a cruel hour of limping back and forth in the cleft, his hands gashed by the jagged walls, at last he found an angle where he was able to ascend, and drew a deep glad breath once more on the top of the treacherous flow.

There was no more running now—he was too sore and lame, and fearful of further pitfalls. He limped cautiously on, until the edge of the lava came down again to the trail. In a few moments more he was back in the grassy "bay." Tex was still there, grazing contentedly at the end of the reata, and gave a joyful neigh.

The sore cowboy saddled the pony, and in five minutes after regaining the "bay" was galloping along the trail northward. The forty miles of the day was nothing to Tex. He was a horse of the plains, and could do forty more, and twenty on top of that. If the rustlers rode anything that could wear Tex out, they were welcome to get away, thought Baby Bones. And if he did catch up with them—well, he would see!

Five miles, ten, fifteen, twenty, fell behind the plucky pony's heels. The reins hung loose on his neck. No one could guide a horse in that darkness—and such a horse needed no guide. A "cowpony" that would lose a trail, or step into a prairie-dog hole by night, would never be tolerated on any self-respecting cow-range. Tex was no "tenderfoot"; and he bounded along as confidently as if he could *smell* his way.

"Orter be closin' up, I reckon," said the cowboy, patting the hot neck and lifting the reins gently.

Tex stood still, and his master leaned forward in the saddle to listen. Yes! There it was, above Tex's hard breathing—the long, low roar!

"We're gettin' there, Tex!" cried Baby Bones. "Keep it up, old boy, an' we'll hev some disappointed rustlers"—and at the word they were off again like an arrow.

Five miles more, the roar swelling louder and louder—until now the pursuer could feel the shake of that multitudinous tread, while its rumble filled the night. As they swept around a turn of the little valley, Tex snorted and wildly rushed into the thunderous cloud of dust. Here were cattle on the run; what else was to be done but "cut them out"?

But Tex's horse-wisdom had led him astray for once. There was a warning yell in Spanish, and an answering chorus from half a dozen sides. A sharp, spiteful flash, a ringing report, and Baby Bones felt a curious numb streak across his leg. A splinter from the horn of his saddle struck his bridle-hand. An instant later there was a flash and a report from below, and a galloping steer plunged forward on its knees. The rustler's bullet had creased Baby's thigh and carried away his saddle-horn. The loosened *fonda,* swinging downward, had dropped his Winchester to the ground, where it was discharged. No time to stop and pick it up now, even had there been light to find it. A stop there would make a target of man and horse, even in that gloom. The only safety was in the indiscriminate crowd of hurrying figures. There was little danger then, unless accident should bring him alongside one of the rustlers. In that case he would "stand an even show, anyhow," as he reflected.

For mile after mile the strange earth-shaking jam of thunderous hoofs swept on. The stolen cattle, the robbers, Baby Bones, were all in one indeterminable jostle; dumb hearts filled with terror, and human ones with hate and deadly thoughts. Baby Bones held his six-shooter cocked down along his hip as Tex galloped on—and he knew well that each of his unseen and outnumbering foes was similarly ready. His eyes were *loose*—looking nowhere, but in that peculiar passive readiness to be called to keenest scrutiny by the least hint from either side.

Once his trained ear detected the firm thud of a horse's hoofs behind him. He turned in his saddle just in time to escape the bullet of one of the desperadoes, who had circled the rear of the herd to discover the interloper. Baby Bones fired even as he wheeled, but the rustler was already lost in the darkness.

Then on a sudden he felt that there was something wrong with the herd—an indefinable change in the roar of hoofs. In another instant he saw in the darkness that the cattle were sweeping to his right and left, like a great torrent suddenly divided by an invisible rock.

Before he could give a thought to this unexpected occurrence, he and Tex seemed to be falling, and a great splash of icy water drenched him from head to foot.

There was another splash beside him, and another on the left, and another, and another, following swifter than thought.

It was the creek, of course; but why did Tex flounder so? And the others! He had heard four of the rustlers ride in, but instead of their hoofbeats on the farther bank now, there was a fearful splashing and cursing— Ah! they were in the Cow Trap!

Poor Tex was struggling with desperate strength, but it was of no avail. The water was already at his shoulders—in a moment he could not even struggle—his feet were gripped in that hideous vise below. The terrified brute, lifting his head high, gave a shriek that was human in its despair. Poor Tex!

Baby Bones had been stunned at first, but he was wide awake now.

To his right, ten feet away, he could make out a dark, struggling mass, from which came wild snorts and husky screams to the saints.

In an instant the cowboy was on his feet in the saddle. Gathering his ungainly frame, he sprang madly out into the air. Those stilt-like, awkward legs had reckoned their tension well. He landed on the withers of a struggling horse, eliciting a new howl from the terrified robber; tottered, caught his poise, and made another desperate bound.

Splash! He had fallen short of the bank, and he felt the deadly sands clasping above his knees. But he threw himself frantically forward, dragging his feet up a little as he went over. And hurra! His hands touched the bank!

He caught a tiny bunch of sedge-grass, held it carefully lest its roots should give way, and pulled gently and steadily. It held. A wave of joy rushed through him as he felt his feet slowly drawing out from that strange clutch. A moment more and he was lying on the bank, weak and trembling with excitement and exertion, but safe.

The struggling in the pool had grown less. There was only a faint splash to be heard now and then above the chorus of shrieks and oaths and prayers of frantic men. The horses were evidently all drowned or already engulfed; and the riders would soon share their fate.

Five minutes before the rough-bred cowboy had had but one desire,—a chance to kill or capture these robbers. But the meaner passions stand aside in the presence of the Great Leveller; and now Baby's only thought was to save his enemies from so hideous a death. He was helpless enough. The reata, with which he could have "roped" them all to safety one by one, had gone down with poor Tex. There was not even a bush, whose helpful branches he might stretch out to the doomed wretches.

He ran up and down the bank, shaking his big fists in despair, yelling, *"Saltan!* Jump flat! I'll help you!"

One Mexican leaped; but, weak with terror, struck upon his feet three yards from the shore. The others did not seem to hear the friendly yell, but went floundering off their submerged saddles beside their disappearing steeds, still shrieking and praying hoarsely.

Baby Bones could see the man who had jumped, already waist-deep. Forgetting his own safety, the youth stooped low and shot his long body out upon the water as if swimming. The sinking rustler made a frantic clutch at him, but the cowboy, turning on his side, dealt him a fearful blow in the face that laid him back motionless upon the water.

Then with great care, lying on his belly in the shallow water, that the treacherous quicksand might get no hold on him, he tugged and hauled first at one leg of the rustler, then at the other. Now that no weight was pushing them down, he soon had them clear.

Twisting one hand in the long hair of the unconscious robber, Baby Bones towed him ashore. Laying his limp captive upon the grass, and finding a faint pulse in the wrist, he cut a couple of thongs from his buckskin jacket and tied the arms and ankles securely. The fellow would soon recover from the stunning, and Baby Bones had no intention that he should get away.

As for the others, there was no help for them. No splash longer disturbed the pool's ripples. The Cow Trap had claimed new victims.

When the foreman and a score of cowboys came with Baby Bones to the deadly pool, just as the day was breaking, it was the same placid, purring, limpid pool of old. There were some fresh hoofprints on its margin, but no more. Even the prisoner was gone.

Soon the sharp-eyed trailers read the whole story in the soil. The foremost cattle had seen and recognized the dreaded pool, and had swerved to either side, blindly followed by those behind. But in the darkness and the stifling dust-cloud the horses had run straight into the trap.

A little farther up the creek one rustler had crossed in safety. He had evidently come back, cut the thongs from Baby Bones's captive, and carried him off on his own horse.

As for the cattle, they were all found in the meadows, worn out with their fearful stampede.

The two surviving rustlers got safely away; but they never raided the T C C again. To this day, if you drop into the home-ranch of an evening, you will have little difficulty in persuading Baby Bones—now with a straggling beard, but still Baby—to tell you about the night when the Cow Trap caught big game.

STEPHEN CRANE

★ ★ ★

A leader in the reaction against genteel-romantic fiction, Stephen Crane (1871-1900) slowly won recognition as a writer of realistic stories in a new impressionistic technique involving objectivity in point of view, accuracy of detail, incisive brevity, rapid yet almost plotless narrative action, and vividly pungent poetic phrasing. After years of free-lance writing and the publication at his own expense of *Maggie: A Girl of the Street* (1892), Crane achieved fame with *The Red Badge of Courage* (1895), a naturalistic account of a private's terrifying experiences in the Civil War. Commissioned to write a series of sketches in 1895, Crane traveled through the Southwest and Mexico; on this trip he wrote "A Man and—Some Others." In 1896 he filibustered in Cuba and barely survived a shipwreck. Later he reported the Greco-Turkish and Spanish-American wars. His best short stories are in *The Little Regiment* (1896) and *The Open Boat and Other Tales of Adventure* (1898). "A Man and—Some Others" is reprinted by permission of Alfred A. Knopf, Inc.

★ ★ ★

A Man and—Some Others

Dark mesquit spread from horizon to horizon. There was no house or horseman from which a mind could evolve a city or a crowd. The world was declared to be a desert and unpeopled. Sometimes, however, on days when no heat-mist arose, a blue shape, dim, of the substance of a specter's veil, appeared in the southwest, and a pondering sheepherder might remember that there were mountains.

In the silence of these plains the sudden and childish banging of a tin pan could have made an iron-nerved man leap into the air. The sky was ever flawless; the manoeuvring of clouds was an unknown pageant; but at times a sheepherder could see, miles away, the long white streamers of dust rising from the feet of another's flock, and the interest became intense.

Bill was arduously cooking his dinner, bending over the fire and toiling like a blacksmith. A movement, a flash of strange color perhaps, off in the bushes, caused him to suddenly turn his head. Presently he arose and, shading his eyes with his hand, stood motionless and gazing. He perceived at last a Mexican sheepherder winding through the brush toward his camp.

"Hello!" shouted Bill.

The Mexican made no answer, but came steadily forward until he was within some twenty yards. There he paused and, folding his arms, drew himself up in the manner affected by the villain in the play. His serape muffled the lower part of his face, and his great sombrero shaded his brow. Being unexpected and also silent, he had something of the quality of an apparition; moreover, it was clearly his intention to be mystic and sinister.

The American's pipe, sticking carelessly in the corner of his mouth, was twisted until the wrong side was uppermost, and he held his frying-pan poised in the air. He surveyed with evident surprise this apparition in the mesquit. "Hello, José!" he said. "What's the matter?"

The Mexican spoke with the solemnity of funeral tollings: "Beel, you mus' geet off range. We want you geet off range. We no like. Un'erstan'? We no like."

"What you talking about?" said Bill. "No like what?"

"We no like you here. Un'stan'? Too mooch. You mus' geet out. We no like. Un'erstan'?"

"Understand? No; I don't know what the blazes you're gittin' at." Bill's eyes wavered in bewilderment, and his jaw fell. "I must git out? I must git off the range? What you givin' us?"

The Mexican unfolded his serape with his small yellow hand. Upon his face was then to be seen a smile that was gently almost caressingly murderous. "Beel," he said, "git out!"

Bill's arm dropped until the frying-pan was at his knee. Finally he turned again toward the fire. "Go on, you doggone little yaller rat!" he said over his shoulder. "You fellers can't chase me off this range. I got as much right here as anybody."

"Beel," answered the other in a vibrant tone, thrusting his head forward and moving one foot, "you geet out or we keel you."

"Who will?" said Bill.

"I—and the others." The Mexican tapped his breast gracefully.

Bill reflected for a time, and then he said: "You ain't got no manner of license to warn me off'n this range, and I won't move a rod. Understand? I've got rights, and I suppose if I don't see 'em through, no one is likely to give me a good hand and help me lick you fellers, since I'm the only white man in half a day's ride. Now, look: if you fellers try to rush this camp, I'm goin' to plug about fifty per cent of the gentlemen present, sure. I'm goin' in for trouble, an' I'll git a lot of you. 'Nuther thing: if I was a fine valuable caballero like you, I'd stay in the rear till the shootin' was done, because I'm goin' to make a particular p'int of shootin' you through the chest." He grinned affably, and made a gesture of dismissal.

As for the Mexican, he waved his hands in a consummate expression of indifference. "Oh, all right," he said. Then, in a tone of deep menace and glee, he added: "We will keel you eef you no geet. They have decide."

"They have, have they?" said Bill. "Well, you tell them to go to the devil!"

II

Bill had been a mine-owner in Wyoming, a great man, an aristocrat, one who possessed unlimited credit in the saloons down the gulch. He had the social weight that could interrupt a lynching or advise a bad man of the particular merits of a remote geographical point. However, the fates exploded the toy balloon with which they had amused Bill, and on the evening of the same day he was a professional gambler with ill fortune dealing him unspeakable irritation in the shape of three big cards whenever another fellow stood pat. It is well here to inform the world that Bill considered his calamities of life all dwarfs in comparison with the excitement of one particular evening when three kings came to him with criminal regularity against a man who always filled a straight. Later he became a cowboy, more weirdly abandoned than if he had never been an aristocrat. By this time all that remained of his former splendor was his pride, or his vanity, which was one thing which need not have remained. He killed the foreman of the ranch over an inconsequent matter as to which of them was a liar, and the midnight train carried him eastward. He became a brakeman on the Union Pacific, and really gained high honors in the hobo war that for many years has devastated the beautiful railroads of our country. A creature of ill fortune himself, he practiced all the ordinary cruelties upon these other creatures of ill fortune. He was of so fierce a mien that tramps usually surrendered at once whatever coin or tobacco they had in their possession; and if afterward he kicked them from the train, it was only because this was a recognized treachery of the war upon the hoboes. In a famous battle fought in Nebraska in 1879, he would have achieved a lasting distinction if it had not been for a deserter from the United States army. He was at the head of a heroic and sweeping charge which really broke the power of the hoboes in that county for three months; he had already worsted four tramps with his own coupling-stock, when a stone thrown by the ex-third-baseman of F Troop's nine laid him flat on the prairie, and later enforced a stay in the hospital in Omaha. After his recovery he engaged with other railroads, and shuffled cars in countless yards. An order to strike came upon him in Michigan, and afterward the vengeance of the railroad pursued him until he assumed a name. This mask is like the darkness in which the burglar chooses to move. It destroys many of the healthy fears. It is a small thing, but it eats that which we call our conscience. The conductor of No. 419 stood in the caboose within two feet of Bill's nose and called him a liar. Bill requested him to use a milder term. He had not bored the foreman of Tin Can Ranch with any such request, but had killed him with expedition. The conductor seemed to insist, and so Bill let the matter drop. He became the bouncer of a saloon on the Bowery in New York. Here most of his fights were as successful as had been his brushes with the hoboes in the West. He gained the complete admiration of the four clean bartenders who stood behind the great and glittering bar. He was an honored man. He nearly killed Bad Hennessy, who, as a matter of fact, had more reputation than ability, and his fame moved up the Bowery and down the Bowery.

But let a man adopt fighting as his business, and the thought grows constantly within him that it is his business to fight. These phrases became mixed in Bill's mind precisely as they are here mixed; and let a man get this idea in his mind, and defeat begins to move toward him over the unknown ways of circumstance. One summer night three sailors from the U.S.S. *Seattle* sat in the saloon drinking and attending to other people's affairs in an amiable fashion. Bill was a proud man since he had thrashed so many citizens, and it suddenly occurred to him that the loud talk of the sailors was very offensive. So he swaggered upon their attention and warned them that the saloon was the flowery abode of peace and gentle silence. They glanced at him in surprise, and without a moment's pause consigned him to a worse place than any stoker of them knew. Whereupon he flung one of

them through the side door before the others could prevent it. On
the sidewalk there was a short struggle, with many hoarse epithets in
the air, and then Bill slid into the saloon again. A frown of false rage
was upon his brow, and he strutted like a savage king. He took a
long yellow night-stick from behind the lunch-counter and started
importantly toward the main doors to see that the incensed seamen
did not again enter.

The ways of sailormen are without speech, and, together in the
street, the three sailors exchanged no word, but they moved at once.
Landsmen would have required three years of discussion to gain such
unanimity. In silence, and immediately, they seized a long piece of
scantling that lay handy. With one forward to guide the battering-ram
and with two behind him to furnish the power, they made a beautiful curve and came down like the Assyrians on the front door of that
saloon.

Strange and still strange are the laws of fate. Bill, with his kingly
frown and his long night-stick, appeared at precisely that moment in
the doorway. He stood like a statue of victory; his pride was at its
zenith; and in the same second this atrocious piece of scantling
punched him in the bulwarks of his stomach, and he vanished like a
mist. Opinions differed as to where the end of the scantling landed
him, but it was ultimately clear that it landed him in southwestern
Texas, where he became a sheepherder.

The sailors charged three times upon the plate-glass front of the
saloon, and when they had finished, it looked as if it had been the
victim of a rural fire company's success in saving it from the flames.
As the proprietor of the place surveyed the ruins, he remarked that
Bill was a very zealous guardian of property. As the ambulance surgeon surveyed Bill, he remarked that the wound was really an ex-
cavation.

III

As his Mexican friend tripped blithely away, Bill turned with a
thoughtful face to his frying-pan and his fire. After dinner he drew
his revolver from its scarred old holster and examined every part of
it. It was the revolver that had dealt death to the foreman, and it
had also been in free fights in which it had dealt death to several or
none. Bill loved it because its allegiance was more than that of man,
horse, or dog. It questioned neither social nor moral position; it
obeyed alike the saint and the assassin. It was the claw of the
eagle, the tooth of the lion, the poison of the snake; and when he
swept it from its holster, this minion smote where he listed, even to

the battering of a far penny. Wherefore it was his dearest possession, and was not to be exchanged in southwestern Texas for a handful of rubies, nor even the shame and homage of the conductor of No. 419.

During the afternoon he moved through his monotony of work and leisure with the same air of deep meditation. The smoke of his supper-time fire was curling across the shadowy sea of mesquit when the instinct of the plainsman warned him that the stillness, the desolation, was again invaded. He saw a motionless horseman in black outline against the pallid sky. The silhouette displayed serape and sombrero, and even the Mexican spurs as large as pies. When this black figure began to move toward the camp, Bill's hand dropped to his revolver.

The horseman approached until Bill was enabled to see pronounced American features and a skin too red to grow on a Mexican face. Bill released his grip on his revolver.

"Hello!" called the horseman.

"Hello!" answered Bill.

The horseman cantered forward. "Good evening," he said, as he again drew rein.

"Good evenin'," answered Bill, without committing himself by too much courtesy.

For a moment the two men scanned each other in a way that is not ill-mannered on the plains, where one is in danger of meeting horse-thieves or tourists.

Bill saw a type which did not belong in the mesquit. The young fellow had invested in some Mexican trappings of an expensive kind. Bill's eyes searched the outfit for some sign of craft, but there was none. Even with his local regalia, it was clear that the young man was of a far, black Northern city. He had discarded the enormous stirrups of his Mexican saddle; he used the small English stirrup, and his feet were thrust forward until the steel tightly gripped his ankles. As Bill's eyes traveled over the stranger, they lighted suddenly upon the stirrups and the thrust feet, and immediately he smiled in a friendly way. No dark purpose could dwell in the innocent heart of a man who rode thus on the plains.

As for the stranger, he saw a tattered individual with a tangle of hair and beard, and with a complexion turned brick-color from the sun and whisky. He saw a pair of eyes that at first looked at him as the wolf looks at the wolf, and then became childlike, almost timid, in their glance. Here was evidently a man who had often stormed the iron walls of the city of success, and who now sometimes valued himself as the rabbit values his prowess.

The stranger smiled genially and sprang from his horse. "Well, sir, I suppose you will let me camp here with you tonight?"

"Eh?" said Bill.

"I suppose you will let me camp here with you tonight?"

Bill for a time seemed too astonished for words. "Well," he answered, scowling in inhospitable annoyance, "well, I don't believe this here is a good place to camp tonight, mister."

The stranger turned quickly from his saddle-girth.

"What?" he said in surprise. "You don't want me here? You don't want me to camp here?"

Bill's feet scuffled awkwardly, and he looked steadily at a cactus-plant. "Well, you see, mister," he said, "I'd like your company well enough, but—you see, some of these here greasers are goin' to chase me off the range tonight; and while I might like a man's company all right, I couldn't let him in for no such game when he ain't got nothin' to do with the trouble."

"Going to chase you off the range?" cried the stranger.

"Well, they said they were goin' to do it," said Bill.

"And—great heavens!—will they kill you, do you think?"

"Don't know. Can't tell till afterward. You see, they take some feller that's alone like me, and then they rush his camp when he ain't quite ready for 'em, and ginerally plug 'im with a sawed-off shotgun load before he has a chance to git at 'em. They lay around and wait for their chance, and it comes soon enough. Of course a feller alone like me has got to let up watching some time. Maybe they ketch 'im asleep. Maybe the feller gits tired waiting, and goes out in broad day, and kills two or three just to make the whole crowd pile on him and settle the thing. I heard of a case like that once. It's awful hard on a man's mind—to git a gang after him."

"And so they're going to rush your camp tonight?" cried the stranger. "How do you know? Who told you?"

"Feller come and told me."

"And what are you going to do? Fight?"

"Don't see nothin' else to do," answered Bill, gloomily, still staring at the cactus-plant.

There was a silence. Finally the stranger burst out in an amazed cry. "Well, I never heard of such a thing in my life! How many of them are there?"

"Eight," answered Bill. "And now look-a here: you ain't got no manner of business foolin' around here just now, and you might better lope off before dark. I don't ask no help in this here row. I know your happening along here just now don't give me no call on you, and you'd better hit the trail."

"Well, why in the name of wonder don't you go get the sheriff?" cried the stranger.

"Oh, hell!" said Bill.

IV

Long, smoldering clouds spread in the western sky, and to the east silver mists lay on the purple gloom of the wilderness.

Finally, when the great moon climbed the heavens and cast its ghastly radiance upon the bushes, it made a new and more brilliant crimson of the campfire, where the flames capered merrily through its mesquit branches, filling the silence with the fire chorus, an ancient melody which surely bears a message of the inconsequence of individual tragedy—a message that is in the boom of the sea, the silver of the wind through the grass-blades, the silken clash of hemlock boughs.

No figures moved in the rosy space of the camp, and the search of the moonbeams failed to disclose a living thing in the bushes. There was no owl-faced clock to chant the weariness of the long silence that brooded upon the plain.

The dew gave the darkness under the mesquit a velvet quality that made air seem nearer to water, and no eye could have seen through it the black things that moved like monster lizards toward the camp. The branches, the leaves, that are fain to cry out when death approaches in the wilds, were frustrated by these mystic bodies gliding with the finesse of the escaping serpent. They crept forward to the last point where assuredly no frantic attempt of the fire could discover them, and there they paused to locate the prey. A romance relates the tale of the black cell hidden deep in the earth, where, upon entering, one sees only the little eyes of snakes fixing him in menaces. If a man could have approached a certain spot in the bushes, he would not have found it romantically necessary to have his hair rise. There would have been a sufficient expression of horror in the feeling of the death-hand at the nape of his neck and in his rubber knee-joints.

Two of these bodies finally moved toward each other until for each there grew out of the darkness a face placidly smiling with tender dreams of assassination. "The fool is asleep by the fire, God be praised!" The lips of the other widened in a grin of affectionate appreciation of the fool and his plight. There was some signaling in the gloom, and then began a series of subtle rustlings, interjected often with pauses during which no sound arose but the sound of faint breathing.

A bush stood like a rock in the stream of firelight, sending its long shadow backward. With painful caution the little company traveled along this shadow, and finally arrived at the rear of the bush. Through its branches they surveyed for a moment of comfortable satisfaction a form in a grey blanket extended on the ground near the fire. The smile of joyful anticipation fled quickly, to give place to a quiet air of business. Two men lifted shotguns with much of the barrels gone, and, sighting these weapons through the branches, pulled trigger together.

The noise of the explosions roared over the lonely mesquit as if these guns wished to inform the entire world; and as the grey smoke fled, the dodging company in back of the bush saw the blanketed form twitching. Whereupon they burst out in chorus in a laugh, and arose as merry as a lot of banqueters. They gleefully gestured congratulations, and strode bravely into the light of the fire.

Then suddenly a new laugh rang from some unknown spot in the darkness. It was a fearsome laugh of ridicule, hatred, ferocity. It might have been demoniac. It smote them motionless in their gleeful prowl, as the stern voice from the sky smites the legendary malefactor. They might have been a weird group in wax, the light of the dying fire on their yellow faces and shining athwart their eyes turned toward the darkness whence might come the unknown and the terrible.

The thing in the grey blanket no longer twitched; but if the knives in their hands had been thrust toward it, each knife was now drawn back, and its owner's elbow was thrown upward, as if he expected death from the clouds.

This laugh had so chained their reason that for a moment they had no wit to flee. They were prisoners to their terror. Then suddenly the belated decision arrived, and with bubbling cries they turned to run; but at that instant there was a long flash of red in the darkness, and with the report one of the men shouted a bitter shout, spun once, and tumbled headlong. The thick bushes failed to impede the rout of the others.

The silence returned to the wilderness. The tired flames faintly illumined the blanketed thing and the flung corpse of the marauder, and sang the fire chorus, the ancient melody which bears the message of the inconsequence of human tragedy.

V

"Now you are worse off than ever," said the young man, dry-voiced and awed.

"No, I ain't," said Bill, rebelliously. "I'm one ahead."

After reflection, the stranger remarked, "Well, there's seven more."

They were cautiously and slowly approaching the camp. The sun was flaring its first warming rays over the grey wilderness. Upreared twigs, prominent branches, shone with golden light, while the shadows under the mesquit were heavily blue.

Suddenly the stranger uttered a frightened cry. He had arrived at a point whence he had, through openings in the thicket, a clear view of a dead face.

"Gosh!" said Bill, who at the next instant had seen the thing; "I thought at first it was that there José. That would have been queer, after what I told 'im yesterday."

They continued their way, the stranger wincing in his walk, and Bill exhibiting considerable curiosity.

The yellow beams of the new sun were touching the grim hues of the dead Mexican's face, and creating there an inhuman effect which made his countenance more like a mask of dulled brass. One hand, grown curiously thinner, had been flung out regardlessly to a cactus-bush.

Bill walked forward and stood looking respectfully at the body. "I know that feller; his name is Miguel. He—"

The stranger's nerves might have been in that condition when there is no backbone to the body, only a long groove. "Good heavens!" he exclaimed, much agitated; "don't speak that way!"

"What way?" said Bill. "I only said his name was Miguel."

After a pause the stranger said: "Oh, I know; but—" He waved his hand. "Lower your voice, or something. I don't know. This part of the business rattles me, don't you see?"

"Oh, all right," replied Bill, bowing to the other's mysterious mood. But in a moment he burst out violently and loud in the most extraordinary profanity, the oaths winging from him as the sparks go from the funnel.

He had been examining the contents of the bundled grey blanket, and he had brought forth, among other things, his frying-pan. It was now only a rim with a handle; the Mexican volley had centered upon it. A Mexican shotgun of the abbreviated description is ordinarily loaded with flatirons, stove-lids, lead pipe, old horseshoes, sections of chain, window weights, railroad sleepers and spikes, dumbbells, and any other junk which may be at hand. When one of these loads encounters a man vitally, it is likely to make an impression upon him, and a cooking-utensil may be supposed to subside before such an assault of curiosities.

Bill held high his desecrated frying-pan, turning it this way and that way. He swore until he happened to note the absence of the stranger. A moment later he saw him leading his horse from the bushes. In silence and sullenly the young man went about saddling the animal. Bill said, "Well, goin' to pull out?"

The stranger's hands fumbled uncertainly at the throat-latch. Once he exclaimed irritably, blaming the buckle for the trembling of his fingers. Once he turned to look at the dead face with the light of the morning sun upon it. At last he cried, "Oh, I know the whole thing was all square enough—couldn't be squarer—but—somehow or other, that man there takes the heart out of me." He turned his troubled face for another look. "He seems to be all the time calling me a—he makes me feel like a murderer."

"But," said Bill, puzzling, "you didn't shoot him, mister; I shot him."

"I know; but I feel that way, somehow. I can't get rid of it."

Bill considered for a time; then he said diffidently, "Mister, you're a eddycated man, ain't you?"

"What?"

"You're what they call a—a eddycated man, ain't you?"

The young man, perplexed, evidently had a question upon his lips, when there was a roar of guns, bright flashes, and in the air such hooting and whistling as would come from a swift flock of steam-boilers. The stranger's horse gave a mighty, convulsive spring, snorting wildly in its sudden anguish, fell upon its knees, scrambled afoot again, and was away in the uncanny death-run known to men who have seen the finish of brave horses.

"This comes from discussin' things," cried Bill, angrily.

He had thrown himself flat on the ground facing the thicket whence had come the firing. He could see the smoke winding over the bush-tops. He lifted his revolver, and the weapon came slowly up from the ground and poised like the glittering crest of a snake. Somewhere on his face there was a kind of smile, cynical, wicked, deadly, of a ferocity which at the same time had brought a deep flush to his face, and had caused two upright lines to glow in his eyes.

"Hello, José!" he called, amiable for satire's sake. "Got your old blunderbusses loaded up again yet?"

The stillness had returned to the plain. The sun's brilliant rays swept over the sea of mesquit, painting the far mists of the west with faint rosy light, and high in the air some great bird fled toward the south.

"You come out here," called Bill, again addressing the landscape, "and I'll give you some shootin' lessons. That ain't the way to shoot."

Receiving no reply, he began to invent epithets and yell them at the thicket. He was something of a master of insult, and moreover he dived into his memory to bring forth imprecations tarnished with age, unused since fluent Bowery days. The occupation amused him, and sometimes he laughed so that it was uncomfortable for his chest to be against the ground.

Finally the stranger, prostrate near him, said wearily, "Oh, they've gone."

"Don't you believe it," replied Bill, sobering swiftly. "They're there yet—every man of 'em."

"How do you know?"

"Because I do. They won't shake us so soon. Don't put your head up, or they'll get you, sure."

Bill's eyes, meanwhile, had not wavered from their scrutiny of the thicket in front. "They're there, all right; don't you forget it. Now you listen." So he called out: "José! Ojo, José! Speak up, *hombre!* I want have talk. Speak up, you yaller cuss, you!"

Whereupon a mocking voice from off in the bushes said, "Señor?"

"There," said Bill to his ally; "didn't I tell you? The whole batch." Again he lifted his voice. "José—look—ain't you gittin' kinder tired? You better go home, you fellers, and git some rest."

The answer was a sudden furious chatter of Spanish, eloquent with hatred, calling down upon Bill all the calamities which life holds. It was as if some one had suddenly enraged a cageful of wildcats. The spirits of all the revenges which they had imagined were loosened at this time, and filled the air.

"They're in a holler," said Bill, chuckling, "or there'd be shootin'."

Presently he began to grow angry. His hidden enemies called him nine kinds of coward, a man who could fight only in the dark, a baby who would run from the shadows of such noble Mexican gentlemen, a dog that sneaked. They described the affair of the previous night, and informed him of the base advantage he had taken of their friend. In fact, they in all sincerity endowed him with every quality which he no less earnestly believed them to possess. One could have seen the phrases bite him as he lay there on the ground fingering his revolver.

VI

It is sometimes taught that men do the furious and desperate thing from an emotion that is as even and placid as the thoughts of a village clergyman on Sunday afternoon. Usually, however, it is to be believed that a panther is at the time born in the heart, and that the subject does not resemble a man picking mulberries.

"B' Gawd!" said Bill, speaking as from a throat filled with dust, "I'll go after 'em in a minute."

"Don't you budge an inch!" cried the stranger, sternly. "Don't you budge!"

"Well," said Bill, glaring at the bushes—"well."

"Put your head down!" suddenly screamed the stranger, in white alarm. As the guns roared, Bill uttered a loud grunt, and for a moment leaned panting on his elbow, while his arm shook like a twig. Then he upreared like a great and bloody spirit of vengeance, his face lighted with the blaze of his last passion. The Mexicans came swiftly and in silence.

The lightning action of the next few moments was of the fabric of dreams to the stranger. The muscular struggle may not be real to the drowning man. His mind may be fixed on the far, straight shadows in back of the stars, and the terror of them. And so the fight, and his part in it, had to the stranger only the quality of a picture half drawn. The rush of feet, the spatter of shots, the cries, the swollen faces seen like masks on the smoke, resembled a happening of the night.

And yet afterward certain lines, forms, lived out so strongly from the incoherence that they were always in his memory.

He killed a man, and the thought went swiftly by him, like the feather on the gale, that it was easy to kill a man.

Moreover, he suddenly felt for Bill, this grimy sheepherder, some deep form of idolatry. Bill was dying, and the dignity of last defeat, the superiority of him who stands in his grave, was in the pose of the lost sheepherder.

VII

The stranger sat on the ground idly mopping the sweat and powder-stain from his brow. He wore the gentle idiot smile of an aged beggar as he watched three Mexicans limping and staggering in the distance. He noted at this time that one who still possessed a serape had from it none of the grandeur of the cloaked Spaniard, but that against the sky the silhouette resembled a cornucopia of childhood's Christmas.

They turned to look at him, and he lifted his weary arm to menace them with his revolver. They stood for a moment banded together, and hooted curses at him.

Finally he arose and, walking some paces, stooped to loosen Bill's grey hands from a throat. Swaying as if slightly drunk, he stood looking down into the still face.

Struck suddenly with a thought, he went about with dulled eyes on the ground, until he plucked his gaudy blanket from where it lay, dirty from trampling feet. He dusted it carefully, and then returned and laid it over Bill's form. There he again stood motionless, his mouth just agape and the same stupid glance in his eyes, when all at once he made a gesture of fright and looked wildly about him.

He had almost reached the thicket when he stopped, smitten with alarm. A body contorted, with one arm stiff in the air, lay in his path. Slowly and warily he moved around it, and in a moment the bushes, nodding and whispering, their leaf-faces turned toward the scene behind him, swung and swung again into stillness and the peace of the wilderness.

VIRGINIA FRAZER BOYLE

★ ★ ★

Best known for her public activity in Confederate and World War memorial organizations, Virginia Frazer Boyle (1863-1938) achieved distinction early with narratives of Tennessee, in which state she resided most of her life. Her stories are tales of imagination and Negro folklore, such as *Devil Tales* (1900), originally printed in *Harper's Magazine*. Others were contributed to *Harper's Weekly, Atlantic Monthly, Delineator, Century, Good Housekeeping,* and *Congregationalist;* best are those uncollected from the *Century,* stories of before-the-war plantation life, with revivals, auctions, and fires, of the prophecies of old 'Bias, and of the ebony Colossus, Black Silas. From this series "The Triumph of Shed" has been chosen. Later Mrs. Boyle turned her hand to centenary pieces and inscriptions. One novel, *Serena* (1905), demonstrated that her real forte was short fiction. In her stories superstition, magic, and witchery powerfully stir the reader; she effectively conveys the air of credulity and wonder, necessary for the zestful reading of such fiction. "The Triumph of Shed" is reprinted by permission of Miss Phoebe Frazer.

★ ★ ★

The Triumph of Shed

FROM time immemorial, as far as Shed was concerned, corn had been planted on the hillside and cotton in the valley; but Young Marse, believing that a sameness in the crops was wearing out the land, decided to reverse it. This was the beginning of all Shed's troubles, for Shed was very fixed in his views agricultural, and Young

Marse had not been bred as a planter, Ole Marse having professional ambitions for his only son.

But the close of the war and the death of the father left the plantation without a manager, and, as nothing better offered, Young Marse assumed the burden, and the land was apportioned among the remaining Negroes "on shares," Young Marse to maintain a general supervision.

All the Negroes were docile enough with the exception of Shed, who, holding the fixed views aforesaid, as well as a profound contempt for Young Marse's books on farming, went about grumbling, and when cornered by Young Marse, copiously quoted Ole Marse and Ole Marse's ways, which was always an unfailing weapon.

Young Marse's idea of a reversal of crops had not been put in operation, for twice Shed had evaded, the first season upon a pretext of stupidity. But the second evasion was accepted as a direct act of disobedience, and Young Marse resolved to take the matter in hand in due time, that Shed should not be allowed to set such an example.

So, on the day of settlement, Shed, hot and uncomfortable, pulling sullenly at his single "gallus," heard the close of Young Marse's harangue.

"Mind, I'll stand this trifling no longer. You shall do as I command you."

Shed shuffled painfully, and hitched his gathered trousers over his rotundity.

"I's mighty ole, an' I been here er mighty long time, Marse Oscar, to be hollered at dat erway by er young pusson. Ole Marse nebber done hit."

There was a limit to patience, and Young Marse knew that the quotations were coming. "*I* am master here now, and I want you to know it."

"But Ole Marse nebber done hit," persisted Shed; "he nebber plant de cotton an' de corn dat erway. He allus say, 'Shed, plant de corn on de hill an' de cotton in de bottom.' An' he done in he grabe now, po' Ole Marse!"

"Shed," said Young Marse, gravely, "I tell you that I am master here now, and if you don't obey me this time, there's going to be trouble between us. Now go!"

All through the winter Shed was very silent; night after night, by the warmth of his hickory fire, he was weighing the portent of Young Marse's words, as well as roasting sweet potatoes. There was a threat implied, and Shed must be ready to meet it. His plan of procedure as yet was rather hazy, for Shed was averse to the making of any kind of effort; but this much was clear: he would never leave the plantation. As he was born and bred there, he argued, the old place "owed him a living," and he intended to stay right there and get it; for elsewhere, Shed knew to his cost, it required a much greater exertion.

At last planting-time came again, and Young Marse, who, upon this occasion, was intent upon seeing in person the innovation established, was called away by business, and Shed was very thoughtful; but on the day appointed for planting, his mood changed. Never in the whole course of his life had Shed been so brisk. Even the mule, under his manipulation, seemed to share in the awakening; for by the second day all of the seed-cotton had been planted, and the third found Shed busily dropping corn.

Young Marse, riding home from the station, was in a contemplative mood. His trip in the interest of some new schemes had not been very profitable. In his heart he was beginning to wonder if some old things were not the best, after all, so he welcomed with pleasure the camp-meeting hymn rolling out upon the still air, in peculiar jerks like those of a large and badly punctured bellows.

"I'll just ride by and see how he is putting in that cotton. The last *Southern Farmer* says it ought to be covered deeper on a hill than in a bottom."

> He—er—plants His—footsteps—in de s-e-ah,
> An' rides—erpun—de—er storm.

"Darn him! If he didn't always sing so loud he'd work a blamed sight faster."

> Blin' um-be-li-ef am—sho ter err,
> An' sc-a-n—His wuk in—vain.

The jerky bellows continued until Young Marse smiled in spite of himself.

"Whoa!" Young Marse reined, and there stood Shed as he had stood at that season from time running back through the memory of the plantation, industriously doing the same thing.

"Didn't I tell you, Shed, not to plant corn here again? I am tired of your nonsense, and if you don't propose to do as I tell you, we've got to part company, that's all."

A single white cloud was floating in the unbroken blue. Shed watched it a moment, then laboriously plucked an imaginary pebble out of the row.

"Looks lak hit mout rain 'twixt now and Sunday—what *you* think 'bout hit, Marse Oscar?"

"I say," thundered Young Marse, "if you can't do as I bid you, we've got to part company!"

Carefully the old man made observation of the cloud again, then with his arms akimbo, and with all of the reserved force of a winter of introspective philosophy, he opened his eyes wide upon the son of his old master.

"W'y, Marse Oscar, whar you thinkin' 'bout gwine?"

"It's *you* who will have to go, and pretty quick, I'm thinking."

Old Shed slowly smoothed the gunny-sack hanging from his neck, then stooped and dropped a grain of corn.

"W'y, Marse Oscar, yo' paw done put me here 'fore *you* was borned! Dis lan' done growed me lak hit growed dis seed-corn, an' hit growed my daddy an' my gran'daddy. No, sar,"—Shed shook his head reproachfully,—"I cain't leabe dis here place. But I's mighty sorry *you* hain't gwine stay, Marse Oscar."

The New South had met the Old, and the Old South had conquered.

Something was stirring in Young Marse's heart that he could not fathom, and he turned and rode away in silence.

With much deliberation a handful of corn was gathered from the sack, and the jerky bellows began to work again.

It was past ten o'clock, and Shed was usually in the field by six, but this morning he was sitting on the overturned water-barrel, leaning against his cabin, with his hat slouched over his eyes, and giving utterance to all of the doleful hymns generally employed to bring the most hardened of sinners to the seat of repentance; for an end had come at last to Shed's Arcadia.

Unused to the new conditions and a restricting poverty, year after year Young Marse had found the plantation more deeply involved in debt, and finally, giving up the struggle as hopeless, he surrendered his patrimony, under a deed of trust, to a great English syndicate then making extensive investments in the Southwest.

Shed received five dollars for his share of the standing crop, and the greatest shock he had ever experienced in his life. Then, adding insult to injury, the syndicate imported a lot of foreign laborers, and Shed, with all of the Negroes in the quarters, was ordered to vacate

upon short notice. Some of them, like Shed, were the result of generations upon the same land, and it was a day of hard reckoning, though
Shed was the only one to rebel.

In little groups the others took their departure in silence, some to
the neighboring plantations, where their presence was an acquisition,
and some crossed the river to seek employment in "town."

Shed watched his fellows out of sight; then, as he turned toward
home, his indignation grew apace.

"*Me* leabe! Ole Shed go easy lak de whi' folks an' de niggers gone?
No, sar! How dis place ebber mobe on 'dout Shed? Hit des bardaciously *cain't!*"

Shed cooked a lonesome hoecake that night and dreamed doleful
dreams. Still he lingered until the new machinery was brought in—
harrows, reapers, binders, all to be run by a new power. But the crown
of sorrow came when they took his mule. Then old Shed got the
"blues," and concluded to go to "town."

"I's stood er heap, but I cain't stan' dis. Marse Oscar done gone ter
hunt fer sumpen ruther ter do, an' de nigger gwine ter follow. I's
mighty ole ter go kerhootin' wid myse'f in er big strange place, but I
cain't hope hit. Wouldn' er happin dis erway if Old Marse wa'n't in
he grabe. Dey des couldn' tech him wid dey jimcrack notions. An'
hit all come erbout frough Marse Oscar wantin' ter tu'n dis here old
lan' wrong side out, hit do; I des knowed hit 'u'd fotch sumpen. But
his gittin' too hot here wid all dem quare-talkin', cuissome folks dat
ain' know de business eend uv er muel f'om t'other. An' sech es dem
er-gwine ter pick cotton—dem, my Lord!"

So, with many a groan within his fat self, and jingling his money
in his pocket by way of comfort, Shed made a long, last dismal farewell, and paid his ferry passage over to "town."

The day in the city was one of intense excitement to Shed. Wider
and wider his eyes opened, both as to the enlightenment of his mind
and the lightening of his purse; for there were many kind friends who
pleaded previous acquaintance, and were more than anxious to introduce him to their social world, though Shed could not remember having met any of them before. However, as they were solicitous, and
inquired particularly after his folks and his health, Shed was induced
to follow, and was initiated into a game of craps, as played by the
Mississippi roustabouts, and several other nefarious schemes of chance,
slyly conducted by thrifty Negroes in the neighborhood of the landing.
Of course Shed did not win the bright silver watch that hung temptingly before him,—"so perzackly lak Ole Marse's, only Ole Marse's
were gole,"—and after staking dime after dime on chances, a great

wave of homesickness came over him as he felt the single dollar that was left in his pocket.

"Dis all I got lef' er de fiver," he sighed, "an' I dunno what bercome uv hit. Better be movin' on somers, 'ca'se if I done git de watch, what good hit gwine do me, 'cep'in' ter gib out de time fer er fool lak I is ter leabe yere—an' I cain't eben tell *dat* time by hit!" And Shed held fast to his remaining dollar as he passed through the mysterious portals, followed to the door by an eager trio, that urged him to "tek des one mo' chance."

Once rid of the sharks and their fetid atmosphere, the old Negro sat down on the curbing to collect his scattered senses. But the noise and the ceaseless wave of movement were confusing, and he longed for his seat on the old water-barrel.

It was in the shadows now, for he had been gone nearly a whole day, and he knew just how they were falling through the trees. He could smell the grass and the cooling weeds; the queer people would soon be gathering in the old quarters, and the cows would come home.

"An' I done lef' hit, done driv off," mused Shed, as he mopped his brow, moist from thought rather than from heat. "But Ole Shed don' wanter call *dis* home; folks in too mighty herry here; an' dey mus' be mighty behin' wid dey haulin', 'ca'se dey nebber 'pear ter git frough. Hain't much uv er place fer er ole nigger lak I is ter 'bide in; done too ole an' too settled ter larn new tricks. Hatter mobe too fas'—my Lord! Shed plumb lose he bref in dis ole town!"

It was surely a melancholy picture that Shed contemplated mentally for a moment; then a peculiarity of the live, bustling town, that had recently taken advantage of the modern innovations, impressed itself upon him, and Shed was sadly lonesome.

"Dem niggers nebber gib me no time ter tek notice erfore, but what dis town done gone an' done wid de muels? I gwine watch fer 'em, 'ca'se I hain't seed nary one sence I landed at de ribber."

But the street-cars, laden with their human freight and moved by an unseen power, whirled past Shed; heavily laden trucks swept by without harness or rein, leaving away in the rear a few massive draft-horses, that, by contrast, were dragging slowly up the levee; but not a mule could old Shed discover. Then, with that instinct of fear, perhaps, which prompts even the scrubbiest and slowest of the horse variety to "shy" at any kind of wheeled wreck by the road, bereft of the sight of his wonted companion in labor, a panic seized upon the old Negro; for, grown weary after several hours of intense watching, Shed was convinced that the positions were identical: both were being spirited out of their natural possessions, and he resolved to give search on behalf of the mule before taking action upon his own case.

"I des bardaciously wants ter see what dey done wid 'em, 'ca'se dey uster hab 'em oncet."

Through the town he wandered, past all of the new-found wonders and terrors, which he dodged, out into the sparsely settled outskirt, without seeing a single specimen for which he so eagerly sought, and at last, hungry and disappointed, he was about to abandon the quest, when just across an open common a long, lean, spavined mule, lazily nibbling the indifferent grass, came into his line of vision.

In an instant Shed recovered himself, intent upon maintaining his own superior dignity.

"Dar you is, you ole curmudgeon!" and Shed shook his head despondently. "All dis day er-lookin' an' des one lef'—an' sech er one! You need n' herry wid yo' eatin', fer dey gone an' lef' you, Jinny. Hain't got no mo' use fer you. W'ar you out fust, twel you hain't no use ter nobody, den flung you erway!"

The voice of the old Negro was soothing, and the mule stopped nibbling her short rations and listened.

"I knows you lonesome, I knows hit, but hit cain't do any good. Dey lay down dey rocks an' dey bricks an' dey tracks, an' dey des skedaddle ober 'em; but dey's lef' you 'way behin', Jinny muel."

The soft voice of the Negro was tremulous as the picture of the improved cultivators rose before his mental vision, together with the swarthy horde of imported labor. Then, as the injustice of his fallen state pressed sore upon him, his superiority was forgotten, and the plaint became almost a wail: "But dey lef' de nigger, too!"

Shed paused in self-commiseration, and he was nearer to giving way than ever before; but the chord of fellowship had been somewhere touched, and the forlorn mule came and rubbed her nose against the old man's arm.

At once dignity and self-possession returned. "Dat's hit, Jinny; you struck de right pardner dis time; but cryin' hain't gwine ter fetch you fodder, ner me corn." And giving the mule a patronizing pat, the dusky philosopher sat down before the companion of his sorrows, to work out the problem that confronted both.

The day was wearing into sunset, and the grazing animal cast long shadows across the common before Shed rose. Deliberately replacing his hat, he tied the rope halter into a rude bridle, and mounting the mule, rode slowly through the gathering dusk in the direction of the river.

"Gee up, Jinny, if you wants ter sleep in Arkansaw dis night! You 's er mighty po' creetur ter tie ter, but one time de Lord done put mo' sense in de ass's head 'n he put in Baalim's, an' I sho gwine trus' de Lord."

Captain Eagan, the new manager of the Greenwood plantation, was waiting at the landing for the second shipment of foreign laborers. All day he had been getting the new machinery, human and other, into position. The work had been very trying, and he had lost patience more than once; but sitting alone in the shadow, watching the twinkling lights far down the river, and waiting for the little packet that never came on time, the pathos of the situation dawned upon him. He was wiping out old customs, traditions, and homes, humble as they were, with as much unconcern as if they had been a colony of ant-hills; but, then, he was only acting under orders.

After much delay, interminably long to a healthy, hungry man, the little packet steamed in, fussing and fuming, and lowering her stage-plank, discharged her human freight. When the last immigrant had been enrolled and sent forward up the levee, Captain Eagan, with a yawn, mounted his horse, considering with a keen relish the prospect of his belated supper. His horse with similar considerations in view cantered briskly, when just at the bend by a clump of osage tangle he stopped suddenly and shied at a shadow across the road.

The captain had heard stories of this wild Arkansas country; he was alone in the midst of a peculiar people, and his hand instinctively sought his pistol.

"Don', Marse Eagan! Don' shoot!" The low musical voice rolled on the still air with the rich melody of reedy notes.

"Hain't nuffin in de way, Marse Eagan, but Baalim an' de ass, an' hit de ass dat gwine ter do de talkin'. Maybe hit 'pear ter be de voice er Baalim, but hit de ass, Marse Eagan; fer de po' fool nigger hain't got sense ernough an' hain't fitten ter speak, fer he sell he birfright ter you yistiddy fer five po' miserbul silber dollars. I hain't nuffin but er po' ole ass, Marse Eagan, but I done fotch all de silber back dat dey didn' cheat him outen in dat town, 'ca'se hit burn we-all lak coals er fire. An' I done fotch de nigger back too, lak de p'odigul son, 'ca'se dar hain't no room fer him on dis here yeth but here on de lan' dat growed him.

"Put him anywhar, mek him do anything, fer dar hain't no dirt dat'll feel de same ter de plow lak ter dis. You won' dribe er cat f'om yo' h'a'th, Marse Eagan, eben er po' stray cat, 'ca'se you 'feard er de luck hit'll fotch; an' dis nigger's mo' 'n er cat, 'ca'se dis de lan' dat borned him. De odder niggers kin mek er place in er new kentry, an' git uster hit, but all Ole Shed got am right here—de grabe uv he Ole Marster, Gord res' him! de grabe uv he daddy an' he mammy, de sunshine uv he youf an' de joy uv he ole age!

"Tek him, Marse Eagan! Let de ole lan' keep him des er little while, —it cain't be fer long,—'ca'se he cain't breabe easy anywhar else! I hain't nuffin but er muel,—I means er ass, Marse Eagan,—but tek us bofe, fer de lub er Gord, tek us bofe, Marse Eagan, 'ca'se we's des er-stan'in' in de dirt road waitin', an' de worl' done passed us by."

For the first time during his oration Shed paused for breath, and, wiping the perspiration that was rolling in great beads down his face, he pulled up the mule, that had stumbled from weakness or perhaps from hunger.

Captain Eagan blinked; then, as he slowly replaced his pistol in his pocket, his face assumed the lines of severity.

"Shed, you rascal, go right on to the kitchen and get your supper!"

With the music of the order ringing in his ears, the old man dismounted with alacrity, and led the ass that had spoken on through the big gate.

Next day Captain Eagan paid for the mule, which had been tracked to the landing, but made no mention of the matter, not even to Shed, though the general expense-book of that date bore a separate entry: "Ten dollars in the cause of religion."

HARRY STILLWELL EDWARDS

★ ★ ★

Journalist, novelist, short story writer, Harry Stillwell Edwards (1855-1938) wrote and published from 1886, when "Two Runaways" appeared, until 1933, five years before his death at eighty-three. From 1879 to 1889, while connected with three newspapers, he composed humorous, sympathetic tales of the effect of the Reconstruction on plantation life in Georgia. In the next decade he published *Sons and Fathers* (1896), a prize novel; *The Marbeau Cousins* (1897), *His Defense and Other Stories* (1899), and some sixty stories in *Harper's, Century, Scribner's,* and *Atlantic.* He turned in 1900 to political activity, serving as Macon's postmaster for twelve years and running in 1920 as an independent candidate for the Senate. Winner of prizes up to $10,000 from stories submitted to the *Chicago Record, Life,* and *Black Cat,* Edwards is best known for a justly famous story in letter form of a Negro's wanderings in search of his master, "Aeneas Africanus" (1920), which in pamphlet form has had a world-wide circulation of nearly one and a half million copies. "His Defense" is reprinted by permission of D. Appleton-Century Company, publishers.

★ ★ ★

His Defense

"WHAT?"

Colonel Rutherford shot a swift glance from the brief he was examining at the odd figure before him, and resumed his occupation quickly, to hide the smile that was already lifting the heavy frown from his face. "Indicted for what?"

"For the cussin' of my mother-in-law; an' I want you ter be on hand at court ter make er speech for me when hit comes up."

"Did you cuss her?"

The lawyer fell easily into the vernacular of his visitor, but he was afraid to lift his eyes again higher than the tips of his own polished boots, resting upon the table in front of him, in the good old Georgia fashion.

"Did I?" The stranger shifted his hat to the other hand and wiped his brow with a cotton handkerchief. His voice was low and plaintive. "I sho'ly did cuss. I cussed 'er comin' an' goin', for'ards and back'ards, all erroun' an' straight through. Ain't no use ter deny hit. I done hit."

He was tall, and in old age would be gaunt. He was also sunburned, and stooped a little, as from hard labor and long walking in plowed ground or long riding behind slow mules. One need not have been a physiognomist to discover that, although yet young, the storms of life had raged about him. But the lawyer noticed that he was neat, and that his jeans suit was homemade, and his pathetic homespun shirt and sewed-on collar—the shirt and collar that never will sit right for any country housewife, however devoted—were ornamented with a black cravat made of a ribbon and tied like a schoolgirl's sash.

The defendant leaned over the table as he finished speaking, resting his hands thereon, and thrusting forward his aquiline features, shame and excitement struggling for expression in his blue eyes.

"Did she cuss you first?"

The stranger looked surprised.

"No."

"Did she abuse you, strike you, insult you—did she ever chuck anything at you?"

"Why, no!—you see, hit wasn't edzactly the words—"

"Then it seems to me, my friend, that you have no use for a lawyer. I never take any kind of a criminal case for less than one hundred dollars, and the court will hardly fine you that much if you plead guilty. By your own statement, you see, you are guilty, and I can't help you. Better go and plead guilty and file an exculpatory affidavit—"

"No, sir. That'll do for some folks, but not for me. I never dodged in my life, and I ain't goin' ter dodge now. All you got ter do is ter make er speech. I want you ter tell them for me—"

"But what is the use, my friend? Can't you see—"

"Don't make no difference. You go. I'll be thar with your money."

"All right," was the laughing rejoinder; "but you are simply wasting time and money."

"That's my business. No man ever wasted his time or money when he was settin' himself right before his folks."

Lifting his head with an air the memory of which dwelt with the attorney for many a day, the novel client departed, leaving him still laughing. He opened his docket and wrote, in the absence of further information: "The man who cussed his mother-in-law, Crawford Court, $100."

Court opened in Crawford County as usual. The city lawyers followed the judge over from Macon in nondescript vehicles, their journey enlivened by many a gay jest and well-told tale, to say nothing of refreshments by the way. The autumn woods were glorious in the year's grand sunset. Like masqueraders in some wild carnival, the gums and sumacs and hickories and persimmons and maples mingled their flaunting banners and lifted them against the blue and cloudless skies. Belated cotton-pickers stole the last of the fields' white lint, and sang in harmonies that echoed from the woodlands, seeming to voice the gladness of unseen revelers.

And Knoxville, waking from its dull dreams, took on life and color for the week. Horses tugged at the down-sweeping limbs or dozed contentedly beside the racks; and groups of country folks, white and black, discussed solemnly or with loud jest the ever-changing situation. The session of court, brief though it be, is fraught with meaning for many families, the chief points of friction being the issues between landlord and tenant, factor and farmer, loan associations and delinquent debtors. And there is always the criminal side of court, with its sable fringe of evildoers.

The sheriff, in obedience to time-honored custom, had shouted from the front steps the names of all parties concerned in the case of the State *versus* Hiram Ard, and the State, through its urbane solicitor, the Hon. Jefferson Brown, had announced "Ready," when Colonel Rutherford felt a hand upon his shoulder, and, looking up, saw a half-familiar face earnestly bent toward his own.

"Hit's come," said the stranger, his blue eyes full of excitement; "an' thar's your hunderd."

"Beg your pardon," said the lawyer; "some mistake! I—don't think —I can exactly locate you."

"What? I'm the man they say that cussed his mother-in-law!"

"Why, of course, of course! One moment, your Honor, until I can consult my client."

The consultation was brief. The lawyer urged a plea of guilty. The client was determined to go to trial.

"Ready for the defense!" said Colonel Rutherford, in despair, waving his client to his seat with a gesture that seemed to disclaim responsibility for anything that might happen.

The usual preliminaries and formalities were soon disposed of, and the jury stricken, twelve good men and true, as their names will show; for to adjudge this case were assembled there Dike Sisson, Bobby Lewis, Zeke Cothern, Tony Hutt, Hob Garrett, Jack Dermedy, Tommie Liptrot, Jack Doozenbery, Abe Ledzetter, Cran Herringdine, Bunk Durden, and Tim Newberry.

The State, upon this occasion, had but one witness. Mrs. Jessy Gonder was called to the stand. The lady was mild-looking and thin, and something in her bearing unconsciously referred one to a happier past. But the good impression—perhaps it is better to say the soft impression—vanished when she loosened her bonnet-strings and tongue, and with relentless, drooping mouth corners—those dead smiles of bygone days—began to relate her grievance.

Well, Mrs. Gonder was one of those unfortunate women whom adversity sours and time cannot sweeten; and that is all there is of it. In sharp, crisp tones and bitter words she told of her experience with the defendant. The narrative covered years of bitterness, disappointment, wounded vanity, and hatred, and was remarkable for its excess of feeling. It was, from a professional standpoint, overdone. It was an outburst. Members of the admirable jury who had looked with surprise and animosity upon Hiram Ard began to regard him with something like sympathy; for, disguise it as she might, it was plain to all men that the overwhelming cause of her grievance was Hiram's conquest of her only daughter. Bobby Lewis leaned over and whispered to Bunk Durden, and both young men laughed until their neighboring jurors were visibly affected, and the court knocked gently with its gavel. When she came to the cause of war wherein this low-bred son-in-law had cursed around her,—her, Jessy Gonder,—had entered the house she occupied and had forcibly taken away a sewing-machine loaned by her own daughter, her voice trembled and she shook her clenched fist above the rail, her eyes, the while, fairly blazing in the shadow of her black bonnet. She sank back at last, exhausted.

While the witness was testifying the defendant looked straight ahead of him, settling slowly in his seat, until his matched hands, supported by his elbows that rested upon the chair, almost covered his face. From time to time a wave of color flushed his cheeks and brow. Then he seemed to wander off to scenes the woman's words recalled, and he became oblivious to his surroundings. When at last his attorney touched him and called him to the witness-stand, he started violently, and with difficulty regained his composure.

"Tell the jury what you know of this case," said Rutherford; and then to the court: "This seems to be purely a family quarrel, your Honor, and I trust the defendant will be allowed to proceed without interruption of any kind. Go on, sir," he concluded, to the latter.

The defendant seated himself in the witness-stand, his arm on the rail, and said:

"Hit's er long story, my friends, an' if thar warn't nothin' in the case but er fine I wouldn't take your time. But thar's er heap more, an' ef you'll all hear me out, I don't think any of you'll believe I'm much ter be blamed. So far as the cussin' is concerned, thar ain't no dispute erbout that. I done hit, an' I oughtn't er done hit. No gentle-man can cuss erroun' er woman, an' for the first time in my life I warn't er gentleman. I could er come here an' pleaded guilty an' quit, but that don't square er gentleman's record. I hired er lawyer ter take my case, an' did hit ter have him put me up here where I could get er chance ter face my people, an' say I was wrong, an' sorry for hit, an' willin' ter take the consequences. That's the kind of man Hiram Ard is."

All the shamefacedness was gone from the man. He had straight-ened up in his chair, and his blue eyes were beaming with earnestness. His declaration, simple and direct, had penetrated every corner of the room. In a moment he had caught the attention of the crowd, for all the world loves a manly man, and from that moment their attention never wavered.

"But," he continued, when the silence had become intense, "I ain't willin' for you ter think that Hiram Ard could cuss erroun' any woman offhand an' for er little matter.

"Some of you knowed me when I was er barefooted boy, with no frien' in the worl' 'ceptin' ma an' pa, an' not them long. This trouble started away back thar—when I was that kind er boy an' goin' ter school. I was 'mos' too big ter go ter school, an' she—I mean Cooney, Cooney Gonder—was 'mos' too young. Somehow I got ter sorter lookin' out for her on the road, gentlemen, an' totin' her books, an' holdin' her steady crossin' the logs over Tobysofkee Creek an' the branches. An' at school, when the boys teased her an' pulled her hair an' hid her dinner-bucket, I sorter tuk up for her; an' the worst fight I ever had was erbout Cooney Gonder.

"Well, so it went on year in an' out. Then pa died, an' the ole home was sold for his debts. An' then ma died. All I had left, gentlemen, was erbout sixty acres on Tobysofkee an' thirty up in Coldneck dees-tric'; an' not er acre cleared. But I went ter work. I cut down trees an' made er clearin', an' I hired er mule an' planted er little crop. Cotton fetched er big price that year, an' I bought the mule outright. An' then er feller come erlong with er travelin' sawmill, an' I let him saw on halves ter get lumber ter build my house. Hit was just er two-room house, but hit war mine, an' I was the proudes'! I bought ernother mule on credit, an' the new lan' paid for hit too an' lef' me money besides. An' then I put on ernother room.

"Well, all this time I was tryin' ter keep comp'ny with Cooney, gentlemen—I say tryin', 'cause her folks didn't think much of me. My family warn't much, an' Cooney's was good blood an' er little stuckup. An' Cooney—well, Cooney had done growed ter be the prettiest an' sweetest in all the Warrior deestric', as you know, an' they had done made her er teacher, for she was smart as she was pretty. An' she was good—too good for me. Ter this day I don't understan' hit. Cooney say hit was because I was honest an' er man all over; that was the excuse she gave for lovin' me. But I do know that when she said yes, two things happened: I kissed her, an' there was er riot in Cooney's family. Cooney's ma was the last ter come roun', an' I don't think she ever did quite come roun', for she warn't at the wedding; but, so help me God, I never bore her no ill will. Hit must have been hard ter give Cooney up.

"I will never forget the day, gentlemen, she come into that little home. Hit was like bein' born ag'in; I was that happy. I made the po'est crop I ever made in my life; but, bless you, the whole place changed. Little vines come up an' made er shade on the po'ch, an' flowers growed about the yard in places that look like they had been waitin' for flowers always. An' the little fixin's on the bureau and windows, an' white stuff hangin' ter the mantelpieces—well, I never knowed what hit was ter live before.

"Then at last I went ter work. It was four mules then, an' me in debt for two, an' some rented land; but no man who had Cooney could honestly call himself in debt. I worked day in an' out, rain or shine, hot or cold, an' I struck hit right. Cooney was sewin' for two an' sewin' on little white things for another, and we were the happiest. One day I come home 'fo' dark ter find Cooney was gone ter her neighbor's. I slipped in on her, an' thar she was er-sewin' on er sewin'-machine, an' proud of the work as I was of the first land I ever laid off. Hit was hard ter pull her away. Well, I didn't say nothin'; I thought, an' I kept hit all ter myself. I went ter town that fall with my cotton, an' when I had done paid my draft at the warehouse I had seventy dollars left. What did I do with hit? What do you reckon I did with hit?"

The aquiline face took on a positively beautiful smile. The speaker leaned over the rail and talked confidentially to the jury.

"Well, here's what I did, gentlemen. I went ter whar that one-arm old soldier stays what keeps sewin'-machines an' the tax-books, an' I planked down sixty of my pile for one of them. An' then I went home an' set the thing in the settin'-room while Cooney was gettin' supper; an' I let her eat, but I couldn't hardly swaller, I was so full of that machine."

He laughed aloud at this point, and several of the jury joined him. The court smiled and lifted a law-book in front of his face.

"When I took her in thar an' turned up the light, Cooney like ter fainted. 'My wife don't have ter sew on no borrowed machine no more,' says I, just so; an' she fell ter cryin' an' huggin' me; an' by an' by we got down ter work. I'll be doggoned if we didn't set up tell one er'clock playin' on that thing! She'd sew, an' then I'd sew, an' then I'd run the wheel underneath an' she'd run the upper works. We hemmed and hawed all the napkins over, an' the table-cloths; an' tucked all the pillow frills; an' Cooney made me er handkerchief out of something. Gentlemen, next ter gettin' Cooney, hit was the happiest night of my life!"

II

Hiram paused to take breath, and the tension on the audience being relieved, they moved, looked into one another's faces, and, smiling, exchanged comments. A breath of spring seemed to have invaded the autumn.

"Wouldn't believe he was guilty ef he swore hit," said a voice somewhere, and there was applause, which was promptly suppressed. Hiram did not hear the comment. He was lost in his dream.

"Then the baby come. But before he come I saw Cooney begin ter change. She'd sit an' droop, an' brighten up an' droop erg'in, lookin' away off; an' her step got slow. Then, one day, hit come ter me: she was homesick for her ma. Well, gentlemen, I reck'n 'twas natchul at that time. She never had said nothin', but the way her ma had done an' the way she had talked about me was the grief of her life. She couldn't see how she was goin' ter meet the new trouble erlone. I fixed hit for her. I took her out on the po'ch where she could break down without my seemin' ter know hit, an' I tole her as how hit did look like hit was a shame for her ma ter have ter live off at her sister's, an' her own chile keepin' house, with a comp'ny room; an' I believed I'd drive over an' tell her ter let bygones be bygones, an' come an' live with us; that I didn't set no store by the hard things she's said, an' we would do our best for her. Well, that got Cooney. She dropped her head down in my lap, an' I knowed I'd done hit the nail on the head. Natchully I was happy erlong with her.

"Well, I went an' made my best talk, an' when I got done, gentlemen, what you reck'n Cooney's ma said—what do you reck'n? She said: 'How's Cooney?' 'Po'ly,' says I. 'I thought so,' says she, 'er you wouldn't er come. I'll get my things an' go.' But Cooney was so happy when she did come, I caught the fever too, an' thought me an' the old lady would get on all right at last. But we didn't. Seemed like pretty soon ma begin ter look for things ter meddle in, an' she got er new name for me ev'y time I come erroun'. I didn't answer back, because she was Cooney's ma. I grit my teeth an' went on. But she'd come out an' lean on the fence, even, when I was plowin', an' talk. 'Look like any fool,' she said one day, 'look like any fool would know better 'n ter lay off land with er twister. Whyn't yer git er roun' p'inted shovel?' My lan' was new, gentlemen, an' full of roots; that's why.

"An' she'd look at my hogs an' say: 'I allus did despise Berkshires. Never saw er sow that wouldn't eat pigs after er while. Whyn't you cross 'em on the big Guinea?' An' then, the chickens. 'Thar's them Wyandottes! Never knew one ter raise er brood yet; an' one rooster takes more pasture than er mule.' An' I paid ten dollars for three, gentlemen. An' then, Cooney's mornin'-glories made her sick. An' she didn't like sewin'-machines; they made folks want more clothes than they ought ter have, an' made the wash too big. An' what she called 'jimcracks' was Cooney's pretties in the sittin'-room.

"But I stood it; she was Cooney's ma. Only, when the mockin'-bird's cage door was found opened an' he gone, I like to have turned my mind loose, for I had my suspicions, an' have yet. He was a little bird when I found him. I was clearin' my lan', an' one of these new niggers come erlong with er single-barrel gun, an' shot both the old birds right before my eyes with one load. I was that mad I took up er loose root an' frailed him tell he couldn't walk straight, an' I bent the gun roun' er tree an' flung hit after him. Then I went ter the nest in the haw-bush, an' started out ter raise the four young ones. I couldn't find er bug ter save me, though it looked easy for the old birds, so I took them home an' tried eggs an' potato. Well, one by one they died, until but one was left. When Cooney come he was grown, an' with the dash of white on his wings all singers have. But he never would sing—I think he was lonesome. The first night she come, I woke ter hear the little feller singin' away like his heart was too full ter hold hit all. I turned over ter wake Cooney, that she might hear him too, an' what do you reck'n? The moonlight had found er way in through the half-open blinds an' had fell across her face. Hit shone out there in the darkness like an angel's, an' that little lonesome bird had seen hit for the first time. Hit started the song in him just like hit had in me, an' God knows—" His voice quivered a moment and he looked away, a slight gesture supplying a conclusion.

"Then the baby come, an' when Cooney said, 'We'll name hit Jessy, after ma,' I said, 'Good enough, Cooney. Hit's natchul.'

"Looks like that ought ter have made it easier all erroun', but hit didn't. Hit all got worse. An' ter keep the peace, I got not ter comin' inter the house tell the dinner-bell would ring. I'd jus' set on the fence, pretendin' I was er-watchin' the stock feed. An' after dinner I'd go out erg'in an' set on the fence ter keep the peace. Not that I blamed Cooney's ma so much, for I didn't. Nobody ever said hit for her but me, an' I don't mind sayin' hit now: but she has had trouble ernough for four women; an' her boy died. He was er good boy, if thar ever was one. I remember the time we went ter school together; an' when he died of the fever, why, hit was then I sorter took his place an' looked out for Cooney all the time. Her boy died, an' I think er heap er 'lowance ought ter be made for er widow when her boy is buried, for I don't believe there is much else left for her in this world."

The stillness in the room was absolute when the witness paused a moment and for some reason studied his fingers, his face bent down. All eyes were unconsciously turned then toward the prosecutrix. She had moved uncomfortably many times during this narrative, and now lowered her veil, as if she felt the focus of their attention. Afterward she did not look up again. Hiram, whose face had grown singularly tender, raised his eyes, somewhat wearily, at last.

"I know what hit is to lose a child," he said gently, "for I lost Jessy. The fever came; she faded out, an'—well—we jus' put her ter sleep out under the two cedars I had left in the corner of the yard. Then hit was worse than ever, for I had Cooney ter comfort, my own load ter tote, an'—Cooney's ma was harder ter stan' than before. I studied an' studied, an' then I took Cooney out with me ter the field an' tole her what was on my mind. 'Let's go up ter Coldneck,' says I, 'an' build us a little house jus' like the one we started with, an' plant mornin'-glories on the po'ch, an' begin over. Let's give ma this place for life, an' two mules, an' split up. An' let's do hit quick, 'cause I can't hold out much longer.' You see, I was 'fraid er myself. Well, Cooney hugged me, an' I saw her heart was happy over the change.

"So we went. Her ma said we were fools, an' settled down ter run her end of the bargain. An' I'm boun' ter say she made good crops, an', with her nephew ter help her, got erlong well tell he married an' went ter his wife's folks.

"Hit looked like hit was goin' ter be easy, gentlemen, leavin' the little home; an' hit was tell Cooney got in the wagon an' looked back —not at the house, an' the flowers she had planted, an' the white curtains in her winders, but at the two little cedars where Jess was sleepin', an' the mockin'-bird balancin' an' singin' on the highest limb. Hit was easy tell then. Her heart jus' broke, an' she cried out ter herself: 'Ma! ma! I wouldn't er treated you that-er-way—I wouldn't er done hit!'" He pointed his finger at the prosecutrix. "She didn't know Cooney felt that-er-way, gentlemen; this is the first time. An' she didn't know that when I came back from Macon, next fall, an' brought er little marble slab with Jess's name on hit, an' put hit up under the cedars, I got one with her Tom's name on hit, too, an' went ter her ole home, an' cleared away the weeds, an' put hit over Tom's grave. He was er good boy—an' he was Cooney's brother.

"Well," continued the defendant, after a pause, "we did well. I cleared the land an' made er good crop. An' then our own little Tom come. That's what we named him. An' one day Cooney asked me ter go back an' get her sewin'-machine from her ma's. Hit was the first plantin' day we had had in April, an' I hated mightily ter lose er day; but Cooney never had asked me for many things, so I went. When I rode up, ma come out, an', restin' her hands on her sides, she said: 'I did give you credit for some sense! What you doin' here, an' hit the first cotton-plantin' day of the year? I'll be boun' you picked out this day ter come for that ar sewin'-machine.' I tolè her I had; an' then she answered back: 'Nobody but er natchul-born fool would come for er sewin'-machine in that sort er wagon. You can't get hit. Thar wouldn't be er whole j'int in hit when you got back!' Well, seein' as how I had brought the thing from Macon once in the same wagon, hit did look unreasonable I couldn't take hit further. But the road ter Coldneck was rougher, an' I couldn't give her no hold on me, so back I went, twelve miles, an' er whole day sp'iled. But Cooney was sorry, I could see; an' she never did ask me for many things, so I borrowed Buck Drawhorn's spring-wagon, an' next day, bright an' early, I put out erg'in. When I got back ter the ole home, she was stan'in' jus' like I left her, with her hands on her sides. I didn't get time ter put in 'fo' she called out: 'Nobody but er natchul-born fool would come here for er machine, an' clouds er-risin' in the rain quarter. Don't you know ef that machine gets wet hit won't be worth hits weight in ole iron? You can't git hit!' Well, gentlemen, seems ter me that with all our kiver mos' still in the house, she might er loant me some ter put on that machine; but she didn't; an' bein' 'fraid er myself, I wheeled roun' an' went back them twelve miles erg'in. Ernother day sp'iled, an' no machine. An' I won't do nobody er injustice, gentlemen. Hit did rain like all-fire, though whar hit come from I don't know tell now, an' I got wet ter the bones.

"But I was determ' then ter git that machine, if I didn't never plant er cotton-seed. Next day I rode up bright an' early, an' thar she was. I hadn't got out the wagon 'fo' she opened: 'You can't git that machine! You go back an' tell Cooney I'm er-sewin' for Hester Bloodsworth, an' when I git done I'll let her know. An' don't you come back here no more tell I let you know!' Well, gentlemen, then I knowed I hadn't been 'fraid of myself for nothin'. I started ter cussin'! I cussed all the way up the walk, an' up the steps, an' inter the room, an' while I was shoulderin' that ar machine, an' while I was er-totin' hit out, an' while I was er-loadin' hit in the wagon, an' while I was er-drivin' off. An' when I thought of them seventy-odd miles, an' the three days plantin' I'd done lost, I stopped at the rise in the road an' cussed back erg'in. I did hit, an', as I said, hit was ongentlemanly, an' I'm sorry. The only excuse I've got, gentlemen, is I did hit in self-defense, for if I hadn't cussed, so help me God, I'd er busted wide open then an' thar!"

The sensation that followed this remarkable climax was not soon stilled; but when quiet was at length restored, everybody's attention was attracted to the prosecutrix. She had never lifted her face from the time the defendant had mentioned the dead boy. She was still sitting with her face concealed, lost in thought, and it is likely that she never knew the conclusion of the defendant's statement. She looked up at last, impressed by the silence, and seeing the court gazing toward her as he fingered his books, she arose wearily and unsteadily.

"Can I say a few words, judge?" Her voice was just audible at first. He nodded gravely. "Then I want to say that—I have—probably been wrong—all the way through. I have had—many troubles—many disappointments. Cooney's husband has been a good husband to her, and has always treated me kindly. I don't believe he intended to curse me, and I think if you will let me take it all back—" She hesitated and faltered.

"Be seated, madam," said the court, with something like tenderness in his voice. "Gentlemen of the jury, this case is dismissed."

The defendant came down from the stand, and paused before the woman in black a moment. Then he bent over her, but the only words any one caught were "Cooney" and "little Tom." He patted her shoulder with his rough, sunburnt hand. She hesitated a moment, and then, drawing down her veil, she took his arm and in silence left the courtroom. There was a sudden burst of applause, followed by the sound of the judge's gavel. At the door, Colonel Rutherford, leaning over the rail which separated the bar from the audience, thrust something into Hiram Ard's hand. "The fee goes with the speech," he said, smiling. "Keep it for little Tom."

PHILIP VERRILL MIGHELS

★ ★ ★

Son of Henry Rust Mighels, a writer of the "Sagebrush School," Philip Verrill Mighels (1869-1911) tried five years of law and journalism in Nevada and California before moving to New York in 1895. He began to paint, and under the influence of his wife, Ella Sterling Clark Cummins, whom he married in 1896, he also tried fiction. His first novel, *Nella* (1900), was published in London after a residence abroad of two and a half years. Mighels, exceedingly ambitious, planned to write a great poem, to produce a great book, and to complete a superb painting, but he gave up art, and in his need for money he acceded to publishers' requests for popular fiction. A tireless worker, he turned out a book a year to a total of eleven, tailoring them to the demands of the market and then losing the returns in stock speculation. After 1900 he gained entrance into *Harper's Magazine,* and published therein the short stories which are his only enduring work. The best of these treat Nevada scenes. From his own background and that of his wife, daughter of a forty-niner, from their experiences in mines and quartz mills, and from later observations during brief sojourns in Nevada, he produced several graphic tales of the arid, alkali country about Carson City. "The Tie of Partnership" is reprinted by permission of Mrs. Adolph Uhl.

★ ★ ★

The Tie of Partnership

THE midnight puff and grind and shriek of machinery, telling off the fevered annals of the mining-camp of Goldenville, fell on deadened ears, as Bronson sat there in his cabin slowly accepting the all that it meant if his partner's words were true.

The light of the candle fell on his flannel shirt, his faded overalls, and wrinkled boots, revealing lines of rugged young manhood, more eloquent for the very weariness which the day of toil had brought upon him. On his face there was more than pallor—there was anguish.

Larry Mott stood silently before him, watching his partner. For a moment he felt a pang of regret to behold the blighting effect upon the unsuspecting Bronson of the lie that love and jealousy had prompted him to tell. But a madness screamed in his brain that with Bronson gone a change would come, and she—she must—she would forget that Bronson had ever existed! Even now Mott beheld her, in her beauty, as she crimsoned with her half-confessed rapture over Bronson's attentions.

He observed his comrade's every phase of pain. Bronson did not lift his head, even when he spoke.

"No," he presently said, as if after cruel reflection, "no—I wouldn't care to see her again. I'd rather not."

Mott made no response.

"We've wanted to get out prospecting anyhow," added Bronson, after another moment of silence. "We might as well start in the morning."

Mott felt his heartbeats quicken. So many of their miner-kind had gone forth into the desolation of the mountains never to return.

"Where shall we go?" he said.

"I don't care, Larry," Bronson replied, in his spiritless way. "Yellow Buttes, Iron Valley, or the Death-trap Range—it's all the same to me."

" 'Lost Gold' is over in the Death-trap hills," suggested Mott.

"And no water," supplemented his partner.

Mott's face flushed, as if he had been detected in a sinister thought, but Bronson's gaze was fixed upon the floor.

"No one knows whether there's water or not," Larry answered. "Anyway, there's gold."

" 'Lost Gold'!" said Bronson, bitterly. " 'Lost Gold' that I shall never find! . . . Larry, perhaps the Death-trap Range is the best—for all concerned. Let's tackle the game."

Again that heavy, quickened beat was swinging Larry's heart. "All right," said he. "We'll get an early start tomorrow morning."

He could not refuse to shake the hand that Bronson extended, but he made no attempt to look his partner in the eye.

Mountains in conclave, mountains numerous as waves upon a sea, mountains everywhere—prodigiously ribbed with rock, and incredibly nude in their treeless, barren desolation—wrinkled, folded, and encompassed all the world where Mott and Bronson blazed a virgin trail.

How utterly insignificant the three living creatures appeared— Bronson, his partner, and the gray little donkey, laden with blankets, provisions, and implements—toiling forward among these giant upheavals of earth! They seemed but illusions evolving from the shimmer and quiver of the heated air.

The day was fearfully hot. It was heat, heat, heat wheresoever a man could turn. The glare was crudely brassy. The sun beat down nakedly as if the intervening veil of atmosphere were gone. The rocks flung irradiated heat from hill to hill incessantly. The sand was as scorching hot as living ashes. Dryness could be tasted in the air. The whole vast universe of rumpled planetary surface was desiccated. In the stunted brush an occasional locust sang as if he spun the heat into vibratory sound. Black, shining lizards lay upon the granite fragments, panting in the glow.

The ravine up which the men were pushing was narrow, winding, monotonous. Bronson was leading the way. Presently halting, he shifted his hat on his head and stood there scanning the scene of barren hills in the quivering air.

It was fifteen miles rearward to the nearest spring of water, and yet they were scarcely more than on the edge of the region wherein the gold was reputed to abound. Despite himself Bronson felt a dread of all the region.

"Larry," said he, "the thing for us to do will be to make a camp in the first good place we find, and then prospect around in the cool of the evening and at daybreak every morning."

"I've got to fill again," said Mott, and going to the donkey, he drew the plug from a hot little keg in the load and filled his canteen with tepid water.

"We'll have to go as slowly as possible on the water," cautioned Bronson. "There was only enough for a couple of days when we left the spring."

"I'll die if I don't have a drink," answered Mott, and he poured at least a pint down his throat, whereas a sip should have been sufficient.

"We'll camp at the first good place," repeated his partner, and again he led the way.

For half an hour they plodded onward in silence. Twice in this time Mott drank from his can in his prodigal fashion. As a matter of fact, his thirst was consuming, for to nerve himself to some deed of finality the man had swallowed a dose of whiskey from a flask he had fetched in his pocket. Moreover, he hated these horrible hills. He feared the place. He loathed the heat, the deprivations, the inclose of the desolate mountains. His one mad thought was to flee back to Goldenville—and to go alone. Hour by hour, day by day, he had stared at the barren region, contenting himself with the one reflection —what a place it was in which to be rid of a partner!

On and on plodded Bronson meantime, searching eagerly for a tolerable spot whereon to make a camp.

They were nineteen miles from the water they had left behind, and men and donkey were alike exhausted, when at length they came to a deep-cut gorge, in the depth of which a towering cliff threw a cooling shadow. Here they halted, Bronson unpacking the burro and heaping the blankets and provisions on the earth.

"There is mighty little water in the keg," he said, as he lifted the precious supply from the pack. "You must have been drinking it faster than you thought."

"Oh, there's plenty," answered Mott. "Don't be fussy."

His partner made no reply. He simply determined they would start back out of the Death-trap Mountains in the morning.

Their supper was cooked and eaten early. Darkness came upon the gorge while the sun was blazing still on the western ridges. The beds were made by seven o'clock, and at nine the weary Bronson was sleeping heavily.

Mott was fearfully awake. For another hour he waited, his madness burning more and more fiercely in his brain. He arose from his blankets at last and paused beside them, listening, his heart pounding dully in his breast. Bronson's breathing was regular and slow. How fearfully still was all that world!

Noiselessly the man glided over to the pack where it lay upon the earth. His mouth was gluey with nervous thirst and dryness. He drank, and then he filled not only his can, but a number of empty flasks as well, with water from the keg. Again he listened. Bronson slept like a child.

Having laid in his own provision of water, Mott now deliberately turned out all that remained, and craftily adjusted the keg above the dampened earth in such a manner as to make it appear that the thing had leaked.

The sweat was beaded on his forehead. He drank again, and sneaking like a thief to the stake to which the donkey was tethered, he tore it from the ground. Coiling up the length of rope, he led the little animal silently away from the camp, up the nearest slope, over the ridge, and down in a hollow, where at last he halted. For a moment then remorse all but checked his madness. He was swayed again by his passion, however, almost at once. Not even the burro could be left for Bronson's possible use. With the butt of his heavy revolver he felled the faithful creature to the earth, and when he turned away at the end the burro was dead in the sand, but without a sign of violence upon its body. Should Bronson find it lying there, he could think of a hundred accidents before he would dream of treachery.

Like a criminal, Mott returned to the base of the cliff, where his partner still remained asleep. With a shiver of dread at the things he had done, the man crept silently into his blankets and waited sleeplessly for the dawn.

A thousand times before the morning came the man would have given almost life itself to alter his work of the night. The silence awed his spirit; Bronson's trust and confidence weighed fearfully upon him; the thought of daylight and detection assumed all the guises of nightmare. From the troubled sleep that came at length upon him Mott awoke in a fever, fighting off a horrible horde of demons that peopled his dreams. By then the eastern sky was paling.

Bronson was roused by the daylight. He was promptly out of his bed. Mott was intently listening, even as he lay there still, pretending sleep. He heard his partner rise, and heard the note of concern he uttered when he presently discovered the absence of the donkey.

"Larry!" said Bronson. "Larry!"

Mott sat up in his blankets and rubbed his eyes. "Hullo!" he answered.

"The burro is gone—escaped," said Bronson. "I don't see how he managed to pull up the stake."

With well-acted anger Mott was instantly out of his bed, cursing the animal roundly.

"He can't be very far away," said Bronson. "But in all these rocks we can't expect to pick up his trail. We'll have to hunt for him blindly."

The sudden success of his scheming had fired Mott anew with madness, craft, and determination.

"What about breakfast?" he presently inquired.

"Grub can wait," replied his partner. "We'd better get the burro back before the sun begins to bake the hills."

"All right," Mott agreed, controlling his nervous tension by a mighty effort. "You hunt upwards and I'll hunt down the canyon. The one who finds him first can fire a shot as a signal."

"He can't be very far away, with all that rope on his neck," repeated Bronson. "I hope we'll find him before it gets too hot."

With blazing eyes Mott watched his partner swing his half-filled canteen across his shoulder, as his sole preparation for striking out in the wrong direction to search for the donkey. If in his thirst as he climbed the hills the man would only consume what little water his can contained, no power on earth could keep him alive to walk those nineteen miles of parching rocks and acclivities that lay between this camp and the water back there on the way to Goldenville.

Unsuspiciously Bronson started up the gorge. For a moment after he had gone Mott remained in camp. A feeble impulse to run and call his partner back—to give him at least a chance for his life—stirred for a moment in Larry's breast. Then the all that a mad, blind love had prompted possessed him more powerfully than ever before. Quickly selecting a fair supply of food from the pack, he started, as swiftly as he could travel, back the way they had come. He knew that he had a sufficient quantity of water to last him to the spring, and that Bronson had not.

In the hour and a half that Mott had been hastening onward in his treachery the sun had lifted up above the barren ridges and was scorching all the world again with its merciless fire.

The man was walking less swiftly. He paused very often to drink from the second of his flasks of water. One he had emptied already and thrown away. Somewhat desperately now he scanned the lifeless mountains. There was nothing in all the prospect that he thought he had seen before. Yet it was utterly absurd to suppose a man could make a mistake in directions. He remembered climbing and descending a number of insignificant hills with his partner—just such ridges as the one before him here.

How horribly hot the rocks and earth were becoming! He drank all the water remaining in his second flask and flung the bottle away. Up the acclivity before him he labored. The air was filled as with the buzz of heat where the locusts droned. Wavering semi-visible fume arose from the hills. He reached the summit of the rise, and descending on the farther side, came abruptly into a meager amphitheater, where he almost stumbled over the body of an animal—the gray little burro, dead where he himself had slain him.

The man staggered backward from the sight. For a moment he could not believe that such a thing could be. How could this carcass be here? Then a feeling of horror crept swiftly upon him. After all his haste to get out of the desolation of mountains to the spring—he had circled about, and was almost back at the camp!

The sweat oozed out on his brow. A fever of fear was on him. The water he had remaining might not be sufficient to last him out of this hideous world of rocks and hills, unless he hurried with all his might! He tried to think—to map out a course. Since the burro was here, then the camp was just over there, and the trail to the outside world must lay a little to the right!

For a time that seemed eternal he hastened on. Then fairly racing down a fold in the heated upheaval of granite and gravel, he presently halted and uttered a guttural cry of dismay.

There before him, in the dizzy glare of the amphitheater, lay the body of the burro.

Mott nearly went crazy. His water was half consumed and he had circled again! The hills seemed swinging about him through the shimmering air. The drone of the locusts was so horribly monotonous, persistent—mocking! But one clear thought remained in his brain— Bronson! Bronson could save him!

He ran up the barren slope in the heat and sped downward on the farther side of the ridge. As he went he looked about him for the cliff of rocks beneath which the camp had been made. No cliff could he find. On and on he ran. His lips were swelling. He drank from his can in his feverish extravagance.

At length he remembered the signal on which they had agreed should the donkey be found. Hurriedly drawing his revolver, he fired every chamber, in his panic.

But he ran on, panting, glaring about at the barren mountains, pausing only to drink. His pistol he loaded and fired repeatedly. The weapon grew unbearably hot. The shots rang out with startling detonations, till the echoes clattered from the hills; yet silence—save for that dull, hot droning of the locusts—succeeded always when the last faint return of sound had died away.

He was blundering farther and farther from the camp. The moment came when his last drop of water was gone. He still raced onward, up hill and down, firing his heated pistol like a madman.

When an answering shot came from far to the left, the man became as weak as a child. He tried to shout, to call on Bronson's name, but his throat was parched and his strength had wilted. He could merely stumble up the slope, from the farther side of which the sound had come. As fast as he could load and fire he signalled with his pistol. But when at length he came in sight of his partner, he fell to the earth in a heap.

It was Bronson's canteen of water at his lips at which Mott was presently gulping. It was Bronson's arm that helped him to his feet.

"Larry, try to help yourself a little," he said. "We'll have to get back to the camp and the shade."

Mott's one thought was that of fleeing from the place. "Can we make the spring?" he demanded, in his fear. "Can you get us out?"

There was no concealment of his terror, his helplessness.

"I don't know," answered Bronson. "Perhaps we can, after sunset, when it's cooler. I went to the camp, but found you had not come back, and I started out again to hunt you up. The water in the keg has leaked away."

Mott groaned in his guilt. He could make no other answer. Something like a chill of horror at his own blind folly shook him from head to foot. He suffered himself to be led where Bronson listed, but he limped.

With an instinct for directions as unerring as an Indian's, Bronson chose the straightest cut for the cliff in the gorge. It was more than two miles away. They could make but wretched progress, for the fearful heat momentarily increased, the way was rough, and the hill they were breasting was steep. In half an hour they had gone no more than a mile of the distance. By then their condition was growing desperate.

Together they came down a sloping field of rocks, dull black from the fires of bygone centuries. Not even the stunted brush could grow upon this smitten hill. Up the slope beyond they toiled with painful slowness. Its ridge was traversed in the glare and shimmer of a heat that seemed insupportable. Beyond it lay a basin, scooped in blistered adamant, yet down at the bottom of this dead arena something greenish appeared to be growing.

Toward this spot the two men descended. Then they presently halted at the edge of a jump-off, six to eight feet high, and stared in unbelief at the sight before them. Fifty feet from where they stood, spread out in the unobstructed glare of the sun, lay a limpid pool of water.

Mott for a moment felt he had suddenly surrendered his senses. The thing could not be true! Bronson, in his sanity, thought of mirage—of anything save that this could be reality. And then a chilling breath of horror swept through his being.

About the well lay a dreadful company—skeletons and carcasses of birds, rabbits, chipmunks, coyotes. A buzzard, recently perished, was there upon its back, its talons stiffened in an attitude of torture—a mute, grim witness pinned to the ground in some hopeless fight with death. A squirrel lay doubled over, its head half buried in the sand, but the grim destroyer held it fast in its clutch, forever.

Bronson was staggered. Then all the tales he had ever heard—of poisonous springs, of caldrons of natural acid spewed from the venomous caverns of the earth—rushed in tumult to his mind. Those still, drawn forms could never in their torture have screamed out a story more awful than they told in their silent poses, about the hole. Death in a score of fantastic grimaces had frozen the unsuspecting creatures, come here out of the parching desolation to sip from a seeming oasis! The man was cold with awe.

But Mott had eyes for water only. His reason, no better than a famishing squirrel's, could drive his muscles only. He uttered a cry of delirious joy and started madly for the well.

Momentarily Bronson failed to realize what his partner meant to do. Then he knew the full extent of the man's frenzy.

"Larry! Larry!" he bawled. "Don't touch it! It's poisonous! It's death!"

But Mott was not to be halted. Bronson beheld him, with outstretched arms, running to fling himself down at the brink of the pool and sink his face in the deadly potion.

"Larry!" he shouted once again.

In a sudden decision he leaped from the granite bank, and darting down upon his partner, heaved his weight in violence against him. Mott went down, but he staggered to his feet at once.

"Let me drink!" he screamed, in a thickened utterance. "Let me drink!"

"No! It's poison! Can't you see it's poison?" cried Bronson. "Look at the dead things—"

"Water! It's water," interrupted Mott. He lurched toward the hole.

Bronson himself was wild for a great long draught. He knew how his partner was burning. But he hurled himself once more against him to fend him away from the deadly well.

Mott hit out at him madly. He missed, and Bronson caught him in his arms. But Larry was strong in his mania. They wrestled in the fearful heat of the sun and rocks. They swayed towards the poisonous spring; they scuffled backward from its brink, raucously panting.

Mad and more mad grew Mott to get to the water. Thickly cursing between his violent catches of breath, he was gaining the mastery. His face had become diabolical. Clutching his partner, he choked him backward. About to fling him off, he felt a rock give way beneath his foot. He nearly fell; his hold relaxed. Instantly Bronson struck him on the chin. Down he went, in a limber heap, beside a dead coyote.

All but overcome himself, Bronson stood above his comrade, pressing his hand to his throat, and breathing with labor.

"It—would kill you—Larry," he said.

Afraid to moisten Larry's lips with the water from his can lest Mott return to consciousness and again make an effort to drink from the pool, he took the merest sip himself; then, by exerting the utmost of his failing strength, he carried and dragged the inert form away from the horrible spot, up the slope, and over the ridge. Thus he came at length upon a ledge of rock, in the narrow shade of which he dropped his partner to the sand.

The meager hoarding of water remaining between the men and death was again reduced when Mott once more opened his eyes. He was weak, yet a certain muscular energy was in him that the heat served only to increase. No sooner had he staggered once more to his feet than he fell to cursing his comrade, and demanding that Bronson direct him back to the well of poison.

Bronson heard him threaten, beg, and pray, unmoved.

"Larry, don't be a fool," he said. "It would kill you in fifteen minutes—maybe less."

"A drink is worth it!" answered Mott, in his thickened voice. "I'll die as it is! I'd rather have it over! I want a drink!"

"If we sit here and wait for night, we may be able to save our lives," said Bronson, who was suffering intensely, not only from thirst, but also from his recent exertions. He added, "This is our only chance."

Mott regarded his partner in fury. Had he dared to face the mountains alone he would simply have slain Nick Bronson on the spot, snatched the can of water, and fled from the place, so desperate was his state of mind. But to lose himself as he had before and to perish alone—the thought nearly drove the man insane.

"We'll never get out! We'll never get out!" he said.

Bronson made no answer. Idly he fingered the rock of the ledge in the shade of which he was sitting. It was rotten quartz. A piece came away in his hand. He looked at it dully. Then he held it up for Mott to see, a faint, grim smile upon his lips.

"The stuff is rich," he said. "We've found the 'Lost Gold' ledge."

For a moment Mott regarded the glittering particles of yellow metal sprinkled through the dross, then again he cursed. He cursed the gold, the mountains, the world. He cursed himself and he cursed his partner, but he dared not curse his God. The fearful heat, the appalling region, the merciless hills cast fear and awe upon his helpless being. He shivered at the thought of a God whose wrath could have touched this stricken place.

"Gold!" he cried. "Gold! gold! gold!—when all I want is water!"

"I'll give you a sip," said Bronson; "then, Larry, for Heaven's sake sit down and be quiet—or you'll never live to make a try tonight."

"A sip!" answered Mott. "A sip!"

Yet he took it, and flung himself down on the earth.

For an hour they lay there, beholding the slender margin of shade diminish as the sun climbed nearer and nearer to meridian. By then the radiation from the rocks and sand was overpowering. The visible atmosphere rose in a dizzying dance. Madness was certainly coming with this inactivity. To forge ahead was to hasten towards the open arms of death; to wait was only to invite an end more lingering.

"We'll have no shade in fifteen minutes more," said Bronson, finally. "We can't stay here."

"Come on!" cried Mott, in his thickened utterance. "Come on!" and he started to his feet.

"We can't go—far," replied his partner.

"Come on! What else can we do?" demanded Mott.

"Larry," answered Bronson, "there is one slim chance—for you—or me. We can't live it out till night sitting still, and we can't both make it back to decent water. We tackled this game as pards—let's look it in the face as partners still."

Mott said, "Well?"

Bronson looked at him with boyish affection in his eyes. "There may be water enough for one, if it's carefully used," he said. "And it's better one should be saved than both should croak. Draw straws with me, Larry, to see which one of us takes the can and strikes out for home."

Mott regarded him wildly for a second, then cunning altered the look in his eyes. A vision of Goldenville arose before his mind—Goldenville and water!—Goldenville and Agnes!—Goldenville and life! But a sudden fear of getting lost shattered all of his dream.

"If I won—I couldn't find the way," he answered, hoarsely.

"I can point it out so you can't go wrong," replied his partner. "What do you say?"

Larry's heart was pumping madly. That can of water! And the heat was driving him crazy.

"All right," he said. "I'll hold the straws. The long one wins."

In excitement he turned his back, and elaborately selecting and arranging two brittle twigs from a stunted shrub, he held them in his fists as he turned to face his companion.

Bronson was pale, but Mott was paler.

"There is nothing better we can do, is there, Larry?" said Nick.

"No," muttered Mott. "And there's no going back on the game. It's your suggestion and what you want!"

"It's all there is," replied his friend.

For a moment the two men faced each other in silence. Mott held forth his hands, each with a bit of the slender gray "straw" protruding above his fingers.

"Take either one," he said, raucously.

Bronson laid his hand on Larry's arm—the left.

"This one," was all he said.

Mott held his partner's gaze with his feverish eyes, while he craftily broke Bronson's straw in his hand by the slightest pressure.

"Take it," he muttered.

Bronson drew it forth. Broken short off, it was barely an inch in length.

"There is the other," said Larry, and as Bronson's gaze was swinging to the second twig, over two inches in length, Mott quickly dropped the bit retained in the hand from which his partner had taken his fate.

A paler cast spread for a moment on Bronson's countenance. "It's all right, Larry," he said. "I'm glad you won."

He took the precious canteen from his shoulder and gave it over to his partner. Then lucidly and briefly he explained the path that Mott was to travel to win his way from the Death-trap Range.

"Don't drink the water too fast, old man," he instructed. "Just plod ahead and only sip it when you feel you absolutely must. It ought to last you through, but you'd better start at once. . . . So-long." He held out his hand for a farewell shake.

"What—are you going to do?" stammered Mott, thickly.

"I'll take it—the best I can," said Bronson, smiling faintly. "If the worst comes—I know the way to the poison hole. Go on. Don't waste your time—and, Larry, don't drink up the water too fast."

Mott felt nothing for the moment save the weight of that small canteen of water on the strap. Goldenville and Agnes—Goldenville and life! cried his fevered brain. He gripped the outstretched hand of his partner, but he did not look him in the eyes.

"So-long," he said, and he started away across the blistering path of rock and gravel.

At the brow of the hill, the descent of which would forever hide his partner from his gaze, Mott came to a halt and turned about.

Back there through the shimmering waves of heat, standing alone by the ledge of gold, was Bronson, watching unflinchingly. He raised his hand and waved good-by.

How terribly alone he seemed! How horribly hot was all that fur-

nace of mountains about him! He had no water! Larry's thought was
shrieking—he had no water!

Something suddenly snapped in Larry's bosom. Something was
flooding his being. Boyhood memories, chummings and affections, and
manhood's thoughts of Bronson's tenderness and sacrifice of self,
surged in upon his heart overwhelmingly. He stood revealed to himself in all his perfidy, all his selfishness, all his shame. And the tie
of partnership refused to sever.

"Oh, Nick—I can't—I can't!" he cried out, hoarsely, in sudden anguish, and dizzily running, back he came, the precious canteen
stripped off and held before him in his hands. "I can't!" he repeated
in self-accusation, as he ran. "Nick, I cheated! I cheated! I cheated!"

Despite the somewhat wild revulsion of feeling upon him, Mott
could confess to nothing but the trickery by which he had robbed his
partner of the can of water. He could not reveal his former treach-
eries. A boyish eagerness to hold to Bronson's affections, a yearning
for friendship, a dread of being hated, shunned, mistrusted, here in
this terrible place, put an absolutely unbreakable seal upon his lips.
He could only think of a strange semi-prayer that God might give
him a chance to redeem himself before the hour should pass forever.

In all that he told he scathed himself without mercy. He begged
his partner to take the water and to go—to leave him there to the
fate he had earned. He was shaken by sobs that were parched to
distressing dryness.

It was almost more than Bronson could endure. He could not take
the can of water and save himself. His affection for Larry had increased a thousandfold in the stress of the moment.

"Larry," said he—"Larry—come on, old man. Let's stick together
and make one last try at least." He held forth his hand, and Mott
took it eagerly.

"Nick," he said, in his thickened utterance, "I'm not worth trying
to save. I'll follow—that's all. If I drop—go on. You could save yourself, I know—if it weren't for me."

The sky was quivering wheresoever their blearing gaze could turn.
A million specks of mica blazed from the rocks and gravel—micro-
cosms of the glaring sun. Exhausted before they started, and suffering
extremely from thirst, the partners nevertheless toiled slowly up the
hill before them, the hot canteen with its meager supply of heated
water brought soon into requisition, despite the conserving fanaticism
now aflame in the mind of either man.

They dragged themselves across a barren ridge, down through a glowing depression, and then along a shallow channel, where the air seemed fairly hurtling with sun-blaze, flung from granite to right and left.

"Larry—take a decent drink—or you're—going to drop," said Bronson, at last, speaking with obvious difficulty. "Take it all. It—can't make but—little difference—now."

Mott refused the can. "Sooner I go—the better," he answered, with a dreadful but an honest smile on his swollen lips. Raising his hand, however, he pointed. "Shade," he said.

A huge, projecting shelf of rock hung so far outward from the sidehill that even the noonday sun could not attack the patch of shade beneath its bulk. Towards this the two men staggered. It was somewhat up the slope, however, and the way was steep. Before they could make the refuge, Bronson abruptly sank to the earth, unconscious.

It was almost a crazed sort of joy with which Larry Mott poured the last remaining half-cup of water down his partner's throat. Bronson was partially revived. Mott supported his weight and urged him again to his feet. In a frenzy of superhuman effort the two reeled drunkenly up the acclivity and reached the shelter of the ledge.

Mott collapsed at once. He fell without a sound, and Bronson sank into helplessness beside him in the sand. From the opposite slope the irradiating heat came dizzily across. The sky was like a monstrous cover that shut the sun and the two men into the furnace of the mountains together.

Bronson, finally responding a little to the cooler breath of the shaded cliff of rock, was presently aware that Mott was gone in a stupor from which he might never recover. Heedless of his partner now, heedless of the end which he felt to be close upon him, Bronson closed his eyes, his thought a vagary of golden heat and fury.

How long a semi-dreaming condition was upon him he could not have known. He was conscious at last of a certain impatience that life could cling to a dried-out, suffering body so stubbornly. Then he was dully aware that something was prodding his brain to activity.

It was sound.

From somewhere out of the awful heat and desolation came a faint, elusive note of whistling—a single note, repeated in a quick staccato manner.

For a moment the man felt his pulses quicken. Then he smiled in a grim, sardonic manner. It was nothing but the torture of a dream.

But the sound came once again, and with crazy leaping of his blood in his veins, the man knew the call of the mountain-quail!

Had a patter of rain been sounding on the earth he could scarcely have felt a more intense excitement.

Quail!—in such a place as this! The brown little travelers—here! —and their tongues so wet they could whistle!

It was noon—the hour when quail come down to drink. They must have knowledge of a spring!

With a chill of nervous excitement shivering through his being, Bronson rose to his feet and started from the shade, his senses all on edge to catch that faint, sweet sound of calling.

It came once more, from down the ravine below the cliff. Cautiously, silently, the man stole out upon the heated sand and rocks and began to descend the canyon.

In its merciless glare the sun beat down upon him. Famishing before he left the shelter, he was presently ready to fall again for want of water. His strength was gone. He fell repeatedly, but staggered on. The sound of the quail calling ceased. His desperation then was boundless. He puckered his lips in an effort to imitate the call. Not a sound could he make. Again he dropped to the earth. Crawling on hands and knees over blistering gravel and fragments of granite, he summoned all the force of will remaining in his body to make one sound of whistling.

Three—four notes, in the clear staccato of the quail-call, came from his lips.

From over a rise of earth and rock a brown little pilgrim made reply.

A mighty hope leaped in the breast of the man. He stumbled to his feet once more in the strength of a heaven-sent impulse, and reeling, toiling upward, came presently in sight of a spot of green, where a dwarfed and drying willow reared its leaves above the bed of the gulch.

Bronson could have cried, had the moisture remained in his body. Bruised from falling, blinded by the shimmer of the air, he plunged insanely towards the willow, startling half a dozen of the quail from cover as he stumbled through the stunted brush and fell face downwards on the earth.

Like a madman he crept to the willow, wildly searching the sand for a trickle of water.

Above the willow there was nothing. Below, the gravel burned with heat. Beneath the pitiful growth there was just an ooze of moisture, where a bird might catch up a crystal drop, but the jealous sun and sand were drinking here with rivalry insatiate.

Bronson thrust his face in the dampened earth and drew in a breath. It was moist—it was sweeter than wine!

With his fingers he dug in the gravel, unearthing a root of the willow. For a moment the hollow in the sand almost filled, but the gravel absorbed the water, even as the man's parched lips descended for a drink. He dug again madly, but the heat was already in his shallow well, and the trickle disappeared.

"If it only were shaded!" said the man, in despair.

In the frenzy of strength that hope was inspiring in his breast, he tore up stunted brush and bent down the willow to form a crude, inadequate tent, as it were, above the dampened spot.

Time after time he thrust his face in the scooped-out hole and got at least a breath that did not scorch his swollen lips. But the shade he had formed could not, it seemed, woo back the ooze of water. With returning strength he toiled to make the shelter more complete.

"Tonight the water will drip," he told himself repeatedly. "Tonight —tonight!"

In the shade he created, the sand cooled off by the end of an hour. A single drop of water trembled forth from the end of an uncovered root and fell to the earth.

With a cry of disappointment Bronson would have snatched it back, but it sank immediately. He placed his hot canteen beneath the root, however, and waited.

A second drop came forth and fell within the can. A third and a fourth were similarly caught. Like a mother-creature sitting there to brood and watch, Bronson remained beside the willow garnering those crystal drops, one by one, as they issued from the earth.

It was over an hour more before he had enough to take to Larry, back there unconscious in the shade. Bronson by then had recovered much of his strength. He hastened up the slope to the cliff, and had the joy of reviving his partner sufficiently to get him to his feet. Then together the two descended to the spring, where they lay upon the earth, alternately wetting their lips from the slowly dripping root and breathing from the moisture of the sand.

All afternoon the broiling sun and the hungering gravel fought with the men for the water. All afternoon the locusts droned, the air ascended in its awful dance, the desolation baked.

But the shadows crept silently eastward at last, and the twilight came as a sweetening presence to the world. In the night the rocks still radiated heat, but the air was cool, and the drop, drop, drop at the tiny spring increased. At twelve o'clock the stars were lending the majesty of their pageant to all the world of mountains.

"The cans are full," said Bronson. "We can make it out to safety by the morning."

They were two haggard, toil-worn men who limped down the trail to Goldenville at last, as one of those hot, dry days was coming to an end. Privation had chiseled its furrows on their faces; suffering still held them in its grip, yet a certain light of joy was burning in Bronson's eyes.

They were almost come to the mining-camp. The grind and puff and shriek of engines came on the air with a sweetness inconceivable. Man was there!—man whose tumult is the voice of life!—man whose symbol is a home!

And yet Larry Mott felt his heart grow ill, even as some little sound of joy escaped the lips of his partner. He had toiled and endured and sacrificed unremittingly, day after day, to atone a little for the wrongs he had done, and peaks of anguish he had climbed without complaint; yet now before him loomed the steepest, hardest, most forbidding peak of all—the struggle with himself.

"Nick," he said, hoarsely, as he paused in the trail,—"Nick—there is something I feel I've got to tell. You've fetched me home—you've saved my life—you've been a partner all the time—but you may not want to shake my hand—not ever again—when I tell you what I did."

"Why, Larry, what's the matter?" Bronson answered. "If you mean about the day we drew straws for the water—"

"No—I don't mean that," said Mott, interrupting. "It was worse than that. I lied to you, Nick, before we started off. I lied about Agnes. She loves you. I was jealous—crazy—everything low and sneaking. I hoped you would go to the Death-trap hills, and when we were there at the cliff I killed the burro and ran off the water in the keg, and tried to get out of the mountains ana leave you there to die. I did it all for a crazy love. I love her now! I can't help loving her, Nick, with all my wretched heart; but—God knows I love my partner!—I had to tell you—now that we are home—but you'll never want to see my face again!"

He leaned against a granite boulder that lay beside the road, and hiding his face in the curve of his arm, was shaken convulsively.

Bronson looked at him strangely as the meaning of the bald confession slowly worked through his brain. Then he presently came and laid his hand on Larry's shoulder.

"We're pards," he said; "don't forget that, Larry—don't. We're better friends than ever. I might have done the same myself. It's over now. Come on, shake hands, and begin to forget. It's past, old man, like that day in the hills—that awful day when we found the 'Lost Gold' ledge."

And after a time, when they had started again for the camp, poor Mott took heart to speak.

"Please don't tell it to Agnes," he said. "I hope she'll some day let me be a friend."

ALICE BROWN

★ ★ ★

An individual's right to live his own life, freed from the tyranny of controls beyond his own innate need, is the theme of many of the narratives of Alice Brown (1857-   ), whose characters, especially in second marriage, frequently batter themselves against life's fences in pursuit of the fulfillment of love, independence, sense of power, or success. However much the actor suffer from his lack of disciplined endeavor, human passion must be permitted free outlet. Humor affords relief to pathos, and a quiet realism is enriched with poetic nature descriptions. Born in Hampton Falls, New Hampshire, Miss Brown attended Robinson School at Exeter, taught for several years, and in 1885 joined the staff of *Youth's Companion*. *Meadow Grass* (1895), *Tiverton Tales* (1899), and *The Country Road* (1906) contain her best short stories. *The Story of Thyrza* (1909) and *The Prisoner* (1916) are perhaps her best novels. "Mis' Wadleigh's Guest" is reprinted from *Meadow Grass* by permission of Houghton Mifflin Company.

★ ★ ★

Mis' Wadleigh's Guest

CYRUS PENDLETON sat by the kitchen fire, his stockinged feet in the oven, and his hands stretched out toward the kettles, which were bubbling posperously away, and puffing a cloud of steam into his face. He was a meager, sad-colored man, with muttonchop whiskers so thin as to lie like a shadow on his fallen cheeks; and his glance, wherever it fell, seemed to deprecate reproof. Thick layers of flannel swathed his throat, and from time to time, he coughed

wheezingly, with the air of one who, having a cold, was determined
to be conscientious about it. A voice from the buttery began pouring
forth words only a little slower than the blackbird sings, and with no
more reference to reply.

"Cyrus, don't you feel a mite better? Though I dunno how you
could expect to, arter such a night as you had on't, puffin' an'
blowin'!" Mrs. Pendleton followed the voice. She seemed to be
borne briskly in on its wings, and came scudding over the kitchen
sill, carrying a pan of freshly sifted flour. She set it down on the
table, and began "stirrin' up." "I dunno where you got such a cold,
unless it's in the air," she continued. "Folks say they're round, nowadays, an' you ketch 'em, jest as you would the mumps. But there!
nobody on your side or mine ever had the mumps, as long as I can
remember. Except Elkanah, though! an' he ketched 'em down to
Portsmouth, when he went off on that fool's arrant arter elwives.
Do you s'pose you could eat a mite o' fish for dinner?"

"I was thinkin'—" interposed Cyrus, mildly; but his wife swept
past him, and took the road.

"I dunno's there's any use in gittin' a real dinner, jest you an' me,
an' you not workin' either. Folks say there's more danger of eatin'
too much 'n too little. Gilman Lane, though, he kep' eatin' less an'
less, an' his stomach dried all up, till 'twa'n't no bigger'n a bladder.
Look here, you! I shouldn't wonder a mite if you'd got some o'
them stomach troubles along with your cold. You 'ain't acted as if
you'd relished a meal o' victuals for nigh onto ten days. Soon as I
git my hands out o' the flour, I'll look in the doctor's book, an' find
out. My! how het up I be!" She wiped her hands on the roller towel,
and unpinned the little plaid shawl drawn tightly across her shoulders. Its removal disclosed a green sontag, and under that manifold
layers of jacket and waist. She was amply protected from the cold.
"I dunno's I ought to ha' stirred up rye 'n' Injun," she went on, returning to her vigorous tossing and mixing at the table. "Some might
say the steam was bad for your lungs. Anyhow, the doctor's book
holds to 't you've got to pick out a dry climate, if you want to go
into a decline. Le' me see! when your Aunt Mattie was took, how
long was it afore she really gi'n up? Arter she begun to cough, I
mean?"

Cyrus moved uneasily.

"I dunno," he said hastily. "I never kep' the run o' such things."

But Mirandy, pouring her batter into the pan, heeded him no more
than was her wont.

"I s'pose that was real gallopin' consumption," she said, with relish.

"I must ask Sister Sarah how long 'twas, next time I see her. She set it down with the births an' deaths."

Cyrus was moved to some remonstrance. He often felt the necessity of asserting himself, lest he should presently hear his own passing-bell and epitaph.

"I guess you needn't stop steamin' bread for me! I ain't half so stuffed up as I was yesterday!"

Mrs. Pendleton clapped the loaf into the pot, wrinkling her face over the cloud of steam that came puffing into it.

"There!" she exclaimed. "Now perhaps I can git a minute to se' down. I 'ain't bound a shoe today. My! who's that out this weather?"

The side door was pushed open, and then shut with a bang. A vigorous stamping of snow followed, and the inner door swung in to admit a woman, very short, very stout, with a round, apple-cheeked face, and twinkling eyes looking out from the enveloping folds of a gray cloud.

"Well!" she said, in a cheery voice, beginning at once to unwind the cloud, "here I be! Didn't think I'd rain down, did ye? I thought myself, one spell, I should freeze afore I fell!"

Mrs. Pendleton hurried forward, wiping her hands on her apron as she went.

"For the land's sake, Marthy Wadleigh!" she cried, laying hold of the newcomer by the shoulders, and giving her an ineffectual but wholly delighted shake. "Well, I never! Who brought you over? Though I dunno which way you come. I 'ain't looked out—"

"I walked from the corner," said Mrs. Wadleigh, who never felt any compunction about interrupting her old neighbor. She was unpinning her shawl composedly, as one sure of a welcome. "How do, Cyrus? Jim Thomas took me up jest beyond the depot, an' give me a lift on his sled; but I was all of a shiver, an' at the corner, I told him he better let me step down an' walk. So I come the rest o' the way afoot an' alone. You ain't goin' to use the oven, be ye? I'll jest stick my feet in a minute. No, Cyrus, don't you move! I'll take t'other side. I guess we sh'n't come to blows over it."

She seemed to have brought into the kitchen, with that freshness of outdoor air which the newcomer bears, like a balsam, in his garments, a breath of fuller life, and even of jollity. As she sat there in her good brown dress, with her worked collar, fastened by a large cameo, her gold beads just showing, and her plump hands folded on a capacious lap, she looked the picture of jovial content, quite able to take care of herself, and perhaps apply a sturdy shoulder to the lagging machinery of the world.

"Didn't you git word I was comin' this week?" she asked. "I sent you a line."

"No, we 'ain't been so fur's the post-office," answered Mirandy, absently. She was debating over her most feasible bill of fare, now that a "pick-up dinner" seemed no longer possible. Moreover, she had something on her mind, and she could not help thinking how unfortunate it was that Cyrus shared her secret. Who could tell at what moment he might broach it? She doubted his discretion. "The roads wa'n't broke out till day before yisterday."

"I shouldn't think they were!" said Mrs. Wadleigh, scornfully, testing the heat with a hand on her skirt, and then lifting the breadths back over her quilted petticoat. "I thought that would be the way on't, but I'd made up my mind to come, an' come I would. Cyrus, what's the matter o' you? Nothin' more'n a cold, is it?"

Cyrus had withdrawn from the stove, and was feeling his chin, uncertainly.

"Oh, no, I guess not," he said. "We've been kind o' peaked, for a week or two, all over the neighborhood; but I guess we shall come out on't, now we've got into the spring. Mirandy, you git me a mite o' hot water, an' I'll see if I can't shave."

Mirandy was vigorously washing potatoes at the sink, but she turned, in ever-ready remonstrance.

"Shave!" she ejaculated. "Well, I guess you won't shave, such a day as this, in that cold bedroom, with a stockin'-leg round your throat, an' all! You want to git your death? Why, 'twas only last night, Marthy, he had a hemlock sweat, an' all the ginger tea I could git down into him! An' then I didn't know—"

"Law! let him alone!" said Marthy, with a comfortable, throaty laugh. "He'll feel twice as well, git some o' them things off his neck. Here, Cyrus, you reach me down your mug—ain't them your shavin' things up there?—an' I'll fill it for you. You git him a piece o' flannel, Mirandy, to put on when he's washed up an' took all that stuff off his throat. Why, he's got enough wool round there, if 'twas all in yarn, to knit Old Tobe a pair o' mittens! An' they say one o' his thumbs was bigger'n the hand o' Providence. You don't want to try all the goodness out of him, do ye?"

Cyrus gave one swift glance at his wife. "There! you see!" it said plainly. "I am not without defenders." He took down his shaving-mug, with an air of some bravado. But Mirandy was no shrew; she was simply troubled about many things.

"Well," she said, compressing her lips, and wrinkling her forehead in resignation. "If folks want to kill themselves, I can't hender 'em!

But when he's down ag'in, I shall be the one to take care of him, that's all. Here, Cyrus, don't you go into that cold bedroom. You shave you here, if you're determined to do it."

So Cyrus, after honing his razor, with the pleasure of a bored child provided at last with occupation, betook himself to the glass set in the lower part of the clock, and there, with much contortion of his thin visage, proceeded to shave. Mirandy put her potatoes on to boil, and set the fish on the stove to freshen; then she sat down by the window, with a great basket beside her, and began to bind shoes.

"Here," said Mrs. Wadleigh, coming to her feet and adjusting her skirt, "you give me a needle! I've got my thimble right here in my pocket. It's three months sence I've seen a shoe. I should admire to do a pair or two. I wish I could promise ye more, but somehow I'm bewitched to git over home right arter dinner!"

Mrs. Pendleton laid down her work and leaned back in her chair. Cyrus turned, cleared his throat, and looked at her.

"Marthy," said the hostess, "you ain't goin' over there to that lonesome house, this cold snap?"

"Ain't I?" asked Mrs. Wadleigh, composedly, as she trimmed the top of her shoe preparatory to binding it. "Well, you see 'f I ain't!"

"In the first place," went on Mrs. Pendleton, nervously, "the crossroad ain't broke out, an' you can't git there. I dunno's a horse could plough through; an' s'posin' they could, Cyrus ain't no more fit to go out an' carry you over 'n a fly."

"Don't you worry," said Mrs. Wadleigh, binding off one top. "While I've got my own legs, I don't mean to be beholden to nobody. I've had a proper nice time all winter, fust with Lucy an' then with Ann,—an' I tell ye 'tain't everybody that's got two darters married so well!—but for the last fortnight, I've been in a real tew to come home. They've kep' me till I wouldn't stay no longer, an' now I've got so near as this, I guess I ain't goin' to stop for nobody!"

Mrs. Pendleton looked despairingly at her husband; and he, absently wiping his razor on a bit of paper, looked at her.

"Marthy!" she burst forth. "No, Cyrus, don't you say one word! You can't go! There's somebody there!"

Mrs. Wadleigh, in turn, put down her work.

"Somebody there!" she ejaculated. "Where?"

"In your house!"

"In my house? What for?"

"I dunno," said Mirandy, unhappily.

"Dunno? Well, what are they doin' there?"

"I dunno that. We only know there's somebody there."

Here the brown-bread kettle boiled over, creating a diversion; and Mirandy gladly rose to set it further back. A slight heat had come into Mrs. Wadleigh's manner.

"Cyrus," said she, with emphasis, "I should like to have you speak. I left that house in your care. I left the key with you, an' I should like to know who you've been an' got in there."

Cyrus opened his mouth, and then closed it again without saying a word. He looked appealing at his wife; and she took up the tale with some joy, now that the first plunge had been made.

"Well," she said, folding her hands in her apron, and beginning to rock back and forth, a little color coming into her cheeks, and her eyes snapping vigorously. "You see, this was the way 'twas. Cyrus, do let me speak!" Cyrus had ineffectually opened his mouth again. "Wa'n't it in November you went away? I thought so. Jest after that first sprinklin' o' snow, that looked as it 'twould lay all winter. Well, we took the key, an' hung it up inside the clock—an' there 'tis now!—an' once a week, reg'lar as the day come round, Cyrus went over, an' opened the winders, an' aired out the house."

Mrs. Wadleigh sat putting her thimble off and on.

"I know all about that," she interposed, "but who's in there now? That's what I want to find out."

"I'm comin' to that. I don't want to git ahead o' my story. An' so 't went on till it come two weeks ago Friday, an' Cyrus wen over jest the same as ever. An' when he hitched to the gate, he see smoke comin' out o' the chimbly, an' there was a man's face at one square o' glass." She paused, enjoying her climax.

"Well? Why don't you go ahead? Mirandy Jane Pendleton, I could shake you! You can talk fast enough when somebody else wants the floor! How'd he git in? What'd he say for himself?"

"Why, he never said anything! Cyrus didn't see him."

"Didn't see him? I thought he see him lookin' out the winder!"

"Why, yes! so he did, but he didn't see him to speak to. He jest nailed up the door, an' come away."

Mrs. Wadleigh turned squarely upon the delinquent Cyrus, who stood, half-shaven, absently honing his razor.

"Cyrus," said she, with an alarming decision, "will you open your head, an' tell me what you nailed up that door for? an' where you got your nails? I s'pose you don't carry 'em round with you, ready for any door 't happens to need nailin' up?"

This fine sarcasm was not lost on Cyrus. He perceived that he had become the victim of a harsh and ruthless dealing.

"I had the key to the front door with me, an 'I thought I'd jest step round an' nail up t'other one," he said, in the tone of one conscious of right. "There was some nails in the woodshed. Then I heard somebody steppin' round inside, an' I come away."

"You come away!" repeated Mrs. Wadleigh, rising in noble wrath. "You nailed up the door an' come away! Well, if you ain't a weak sister! Mirandy, you hand me down that key, out o' the clock, while I git my things!"

She walked sturdily across to the bedroom, and Mirandy followed her, wringing her hands in futile entreaty.

"My soul, Marthy! you ain't goin' over there! You'll be killed, as sure as you step foot into the yard. Don't you remember how that hired man down to Sudleigh toled the whole fam'ly out into the barn, one arter another, an' chopped their heads off—"

"You gi' me t'other end o' my cloud," commanded Mrs. Wadleigh. "I'm glad I've got on stockin'-feet. Where's t'other mitten? Oh! there 'tis, down by the sto'-leg. Cyrus, if you knew how you looked with your face plastered over o' lather, you'd wipe it off, an' hand me down that key. Can't you move? Well, I guess I can reach it myself."

She dropped the house key carefully into her pocket, and opened the outer door; both Cyrus and his wife knew they were powerless to stop her.

"O Marthy, do come back!" wailed Mrs. Pendleton after her. "You 'ain't had a mite o' dinner, an' you'll never git out o' that house alive!"

"I'd ruther by half hitch up myself," began Cyrus; but his wife turned upon him, at the word, bundled him into the kitchen, and shut the door upon him. Then she went back to her post in the doorway, and peered after Mrs. Wadleigh's square figure on the dazzling road, with a melancholy determination to stand by her to the last. Only when it occurred to her that it was unlucky to watch a departing friend out of sight, did she shut the door hastily, and go in to reproach Cyrus and prepare his dinner.

Mrs. Wadleigh plodded steadily onward. Her face had lost its robustness of scorn, and expressed only a cheerful determination. Once or twice her mouth relaxed, in retrospective enjoyment of the scene behind her, and she gave vent to a scornful ejaculation.

"A man in my house!" she said once, aloud. "I guess we'll see!"

She turned into the crossroad, where stood her dear and lonely dwelling, with no neighbors on either side for half a mile, and stopped a moment to gaze about her. The road was almost untravelled, and the snow lay encrusted over the wide fields, sparkling on the heights and blue in the hollows. The brown bushes by a hidden stone-wall broke the sheen entrancingly; here and there a dry leaf fluttered, but only enough to show how still such winter stillness can be, and a flock of little brown birds rose, with a soft whirr, and settled further on. Mrs. Wadleigh pressed her lips together in a voiceless content, and her eyes took on a new brightness. She had lived quite long enough in the town. Rounding a sweeping bend, and ploughing sturdily along, though it was difficult here to find the roadway, she kept her eyes fixed on a patch of sky, over a low elm, where the chimney would first come into view. But just before it stepped forward to meet her, as she had seen it a thousand times, a telltale token forestalled it; a delicate blue haze crept out, in spiral rings, and tinged the sky.

"He's got a fire!" she exclaimed loudly. "He's there! My soul!" Until now the enormity of his offense had not penetrated her understanding. She had heard the fact without realizing it.

The house was ancient but trimly kept, and it stood within a spacious yard, now in billows and mounds of snow, under which lay the treasures inherited by the spring. The trellises on either side the door held the bare clinging arms of jessamine and rose, and the syringa and lilac bushes reached hardily above the snow. As Mrs. Wadleigh approached the door, she gave a rapid glance at the hoppole in the garden, and wondered if its vine had stood the winter well. That was the third hop vine she'd had from Mirandy Pendleton! Mounting the front steps, she drew forth the key, and put it in the door. It turned readily enough, but though she gave more than one valiant push, the door itself did not yield. It was evidently barricaded.

"My soul!" said Mrs. Wadleigh.

She stepped back, to survey the possibilities of attack; but at that instant, glancing up at the window, she had Cyrus Pendleton's own alarming experience. A head looked out at her, and was quickly withdrawn. It was dark, unkempt, and the movement was stealthy.

"That's him!" said Mrs. Wadleigh, grimly, and returning to the charge, she knocked civilly at the door. No answer. Then she pushed again. It would not yield. She thought of the ladder in the barn, of the small cellar-window; vain hopes, both of them!

"Look here!" she called aloud. "You le' me in! I'm the Widder Wadleigh! This is my own house, an' I'm real tried stan'in' round here, knockin' at my own front door. You le' me in, or I shall git my death o' cold!"

No answer; and then Mrs. Wadleigh, as she afterwards explained it, "got mad." She ploughed her way round the side of the house,—

not the side where she had seen the face, but by the "best-room" windows,—and stepped softly up to the back door. Cyrus Pendleton's nail was no longer there. The man had easily pushed it out. She lifted the latch, and set her shoulder against the panel.

"If it's the same old button, it'll give," she thought. And it did give. She walked steadily across the kitchen toward the clock-room, where the man that moment turned to confront her. He made a little run forward; then, seeing but one woman, he restrained himself. He was not over thirty years old, a tall, well-built fellow, with very black eyes and black hair. His features were good, but just now his mouth was set, and he looked darkly defiant. Of this, however, Mrs. Wadleigh did not think, for she was in a hot rage.

"What under the sun do you mean, lockin' me out o' my own house?" she cried, stretching out her reddened hands to the fire. "An' potaters b'iled all over this good kitchen stove! I declare, this room's a real hog's nest, an' I left it as neat as wax!"

Perhaps no man was ever more amazed than this invader. He stood staring at her in silence.

"Can't you shet the door?" she inquired, fractiously, beginning to untie her cloud. "An' put a stick o' wood in the stove? If I don't git het through, I shall ketch my death!"

He obeyed, seemingly from the inertia of utter surprise. Midway in the act of lifting the stove-cover, he glanced at her in sharp suspicion.

"Where's the rest?" he asked, savagely. "You ain't alone?"

"Well, I guess I'm alone!" returned Mrs. Wadleigh, drawing off her icy stocking-feet, "an' walked all the way from Cyrus Pendleton's! There ain't nobody likely to be round," she continued, with grim humor. "I never knew 'twas such a God-forsaken hole, till I'd been away an' come back to't. No, you needn't be scairt! The road ain't broke out, an' if 'twas, we shouldn't have no callers today. It's got round there's a man here, an' I'll warrant the selec'men are all sick abed with colds. But there!" she added, presently, as the soothing warmth of her own kitchen stove began to penetrate, "I dunno's I oughter call it a God-forsaken place. I'm kind o' glad to git back."

There was silence for a few minutes, while she toasted her feet, and the man stood shambling from one foot to the other and furtively watching her and the road. Suddenly she rose, and lifted a pot-cover.

"What you got for dinner?" she inquired, genially. "I'm as holler's a horn!"

"I put some potatoes on," said he, gruffly.

"Got any pork? or have you used it all up?"

"I guess there's pork! I 'ain't touched it. I 'ain't eat anything but potatoes; an' I've chopped wood for them, an' for what I burnt."

"Do tell!" said Mrs. Wadleigh. She set the potatoes forward, where they would boil more vigorously. "Well, you go down sullar an' bring me up a little piece o' pork—streak o' fat an' streak o' lean— an' I'll fry it. I'll sweep up here a mite while you're gone. Why, I never see such a lookin' kitchen! What's your name?" she called after him, as he set his foot on the upper stair.

He hesitated. "Joe!" he said, falteringly.

"All right, then, Joe, you fly round an' git the pork!" She took down the broom from its accustomed nail, and began sweeping joyously; the man, fishing in the pork-barrel, listened meanwhile to the regular sound above. Once it stopped, and he held his breath for a moment, and stood at bay, ready to dash up the stairs and past his pursuers, had she let them in. But it was only her own step, approaching the cellar door.

"Joe!" she called. "You bring up a dozen apples, Bald'ins. I'll fry them, too."

Something past one o'clock, they sat down together to as strange a meal as the little kitchen had ever seen. Bread and butter were lacking, but there was quince preserve, drawn from some hidden hoard, the apples and pork, and smoking tea. Mrs. Wadleigh's spirits rose. Home was even better than her dreams had pictured it. She told her strange guest all about her darter Lucy and her darter Ann's children; and he listened, quite dazed and utterly speechless.

"There!" she said at last, rising, "I dunno's I ever eat such a meal o' victuals in my life, but I guess it's better'n many a poor soldier used to have. Now, if you've got some wood to chop, you go an' do it, an' I'll clear up this kitchen; it's a real hurrah's nest, is ever there was one!"

All that afternoon, the stranger chopped wood, pausing, from time to time, to look from the shed door down the country road; and Mrs. Wadleigh, singing "Fly like a Youthful," "But O! their end, their dreadful end," and like melodies which had prevailed when she "set in the seats," flew round, indeed, and set the kitchen in immaculate order. Evidently her guest had seldom left that room. He had slept there on the lounge. He had eaten his potatoes there, and smoked his pipe.

When the early dusk set in, and Mrs. Wadleigh had cleared away their supper of baked potatoes and salt fish, again with libations of quince, she drew up before the shining stove, and put her feet on the hearth.

"Here!" she called to the man, who was sitting uncomfortably on one corner of the woodbox, and eyeing her with the same embarrassed watchfulness. "You draw up, too! It's the best time o' the day now, 'tween sunset an' dark."

"I guess I'd better be goin'," he returned, doggedly.

"Goin'? Where?"

"I don't know. But I'm goin'."

"Now look here," said Mrs. Wadleigh, with vigor. "You take that chair, an' draw up to the fire. You do as I tell you!"

He did it.

"Now, I can't hender your goin', but if you do go, I've got a word to say to you."

"You needn't say it! I don't want nobody's advice."

"Well, you've got to have it jest the same! When you bile potaters, don't you let 'em run over onto the stove. Now you remember! I've had to let the fire go down here, an' scrub till I could ha' cried. Don't you never do such a thing ag'in, wherever you be!"

He could only look at her. This sort of woman was entirely new to his experience.

"But I've got somethin' else to say," she continued, adjusting her feet more comfortably. "I ain't goin' to turn anybody out into the snow, such a night as this. You're welcome to stay, but I want to know what brought ye here. I ain't one o' them that meddles an' makes, an' if you 'ain't done nothin' out o' the way, an' I ain't called on for a witness, you needn't be afraid o' my tellin'."

"You will be called in!" he broke in, speaking from a desperation outside his own control. "It's murder! I've killed a man!" He turned upon her with a savage challenge in the motion; but her face was set placidly forward, and the growing dusk had veiled its meaning.

"Well!" she remarked, at length, "ain't you ashamed to set there talkin' about it! You must have brass enough to line a kittle! Why 'ain't you been, like a man, an' gi'n yourself up, instid o' livin' here, turnin' my kitchen upside down? Now you tell me all about it! It'll do ye good."

"I'm goin'," said the man, breathing hard as he spoke, "I'm goin' away from here tonight. They never'll take me alive. It was this way. There was a man over where I lived that's most drunk himself under ground, but he ain't too fur gone to do mischief. He told a lie about me, an' lost me my place in the shoe shop. Then one night, I met him goin' home, an' we had words. I struck him. He fell like an ox. I killed him. I didn't go home no more. I didn't even see my wife. I couldn't tell her. I couldn't be took *there*. So I run away. An' when I got starved out, an' my feet were most froze walkin', I see this house, all shet up, an' I come here."

He paused; and the silence was broken only by the slow, cosey ticking of the liberated clock.

"Well!" said Mrs. Wadleigh, at last, in a ruminating tone. "Well! well! Be you a drinkin' man?"

"I never was till I lost my job," he answered, sullenly. "I had a little then. I had a little the night he sassed me."

"Well! well!" said Mrs. Wadleigh, again. And then she continued, musingly: "So I s'pose you're Joe Mellen, an' the man you struck was Solomon Ray?"

He came to his feet with a spring.

"How'd you know?" he shouted.

"Law! I've been visitin' over Hillside way!" said Mrs. Wadleigh, comfortably. "You couldn't ha' been very smart not to thought o' that when I mentioned my darter Lucy, an' where the children went to school. No smarter'n you was to depend on that old wooden button! I know all about that drunken scrape. But the queerest part on't was—Solomon Ray didn't die!"

"Didn't die!" the words halted, and he dragged them forth. "Didn't die?"

"Law, no! you can't kill a Ray! They brought him to, an' fixed him up in good shape. I guess you mellered him some, but he's more scairt than hurt. He won't prosecute. You needn't be afraid. He said he dared you to it. There, there now! I wouldn't. My sake alive! le' me git a light!"

For the stranger sat with his head bowed on the table, and he trembled like a child.

Next morning at eight o'clock, Mrs. Wadleigh was standing at the door, in the sparkling light, giving her last motherly injunction to the departing guest.

"You know where the depot is? An' it's the nine o'clock train you've got to take. An' you remember what I said about hayin' time. If you don't have no work by the middle o' May, you drop me a line, an' perhaps I can take you an' your wife, too. Lucy's children al'ays make a sight o' work. You keep that bill safe, an'—Here, wait a minute! You might stop at Cyrus Pendleton's—it's the fust house arter you pass the corner—an' ask 'em to put a sparerib an' a pat o' butter into the sleigh, an' ride over here to dinner. You tell 'em I'm as much obleeged to 'em for sendin' over last night to see if I was alive, as if I hadn't been so dead with sleep I couldn't say so. Good-bye! Now, you mind you keep tight hold o' that bill, an' spend it prudent!"

HELEN R. MARTIN

★ ★ ★

To Southeastern Pennsylvania, at the invitation of William Penn, came groups of Mennonites and Amish who had refused to submit to the religious regulations of Switzerland and Germany. Clinging tenaciously to their ancient beliefs, these people maintain a strict discipline and enforce separation from the world by a stringent use of excommunication. They prohibit marriage outside the brotherhood, refuse to bear arms or take an oath, and, in some congregations, wear a distinctive garb, use hooks and eyes instead of buttons, and disallow modern machinery and automobiles. Belief in witchcraft and exorcism by powwow are still common. Besides these sects are many other people of German origin, who also preserve the original German dialects, now modified by contact with English into Pennsylvania Deitsch. Earliest to place these people in fiction was Helen Reimensnyder Martin (1868-1939), author of some thirty volumes. "Ellie's Furnishing" is reprinted from *The Betrothal of Elypholate* by permission of D. Appleton-Century Co.

★ ★ ★

Ellie's Furnishing

THE schoolteacher, Eli Darmstetter, had "composed" the form of invitation to be sent to those friends and relatives who lived too far away to be invited by word of mouth.

CANAAN, LANCASTER CO., PA.
May 10, 1895

DEAR FRIEND:
Inclosed please find an Invitation to our Daughter Ellie Furnishing Party, it was to take place on May 5, 1895. But oweing to Some of her

Prominent Friends being away and Some had former engagements, We
Concluded to postpone the affair until the 10th inst. So I hope it will be
Convenient for you and your Esteemable Wife to confer us a favor and
pleasure by being present at that Evening.

With Regards and Respects

I Remain

Truly yours

DANIEL SEIDENSTICKER

Mr. Seidensticker had this form, with some variations to suit individual cases, copied and sent far and wide to all his friends, acquaintance, kith and kin; and the replies that they brought during
the several weeks following afforded high entertainment, not to say
mad dissipation, to the Seidenstickers. Indeed, so broken up was the
dull monotony of their lives by the unaccustomed daily arrival of
mail, and by preparations for the Furnishing Party and expeditions
to town to buy the furniture for Ellie's parlor, that the nerve and
brain of the family were strained to a severe tension in sustaining all
this unwonted mental and physical activity.

"This here'n is from Bucks County," Mrs. Seidensticker one evening announced to her assembled family as she opened a letter which
Jakey, her nine-year-old son, had just brought from the post-office
at Canaan. It was a mild evening in early May, and they were all
gathered on the kitchen porch to enjoy the budget of mail which,
since the sending forth of the invitations, had come to be the most
important feature of their day: Ellie, the grown-up daughter; Silas,
her elder brother, who shared his father's labors on their large farm;
Jakey, the little brother; and Mr. and Mrs. Seidensticker.

Mrs. Seidensticker, a large, stout woman a little past middle age,
wore the New Mennonite plain dress and white cap, but her fat,
dull countenance did not bear that stamp of other-worldliness so characteristic of many New Mennonites. Her pretty, dainty daughter Ellie,
who was dressed "fashionable," had—much more than her mother
—the pensive, nun-like face so often seen behind the black sunbonnets
of the wives of Lancaster County farmers.

Mr. Seidensticker, a hard-working Pennsylvania Dutch farmer, did
not wear the Mennonite garb. He had never "turned plain" and
"given himself up," and he still "remained in the world."

"It's from Cousin Elipholat," Mrs. Seidensticker continued. "Ellie,
you read it oncet," she added, leaning forward in her chair and passing the letter to her daughter, who sat near her on the porch. "You're
handier at readin' writin' than what I am still."

"Leave Si read it," Ellie indifferently returned.

Her mother looked at her inquiringly. "What's the matter of you, Ellie? Ain't you mebbe feelin' just so good or what?"

"Oh, I'm feelin' just so middlin'; I don't want for to read. Leave Si."

Mrs. Seidensticker had been vaguely conscious, in the past few days, of the fact that something was troubling Ellie. The girl was not like herself; ever since she and Sam Shunk, her "gentleman friend," had gone to town together to buy the furniture for the parlor in which Ellie was to "set up Sa'urdays and keep company" with him, she had been pale and listless, and at times she wore a look of suffering that troubled the mother deeply. Could something have gone wrong between Ellie and Sam? Mrs. Seidensticker's questionings had brought no confidences from Ellie. What a mortification it would be if, when all the preparations were made for the "Furnishing" party, at which the engagement of Ellie and Sam was to be "put out," it should transpire that "one of 'em wasn't satisfied with the other"!

Mrs. Seidensticker was greatly troubled.

"Then, Si, you read it," she said with a sigh, giving the letter to her grown son, who sat on the porch-step at her feet.

Silas, bending to the task allotted to him, strenuously grasped the sheet with both his hands.

Dear cousins my Pop he can't come, Because he ain't no more alive. He died. He was layin' for 22 weeks. It's five years back already that he died for me I'm sorry he can't come. But he's dead. I would come but I'm turned plain and wear the garb now and so parties and such things like them don't do me no good, and I'd best not addict to them things. Pop he would of like to come. But he is dead this five years now.

Your Well Wisher

ELIPHOLAT HINNERSHIZ

"Now, think!" said Mrs. Seidensticker with a long sigh. "I didn't never hear that Cousin Jake passed away. He was a good man," she said mournfully. "If yous could see him right now here on this porch, you'd know he was one of the finest men settin'! He was just comin' forty years old when I seen him last; that was mebbe fifteen years back already. I ain't sure it was just to say fifteen—but we won't stop at fifteen, but we'll give it that anyhow. Do you mind of him, Pop?" she asked her husband.

Mr. Seidensticker drew his long, thin length up from the pump-bed and leaned against a pillar of the porch.

"Ach, yes, I mind of *him*. He had sich a long beard that way. He was very proud of hisseff with his beard, Mom."

"Yes," she said, thoughtfully reminiscent; "he was the high-feel-ingest man! You see," she explained to her children, "he married sich a tony wife! She was wonderful tony. Her pop was a headwaiter in a hotel, and she was, oh, a way-up woman. If she got mad, I want you to notice of the sparks didn't fly!"

"And do you mind, Mom," said Ellie's soft voice, "how oncet when you took me to Bucks County to see her when I was a little girl, she used to use napkins on the table for every day still?"

"Yes," nodded her mother. "She sayed she was raised that way. But people's ways is different in Bucks County to what they are here. I've took notice of that whenever I traveled to Bucks County. Yes, the world changes a heap in thirty or forty miles already. She was so much for makin' the windows open in summertime. I ain't. We ain't raised to that in Lancaster County. It draws flies. And she didn't raise her babies like what I did. She sayed I was too much for keepin' 'em covered up and hot. She wasn't in for that. She did, now, have queer ways to herself. She didn't have no children but only Elipholat and another one that was born dead. She didn't want no more, she sayed, still; she wasn't no friend to children. But I tole her when you're married, you ain't ast do you favor children or no. And she sayed the Lord didn't give but the two children; and she must say she didn't never disagree with the Lord that He did not treat her like them Stuffenkind fambly that had nineteen, so they never could stay in the house all together mit, but two had to take turn staying outside. Yes, that's the way she'd talk still; like they all in Bucks County, makin' joke of what they hadn't should."

"Who's the other letter from, Mom?" asked Jakey from his perch on the porch railing. "I brung two and a postal card. When John Doen give me our mail, he sayed he couldn't make out the writin' on that there postal card, only he could see it was from Ebenezer Duttonhoffer."

"Oh, him," nodded Mrs. Seidensticker. "Here, Si, read it oncet."

The early shades of the May evening were gathering and Silas was obliged to hold the postal card close to his eyes in order to decipher its faintly-penciled message.

Friend Mary:

Pete he has fallin' fits now and he's often took worse, so it don't suit just so very convenynt and the horse he has bots and this after the mare she got pink eye for me but if the weather ain't inclement and we can make it so it suits yet for one of the horses we will come then if Sally's foot gets better she's got it so bad in her foot.

Respectfullie
Ebenezer Duttonhoffer

"Ach," said Mr. Seidensticker; "them Duttonhoffers was always a ridic'lous fambly for havin' things happen of 'em. They'll all be here, you mind if they ain't! Pete with his fallin' fits and Sally with her leg or foot or whatever—and every one of 'em. They're always close by when they know a body's goin' to have entertainment. And when you go to *their* place they're just that near they never ast you to eat. Ach, mebbe they'll ast you to pick a piece—but they ain't givin' you no square meal."

"Here's one from Cocalico," said Mrs. Seidensticker. "That must be from Sister Lizzie Miller. Here, Si."

"You'd better make the lamp lit then. I can't hardly see no more," said Silas.

"There's just only this one any more; I guess you can make out to read that."

"Gimme here, then."

Silas changed his position a bit and strained his eyes to read.

SISTER MARY:
I wish you the grace and Piece of the Lord. Mamie got Daniel's Invitation all right she was snitzing the apples and cut herself so ugly in the thumb I'm writing for her I'd leave her come if I otherwise could but I don't know what to wear on her. I'd sooner she'd go as stay for all we're getting strangers Thursdays and we've made out to clean the kitchen to-morrow, so I don't know how long it will go before I can get time to make her a new dress already. It would be wishful for her to have a new dress her other one where she bought off of Haverbushes is wore out yet.
                                                              SISTER LIZZIE

"Sister Lizzie's a wonderful hard-workin' woman," remarked Mrs. Seidensticker. "And now her children's all growed up over her, she works as hard as ever she did still. And her man, he always used her so mean that way."

"Does he farm yet?" inquired Mr. Seidensticker, who, having washed his hands at the pump close by the porch, while listening to the letters, was now drying them on one of the roller-towels which hung on the brick wall of the house.

The Seidensticker towel-system was unique. Two towels always hung on the side of the house, one of them doing its second week of service for the entire family, the other its first—the former being used exclusively for hands, and the fresher one for faces. The pump, the two roller-towels, and one "wash rag" hanging over the top of the pump (and known in the family as *the* wash rag) constituted the only toilet appointments of the household.

"Whether Sister Lizzie's man farms?" inquiringly repeated Mrs. Seidensticker. "No, he don't carry on nothin' now. He's such a wonderful man for snitz pie. I guess that's why they're snitzing so early. Their winter snits mebbe give out for 'em. Yes, Lizzie's man was always a friend to pie. And he always sayed to Lizzie, 'Put right much sugar on it.' Lizzie thought that's what made his teeth go so fast, so's he had to get his store ones already. He's got his store teeth better'n thirty years now."

The sound, at this minute, of wheels in the distance, on the road which passed their gate, suddenly set the whole family on the *qui vive* of expectation. Jakey leaped like a squirrel from the porch railing and ran to the front fence. Mr. Seidensticker dropped the family hand-towel and craned his long thin neck around the pump; Silas, Ellie, and Mrs. Seidensticker leaned forward expectantly.

Not that they were dreading or pleasantly anticipating (as might have appeared) either a foe or a friend in the approaching vehicle; but in the dull monotony of their lives the passing of a wagon was an episode of exciting interest. For a wagon to pass a Lancaster County farmhouse, and the inmates thereof to miss seeing whose wagon it was, was a mishap to be lamented for days to come.

"It's John Herr's!" Jakey called, as soon as the horse was near enough for him to recognize it.

"Oh, him!" Mrs. Seidensticker said in a tone of satisfied curiosity. "I guess he's been in to Canaan for his mail, mebbe."

When John Herr's buggy had passed and disappeared, Jakey came back to the porch.

"Did you fetch the mail for Abe's this evening?" Mrs. Seidensticker inquired of the child.

"Abe's" was their designation for the household, a half-mile distant, belonging to the young married sister of Mrs. Seidensticker, who had married a farmer named Abe Kuhns.

"Whether I fetched the mail for Abe's?" repeated Jakey. "Yes, I fetched it down to 'em then."

"What did they get?"

"Nothin' but the *Weekly Intelligencer*," Jakey replied, taking a handful of dried apples out of a pan on the porch bench and beginning to eat them.

"You're to leave them snits be now," admonished his mother.

"I didn't eat very hearty at supper," argued Jakey. "I had to hurry to get done once, to go for the mail already, and I had only butter-bread and coffee soup."

"Well, if you feel for some more supper, go to the cupboard and get a piece. Don't eat them snits. They're unhealthy when they ain't cooked."

"I like 'em better'n a piece," protested Jakey, though he obediently put them back into the pan; the children of the Pennsylvania Dutch are reared in old-fashioned implicit obedience to parental authority.

"But you wouldn't like the stomeek ache you'd mebbe get if you eat 'em," said his father. "A body must be a little forethoughted that way about what they eat still."

Mrs. Seidensticker's stout figure rose heavily from her rocking-chair.

"I'd mebbe better come in now. You just stay settin'," she added to Ellie. "You seem like as if you was a little tired. You're so quiet this evening. Ain't you mebbe feelin' good, Ellie?"

"Oh, I'm feelin' just so middlin'," Ellie softly answered.

"Is Sam comin' tonight?"

Ellie rose from her straight-backed seat and took her mother's low rocking-chair. "He didn't speak nothin' about when he'd come over again," she answered.

"Well, I'm goin' to bed," her mother announced with a yawn as she walked to the kitchen door. "Are you comin', Pop?"

"I might as well, I guess."

Silas and Jakey, without comment, followed their parents indoors and left Ellie alone on the porch. It was generally understood that the coast must be clear for a possible visit from Sam.

Sam Shunk had been Ellie Seidensticker's "steady regular gentleman friend," not only for the past four months, since her eighteenth birthday, but he had "kept steady comp'ny" with her even before either he or she had reached the age or the worldly condition when "settin' up Sa'urdays" was, according to the social rubrics of Canaan Township, the proper and conventional procedure. Time had, therefore, established his prerogative to the sobriquet of "Friend" with a capital F and an especial significance.

Left alone on the porch in the gathering spring twilight, Ellie's pretty head drooped upon her breast, and a long, tired sigh swelled her young bosom. Presently two big tears trickled over her pale cheeks and a little gasping sigh came from her throat. The measure of her Spartan self-control in the presence of her family was the exceeding trouble and distress manifest just now in every line of her relaxed form and delicate face.

The secret grief that was rending her was the realization that she must give up Sam. In anguish of spirit she asked herself how she could ever bring herself to do it. For, oh, she loved him! He was so kind, so strong, so handsome! In all the township, where was his peer? Her soul was knit to his and she did not, she did not, want to give him up!

But she must. Sam belonged to the World. And she—she was about to give herself to the service of her Lord and Master, who forbade that His children be unequally yoked together with unbelievers.

It was the "Furnishing" that had brought Ellie to this state of self-abnegation. Her mother, as has been said, was a New Mennonite. The creed of this sect, forbidding not only gay apparel, but also any but the plainest and simplest of household furnishings, the custom has grown up among its members of leaving the "front room" of their homes unfurnished until the eldest daughter shall have come of age, when, if by that time she has not been moved by the spirit to "give herself up," that is, to abandon the vain pomps and glories of this wicked world, "turn plain" and join the New Mennonites, her parents give vent to their long repressed human instincts for adornment and fit up the parlor for her in the best style they can afford.

New Mennonites never force their own convictions upon their children, for since it is the Spirit only, and not any human agent, which can teach men the way of salvation, and as the "mere morality" of the unconverted can never be counted unto a man for righteousness, either he must, of his own free will and accord and without outside influence, give himself absolutely and entirely to the Lord's service, or else be a child of "the Enemy" outright. There is no medium course. It is thus that the New Mennonites explain the seeming inconsistency of freely allowing to their children the "vanities" which they themselves eschew as sinful.

The event regularly known in Lancaster County as "Furnishing" is, next to marriage, the most auspicious time in a young girl's life. As soon as her parents have "furnished" for her, she is expected to enter upon her matrimonial campaign and, anon, settle down to "keep comp'ny" with one especial "Friend," whom, as soon as convenient, she marries, and then the furniture of her parlor is taken with her into her own new home.

Now Ellie had always anticipated with delight the time of her "Furnishing," and when it had at last arrived, she threw herself, heart and soul, into the joy of choosing her "things"—the cabinet organ, the "stuffed" sofa and chairs, the marble-topped table, plush album, gilt-framed "Snow Scene," and Brussels carpet. Sam had gone with her, one Saturday morning, to Lancaster, to help her do her choosing. Later in the day he and she had gone to the Vaudeville

Show at the Park, and it had been the shock of the latter, combined with what she had suddenly felt to be the wicked selfishness of her enormous expenditures for things unnecessary for the soul and only pleasing to the worldly eye, that had brought her to a realization of the frivolity and error of temporizing with the World, and had convinced her of her duty to abandon its pomps and hollowness; to seek and hold fast to the Truth that the Saviour had died to reveal to cold and indifferent man. Her religious nature was awakened, and with clear vision she saw the real things of her life in their true contrast to its vanities. She knew, with a fatal certainty, that never again would she find joy in the things that heretofore had absorbed her to the neglect of her soul's salvation. She must give herself up. And she must therefore abandon Sam.

How was she ever to break it to him, loving and trusting her as he did?

"What'll he think of me, comin' with somepin' like this and my promise passed only four weeks a'ready. And he's so much for me to dress! And I was always so wonderful stylish! How will I ever tell him I'm turnin' plain as soon as I otherwise can?"

But this weakness, she knew, was only a temptation of the Enemy of her soul, who watched every thought of her heart, to trip her up and drag her back into the World at the least opportunity.

Meanwhile, while Ellie was sitting on the porch in the May twilight, battling with the weakness of the flesh in the sacrifice which she was called upon to make for the faith that was in her, Sam Shunk was trudging down the road, towards the home of his sweetheart, on an errand that made every step of this usually blissful walk one of pain and effort.

He found Ellie alone on the porch where, a few moments before, her family had left her.

The new pink shirtwaist which she wore made her cheeks look so like ripe peaches that, for a forgetful instant, he anticipated with satisfaction the kisses he would presently press upon their downy softness. But only for an instant. The chilling remembrance came to him of the sad purport of his visit to her tonight.

With a heavy heart he seated himself in the rocking-chair at her side.

So absorbed was he in his own mental burden that he failed to notice how subdued and reserved was the greeting which she gave him.

From force of habit he began with his usual form of social intercourse in opening up his customary weekly stint of courting.

"Nice evening, this evening; say not?"

"Ain't!" Ellie's low soft voice agreed.

"How's the folks?"

"*They're* pretty well."

A faint impression of something unaccustomed in her tone caused Sam to steal a glance at her fair and delicate face at his side.

"How's your Mom?" he inquired conversationally. Sam was not brilliant in dialogue, and as Ellie herself was usually not remarkably articulate, their social intercourse was sometimes a little difficult.

"She's pretty well, too," she replied.

"How's your Pop?"

"*He's* old-fashioned."

Sam gently rocked his chair and gazed out across the darkening lawn.

"Nice evening, this evening, ain't it is," he returned to the charge.

"Yes, anyhow," sweetly agreed Ellie.

"How's Jakey?"

"He's pretty well."

"Is Si well, too?" Sam asked by way of variety.

"Yes, he's pretty well."

They rocked in silence for a few minutes.

"I'm glad the folks is all well."

"Yes, they're all right good," Ellie consented with complacent absence of originality.

"It's right warm, ain't?"

"Yes, Pop he sayed it would make somepin' down before morning, he thought."

"Say, Ellie! I don't trust to be on them trolley cars in Lancaster when it's goin' to give a gust. Last time I was goin' to take a trolley ride, I seen it was thunderin' and I tole the conductor I wanted off right away at the corner already."

"I guess!" Ellie nodded.

Sam now fell into a temporary silence as he gloomily contemplated the dread task at his hands of telling Ellie the object of his visit. Again he stole a side glance at her, and the strange, plaintive look he detected about her sweet eyes smote his big, generous heart. How could he make her unhappy? She trusted him and believed in his love for her. What should he do?

"Say, Ellie?"

"What, Sam?"

"That man in the dime matynee in there at Lancaster, last Sa'urday, that could twist himself so queer, still, say, Ellie, that was false hair he had on!"

"You think!"

"I'm pretty near sure."

"Now think!" Ellie said wonderingly.

"And that colored lady you mind of—that sung sich a touchin' piece about 'I wisht my color would fade'; say, Ellie, she was only a white person with shoe-blacking or whatever on her face!"

"I say!" cried Ellie in surprise.

"A body hadn't ought to give their countenance to sich shows like what them is, Ellie. It don't do a person no good."

"No, Sam, I don't think so nuther. And if you feel a little conscientious, you'd better let sich things be, then."

"Ellie, I got to tell you somepin'!"

"Don't tell me tonight, Sam," Ellie pleaded, feeling sure he was going to press her to name their wedding-day, as he had lately been doing most strenuously. "I ain't feelin' good tonight. Don't speak nothin' to me tonight."

"I can't help for that—I got to tell you this here. Say, Ellie, it ain't that I haven't got no love to you—but indeed, Ellie, I can't marry you."

Ellie slowly turned in her chair and gazed at him in the deepening darkness

"Why not, Sam?" she asked, in a voice so low that he scarcely caught her words.

"Ellie, I'm going to give myself up!"

"Oh, Sam!"

"Don't tempt me not to!" he cried almost piteously. "I want you —you know how bad I want you—but you're in the World, Ellie, and I can't marry you! If it breaks my heart and yours, I've got to leave you and cleave unto Christ! It was goin' with you to town done it—and buyin' them things for your 'Furnishing' and then seein' the dime matynee. I seen, Ellie, how pleasing to the eye it was, but not for the glory of Gawd. And I can't never no more give my countenance to fashionable things. I'm turnin' plain as soon as I can get to town to get my plain clo'es once. Servin' the Lord ain't easy, it ain't easy," he said. "You mind where the Bible says, 'If a man smite thee, turn him the other cheek.' That's pretty hard, and it wouldn't suit me so well to do it. Indeed, I say that. But I must do all them things if I'm a child of Gawd. And John Souders preached how he seen 'em die horrible already when they was unconverted."

"But, Sam—"

"Ellie!" Sam quickly interrupted, as though dreading the effect of her pleading, "it's like dyin' to me to give you up. I'd most ruther *be* dead. But it's my duty. Last night my sins opened up before me and I was wonderful concerned; and at last, after a great struggle, I made up my mind I'd give myself to the guidance of the Spirit. Then, here this mornin', already, when I fell awake, the Enemy was temptin' me, and he tole me how pretty you was and how sweet, Ellie. But," Sam solemnly added, "I've overcome the Enemy, and I come here tonight yet to give you good-bye."

Only "the angels in the heavens above and the demons down under the sea" could measure the sacrifice which the stalwart youth was thus making in his loyalty to what he felt to be a larger truth of life than any mere personal relation of his own.

"Sam! Sam! Listen at me."

Ellie leaned forward in her eagerness and clasped his big arm with both her hands.

"*I* got in trouble, too, Sam, about my sins, after we'd been to town. I was in wonderful trouble, Sam. And that evening," she eagerly went on, "the sky got so red I thought the world would go to an end. And next day I seen how nice and humble Mom looked in her plain dress—and, Sam, I *hated* my Furniture and my fashionable clo'es! And that next evening, the sky was redder than ever! And Sam, I let loose of everything—my clo'es, my Furniture, the party —and you—and joined to the Lord! And this morning I went over to Mamie Herr's that I got mad at 'cause she talked down on you —and I knowed I must be made satisfied with all my enemies, so I tole her I wasn't any more mad yet. And, oh, Sam, it never suspicioned me that the Spirit was guidin' *you,* too!"

Sam's arms were about her now, and she was clinging to him:

> "'Gawd works in a mysterious way
> His wonders to perform.'"

"Ain't he does, Ellie!" he whispered, pressing an ecstatic kiss upon her lips.

"Ain't he does!" was Ellie's rapturous response.

ZONA GALE

★ ★ ★

The struggle of women to maintain a courageous independence in the face of bereavement, of loneliness, and of poverty is described in many stories by Zona Gale Breese (1873-1939). Although she limited herself to small towns and their people, a revolutionary change in attitude is noticeable in the course of her career. Similar in substance and in sparse, poetic style are *Friendship Village* (1909), affirmative of the goodness of small-town life; *Miss Lulu Bett* (1920), in which a spinster revolts against the tyranny of a brother-in-law; and *Yellow Gentians and Blue* (1927), bitter revelations of man's inhumanity to his fellows; yet the mood of contentment in her first volume alters into one of dissatisfaction. These faithful records of inhibited lives penetrate beneath the surface of life with the mercy of a surgeon's scalpel: hope is not entirely denied. "Nobody Sick, Nobody Poor" is reprinted from *Friendship Village* by permission of The Macmillan Company.

★ ★ ★

Nobody Sick, Nobody Poor

Two days before Thanksgiving the air was already filled with white turkey feathers, and I stood at a window and watched until the loneliness of my still house seemed like something pointing a mocking finger at me. When I could bear it no longer I went out in the snow, and through the soft drifts I fought my way up the Plank Road toward the village.

I had almost passed the little bundled figure before I recognized

Calliope. She was walking in the middle of the road, as in Friendship we all walk in winter; and neither of us had umbrellas. I think that I distrust people who put up umbrellas on a country road in a fall of friendly flakes.

Instead of inquiring perfunctorily how I did, she greeted me with a fragment of what she had been thinking—which is always as if one were to open a door of his mind to you instead of signing you greeting from a closed window.

"I just been tellin' myself," she looked up to say without preface, "that if I could see one more good old-fashion' Thanksgivin', life'd sort o' smooth out. An' land knows, it needs some smoothin' out for me."

With this I remember that it was as if my own loneliness spoke for me. At my reply Calliope looked at me quickly—as if I, too, had opened a door.

"Sometimes Thanksgivin' *is* some like seein' the sun shine when you're feelin' rill rainy yourself," she said thoughtfully.

She held out her blue-mittened hand and let the flakes fall on it in stars and coronets.

"I wonder," she asked evenly, "if you'd help me get up a Thanksgivin' dinner for a few poor sick folks here in Friendship?"

In order to keep my self-respect, I recall that I was as ungracious as possible. I think I said that the day meant so little to me that I was willing to do anything to avoid spending it alone. A statement which seems to me now not to bristle with logic.

"That's nice of you," Calliope replied genially. Then she hesitated, looking down Daphne Street, which the Plank Road had become, toward certain white houses. There were the homes of Mis' Mayor Uppers, Mis' Holcomb-that-was-Mame-Bliss, and the Liberty sisters,—all substantial dignified houses, typical of the simple prosperity of the countryside.

"The only trouble," she added simply, "is that in Friendship I don't know a soul rill sick, nor a soul what you might call poor."

At this I laughed, unwillingly enough. Dear Calliope! Here indeed was a drawback to her project.

"Honestly," she said reflectively, "Friendship can't seem to do anything like any other town. When the new minister come here, he give out he was goin' to do settlement work. An' his second week in the place he come to me with a reg'lar hang-dog look. 'What kind of a town is this?' he says to me, disgusted. 'They ain't nobody sick in it an' they ain't nobody poor!' I guess he could 'a' got along without the poor—most of us can. But we mostly like to hev a few sick

to carry the flowers off our house plants to, an' now an' then a
tumbler o' jell. An' yet I've known weeks at a time when they wasn't
a soul rill flat down sick in Friendship. It's so now. An' that's hard,
when you're young an' enthusiastic, like the minister."

"But where are you going to find your guests then, Calliope?"
I asked curiously.

"Well," she said brightly, "I was just plannin' as you come up
with me. An' I says to myself: 'God give me to live in a little bit of a
place where we've all got enough to get along on, an' Thanksgivin'
finds us all in health. It looks like He'd afflicted us by lettin' us hev
nobody to do for.' An' then it come to me that if we was to get up
the dinner,—with all the misery an' hunger they is in the world,—
God in His goodness would let some of it come our way to be fed.
'In the wilderness a cedar,' you know—as Liddy Ember an' I was
always tellin' each other when we kep' shop together. An' so to-day
I said to myself I'd go to work an' get up the dinner an' trust there'd
be eaters for it."

"Why, Calliope," I said, "Calliope!"

"I ain't got much to do with, myself," she added apologetically;
"the most I've got in my sullar, I guess, is a gallon jar o' watermelon
pickles. I could give that. You don't think it sounds irreverent—
connectin' God with a big dinner, so?" she asked anxiously.

And, at my reply:—

"Well, then," she said briskly, "let's step in an' see a few folks that
might be able to tell us of somebody to do for. Let's ask Mis' Mayor
Uppers an' Mis' Holcomb-that-was-Mame-Bliss, an' the Liberty girls."

Because I was lonely and idle, and because I dreaded inexpressibly
going back to my still house, I went with her. Her ways were a kind
of entertainment, and I remember that I believed my leisure to be
infinite.

We turned first toward the big shuttered house of Mis' Mayor
Uppers, to whom, although her husband had been a year ago removed from office, discredited, and had not since been seen in Friendship, we yet gave her old proud title, as if she had been Former
Lady Mayoress. For the present mayor, Authority Hubblethwaite,
was, as Calliope said, "unconnect'."

I watched Mis' Uppers in some curiosity while Calliope explained
that she was planning a dinner for the poor and sick,—"the lame
and the sick that's comfortable enough off to eat,"—and could she
suggest some poor and sick to ask? Mis' Uppers was like a vinegar
cruet of mine, slim and tall, with a little grotesquely puckered face
for a stopper, as if the whole known world were sour.

"I'm sure," she said humbly, "it's a nice i-dee. But I declare, I'm put to it to suggest. We ain't got nobody sick nor nobody poor in Friendship, you know."

"Don't you know of anybody kind o' hard up? Or somebody that, if they ain't down sick, feels sort o' spindlin'?" Calliope asked anxiously.

Mis' Uppers thought, rocking a little and running a pin in and out of a fold of her skirt.

"No," she said at length, "I don't know a soul. I think the church'd give a good deal if a real poor family'd come here to do for. Since the Cadozas went, we ain't known which way to look for poor. Mis' Ricker gettin' her fortune so puts her beyond the wolf. An' Peleg Bemus, you can't *get* him to take anything. No, I don't know of anybody real decently poor."

"An' nobody sick?" Calliope pressed her wistfully.

"Well, there's Mis' Crawford," admitted Mis' Uppers; "she had a spell o' lumbago two weeks ago, but I see her pass the house to-day. Mis' Brady was laid up with toothache, too, but the *Daily* last night said she'd had it out. An' Mis' Doctor Helman did have one o' her stomach attacks this week, an' Elzabella got out her dyin' dishes an' her dyin' linen from the still-room—you know how Mis' Doctor always brings out her nice things when she's sick, so't if she should die an' the neighbours come in, it'd all be shipshape. But she got better this time an' helped put 'em back. I declare it's hard to get up anything in the charity line here."

Calliope sat smiling a little, and I knew that it was because of her secret certainty that "some o' the hunger" would come her way, to be fed.

"I can't help thinkin'," she said quietly, "that we'll find somebody. An' I tell you what: if we do, can I count on you to help some?"

Mis' Uppers flushed with quick pleasure.

"Me, Calliope?" she said. And I remembered that they had told me how the Friendship Married Ladies' Cemetery Improvement Sodality had been unable to tempt Mis' Uppers to a single meeting since the mayor ran away. "Oh, but I couldn't though," she said wistfully.

"No need to go to the table if you don't want," Calliope told her. "Just bake up somethin' for us an' bring it over. Make a couple o' your cherry pies—did you get hold of any cherries to put up this year? Well, a couple o' your cherry pies an' a batch o' your nice drop sponge cakes," she directed. "Could you?"

Mis' Mayor Uppers looked up with a kind of light in her eyes.

"Why, yes," she said, "I could, I guess. I'll bake 'em Thanksgivin' mornin'. I—I was wonderin' how I'd put in the day."

When we stepped out in the snow again, Calliope's face was shining. Sometimes now, when my faith is weak in any good thing, I remember her look that November morning. But all that I thought then was how I was being entertained that lonely day.

The dear Liberty sisters were next, Lucy and Viny and Libbie Liberty. We went to the side door,—there were houses in Friendship whose front doors we tacitly understood that we were never expected to use,—and we found the sisters down cellar, with shawls over their head, feeding their hens through the cellar window, opening on the glassed-in coop under the porch.

In Friendship it is a point of etiquette for a morning caller never to interrupt the employment of a hostess. So we obeyed the summons of the Liberty sister to "come right down"; and we sat on a firkin and an inverted tub while Calliope told her plan and the hens fought for delectable morsels.

"My grief!" said Libbie Liberty tartly, "where you goin' to *get* your sick an' poor?"

Mis' Viny, balancing on the window ledge to reach for eggs, looked back at us.

"Friendship's so comfortable that way," she said, "I don't see how you can get up much of anything."

And little Miss Lucy, kneeling on the floor of the cellar to measure more feed, said without looking up:—

"You know, since mother died we ain't never done anything for holidays. No—we can't seem to want to think about Thanksgiving or Christmas or like that."

They all turned their grave lined faces toward us.

"We want to let the holidays just slip by without noticin'," Miss Viny told us. "Seems like it hurts less that way."

Libbie Liberty smiled wanly.

"Don't you know," she said, "when you hold your hand still in hot water, you don't feel how hot the water really is? But when you move around in it some, it begins to burn you. Well, when we let Thanksgiving an' Christmas alone, it ain't so bad. But when we start to move around in 'em—"

Her voice faltered and stopped.

"We miss mother terrible," Miss Lucy said simply.

Calliope put her blue mitten to her mouth, but her eyes she might not hide, and they were soft with sympathy.

"I know—I know," she said. "I remember the first Christmas after my mother died—I ached like the toothache all over me, an' I couldn't bear to open my presents. Nor the next year I couldn't either—I couldn't open my presents with any heart. But—" Calliope hesitated, "that second year," she said, "I found somethin' I could do. I saw I could fix up little things for other folks an' take some comfort in it. Like mother would of."

She was silent for a moment, looking thoughtfully at the three lonely figures in the dark cellar of their house.

"Your mother," she said abruptly, "stuffed the turkey for a year ago the last harvest home."

"Yes," they said.

"Look here," said Calliope; "if I can get some poor folks together, —or even *one* poor folk, or hungry,—will you three come to my house an' stuff the turkey? The way—I can't help thinkin' the way your mother would of, if she'd been here. An' then," Calliope went on briskly, "could you bring some fresh eggs an' make a pan o' custard over to my house? An' mebbe one o' you'd stir up a sunshine cake. You must know how to make your mother's sunshine cake?"

There was another silence in the cellar when Calliope had done, and for a minute I wondered if, after all, she had not failed, and if the bleeding of the three hearts might be so stanched. It was not self-reliant Libbie Liberty who spoke first; it was gentle Miss Lucy.

"I guess," she said, "I could, if we all do it. I know mother would of."

"Yes," Miss Viny nodded, "mother would of."

Libbie Liberty stood for a moment with compressed lips.

"It seems like not payin' respect to mother," she began; and then shook her head. "It ain't that," she said; "it's only missin' her when we begin to step around the kitchen, bakin' up for a holiday."

"I know—I know," Calliope said again. "That's why I said for you to come over in my kitchen. You come over there an' stir up the sunshine cake, too, an' bake it in my oven, so's we can hev it et hot. Will you do that?"

And after a little time they consented. If Calliope found any sick or poor, they would do that.

"We ain't gettin' many i-dees for guests," Calliope said, as we reached the street, "but we're gettin' helpers, anyway. An' some dinner, too."

Then we went to the house of Mis' Holcomb-that-was-Mame-Bliss —called so, of course, to distinguish her from the "Other" Holcombs.

"Don't you be shocked at her," Calliope warned me, as we closed

Mis' Holcomb's gate behind us, "she's dreadful diff'r'nt an' bitter since Abigail was married last month. She's got hold o' some kind of a Persian book, in a decorated cover, from the City; an' now she says your soul is like when you look in a lookin'-glass—that there ain't really nothin' there. An' that the world's some wind an' the rest water, an' they ain't no God only your own breath—oh, poor Mis' Holcomb!" said Calliope. "I guess she ain't rill balanced. But we ought to go to see her. We always consult Mis' Holcomb about everything."

Poor Mis' Holcomb-that-was-Mame-Bliss! I can see her now in her comfortable dining room, where she sat cleaning her old silver, her thin, veined hands as fragile as her grandmother's spoons.

"Of course, you don't know," she said, when Calliope had unfolded her plans, "how useless it all seems to me. What's the use —I keep sayin' to myself now'-days; what's the use? You put so much pains on somethin', an' then it goes off an' leaves you. Mebbe it dies, an' everything's all wasted. There ain't anything to tie to. It's like lookin' in a glass all the while. It's seemin', it ain't bein'. We ain't certain o' nothin' but our breath, an' when that goes, what hev you got? What's the use o' plannin' Thanksgivin' for anybody?"

"Well, if you're hungry, it's kind o' nice to get fed up," said Calliope, crisply. "Don't you know a soul that's hungry, Mame Bliss?"

She shook her head.

"No," she said, "I don't. Nor nobody sick in body."

"Nobody sick in body," Calliope repeated absently.

"Soul-sick an' soul-hungry you can't feed up," Mis' Holcomb added.

"I donno," said Calliope thoughtfully, "I donno but you can."

"No," Mis' Holcomb went on; "your soul's like yourself in the glass: they ain't anything there."

"I donno," Calliope said again; "some mornin's when I wake up with the sun shinin' in, I can feel my soul in me just as plain as plain."

Mis' Holcomb sighed.

"Life looks dreadful footless to me," she said.

"Well," said Calliope, "sometimes life *is* some like hearin' firecrackers go off when you don't feel up to shootin' 'em yourself. When I'm like that, I always think if I'd go out an' buy a bunch or two, an' get somebody to give me a match, I could see more sense to things. Look here, Mame Bliss; if I get·hold o' any folks to give the dinner for, will you help me some?"

"Yes," Mis' Holcomb assented half-heartedly, "I'll help you. I ain't nobody much in family, now Abigail's done what she has. They's only Eppleby, an' he won't be home Thanksg'vin this year. So I ain't nothin' else to do."

"That's the i-dee," said Calliope heartily; "if everything's foolish, it's just as foolish doin' nothin' as doin' somethin'. Will you bring over a kettleful o' boiled potatoes to my house Thanksgivin' noon? An' mash 'em an' whip 'em in my kitchen? I'll hev the milk to put in. You—you don't cook as much as some, do you, Mame?"

Did Calliope ask her that purposely? I am almost sure that she did. Mis' Holcomb's neck stiffened a little.

"I guess I can cook a thing or two beside mash' potatoes," she said, and thought for a minute. "How'd you like a pan o' 'scalloped oysters an' some baked marcaroni with plenty o' cheese?" she demanded.

"Sounds like it'd go down awful easy," admitted Calliope, smiling. "It's just what we need to carry the dinner off full sail," she added earnestly.

"Well, I ain't nothin' else to do an' I'll make 'em," Mis' Holcomb promised. "Only it beats me who you can find to do for. If you don't get anybody, let me know before I order the oysters."

Calliope stood up, her little wrinkled face aglow; and I wondered at her confidence.

"You just go ahead an' order your oysters," she said. "That dinner's goin' to come off Thanksgivin' noon at twelve o'clock. An' you be there to help feed the hungry, Mame."

When we were on the street again, Calliope looked at me with her way of shy eagerness.

"Could you hev the dinner up to your house," she asked me, "if I do every bit o' the work?"

"Why, Calliope," I said, amazed at her persistence, "have it there, of course. But you haven't any guests yet."

She nodded at me through the falling flakes.

"You say you ain't got much to be thankful for," she said, "so I thought mebbe you'd put in the time that way. Don't you worry about folks to eat the dinner. I'll tell Mis' Holcomb an' the others to come to your house—an' I'll get the food an' the folks. Don't you worry! An' I'll bring my watermelon pickles an' a bowl o' cream for Mis' Holcomb's potatoes, an' I'll furnish the turkey—a big one. The rest of us'll get the dinner in your kitchen Thanksgivin' mornin'. My!" she said, "seems though life's smoothin' out fer me a'ready. Goodby—it's 'most noon."

She hurried up Daphne Street in the snow, and I turned toward my lonely house. But I remember that I was planning how I would make my table pretty, and how I would add a delicacy or two from the City for this strange holiday feast. And I found myself hurrying to look over certain long-disused linen and silver, and to see whether my Cloth-o'-Gold rose might be counted on to bloom by Thursday noon.

II

"We'll set the table for seven folks," said Calliope, at my house on Thanksgiving morning.

"Seven!" I echoed. "But where in the world did you ever find seven, Calliope?"

"I found 'em," she answered. "I knew I could find hungry folks to do for if I tried, an' I found 'em. You'll see. I sha'n't say another word. They'll be here by twelve sharp. Did the turkey come?"

Yes, the turkey had come, and almost as she spoke the dear Liberty sisters arrived to dress and stuff it, and to make ready the pan of custard, and to "stir up" the sunshine cake. I could guess how the pleasant bustle in my kitchen would hurt them by its holiday air, and I carried them off to see my Cloth-o'-Gold rose which had opened in the night, to the very crimson heart of it. And I told them of the seven guests whom, after all, Calliope had actually contrived to marshal to her dinner. And in the midst of our almost gay speculation on this, they went at their share of the task.

The three moved about their office gravely at first, Libbie Liberty keeping her back to us as she worked, Miss Viny scrupulously intent on the delicate clatter of the egg-beater, Miss Lucy with eyes downcast on the sage she rolled. I noted how Calliope made little excuses to pass near each of them, with now a touch of the hand and now a pat on a shoulder, and all the while she talked briskly of ways and means and recipes, and should there be onions in the dressing or should there not be? We took a vote on this and were about to chop the onions in when Mis' Holcomb's litle maid arrived at my kitchen door with a bowl of oysters which Mis' Holcomb had had left from the 'scallop, an' wouldn't we like 'em in the stuffin'? Roast turkey stuffed with oysters! I saw Libbie Liberty's eyes brighten so delightedly that I brought out a jar of seedless raisins and another of preserved cherries to add to the custard, and then a bag of sweet almonds to be blanched and split for the cake o' sunshine. Surely, one of us said, the seven guests could be preparing for their Thanksgiving dinner with no more zest than we were putting into that dinner for their sakes. "Seven guests!" we said over and again.

"Calliope, how did you do it! When everybody says there's nobody in Friendship that's either sick or poor?"

"Nobody sick, nobody poor!" Calliope exclaimed, piling a dish with watermelon pickles. "Land, you might think that was the town motto. Well, the town don't know everything. Don't you ask me so many questions."

Before eleven o'clock Mis' Mayor Uppers tapped at my back door, with two deep-dish cherry pies in a basket, and a row of her delicate, feathery sponge cakes and a jar of pineapple and pie-plant preserves "to chink in." She drew a deep breath and stood looking about the kitchen.

"Throw off your things an' help, Mis' Uppers," Calliope admonished her, one hand on the cellar door. "I'm just goin' down for some sweet potatoes Mis' Holcomb sent over this morning, an' you might get 'em ready, if you will. We ain't goin' to let you off now, spite of what you've done for us."

So Mis' Mayor Uppers hung up her shawl and washed the sweet potatoes. And my kitchen was fragrant with spices and flavourings and an odorous oven, and there was no end of savoury business to be at. I found myself glad of the interest of these others in the day and glad of the stirring in my lonely house. Even if their bustle could not lessen my own loneliness, it was pleasant, I said to myself, to see them quicken with interest; and the whole affair entertained my infinite leisure. After all, I was not required to be thankful. I merely loaned my house, cosey in its glittering drifts of turkey feathers, and the day was no more and no less to me than before, though I own that I did feel more than an amused interest in Calliope's guests. Whom, in Friendship, had she found "to do for," I detected myself speculating with real interest as in the dining room, with one and another to help me, I made ready my table. My prettiest dishes and silver, the Cloth-o'-Gold rose, and my yellow-shaded candles made little auxiliary welcomes. Whoever Calliope's guests were, we would do them honour and give them the best we had. And in the midst of all came from the City the box with my gift of hothouse fruit and a rosebud for every plate. "Calliope!" I cried, as I went back to the kitchen, "Calliope, it's nearly twelve now. Tell us who the guests are, or we won't finish dinner!"

Calliope laughed and shook her head and opened the door for Mis' Holcomb-that-was-Mame-Bliss, who entered, followed by her little maid, both laden with good things.

"I prepared for seven," Mis' Holcomb said. "That was the word you sent me—but where you got your seven sick an' poor in Friendship beats me. I'll stay an' help for a while—but to me it all seems like so much monkey work."

We worked with a will that last half-hour, and the spirit of the kitchen came upon them all. I watched them, amused and pleased at Mis' Mayor Uppers's flushed anxiety over the sweet potatoes, at Libbie Liberty furiously basting the turkey, and at Miss Lucy exclaiming with delight as she unwrapped the rosebuds from their moss. But I think that Mis' Holcomb pleased me most, for with the utensils of housewifery in her hands she seemed utterly to have forgotten that there is no use in anything at all. This was not wonderful in the presence of such a feathery cream of mashed potatoes and such aromatic coffee as she made. *There* was something to tie to. Those were real, at any rate, and beyond all seeming.

Just before twelve Calliope caught off her apron and pulled down her sleeves.

"Now," she said, "I'm going to welcome the guests. I can—can't I?" she begged me. "Everything's all ready but putting on. I won't need to come out here again; when I ring the bell on the sideboard, dish it up an' bring it in, all together—turkey ahead an' vegetables followin'. Mis' Holcomb, you help 'em, won't you? An' then you can leave if you want. Talk about an old-fashion' Thanksgivin'. My!"

"Who *has* she got?" Libbie Liberty burst out, basting the turkey. "I declare, I'm nervous as a witch, I'm so curious!"

And then the clock struck twelve, and a minute after we heard Calliope tinkle a silvery summons on the call-bell.

I remember that it was Mis' Holcomb herself—to whom nothing mattered—who rather lost her head as we served our feast, and who was about putting in dishes both her oysters and her macaroni instead of carrying in the fair, brown, smoking bake pans. But at last we were ready—Mis' Holcomb at our head with the turkey, the others following with both hands filled, and I with the coffee-pot. As they gave the signal to start, something—it may have been the mystery before us, or the good things about us, or the mere look of the Thanksgiving snow on the window-sills—seemed to catch at the hearts of them all, and they laughed a little, almost joyously, those five for whom joy had seemed done, and I found myself laughing too.

So we six filed into the dining room to serve whomever Calliope had found "to do for." I wonder that I had not guessed before. There stood Calliope at the foot of the table, with its lighted candles and its Cloth-o'-Gold rose, and the other six chairs were quite vacant.

"Sit down!" Calliope cried to us, with tears and laughter in her voice. "Sit down, all six of you. Don't you see? Didn't you know?

Ain't we soul-sick an' soul-hungry, all of us? An' I tell you, this is goin' to do our souls good—an' our stomachs too!"

Nobody dropped anything, even in the flood of our amazement. We managed to get our savoury burden on the table, and some way we found ourselves in the chairs—I at the head of my table where Calliope led me. And we all talked at once, exclaiming and questioning, with sudden thanksgiving in our hearts that in the world such things may be.

"I was hungry an' sick," Calliope was telling, "for an old-fashion' Thanksgivin'—or anything that'd smooth life out some. But I says to myself, 'It looks like God had afflicted us by not givin' us anybody to do for.' An' then I started out to find some poor an' some sick— an' each one o' you knows what I found. An' I ask' myself before I got home that day, 'Why not them an' me?' There's lots o' kinds o' things to do on Thanksgivin' Day. Are you ever goin' to forgive me?"

I think that we all answered at once. But what we all meant was what Mis' Holcomb-that-was-Mame-Bliss said, as she sat flushed and smiling behind the coffee-cups:—

"I declare, I feel something like I ain't felt since I don't know when!"

And Calliope nodded at her.

"I guess that's your soul, Mame Bliss," she said. "You can always feel it if you go to work an' act as if you got one. I'll take my coffee clear."

And as we laughed, and as I looked down my table at my guests, I felt with a wonder that was like belief. How my heart leaped up within me and how it glowed! And I knew a mist of tears in my eyes, and something like happiness possessed me.

And I understood, with infinite thanksgiving, that, if I would have it so, my little house need never be wholly lonely any more.

APPENDIX

Table of Contents

arranged by regions represented

MAINE:

SARAH ORNE JEWETT:
A Lost Lover (1878) 329
Miss Debby's Neighbors (1883) 344
A White Heron (1886) 354

NEW HAMPSHIRE:

ALICE BROWN:
Mis' Wadleigh's Guest (1895) 806

MASSACHUSETTS:

HARRIET BEECHER STOWE:
The Minister's Housekeeper (1871) 72
MARY E. WILKINS FREEMAN:
Gentian (1887) 514
A New England Nun (1891) 525
A Village Singer (1891) 536
SARAH ORNE JEWETT:
The Gray Mills of Farley (1898) 363

CONNECTICUT:

ROSE TERRY COOKE:
Uncle Josh (1857) 84
Grit (1877) 99

UPPER NEW YORK STATE; THE ADIRONDACKS:

PHILANDER DEMING:
Lost (1873) 179

PENNSYLVANIA:

MARGARET DELAND:
The Child's Mother (1898) 677
HELEN R. MARTIN:
Ellie's Furnishing (1903) 819

VIRGINIA:

   THOMAS NELSON PAGE:
      Polly: A Christmas Recollection (1886) 447
      P'laski's Tunaments (1890) 470

   F. HOPKINSON SMITH:
      Six Hours in Squantico (1890) 572

NORTH CAROLINA:

   CHARLES W. CHESNUTT:
      Sis' Becky's Pickaninny (1899) 666

SOUTH CAROLINA:

   CONSTANCE FENIMORE WOOLSON:
      King David (1878) 225

TENNESSEE:

   MARY NOAILLES MURFREE (Charles Egbert Craddock):
      Taking the Blue Ribbon at the County Fair (1880) . . . 294
      Over on the T'other Mounting (1881) 311

   VIRGINIA FRAZER BOYLE:
      The Triumph of Shed (1901) 767

GEORGIA:

   AUGUSTUS BALDWIN LONGSTREET:
      The Horse-Swap (1835) 28
      The Gander-Pulling (1835) 35

   RICHARD MALCOLM JOHNSTON:
      How Mr. Bill Williams Took the Responsibility (1871) . . . 118

   JOEL CHANDLER HARRIS:
      Trouble on Lost Mountain (1886) 409
      Ananias (1888) 430

   HARRY STILLWELL EDWARDS:
      His Defense (1899) 776

OHIO:

   CONSTANCE FENIMORE WOOLSON:
      Solomon (1873) 188

   MARY HARTWELL CATHERWOOD:
      The Stirring-Off (1883) 383

UPPER MICHIGAN PENINSULA AND MACKINAC:

   CONSTANCE FENIMORE WOOLSON:
      Peter, the Parson (1874) 206

Mary Hartwell Catherwood:
  Pontiac's Lookout (1894) 393

MICHIGAN:
  Caroline Matilda Kirkland:
    The Land-Fever (1845) 42
    The Bee-Tree (1841) 54

WISCONSIN:
  Hamlin Garland:
    The Return of a Private (1890) 590
  Zona Gale:
    Nobody Sick, Nobody Poor (1907) 831

KANSAS:
  William Allen White:
    The Story of Aqua Pura (1893) 728

IOWA:
  Hamlin Garland:
    Lucretia Burns (1893) 613

KENTUCKY:
  James Lane Allen:
    Two Gentlemen of Kentucky (1888) 548

ILLINOIS:
  James Hall:
    The French Village (1829) I

ARKANSAS:
  Alice French (Octave Thanet):
    The Mortgage on Jeffy (1887) 484
    The Loaf of Peace (1888) 503
  Ruth McEnery Stuart:
    Aunt Delphi's Dilemma (1891) 735

LOUISIANA and NEW ORLEANS:
  George Washington Cable:
    'Tite Poulette (1874) 242
    Belles Demoiselles Plantation (1874) 260
    Jean-ah Poquelin (1875) 275

GRACE ELIZABETH KING:
A Drama of Three (1892) 635
La Grande Demoiselle (1893) 640
KATE CHOPIN:
Désirée's Baby (1894) 646
A Gentleman of Bayou Têche (1894) 651
Nég Créol (1897) 657
Suzette (1897) 662

NEW MEXICO:
ALBERT PIKE:
The Inroad of the Nabajo (1834) 15
THOMAS ALLIBONE JANVIER:
The Lost Mine (1884) 703
CHARLES F. LUMMIS:
Bogged Down (1897) 744

NEVADA:
PHILIP VERRILL MIGHELS:
The Tie of Partnership (1904) 788

IDAHO:
MARY HALLOCK FOOTE:
Maverick (1894) 583

TEXAS:
STEPHEN CRANE:
A Man and—Some Others (1897) 753

CALIFORNIA:
BRET HARTE:
Tennessee's Partner (1870) 139
The Romance of Madroño Hollow (1873) 147
The Iliad of Sandy Bar (1873) 157
How Santa Claus Came to Simpson's Bar (1873) 166
FRANK NORRIS:
The Third Circle (1895) 720